The Dorling Kindersley SCIENCE Encyclopedia

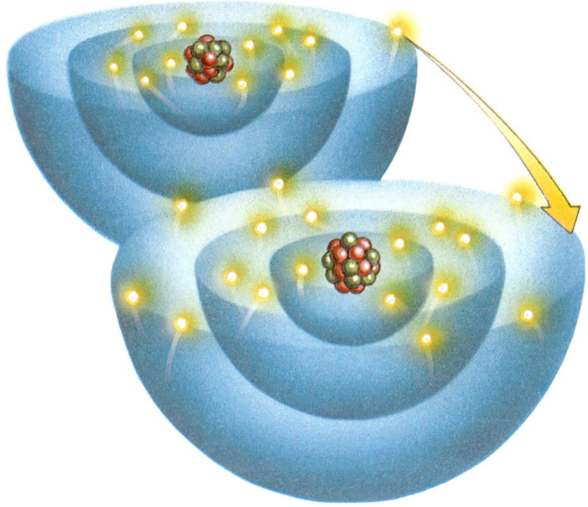

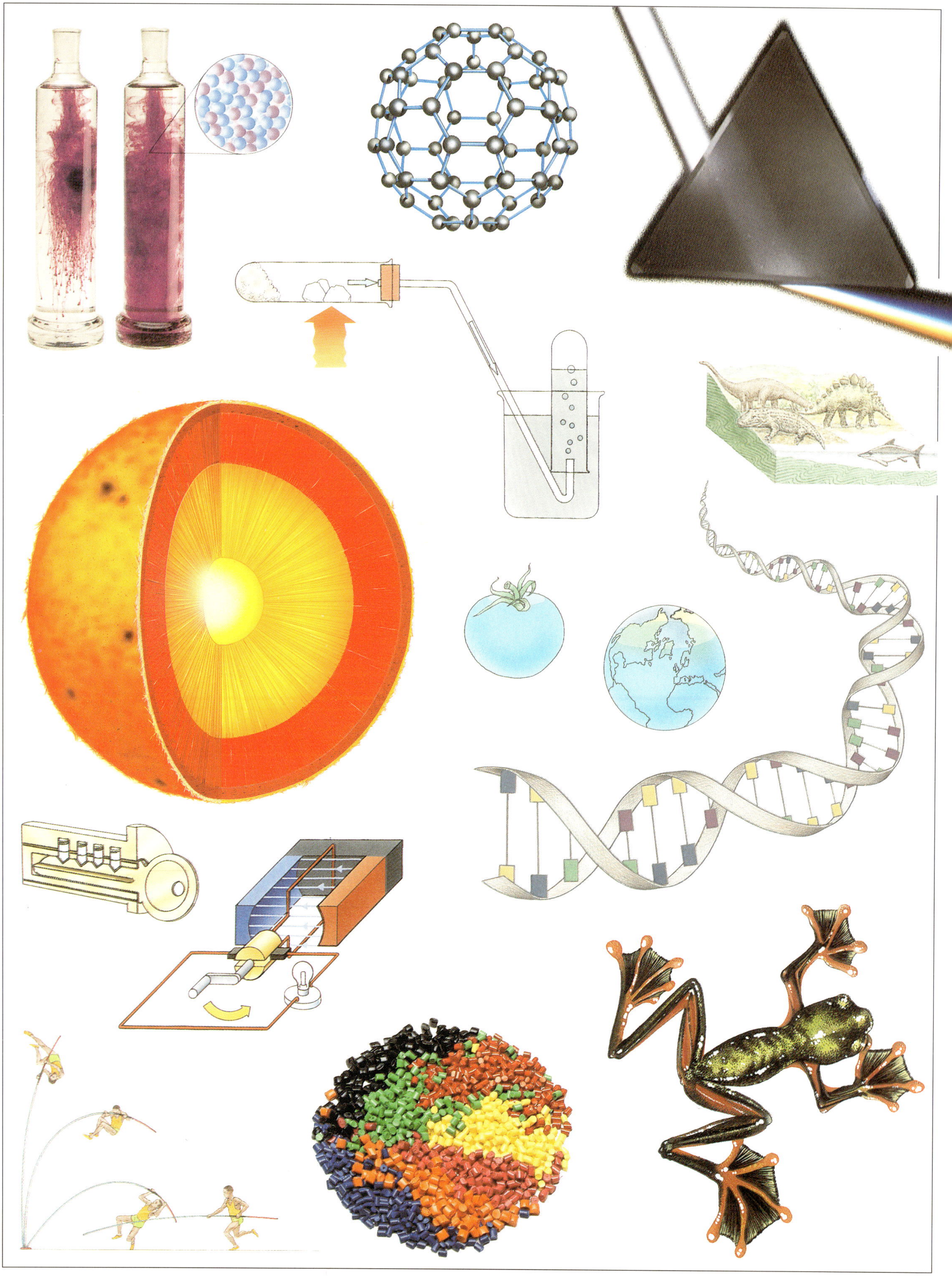

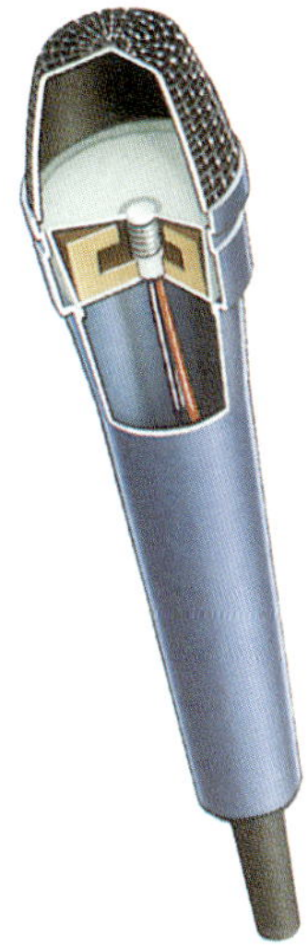

The Dorling Kindersley

SCIENCE Encyclopedia

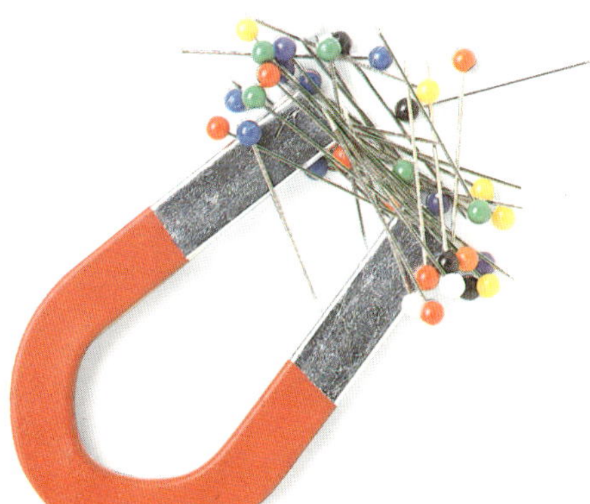

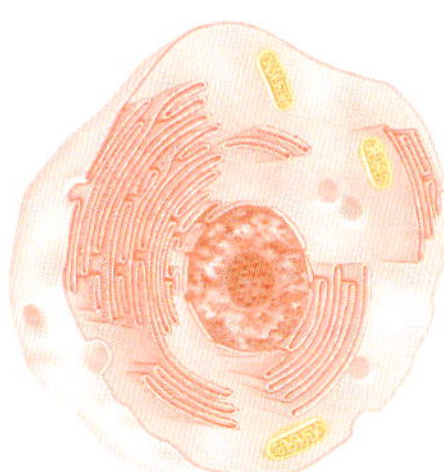

DORLING KINDERSLEY EDUCATION

A DORLING KINDERSLEY BOOK

Senior Editor Susan McKeever **Senior Art Editor** Martyn Foote

Editors
Caroline Beattie, Helen Dowling, Linda Martin,
Mina Patria, Louise Pritchard, Jackie Wilson

Art Editors
Alexandra Brown, Wayne Holder, Marcus James, Rebecca Johns,
Carole Orbell, Tina Robinson, Simon Yeomans, Dominic Zwemmer

Managing Editor Sophie Mitchell **Managing Art Editor** Miranda Kennedy
Picture Research Lorna Ainger, Caroline Brooke, Anne Lyons,
Catherine O'Rourke, Christine Rista
Production Louise Barratt, Ruth Cobb

Editorial consultants
Heather Couper BSc, FRAS, Hon. D. Litt
Nigel Henbest BSc, MSc, FRAS

Contributors
David Burnie BSc; Karen Davies BSc PGCE; Dougal Dixon BSc PhD; David Glover BSc PhD; John Gribbin MSc PhD; Mary Gribbin BA; Ian Harrison BSc PhD MBA; Robin Kerrod FRAS; Peter Lafferty BSc MSc PGCE; Peter Riley BSc C. Biol PGCE; Carole Stott BA FRAS; Barbara Taylor BSc; Keith Wicks

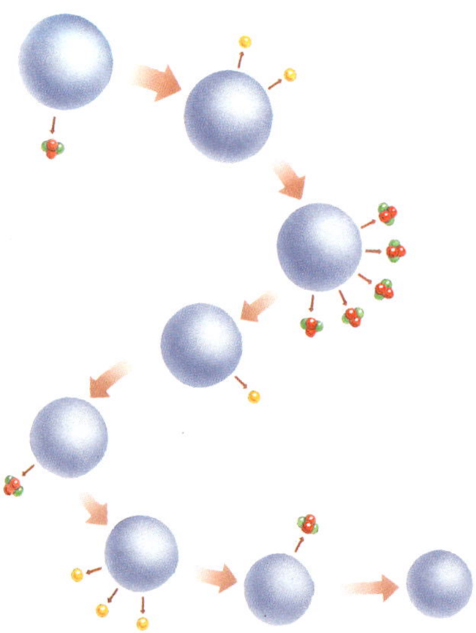

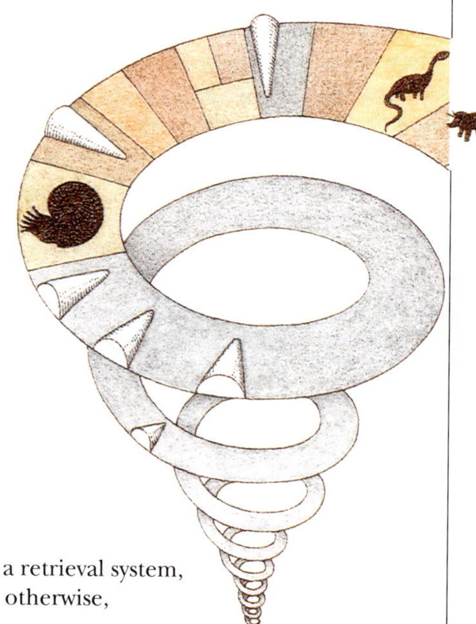

Educational consultants
David Evans BSc, C. Biol, M. I. Biol
Kimi Hosoume BA

History of science consultant
Patricia Fara BSc, MSc

Natural history consultant
Steve Parker BSc

This is a Dorling Kindersley Education edition, 1994
First published in Great Britain in 1993
by Dorling Kindersley Limited
9 Henrietta Street
Covent Garden London WC2E 8PS

A CIP catalogue record for this book is available from the British Library

ISBN 0 7513 5056 7 (trade edition)
ISBN 0 7516 0805 X (school edition)
Colour reproduction by Colourscan, Singapore
Printed and bound in Italy by A. Mondadori Editore, Verona

CONTENTS

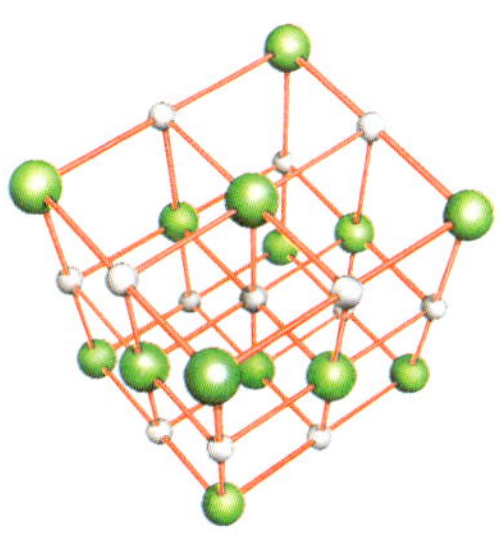

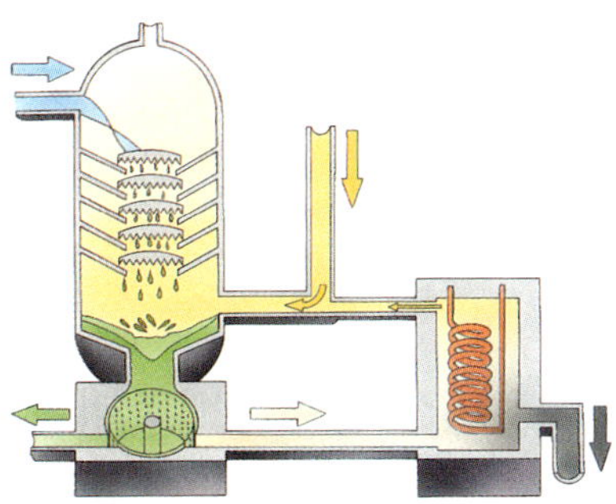

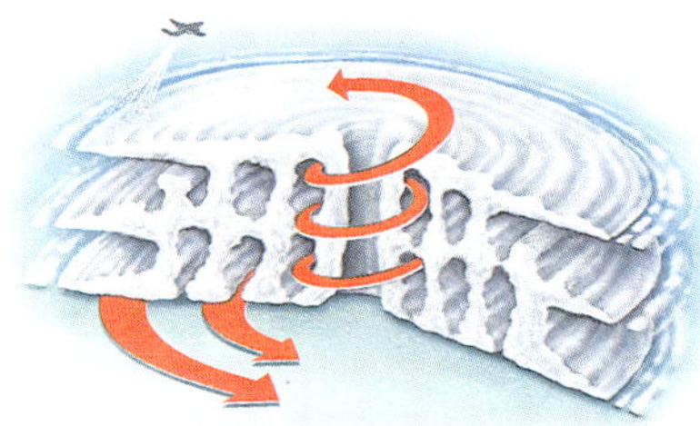

273 SPACE

305 LIVING THINGS

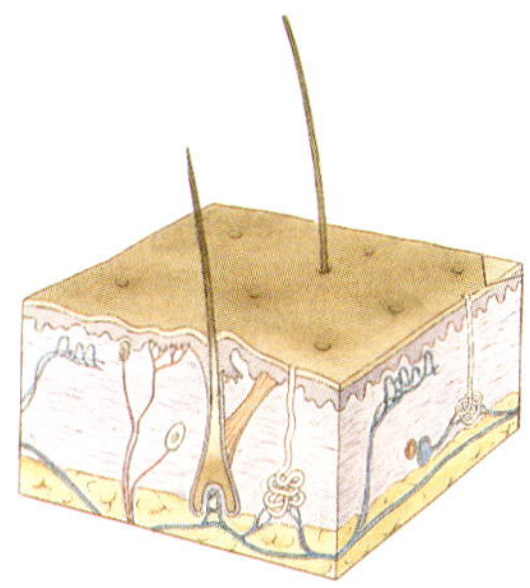

337 HOW LIVING THINGS WORK

369 ECOLOGY

How to use this book

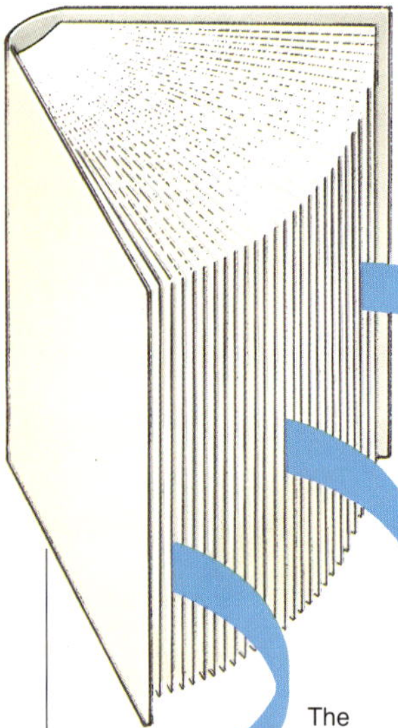

These pages show you how to use *The Dorling Kindersley Science Encyclopedia*. The enyclopedia is divided into 12 thematic sections, such as Reactions and Living Things. Within each section are main entries on the subject, such as the Chemistry of Food or Reptiles. To find an entry, look on the contents pages, where the heading of each page is listed, or turn to the index, which tells you which pages contain information on the subject you are looking up.

The index lists all the subjects in *The Science Encyclopedia*, with the pages they appear on.

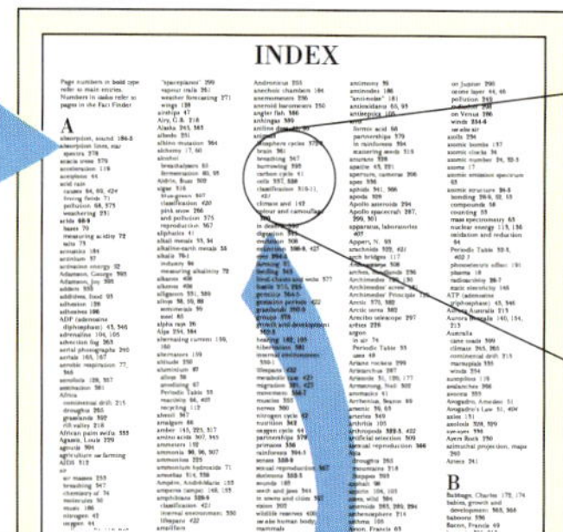

The 12-page index is at the back of *The Science Encyclopedia*. The numbers refer to page numbers.

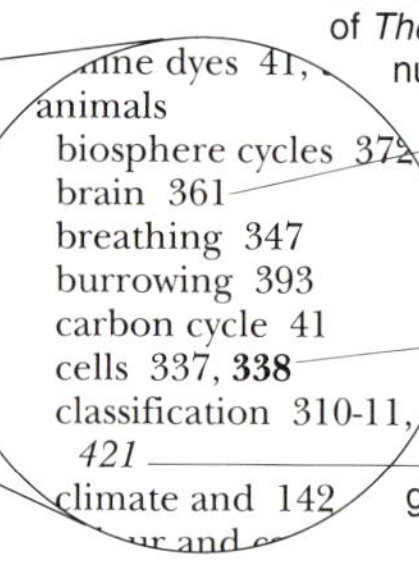

The page number in normal type gives general references within *The Science Encyclopedia*.

The page number in **bold** type gives the main entry.

The page number in *italic* type gives pages in the *Fact finder*.

Each main entry is either one or two pages long.

The contents pages list each page subject under its thematic section head.

SCIENCE THEMES
Information in the encyclopedia is arranged in a thematic way. Each entry gives detailed information on one topic, making it ideal for project work. Reading other pages in the same section enables you to explore and understand the subject fully. This page on Chemical Analysis is from the Reactions section. The words and pictures describe subjects such as Chromatography and Flame Tests in a clear and exciting way.

TIME CHARTS
There are four different time charts at the front of *The Science Encyclopedia*. Each one has a theme: Matter, Energy, Earth and Space, and Living Things. The time charts trace the development of different branches of science, from the earliest times to the present day.

Atomic Structure tells you what atoms are made of.

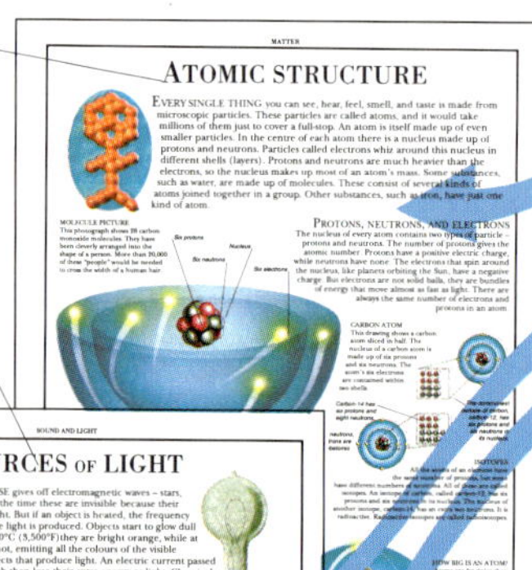

Find out more

Atomic structure p.24
Compounds and mixtures p.58
Separating mixtures p.61
Sources of light p.193
Genetics p.364
Fact finder p.404

Sources of Light explains why atoms give out light when heated – a method of identifying an element.

FIND OUT MORE
There is a *Find out more* box in the bottom right-hand corner of each entry page. This box lists other pages in *The Science Encyclopedia* where you can find out more about your subject. For example, the *Find out more* box on the Chemical Analysis page lists six related entries and their page numbers.

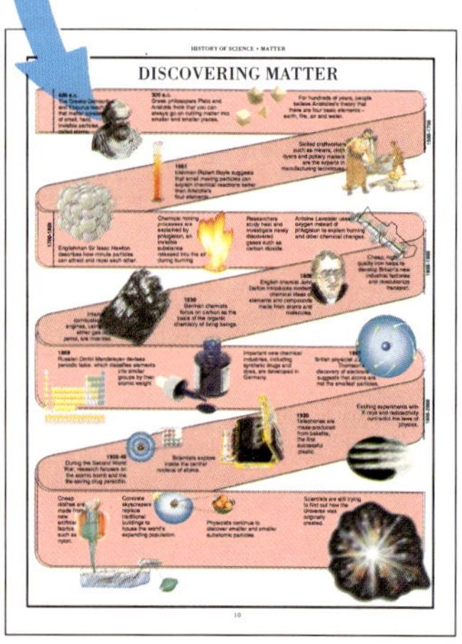

Genetics tells you how a chemical code in DNA makes each being unique.

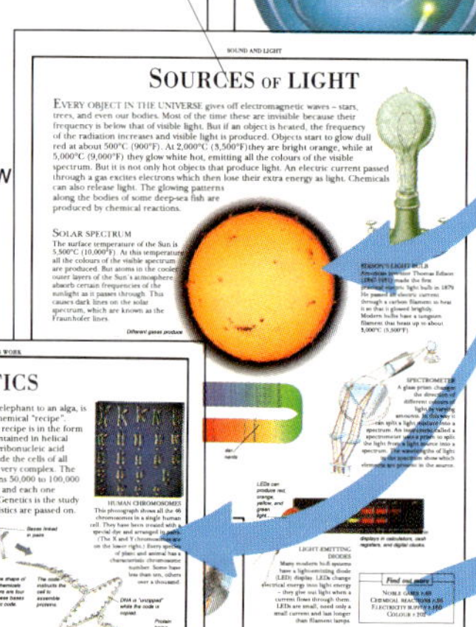

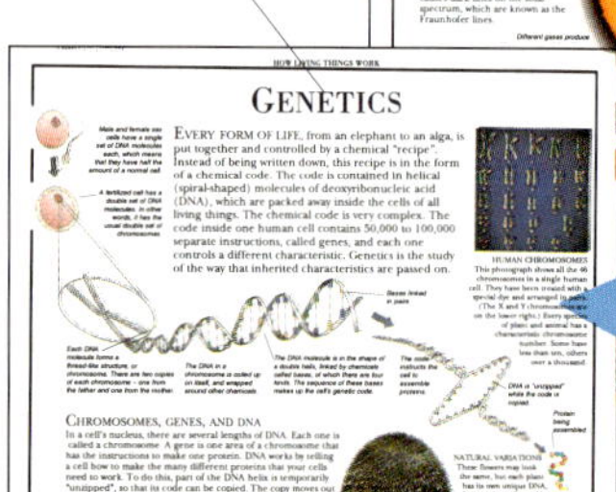

The *Find out more* box on Sources of Light leads you to four related entries: Noble Gases, Chemical Reactions, Electricity Supply, and Colour.

MAIN ENTRIES

The information on each page is presented in a way that makes it easy to understand what is going on. Start reading at the introduction, move on to the sub-entries and then read the captions and annotations.

Introduction
Each main entry starts with an introduction that provides a clear explanation of the subject. After reading this, you should have a good idea of what the page is all about.

Entry heading
This big heading at the top of the page describes a main entry.

Running head
This reminds you which section you are in. This entry on Kinetic Theory is in the Reactions section.

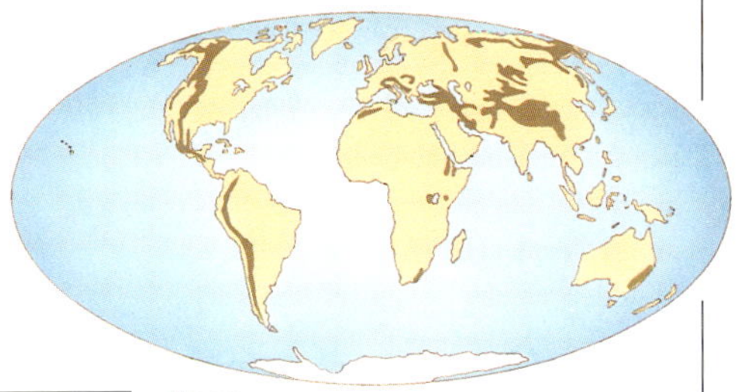

Maps
The maps in *The Science Encyclopedia* give at-a-glance geographical information. For example, this map appears on a page about mountain ecosystems. It shows where the main mountain ranges of the world are.

Sub-entry
A sub-entry is under the second-largest heading on the page. It examines aspects of the main entry in detail. For example, the sub-entries on Kinetic Theory are about diffusion and expansion, both important examples of kinetic theory.

Photographs
All the pages in *The Science Encyclopedia* have photographs. This photograph of bromine diffusion was specially taken in a studio, so that you can see exactly what really happens.

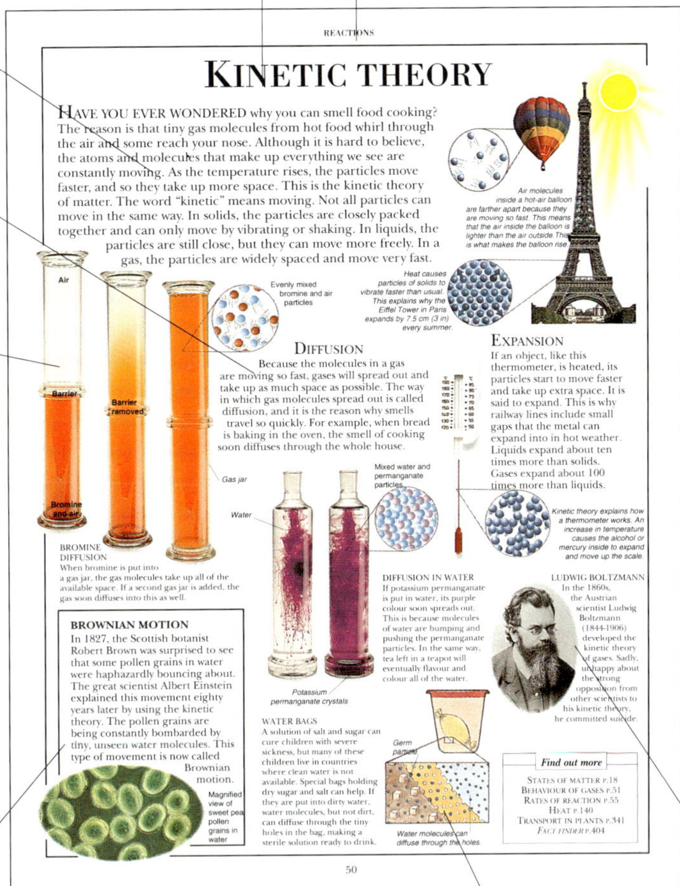

REACTIONS

KINETIC THEORY

HAVE YOU EVER WONDERED why you can smell food cooking? The reason is that tiny gas molecules from hot food whirl through the air and some reach your nose. Although it is hard to believe, the atoms and molecules that make up everything we see are constantly moving. As the temperature rises, the particles move faster, and so they take up more space. This is the kinetic theory of matter. The word "kinetic" means moving. Not all particles can move in the same way. In solids, the particles are closely packed together and can only move by vibrating or shaking. In liquids, the particles are still close, but they can move more freely. In a gas, the particles are widely spaced and move very fast.

Air molecules inside a hot-air balloon are farther apart because they are moving so fast. This means that the air inside the balloon is lighter than the air outside. This is what makes the balloon rise.

Heat causes particles of solids to vibrate faster than usual. This explains why the Eiffel Tower in Paris expands by 7.5 cm (3 in) every summer.

DIFFUSION
Because the molecules in a gas are moving so fast, gases will spread out and take up as much space as possible. The way in which gas molecules spread out is called diffusion, and it is the reason why smells travel so quickly. For example, when bread is baking in the oven, the smell of cooking soon diffuses through the whole house.

EXPANSION
If an object, like this thermometer, is heated, its particles start to move faster and take up extra space. It is said to expand. This is why railway lines include small gaps that the metal can expand into in hot weather. Liquids expand about ten times more than solids. Gases expand about 100 times more than liquids.

Kinetic theory explains how a thermometer works. An increase in temperature causes the alcohol or mercury inside to expand and move up the scale.

BROMINE DIFFUSION
When bromine is put into a gas jar, the gas molecules take up all of the available space. If a second gas jar is added, the gas soon diffuses into this as well.

BROWNIAN MOTION
In 1827, the Scottish botanist Robert Brown was surprised to see that some pollen grains in water were haphazardly bouncing about. The great scientist Albert Einstein explained this movement eighty years later by using the kinetic theory. The pollen grains are being constantly bombarded by tiny, unseen water molecules. This type of movement is now called Brownian motion.

Magnified view of sweet pea pollen grains in water

Potassium permanganate crystals

DIFFUSION IN WATER
If potassium permanganate is put in water, its purple colour soon spreads out. This is because molecules of water are bumping and pushing the permanganate particles. In the same way, tea left in a teapot will eventually flavour and colour all of the water.

LUDWIG BOLTZMANN
In the 1860s, the Austrian scientist Ludwig Boltzmann (1844-1906) developed the kinetic theory of gases. Sadly, unhappy about the strong opposition from other scientists to his kinetic theory, he committed suicide.

WATER BAGS
A solution of salt and sugar can cure children with severe sickness, but many of these children live in countries where clean water is not available. Special bags holding dry sugar and salt can help. If they are put into dirty water, water molecules, but not dirt, can diffuse through the tiny holes in the bag, making a sterile solution ready to drink.

Germ particle

Water molecules can diffuse through the holes.

Find out more
STATES OF MATTER P.18
BEHAVIOUR OF GASES P.51
RATES OF REACTION P.55
HEAT P.140
TRANSPORT IN PLANTS P.341
FACT FINDER P.404

50

Date boxes
Many pages have a date box. These give landmarks of achievement in date order. This date box appears on a page called Optical Instruments. It gives the dates of when the most important telescopes were built.

IMPORTANT TELESCOPES

1789 William Herschel telescope, England, 1.23 m (4 ft) diameter.

1845 Lord Rosse telescope, Ireland, 1.83 m (6 ft) diameter.

1917 Mount Wilson telescope, California, USA, 2.54 m (8 ft) diameter.

1948 Hale Reflector, Palomar, California, USA, 5 m (16 ft) diameter.

1976 Mount Semirodriki telescope, CIS, 6 m (19.5 ft) diameter.

1992 Keck telescope, Hawaii, 10 m (33 ft) diameter.

Cutaway illustrations
Some pages have illustrations that reveal the insides of objects and living things. This illustration of a toadstool shows what it is made up of and how it works.

Special information boxes
On some pages, you will find information boxes, which highlight particular aspects of a main entry. This box tells you about Brownian motion, which can be explained by kinetic theory.

Captions and annotations
Every illustration has a caption. They often have annotations (in *italics*) as well. These point out important details within an illustration or photograph.

Illustrations
Most pages in *The Science Encyclopedia* contain clear, detailed illustrations that help you to understand scientific concepts.

Biographies
Many pages contain biographical details of notable scientists and inventors. Biographies tell you about the life of the scientist or inventor, when they lived, and what they did.

FACT FINDER

The *Fact finder* pages at the back of *The Science Encyclopedia* are packed with useful charts, facts, and figures on all the topics in the encyclopedia. These pages are from the Reactions section.

A chart shows you the reactivity series, and illustrates what happens to different metals when they are mixed with various substances.

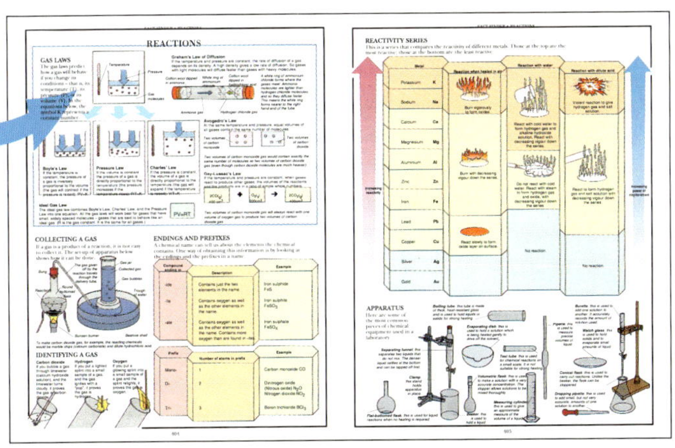

The gas laws are clearly stated and illustrated.

The different laws for identifying gases are explained.

A table shows you what endings and prefixes of chemical names mean.

The chemical equipment you might use in a science laboratory is illustrated and explained.

ABBREVIATIONS

Some words are abbreviated (shortened) in *The Science Encyclopedia*. The following list explains what the abbreviations stand for:

°C = degrees Celsius
°F = degrees Fahrenheit
mm = millimetre
cm = centimetre
m = metre
km = kilometre
sq km = square kilometre
km/h = kilometres per hour
g = gram
kg = kilogram
l = litre
in = inch
ft = foot
yd = yard
mph = miles per hour
oz = ounce
lb = pound
c. before a date = about
B.C. = before Christ
A.D. = anno Domini, after the birth of Christ

DISCOVERING MATTER

400 B.C.
The Greeks Democritus and Epicurus teach that matter consists of small, hard, invisible particles called atoms.

Democritus

For hundreds of years, people believe Aristotles' theory that there are four basic elements – earth, fire, air and water.

Plato considered these solids represented the atoms of the four elements: earth, air, fire, and water.

300 B.C.
Greek philosophers Plato and Aristotle believe that you can always go on cutting matter into smaller and smaller pieces.

1500-1700

Skilled craftworkers such as miners, cloth dyers and pottery makers are the experts in manufacturing techniques.

Gas molecules diffuse (spread out) into the air in a gas jar.

1661
Irishman Robert Boyle suggests that small moving particles can explain chemical reactions better than Aristotle's four elements.

1700-1800

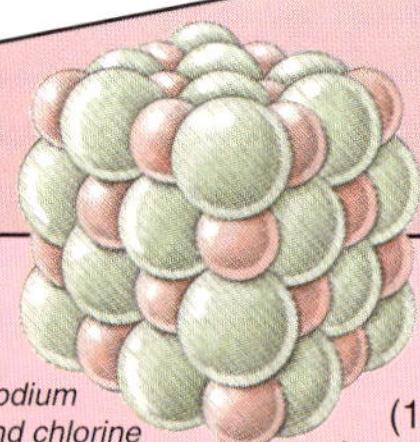

Sodium and chlorine atoms join together to form sodium chloride.

Englishman Sir Isaac Newton (1643-1727) describes how minute particles can attract and repel each other.

Chemical processes are explained by phlogiston, an invisible substance released into the air during burning.

Researchers study heat and investigate newly discovered gases such as carbon dioxide.

Antoine Lavoisier (1743–94) uses oxygen instead of phlogiston to explain burning and other chemical changes.

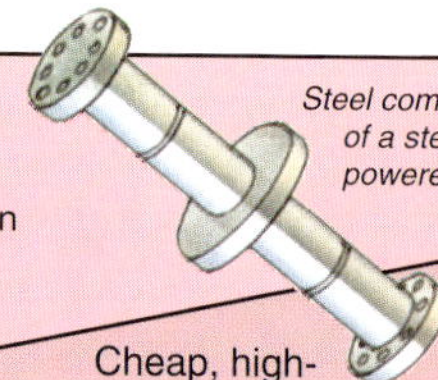

Steel component of a steam-powered ship.

1800-1900

Cheap, high-quality iron is used to make steel.

1808
English chemist John Dalton introduces modern chemical ideas of elements and compounds made from atoms and molecules.

Coal consists mainly of carbon.

1830
German chemists focus on carbon as the basis of the organic chemistry of living beings.

Internal combustion engines, using either gas or petrol, are invented.

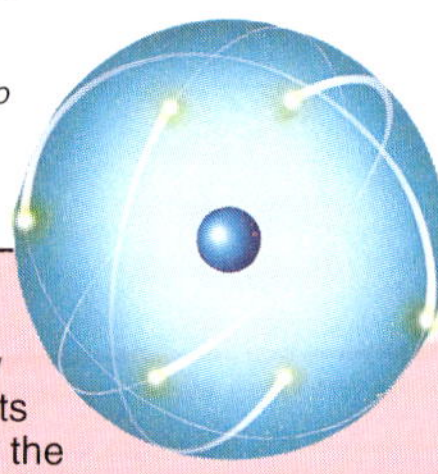

In 1913 atoms shown to contain a small nucleus, surrounded by even smaller electrons.

1869
Russian Dmitri Mendeleyev devises the Periodic Table, which classifies elements into similar groups by their atomic weight.

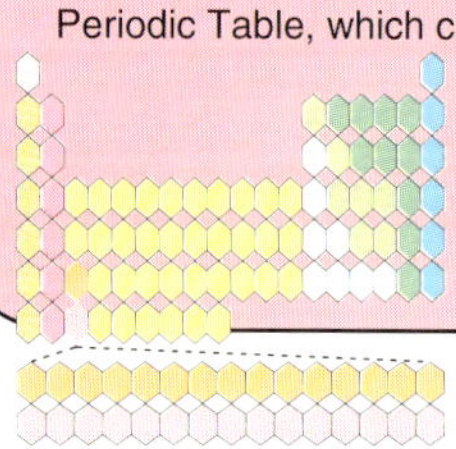

The Periodic Table

Artificial pigments and dyes are added to ink to give it colour.

Important new chemical industries, including synthetic drugs and dyes, are developed in Germany.

1897
British physicist J.J. Thomson's discovery of electrons suggests that atoms are not the smallest particles.

1900-2000

Potentially harmful X-rays are modified to provide beneficial medical information. They enable doctors to see the body beneath the skin.

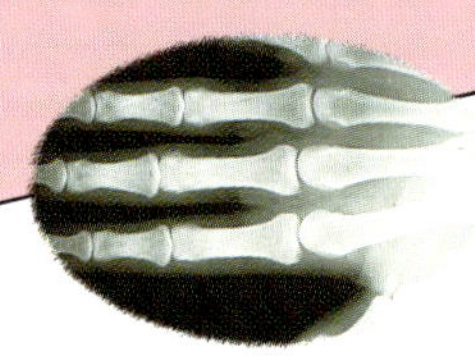

Telephones are mass-produced from Bakelite, a synthetic plastic. The plastic industry begins to grow into one of the world's largest.

Many objects are made from plastic.

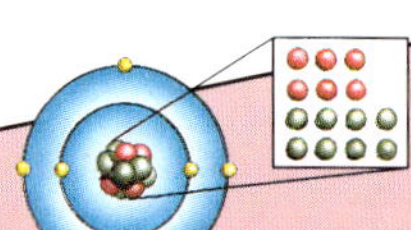

1939-45
During the Second World War, research focuses on the atomic bomb and the life-saving drug penicillin.

Scientists explore inside the central nucleus of atoms. Even smaller particles, protons and neutrons, are discovered.

Cheap clothes are made from new artificial fabrics such as nylon.

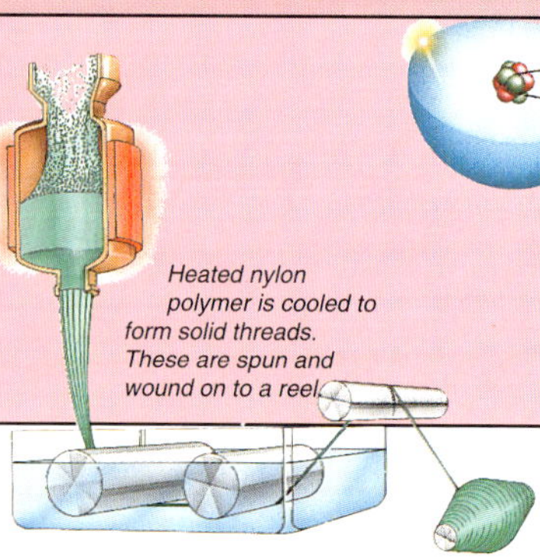

Heated nylon polymer is cooled to form solid threads. These are spun and wound on to a reel.

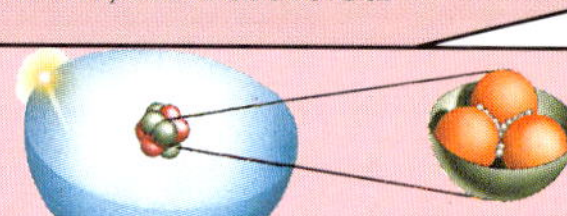

Quarks are discovered inside protons and neutrons.

Physicists continue to discover smaller and smaller subatomic particles called quarks.

Scientists are still trying to find out how the Universe was originally created.

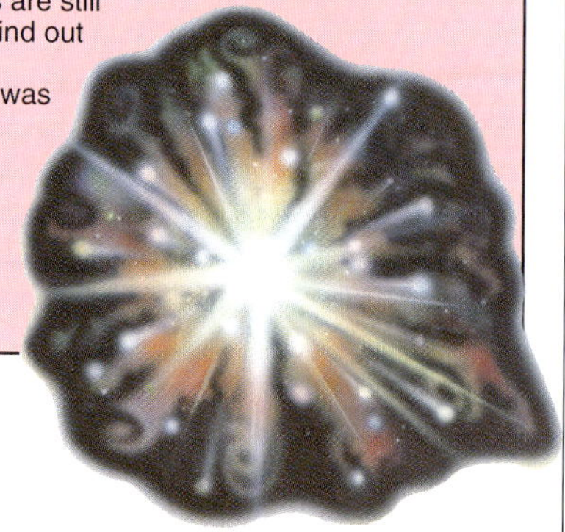

DISCOVERING ENERGY

Early civilizations rely on wind and muscle power for travelling and building, and use wood for heat.

The Greek mathematician Archimedes establishes the principles of mechanics and invents many important devices.

Archimedes' screw

For hundreds of years, ideas are dominated by the work of the Greek philosopher Aristotle.

1500-1700

The Italian physicist and astronomer Galileo insists on using experiments and mathematics for exploring nature.

Apparatus to show Galileo's projectile experiment.

1687
Isaac Newton publishes his theory of gravity, a single mathematical law describing the movement of distant planets as well as objects on Earth.

1700-1800

For many years, argument rages between supporters of Newton's idea that light consists of tiny particles and Dutch physicist Huygen's suggestion that light is made from waves.

1745
The invention of the Leyden jar, which can store static electricity, enables new electrical experiments to be carried out.

1760-70
The earliest steam engines replace horses for pumping water out of tin mines. Steam engines are later developed into locomotives.

1799
In Italy, Alessandro Volta invents the battery, the first source of current electricity.

1800-1900

Using advanced mathematical techniques and delicate experiments, French researchers establish the wave theory of light.

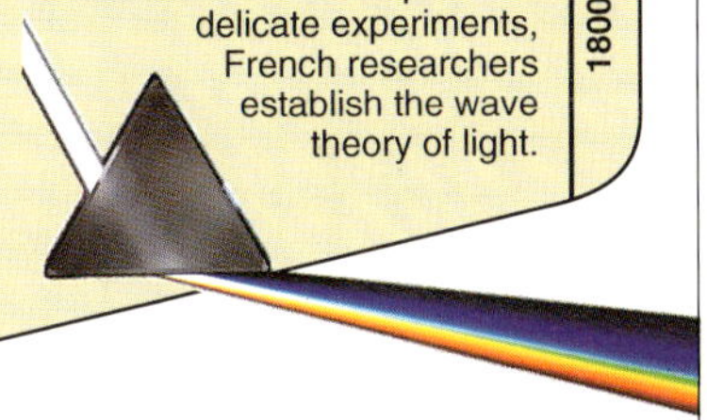

1820-31
English scientist Michael Faraday uses attracting and repelling magnetic forces as a basis for the dynamo, crucial for supplying domestic and industrial electricity.

Steam engines power the new factories and trains, making Britain the world's first industrialized nation.

As machines become more important, physicists and engineers study the relationships between heat, power, and work.

James Joule (1818-89) realizes that work produces heat.

1888
German physicist Heinrich Hertz creates radio waves in his laboratory, a discovery vital for science.

Public gas and electricity networks start to transform industry as well as people's daily lives.

Phonographs and moving films are invented: the entertainment industry is born.

1900-2000

1915
German-born Albert Einstein revolutionizes our views of the Universe by introducing his general relativity theory.

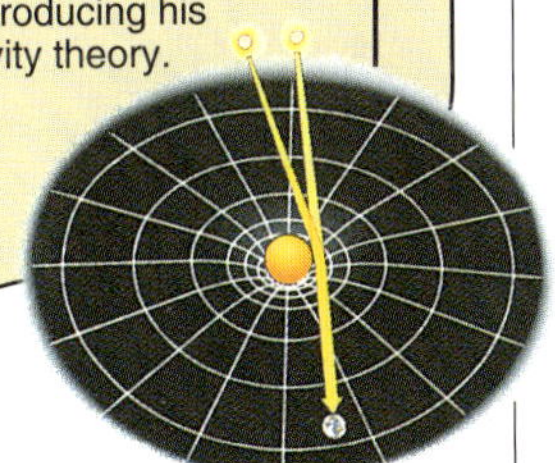

In 1919 Einstein proposes that light is bent by gravity. Light from a star is bent by the Sun.

New theories called quantum mechanics explain that light is a stream of tiny photons that act as waves and particles.

Scientists learn more about radioactivity as they investigate the internal structure of the atomic nucleus.

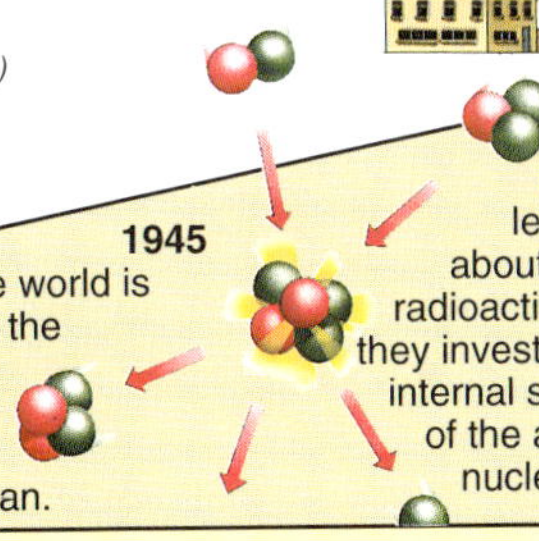

1945
The world is shocked by the destructive power of the atomic bomb as two American bombs fall on Japan.

New electricity generating stations harness nuclear energy for more peaceful purposes.

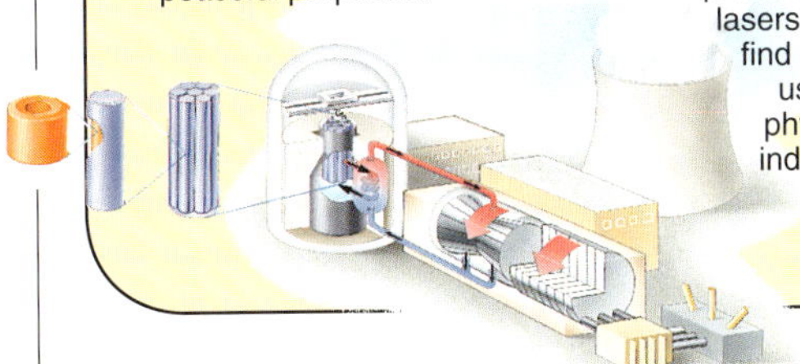

The powerful beams of light produced by lasers soon find many uses in physics, industry, and medicine.

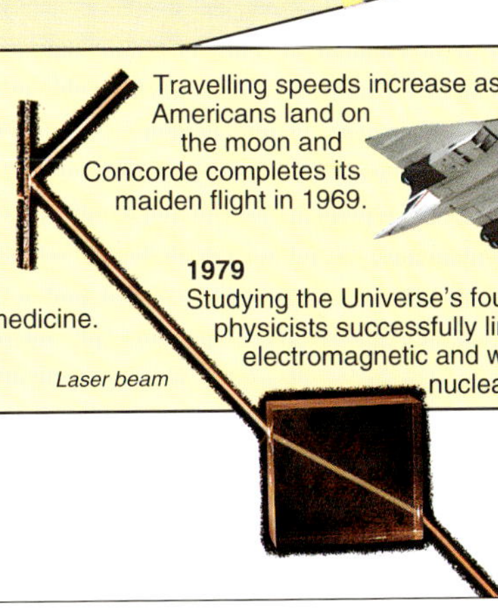

Laser beam

Travelling speeds increase as Americans land on the moon and Concorde completes its maiden flight in 1969.

1979
Studying the Universe's four forces, physicists successfully link the electromagnetic and weak nuclear forces.

Ecologists become increasingly concerned about using safer sources of power which will not damage the environment.

Scientists continue to investigate whether all the galaxies in the Universe are ruled by the same laws of physics.

DISCOVERING EARTH AND SPACE

Early civilizations have differing ideas about the Universe. Hindus believe that the Earth is supported by four elephants on top of a giant turtle.

Most Ancient Greek philosophers believe that the Earth is stationary at the centre of the Universe.

The Ancient Greeks devised elaborate maps of the sky based on their belief of mythological creatures.

1500-1700

1543
The Polish astronomer Copernicus suggests that the behaviour of the heavenly bodies could be better explained if the Earth moved round the Sun.

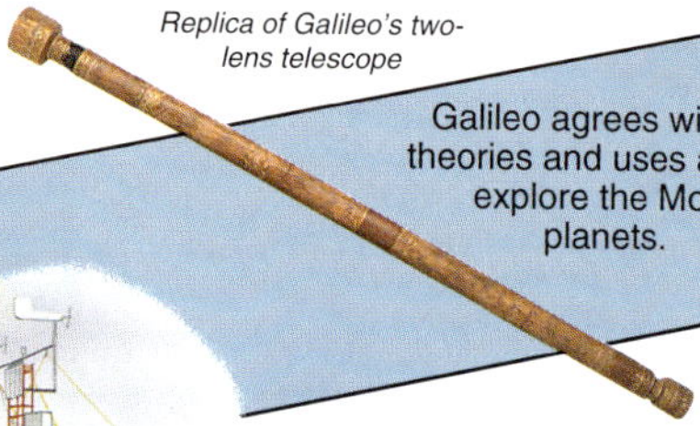

Replica of Galileo's two-lens telescope

Galileo agrees with Copernican theories and uses a telescope to explore the Moon and the planets.

1781
The British astronomer William Herschel maps the stars and discovers a new planet called Uranus.

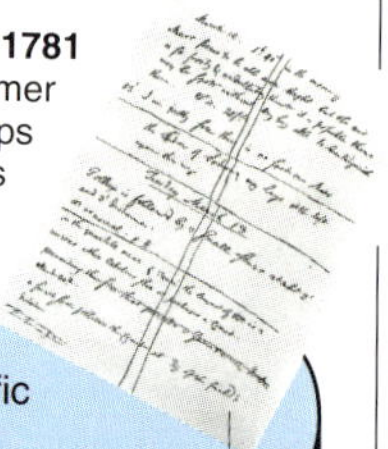

Page from Herschel's diary

1700-1800

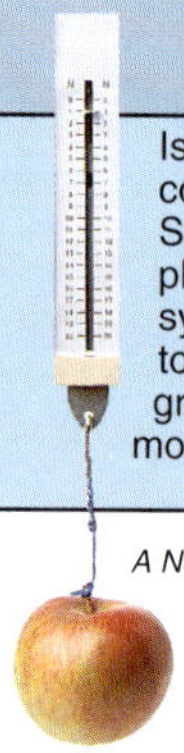

A Newton meter

Isaac Newton's concept of a Sun-centred planetary system held together by gravity becomes more popular.

New and more accurate instruments enable people to record and collect information about the earth's atmosphere. This new science is called meteorology.

H.M.S. Endeavour

As explorers like James Cook undertake long scientific expeditions, maps improve and information is gathered about many plants, animals and societies.

1800-1900

As European powers expand their empires, extensive projects are launched to map and measure the world.

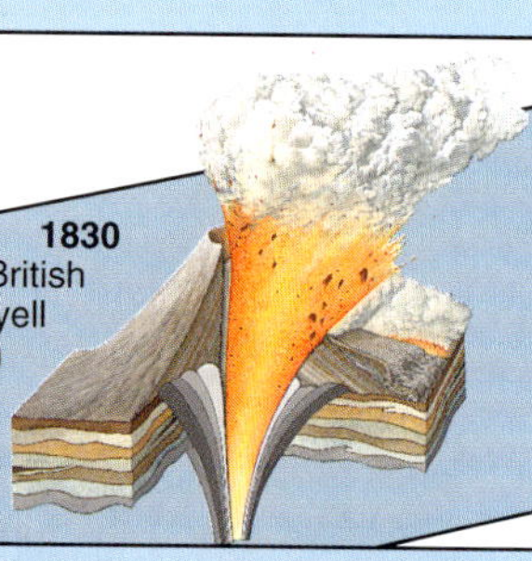

1830
The British geologist Charles Lyell suggests that the Earth has been gradually changing over a long period of time.

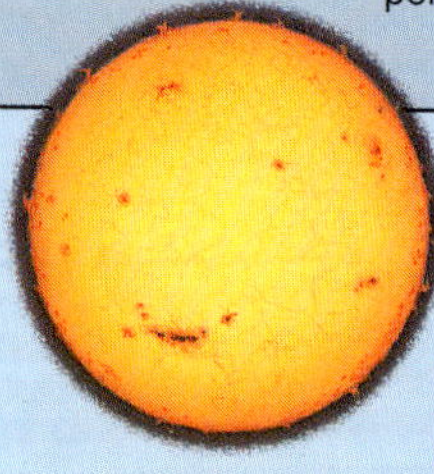

1868
The gas helium, one of the Earth's lightest elements, is first seen in the spectrum of the Sun.

Fraunhofer lines in the Sun's spectrum show which elements are present in the Sun's atmosphere.

1880s
Most scientists believe that light and electricity are transmitted through an invisible medium called the aether surrounding the Earth.

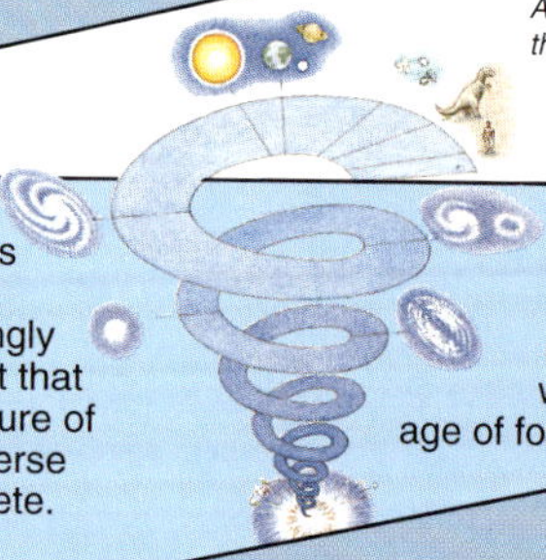

A visual history of the Universe

Scientists become increasingly confident that their picture of the Universe is complete.

1896
The French physicist Henri Becquerel discovers radioactivity, which can measure the age of fossils.

1900-2000

1908
An enormous new telescope is built at Mount Wilson Observatory in California, United States.

Radiotelescopes enable the distant Universe to be surveyed. Scientists discuss theories about its creation.

Pluto with its moon, Charon.

1935
Knowledge of the Universe continues to grow, as Pluto is discovered and other galaxies are studied.

Although ridiculed, the German geophysicist Alfred Wegener keeps finding evidence to support his novel ideas of continental drift.

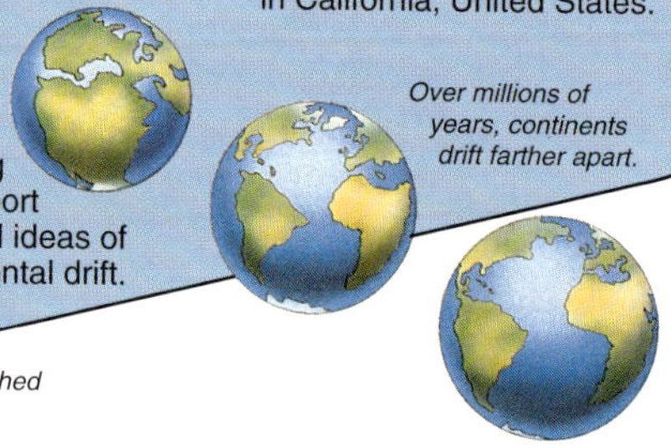

Over millions of years, continents drift farther apart.

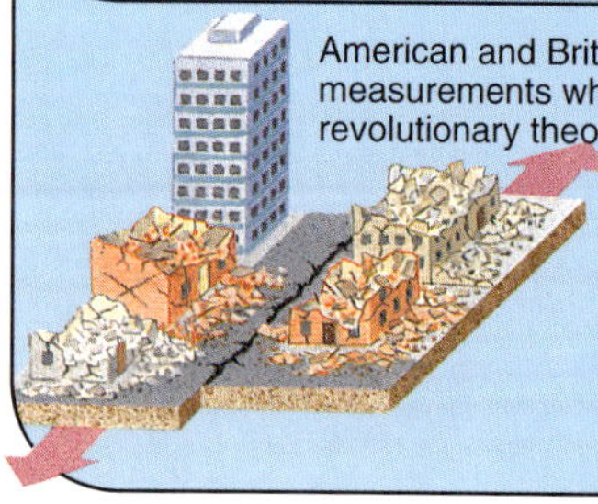

American and British scientists take measurements which confirm the revolutionary theories of continental drift and plate tectonics.

The Russians and the Americans launch manned spacecraft to explore the Moon and send probes far out into space.

An Apollo lunar module departing from the surface of the Moon in1969.

Satellite launched far into space

Weather forecasting becomes far more accurate with the assistance of powerful computers and satellites orbiting round the Earth.

Scientists develop complex theories that describe the creation of the Universe in a single event called the Big Bang.

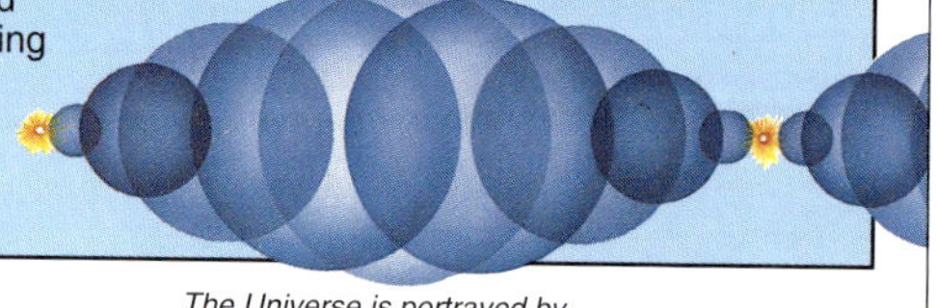

The Universe is portrayed by scientists as a huge "bubble", expanding from a small point, where the Big Bang occurred.

DISCOVERING LIVING THINGS

1500–1700

Early Egyptian civilizations believe that gods linked with plants and animals can influence their lives.

The Ancient Egyptian Goddess Bastet – a cat.

The Greek philosopher Aristotle teaches the importance of carefully studying and classifying animals.

Early chemists known as "alchemists" attempt to turn ordinary substances into gold. Experiments with medical cures are also carried out.

A 14th century manuscript showing an alchemist at work

The Italian Andreas Vesalius (1514-64) dissects dead bodies to find out how human anatomy works.

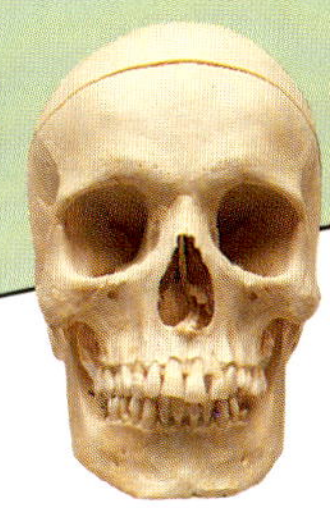

1628
In England, William Harvey describes how the heart continually pumps blood around the body.

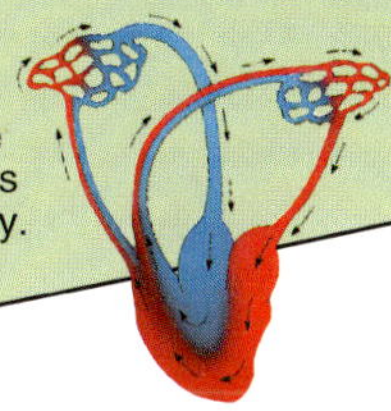

1700–1800

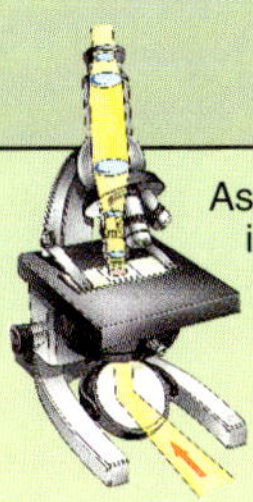

As instruments improve, the microscopic structure of a wide variety of plants and animals is examined in finer detail.

Chart showing how the Roman snail (Helix pomatia) is classified.

1749
The Swedish botanist Carl Linnaeus invents his influential system for classifying plants and animals using two Latin names.

The French naturalist Georges-Louis Buffon (1707-88) suggests that living things might have been slowly changing since the Earth was created.

1800–1900

The existence of new fossils allows Georges Cuvier to prove that species can become extinct and be created.

Jean Lamarck's theory that animals pass on environmental adaptations to their offspring is influential well into the 20th century.

Foxes living in the same habitats in different parts of the world often look similar because they have adapted to survive in the same kind of ecosystem.

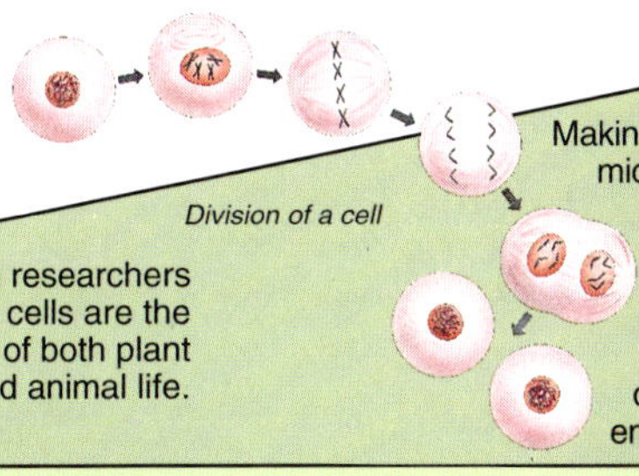

Division of a cell

Making detailed microscopic examinations, German biologists put forward new theories about the development of embryos.

German researchers show that cells are the basic unit of both plant and animal life.

1859
The English naturalist Charles Darwin publishes the massive *Origin of Species* to support his theory of evolution.

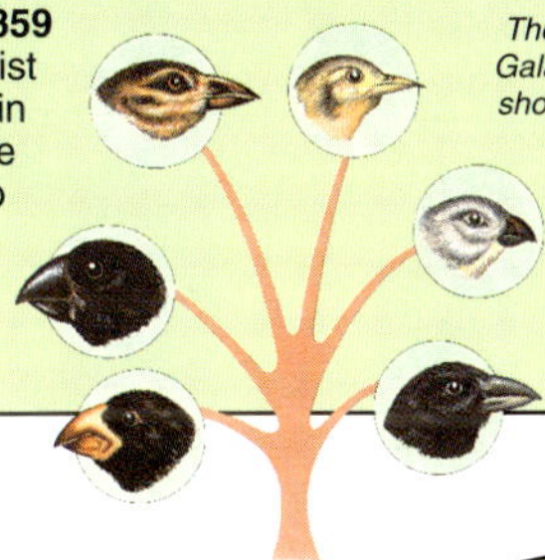

The finches of the Galapagos Islands show distinct beak variations brought about by particular environments.

From his careful experiments, the French chemist Louis Pasteur shows that fermentation is due to micro-organisms.

Important fossil discoveries, including that of the dinosaurs, are made during the 1800s. The fossil bird *Archaeopteryx* shows that birds may have evolved from reptiles.

Archaeopteryx

1900–2000

Modern genetic theory begins with the rediscovery of Gregor Mendel's (1822-84) forgotten work on heredity in peas.

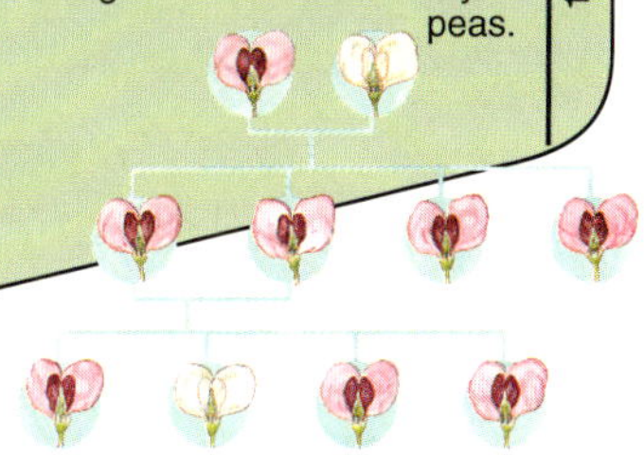

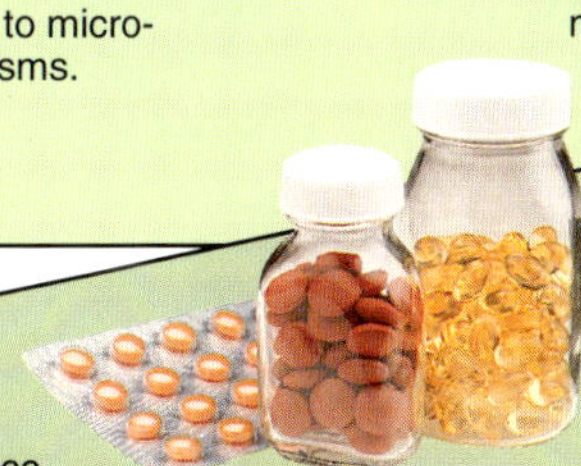

Biochemists demonstrate the vital importance for health of minute quantities of chemicals like vitamins and hormones.

1940s
Health care is improved dramatically with the mass-production of antibiotics.

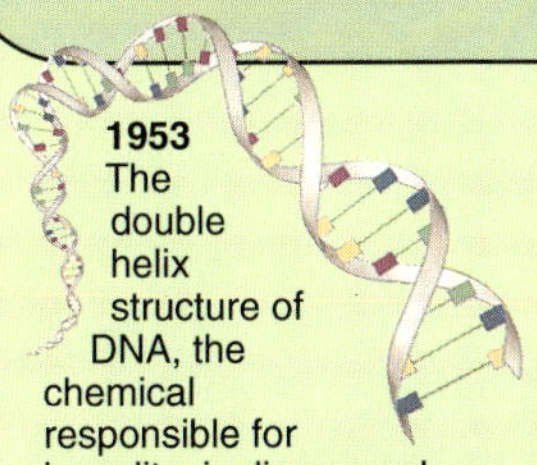

1953
The double helix structure of DNA, the chemical responsible for heredity, is discovered. This revolutionizes biology.

The new science of molecular biology grows as scientists explore the nature of genes and reproduction.

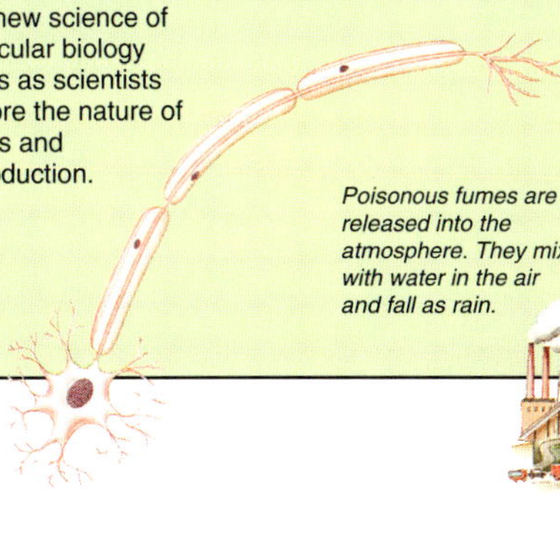

Poisonous fumes are released into the atmosphere. They mix with water in the air and fall as rain.

1980s
Ecologists realise that the pollution from one country can cause acid rain in another destroying vast areas of natural vegetation.

1990s
Controversial new techniques of genetic engineering enable scientists to "design" disease-free animals, therefore providing a larger yield of meat.

How scientists work

Men and women leading very different lives and interested in a range of different topics describe themselves as scientists. The hospital technician examining blood samples, the mathematician thinking about the origins of the Universe, the botanist collecting rare plant specimens, and the chemist developing a new type of food flavouring are all scientists who share a belief in studying the world to discover how it works and to find ways to improve our lives.

What is a scientist?

Modern scientists are professional men and women who earn their living by investigating the Universe around us and inventing new ways of using its resources. A few scientists become famous by making spectacular discoveries, but millions more make important contributions to scientific knowledge by their careful and patient work.

Louis Pasteur (1822–95), who discovered a vaccine for rabies.

The research team

Modern scientific experiments are so complex that people often work in teams. Each team member contributes his or her own particular knowledge and skills. Some scientists organize the team and their apparatus.

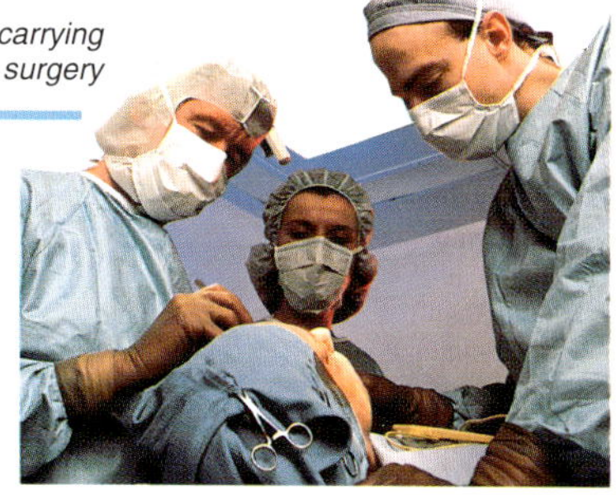

Surgeons carrying out plastic surgery

THE REWARDS OF SCIENCE

Scientists value their work because it is personally satisfying, and because scientific advances can benefit society.

Nuclear bomb test in the Nevada Desert, U.S.A.

POSITIVE AND NEGATIVE

Our modern world depends on telephones, electricity, cars, and countless other scientific discoveries and inventions. Millions of lives have been saved by drugs such as penicillin and the smallpox vaccine. But some people hold science responsible for worldwide disasters like the atomic bomb, pollution, and the thinning of the ozone layer.

Nuclear plant in Sellafield, England

PERSONAL REWARDS

Many people choose science as a career because it offers them an exciting challenge. Making an outstanding scientific discovery can bring international fame, wealth, and important awards like the Nobel Prize.

Alfred Nobel (1833–96)

RESPONSIBILITY

Politicians, economists, scientists, and other social planners must jointly decide whether experiments such as setting up reactions in a nuclear reactor, or trying to correct a baby's inherited defects are going to harm or benefit society.

WORKING ENVIRONMENTS

We usually picture scientists working in a laboratory, but many scientific studies need to be conducted outside. Ecology (the study of plants and animals in their habitat), meteorology (the study of the weather), and horticulture (the study of crop-growing) are all areas of science that require experimental work outside.

This scientist is calculating the photosynthetic rate in an oilseed rape field.

SCIENTIFIC EQUIPMENT

Helium-filled balloons like this carry instruments into the air to collect data on temperature, pressure, and wind speed at different heights.

Scientist working on experiments in genetic engineering.

COMPUTERS

Scientific experiments often use computers to work out lengthy mathematical calculations quickly and accurately. They are also able to store and organize vast collections of data.

Scientific experiments

Experiments are central to the success of science. By trying out what happens when they slightly alter the natural world, scientists can collect information that gives them ideas about how the world works. They can test and compare different theories to see which one is the most useful for describing the world's behaviour, and can develop effective new equipment, chemicals, and techniques.

OBSERVATION

Some important discoveries – such as the invention of electric batteries which originated in 18th-century experiments on frogs – are the result of scientists observing an unusual event and appreciating its significance.

Alessandro Volta with his early battery, 1799.

The bending of light from a star by the Sun.

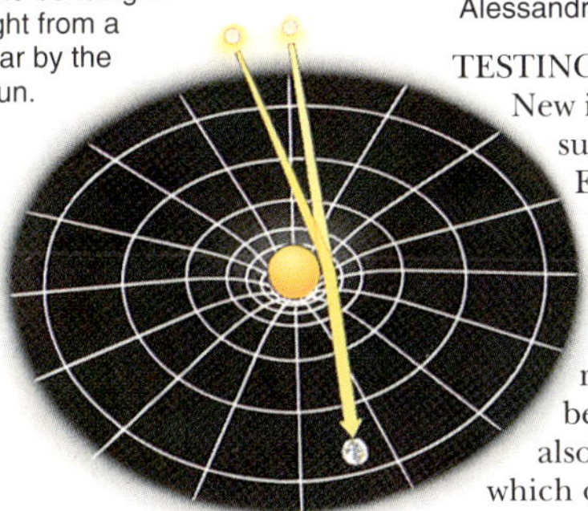

TESTING

New ideas must be tested to make sure that they work. Albert Einstein's relativity theory was tested during an eclipse of the Sun to see if the light from a distant star was curved – it was. Louis Pasteur tested his new rabies vaccine on a boy who had been bitten by a dog. Scientists also design experiments to show which of two competing theories is better at explaining the world.

COLLECTING INFORMATION

Working like detectives, scientists must carefully gather together and share detailed information on everything in the world around them. Scientific theories are based on interpreting and explaining this enormous collection of data. Computerized systems have helped to make the gathering of information and its analysis more efficient.

EXPLORATION

Whether they are investigating the effects of a new drug, the internal structure of an atom, the life of a dolphin, or the nature of the Sun, scientists use experiments to explore the nature of the world.

DEMONSTRATION

Experiments can be useful for convincing other people about a scientific theory. In a dangerous and dramatic experiment designed to demonstrate that lightning discharges are a form of electricity, Benjamin Franklin (1706–1790) flew a kite during a thunderstorm to draw electricity down from the sky.

Sparks jumped when lightning flowed along the kite string to which Franklin had attached a key.

SCIENTIFIC TECHNIQUES

All scientific work is carried out systematically and methodically. Scientists have developed various ways of dealing with different types of information.

Charles Darwin divided finches he saw on the Galapagos Islands into different species.

CLASSIFICATION

Scientists classify objects to give nature some kind of order. Plants and animals are grouped into families. In the chemical world, the periodic table puts the elements into groups to show the relationships between them.

MEASUREMENT

Accurate measurement is crucial for modern science and engineering. Scientists must find ways of measuring enormous distances, such as those between stars, as carefully as measuring the size of tiny biological cells, and the tiny dimensions of atoms and molecules.

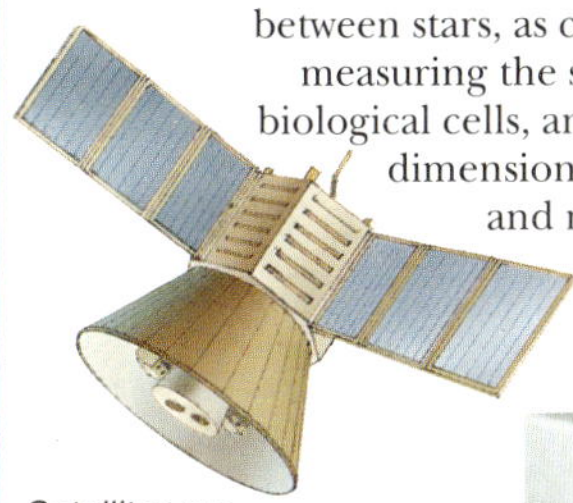

Satellites are sophisticated robots that are sent into space.

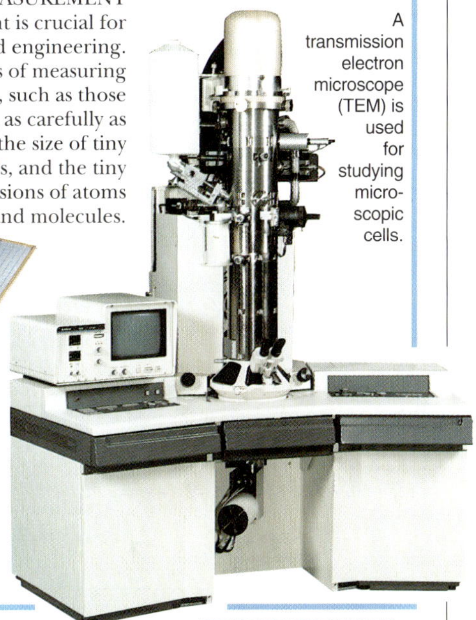

A transmission electron microscope (TEM) is used for studying microscopic cells.

EQUIPMENT

Sophisticated apparatus enables scientists to peer into tiny atoms, distant galaxies, and the hidden secrets of living nature.

MODELS AND THEORIES

Just as globes are used as miniature models of the Earth, scientists develop theories, construct laws of nature, and build mathematical models to describe how the Universe works.

THEORIES

Scientists aim to produce theories which will not only successfully describe the information they have collected, but which will also explain how different events are related to each other, and that can predict the results of future experiments.

MATHEMATICAL MODELS

Isaac Newton's famous law of gravity is a mathematical model describing how the Universe is held together.

Isaac Newton (1643–1727)

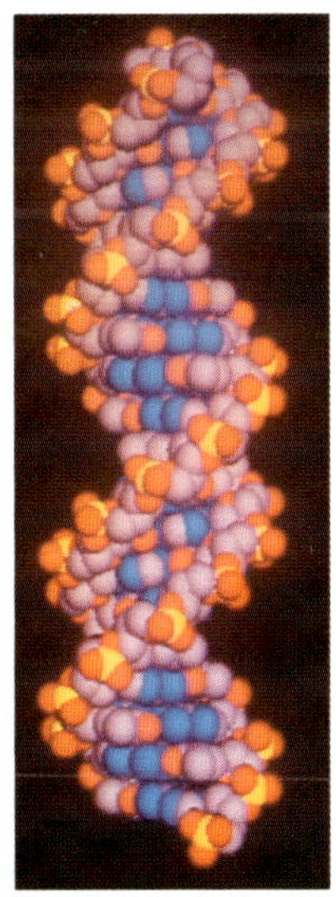

Molecular computer graphic of DNA model showing the double helix structure.

PHYSICAL MODELS

The double helix is a physical model of DNA. It shows the structure of the chemical that lies at the heart of heredity.

Safety codes

We all come across dangerous and poisonous substances in our everyday lives, but they are not always obvious. To help us identify them, safety codes – a combination of pictures and words – are used as warning symbols. It is essential for your health and safety that you follow these.

In the home

Many cleaning materials used in the home have safety codes printed on them to show that they are poisonous if swallowed, breathed in, or allowed to stay on the skin. You should always wash your hands after using chemicals. Sometimes protective clothing is necessary.

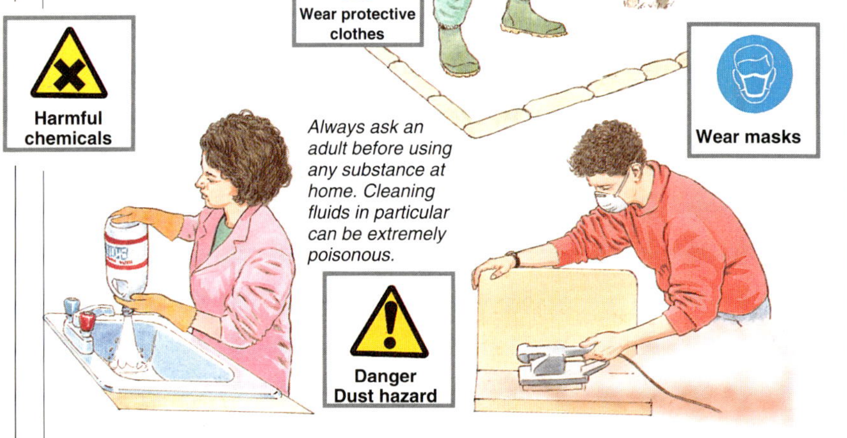

Always ask an adult before using any substance at home. Cleaning fluids in particular can be extremely poisonous.

In the school laboratory

Care must be taken when conducting experiments in the school laboratory. Some laboratory chemicals are toxic. Heating others over a Bunsen burner can be dangerous if the correct procedures are not carried out. Many substances have very strong smells, and can cause unpleasant symptoms if inhaled.

Always wear protective glasses, tie back long hair and be careful of loose clothes.

In the street

Look out for safety codes when you are out walking in the street. In particular, building sites and petrol stations can be very dangerous. Safety codes help you to avoid accidents.

It is against the law for pedestrians to cross some roads such as motorways as traffic speeds are high.

MATTER

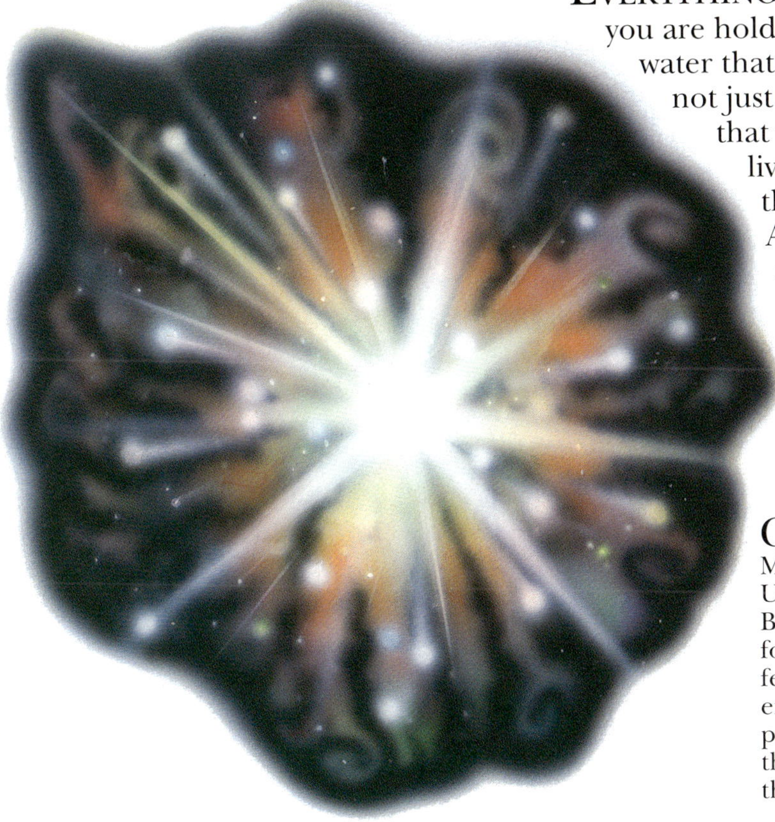

EVERYTHING YOU CAN THINK of, from the book that you are holding, to the chair that you are sitting on, to the water that you drink, is made up of matter. But matter is not just things that you can touch. It includes the air that you breathe. The planets in the Universe, living things such as insects, and non-living things such as rocks are also made of matter. All matter is made of tiny particles called atoms, which are themselves made up of even smaller particles, called subatomic particles. Chemistry involves studying what matter is made of, and how atoms join together to make different things.

CREATION OF MATTER

Most scientists believe that all the matter in the Universe was created in an explosion called the Big Bang (left). Great heat and energy followed the explosion. Then, after just a few seconds, some bundles of the energy turned into tiny particles. The particles turned into the atoms that make up the Universe that we live in today.

ORIGINS OF CHEMISTRY

Hundreds of years ago, before anyone knew about atoms, people called alchemists tried to find out what things were made of. They tried to turn metals such as lead into gold. They also searched for a medicine that would give eternal life. They tried without success. Many alchemists were women. One name for alchemy, *opus mulierum*, is Latin for women's work.

This page is from a 14th-century Arab manuscript.

These pictures show alchemists at work.

NON-LIVING MATTER

Most matter in the Universe is non-living. This means that it does not grow, reproduce, or move itself about. A good example of non-living matter is the rock that makes up the Earth that we live on.

LIVING MATTER

The Earth is home to many living things, including plants and animals of all kinds. Although a butterfly seems very different from a rock, they are both made out of atoms. The atoms just join up in a different way to create something else.

FOUNDERS OF CHEMISTRY

The French chemist Antoine Lavoisier (1743-94) is thought of as the founder of chemistry. Antoine showed that burned substances are heavier than unburned substances. He concluded that this was because the burned substances gained a gas, oxygen. Marie Lavoisier (1758-1836) worked with her husband by translating scientific works and campaigning for acceptance of their ideas.

PARTICLES OF MATTER

Scientists use a bubble chamber to identify subatomic particles. The bubble chamber contains liquid hydrogen near its boiling point. Subatomic particles travelling through the liquid cause it to boil, leaving trails of bubbles. Although the particles are invisible, the trails that they leave can be seen, and are different for each type of particle.

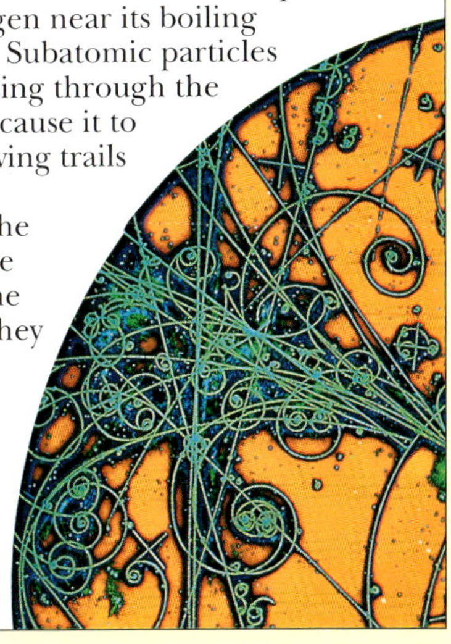

STATES OF MATTER

IMAGINE A MOUNTAIN, a lake, and the air around them. These three things represent the three states in which matter occurs. Mountains are made of rock, which is solid. A lake is made of water, which is liquid. And the air that we breathe is made of gas. Solids have a definite volume and shape, but some, such as rubber, have a shape that can be changed. Most solids are hard. Liquids have a fixed volume but no definite shape, and they can flow. Gases have no definite volume or shape, and they can also flow. And you can't see most gases. Because they can flow, liquids and gases are called fluids. The three states of matter behave the way they do because the particles that make them up move in different ways.

THREE STATES
This picture of hot springs, at Waiotapu in New Zealand, shows the three states of matter, all together in one place. The rock is a solid, the water is a liquid, and the rising vapour is a gas.

LIQUID

Next time you have a drink, notice what is happening inside your glass. The liquid takes on the shape of the glass. But if you spill it, the shape of the liquid changes. If you pour the liquid into a different container, the shape of the liquid changes, but the volume remains the same.

SOLID

A solid, such as a book, has a definite shape that is not easy to change. This is because the particles of a solid are linked to one another by strong bonds into a firm structure.

GAS

A gas quickly fills any space it is put in because its particles move fast. This means that a gas has no shape or volume of its own, but takes the shape of its container. For example, this balloon is filled up with the gas helium. Objects can pass through a gas easily because its particles are far apart. We can walk through air and not feel a thing.

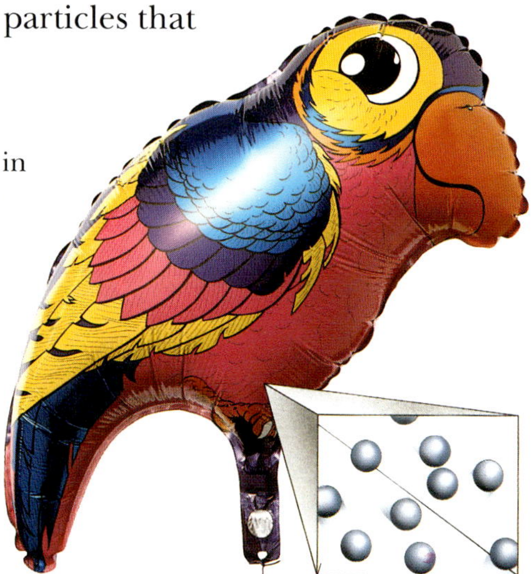

Particles in gases are far apart and move at high speed. They have little effect on one another.

Particles in liquids attract each other and stick together in bundles. These slide past each other and move about.

Particles in solids are tightly packed together. They attract one another so strongly that they cannot move about: they only vibrate.

PLASMA

There is a fourth state of matter, called plasma, but it is not often seen. It only exists at very high temperatures inside the Sun and other stars, or on Earth at low pressures. It consists of atoms split up by great heat or electricity. This ball contains a central electrode surrounded by plasma. If you touch the surface, flashes will jump to your hand from the centre. The flashes travel up paths in the plasma created by the split atoms.

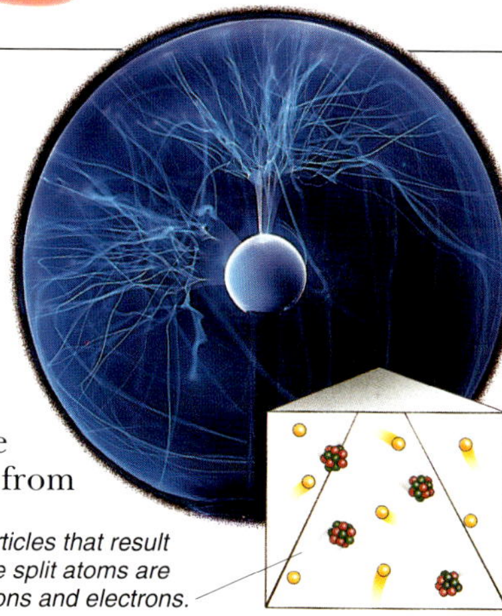

The particles that result from the split atoms are called ions and electrons.

Using states of matter

Solids, liquids, and gases are all around you and are used in many ways. If you have a bicycle, you can see the three states of matter working together in harmony. Many parts of the bicycle are made of solids. Even the rubber of the tyres is a solid, although it is flexible, and will change shape if you go over a bump. The tyres are filled with air. And the oil on your bicycle chain is a liquid.

SOLIDS IN USE

A bicycle frame is solid, as are the rim and the spokes of the wheels. The frame has to be solid to keep the bicycle together. And the steel rim and spokes on the wheels ensure that they keep their round shape, which is important if you want to cycle properly.

LIQUIDS IN USE

All liquids can flow, and some can flow more easily than others. A liquid's viscosity is a measure of how fast or slowly it flows. Water flows easily because it has low viscosity. Oils flow more slowly, and have higher viscosity. A viscous liquid such as an oil is used between metal parts to stop them rubbing against each other. This is called lubrication.

You can reduce the volume of a gas by squeezing it into a smaller space. Or you can squeeze more and more gas into the same space. This is what happens when you pump up a bicycle tyre.

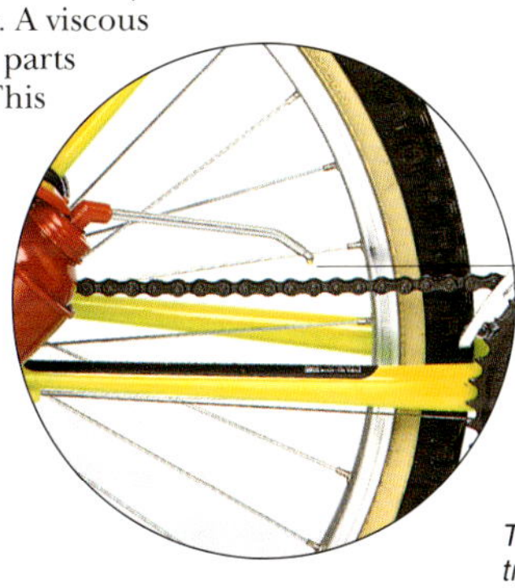

Oil on a bicycle chain keeps all the parts moving easily and prevents them from wearing down.

GASES IN USE

Unlike solids and liquids, gases do not have a fixed volume. This means that you can compress them, or reduce their volume. Gases are compressible because there is plenty of space between gas particles. When you cycle over a bump, the air in your tyre is compressed. So it absorbs the shock of the bump instead of passing it through the bicycle.

Pondskaters are so light that the surface tension of water holds their weight. Their feet just cause little dents on the surface.

SURFACE TENSION

Particles in water attract each other – they pull towards each other equally in all directions. But particles on the surface can only be pulled into the water by particles underneath – there are no particles to pull in the opposite direction. This tension creates a stretchy skin around water that is strong enough to support the weight of tiny insects.

The piston transmits the pressure from the brake pedal.

Brake pads are forced against the wheel by liquid pressure.

Pressure is applied to the brake pedal.

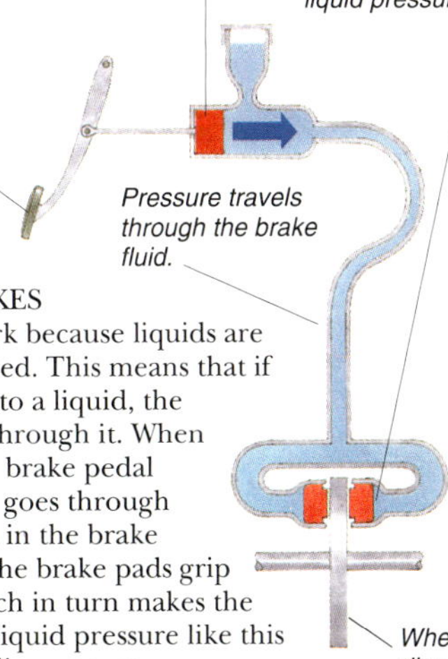

Pressure travels through the brake fluid.

Wheel disc

HYDRAULIC BRAKES

Car foot-brakes work because liquids are not easily compressed. This means that if you apply pressure to a liquid, the force will go right through it. When a driver presses the brake pedal down, the pressure goes through the piston to liquid in the brake pipes. This makes the brake pads grip the wheel disc, which in turn makes the wheels stand still. Liquid pressure like this is known as hydraulic pressure.

Find out more

Changes of state p.20
Properties of matter p.22
Bonding p.28
Kinetic theory p.50
Behaviour of gases p.51
Forces in fluids p.128
Sun p.284

CHANGES OF STATE

IF YOU TRIED TO STIR hot cooking oil with a plastic spoon, the plastic would melt. Plastic is solid. This means that it will remain solid at temperatures and pressures normally found on Earth. But change the circumstances, and you can change the normal state of a substance. In the same way, if you put orange juice, normally a liquid, into a freezer, it will go solid. And if you breathe onto a cold windowpane, the water vapour in your breath (normally a gas) will condense into drops of liquid. If the Sun shines on them, the heat turns them back into a gas and they evaporate into the air again. Even the hardest rocks melt at the very high temperatures and pressures found underneath the Earth's crust. Most substances that we know will change state when the temperature or the pressure changes enough.

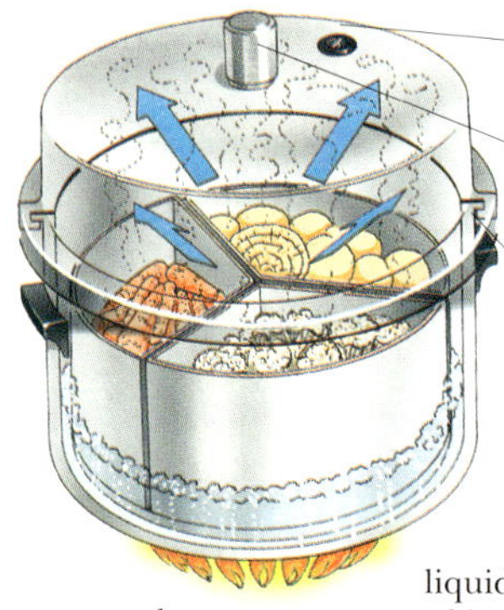

PRESSURE COOKING
The temperature at which a liquid boils (boiling point) depends on the pressure around it. When the pressure goes down, the boiling point goes down, because the molecules can escape as a gas more easily. When the pressure goes up, the boiling point goes up, because it is more difficult for the molecules to escape. In pressure cookers, the increased pressure raises the water's boiling point. At the higher temperature, the food cooks more quickly.

FROM SOLID TO GAS

If you heat a solid to a special temperature called the melting point, it will melt into liquid. If you heat it even more, it gets to a point when the liquid changes into a gas. This is the boiling point. At the boiling point, all the particles in a liquid get enough energy from the heat to break free from each other. Then bubbles of gas form in the liquid. Liquids are always slowly changing to gas, even below boiling point. This is called evaporation.

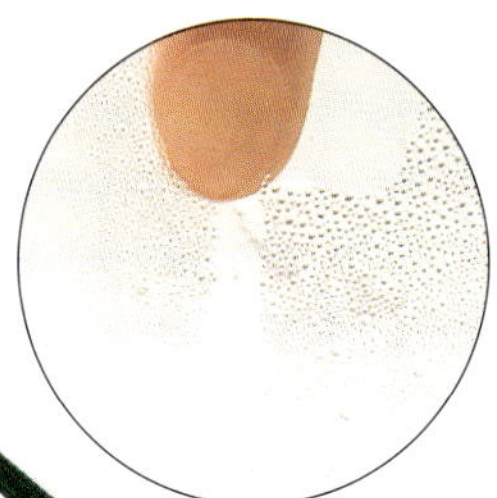

CONDENSATION
Cold glasses get little droplets of water on them because water vapour from the air turns back into water on the cold glass. Cold glass removes energy from particles and so turns them into liquid.

EVAPORATION
Why does wet ink dry? Because the water in it turns into water vapour and evaporates into the air. Some of the water particles get enough energy to escape and form the gas.

SUBLIMATION
Sometimes a solid turns straight into a gas. This is called sublimation. It is what happens with dry ice, used to make dramatic-looking clouds on stage in a theatre. Dry ice is really frozen carbon dioxide. It is called dry because it does not become liquid before turning into a gas.

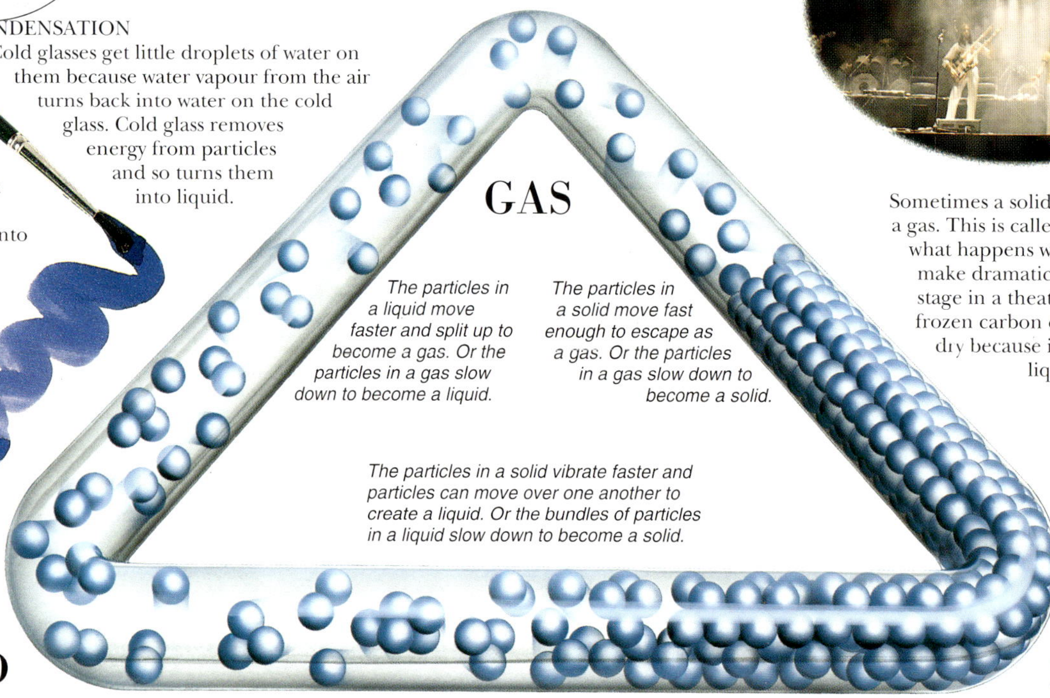

MELTING
Particles in a solid are packed tightly together. But when heated, they vibrate more and more until they can break free of fixed positions, and move freely over each other. The solid turns into a liquid. This is what happens when chocolate melts.

FREEZING
A dripping candle will soon freeze into a solid if you blow it out. This is because the particles, speeded up by the heat of the flame, slow down again and move closer together when the heat is removed. When they slow down enough, they get locked into position again, forming a solid.

STATES OF WATER

Water is unusual because it can be found in all three states of matter in everyday life. In solid form it is ice, in liquid form, water, and in gaseous form, water vapour. The properties of water in these three states are important to everything on Earth. For example, plants and animals need water regularly to survive.

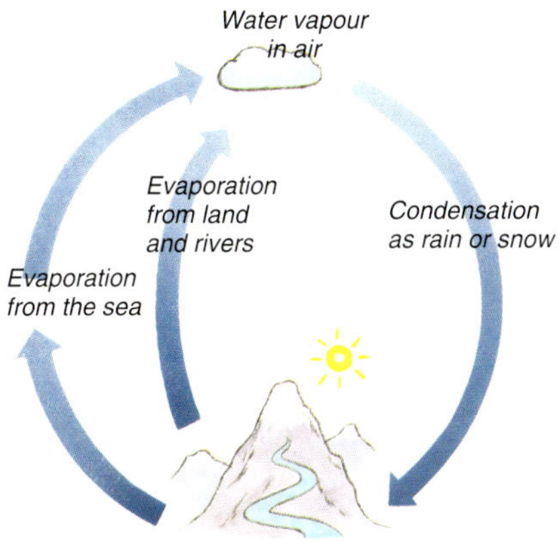

WATER CYCLE
The never-ending cycle between the different states of water is essential to everything on Earth. Liquid water evaporates and solid snow sublimes into the air. Water vapour condenses into droplets to form clouds. Water droplets fall back to Earth as rain or snow.

WATER VAPOUR
When the temperature is high, water evaporates quickly. In the warm tropical forests of South America there is plenty of rain, and because the temperature is high, water evaporates all the time. The water vapour in the air makes it very humid, and means that special types of plants, such as certain orchids, can thrive. They take all the moisture they need straight from the air, not from the ground.

STEAM POWER
When water boils, it turns into steam. Steam is water vapour that is hot. Being a gas, it takes up much more space than the liquid it came from. It is full of energy and can be used to drive heat engines such as the steam turbine. It enters the turbine at high temperature and pressure, and drives the turbine wheels round.

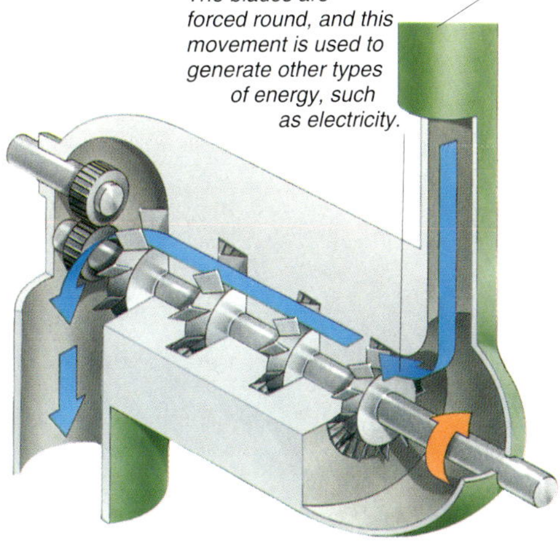

EXPANDING ICE
Have you noticed how pipes often burst in freezing weather? This is because the water inside them expands as it freezes into a solid.

CHANGES WITH PRESSURE

Pressure can bring about a change of state. It is possible to ice skate because skates move over the ice on a thin layer of water. The weight of the skater is concentrated into the blade. This causes pressure under the blade which makes the ice melt as the skate moves over it.

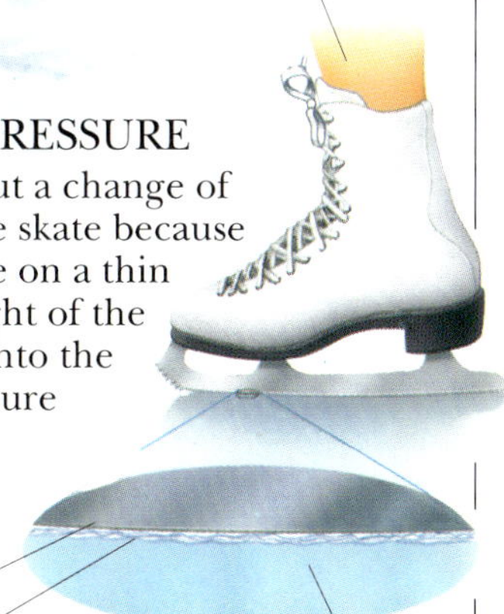

Find out more

STATES OF MATTER P.18
SOLUTIONS P.60
CHEMISTRY OF WATER P.75
WATER INDUSTRY P.83
FORMATION OF THE EARTH P.210
CYCLES IN THE BIOSPHERE P.372

PROPERTIES OF MATTER

A SAUCEPAN IS MADE OF STEEL and plastic for a very good reason. The handle is plastic because plastic is a good insulator and it stops the handle getting too hot and burning your hand. The pan is steel because it is a good conductor and lets the heat go through to the food. Good insulation or good conductivity is an example of a particular property of matter. Some properties, such as conductivity, can be measured. Others, such as the smell of an object, can only be described. Scientists measure the properties of many different materials. They do this at room temperature and pressure so that they can make accurate comparisons between them.

You can describe an orange by its colour and shape, how it feels to the touch, how it smells, and how it tastes.

SENSING MATTER

In the everyday world, people do not usually describe objects in the same way as scientists do. We rely more on our senses than on measurements with instruments. But human senses are not consistent. They cannot measure how much something smells, or exactly what it tastes like, and one person may sense things in quite a different way from another.

NEUTRON STAR

The metal osmium is the densest substance on Earth. It is twice as dense as lead and over 22 times as dense as water. But the densest material in the Universe is a neutron star. A pinhead of a neutron star weighs a million tonnes.

Neutron star

A pinhead of a neutron star

A hydrometer is used to measure the density of a liquid. It floats in a container full of the pure liquid, and the reading is taken at the top of the liquid. The hydrometer floats high up in a dense liquid, but lower in a less dense liquid.

Water has a density of 1. Liquids with a lower density float on top of it, and those with a higher density sink below it.

Gases always bubble to the surface of a liquid because they have such a low density. Air has a relative density of only 0.0012.

Methylated spirits: relative density 0.8

Corn oil: relative density 0.9

Water: density 1

Mercury: relative density 13.6

DENSITY

Different materials have a different mass for the same volume. The mass (in grammes) of a cubic centimetre of something is its density. Densities of all solids, liquids, and gases are sometimes given as their density relative to water (relative density).

WEIGHT, MASS, AND VOLUME

You can measure the amount of something in two ways: by its volume or by its mass. You buy petrol by its volume (in litres or gallons) – that is the amount of space it occupies. But you buy potatoes by mass (in kilograms or pounds) – that is a measure of the amount of matter in the bag of potatoes. The volume of something can be changed by compressing or heating it, but the mass stays constant. When gravity pulls on an object, it creates a force called weight which depends on the mass of the object.

The cube of lead is as heavy as a piece of wax with a volume 13 times greater, and a piece of balsa wood with a volume 56 times greater.

Lead: density 11.3

Wax: density 0.9

Balsa wood: density 0.2

STRENGTH

Most metals are strong when they are pulled, so they can be used to build structures such as this cable-stayed bridge. The road is held by cables made of steel, which do not break when they are pulled by the downwards force of the road. The pillars that hold up the bridge are made of concrete because it is strong enough not to break up when it is squashed by the force of the bridge pushing it down.

A tower holds the cables in place.

PLASTICITY

If you press some materials, such as dough or putty, they change shape and stay that way. These materials are called plastic materials. There are different kinds of plasticity, called malleability and ductility. If a metal can be beaten into thin sheets without breaking, it is malleable. If it can be drawn into a fine wire, it is ductile.

Copper and some other metals can be drawn into wire finer than a human hair. This means that copper is ductile.

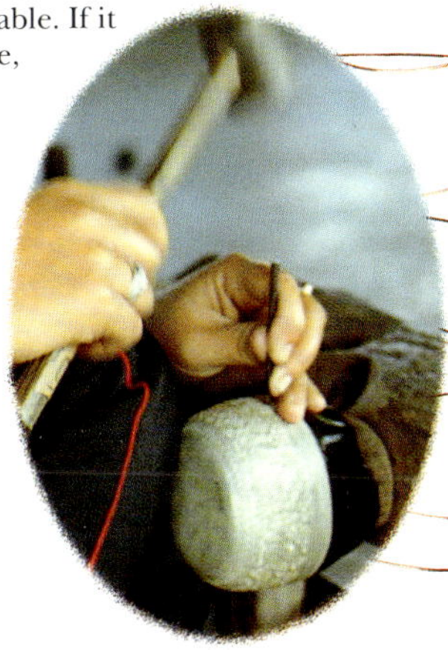

This silversmith is making a bowl by beating out the silver into the right shape. This means that silver is malleable.

If you press wax onto the end of a metal spoon and onto the end of a plastic spoon in hot water, the wax on the end of the metal spoon will start to melt first.

Water is a good thermal conductor. It transmits heat to the metal spoon.

CONDUCTING HEAT

Metals conduct (pass on) heat well. They have high thermal (heat) conductivity because of their atomic structure. Materials such as plastics and wood have poor thermal conductivity, so they are good insulators. This makes them very useful for covering thermal conductors. This is why the handles of kitchen utensils and saucepans are usually plastic.

ELASTICITY

Rubber has an interesting property. When you pull it, it stretches. When you let go, it shrinks back to its original size. This property is called elasticity. Most materials, even metals, are elastic. Some materials have an elastic limit, which means that they do not return to the original shape and size if they are stretched too far.

A rubber balloon stretched out as far as possible

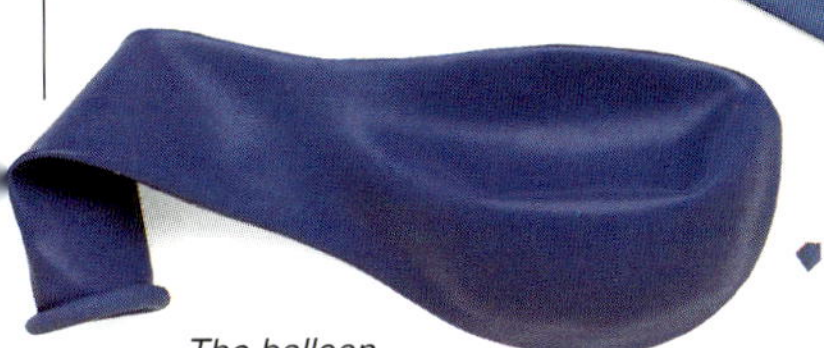

The balloon has returned to its original shape after being stretched.

BRITTLENESS

Rubber is elastic at normal temperatures. But this balloon was dipped in liquid nitrogen, which has a temperature of –196°C (–385°F). The balloon became brittle and shattered into pieces when tapped with a hammer. Some substances, such as glass, are brittle at normal temperatures. Other substances, such as clay, are normally plastic, but are brittle after being baked in a kiln.

CONDUCTING ELECTRICITY

Electricity can flow easily through metals, meaning that metals can conduct electricity. This is because metals have free-flowing electrons on their atoms. Plastics, glass, wood, and most other solid materials, except for carbon, are very poor conductors. They are electrical insulators, which is why plastic is used to cover conductors such as the wire in a cable.

Copper wire

The plastic completely covers the copper wires.

Some substances are more soluble than others. Chalk hardly dissolves in cold water. But sugar dissolves easily, even in cold water.

Chalk in cold water

Sugar in cold water

Chalk is not very soluble even in hot water. But sugar is much more soluble in hot water. The hotter the water, the more soluble sugar becomes.

Chalk in hot water

Sugar in hot water

SOLUBILITY

Many solids, liquids, and gases dissolve in water and other liquids to form a solution: they are soluble. Sugar dissolves in tea, and salt dissolves in water. The dissolving substances are called solutes, and the liquids that they dissolve in are called solvents. Water is often called the universal solvent because so many things dissolve in it. This property is vital to life. Water carries dissolved substances around in blood and sap. Animals that live in water get their oxygen as the gas dissolved in water.

The boiling point: liquid turns into vapour, or vapour condenses into liquid. It is always higher than the melting point.

The melting (or freezing) point: solid melts into liquid, or liquid freezes into solid.

MELTING AND BOILING POINTS

Every pure substance has a constant melting point and boiling point at normal air pressure. But if the substance is not pure, the melting and boiling points change. Salt on snow lowers the melting point, so it melts to water, and the weather has to be much colder before it freezes again.

Find out more

ATOMIC STRUCTURE P. 24
TRANSITION METALS P.36
CARBON P.40
SOLUTIONS P.60
CHEMICAL ANALYSIS P.62
FLOATING AND SINKING P.129
CURRENT ELECTRICITY P.148
FACT FINDER P.402

ATOMIC STRUCTURE

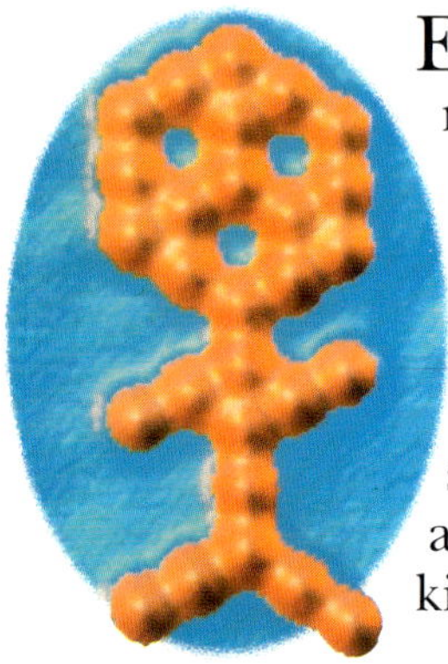

EVERY SINGLE THING you can see, hear, feel, smell, and taste is made from microscopic particles. These particles are called atoms, and it would take millions of them just to cover a full-stop. An atom is itself made up of even smaller particles. In the centre of each atom there is a nucleus made up of protons and neutrons. Particles called electrons whiz around this nucleus in different shells (layers). Protons and neutrons are much heavier than the electrons, so the nucleus makes up most of an atom's mass. Some substances, such as water, are made up of molecules. These consist of several kinds of atoms joined together in a group. Other substances, such as iron, have just one kind of atom.

MOLECULE PICTURE
This photograph shows 28 carbon monoxide molecules. They have been cleverly arranged into the shape of a person. More than 20,000 of these "people" would be needed to cross the width of a human hair.

PROTONS, NEUTRONS, AND ELECTRONS

The nucleus of every atom contains two types of particle – protons and neutrons. The number of protons gives the atomic number. Protons have a positive electric charge, while neutrons have none. The electrons that spin around the nucleus, like planets orbiting the Sun, have a negative charge. But electrons are not solid balls, they are bundles of energy that move almost as fast as light. There are always the same number of electrons and protons in an atom.

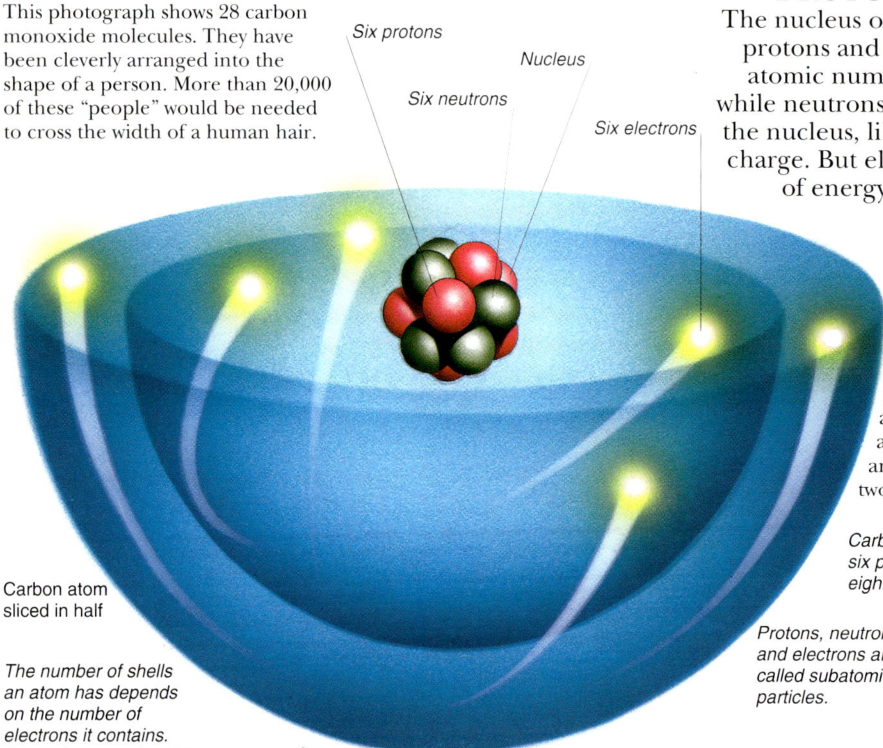

Carbon atom sliced in half

CARBON ATOM
This drawing shows a carbon atom sliced in half. The nucleus of a carbon atom is made up of six protons and six neutrons. The atom's six electrons are contained within two shells.

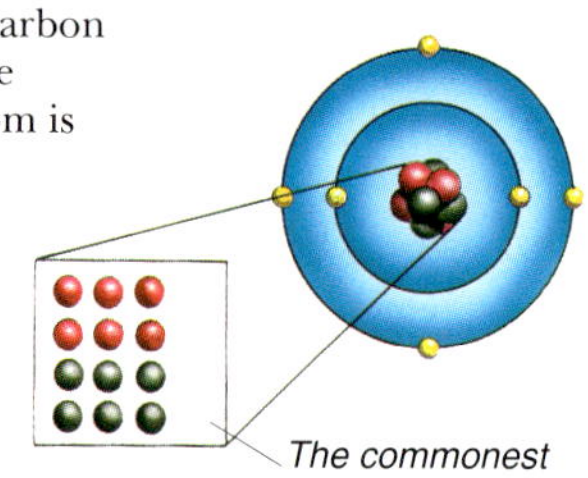

The commonest isotope of carbon, carbon-12, has six protons and six neutrons in its nucleus.

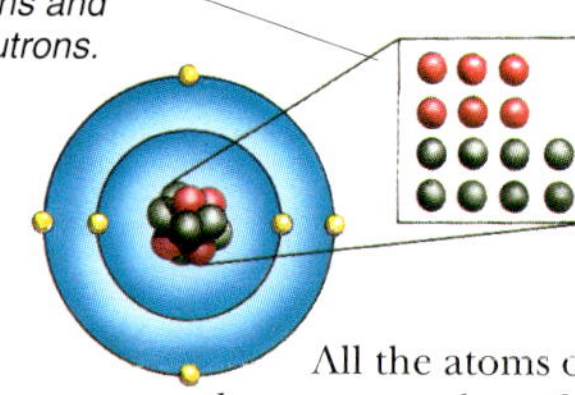

Carbon-14 has six protons and eight neutrons.

Protons, neutrons, and electrons are called subatomic particles.

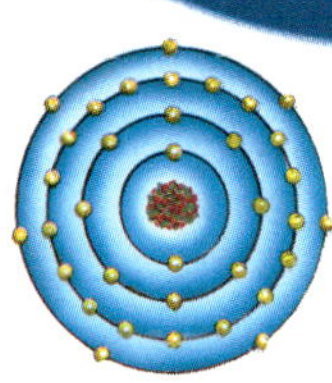

The number of shells an atom has depends on the number of electrons it contains. A bromine atom has 35 electrons in four shells. Some atoms have as many as seven shells.

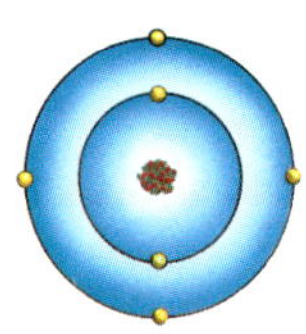

The first shell of a carbon atom contains two electrons. The other four electrons are in the second shell.

ISOTOPES
All the atoms of an element have the same number of protons, but some have different numbers of neutrons. All of these are called isotopes. An isotope of carbon, called carbon-12, has six protons and six neutrons in its nucleus. The nucleus of another isotope, carbon-14, has an extra two neutrons. It is radioactive. Radioactive isotopes are called radioisotopes.

JOHN DALTON

A Greek philosopher, Democritus (c.460-361 B.C.), put forward the idea that the Universe was made of tiny, indivisible particles he called atoms. His concept was discussed for hundreds of years. Then, in 1808, the English chemist John Dalton (1766-1844) suggested from his experimental work that each chemical element is made up of identical atoms, and that elements are different because they are each made of different atoms. This became known as Dalton's atomic theory.

Even in atoms with many particles, most of the atom is empty space.

HOW BIG IS AN ATOM?
Atoms are far tinier than anyone can imagine. It would take as many as 10 million of them side by side to measure one millimetre. Even though they are so small, atoms are mostly made of space, because the electrons are so far from the nucleus. If the nucleus were the size of a tennis ball, the whole atom would be as big as the Empire State Building in New York.

ERNEST RUTHERFORD

The New Zealand-born physicist Ernest Rutherford (1871-1937) discovered in 1911 that atoms have a tiny, dense nucleus. Rutherford and his colleagues were shooting positively charged alpha particles at a very thin sheet of gold foil. Alpha particles consist of two protons and two neutrons and so have a positive charge. Most of the alpha particles went straight through, but some changed path and some even bounced back. This showed that the atom's positive charge is concentrated in a small nucleus, which was changing the paths of the alpha particles. Most of the atom is made up of empty space.

SUBATOMIC PARTICLES

The protons, neutrons, and electrons that make up an atom are just three of more than 200 subatomic particles that are now known. Scientists are discovering new particles all the time. They use powerful machines called particle accelerators to smash atoms or subatomic particles together, at high speed, to make other subatomic particles. They give the particles weird and wonderful names such as kaon, upsilon, and charmed lambda.

INVENTORS
John Cockcroft (1897–1967) and Ernest Walton (born 1903) were the first to develop a particle accelerator, in 1932. For this they won the Nobel Prize for Physics in 1951. In the picture, Ernest Walton is seated inside the counting room, where the particles are detected. The long tube above it is the accelerating tube, and the hat-shaped part above that is where the particles start off.

PARTICLE ACCELERATOR
In accelerators such as a synchrotron (right), beams of subatomic particles are sent round in circles by powerful electromagnets, and speeded up by pulses of electricity. When the particles are travelling fast enough, they are extracted and made to smash into each other. Scientists can then analyse the particles produced.

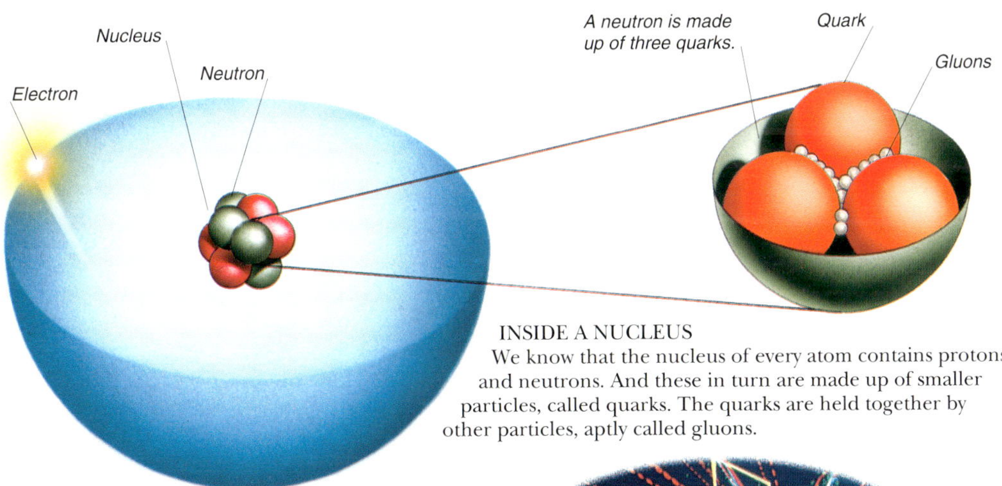

INSIDE A NUCLEUS
We know that the nucleus of every atom contains protons and neutrons. And these in turn are made up of smaller particles, called quarks. The quarks are held together by other particles, aptly called gluons.

SUBATOMIC PARTICLES

1897 J.J. Thomson (1856–1940) discovers the electron.

1909 Robert Millikan (1868–1953) measures the negative charge on the electron.

1911 Ernest Rutherford (1871–1937) discovers that atoms have a nucleus.

1913 Niels Bohr (1885–1962) discovers electron shells.

1932 James Chadwick (1891–1974) discovers the neutron.

1963 Murray Gell-Mann (born 1929) suggests the existence of quarks.

Particle tracks in a bubble chamber

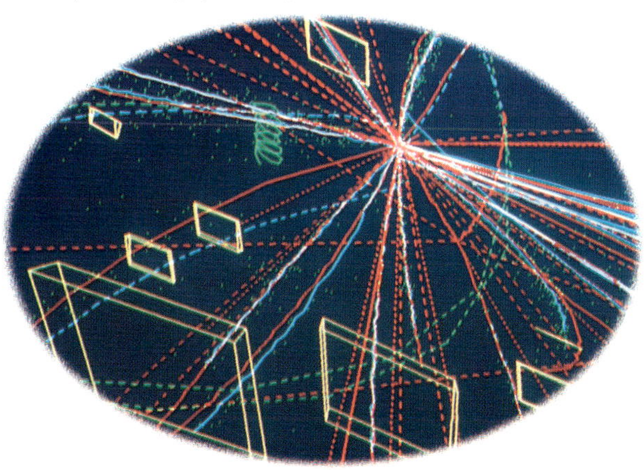

PARTICLE TRACKS
Scientists often use electronic detectors to pick up the tracks of particles created by collisions in particle accelerators. A computer processes the information and displays the tracks on a screen. From the tracks, scientists can work out the mass and electric charge of the particles that made them. For example, the green spiral is the track of a low-energy electron.

Find out more

RADIOACTIVITY P.26
BONDING P.28
ELEMENTS P.31
CARBON P.40
NUCLEAR ENERGY P.136
LIGHT P.190
FACT FINDER P.402

Radioactivity

RADIOACTIVITY

1896 Antoine Becquerel (1852-1908) discovers radioactivity.

1898 Marie Curie(1867-1934)and Pierre Curie (1859-1906) discover radium and polonium.

1934 Pavel Cherenkov (born 1904) discovers Cherenkov radiation.

1934 Irène Joliot-Curie (1897-1956), Marie and Pierre's daughter, and her husband, Frédéric (1900-1958), show that radioactivity can be produced artificially.

THE RADIATION THAT IS USED in hospitals to treat disease is caused by atomic nuclei (plural of nucleus) breaking up. Most atoms have stable nuclei – meaning that the number of neutrons and protons stays the same. But some nuclei are unstable and can split up: they are radioactive. These unstable nuclei have a different number of neutrons from stable nuclei, and are called radioisotopes. When they break up, the nuclei give out radiation. This process is known as radioactive decay. The larger the number of subatomic particles in an atom, the more likely it is to be radioactive. Uranium, for example, has 238 subatomic particles and is highly radioactive.

RADIATION GLOW

Radioactive materials are often stored in water. The water acts as a shield to absorb the radiation. As the particles travel through the water, they make it emit a bluish light. This is called Cherenkov radiation, after the Soviet physicist Pavel Cherenkov, who won a Nobel Prize for its discovery.

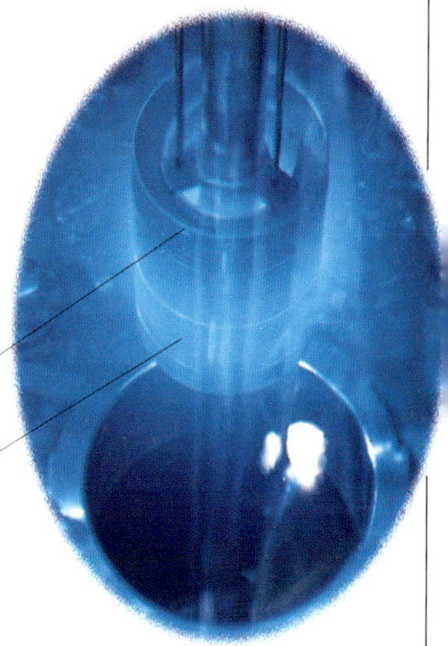

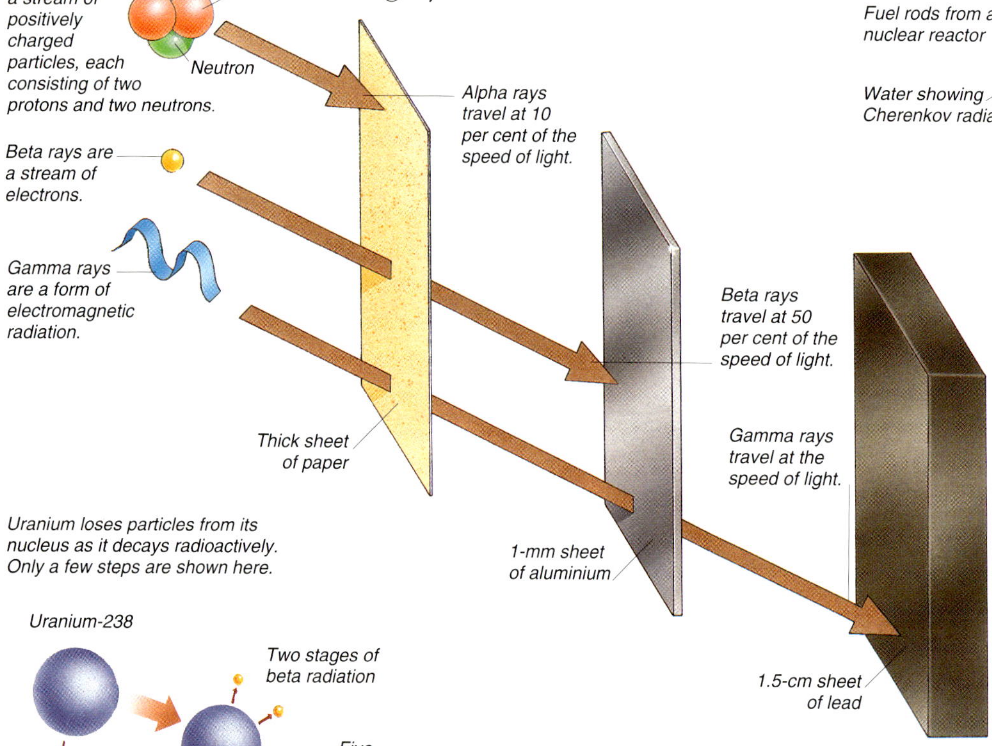

Penetrating power

Three types of radiation are given out by radioisotopes: alpha, beta, and gamma. They are all dangerous to living things. They can pass into living tissue and damage it. If you are exposed to too much radiation, it can kill you. Alpha radiation is the least harmful. Its particles cannot even pass through a sheet of paper. Metal is needed to stop the beta particles. But only thick lead or concrete can stop the powerful gamma rays.

Uranium loses particles from its nucleus as it decays radioactively. Only a few steps are shown here.

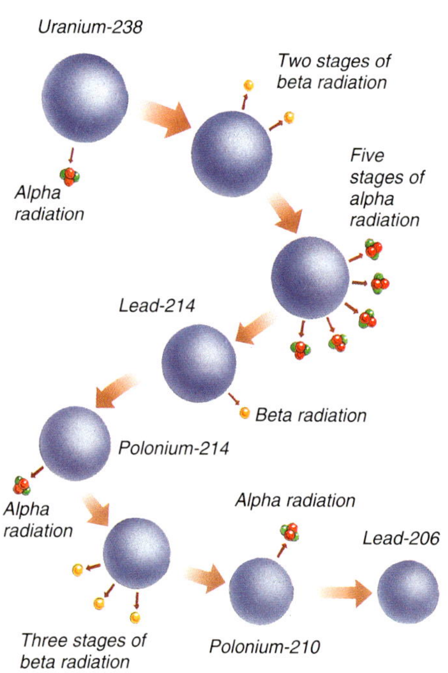

RADIOACTIVE DECAY

Uranium-238 is the most common isotope of uranium. It has 238 particles in its nucleus. The number of nuclear particles goes down as radiation is given off in a series of steps. At each step, a new element is formed. The rate of this radioactive decay is called the half-life; the time it takes for half the atoms in a radioactive substance to decay. The half-life of uranium-238 is 4,500 million years, because it takes 4,500 million years for half the atoms in any amount of uranium-238 to decay radioactively.

MARIE CURIE

The French physicist Antoine Becquerel discovered the radioactivity of uranium when uranium salts unexpectedly clouded a photographic plate. Marie Curie and her husband Pierre Curie then investigated uranium. They found that its ore, pitchblende, was so radioactive that another radioactive element must be present. They found two, radium and polonium, and Becquerel and the Curies shared the 1903 Nobel Prize for Physics for isolating radium. Marie Curie died of leukaemia, probably caused by exposure to so much radiation.

USEFUL RADIATION

The radiation from radioactive materials can be deadly, so it always needs to be treated with care. But it can be put to good use. Heart pacemakers contain nuclear batteries, because they last so much longer than ordinary batteries. Cancers are detected and destroyed using radioactivity.

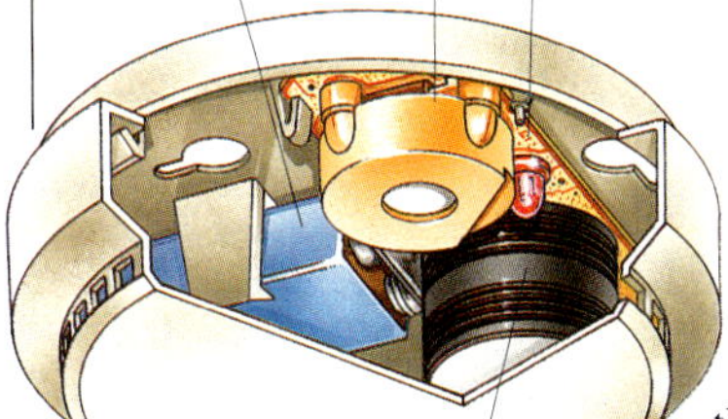

SMOKE ALARMS

Many smoke alarms have a weak radioactive source such as americium-241. Its rays split the atoms inside a chamber into ions, which makes them pass a slight electric current. If smoke enters this chamber, it disturbs the ions and reduces the current. A microchip senses this and triggers the alarm.

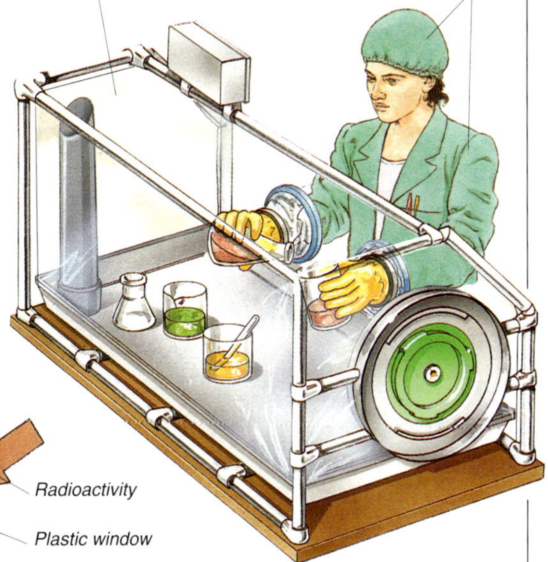

HANDLING RADIOACTIVE SUBSTANCES

Radioactive materials must be handled with care. In the nuclear industry the workers handle the materials through special gloves fitted into a cabinet. Sometimes people have to work outside a room with the deadly materials in it, so they use remote-handling instruments that mimic the action of their own hands. All nuclear workers wear a special badge called a dosimeter, which records the amount of radiation they receive over a certain period.

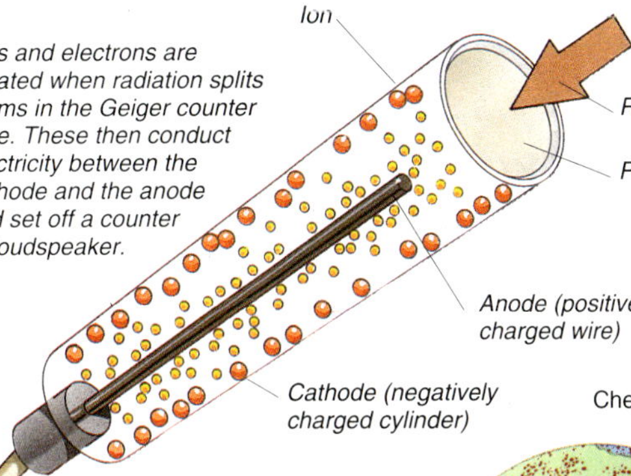

GEIGER COUNTER

A Geiger counter detects and measures the intensity of radiation. It is named after Hans Geiger (1882–1945), the German physicist who perfected it. The detecting probe is filled with gas at low pressure. The radioactivity splits the gas into ions, which produce a pulse of electricity. The needle on the dial or the speed of the clicks produced indicate the amount of radioactivity.

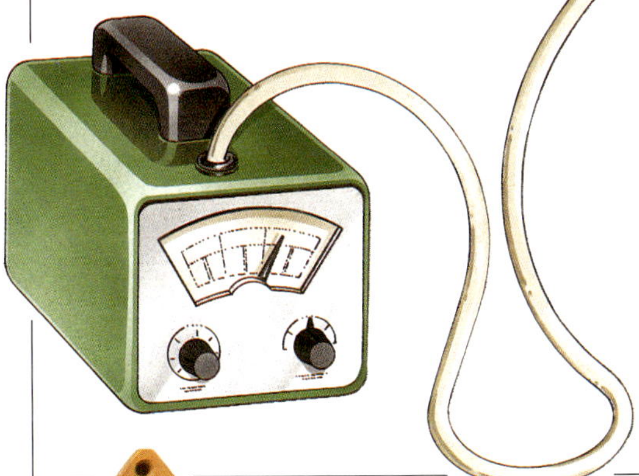

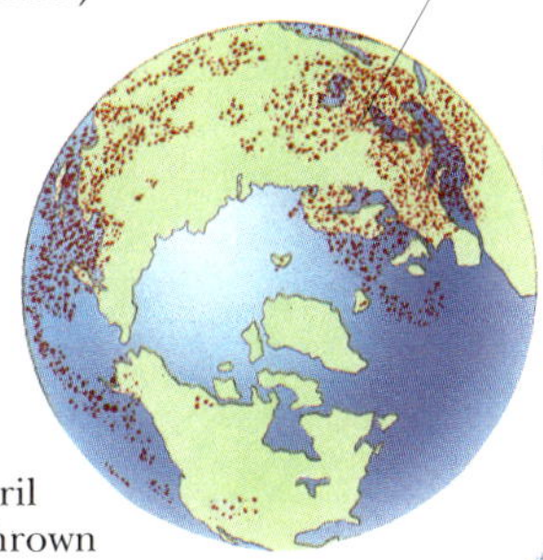

RADIOACTIVE FALLOUT

Nuclear power stations hold large quantities of radio-active material, which is usually quite safe. But one of the world's worst nuclear accidents was the explosion at the Chernobyl nuclear reactor in the Ukraine in April 1986. Radioactive material thrown into the air eventually returned to the ground as fallout, contaminating large areas of Europe. This map shows the contamination ten days after the explosion.

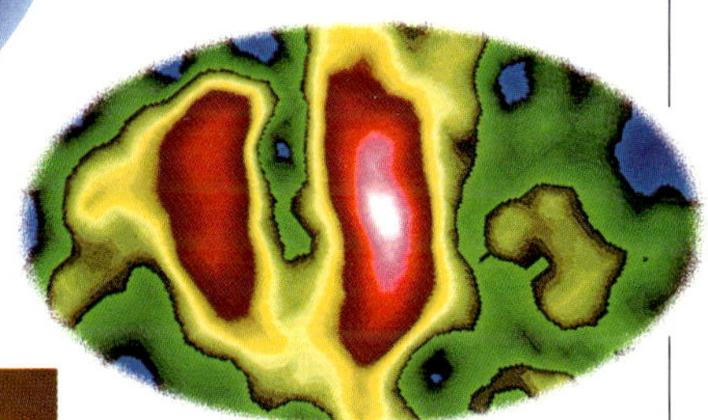

RADIOISOTOPE LABELLING

When certain radioisotopes are injected into the body, they collect in, or label, particular organs. This allows doctors to examine the organs more easily. The radiation that the isotopes give off may reveal damaged tissue. In this false-colour image of a human heart, the damaged tissue is the horseshoe shape on the right of the picture.

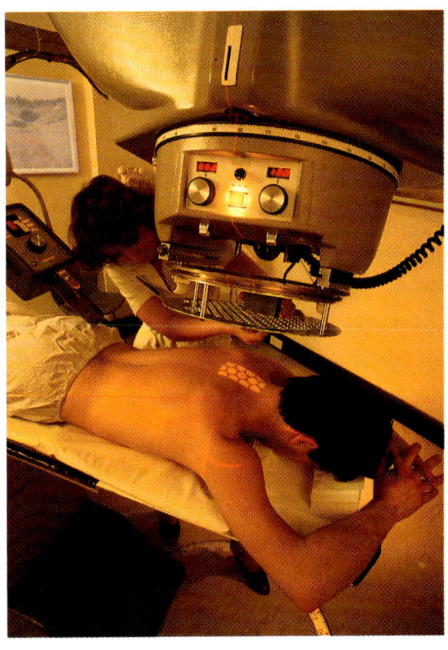

CARBON DATING

Animals and plants have a known proportion of a radioisotope of carbon, carbon-14, in their tissues. When they die they stop taking carbon in, and the amount of carbon-14 goes down at a known rate (the half-life). Using the half-life, the age of ancient organic materials can be found by measuring the amount of carbon-14 that is left. This wooden mummy label is about 2,500 years old.

RADIOTHERAPY

Hospitals use radiotherapy to treat patients suffering from cancer. In this machine, gamma rays from a cobalt radioisotope are being focused on a cancer to kill the cells and prevent the cancer spreading to other parts of the body. Gamma rays are also used to sterilize medical equipment.

Find out more

ATOMIC STRUCTURE P.24
BONDING P.28
ELEMENTS P.31
HYDROGEN P.47
NUCLEAR ENERGY P.136
ELECTROMAGNETIC SPECTRUM P. 192
FACT FINDER P.402

BONDING

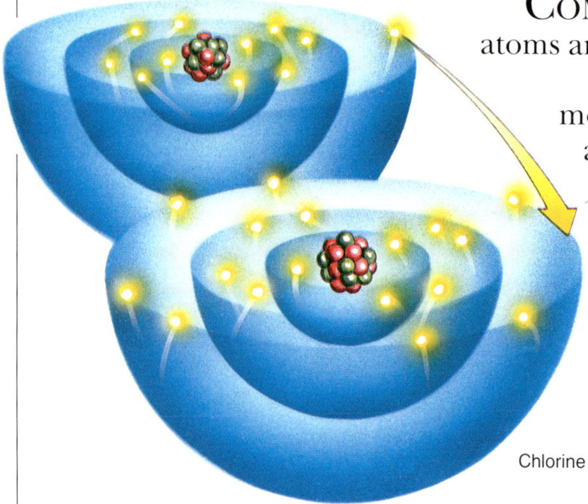

COMMON SALT IS MADE OF sodium and chlorine atoms. These atoms aren't just mixed with each other, they are stuck together with a chemical "glue", known as a bond. All bonding involves the movement of electrons in the outermost shells of the atoms. But atoms use these electrons to bond in different ways. In salt, for example, atoms give away or take in electrons; this forms what is called an ionic bond. In a compound such as water, atoms share their electrons; this forms what is called a covalent bond. And in metals, the electrons flow around all the atoms; this is called a metallic bond. Different atoms stuck together with different bonds make up the millions of different substances found on Earth.

IONIC BONDS

An ionic bond happens when an atom loses or gains one or more electrons from its outer shell. Each atom becomes electrically charged in the process, and is then called an ion. Ions are either cations or anions. The atom that has lost electrons is called the cation, and has a positive charge. The atom that has gained electrons is called the anion, and has a negative charge. These opposite electrical charges attract the ions to each other very strongly. So most ionic bonds are very difficult to break. Ionic compounds are usually solids, and will only melt at a very high temperature. When sodium and chlorine atoms form an ionic bond together, they become the ionic compound sodium chloride (common salt).

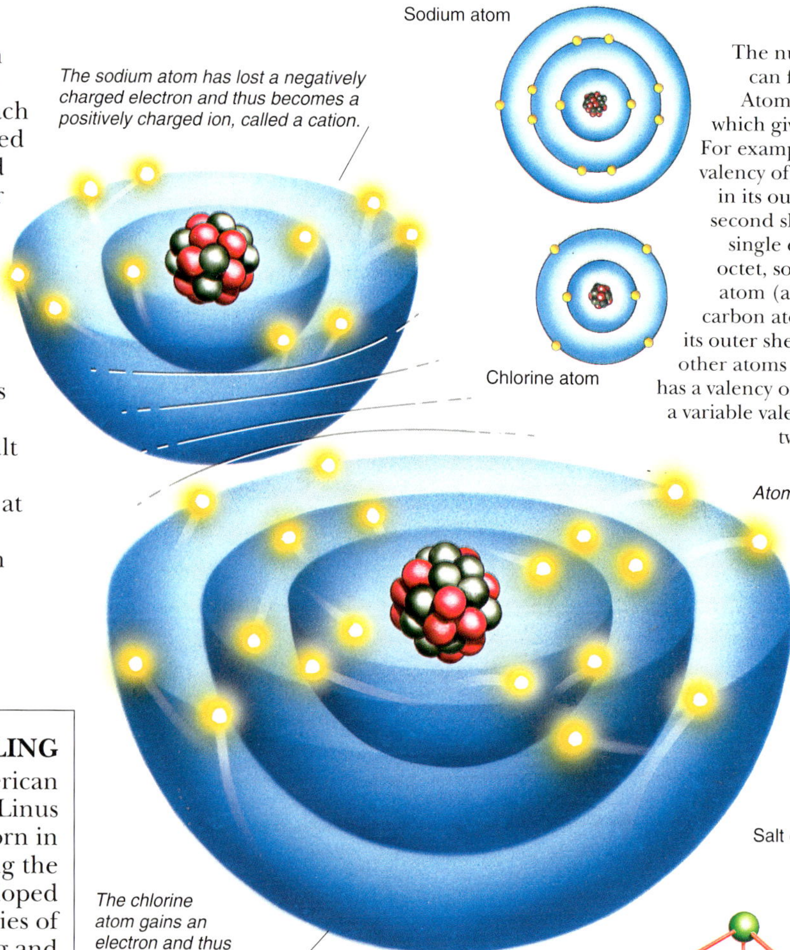

VALENCY

The number of bonds an atom can form is called its valency. Atoms have a valency number which gives you this information. For example, a sodium atom has a valency of one. It has one electron in its outer shell, and eight in its second shell. It has to give away a single electron to leave a stable octet, so it bonds with one other atom (as in sodium chloride). A carbon atom has four electrons in its outer shell. It can bond with four other atoms to form a stable octet. It has a valency of four. Some atoms have a variable valency: iron can bond with two or three other atoms.

LINUS PAULING

The American chemist Linus Pauling was born in 1901. During the 1930s, he developed important theories of chemical bonding and molecular structure. He calculated energies needed to make bonds and angles of bonds, and measured distances between atoms. For this work he was awarded the 1954 Nobel Prize for Chemistry. He was also awarded the 1962 Nobel Prize for Peace for his efforts to stop the testing of nuclear bombs.

Salt crystals

IONIC STRUCTURE

In the ionic compound sodium chloride, all the ions are arranged in a regular structure called a giant ionic lattice. The crystals of salt are cubes, because of the basic structure of the lattice. All ionic compounds form a lattice, but their ions may be arranged in a different way. This will give the lattice a different structure, and the crystal a different shape.

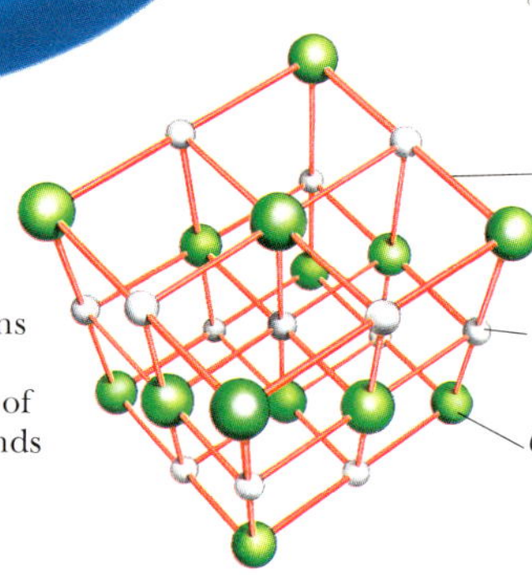

COVALENT BONDS

A lot of atoms do not easily lose or gain electrons to form ionic bonds. Instead they share electrons between them. The electrons are shared in pairs called electron pairs. This type of bond is called a covalent bond. The smallest part of a compound with covalent bonds is called a molecule. The forces that attract the molecules to each other are quite weak. That is why so many covalent compounds are gases or liquids. They have low melting and boiling points because it does not take much energy to break the bonds between them.

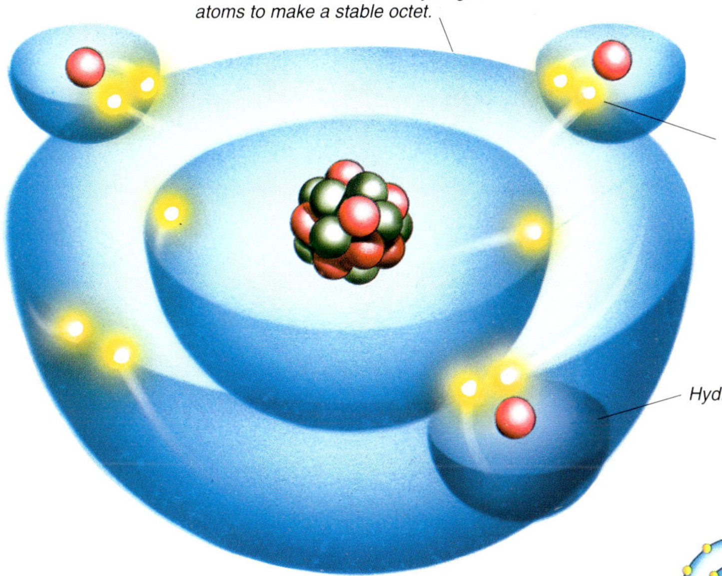

Nitrogen has five electrons in its outer shell and bonds with three hydrogen atoms to make a stable octet.

COVALENT MOLECULES
This computer simulation shows the three-dimensional structure of the carbon compound butane (bottled gas). Butane is a typical covalent compound. Because its molecules bond to each other with weak forces, called Van der Waals' forces, liquid butane easily becomes a gas.

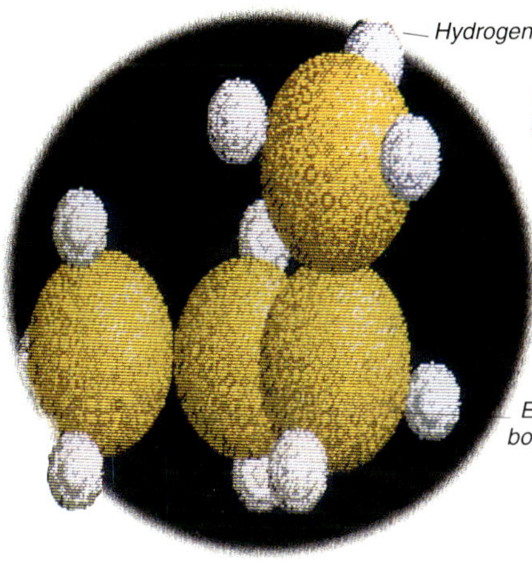

Each carbon atom is bonded to other atoms.

Butane flame from bottled gas in a camping stove

DOUBLE BONDS
In covalent bonds, sometimes atoms share two pairs of electrons between them, instead of one. The oxygen that exists in the atmosphere consists of two atoms linked together by a double bond.

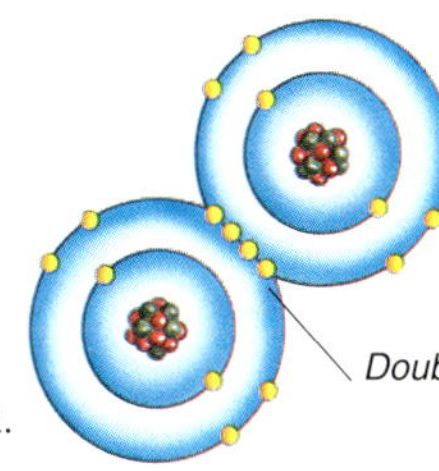

Oxygen atoms

HYDROGEN BONDS

A molecule of water (H_2O) is made up of two hydrogen atoms linked to one oxygen atom by covalent bonds. As well as sticking together with Van der Waals' forces, water molecules are held together with hydrogen bonds. These occur when hydrogen atoms that are slightly positively charged are attracted to slightly negatively charged oxygen atoms. The oxygen atoms are slightly negative because they attract electrons in the covalent bond more strongly than the hydrogen atoms do.

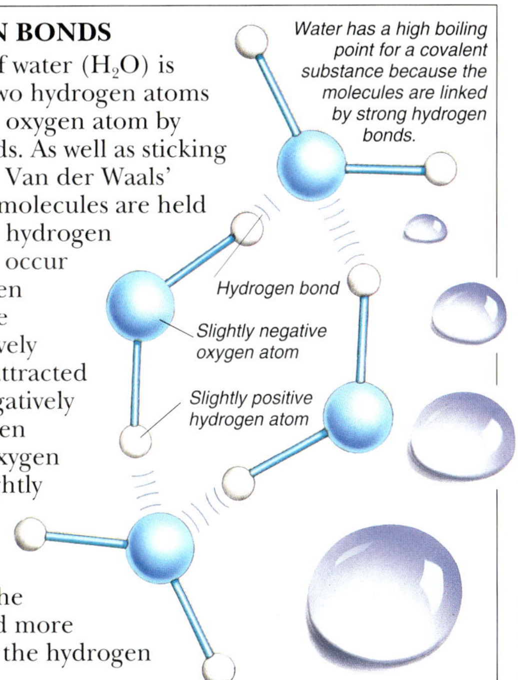

Water has a high boiling point for a covalent substance because the molecules are linked by strong hydrogen bonds.

METALLIC BONDS

In the atoms that make up a metal, the electrons in the outer shell are only loosely attached. These electrons float around in a common pool, or "sea" of electrons. This is metallic bonding. The sea of electrons can flow around easily. This explains why metals can conduct electricity so well. When heat or electricity is applied to one part of the metal, the electrons quickly carry it to all the other parts.

A false-colour image of a gold lattice. Each yellow dot represents a gold atom.

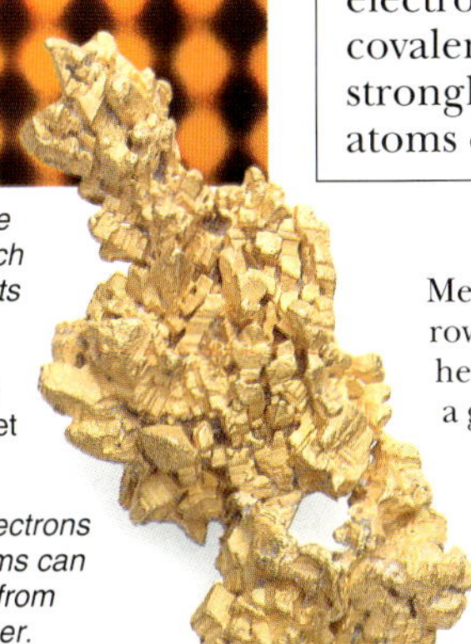

Crystalline gold nugget

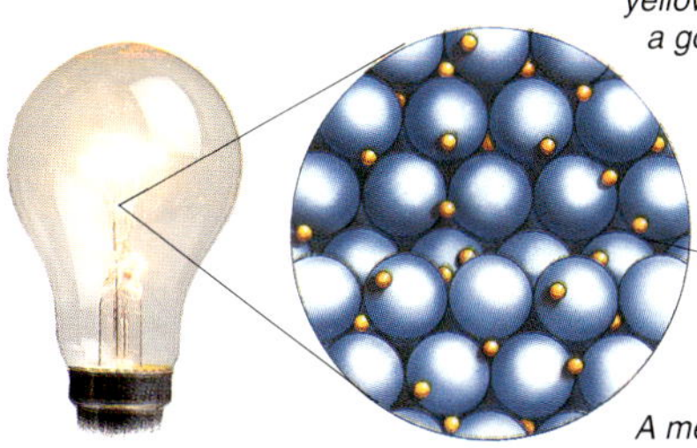

The outer electrons of metal atoms can move freely from one to another.

A metal bulb filament glows as electricity passes through it.

METAL STRUCTURE
Metal atoms are arranged in rows that fit neatly together, held by a sea of electrons in a giant metallic lattice. The sea of electrons means that no atom is bonded to its neighbours, so the atoms can move around and still form strong bonds in a new position. This is why metals are easily bent and hammered.

Find out more

ATOMIC STRUCTURE P.24
CRYSTALS P30
PERIODIC TABLE P.32
CHEMICAL REACTIONS P.52
DESCRIBING REACTIONS P.53
COMPOUNDS AND MIXTURES P.58
CHEMISTRY OF WATER P.75
CURRENT ELECTRICITY P.148

CRYSTALS

IF YOU LOOK at sugar under a magnifying glass, you will see tiny, glassy cubes. These are sugar crystals. Gems such as rubies and sapphires are also crystals. Most solids, including metals, are made up of lots of crystals. Sometimes you cannot see them because they are too small or stuck together, but you can often see them in rocks. Crystals in rocks often have no definite shape because they are packed together. But when they grow freely in rock cavities, they form beautiful, regular shapes. There are seven main crystal shapes, or systems. These shapes reflect the arrangement of the atoms or ions that the crystal is made of, called the crystal lattice. Scientists investigate this lattice with X-rays.

CRYSTAL COLOUR
Some crystals, such as sulphur, are almost always the same colour. But quartz (silicon dioxide) comes in different colours. This is because it gets coloured by impurities. In its pure form, quartz is transparent and is called rock crystal. But it can be white (milky quartz), pink (rose quartz), or yellow (citrine). In this purple variety (amethyst), the colour comes mainly from iron.

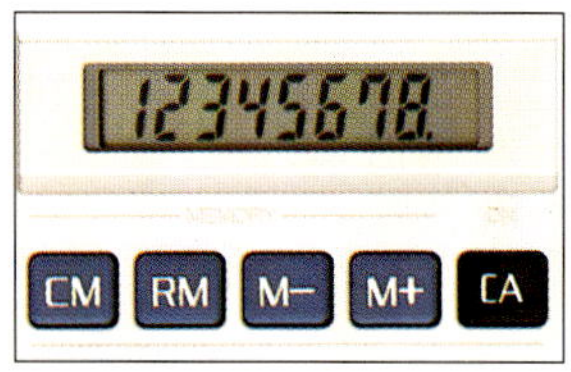

LIQUID CRYSTALS
The displays you see on digital watches and calculators consist of transparent liquid crystal held between two sheets of glass in a certain pattern. When electricity is passed through the liquid crystal, it appears darker in the segments needed to show the right number, while the other segments stay transparent. This type of display is called a liquid crystal display (LCD).

PEGMATITE
The crystals in this rock, called pegmatite, are large because the rock cooled slowly. The crystal shapes are not regular because the crystals formed right next to each other, not in a free space.

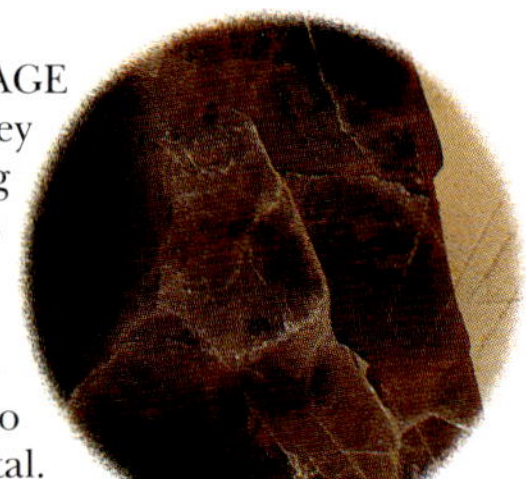

CLEAVAGE
When crystals break, they tend to cleave (split) along certain planes. The planes are related to the basic crystal lattice. Mica, for example, cleaves into thin sheets parallel to the base of the crystal.

Galena (lead ore) has cubic symmetry.

Topaz (right) has rhombic symmetry.

Emerald has hexagonal symmetry.

Idocrase has tetragonal symmetry.

Gypsum has monoclinic symmetry.

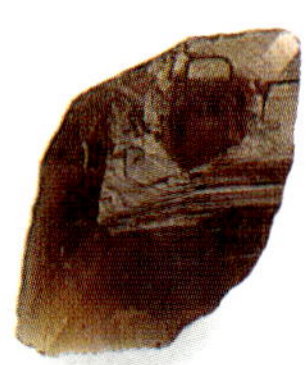

Axinite has triclinic symmetry.

Quartz has trigonal symmetry.

MAKING CRYSTALS
This pattern of different crystals was made from ammonium iron sulphate crystals (brown), cobalt chloride crystals (dark blue), and copper nitrate crystals (light blue). Crystals are easy to grow by hanging a string in water into which you have stirred a lot of sugar or bath crystals.

CRYSTAL SYSTEMS

The seven basic systems of crystals are shown above. Perfectly shaped crystals are rare, but whatever the shape of the crystal, its symmetry can be measured. This helps scientists to identify it.

WILLIAM BRAGG

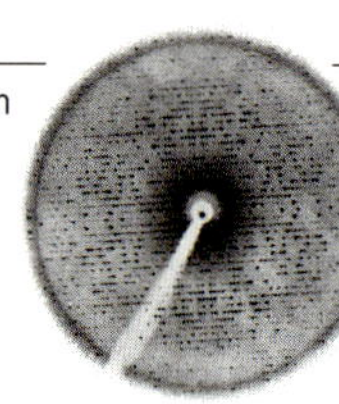

X-ray crystallogram of a protein

William Henry Bragg (1862-1942) and his son William Lawrence Bragg (1890-1971) were the first to study the structure of crystals using X-rays. They won the Nobel Prize for Physics in 1915 for their work. If a beam of X-rays is passed through a crystal, it makes a pattern on a photographic plate. This pattern is called a crystallogram. It reveals the crystal's internal structure, which is the arrangement of the atoms. Each crystal has its own crystallogram.

Find out more

STATES OF MATTER P.18
BONDING P.28
SULPHUR P.45
SALTS P.73
CHEMISTRY OF WATER P.75
ROCKS AND MINERALS P.221
FACT FINDER P.402

ELEMENTS

A GOLD BAR is made of atoms of one kind only, gold atoms, which means that gold is an element. Most things in the Universe consist of combinations of different elements, called compounds. Only a few elements can be found in the pure state, such as gold, copper, and silver. So far 109 elements are known, of which 89 occur naturally on Earth. About ten of these were known before the 18th century, but most were discovered in the 18th and 19th centuries. It was then that chemists seriously began to investigate chemical elements and compounds. Today, 20 artificial elements have been created that do not exist in nature. All are radioactive. Some only exist for a few millionths of a second.

ANCIENT ELEMENTS

During the 4th century B.C., Ancient Greek philosophers such as Aristotle believed that all forms of matter were made up of just four elements, arranged in different proportions. These were fire, air, water, and earth. Bone, for example, was made up of four parts fire, two parts water, and two parts earth. This illustration, from a 17th-century German poem on alchemy, shows four characters symbolizing earth (*Terra*), water (*Aqua*), air (*Aer*), and fire (*Ignis*).

ELEMENTS IN PREHISTORY
Iron was one of the elements familiar to ancient people from about 1500 B.C. The Hittites, in what is now central Turkey, found that they could obtain it by heating iron ores and extracting the iron. Their knowledge then spread across Europe. This iron reaping hook is over 2,000 years old.

Iron blade fitted into handle made from antler.

BIRTH OF THE ELEMENTS
The simplest element, hydrogen, was the first to form, shortly after the Big Bang, which created the Universe thousands of millions of years ago. It was followed by helium. All the elements that now make up the Earth were created in the heart of giant stars. The elements were scattered through space when these stars exploded.

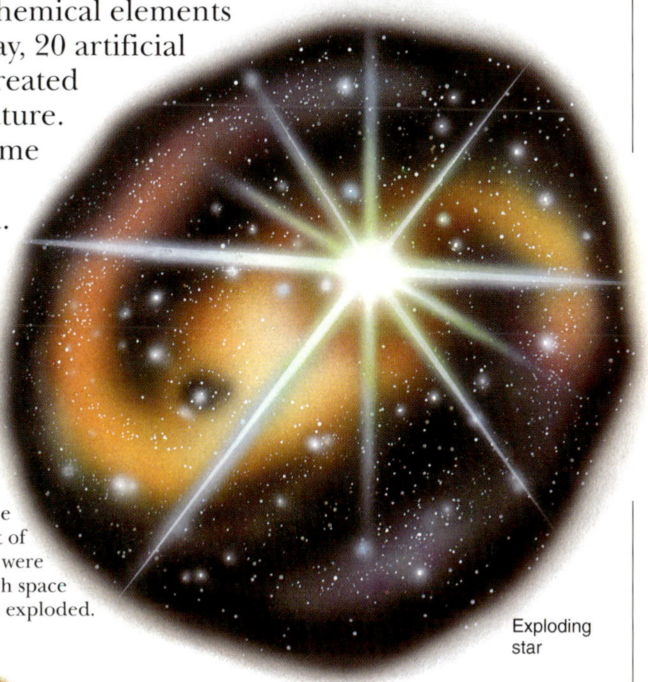

Exploding star

AGE OF THE ELEMENTS
In 1669 a German man called Hennig Brand was probably the first to extract an element when he discovered phosphorus. But it was nearly a century later before others followed him and heated substances to extract the elements from their compounds. Others separated elements by electrolysis, which means passing electricity through a substance.

A 19th-century laboratory

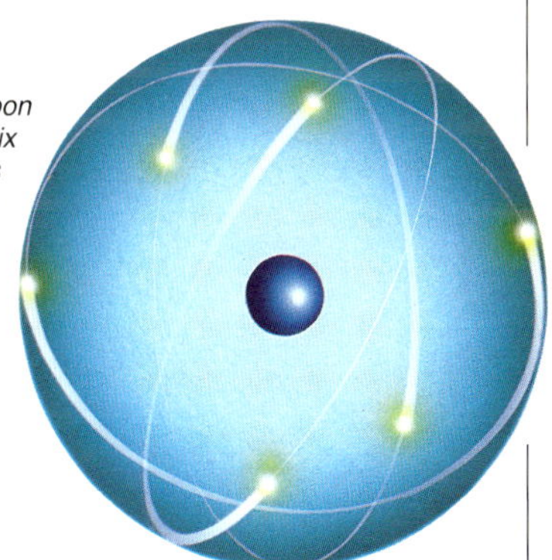

In this carbon atom, the six electrons spin around constantly ready to bond with other atoms.

ATOMS
All the atoms of an element have the same numbers of electrons in their shells and protons in the nucleus. This gives each element its unique chemistry.

LINEAR ACCELERATOR
Nuclear physicists can create a new element by bombarding an existing element with high-speed particles in a linear accelerator. By adding to the number of protons in the nucleus, a new element is made.

COMMON ELEMENTS
In the Universe as a whole, hydrogen and helium are by far the most common elements. They are the main elements in the stars, making up 98 per cent of their matter. In the Earth's crust, there is more oxygen than any other element, followed by silicon. Together they account for nearly three-quarters of the crust. Carbon, hydrogen, and oxygen are the most common elements in the human body, because they make up the compounds in all the body cells.

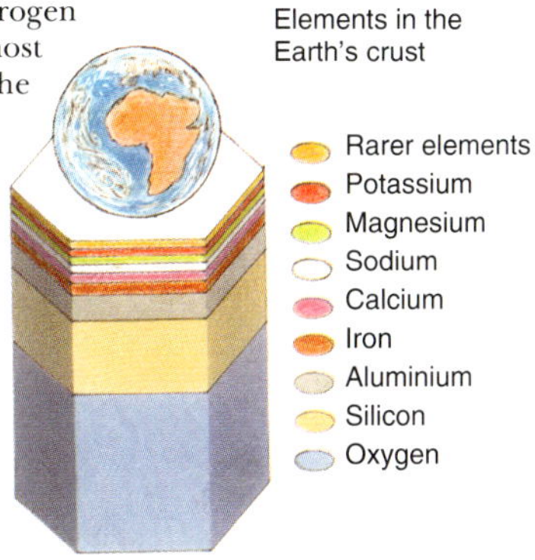

Elements in the Earth's crust

Find out more

ATOMIC STRUCTURE P.24
RADIOACTIVITY P.26
PERIODIC TABLE P.32
COMPOUNDS AND MIXTURES P.58
FACT FINDER P.402

PERIODIC TABLE

THIS COMPLICATED-LOOKING TABLE is really a simple list of all the elements. They are arranged in rows in order of increasing atomic number, or number of protons in the nucleus. During the 1860s chemists noticed that certain groups of elements behaved in similar ways, and tried to set the groups out clearly in a table. In 1869 Dimitri Mendeleyev published the best table, which is still used today. A chemist can tell a lot about an element just by looking at its position in the periodic table.

Calcium

Silicon

Sulphur

Titanium

Tungsten

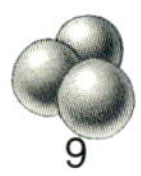
Cobalt

Copper

1	2	3	4	5	6	7	8	9	10	11	12	13	14	15	16	17	18
1 H Hydrogen 1																	2 He Helium 4
3 Li Lithium 7	4 Be Beryllium 9											5 B Boron 11	6 C Carbon 12	7 N Nitrogen 14	8 O Oxygen 16	9 F Fluorine 19	10 Ne Neon 20
11 Na Sodium 23	12 Mg Magnesium 24											13 Al Aluminium 27	14 Si Silicon 28	15 P Phosphorus 31	16 S Sulphur 32	17 Cl Chlorine 35	18 Ar Argon 40
19 K Potassium 39	20 Ca Calcium 40	21 Sc Scandium 45	22 Ti Titanium 48	23 V Vanadium 51	24 Cr Chromium 52	25 Mn Manganese 55	26 Fe Iron 56	27 Co Cobalt 59	28 Ni Nickel 58	29 Cu Copper 63	30 Zn Zinc 64	31 Ga Gallium 69	32 Ge Germanium 74	33 As Arsenic 75	34 Se Selenium 80	35 Br Bromine 79	36 Kr Krypton 84
37 Rb Rubidium 85	38 Sr Strontium 88	39 Y Yttrium 89	40 Zr Zirconium 90	41 Nb Niobium 93	42 Mo Molybdenum 98	43 Tc Technetium 97	44 Ru Ruthenium 102	45 Rh Rhodium 103	46 Pd Palladium 106	47 Ag Silver 107	48 Cd Cadmium 114	49 In Indium 115	50 Sn Tin 120	51 Sb Antimony 121	52 Te Tellurium 130	53 I Iodine 127	54 Xe Xenon 132
55 Cs Caesium 133	56 Ba Barium 138	57-71	72 Hf Hafnium 180	73 Ta Tantalum 181	74 W Tungsten 184	75 Re Rhenium 187	76 Os Osmium 192	77 Ir Iridium 193	78 Pt Platinum 195	79 Au Gold 197	80 Hg Mercury 202	81 Tl Thallium 205	82 Pb Lead 208	83 Bi Bismuth 209	84 Po Polonium 209	85 At Astatine 210	86 Rn Radon 222
87 Fr Francium 223	88 Ra Radium 226	89-103	104 Unq Unnil-quadium 260	105 Unp Unnil-pentium 262	106 Unh Unnil-hexium 263	107 Uns Unnil-septium 262	108 Uno Unnil-octium 265.	109 Une Unnil-ennium 266									

Mercury

Iodine

57 La Lanthanum 139	58 Ce Cerium 140	59 Pr Praseodymium 141	60 Nd Neodymium 142	61 Pm Promethium 145	62 Sm Samarium 152	63 Eu Europium 153	64 Gd Gadolinium 158	65 Tb Terbium 159	66 Dy Dysprosium 164	67 Ho Holmium 165	68 Er Erbium 168	69 Tm Thulium 169	70 Yb Ytterbium 174	71 Lu Lutetium 175
89 Ac Actinium 227	90 Th Thorium 232	91 Pa Protactinium 231	92 U Uranium 238	93 Np Neptunium 237	94 Pu Plutonium 244	95 Am Americium 243	96 Cm Curium 247	97 Bk Berkelium 247	98 Cf Californium 251	99 Es Einsteinium 254	100 Fm Fermium 257	101 Md Mendelevium 258	102 No Nobelium 255	103 Lr Lawrencium 256

Uranium

Plutonium

6 C Carbon 12

The atomic number is the number of protons in the nucleus. It goes up one by one along each period.

The symbol is a shorthand way of writing the element used in chemical equations.

The relative atomic mass is the mass of the atom compared with the mass of carbon-12, taken as 12.

KEY

- Alkali metals
- Alkaline-earth metals
- Transition metals
- Lanthanides
- Actinides
- Poor metals
- Semimetals
- Non-metals
- Noble gases

DIMITRI MENDELEYEV

A Russian schoolteacher, Dimitri Mendeleyev (1834–1907), collected all the information about the known elements and wrote out a card for each one. Then he arranged the cards in the order of their atomic weights to create the periodic table. He left gaps for elements he predicted would be discovered, and the three found in his lifetime proved him right.

Groups and periods

How does the periodic table work? The 109 known elements are arranged in horizontal rows, called periods. The atomic number goes up as you move across. The periods start with an alkali metal on the left and end with a noble gas on the right. The atoms of the elements on the left, at the beginning of each period, have only one electron in their outer shell. By the end of the period the outer shell is filled with eight electrons. The vertical columns, called groups, each contain elements that have the same number of electrons in the outer shell. So they have the same valency and behave in a similar way chemically.

PERIODIC TABLE

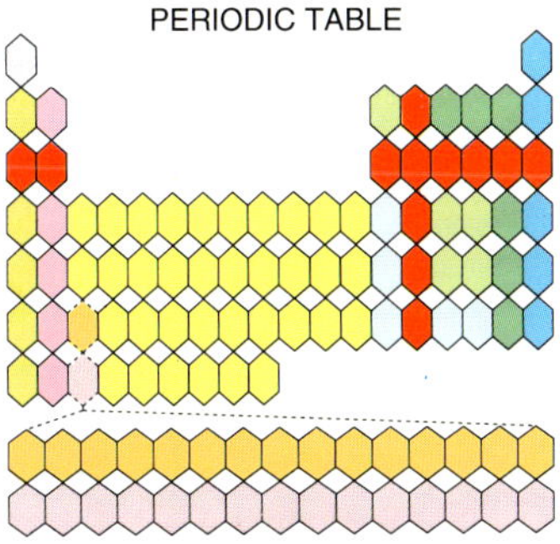

Group 14: carbon (C), silicon (Si), germanium (Ge), tin (Sn), lead (Pb)

Period 3: sodium (Na), magnesium (Mg), aluminium (Al), silicon (Si), phosphorus (P), sulphur (S), chlorine (Cl), argon (Ar)

METALS AND NON-METALS

Most of the chemical elements are metals. The non-metals are in a triangle on the right of the periodic table. Between the two are the semimetals, which have some properties of metals and some of non-metals. There are several big differences between metals and non-metals. Metals are solid (the one exception is mercury, a liquid). They conduct heat and electricity well, and usually have high melting and boiling points. They form positive ions (cations) when they bond with other elements. Most non-metals are gases, with low melting and boiling points. They are not good conductors, except for carbon. They form negative ions (anions) when they bond with other elements.

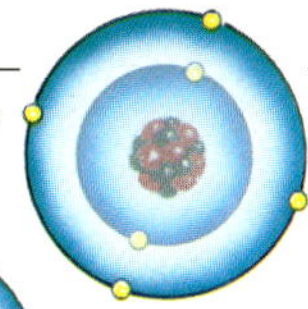

Carbon has two shells.

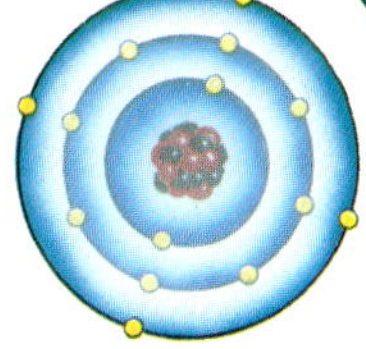

Silicon has three shells.

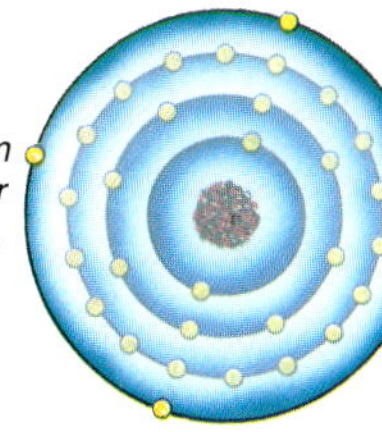

Germanium has four shells.

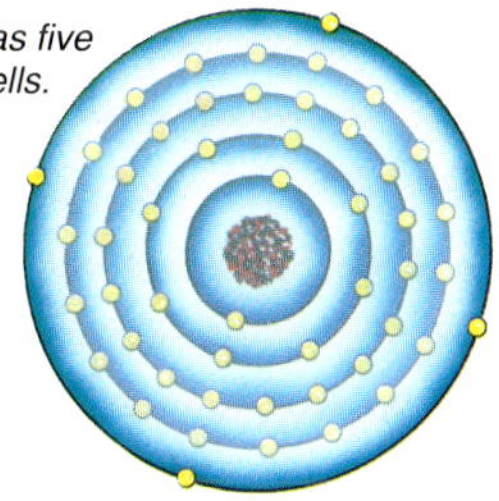

Tin has five shells.

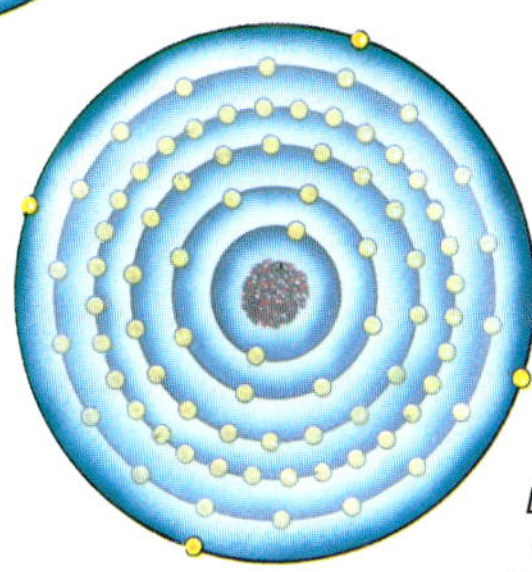

Lead has six shells.

DOWN A GROUP

In some groups, such as Group 1, the alkali metals, Group 2, the alkaline-earth metals, and Group 18, the noble gases, the group relationship is very obvious: the elements are similar in appearance and reactivity (ability to bond). In other groups, such as Group 14, the chemical properties remain similar, but the elements change from a non-metal at the top to metals at the bottom. Carbon (C) is a typical non-metal, silicon (Si) and germanium (Ge) are both semimetals, and tin (Sn) and lead (Pb) are both metals.

6	C	Carbon	12
14	Si	Silicon	28
32	Ge	Germanium	74
50	Sn	Tin	120
82	Pb	Lead	208

Down a group, the number of shells increases by one with each element. An atom can have up to seven shells. The number of electrons in the outer shell is always the same as the other elements in the group.

The number of electrons for each element is the same as the atomic number.

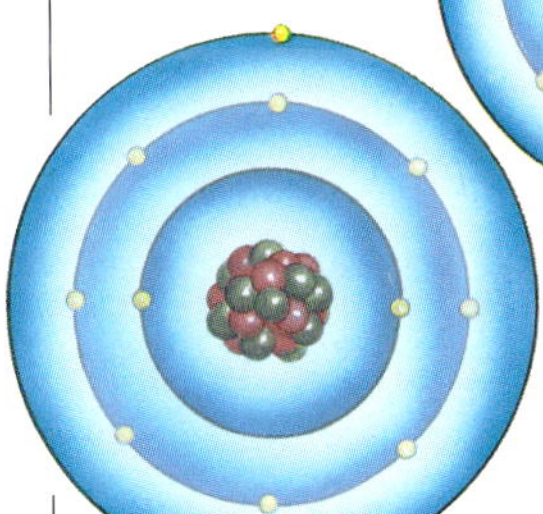

Sodium, from Group 1, has 11 electrons, with one in its outer shell.

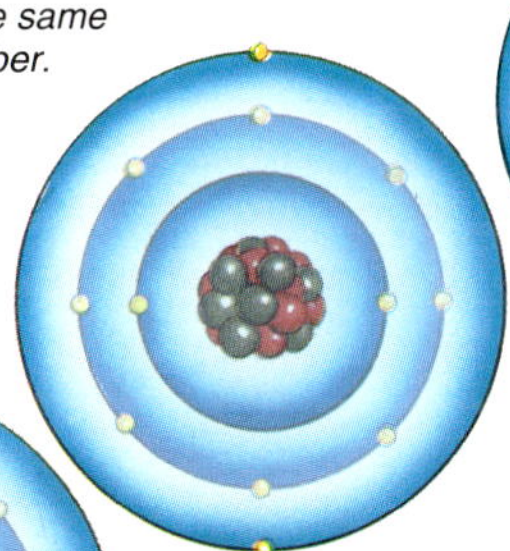

Magnesium, from Group 2, has 12 electrons, with two in its outer shell.

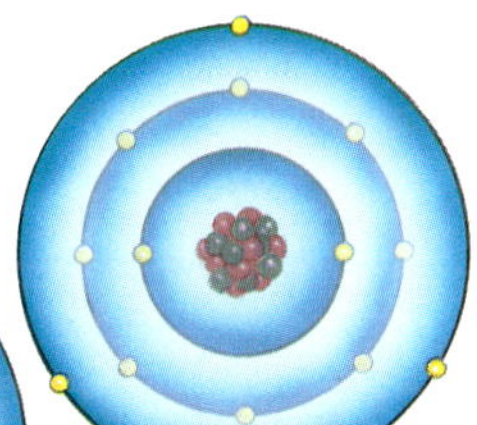

Aluminium, from Group 13, has 13 electrons, with three in its outer shell.

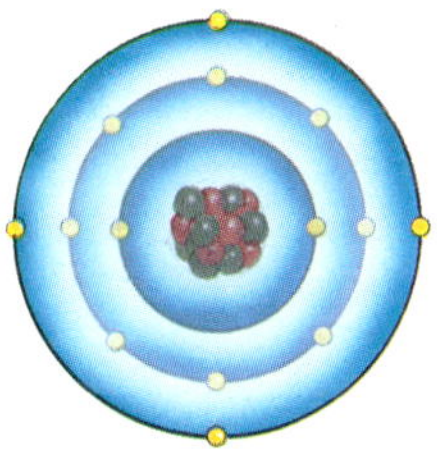

Silicon, from Group 14, has 14 electrons, with four in its outer shell.

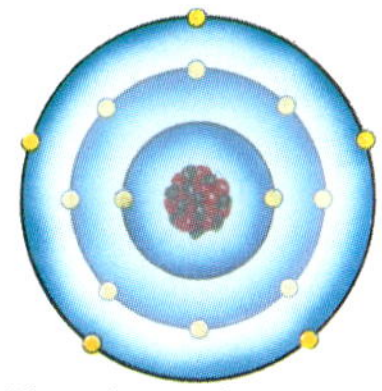

Phosphorus, from Group 15, has 15 electrons, with five in its outer shell.

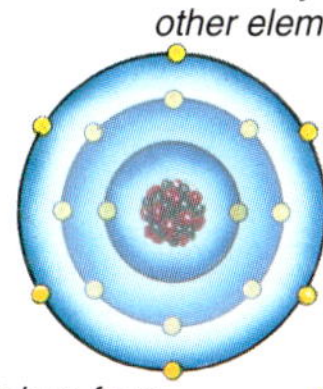

Sulphur, from Group 16, has 16 electrons with six in its outer shell.

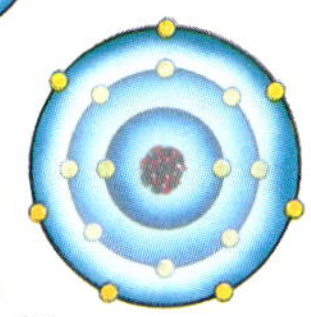

Chlorine, from Group 17, has 17 electrons, with seven in its outer shell.

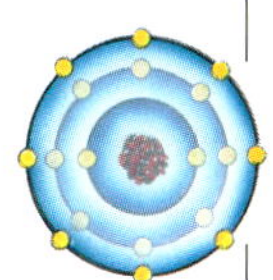

Argon, from Group 18, has 18 electrons, with eight in its outer shell.

ACROSS A PERIOD

Going across the period, the number of electrons increases by one with each element, and the chemical properties of the elements show a gradual change. In Period 3, the elements change from the metal sodium (Na), through the semimetal silicon (Si), to the non-metal Argon (Ar). The elements change from forming cations to forming anions.

DECREASING SIZE

The number of shells remains the same across a period, but as the number of electrons increases, the size of the atom decreases. This is because the extra protons in the nucleus pull the extra electrons closer to it.

11	12	13	14	15	16	17	18
Na	Mg	Al	Si	P	S	Cl	Ar
Sodium	Magnesium	Aluminium	Silicon	Phosphorus	Sulphur	Chlorine	Argon
23	24	27	28	31	32	35	40

Find out more

ATOMIC STRUCTURE P.24
BONDING P.28
ELEMENTS P.31
ALKALI METALS P.34
SEMIMETALS P.39
NOBLE GASES P.48
REACTIVITY SERIES P.66
FACT FINDER P.402

ALKALI METALS

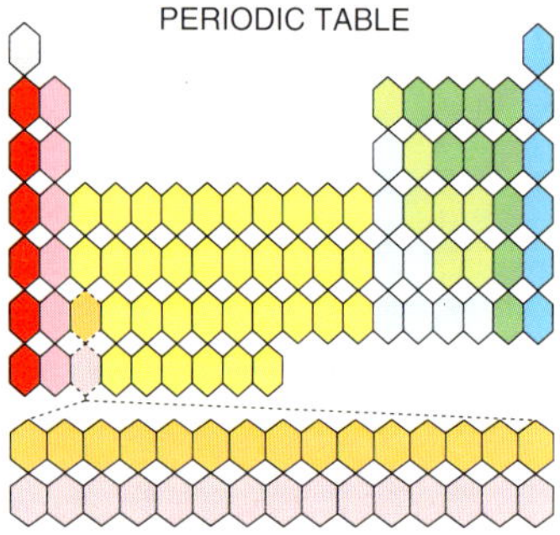

Group 1: lithium (Li), sodium (Na), potassium (K), rubidium (Rb), caesium (Cs), and radioactive francium (Fr)

THE SALT THAT YOU EAT on your food contains sodium, the most common element of Group 1 of the periodic table. All the members of this group are called the alkali metals, because they react with water to form alkaline solutions. Potassium, another member, is an ingredient in fertilizers, as potassium sulphate, or potassium nitrate (also called saltpetre). Doctors use compounds of lithium to treat manic depression, a mental illness. Also, lithium is mixed with aluminium to make a light but strong alloy (metal mixture) used in aeroplanes. All the alkali metals are a silvery-white colour. Their reactivity increases going down the group. All have one electron in their outer shells.

SOAPMAKING
Sodium hydroxide and potassium hydroxide are boiled with fat to make hard soap and liquid soap. It is thought that soap was first made by the Ancient Egyptians.

Alkali metals are soft enough to cut with a knife.

Sodium reacts so quickly with oxygen in the air that a cut surface tarnishes within minutes. Alkali metals are stored in oil to prevent this reaction.

Potassium reacts even faster than sodium with oxygen in the air.

SODIUM LAMPS
Street lamps glow a vivid orange-yellow because they contain sodium vapour. The colour is produced when electricity passes through this vapour. Sodium compounds give a similar colour when they are held in a flame.

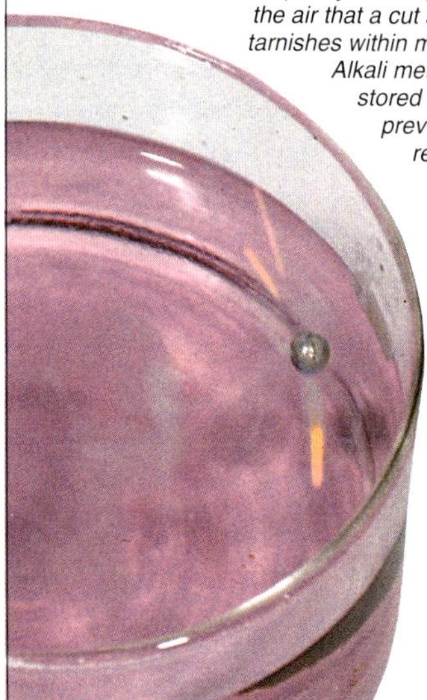

REACTION WITH WATER
A piece of potassium metal reacts so vigorously with water that it zooms all over the surface, creating bubbles of gas. This gas is hydrogen, which burns with a pink-blue flame. The potassium and the water react to form potassium hydroxide, which makes an alkaline solution in water. When all the metal has reacted with the water, the water is warm because of the heat given out during the reaction. All the alkali metals react in a similar way with water. However, rubidium and caesium explode as they touch it.

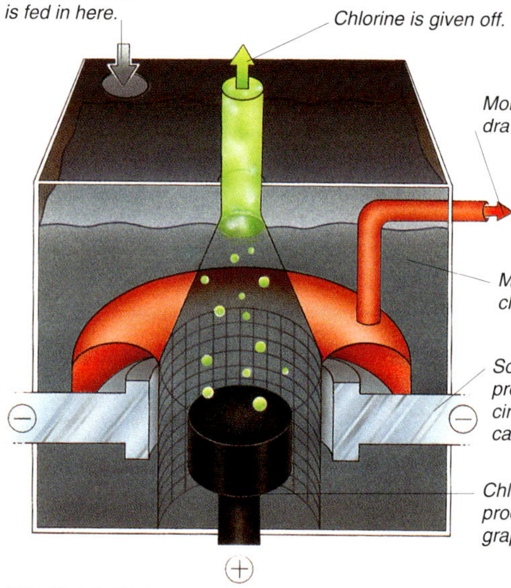

MAKING SODIUM
Sodium can be extracted from salt (sodium chloride), using a Down's cell. The salt is heated to 800°C (1760°F) to make it melt. Electricity travels through the molten salt, via two rods called a cathode and an anode, to make it separate into sodium and chlorine. This process is called electrolysis, and was first carried out by Humphry Davy (1778–1829).

CAESIUM ATOMIC CLOCK

Clocks keep time by "counting" some kind of rhythm, such as the swinging of a pendulum. Atomic clocks "count" the natural vibrations of caesium atoms. Scientists know that caesium atoms vibrate at 9,192,631,770 times per second, so fractions of a second can be measured very accurately using this clock. The vibrations are detected with the help of an electromagnetic field.

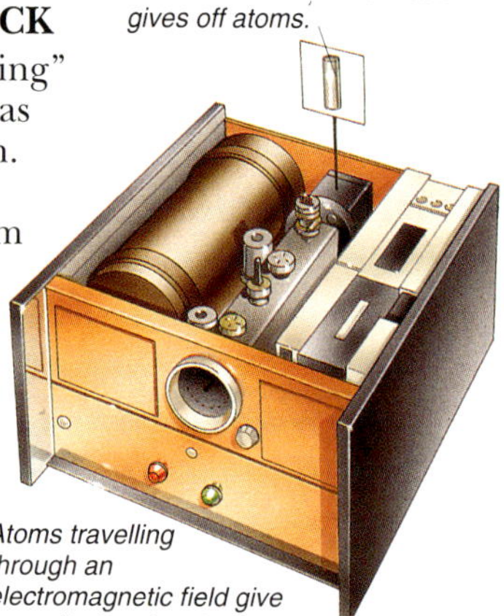

Find out more

BONDING P.28
PERIODIC TABLE P.32
ELECTROLYSIS P.67
ALKALIS AND BASES P.70
CHEMISTRY IN FARMING P.91
ALKALI INDUSTRY P.94
ELECTROMAGNETISM P.156
FACT FINDER P.402

ALKALINE-EARTH METALS

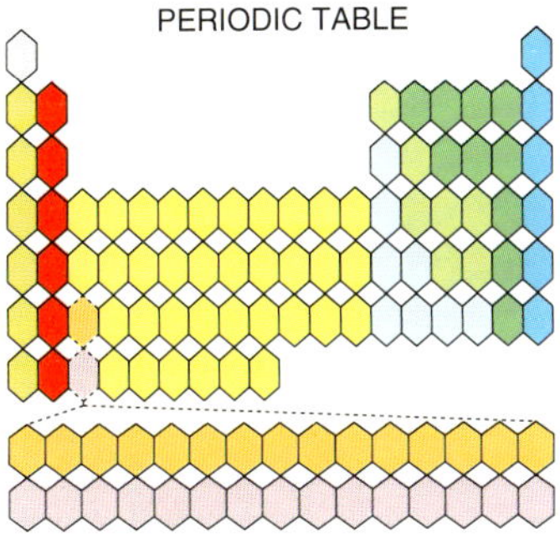

Group 2: beryllium (Be), magnesium (Mg), calcium (Ca), strontium (Sr), barium (Ba), and radioactive radium (Ra)

CALCIUM, FOUND IN CHALK, milk, and your bones, is one of the most familiar elements in Group 2 of the periodic table. All these elements are called alkaline-earth metals because they react with water to produce alkaline solutions and their compounds occur widely in nature. For example, beryllium is found in the semi-precious gem beryl. Radium is the radioactive element discovered by Marie Curie. A radioisotope of strontium, strontium-90, is a dangerous part of nuclear fallout, but it is also used to treat skin cancers. In their pure form, alkaline-earth metals are silvery-white. They have a similar chemistry to the alkali metals, but they are less reactive. They all have two electrons in their outer shells.

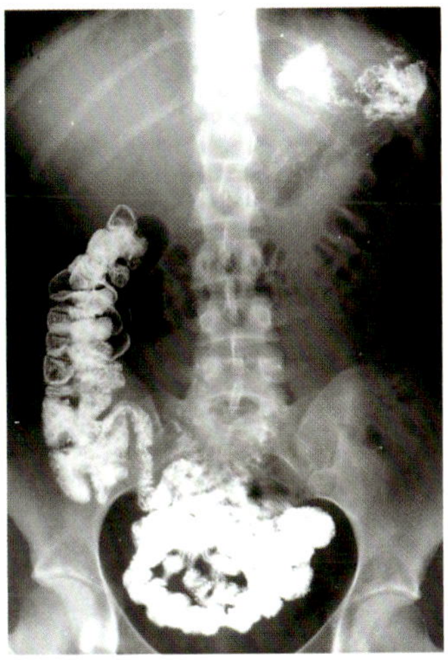

BARIUM MEAL
In hospitals, some patients have a "barium meal", which contains barium sulphate, before they have an X-ray. The barium sulphate blocks X-rays and makes the digestive system show up on X-ray photographs. Doctors can then see if there is anything wrong.

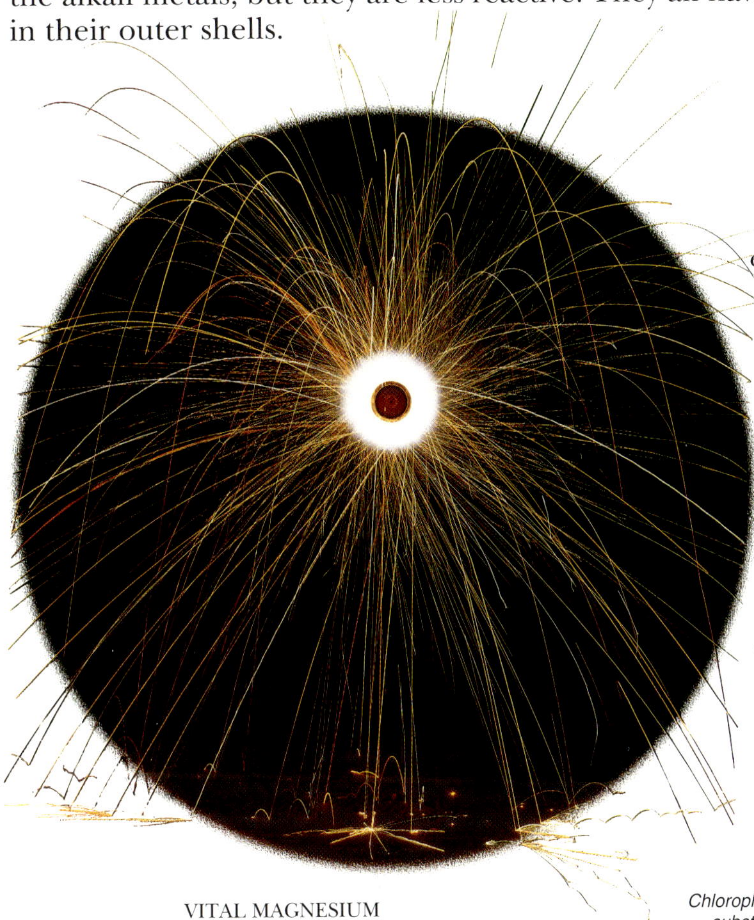

FIREWORK COLOURS

The vivid colours we see in fireworks are mainly produced by alkaline-earth metals. Magnesium metal is used in some fireworks to produce a brilliant white light. Strontium compounds are used to produce crimsons, and barium compounds are used to produce greens.

LIGHTWEIGHT ALLOYS
Magnesium is widely used in alloys for bicycle frames, which also contain such metals as aluminium and zinc. This makes them light but strong.

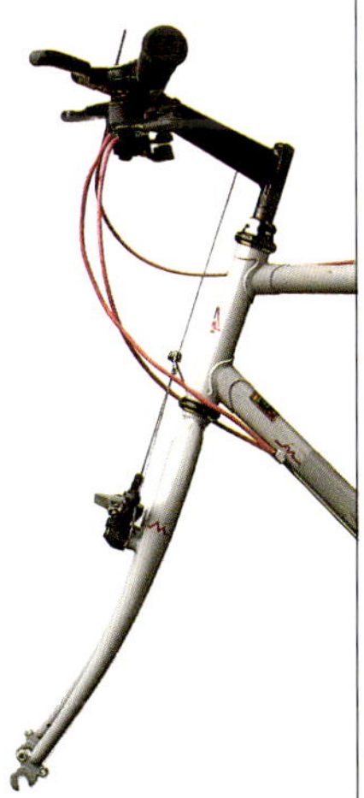

VITAL MAGNESIUM
The green pigment chlorophyll is essential for plants to be able to make food. Chlorophyll contains magnesium compounds, which help capture the energy in sunlight. This energy is used in the food-making process called photosynthesis.

Chlorophyll is the substance that makes plants green.

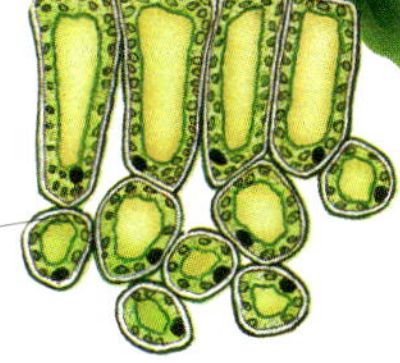
Chlorophyll is found in chloroplasts, tiny bodies in plant cells.

CHALKY FALLS
In hot springs, like Pammukale Falls in Turkey, warm water bubbles to the surface and cascades over the surrounding rocks. If it contains a lot of dissolved chalk (calcium carbonate), this will come out of solution as the water evaporates, and be deposited as chalky "icicles".

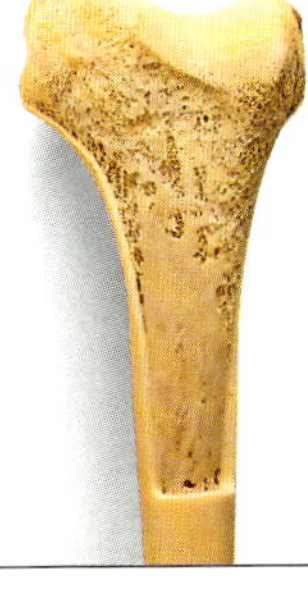

BONE CALCIUM
Calcium is a major ingredient of bone, where it is present as calcium phosphate. This makes bones hard, so that they can give structure and protection to other parts of the body.

Find out more

PERIODIC TABLE P.32
COMPOUNDS AND MIXTURES P.58
ALKALIS AND BASES P.70
PHOTOSYNTHESIS P.340
SKELETONS P.352
FACT FINDER P.402

TRANSITION METALS

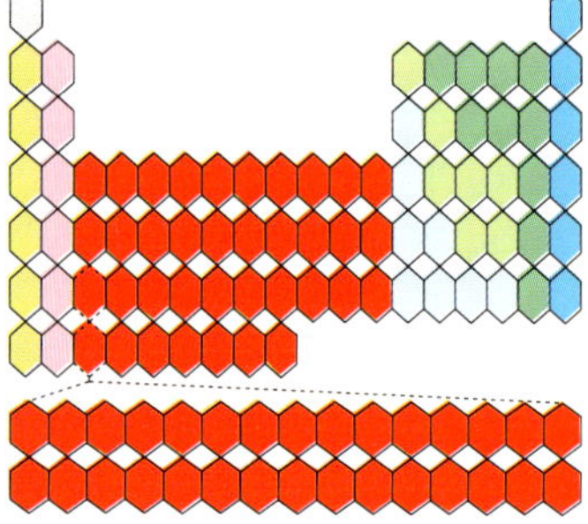

There are a lot of transition metals. Some are very well known, but some are very rare. The more familiar ones include iron (Fe), cobalt (Co), nickel (Ni), copper (Cu), zinc (Zn), silver (Ag), cadmium (Cd), tungsten (W), platinum (Pt), gold (Au), and mercury (Hg).

IRON, NICKEL, SILVER, AND GOLD are typical metals. They are shiny, hard, and strong. They have high melting points, and conduct heat and electricity well. In the periodic table these and most of the other typical metals form part of a central block of elements called the transition metals. Each of the elements is very similar to those near it in the table. As well as being typical metals, the transition elements have other things in common. Many have variable valencies, many are good catalysts, they form alloys with other metals, and many of their compounds are coloured.

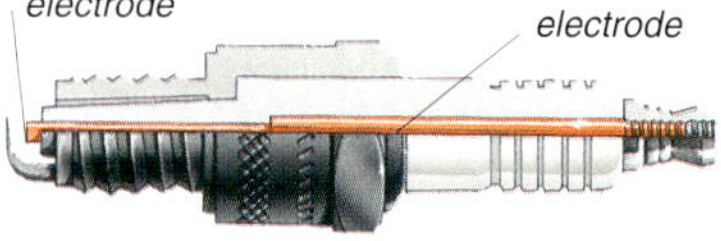

SPARK PLUG
The main body and lower electrode of a spark plug are made of iron. The central electrode is usually made of a copper alloy.

TRANSITION METALS IN CARS

A car is a good example of something that is made of many transition metals. The body shell is made of mild steel, which is iron with a little carbon. The steel also contains traces of manganese, to improve its quality and strength. Sometimes the steel shell is galvanized (coated with zinc), to protect the steel from rusting.

Valve springs, which control the valves that regulate the flow of fuel mixture, are made of steel alloyed with chromium and vanadium, so that they can resist high temperatures and last for a long time.

Suspension springs are made of steel with a high percentage of carbon in it, hardened and heat-treated to give increased strength.

Most engine blocks (containing the cylinders, where the fuel mixture is fired) are made of cast iron, which contains a high percentage of carbon and other impurities. It is cheap and resists shock well.

The generator, the part of a car which produces electricity, contains coils of fine copper wire. Elsewhere, perhaps as much as 100 m (110 yards) of copper wire connect the car's electrical components.

The bearings in the gear box are layered, with an inner lining of relatively soft bearing alloy containing metals such as copper, tin, and lead, and an outer shell of steel.

Stainless steel, which is iron alloyed with chromium and nickel, is used for the trim in various places and sometimes for the exhaust system.

Car paints are often made using transition metal compounds. White paint may contain titanium dioxide, and red and yellow paints may contain cadmium sulphides.

The headlamp reflector is usually chromium plated. Chromium provides the final hard shiny coating over base layers of nickel and copper.

The light bulb contains tungsten in the coiled filament. It retains its strength when white hot, and is long-lasting.

ZINC
Zinc is often used in batteries. In the type of battery you would use in a torch, the zinc makes up the casing. In the pill-sized mercury battery, the zinc is inside.

An ordinary battery with the outside label stripped off to show the zinc casing.

This battery is the type you would find inside a watch.

MAGNETIC METALS
Iron, cobalt, and nickel are the only transition metals that can be made into strong magnets. Electromagnets have an iron core that becomes strongly magnetic when electricity is passed through surrounding coils. They are used to move waste iron in scrapyards. The electricity is switched on to pick up the iron, then switched off to drop it.

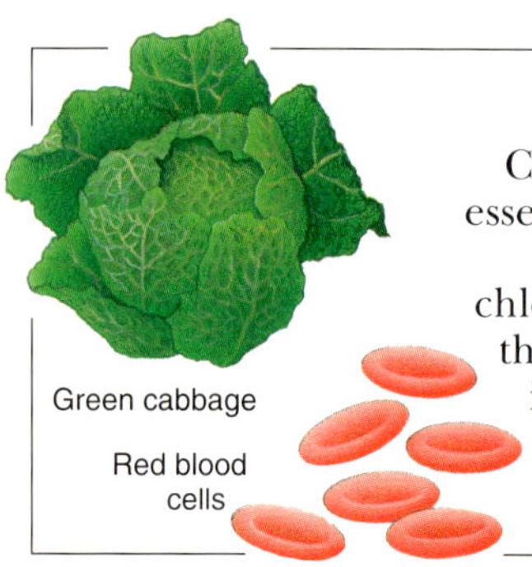

Green cabbage

Red blood cells

IRON FOR LIFE

Compounds containing iron are essential to living things. In plants, iron compounds help to make chlorophyll, the green compound that produces food. In mammals iron is found in red blood cells in haemoglobin, which carries oxygen round the body.

These pellets are pure nickel.

SILVER

The precious metal silver has been used to make jewellery for thousands of years. Today it is used most in the photographic industry. This is because the compounds it forms with chlorine, bromine, and iodine are sensitive to light. They are the active ingredients on a photographic film. The silver compounds change chemically when light hits them. This change is made visible during the developing process, which turns the light-affected compounds to pure silver. Tiny grains of silver make up the dark areas on a photographic negative.

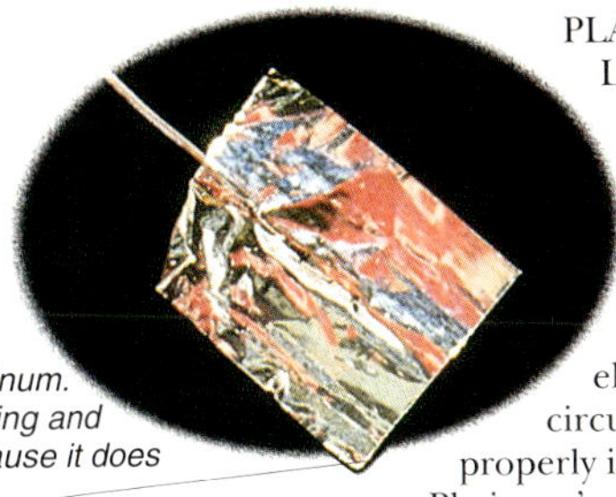

This small, square electrode is made of platinum. It is long-lasting and efficient because it does not corrode.

PLATINUM

Like gold and silver, platinum is a precious metal, used to make jewellery. It is precious because it is rare and attractive. It also never corrodes or wears away. This is also why it is used to make electrodes and electronic circuits – they would not work properly if their circuit metal tarnished. Platinum's main use in industry is as a catalyst, meaning it speeds up reactions such as the breakdown of oil products.

NICKEL ALLOYS

Silver-coloured coins are made from cupronickel, an alloy of copper and nickel. Nickel is also used, along with two other transition metals, iron and chromium, to make stainless steel. Nickel is a shiny metal that does not corrode or tarnish, and it gives these properties to its alloys. Another interesting nickel alloy, with iron, is Invar. This is used in precision measuring instruments because it scarcely expands or contracts at all when the temperature changes.

Each gold bar is numbered for security reasons.

NATIVE METALS

Most elements are not found native (in a pure state) in the Earth's crust, but a few of the transition metals are. The most important of these include copper, silver, gold, and platinum. Gold has been the most prized metal of all for centuries. It is one of the most chemically unreactive elements there is. These gold bars are almost 100 per cent pure and will never lose their shine.

GALILEO'S BATTERIES

The U.S. space probe *Galileo*, heading for Jupiter, has nuclear batteries, called RTGs (radioisotope thermoelectric generators), which are powered by plutonium.

INNER TRANSITION SERIES

Part of the transition metals, the inner transition series consists of two periods on the periodic table. The lanthanides are in Period 6, so called because of their first element, lanthanum. The actinides are in Period 7 and are named after their first element, actinium. Within each of these groups, the elements behave in a similar way chemically. The lanthanides are so similar that chemists had difficulty telling them apart. And besides having similar properties, the actinides are all radioactive.

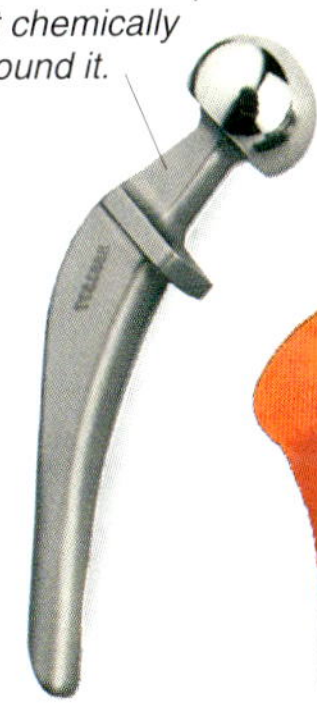

Once in place, this titanium hip joint will not react chemically with the tissues round it.

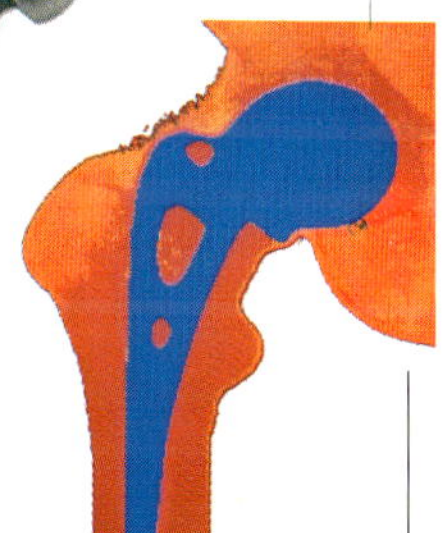

Coloured X-ray of a titanium hip joint in place.

TITANIUM

Titanium is a very strong, unreactive metal. This makes it useful for hip joints and other parts implanted in the body to repair or replace damaged bones.

SAMARIUM IN MAGNETS

Magnets in a loudspeaker help to transmit the sound. Samarium, one of the lanthanides, and cobalt make powerful magnets, and so smaller loudspeakers can be made using magnets containing these metals.

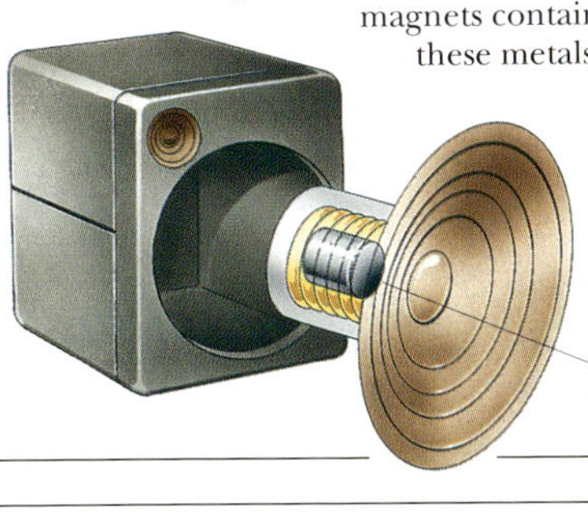

Samarium magnet

Uranium

REFINED URANIUM

The best-known actinide, uranium, is the fuel used in nuclear reactors. It is extracted from the ore pitchblende. The mining of this ore is carefully controlled because it is so valuable.

Find out more

RADIOACTIVITY P.26
CATALYSTS P.56
IRON AND STEEL P.84
ALLOYS P.88
DYES AND PIGMENTS P.102
NUCLEAR ENERGY P.136
ELECTROMAGNETISM P.156
PHOTOGRAPHY P.206
FACT FINDER P.402

POOR METALS

PERIODIC TABLE

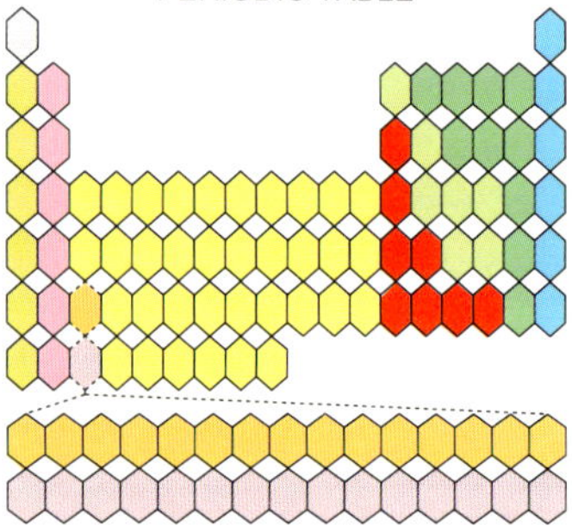

Aluminium (Al), gallium (Ga), indium (In), thallium (Tl), tin (Sn), lead (Pb), bismuth (Bi), and polonium (Po)

SOME METALS ARE QUITE SOFT AND WEAK, and melt easily. Although these are known as the poor metals, they are very useful. Tin and lead were two of the earliest metals used by people because they are easily extracted from their ores (minerals). They are especially useful in alloys. Bronze, a mixture of tin and copper, was the first alloy to be made, in about 3500 B.C. Pewter and solder are tin-lead alloys. Lead is one of the densest (heaviest) metals in common use. The Romans made drains out of lead, and their word for lead was *plumbum*, which is why we still call our drainage systems "plumbing". But lead is a serious health hazard because it gradually builds up in the body and is poisonous. Another poor metal, aluminium, is one of the least dense (lightest) of all metals.

The skin of an aeroplane is made of sheets of aluminium alloy riveted together. The aluminium quickly reacts with oxygen to form a protective coating of its own, so it does not need to be painted for protection as iron does.

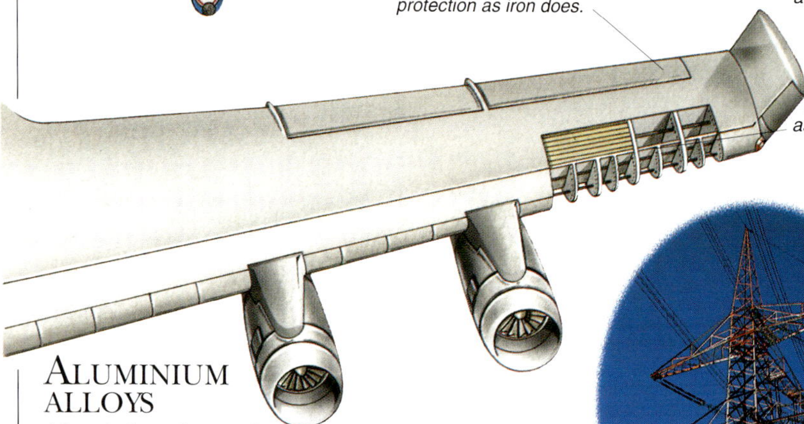

The inside of an aeroplane wing is mostly empty, with a few "ribs" that hold the outer aluminium skin in place. This is to keep the aeroplane as light as possible.

ALUMINIUM ALLOYS

Aluminium is a soft and weak metal. It is the metal used to make kitchen foil. But when aluminium is alloyed with metals such as copper, it becomes hard and as strong as steel. Aluminium alloys are used to build aeroplanes because of their combination of lightness and strength.

ELECTRICAL USES
Aluminium is a good conductor of electricity. It is used for the transmission lines that carry mains electricity across the country on pylons. The lines have a core of steel to give them strength.

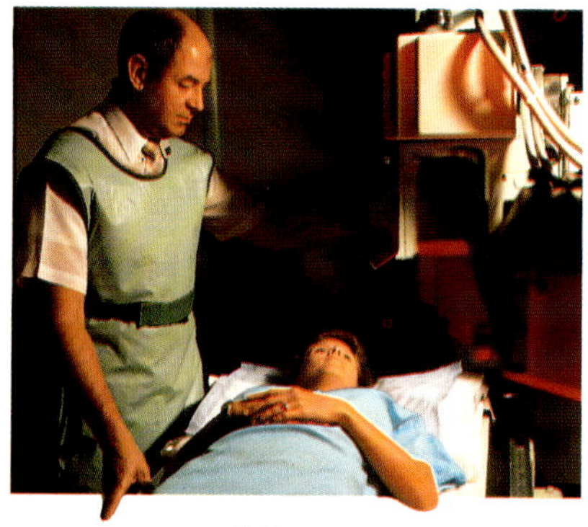

HEAVY AS LEAD

Lead has a high density. For this reason it is a good barrier to radiation. This is put to use in the nuclear industry and hospital X-ray departments, where the staff wear lead aprons. These aprons are made by baking a mixture of fine lead powder and plastic to make a flexible sheet. This is then cut out to the right shape.

Lead shot can cause pollution in the wild. Birds that swallow it are gradually poisoned by it.

LEAD IN GLASS
The sparkle of crystal is the result of adding lead oxide to glass. The lead also makes crystal softer. This means that designs that will glitter can be cut into it.

TIN–LEAD ALLOYS
Pewter, a tin-lead alloy, is used to make tankards and ornaments. Solder is another tin-lead alloy, used to join metals in plumbing and electrical circuiting.

TIN CANS

As the pure metal, tin is most used as a coating on steel, to make tinplate. The tin is applied by dipping or electrolysis. Ordinary tin cans are made of tinplate. Most drinks cans are made out of aluminium.

Tin has two forms, white and grey. The white form turns into the powdery grey form at low temperatures. Tin was one of the elements known to ancient civilizations, who combined it with copper to make bronze. Bronze was used to make jewellery and, later, tools.

Find out more

ATOMIC STRUCTURE P.24
PERIODIC TABLE P.32
REACTIVITY SERIES P.66
ELECTROLYSIS P. 67
ALUMINIUM P.87
ALLOYS P.88
FACT FINDER P.402

SEMIMETALS

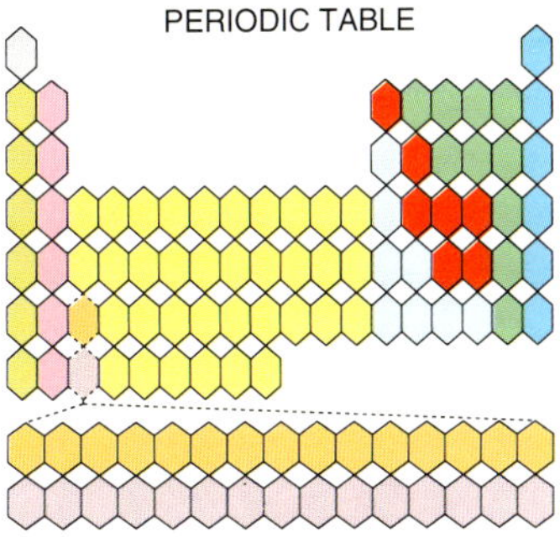

Boron (B), silicon (Si), germanium (Ge), arsenic (As), antimony (Sb), selenium (Se), and tellurium (Te)

MOST OF THE CHEMICAL ELEMENTS have definite properties that identify them either as a metal or a non-metal. But a few elements have properties that place them in between. These are the semimetals, or semiconductors. For example, arsenic looks metallic, but it is a poor conductor of heat and electricity. Like a non-metal, it forms compounds with many metals. Several semimetals are used in alloys. Silicon forms part of steel, and antimony forms part of an alloy used to make ball bearings. But the most important use of semimetals is in semiconductors. These are used to make microchips and other electronic components (parts).

These solar cells are cut from a cylinder of solid silicon.

SOLAR CELLS
Satellites are often designed to stay up in space for years. Ordinary batteries would not last long, so large panels of solar batteries are used instead. The solar panels contain thousands of tiny cells of silicon, which convert the energy of sunlight into electricity. The panels are positioned so that they always face the Sun, and as the satellite travels round the Earth, the maximum amount of sunlight can be used to provide energy.

SILICATES
Silicon is the most plentiful solid element on Earth. It is most commonly found in the form of complex compounds called silicates in clays and rocks. This crystal is a feldspar, a potassium aluminium silicate, one of the commonest minerals on Earth.

BORON AND SILICON
Glass is made from sand, which is one mineral form of silica or silicon dioxide. Quartz is another common silica mineral, often found as attractive crystals. Heatproof glass contains another semimetal, boron. The addition of the boron prevents the glass from expanding too much and cracking when it is heated. Borosilicate glass saucepans can be put straight onto a flame. Glassware in laboratories is also made of this type of glass.

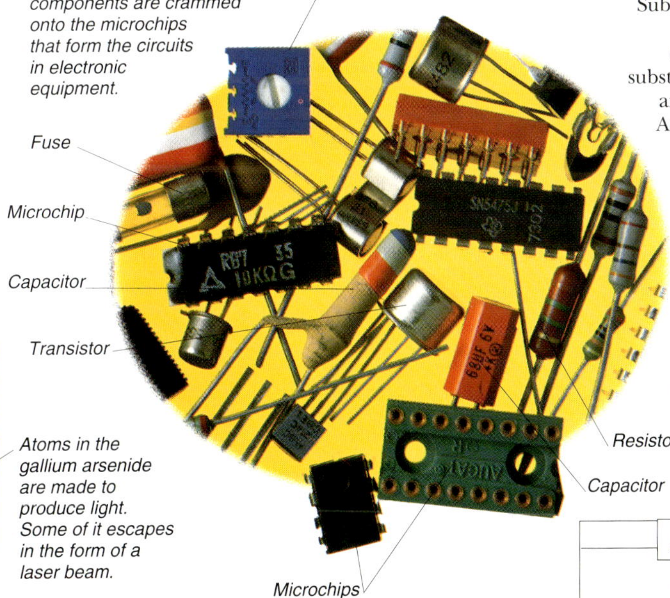

SEMICONDUCTORS
Substances that can be either conductors or insulators, depending on what other substances are added to them, are called semiconductors. Adding substances to them is called doping. The most widely used semiconductor is silicon, which is doped with boron or phosphorus. Semiconductors are used to create devices such as diodes and transistors, which can pass, strengthen, or block an electric current.

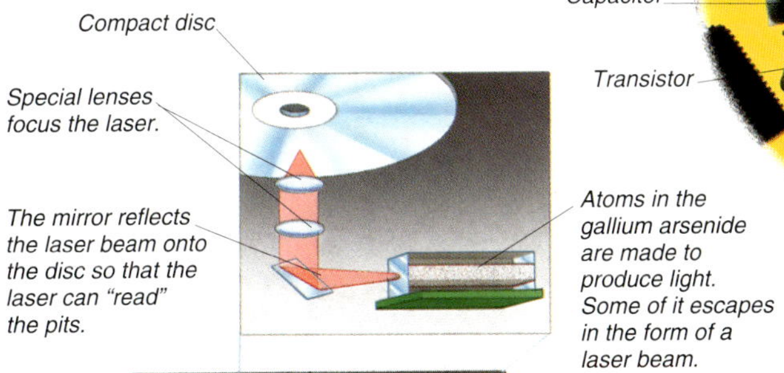

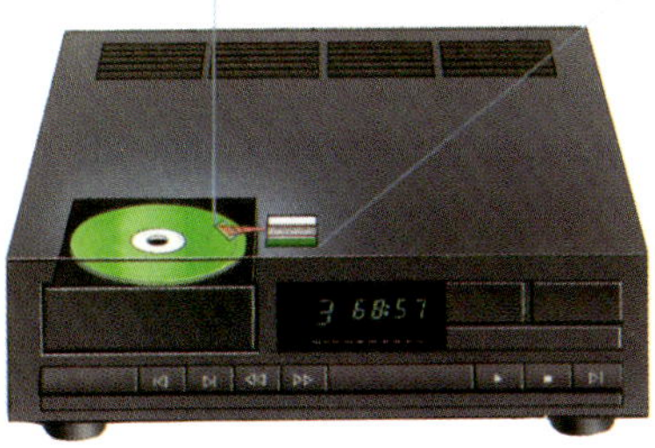

COMPACT DISC
Music is recorded as pits on a compact disc, and these are "read" by a low-powered laser beam. The laser is a semiconductor, or diode, laser produced from gallium arsenide, a compound of arsenic. A diode is a device that has been doped to allow electricity to flow in one direction only. Diode lasers also transmit signals in fibreoptic telephone lines.

Find out more

CRYSTALS P.30
PERIODIC TABLE P.32
GLASS P.110
MATERIAL DESIGN P.111
CURRENT ELECTRICITY P.148
ELECTRONIC COMPONENTS P.168
ROCKS AND MINERALS P.221
FACT FINDER P.402

CARBON

PERIODIC TABLE

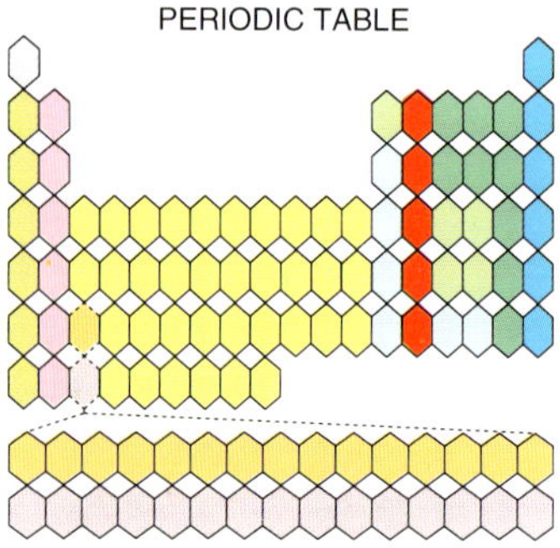

Group 14: carbon (C), silicon (Si), germanium (Ge), tin (Sn), and lead (Pb)

WITHOUT CARBON, no living thing could survive. We all have carbon in our bodies, and take it in when we eat our food every day. The carbon atom can bond with as many as four other atoms from other elements, as well as other carbon atoms, so there are hundreds of thousands of different carbon compounds. Carbon is a non-metal. In nature it occurs in its pure form as diamond and graphite. In compounds it occurs in carbonate rocks such as chalk, fossil fuels such as coal, and carbon dioxide in the air. When fuels burn, the carbon in them reacts with the oxygen in the air to form carbon dioxide. But too much carbon dioxide in the air traps heat like the glass of a greenhouse. This is called the greenhouse effect.

FIZZY DRINKS
The fizz in drinks is carbon dioxide. The gas dissolves in the liquid under pressure, and bubbles come out when the pressure is released.

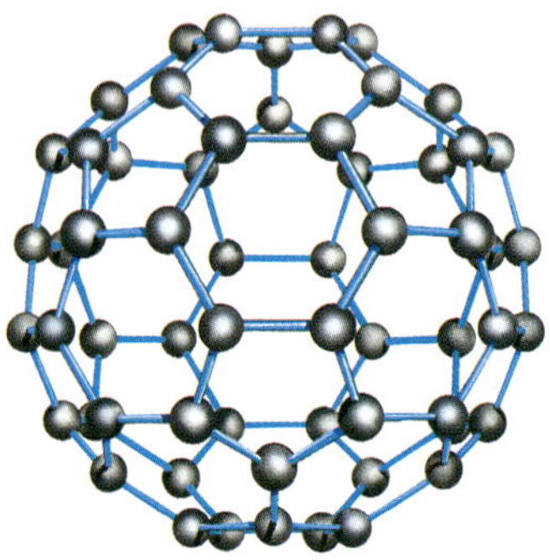

CARBON BUCKYBALLS
In 1990 scientists discovered a third allotrope of carbon, besides diamond and graphite. Its molecular structure looks like a football or the domed roof of the stadium developed by American engineer Buckminster Fuller. This form of carbon was therefore named buckminsterfullerene, and one molecule is sometimes called a "buckyball".

Anthracite, the best coal, is over 90 per cent carbon.

Diamond is the hardest mineral known.

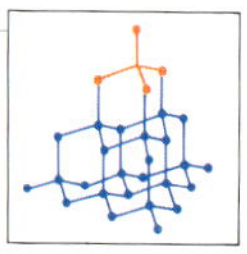

In diamond, each carbon atom is attached to four other carbon atoms.

When you draw a line with a pencil, graphite is left as a mark because the sheets of carbon atoms are easily pulled apart.

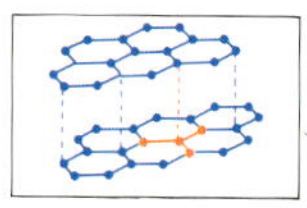

In graphite, each carbon atom is attached to only three other carbon atoms in flat sheets that are weakly attracted to each other.

DIFFERENT FORMS OF CARBON

At first sight, diamond and graphite seem to have nothing in common. Diamond is hard and clear and graphite is soft and grey. But they are both forms (allotropes) of carbon. Carbon also makes up a large part of coal. When coal is heated out of contact with air, it turns to coke, a smokeless fuel. The charcoal used in barbeques is carbon made by partly burning wood or bones.

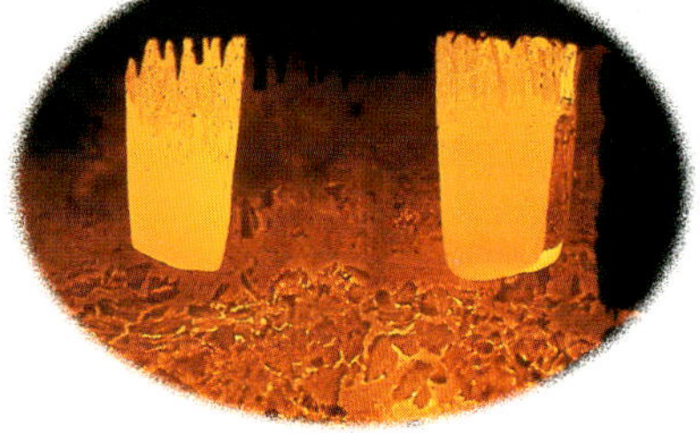

ELECTRIC CARBON
Carbon is unusual among non-metals because it is a good conductor of electricity. In steelmaking, the electrodes in the electric arc furnace are graphite blocks. Electricity arcs (jumps) between the electrodes and the metal scrap. The heat produced melts the metal.

CARBON FIBRES

Organic textile fibres are heated to make silky threads of pure carbon. These fibres are combined with other materials such as plastic to make very strong and light composite materials. Carbon-fibre composites are useful for objects where lightness and strength are important, from tennis rackets to small aeroplanes.

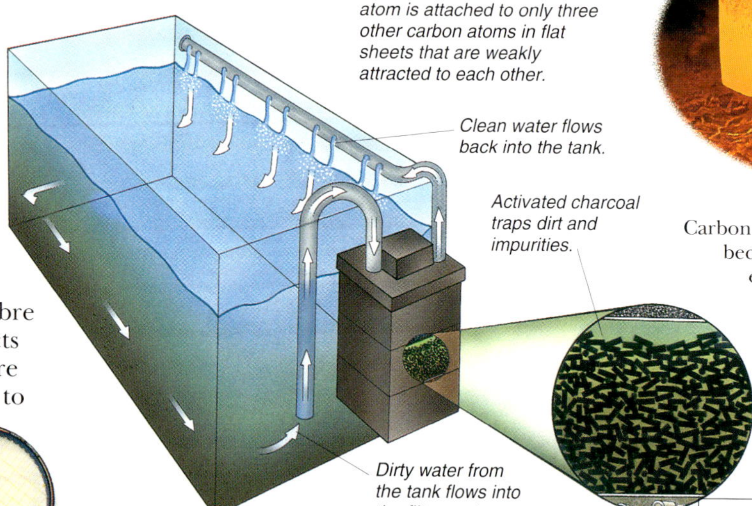

Clean water flows back into the tank.

Activated charcoal traps dirt and impurities.

Dirty water from the tank flows into the filter canister.

ACTIVATED CHARCOAL
When specially treated, or activated, charcoal has great powers of adsorption, meaning it attracts materials to its surface. It can remove poisonous gases or unpleasant odours from the air. It forms part of gas masks, spacecraft ventilation systems, and cooker hoods. It is also used to purify liquids, including the water in fish tanks. The water in the tank passes over the charcoal, which removes the dirt. The cleaned water then goes back into the tank.

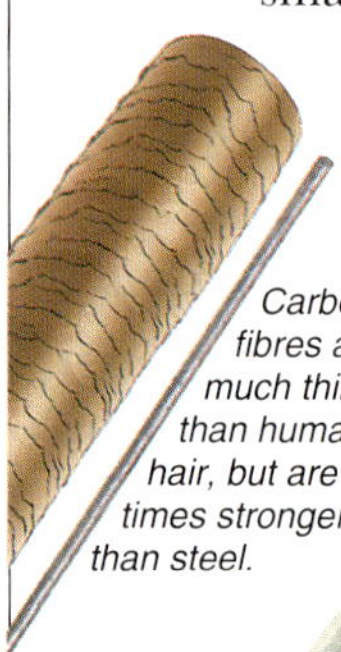

Carbon fibres are much thinner than human hair, but are eight times stronger than steel.

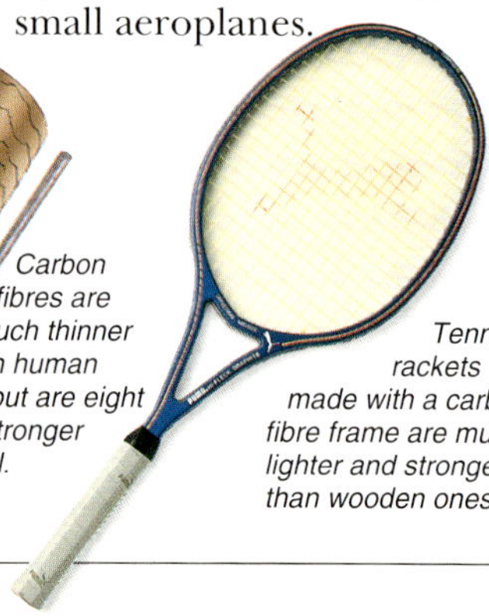

Tennis rackets made with a carbon-fibre frame are much lighter and stronger than wooden ones.

Find out more

PERIODIC TABLE P.32
ORGANIC CHEMISTRY P.41
IRON AND STEEL P.84
COAL PRODUCTS P.96
MATERIAL DESIGN P.111
CYCLES IN THE BIOSPHERE P.372
FACT FINDER P.402

ORGANIC CHEMISTRY

CARBON IS SO IMPORTANT that there is a whole area of science that studies it. This is organic chemistry. It is called "organic" because it used to be the study of living organisms (living things consist of carbon compounds). But now it is the study of all compounds that contain carbon, except for "inorganics" such as carbonates and carbon dioxide. Carbon is different from all the other elements because it has a unique ability: it can form very stable bonds with itself. Because of this, there are long chains containing hundreds of thousands of carbon atoms. Organic compounds can be divided into families such as proteins, fats, and sugars.

Brightly coloured fabrics that do not fade became possible with aniline dyes.

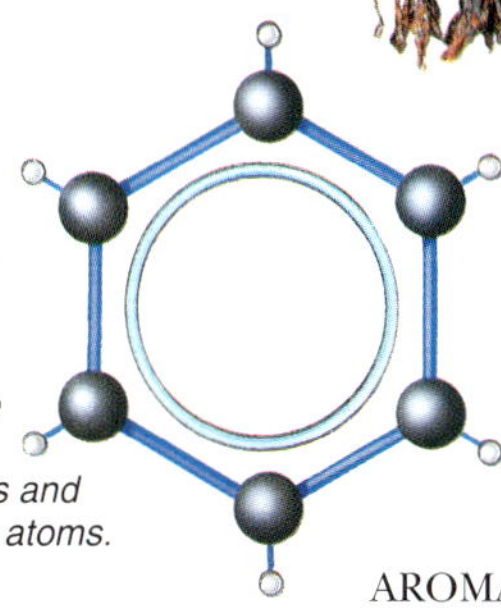

The benzene ring has six carbon atoms and six hydrogen atoms.

LIVING CHEMISTRY
Carbon compounds hold the key to plant and animal life on Earth. Life is only possible because of the extremely complex and varied chemistry of carbon that goes on in all living cells.

CARBON CYCLE
Carbon circulates through the air, animals, plants, and the soil all the time. This is called the carbon cycle.

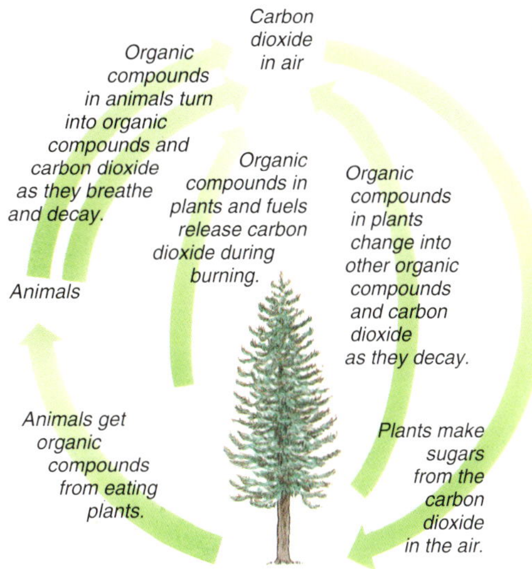

AROMATICS AND ALIPHATICS
Benzene is an organic liquid with a powerful aroma. Organic compounds that contain the benzene ring structure are called the aromatics. The aromatic compound aniline, also called aminobenzene, is the starting point for a whole range of vivid dyes, called the aniline dyes. Organic compounds that are made up of chains of carbon atoms, with no rings, are called aliphatics.

ORGANIC CHEMISTRY

1808 The Swedish chemist Jöns Berzelius (1779–1848) uses the term organic chemistry to refer to the chemistry of living things.

1828 The German chemist Friedrich Wöhler (1800–82), succeeds in recreating a natural carbon compound in his laboratory. The meaning of organic chemistry now changes to refer to the chemistry of most carbon compounds, not just the natural ones.

1865 The German chemist Friedrich Kekulé von Stradonitz (1829–96) thinks up the idea of a ring structure for benzene after dreaming about a snake biting its tail.

ISOMERS
Some carbon compounds contain the same atoms, but have different properties. This is because the atoms are arranged in a different way. Such compounds are called isomers. Butane and 2-methyl propane are isomers of each other. Bottled gas always contains some 2-methyl propane as well as butane. They are both made up of four carbon atoms and ten hydrogen atoms.

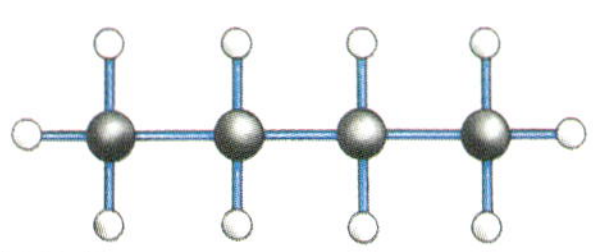

Butane

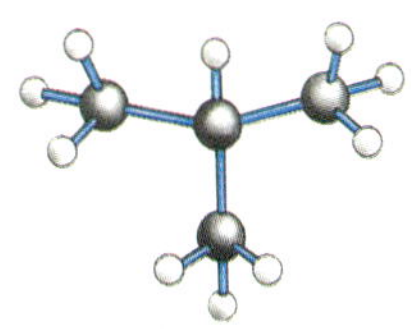

2-methyl propane

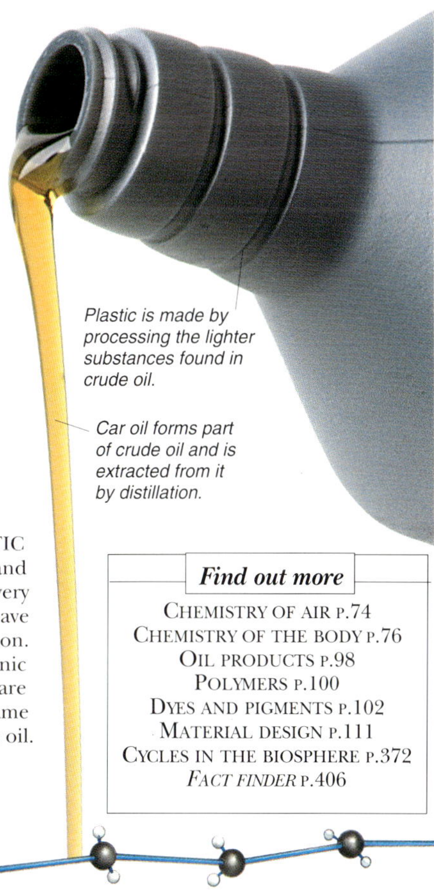

Plastic is made by processing the lighter substances found in crude oil.

Car oil forms part of crude oil and is extracted from it by distillation.

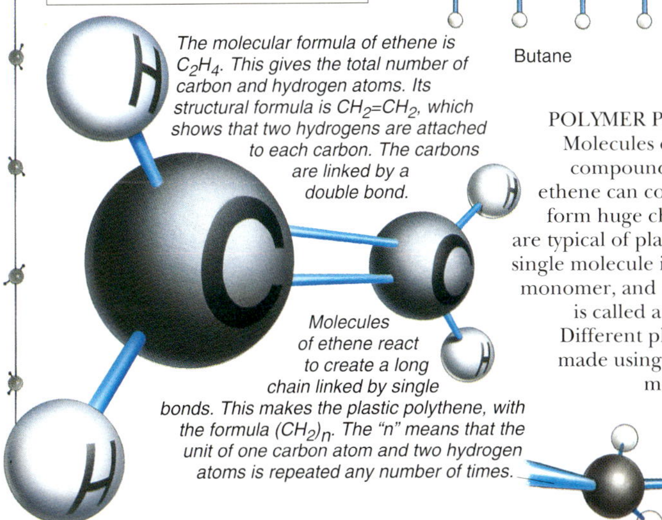

The molecular formula of ethene is C_2H_4. This gives the total number of carbon and hydrogen atoms. Its structural formula is $CH_2=CH_2$, which shows that two hydrogens are attached to each carbon. The carbons are linked by a double bond.

Molecules of ethene react to create a long chain linked by single bonds. This makes the plastic polythene, with the formula $(CH_2)_n$. The "n" means that the unit of one carbon atom and two hydrogen atoms is repeated any number of times.

POLYMER PLASTICS
Molecules of carbon compounds such as ethene can combine to form huge chains that are typical of plastics. The single molecule is called a monomer, and the chain is called a polymer. Different plastics are made using different monomers.

OIL AND PLASTIC
Car lubricating oil and plastic don't seem very alike. But they have something in common. They are both organic materials, and are produced from the same source, crude oil.

Find out more

CHEMISTRY OF AIR P.74
CHEMISTRY OF THE BODY P.76
OIL PRODUCTS P.98
POLYMERS P.100
DYES AND PIGMENTS P.102
MATERIAL DESIGN P.111
CYCLES IN THE BIOSPHERE P.372
FACT FINDER P.406

NITROGEN

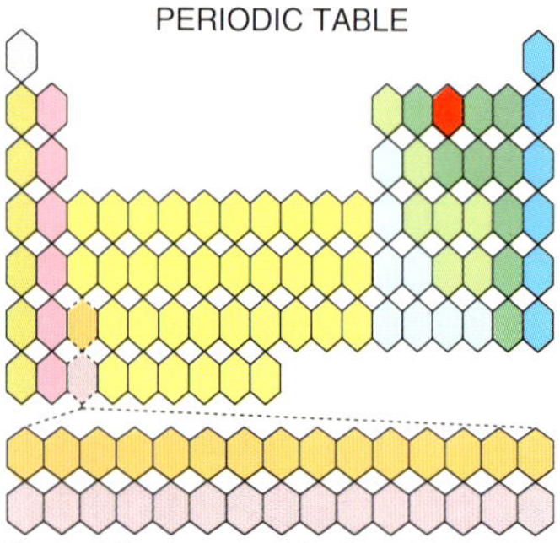

Group 15: nitrogen (N), phosphorus (P), arsenic (As), antimony (Sb), and bismuth (Bi)

THERE IS AN ELEMENT that is vital to life, and forms almost 80 per cent of the air around us. This element is nitrogen. It is a colourless gas with no taste or smell, and it forms part of the proteins in every living cell. A constant cycle keeps nitrogen in our lives. Plants get nitrogen from the soil. Animals get nitrogen by eating plants or other animals. When plants and animals die, they rot and return nitrogen to the soil. Nitrogen is also in the Earth as minerals such as sodium nitrate. Like oxygen, nitrogen in the air is made up of molecules with two atoms, which have the symbol N_2. Nitrogen forms several compounds with oxygen. These include the gases that come out of car exhausts and damage the environment.

NITROGEN EXPLOSIVES

Explosives are unstable substances that release a huge volume of gases quickly. The gases expand very rapidly and this produces a devastating shock wave. Most chemical explosives contain nitrogen, including nitroglycerine and trinitrotoluene (TNT). Nitroglycerine is an oily liquid that is highly unstable. It is made safer by being mixed with a sort of clay to make dynamite. Explosives are used to make bombs.

Explosives can be used in a very controlled way to bring down a building without damaging others nearby.

Nitrogen fertilizers help crops to grow

NITROGEN FERTILIZERS

Farmers and gardeners apply fertilizers containing nitrogen to their soil, to put back the nitrogen that plants take out. In the past, rotted manure, which is rich in nitrogen, was used. Today, many people prefer to use artificial fertilizers such as nitrates and ammonium sulphate.

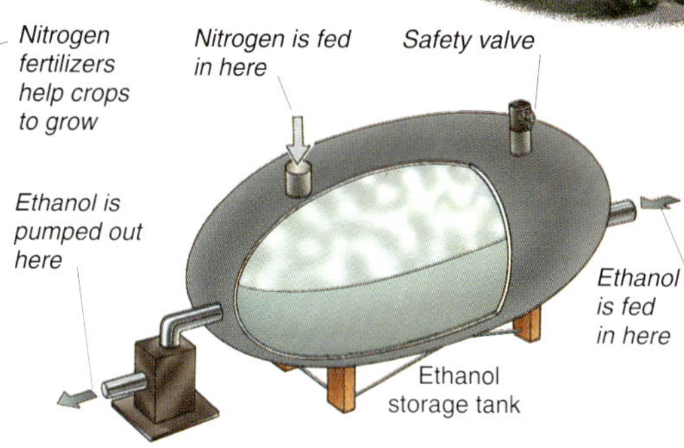

UNREACTIVE NITROGEN

Nitrogen is unreactive, so it is used to exclude oxygen, which is very reactive, from a range of containers. Ethanol (ordinary alcohol) is likely to catch fire if it comes into contact with oxygen, so nitrogen is used to exclude it from the storage tanks. Crisp packets are filled with nitrogen. This excludes oxygen, which would react with fat in the crisps and make them go stale.

NITROGEN CYCLE

There is a continuous exchange of nitrogen between the atmosphere, animals, and plants. This is called the nitrogen cycle.

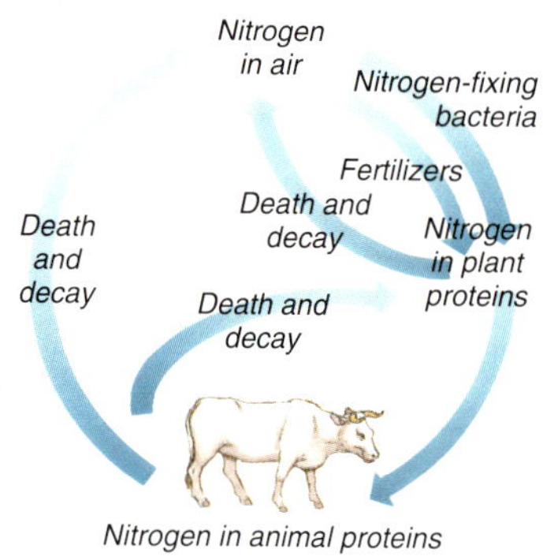

LIQUID NITROGEN

Food is quick-frozen using liquid nitrogen. Foods such as cheesecakes are loaded onto a conveyor belt in a tunnel freezer (left). As they move along, they are first cooled by nitrogen gas, then sprayed with liquid nitrogen, which freezes them.

ANAESTHETIC NITROGEN

Dinitrogen oxide is a sweet-smelling gas used as an anaesthetic. It is called "laughing gas" because it makes some patients laugh before and after they are unconscious. In the 19th century, demonstrations of the effects of laughing gas were given in private houses in London, England, just for fun. Later scientists realized how useful the gas could be as an anaesthetic.

Find out more

BONDING P.28
PERIODIC TABLE P.32
CHEMISTRY OF AIR P.74
AMMONIA P.90
CHEMISTRY IN FARMING P.91
RAIN P.264
CYCLES IN THE BIOSPHERE P.372
FACT FINDER P.402

PHOSPHORUS

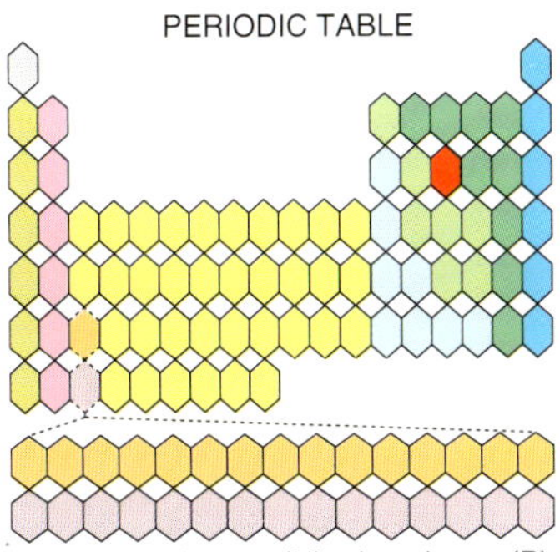

Group 15: nitrogen (N), phosphorus (P), arsenic (As), antimony (Sb), and bismuth (Bi)

HAVE YOU EVER WONDERED why cola has a sharp taste? The sharpness comes from phosphoric acid, a compound of phosphorus. In its common form, phosphorus is a yellowish, waxy, and slightly see-through solid. It glows in the dark, an effect called phosphorescence. Yellow phosphorus is so reactive that it must be kept under water to stop it reacting with oxygen and catching fire. Phosphorus is important in living things. Plants extract phosphorus from the soil. Animals get it from plants. In the Earth, phosphorus occurs mainly in mineral phosphates, most of which are made into fertilizers.

MINING PHOSPHORUS
In the Earth, phosphorus occurs in apatite (calcium phosphate), which exists in several forms. The main deposits are in North Africa. Phosphate rock is used in huge quantities in the chemical industry to make fertilizers. The rock is treated with sulphuric acid to make superphosphate, a fertilizer that is easily absorbed by plants.

PHOSPHORUS AND LIGHT
Red phosphorus is made by heating yellow phosphorus at high temperatures. It is then rolled into sheets. Red phosphorus is used in marine distress flares to create a very bright light. It is also an active ingredient in matches. A safety match will only strike on a surface containing red phosphorus. A strike-anywhere match has a phosphorus compound in the tip.

PHOSPHORUS ALLOTROPES
There are three main forms (allotropes) of the element phosphorus. Pictured left are sticks and chunks of yellow phosphorus. But they are slowly changing into red phosphorus because it is much more stable. You can see the dark patches on the sticks. Black phosphorus, the most stable form, can be made by heating the yellow under pressure.

Calcium phosphate is part of bones and teeth, but in nature it appears as crystals in a variety of colours and is called apatite.

PHOSPHORUS FOR LIFE

Bones and teeth are mainly made of calcium phosphate, which makes them hard. Phosphate groups form part of DNA (deoxyribonucleic acid) in the nucleus of cells, which controls each cell. A phosphate called ATP (adenosine triphosphate) provides energy in the body. When it breaks down to ADP (adenosine diphosphate), energy is released for doing something energetic or for body functions such as making muscle protein.

PHOSPHATES
The washing powder or liquid used to wash clothes contains sodium tripolyphosphate. This softens the water. Phosphates from sewage, fertilizers, and detergents pollute rivers because it makes a lot of algae grow. These then use up the oxygen in the water. Organic phosphates are used as pesticides.

DISCOVERING PHOSPHORUS
A German alchemist named Hennig Brand (17th century) extracted phosphorus from 50 buckets of urine. He boiled the urine down and heated it with sand. Brand chose the name phosphorus, which means light-bearer in Greek, because the element glows in the dark. Brand kept his method secret, but the Irish chemist Robert Boyle (1627–91) rediscovered phosphorus a few years later.

Find out more

PERIODIC TABLE P.32
ALKALINE-EARTH METALS P.35
NITROGEN P.42
CHEMISTRY OF THE BODY P.76
CHEMISTRY IN FARMING P.91
SOAPS AND DETERGENTS P.95
CELLS P.338
FACT FINDER P.402

OXYGEN

PERIODIC TABLE

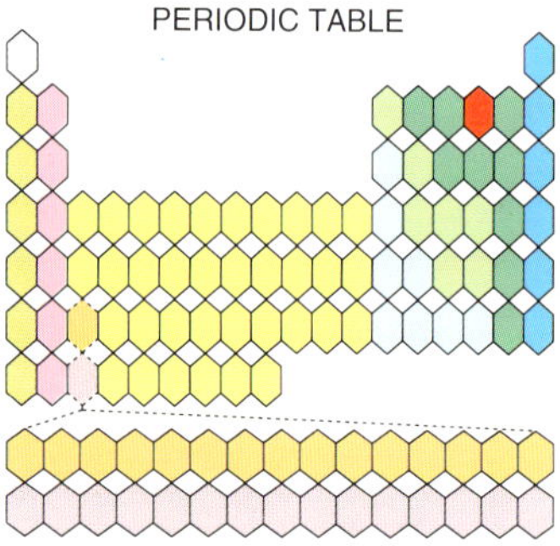

Group 16: oxygen (O), sulphur (S), selenium (Se), tellurium (Te), and polonium (Po)

THERE IS MORE OXYGEN on Earth than any other element. It is an invisible and odourless gas, and without it we would all die. We breathe it in all the time in air, where it is mixed with other gases. Oxygen is found in many things. In the oceans, it is dissolved in, and forms part of, water. In the rocks, it is found in most minerals. Ordinary oxygen is made up of molecules with two atoms, which have the symbol O_2. High in the atmosphere, a three-atom form called ozone is more common. A protective layer of ozone shields the Earth from dangerous radiation from space. Oxygen is very reactive. Burning, rusting, and respiration are just some of the chemical reactions that happen when substances combine with oxygen in the air.

RED ROCKS
The atmosphere has not always contained oxygen. But we know when it first arrived because it reacted with the iron in these rocks and turned them red. The rocks are about 2,000 million years old.

CUTTING WITH OXYGEN
Oxygen can be used to cut steel. In a special type of torch called an oxyacetylene torch, the gas acetylene is made to burn in pure oxygen to produce a temperature of over 3000°C (8600°F). This melts the steel underneath the flame and leaves a cut. Oxyacetylene torches are also used to weld steel. The two edges of the steel melt in the torch flame, and join up as they cool.

LIVING EARTH

The atmosphere contains about 21 per cent oxygen. When animals breathe, they take oxygen from the atmosphere. Plants put it back again as they make their food by photosynthesis. Fish and many other aquatic creatures breathe the oxygen that is dissolved in water.

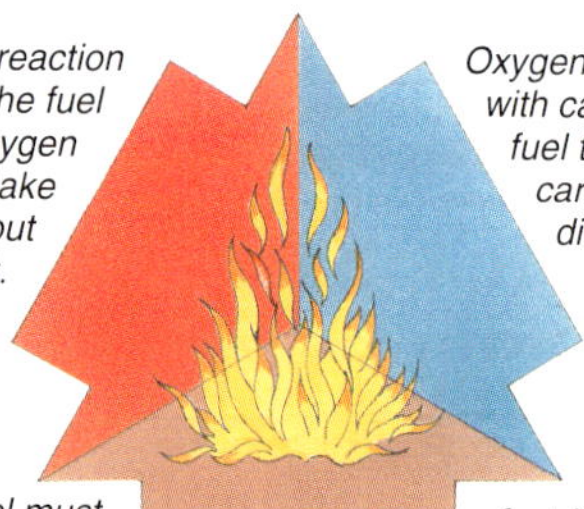

BURNING
The fire triangle shows what is needed to make a fire: heat, oxygen, and a fuel. If any one of these things is missing, the fire cannot start or will quickly go out. That is why covering a camp fire with sand or stones will make it go out. The sand or stones exclude oxygen, and so the fire cannot burn.

DISCOVERING OXYGEN
The English chemist Joseph Priestley (1733–1804) announced his discovery of oxygen in 1774, not knowing that the Swedish chemist Carl Scheele (1742–86) had found it first one or two years earlier. They proved that air is not one element. But neither quite realized what he had discovered. It was the French chemist Antoine Lavoisier (1743–94) who proved, in 1775, what oxygen is.

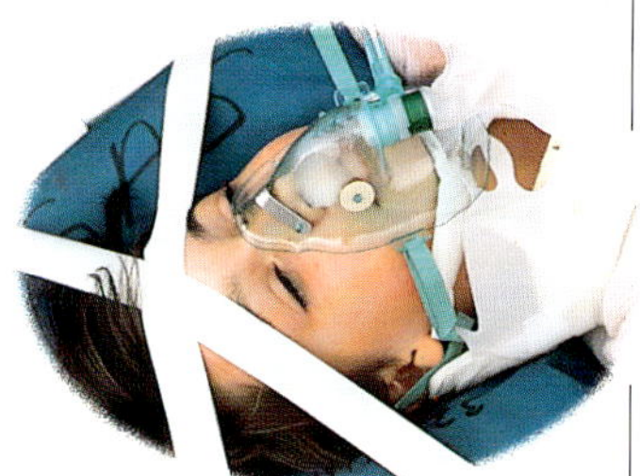

EMERGENCY OXYGEN
Patients with breathing problems or those who are very ill are given extra oxygen. Their lungs do not have to work so hard, and so the patients recover more quickly.

RUST

Iron and steel left in the air and the wet soon become covered with an orange-brown deposit called rust. Rust is iron oxide, the result of a chemical reaction between iron, oxygen, and moisture.

Find out more

BONDING P.28
PERIODIC TABLE P.32
OXIDATION AND REDUCTION P.64
CHEMISTRY OF AIR P.74
CELLULAR RESPIRATION P.346
CYCLES IN THE BIOSPHERE P.372
FACT FINDER P.402

Sulphur

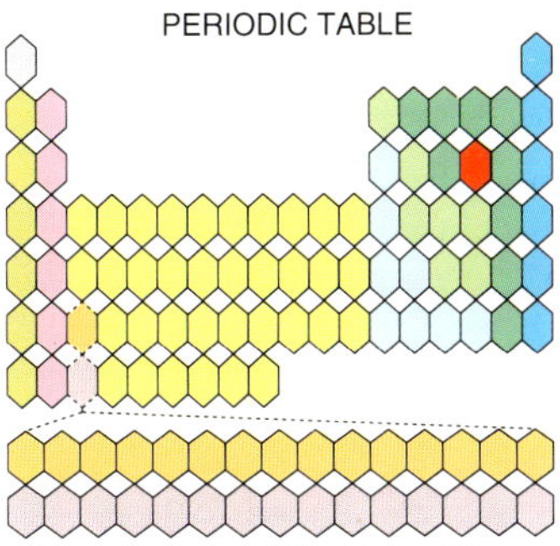

Group 16: oxygen (O), sulphur (S), selenium (Se), tellurium (Te), and polonium (Po)

WITHOUT SULPHUR, substances such as paint and detergents could not exist. They are made by a process that uses sulphuric acid, a major industrial ingredient made from sulphur. Sulphur is a bright yellow solid. In the ground, sulphur minerals include sulphides such as galena (lead ore) and sulphates such as gypsum. Sulphur is one of the most reactive of all the elements. It reacts with oxygen to form sulphur dioxide. This gas is given off in huge amounts by coal-burning power stations because coal contains sulphur. This causes pollution in the air. Sulphur is used to vulcanize (harden) rubber. This makes rubber hard enough to be made into tyres.

PROTEIN SULPHUR
Egg yolk contains sulphur, which moves out to the edge of the yolk to make a grey band if the egg is boiled for too long. Sulphur is a vital part of body-building proteins. When these break down, they produce hydrogen sulphide, a poisonous gas that smells of rotten eggs.

Sulphur crystals

Fine crystals of sulphur are found among the rocks in volcanic regions of the world. These are the rhombic shape. Volcanic vents (cracks) are a major source of sulphur in countries such as Sicily, Java, and the United States. The sulphur comes from gases in the Earth's interior.

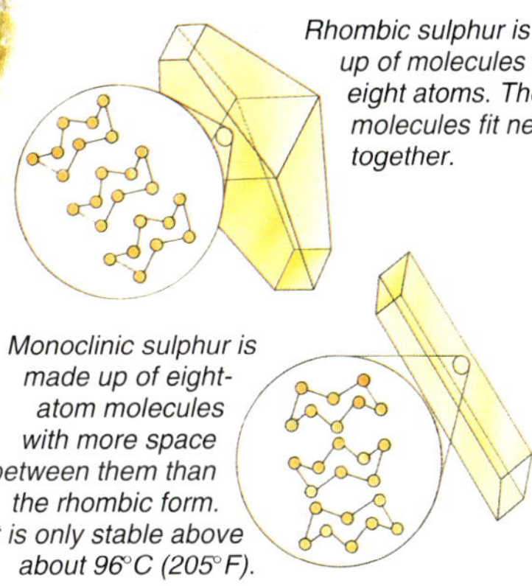

SULPHUR ALLOTROPES
There are two main forms, or allotropes, of sulphur. The stable form at normal temperatures is the rhombic form. In both forms the sulphur atoms are arranged in rings of eight.

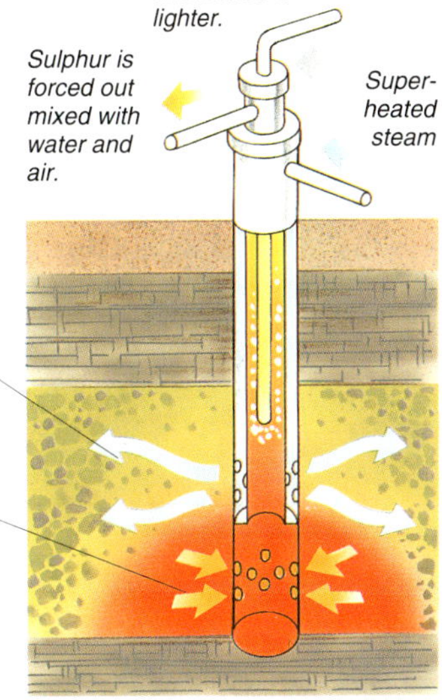

EXTRACTING SULPHUR
Sulphur can be extracted from underground deposits by the Frasch process. Three pipes are forced down into the sulphur deposit. Superheated steam is pumped down the outside pipe, which melts the sulphur. Compressed air is then sent down the central pipe. It forces frothy liquid sulphur up to the surface.

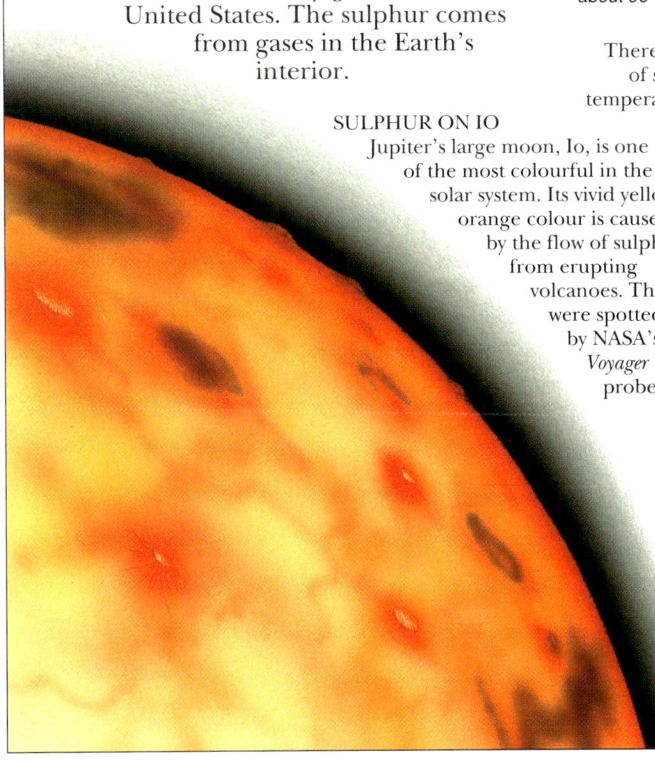

SULPHUR ON IO
Jupiter's large moon, Io, is one of the most colourful in the solar system. Its vivid yellow-orange colour is caused by the flow of sulphur from erupting volcanoes. These were spotted by NASA's *Voyager* probes.

SULPHUR BACTERIA
Some bacteria use sulphur instead of oxygen for energy, so they can only live on dissolved sulphur compounds. In the United States they are being used to release pure copper, and other transition metals, from their compounds with sulphur.

Find out more

CRYSTALS P.30
PERIODIC TABLE P.32
CHEMISTRY OF AIR P.74
SULPHURIC ACID P.89
GAS PRODUCTS P.97
INDUSTRIAL POLLUTION P.112
RAIN P.264
FACT FINDER P.402

HALOGENS

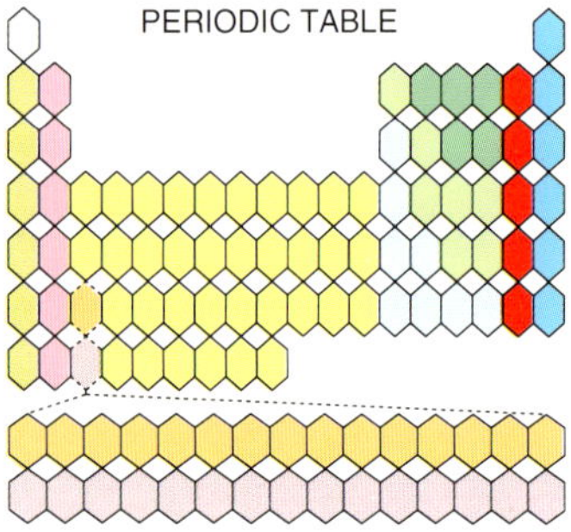

Group 17: fluorine (F), chlorine (Cl), bromine (Br), iodine (I), and radioactive astatine (At)

THE STRONG SMELL in swimming pools is caused by chlorine, one of the best-known elements in Group 17, the halogens. Chlorine also forms part of sodium chloride (common salt). Fluorides, compounds of fluorine, help prevent tooth decay, so they are added to toothpaste and tap water. Organic chlorine and fluorine compounds (CFCs) are also used as pesticides, and in refrigerators as the cooling agent. But they are harmful to the environment, so alternatives are being found. All the silver halides (halogen compounds) are light-sensitive, so they are used to make photographic film and paper. Silver bromide is the most commonly used. All the halogens are highly reactive. All have seven electrons in their outer shells.

CHLORINATING WATER

Chlorine can be extracted from concentrated brine (salt water), using electrolysis. It is a strong bleach and disinfectant, killing harmful bacteria. For this reason it is used to treat water in swimming pools and at water supply plants. Chlorine is turned into a liquid for this purpose.

FLUORESCING FLUORITE

Fluorine occurs naturally in minerals such as fluorite (fluorspar). Fluorite forms cubic crystals in a variety of colours due to impurities. Many fluoresce (glow) in ultraviolet light.

CHLORINE

Chlorine is a yellow-green, poisonous gas. Like all the halogens, it readily combines with hydrogen and water. Together they make hydrochloric acid, a very strong acid.

SEAWEED IODINE

Traces of iodine occur in sea water and in seaweed. It is also important in the thyroid gland, which controls energy levels and growth in young mammals. People lacking iodides develop a swollen thyroid gland, called a goitre, on their neck.

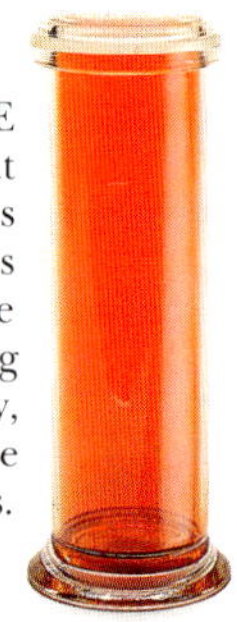

BROMINE

Bromine is a dark red liquid that gives off a choking and poisonous red-brown vapour. Bromine is one of only two liquids in the periodic table. As well as being used in photography, bromine compounds are used as mild sedatives.

SLIPPERY PLASTIC

A fluorine compound, PTFE (polytetrafluoroethene), is used as the non-stick coating on pans because it is so slippery. Although it is a plastic, it is not affected by heat and is very unreactive. This makes it ideal for saucepans and ovenware.

IODINE

Iodine is a purple-black solid that turns to gas very easily, giving off a purple vapour. Iodine compounds, known as iodides, are used in dyes and as industrial catalysts. Iodine dissolved in water is used as a test for starch.

PTFE (also known as Teflon) works by actively repelling other chemicals. Even an egg cannot stick to a Teflon frying pan.

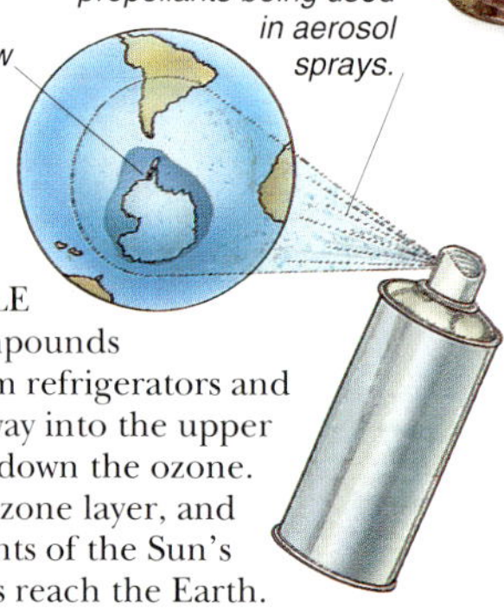

Clear evidence about the harmful effect of CFCs has led to alternative propellants being used in aerosol sprays.

An ozone hole now regularly appears in winter in the Antarctic over the South Pole.

THE OZONE HOLE

CFCs (chlorine and fluorine compounds with carbon) escape into the air from refrigerators and aerosol sprays. They find their way into the upper atmosphere, where they break down the ozone. This is causing holes in the ozone layer, and means that harmful amounts of the Sun's ultraviolet rays reach the Earth.

Find out more

BONDING P.28
PERIODIC TABLE P.32
OXYGEN P.44
ALKALI INDUSTRY P.94
INDUSTRIAL POLLUTION P.112
PHOTOGRAPHY P.206
CYCLES IN THE BIOSPHERE P.372
FACT FINDER P.402

HYDROGEN

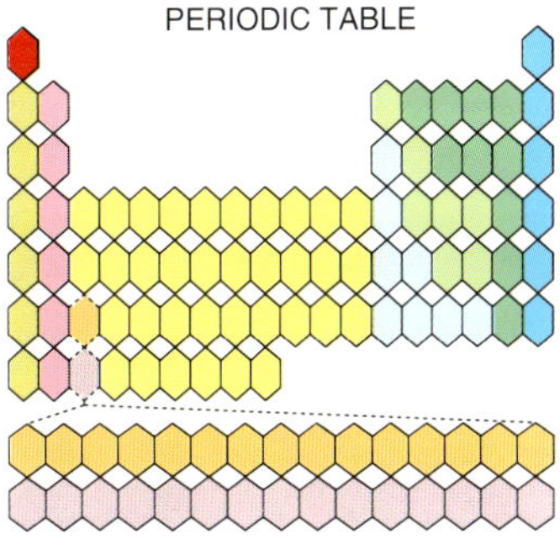

Hydrogen (H)

IMAGINE A WORLD without sunlight or heat. This is what would happen if there were no hydrogen. You cannot see, taste, or smell hydrogen, yet it is the most plentiful element in the Universe. It is a gas, with many uses. Much is made into ammonia, which is used to produce fertilizers and other chemicals. Hydrogenation (treatment with hydrogen) is used to harden vegetable oils and fats into margarine in the food industry. It also increases the amount of petrol produced from crude oil. All acids owe their acidity to hydrogen ions.

IN THE UNIVERSE
Hydrogen is present not only in the stars but in the clouds, or nebulae, that exist in the space between them.

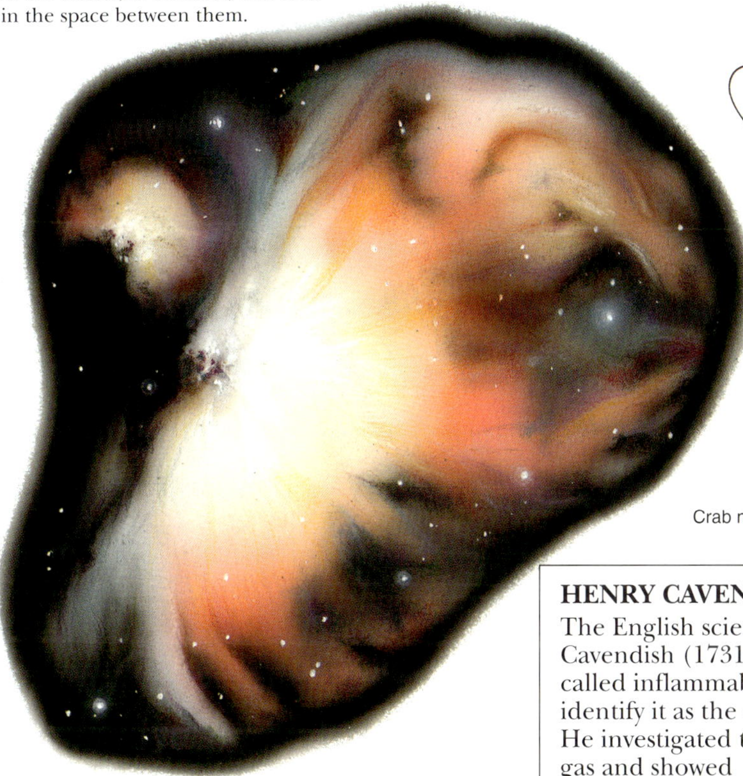

IN THE SUN
Hydrogen makes the Sun shine. A huge amount of energy is given out when the nuclei of atoms of hydrogen join up, or fuse together, in the Sun's searingly hot interior. This process is called nuclear fusion. It is also used in the destructive hydrogen bomb.

Crab nebula

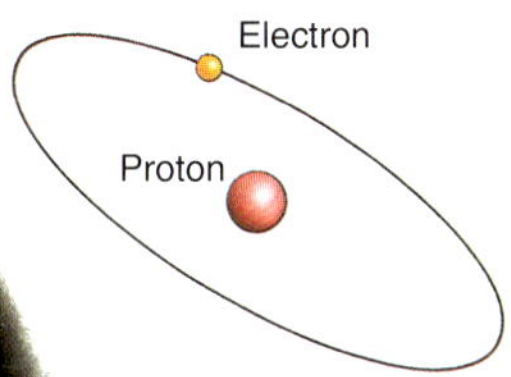

SIMPLE STRUCTURE
Hydrogen has the simplest atom there is, with one proton, which forms the nucleus, and one electron.

ON EARTH
There is a lot of hydrogen on Earth because it forms part of water (H_2O). It is the commonest element, with carbon, in living things and fossil fuels.

HENRY CAVENDISH

The English scientist Henry Cavendish (1731–1810) found a gas he called inflammable air. But he did not identify it as the element hydrogen. He investigated the properties of the gas and showed that water is formed when it is burned in air. This proved that water is not, as had been thought, a separate element. Later, the gas was called hydrogen.

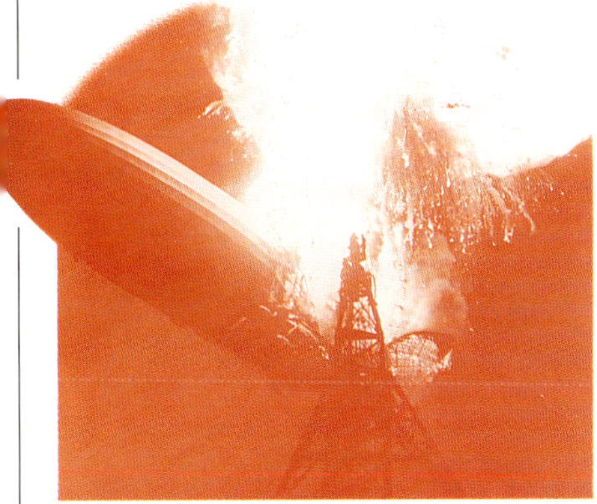

BALLOONS AND AIRSHIPS
Hydrogen explosions were the cause of airship disasters in the 1930s, like that of the *Hindenburg* on 6 May 1937. Because it is so light, hydrogen should be ideal for filling balloons and airships. The drawback is that it easily bursts into flame, forming an explosive mixture with the oxygen in the air.

FUEL OF THE FUTURE

Experimental cars that run on hydrogen have already been built. The fuel source is a hydrogen compound that is heated to release the hydrogen. The advantage of these cars is that they cause no pollution because hydrogen forms water when it burns.

Hydrogen-powered car

Find out more

ATOMIC STRUCTURE P.24
PERIODIC TABLE P.32
OXIDATION AND REDUCTION P.64
MEASURING ACIDITY P.72
AMMONIA P.90
ENERGY SOURCES P.134
NUCLEAR ENERGY P.136
SUN P.284
FACT FINDER P.402

NOBLE GASES

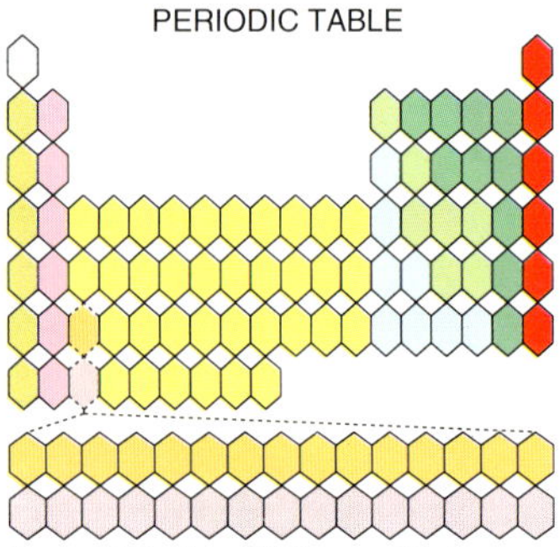

Group 18: helium (He), neon (Ne), argon (Ar), krypton (Kr), xenon (Xe), and radioactive radon (Rn)

BALLOONS THAT SOAR into the air when you let them go are filled with helium, one of the six gases that fill Group 18 of the periodic table. These are the noble gases, and they make up about one per cent of the air. Neon, used in brightly coloured neon lights, is another well-known noble gas. Radon is radioactive and is produced by the decay of radium. It makes up much of the background radiation that occurs in areas where there are granite rocks. Noble gases are also called the rare or inert gases because chemists have been able to make only a few compounds from them. They rarely react with anything because they are so stable: their outer shells are totally filled with electrons.

HELIUM
After hydrogen, helium is the lightest gas. It is lighter than air. That is why it is used to fill modern balloons and airships. It is safer than hydrogen because it does not burn. Only a faint trace of helium is present in the atmosphere. But some deposits of natural gas contain quite large amounts, and these are the main commercial source of the gas.

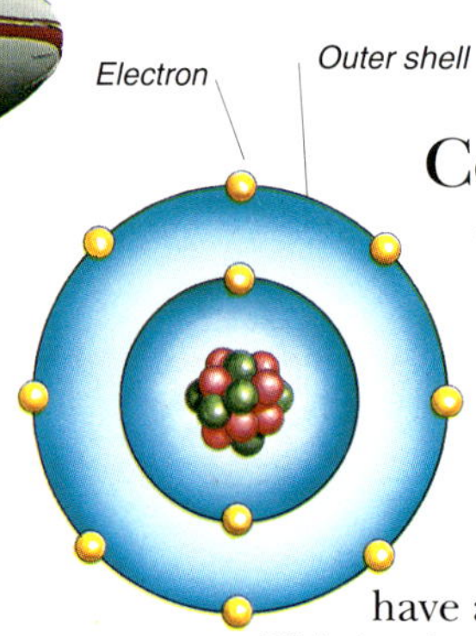

COMPLETE SHELLS

A neon atom has eight electrons in its outer shell. With these, the shell is complete. The atom does not need to lose or gain electrons by bonding with other atoms. All noble gases have a complete outer shell. This is why they are so unreactive.

NEON LIGHTS
The colours of this neon rainbow are produced by passing electricity through the tubes, which contain a noble gas and other substances at low pressure. Each noble gas produces a different colour, and other substances are added for more colours. Helium gives a yellow light, neon gives a brilliant red-orange light, argon gives a blue light, and krypton gives a violet light.

WILLIAM RAMSAY

In 1894, Lord Rayleigh (1842–1919) and William Ramsay (1852–1916) discovered the noble gas argon. Helium had already been found in the Sun, and in 1895 Ramsay found it existed on Earth. He went on to discover krypton, neon, and xenon in 1898. He prepared the last three by the distillation of liquid air. For this work he was awarded the 1904 Nobel Prize for Chemistry. In 1910, he discovered radon.

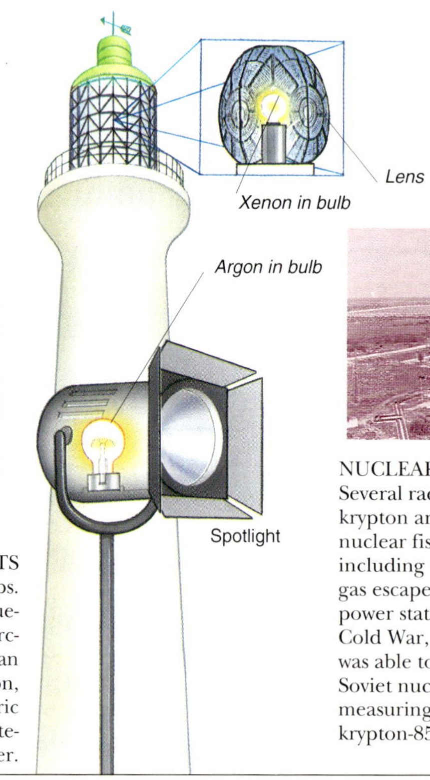

GAS LIGHTS
Argon and xenon are used in electric lamps. Lamps filled with xenon produce an intense blue-white light. Lighthouses often use xenon arc-lamps, in which the light is produced by an electric arc, a sort of continuous spark. Argon, mixed with nitrogen, is used in ordinary electric light bulbs. The inert mixture makes the white-hot tungsten filament inside a bulb last longer.

Novovoronezhskaya nuclear power plant in Russia

NUCLEAR BY-PRODUCT
Several radioisotopes of krypton are produced in the nuclear fission of uranium, including krypton-85. This gas escapes from nuclear power stations. During the Cold War, the United States was able to keep track of Soviet nuclear activity by measuring the amount of krypton-85 in the air.

Find out more

ATOMIC STRUCTURE P.24
RADIOACTIVITY P.26
PERIODIC TABLE P.32
CHEMISTRY OF AIR P.74
NUCLEAR ENERGY P.136
FACT FINDER P.402

REACTIONS

EVERY MINUTE OF EVERY DAY, millions of chemical reactions are taking place around us. Some are natural processes, while others are the result of human activities. Inside our bodies, the food we eat is broken down in a complex series of reactions to provide us with energy. Plants are busy using the Sun's energy to convert carbon dioxide and water into carbohydrates and oxygen – a reaction called photosynthesis. Meanwhile, chemical reactions in the Earth's atmosphere constantly remove the Sun's harmful ultraviolet rays which would make life impossible. In the laboratory, scientists use chemical reactions in many different ways: to make new drugs, to prevent food rotting too quickly, to convert crude oil into petrol, or to provide many of the materials that make our clothes and our homes.

A chemical in plants called chlorophyll uses sunlight to convert carbon dioxide and water into carbohydrates and oxygen.

Silver objects gradually become dull and blackened because hydrogen sulphide in the air reacts with the silver to produce a thin layer of silver sulphide.

When we wash dishes, the detergent in the washing-up liquid breaks down any dirt and grease and helps them dissolve in the water.

The baked cake no longer resembles its ingredients of flour, eggs, butter, and sugar. They have been changed by a chemical reaction.

Baked cake

Melting ice lollies

CHEMICAL CHANGE

Baking a cake is an example of a chemical change. Once cooked, the cake does not taste like its ingredients any more – it is chemically different. Most chemical changes are permanent or irreversible – you cannot turn the baked cake back into flour, butter, eggs, and sugar. However, there are a few chemical changes which are reversible.

PHYSICAL CHANGE

A melting ice lolly is an example of a physical change. The lollipop has not changed chemically – it may look different, but it still tastes the same. Physical changes are not permanent, they are reversible. The ice lolly can be made solid again by cooling it down in a freezer compartment.

FRANCIS BACON

Francis Bacon (1561-1626) was a lawyer, experimenter, and great English political figure. In 1620, he wrote a book called *New Method*, in which he said that theories about how matter works were only useful if they were supported by experiments.

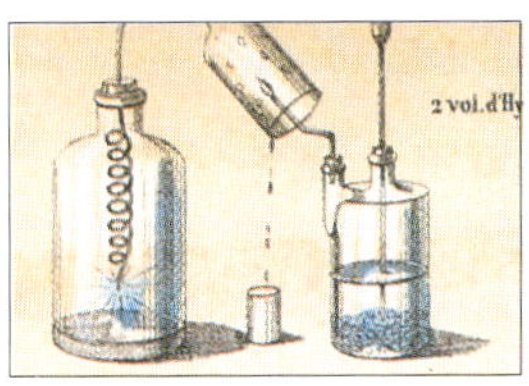

Scientific equipment from the 18th century

ROBERT BOYLE

The Irish chemist Robert Boyle (1627-91) was one of the first modern chemists. In 1661, he published a famous book, *The Sceptical Chymist*, in which he said that ideas should always be tested by experiment to see if they are really true. While experimenting with gases, he discovered a rule about how they behave, known as Boyle's law.

MODERN LABORATORY

Many scientific laboratories contain a range of equipment that scientists use to carry out different experiments. For example, some scientists might study the reactions involved in making acid rain so they can develop ways to prevent it. Other scientists may use chemical reactions to make new materials or to find cures for diseases.

KINETIC THEORY

HAVE YOU EVER WONDERED why you can smell food cooking? The reason is that tiny gas molecules from hot food whirl through the air and some reach your nose. Although it is hard to believe, the atoms and molecules that make up everything we see are constantly moving. As the temperature rises, the particles move faster, and so they take up more space. This is the kinetic theory of matter. The word "kinetic" means moving. Not all particles can move in the same way. In solids, the particles are closely packed together and can only move by vibrating or shaking. In liquids, the particles are still close, but they can move more freely. In a gas, the particles are widely spaced and move very fast.

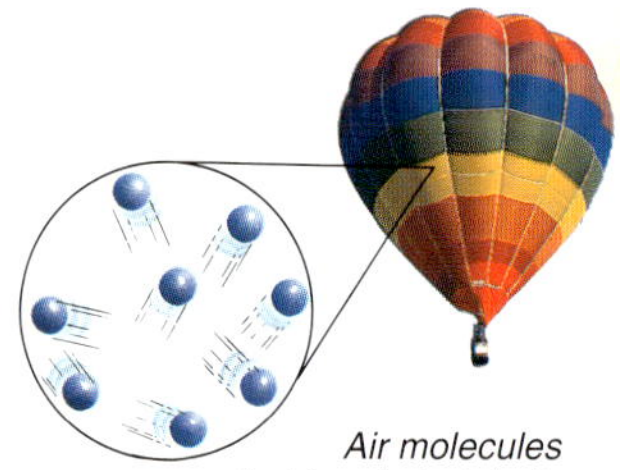

Air molecules inside a hot-air balloon are farther apart because they are moving so fast. This means that the air inside the balloon is lighter than the air outside. This is what makes the balloon rise.

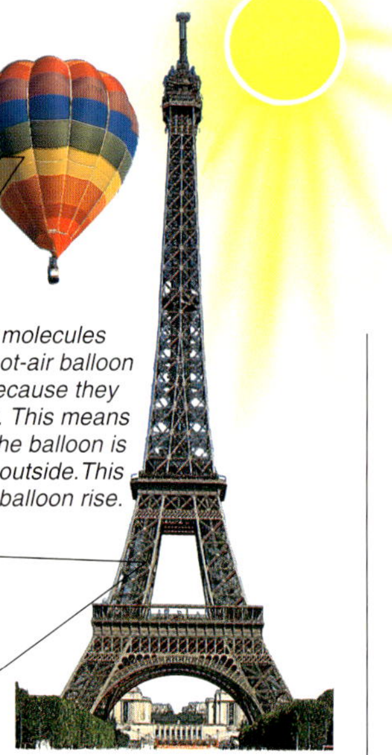

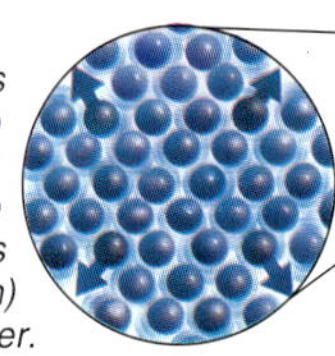

Heat causes particles of solids to vibrate faster than usual. This explains why the Eiffel Tower in Paris expands by 7.5 cm (3 in) every summer.

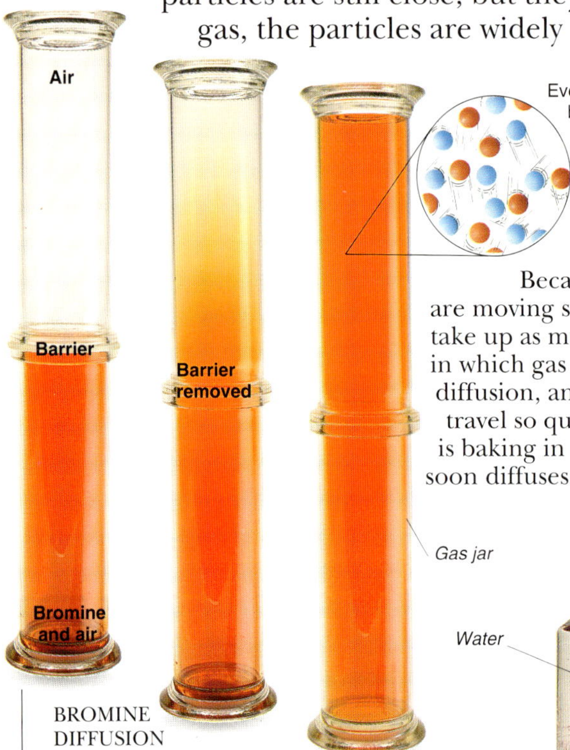

Evenly mixed bromine and air particles

Gas jar

BROMINE DIFFUSION
When bromine is put into a gas jar, the gas molecules take up all of the available space. If a second gas jar is added, the gas soon diffuses into this as well.

DIFFUSION

Because the molecules in a gas are moving so fast, gases will spread out and take up as much space as possible. The way in which gas molecules spread out is called diffusion, and it is the reason why smells travel so quickly. For example, when bread is baking in the oven, the smell of cooking soon diffuses through the whole house.

EXPANSION

If an object, like this thermometer, is heated, its particles start to move faster and take up extra space. It is said to expand. This is why railway lines include small gaps that the metal can expand into in hot weather. Liquids expand about ten times more than solids. Gases expand about 100 times more than liquids.

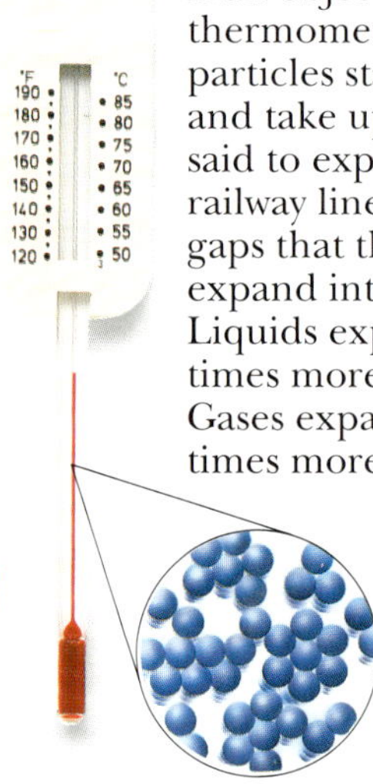

Kinetic theory explains how a thermometer works. An increase in temperature causes the alcohol or mercury inside to expand and move up the scale.

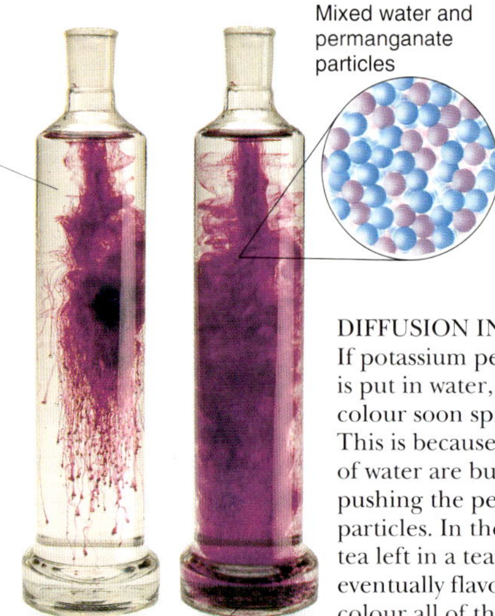

Water

Mixed water and permanganate particles

Potassium permanganate crystals

DIFFUSION IN WATER
If potassium permanganate is put in water, its purple colour soon spreads out. This is because molecules of water are bumping and pushing the permanganate particles. In the same way, tea left in a teapot will eventually flavour and colour all of the water.

LUDWIG BOLTZMANN
In the 1860s, the Austrian scientist Ludwig Boltzmann (1844-1906) developed the kinetic theory of gases. Sadly, unhappy about the strong opposition from other scientists to his kinetic theory, he committed suicide.

BROWNIAN MOTION

In 1827, the Scottish botanist Robert Brown was surprised to see that some pollen grains in water were haphazardly bouncing about. The great scientist Albert Einstein explained this movement eighty years later by using the kinetic theory. The pollen grains are being constantly bombarded by tiny, unseen water molecules. This type of movement is now called Brownian motion.

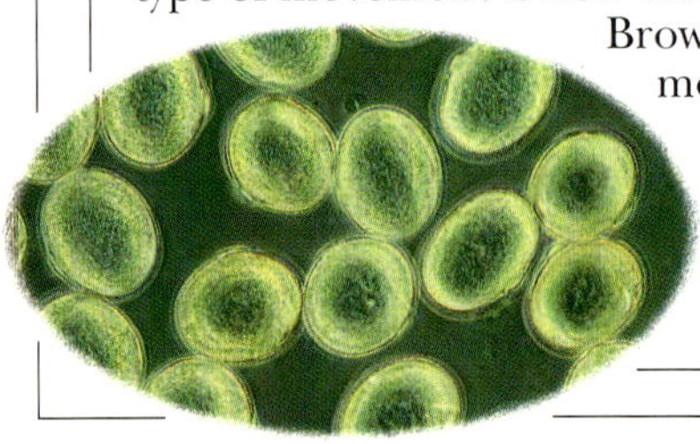

Magnified view of sweet pea pollen grains in water

WATER BAGS
A solution of salt and sugar can cure children with severe sickness, but many of these children live in countries where clean water is not available. Special bags holding dry sugar and salt can help. If they are put into dirty water, water molecules, but not dirt, can diffuse through the tiny holes in the bag, making a sterile solution ready to drink.

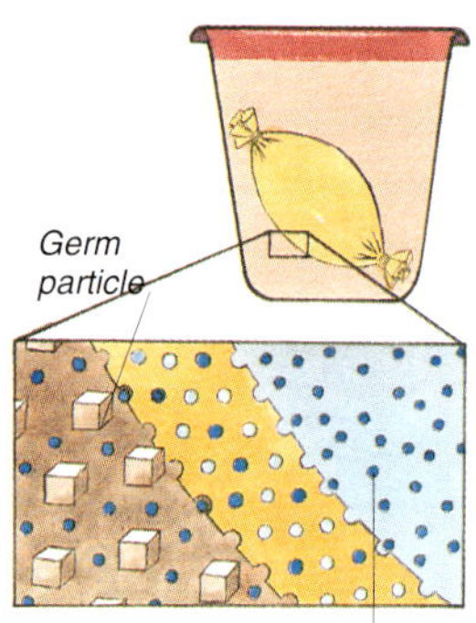

Germ particle

Water molecules can diffuse through the holes.

Find out more

STATES OF MATTER P.18
BEHAVIOUR OF GASES P.51
RATES OF REACTION P.55
HEAT P.140
TRANSPORT IN PLANTS P.341
FACT FINDER P.404

BEHAVIOUR OF GASES

GAS PARTICLES MOVE around freely and very fast. This is why they can produce dramatic effects if their temperature, volume, or pressure are changed. For example, it may be dangerous to leave a spray can in a hot place. As they become hotter, the gas particles inside will move faster and so push harder against the sides of the can. They may even cause the can to explode. Heating the can has increased the pressure of the gas inside. Similar effects were observed in the 17th and 18th centuries by scientists. They devised laws that are still used to predict how a gas will behave.

Boyle's law explains why bubbles from a diver get bigger as they rise to the water surface.

BOYLE'S LAW

Have you noticed that bubbles of gas are smaller at the bottom and get bigger as they rise through a liquid? This is because there is more liquid pressing on the bubbles and making them smaller when they are at the bottom than when they are near the surface of the liquid. This is an example of Boyle's law in practice. It was discovered in 1662 by the Irish chemist Robert Boyle. The law states that, at constant temperature, the volume of a gas is inversely proportional to the pressure – if the pressure increases, the volume decreases.

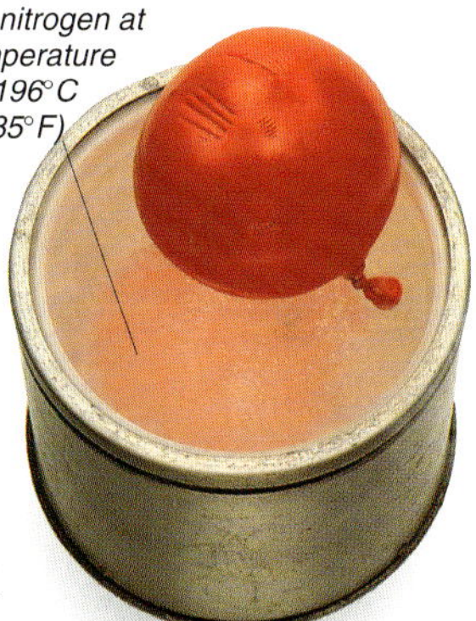

Liquid nitrogen at a temperature of -196°C (-385°F)

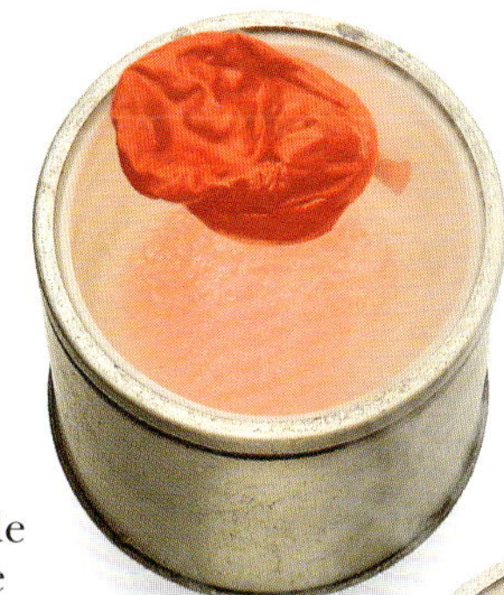

The balloon deflates in the cold liquid.

CHARLES' LAW

A balloon full of air shrivels up when it is put in a container of liquid nitrogen. The very low temperature causes the air molecules inside the balloon to slow down. As a result, there are fewer collisions with the walls of the balloon and the balloon shrinks. This relationship between the temperature and volume of a gas was discovered by the French scientist Jacques Charles in 1787. His law says that, at constant pressure, the volume of a gas is proportional to the temperature – if the temperature is halved, then the volume is halved too.

REFRIGERATOR

Inside the pipes of a refrigerator, a fluid called a refrigerant continually flows around. When it passes through a narrow opening, it rapidly expands to a gas. To become a gas, the liquid molecules must take in heat from their surroundings (the inside of the refrigerator), which become cold. The gas then flows to a compressor which forces it back to a liquid. This process gives out heat, which is why the back of a refrigerator feels warm.

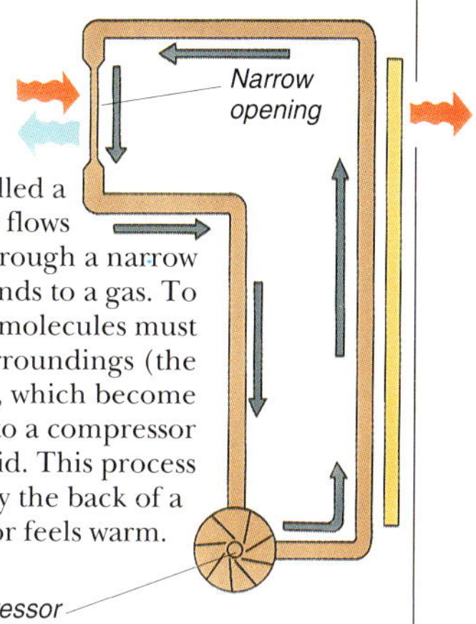

The burst balloon holds very few air molecules and so is lighter than the full balloon.

HEAVY GASES

It is easy to think that as most gases are invisible, they weigh nothing. This is not true. All gases have some mass as they are made of particles. If two balloons full of air are balanced and then one is burst, the mass of the air in the remaining balloon pulls it down.

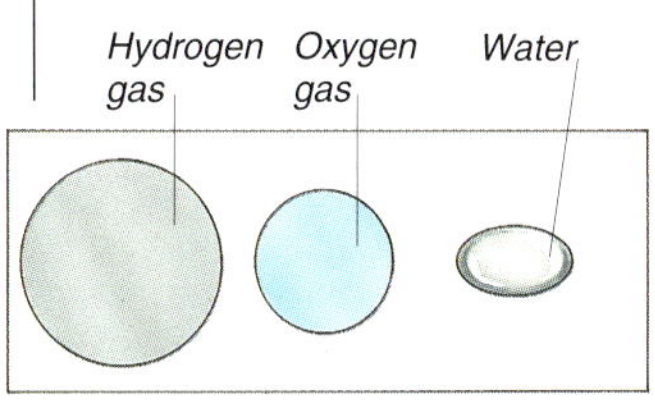

GAY-LUSSAC'S LAW

In 1808, the French chemist Joseph Louis Gay-Lussac found that when hydrogen and oxygen react to make water, two volumes of hydrogen always react with one of oxygen. He went on to discover that when any gases react together, the volumes in which they do so are in a ratio of simple whole numbers. This is known as Gay-Lussac's law.

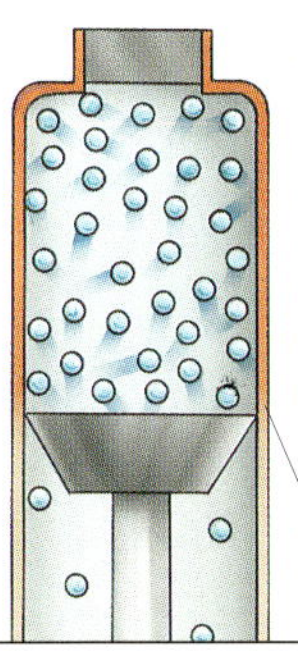

The wall of the pump becomes warm as faster molecules bump against it.

BICYCLE PUMP

A bicycle pump always feels warm when it is used. This is because the air molecules inside it are forced closer together and so they collide faster with the walls of the pump, which get hotter.

The balloon starts to expand as the gas molecules speed up in the warmer air.

AVOGADRO'S LAW

If a container is filled with chlorine and another identical one with oxygen, the two containers will contain the same number of molecules. This is true even though each chlorine molecule weighs twice as much as each oxygen molecule. This principle was discovered in 1811 by the Italian physicist Amedeo Avogadro. His law says that equal volumes of gases at the same temperature and pressure contain the same number of molecules.

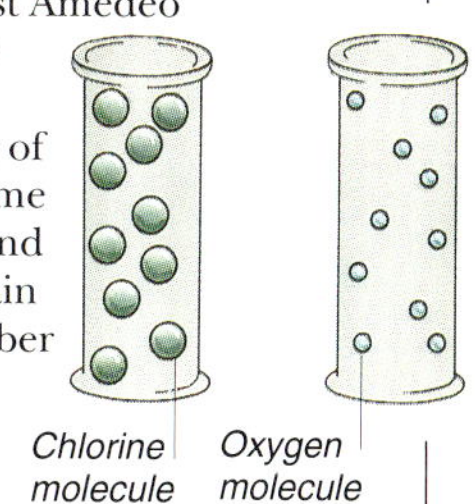

Find out more

STATES OF MATTER P.18
CHANGES OF STATE P.20
KINETIC THEORY P.50
CHEMISTRY OF AIR P.74
PRESSURE P.127
FORCES IN FLUIDS P.128
HEAT P.141
FACT FINDER P.404

CHEMICAL REACTIONS

WHAT IS A CHEMICAL REACTION? It is simply breaking substances apart and making new ones from the pieces. Whenever a reaction takes place, new substances, the products, are made. These have very different properties from the original starting materials, the reactants. For these new substances to be made, atoms and molecules must be rearranged. This requires the breaking and making of chemical bonds. For a bond to break, energy is needed, while making a bond releases energy. Both occur in every chemical reaction. The energy can be in the form of heat, light, or electricity. Reactions that release heat are said to be exothermic. Those in which heat is taken in are called endothermic.

EXOTHERMIC REACTIONS
When wood burns, its chemical energy is released in the form of heat. The reaction involves bond-breaking and bond-making, but the amount of heat given off by making bonds is greater than that absorbed by bonds breaking. As a result, heat is given off and the surroundings become hotter. This is an example of an exothermic reaction.

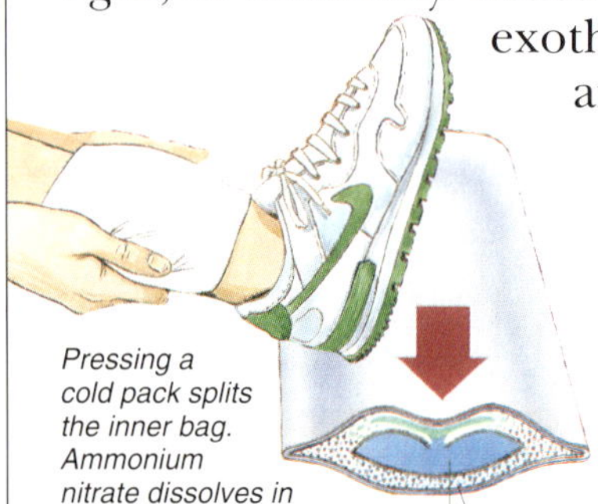

Pressing a cold pack splits the inner bag. Ammonium nitrate dissolves in the water, making the solution very cold.

ENDOTHERMIC REACTIONS
Cold packs are used by athletes to cool down injuries. The cold pack uses a reaction to take heat from the athlete's body. The heat absorbed by bond-breaking is greater than that given out by bond-making. This is an example of an endothermic reaction.

Methane and oxygen react to make carbon dioxide and water. This diagram shows how the bonds between atoms break and rejoin.

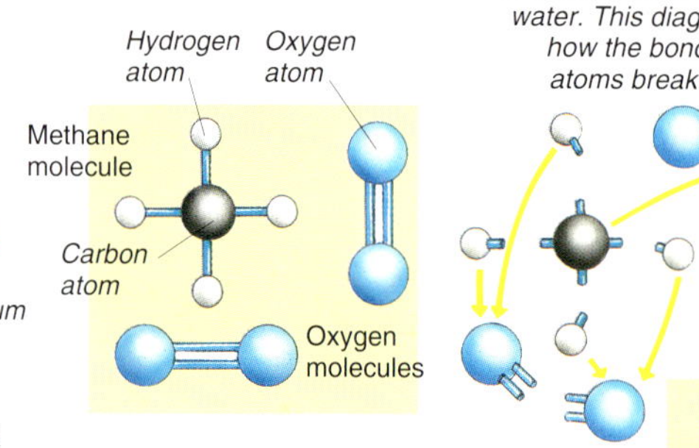

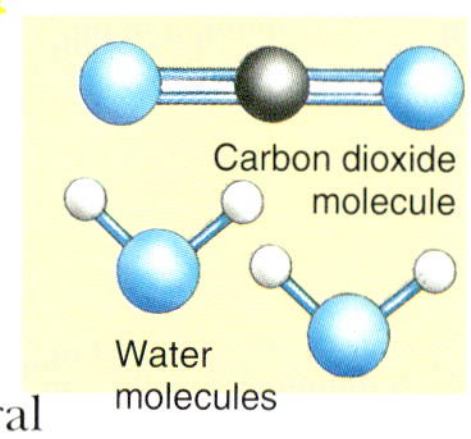

CHANGING BONDS

In every chemical reaction, bonds are broken so that new ones can be made. Methane, the main component of natural gas, has four hydrogen atoms bonded to one carbon. When burned, it reacts with oxygen in the air and all the bonds between the atoms are broken. New bonds form to make carbon dioxide and water. As these new bonds have less stored energy than the original ones, the reaction gives out energy as heat.

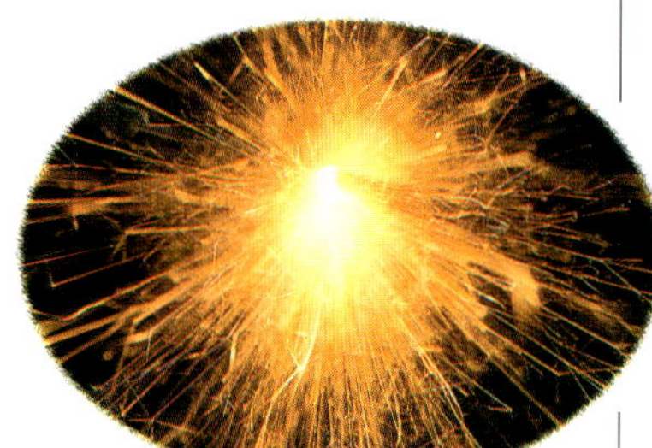

The magnesium in a sparkler reacts with oxygen in the air to form magnesium oxide. This reaction gives out energy as light.

A book cover fades because light is taken in by the dye molecules and destroys some of the chemical bonds.

ACTIVATION ENERGY

Most reactions need a certain amount of energy to start. This is why a match will not light until it is activated by striking it. A candle will not burn until a match is held to it. The amount of energy needed to get a reaction started is called the activation energy.

The activation energy is like a hill that the reactants have to get over.

A lighted match starts the reaction between oxygen in the air and candle wax. Once started, the reaction continues without help.

*This electric ray (*Hypnos monopterygium*) uses a reaction that gives out energy as electricity. This is used by the ray to stun its prey.*

Lightning causes a reaction between nitrogen and oxygen to make nitrogen dioxide. This dissolves in water and falls to Earth as nitric acid, a component of acid rain.

REACTIONS WITH ELECTRICITY
Some chemical reactions use electricity, others produce it. An electric ray, for example, can kill small fish with a 200-volt shock, through a reaction in its cells. Lightning is an electric spark. The energy it produces can cause reactions in the air. It causes nitrogen dioxide to be made from oxygen and nitrogen, and ozone from oxygen.

REACTIONS WITH LIGHT
When a chemical reaction gives out or takes in energy, it may do so as light. A burning sparkler gives out an intense white light. Posters and clothes fade in strong sunlight because a reaction occurs when light is taken in. Sunlight also sets off a reaction in our skin to form the pigment melanin. This is how people tan.

Find out more

BONDING P.28
DESCRIBING REACTIONS P.53
RATES OF REACTION P.55
CATALYSTS P.56
ENERGY CONVERSION P.138
FACT FINDER P.404

DESCRIBING REACTIONS

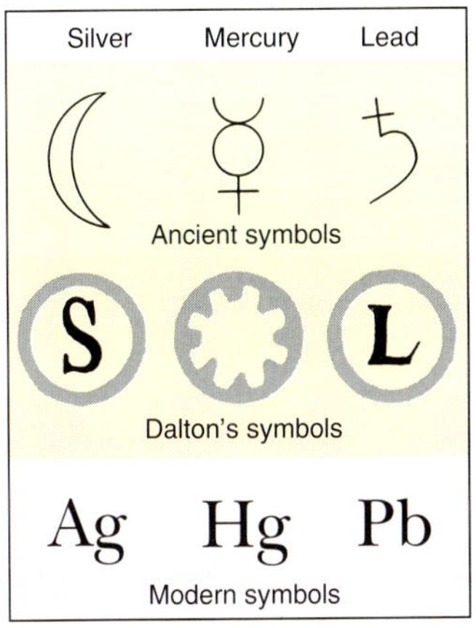

CHEMICAL FORMULAE and chemical equations are the chemist's equivalent of shorthand writing. They are used to describe chemicals and their reactions. The chemical formula of a compound (combination of elements) shows which atoms it contains and in what proportions. A chemical equation is used to describe a chemical reaction. Like a cookery recipe, an equation gives a list of ingredients and the proportions in which they need to be mixed. It also shows what will be produced during the reaction. Chemical equations overcome problems of language. They are used by chemists to tell other scientists all over the world about what they have seen during their experiments.

The two clear solutions are mixed and a yellow solid, lead iodide, is formed.

SYMBOLS AND FORMULAE
In ancient times, seven elements were known, each of which was depicted by a different planet. Around 1800, the English chemist John Dalton devised a set of picture symbols for the known elements. In 1811, Swedish chemist Jöns Berzelius invented the system we now use where letters represent elements. These letters can be put together to show a compound's chemical formula.

Solution of potassium iodide in water

Solution of lead nitrate in water

This is an example of a double decomposition reaction in which two compounds in solution swap partners.

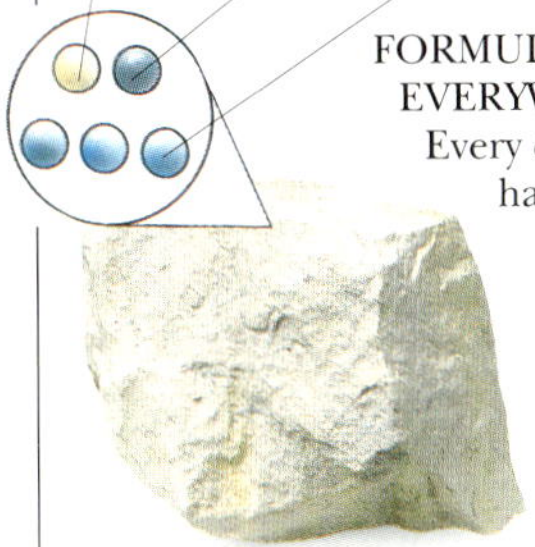

FORMULAE EVERYWHERE
Every compound has a chemical name as well as a formula showing the elements it contains. For example, the chemical name of chalk is calcium carbonate. Its chemical formula is $CaCO_3$. This tells us that in chalk, for every atom of calcium (Ca), there will be one atom of carbon (C) and three atoms of oxygen (O).

Word equation: potassium iodide + lead nitrate → lead iodide + potassium nitrate

Symbolic equation: $2KI(aq) + Pb(NO_3)_2(aq) \rightarrow PbI_2(s) + 2KNO_3(aq)$

To make a balanced equation, the number of KI molecules (and the number of KNO_3 molecules) must be doubled.

Chemists use symbols that show what state the chemical is in. (s) means solid, (l) means liquid, (g) means gas, and (aq) means dissolved in water.

This 2 shows there are two nitrate groups joined to each lead atom.

LAW OF CONSERVATION OF MASS

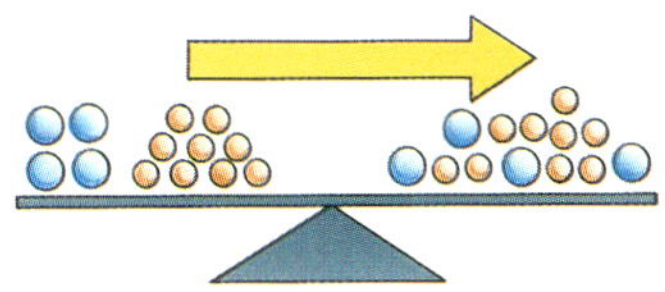

When a chemical reaction occurs, nothing disappears, the atoms are just rearranged. An equation must therefore be balanced. The number of atoms on each side must be the same. This is the law of conservation of mass. It says that the total mass of the substances produced in a reaction equals the total mass of materials used.

MOLES
Because atoms and molecules are so tiny, chemists count them by mass. The mole is their counting unit. A mole of any substance contains 6×10^{23} particles, but each substance has a different mass (its molecular or atomic mass). Using the mole to count particles is just the same as a banker counting coins by weighing them.

One mole of lead tetraoxide contains 6×10^{23} molecules. It has a mass of 685 g.

One mole of aluminium contains 6×10^{23} atoms. It has a mass of 27 g. 6×10^{23} is known as Avogadro's constant.

EQUATIONS
A reaction can be described in different ways. One way is to write an equation. This can be in words or with chemical formulae. If chemical formulae are used, the equation must balance; that is, it must have the same numbers of the same atoms on each side. Only a balanced equation can show the proportions in which the chemicals react together.

VALENCY
The number of chemical bonds an atom can make is called its valency. It is the number of electrons an atom gains, loses, or shares when it forms a bond. To form a compound, the total of the valencies of each element must add up to the same number.

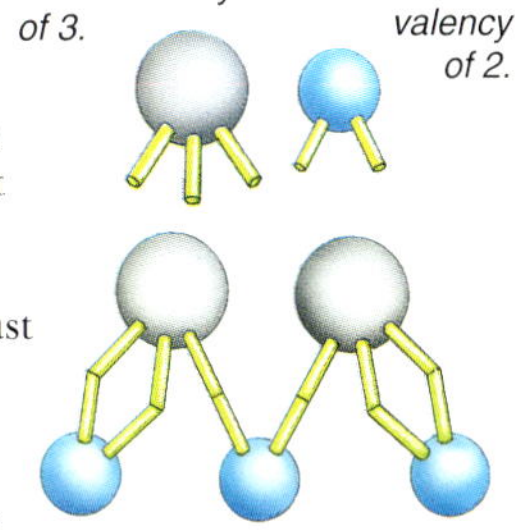
Aluminium (Al) has a valency of 3.

Oxygen (O) has a valency of 2.

When the compound aluminium oxide (Al_2O_3) is made, 2 atoms of aluminium combine with 3 of oxygen.

Find out more

BONDING P.28
PERIODIC TABLE P.32
CHEMICAL REACTIONS P.52
COMPOUNDS AND MIXTURES P.58
FACT FINDER P.404

REVERSIBLE REACTIONS

IMAGINE TRYING TO MAKE a log of wood from its smoke and ashes. Most chemical reactions, like burning, only go in one direction. Once they have happened, they cannot be reversed. They are irreversible. But not all chemical reactions are like this. Sometimes it is possible to reverse the change that has occurred. For example, when an alkali such as washing soda is added to red cabbage juice, the juice turns green. If an acid, such as vinegar, is then added to this green juice, the juice is turned back to its red colour. Such reactions are reversible. Reversible reactions have a forward reaction (red juice to green juice) and a backward reaction (green juice to red juice). In fact, both reactions are happening at the same time, but depending on the conditions, one may be stronger than the other.

EQUILIBRIUM

In a reversible reaction, after a time it will look as if nothing is happening. In fact, both the forward and backward reactions are continuing, but at the same speed. This is chemical equilibrium. In the same way, if you are using a running machine, you will stay in the same position if you run at the same speed as the machine. If the machine speeds up, you will move backwards. To reach equilibrium again, you need to speed up too.

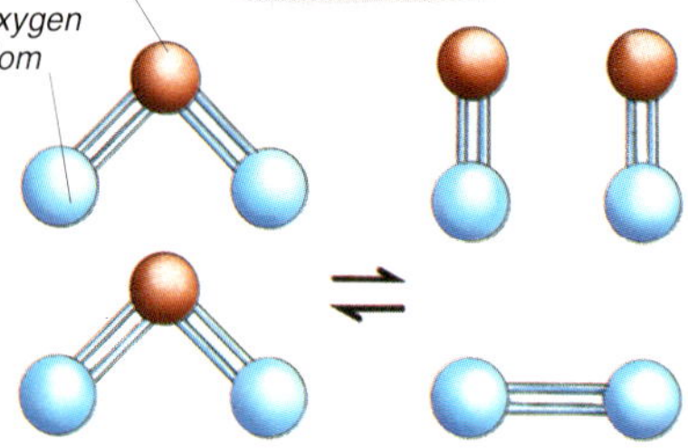

NITROGEN DIOXIDE
If brown nitrogen dioxide gas is heated, the colour becomes lighter and lighter until at 620°C (1148°F), the gas is totally colourless. This is because it has broken down into nitrogen monoxide and oxygen, both of which are colourless gases. On cooling, the changes are reversed.

IRREVERSIBLE CHANGE
When paper burns, carbon dioxide gas, water, and black carbon soot are produced. These cannot be turned back to paper again because burning paper is an irreversible reaction.

LE CHATELIER'S PRINCIPLE
A change in temperature, pressure, or concentration during a reversible reaction will change the speed of either the forward or backward reaction. If cooled, for example, the reaction that gives out heat will speed up, so as to cancel out the effect of the cooling. Such effects are summed up in Le Chatelier's principle. This says that if a change is made to a reaction in equilibrium, the reaction will adjust itself to cancel out the effects of that change.

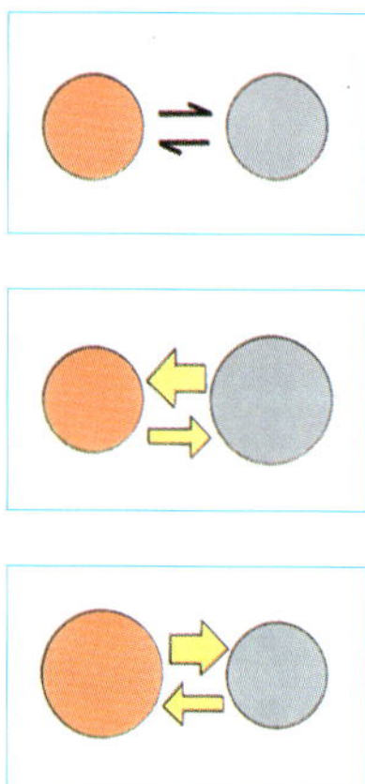

The reaction is in equilibrium. The forward and backward reactions are continuing at the same speed.

If more of the products are added, the backward reaction will speed up so as to use up the extra ingredients.

If more of the reactants are added, the forward reaction will speed up, so that the extra reactants are used up.

HENRI LE CHATELIER
Born in Paris, Le Chatelier (1850-1936) worked for some years as a mining engineer before he took up a teaching post at the University of Paris. He is remembered for his theory, Le Chatelier's principle.

CHEMICAL CLOCKS
Some reversible reactions do not settle down to an equilibrium. Once started, they continue to oscillate backwards and forwards. Sometimes this produces amazing colour changes. One moment a solution may be blue, and the next moment, red. Because these oscillations occur at regular intervals, these reactions have been called chemical clocks.

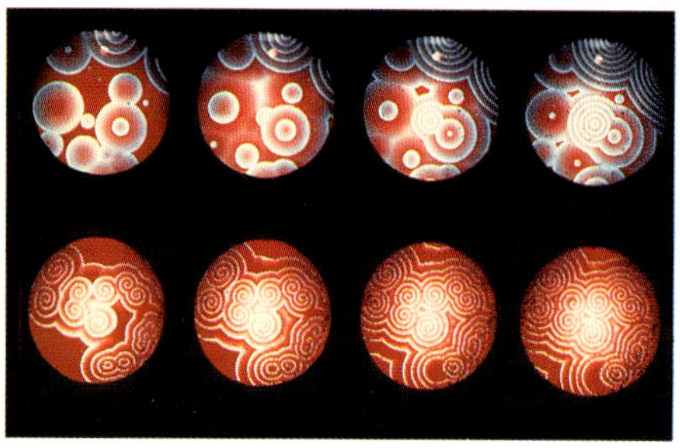

These photographs of two chemical clock reactions were taken at one-minute intervals. They show how waves of colour move through the reaction.

Find out more

CHANGES OF STATE P.20
NITROGEN P.42
OXYGEN P.44
CHEMICAL REACTIONS P.52
RATES OF REACTION P.55
MEASURING ACIDITY P.72
AMMONIA P.90

RATES OF REACTION

EXPLOSIONS OCCUR very quickly. Other reactions occur more slowly – a bicycle might take several years to rust. In our lives, we often want to alter the rate (speed) of a reaction. When we put milk into the refrigerator, we are slowing down the rate at which it turns sour. Chemists also want to control the rate of reactions. Industrial chemists want to speed up reactions to lower costs. Environmental scientists want to slow down reactions that can damage the Earth. Many factors can affect the rate of a reaction. The important ones are temperature, pressure, concentration, light, and surface area.

COAL EXPLOSION
A large piece of coal will not react with air unless we light it. A mixture of coal dust and air, however, can react rapidly and explosively, as in a coal mine explosion. This is because coal dust has a larger amount of surface that can react.

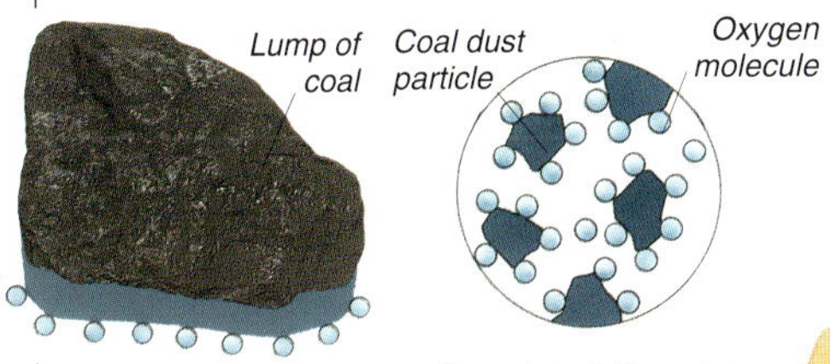

Oxygen molecules can only reach the surface coal particles.

In coal dust, there are many coal particles available to react with the oxygen molecules.

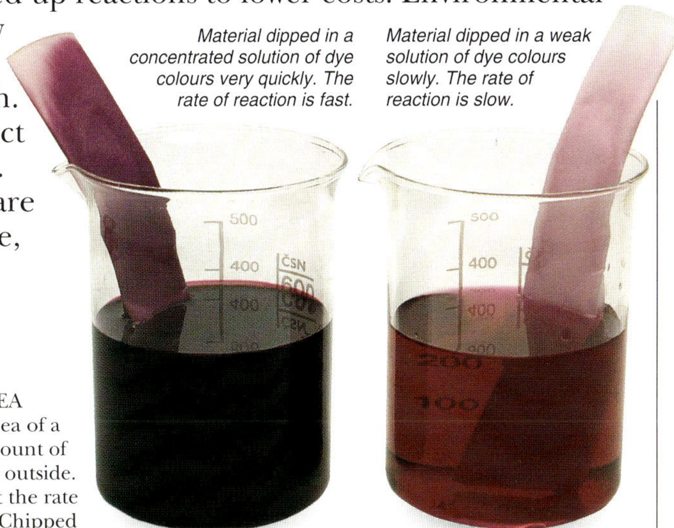

Material dipped in a concentrated solution of dye colours very quickly. The rate of reaction is fast.

Material dipped in a weak solution of dye colours slowly. The rate of reaction is slow.

EFFECT OF SURFACE AREA
The surface area of a solid is the amount of surface on the outside. This can affect the rate of reaction. Chipped potatoes are quicker to fry than whole ones as there are more exposed particles on the surface of the potato chips which can react with the hot oil.

Potato is often cooked in a deep fat fryer. Big chunks take a while to cook, but thinly sliced pieces will cook in seconds as they have a larger surface area for their volume.

EFFECT OF CONCENTRATION
If you wanted to dye some material quickly, you could make the dye solution very concentrated. A concentrated solution has a lot of dye particles dissolved in it, so there are more particles to collide with the material and cause a reaction. A weak solution, on the other hand, contains only a few dye particles and would cause a slow rate of reaction. For the same reason, anything will burn very quickly in air with a high oxygen content.

Ötze, a 5,000-year-old male body found in a glacier between Italy and Austria in 1991, was well preserved. His body would normally have been reduced to bones, but the low temperature slowed down his decomposition.

EFFECT OF TEMPERATURE
Most reactions go faster at higher temperatures. This is because the reacting particles have more energy and move faster. They are more likely to bump into one another with enough energy to cause a reaction. In the cold, all chemical reactions are slowed down. This is why a refrigerator is used to preserve food.

EFFECT OF LIGHT
Biodegradable plastics will decompose more quickly in strong sunlight than in a kitchen cupboard. This is because some reactions are speeded up by light. Light gives the reacting molecules more energy to move.

COLLISION THEORY
For a chemical reaction to happen, the reacting particles must bang into, or collide, with each other with enough force or energy (the activation energy) to break bonds. This is collision theory. If the particles do not have this energy, they will just harmlessly bounce off one another. It is like stock car racing, where two cars need to bump into each other with a lot of force in order to cause damage.

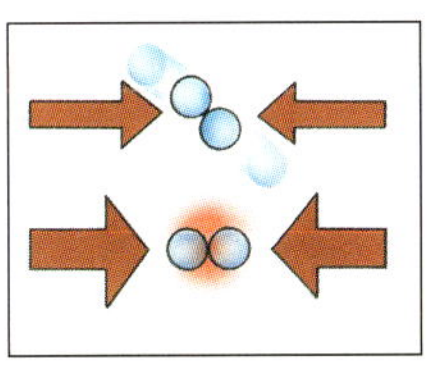

If two particles meet, they may rebound with no reaction, but if they collide with enough force, a chemical reaction will occur.

EFFECT OF PRESSURE
Particles in a gas are wide apart. But if the pressure is raised, they are brought closer together and are more likely to bump into and react with one another. In a machine called an autoclave, high pressure is used so that objects can be very quickly sterilized by steam.

Find out more

KINETIC THEORY P.50
CHEMICAL REACTIONS P.52
CATALYSTS P.56
SOLUTIONS P.60
CHEMICAL INDUSTRY P.82

CATALYSTS

Have you noticed the fizz that sugar makes when it is put into a fizzy drink? The sugar is acting as a catalyst for the dissolved carbon dioxide gas to come out of solution.

THE MAGICIANS of the chemical world, catalysts,can alter the speed of a reaction but are left unchanged once the reaction has finished. They work like an introduction agency, introducing the reactants to one another. Around 90 per cent of all chemicals are made using a catalyst. Artificial catalysts are used in the manufacture of petrol, plastics, fertilizers, medicines, and synthetic fibres for clothing. Enzymes are natural catalysts that control the way our bodies work. Usually, catalysts are used to speed up a reaction. But they can also be used to slow down a reaction, a process known as inhibition. For example, chemicals called antioxidants are added to food to prevent it rotting too quickly. The word catalyst was first used by the Swedish chemist Jöns Berzelius, and means "to break down".

Catalysts lower the activation energy of the reaction.

REACTION PATH

To speed up a reaction, catalysts provide an easier pathway for the reaction to follow. Imagine a cycle race in which one team struggles over the top of the mountain, while the other team freewheels down a lower path. The path over the mountain is like the normal route for the reaction. The lower path is the route the catalyst provides.

Reacting molecule trapped in the pore of a zeolite

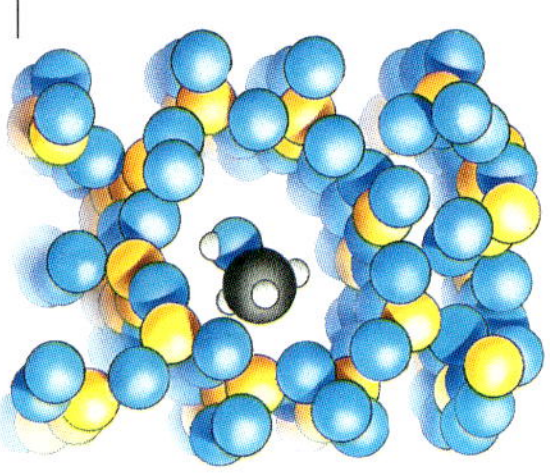

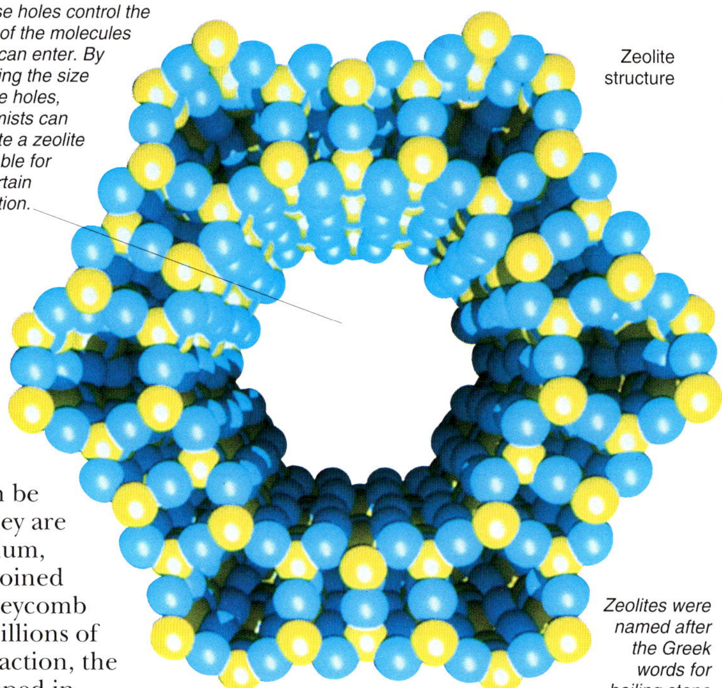

Zeolites were named after the Greek words for boiling stone because when they are heated, water is driven out of the millions of channels that they contain, leaving a very effective catalyst.

This is a selection of different catalysts. They come in all shapes and sizes, but they must always have a large surface area.

ZEOLITES

The zeolites are an amazing family of catalysts. These occur naturally in volcanic rocks, but they can be made artificially as well. They are usually made up of aluminium, silicon, and oxygen atoms joined together in a beautiful honeycomb structure which contains millions of holes or pores. During a reaction, the reacting molecules are trapped in these pores while they react with each other. The size of the pores is very important, as only molecules of a particular size can enter and undergo a chemical reaction.

METHANOL

Methanol is a clear liquid that can be stored in a bottle for a hundred years without changing. But if it is passed over a heated zeolite catalyst, it immediately undergoes a chemical reaction and is converted to petrol. This remarkable reaction is used in New Zealand as part of a process for converting natural gas to petrol.

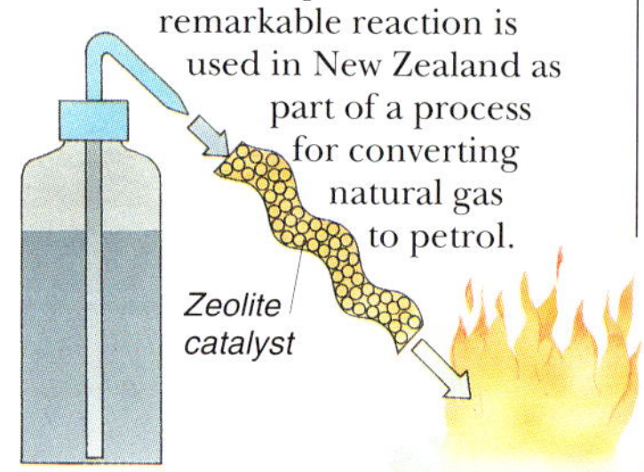

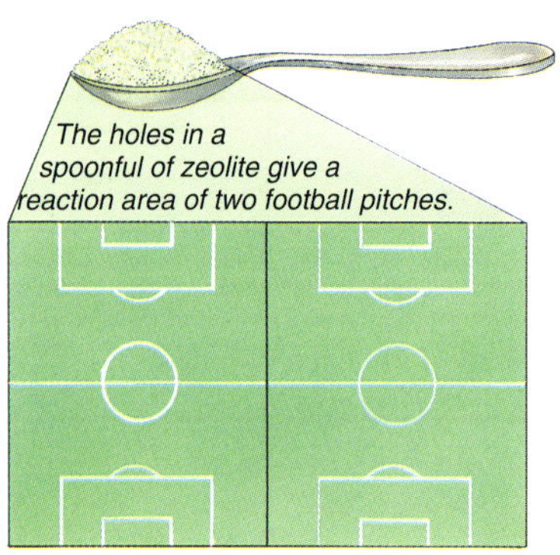

SURFACE AREA

Most catalysts work by bringing the reactants close together. They do this by forming a temporary bond with one or both of the reactants. So it is important for a catalyst to have a large surface area, as this is where the reaction takes place. For instance, a spoonful of a zeolite has the same surface area as two football pitches.

FUEL CELLS

Even astronauts rely on catalysts. To send people into space, you need a power supply for the spacecraft, and a supply of water for the crew. The fuel cell provides both of these. It uses a metal catalyst, usually platinum, to convert hydrogen and oxygen into water. This reaction produces electricity. In this way, a fuel cell can provide all the energy a spacecraft needs, as well as all the water needed for drinking, washing, and rehydrating dried food.

WILHELM OSTWALD
Born in Latvia, Wilhelm Ostwald (1853-1932) spent most of his life in Germany. He carried out research into catalysts at a time when the idea of a chemical that could drastically alter the speed of a reaction seemed ridiculous. Ostwald persevered and showed the world how extremely useful catalysts can be by developing a process for converting ammonia into nitric acid. In 1909, he was awarded the Nobel Prize for Chemistry.

ENZYMES

Nature produces remarkable catalysts called enzymes, without which the thousands of reactions in the human body would be so slow that life could not go on. Enzymes in our bodies catalyze the breakdown of our food and help to make important chemicals such as proteins. Today, enzymes are even used in industry to make washing powder, medicines, and fruit juices.

Cloudy fruit juices are made clear by enzymes.

Enzymes in washing powders help to break down stains.

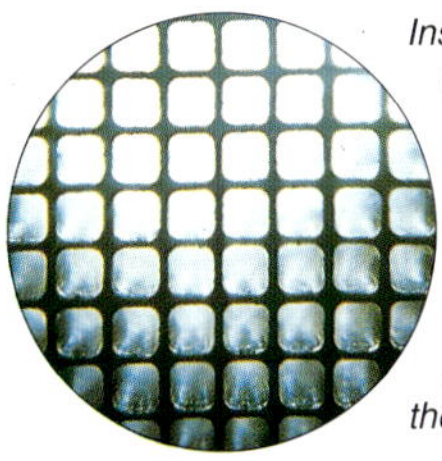

Inside the convertor is a honeycomb structure, coated with a tiny amount of the metals platinum and rhodium. These metals are the catalysts.

Unlike other catalysts, an enzyme will only catalyze one type of reaction. Just as only the correct key will fit a lock, the reacting molecules must be exactly the right shape to fit the enzyme molecule.

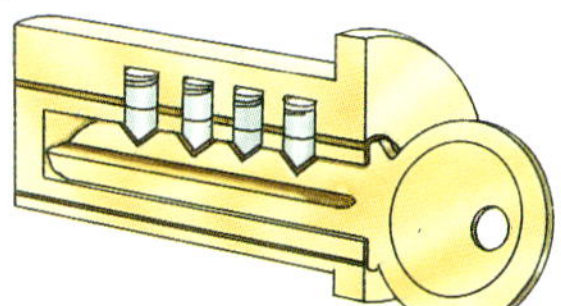

ENZYME WASHING POWDERS
Biological washing powders contain enzyme catalysts that help to break down stains. Because enzymes are destroyed at high temperatures, biological washing powders are not effective in very hot water.

CATALYTIC CONVERTOR
Some cars contain a catalyst called a catalytic convertor. This changes the toxic exhaust gases that would pollute the atmosphere into less harmful gases. It is made of a thin coating of two metals, platinum and rhodium, on a solid honeycomb support. Because lead can poison platinum and rhodium (it will stick to them and prevent any reactions from taking place), cars with catalytic convertors must use lead-free petrol.

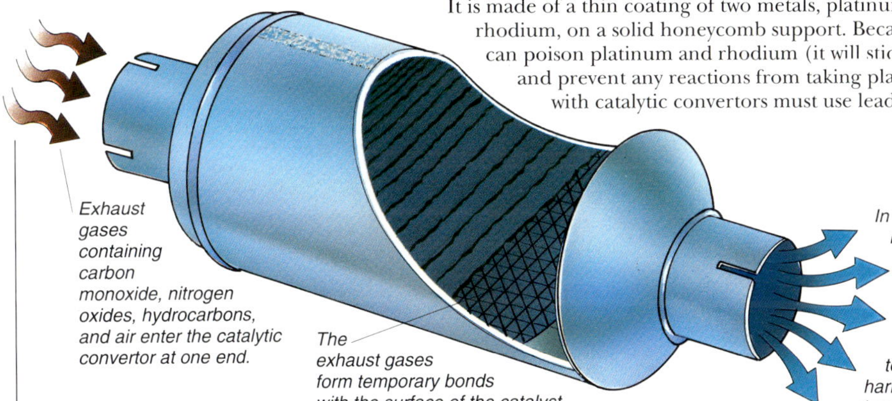

Exhaust gases containing carbon monoxide, nitrogen oxides, hydrocarbons, and air enter the catalytic convertor at one end.

The exhaust gases form temporary bonds with the surface of the catalyst. This brings them into close contact and allows the reactions to occur.

In the convertor, carbon monoxide and the hydrocarbons are converted into carbon dioxide and water. The nitrogen oxides are converted to nitrogen. These less harmful gases are released into the air.

Ozone layer over the Arctic

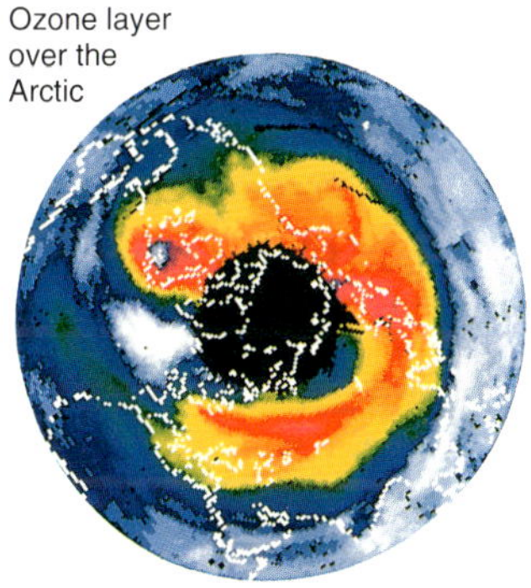

OZONE CATALYST
Chlorine from the decomposition of chlorofluorocarbons (CFCs) is the catalyst for the breakdown of ozone to oxygen in the upper atmosphere. As with all catalysts, the chlorine is left unchanged at the end of the reaction and so can go on to more ozone destruction. This is what is causing a hole in the ozone layer.

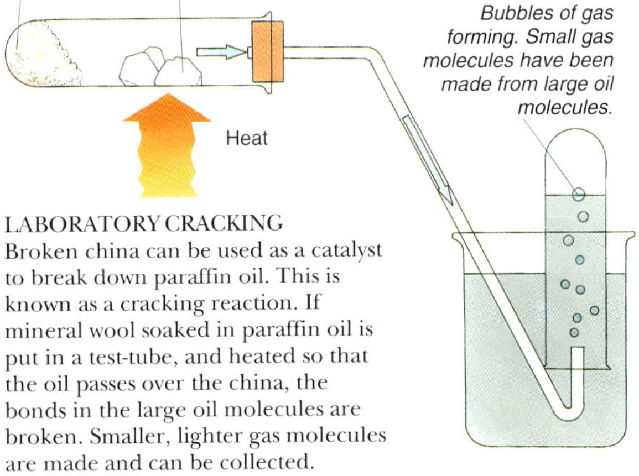

LABORATORY CRACKING
Broken china can be used as a catalyst to break down paraffin oil. This is known as a cracking reaction. If mineral wool soaked in paraffin oil is put in a test-tube, and heated so that the oil passes over the china, the bonds in the large oil molecules are broken. Smaller, lighter gas molecules are made and can be collected.

CATALYTIC CRACKING
Molecules with very long chains of carbon atoms are more useful if they are heated and broken down into smaller pieces, but this process requires very high temperatures. By using a catalyst such as a zeolite, this splitting, or "cracking" process is made much easier and quicker. In this way, large crude oil molecules can be turned into smaller, more useful ones, such as those that make up petrol.

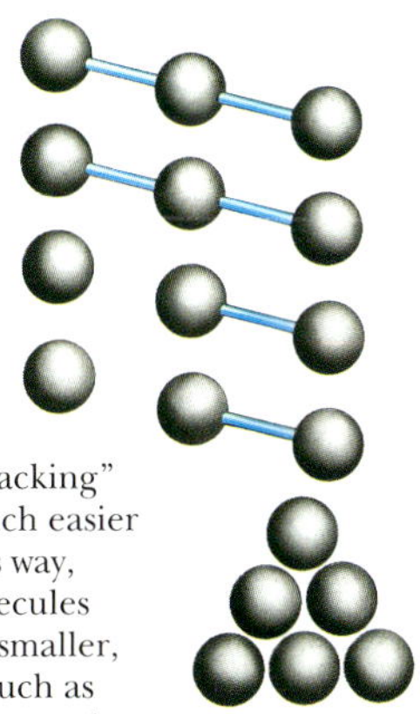

Find out more

CHEMICAL REACTIONS P.52
RATES OF REACTION P.55
COMPOUNDS AND MIXTURES P.58
CHEMISTRY OF THE BODY P.76
OIL PRODUCTS P.98
DIGESTION P.345

COMPOUNDS AND MIXTURES

ELEMENTS THAT EXIST on their own are rarely found in the natural world. Most substances are made up of two or more elements that bond in different ways to form compounds. In a compound, atoms of different elements bond in a chemical reaction. Once this reaction has taken place, it is very difficult to separate the different elements of the compound. Water is a good example of a compound. It is made up of two atoms of hydrogen combined with one of oxygen. Combining elements to form a compound is very different from just mixing them together. Mixtures are combinations of different elements or compounds. Sea water, for example, is a mixture of water with other compounds, such as salt. But unlike compounds, no chemical reaction takes place when the elements or compounds mix together. This means that it is usually possible to separate mixtures into their different parts.

BUILDING BLOCKS
Just as letters of the alphabet can be used in different combinations to make millions of words, the elements can be arranged to make countless different compounds. The elements are nature's building blocks. Like a handful of building bricks, they can be used to build many different chemical structures.

IRON AND SULPHUR
A mixture of iron and sulphur contains separate iron and sulphur atoms. If this mixture is heated, a chemical reaction occurs and a new compound, iron sulphide, is made. Iron sulphide contains iron and sulphur atoms joined together and has very different properties from the mixture.

When iron filings are mixed with sulphur in a watch glass, you can still see the black iron specks in the yellow sulphur powder.

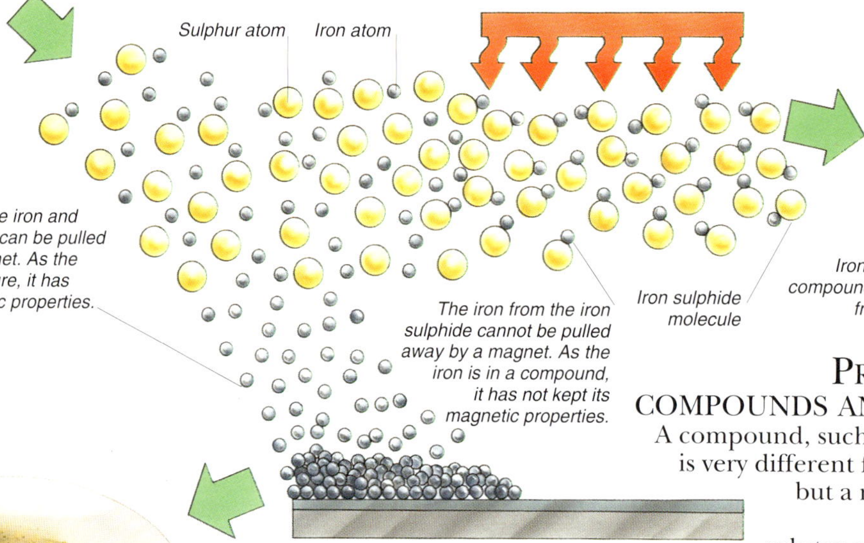

The iron from the iron and sulphur mixture can be pulled away by a magnet. As the iron is in a mixture, it has kept its magnetic properties.

The iron from the iron sulphide cannot be pulled away by a magnet. As the iron is in a compound, it has not kept its magnetic properties.

Iron sulphide is a black shiny compound with different properties from those of its elements.

In a mixture, iron filings can be separated from sulphur using a magnet.

PROPERTIES OF COMPOUNDS AND MIXTURES

A compound, such as iron sulphide, is very different from its elements, but a mixture keeps the properties of the substances it contains. It is difficult to separate a compound into its elements, but a mixture can be separated quite easily. A mixture of iron and sulphur, for example, can be separated by removing the iron with a magnet. A compound always contains the same proportions of its elements. Iron sulphide (FeS) always contains one part of iron to one part of sulphur. The amounts of the different substances in a mixture can vary.

JOSEPH-LOUIS PROUST
French chemist Joseph-Louis Proust (1754-1826) liked to analyse the content of anything that came within his reach. He discovered that the proportions of elements in any compound was always the same. This went against the thinking of respected scientists, but Proust was proved right. He had discovered the law of constant composition.

LAW OF CONSTANT COMPOSITION
Salt (sodium chloride, NaCl) is a compound that is found in sea water, salt mines, or can be made in a laboratory. But it is always the same salt, containing one sodium atom to one chlorine atom. A pure compound always contains the same elements in the same proportions.

Plastics are compounds of mostly hydrogen and carbon.

There are compounds and mixtures everywhere in this city scene from Florida, U.S.A.

Glass is a compound of silicon and oxygen.

Car bodies are made using mixtures of metals, called alloys.

Types of mixture

Solids, liquids, and gases can all be mixed in different combinations. Liquid mixtures, for example, are found in several forms. Alcohol and water mix easily. They are miscible liquids. Immiscible liquids such as vinegar and oil separate into two parts. By adding a substance called an emulsifier, the oil droplets will float suspended in the vinegar to produce a mixture called an emulsion. Mayonnaise is an emulsion of oil in vinegar. The emulsifier used is egg yolk.

Incense smoke is a mixture of solid dust and the air.

Bread is a mixture of a solid and a gas.

In salad dressing, oil floats on top of vinegar. These two liquids will not mix. They are immiscible.

Whisky is a mixture of two miscible liquids, alcohol and water, which is why it does not separate into two parts.

Hair gel is a mixture of a solid, fat, and water. The fat traps the water and stops it from moving around.

Shaving foam is a mixture of a liquid and a gas.

When flour is mixed into water, it stays suspended in the water. Flour and water form a suspension. A colloid is a suspension in which the suspended particles are very tiny.

Fizzy drinks have a gas, carbon dioxide, dissolved in the liquid.

Alloys

Objects such as spacecraft must be made of light yet strong material. Pure metals are not tough enough and so mixtures of metals, called alloys, are used. Alloys are made by adding a small amount of one pure metal to another. As the atoms of the second metal are different in shape, they change the formation of the original metal. This makes it tougher and more difficult to bend.

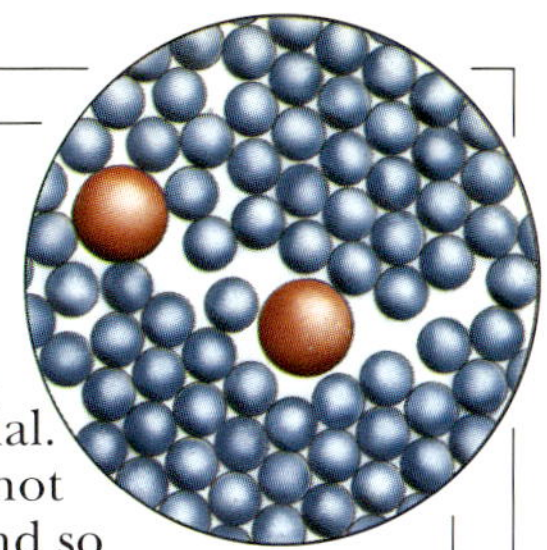

In an alloy, atoms of one metal stop those of another from sliding around.

This space shuttle is made of a titanium alloy.

Synthesis and decomposition

Chemists often build bigger and more useful molecules from smaller ones. This is called synthesis. Sometimes it is necessary to do the opposite and break down the larger molecules into smaller ones. This is called decomposition.

Chlorine is a poisonous green gas.

Sodium is a highly reactive, silvery-grey metal.

When sodium and chlorine combine, they make sodium chloride, or common salt.

Different compounds

Copper and oxygen can make two different compounds. Copper (I) oxide, a red-brown powder, has two parts of copper to one part of oxygen. Copper (II) oxide has one part of copper to one part of oxygen and is grey-black.

Copper (I) oxide (Cu_2O)

Copper (II) oxide (CuO)

Making a compound

Compounds are very different from the elements which make them. Common salt is a compound of sodium and chlorine. Sodium is a metal that is stored in oil as it reacts dangerously with air or water. Chlorine, a reactive green gas, is poisonous in large quantities. When sodium and chlorine atoms join, they lose their dangerous and poisonous properties. They form a new compound, sodium chloride, which is the familiar salt that we use to flavour our food.

A sodium atom gives one electron to a chlorine atom so that each ends up with eight electrons in their outer shell.

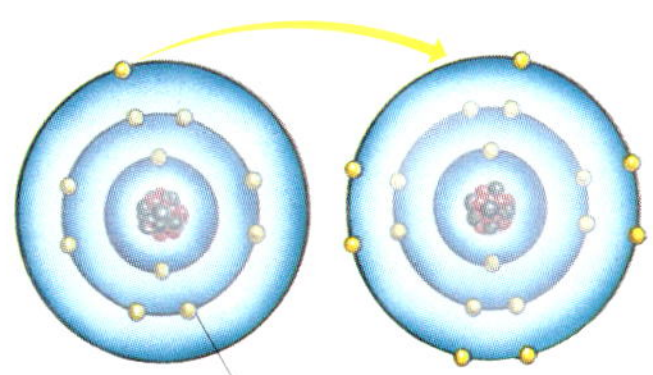

Moving electrons

Atoms are made of a nucleus with electrons moving around it in different levels or shells. An atom is generally most stable if it has eight electrons in its outer shell. If it has fewer than this, the atom is reactive and may be dangerous. When sodium and chlorine combine, electrons move places so that both sodium and chlorine each have a stable outer shell of electrons and the compound they make, salt, is stable and unreactive.

Purity

In chemical terms, pure substances contain only one type of atom or molecule. Pure gold is made up of gold atoms and nothing else. Some drinks are described as "pure juice", which means that nothing artificial has been added to them. To a chemist, however, the juice is not a pure substance as it is a mixture of compounds like water and sugar. Mixtures are not pure, unlike compounds, which contain only one kind of molecule.

Although freshly squeezed orange juice contains no additives, a chemist would not call it pure as it is made of more than one kind of molecule.

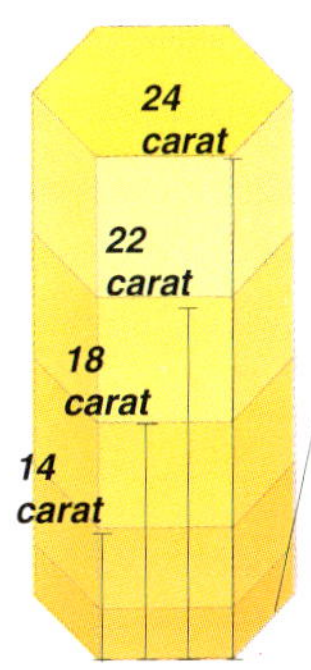

Only 24 carat gold is pure gold. Lower carats of gold are mixtures of gold with other, cheaper metals.

9 carat gold contains only 37% gold.

9 carat gold ring

Find out more

Atomic structure p.24
Bonding p.28
Elements p.31
Chemical reactions p.52
Solutions p.60
Separating mixtures p.61
Chemical analysis p.62
Alloys p.88
Cosmetics p.103

SOLUTIONS

SEA WATER LOOKS CLEAR, but it contains many substances, such as salt and oxygen, which have dissolved in the water and become invisible. It is an example of a solution, a special type of mixture in which different molecules are evenly mixed. Solutions are often made by dissolving a solid into a liquid, like when sugar is stirred into tea. Sugar is called the solute and tea is called the solvent. There are other kinds of solutions too. Gases, liquids, and solids can all be solutes or solvents. Concentrated solutions contain a large amount of solute in a solvent, while in dilute solutions there is only a little solute. Orange squash is a concentrated solution that is diluted by adding water.

A fizzy fruit drink is a solution of fruit juice, sugar, and carbon dioxide.

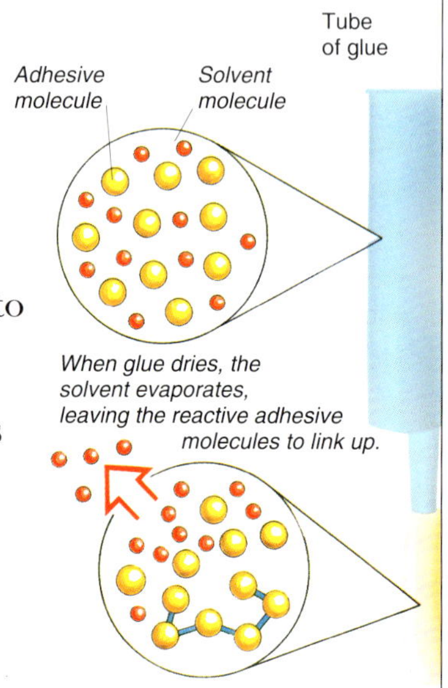

When glue dries, the solvent evaporates, leaving the reactive adhesive molecules to link up.

ATTRACTING MOLECULES

Whether a substance will dissolve depends on how much the molecules of solute and solvent are attracted to each other. Water is a good solvent as it has a slight electric charge and can form weak bonds with other charged particles. Certain compounds, such as salt, break down in water into two particles, one with a positive charge and one with a negative charge. These particles, called ions, can form weak bonds with the water molecules.

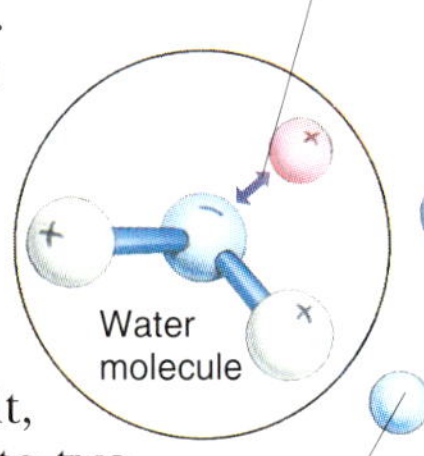

A positively charged ion is attracted to the negative end of a water molecule.

NON-LIQUID SOLUTIONS

Air is a solution of oxygen and other gases dissolved in nitrogen. Boats are made from alloys that are solid solutions of one metal dissolved in another metal.

DIFFERENT SOLVENTS

Some substances will not dissolve in water. Some types of glue, for example, have to be dissolved in another type of solvent called an organic solvent, such as acetone. When glue dries, the solvent evaporates, leaving behind the sticky solid that binds the surfaces together.

Water molecule

Dissolved particles mix with water molecules.

The air that deep-sea divers breathe dissolves in their blood to form a solution. If the diver surfaces too quickly, the air can come out of solution to form bubbles in the blood. This is a dangerous condition known as "the bends".

Fish use the small amounts of oxygen dissolved in water to stay alive. Unlike solids, gases dissolved in liquids come out of solution when the liquid is heated. This is one reason why fish cannot survive in very warm water.

SATURATED SOLUTION

The Dead Sea between Israel and Jordan contains a massive amount of salt. The water evaporates in the hot Sun, leaving the same amount of salt but less water. There is no longer any room for all the dissolved salt, and it forms solid crystals. When solutions cannot hold any more solute, they are said to have become saturated.

UNIVERSAL SOLVENT

Alchemists were early chemists. In the course of their experiments, they discovered ways to purify metals by dissolving them in solvents. The alchemists dedicated themselves to the search for a "universal solvent", a substance in which all things would dissolve. They never found it. If they had, what would they have kept it in?

INSOLUBLE SOLIDS

Substances that dissolve in water, such as salt, are said to be soluble in water. Insoluble substances, such as sand and oil, will not dissolve. This is because the water cannot overcome the forces holding the molecules of sand or oil together. These molecules prefer to stay bonded to each other, rather than separate and mix with the water molecules.

Find out more

PROPERTIES OF MATTER P.22
BONDING P.28
ORGANIC CHEMISTRY P.41
COMPOUNDS AND MIXTURES P.58
SEPARATING MIXTURES P.61
CHEMISTRY OF WATER P.75
ADHESIVES P.106

SEPARATING MIXTURES

WHEN YOU COOK RICE, you use a sieve to separate the rice from the water, a method known as filtration. Chemists use this and other familiar techniques to separate mixtures in a laboratory so that they can study one particular substance. The method they choose depends on the type of mixture and the different properties of the substances it contains. For example, since tea leaves do not dissolve in tea, you can use a strainer to filter them. If the tea leaves were fairly large, you might just leave them to settle before drinking the tea. This is another technique known as decanting.

DECANTING
To search for gold in rivers, huge pans were once used to scoop up a mixture of sand, gravel, and river water. The mixture was swirled around, and any heavy gold particles sank to the bottom. The unwanted muddy liquid could then be decanted (poured) off. Decanting separates two substances with different densities. As cream is less dense than milk, for example, it can easily be decanted off.

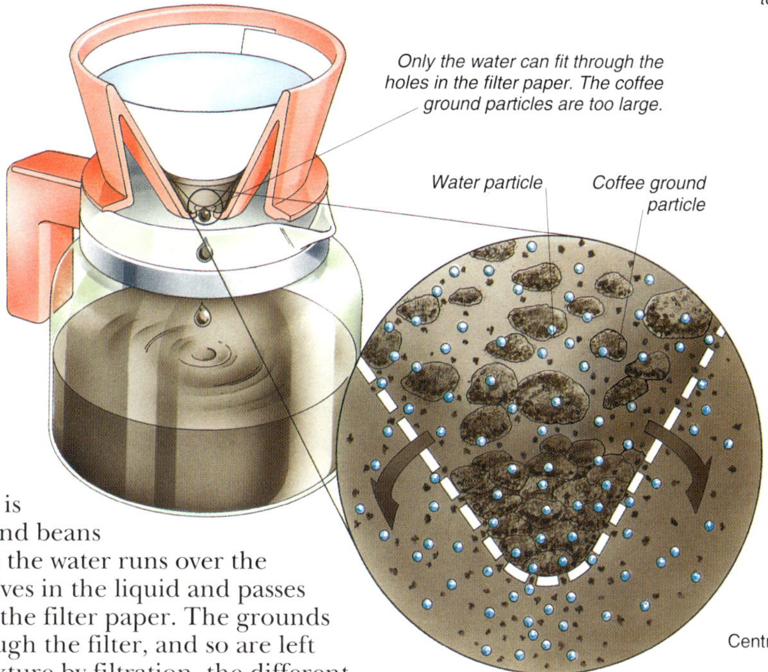

DESICCATION
To keep substances dry in the laboratory, chemists might put them in a desiccator. This sealed dish contains a solid, such as silica gel, that absorbs the moisture in the air. Packets of silica gel are often put inside camera cases so that moisture will not ruin the lens. Desiccation is simply a separating technique that removes water from a solid.

FILTRATION
In a coffee maker, a filter is used to separate the ground beans from the liquid coffee. As the water runs over the grounds, the coffee dissolves in the liquid and passes through the tiny holes in the filter paper. The grounds are too large to pass through the filter, and so are left behind. To separate a mixture by filtration, the different parts of the mixture must be present in different-sized pieces.

Centrifuge

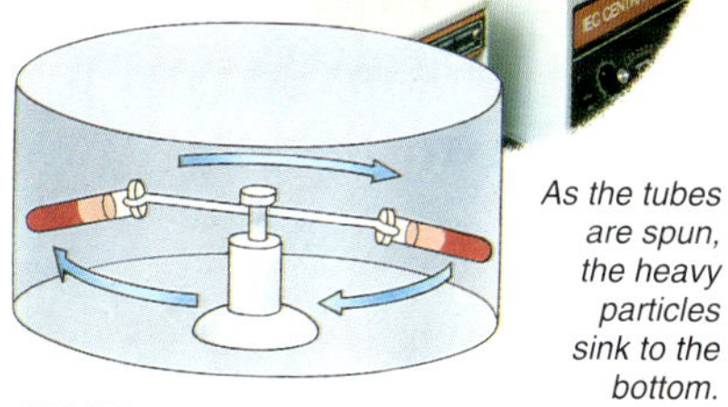

As the tubes are spun, the heavy particles sink to the bottom.

Drying crops in the Sun

DISTILLATION
If you were marooned on a desert island, how would you obtain pure water to drink? If sea water is boiled, the water comes off as steam. If this is then cooled, pure liquid water can be collected. This is a separating method called distillation that is used whenever the liquid part of a mixture is needed. The method can also be used if a mixture of liquids needs to be separated. This is fractional distillation. By heating the mixture, the liquid with the lowest boiling point will come off first. The liquid fraction with the highest boiling point will come off last.

CENTRIFUGING
A centrifuge is like a spin-dryer. It separates mixtures of liquids and solids by spinning them around at high speed. Dense substances sink to the bottom, while the less dense substances rise to the top. Test tubes of blood are centrifuged to separate the heavier blood cells from liquid plasma.

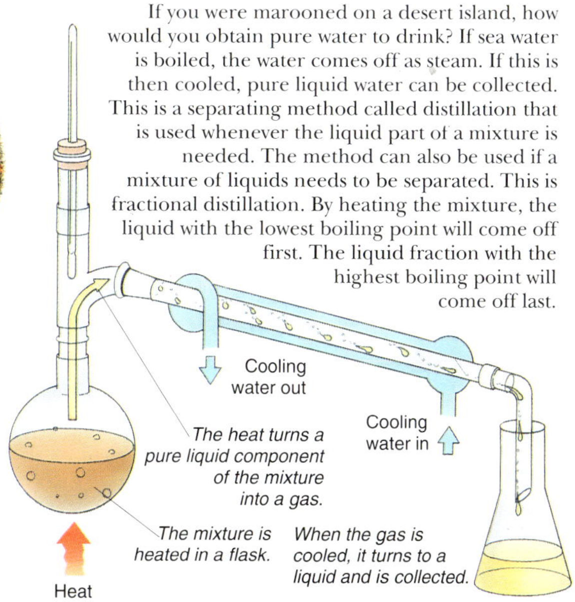

EVAPORATION
Fruit such as grapes can be left outside to dry in the Sun. The heat turns the liquid water in grapes into water vapour which is lost to the air, leaving wrinkled sultanas. This process of removing a liquid by heat is known as evaporation. Drying your hair with a hair drier is another example of evaporation.

Find out more

CHANGES OF STATE P.20
PROPERTIES OF MATTER P.22
COMPOUNDS AND MIXTURES P.58
SOLUTIONS P.60
CHEMICAL ANALYSIS P.62
OIL PRODUCTS P.98
CIRCULAR MOTION P.125

Chemical analysis

CHEMISTS OFTEN WORK like detectives. They look for clues to reveal the true identity of a substance. Food chemists carry out experiments to find whether food contains poisons or bacteria. Medical chemists examine fluids such as blood and urine for signs of disease in our bodies. Environmental chemists measure the health of the environment by testing samples of air, water, and soil, so that they can record levels of pollution. Scientists can use a wide range of techniques to analyse substances. Identifying the ingredients of a substance is called qualitative analysis. Finding out exactly how much of each ingredient it contains is called quantitative analysis.

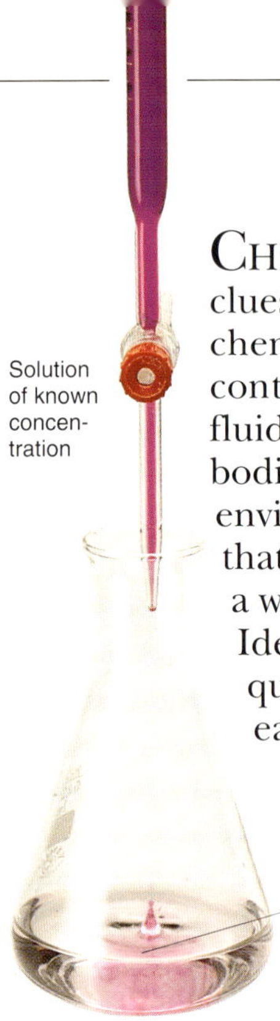

Solution of known concentration

The test solution turns from colourless to pink when it has all reacted.

TITRATION
To find out the concentration of a solution, chemists use a method called titration. They make the solution react with a chemical whose concentration is known. When all of the solution has reacted, a colour change occurs. Its concentration can then be worked out by measuring how much of the chemical was used.

GAS CHROMATOGRAPHY
To separate a mixture of gases, chemists sometimes use a technique called gas chromatography. The mixture is made to travel through a solid, and because some parts of the mixture are more strongly held by the solid than others, the mixture is separated into its components.

The blue dye stays near to the centre of the paper because it is more attracted to the paper than the other dyes.

The yellow dye travels on to the edge of the paper as it is more attracted to the water than the other dyes.

CHROMATOGRAPHY
Black ink may be a mixture of different dyes. When you put a drop onto filter paper and then add water, the blot spreads out into different coloured rings. Each separate ring contains a different dye. The dyes separate because some stick to the paper, and so remain near the centre, while others stay dissolved in the water and are taken farther out. This is a technique known as chromatography. Chemists often use chromatography to test a substance for purity, and doctors use it to analyse urine samples for traces of sugar (which would indicate diabetes).

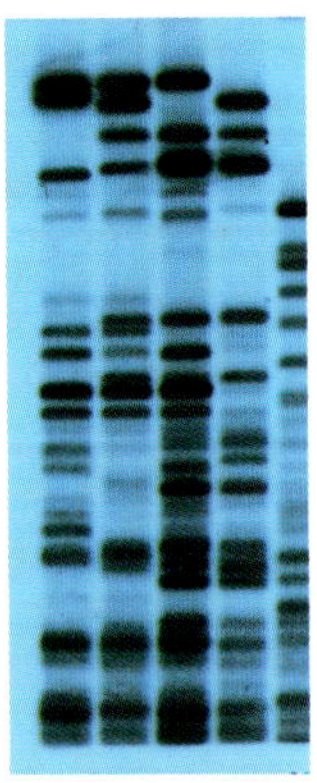

Every person has a DNA profile that is unique to them.

FORENSIC SCIENCE
Forensic scientists use many tests to solve crimes. A new test, known as DNA profiling, can be used to identify which person a trace of blood, or skin cells such as those in the roots of hairs, belongs to. It uses a method called electrophoresis, similar to chromatography, but which uses electricity. The genetic material is separated from the sample. Because this material is unique to one person, just like their fingerprints, it can be used for identification. This is why the method is sometimes called genetic fingerprinting.

Scientists, like cooks, need weighing scales so that they can make accurate measurements of the substances they use in the laboratory. This is a type of quantitative analysis.

Fool's gold

When fool's gold is dragged across a white tile, it leaves a black trail. Real gold leaves no mark.

DESTRUCTIVE TESTING
Real gold or fool's gold? Fool's gold is a compound of iron and sulphur that looks like gold. To test a sample, chemists can weigh it (fool's gold is lighter), drop acid onto it (fool's gold will dissolve), or drag it across a white tile (fool's gold leaves a black streak). The acid test and the white tile test damage the sample. They are destructive testing methods. Non-destructive testing, such as weighing, leaves the sample intact.

FRANCIS ASTON

English chemist Francis William Aston (1877-1945) invented the mass spectrometer in 1919. Aston worked as assistant to J. J. Thomson at the Cavendish Laboratory, Cambridge University, where he studied positively charged rays. The invention of the mass spectrometer led Aston to discover many new isotopes. This work won him the Nobel Prize for Chemistry in 1922.

MASS SPECTROMETER

Although the masses of atoms are too small to be measured, they can be compared. A very accurate piece of equipment that does just this is the mass spectrometer. It separates the atoms in a sample according to their mass and shows the amounts of the different atoms that are present. It does this by turning the atoms into ions and deflecting them in a magnetic field. Heavier ions are deflected more than light ones. The ions are therefore separated and can be identified.

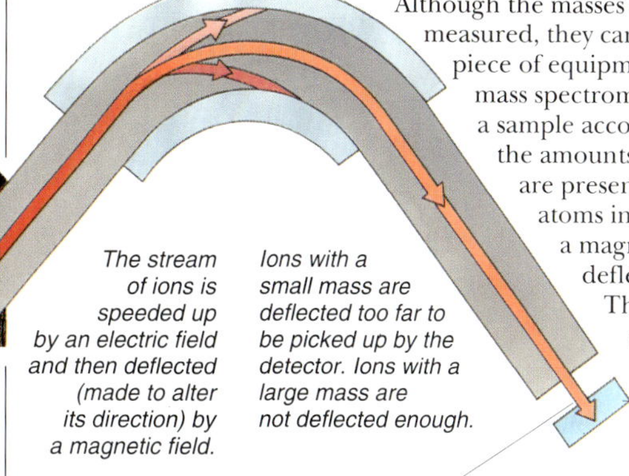

The stream of ions is speeded up by an electric field and then deflected (made to alter its direction) by a magnetic field.

Ions with a small mass are deflected too far to be picked up by the detector. Ions with a large mass are not deflected enough.

Detector

The sample is turned into a gas, and its atoms are converted into ions.

Only one type of ion is deflected by the right amount. By changing the strength of the magnetic field, different ions are recorded by the detector.

Reading from mass spectrometer

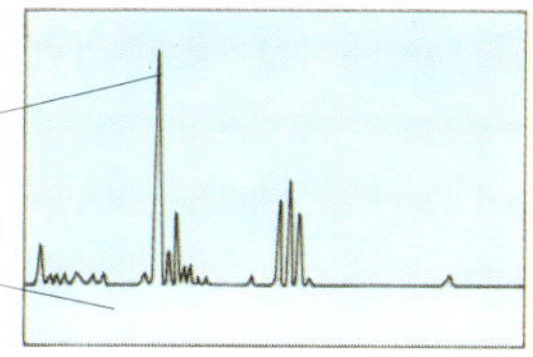

The height of the peak gives the number of each ion present.

The bottom scale gives the mass of each ion.

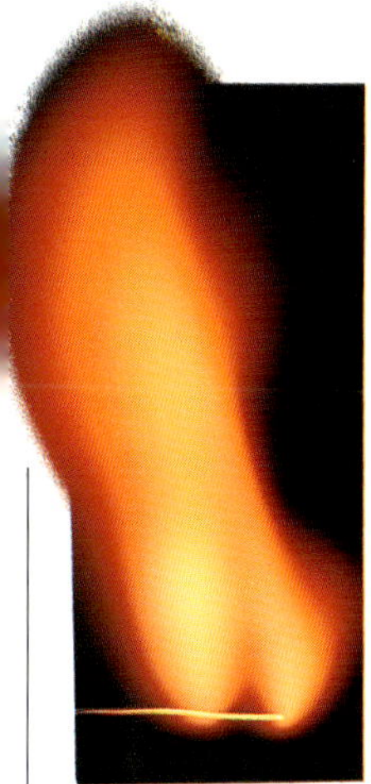

Sodium compounds burn with an orange flame.

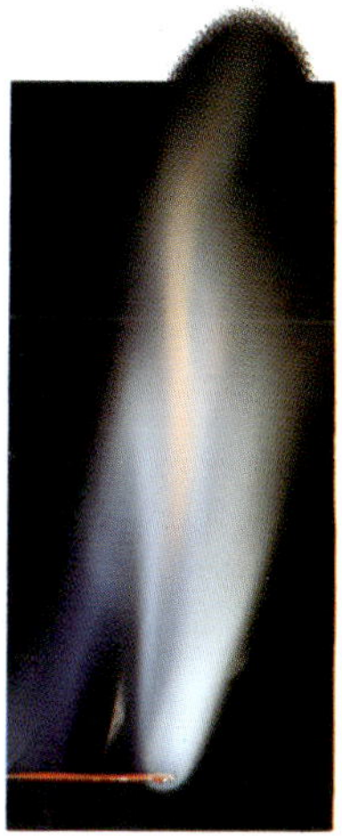

Lead compounds burn with a blue flame.

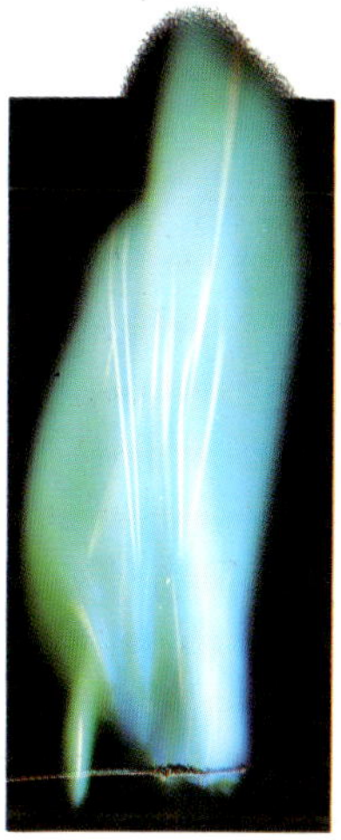

Copper compounds burn with a green-blue flame.

Atomic emission spectrum of the element helium

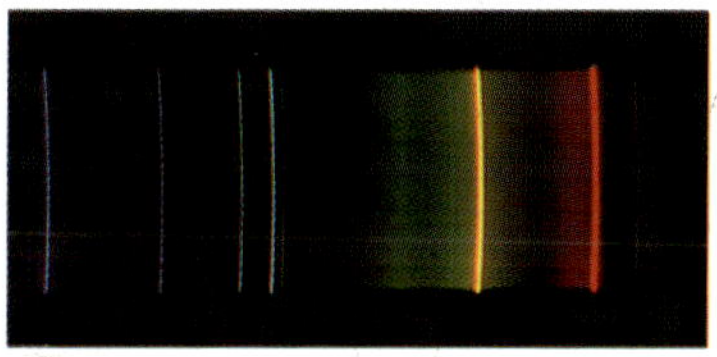

ATOMIC EMISSION SPECTRUM

The coloured light given out, or emitted, by an atom during a flame test is only part of the story. The atom actually emits a whole range of different lights when it is heated, but only some light is visible to us. The other frequencies of light can be picked up by an instrument called a spectroscope to give the atomic emission spectrum. This is the fingerprint of an atom. Each element has a different spectrum.

Barium compounds burn with a brown-green flame.

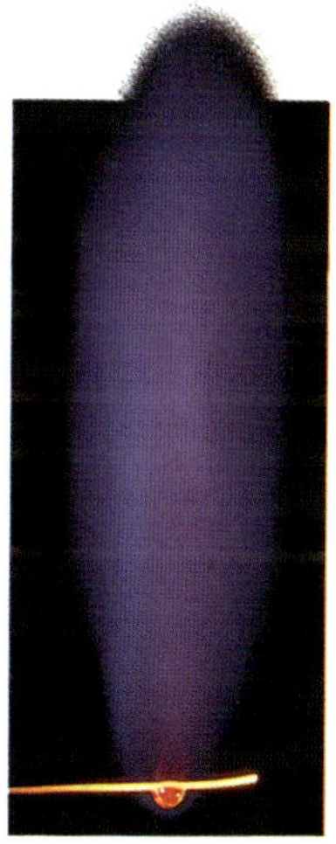

Potassium compounds burn with a lilac flame.

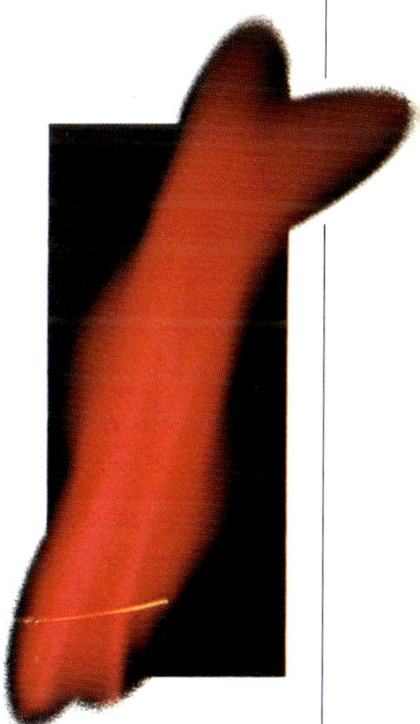

Lithium compounds burn with a red flame.

FLAME TESTS

When a metal compound is heated in a flame, it burns to give the flame a particular colour. This happens because the heat of the flame makes the electrons in the atom move around, and as they do so they give off light. Different metals give different colours of light to the flame and so this colour identifies the metal. Copper compounds, for example, always give a green-blue colour to a flame. These characteristic colours of metal compounds are also responsible for the beautiful colours of fireworks.

Environmental chemist testing the purity of a river

WATER TESTING

Environmental scientists use chemical analysis to test the quality and safety of water. A river may be polluted with fertilizers, detergents, waste, sewage, or acid rain. A scientist can use titration methods, for example, to find out how much of a dissolved substance a sample of water contains.

ANALYSING NAPOLEON

After his death, chemists analysed hair samples from the French emperor Napoleon Bonaparte (1769-1821) and found traces of arsenic, a poison. Murder was suspected. But recently it was discovered that the colouring in his wallpaper contained high levels of arsenic. Dampness and mould may have turned it into a deadly gas.

Find out more

ATOMIC STRUCTURE P.24
COMPOUNDS AND MIXTURES P.58
SEPARATING MIXTURES P.61
SOURCES OF LIGHT P.193
GENETICS P.364
FACT FINDER P.404

OXIDATION AND REDUCTION

Every time something burns, it combines with oxygen from the air. Burning is an oxidation reaction.

IF YOU FELT COLD ON THE MOON, you would never be able to light a fire to keep warm. This is because burning is a reaction in which a substance combines with oxygen – an oxidation reaction – and there is no oxygen around the Moon. Many important, everyday chemical reactions involve oxidation. It occurs when substances burn, when metals rust, and even when we breathe. The food that we eat is converted into energy by combining with the oxygen that we breathe in. Substances that combine with oxygen or that lose hydrogen are said to be oxidized. The process where a substance loses oxygen or gains hydrogen is called reduction, and it always happens at the same time as oxidation: when one substance gains oxygen, another must give it up.

REDUCTION

When a substance loses oxygen or gains hydrogen in a chemical reaction, it is reduced. This is caused by another substance removing oxygen or giving hydrogen. This other substance is known as a reducing agent. One example of this is the gas carbon monoxide given out by car exhausts. This will readily gobble up oxygen to form carbon dioxide.

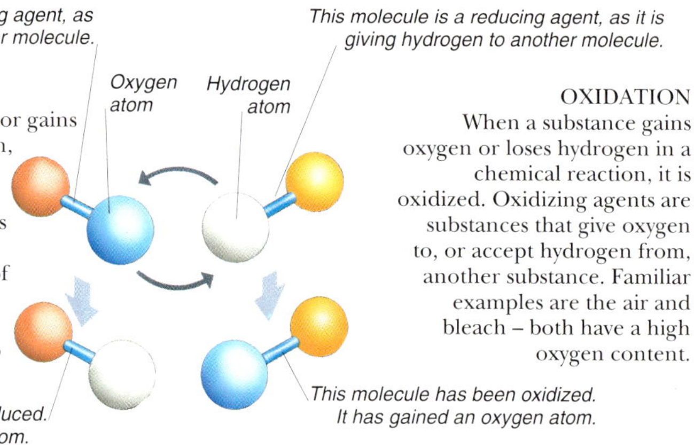

OXIDATION

When a substance gains oxygen or loses hydrogen in a chemical reaction, it is oxidized. Oxidizing agents are substances that give oxygen to, or accept hydrogen from, another substance. Familiar examples are the air and bleach – both have a high oxygen content.

RUSTING

If iron or steel are exposed to air and moisture, they will rust. Rusting is a destructive example of an oxidation reaction. The iron is oxidized to form iron oxide (rust). Once the top layer of metal has rusted, oxygen from the air can reach the inner layers. Rust will therefore quickly eat its way through the metal. Applying a coat of protective paint to a surface such as the hull of a ship prevents rust from forming, because the oxygen in the air cannot reach the iron.

OXIDATION IN KILNS

Potters may put a glaze on their pots that contains a metal – iron, for example. When the pot is baked in a kiln containing a lot of oxygen, the iron is oxidized to one form of iron oxide, Fe_2O_3, which is red. If the pot is baked in a kiln containing only a little oxygen, another form of iron oxide, FeO, is formed, which is black.

PHLOGISTON THEORY

Watching flames leaping from wood inspired a German doctor, Georg Stahl (1660-1734). He suggested that everything that burned gave out a substance called phlogiston. Later, Antoine Lavoisier (1743-94), a French chemist, dismissed this theory. He proved that when something burns, it combines with oxygen from the air.

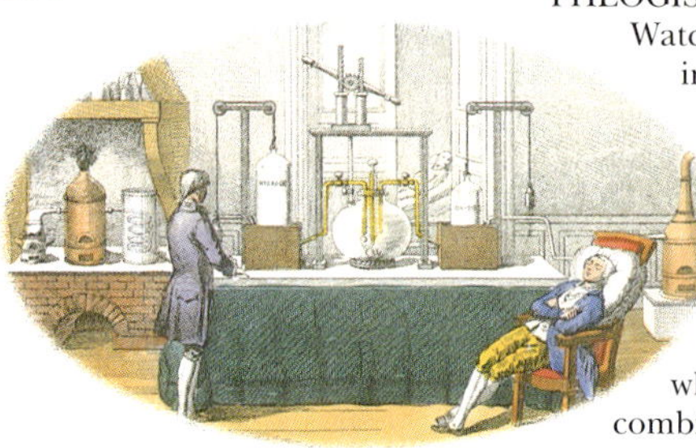

OXIDES

When non-metals combine with oxygen, they form oxides which make acid solutions in water. Nitrogen oxide and sulphur dioxide, for example, are non-metal oxides produced by power stations. When these oxides dissolve in the moist air, they fall as acid rain, harming trees, lakes, and buildings. This is why power stations are now trying to control their emissions. Metals, on the other hand, combine with oxygen to form oxides which make alkaline solutions in water.

ELECTRON TRANSFER

During the oxidation and reduction processes, there is always a movement of electrons between the atoms. Atoms that gain electrons are said to be reduced. Atoms that lose electrons are said to be oxidized. Nowadays, chemists call these processes oxidation and reduction, even when oxygen and hydrogen are not involved in the reaction.

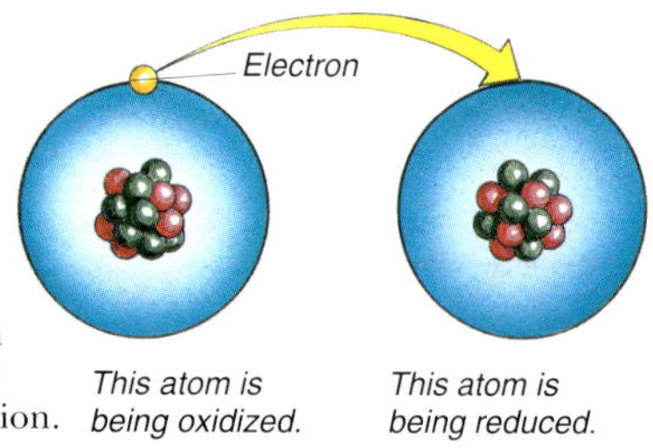

GUNPOWDER

Gunpowder was discovered accidentally by Chinese alchemists in the 7th century. Its main ingredients are saltpetre (potassium nitrate), sulphur, and carbon. Setting light to gunpowder is an example of an explosive oxidation reaction. While most substances burn by taking oxygen from the air, gunpowder burns by taking oxygen from the saltpetre. The chemical formula for saltpetre, KNO_3, shows it contains a lot of oxygen.

MAKING MARGARINE

The margarine that you spread on your bread is made from liquid vegetable oils, such as sunflower oil. To turn these liquids into solid fats, the oil is combined with hydrogen. This process is called hydrogenation and is an example of a reduction reaction. By controlling the amount of hydrogen added to the oils, the margarine can be made as soft or as hard as needed.

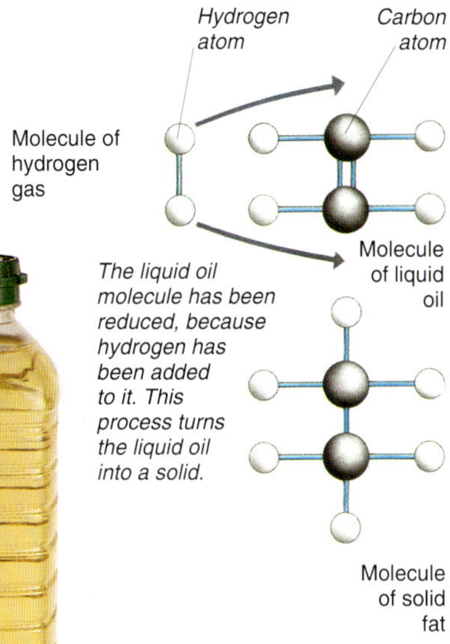

ANTIOXIDANTS

Food can go bad by reacting with oxygen in the air. To prevent this, chemicals called antioxidants are added to the food when it is made. It is these, rather than the food, which will react with the oxygen and so the food is kept fresh. Antioxidants are often found in fatty foods such as vegetable oils because fats are very quick to oxidize.

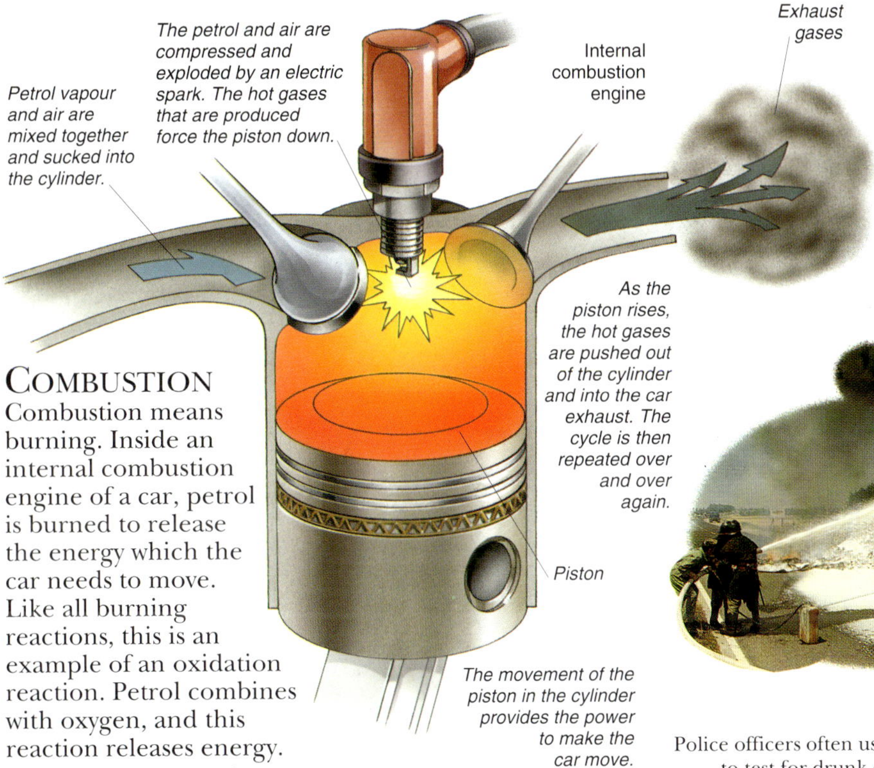

COMBUSTION

Combustion means burning. Inside an internal combustion engine of a car, petrol is burned to release the energy which the car needs to move. Like all burning reactions, this is an example of an oxidation reaction. Petrol combines with oxygen, and this reaction releases energy.

FIRE-FIGHTING

To burn, a fire needs a fuel (the burning substance) and heat. Since burning is an oxidation reaction, a fire also needs a supply of oxygen to keep going and by taking this away, the fire can be stopped. This can be done either by smothering the flames with a blanket, or by covering them with foam or carbon dioxide from an extinguisher.

BREATHALYSER

Police officers often use an oxidation reaction to test for drunk drivers. When someone breathes into a breathalyser, any alcohol (ethanol) in their breath is oxidized to make ethanoic acid. This produces an electric current. The strength of the current shows the amount of alcohol present in the driver's breath.

BLEACHING

Household bleaching fluids contain powerful oxidizing agents that oxidize the coloured substances in cloth and make them colourless. Modern bleaches contain hydrogen peroxide, H_2O_2. Its formula shows that it contains a lot of oxygen.

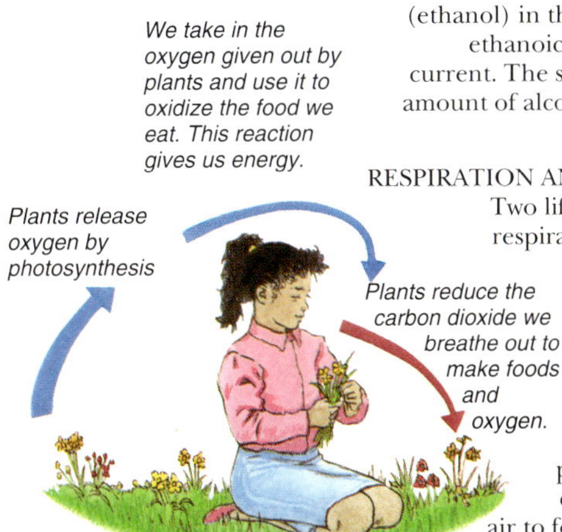

RESPIRATION AND PHOTOSYNTHESIS

Two life-giving reactions called respiration and photosynthesis are oxidation and reduction reactions. In respiration, the food we eat is oxidized. This releases the energy our bodies need. Plants use a reaction called photosynthesis to reduce carbon dioxide from the air to form sugars and starches.

Find out more

ATOMIC STRUCTURE P.24
OXYGEN P.44
HYDROGEN P.47
CHEMICAL REACTIONS P.52
CHEMISTRY OF AIR P.74
ENGINES P.143
PHOTOSYNTHESIS P.340
CELLULAR RESPIRATION P.346
FACT FINDER P.404

REACTIVITY SERIES

POTASSIUM IS SO REACTIVE that it is rarely found on its own. It is usually tightly bonded to other elements. Silver, on the other hand, is such a remarkably unreactive element that it can be safely used for cutlery as it will not react with food. By comparing the way they react, a league table of metals can be drawn up. This is called the reactivity series. The metals at the top of the series are the most reactive; the metals at the bottom are the least reactive. The series is used to predict what will happen when different metals react together. For example, if potassium and silver were competing to react with chlorine, potassium would win and potassium chloride would be formed. A metal will win any competition between it and another metal lower in the series.

UNREACTIVE GOLD
Archaeologists frequently discover gold objects, such as jewellery or masks. These are often as good as new, even though they have been buried for thousands of years. Unlike most metals, which would have corroded, gold is an unreactive metal. This is why it is placed at the bottom of the reactivity series.

DISPLACEMENT

When copper is dropped into a solution of silver nitrate, the two metals compete for the nitrate ions. Because copper is higher in the reactivity series, it is able to "grab" the nitrate ions from the silver. The result is a blue solution of copper nitrate and needles of silver metal. This is called a displacement reaction, as the copper metal has displaced the silver from solution.

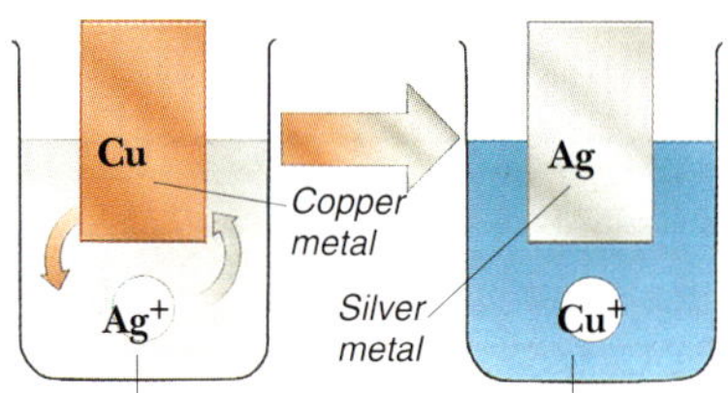

The silver and the copper have swapped positions.

If aluminium's oxide layer is removed, the exposed aluminium reacts violently with air.

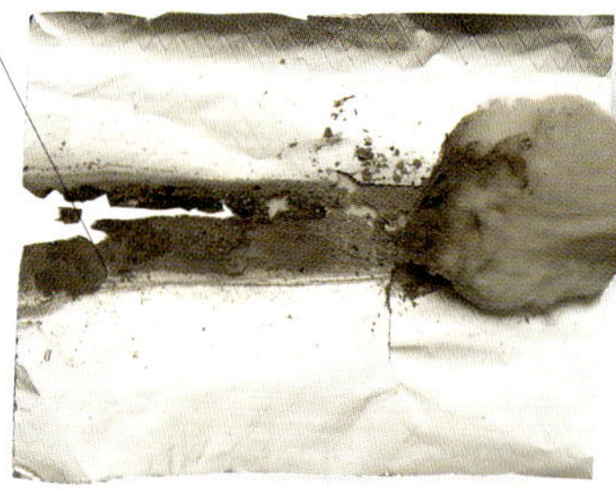

ALUMINIUM
Aluminium is an odd metal. It is high in the reactivity series, and yet aluminium saucepans are used to cook food. This is because it reacts with oxygen in the air to form a protective layer of aluminium oxide. But if this layer is broken down, for example by rubbing aluminium foil with a chemical called mercury chloride, the exposed aluminium is extremely reactive.

GALVANIZING
Objects made of steel, which is mostly iron, can be protected against rusting by a coating of a more reactive metal, usually zinc. This process is called galvanizing. Oxygen in the air will react with the zinc rather than with the iron, even if the zinc layer is scratched. This is sometimes called sacrificial protection, since the zinc has been sacrificed to protect the iron.

HISTORY OF METALS

The use of metals came late in history. Early people used only bones, stone, and wood. Since copper, silver, and gold are at the bottom of the reactivity series, they were easily found, and were the first metals ever used. By 2000 B.C., iron, a more reactive metal, could be extracted from its ores by heat. The Iron Age had begun. Aluminium is a common but very reactive metal that could not be extracted until the 19th century.

Iron tongs from the Iron Age

THE SERIES
This is the reactivity series. It shows the order of reactivity of different metals. Those at the top, such as sodium and potassium, react violently with air. Those at the bottom, such as silver and gold, are unaffected by air. Those in between, such as iron and zinc, react slowly. The way a metal is extracted from its ores (naturally occurring compounds) depends on its position in the reactivity series.

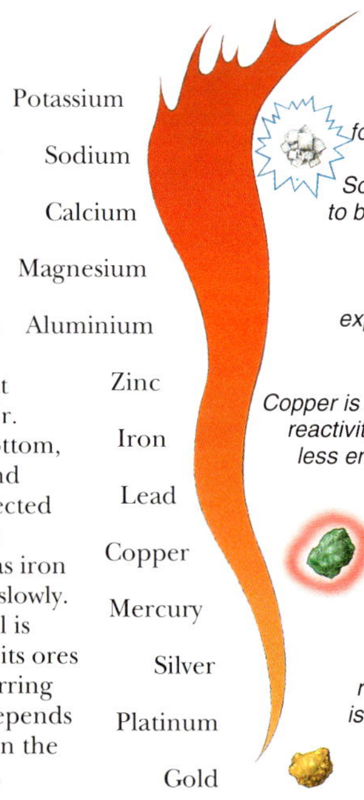

Sodium is high in the reactivity series and so forms very stable compounds. Sodium metal has to be obtained from molten sodium chloride by the powerful but expensive method of electrolysis.

Copper is lower down the reactivity series and so less energy is needed to extract it. Copper can be obtained by just heating its ores.

Gold, at the bottom of the reactivity series, is unreactive and can be found uncombined in nature.

Find out more

ALKALI METALS P.34
TRANSITION METALS P.36
SOLUTIONS P.60
ELECTROLYSIS P.67
IRON AND STEEL P.84
COPPER P.86
ALUMINIUM P.87
FACT FINDER P.404

ELECTROLYSIS

TEARING A COMPOUND APART using electricity is a process called electrolysis. For this to work, the compound has to conduct electricity – it must be either molten or in solution, and it must contain electrically charged ions that are free to move. Two metal or carbon rods, the electrodes, are placed in the substance to be split (the electrolyte). When a battery is connected, electricity flows through the liquid. The positive ions of the compound move to the negatively charged electrode (the cathode). The negative ions move to the positively charged electrode (the anode). The compound is split into two parts.

ELECTROREFINING
Electrolysis can be used to purify copper. This process is called electrorefining. Impure copper is the anode, a sheet of pure copper is the cathode, and the electrolyte is copper sulphate solution. When electricity is passed through the solution, pure copper is transferred from the impure to the pure sample. The impurities fall to the bottom of the solution.

ANODIZING
If electricity is passed through acid with aluminium as the anode, oxygen is formed at this anode and reacts with the aluminium to form a protective coating of aluminium oxide. This is called anodizing. Coloured foils are made by dyeing this oxide layer.

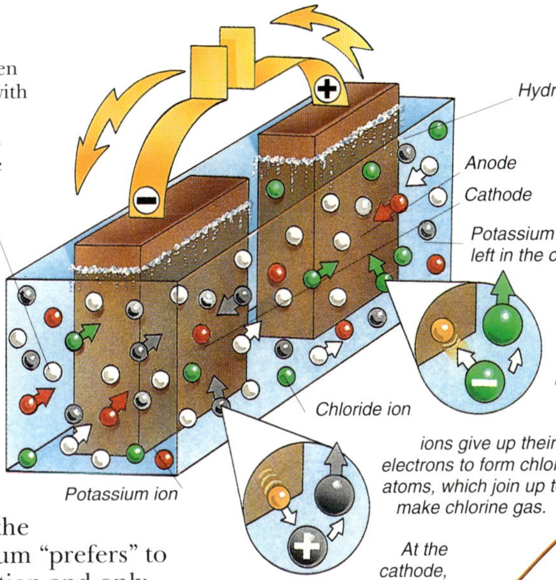

MOVING IONS

When electricity is passed through a solution of potassium chloride (KCl) in water (H_2O), not only is the potassium chloride pulled apart, but also the water. The potassium ions and hydrogen ions, both positively charged, move to the cathode but because potassium "prefers" to stay as an ion, it stays in solution and only hydrogen gas is given off. Chloride ions and hydroxide ions, both negatively charged, move to the anode. The hydroxide ions stay in solution and only chlorine gas is given off.

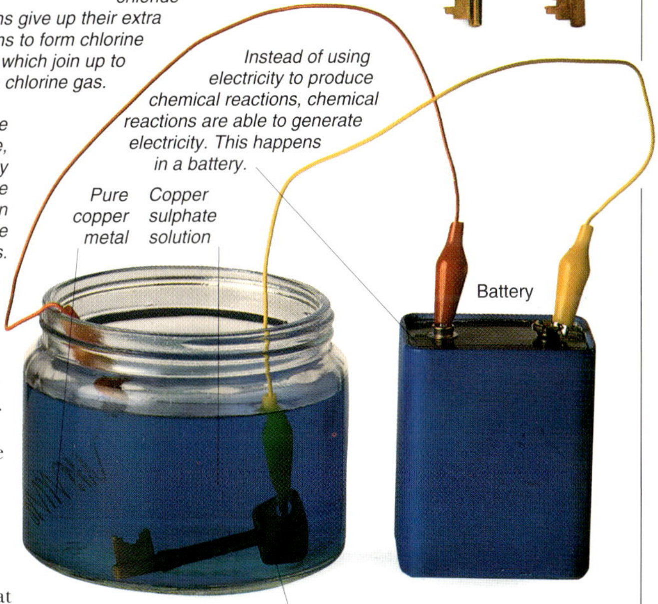

HUMPHRY DAVY

The English chemist Humphry Davy (1778-1829) is best known for his invention of the miner's safety lamp, but he was also one of the first to use electrolysis. He discovered sodium, potassium, calcium, and a number of other metals because he was able to separate them from their compounds by electrolysis. Davy appointed an assistant called Michael Faraday in 1813, who continued Davy's work and went on to become a very famous scientist himself.

ELECTROPLATING
Coating an object, like a key, with a thin layer of metal is a process called electroplating. The object is made the cathode. The anode is a pure piece of plating metal, such as copper. The electrolyte contains a compound of this metal (copper sulphate, for example). Metal ions move through the solution and coat the object. Tin cans are made by electroplating tin onto steel.

WATER
When electricity is passed through water (H_2O), hydrogen gas forms at the cathode and oxygen at the anode. Because water contains two hydrogen atoms for every oxygen atom, twice as much hydrogen as oxygen is produced.

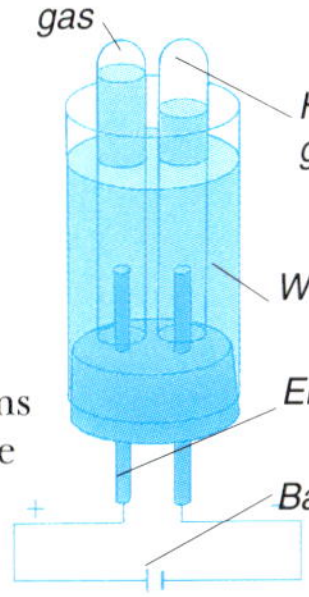

Find out more

BONDING P.28
SOLUTIONS P.60
REACTIVITY SERIES P.66
COPPER P.86
CELLS AND BATTERIES P.150
FACT FINDER P.404

Scientists use the pH scale to describe the strength of acids and alkalis. It runs from 1 to 14. The more hydrogen ions it contains, the stronger it is, and the lower its pH. All acids have a pH of less than 7.

ACIDS

Acid half of the pH scale

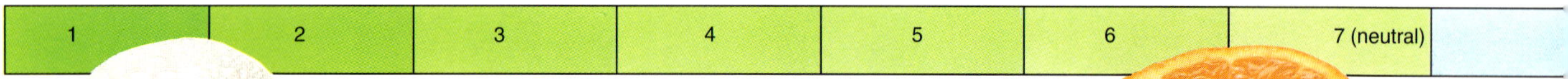

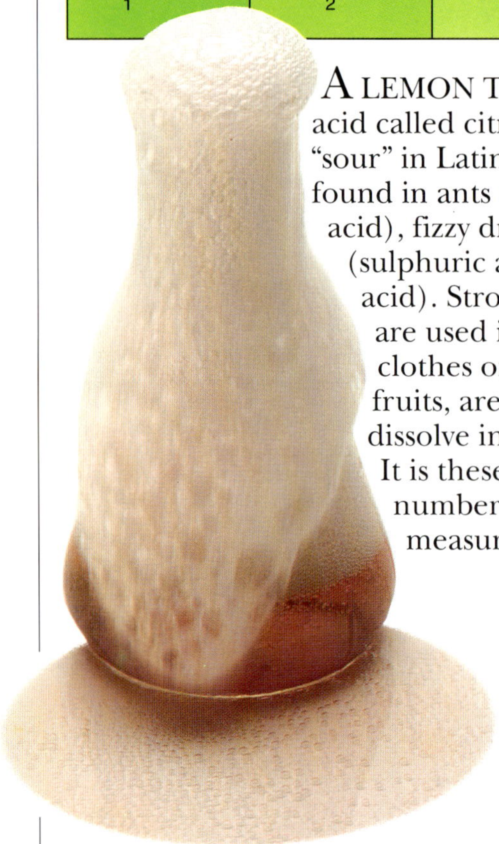

A LEMON TASTES SOUR because it contains an acid called citric acid. In fact, the word acid means "sour" in Latin. Acids are everywhere. They are found in ants (methanoic acid), grapes (tartaric acid), fizzy drinks (carbonic acid), car batteries (sulphuric acid), and even in our stomachs (hydrochloric acid). Strong acids such as sulphuric and nitric acids, which are used in laboratories, are very dangerous and will burn clothes or skin. Some weak acids, such as those found in fruits, are safe to eat. All acids contain hydrogen and dissolve in water to form positively charged hydrogen ions. It is these ions that give acids their special properties. The number of hydrogen ions an acid can form in water is a measure of its strength, known as its pH.

HIGH pH
Citrus fruits such as lemons and oranges contain citric acid. This is a weak acid. It has a fairly high pH, but still under 7.

STRONG ACIDS
Some acids, such as nitric acid and sulphuric acid, are strong. Their molecules completely dissociate (split up) into hydrogen and other ions in water. The strength of an acid tells us how many of these split-off hydrogen ions are present in the solution. Just as you dilute orange squash with water, you can dilute strong acids with water, so there are fewer hydrogen ions in solution. This lowers their acidity (increasing the pH).

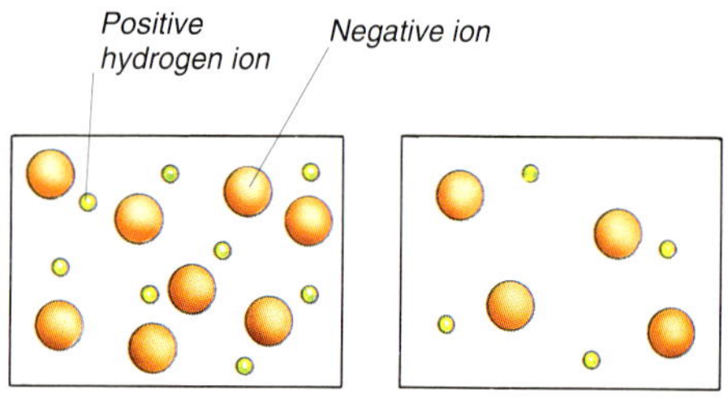

Concentrated strong acid
Dilute strong acid

LOW pH
Acids found in the laboratory, such as sulphuric acid, are strong. They have a low pH. We have a strong acid, hydrochloric acid, in our stomachs to help digest our food.

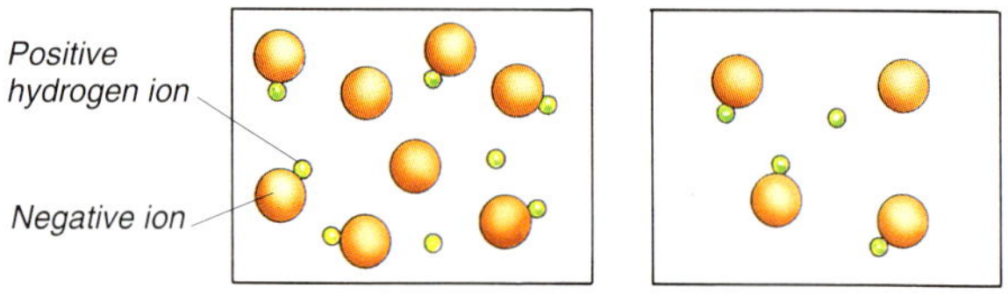

Concentrated weak acid
Dilute weak acid

WEAK ACIDS
Some acids, such as the citric acid found in oranges and lemons, are weak acids. When dissolved in water, only a very small number of their molecules will dissociate to form hydrogen ions. You can make concentrated or dilute solutions of a weak acid by either removing or adding water. A very concentrated solution of a weak acid and a very dilute solution of a strong acid may well have the same pH.

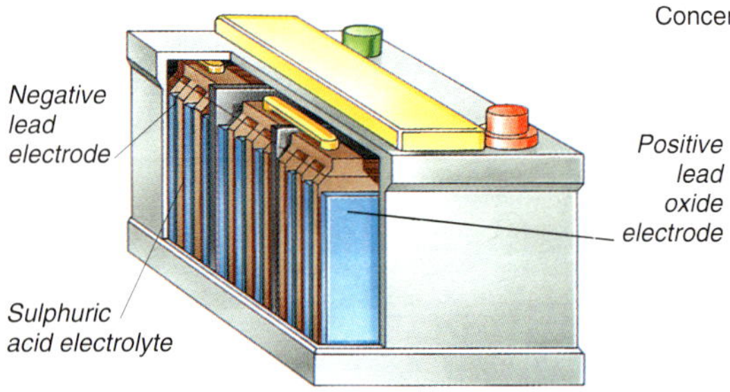

ACID FROM ANTS
An acid called methanoic acid (formic acid) is produced naturally by both stinging ants and stinging nettles. Long ago, people made formic acid by boiling ants in a big pot. Today, it is made from other chemicals. It is used to preserve silage (crops stored for animal fodder) and to make paper and textiles.

LEAD-ACID BATTERY

Strong acids make good electrolytes (liquids that conduct electricity). This is because in water they are almost completely split up into positive hydrogen ions and negative ions. These electrically charged ions can carry an electric current. Sulphuric acid is used as the electrolyte in the lead-acid batteries found in cars. Lead plates act as the electrodes. These batteries produce the energy to start the car.

A clam will die if the pH of its water falls below 6. *A salamander will die if the pH of its water falls below 5.* *A brook trout will die if the pH of its water falls below 4.5.* *A wood frog will die if the pH of its water falls below 4.*

ACID WATER
Lakes and rivers can be polluted by acid rain. This increases the acidity, or lowers the pH of the water, and so may be harmful to fish and other aquatic life. Some animals are more sensitive to these pH changes than others. A clam, for example, cannot survive if the pH of its water falls below 6. Wood frogs, on the other hand, can survive in water with a pH as low as 4.

ACID ON PAPER

Concentrated sulphuric acid is very corrosive. It acts as a dehydrating agent, which means that it removes water from any substance it comes into contact with. Paper is made from cellulose, a plant material that contains carbon, hydrogen, and oxygen. When sulphuric acid reacts with paper, it removes the water (hydrogen and oxygen), and leaves the black carbon behind. This is why the paper looks burnt.

The cork flies out of the bottle. It is pushed by the carbon dioxide gas created during the chemical reaction between the vinegar and the bicarbonate of soda.

Vinegar mixed with bicarbonate of soda

A compound called sodium ethanoate is left behind in the bottle. This is a salt.

YELLOWING PAGES

Have you noticed that the pages in new books look very white, while those in older books have turned yellow? Paper contains tiny amounts of an acid. Over years and years, this acid very slowly starts to break down the cellulose fibres in the paper. This changes the colour of the paper from white to yellow. The reaction is speeded up by sunlight, and the paper may turn brown and become brittle.

ACID ON CARBONATE

If you add vinegar (ethanoic acid) to bicarbonate of soda (sodium hydrogen carbonate) in a corked bottle, a fizzy reaction occurs. The acid breaks down the carbonate to make carbon dioxide gas. So much gas is produced that it fills up the bottle, and then forces the cork out like a cannonball. Acids will always break down carbonates to form carbon dioxide. This reaction is used in cookery. Baking powder is a mixture of cream of tartar (a form of tartaric acid) and bicarbonate of soda. In water, they make carbon dioxide, which is the gas that makes cakes rise.

A furious bubbling of hydrogen gas is given off.

Hydrochloric acid

Chippings of zinc metal

ACID ON METAL

You should never store vinegar in a metal bottle. It can create a slight fizzing of hydrogen gas. The hydrogen that all acids contain can be driven off when the acid meets a reactive metal. This is why acids are never kept in metal containers. When hydrochloric acid is poured on zinc (above), there is a fizzing of hydrogen gas. The zinc replaces the hydrogen in the acid to form zinc chloride.

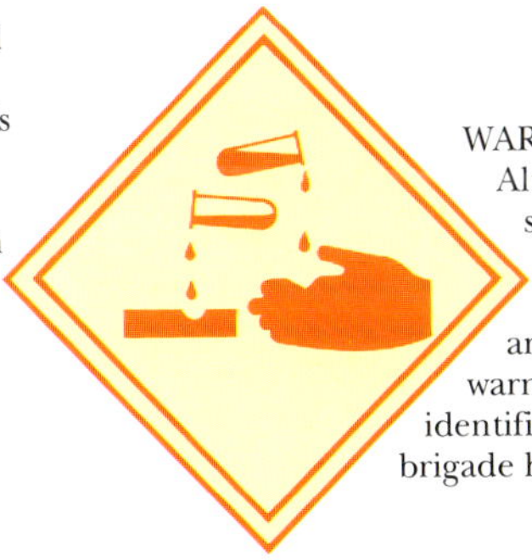

WARNING SYMBOL

Although acids often look like water, strong acids are corrosive and cause severe burns. Because of this, the containers in which acids are transported carry a hazard warning sign. This has a code that identifies the acid and tells the fire brigade how to deal with a spillage.

PICKLING

Since acids are dangerous to living things, they can be used as preservatives to kill bacteria. Many foods, like onions and beetroot, are preserved by soaking in vinegar (ethanoic acid). This process is called pickling. The acid kills any micro-organisms and so stops the food going bad. Pickling was widely used before the invention of refrigerators.

ACID DISCOVERIES

11th century Arabic chemists find out how to make sulphuric, nitric, and hydrochloric acids.

1675 Irish chemist Robert Boyle wrongly suggests that acids contain special particles that squeeze into gaps in metals, breaking them apart.

1854 The writing of French chemist Auguste Laurent proves that all acids contain hydrogen.

1887 Swedish chemist Svante Arrhenius proposes that all acids contain hydrogen ions and these give acids their special properties.

ACID IN RAIN

Rainwater has always been slightly acidic, as carbon dioxide in the air dissolves in rain to form carbonic acid. But the acidity of rain has increased since the world became industrialized. This is because fossil fuels such as coal release sulphur dioxide and nitrogen dioxide when they are burned. These gases react with the water in clouds to form sulphuric acid and nitric acid. Acid rain threatens many buildings, especially those made of limestone, which is calcium carbonate. This is because acids easily break down carbonates into carbon dioxide gas.

Find out more

BONDING P.28
HYDROGEN P.47
SOLUTIONS P.60
ALKALIS AND BASES P.70
MEASURING ACIDITY P.72
SALTS P.73
SULPHURIC ACID P.89
CELLS AND BATTERIES P.150

ALKALIS AND BASES

WHEN YOU ARE STUNG by a nettle, the first thing you reach for is a dock leaf. The leaf contains a natural base that counteracts the acid in the nettle sting. Bases are substances that can cancel out acidity. They are said to neutralize acids. Alkalis are bases that can dissolve in water. Bases and alkalis are all around us – in oven cleaners, polish, baking powder, indigestion tablets, saliva, and chalk. Like acids, some alkalis are very dangerous and can cause burns if splashed onto the skin. All alkalis dissolve in water to form hydroxide ions (OH^-). These ions react with the hydrogen ions (H^+) in acids to cancel out acidity. The number of hydroxide ions an alkali can make in water is a measure of its strength. This is measured on the pH scale.

SOAP
Alkalis feel soapy when rubbed between the fingers. This is because they react with the oils in our skin and start to dissolve them. Soap is made by boiling animal fats or vegetable oils with the strong alkali sodium hydroxide (NaOH).

ALKALI FROM ASHES
The word alkali is Arabic and means the "ashes of a plant". Alkalis used to be made by burning wood and other plants – sodium carbonate from sea plants and potassium carbonate from land plants. Alkalis can now be made by electrolysis.

ALKALIS IN SPACE
Astronauts in the Apollo space missions used the alkali lithium hydroxide to neutralize the dangerous levels of carbon dioxide gas they were breathing out. This type of neutralization is also used to remove carbon dioxide from air-conditioned buildings.

This is a type of alkaline battery you might find in a watch or a calculator.

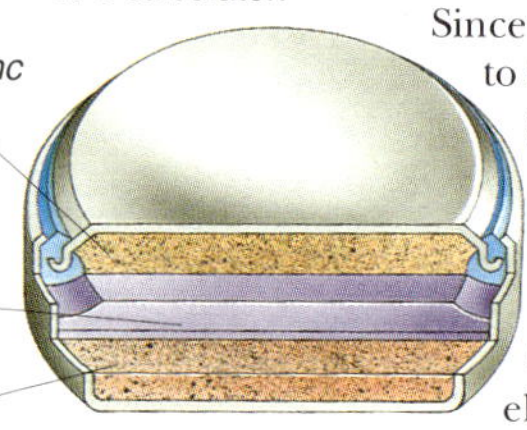

ALKALI CONDUCTORS
Since alkalis break up in water to form ions, alkalis are good conductors of electricity. In an alkaline battery, the strong alkali potassium hydroxide is used to conduct electricity between two electrodes.

WARNING SYMBOL
Concentrated solutions of alkali are corrosive and can cause severe burns. Because of this, the containers in which they are stored and transported always carry a hazard warning sign.

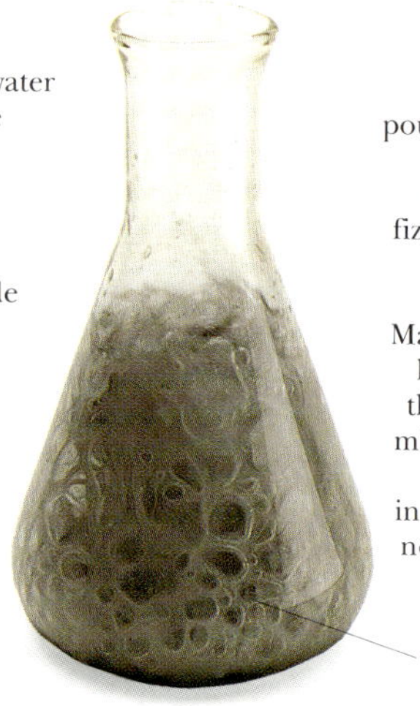

Sodium hydroxide mixed with magnesium pieces

ALKALI ON METAL
When a solution of sodium hydroxide is poured onto some pieces of magnesium metal, there is a tremendous fizzing. This is hydrogen gas that has formed during the reaction. Magnesium hydroxide is left in the flask. This is the active ingredient in milk of magnesia, which people take to cure indigestion – it works by neutralizing excess acid in the stomach.

CALCIUM CARBONATE

Seashells, coral, chalk, limestone, and marble are all made of the base calcium carbonate. It is a very important and useful compound in the chemical industry for making fertilizer, glass, cement, and steel. By heating calcium carbonate, calcium oxide (quicklime) is made. Just by adding water, this can be made into calcium hydroxide (slaked lime), which is used to neutralize acid in water supplies. Slaked lime can be mixed with sand and water to make mortar.

Limestone processing plant

The more hydroxide ions an alkali contains, the stronger it is, and the higher its pH. All alkalis have a pH greater than 7.

Alkali half of the pH scale

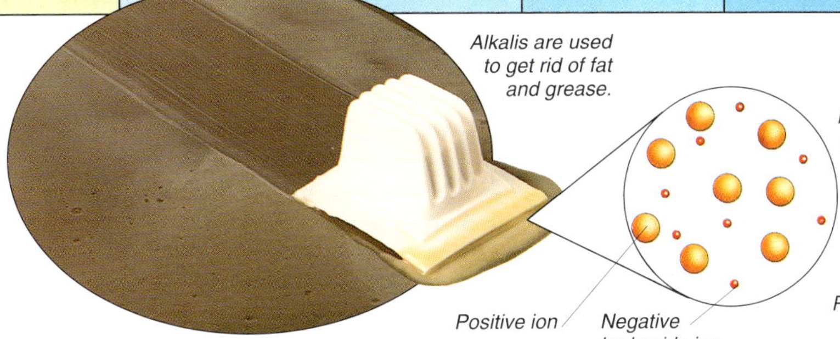

Alkalis are used to get rid of fat and grease.

In a strong alkali, many hydroxide ions have split off from the positive ions.

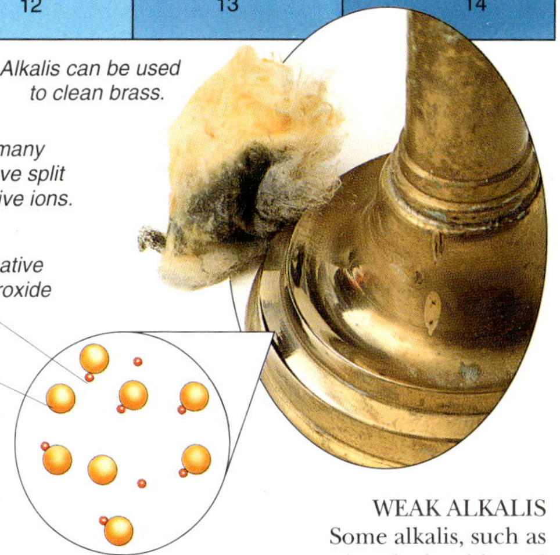

Alkalis can be used to clean brass.

In a weak alkali, only a few hydroxide ions have split off from the positive ions.

STRONG ALKALIS

Some alkalis, such as sodium hydroxide and potassium hydroxide, are called strong alkalis. When they dissolve in water, all their molecules dissociate (split up) into ions. This means they contain many hydroxide ions, and so have a high pH. Oven cleaners, for example, contain the strong, corrosive alkali sodium hydroxide. This reacts with the burnt, fatty deposits that form on the oven walls during cooking.

WEAK ALKALIS

Some alkalis, such as ammonium hydroxide and bicarbonate of soda (sodium hydrogen carbonate), are weak alkalis. In solution, only a few molecules dissociate into ions. They therefore contain only a few hydroxide ions, and so have a low pH. Brass cleaner is a weak alkaline solution. It works by breaking down the oxide layer that forms on the surface of the brass when brass is left exposed to the air.

A bee sting is very painful as it contains an acid. This can be neutralized by an alkali such as soap.

Close-up view of the sting of a bee

LIMING FIELDS AND LAKES

Acid rain increases the acidity of the lakes and soils on which it falls. This takes out essential nutrients from the soil. To fix this, farmers spread powdered lime (calcium hydroxide) on their fields. The lime is a base which neutralizes the acidity. Lime can also be added to lakes to reduce acidity. Adding lime to lakes and fields can relieve the damage caused by acid rain, but it does not stop the cause of the pollution.

Farmer liming field

NEUTRALIZATION

Every time a base meets an acid, neutralization occurs, and water and a compound called a salt are produced. This reaction can be used to treat some animal and plant stings. If you are stung by a wasp which has a basic sting, you can neutralize it with an acid such as lemon juice or vinegar. If you are stung by a bee or an ant, you can neutralize the acid sting with an alkali such as bicarbonate of soda. Nettles also give acidic stings which can be treated by rubbing with a dock leaf, which contains an alkali.

A wasp sting is very painful because it contains an alkali. This can be neutralized by an acid such as vinegar.

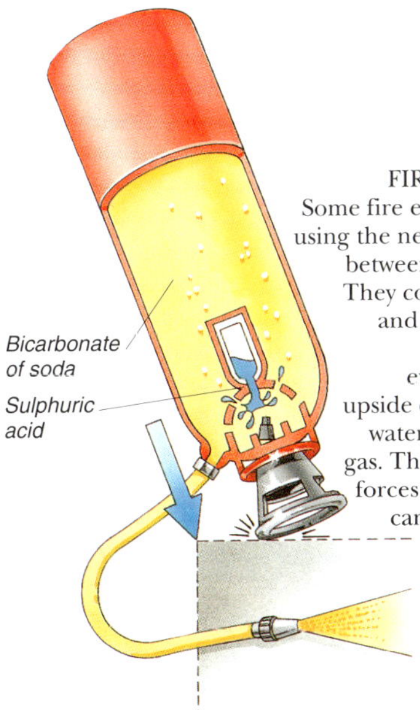

FIRE EXTINGUISHER

Some fire extinguishers work by using the neutralization reaction between an acid and a base. They contain sulphuric acid and bicarbonate of soda, which mix when the extinguisher is turned upside down. This produces water and carbon dioxide gas. The pressure of this gas forces a foam of liquid and carbon dioxide bubbles out of the nozzle.

The fizzy reaction between the acid and the alkali forces out a foam, which can be used to put out fires.

ALKALI IN THE PLAGUE

Seventeenth-century London, England was an unhealthy place to live in and was continually ravaged by plague – the plague of 1665 killed 80,000 people. The bodies were buried in mass graves which were covered with a strong alkali, lime, to speed up the rate of decomposition (rotting).

Find out more

BONDING P.28
SOLUTIONS P.60
ACIDS P.68
MEASURING ACIDITY P.72
SALTS P.73
ALKALI INDUSTRY P.94

MEASURING ACIDITY

HAVE YOU NOTICED how the colour of tea changes slightly when you add a slice of lemon? The tea is acting as an indicator, showing that the lemon has increased the acidity. Some coloured chemicals are used in the same way to show whether a solution is acid or alkaline. A measure of the acidity or alkalinity of a solution is called pH, short for "power of hydrogen". This is a scale that runs from 1 to 14. It is based on the number of hydrogen ions a solution contains. A pH of 1 shows the solution contains many hydrogen ions and is a strong acid. A pH of 14 indicates that the solution contains few hydrogen ions and is a strong alkali. Neutral solutions have a pH of 7.

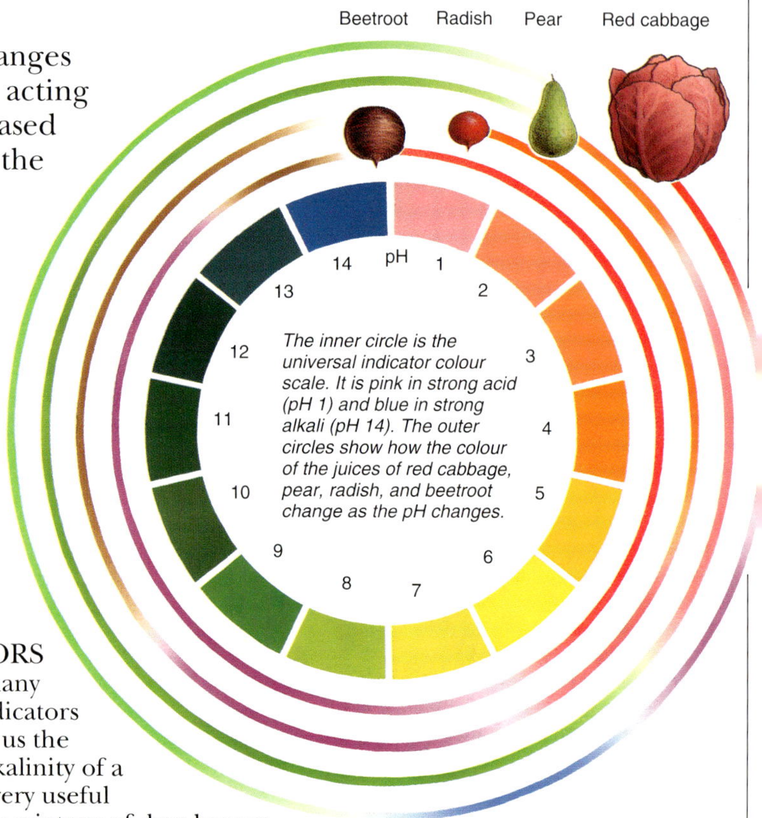

The inner circle is the universal indicator colour scale. It is pink in strong acid (pH 1) and blue in strong alkali (pH 14). The outer circles show how the colour of the juices of red cabbage, pear, radish, and beetroot change as the pH changes.

SOIL ACIDITY

Gardeners often have to worry about the pH of their soil. Some plants will only grow in a certain pH range. Soils in chalk and limestone regions are usually alkaline (pH 7 to 7.5). Soils in sandstone, clay, moorland and peat areas are usually acidic (pH 6.5 to 7). Heather prefers to grow on acidic soils, and that is why it often covers open moorland.

Phenolphthalein is deep pink above pH 9.5.

Phenolphthalein is colourless below pH 8.5.

INDICATORS

There are many different indicators that can tell us the acidity or alkalinity of a solution. A very useful indicator is a mixture of dyes known as universal indicator. This gives a range of colour changes from red for pH 1 (very strong acid) to blue for pH 14 (very strong alkali). The dyes obtained from fruits and vegetables, such as pears, onions, and red cabbage, can also be used as indicators. They change colour as the pH changes. The juice of a red cabbage, for example, turns from red in strong acid, through to pink, purple, blue, and green in strong alkali.

Hydrangeas grown in alkali soil produce red flowers.

Hydrangeas grown in acid soil produce blue flowers.

NATURAL INDICATORS

Some plants are natural indicators. The colour of hydrangeas depends on whether the soil is acid or alkaline. Litmus is an indicator obtained from a plant called a lichen. Litmus paper is made by soaking paper in litmus solution. It turns red in acid and blue in alkali.

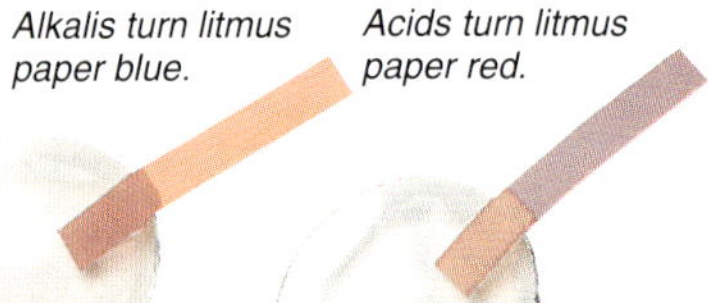

Alkalis turn litmus paper blue. *Acids turn litmus paper red.*

LABORATORY INDICATORS

Scientists often use special laboratory indicators to help find when just enough acid has been added to neutralize all the alkali in a reaction. Two examples are methyl orange and phenolphthalein. These change colour at a precise pH.

Methyl orange is orange between pH 4 and 8.

Methyl orange is yellow above pH 8.

Methyl orange is red below pH 3.

Contact lens solutions and injections have to be buffered so the pH of your body fluids is not altered.

BUFFERS

Sometimes, we don't want the pH of a solution to change. In the body, for example, most reactions will only take place within a narrow range of pH. A change of just 0.5 in the pH of your blood could kill you. To prevent this from happening, the body produces substances (called buffers) that neutralize any changes in acidity or alkalinity and keep the pH of the blood constant. For the same reason, intravenous injections have to be carefully buffered.

pH METER

A very accurate measure of the pH of a solution can be found by using a pH meter. It uses an electrode to measure the concentration of hydrogen ions in solution and displays the pH of the solution, either digitally or by a needle on a scale.

Find out more

BONDING P.28
HYDROGEN P.47
REVERSIBLE REACTIONS P.54
SOLUTIONS P.60
CHEMICAL ANALYSIS P.62
ACIDS P.68
ALKALIS AND BASES P.70

SALTS

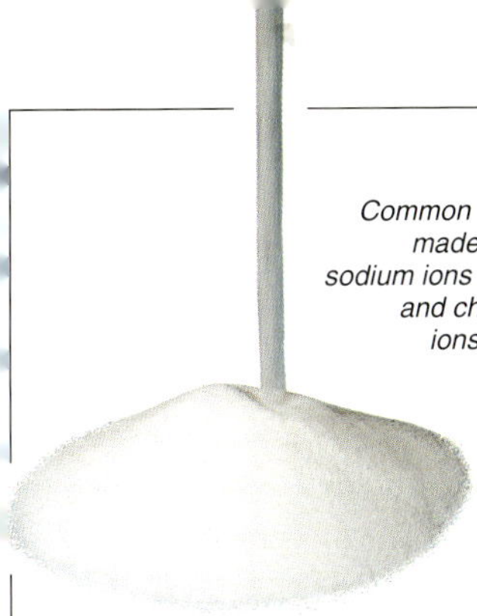

Common salt is made up of sodium ions (Na^+) and chloride ions (Cl^-).

HAVE YOU WONDERED why the sea is salty? Salts are naturally occurring compounds that are often soluble in water. Rivers dissolve salts from the earth and carry them down to the sea. The salt we put on food is just one type of salt. But there are many others. In fact, salts are very common and useful chemicals. Plaster of Paris, gunpowder, chalk, paint pigments, garden insecticide, and fertilizers are all examples of salts. They are compounds of a metal and a non-metal joined together by an ionic bond. A salt is made whenever an acid reacts with a metal or a base, and they usually form beautiful crystals.

IONS

All salts are made up of ions. It is because of these ions that salts are able to dissolve in water, and their solutions will conduct electricity. The strong ionic bond explains why salts usually have such high melting and boiling points.

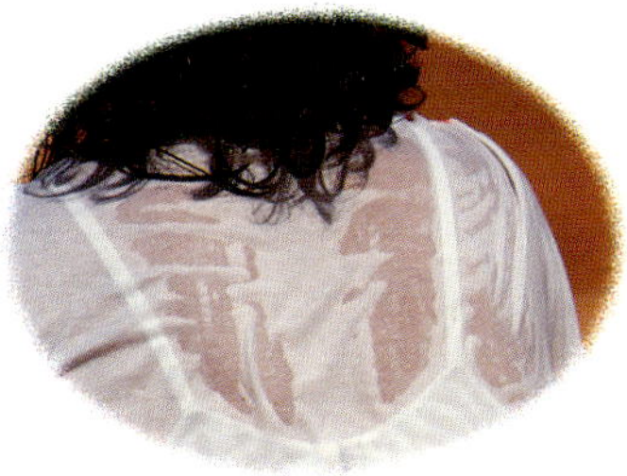

BODY SALTS

The next time you sweat, see how salty the sweat tastes. Every time you sweat, you lose salt from your body. Because salt is vital to the healthy running of the body, this can lead to dehydration and collapse. This is why doctors advise people to take salt tablets when they visit hot countries. This replaces the salt that is lost in sweat.

Dilute sulphuric acid

When the acid mixes with the black copper oxide, a blue solution of copper sulphate is made.

Tiny blue crystals of the salt, copper sulphate, start to appear once the solution is heated.

Bunsen burner

The heat from the bunsen burner drives off the water from the solution, leaving the salt behind.

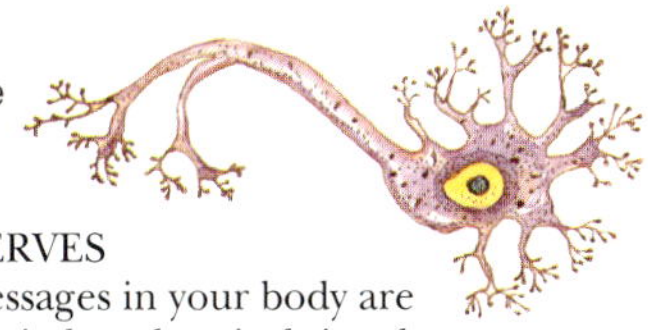

Nerve cell

NERVES

Messages in your body are carried as electrical signals along nerve fibres. When there is a gap between two fibres, the signal is carried across by potassium and sodium ions in the cell fluid. These vital ions come from the salts you eat.

MAKING A SALT

Every time an acid and a base are mixed, a salt is made. If black copper oxide (a base) is mixed with dilute sulphuric acid and heated, a blue solution is created. The base has neutralized the acid and a dissolved salt, copper sulphate, has been formed. The water from this solution can be boiled away, until the blue crystals of copper sulphate slowly start to appear.

Blue copper sulphate crystals

SALT FAMILIES

In a salt, the metal (copper) comes from the base (copper oxide) and the non-metal part (sulphate) comes from the acid (sulphuric acid). Each acid therefore has its own family of salts. Sulphuric acid makes sulphates, citric acid makes citrates, and so on. Each base also forms a family of salts. Copper oxide, for example, always makes copper salts.

Tarnished copper

The copper is cleaned by a lemon. In doing so, a salt is made that dissolves in the lemon juice.

COPPER SALT

Copper easily reacts with oxygen from the air to form a thin coating of copper oxide. Copper that has tarnished in this way can be cleaned with lemon juice. The acid in the lemon juice (citric acid) reacts with the copper oxide (a base) to form a salt (copper citrate) and water. This salt will dissolve in water, leaving the copper clean and shiny.

Salts often make beautiful crystals.

Fluorite crystal

NATURAL SALTS

Many ores and minerals are made of salts. These include limestone (calcium carbonate), gypsum (calcium sulphate), and fluorite (calcium fluoride). If they grow in the right conditions, all salts will form beautiful crystals.

Find out more

BONDING P.28
CRYSTALS P.30
COMPOUNDS AND MIXTURES P.58
SOLUTIONS P.60
ACIDS P.68
ALKALIS AND BASES P.70

CHEMISTRY OF AIR

Air contains many different colourless gases.

THE INVISIBLE BUT VITAL AIR surrounds us all the time. It is a mixture of different gases, mainly nitrogen and oxygen. We are constantly changing the composition of the air around us – just by breathing, we are reducing the amount of oxygen it contains. The air in the atmosphere is like a protective shield. It filters out the Sun's harmful ultraviolet rays but allows the visible and infrared rays, on which we depend for light and heat, to pass through. The air in the atmosphere also acts like an insulating blanket, preventing extremes of temperature. Without it, the Earth would be like the Moon – boiling hot by day, and freezing cold at night.

Nitrogen makes up 78% of the air.

Oxygen makes up 21% of the air.

Argon makes up 0.9% of the air.

Carbon dioxide makes up 0.03% of the air.

Small amounts of other gases make up the remaining 0.07% of the air.

Petrol-driven cars cannot be used on the moon. Astronauts must use electric cars.

On Earth, a car continually takes in air. The oxygen in the air is needed to burn petrol – the energy released in the reaction drives the car.

LIFE-GIVING AIR

All life depends on air for its survival. We use the oxygen in air to convert food into energy, and we breathe out carbon dioxide. Plants use a reaction called photosynthesis to convert the carbon dioxide from the air into foods, such as sugars, which they need to grow.

ESSENTIAL AIR

It is easy to forget that we are surrounded by air. But without it, many of the things that we take for granted could not happen. For example, if you took a car to the Moon, it would not work because there is no air there. This is why astronauts have to use an electric car when they explore the Moon.

FRACTIONAL DISTILLATION OF AIR

Air contains some very useful gases. They can be separated by a process called fractional distillation. Air is made into a liquid by being cooled to a very low temperature. When it is left to warm up, the gases boil off the liquid at different times since they have different boiling points. The gases can therefore be collected separately.

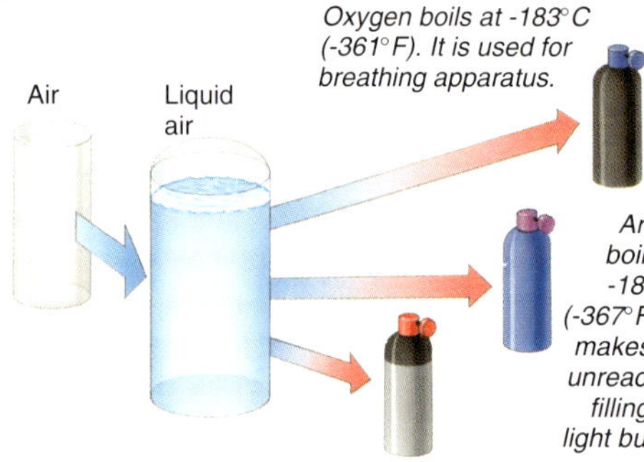

Oxygen boils at -183°C (-361°F). It is used for breathing apparatus.

Argon boils at -186°C (-367°F). It makes an unreactive filling for light bulbs.

Nitrogen boils at -196°C (-305°F). It is used to make fertilizers, and nitric acid.

DISCOVERIES

1754 Scottish doctor Joseph Black finds carbon dioxide in air.

1772 Scottish physician Daniel Rutherford finds nitrogen in air.

1774-79 Joseph Priestley (English) and Antoine Lavoisier (French) find oxygen in air.

1892-98 British scientists Sir William Ramsay and Lord Rayleigh find air contains inert gases.

AIR QUALITY

Human activities have caused changes in the composition of the air. For example, it wasn't necessary to clean silver until around 1600, when the levels of sulphur in the air started to rise. The biggest changes have occurred since the Industrial Revolution in the 19th century, when people started burning carbon fuels on a large scale. Carbon dioxide makes up a larger part of air today than it ever did before. We must control the levels of pollution released into the air to protect life on Earth.

Find out more

NITROGEN P.42
OXYGEN P.44
NOBLE GASES P.48
BEHAVIOUR OF GASES P.51
COMPOUNDS AND MIXTURES P.58
OXIDATION AND REDUCTION P.64
INDUSTRIAL POLLUTION P.112
ATMOSPHERE P.248

CHEMISTRY OF WATER

DON'T BE FOOLED BY WATER. What appears to be just a colourless, odourless, and tasteless liquid, is actually a hard-working chemical whose reactions are vital to life. Water is a compound of hydrogen and oxygen. Its chemical formula, H_2O, shows that each molecule of water contains two atoms of hydrogen and one atom of oxygen. Water is not only all around us, in rain, clouds, and the seas; it is inside us as well. Water carries nutrients to your cells, and waste products from your body. Water is very good at dissolving substances. Because of this, it is hardly ever found in its pure form. The water from a tap, for example, has been in contact with rocks, soil, and air before it reaches us and therefore contains many dissolved chemicals.

At room temperature, pure water is a colourless liquid. It boils at 100°C (212°F), freezes at 0°C (32°F), and has a neutral pH of 7.

There are more molecules of water in just one drop than all the millions of stars we can see in the sky.

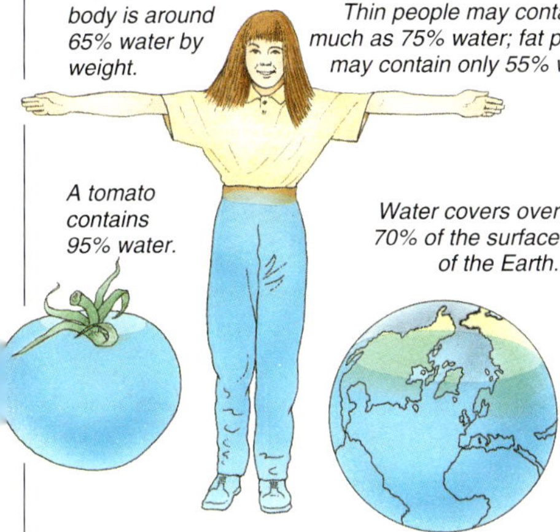

The human body is around 65% water by weight.

Thin people may contain as much as 75% water; fat people may contain only 55% water.

A tomato contains 95% water.

Water covers over 70% of the surface of the Earth.

Close-up of kettle scale

HARD WATER

Certain dissolved chemicals make water "hard". Hard water does not easily form a lather with soap. Instead, a white precipitate, scum, is formed. There are two types of hardness in water. Calcium and magnesium hydrogen carbonates cause temporary hardness, which can be removed by boiling. This makes a solid (calcium carbonate) – the scale found in kettles. Permanent hardness is caused by calcium and magnesium sulphates. These can be removed by passing the water through a water softener, which swaps the magnesium and calcium ions for sodium ions.

WATER EVERYWHERE

Water is the most common chemical compound, and covers over 70 per cent of the Earth's surface. On average, the human body is about 65 per cent water. Some foods are almost all water. A ripe tomato, for example, is 95 per cent water. In all these places, the water is busy carrying out important chemical functions.

WATER IN AIR

On a humid day, the air contains a lot of water vapour. Humidity is a measure of the amount of water in the air. Dry air, such as that in a desert, contains very little water vapour.

Deserts contain too little water to support very much life.

Adding water to white copper sulphate crystals turns them blue.

SOLID WATER

Unlike most other substances, water expands when it freezes. When water molecules join up to form ice, a hydrogen atom from one molecule joins to an oxygen atom from another. This creates a hexagon (six-sided) shape, with an empty space in the middle. This explains both why ice is less dense than water and why snowflakes are based on this hexagonal shape.

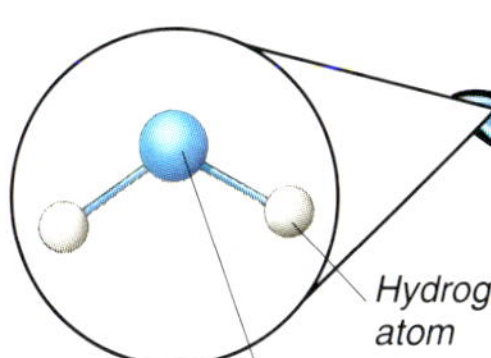

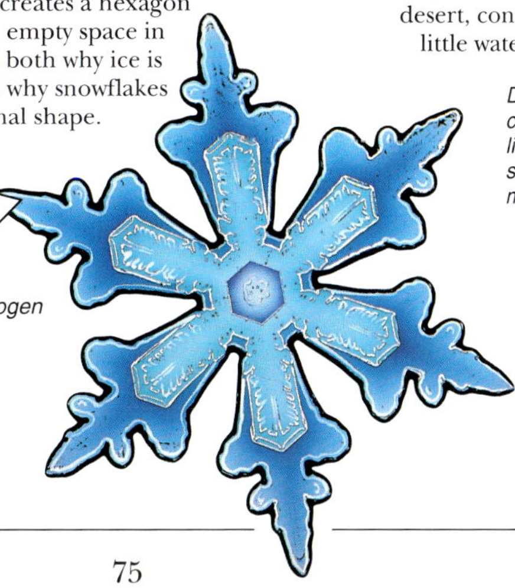

WATER OF CRYSTALLIZATION

Many compounds contain water molecules trapped in their crystals. This is the water of crystallization. It can be driven off by heating. If blue copper sulphate crystals are heated, they lose their water of crystallization and turn white. Adding water to these white crystals turns them blue again. Because only water can produce this colour change, the process is used as a chemical test for water.

Find out more

CHANGES OF STATE p.20
BONDING p.28
CRYSTALS p.30
SOLUTIONS p.60
WATER INDUSTRY p.83
HUMIDITY p.252
SNOW p.266

CHEMISTRY OF THE BODY

YOUR BODY IS A MOBILE CHEMICAL FACTORY that processes raw materials, such as food, water, and oxygen. After being fed in, these raw materials go through a series of complicated chemical reactions, known as metabolism. This produces the energy the body needs to function. One series of reactions breaks down large molecules of food into smaller ones, such as glucose, that can pass into the bloodstream. This process is called digestion. The blood transports the glucose to the liver, where it is stored as the body's fuel. The cells release the energy in this fuel by a reaction called respiration. Waste products are taken for disposal to the end of the body's factory line.

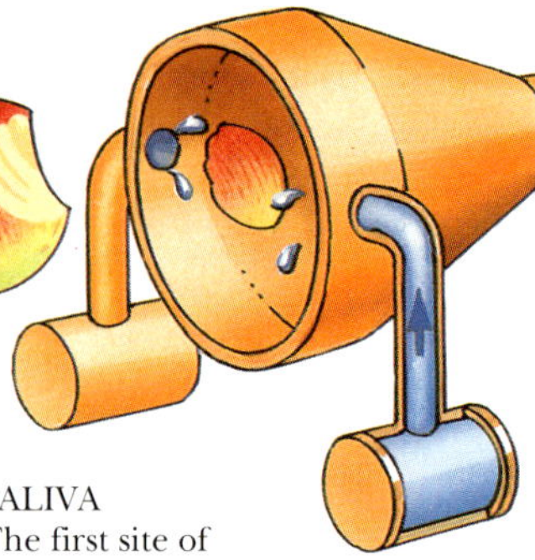

SALIVA
The first site of chemical attack on the food that we eat is our mouth. Here, saliva pours out of the salivary glands and onto the food, which is being ripped apart by our teeth. The saliva is a watery mix that contains an enzyme called amylase. This enzyme starts to break down the starch in food. Since amylase will only work in alkaline conditions, saliva is very slightly alkaline.

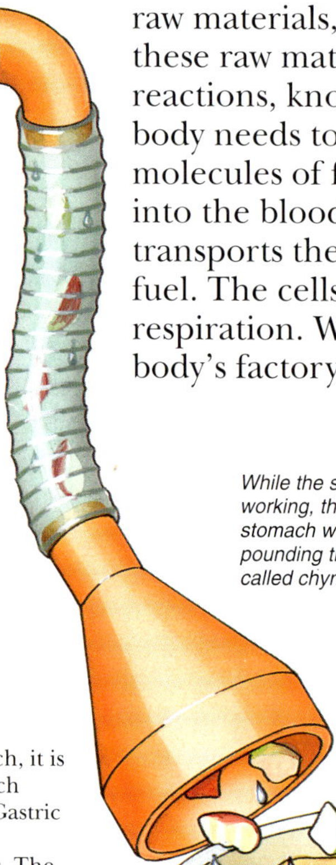

While the stomach enzymes are working, the contractions of the stomach wall work like a liquidizer, pounding the food into a fluid called chyme.

MAKING GLUCOSE

In the intestine, the food is bombarded by a mix of chemicals called bile. This is piped in from the liver, via the gall bladder. It contains bile salts which help to break down fats. Enzymes to complete the digestion of food come from the pancreas and the intestine wall. Glucose, one of the products of all these reactions, is transported to the liver.

STOMACH
Once the food has reached the stomach, it is swirled around with gastric juices, which have poured from the gastric glands. Gastric juices contain a strong acid called hydrochloric acid and several enzymes. The acid kills germs in the food and activates an enzyme called protease, which breaks down proteins.

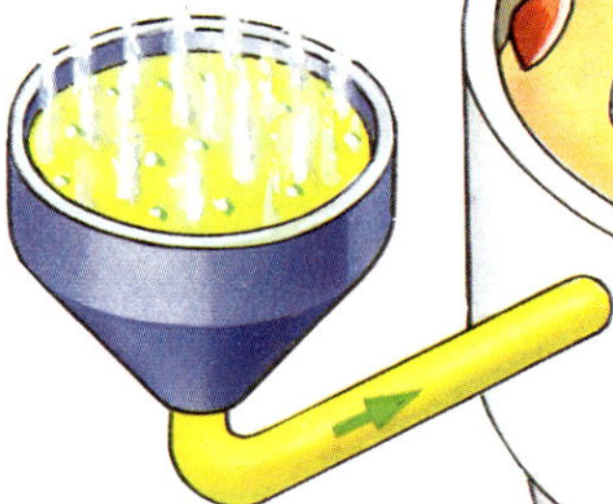

Hydrochloric acid is made in the gastric glands by a chemical reaction involving carbon dioxide, water, and salt.

Gall bladder

The bile contains bicarbonate of soda (sodium hydrogen carbonate), which neutralizes the acid from the stomach.

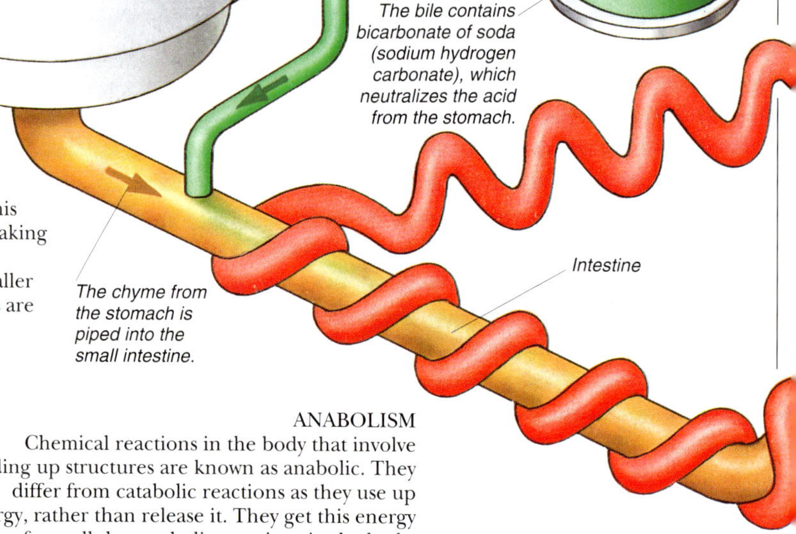

The chyme from the stomach is piped into the small intestine.

Intestine

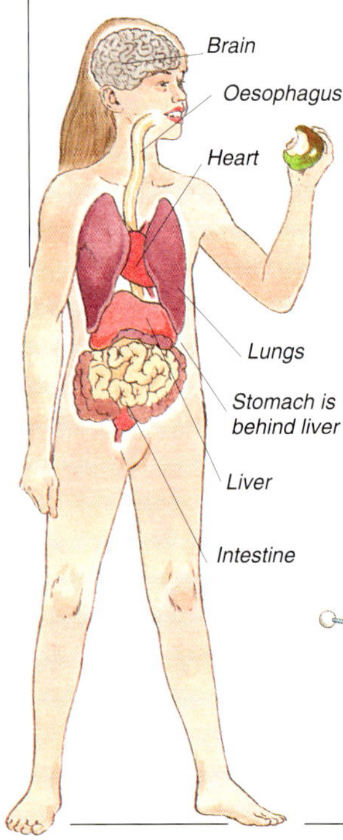

CATABOLISM
Some chemical reactions in the body produce energy. Respiration, for example, releases energy by breaking down glucose into smaller molecules. This energy is not produced as a result of breaking the glucose bonds but is released when stronger bonds are formed in the smaller molecules. Energy-releasing reactions are called catabolic reactions, and the process itself is called catabolism.

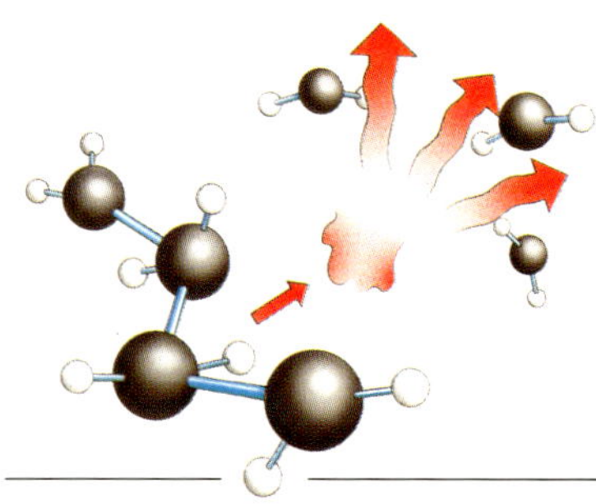

ANABOLISM
Chemical reactions in the body that involve building up structures are known as anabolic. They differ from catabolic reactions as they use up energy, rather than release it. They get this energy from all the catabolic reactions in the body. Making blood proteins involves building large, complex molecules from simple ones. It uses a great deal of energy and is an anabolic reaction. The process itself is called anabolism.

ENZYMES

Many chemical reactions in the body are speeded up by special catalysts called enzymes. Each enzyme helps with one particular reaction. They are cleverly able to distinguish between molecules that are very similar, so they will not speed up the wrong reaction. Enzymes are remarkably efficient and fast-working catalysts. Without them, our body reactions would be so slow that we would certainly die.

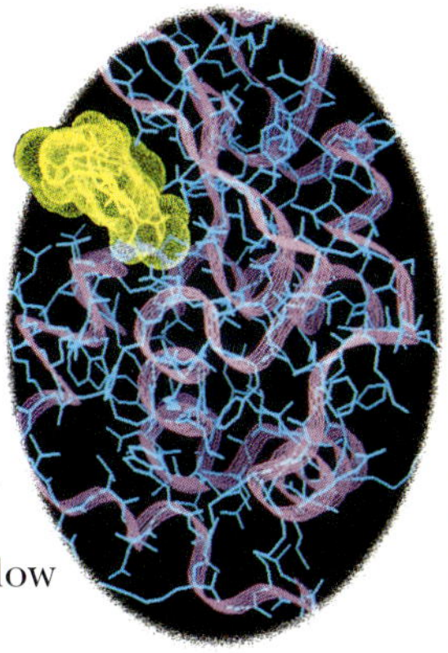

BODY ELEMENTS

Your body is made up of many different chemical elements. Oxygen, carbon, and hydrogen are found in the fats, proteins, and carbohydrates that make up most of the body tissues. Nitrogen is found in proteins, and bones contain calcium. Trace elements in the body include iron, sodium, potassium, copper, zinc, magnesium, phosphorus, iodine, chlorine, silicon, and sulphur. These elements, although present in only minute amounts, are essential for keeping the body healthy.

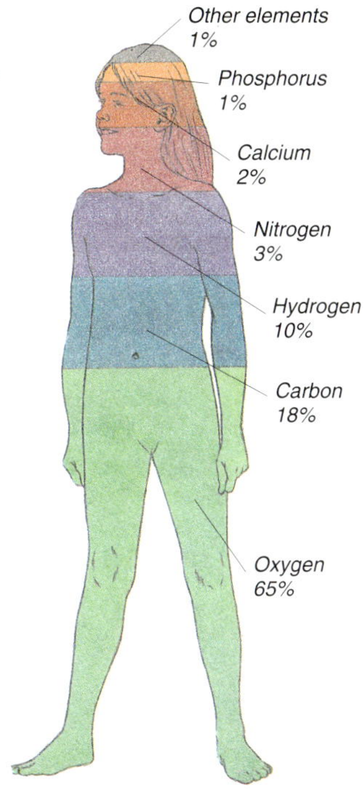

LIVER

The liver is the body's chemical powerhouse. It produces a green liquid, bile, that aids digestion, and it keeps a store of glucose, vitamins, and minerals. Poisons from drugs and alcohol are also removed from the blood by the liver. The reactions that occur in the liver are mostly exothermic, which means they give out heat. This heat is spread around the body by the blood to keep us warm.

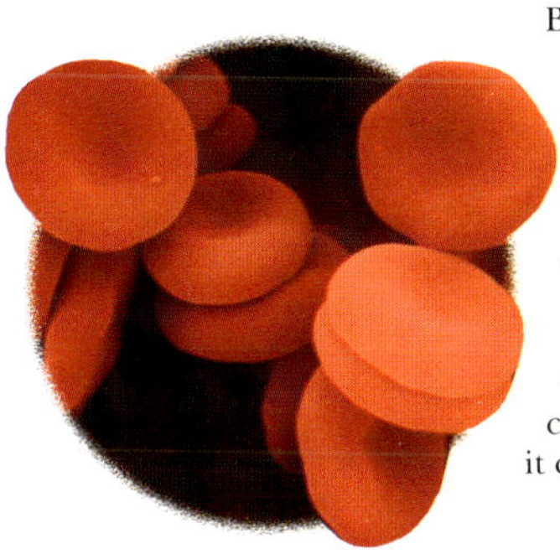

BLOOD

Red blood cells contain haemoglobin, a compound of protein and iron, which combines with oxygen in the lungs and transports it to all the body's cells. When the oxygen has been released for cell respiration, haemoglobin loses its bright red colour and becomes purplish. It then combines with the waste carbon dioxide produced by the cells and deposits it in the lungs so that it can be breathed out.

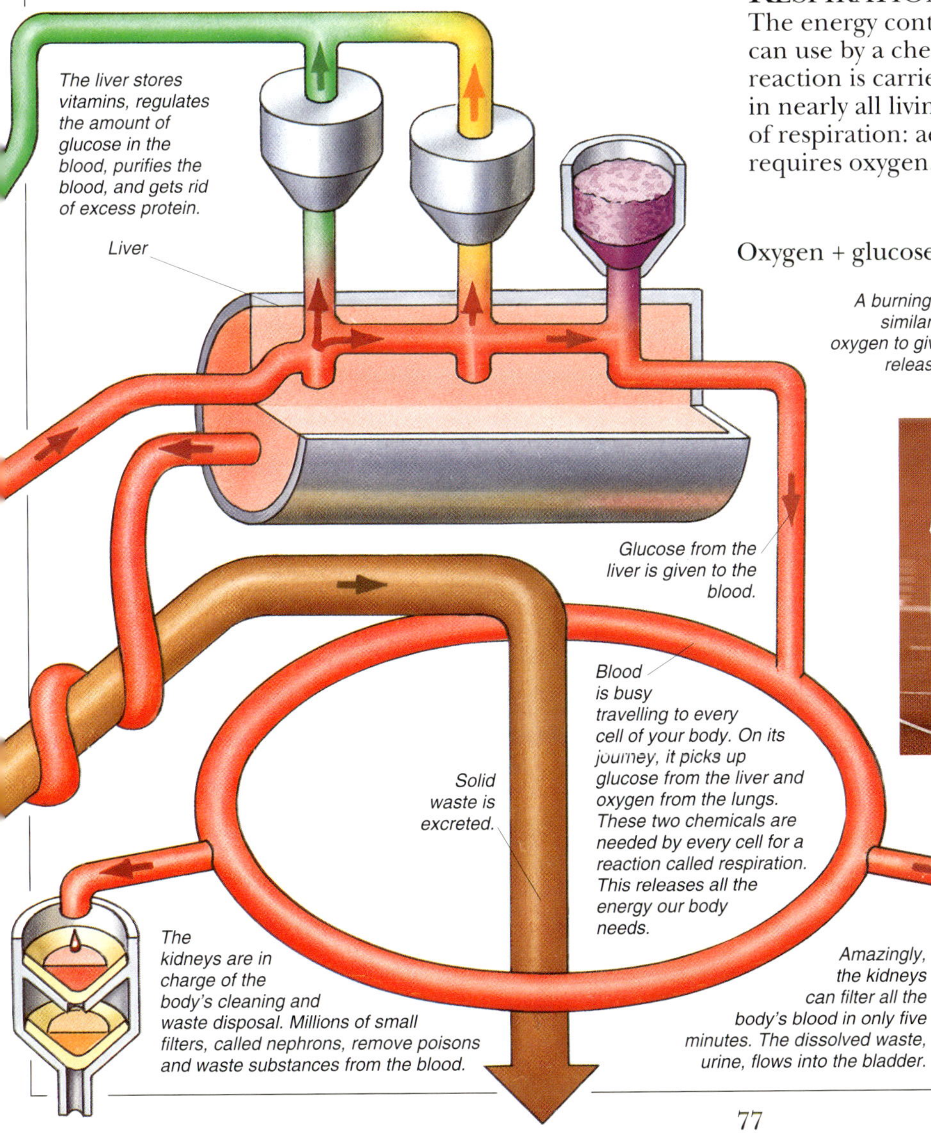

RESPIRATION

The energy contained in food is converted into energy we can use by a chemical reaction called respiration. This reaction is carried out in every single cell of our body and in nearly all living cells in the world. There are two kinds of respiration: aerobic and anaerobic. Aerobic respiration requires oxygen. It releases a great deal of energy.

Oxygen + glucose → carbon dioxide + water + ENERGY

A burning nut gives out heat and light energy. This reaction is very similar to aerobic respiration. In both cases, food combines with oxygen to give energy. But inside your body, the energy is not suddenly released as a flame, it is released more gradually in chemical form.

ANAEROBIC RESPIRATION

If you are running fast in a race, your muscles are using up oxygen faster than your lungs can take it in. The cells start to use anaerobic respiration to give you extra energy. This reaction does not require oxygen but produces less energy than aerobic respiration does.

Glucose → lactic acid + energy

Lactic acid causes muscle ache and cramp. This is why athletes take deep breaths at the end of a race, to replace oxygen supplies and to get rid of the lactic acid.

Find out more

CATALYSTS P.56
CHEMISTRY OF FOOD P.78
DIGESTION P.345
CELLULAR RESPIRATION P.346
BLOOD P.348
INTERNAL ENVIRONMENT P.350

CHEMISTRY OF FOOD

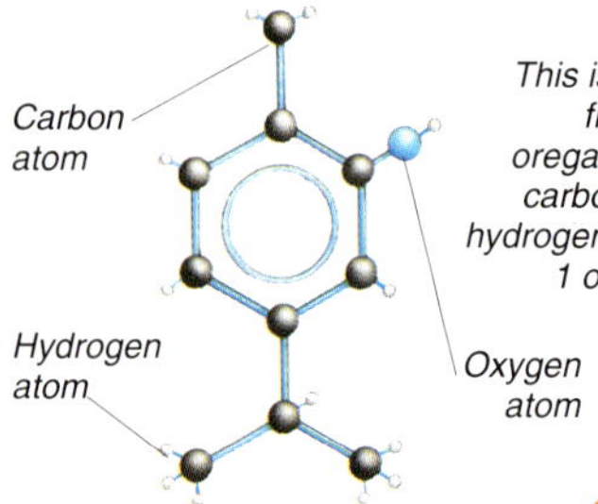

This is a molecule from the herb oregano. It has 10 carbon atoms, 14 hydrogen atoms, and 1 oxygen atom.

THERE ARE MORE CHEMICALS in the food you eat than you would ever find in a laboratory. Many of the chemicals contained in food are vital to life. Groups of chemicals called proteins, carbohydrates, fibre, fats, vitamins, minerals, and water are all needed for a healthy diet. Other chemicals may be responsible for the flavour, while still more may give the food colour. Just the oil from orange peel contains around 50 different chemical compounds. Whenever food is cooked, reactions occur that change these chemicals. In fact, cookery and chemistry have a lot in common. Many of the processes they use, such as heating, mixing, and filtering, are very similar.

CHEMICAL PIZZA
A pizza is really just a plate of chemicals, and most of them are good for you. The hundreds of different chemicals present have very complicated formulae. Just look at the complicated chemical above which gives the herb oregano its flavour.

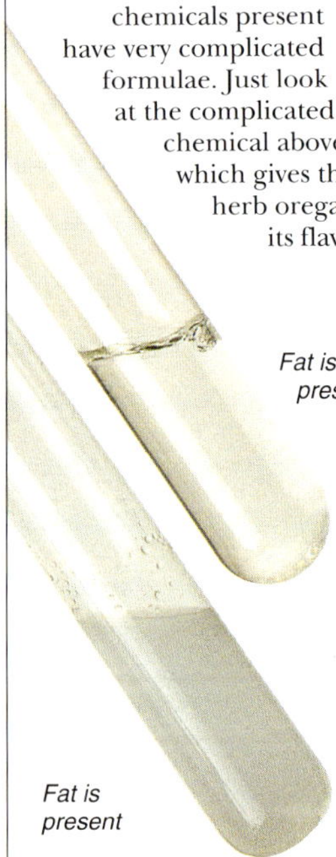

Fat is not present

Fat is present

FAT TEST
Fats are large molecules of carbon, hydrogen, and oxygen found in foods such as cheese, peanuts, and butter. A food sample can be tested for fat by shaking it in ethanol (a type of alcohol). Any fats in the food will dissolve to give a clear solution. This is then poured into a tube of water. Because fats are insoluble in water, tiny droplets of fat will cloud the water if fats are present in the food.

PROTEIN TEST
Food scientists test a food for proteins by crushing up a sample with water. If dilute sodium hydroxide, followed by a few drops of copper sulphate solution are added, the colour will change from pale blue to pale purple if protein is present in the food.

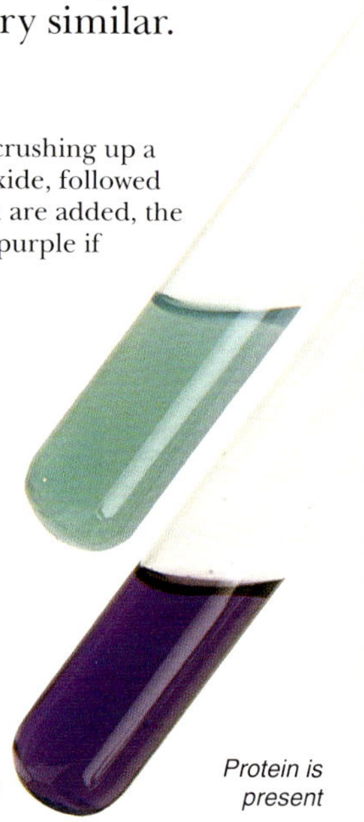

Protein is not present

Protein is present

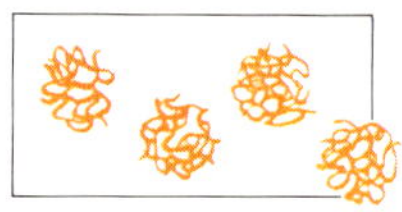

The protein chains in a raw egg are neat spiralled chains.

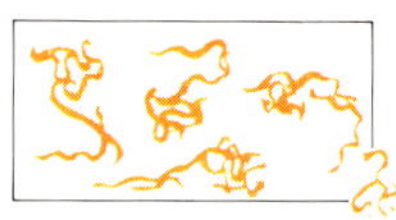

As the egg is heated, the protein chains start to unravel.

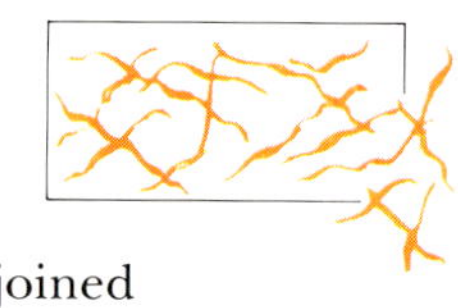

When the chains are unravelled, they become tangled with each other and form a solid mesh.

PROTEINS

Life-building chemicals called proteins are found in foods such as eggs, meat, and nuts. They are made up of carbon, nitrogen, sulphur, oxygen, and hydrogen atoms. Some protein molecules are joined together in long, spiralled chains. As you cook an egg, the protein molecules first unravel (called denaturation) and then tangle up together to form a solid mesh. This is why the protein white of an egg becomes solid when cooked.

ONION CHEMICALS
Why does chopping up an onion make you cry? Onions contain a number of unusual sulphur compounds. When the onion is cut, these react with oxygen in the air to form strong-smelling chemicals that cause your eyes to water. Scientists have recently discovered that some of the sulphur compounds may be useful for treating asthma.

MINERALS
The tiny amounts of inorganic substances we need in our diet are known as minerals. Water dissolves these minerals, containing the elements calcium, iron, potassium, and magnesium, out of the soil. They are then taken up through the roots of the plants growing in the soil. By eating these plants, we also eat the minerals they contain.

VITAMINS

The vitamins are a mixed assortment of chemicals that are only needed by the body in small amounts. They are found in many foods, such as citrus fruits (vitamin C), green vegetables (vitamins A and K), carrots (vitamin A), wholemeal bread (vitamin B), and oily fish (vitamin D).

LEMON PRESERVATIVE

Freshly cut fruits, such as apples and bananas, soon become brown when they are exposed to the air. This is a reaction between chemicals in the fruit and oxygen, speeded up by an enzyme in the fruit. As enzymes are very sensitive to changes in acidity, the browning reaction is slowed down by adding an acid, such as lemon juice, to the freshly cut fruit.

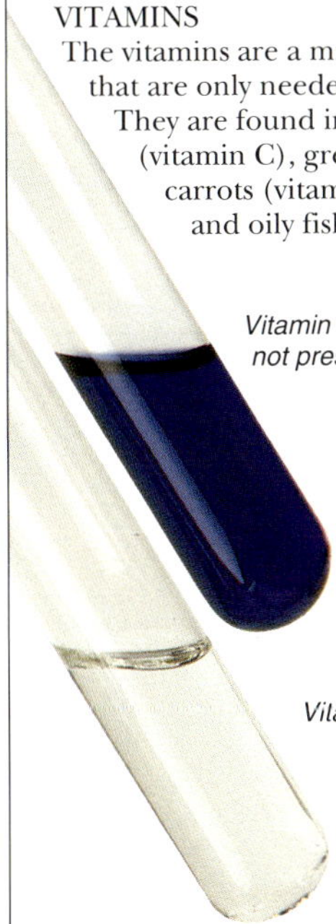

Vitamin C is not present

Vitamin C is present

VITAMIN C TEST

There is a blue dye, called DCPIP, which vitamin C can turn colourless. If this change happens when a sample of food (crushed in water) is added to the dye, it proves that the food contains vitamin C.

SUGARS

The sweetness of jams and cakes is due to a group of chemicals called sugars. These are compounds of carbon, hydrogen, and oxygen. One of the simplest sugars is glucose. Its chemical formula is $C_6H_{12}O_6$. Other simple sugars include lactose, which is found in milk, and fructose, which is found in fruits. Sugars are not confined to the kitchen any more. Industrial chemists have started to convert sugars into industrial chemicals, which are used to make paints and detergents.

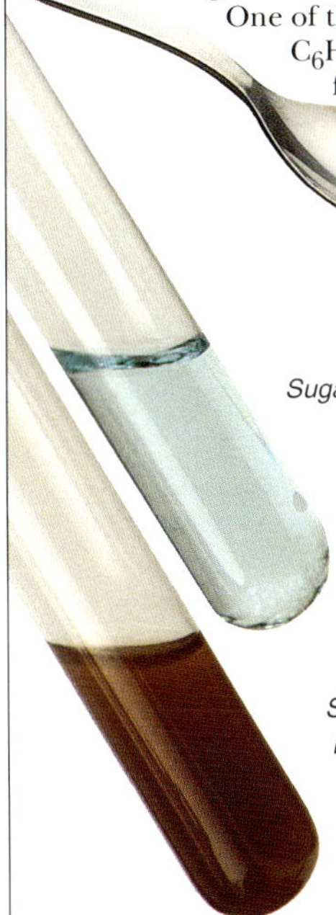

Sugar is not present

Sugar is present

CARAMELIZING SUGAR

When sugar is heated the sugar molecules start to break down, giving off water. If the heating is continued the sugar caramelizes, becoming dark brown and sticky. Caramel is used as a colouring for vinegar, gravies, and other foodstuffs.

Caramelized sugar

SUGAR TEST

A food can be tested for sugar by crushing it with water and adding a special chemical called Benedict's solution. If an orange-brown precipitate (tiny solid particles) forms when this mixture is heated, it shows that sugar is in the food.

Sugary foods

PRESERVING FOOD

Fresh foods, such as fish, soon go bad if they are left in the open air, because harmful microbes start to grow on them and inside them. But food can be preserved by killing the microbes or by slowing down their growth. There are a number of common methods for doing this. Freezing, salting, smoking, and pickling all slow down, or even stop, the microbes from multiplying. Heating or passing radiation through the food are the only ways to kill all the microbes.

Fish are smoked by holding them over a wood fire. The heat from the fire and the chemicals in the smoke slow down the rate at which microbes grow. Smoking also adds flavour and changes the texture of food.

STARCH TEST

Starch can be detected by crushing up a food sample with water and adding a few drops of iodine solution. If this turns to a blue-black colour, it shows that the food contains starch.

Pasta, potatoes, and rice all contain starch.

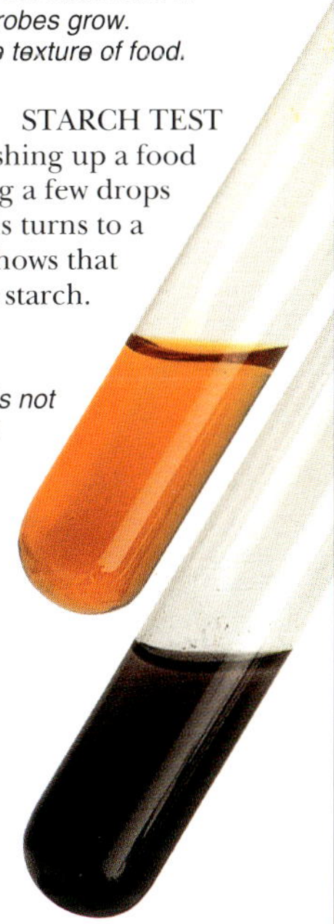

Starch is not present

Starch is present

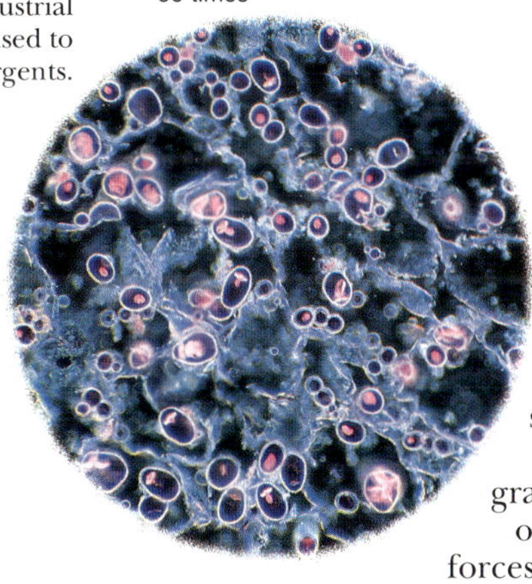

Starch granules in water, magnified 60 times

STARCH

Starchy foods, such as bread, potatoes, rice, and pasta, are made up of sugar molecules joined together in long chains. Starch and sugar are sometimes called carbohydrates. The starch in flour is used to thicken sauces like gravy. When starch granules are heated in water, some of the water gets inside them and forces the individual starch molecules inside the granules apart. This causes the granules to swell up until they burst, leaking the starch molecules into the surrounding liquid, and thickening the sauce.

FOOD POISONS

Some foods naturally contain tiny amounts of poisons, which in very large doses can make us ill. Bananas contain a chemical that can produce hallucinations. Green potatoes contain a poison, solanine, which causes stomach ache. Cheeses can contain tyramine, a chemical related to the body hormone adrenaline. This affects our pulse rate and can cause nightmares.

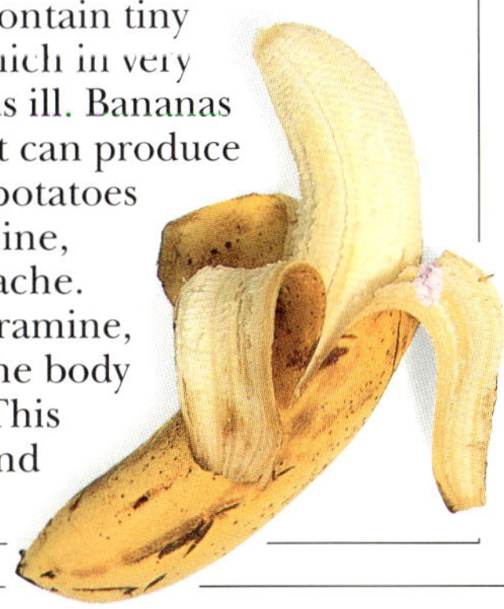

Find out more

ORGANIC CHEMISTRY P.41
CHEMICAL ANALYSIS P.62
CHEMISTRY OF THE BODY P.76
FERMENTATION P.80
FOOD INDUSTRY P.92
NUTRITION P.342
FEEDING P.343

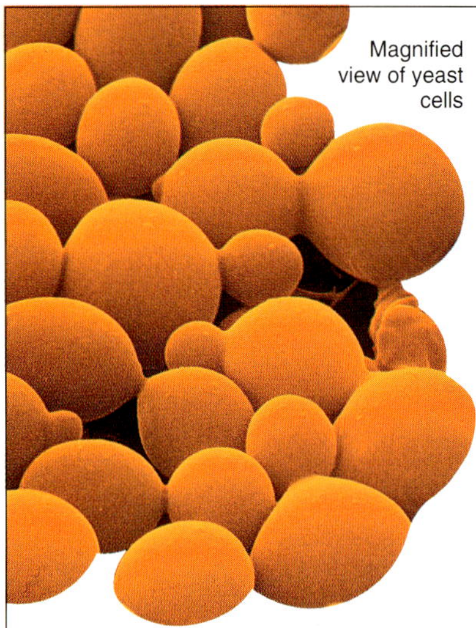

Magnified view of yeast cells

FERMENTATION

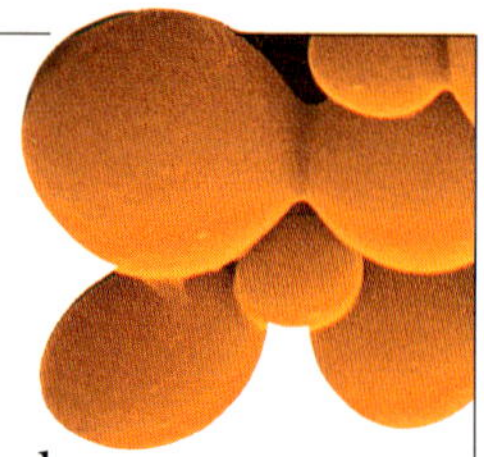

FOR THOUSANDS OF YEARS, fermentation has been used to make bread, beer, and wine. Today, it is used to make foods such as bread and yoghurt, alcoholic drinks such as wine, drugs such as penicillin, and chemicals such as methanol and citric acid. Fermentation is a chemical process. Tiny organisms called microbes grow by converting the sugars in foods, such as fruits and grain, into alcohol and carbon dioxide. Microbes can live almost anywhere. It is likely that fermentation was discovered by accident when fruits or grain were stored in containers. One safe and commonly used microbe is yeast. Not all microbes are safe to eat – many are harmful and poisonous.

Yeasts are tiny living organisms that are only visible through a microscope. Yeasts grow on the skins of fruits, such as grapes and apples, by feeding on sugars. Each yeast cell divides rapidly as it feeds.

The gas given off travels through this tube to the limewater.

Airtight stopper

Yeast converts the sugar into alcohol, which is left in the flask, and carbon dioxide gas.

Bubbles of gas forming

Yeast mixed with warm water and sugar

The clear limewater turns cloudy after mixing with the gas. This proves the gas is carbon dioxide.

When water is mixed with the flour and the dough is kneaded, some of the proteins in the flour combine to form a network of molecules that is strong and elastic.

MAKING BREAD

One of the ingredients of bread is yeast. After the dough has been kneaded, it is put in a warm place. The yeast respires with oxygen by feeding on the sugars and breaking them down into carbon dioxide and water. These gases cause the dough to rise. As you bake the dough, the yeast is killed, and the gases expand to give the bread a spongy texture. If dough without yeast is used, it will not rise. The bread it makes is called unleavened bread.

FIRST FERMENTATION

The Ancient Egyptians were the first to make leavened bread 5,000 years ago. They used to keep a store of sour fermented dough (called sourdough) that was added to each mix to make the bread rise. Sourdough was probably discovered when yeast spores were blown onto dough that had been mixed and put to one side before baking.

YEAST

If a mixture of yeast, sugar, and warm water is left to stand, bubbles of gas appear as the yeast ferments. If this gas is bubbled through limewater (a solution of calcium hydroxide in water), it turns the limewater cloudy. This result proves that the gas is carbon dioxide – the cloudiness in the limewater is the insoluble compound calcium carbonate suspended in the water. The yeast is respiring without oxygen. This means it feeds on the sugar, converting it to carbon dioxide and alcohol, which is left in the flask.

ALCOHOL

Microbes will normally produce carbon dioxide and water by respiration (as in bread-making). However, if the microbes do not have a good supply of air, they make carbon dioxide and alcohol. This is why alcoholic drinks are made by carrying out the fermentation in sealed containers. When the solution contains around 14 per cent alcohol, the microbes become poisoned, and fermentation stops. This is why alcoholic drinks with more than 14 per cent alcohol cannot be made just by fermentation.

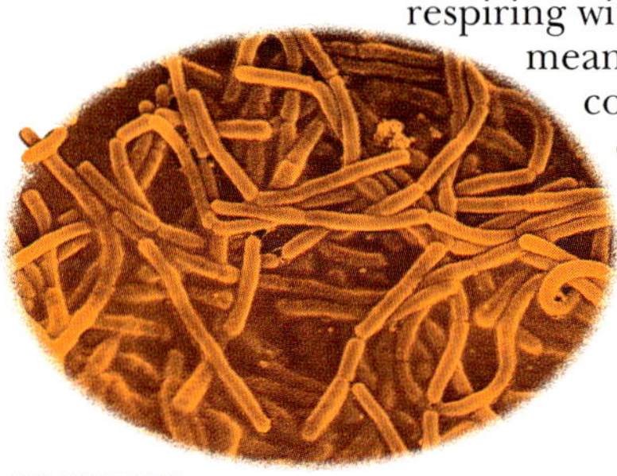

Lactobacillus bulgaricus bacteria, magnified

YOGHURT

Yoghurt is made by adding certain bacteria (lactobacilli) to milk and allowing this to ferment without oxygen. The bacteria multiply and cause the milk to thicken. They reduce the sugar content by converting the milk sugar, lactose, into lactic acid. This is why natural yoghurt tastes sour.

BLUE CHEESES

A special type of penicillin mould is added to blue cheese to give it its colour and taste. As the cheese matures, small holes are made in it with stainless steel needles to ensure that the mould has enough oxygen to grow.

Find out more

CHEMISTRY OF THE BODY P.76
CHEMISTRY OF FOOD P.78
SINGLE-CELLED ORGANISMS P.314
FUNGI P.315
ASEXUAL REPRODUCTION P.366

MATERIALS

IMAGINE WHAT LIFE would be like if you wore concrete shoes and rode bicycles made of glass. These are just two of the many materials we use in our daily lives – but not for walking or cycling! Most of the materials around us have been changed from their natural state. The original materials come from substances in the ground, in water, or even in the air. Chemical processes change these raw materials into materials with special properties that we can use. For example, the materials in our clothes are made from fibres that are stretchy, soft, and strong. This makes our clothes comfortable and hard-wearing.

A sports cap is made of cotton for keeping cool.

Sunglasses made from chemicals in oil are light and safe to wear.

Racket frame is made of plastic containing graphite, synthetic leather-cushioned grips, and synthetic strings.

Sports socks are made of natural fibres to keep feet cool.

Wood is a tough and hard natural material made from trees.

Sports clothes are made from strong, comfortable materials, such as polyester, cotton, and nylon.

Paper consists of natural fibres made from trees.

Tennis balls are made from rubber, nylon, and natural fibres.

Sports shoes are made from leather or canvas, with rubber soles for flexibility.

MATERIALS FOR TENNIS

All the materials used in a game of tennis are perfectly suited to their functions. Rackets are strong because they need to stop balls that are travelling very fast. Balls are made from materials that do not tear when they collide with the racket or the court. Tennis shoes and the court surface are both made of tough materials to withstand the wear and tear caused by players running all over the court.

TERRACOTTA

About 7,000 years ago, people found that if they heated clay it changed into a hard, brittle substance. By shaping the clay before baking, people could make bowls, cups, and urns to hold food and drink. They called this material terracotta, which means baked earth. This was one of the first manufactured materials.

EXTRACTING IRON

The Hittites of Turkey discovered how to extract iron 3,500 years ago. The secret was to heat rock containing iron with burning charcoal. This made the metal soft enough to hammer into weapons and tools.

FROM IRON TO STEEL

Early metalworkers knew that carbon could make iron hard. Then, in 1740, a British steelmaker called Benjamin Huntsman found a way to control the amount of carbon to produce a strong metal called steel. Steel is now used to make a range of products from needles to car bodies.

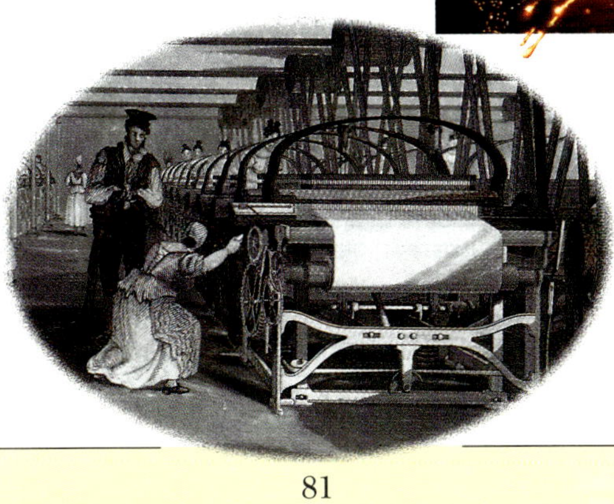

CLOTH STEAMS AHEAD

Since 8000 B.C. people have been spinning natural fibres to make threads, and weaving or knitting them together to make cloth. In the late 18th century, Europeans invented machines that could spin and weave using steam power.

AGE OF PLASTICS

In the 1850s, Alexander Parkes, an English chemist, made the first plastic material. Today, plastics are made from the chemicals in oil. They are used to make toys, as well as many household products, such as bins and chairs.

CHEMICAL INDUSTRY

MATERIALS MADE IN THE CHEMICAL INDUSTRY are all around you and some are inside you, too. These materials range from the paint on cars to the food you eat. Each material is made in a factory called an industrial plant. Raw materials, such as minerals, oil, water, coal, and gas, enter the industrial plant where chemical reactions take place. These reactions change the raw materials into useful materials. The useful materials are then transported to be used by people all over the world. Industrial plants are very expensive to build and to run. They are one of the largest industries in the world, and their aim is to make materials at prices people can afford.

IN THE PIPELINE
Colour-coded pipes transport cooling water, steam, liquid, and chemical gases around modern industrial plants.

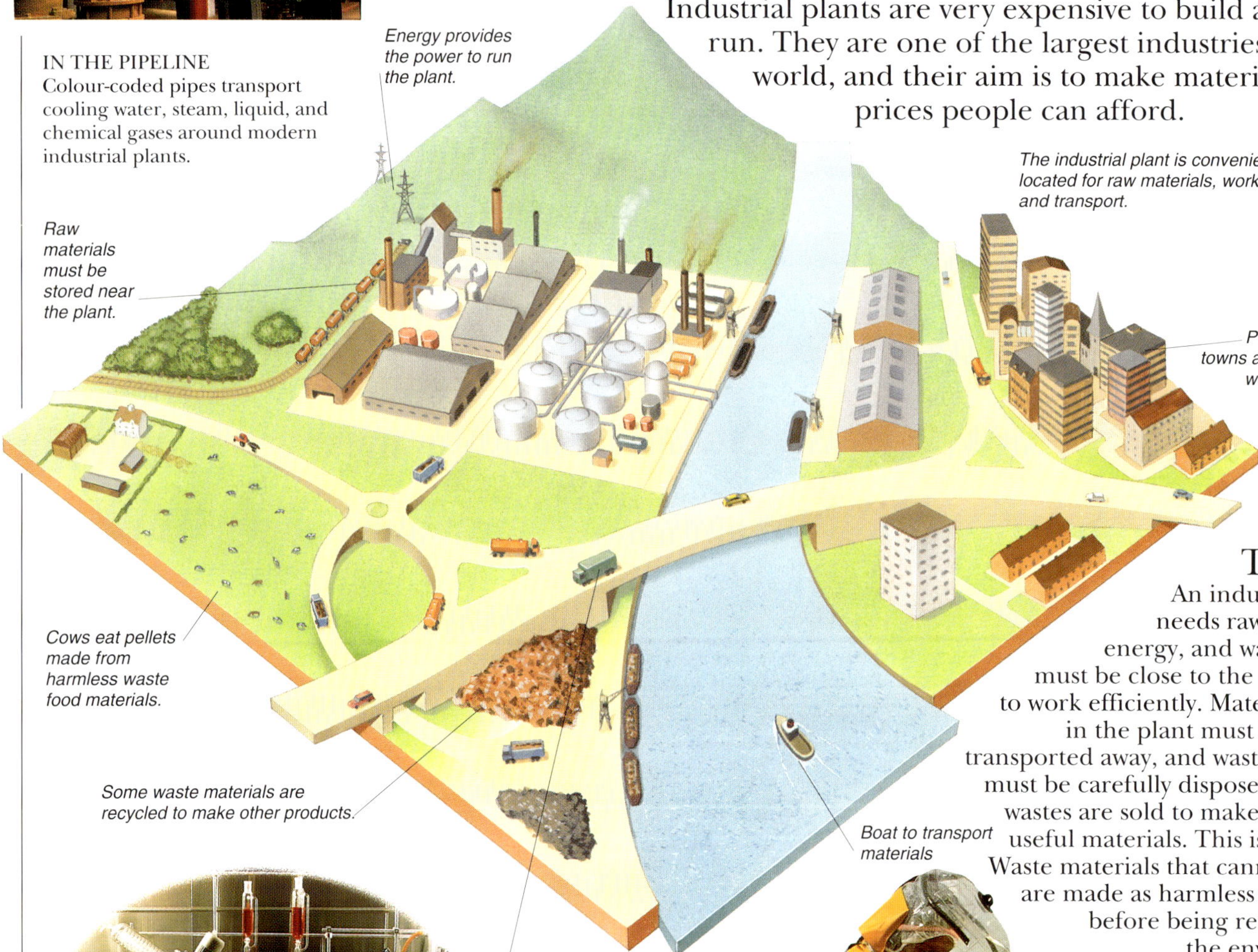

THE SITE

An industrial plant needs raw materials, energy, and water. These must be close to the plant for it to work efficiently. Materials made in the plant must be cheaply transported away, and waste materials must be carefully disposed of. Some wastes are sold to make into other useful materials. This is recycling. Waste materials that cannot be sold are made as harmless as possible before being released into the environment.

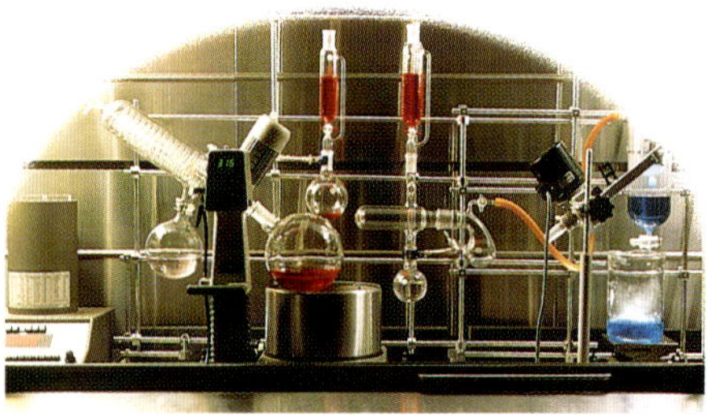

KEEPING SAFE
Chemical reactions can produce poisonous fumes, start fires, and cause explosions. Industrial workers are protected from such hazards by safety equipment and warning systems in the plant. Special protective clothing is provided in case of such emergencies.

SMALL SCALE MODEL
Before building an industrial plant, a small scale model is built in a laboratory. Chemicals are passed through glass apparatus to make each stage of the process easy to see and check. When the scientists are sure the chemical reactions and equipment work safely, this model is scaled up.

SCALING UP
When the small scale model is running well, and ways have been investigated to make the material cheaply, the equipment and processes are scaled up to make a full-size plant.

Find out more

CHEMICAL REACTIONS P.52
WATER INDUSTRY P.83
INDUSTRIAL POLLUTION P.112
ENERGY SOURCES P.134
FACT FINDER P.406

WATER INDUSTRY

A PERSON CAN LIVE for about six days without water, but most of industry would stop working straight away. Industry needs large amounts of water to make almost all the materials we use. Every day, the world's industries use on average four times as much water as people use in their homes. Rain is the main source of all this water, but before we use it, it must be cleaned. When rain hits the ground, it rushes into streams and rivers, or sinks into rock beneath the ground. On its journey, the water picks up small particles of rock, bacteria from the soil, and dissolved chemicals from almost everything it flows over.

DESALINATION
In places where there is little rain, such as the Middle East, people obtain water from the sea. The sea water is heated, at low pressure. Only pure water evaporates, and is condensed in collecting trays. The salt is left as a concentrated solution.

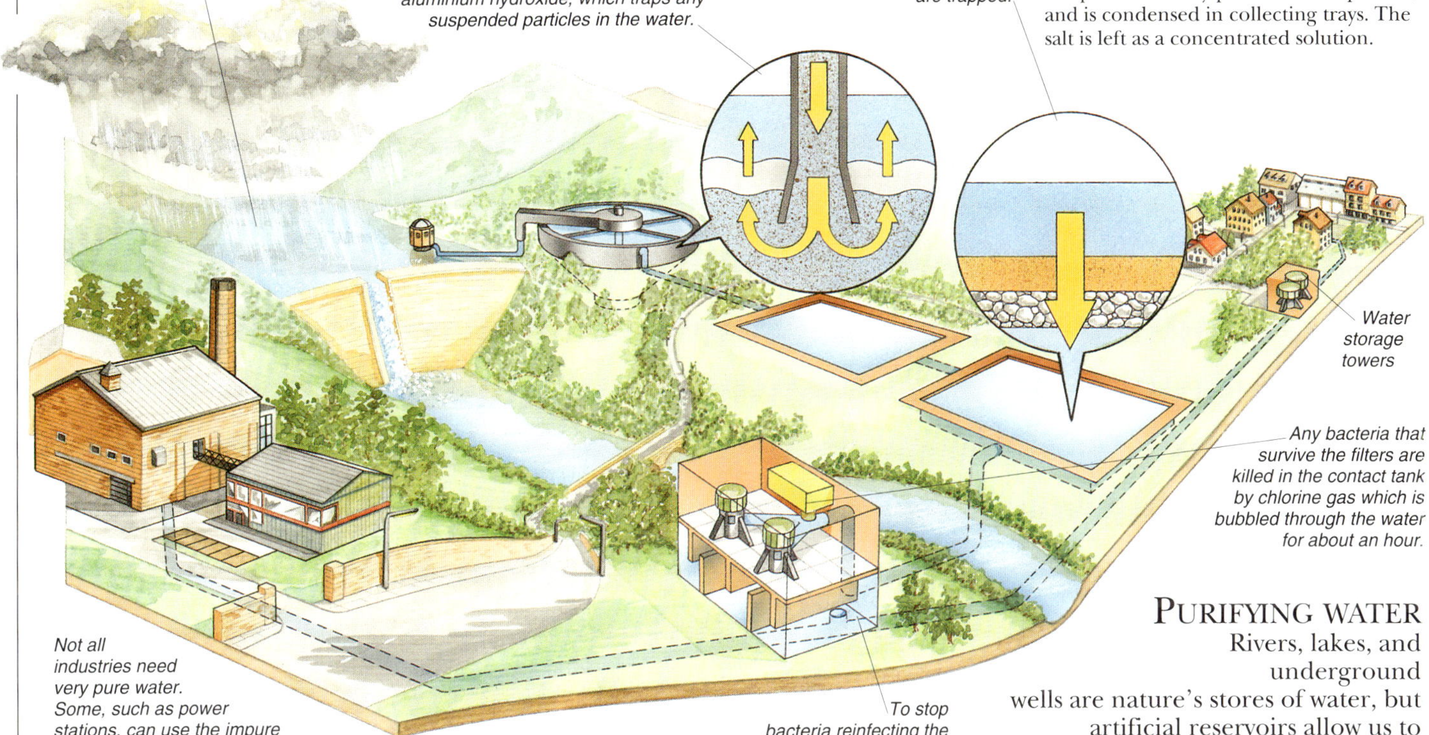

PURIFYING WATER

Rivers, lakes, and underground wells are nature's stores of water, but artificial reservoirs allow us to store large amounts of water near to factories and homes. As the water leaves the reservoir, it passes through a screen to remove objects such as rubbish and twigs. Filters made from chemicals, sand, and gravel remove smaller particles that could scour (wear away) the inside of water pipes, damage industrial equipment, or make drinking water cloudy. Bacteria or viruses, which may cause disease and death, are dealt with by bubbling toxic gases, such as chlorine or ozone, through the water.

HOW INDUSTRY USES WATER
Industry uses large amounts of water. The water cools furnaces where chemical reactions release heat, provides the heat to start a chemical reaction, or generates steam to drive a pump or electrical generator. Used as a solvent, water dissolves many substances, making the diluted solution easier to handle. Finally, water cleans materials, equipment, and the workplace.

Manufacturing a car involves a surprising amount of water.

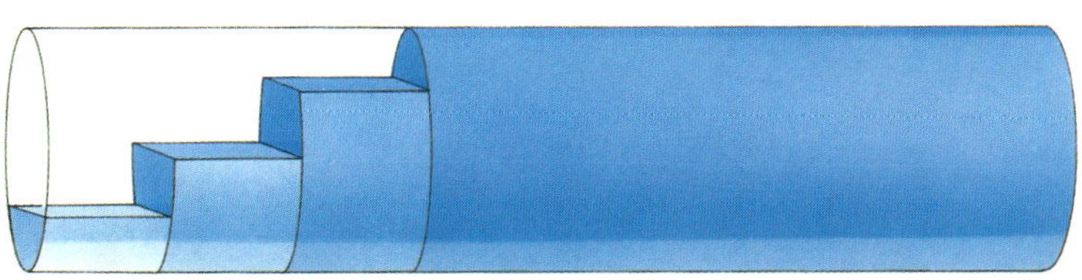

WATER FACTS
To make a car requires 30,000 litres (8,000 gallons) of water. To make 1 tonne of steel requires 4,500 litres (1,125 gallons) of water, but a shower uses only 35 litres (9 gallons). 1 litre of lemonade uses 8 litres (2 gallons) of water.

Find out more

CHANGES OF STATE P.20
SOLUTIONS P.60
SEPARATING MIXTURES P.61
CHEMISTRY OF WATER P.75
CHEMICAL INDUSTRY P.82
FACT FINDER P.406

IRON AND STEEL

CAST IRON
The dome of the Capitol, in Washington D.C., contains 4,000 tonnes of cast iron. The different parts were made by being cast in a mould.

WITHOUT IRON AND STEEL, what would we use for making cars, supporting tall buildings, or producing machines to make nearly every product there is? Iron is the cheapest and most important metal we use. Iron is extracted from a rocky material called iron ore, and most iron is then made into steel. Like many elements, iron is too reactive to exist on its own in the ground. Instead, it combines with other elements, especially oxygen, in ores. The chemical process for extracting a metal from its ore is called smelting. Iron ore is heated with limestone and coke, which is mostly made up of carbon. Coke and limestone remove the unwanted parts of the iron ore to leave almost pure iron, which still contains some carbon. Steel is made by removing more carbon and adding other metals.

THE BLAST FURNACE

Iron is extracted from iron ore in blast furnaces. The biggest are 60 m (200 ft) high, produce 10,000 tonnes of iron a day, and work non-stop for 10 years. The furnace gets its name from the blast of hot air that heats up the raw materials. These are iron ore, limestone, and coke (a form of carbon). As carbon is more reactive than iron, it grabs the oxygen from the iron ore, leaving iron metal behind.

HENRY BESSEMER
Steel is the most useful form of iron, but removing the carbon from the iron used to be an expensive process. In 1856, a British inventor, Henry Bessemer (1813-1898), devised a cheap way of removing most of the carbon. Air was blown through the molten metal in a furnace called a converter. The oxygen in the air removed the carbon.

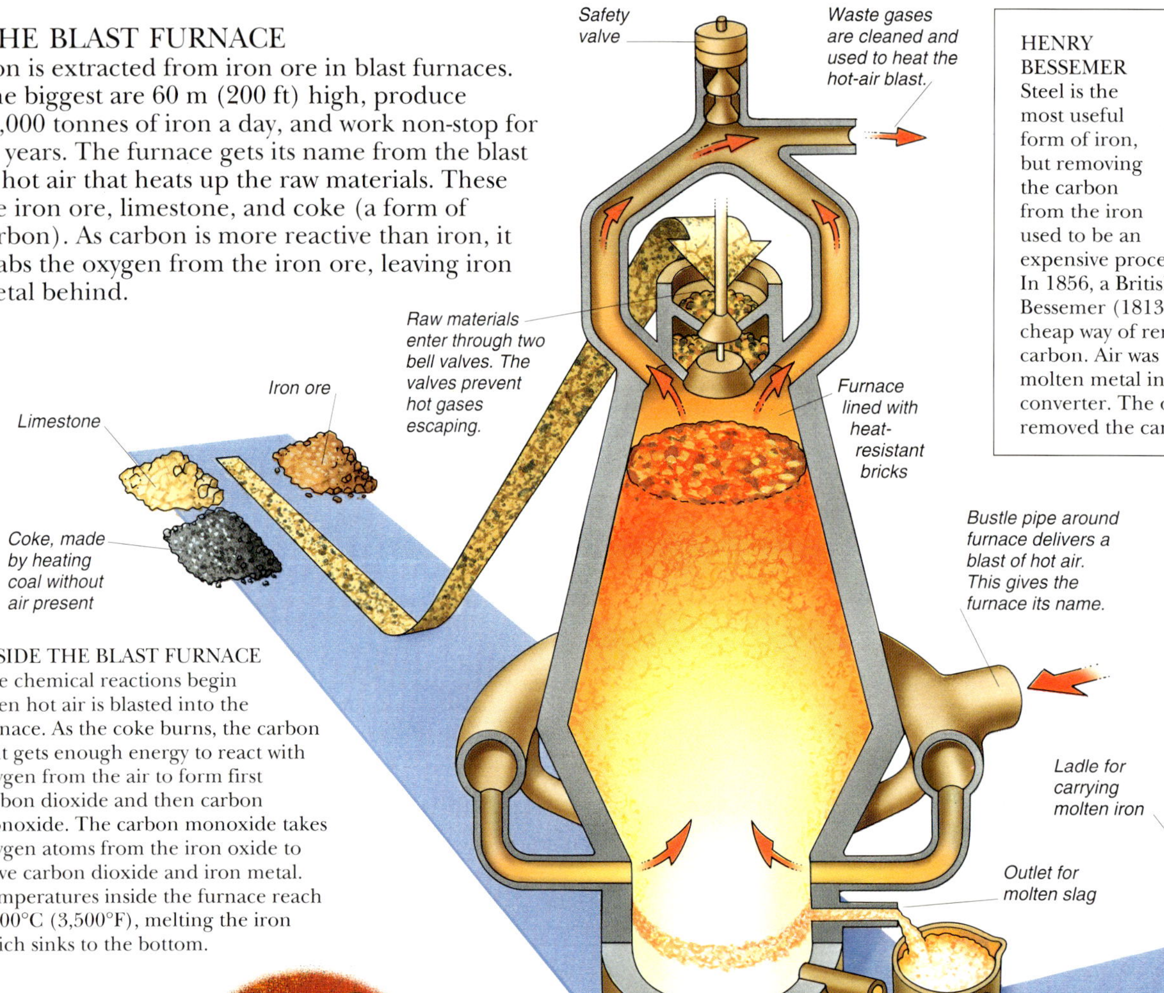

INSIDE THE BLAST FURNACE
The chemical reactions begin when hot air is blasted into the furnace. As the coke burns, the carbon in it gets enough energy to react with oxygen from the air to form first carbon dioxide and then carbon monoxide. The carbon monoxide takes oxygen atoms from the iron oxide to leave carbon dioxide and iron metal. Temperatures inside the furnace reach 1,900°C (3,500°F), melting the iron which sinks to the bottom.

IRON IN CLOSE-UP
When cast iron is magnified 200 times, you can see crystals of carbon (blue) in it. The smooth red background is pure iron (called ferrite). The carbon crystals make the metal brittle.

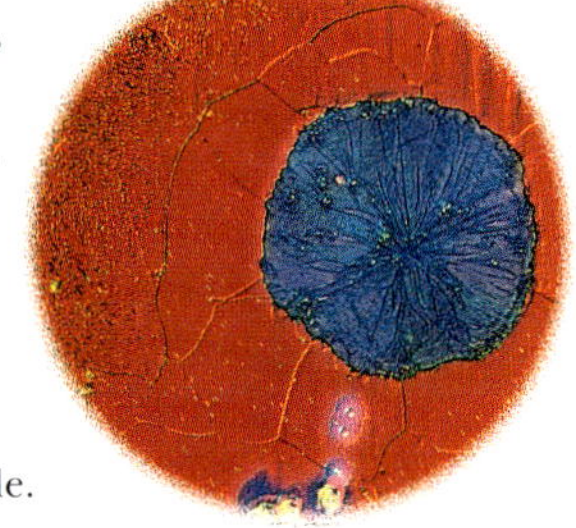

SLAG
Limestone is included in the furnace because it mixes and combines with sand, clay, and stones in the ore. They form a waste material, called slag, which floats on top of the molten metal.

IMPURITIES
Iron from a blast furnace is 90-95 per cent pure. The main impurity is carbon, absorbed from the coke in the blast furnace. Carbon makes the iron hard but not very strong. Most iron is converted into steel, a form of iron that contains less than 1.7 per cent of carbon.

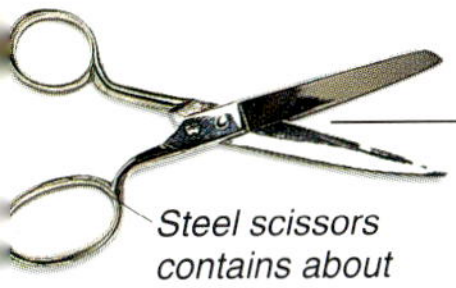

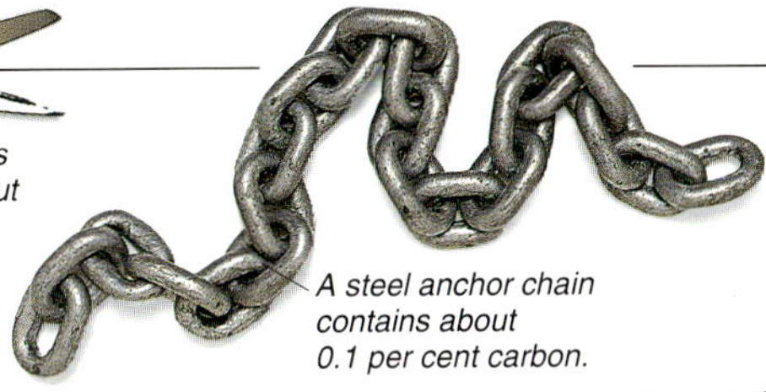

Stainless steel in the laboratory

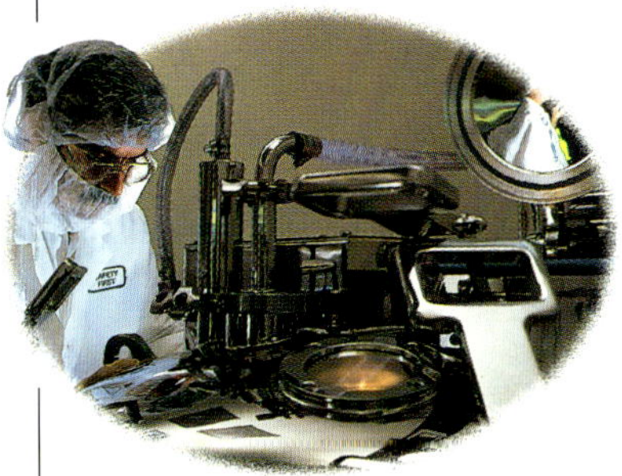

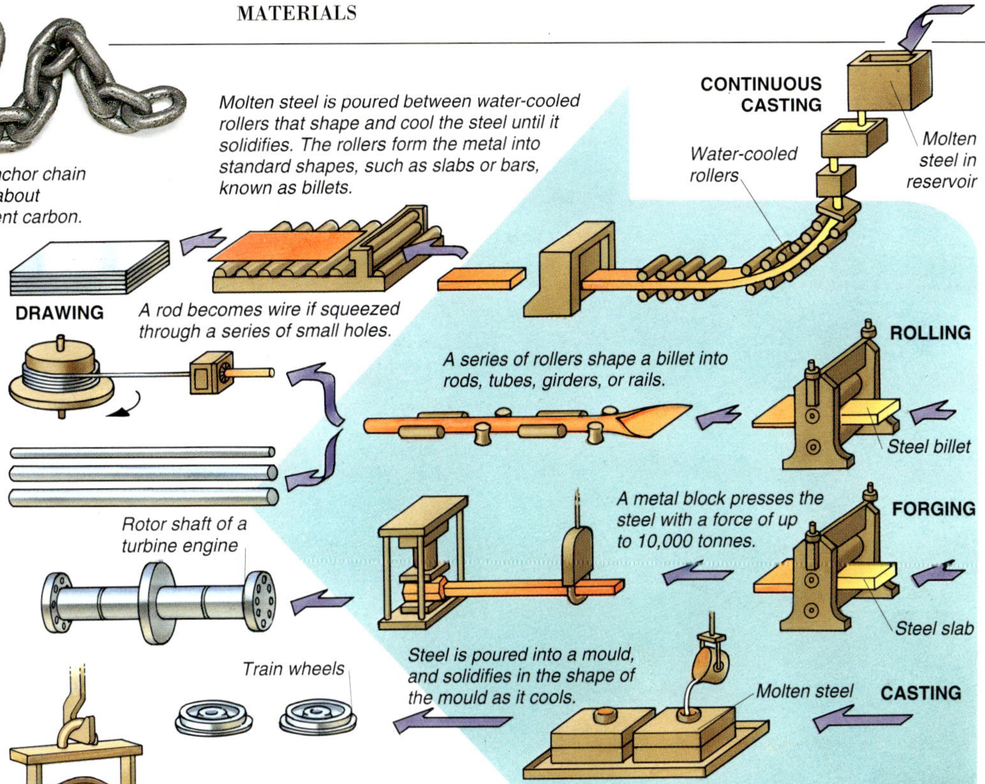

MORE THAN ONE STEEL

There are carbon steels and alloy steels. Low-carbon steels are tough yet easy to shape. High-carbon steels are hard and brittle, but can be given sharp cutting edges. Alloy steels contain a range of metals, each giving the steel a special property. Chromium, nickel, and steel make stainless steel, which is hard-wearing and does not rust.

SHAPING STEEL

Steel can be shaped in a variety of ways. Rolling stretches and squeezes ingots of steel into sheets, tubes, or strips. In drawing, rolled steel is pulled through a hole to make a wire. In casting, it is left to cool in a mould. Forged steel is made by squeezing hot steel.

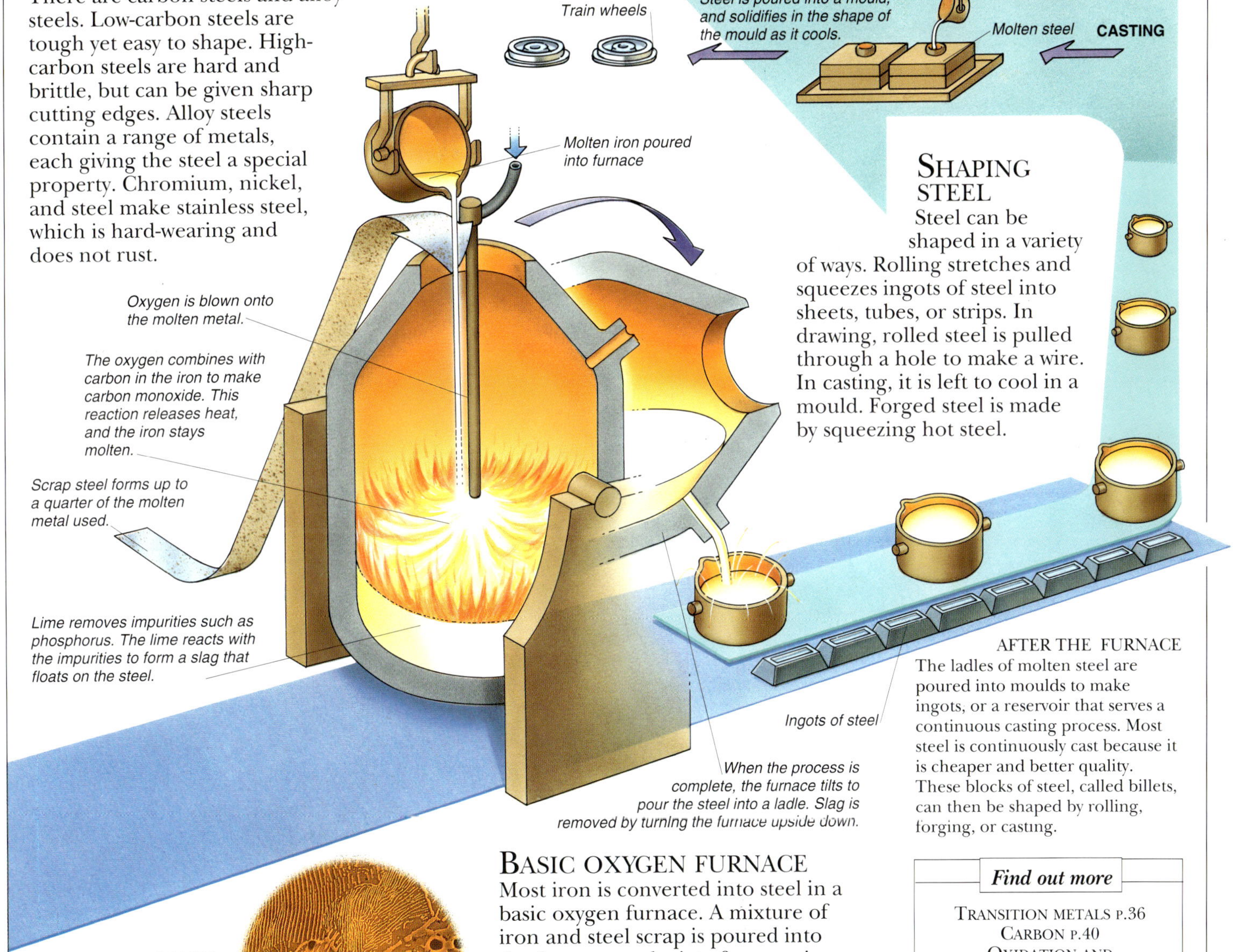

AFTER THE FURNACE

The ladles of molten steel are poured into moulds to make ingots, or a reservoir that serves a continuous casting process. Most steel is continuously cast because it is cheaper and better quality. These blocks of steel, called billets, can then be shaped by rolling, forging, or casting.

BASIC OXYGEN FURNACE

Most iron is converted into steel in a basic oxygen furnace. A mixture of iron and steel scrap is poured into the furnace, and a jet of oxygen is blown over it. Oxygen combines with the carbon in the iron, carrying it away as carbon monoxide. It takes a basic oxygen furnace just 40 minutes to produce 350 tonnes of steel.

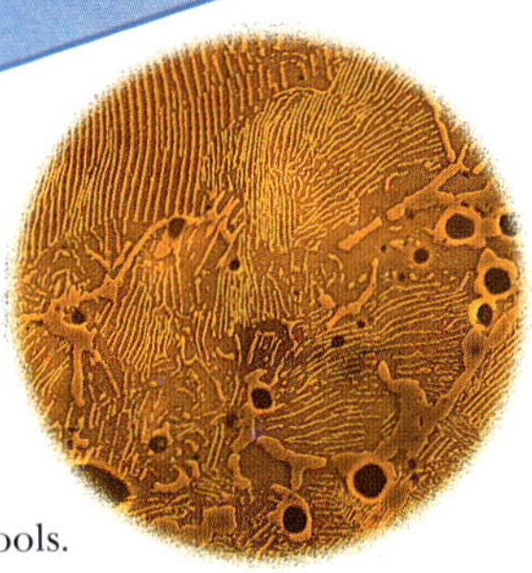

STEEL IN CLOSE-UP

This picture shows a low-carbon steel, containing 0.87 per cent carbon. The structure of steel is varied with different amounts of carbon and by the way it cools.

Find out more

TRANSITION METALS P.36
CARBON P.40
OXIDATION AND REDUCTION P.64
REACTIVITY SERIES P.66
COAL PRODUCTS P.96
SEDIMENTARY ROCKS P.223
FACT FINDER P.406

Copper

YOU MAY NOT BE ABLE TO SEE IT, but copper is all around you. The walls and ceilings of almost every room contain copper wire leading to light fittings and plug sockets. These wires carry the electricity that provides light and power in our homes. In its natural form, copper occurs in the ground as copper ore, a mineral. But this ore contains only 0.5–1 per cent of the metal. The rest is rock. The world produces 9.6 million tonnes of copper a year. This means that more than a thousand million tonnes of ore have to be removed from the ground and the pure copper extracted.

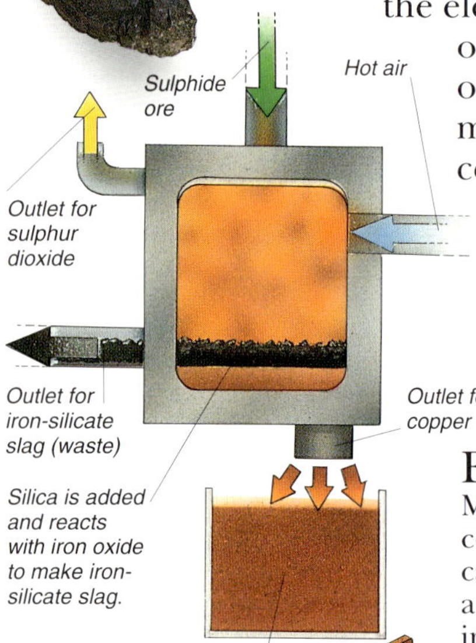

LEACHING
In some ores, the copper is combined with oxygen. In a process called leaching, sulphuric acid is sprayed over these copper oxide ores, which dissolves the copper but not the rock. The copper and sulphuric acid form a solution of copper sulphate, which is purified by electrolysis.

Extracting copper

Most copper is extracted from a compound of iron, sulphur, and copper called sulphide ore. Hot air is blown into a furnace to separate the copper from the iron and sulphur. The iron and sulphur react with the oxygen to form iron oxide and sulphur dioxide, leaving molten copper metal. This copper, known as blister copper, is about 98 per cent pure. A process called electrolysis is needed to separate the remaining impurities.

Carrie Everson

CARRIE EVERSON
Ores contain a mixture of valuable metallic substances and worthless rock. An American schoolteacher, Carrie Everson, invented a way of separating the two in 1886. She ground up ore and mixed it with oil and acid. This produced a froth in which the metallic substances floated while the rocky materials sank.

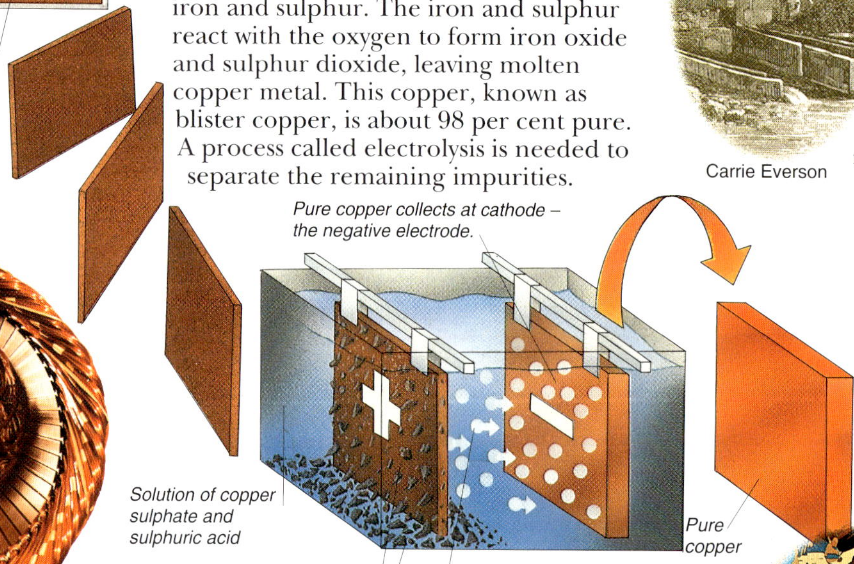

ELECTROLYSIS
A slab of blister copper can be transformed into pure copper by electrolysis. The slab is suspended in a solution of copper sulphate and sulphuric acid, where it acts as a positive electrode (anode). When electricity is passed through the solution, the copper in the anode is dissolved. The pure copper collects at the negative electrode (cathode) and the impurities fall below.

Electric coils in motor

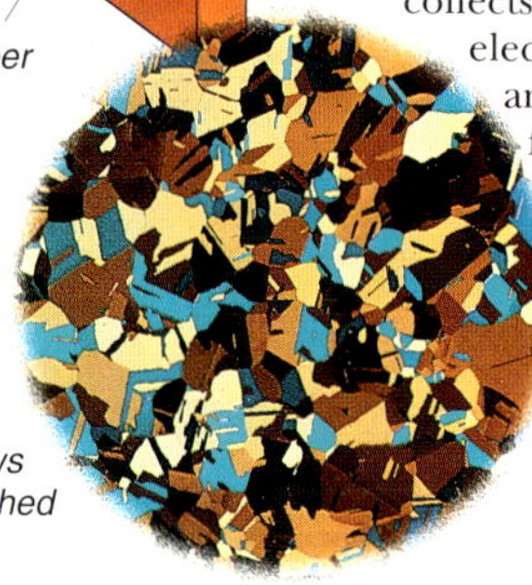
Micrograph of copper

Atoms of copper stack together in a regular way as the metal forms to make crystals. The way the crystals interlock allows the metal to be easily pushed or pulled into shape.

USES OF COPPER
Copper is a good conductor of heat and electricity. We use it to make cooking utensils and all sorts of pipes for carrying hot water, both in homes and in industry. We also use it to make different kinds of electrical devices, such as lightning conductors and the electric coils in motors. Copper does not rust easily, so it lasts a very long time.

COPPER BY-PRODUCTS
Gold, silver, and platinum can be found in their pure state in the Earth's crust, so they do not have to be extracted from ores. However, useful amounts are found in the slimes that form during the electrolysis of copper.

Find out more

TRANSITION METALS P.36
REACTIVITY SERIES P.66
ELECTROLYSIS P.67
ALLOYS P.88
SULPHURIC ACID P.89
FACT FINDER P.406

ALUMINIUM

The Emperor of France, Napoleon III (1808-1873), used aluminium plates to impress his most important guests. Today we use aluminium foil to wrap food because it is so cheap.

YOU'VE PROBABLY SEEN aluminium in the form of soft drink cans or thin sheets of foil. It is the most common metal on Earth. It occurs naturally in many different kinds of rock. But most of the aluminium we use is extracted from an ore called bauxite. Because aluminium easily combines with other elements, a great deal of energy is needed to separate it into its metallic (pure) form. Chemists discovered a cheap way of extracting aluminium in 1886. Before this, the metal was much more expensive than silver and gold.

CYCLE SUPPORT
Aluminium is easy to work and shape. As a tubular frame, it provides a very lightweight support for the racing cyclist.

Huge wheel extracts bauxite ore from the Earth's crust.

The major aluminium ore, bauxite, is formed over long periods by the weathering of rocks containing aluminium silicates (aluminium, silicon, and oxygen).

EXTRACTING ALUMINIUM

Aluminium is extracted from bauxite by the Bayer process and electrolysis. In the Bayer process, bauxite is mixed with caustic soda and heated. This produces sugar-like crystals of pure aluminium oxide. These are dissolved in molten sodium aluminium fluoride, called cryolite. Electrolysis is then used to split up the aluminium and oxygen.

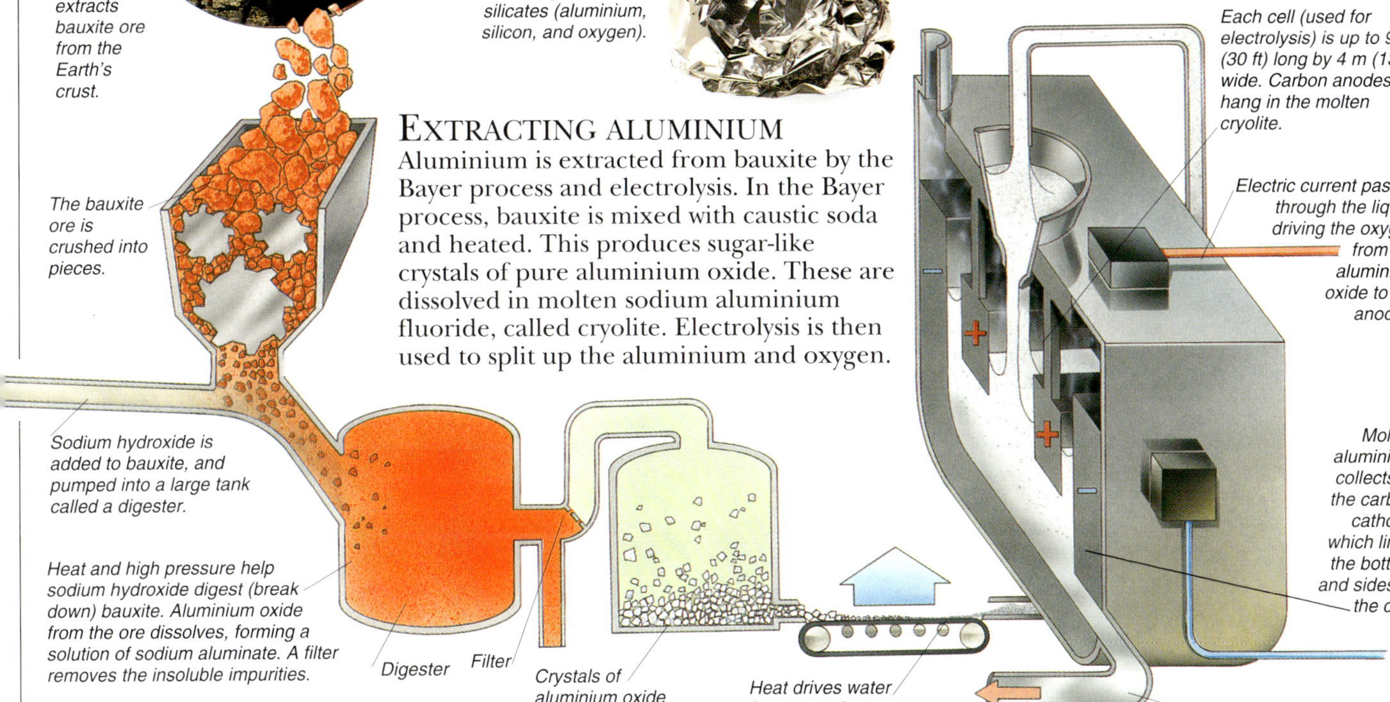

The bauxite ore is crushed into pieces.

Sodium hydroxide is added to bauxite, and pumped into a large tank called a digester.

Heat and high pressure help sodium hydroxide digest (break down) bauxite. Aluminium oxide from the ore dissolves, forming a solution of sodium aluminate. A filter removes the insoluble impurities.

Digester

Filter

Crystals of aluminium oxide form as the solution cools, leaving sodium hydroxide.

Heat drives water from crystals, to leave a fine powder.

Each cell (used for electrolysis) is up to 9 m (30 ft) long by 4 m (13 ft) wide. Carbon anodes hang in the molten cryolite.

Electric current passes through the liquid, driving the oxygen from the aluminium oxide to the anodes.

Molten aluminium collects at the carbon cathode which lines the bottom and sides of the cell.

Aluminium is collected and used to make many products. It can also be easily recycled.

COINCIDENTAL CHEMISTS
In 1886, two chemists independently discovered how to extract aluminium using electricity. Their discovery reduced the price of aluminium to a fraction of the price of silver in four years. The two chemists were Charles Martin Hall (1863-1914), a student at Oberlin College in the USA, and P.L.T. Heroult (1863-1914), a young chemist working in France. By coincidence, they were not only the same age when they made their discovery, but also died within eight months of each other.

C.M. Hall

P.L.T. Heroult

USING ALUMINIUM
When the surface of aluminium reacts with oxygen in the air, a thick coating of aluminium oxide forms. This seals the metal from the air and stops it corroding. Aluminium is also durable, light, and a good conductor of electricity. We use it to make parts for planes, cars, and lorries, and to make electric cables.

Find out more

POOR METALS P.38
REACTIVITY SERIES P.66
ELECTROLYSIS P.67
CHEMICAL INDUSTRY P.82
ALLOYS P.88
FACT FINDER P.406

ALLOYS

IF YOU HAD BEEN A SOLDIER in Ancient Greece you would have had to stop in battle to straighten your bronze sword. But bronze was a great improvement on copper, which bends even more easily. Most pure metals are weak and soft. But two soft metals mixed together make a harder metal called an alloy. Bronze is an alloy of copper and tin. By changing the amounts and combinations of the metals, the properties of an alloy can be altered. Most alloys consist of two or more metals, but some contain a non-metal, such as carbon. The most widely used alloy of this type is steel.

THE FIRST ALLOY
About 6,000 years ago, people discovered that copper could be made harder if mixed with tin. This alloy is called bronze. It was so widely used for many years that this period of time became known as the Bronze Age.

Aluminium mixed with magnesium and copper provides a lightweight body that is strong enough to stand up to high-speed winds and the impact of landing.

HIGH TEMPERATURES
A drill bit cuts its way through hard material, spinning thousands of times a minute. A tungsten carbide alloy, with a melting point of over 2,900°C (5,250°F), provides the hardness and strength to do this.

LOW TEMPERATURES
Solder, an alloy of tin and lead, is perfect for joining metal parts together. It has a lower melting point than either of its pure metals, so it does not damage any of the parts. It creates a bridge between the two metal parts.

In a jet engine, metal discs hold the turbine blades in place. Discs are made from a superalloy of 11 elements including nickel and titanium.

ALLOYS IN AIRCRAFT

Jet aircraft need lightweight alloys for their bodies to make take off easier and to keep fuel consumption down. Their engines need special alloys designed to withstand very high temperatures. Rapidly spinning turbine blades at the front of the engine suck in air at temperatures of up to 600°C (1,100°F).

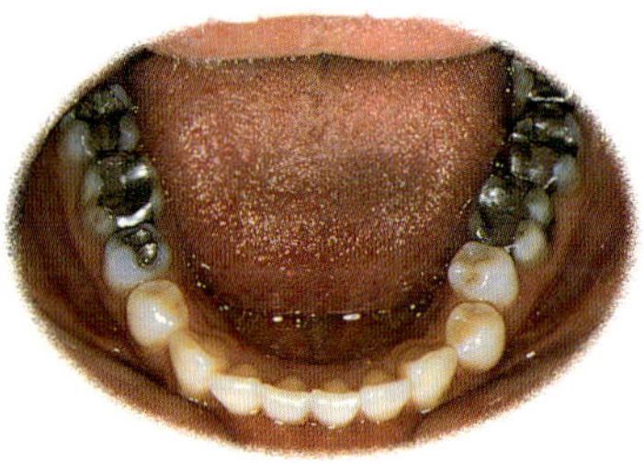

DENTAL ALLOY
You may have an alloy in your teeth. Dentists use amalgam – the alloy of mercury, silver, tin, zinc, and copper – to fill cavities. It forms a solid that can be shaped like putty to match the contours of the teeth before it hardens.

MAKING ALLOYS
Most alloys are made by melting metals and mixing them together. Care must be taken to make sure that one metal does not boil before the other melts. When making brass, for example, solid zinc is dropped into molten copper. If the zinc were heated to the same temperature as the copper, it would boil away into a vapour.

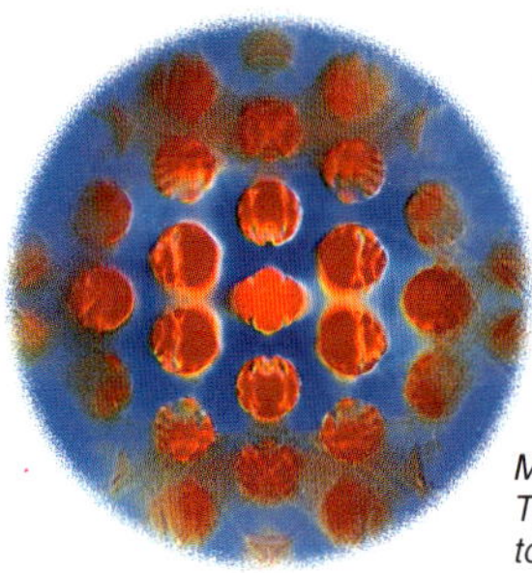

Metals in an alloy dissolve in each other. Their atoms mix freely and lock together to make strong crystals when they cool.

Find out more

BONDING P.28
ALKALI METALS P.34
TRANSITION METALS P.36
POOR METALS P.38
REACTIVITY SERIES P.66
FACT FINDER P.406

SULPHURIC ACID

Sulphur (a solid element), is the key raw material in sulphuric acid. But water and air are also needed.

WHAT DO FERTILIZERS, PAINTS, explosives, and detergents have in common? They are all made with sulphuric acid. In fact, many of the items we use every day would not exist without it. Sulphuric acid does not occur naturally; it has to be manufactured. The chemical industry produces about 150 million tonnes of it each year. Fortunately, sulphuric acid is cheap to make because the waste heat from one stage of the process can be used to provide heat for the next stage.

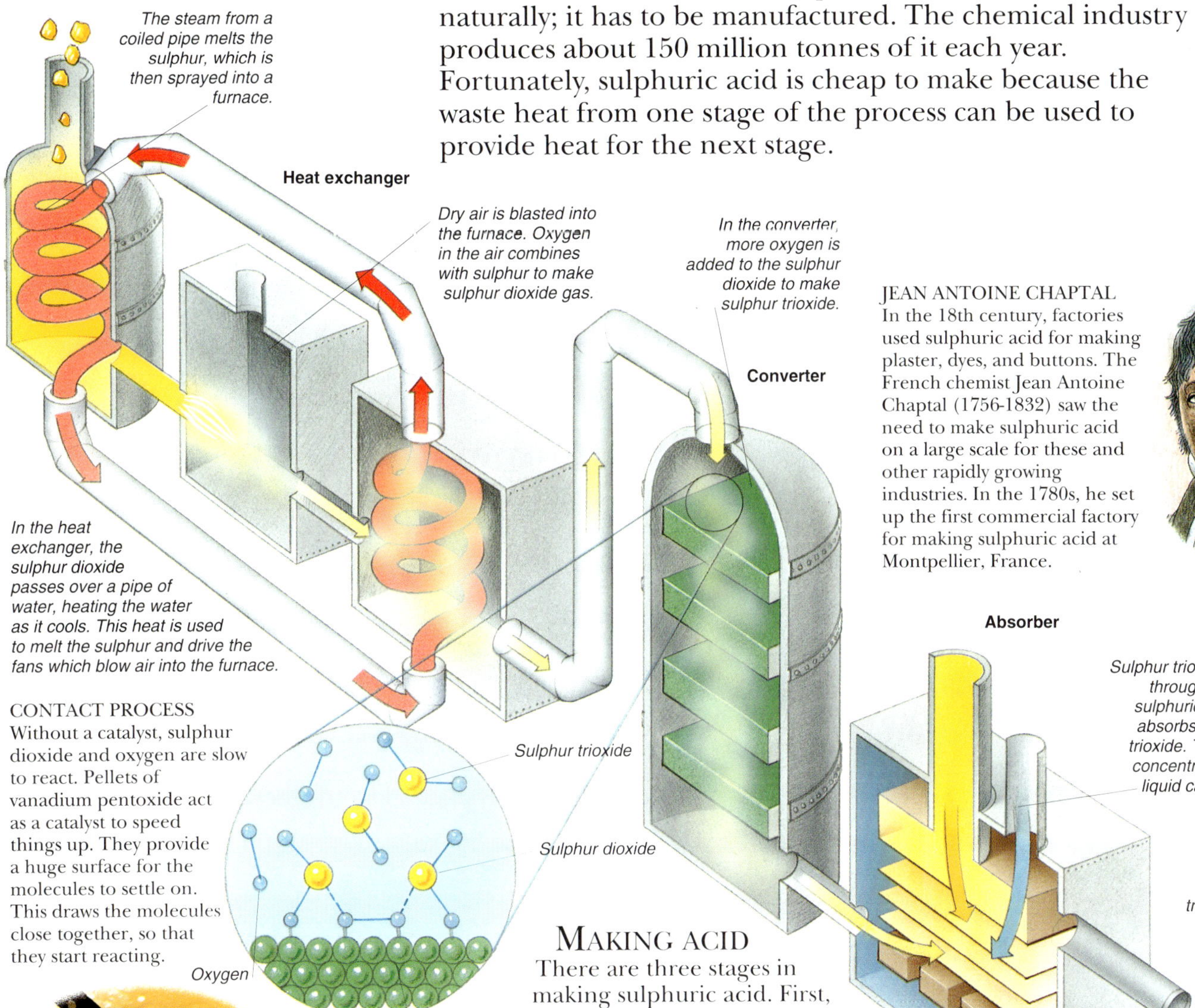

The steam from a coiled pipe melts the sulphur, which is then sprayed into a furnace.

Dry air is blasted into the furnace. Oxygen in the air combines with sulphur to make sulphur dioxide gas.

In the converter, more oxygen is added to the sulphur dioxide to make sulphur trioxide.

In the heat exchanger, the sulphur dioxide passes over a pipe of water, heating the water as it cools. This heat is used to melt the sulphur and drive the fans which blow air into the furnace.

Sulphur trioxide passes through a spray of sulphuric acid which absorbs the sulphur trioxide. This forms a concentrated fuming liquid called oleum.

Sulphur trioxide could be added directly to water to produce sulphuric acid. But the reaction would be too violent.

The oleum is diluted with water to make sulphuric acid of the right strength.

JEAN ANTOINE CHAPTAL

In the 18th century, factories used sulphuric acid for making plaster, dyes, and buttons. The French chemist Jean Antoine Chaptal (1756-1832) saw the need to make sulphuric acid on a large scale for these and other rapidly growing industries. In the 1780s, he set up the first commercial factory for making sulphuric acid at Montpellier, France.

CONTACT PROCESS

Without a catalyst, sulphur dioxide and oxygen are slow to react. Pellets of vanadium pentoxide act as a catalyst to speed things up. They provide a huge surface for the molecules to settle on. This draws the molecules close together, so that they start reacting.

MAKING ACID

There are three stages in making sulphuric acid. First, sulphur and air are heated to make sulphur dioxide. In the second stage, known as the contact process, sulphur dioxide and air are mixed to produce sulphur trioxide. Finally, this gas is dissolved in sulphuric acid to give oleum, a super concentrated form of sulphuric acid.

MAKING RAYON

A bath of sulphuric acid is essential for making rayon, a synthetic fibre. Strands of syrup, made from wood pulp, pass through 10,000 holes in this head. The acid in the bath hardens the strands into 10,000 solid threads of rayon.

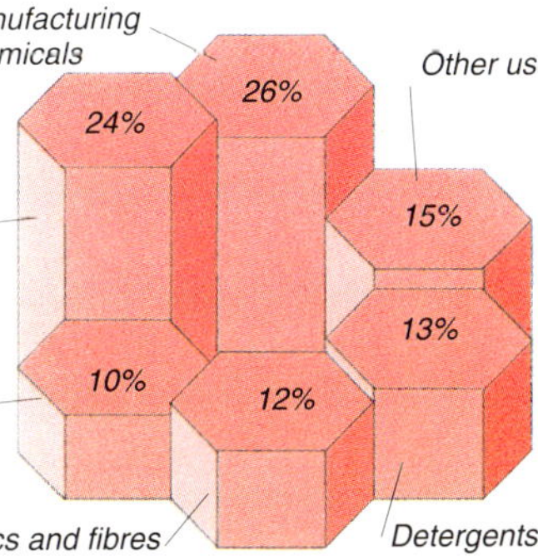

USING SULPHURIC ACID

Industrially, sulphuric acid is a very useful chemical because it reacts readily with other materials, removing metals, oxygen, water, and other unwanted substances. Apart from manufacturing other chemicals, sulphuric acid is also used in car batteries, oil refining, and for cleaning metals.

Find out more

SULPHUR P.45
CATALYSTS P.56
OXIDATION AND REDUCTION P.64
ACIDS P.68
AMMONIA P.90

AMMONIA

RAW MATERIALS
Hydrogen and nitrogen are the raw materials for ammonia. Hydrogen is made by reacting methane in natural gas with steam. Nitrogen is extracted from the air.

IF YOU'VE EVER HAD a whiff of ammonia, then you know how strong the smell is. In the 19th century, ammonia (a compound of nitrogen and hydrogen) was used in smelling salts to revive people who had fainted. Today, ammonia is an important raw material for many chemical processes and products – especially fertilizer. Much of the 140 million tonnes of ammonia produced each year is used to make fertilizers. These give plants the nitrogen they need to grow. In fact, it was the shortage of nitrogen fertilizers that led to the development of a process for manufacturing ammonia on a large scale. Modern ammonia plants make hundreds of tonnes of this colourless, strong-smelling gas every day.

Fritz Haber

Carl Bosch

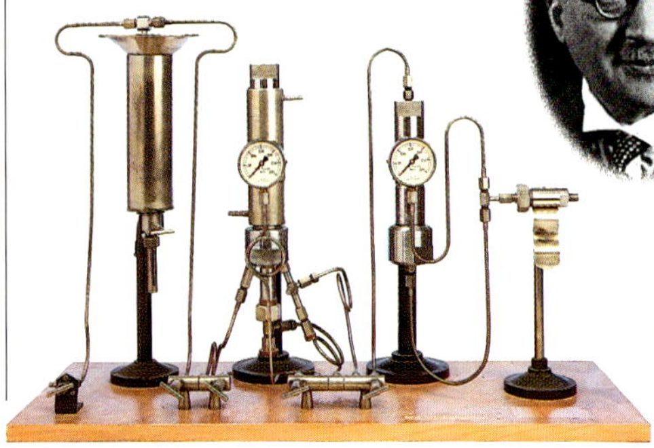

Haber's apparatus for making ammonia

FRITZ HABER AND CARL BOSCH
In 1908, the German chemist Fritz Haber (1868-1934) used this apparatus (left) to produce ammonia. Making nitrogen and hydrogen react together was not easy, but Haber calculated how to make the reaction work. Five years later, Carl Bosch (1874-1940) had scaled the experimental apparatus up to industrial size. Bosch, a German industrial chemist, had to design large pieces of equipment that would endure the high pressures and temperatures needed to make ammonia.

Modern ammonia plants are huge. This equipment removes carbon dioxide from hydrogen – just one stage in preparing one of the raw materials from methane.

MAKING AMMONIA

Today, ammonia is still made in plants that have Bosch's basic design. The process is very complicated. It involves several stages, including purifying the nitrogen and hydrogen. The most important stage, though, is converting nitrogen and hydrogen to ammonia. Bosch did 6,500 experiments to find that the best catalyst for speeding up the reaction was iron.

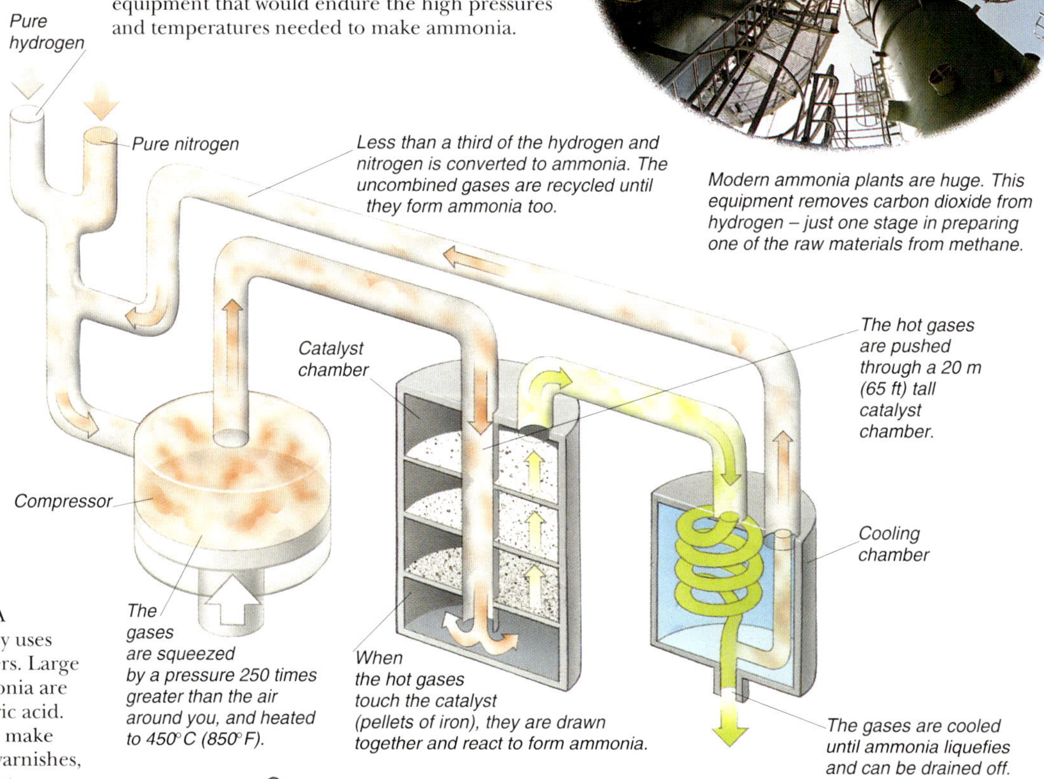

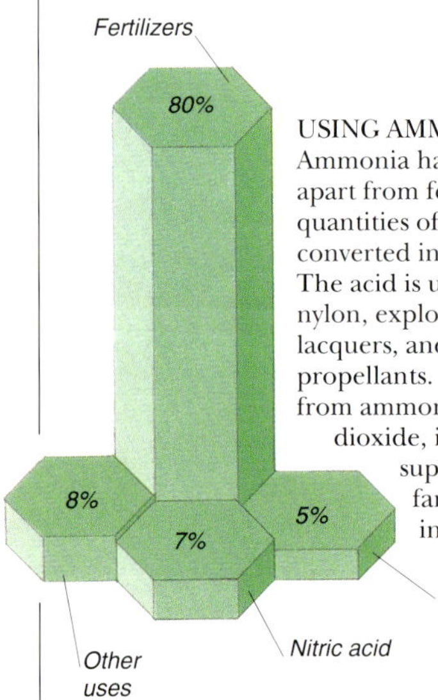

USING AMMONIA
Ammonia has many uses apart from fertilizers. Large quantities of ammonia are converted into nitric acid. The acid is used to make nylon, explosives, varnishes, lacquers, and rocket propellants. Urea, made from ammonia and carbon dioxide, is used as a food supplement for farm animals and in plastics.

ACID TO FERTILIZER
Farmers use ammonium salts as a fertilizer. These are made by mixing ammonia gas with hot nitric acid, and then spraying the solution into the top of a tower. The droplets fall into a rising current of cold air and form pellets.

Find out more

BONDING P.28
NITROGEN P 42
HYDROGEN P.47
CATALYSTS P.56
FACT FINDER P.406

Chemistry in Farming

Much of the food you eat has been grown with the help of chemicals. In order to provide this food, farmers need the help of the chemical industry. This industry produces fertilizers that contain minerals for plants. Without minerals, plant growth is poor, and food production is low. Some chemicals control the ripening of fruit, so it doesn't go bad before you eat it. Chemical food supplements for farm animals help them grow faster and avoid disease. But many people are concerned about the amount of chemicals we use to produce food. Too much fertilizer can lead to water pollution, and some pesticides can kill harmless plants and animals, and can be dangerous to people's health.

CHEMICAL FOOD
In addition to their natural food, farm animals eat pellets of chemicals. These contain extra nitrogen to help build strength and speed up growth.

INSECT KILLERS
Insecticides kill in three different ways. If an insect touches contact insecticides, eats stomach poisons, or breathes in fumigants (poison gases), it will die.

Organic Farming

The crops and livestock on an organic farm do not receive any synthetic chemicals in fertilizers and food supplements. Organic farmers treat the soil with manure, to provide minerals for the crops. Every year, they grow a different crop in each field, so that all the plants can benefit from the range of minerals in the manure. This also disrupts the lives of pests and keeps their numbers low. Organic farm animals get supplements from natural chemicals found in seaweed.

FUNGUS KILLERS
Fungicides are organic chemicals that may contain zinc, manganese, and copper. Farmers spray them on to crops or put them in the soil. This stops the fungus from spreading and destroying the whole crop.

WEEDKILLERS
Herbicides kill weeds in a variety of ways. Some interfere with photosynthesis and stop the weed making food. Others work by poisoning the growing cells at the tips of the roots and shoots.

Pest Killers

Any living thing that disrupts the growth of crops or livestock is a pest. It may be a weed competing with crop plants for space, water, and minerals. It could also be a fungus sending out its feeding threads to destroy plant tissue, or an insect eating its way through leaves, fruits, and roots. Farmers reduce the number of pests by using pesticides – chemicals designed to stop one or more life-giving reactions in a pest's body.

CHEMICALS TO GROW CROPS
Fertilizers provide the range of minerals that plants need. Each mineral helps the plant to grow in a different way. To test the effects of a fertilizer, farmers grow two groups of plants and give fertilizer to one group. Then they compare the two groups at the end of the growing period.

Find out more

Alkali metals p.34
Nitrogen p.42
Phosphorus p.43
Alkalis and bases p.70
Fact finder p.406

FOOD INDUSTRY

MOST OF THE FOOD in your last meal was probably harvested on a farm many weeks ago, but it still tasted good. The food industry processes much of our food with chemicals so that it remains edible and safe, and looks attractive, for a long time. Without these chemicals, microbes (bacteria and fungi) would get to your food before you had a chance to eat it. Microbes produce compounds that taste and look unpleasant, and may be toxic. Food processing began thousands of years ago to help people keep food through the lean winter months. Today, food processing allows food from other parts of the world to be transported to our local shops so that we can enjoy a great variety of things to eat all through the year.

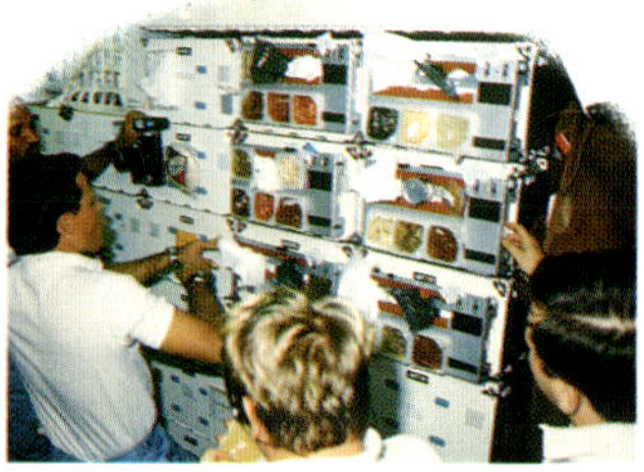

FREEZE THEN DRY
Astronauts rely on freeze-dried food. In the freeze-drying process, the food is frozen, and then the water is removed. You can keep freeze-dried food at room temperatures because bacteria cannot live without water.

IN THE CAN
Walk into any supermarket and you'll see lots of canned food. Canning is the most popular way of preserving food. Fresh foods are first boiled for a short time, to destroy their enzymes, and then put in cans and heated to kill bacteria. Finally, the cans are sealed to prevent air bringing oxygen and bacteria to the food again.

QUICK FREEZING
Bacteria cannot feed and breed if the food is frozen. In fluidized freezing, small items of food, such as peas, pass over a blast of cold air (-34°C or -29°F) on a conveyor belt. The air makes the peas rise and move freely over one another like particles in a fluid. The peas freeze in minutes.

After cows are milked, a tanker transports their milk to the dairy.

PASTEURIZATION
Boiling kills bacteria, but also destroys nutrients. In the pasteurization process, liquids such as milk are heated to 70°C (160°F) for 15 seconds and then cooled quickly. The flavour is preserved while the bacteria are destroyed.

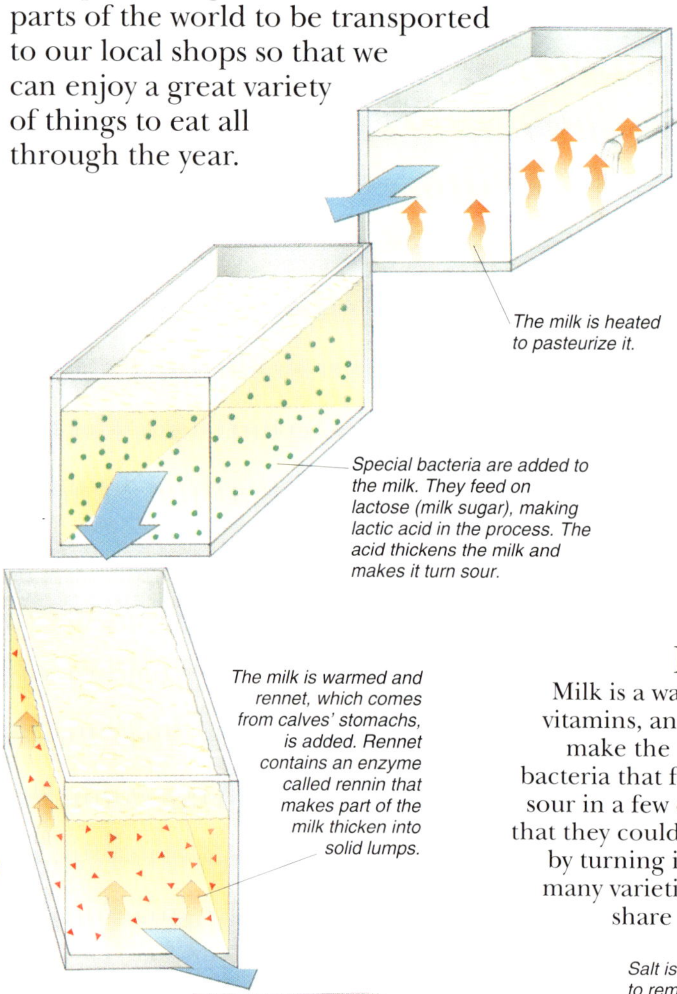

The milk is heated to pasteurize it.

Special bacteria are added to the milk. They feed on lactose (milk sugar), making lactic acid in the process. The acid thickens the milk and makes it turn sour.

The milk is warmed and rennet, which comes from calves' stomachs, is added. Rennet contains an enzyme called rennin that makes part of the milk thicken into solid lumps.

FROM MILK TO CHEESE

Milk is a watery solution of protein, sugar, vitamins, and minerals, with fat droplets to make the milk white. But it also contains bacteria that feed, breed, and make the milk sour in a few days. Our ancestors discovered that they could preserve the nutrients in milk by turning it into cheese. Today, there are many varieties of cheese, but most of them share the basic stages of production.

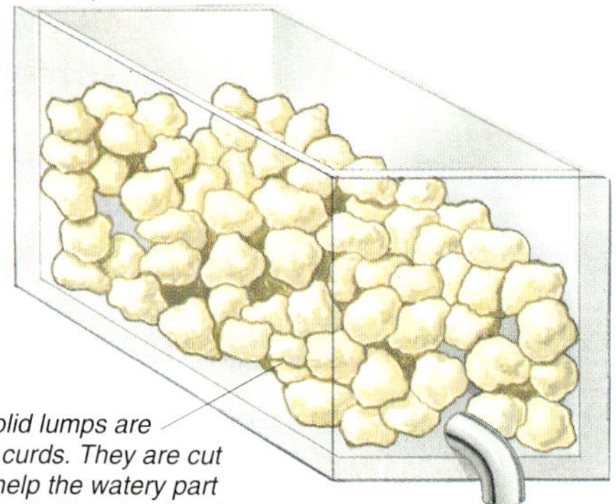

The solid lumps are called curds. They are cut up to help the watery part of the milk (the whey) drain away. The whey is made into food for farm animals.

Salt is added to the curds, and they are pressed to remove any remaining whey. The curds are shaped into moulds and stored on cool shelves and left to ripen into cheese.

Additives

It does not take long to collect the foods shown here for a snack. Snacks should only be eaten occasionally because of the high level of fats and sugar they contain. They also contain chemicals called additives. The food industry uses additives to stop food from going bad before we eat it. Additives also keep food looking attractive and tasting good. There are hundreds of different additives, some natural and some synthetic.

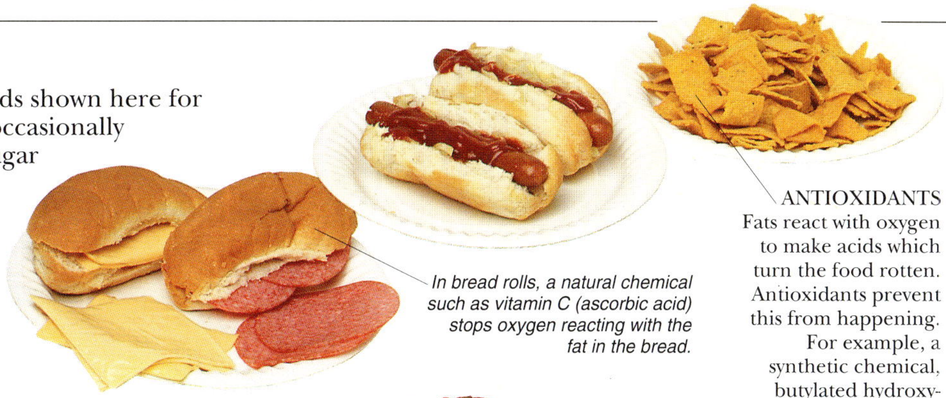

In bread rolls, a natural chemical such as vitamin C (ascorbic acid) stops oxygen reacting with the fat in the bread.

ANTIOXIDANTS
Fats react with oxygen to make acids which turn the food rotten. Antioxidants prevent this from happening. For example, a synthetic chemical, butylated hydroxytoluene (BHT), will stop the fat in corn chips going rotten.

In biscuits, bases such as sodium and ammonium hydrogen carbonate improve flavour and prevent changes in acidity and colour.

FLAVOURINGS
Drinks such as cola contain natural flavouring chemicals. But if the chemicals break up, flavour is lost. So synthetic chemicals, which are stronger tasting and less likely to break up, copy the natural chemicals.

EMULSIFIERS
Normally fat and water quickly separate. But emulsifiers, such as lecithin from egg yolk, keep them in place in yoghurt, chocolate, and ice cream.

COLOURINGS
Natural pigments may break up, leaving the food looking pale and unappetising. A stronger natural colouring, such as beta carotene from carrots, keeps your orange juice looking orange.

Sweets have synthetic colourings from dyes which tempt us to eat them.

PRESERVATIVES
Salts and sugar can poison and kill bacteria and fungi. This is why sodium nitrite is added to salami and hot dogs, and potassium sorbate to chilli dip. These preservatives make your food last longer.

FOOD PROCESSING

4000 B.C. Salt and chemicals in smoke are used to preserve food.

3000 B.C. Yeast is used to make alcoholic drinks by fermentation.

A.D. 200 Bacteria is used to make yoghurt by fermentation.

1810 Nicolas-François Appert (1752-1841) discovers a way of preserving food in sealed containers. Canning industry is developed from his discovery.

1860s Louis Pasteur (1822-95) invents a way of killing harmful microbes in wine and beer.

1920s Clarence Birdseye (1886-1956) develops a method for quick-freezing food.

Irradiation

Irradiation uses radiation to preserve foods. Radiation passes through the food, killing any organisms. But in fruits and vegetables, irradiation slows ripening and stops further growth. The technique also alters the molecules of the food itself, and can destroy vitamins and other nutrients. Because of this, and because fears about levels of radioactivity in treated food, irradiation remains a controversial technique.

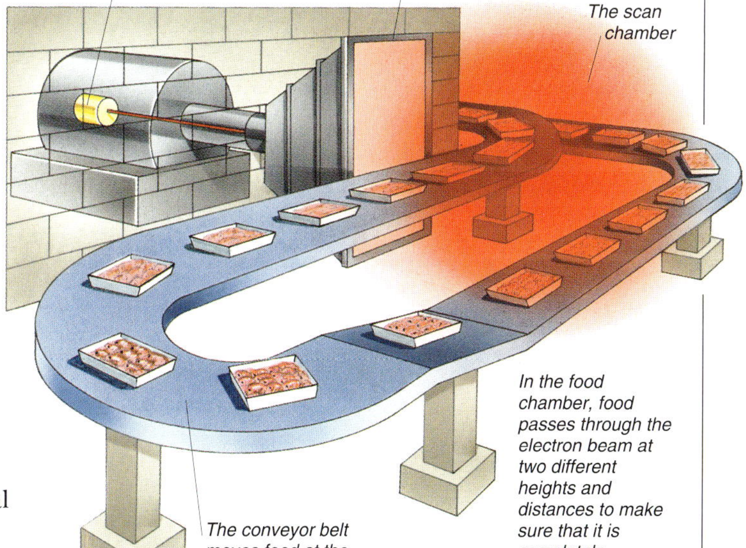

Electron gun releases high-energy electrons.

Scan horn keeps the electron beam in a small area of the processing plant.

The scan chamber

In the food chamber, food passes through the electron beam at two different heights and distances to make sure that it is completely irradiated.

The conveyor belt moves food at the correct speed to receive the permitted dose of radiation.

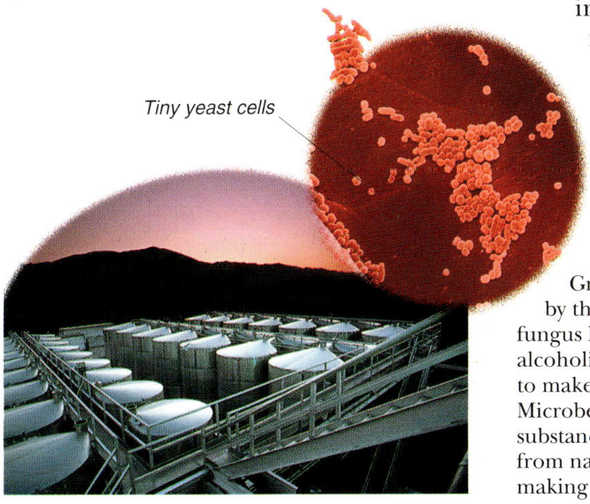

Tiny yeast cells

HELPFUL MICROBES
Grape juice in these vats is being turned into wine by the action of millions of tiny yeast cells. This fungus has been used for thousands of years in making alcoholic drinks and bread. Today, the use of microbes to make materials for us is called biotechnology. Microbes can make useful materials from unlikely substances. Some microbes can turn methanol, made from natural gas and waste products from the paper-making industry, into food for farm animals.

Find out more

Radioactivity p.26
Oxidation and reduction p.64
Chemistry of food p.78
Fermentation p.80
Fact Finder p.406

ALKALI INDUSTRY

THE SALT WE SPRINKLE on our food can also be used to make the soap that we rub on our skin. Salt, also known as sodium chloride, can be made into two different alkalis: sodium hydroxide and sodium carbonate. These are used to make many products. Of all the alkalis produced in the industry, these two are the most important. Each year, chemical plants throughout the world produce about 35 million tonnes of each alkali. Sodium hydroxide is made by passing a current of electricity through a salt solution called brine. This also produces chlorine, which is why the alkali industry is also known as the chlor-alkali industry. Sodium carbonate can be made from brine and carbon dioxide.

Sodium hydroxide is made by passing electricity through brine in these cells.

SODIUM HYDROXIDE

Salt dissolved in water consists of four different ions (particles): sodium, chloride, hydrogen, and hydroxide. During electrolysis, a current of electricity draws the negative ions (chloride and hydroxide) to the anode, and the positive ions (sodium and hydrogen) to the cathode. When separated from the chloride, sodium reacts with the water to form sodium hydroxide.

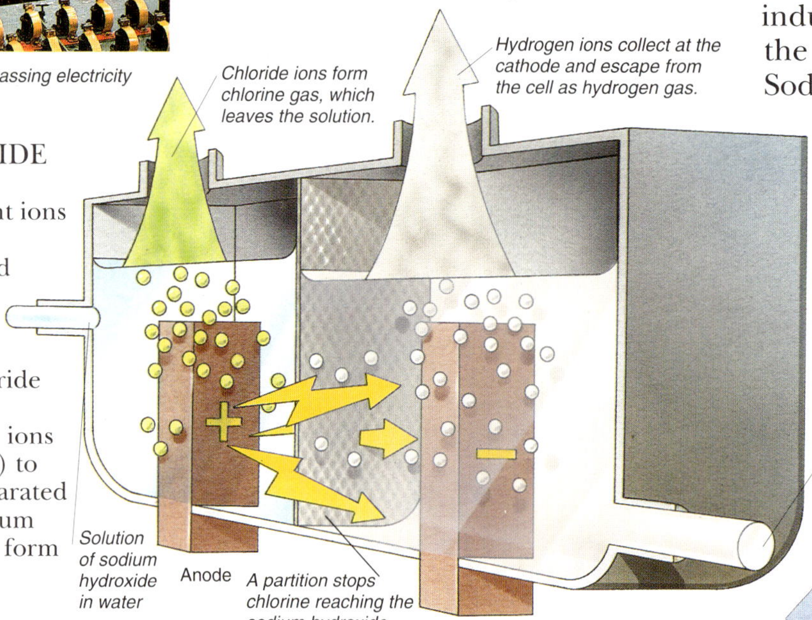

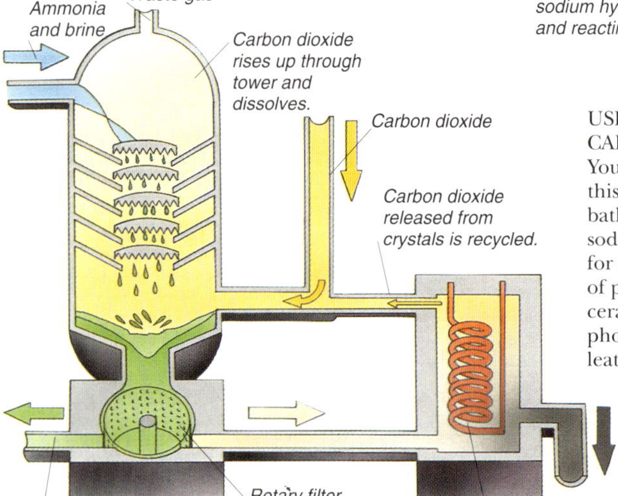

USING SODIUM CARBONATE

You've probably seen this alkali in the form of bath crystals or washing soda. But it is also used for making a wide range of products from ceramics and textiles to photographs and leather goods.

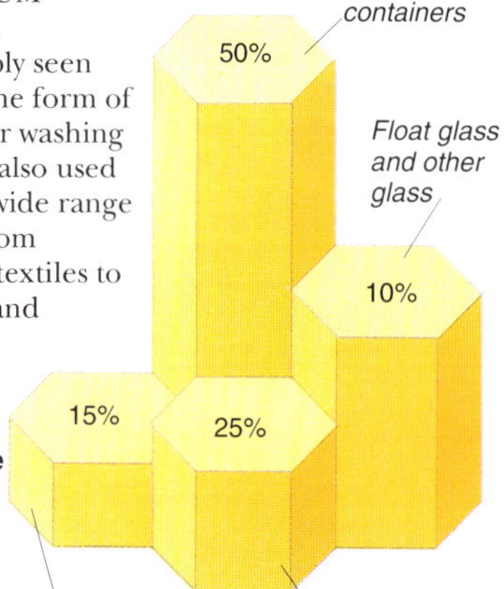

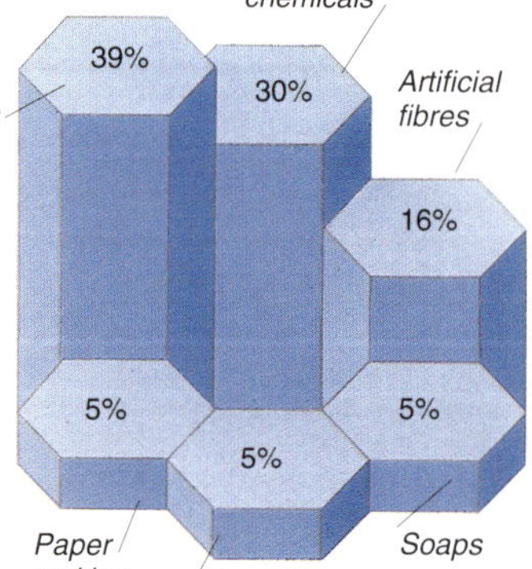

USING SODIUM HYDROXIDE

Alkalis are well known for neutralizing acids. But in industry, sodium hydroxide has many other uses, including making bleaches, drugs, dyes, and oil products, as well as processing foods, metals, and rubber.

SODIUM CARBONATE

Brine will absorb carbon dioxide to form sodium carbonate. In a process called the Solvay process, carbon dioxide is dissolved in brine and ammonia. This produces crystals of sodium hydrogen carbonate and ammonium hydroxide solution. The crystals are then heated to form sodium carbonate.

TRONA ORE
In parts of the United States and Africa, trona ore provides a source of sodium carbonate. Trona ore is sodium hydrogen carbonate, and is easily refined without using the Solvay process.

Find out more

BONDING P.28
ALKALI METALS P.34
HALOGENS P.46
ELECTROLYSIS P.67
ALKALIS AND BASES P.70
FACT FINDER P.406

SOAPS AND DETERGENTS

IMAGINE HOW DIRTY you would be without soap. Water can dissolve many dirty substances, but not grease. Certain salts of sodium, known as soap, can break up the grease so that the water can wash it away. Soap is made by reacting sodium hydroxide with animal and vegetable fats, or oils. Some kinds of water, however, contain chemicals that react with the soap to form a white insoluble powder, called scum. Detergents copy the action of soap without making scum. To make detergents, chemicals from crude oil are reacted with sulphuric acid.

DIFFERENT CLEANERS
Cleaners help us in many different ways. Soap coats your skin in grease-removing molecules. Shampoo has extra chemicals that make the lather stay in place on your hair while attacking the grease. Floor cleaner has chemicals called builders that clear away gritty dirt, while washing-up liquid has other chemicals to clear away greasy scraps of food.

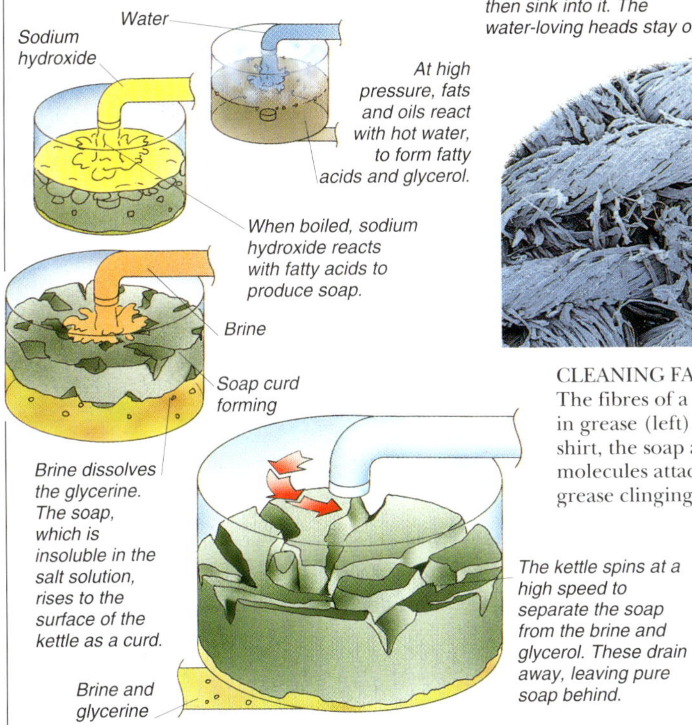

MAKING SOAP
To make soaps, fats or oils are heated to break them up into fatty acids and glycerol. The fatty acids will react with an alkali, such as sodium hydroxide, to produce soap. Brine removes the glycerol from the soap. Before the soap is made into blocks, flakes, or powders, chemicals are added to kill germs, add colour and scent, and soften water. Manufacturing a bar of soap from raw materials takes just 15 minutes.

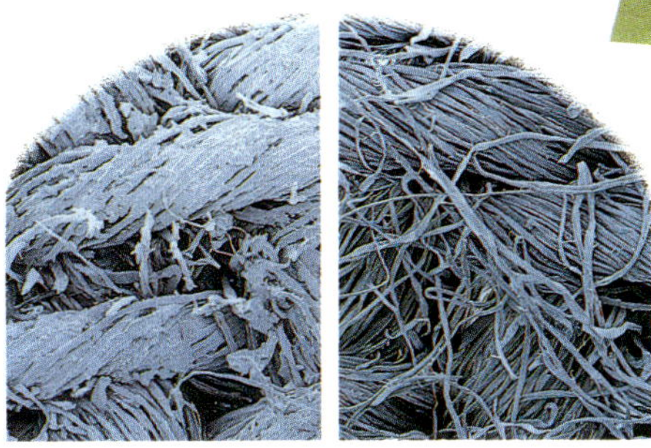

CLEANING FABRICS
The fibres of a cotton shirt are covered in grease (left). But when you wash the shirt, the soap and detergent molecules attack and remove the grease clinging to the fibres (right).

CLEANING IN ACTION

When you mop a floor, the soap or detergent works as hard as you do. Soap and detergent molecules have a head that is attracted to water and a tail that is attracted to grease. When you mix soap or detergent with water, the water-loving heads dissolve, while the grease-loving tails attach themselves to grease and lift it away from any surface.

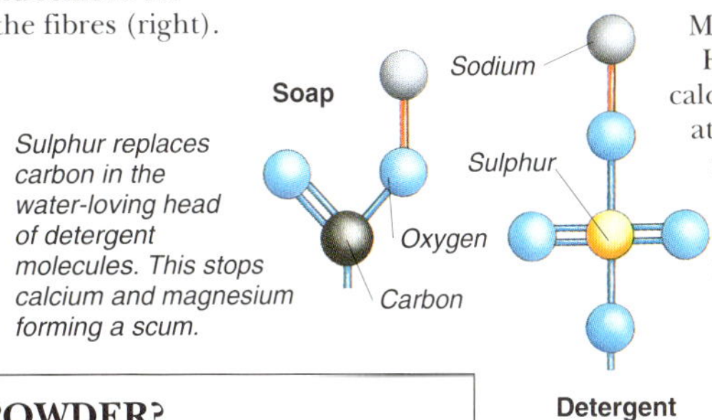

MOLECULE HEADS
Hard water contains calcium or magnesium atoms. These replace the sodium atom in the water-loving head of soap molecules, forming a powdery scum.

WHAT'S IN A WASHING POWDER?
Most powders contain enzymes to break down the molecules in sweat and bloodstains. Dyes, called brighteners, make clothes look brighter. Builders stop dirt settling back on cleaned clothes, soften the water, and keep the acidity constant for all the chemical reactions.

Find out more

PHOSPHORUS P.43
COMPOUNDS AND MIXTURES P.58
SOLUTIONS P.60
ALKALIS AND BASES P.70
CHEMISTRY OF WATER P.75
FACT FINDER P.406

COAL PRODUCTS

WHEN WE BURN COAL, we release energy and chemicals that were trapped for 250 million years. Back then, huge numbers of dying plants decomposed slowly to form coal. We use coal to provide the energy to spin electrical generators in power stations. Heating coal without air turns it into coke, which provides the energy in blast furnaces for making metals. When we process coke, it releases other chemicals – ammonia, a flammable gas, and tar. These can be changed into new chemicals to produce many different products, including dyes, paints, and medicine. In fact, more than 2,000 chemicals can be made from coal.

COAL IN THE MAKING
Swamp plants used the Sun's energy, and chemicals in their surroundings to make chemical energy in their cells. When the plants died, their remains turned into coal.

Coal gas contains hydrogen, methane, and carbon monoxide. It was first used for lighting in 1792. In the 19th century, coal gas provided energy for both lighting and cooking in many towns.

Ammonia gas is dissolved in sulphuric acid where it reacts to form crystals of ammonium sulphate. Until 1913, these crystals were the main source of fertilizers.

FROM COAL TO COKE

When coal is heated to a temperature between 900° – 1,300°C (1,650°–2,400°F) in ovens, without any air, a mixture of gases and liquids escape from it. These are separated into coal gas, a watery solution of ammonia called ammoniacal liquor, and coal tar. The solid left behind is called coke. It contains more than 80 per cent carbon.

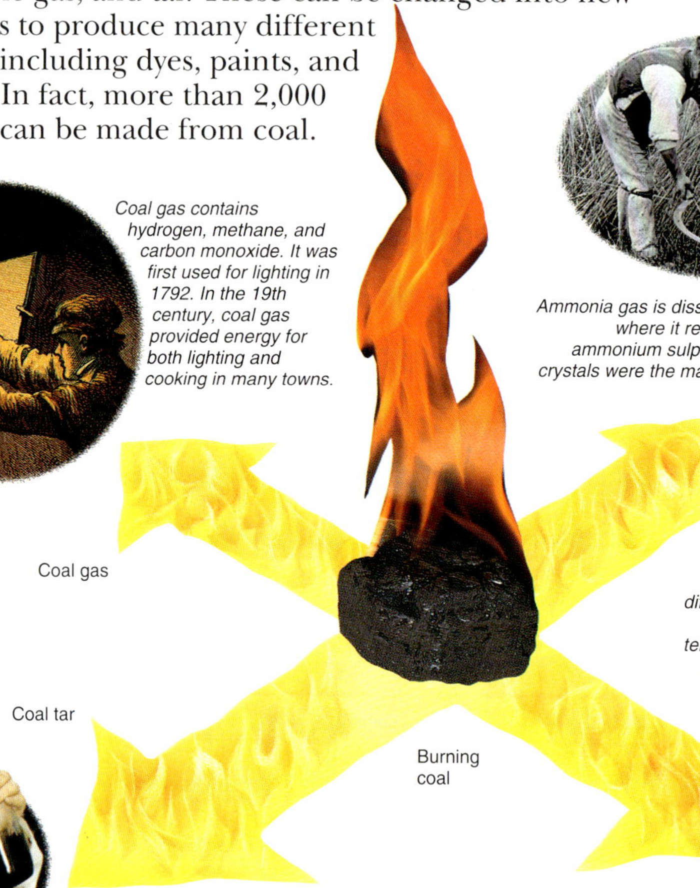

A range of cokes are made by heating different kinds of coal at either a low or high temperature. The cokes produced provide fuel for heating in homes and industries.

COAL TAR CHEMICALS
Coal tar contains several useful chemicals. These are separated by distillation, because each has a different boiling point. Chemicals with high boiling points include pitch and creosote. Those with lower boiling points include benzene and carbolic acid.

Spraying fruit trees with pesticides made from coal tar

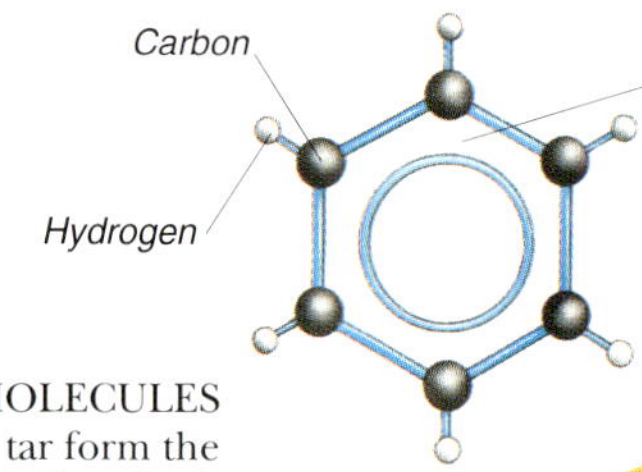

Benzene is a ring compound of hydrogen and carbon atoms.

Early dyes made from aniline – one of the compounds in coal tar.

Coal tar soap

USEFUL MOLECULES
The molecules in coal tar form the raw materials for making hundreds of new chemicals. By adding other chemicals to these molecules, thousands of useful products can be made. Creosote in its unrefined state is a wood preservative. If the different molecules in it are separated, they can be used for making pesticides and drugs.

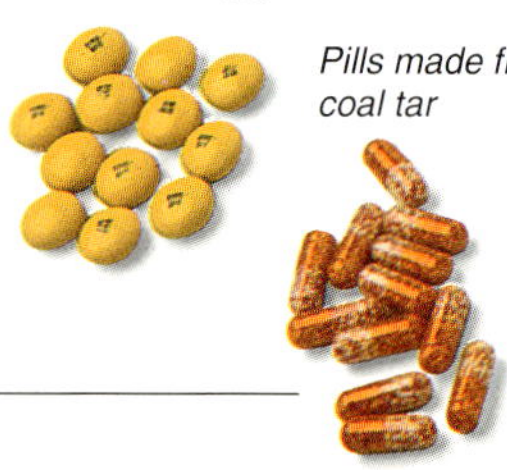

Pills made from coal tar

COLOURS AND KILLERS
In the 1850s, chemists made the first synthetic dyes from coal tar chemicals. They were brighter than most natural dyes, and did not fade in light or easily wash out of fabrics. When carbolic acid (a coal tar chemical) was discovered to have antiseptic properties, it was added to soap to kill germs.

Find out more

CARBON P.40
AMMONIA P.90
GAS PRODUCTS P.97
OIL PRODUCTS P.98
DYES AND PIGMENTS P.102
FACT FINDER P.406

GAS PRODUCTS

THE FLAME BURNING on a gas cooker marks the end of a long journey for a chemical called methane. The trip began millions of years ago, when the remains of tiny marine plants and animals formed natural gas that became trapped in rock. Most of this gas is methane, but there are many other chemicals in it too. In the 1930s, natural gas was cleaned of any impurities, and we began to use it as a fuel. Chemists soon discovered that these impurities could be used as raw materials in other industrial plants. Methane itself is also used as a raw material to produce hundreds of different products, from fertilizers to detergents. It can even be used to make protein.

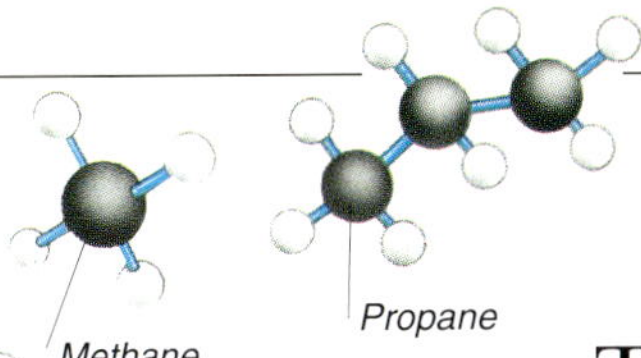

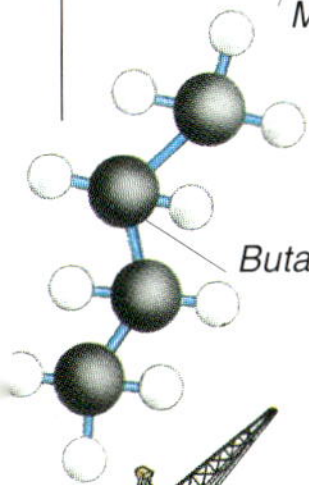

MIX OF GASES
There are four main gases in natural gas. The proportions vary, but a typical ratio is 80 per cent methane, 7 per cent ethane, 6 per cent propane, and 2.5 per cent butane.

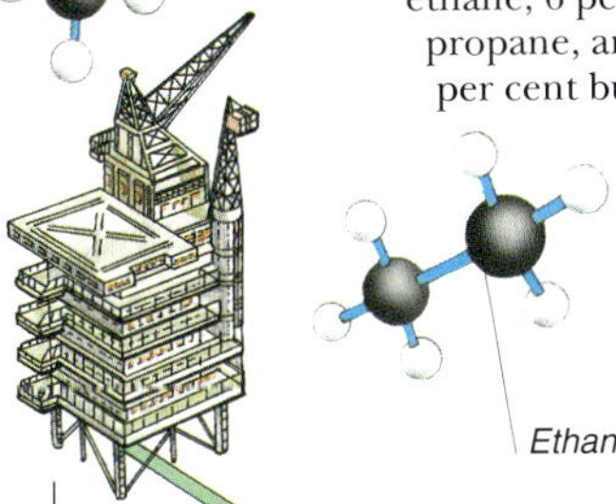

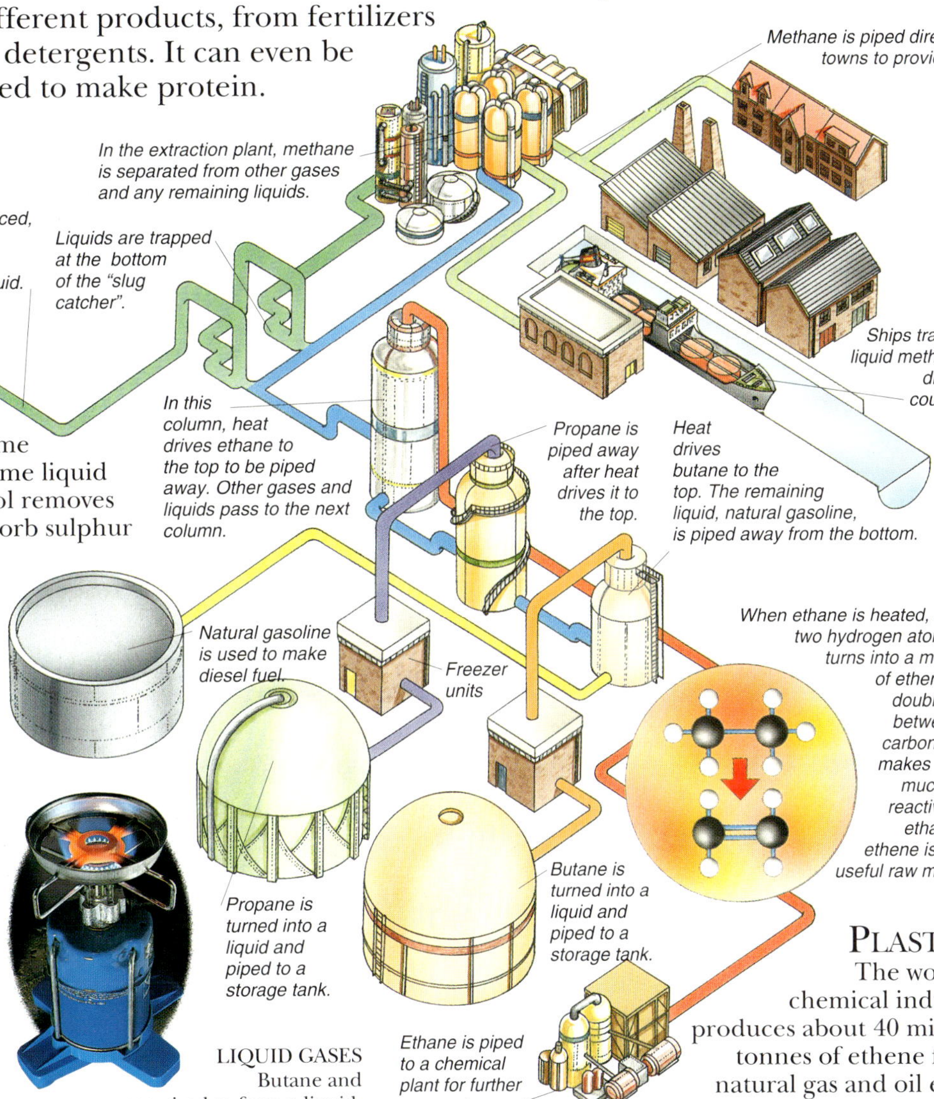

GAS SEPARATION

Impurities are removed from natural gas in a variety of ways. When the pressure is reduced, some of the heavier hydrocarbons become liquid and separate from the gas. Alcohol removes water, while special chemicals absorb sulphur and carbon dioxide from the gas.

LIQUID GASES
Butane and propane are pressurized to form a liquid. When the pressure is released, the liquid becomes a gas once more. Camping cookers, lanterns, and cigarette lighters rely on these liquefied gases.

USEFUL IMPURITIES
The chemicals removed as natural gas is purified have their uses too. Sulphur provides the raw material for making sulphuric acid. Hydrogen is used to make ammonia. And the uses of helium, a very light and unreactive gas, include filling balloons and controlling the pressure of rocket fuel.

PLASTICS

The world's chemical industry produces about 40 million tonnes of ethene from natural gas and oil every year. Ethene reacts easily with other chemicals, or even with itself, to form a range of plastic materials.

Plastic ducks and ski boots are just two of the many plastic products formed from ethene.

Find out more

CARBON P.40
BEHAVIOUR OF GASES P.51
SEPARATING MIXTURES P.61
COAL PRODUCTS P.96
OIL PRODUCTS P.98
OIL AND GAS P.239
FACT FINDER P.406

OIL PRODUCTS

OIL DOES NOT JUST PROVIDE the power to turn the wheels of a car, it covers the roads they run on too. Crude oil is a sticky, dark liquid that occurs naturally under the ground or the sea and has a pungent smell. Most of the substances found in crude oil are hydrocarbons: compounds of hydrogen and carbon atoms joined together in chains. They formed over 200 million years ago as the remains of marine plants and animals decayed. Early this century, chemists discovered that they could separate the different hydrocarbons in oil by heating them. Chemists now make thousands of products from crude oil.

Heavy, or long chain, hydrocarbons are black, thick, and waxy.

Light, or short chain, hydrocarbons are relatively pale and thin.

CRUDE OILS
Oil contains a mixture of hydrocarbons, each with a different number of carbon atoms in its chain. The proportion of hydrocarbons in oil varies from one place to another. Middle East oil has more long molecules, which makes the oil thick. North Sea oil has fewer long molecules and is thinner.

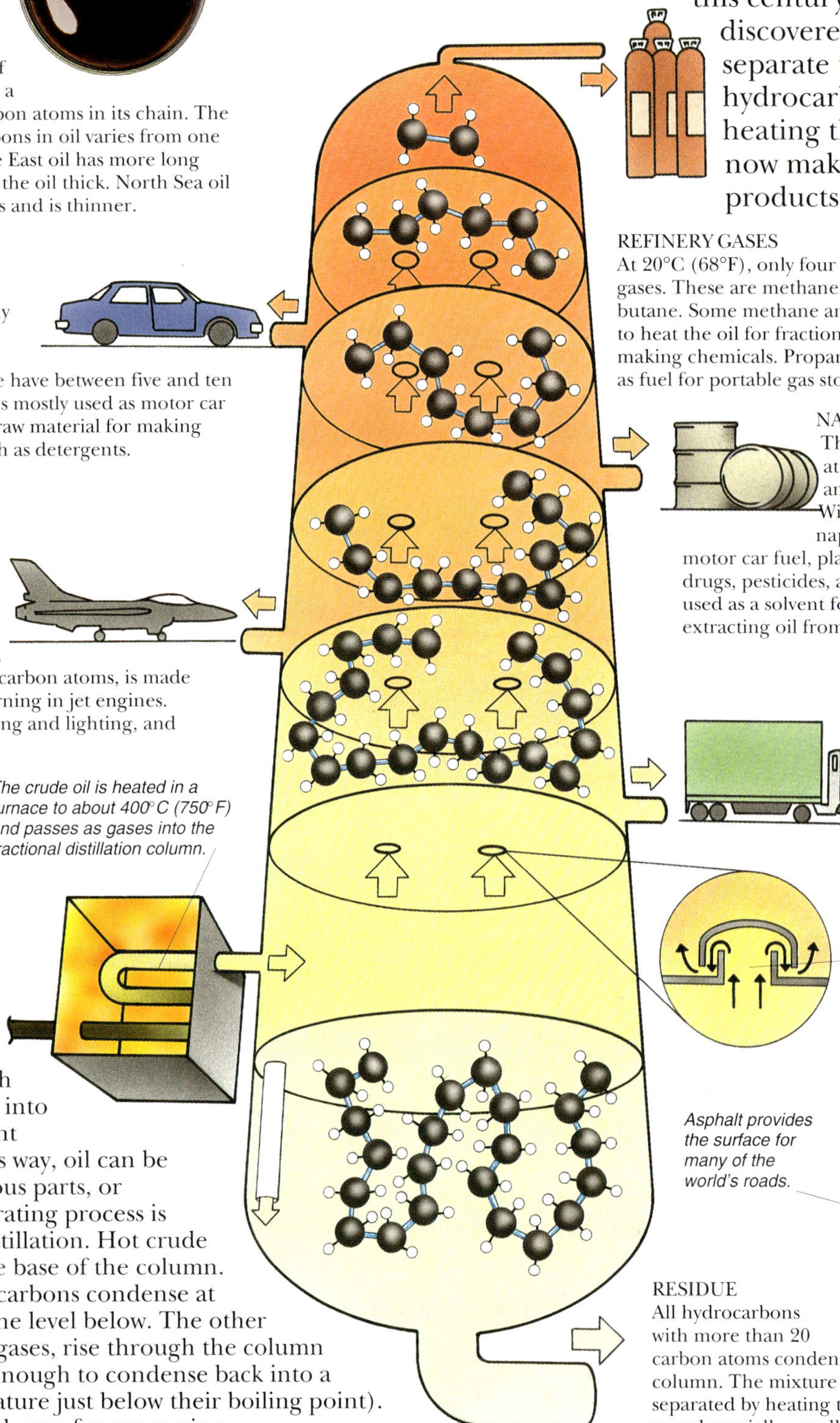

REFINERY GASES
At 20°C (68°F), only four hydrocarbons remain as gases. These are methane, ethane, propane, and butane. Some methane and ethane is used as a fuel to heat the oil for fractionating, but most is used for making chemicals. Propane and butane are bottled as fuel for portable gas stoves and lights.

GASOLINE
Between 20° and 70°C (70°–160°F) a thin, runny liquid runs out. This is called gasoline. The hydrocarbons in gasoline have between five and ten carbon atoms. Gasoline is mostly used as motor car fuel, but it also acts as a raw material for making plastics or chemicals such as detergents.

NAPHTHA
This yellow liquid condenses at temperatures between 70° and 160°C (150°–320°F). With 8–12 carbon atoms, naphtha can be made into motor car fuel, plastics, and chemicals for drugs, pesticides, and fertilizers. It is also used as a solvent for processing rubber or extracting oil from seeds.

KEROSENE
A light oily liquid called kerosene condenses at temperatures between 160° and 250°C (320°–480°F). Kerosene, with between 10 and 16 carbon atoms, is made into aviation fuel for burning in jet engines. Paraffin is used for heating and lighting, and in solvents for paints.

GAS OIL
At this level, which is kept at 250°–350°C (480°–660°F), gas oil condenses. It has between 14 and 20 carbon atoms. Gas oil is used to make diesel fuel and central heating oil. It also makes asphalt softer and easier to spread.

The crude oil is heated in a furnace to about 400°C (750°F) and passes as gases into the fractional distillation column.

Gases pass up the column through bubble caps. If the temperature is cool enough, the gas condenses on the cap and runs off as a liquid.

FRACTIONAL DISTILLATION

When crude oil is heated to a certain temperature, the hydrocarbons in it turn into different gases. Each gas condenses back into a liquid at a different temperature. In this way, oil can be separated into various parts, or fractions. The separating process is called fractional distillation. Hot crude oil is fed in near the base of the column. The heaviest hydrocarbons condense at once and fall into the level below. The other hydrocarbons, still gases, rise through the column until they cool off enough to condense back into a liquid (at a temperature just below their boiling point). They are then piped away for processing.

Asphalt provides the surface for many of the world's roads.

RESIDUE
All hydrocarbons with more than 20 carbon atoms condense as soon as they enter the column. The mixture of heavy hydrocarbons is separated by heating to produce lubricating oil, petroleum jelly, candle wax, and bitumen.

BREAKING UP MOLECULES

Separating the hydrocarbons in oil by fractional distillation gives more long chain molecules than we can use and not enough small ones such as naphtha and gasoline. Catalytic cracking splits, or cracks, the larger molecules into more useful, smaller ones. Cracking involves heating the heavy oil under pressure in a special cracking chamber. Some of the bonds between the carbon atoms break to leave a mixture of shorter chain hydrocarbons. By using a catalyst, the process is speeded up and cracking can take place at a lower temperature.

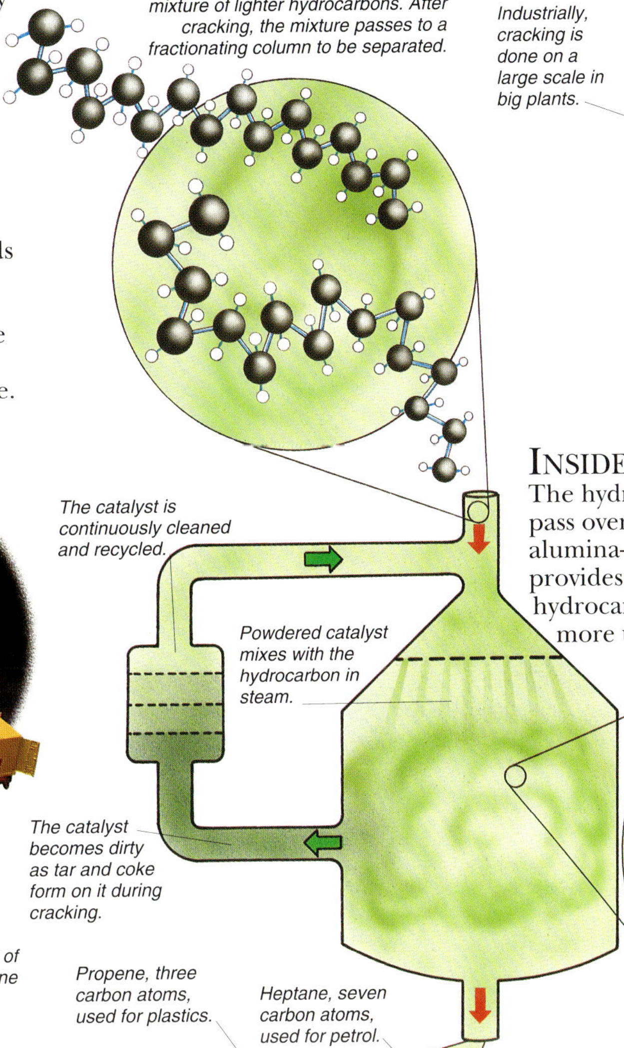

Industrially, cracking is done on a large scale in big plants.

INSIDE THE CRACKER

The hydrocarbons, heated by steam, pass over the hot catalyst of powdered alumina-silica gel. The catalyst provides a huge surface on which the hydrocarbons break up into smaller, more useful hydrocarbons.

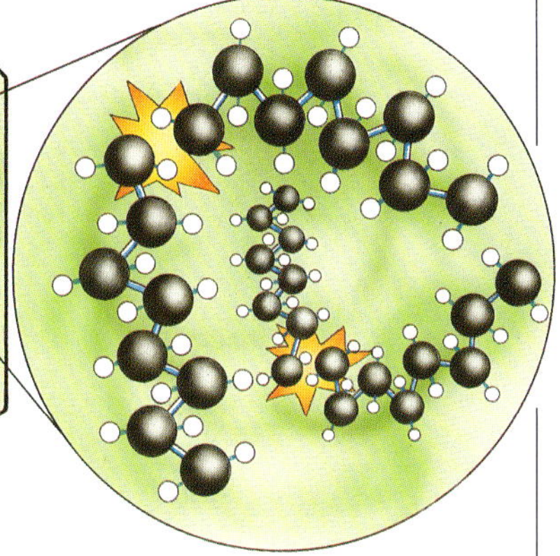

Polyethene toys

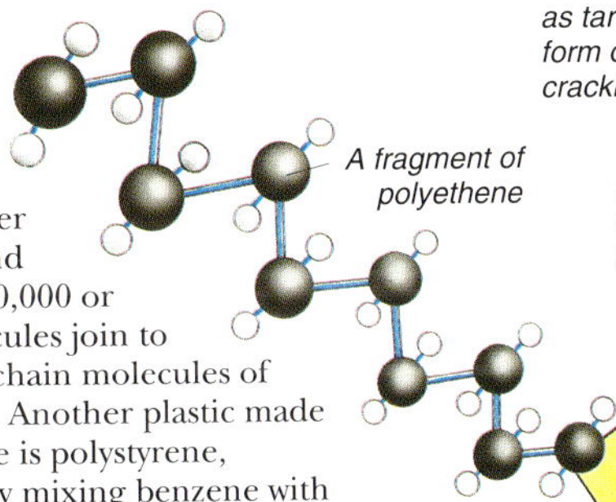

A fragment of polyethene

PLASTICS
Heat ethene under pressure, and groups of 30,000 or more molecules join to make long chain molecules of polyethene. Another plastic made from ethene is polystyrene, produced by mixing benzene with ethene. One use of polystyrene is to make safe toys for children. Ethene and chlorine make polyvinyl chloride (PVC).

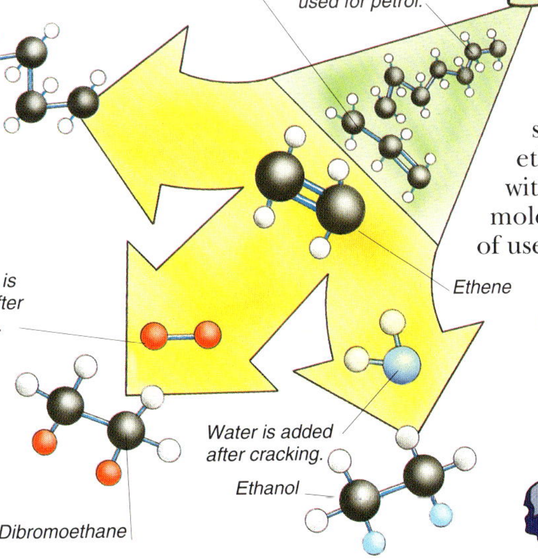

ETHENE'S MANY USES

After cracking, the compounds are separated by fractionation. One of them, ethene, is so reactive that it can easily join with many chemicals, and even other ethene molecules, to be converted into a wide range of useful liquids and solids.

Ethene reacts with water to provide a solvent for paints and perfumes.

PETROL ADDITIVE
Adding bromine to ethene produces dibromoethane which is used as an octane booster for motor fuels. It prevents petrol igniting too quickly in the engine and causing "knocking" which reduces the engine's performance.

ETHANOL
Ethene and water combine to produce ethanol, a solvent used for manufacturing many paints, cosmetics, perfumes, soaps, and dyes. Adding oxygen to ethanol produces ethanoic acid, used in making synthetic fibres.

Find out more

ATOMIC STRUCTURE P.24
BONDING P.28
CRYSTALS P.30
ROCKS AND MINERALS P.221
FACT FINDER P.406

POLYMERS

Table tennis balls are still made from celluloid.

IS THAT A POLYMER GROWING out of your head? The fibres that make up your hair are made of long, strong, flexible molecules. They are polymers – long, winding chains made up of thousands of smaller molecules, called monomers, linked together. Polymers are common and useful molecules. Natural polymers not only make up hair, but also the cellulose in plants, and the wool of sheep. Polymers can also be made from chemicals. All plastics and many of the clothes we wear are made in this way. The first synthetic polymer, Parkesine, was made by English chemist Alexander Parkes in the 1850s. Today, chemicals are made into a wide range of polymers. They can be designed for particular jobs.

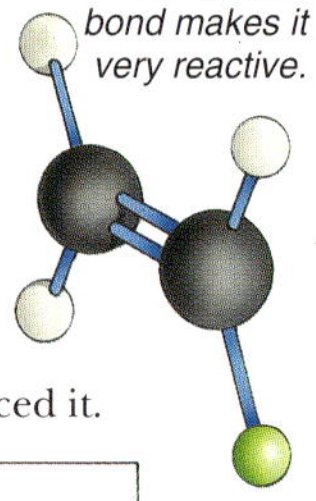

This is vinyl chloride, the monomer that makes PVC. The double bond makes it very reactive.

CELLULOID

By changing the ingredients of Parkesine, an American chemist, John Hyatt, made celluloid. This was used for making spectacle frames and photographic film, but other plastics have now replaced it.

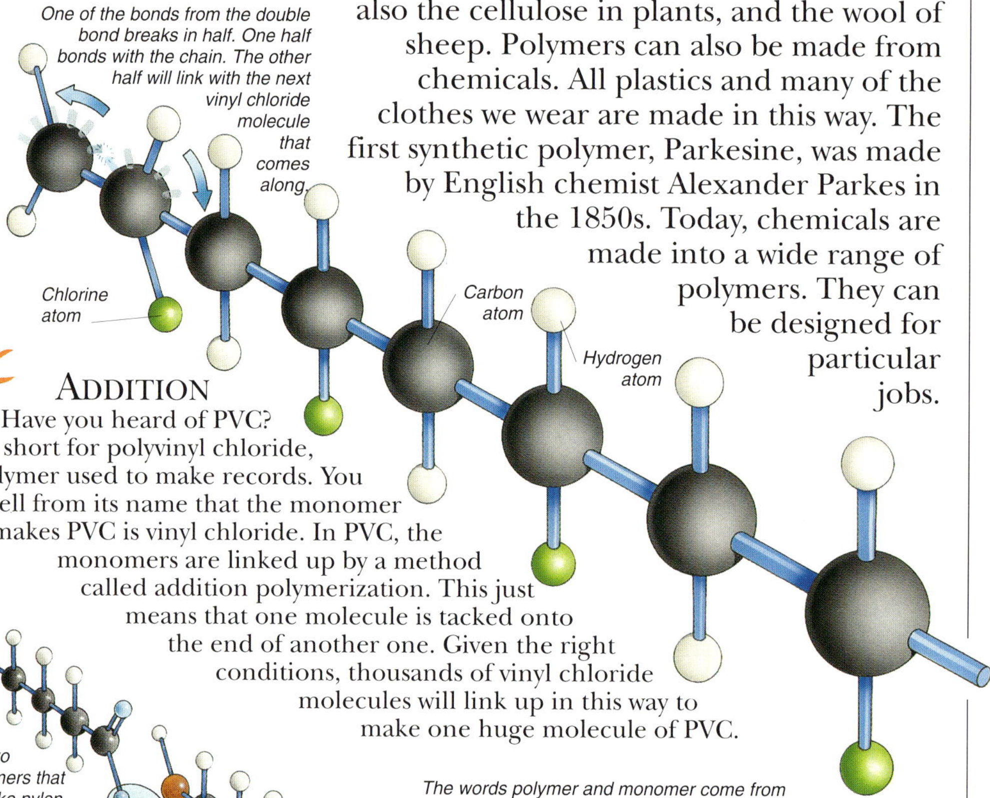

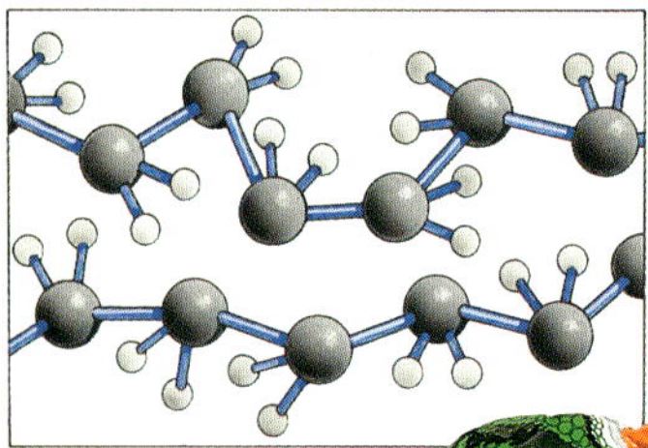

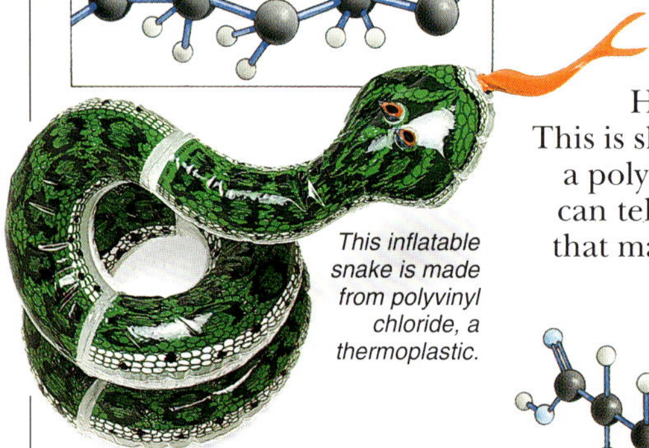

This inflatable snake is made from polyvinyl chloride, a thermoplastic.

ADDITION

Have you heard of PVC? This is short for polyvinyl chloride, a polymer used to make records. You can tell from its name that the monomer that makes PVC is vinyl chloride. In PVC, the monomers are linked up by a method called addition polymerization. This just means that one molecule is tacked onto the end of another one. Given the right conditions, thousands of vinyl chloride molecules will link up in this way to make one huge molecule of PVC.

THERMOPLASTIC

The way that polymer chains are arranged affects the way a plastic behaves when it is heated. In a thermoplastic, the chains are arranged side by side, with no links between them. When heated, the chains slide over each other, and the plastic melts. It sets again when the temperature falls.

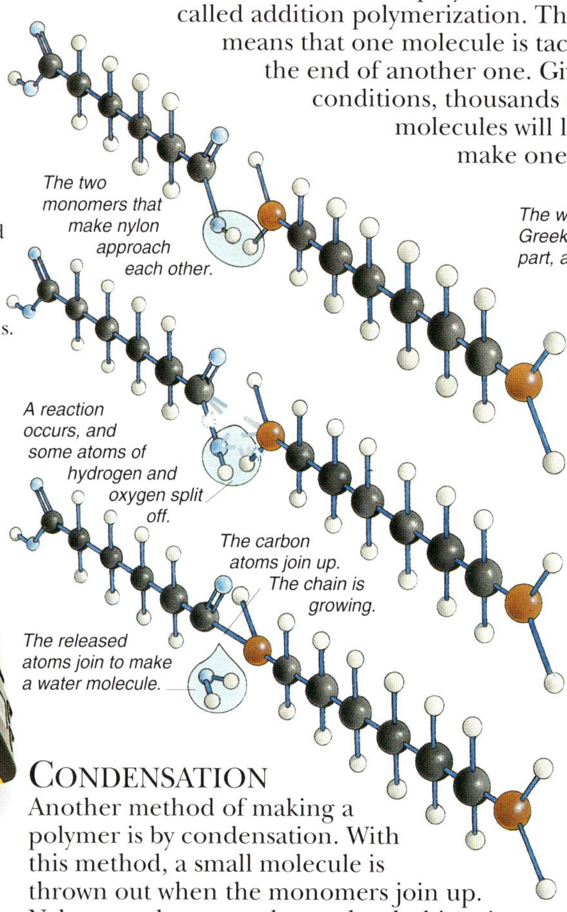

The words polymer and monomer come from Greek words. "Poly" means many, "mer" means part, and "mono" means one.

PLASTIC PELLETS

Most plastics are produced in the form of granules or pellets. Polystyrene granules are white, polyethene granules are transparent. When these pellets are melted, they can be coloured and made into whatever object is required.

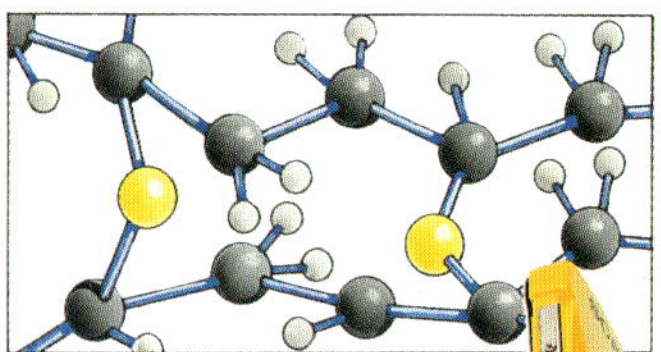

The delicate electronic components of this personal stereo are protected in a case made from a thermoset.

THERMOSET

Polymers such as melamine and silicone are thermosets. Their polymer chains are linked together to form a strong network. When heated, the chains cannot move, and so the plastic does not melt.

CONDENSATION

Another method of making a polymer is by condensation. With this method, a small molecule is thrown out when the monomers join up. Nylon, a polymer used to make clothing, is made in this way. It is made from the linking of two monomers. Every time one monomer joins onto the chain, a molecule of water is released.

BAKELITE

During an experiment, American chemist Leo Baekeland (1863-1944) found a sticky mess in the bottom of his apparatus. On heating, this softened and then set into a hard solid. He improved its properties to make a tough, resistant plastic that could be moulded into different shapes. He called it Bakelite. It was used to make cameras, telephones, and plugs.

Using polymers

Freshly made polymer granules have little use on their own. But if they are heated, they will fuse together to make a substance that can be easily shaped. The types of material that polymers make are very useful because they are very strong, and yet very light in weight.

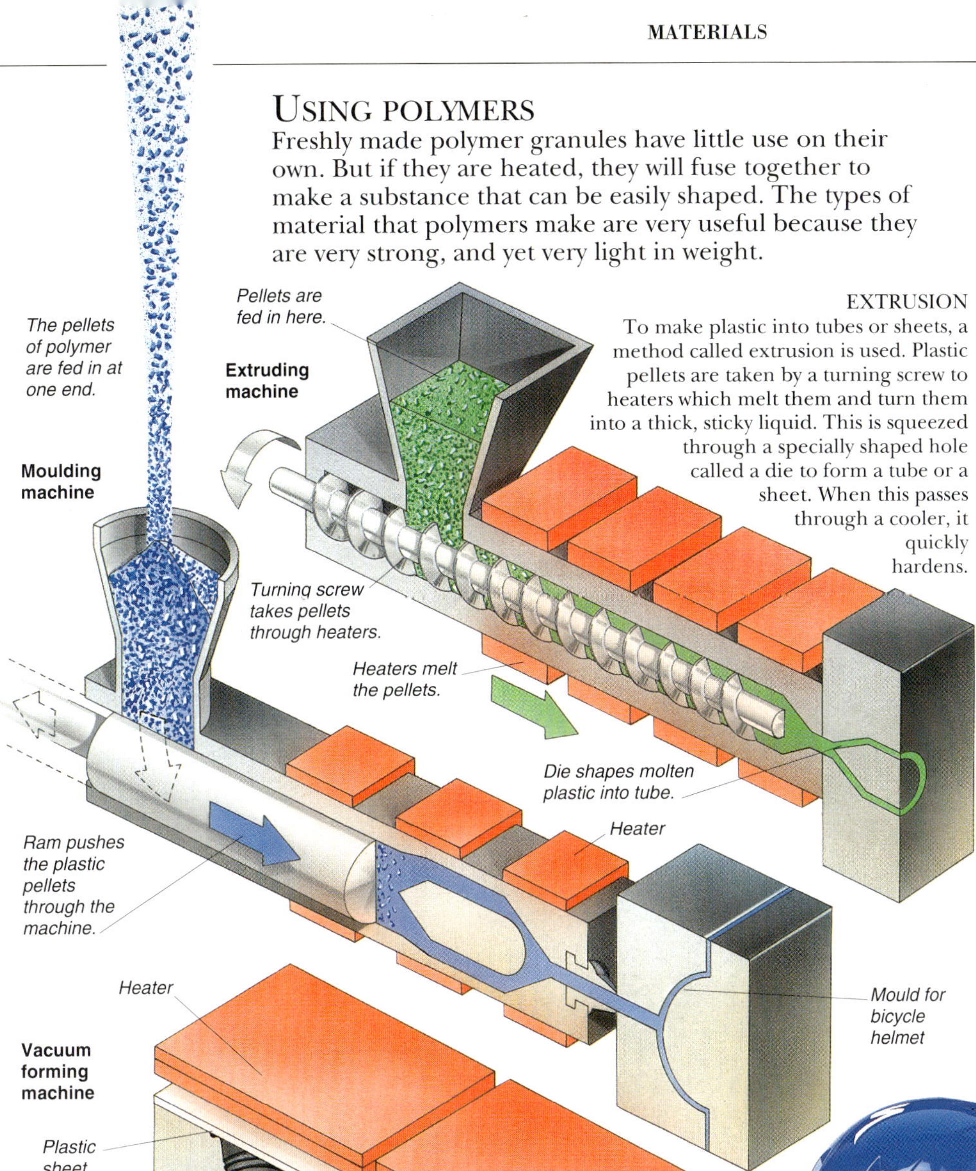

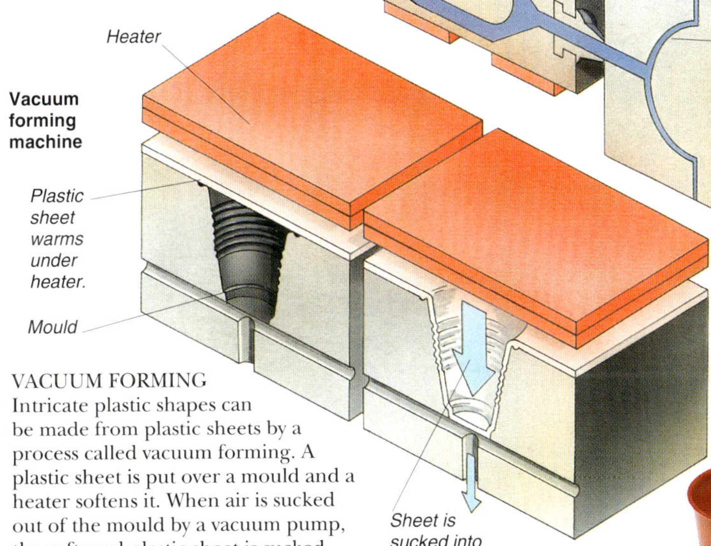

EXTRUSION

To make plastic into tubes or sheets, a method called extrusion is used. Plastic pellets are taken by a turning screw to heaters which melt them and turn them into a thick, sticky liquid. This is squeezed through a specially shaped hole called a die to form a tube or a sheet. When this passes through a cooler, it quickly hardens.

RUBBER

Rubber, a gum extracted from tropical trees, is a natural polymer. Its molecules have twists and loops in them which give rubber its elasticity. Raw rubber is weak, as its molecules are not linked together. To make these links, it is heated with sulphur in a process called vulcanization. This toughened rubber allows tyres to squash and stretch without breaking.

Miles of tubing can be made by an extruding machine.

MOULDING

One way of turning plastic into special shapes is by a method called moulding. A ram pushes the pellets through a machine where heaters melt them. The hot, liquid plastic is then forced into a mould. Water cools the mould and makes the plastic set.

Up to 90 bicycle helmets an hour can be made on one moulding machine.

VACUUM FORMING

Intricate plastic shapes can be made from plastic sheets by a process called vacuum forming. A plastic sheet is put over a mould and a heater softens it. When air is sucked out of the mould by a vacuum pump, the softened plastic sheet is sucked into the mould by the air pressure above. When it is cooled, the plastic shape can be turned out of the mould.

This quick and simple process makes millions of plastic cups every day.

STEPHANIE KWOLECK

An American research chemist, Stephanie Kwoleck (born 1923) has made many discoveries about polymers. She discovered a solvent that could make Kevlar aramid fibre. Its threads are stronger than steel, yet very light. It is used to build spacecraft and bullet-proof vests.

RECYCLING PLASTICS

Some plastics can be recycled. Polyethene terephthalate (PET), used for drink bottles, is collected into bales, cleaned, and then shredded into chips that can be used again. Biodegradable plastic bottles are made from a polymer of a sugar, glucose. Microbes on a rubbish tip will break them down into carbon dioxide and water.

Find out more

Carbon p.40
Organic chemistry p.41
Chemical reactions p.52
Oil products p.98
Fibres p.107
Fact finder p.406

DYES AND PIGMENTS

It took 9,000 whelk shells to make just one gram of purple dye for a Roman Emperor's toga.

WE LIVE IN A COLOURFUL WORLD. Most of the objects around us have been coloured by dyes or pigments. Dyes colour the fibres in our clothes, in paper, leather, and even food. Dyes can dissolve in water so they can get into the nooks and crannies of a fibre. Here, they bond to the fabric in a chemical reaction. Pigments are coloured particles which do not dissolve in water. This means they can only coat the surface of a material and they do not react chemically with it. They are used to make paints, printing inks, and for colouring plastics.

Shell of the murex whelk

The cuttlefish is not a fish, but a mollusc, related to the octopus. Its ink contains a natural pigment.

The pigments in this ink are made from organic chemicals.

PIGMENTS

The cuttlefish escapes from its predators by squirting a cloud of black ink into their path. The pigment in this ink was used to give photographs a brown tint in the 19th century. Today, however, most pigments are made from organic chemicals that give bright colours and do not fade too quickly.

NATURAL OR SYNTHETIC

There are thousands of different dyes. Natural dyes are made from plants such as the woad or madder, or shellfish such as the murex whelk. Synthetic dyes are made by adding sulphur or chlorine to the colourless chemicals made by distilling petroleum or coal tar.

Mordant dyeing process

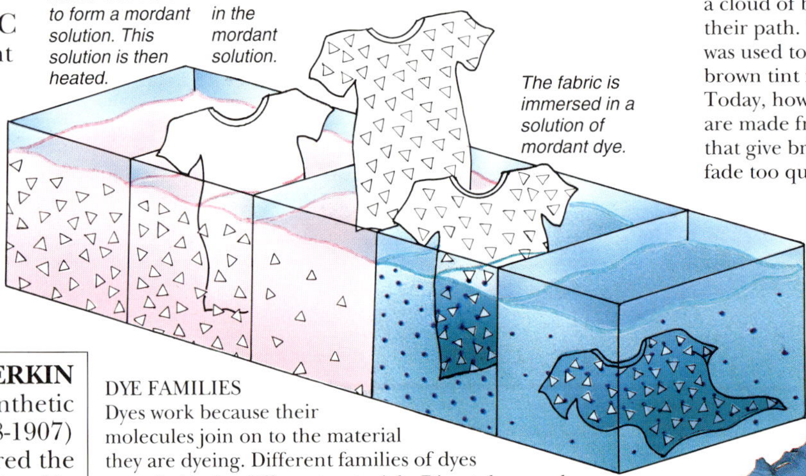

The dye will hold fast, which means it will not fade when the fabric is washed.

WILLIAM PERKIN

While trying to make synthetic quinine, William Perkin (1838-1907) accidentally discovered the first synthetic dye. He extracted a purple substance from the mixture he was working on and found it could dye silk. He called it mauve. Perkin went on to build a dye-works. This was the start of the dye industry.

DYE FAMILIES

Dyes work because their molecules join on to the material they are dyeing. Different families of dyes are suitable for different materials. Direct dyes work best on fabrics that are only washed occasionally, such as curtains. Vat dyes are ideal for fabrics that need frequent washes. Mordant dyes will not colour a fabric on their own. In the mordant dyeing process, an extra chemical (a metal compound) fixes the dye molecules to the fabric.

PAINTS

All paints contain a pigment to give them colour. But they also need a chemical called a binder to hold the pigment in place, and a solvent so the paint can flow easily. Some paints have water as their solvent. Gloss paints, however, have a white spirit solvent. This is why they have such a strong smell.

1. Pigment particles give the paint its colour. Each particle in this powder may be as small as a millionth of a centimetre across.

2. The pigment is mixed with the binder so that the particles can spread out evenly.

DRYING PAINT

When a surface is painted and left to dry, the solvent in the paint evaporates into the air. This leaves the binder and the pigment close together. They react to form a tough weather-resistant film. Paint may also contain a white pigment. This scatters light back to our eyes so that we can clearly see the paint colour.

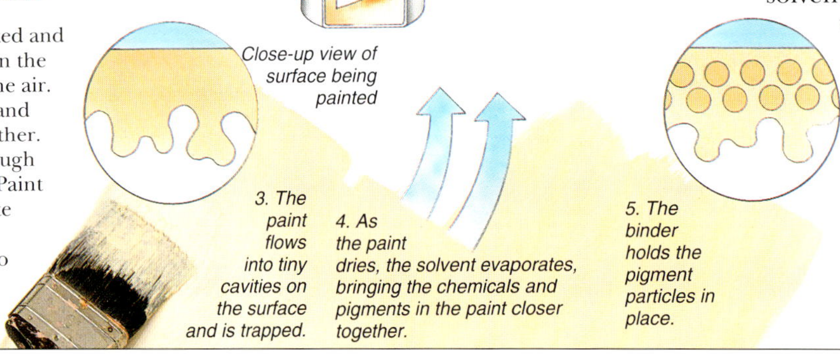

Find out more

BONDING P.28
ORGANIC CHEMISTRY P.41
SOLUTIONS P.60
COAL PRODUCTS P.96
COSMETICS P.103
FACT FINDER P.406

COSMETICS

AS LONG AGO as 5000 B.C., the Ancient Egyptians used cosmetics to change their looks. Their cosmetics were made from ground-up minerals. The cosmetics we use today are made from a mixture of chemicals. Many of these come from the petroleum industry. They are mixed with plants, oils, waxes, talcs, clays, and various metal compounds. When a new cosmetic is made, great care is taken to make sure the chemicals it contains do not harm the skin. There are tighter controls on make-up such as lipsticks, as these may accidentally get into the mouth. In the past, the chemicals were tested on animals but today, more companies are finding new ways to test the chemicals.

ANCIENT COSMETICS
Fashionable Egyptian women wore kohl to blacken their hair, eyebrows, and eyelashes. They also used malachite powder as eye-shadow. Kohl is made from naturally occurring lead sulphide, called galena. Malachite is made from ground copper carbonate.

BEFORE AND AFTER
Cosmetics were applied to one half of this model's face to show how they can change a person's appearance. The first step was to apply the foundation cream to help keep the make-up in place. Next, a mixture of peach, yellow, and white powders was applied to the skin. These cover marks on the skin such as blueness below the eyes or redness caused by blood vessels close to the surface of the skin.

ANCIENT TRADITIONS
For many years, people have coloured their skins with substances from plants, animals, clays, and minerals. The reasons for doing this ranged from showing the rank of a person in society, to preparation for a special ceremony. Today, the people of New Guinea still keep these ancient traditions alive.

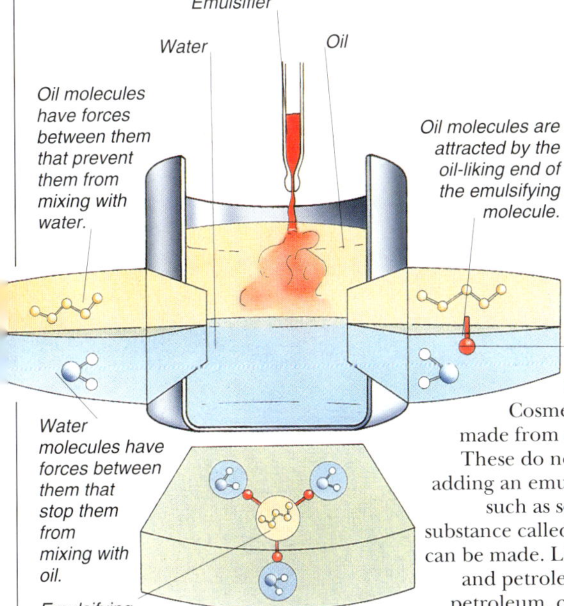

Emulsifying molecules link the oil and water together. This forms an oil-in-water emulsion.

These are some of the cosmetics you'll see in any department store. Each one comes in a variety of shades to match your skin type.

As nails are a fairly tough part of the body, nail varnish contains chemicals that cannot be used elsewhere. It consists of a pigment in an organic solvent such as acetone.

EMULSIONS
Cosmetics are often made from oil and water. These do not mix, but by adding an emulsifying agent such as soap, a creamy substance called an emulsion can be made. Liquid paraffin and petroleum jelly from petroleum, castor oil from beans, and lanolin from wool grease make up the oily part of an emulsion.

WHAT ARE COSMETICS MADE OF?
Every cosmetic contains a mix of chemicals. Nail varnish has at least 11 chemicals. It usually contains resin, plasticizer, solvents, and pigments. Foundation cream contains up to 23 chemicals. It is an oil-in-water emulsion that contains a complex mixture of acids and alcohols.

Find out more

COMPOUNDS AND MIXTURES P.58
SOLUTIONS P.60
SOAPS AND DETERGENTS P.95
COAL PRODUCTS P.96
DYES AND PIGMENTS P.102
FACT FINDER P.406

CHEMISTRY IN MEDICINE

Over 200 years ago, a brew containing foxglove leaves was used to treat people with heart failure. Many years later, these leaves were found to contain the drug called digitoxin. Today, digitoxin is still used to treat heart failure.

Foxglove plant

Chunks of willow bark

YOUR BODY IS MADE from thousands of different chemicals. If these are not working properly, you become ill. A doctor may treat you by giving you more chemicals in the form of medicines. This treatment of illness is not new. Over 2,000 years ago, the people of Ancient Mesopotamia used 250 different plants and 120 minerals to treat ailments. Many of these were still used in the 19th century, when the chemicals from plants were put into tablets. But some of these gave people a second illness, called a side-effect. Today, scientists are able to make chemicals similar to the natural ones. By altering the molecules slightly, they can prevent side-effects.

NATURAL DRUGS
The Greek doctor Hippocrates used willow bark as long ago as 400 B.C. to relieve the pain of his patients. But it also caused stomach irritation. The bark contains a chemical called salicylic acid. In 1893, a German chemist, Felix Hoffman, made a very similar chemical from coal tar, which had fewer side-effects. This drug is now known as aspirin. Over 100,000 million aspirin tablets are taken every year throughout the world.

DEVELOPING A DRUG

A new drug is made to treat a specific illness. Up to 30 chemicals may be selected for the first set of drug tests. These may have been made from chemicals in plants, or chemicals from the laboratory. The chemicals are tested for poisonous effects. For example, they may break down to form harmful substances. The tests take three years and only very few chemicals will pass them.

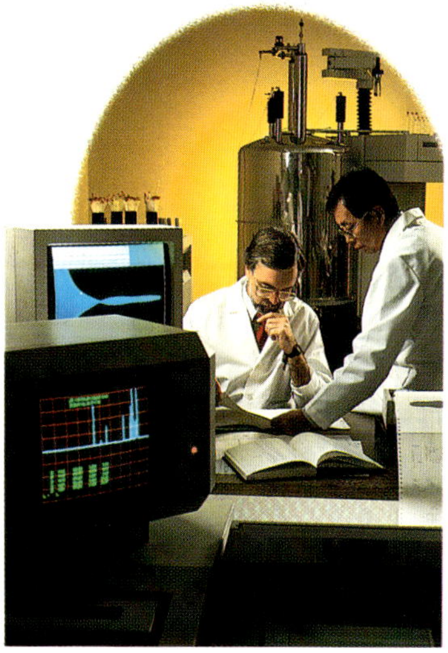

TRACKING THE DRUG
The chemicals that pass the first drug tests are carefully tested on healthy humans to investigate any side-effects they may give. Samples of each chemical are made slightly radioactive, so that their movement through the body can be tracked with an instrument called a Geiger counter.

PAUL EHRLICH
The German doctor Paul Ehrlich (1854-1915) sought a "magic bullet" which would kill disease-giving bacteria, but would leave human cells undamaged. He thought that dyes that could stain bacteria but not other cells might be a good starting point.
The first synthetic drug he discovered was the dye trypan red for treating sleeping sickness. Ehrlich later found that a very similar chemical, salvarsan, could cure syphilis.

DRUG TEST
After eight years of testing, one drug is selected. One group of patients is given tablets that contain the drug. A second group is given placebos (inactive drugs). The effectiveness of the drug can be assessed by comparing these two groups.

HOW DRUGS WORK
Every cell of your body has receptors on its surface. Some drugs are thought to work by their interaction with these receptors. Adrenaline is a chemical your body produces. It makes your heart beat faster in times of stress. A drug called salbutamol relaxes lung muscles by joining adrenaline on the receptors of lung muscle cells. But another drug called propranolol blocks off receptors on heart muscle cells. This prevents adrenaline from reaching the receptors. In this way, it prevents a heart from beating dangerously fast.

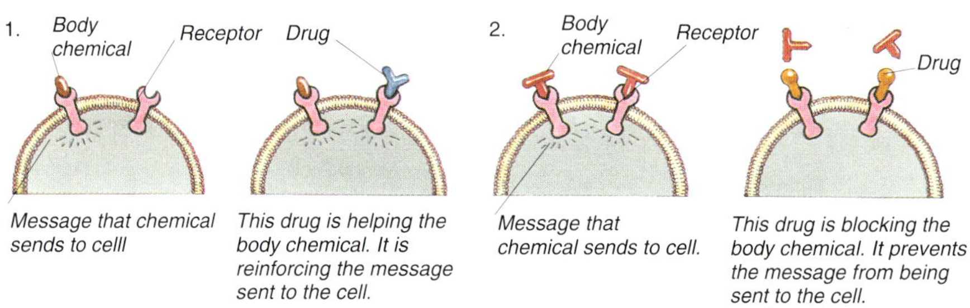

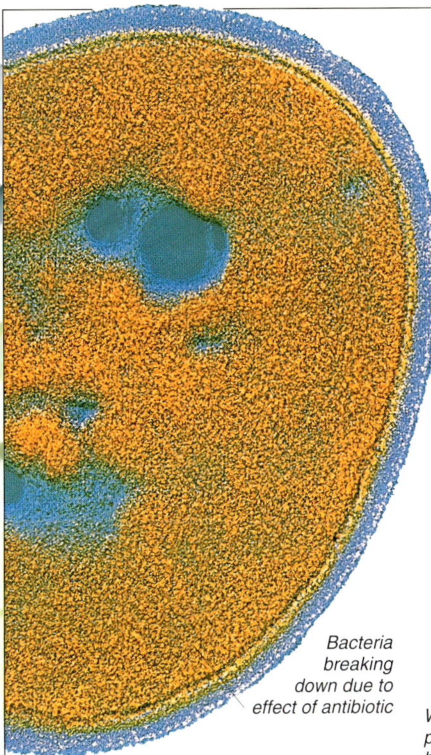

Bacteria breaking down due to effect of antibiotic

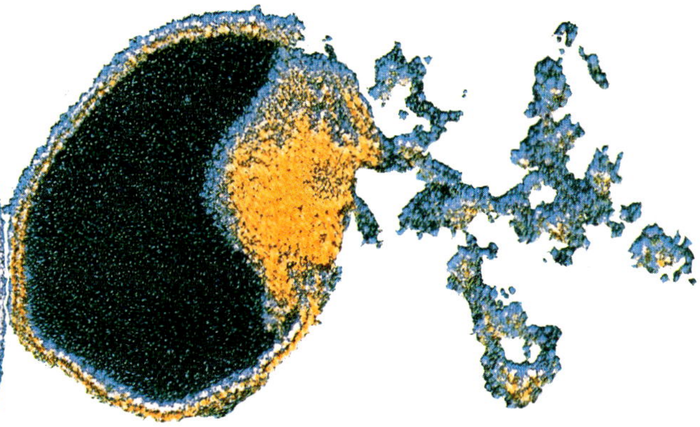

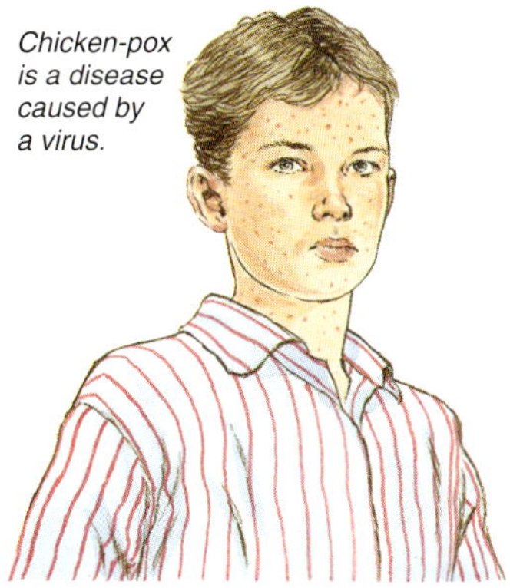

Chicken-pox is a disease caused by a virus.

BACTERIA

Organisms called bacteria cause diseases such as tonsillitis. They can be killed by chemicals called antibiotics. Early antibiotics, such as one called penicillin, were all made from moulds and fungi. Today, most are created from other chemicals. There are two main ways in which antibiotics work. One type prevents the bacteria from making its cell walls. Another type interferes with the chemical activities in the cells of bacteria.

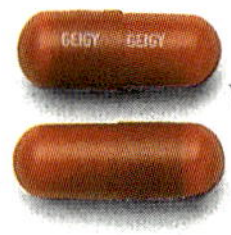

Viruses cannot be killed by antibiotics. Antiviral drugs must be used.

VIRUSES

Micro-organisms called viruses cause diseases such as chicken-pox and colds. Because they inhabit body cells, it is difficult to create drugs that kill them, yet do not harm the person. Antiviral drugs work by blocking the chemicals the virus needs to reproduce. AIDS is caused by a very tough virus. It may take many years before a drug can control it.

BODY CHEMICALS

A healthy body makes many different chemicals that control the action of the different body systems. Some illnesses occur because the body produces too much or too little of one of these chemicals. Many drugs are chemicals designed to treat a particular illness. They work with the appropriate body chemical to bring the system back under control.

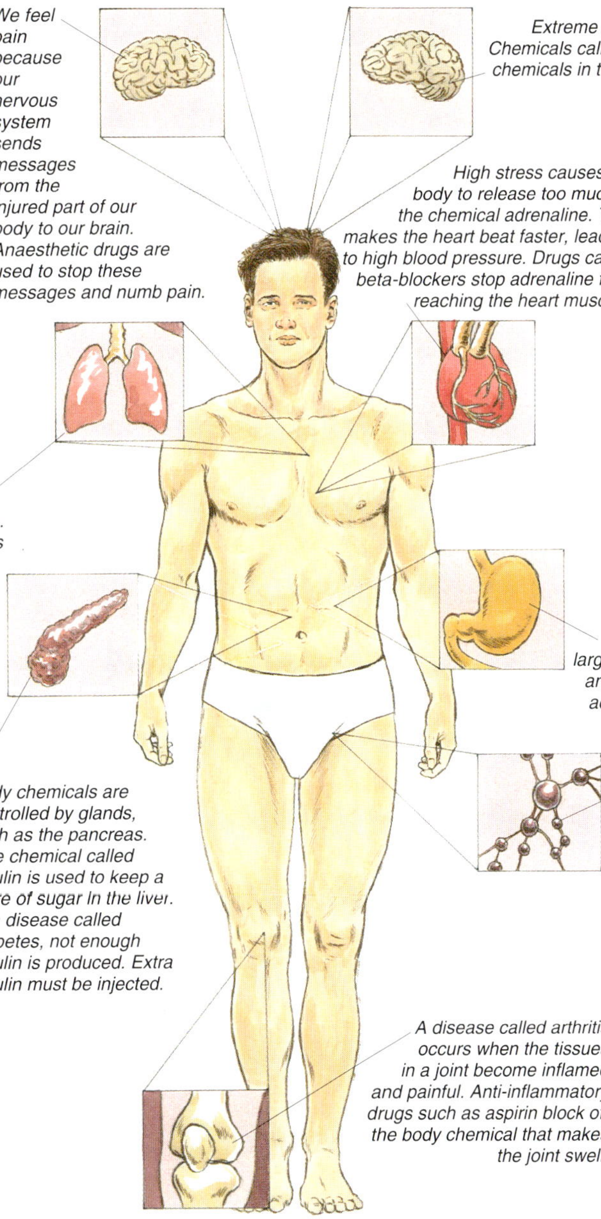

We feel pain because our nervous system sends messages from the injured part of our body to our brain. Anaesthetic drugs are used to stop these messages and numb pain.

Extreme anxiety is sometimes eased with drugs. Chemicals called diazepam and nitrazepam work with chemicals in the brain. These drugs can be addictive.

High stress causes the body to release too much of the chemical adrenaline. This makes the heart beat faster, leading to high blood pressure. Drugs called beta-blockers stop adrenaline from reaching the heart muscles.

In an asthma attack, tiny muscles in the lungs squeeze the airways, making it difficult to breathe. When the drug salbutamol is inhaled, the muscles relax, and breathing becomes easier.

Stress can make the stomach produce large quantities of acid, which can result in an ulcer. Anti-acid tablets can reduce the acidity. Special drugs called H2 blockers can stop the production of the acid.

Body chemicals are controlled by glands, such as the pancreas. One chemical called insulin is used to keep a store of sugar in the liver. In a disease called diabetes, not enough insulin is produced. Extra insulin must be injected.

White blood cells are made by cell division in the lymphatic system. If they do not divide correctly, cancer cells develop which produce a disease called leukaemia. This can be controlled by cytotoxic drugs that interfere with the way the cancer cells divide and grow.

A disease called arthritis occurs when the tissues in a joint become inflamed and painful. Anti-inflammatory drugs such as aspirin block off the body chemical that makes the joint swell.

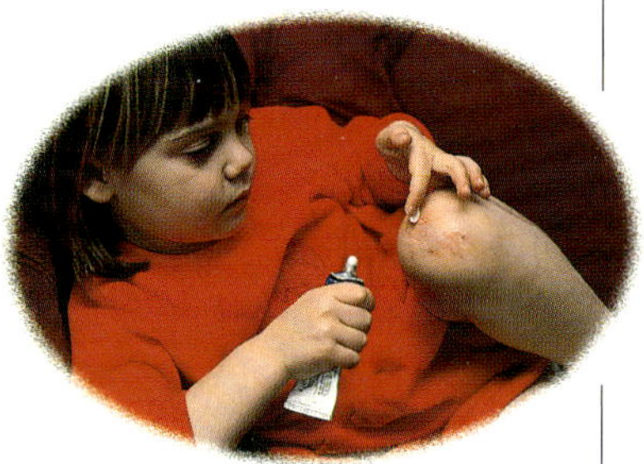

ANTISEPTICS

Wounds can become infected with harmful bacteria if an antiseptic is not applied to kill them. Antiseptics are able to kill bacteria in many ways. The alcohol rubbed onto your skin by a doctor before an injection kills bacteria by breaking up the protein that makes up their cells.

FIGHTING DISEASE

1796 English doctor Edward Jenner performs first vaccination against smallpox.

1867 English scientist Joseph Lister discovers first widely used antiseptic – carbolic acid.

1928 Scottish scientist Alexander Fleming discovers that *penicillium* kills bacteria. This leads to further developments on the antibiotic by Florey and Chain.

1932 German chemist Gerhard Domagk develops first synthetic drug to kill bacteria (sulfa drug).

1941 Australian doctor Howard Florey and German doctor Ernst Chain develop penicillin.

Find out more

CHEMISTRY OF THE BODY P.76
VIRUSES P.312
BACTERIA P.313
PRIMATES P.336
CELLS P.338
INTERNAL ENVIRONMENT P.350
FACT FINDER P.406

ADHESIVES

IMAGINE TRYING TO WALK in your shoes if you did not have adhesives holding them together. Adhesives have a wide variety of uses. They range from the sticky substances on the back of postage stamps and on the flaps of envelopes, to the substances that hold together the pages of this book, and that strengthen the joints in your chair. Many different materials are used as adhesives. The first adhesives came from plants and animals. In the 19th century, rubber was a major ingredient in adhesives. Today, polymers are widely used. Every adhesive sticks because its molecules form bonds with the objects it is joining together. These bonds can be as strong as those that hold together the molecules in a piece of rock.

RESIN AS GLUE
Liquid oozes from the cut branch of a pine tree. This contains a resin that has been used as a glue for hundreds of years.

The yellow car is stuck to the board with a strong epoxy resin.

EPOXY RESIN
Industries often use epoxy resin glues. Epoxy resins are chemically manufactured synthetic glues. They are popular because they stick a wide range of materials together, and can form very strong bonds that are resistant to both heat and weather.

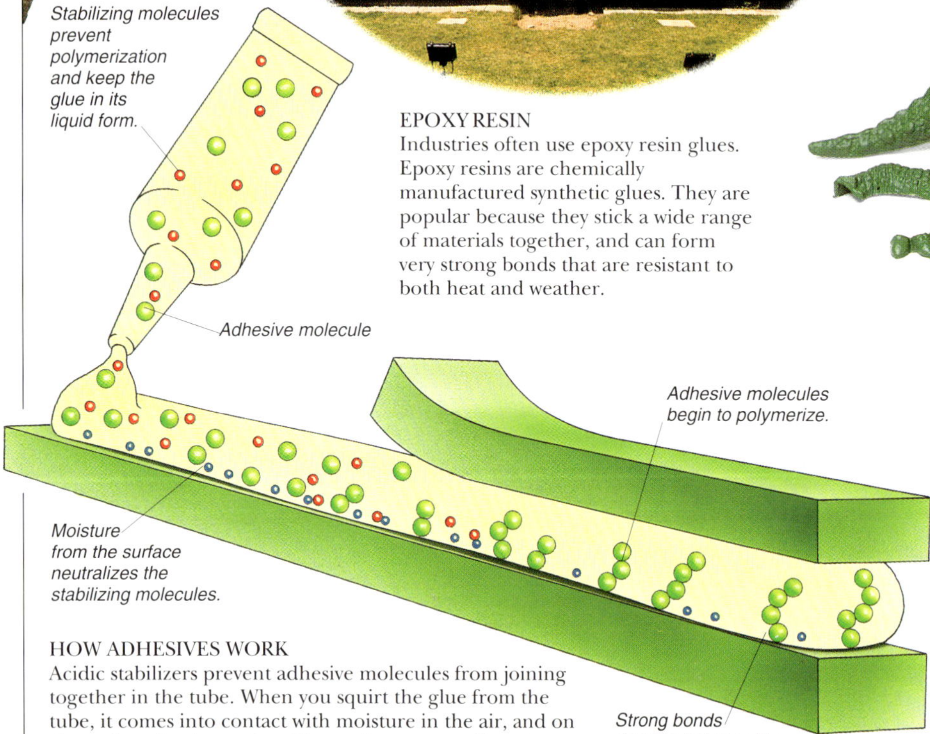

HOW ADHESIVES WORK
Acidic stabilizers prevent adhesive molecules from joining together in the tube. When you squirt the glue from the tube, it comes into contact with moisture in the air, and on the surface that it touches. The moisture neutralizes the stabilizer, leaving the adhesive molecules to join together. Polymers, which are chains of molecules, form strong, solid bonds between the surfaces in contact with the glue.

THERMOPLASTIC GLUE
This glue is used in model-making. It contains polystyrene molecules dissolved in a solvent such as acetone. The solvent evaporates when the glue is applied to a joint, and the polystyrene molecules combine to form a bond. If the joint is warmed, the molecules slide over each other as the glue melts, allowing the joint to be reshaped.

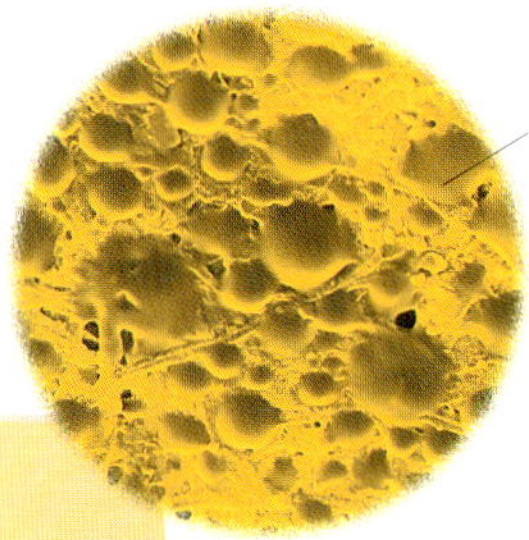

A photograph of magnified molecules joining together in an adhesive

A TWO-PART GLUE
Some epoxy resins need a catalyst or a hardener to make them set. The resin and catalyst are kept in separate tubes and mixed together when needed. The mixture quickly forms a bond that will not melt when heated.

RE-USABLE LABELS
The sticky strip on a re-usable label has thousands of tiny adhesive bubbles. A few bubbles burst each time it is stuck to a surface, making it removable and re-usable.

Find out more

CHANGES OF STATE P.20
CATALYSTS P.56
SEPARATING MIXTURES P.61
POLYMERS P.100
FACT FINDER P.406

Fibres

WHEN YOU GET DRESSED, you cover your body in clothes made of fibres. Natural fibres come from the seeds of a plant or from the fur of an animal. Other fibres are artificial. For example, nylon is made from chemicals found in oil. The first clothes were just animal skins. Then, five thousand years ago, people began to use natural fibres to make strong fabrics. They spun (twisted) cotton and wool fibres to make threads of yarn. The first process of interlocking the yarn into a fabric was weaving. This is still a major fabric-making process today. Later, the knitting process developed, producing warm, flexible clothes. During the 19th century, people became more aware of how natural fibres were formed, and soon chemicals were being used to make fibres too.

Making nylon

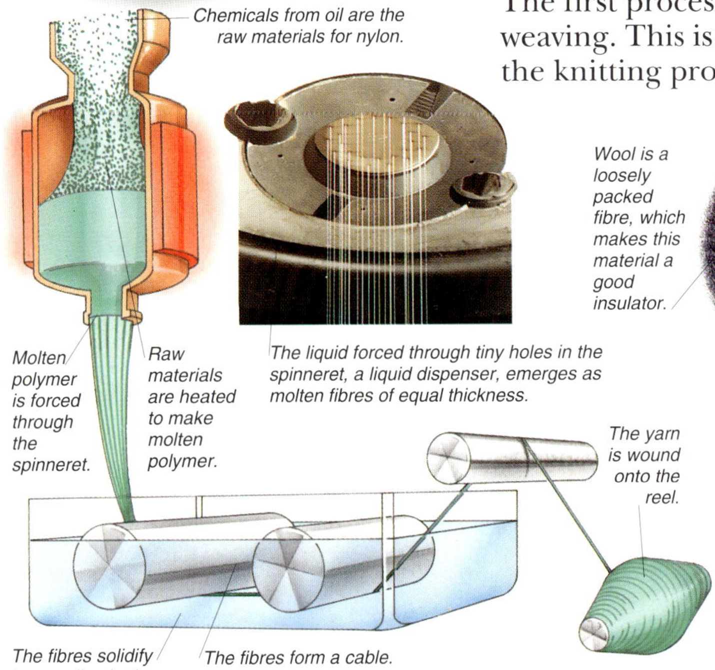

MAKING NYLON
Nylon was the first synthetic fibre to be made entirely of chemicals. Nylon pellets are heated to 260°C (500°F) to form a molten polymer solution. This is forced through the spinneret: a process known as extrusion. As the polymer comes out of the tiny holes into the cool atmosphere, they begin to form solid threads of nylon. These are treated in a special cooling bath, spun into a long yarn, and wound onto the reel.

NATURAL AND SYNTHETIC FIBRES
The original fibres used for clothing, such as wool, cotton, and silk, came from plants and animals. Today, people also use chemicals, known as petrochemicals, to make synthetic fibres. These include polyester, acrylic, and nylon, which are cheaper and stronger than natural materials.

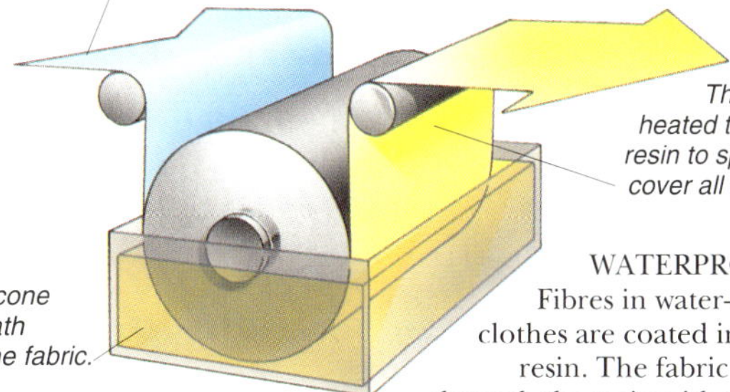

WATERPROOFING
Fibres in water-repellent clothes are coated in silicone resin. The fabric is passed through the resin with the aid of rollers. Heat is then applied to it to help the resin coat the fabric evenly. The resin prevents the fabric from absorbing water, making it an ideal material for raincoats and tents.

RAYON MANUFACTURE
Rayon is an artificial fibre made from cellulose in wood pulp. It is a reconstituted fibre because the original raw ingredient, cellulose, is broken down and then re-formed. This creates a superior form of the orginal material: it is stronger and easier to dye. There are different types of rayon. The most important is called viscose.

CHARDONNET
The French chemist, Count Hilaire Chardonnet (1839-1924), treated cotton fibres with chemicals and alcohol, then forced them through a spinneret. The alcohol evaporated, leaving shiny fibres that appeared to give out rays of light. These new fibres were called rayon or "Chardonnet silk" and became very popular at the beginning of the 20th century.

Find out more

CHANGES OF STATE P.20
BONDING P.28
SOLUTIONS P.60
POLYMERS P.100
DYES AND PIGMENTS P.102
MATERIAL DESIGN P.111

PAPER

EARLY PAPER
Making paper from wood began in China in about A.D. 105 using the fibres from the mulberry tree. But the idea is thought to have come from someone watching wasps building their nests from tiny wood chips.

NEARLY ONE THIRD OF THE EARTH is covered in trees. Many of these trees supply us with paper. The lines you can see in a piece of wood are called the grain. They are made by thousands of tiny fibres that the tree produces as it grows. The tree uses these fibres to carry water through its trunk and to support the weight of its branches. In the paper-making industry the fibres are separated, then joined together in a criss-cross pattern to make thin sheets like the one these words are printed on. Try tearing a sheet of paper – you will see tiny fibres that have been stuck together to make it. By replanting trees to replace those chopped down for paper, this supply of raw material should not run out.

MAKING PAPER

Paper is made in a factory called a paper mill. Wood is broken into small pieces to help chemicals to attack it and release the fibres. The lignin, which gives the fibres their strength, is dissolved in hot chemical liquids. Then chemicals are added to the fibres to make the paper smooth, strong, and opaque. Sizing, made from rosin or wax, is added to make the paper water-resistant.

Making paper

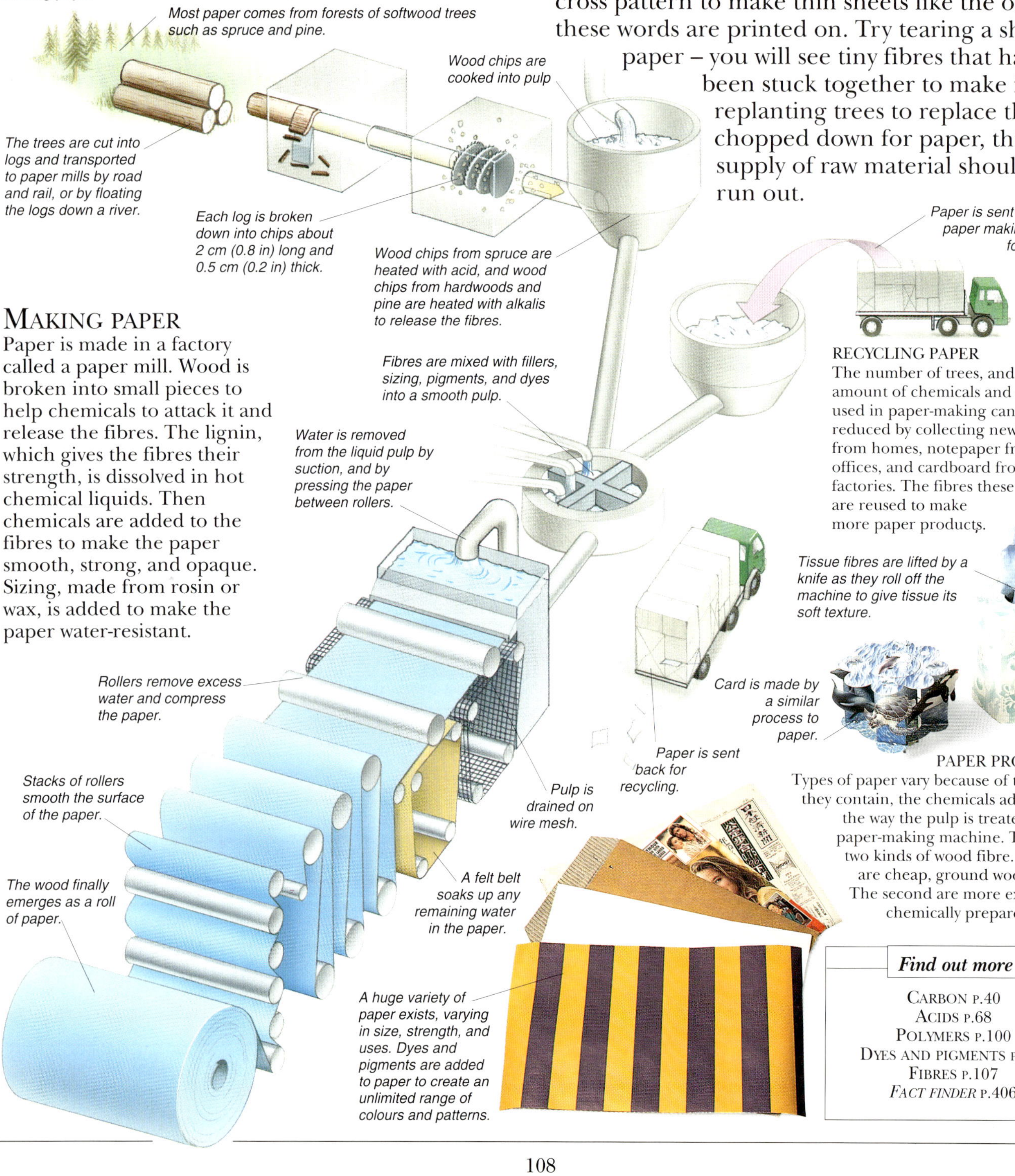

RECYCLING PAPER
The number of trees, and the amount of chemicals and energy used in paper-making can be reduced by collecting newspapers from homes, notepaper from offices, and cardboard from factories. The fibres these contain are reused to make more paper products.

Tissue fibres are lifted by a knife as they roll off the machine to give tissue its soft texture.

Card is made by a similar process to paper.

A huge variety of paper exists, varying in size, strength, and uses. Dyes and pigments are added to paper to create an unlimited range of colours and patterns.

PAPER PRODUCTS
Types of paper vary because of the fibres they contain, the chemicals added, and the way the pulp is treated on the paper-making machine. There are two kinds of wood fibre. The first are cheap, ground wood fibres. The second are more expensive, chemically prepared fibres.

Find out more

CARBON P.40
ACIDS P.68
POLYMERS P.100
DYES AND PIGMENTS P.102
FIBRES P.107
FACT FINDER P.406

CERAMICS

POTTER'S CLAY
Pottery clay is a mixture of two clays. Kaolin (china clay) gives pottery its smooth texture. Ball clay gives the pottery its strength.

YOU ARE SURROUNDED by ceramics. Many of the objects you handle every day are made out of a ceramic material. Ceramics have a range of uses from making the walls of your home, insulating cables on overhead power lines, to mending broken teeth. Ceramics are divided into two groups. In the first group are materials that are moulded into their shape before being heated. Pottery and bricks are examples of this first group. The second group consists of materials that are shaped after being treated by heat. These include glass and cement.

Water molecules in wet clay

Fired clay loses its water, forming a tighter, stronger structure.

INSIDE A KILN
Moist pottery clay is moulded and then placed in a kiln until it hardens. Reactions take place in the clay in which chemicals separate and then join together again to form stronger substances.

USING CERAMICS

Ceramics are the hard, brittle substances made by firing clay. Clay has been used to make pottery for thousands of years. It was originally baked in an open oven, but it is now heated in a kiln or furnace until it hardens. New ceramics are being developed for use in car and aircraft engines. These last longer and are able to withstand very high temperatures.

Strong, weather-resistant bricks are ideal building materials.

The shiny glazes on clay beads are also made out of clay.

Cement holds pieces of rock together in a concrete mixture.

The porous clay of a plant pot lets water evaporate from the soil and keeps the plant roots cool.

The glazed surface of a tile is easy to clean.

Glass is a hard, transparent material made from metal silicates. It is shaped from a molten state.

Crockery holds your drink because it is watertight.

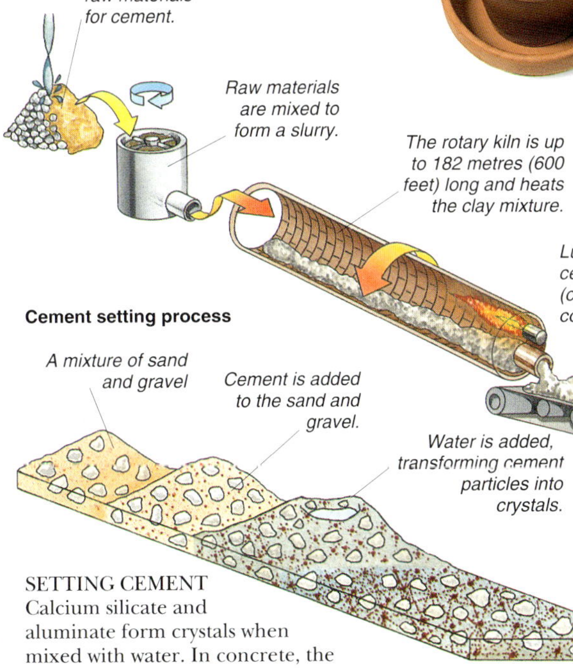
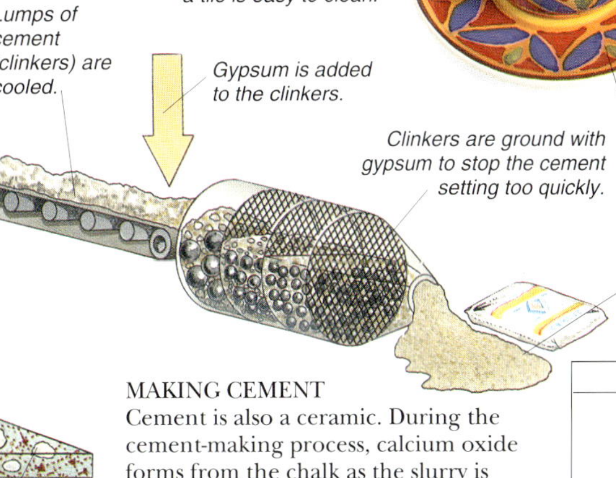

SETTING CEMENT
Calcium silicate and aluminate form crystals when mixed with water. In concrete, the crystals grow in the spaces between the sand and gravel. As the crystals grow, they surround the sand and gravel forming strong bonds to hold the cement together.

MAKING CEMENT
Cement is also a ceramic. During the cement-making process, calcium oxide forms from the chalk as the slurry is heated. This joins with silicon and aluminium in the clay to form calcium silicate and aluminate. The clinkers are ground up with gypsum to stop the cement setting too quickly for the builders to use.

Find out more

CHANGES OF STATE P.20
BONDING P.28
ORGANIC CHEMISTRY P.41
MATERIALS P.81
DYES AND PIGMENTS P.102
FIBRES P.107

GLASS

HAND-MADE GLASS
To make glass by hand, molten glass is collected onto the end of a hollow blowing iron and a small bubble is blown. The glass is then cooled by rolling it on an iron slab and it is shaped with tools. The glass is reheated during shaping, so it is easier to handle.

RAW MATERIALS
Sand usually melts at 1700°C (3090°F). But if it is mixed with sodium carbonate (soda), the melting point is reduced, saving energy. Calcium carbonate (limestone) is added to stop the glass from dissolving in water. Waste glass is also added, and melted down for reuse.

ONE OF THE OLDEST ARTIFICIAL MATERIALS, glass was first made around 5,000 years ago. Glass is actually cooled liquid sand. Like thick treacle, it is a liquid that has never set – an old sheet of glass is always slightly thicker at the bottom than at the top. Glass is very useful as it is easily shaped, rust-proof, and forms hard, transparent objects that are not affected by chemicals. It is also very cheap to make and can be recycled over and over again. Glass has a wide range of uses from holding our drinks to helping us to see. Its properties can be changed by adding chemicals, by adding other materials such as wire, and by controlling the way glass cools down.

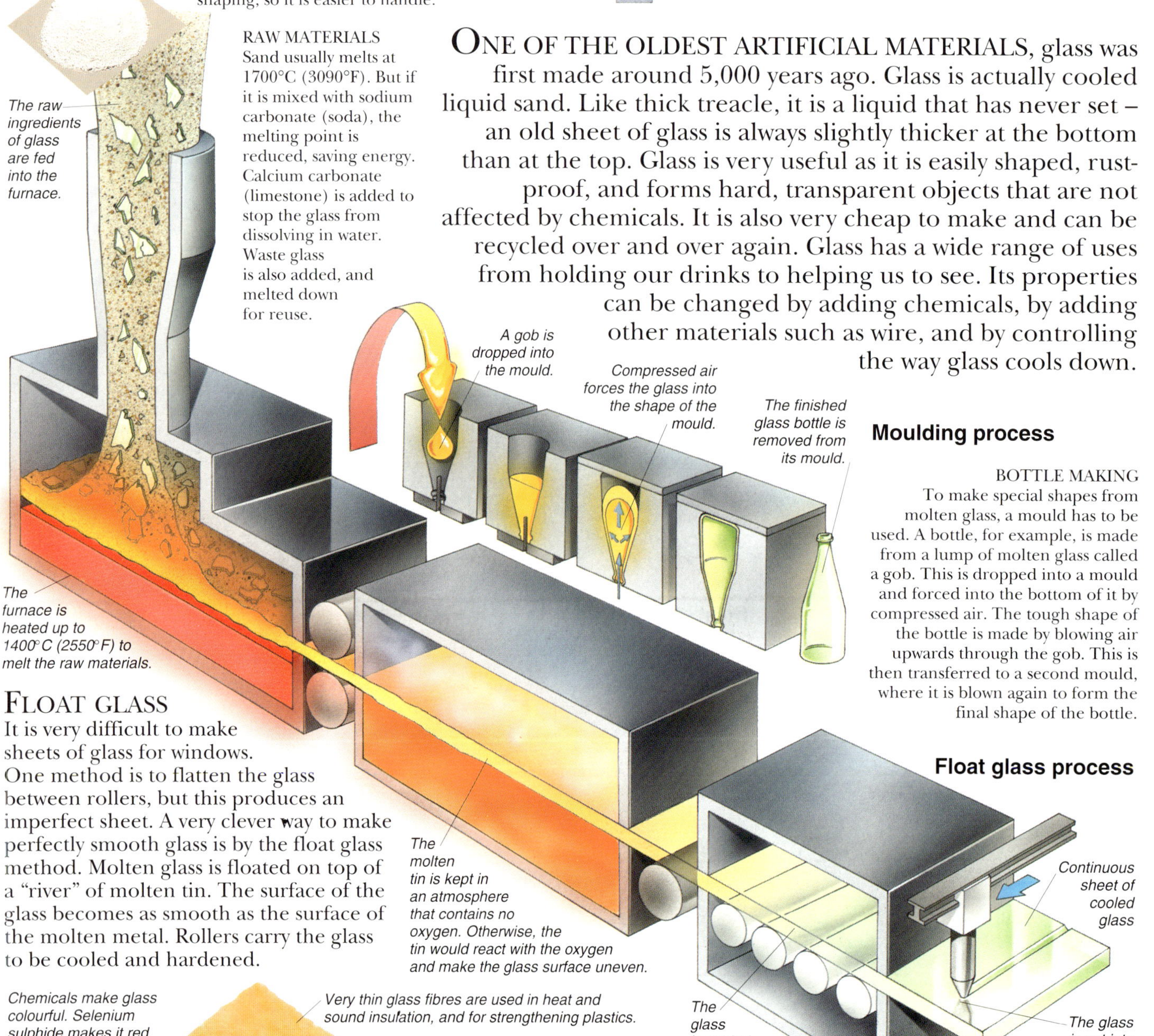

BOTTLE MAKING
To make special shapes from molten glass, a mould has to be used. A bottle, for example, is made from a lump of molten glass called a gob. This is dropped into a mould and forced into the bottom of it by compressed air. The tough shape of the bottle is made by blowing air upwards through the gob. This is then transferred to a second mould, where it is blown again to form the final shape of the bottle.

FLOAT GLASS

It is very difficult to make sheets of glass for windows. One method is to flatten the glass between rollers, but this produces an imperfect sheet. A very clever way to make perfectly smooth glass is by the float glass method. Molten glass is floated on top of a "river" of molten tin. The surface of the glass becomes as smooth as the surface of the molten metal. Rollers carry the glass to be cooled and hardened.

Chemicals make glass colourful. Selenium sulphide makes it red, copper oxide makes it blue, phosphates and alumina make it milky.

Very thin glass fibres are used in heat and sound insulation, and for strengthening plastics.

CHANGING GLASS
The way glass is treated after it has emerged from the furnace changes its properties, making it suitable for a particular job. By rapidly cooling the glass with jets of air, toughened glass suitable for car windows can be made. The green tint in raw glass can be removed by adding cobalt and selenium oxide.

Boron oxide is added to the raw materials of glass to make borosilicate glass. This is used in oven dishes and laboratory glassware because it is able to resist temperature changes.

Find out more

CHANGES OF STATE P.20
SEMIMETALS P.39
FIBRES P.107
MATERIAL DESIGN P.111
REFLECTION P.194
FACT FINDER P.406

MATERIAL DESIGN

IMAGINE WHAT YOUR HOME would look like if everything were made out of just one material, such as steel. A wide range of materials need to be used in the home. A window-frame is made from wood for strength, while the window glass lets in light, but keeps out rain. Today, the wood may be replaced by plastic, and two panes of glass are often used to stop heat escaping. People are always looking for new materials to make life easier and cheaper. This search may involve using an old material in a new way, joining different materials together, or experimenting with chemicals to make a completely new material. Every new material or new combination of materials must be thoroughly tested to check it can stand up to the job.

GLASS-REINFORCED PLASTICS
If glass fibres are embedded in plastic, they reinforce it, and give it extra strength. This glass-reinforced plastic, known as fibreglass, is used to build boats. It is an example of a composite material, in which the properties of two common materials are combined.

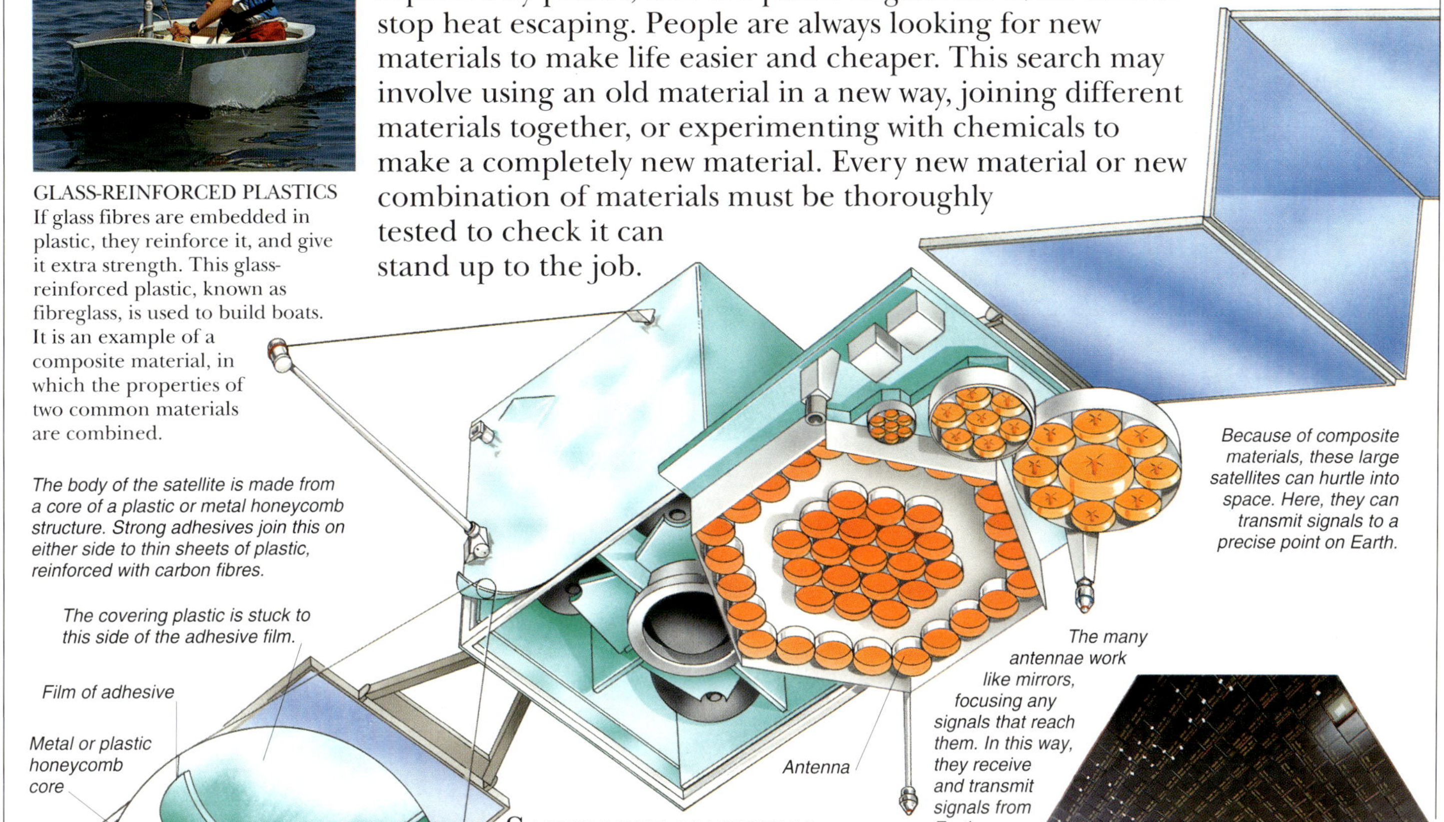

SATELLITE MATERIAL

If you need to send something into the harsh conditions of space, it needs to be built out of a material much more resilient than wood or metal. Satellites are made from specially developed materials. These are light enough to be launched, but can withstand the stresses and strains produced when the satellite is put into orbit.

HEAT-RESISTANT MATERIALS
Extra-tough materials called cermets can withstand incredible heat. They are made by mixing metal and ceramic particles. Cermets are shaped into jet turbine blades and rocket nozzles, which both get extremely hot in use. Over 30,000 cermet tiles protect the space shuttle from the frictional heat produced as it re-enters the Earth's atmosphere.

LIFE-SAVING MATERIALS
Many damaged or diseased body parts can be replaced by synthetic materials. Metal alloys are used to make skull plates. Artificial hip joints are made from a combination of metal alloys and plastics. Blood vessels are made from fibres of fabrics. Today, even artificial hearts are made from a combination of plastic and aluminium.

SEEING STARS
Enormous telescopes are needed to explore the vastness of space. The light they collect must be reflected from a huge mirror to make an image that astronomers can see. The mirror is made from glass mixed with ceramics. This gives a material that is strong, so it does not break under its own weight, and does not change shape as the temperature changes.

Find out more

PROPERTIES OF MATTER P.22
ALLOYS P.88
FIBRES P.107
PAPER P.108
CERAMICS P.109
GLASS P.110
FACT FINDER P.406

INDUSTRIAL POLLUTION

THE PRICE WE PAY for using so many different types of material is pollution. This occurs when we release substances into the environment which harm living things as well as structures. Up until about 200 years ago, there was very little pollution. The population was smaller and people used mostly natural materials. Their wastes could be broken down by microbes in the soil. Today, some of our machines, factories, and power stations disfigure the environment. Some of our wastes do not break up but pollute the land, the water, and the air. Industry is now trying to limit the pollution it creates.

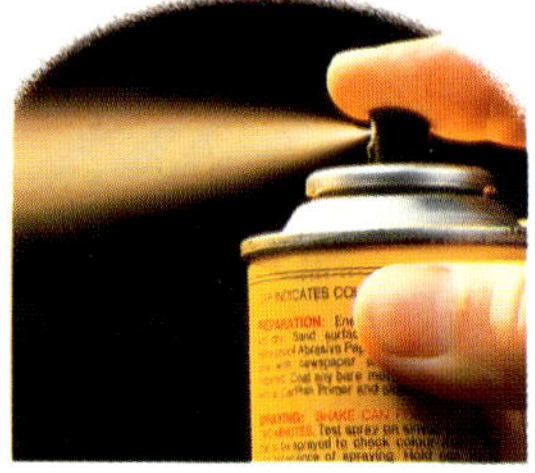

COVERING EYESORES
Quarries near towns can be filled in with rubbish. This is stored on polyethene sheets to control the drainage of water. The methane produced by the decaying rubbish is collected in pipes and used as a fuel. When the quarry is full, the rubbish is covered with soil and appropriate plants to create new habitats for animals.

OZONE LAYER
Chemicals called CFCs in aerosols and refrigerants destroy ozone when they escape into the atmosphere. These are now being replaced with carbon dioxide, and with hydrocarbons that do not destroy ozone.

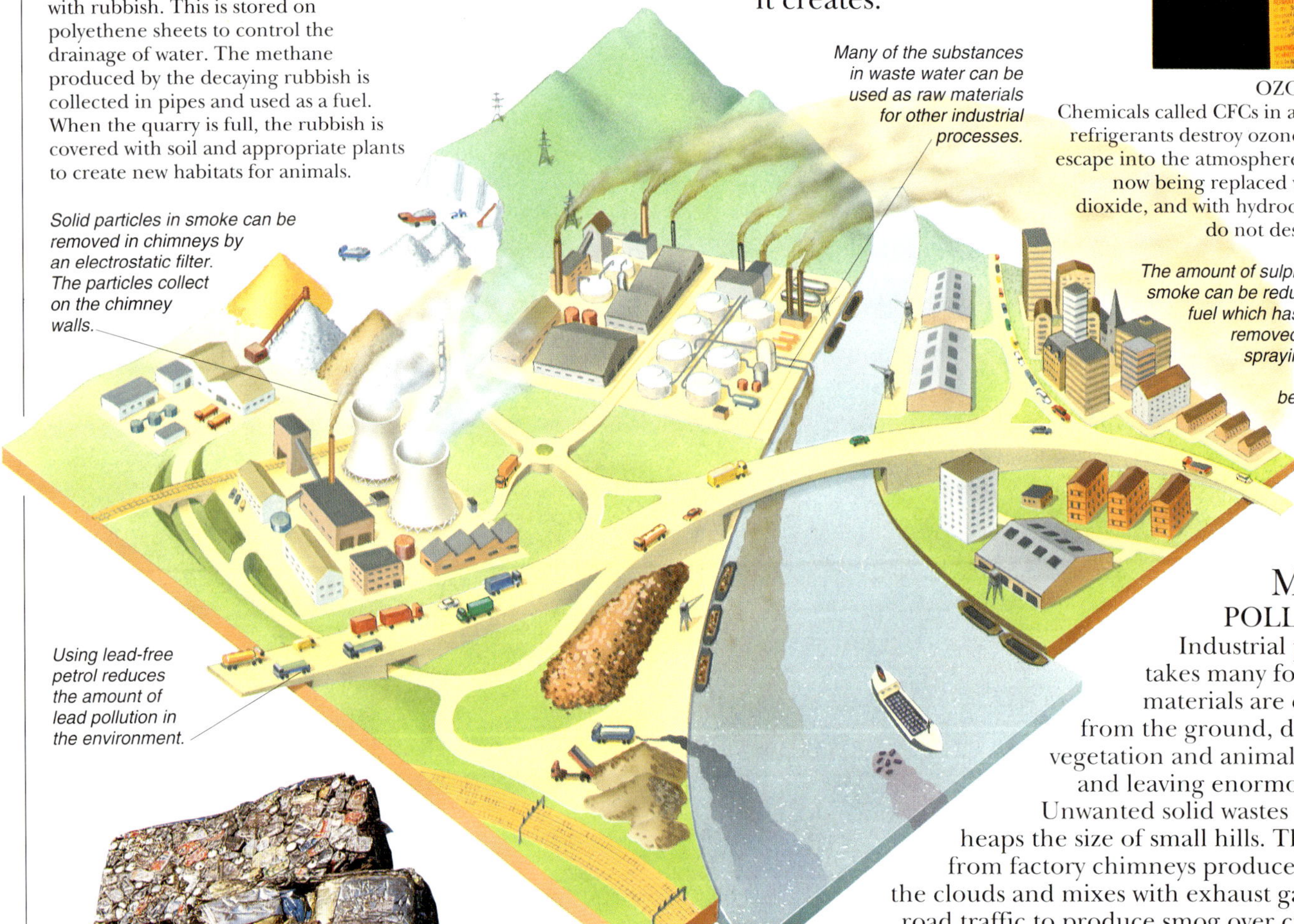

Many of the substances in waste water can be used as raw materials for other industrial processes.

Solid particles in smoke can be removed in chimneys by an electrostatic filter. The particles collect on the chimney walls.

The amount of sulphur dioxide in smoke can be reduced by using fuel which has had sulphur removed from it or by spraying the smoke with water before it leaves the chimney.

Using lead-free petrol reduces the amount of lead pollution in the environment.

MAKING POLLUTION

Industrial pollution takes many forms. Raw materials are extracted from the ground, destroying vegetation and animal habitats, and leaving enormous holes. Unwanted solid wastes can form heaps the size of small hills. The smoke from factory chimneys produces acids in the clouds and mixes with exhaust gases from road traffic to produce smog over cities. The water released from factories can contain wastes that kill aquatic life. Oil slicks may be created when ships are involved in accidents.

RECYCLING MATERIALS
Fewer raw materials need to be used if materials are recycled. This conserves raw materials for the future, reduces pollution, and saves energy. Using recycled materials to make aluminium cans, for example, would give a 95 per cent saving in energy and a 95 per cent fall in pollution.

CONSERVING HEAT
If heat is wasted, more fuel has to be burned to replace it. This causes extra pollution. The loss of heat energy from a building or factory can be revealed by an infrared photograph. The regions losing the most heat, hot spots, show up as white. They can be treated with extra insulation to stop the heat escaping.

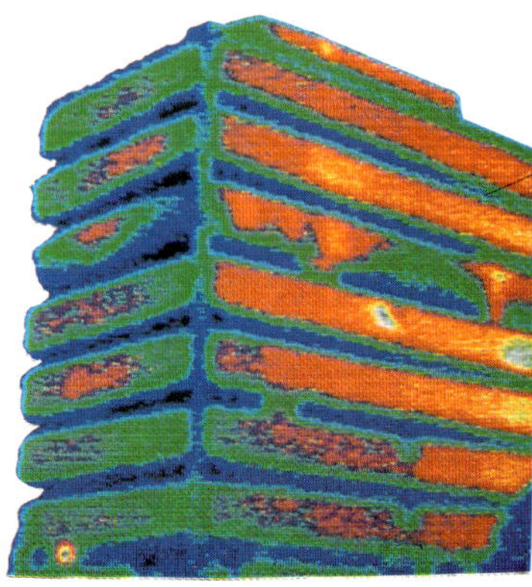

False colour image showing the heat lost from an office block

Find out more

SULPHUR P.45
CATALYSTS P.56
CHEMISTRY OF AIR P.74
CHEMICAL INDUSTRY P.82
BIOSPHERE P.370
FACT FINDER P.406

FORCES AND ENERGY

ENERGY MAKES THINGS HAPPEN, from a bolt of lightning to tying a shoelace. Nothing could live or move without energy. Animals use energy to walk and run; plants use energy to grow. Winds use energy when they blow; waves use energy when they roll across the ocean. And when a car moves, it is using energy stored in its fuel. But none of these things would happen if there were no forces at work. Whenever energy is used, forces are involved. Forces are needed to start things moving, to change the way they move, and to stop them from moving. Forces are also responsible for breaking things and for holding things together. Without forces and energy, nothing would happen in the Universe.

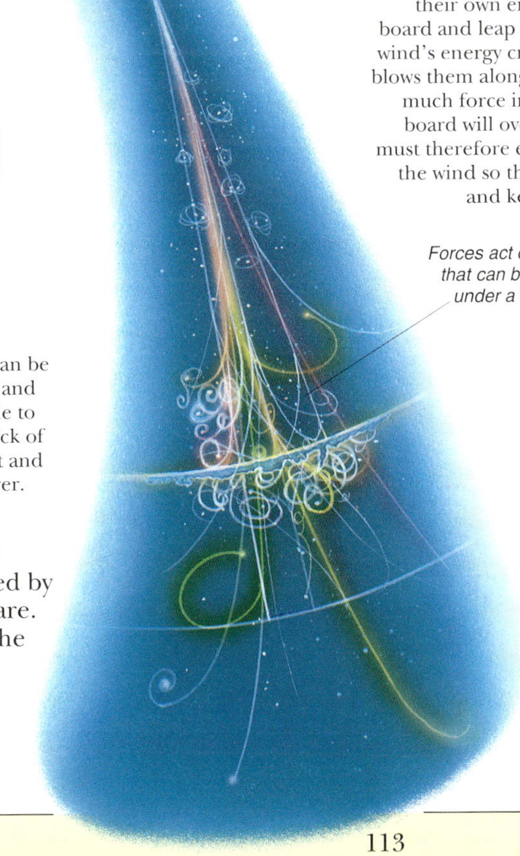

IN SPACE

Forces and energy act on a huge scale in space. The stars shine because they are producing energy in the form of heat and light. The atmosphere of a star is kept in place by the force of gravity – the same force that pulls objects towards the Earth.

USING THE WIND

Windsurfing involves the use of forces and energy. Windsurfers use their own energy to control the board and leap over the waves. The wind's energy creates the force that blows them along. But if there is too much force in one direction, the board will overturn. Windsurfers must therefore exert a force against the wind so that they can balance and keep the sail upright.

ENERGY FROM THE SUN

The Sun provides most of our energy in the form of sunlight. More energy reaches Earth from the Sun in an hour than all of us use in a year. Plants like these sunflowers need the Sun's energy to grow. They store some of it in chemical form. An animal that eats a plant uses this stored energy.

NIGHT LIGHTS

Electricity is a form of energy. It can be generated in large power stations and transmitted long distances by cable to homes, offices, and factories. A flick of a switch easily changes it into heat and light energy, and mechanical power.

SUBATOMIC FORCES

Tiny particles are influenced by forces just as large objects are. The forces that act inside the nucleus, or centre, of an atom are the strongest of all forces. Their energy is released in a nuclear bomb explosion.

FORCES IN BUILDINGS

Buildings must be made to withstand large forces or they would fall down. The roof of the terminal at Jeddah airport in Saudi Arabia is made of fibreglass, which is even stronger than steel. Forces stretch the roof into an unusual shape.

FORCES

THERE ARE FORCES all around us. A force is a push or a pull. It is something that acts on an object. The wind exerts a force when it blows; gravity is a force that pulls everything down towards the centre of the Earth and gives objects their weight. Animals and machines make forces too. When a grasshopper leaps from a leaf, its legs exert a small force on the leaf. Machines are used to produce large forces. A jet engine can produce a force that is millions of times larger than the force produced by a leaping grasshopper.

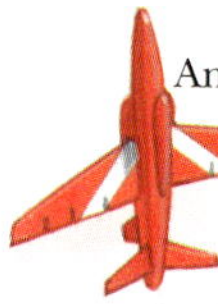

FORCES IN FLIGHT
An aeroplane in flight has four forces acting on it. The engine produces a forward force called thrust, the wings produce an upward force called lift, and the force of gravity pulls the aircraft downwards. A force called drag, caused as the aircraft pushes against the air, slows it down.

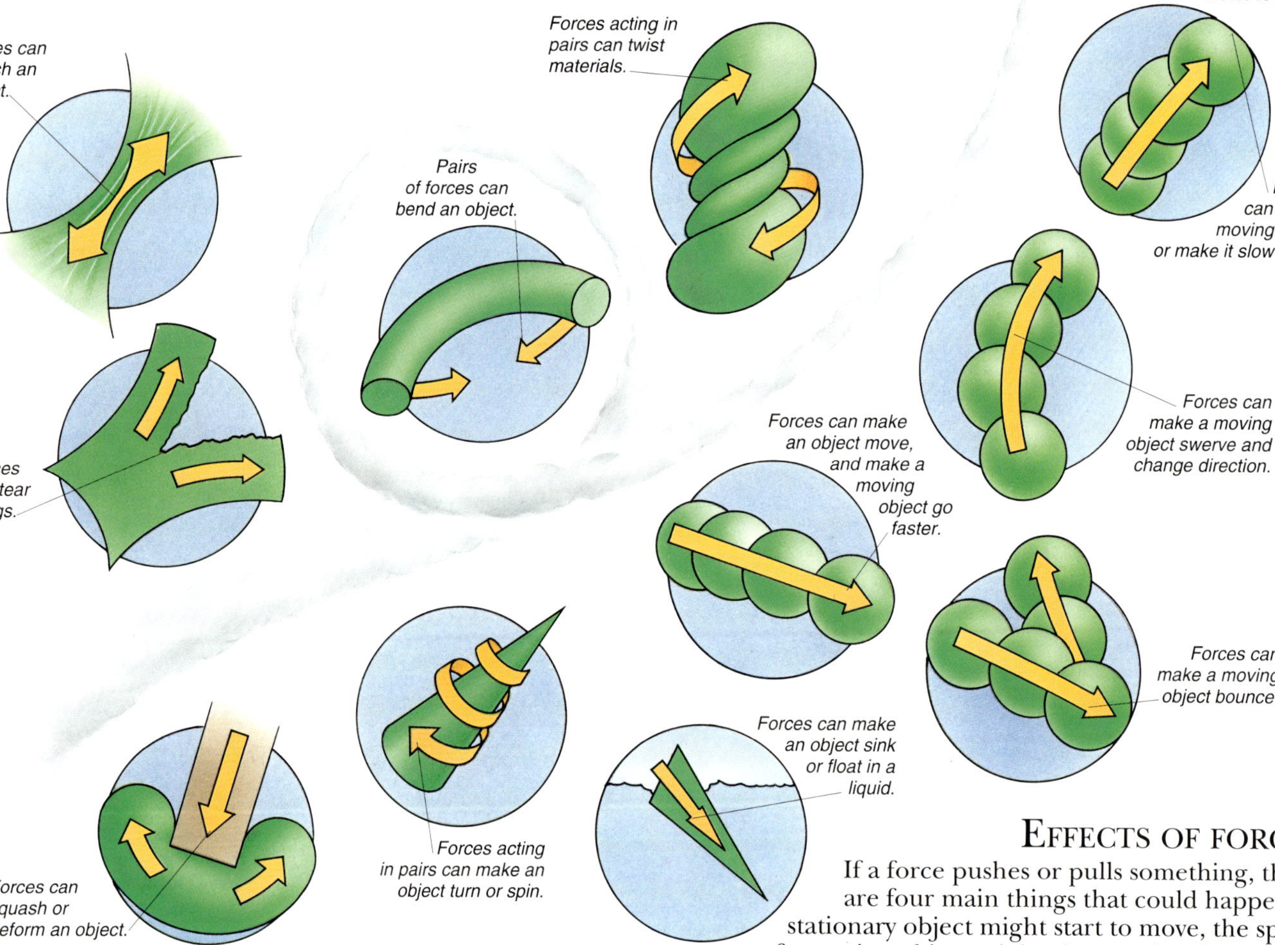

EFFECTS OF FORCES

If a force pushes or pulls something, there are four main things that could happen. A stationary object might start to move, the speed of a moving object might change, the direction of a moving object might change, or the shape or size of an object might change. The greater the force, the greater the effect it has.

FORCE FIELDS

The region in which a force can be felt is called a force field. The strength of a force field is greatest close to its source, such as a magnet. Iron filings scattered on a piece of paper on top of a magnet will gather along the lines of force in the magnet's force field. The lines show how the force field spreads out around the magnet.

FORCES OF NATURE
Some weather conditions create strong forces. A tornado, a whirling spiral of wind, can cause a huge amount of damage. Large tornadoes toss anything in their path – cars, buildings, trees – high into the air and then smash them down hundreds of metres away. The most destructive tornado on record occurred in the United States, in 1925. Hundreds of people were killed as it left a 300 m-(980 ft-) wide trail of demolished buildings, uprooted trees, and overturned cars.

BASIC FORCES

The basic forces are gravity, electricity, magnetism, and two kinds of nuclear force called the weak and strong forces. All other forces come from them. In 1979, Sheldon Glashow, Steven Weinberg, and Abdus Salam received the Nobel Prize for Physics for proving that the magnetic, electric, and weak nuclear forces are really aspects of one force. They called this force the electroweak force. Scientists are now trying to prove the theory that gravity and the strong nuclear force are related to the electroweak force. This theory is called the Grand Unified Theory, or GUT.

ABDUS SALAM

In 1979, the Pakistani scientist Abdus Salam (born 1926) became the first person from his country to receive a Nobel Prize. Salam had wanted to be a civil servant but changed his mind when he won a scholarship to study physics at Cambridge University, England. At Cambridge, he developed the theory of the electroweak force. His ideas were proved correct at CERN, the European research laborarator y near Geneva, Switzerland, in 1973.

CONTACT AND NON-CONTACT FORCES

Some forces are only produced when one object touches another. These are called contact forces. Other forces do not need contact to have an effect. For example, a magnet can pull a piece of iron towards it without touching it. These forces are called non-contact forces.

ELECTRIC FORCES

A plastic ruler can be given an electrical charge, called static electricity, by rubbing it against a T-shirt or a jumper. The static electricity will cause the ruler to attract small pieces of paper to it without touching them.

HITTING WITH FORCE

When a snooker player hits the ball with the cue, a good contact is essential. The push of the cue applies a contact force to the ball. If the moving ball hits another stationary ball, the contact starts the second ball moving.

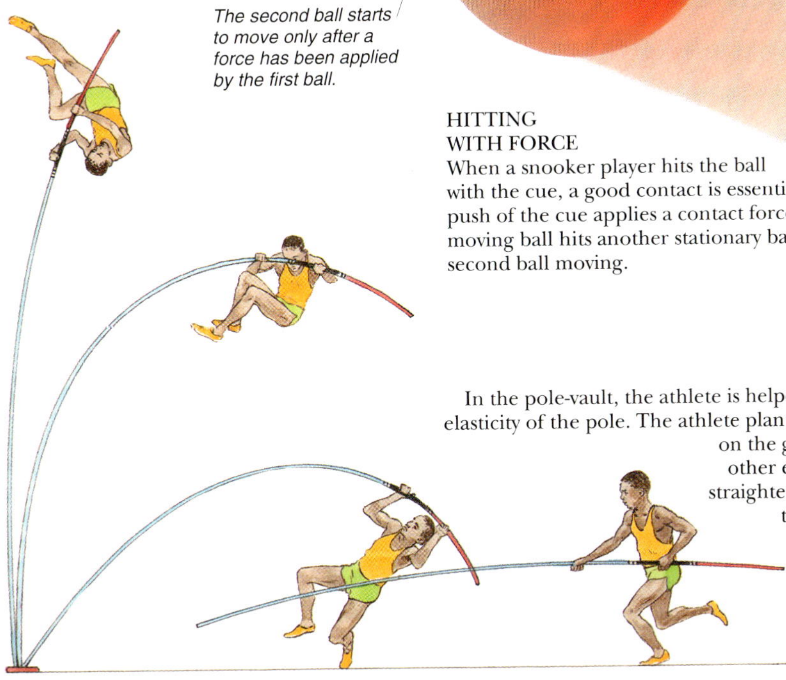

ELASTIC FORCE

In the pole-vault, the athlete is helped over the bar by the elasticity of the pole. The athlete plants one end of the pole on the ground and bends the other end down. As the pole straightens it applies a force to the vaulter, lifting him upwards. The vaulter and pole obviously need to be in contact with each other!

Find out more

FORCES AND MOTION P.120
ENERGY SOURCES P.134
NUCLEAR ENERGY P.136
STATIC ELECTRICITY P.146
MAGNETISM P.154
STRUCTURE OF THE EARTH P.212
TORNADOES P.259

FORCES AND MOTION

ONCE AN OBJECT IS MOVING, it will keep moving until a force halts it. This is proved by spacecraft. They will travel for ever through space at a constant speed until a force acts on them. It has taken people more than 2,000 years to understand this. The Ancient Greek thinker Aristotle thought that an object could only move if pushed by a force, and the movement stopped when the force was removed. But this did not explain why a ball continued to fly through the air after it had left a thrower's hand. A better theory was put forward in the 16th century by Italian experimenter Galileo. He recognized that no force was needed to keep an object moving, only to start, stop, or accelerate it. In 1687, Englishman Isaac Newton built upon Galileo's work. He put forward three laws of motion.

IN THE AIR
When you throw a ball, it moves in two ways at the same time: forwards at a constant speed and downwards due to gravity. The resultant path it takes is caused by a combination of the two motions.

INERTIA
A bobsleigh team has to push hard to make the bob start to move. And they have to keep pushing to make it move faster. This tendency of the bobsleigh to resist having its state of motion changed is called inertia. All objects have inertia and the more mass they have, the greater their inertia.

NEWTON'S FIRST LAW
A frog leaping from a lily pad illustrates Newton's Laws of Motion well. Newton's first law states that if an object is not being pushed or pulled by a force, it will either stay still or move in a straight line at a constant speed.

NEWTON'S SECOND LAW
Newton's second law states that when a force acts on an object the object will start to move, speed up, slow down, or change direction. The greater the force, the greater the change of movement.

NEWTON'S THIRD LAW
The third law states that if you push or pull an object, it will push or pull you to an equal extent. As Newton put it, "to every action there is an equal and opposite reaction".

ISAAC NEWTON

One of the greatest scientists of all time, Isaac Newton (1642-1727) was born in Lincolnshire, England. He was sent to study at Cambridge University in 1661. But during the years 1665-6, Newton returned home because Cambridge was struck by the Plague. It was then that he made his most important discoveries. He formulated his laws of motion and invented a kind of mathematics, called calculus, to express them. He explained how gravity keeps the planets in orbit around the Sun. Newton was honoured by being buried in Westminster Abbey in London, England.

MOMENTUM
A moving object has momentum – it will keep on moving until a force stops it. When you catch a ball, you must exert a force on it to remove its momentum and stop it moving. But when your hand and the ball collide, the ball will exert a force on your hand so the momentum of your hand will change. The momentum gained by your hand is equal to the momentum lost by the ball. The greater the mass and velocity of an object, the larger its momentum.

The best way to catch a ball is to recoil with it so that the collision lasts longer and the force is less.

Find out more

FORCES p.114
ACCELERATION p.119
GRAVITY p.122
ENGINES p.143
JUPITER p.290
SOLAR SYSTEM p.283
AMPHIBIANS p.328

FRICTION

IT IS HARD TO DRAG A HEAVY WEIGHT along a rough surface. This is because there is a force called friction, which slows down the movement of objects sliding over each other. Friction occurs because no surface is perfectly smooth. This means that when any two surfaces press together, the rough pieces, however tiny, catch on each other. The rougher the surfaces, the more friction there is. If there were no friction, it would be easy to drag large weights. But if there were no friction, everything would keep sliding. You would not be able to walk as your shoes would not grip the ground; you would not be able to pick anything up because you would have no grip between your fingers and the object. Friction causes wear and tear which is why even metal wears down.

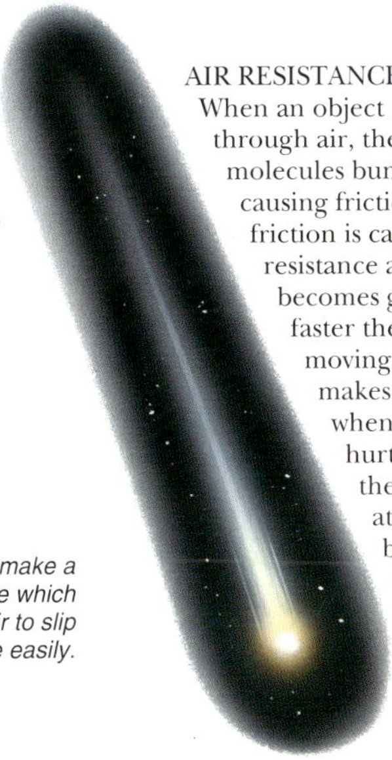

AIR RESISTANCE
When an object moves through air, the air molecules bump against it causing friction. This friction is called air resistance and it becomes greater the faster the object is moving. Friction makes things hot, so when a meteor hurtles through the Earth's atmosphere it becomes so hot it begins to break up.

The rider crouches low to make a streamlined shape which allows the air to slip past more easily.

The helmet is as streamlined as possible.

Handlebars are covered with rough material to increase friction between them and the hands for better grip.

Brake pads press against the rim of the wheel and friction slows the wheel.

Tyres grip the road with friction. They have a pattern of grooves called the tread which allows water to escape from under the wheels. Otherwise, any water on the road would act as a lubricant and reduce the friction and the grip.

Pedals have a rough surface to increase friction and stop the cyclist's feet from slipping off.

Cogs, chain, and gears are lubricated with oil to reduce friction.

FRICTION EVERYWHERE

There are many places on a bicycle where friction acts. In some places, such as between the brake pads and the wheels, it is important to have friction. In other parts, such as the gears, you want as little friction as possible.

Oil flows into the "valleys" in the rough surfaces.

REDUCING FRICTION
Friction can cause machine parts to wear out, but it can be reduced by using ball bearings lubricated, or coated, with oil. The ball bearings work because they roll rather than drag across each other.

STREAMLINING IN NATURE
Objects experience friction moving through water too. This is called drag. A bird diving for a fish puts its wings back to make a streamlined shape. And most fish are streamlined so they can move through the water easily.

CHRISTOPHER COCKERELL

A British engineer, Christopher Cockerell (born 1910) invented the hovercraft in 1955. He thought up the idea of using a strong downward jet of air to push a boat up and away from the water, letting it move without friction. When Cockerell told the British government of his invention, they were so impressed that they placed the invention on the Top Secret list! He was eventually given permission to manufacture the new boat. The first large hovercraft was launched in 1969.

Air is drawn in and forced under the hovercraft. A "skirt" of flexible material around the hull stops air leaking out. The hovercraft rides on this cushion of air which reduces friction between it and the water. Propellers drive the craft forwards.

Find out more

ACCELERATION P.119
MEASURING FORCES P.123
MACHINES P.130
ENGINES P.143
COMETS AND METEORS P.295

GRAVITY

WHEN YOU DROP SOMETHING, it falls to the ground. The force that makes it do this is the Earth's gravity. Gravity is a force that pulls objects together. It is not just the Earth that has gravity. The Moon has gravity too. And the Sun's gravity attracts the Earth and planets and holds them in their orbits. The force of gravitational attraction between two objects depends upon the distance between them – the greater the distance, the smaller the force pulling them together. It also depends upon the masses of the objects – the greater the mass of the objects, the greater the force of gravity.

On the Moon   On Earth

MASS AND WEIGHT

Mass is not the same as weight. Mass is the amount of material in an object; weight is the force exerted on an object's mass by gravity. On the Moon, a pile of strawberries would weigh one-sixth as much as it does on Earth but the mass would be the same. This is because the Moon's surface gravity is one-sixth as strong as the Earth's.

CENTRE OF GRAVITY

The point at which the effect of gravity on an object seems to be concentrated is called the centre of gravity. It is the point where the whole weight of the object seems to act. An object can be balanced if it is supported directly in line with its centre of gravity. But balancing is easiest if the object has a low centre of gravity.

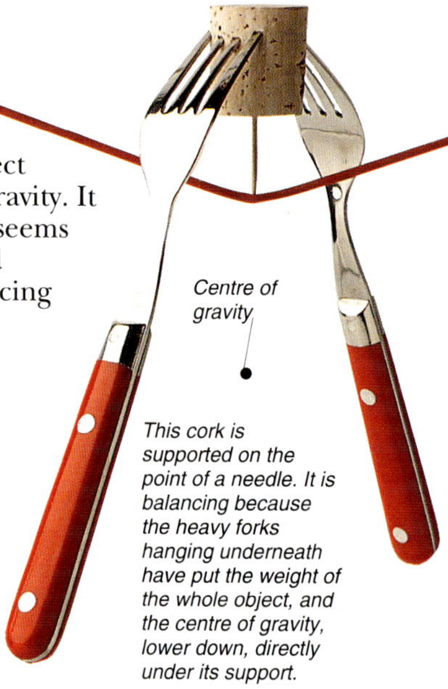

This cork is supported on the point of a needle. It is balancing because the heavy forks hanging underneath have put the weight of the whole object, and the centre of gravity, lower down, directly under its support.

Jumping on the Moon

1. Hang the object and the plumbline together from the same point. Draw a line where the plumbline falls.

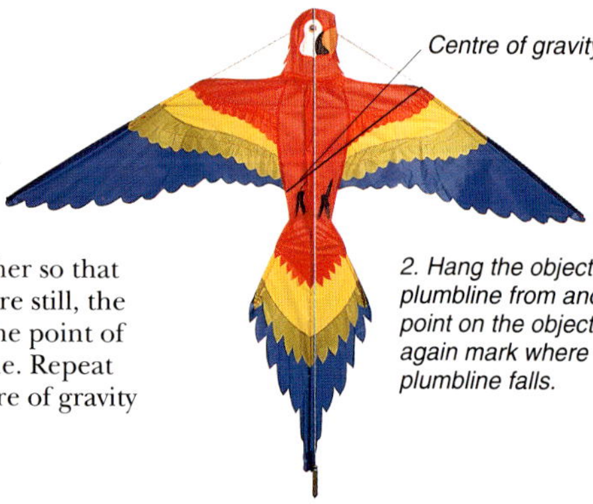

2. Hang the object and plumbline from another point on the object and again mark where the plumbline falls.

FINDING THE CENTRE OF GRAVITY

It is easy to find the centre of gravity of a flat object such as this kite. Hang the object and a plumbline together so that they can both swing freely. When they are still, the centre of gravity will be directly below the point of suspension somewhere on the plumbline. Repeat this from a different point and the centre of gravity will be where the two lines cross.

THE MOON'S GRAVITY

Gravity on the Moon is less than that on the Earth because the Moon is much smaller and has less mass than the Earth. On the Moon, falling objects accelerate downwards at one-sixth the rate they do on the Earth, and a person can jump six times as high on the Moon as on the Earth.

Jumping on the Earth

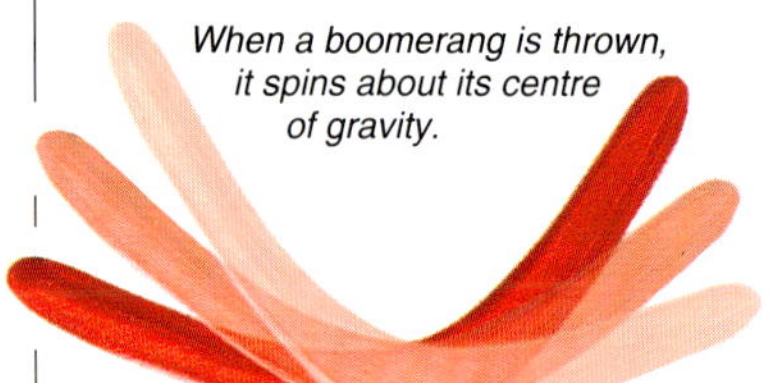

When a boomerang is thrown, it spins about its centre of gravity.

BOOMERANG

Some objects, such as a boomerang, have their centre of gravity outside their body. Because of its shape, a boomerang cannot be balanced by supporting it at one point on its flat side. Edge-on, it will balance when supported at the point of the V.

TIDES

Gravity causes the tides. The ocean on the side of the Earth nearest the Moon is pulled outwards by the Moon's gravity, creating a high tide. It is high tide on the far side of the Earth at the same time because the Earth is pulled towards the Moon more than the water on that side. The Sun has a small effect on tides. When Moon and Sun are in line, their gravity combines to produce a high spring tide.

Find out more

MEASURING FORCES P.123
TURNING FORCES P.124
CIRCULAR MOTION P.125
WAVES, TIDES, AND CURRENTS P.235
SOLAR SYSTEM P.283
ROCKETS P.299

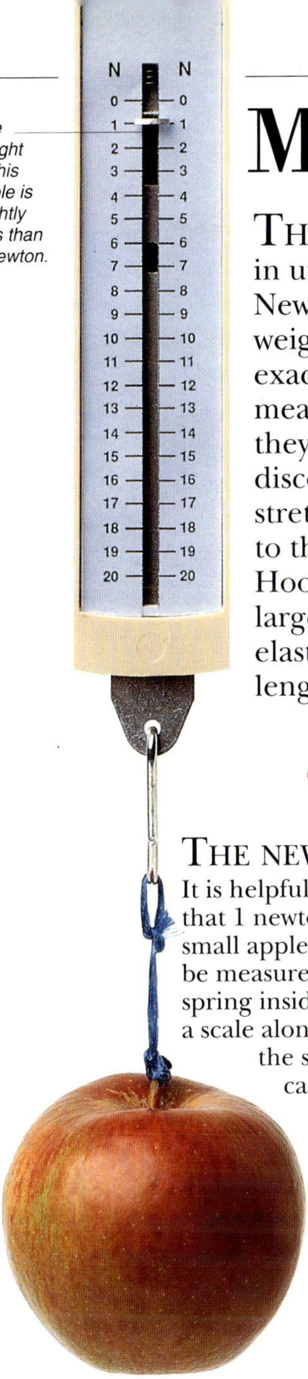

The weight of this apple is slightly less than 1 newton.

MEASURING FORCES

THE SIZE OF A FORCE is usually expressed in units called newtons, named after Sir Isaac Newton. On Earth, a mass of 1 kg (2.2 lb) weighs almost 10 newtons – 9.8 newtons to be exact. A spring balance is often used to measure a force because springs are elastic – they stretch. The inventor Robert Hooke discovered that the amount an elastic body stretches out of shape is in direct proportion to the force acting on it. This is known as Hooke's law. As long as the force is not too large, stretching the spring past its limit of elasticity, the spring will go back to its original length when the force is removed.

Cavendish measured how much the beam moved to calculate the gravity between the balls.

MEASURING GRAVITY

Englishman Henry Cavendish (1731-1810) used this apparatus to calculate the Earth's mass. He hung two lead balls from the ends of a beam which turned horizontally. The balls were attracted by gravity to two larger lead balls nearby. As the small balls moved, they turned the beam. Cavendish calculated the gravity between the balls and, from that, the mass of the Earth.

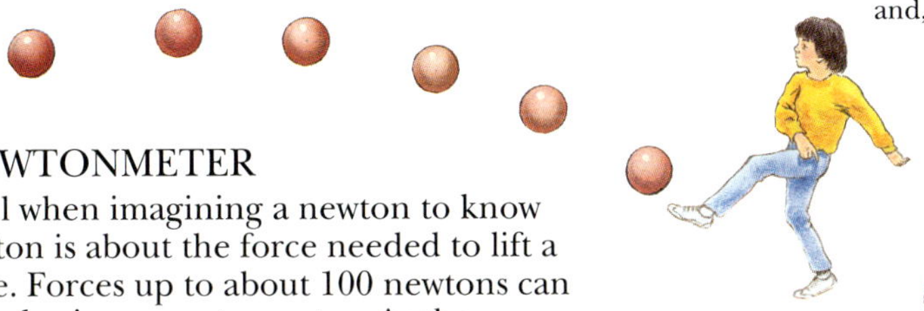

THE NEWTONMETER

It is helpful when imagining a newton to know that 1 newton is about the force needed to lift a small apple. Forces up to about 100 newtons can be measured using a newtonmeter. As the spring inside is stretched, a marker moves down a scale along the side of the meter and indicates the size of the stretching force – in this case the weight of an apple.

COMPARING FORCES

Lifting a ball requires a force of about 4 newtons. A kick applies a force of about 10 newtons to the ball. Compare this with the force of a jet engine – 100,000 newtons. On a small scale, an insect jumping into the air uses a force of about 0.001 newtons.

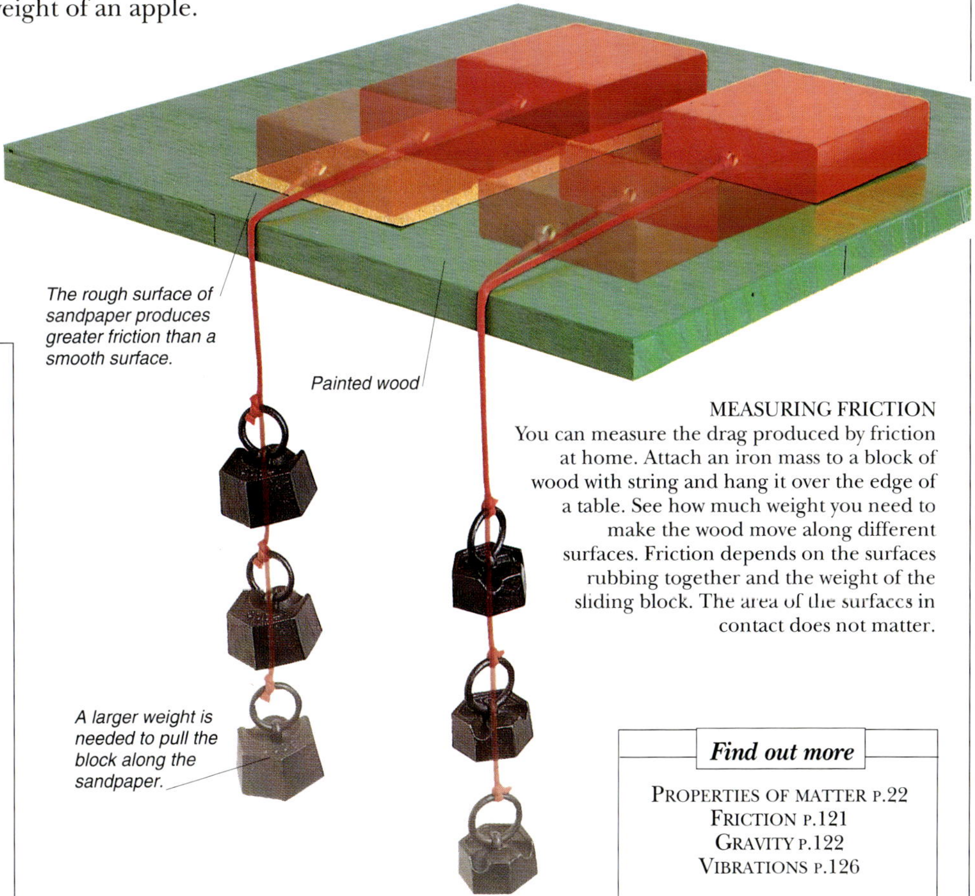

The rough surface of sandpaper produces greater friction than a smooth surface.

Painted wood

A larger weight is needed to pull the block along the sandpaper.

MEASURING FRICTION

You can measure the drag produced by friction at home. Attach an iron mass to a block of wood with string and hang it over the edge of a table. See how much weight you need to make the wood move along different surfaces. Friction depends on the surfaces rubbing together and the weight of the sliding block. The area of the surfaces in contact does not matter.

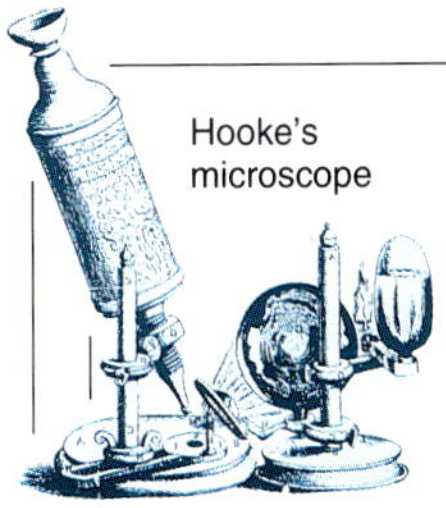

Hooke's microscope

ROBERT HOOKE

English inventor Robert Hooke (1635-1702) is best remembered for discovering how elastic objects stretch. He was a skilled instrument-maker and helped improve scientific instruments such as microscopes, telescopes, and barometers. He designed a telegraph system and a watch regulated by a vibrating spring, rather than a pendulum. In 1665, he published a book containing drawings of insects seen through the microscope.

Find out more

PROPERTIES OF MATTER P.22
FRICTION P.121
GRAVITY P.122
VIBRATIONS P.126

TURNING FORCES

WHEN YOU TURN THE HANDLEBARS of your bicycle, you pull on one side and push on the other. This pair of forces is an example of a couple, or pair of turning forces. The point around which an object turns is called the fulcrum, or pivot. A single force can make an object turn if it acts some distance away from a fixed fulcrum. When you open a door, you apply a single force to the door handle and the door turns as it swings open. The door hinge is the fulcrum around which the door turns. The turning effect of a force depends upon the size of the force and how far away from the fulcrum the force is acting. The further away the force, the greater the turning effect.

BALANCING THE FORCES
When an object is in equilibrium, or balanced, the turning force on one side of the fulcrum is equal to the turning force on the other side. A cyclist in trial riding uses this principle when he stops a plank from seesawing down over a log before he is ready.

MAXIMUM FORCE
In some countries, cattle are used to turn a wheel to raise water. They are harnessed to the end of a pole attached to the wheel. As they walk round, they turn the wheel. It is easier for them if the pole is as long as possible to make their turning force greater.

A bottle containing a small amount of water is stable as it has a low centre of gravity. The centre of gravity remains above the base of the bottle when it is tipped slightly, producing a turning force that returns the bottle to its original position.

STABILITY
An object is said to be in stable equilibrium if, when pushed slightly, its centre of gravity is still lying above its base. Gravity pulls the object back to its original position. If an object falls over when pushed slightly, it is in unstable equilibrium. Its centre of gravity is no longer above its base and gravity pulls the object further. An object is in neutral equilibrium if it remains in its new position when pushed slightly.

WEIGHING SCALES
The Ancient Romans used turning forces to weigh things on a steelyard. Steelyards are still used today. You may get weighed on a steelyard at the doctor's. While you stand on the scales, a bob is moved along a bar until the bar balances. Your weight can then be read from a scale on the bar where the balancing weight stops.

VEHICLE TESTING
Tall vehicles are made safer by putting their wheels wide apart and their engines low down. This keeps their centre of gravity low. This bus is being tested to see how far it will tip before it topples over.

Find out more

FORCES AND MOTION P.120
GRAVITY P.122
MEASURING FORCES P.123
MACHINES P.130

CIRCULAR MOTION

WHEELS, SPINNING TOPS, propellers, and roundabouts all go round in circles. They are really changing direction all the time. Each part of the spinning object is trying to move forwards in a straight line, but a force is pulling them in towards the centre of the circle. This force is called centripetal force. It continually changes the direction of a turning object so that it goes round in a circle and not in a straight line. When an animal, running at speed, makes a tight turn, its feet push into the ground. The ground pushes back and this provides a centripetal force. If the animal was running on ice and could not grip the ground, there would be no centripetal force and the animal would find it extremely difficult to make the turn!

SPINNING GYROSCOPE
Spinning objects have inertia, just as objects moving in a straight line have. They resist having their direction of movement changed. A gyroscope is a device that contains a spinning wheel. If the wheel is spinning fast enough, it resists gravity and it is then very difficult to push the gyroscope over. Electrically driven gyroscopes are used in navigation systems on aeroplanes and ships.

CENTRIFUGAL FORCE
A toy car racing round a loop-the-loop track does not fall off, even when it is upside-down. A force appears to be pushing it upwards. This is sometimes called centrifugal force. But centrifugal force is really inertia trying to make the car go straight on.

As the bowl spins, the water rises up the walls.

Turntable spinning the bowl round.

The water is level when the bowl is not spinning.

CLIMBING WATER
If a bowl of water is spun quickly round and round, the water tries to fly out in a straight line. A force is needed to stop it. This is provided by the walls of the bowl. The faster the bowl spins, the more the water moves outwards. A spin dryer uses this effect to remove water from clothes. The water moves towards the walls of the drum, and if it finds one of the holes it flies straight through.

WEIGHTLESSNESS IN ORBIT

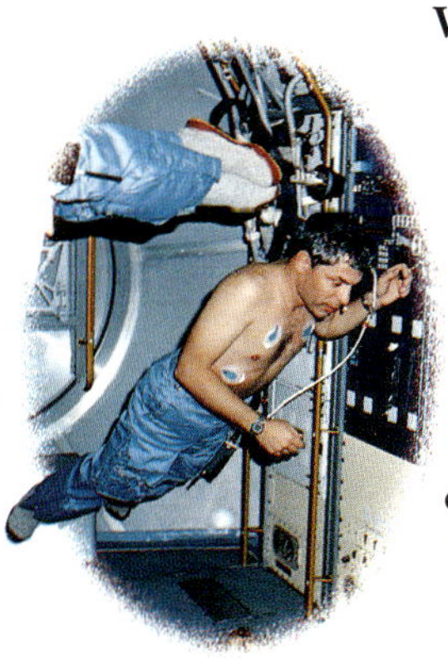

A space shuttle is held in orbit around the Earth because the Earth's gravity provides a centripetal force, which makes it move in a circle rather than fly off into space. Astronauts inside the shuttle are affected by gravity to the same extent. They feel weightless because they are continuously falling. But they are moving forwards at such a speed that they are carried "over the horizon" in a circular path that never gets any nearer the ground.

The faster the thrower spins, the further the hammer will fly when he lets go.

HAMMER THROW
A hammer thrower spins the hammer round as fast as he can before releasing it. The centripetal force needed to keep it spinning round is the pull on the wire. When the thrower lets go of the hammer, he removes the centripetal force and the hammer's inertia makes it fly off in a straight line.

Find out more

FORCES AND MOTION P.120
FRICTION P.121
GRAVITY P.122
ROCKETS P.299

VIBRATIONS

IF YOU HANG A MASS from a piece of string, and push the mass to one side, it will swing from side to side in a regular way. These back and forth movements are called oscillations, or vibrations. The number of times an object vibrates in one second is called the frequency. Everything has a natural frequency. If you force an object to vibrate at its natural frequency, the oscillations get larger. In 1940, the wind made the Tacoma Narrows bridge in Washington State, United States, vibrate at a rate that matched its natural frequency. The vibrations became so violent that the bridge collapsed. But vibrations can also be useful. Pneumatic drills use vibrations to break up materials, and clocks measure time by counting regular vibrations.

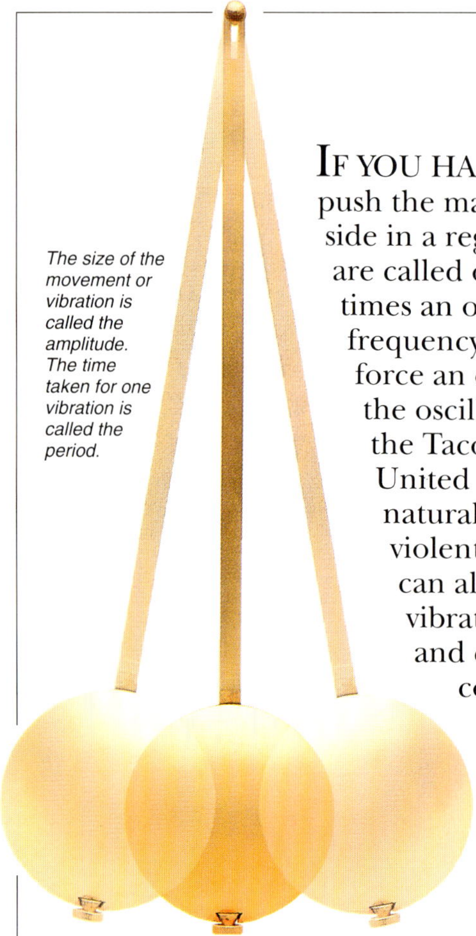

PENDULUM
The swing of a pendulum is a vibration. The time taken for one swing depends only upon the length of the pendulum, provided the swings are small. The weight of the bob on the end does not matter. Italian experimenter Galileo suggested that a clock could be regulated by a pendulum. In a pendulum clock, the pendulum swings and turns a wheel at a regular rate. The wheel turns the hands of the clock.

EARTHQUAKE VIBRATIONS
Vibrations caused by an earthquake can make buildings collapse. This special effects photo symbolizes an earthquake in San Francisco, United States. San Francisco lies on the San Andreas fault, one of the world's great fault lines. A fault line is where earthquakes are likely to happen.

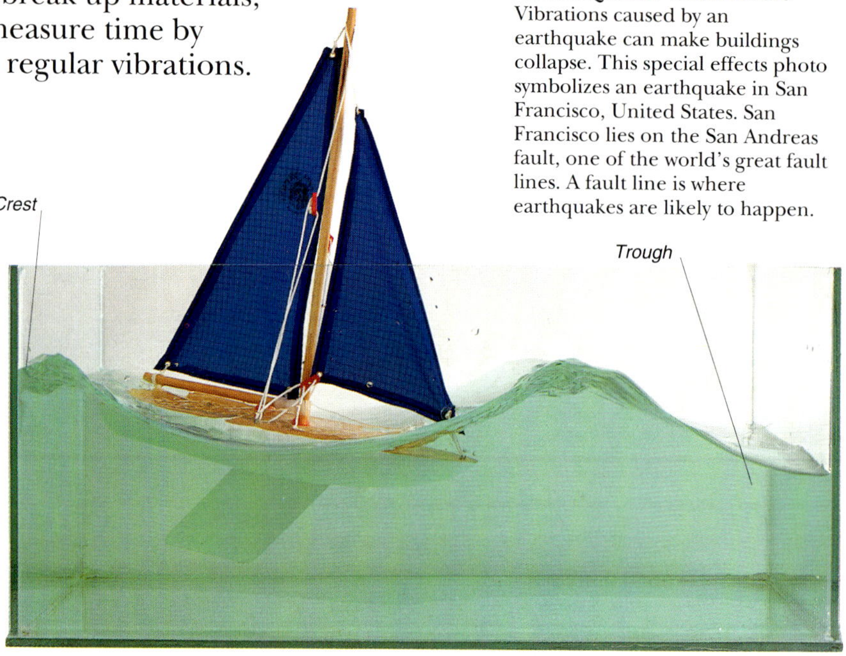

WATER WAVES
Ripples on a pond or waves on the sea are transverse waves. As the wave passes, water particles vibrate up and down at right angles to the direction of the wave.

WAVES

Vibrations cause waves. Some waves are obvious, as on the sea and on the surface of a pond. But some waves are not so easy to see, for example sound waves, which are caused by something vibrating. Waves can be transverse or longitudinal.

SOUND WAVES
When a musical instrument such as the cymbals vibrate, they cause sound waves in the air. In a sound wave, air particles vibrate back and forth in the same direction as the wave is travelling. They are longitudinal waves.

PIEZOELECTRICITY

Quartz has a special property – an electric charge changes its size. Because of this piezoelectric effect, a suitable electric current makes a crystal vibrate at a precise frequency. In a quartz watch, current from a battery makes a micro-thin slice of quartz crystal vibrate 32,768 times each second. A microchip reduces this rate to produce a signal once a second. This signal controls the motor that turns the hands or activates the digital display.

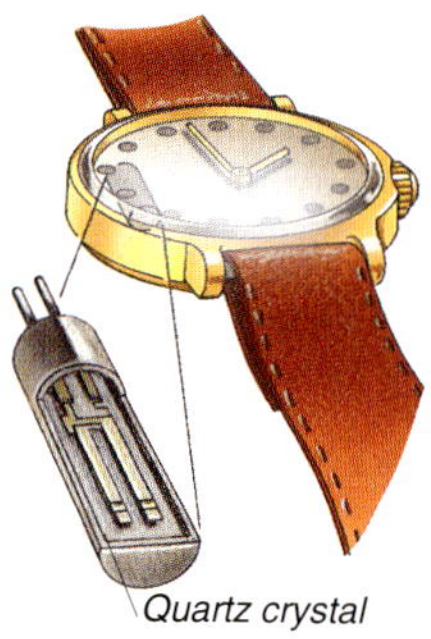

Find out more

CRYSTALS P.30
SOUND P.178
MEASURING SOUND P.180
EARTHQUAKES P.220
WAVES, TIDES, AND CURRENTS P.235

PRESSURE

WHY DO CAMELS have large, flat feet? Why does a pin have a sharp point? The reason is because if you spread a force over a large area, the pressure of the force will be reduced. And by concentrating a force into a small area the pressure will be greater. A camel does not sink into the sand because its weight is spread over a large area. But when you push a drawing pin into a notice board, the sharp point goes into the board easily because the force of your thumb is concentrated into a tiny area.

Pressure is measured by the force acting on a single unit of area.

SPREADING THE LOAD
The jacana bird of South America has exceedingly long toes and claws. Its weight is therefore spread over a large area and it can walk on the floating lily pads without sinking.

SINKING IN
A watering can does not sink into soil because its weight is spread over its base. But a trowel is easy to push into soil as its weight is concentrated into the thin edge. A sharp knife cuts easily for the same reason: the force on the knife is concentrated into a small area along the cutting edge.

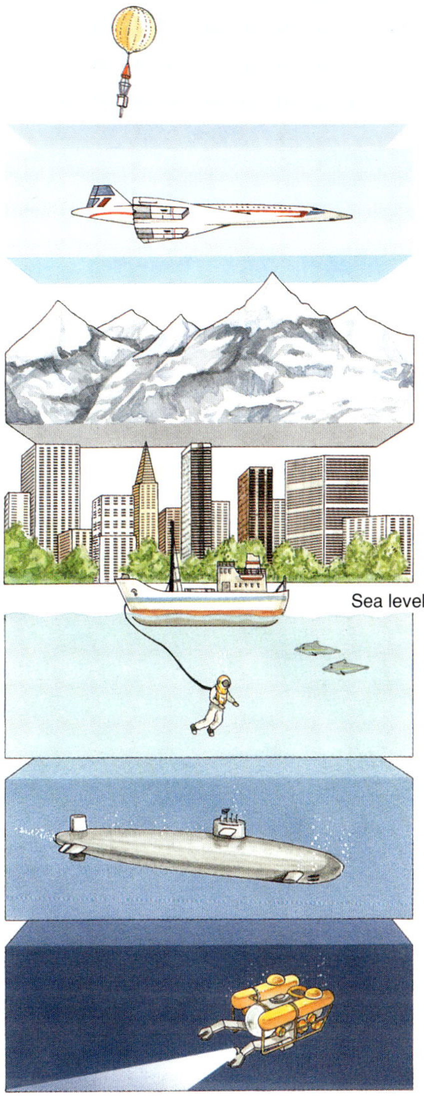

Air pressure at 20,000 m (66,000 ft) is less than one-tenth that at sea level.

Airliners fly at a height where air presssure is less than pressure inside the body. It would be impossible for the body to take in air, so the inside of airliners is pressurized.

On mountain tops, the air is thin so climbers usually use breathing apparatus to give them more oxygen. Air pressure is half that at sea level.

At sea level, air pressure is roughly equal to the weight of a cow sitting on a large dinner plate.

People cannot dive deeper than about 120 m (400 ft) as the water pressure would crush them.

Submarines can dive deep under water. They have thick hulls to withstand the great water pressure.

At a depth of 10,000 m (33,000 ft) under the ocean, the pressure of water is equivalent to seven elephants balanced on a small dinner plate!

UNDER PRESSURE
Liquids and gases, both called fluids, exert pressure on objects. Air exerts pressure on you. If it were not for the fact that the fluids inside your body exert as much pressure as the air outside, the pressure of air at ground level would crush you! Air pressure decreases the higher up you go as there is less and less air.

EVANGELISTA TORRICELLI

Air pressure is measured with a barometer. The mercury barometer was invented by Italian Evangelista Torricelli (1608-47) in 1643. He discovered that the height of mercury in a tube placed upside-down in a cup of mercury varies as air pressure changes. Torricelli learnt from Galileo and eventually succeeded him as court mathematician to the Grand Duke of Tuscany. A unit of pressure, the torr, is named after him. One torr is the pressure that supports 1mm (0.04 in) of mercury in a barometer.

PRESSURE IN LIQUIDS
The pressure in liquids acts in all directions. The water squirts through the holes in the side of this container because of horizontal pressure.

Find out more

BEHAVIOUR OF GASES P.51
FORCES IN FLUIDS P.128
ATMOSPHERE P.248
AIR PRESSURE P.250

Forces in Fluids

LIQUIDS AND GASES both flow when a force acts on them. They are known as fluids. Fluids have no definite shape and take the shape of their container. When fluids are squeezed by a force, the force is transmitted to all other parts of the fluid. This is called Pascal's Principle and it is used to drive some machinery. In the hydraulic brake of a car, for example, the force applied to the brake pedal is transmitted to the wheels by a liquid, called the brake fluid. Another useful property of fluids is that a fast-moving fluid has a lower pressure than a slow-moving one. This is known as Bernoulli's Principle. It enables lumbering aeroplanes to soar high into the sky.

BIRD WINGS
A bird gets most of its lift by flapping its wings which push the air downwards producing an upward reaction force. However, when the bird is just gliding, the wing itself produces some lift because of its shape.

AEROFOIL
The wing of an aeroplane is curved on top and nearly flat underneath. This special shape is called an aerofoil; it rises when air, which is a fluid, flows around it. This is because air flowing over the top of an aerofoil-shaped wing travels faster than air passing underneath. According to Bernoulli's Principle, this means that the pressure under the wing is greater than the pressure over the wing, creating lift. The faster the air flow, the greater the lift. This is why an aircraft must be travelling very fast to take off.

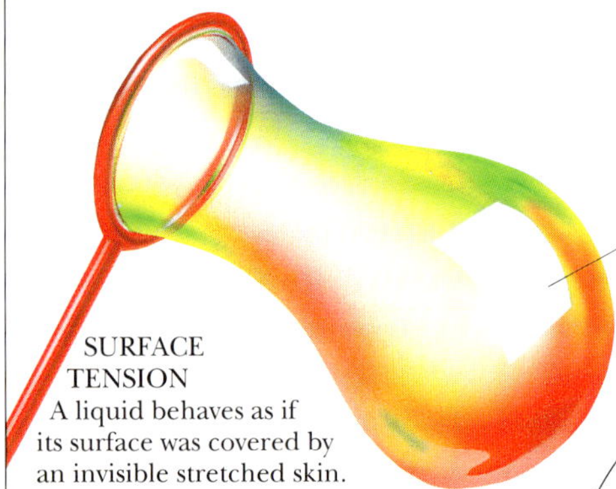

SURFACE TENSION
A liquid behaves as if its surface was covered by an invisible stretched skin. This effect is called surface tension. It is caused by forces between molecules pulling those molecules at the surface inwards. A bubble is normally a sphere because surface tension pulls it into this shape.

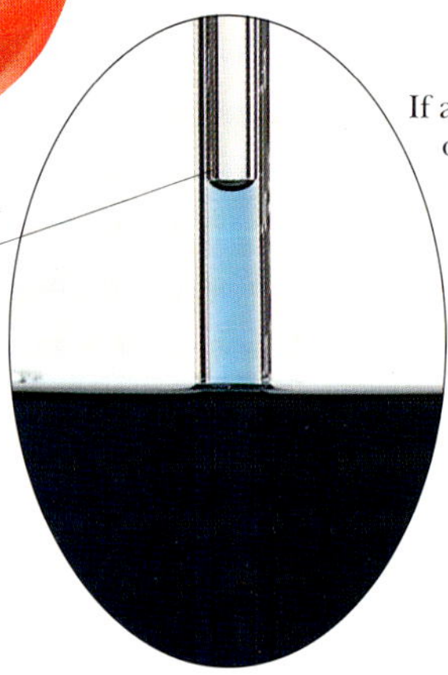

CAPILLARY ACTION
If a liquid is at the bottom of a very narrow tube, it may move up the tube. This is known as capillary action. It will happen if the force of attraction between the liquid molecules and the molecules of the tube is stronger than the attraction between the liquid molecules themselves.

BLAISE PASCAL
Frenchman Blaise Pascal (1623-62) was a brilliant mathematician and religious thinker. He made the first successful calculating machine at the age of 22. In 1646, he made a mercury barometer and later used it to measure air pressure. While studying liquids, he discovered the principle named after him. Pascal's Principle states that, in a liquid or gas, pressure applied to one point is transmitted equally to all parts of the fluid. Pascal's name is given to a unit of pressure. One pascal (Pa) is 1 newton per square metre.

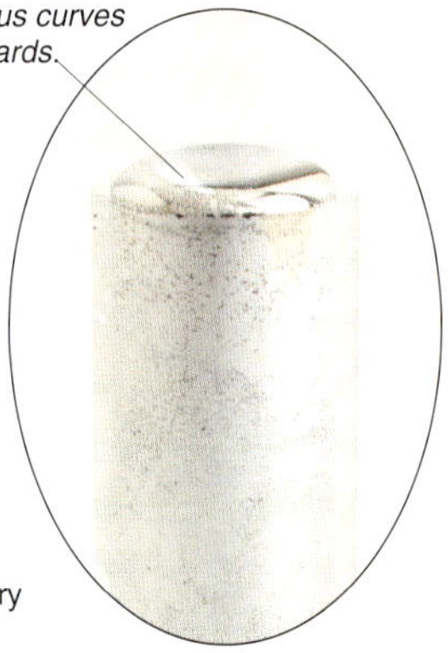

COHESION AND ADHESION
The surface, or meniscus, of water in a tube is curved upwards but that of mercury is curved downwards. This is because the particles of mercury are strongly attracted to each other; they have strong cohesion (and a high surface tension). Cohesion is a force between particles of the same type. The water particles are more attracted to the glass particles of the tube. This force between two different materials is called adhesion. It is the reason why raindrops stick to a windowpane.

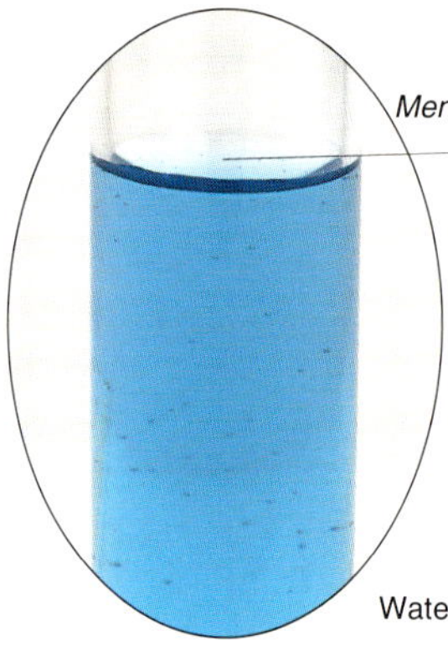

Find out more

PROPERTIES OF MATTER P.22
BONDING P.28
SOAPS AND DETERGENTS P.95
ADHESIVES P.106
PRESSURE P.127
CALCULATORS P.172
AIR PRESSURE P.250
FACT FINDER P.408

FLOATING AND SINKING

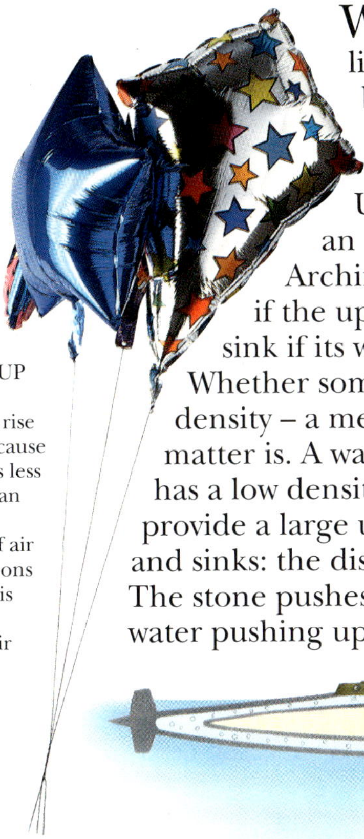

WHY DOES AN OBJECT seem to get lighter as you lower it into water? It is because the water pushes against it, supporting some of its weight. This supporting force is called the upthrust. Upthrust is equal to the weight of fluid an object displaces, or pushes away. This is Archimedes' Principle. An object will float if the upthrust is equal to its weight. It will sink if its weight is greater than the upthrust. Whether something floats, depends on its density – a measure of how packed together its matter is. A wax candle floats on water because it has a low density and displaces enough water to provide a large upthrust. A stone is denser than water and sinks: the displaced water does not equal its weight. The stone pushes away with more force than that of the water pushing up.

GOING UP
Helium balloons rise in air because helium is less dense than air. The weight of air the balloons displace is greater than their weight.

FLOATING IN WATER
A peach floats in water because the weight of water it displaces is equal to its own weight. This means that the force of the upthrust exactly equals the force of the peach's weight pushing down.

SUBMARINES
Inside a submarine there are containers called ballast tanks. If these are full of air, the submarine will float. Even though it is made of steel, the *average* density of the submarine is less than that of water. By pumping water into the ballast tanks, the submarine can sink. This is because with its ballast tanks full of water, the submarine has a higher density than water.

ARCHIMEDES
It is said that Archimedes, a Greek inventor who lived in the third century B.C., discovered his Principle after noticing that his bath overflowed when he got into it. He ran through the streets naked, shouting "Eureka!" ("I've got it!"). With his principle, he helped to prove that the King's goldsmith had tried to cheat him by putting silver into a gold crown. Archimedes made discoveries in hydrostatics (science of stationary fluids), geometry, and mechanics (science of machines).

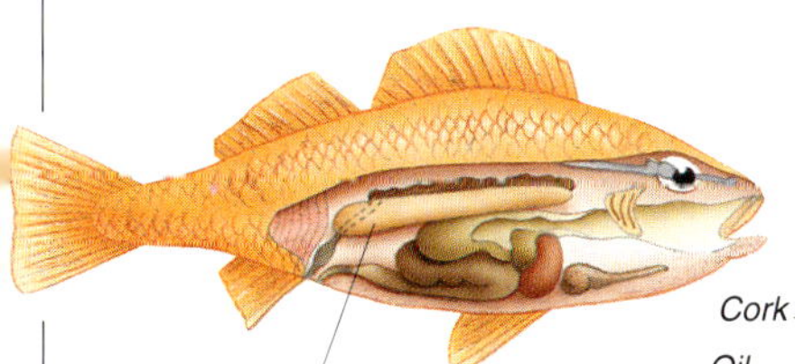

FISH
Some fish have a swim bladder like the ballast tanks of a submarine. Air can enter this bladder either via the fish's mouth, or from the bloodstream. This enables the fish to rise in the water.

HIGHER OR LOWER?
Oil floats on water because it is less dense than water. Water floats on syrup because it is less dense than syrup. A cork is less dense than all three liquids, and so floats on the surface of the oil. A plastic block has a density lower than water but higher than oil. This means it sinks through the oil, but floats on the water. A grape has a higher density than oil or water, but lower than syrup. So the grape floats on the syrup.

Find out more

PROPERTIES OF MATTER P.22
FORCES IN FLUIDS P.128
MACHINES P.130
FISH P.326
FACT FINDER P.408

MACHINES

NOT ALL MACHINES are large and noisy. Many are small and they are used to do simple jobs. But whatever their size, all machines make a particular job easier to do. Some machines can change a small movement into a large one; some can change a small force into a large one; others can change the direction or position of a force, and apply it where it is most needed. The smaller the effort force, the greater distance it must move. This is called the Principle of the Machine. Unfortunately all machines are less than 100 per cent efficient. Some of the effort put in is not used to do the job in hand, but to overcome friction between parts.

COMPLEX MACHINES

A combine harvester is a complex machine, but it is made up of lots of simple machines connected together in many ingenious ways: by gear trains, levers, moving belts, and hydraulic pipe systems. The result is a useful tool that combines the two parts of harvesting – cutting the crop and separating the grain – hence its name.

MAGNIFYING MOVEMENT
When a rowing eight use their oars to move the boat, they are using machines that magnify movement. They move the inner end of the oars a small distance but the other end of the oars moves a larger distance, pulling the boat swiftly through the water.

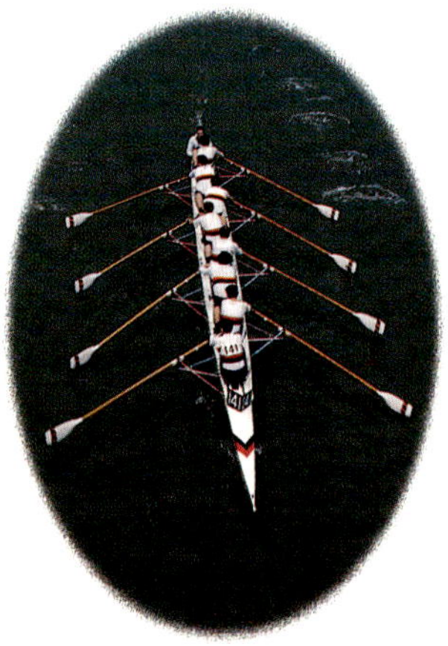

MAGNIFYING FORCE
Archimedes, the Ancient Greek inventor, said, "Give me a lever long enough, and I could move the world". In theory, this statement is true because a lever magnifies force. For example, a claw-hammer, a type of lever, can be used to remove a nail from a piece of wood.

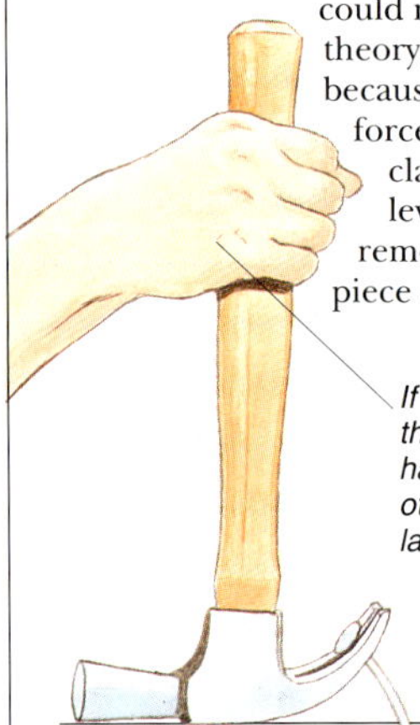

INSIDE A PIANO

A pianist needs to play notes quickly to produce good music. Each key in a piano is linked to a complex system of levers that magnify movement. The pianist has to use only a small finger movement to make the hammer hit the piano wire strongly, and sound a note.

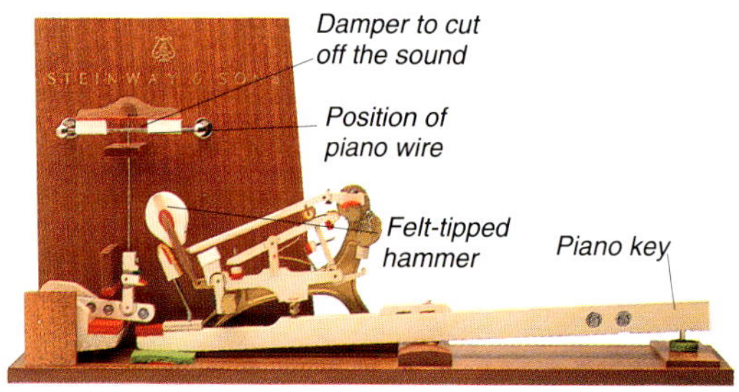

ROUND AND ROUND
It is easier to walk up a mountain by taking the winding road than to try to walk straight up the side. The winding road is acting as a simple machine. It decreases the effort you use to reach the top of the mountain, but increases the distance you must move.

Simple machines

Slopes, wedges, screws, levers, wheels and axles, pulleys, and gears are all called simple machines. They can make a job easier to do because they allow a small force, the effort, to overcome a larger force, the load. Machines that increase force are said to give a mechanical advantage. Mechanical advantage can be calculated by dividing the load by the effort. In machines that are used to increase movement, the advantage, called the velocity ratio, is calculated by dividing the distance the load moves by the distance the effort moves.

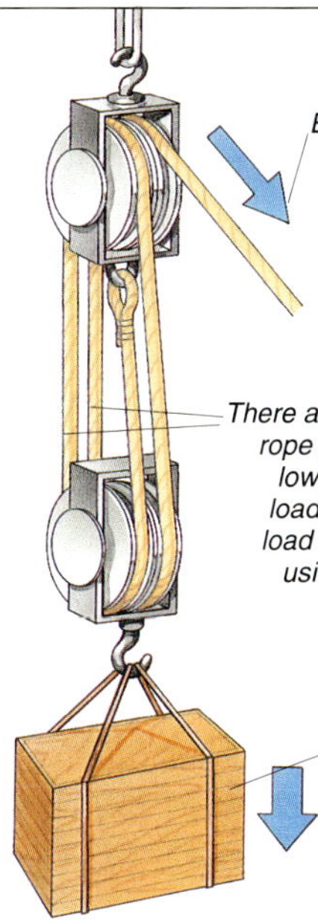

WEDGE

The blade of an axe is a wedge – a machine that magnifies force. When the axe is swung into the wood, the force of the swing is transferred to the blade. The blade moves forwards through the wood, and forces it to split apart. The wood moves a smaller distance than the blade but with more force.

PULLEY

A pulley is useful for lifting things up vertically. It is simply a piece of rope wound round a wheel. One end of the rope is attached to the load, and force is applied at the other end to lift the load. A pulley magnifies force when more than one wheel is used. One wheel is attached to the load and the others to a support, such as a beam.

GEARS, AND WHEEL AND AXLE

A rotary egg whisk contains two kinds of machine: gears, and wheels and axles. Gears are toothed wheels that are interlocked in pairs. They can magnify speed or force. Usually, one wheel is larger than the other. A wheel and axle magnifies force because the wheel is larger than the axle. The axle turns in a smaller circle but with greater force.

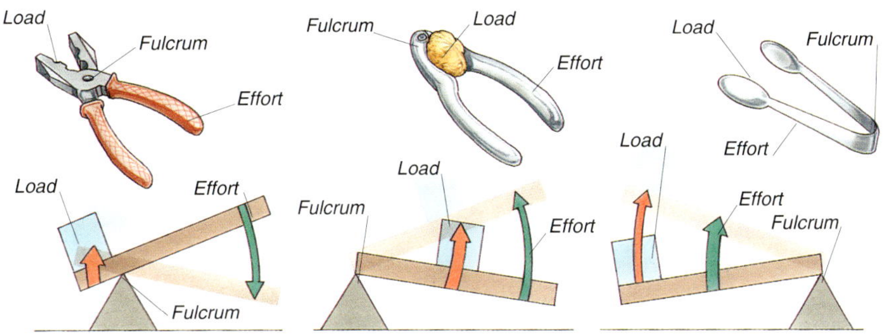

Pliers are a class 1 lever – a force magnifier.

Nutcrackers are a class 2 lever – a force magnifier.

Tongs are a class 3 lever – a distance magnifier.

LEVER

A lever is a rod or bar that turns about a point called the fulcrum, or pivot, to move a load. There are three kinds of lever, with different arrangements of load, effort, and fulcrum. Some levers magnify force, others magnify distance. For a lever to be a force magnifier, the effort must be applied further away from the fulcrum than the load. There are examples of levers in your body. For example, your arm is a class three lever. Your elbow is the fulcrum, the muscles in your arm provide the effort, and your hand is the load.

INCLINED PLANE

It is easier to push something up a slope, or inclined plane, than to lift it straight up. Removers use a ramp to load heavy items into a van. They have to move things further than they would if they lifted them vertically, but they need to use less effort. An inclined plane is therefore a force magnifier.

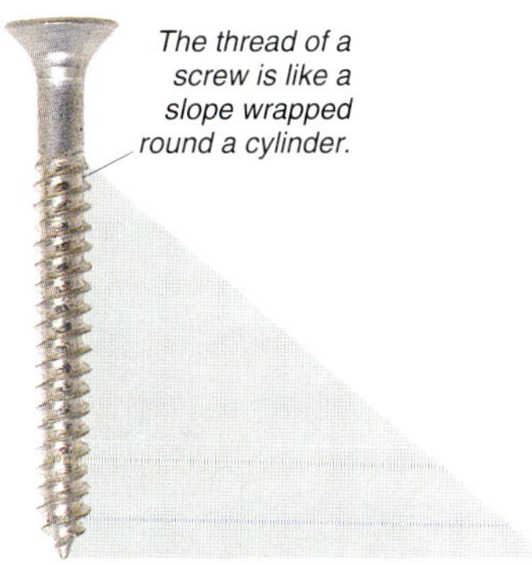

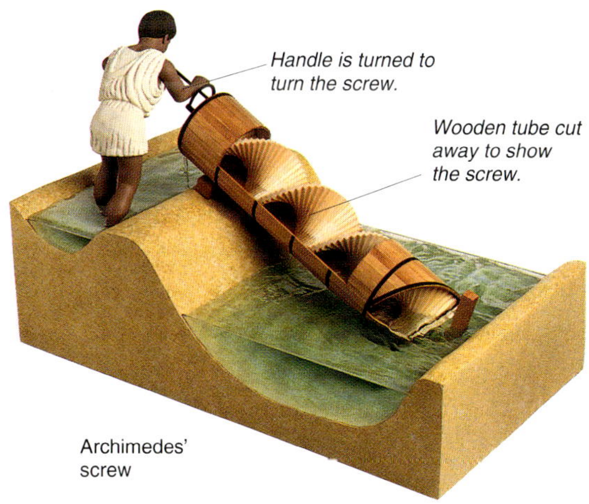

Archimedes' screw

SCREW

The thread of a screw is really an inclined plane. A screw can produce a mechanical advantage because it turns around a greater distance than it moves forwards. This means that it moves forwards with a greater force than is used to turn it. Water is sometimes lifted, for example from a river to irrigate a field, with a device called an Archimedes' screw. Each time the screw turns, it lifts water a little bit higher up inside a tube.

Find out more

Forces and motion p.120
Turning forces p.124
Floating and sinking p.129
Musical sounds p.186
Skeletons p.352
Fact finder p.408

WORK AND ENERGY

When an apple that weighs 1 newton is lifted vertically by 1 m (3.3 ft), a joule of work is done.

TO A SCIENTIST, work is done only when a force moves something. If you lift a heavy object, you do work because you exert a force which moves that object. Work cannot be done without energy. Energy is the ability to do work. When work is done, energy is used, or converted from one form to another. You get your energy from your food; it is called chemical energy. Some machines get their energy in chemical form – from fuels such as petrol or gas. And there are other forms of energy: heat, light, sound, nuclear, and electrical energy. To understand how and why things move we need to know what kind of energy they have, and how much.

MEASURING WORK
When a fork-lift truck lifts crates, it is working to overcome the force of gravity. The heavier the crates, and the further the truck lifts them, the more work is done.

NATURAL ENERGY
A dung beetle uses energy stored in its muscles to do work – in this case, to push a ball of dung up a slope. The heavier the ball is, and the higher it is pushed, the more work the beetle does, and the more energy it uses.

JOULES
The joule is used as the unit for work as well as energy. One joule is the work done when a force of 1 newton moves something a distance of 1 m (3.3 ft) in the direction of the force.

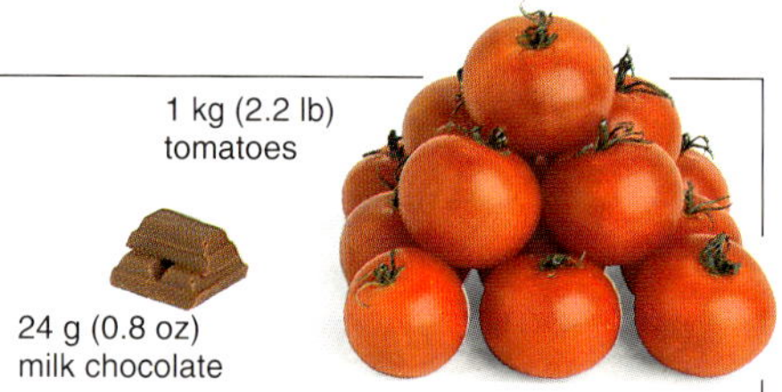

FOOD ENERGY

You would not be able to stay alive without the energy you get from food. But it can be just as bad for you to take in too much energy as too little. Different kinds of food contain different amounts of energy. For example, you would have to eat about 1 kg (2.2 lb) fresh tomatoes to get as much energy as you would from just 24 g (0.8 oz) milk chocolate.

JAMES JOULE

Englishman James Joule (1818-89) was one of the first to realize that work produces heat and that heat is a form of energy. He rotated paddles in a container of water and the water became warmer. The more work that was done to turn the paddles, the hotter the water became. Joule realized that work was changing movement energy into heat energy. Joule loved experimenting. He once found that the water at the base of a waterfall was hotter than the water at the top, proving that the energy of the falling water was being converted into heat.

ENERGY REQUIREMENTS
Energy is measured in units called joules, but the joule is a small unit. There are 1,000 joules in a kilojoule (kJ) – a unit used for measuring the amount of energy in our food. Kilocalories (kcal) are also used. One kilocalorie is equal to 4.2 kilojoules. Males and females, babies, teenagers, and adults, all use different amounts of energy every day, and it depends on what they are doing. A teenage boy needs about 12,600 kJ (3,000 kcal) of energy each day. A teenage girl needs about 10,500 kJ (2,500 kcal).

TYPES OF ENERGY

A moving object has energy, called kinetic energy. The energy of a moving car could demolish a brick wall. Where there are forces, there is also stored energy, called potential energy because it has the potential to turn into kinetic energy. Chemical energy is a form of stored energy. It is stored in the chemical make-up of some substances such as plants, oil, coal, and batteries.The most versatile form of energy is electricity. It can be easily converted into other forms of energy: light, sound, and heat.

A portable television has chemical energy stored in its battery. This is released when an electric current flows through the television to produce heat, light, and sound.

JAMES WATT

Scottish engineer James Watt (1736-1819) became Mathematical Instrument Maker at the University of Glasgow when he was 20. While repairing a model steam engine, he realized how the engine could be improved by having two cylinders. He made a full-scale improved engine which was much more powerful and economical than earlier engines. His engines were soon used in factories and mines all over the country and were exported to Europe and North America.

A kitten has chemical energy stored in its muscles. It uses some of this energy to climb up a tree. As it climbs, it increases its gravitational potential energy – the potential to fall off! When it falls, the kitten will have kinetic energy.

A plant has chemical energy stored in its leaves. This can be released if the chemical make-up of the plant is changed, for example if it is eaten by an animal or burnt to produce heat and light.

It takes two children to lift the weight as quickly as the man.

POWER LIFTING

Power is the rate at which work is done, or how quickly one form of energy is changed to another. A man is more powerful than a child. He can lift a load quickly, but children can only lift it slowly. The unit of power is the watt which equals 1 joule per second.

KINETIC ENERGY

Windmills were originally used to drive a machine such as a millstone. When the sails turned, they moved the millstone converting the kinetic energy of the wind into the movement of the millstone. The amount of kinetic energy that a moving object has increases with the mass and speed of the object. If the mass of a moving object is doubled, its kinetic energy is doubled. If the speed doubles, the kinetic energy increases four times.

A jack-in-the-box has elastic potential energy when it is squeezed into its box.

When the lid of the box is lifted, the jack-in-the-box has kinetic energy as it jumps up.

POTENTIAL ENERGY

Potential energy is the energy that a body has because of its position or because of the state it is in. For example, a jack-in-the-box has potential energy when it is squashed into its box. Types of potential energy are: gravitational potential energy (of a raised object), elastic potential energy (of a stretched or squashed elastic material), electrical potential energy (of an object near an electric charge), and magnetic potential energy (of a piece of iron near a magnet).

Find out more

ENERGY SOURCES P.134
HEAT P.140
ENGINES P.143
ELECTRICITY SUPPLY P.160
SOUND AND LIGHT P.177
FACT FINDER P.408

NUCLEAR ENERGY

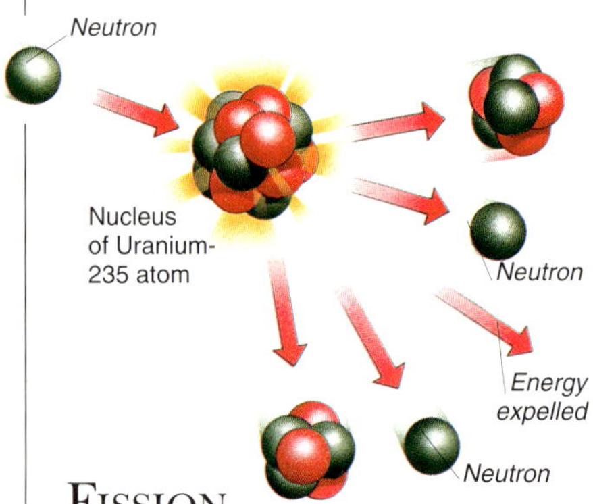

THE ATOM contains a huge amount of energy – nuclear energy. This is due to the strong forces that exist between particles in the nucleus of an atom. Nuclear reactions happen naturally: they power the Sun. Humans have tried to harness nuclear energy, but have only managed to obtain it from certain atoms, such as those of uranium, plutonium. and deuterium (a type of hydrogen). One kilogram (2.2 lb) of deuterium can produce as much energy as three million kilograms (6.6 million lb) of coal. There are two basic processes for releasing nuclear energy: nuclear fission, when the nucleus of an atom splits, and nuclear fusion, when the nuclei of two or more atoms fuse, or join together.

FISSION

Normally, nothing can penetrate an atom's nucleus because it is surrounded by circling electrons. But a high-speed neutron can blast through to be absorbed by the nucleus. If the nucleus is unstable, it will split into two parts. This is nuclear fission. Two or three neutrons are produced, which can go on to blast more nuclei, setting up a chain reaction.

RADIATION
These workers are preparing to replace a fuel rod in the reactor core. The core is under 10.5 m (35 ft) of water to protect the workers from the radiation produced. The blue glow is due to the fact that energetic charged particles travel faster through water than does light.

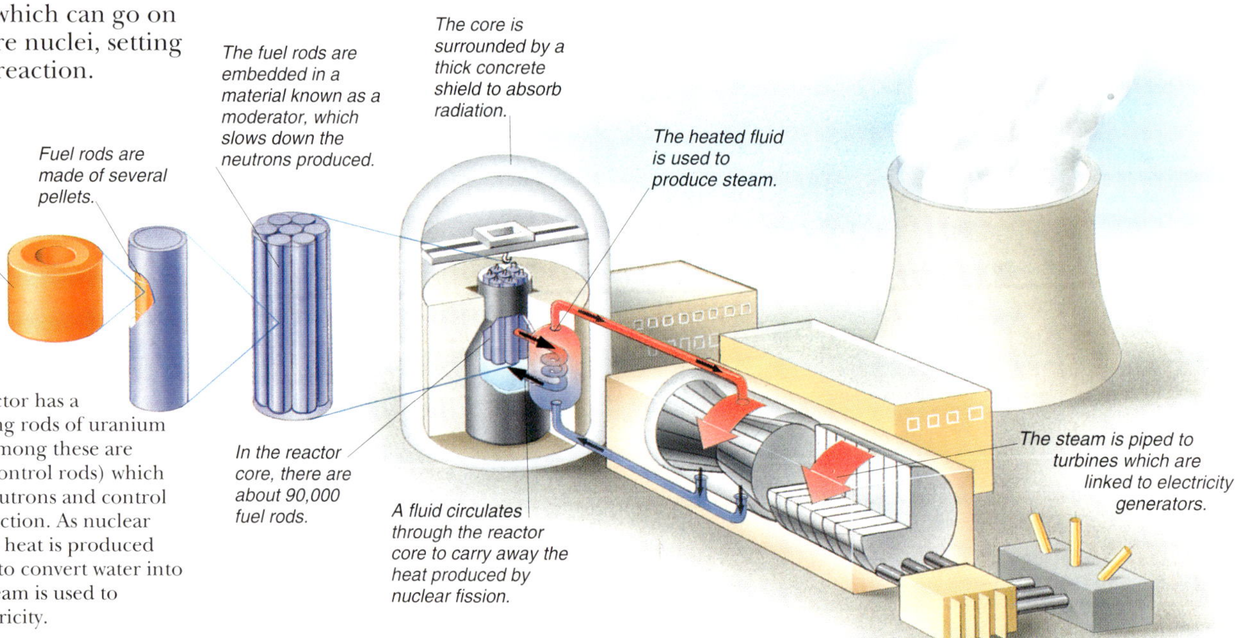

NUCLEAR REACTOR
A nuclear reactor has a core containing rods of uranium (fuel rods). Among these are boron rods (control rods) which can absorb neutrons and control the rate of reaction. As nuclear fission occurs, heat is produced which is used to convert water into steam. The steam is used to generate electricity.

MASS INTO ENERGY

When a nuclear reaction occurs, the mass of the products is less than the starting mass. Some mass has vanished. Albert Einstein showed that this disappearing mass is converted to energy. When a mass, m, disappears, energy, E, is released. $E=mc^2$, where c is the speed of light. As c is a very large number, a tiny loss of mass produces a huge amount of energy. Just 1 kg (2.2 lb) of matter could produce as much energy as a major earthquake, which can cause great damage, as shown here in Mexico City in 1985.

NUCLEAR WASTE
Fuel rods in a nuclear reactor become used up and have to be replaced. But they are highly radioactive and therefore dangerous. Nuclear waste will remain radioactive even after 25,000 years, so must be disposed of carefully. It can be stored as a concentrated liquid in stainless-steel tanks which are surrounded in concrete. The most dangerous nuclear waste can be turned into glass blocks. It is planned to store these blocks in deep mines underground.

NUCLEAR WEAPONS

An atomic bomb uses uncontrolled nuclear fission. If a certain amount of uranium-235 or plutonium-239 is brought together, it will explode. A hydrogen bomb uses nuclear fusion. It is an atomic bomb surrounded by deuterium. When the atomic bomb explodes, the high temperature produced makes the deuterium nuclei fuse. This photo shows the city of Hiroshima in Japan after an atomic bomb was dropped on it in 1945.

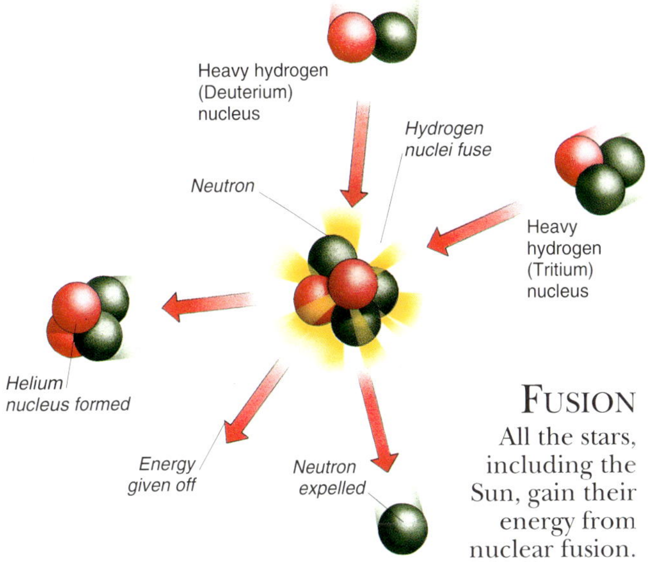

FUSION

All the stars, including the Sun, gain their energy from nuclear fusion. This is when two or more nuclei stick, or fuse together. In the Sun, for example, hydrogen nuclei are fusing to form helium nuclei. In the process, some mass is lost and converted to energy.

HARNESSING FUSION
As yet, fusion is not a practical way to obtain energy on Earth. Most fusion research uses a machine called a tokamak. This holds a doughnut-shaped vessel containing the gas to be fused, called a plasma. The plasma must be heated to a temperature of millions of degrees before fusion occurs. No container could cope with such heat, so magnetic fields are used to keep the hot plasma away from the vessel walls.

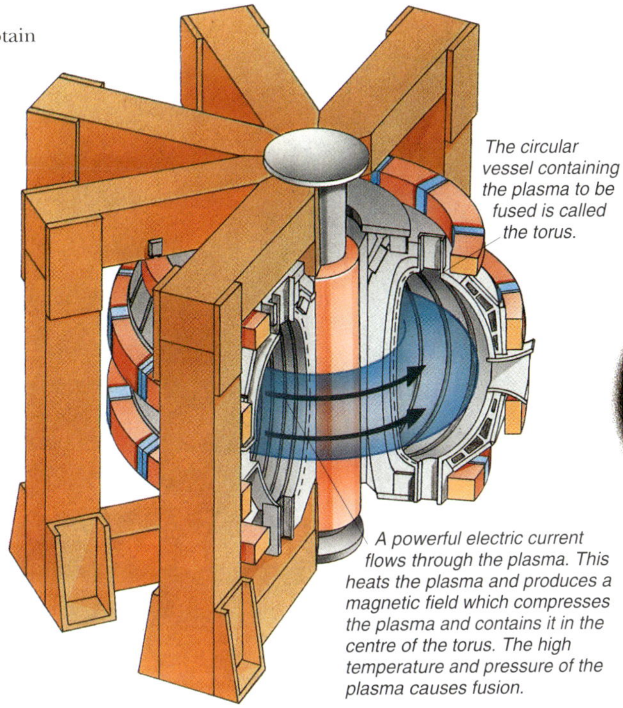

The circular vessel containing the plasma to be fused is called the torus.

A powerful electric current flows through the plasma. This heats the plasma and produces a magnetic field which compresses the plasma and contains it in the centre of the torus. The high temperature and pressure of the plasma causes fusion.

FUSION ACCELERATOR
Other efforts to produce controlled nuclear fusion are carried out in machines called particle beam accelerators. The most powerful one is in Albuquerque, United States. This directs a 100-trillion-watt pulse of electricity towards a pea-sized pellet of deuterium gas. The accelerator sits in a tank of water. As the beam is fired, electric sparks cross the surface. The gas is heated to millions of degrees for a few billionths of a second – not enough to start a fusion reaction, but research is continuing.

NUCLEAR ENERGY

1905 German physicist Albert Einstein shows that mass can be converted into energy.

1919 New Zealander Ernest Rutherford announces he split the nucleus of a nitrogen atom.

1939 German scientists Otto Hahn and Fritz Strassman announce the discovery of nuclear fission.

1942 First nuclear reactor built by Italian Enrico Fermi in a squash court at the University of Chicago, United States.

1951 First nuclear electricity made by an experimental breeder reactor at Idaho, United States.

1956 The first commercial nuclear power station starts up at Calder Hall, England.

1986 An explosion in a reactor at Chernobyl, Russia releases clouds of radioactive material which spread as far as Sweden.

1991 First controlled nuclear fusion in JET (Joint European Torus), at Oxford, England.

LISE MEITNER

Austrian-born Lise Meitner (1878-1968) worked in Berlin from 1907 with a German physicist, Otto Hahn. In 1938, she had to flee from the Nazis and went to Sweden. A few months later, Hahn told her of some puzzling results he and another German, Fritz Strassman, had found in an experiment. Meitner realized that Hahn had split the uranium nucleus. This was the discovery of nuclear fission. When Hahn reported the discovery, he gave little credit to Meitner for her insight. In 1944, Hahn was given the Nobel Prize for the discovery but Meitner did not share the prize she rightly deserved.

Find out more

ATOMIC STRUCTURE P.24
RADIOACTIVITY P.26
SPEED P.118
ENERGY SOURCES P.134
ENERGY CONVERSION P.138
CURRENT ELECTRICITY P.148
MAGNETISM P.154
STARS P.278
FACT FINDER P.408

ENERGY CONVERSION

WHEN LIGHTNING STRIKES, electrical energy is spectacularly converted into light, sound, and heat energy. This is just one example of energy changing from one form to another. Energy conversions are continually happening around us. When you press a light switch, electrical energy is converted into light and heat energy. A glow-worm converts the chemical energy from its food into light energy and, if it needs to move, into movement energy. Energy is converted whenever work is done. When you lift something heavy, chemical energy in your muscles is converted into the potential energy of the raised object. The more work that is done, the more energy that is converted.

ENERGY CHANGES
A drawn bow has elastic potential energy. The bow is like a compressed spring. When the bow is released, the potential energy changes to kinetic energy of the moving arrow. When the arrow hits the target, we hear a "thud"; its kinetic energy has changed into sound energy, and a little heat energy. This Egyptian wall painting shows the pharaoh Rameses II.

Inside the Sun, nuclear energy is converted to heat and light energy.

The green leaves of this carrot convert light energy from the Sun into the chemical energy of sugar by a process called photosynthesis.

If you eat a carrot, the chemical energy it contains is transferred to your body. It is used for activities, such as breathing and moving. Winding up an alarm clock changes this chemical energy to elastic potential energy in the spring.

In an alarm clock, the potential energy of the wound spring is converted to movement energy of its hands and sound energy of its ticks. The clock keeps working until the spring is unwound and has lost its potential energy.

ENERGY CHAIN

Did you realize that your alarm clock is really powered by the Sun? Energy is seldom changed directly from its starting form to its final form. It usually goes through a chain of energy conversions. The Sun's energy makes food grow. By eating this food, we create a store of chemical energy inside us. Among other things, we can use this energy to wind up an alarm clock. This gives the clock potential energy, which it is able to change into movement and sound energy.

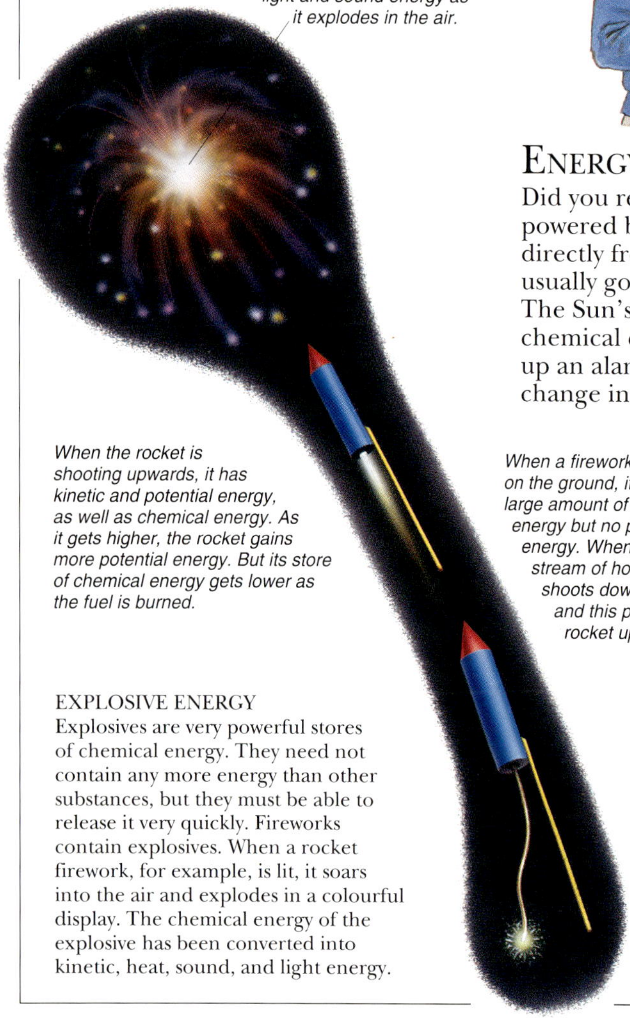

The remainder of the rocket's chemical energy is released as light and sound energy as it explodes in the air.

When the rocket is shooting upwards, it has kinetic and potential energy, as well as chemical energy. As it gets higher, the rocket gains more potential energy. But its store of chemical energy gets lower as the fuel is burned.

When a firework rocket is on the ground, it has a large amount of chemical energy but no potential energy. When ignited, a stream of hot gas shoots downwards and this pushes the rocket up.

EXPLOSIVE ENERGY
Explosives are very powerful stores of chemical energy. They need not contain any more energy than other substances, but they must be able to release it very quickly. Fireworks contain explosives. When a rocket firework, for example, is lit, it soars into the air and explodes in a colourful display. The chemical energy of the explosive has been converted into kinetic, heat, sound, and light energy.

LORD KELVIN
The British physicist William Thomson (1824-1907) was born in Belfast, Northern Ireland. He entered Glasgow University when he was just ten years old and became a professor at the age of 22. He helped to found the new science of thermodynamics, establishing clear relationships between heat, work, and energy. He also invented the absolute temperature scale – the Kelvin scale – and made important discoveries about electricity and magnetism. His title became Lord Kelvin after he was honoured by Queen Victoria.

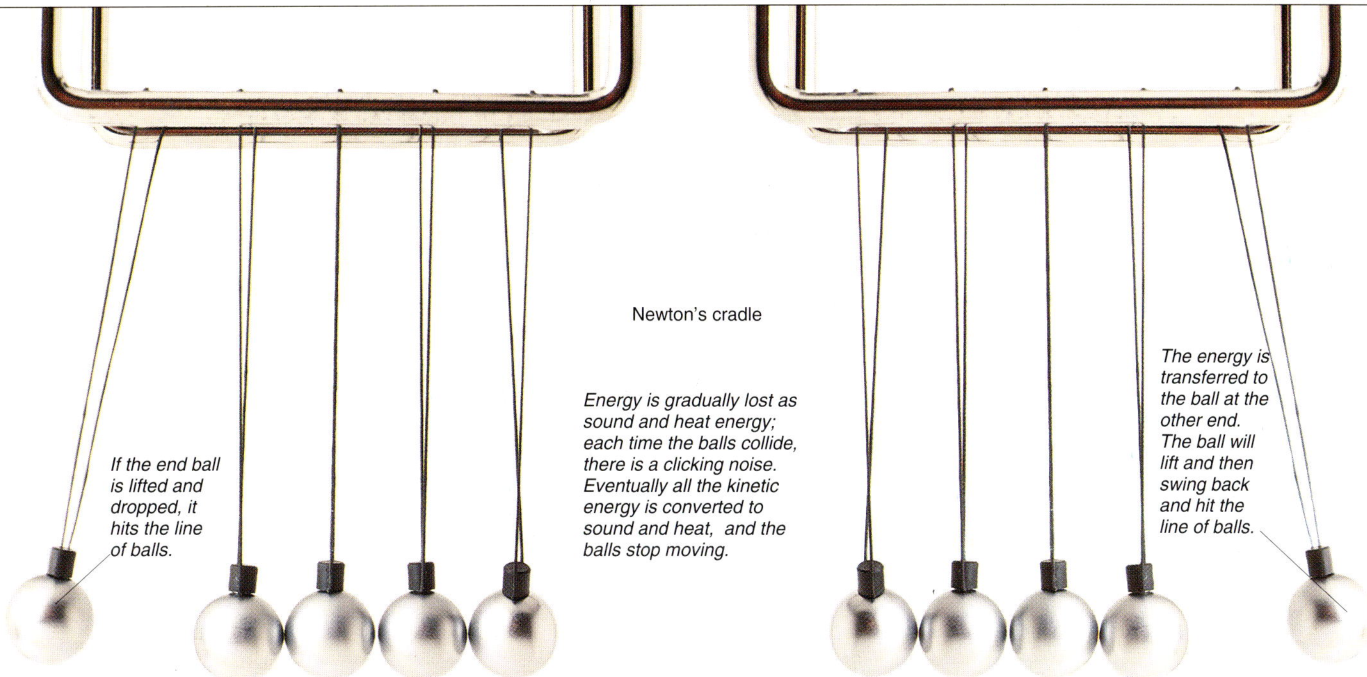

Newton's cradle

If the end ball is lifted and dropped, it hits the line of balls.

Energy is gradually lost as sound and heat energy; each time the balls collide, there is a clicking noise. Eventually all the kinetic energy is converted to sound and heat, and the balls stop moving.

The energy is transferred to the ball at the other end. The ball will lift and then swing back and hit the line of balls.

Conservation of energy

Energy can be neither created nor destroyed; it can only be converted into other forms. When energy is converted, some waste heat is always produced, but if we take this into account, the total amount of energy is unchanged. This is called the Principle of Conservation of Energy. The principle is illustrated by a toy called Newton's cradle. Little energy is lost as sound or heat, so the balls at either end will keep swinging for some time.

A perpetual motion machine proposed in 1834. The weight of the balls moving along the arms was supposed to keep the wheel turning.

PERPETUAL MOTION

Many people have tried to design machines that will go on working forever without an energy source – a perpetual motion machine. This is an impossible dream; all real machines need a continuous source of energy. Not only this, but they always need more energy than they can give out.

USEFUL ENERGY

A steam train produces waste heat from its funnel. It would be hard to use this heat energy to power anything else. Waste heat is not useful energy; it is low-quality energy. Electricity, on the other hand, is useful; it is high-quality energy. Whenever energy changes form, some high-quality energy is lost. This means the amount of useful energy in the Universe is always decreasing.

A conventional stove uses valuable energy to heat the saucepan.

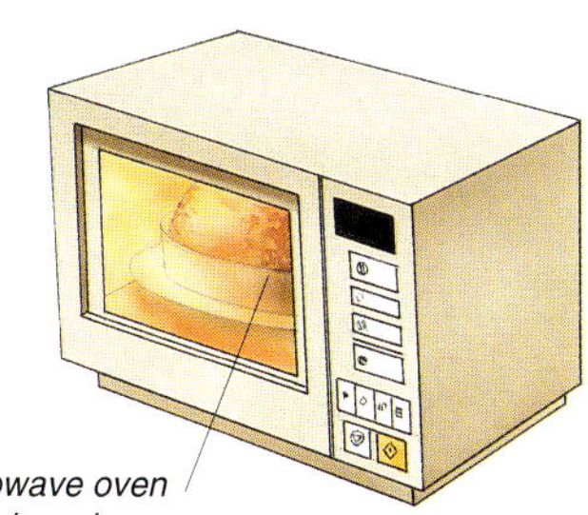

A microwave oven does not waste energy in heating the plate; it just heats the food.

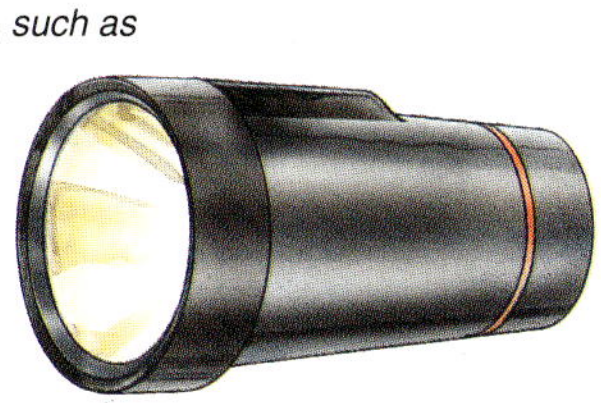

Dry-cell batteries, such as those used in a torch, waste only 10 per cent of the energy they contain.

A light bulb in an electric lamp wastes 95 per cent of the energy it consumes.

ENERGY EFFICIENCY

When we use a form of energy to do work, some of the energy does not go where we want it to go; it is wasted, usually as heat. For example, a light bulb converts only about 5 per cent of the energy that it consumes into light; the rest is converted into waste heat. The efficiency of the light bulb is said to be 5 per cent. No energy converter can ever be 100 per cent efficient.

SAVING ENERGY

We must conserve high-quality energy sources, such as electricity, coal, natural gas, and oil as they are in short supply. Using a microwave oven is one way of saving energy because a microwave oven uses less energy than a conventional oven to cook food. A well-insulated house needs less fuel to heat it, and a machine that is kept in good condition is able to work at its maximum efficiency.

Find out more

CHEMICAL REACTIONS P.52
WORK AND ENERGY P.132
ENERGY SOURCES P.134
NUCLEAR ENERGY P.136
HEAT P.140
CURRENT ELECTRICITY P.148
THUNDER AND LIGHTNING P.257
FACT FINDER P.408

HEAT TRANSFER

IF YOU STAND NEAR A FIRE, heat enters your body from your surroundings. If you are outside on a freezing day, heat escapes from your body into the cold air around you. Heat always travels from something hot to something cold, or from a hot part of something to a cold part. There are three ways that heat can travel: by convection, conduction, or radiation. Convection is how heat travels in moving currents through liquids and gases. Conduction is how heat travels through solids. When one part of a substance is heated, its molecules start to vibrate more violently. They knock against their neighbours and pass their energy on. Radiation is how heat travels through empty space by electromagnetic waves. This is how heat gets to the Earth from the Sun.

RADIATION
All objects emit heat radiation, also called infrared radiation. The hotter the object, the more radiation it emits. Infrared radiation travels at the same speed as light, but has a longer wavelength. Like light waves, infrared radiation is reflected by shiny surfaces and absorbed by dark surfaces. We cannot see infrared rays but cameras with special film can take infrared photographs called thermographs. Different colours indicate different amounts of heat radiating out. The hottest bit shows as white.

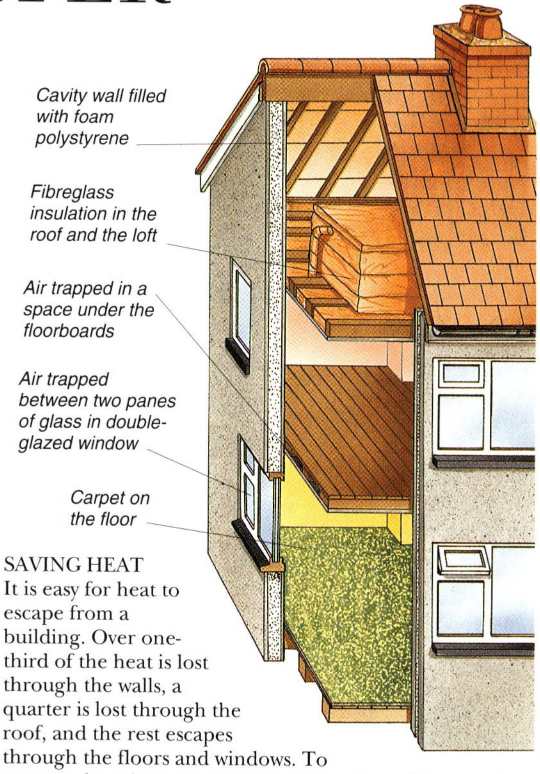

SAVING HEAT
It is easy for heat to escape from a building. Over one-third of the heat is lost through the walls, a quarter is lost through the roof, and the rest escapes through the floors and windows. To prevent these losses, buildings need to be well insulated.

CONVECTION
When the land gets hot, it heats the air above it. The heated air rises because it expands and becomes less dense. Cooler air falls down to take its place. A continuous current of rising and falling air, called a convection current, is set up. Gliders and birds use convection currents called thermals to lift them up in the air.

CONDUCTION
Different materials conduct heat by different amounts. Metals are the best conductors. Saucepans are made of metal so that they heat up quickly. Saucepan handles are made of wood or plastic which are poor conductors. Water is a poor conductor; cork and fibreglass are poor conductors because they are mainly air, and gases are the worst conductors of all.

RIGHT FOR THE CLIMATE
Many animals have shapes and colours to suit the climate in which they live. The fennec fox lives in the North African desert. During the day, the fox's pale fur does not absorb much heat radiation and its huge ears transfer heat to the air by convection. At night, when it is cold, the fox's fur traps air, which stops too much heat escaping from its body by conduction.

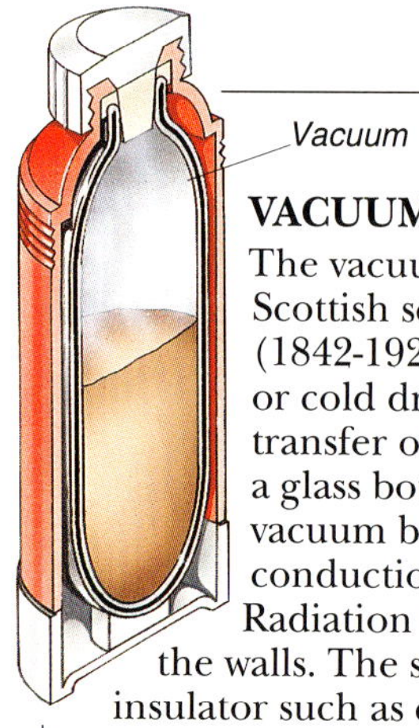

VACUUM FLASK

The vacuum flask was invented by Scottish scientist James Dewar (1842-1923). It keeps hot drinks hot, or cold drinks cold, by stopping the transfer of heat. The flask consists of a glass bottle with double walls. A vacuum between the walls stops conduction and convection. Radiation is prevented by silvering the walls. The stopper is made of a good insulator such as cork or hollow plastic.

Find out more

HEAT P.140
ELECTROMAGNETIC SPECTRUM P.192
WINDS P.254
FORMATION OF CLOUDS P.262
DESERTS P.390
FACT FINDER P.408

ENGINES

THE ROCKET is the most powerful engine. It can lift a heavy spacecraft off the ground and send it into space. Aircraft, cars, boats, motorcycles, and many other machines are driven by a petrol or diesel engine. Without engines, we would have to rely on our own strength and the strength of animals for transport and industry. Every engine converts energy from some sort of fuel into movement. They work on the principle that a hot gas expands. Fuel is burnt to heat gas and the expansion of the gas is harnessed to drive the machine. Some engines have pistons which move back and forth inside cylinders. They are called reciprocating engines. Other engines do not have pistons.

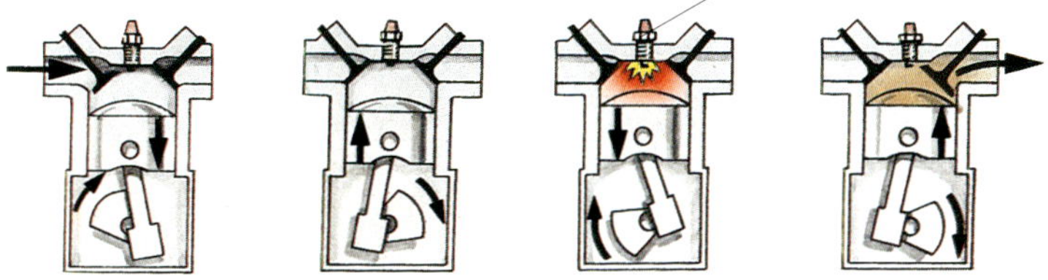

1. Induction – Piston descends, sucking in fuel and air through the open inlet valve.

2. Compression – Piston ascends, compressing the fuel mixture. Both valves are closed.

3. Power – Spark plug ignites the mixture. The exploding fuel forces piston down.

4. Exhaust – Piston ascends, forcing the burnt fuel out through the open exhaust valve.

INTERNAL COMBUSTION ENGINE
A car engine is called an internal combustion engine because the fuel is burnt inside a cylinder ("combustion" meaning burning). Most cars have a four-stroke engine. They produce their power with four movements, or strokes, of the piston. Engines have between four and eight cylinders which move in sequence to produce a continuous output of power.

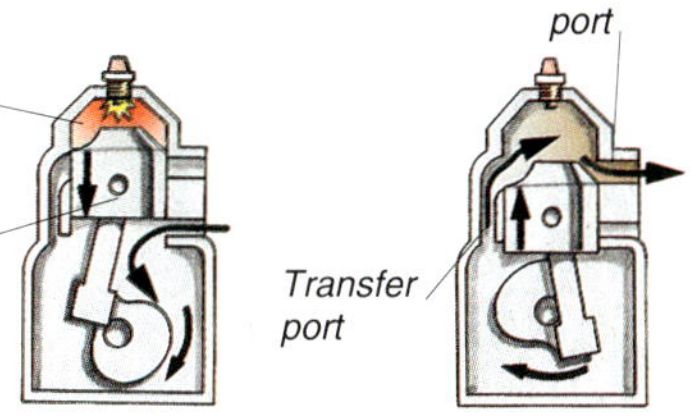

1. Piston rises, sucking fuel mixture into the lower part of the engine. The piston compresses the fuel already in the cylinder. A spark explodes the mixture when it is fully compressed.

2. Piston descends, pushing new fuel into the cylinder through the transfer port. The burnt fuel is pushed out through the exhaust port.

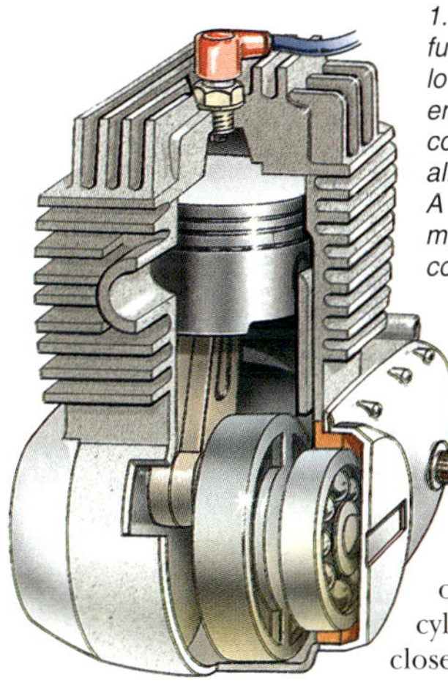

TWO-STROKE ENGINE
Motor cycles have two-stroke engines. These engines are small and powerful but they are noisy. They have no valves. Instead there are openings, called ports, in the side of the cylinder. The moving piston opens and closes the ports.

STEAM ENGINE
Because the fuel is burned outside the cylinder, in a furnace, a steam engine is called an external combustion engine. Hot gases produced by burning coal flow through a boiler and heat water, making steam. The steam is heated, until it is at high pressure and temperature, and fed to the cylinder. There it expands, forcing the piston along. In a locomotive, the moving piston turns the wheels.

GEORGE STEPHENSON

The first successsful steam locomotive was built by British engineer George Stephenson (1781-1848). He began his career caring for the engines and pumps in the mines near Newcastle, England. In 1825, he set up a locomotive factory where he designed and built the first locomotive to pull a passenger train, on the world's first public railway between Darlington and Stockton. Stephenson's most famous locomotive was called the *Rocket*. In 1829, it won a competition, reaching a speed of 46 km/h (29 mph). It was then used on the Liverpool to Manchester line.

Continued on next page

Continued from previous page

ENGINE DEVELOPMENT

1712 Thomas Newcomen builds the first steam engine to use a cylinder and piston.

1765 James Watt builds a steam engine six times as powerful as the Newcomen engine.

1800 Richard Trevithick builds the first high-pressure steam engine.

1860 Etienne Lenoir designs the first internal combustion engine, using coal gas and air as fuel.

1877 Nikolaus Otto develops the four-stroke engine.

1883 Gottlieb Daimler builds the first petrol engine.

1884 Charles Parsons builds the first steam turbine to generate electricity.

1926 Robert Goddard launches the first liquid-fuel-propelled rocket.

1930 Frank Whittle patents the jet engine.

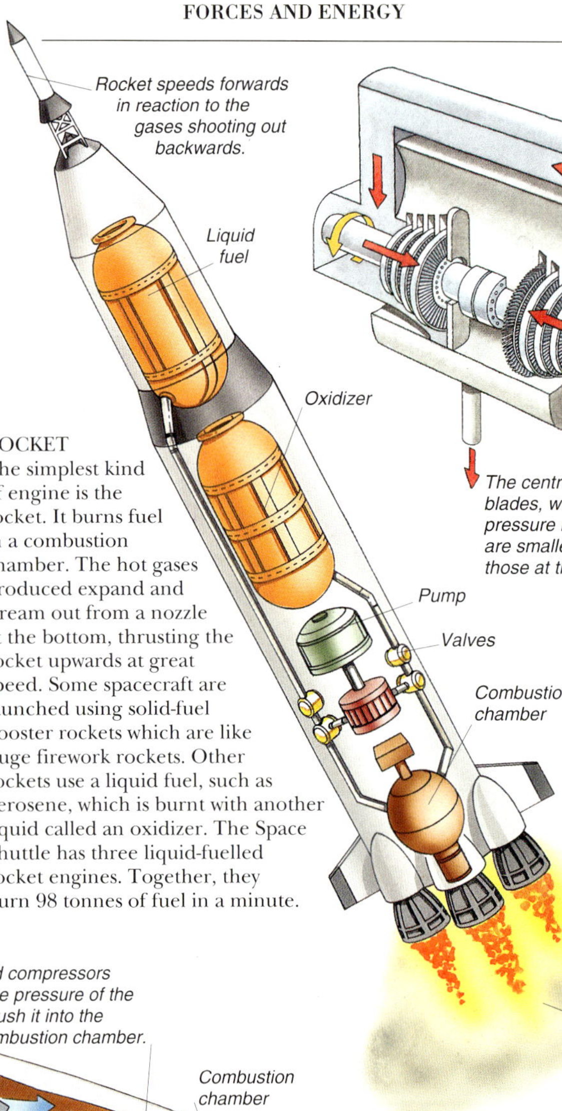

ROCKET
The simplest kind of engine is the rocket. It burns fuel in a combustion chamber. The hot gases produced expand and stream out from a nozzle at the bottom, thrusting the rocket upwards at great speed. Some spacecraft are launched using solid-fuel booster rockets which are like huge firework rockets. Other rockets use a liquid fuel, such as kerosene, which is burnt with another liquid called an oxidizer. The Space Shuttle has three liquid-fuelled rocket engines. Together, they burn 98 tonnes of fuel in a minute.

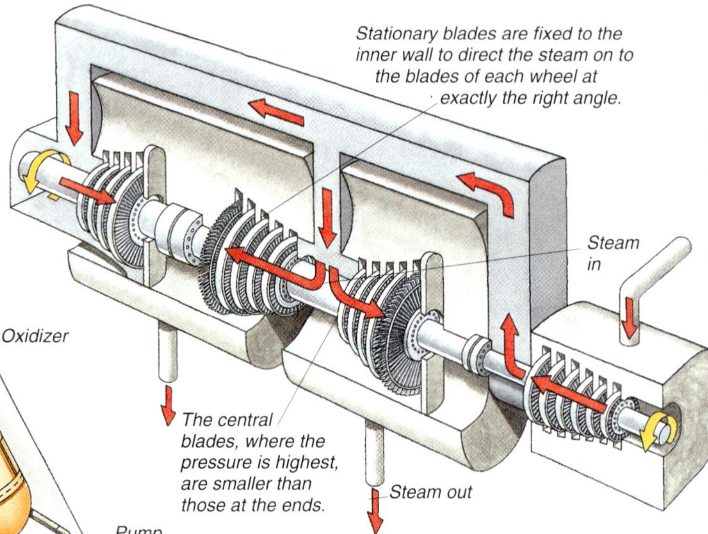

STEAM TURBINE
In its simplest form, a turbine is a wheel with blades mounted on an axle. It can be driven by gas, steam, or water. Steam turbines are used in power stations. Steam is driven at high pressure against the blades to turn the turbine which is connected to the electricity generator. Multi-stage turbines are most efficient, taking nearly all the energy from the steam.

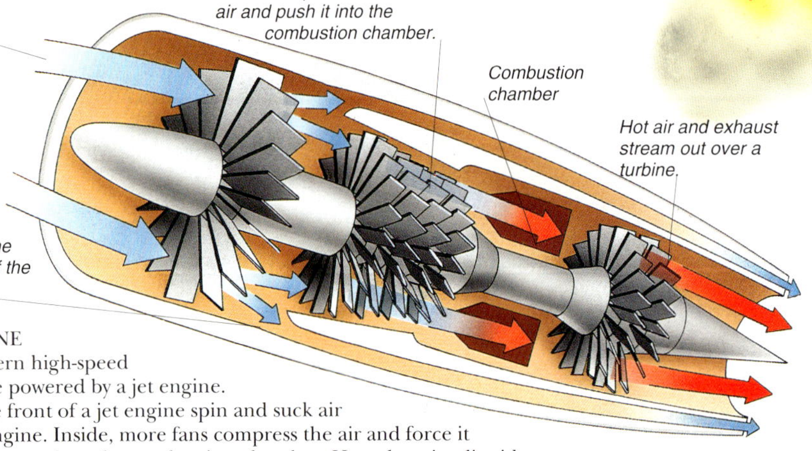

JET ENGINE
Most modern high-speed aircraft are powered by a jet engine. Fans at the front of a jet engine spin and suck air into the engine. Inside, more fans compress the air and force it at high pressure into the combustion chamber. Here, burning liquid fuel heats the air, which expands and rushes towards the tail of the engine. As the air streams out, it spins a turbine which drives the fans at the front. In a turbofan engine, shown here, some air flows through a duct around the main part of the engine. This means there is more air flowing through, giving the engine extra thrust.

FRANK WHITTLE

English test pilot and engineer Frank Whittle (born 1907) invented the jet engine in 1929. He tried to persuade the British Air Ministry that his engine would work, but his ideas were rejected. He set up his own company to make the new engine and, by 1937, the first engine had been built and tested on the ground. In 1941, an experimental aircraft with a Whittle engine made its first flight.

JET PROPULSION
This toy car uses jet propulsion to speed along the floor. A balloon is attached to the car and filled with air. When a valve is opened, air rushes out backwards through the neck of the balloon, thrusting the car forwards.

Find out more

Behaviour of gases p.51
Forces and motion p.120
Work and energy p.132
Energy sources p.134
Electric motors p.158
Rockets p.299

ELECTRICITY AND MAGNETISM

ALMOST ANYWHERE YOU GO, you will find electricity at work, and often magnetism too. Electricity and magnetism have completely changed our lives. Generators use magnetism to produce electricity from motion, so that light and heat are available at the flick of a switch. Electric motors use magnetism to change electricity into motion, so that machines can do tedious work for us, such as washing clothes. Other motorized machines, such as electric drills, help us to carry out tasks quickly and with little effort. Electronics (the use of components, or parts, for controlling electricity in various ways) allows us to use electricity and magnetism in many ways, as in radio, radar, and computers.

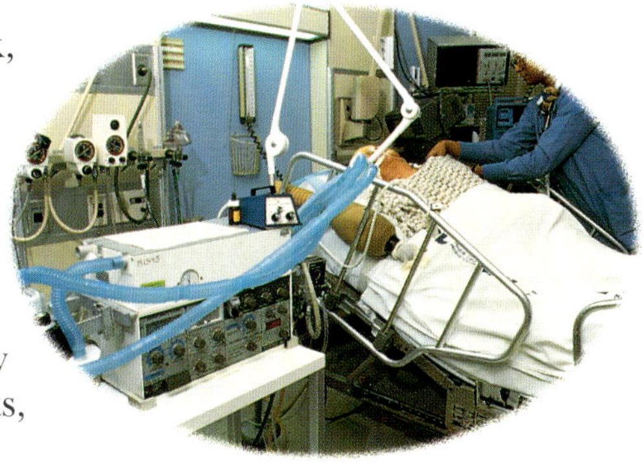

ELECTRONICS THAT CARE
People who are very ill often need constant attention in hospital. Instead of a nurse sitting at the bedside, electronic equipment monitors (constantly checks) their condition. If, for example, a patient's breathing or heartbeat changes, the equipment sounds an alarm to tell nurses and doctors that they are needed.

VERSATILE ENERGY

Electricity is easily generated, transmitted to where it is needed, and converted into other forms of energy. In an office, for example, a fan changes electricity into motion, and a bulb changes electricity into light. A telephone changes electricity into sounds, and also changes sounds into electricity. And a computer changes a steady supply of electricity into pulses to carry out its tasks.

Since electric light bulbs were first used in the late 1800s, they have been made much more reliable and efficient.

Electricity helps to make our surroundings more comfortable. The motor in an electric fan makes the blades turn round to send out a stream of air.

Until the mid-1970s, most people had never seen a computer. Now computers are almost everywhere. The principles of computing were set out more than 150 years ago, but electronic computers could only be made for everyone to buy when the complex circuits could be made small enough.

A modern telephone does more than let us talk to people. Its electronic memory can store different numbers so that we can call them by pressing a single button.

Today's cheap pocket calculator would have amazed scientists in the early 1950s. Then, a whole room full of valves and other bulky components would have been necessary to make a calculator.

LODESTONE
Found in the Earth, lodestone is a mineral that is naturally magnetized. It is a form of the mineral magnetite. Iron filings near it become magnetized and stick to it. Some early sailors used a piece of lodestone, suspended from a string, as a magnetic compass.

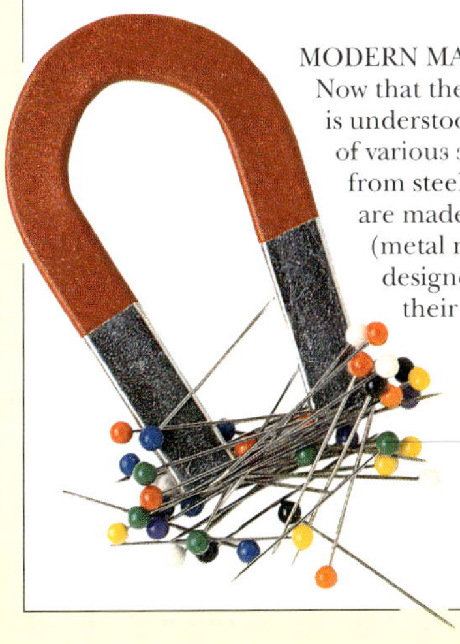

MODERN MAGNETS
Now that the nature of magnetism is understood, powerful magnets of various shapes can be made from steel. The best magnets are made from steel alloys (metal mixtures) specially designed to keep their magnetism.

Steel pins can be temporarily magnetized, which allows them to be picked up with a magnet.

ANCIENT ELECTRICITY
Around 600 B.C., an Ancient Greek philosopher (thinker) called Thales of Miletus found that when he rubbed a piece of amber with a cloth, feathers and other light objects stuck to it. We now know that the amber had become electrically charged by friction. The word "electricity" comes from the Greek for amber – *elektron*.

"ELECTRICS" AND "NON-ELECTRICS"
William Gilbert (1544-1603) did outstanding work in magnetism and electricity. He showed that the Earth must be like a magnet to affect compasses. He recognized the difference between electrical insulators and conductors, and called them "electrics" and "non-electrics".

STATIC ELECTRICITY

A balloon can stick to a jumper because rubbing the two together gives each one an opposite charge.

THE CRACKLING NOISE you sometimes hear when you pull your jumper off over your head happens because of static electricity. If it's dark, you can see flashes of light as well. Static electricity is electricity that doesn't move. The crackles and flashes are the static electricity suddenly flowing away; this is discharging. You sometimes get an electric shock from touching a doorknob, because the static electricity that builds up in your body suddenly flows from your hand to the doorknob. Lightning is static electricity suddenly discharging between clouds or between clouds and the ground. Static electricity builds up with friction, when two different materials rub together.

ELECTROSTATIC INDUCTION
You can use a plastic spoon to make a stream of water from the tap flow sideways by rubbing the spoon on your clothes. Negative charges on the spoon repel negative charges in the water to the far side and attract positive charges in the near side. The spoon induces these charged regions in the water, so the effect is called electrostatic induction.

The charges were built up on the spoon by friction.

CHARGING BY FRICTION

All objects are made of atoms. Each atom has equal numbers of electrons and protons. Electrons have a negative charge; protons have a positive charge. These charges balance each other exactly to make objects neutral (uncharged). But friction, like rubbing a balloon on your jumper, makes electrons rub off from your jumper onto the balloon. This charges the balloon with static electricity. It now has more electrons than protons, so it is negatively charged. And your jumper, with more protons than electrons, is positively charged.

ATTRACTION
A balloon that has been charged by friction will attract small pieces of paper. Like charges repel each other, so the negative charges on the balloon force away the negative charges in the paper. The parts of the paper closest to the balloon become positively charged. They stick to the negatively charged balloon because opposite charges attract.

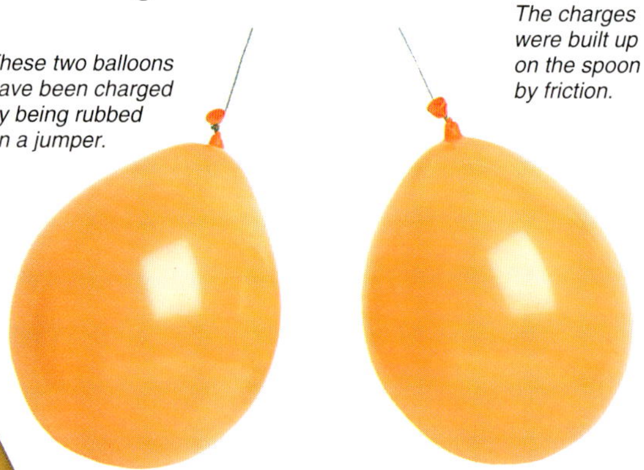

These two balloons have been charged by being rubbed on a jumper.

REPULSION
Two charged balloons hang side by side on threads attached to the same point. They repel each other because they are both negatively charged. If they were both neutral, they would hang next to each other.

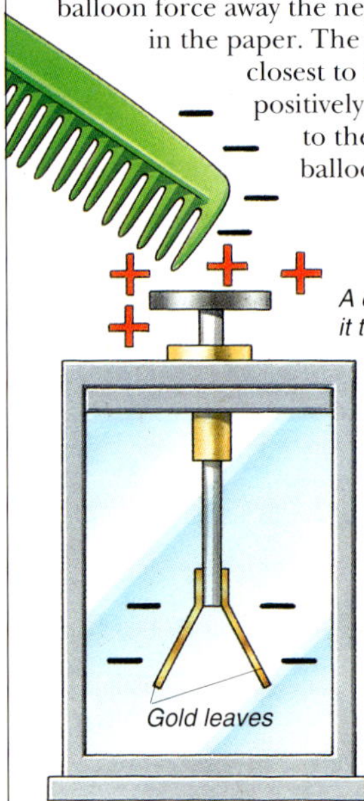

A comb, negatively charged by passing it through hair, repels negative charges to the leaves, making them deflect (alter their direction).

ELECTROSCOPE
The gold-leaf electroscope is an instrument that can show whether or not an object is charged. If you bring a charged object near the metal plate at the top, the gold leaves are both given the same charge by induction. Since like charges repel each other, the hinged leaves spread apart. Gold leaves are extremely thin and light. They are used to make the electroscope very sensitive.

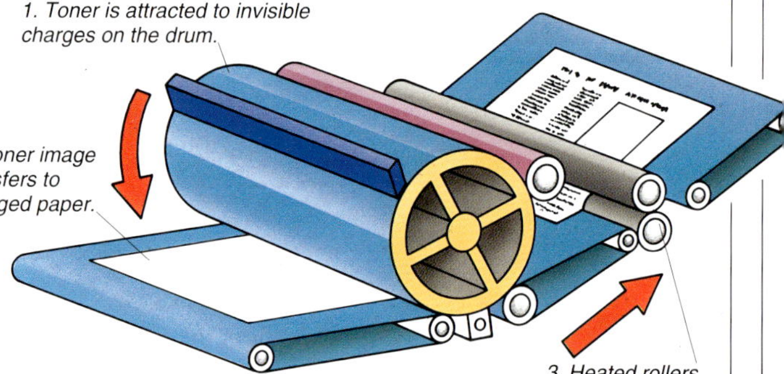

1. Toner is attracted to invisible charges on the drum.

2. Toner image transfers to charged paper.

3. Heated rollers bond toner image to paper.

PHOTOCOPIER
Many photocopiers work by using static electricity. An image of the original forms on the large drum inside the machine as invisible positive charges. These attract particles of fine black powder, the toner, producing a visible image on the drum. The toner is then transferred to electrically charged paper as it passes round the drum. Heated rollers melt the toner, so that it sticks to the paper and forms a permanent image.

GIANT SPARKS
A fork of lightning flashing across the sky is a giant spark leaping between the ground and a cloud. As well as giving out a very bright light, lightning is very hot. The air around it heats up and therefore expands so quickly that it explodes, causing thunder.

CHARGES WITHIN A CLOUD

High in the air, in the clouds, swirling ice particles become charged with static electricity. The top of the cloud becomes positively charged, and the bottom of the cloud becomes negatively charged. Sometimes this electricity discharges as a flash of lightning inside the cloud to balance out the charges once more.

BENJAMIN FRANKLIN

American statesman, author, printer, and inventor Benjamin Franklin (1706-90) showed that lightning is caused by electricity by carrying out a very dangerous experiment. In 1752, he flew a kite in a thunderstorm. Electricity passed down the damp string to a key at the other end. When he put a finger near the key, a spark jumped between them. Franklin concluded that electricity in clouds caused the spark and that lightning is a kind of spark too. In 1753, he announced his invention of the lightning conductor.

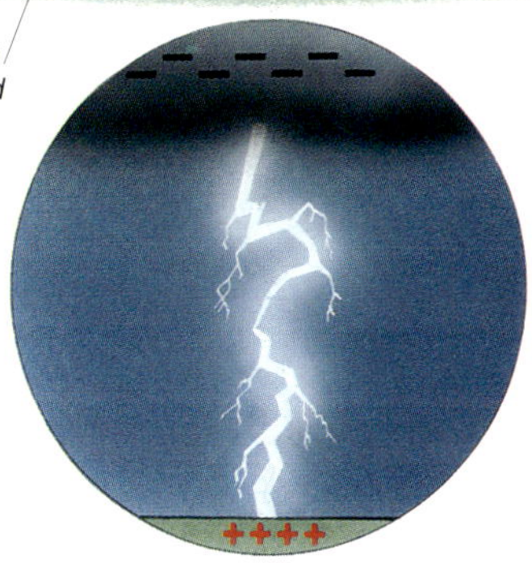

HOW LIGHTNING STRIKES
If the charges in the cloud are strong enough, they force a path to the ground through the air and discharge as a lightning flash. Tall buildings, trees, and people on open ground are prime targets for lightning because they provide a convenient path for the discharge.

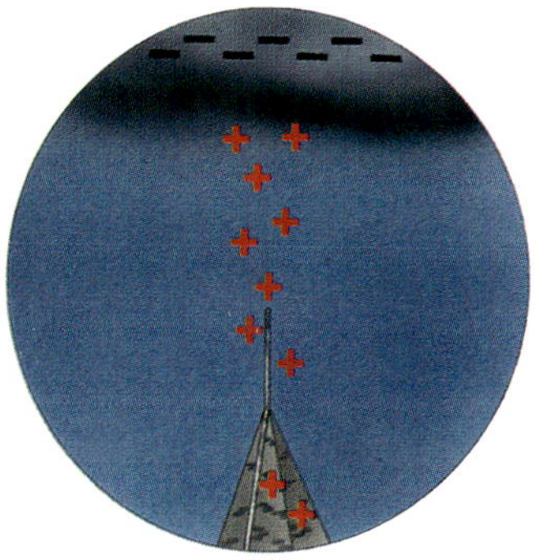

LIGHTNING CONDUCTOR
Most tall buildings have a metal rod called a lightning conductor on the roof. A wire connects the rod to the ground. The negative charges on the underside of the cloud attract positive charges from the ground. A stream of these positive charges flows up to the cloud, where they cancel out some of the negative charges. This may prevent lightning from striking, but if lightning does strike, the electricity flows harmlessly through the rod and wire.

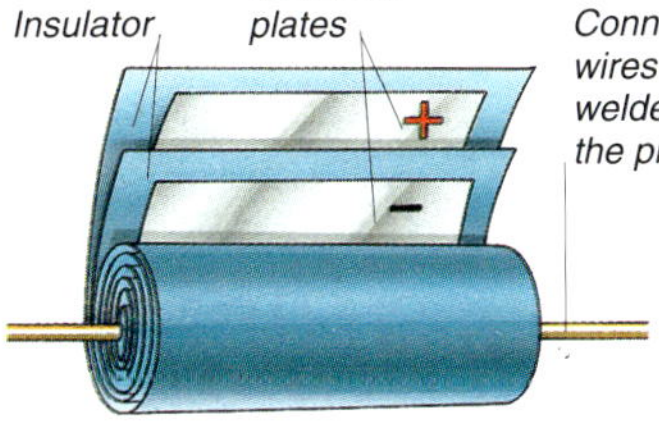

CAPACITORS
Devices called capacitors are used to store an electric charge in electronic equipment such as televisions and computers. For example, electricity supplied as brief pulses is stored in a capacitor so that a steady current can be given out from it. Inside some capacitors, metal foil plates are separated by thin plastic, all rolled up and sealed.

LEYDEN JAR
Early experimenters sometimes stored electricity in a device called a Leyden jar. It was named after the Dutch city where the jar was first used, in 1745. One form consists of a glass jar with a coating of tin foil inside and outside. A metal rod connects to the inner foil. An electric charge can be stored on the tin foil plates. This Leyden jar was an early form of capacitor.

Find out more

ATOMIC STRUCTURE P.25
CURRENT ELECTRICITY P.148
ELECTRONIC COMPONENTS P.168
THUNDER AND LIGHTNING P.257

CURRENT ELECTRICITY

ALMOST EVERYWHERE WE GO we can see current electricity at work. Bulbs change electricity into light, electric heaters change electricity into heat, and electric motors change electricity into motion. Electricity is a form of energy, and it has so many uses because it is easily changed into other forms of energy. Electricity is also very easy to use because it can flow along wires to wherever we need it. We call this flow an electric current. The flow is measured in units called amperes or amps. Most electric currents consist of a stream of electrons, but some currents consist of other kinds of charged particles, called ions.

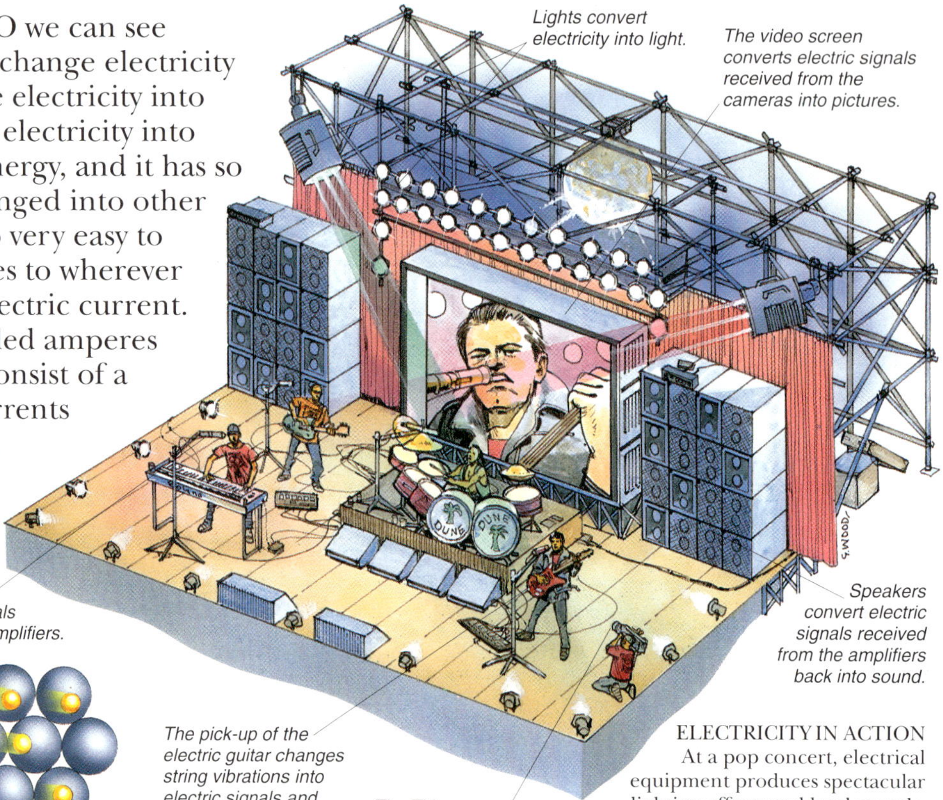

ELECTRICITY IN ACTION
At a pop concert, electrical equipment produces spectacular lighting effects and loud sounds. People a long way from the stage can watch the musicians on the huge screens around the stadium.

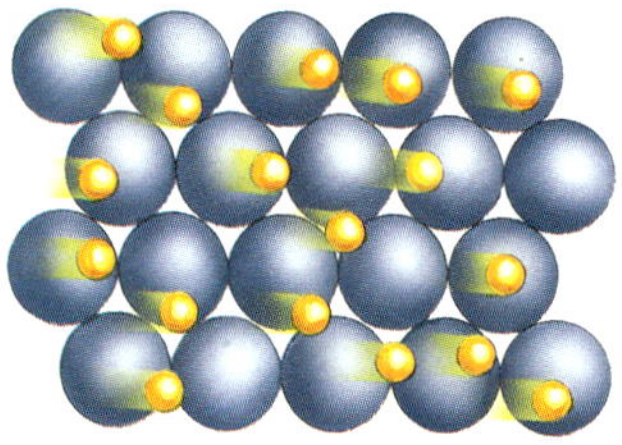

FREE ELECTRONS
Electricity can flow through a metal, such as copper, because the metal contains electrons that are free to move from one atom to another.

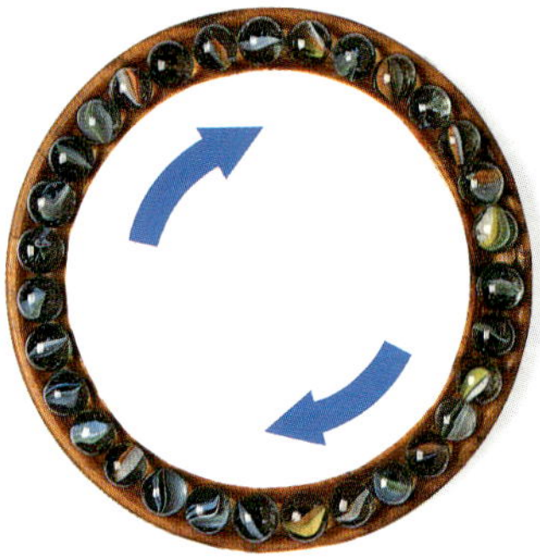

ROUND AND ROUND
Using marbles, you can demonstrate how an electric current flows. If you push a circle of touching marbles, they all move at once. The one at the other end moves as soon as you touch the first marble. A battery forces electrons along wires in a similar way to make an electric current flow.

CONDUCTORS AND INSULATORS

Copper wires in electrical cables are called conductors because they conduct an electric current, which means that they allow it to pass through them. Around the copper wires is plastic, which does not conduct electricity because it has no free electrons. It is called an insulator. It prevents electricity flowing where it is not wanted.

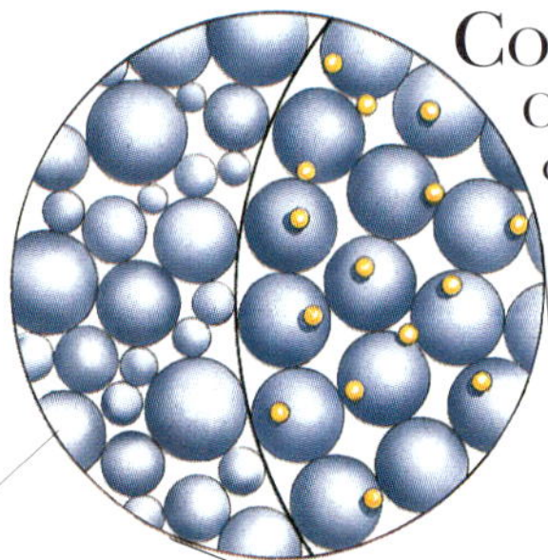

In an insulator, all the electrons stay with their own atoms, so electricity cannot flow through it.

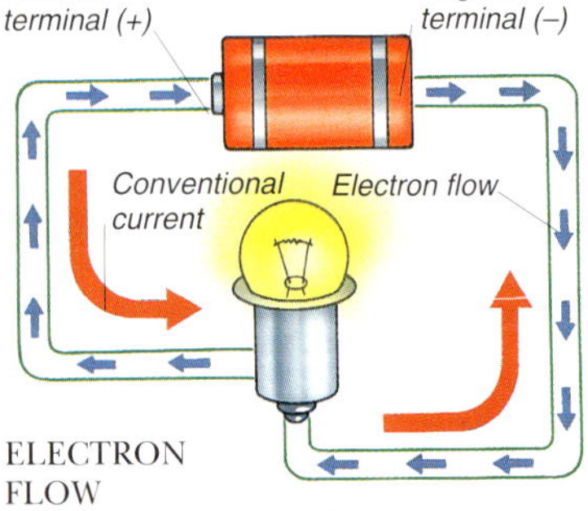

ELECTRON FLOW
People used to think electricity flowed around a circuit from a battery's positive terminal to its negative one. Many useful rules were worked out using this idea, so current is still shown like this. This is called conventional current. In fact, electrons flow from the negative terminal to the positive one.

OVERHEAD SUPPLIES
Some electric trains pick up electricity using arms that slide along cables above the track. These cables must be bare (uninsulated), so that the arms can make electrical contact with them. Current flows to the motor that drives the train. The overhead cables have to be supported using insulators. This prevents electricity from being wasted or dangerous. Conductors and insulators are used together to make electricity safe and efficient.

CHARLES AUGUSTIN COULOMB
Coulomb (1736-1806) was a French physicist, inventor, and engineer. His most important work involved friction, magnetism, and electricity. He devised sensitive instruments for measuring the forces between magnets and between electric charges. The unit for measuring an amount, or charge, of electricity is named after him. One coulomb (symbol C) is the amount of electricity that flows past any point when a current of one amp flows for one second.

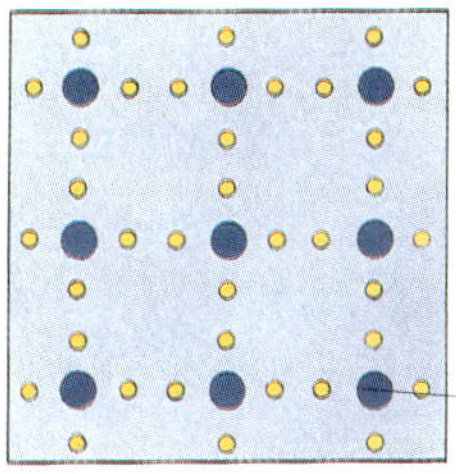

PURE SILICON
In pure silicon, there are four electrons for each of the silicon atoms. The charges of the electrons balance out four positive charges in each nucleus, so silicon is neutral.

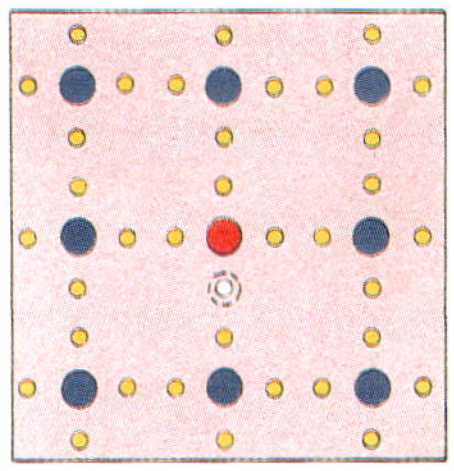

P-TYPE SEMICONDUCTOR
Boron has only three electrons per atom. So if small amounts of boron are added to silicon, this leaves holes, which makes the material positive, and gives a p-type semiconductor.

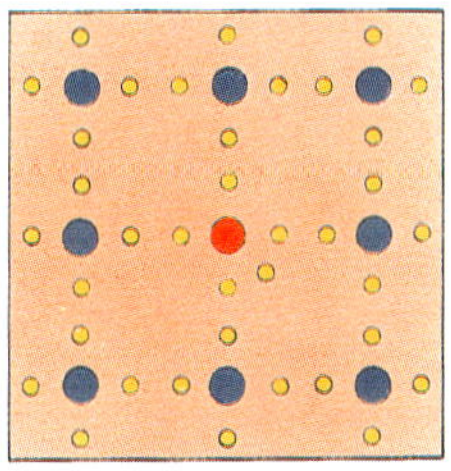

N-TYPE SEMICONDUCTOR
Arsenic and phosphorus have five electrons per atom. So adding a trace of either to silicon introduces free electrons. This gives an n-type semiconductor.

SEMICONDUCTORS

Materials that do not conduct electricity very well are called semiconductors or semimetals. They are used to control current in electronic equipment. Silicon is the most common semiconductor. It is doped (made impure) with tiny amounts of arsenic, phosphorus, or boron to alter its electrical properties and make n-type (negative) or p-type (positive) semiconductors. In n-type semiconductors, electrons carry the current, and in p-type semiconductors holes carry the current. Semiconductors are used to make electronic devices such as silicon chips for computers.

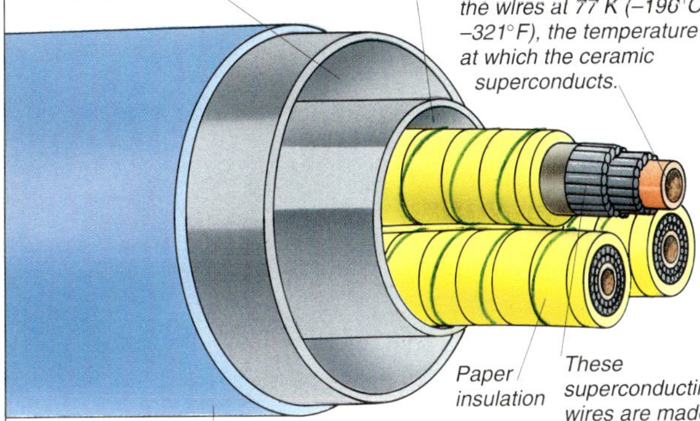

SUPERCONDUCTING CABLES
A material that conducts electricity well has little resistance to the flow of current. In certain metals, such as tin and lead, and some ceramics, the resistance becomes almost zero when they are cooled to a very low temperature. In other words, they become superconductors (almost perfect conductors). Superconductors would be ideal as electricity supply cables, as they would waste hardly any power. But they need to be kept cool with liquid nitrogen or liquid helium, and this is expensive to install and run. Experiments are being done to find superconductors that work at higher temperatures.

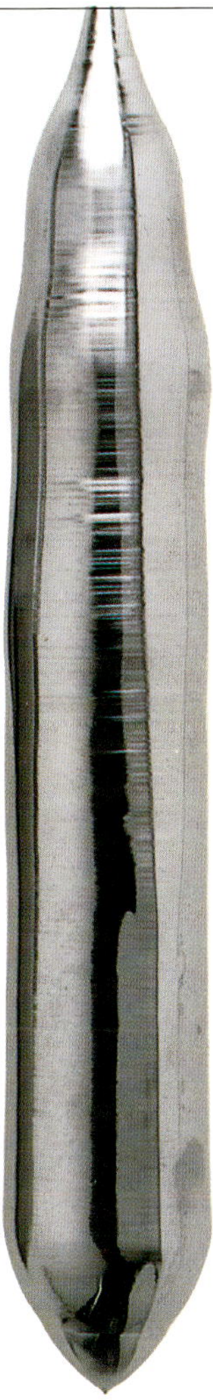

A crystal of pure silicon

ALEX MÜLLER

The main problem with superconductors is that they have to be kept at close to absolute zero. This is the lowest possible temperature, 0 K (–273°C, –460°F). But Swiss physicist Alex Müller (born 1927), helped by Georg Bednorz (born 1950), found that a copper oxide ceramic material containing barium and lanthanum can superconduct at 35 K (–238°C, –396°F). They won the Nobel Prize for Physics in 1987. By 1988, others had made a ceramic material superconduct at 123 K (–150°C, –238°F). But no one has yet made a superconductor that works at room temperature.

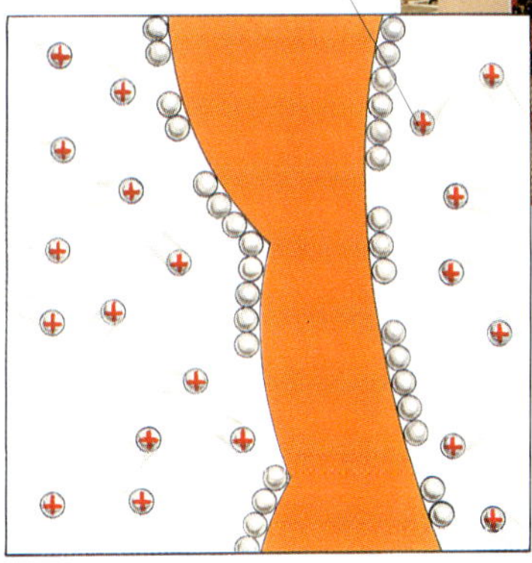

ELECTRICITY AND IONS
A current can flow through a solution not as electrons, but as charged particles called ions. Electroplating is a way of covering an object with a layer of metal using electricity. The object to be coated is connected to the negative side of the electricity supply, which makes it the negative electrode. It attracts positively charged ions (for example silver, copper, or zinc ions) and therefore becomes coated (electroplated) with silver, copper, or zinc.

ELECTROPLATING
These printed circuit boards have been dipped into a solution of copper sulphate. Electricity is run through the solution and the circuit boards. The boards form the anode in the circuit, so the copper ions are attracted to them and become attached to the board to make the copper tracks.

Find out more

PROPERTIES OF MATTER P.22
ATOMIC STRUCTURE P.24
SEMIMETALS P.39
ELECTROLYSIS P.67
CELLS AND BATTERIES P.150
ELECTRONIC COMPONENTS P.168
FACT FINDER P.410

CELLS AND BATTERIES

HOW MANY BATTERY-OPERATED devices are there in your home? Radios, torches, toys, clocks, and watches are a few of the more common items that use batteries. Batteries come in many shapes and sizes. Some are little bigger than a pill, while others are too heavy for a person to lift. But most batteries have one thing in common: they store chemical energy and change it to electrical energy. A cell is the basic unit that produces electricity, and a battery has two or more cells. But we often use the word battery when talking about a single cell too, like a dry cell. The pill-sized battery in a watch is a cell. Cells act like pumps to force electrons to flow along conductors.

Actual size

MERCURY OXIDE CELL
Many electronic watches run on a single mercury oxide cell. This type provides a steady 1.35-volt supply over a long period.

INSIDE A CELL

A typical cell has three main parts. There is a negative electrode, a positive electrode, and between these is a chemical, or a mixture of chemicals, called the electrolyte. This is a moist paste or a liquid that conducts electricity because the chemicals in it split into charged groups of atoms called ions. Chemical reactions in the cell cause electrons to flow out of the negative electrode, through the device being powered and back via the positive electrode.

Actual size

NICKEL CADMIUM CELL
Unlike common cells, nickel cadmium cells can be recharged when they have run down. This makes running a battery-powered toy much cheaper.

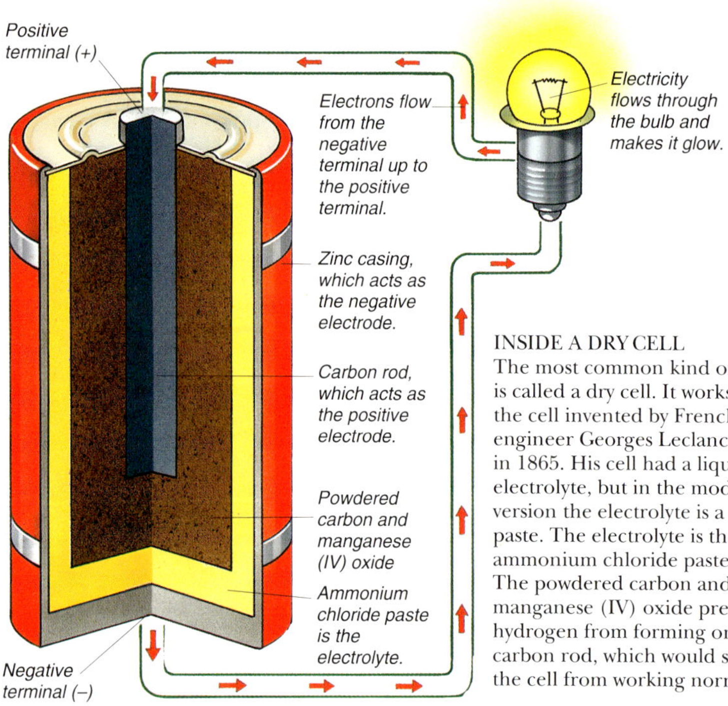

INSIDE A DRY CELL
The most common kind of cell is called a dry cell. It works like the cell invented by French engineer Georges Leclanché in 1865. His cell had a liquid electrolyte, but in the modern version the electrolyte is a moist paste. The electrolyte is the ammonium chloride paste. The powdered carbon and manganese (IV) oxide prevent hydrogen from forming on the carbon rod, which would stop the cell from working normally.

DRY CELLS
Ordinary dry cells are used in most torch batteries. Common dry cells use ammonium chloride as the electrolyte. Cells needed to supply heavier currents use zinc chloride. Alkaline cells, which last longer and can supply even heavier currents, use the alkali potassium hydroxide.

Actual size

ELECTROMOTIVE FORCE
The electrical force of a cell or battery is called its electromotive force (e.m.f.). This force, which makes electrons flow around a circuit, is measured in units called volts (symbol V). Each kind of cell has a particular e.m.f. A dry cell, for example, has an e.m.f. of 1.5 volts.

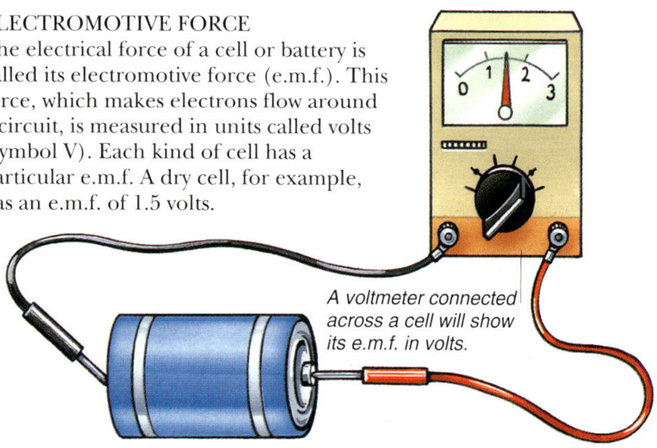

A voltmeter connected across a cell will show its e.m.f. in volts.

ALESSANDRO VOLTA

An Italian count called Alessandro Volta (1745-1827) invented the first battery. Each cell had a copper disc and a zinc disc for the electrodes. Between them was a piece of cloth soaked in salt solution. This was the electrolyte. Each cell had a small e.m.f. But Volta found that a pile of these cells gave a large e.m.f. This, the first true battery, is known as Volta's pile, or a Voltaic pile. The volt, the unit for electromotive force, is named after him.

Cell size

Most electric torches take two or more dry cells. As in Volta's pile, the cells are connected in series, or one after the other. This increases the total e.m.f. For example, two 1.5-volt cells in series have a total e.m.f. of 3 volts. A larger e.m.f. can force a larger current around a circuit. Large, powerful torches may take four or more cells. The size of a cell itself has no effect on its e.m.f. The chemicals in the cell determine its e.m.f. But large cells last longer than small cells of the same basic type.

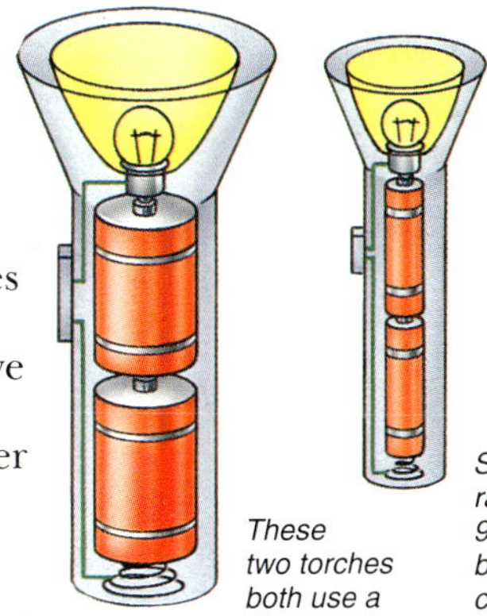

These two torches both use a 3-volt bulb because the batteries in each torch produce an e.m.f. of 3 volts.

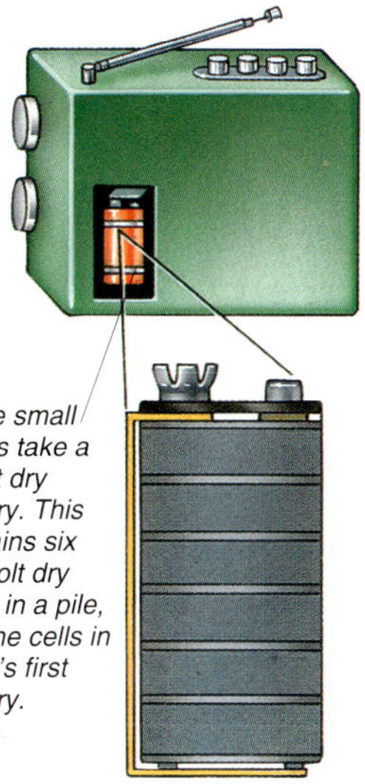

Some small radios take a 9-volt dry battery. This contains six 1.5-volt dry cells, in a pile, like the cells in Volta's first battery.

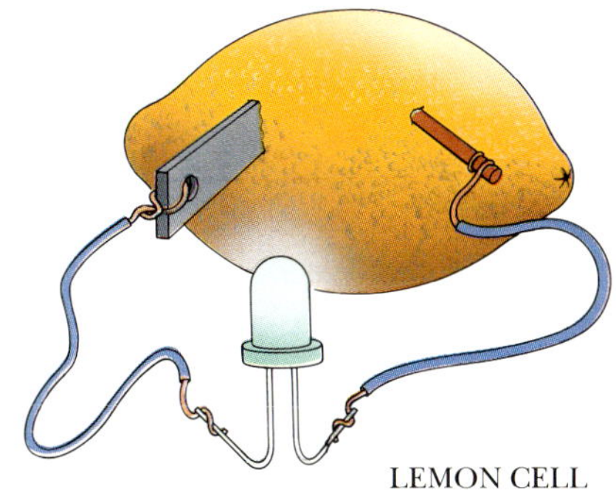

LEMON CELL

You can make a simple cell by pushing objects made of two different metals into a lemon. The metals are the electrodes of the cell. The lemon juice, which is a weak acid, is the electrolyte. A piece of zinc and a piece of copper wire work well as electrodes. The e.m.f. produced lights up an LED (light-emitting diode).

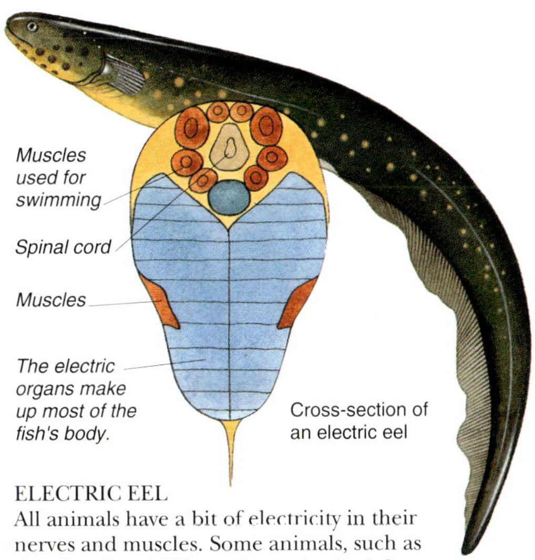

Cross-section of an electric eel

ELECTRIC EEL

All animals have a bit of electricity in their nerves and muscles. Some animals, such as the electric eel (*Electrophorus electricus*) from South America, can produce a powerful blast of electricity, which they use to kill their prey. The organ that produces electricity takes up most of the eel's body, and is made of special muscles. Electricity is built up in the organ by the movement of ions, and then timed to discharge all at once to produce a voltage high enough to stun fish swimming nearby. In some electric eels this voltage can reach 650 volts – enough to stun a person.

SOLAR CELLS

Unlike ordinary cells, solar cells do not use chemical energy. Instead, they change light energy into electricity. Solar cells are also known as photovoltaic (light-voltage) cells. Small solar cells power some pocket calculators. In some places, such as Antarctica, where there is no mains electricity supply, big panels containing many solar cells are sometimes used instead. Most solar cells are devices called silicon diodes.

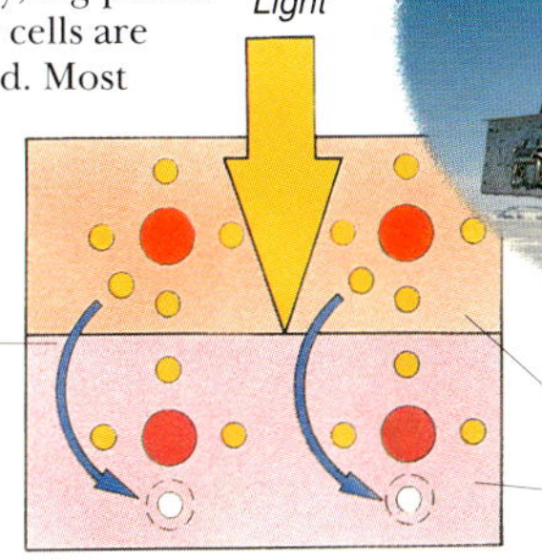

When light hits the area where the two types of semiconductor join, electrons flow through the cell as an electric current.

ELECTRIC CAR

This car has a battery for use in towns and a petrol engine to keep the battery powered up for longer journeys. Some prototype electric cars run on batteries only, but the batteries tend to be large and not last long enough. The batteries are recharged overnight on mains electricity, making the most of a time when few people are using electricity. The great advantage of battery-powered cars is that they produce much less air pollution than those that use petrol or diesel engines. So they are an important way of dealing with pollution problems.

Electricity is produced in the reactions between the plates and the sulphuric acid.

CAR BATTERY

Most cars have a 12-volt battery containing six 2-volt lead-acid cells. Each cell consists of a lead plate, a lead dioxide plate, and sulphuric acid. Unlike dry cells, lead-acid cells can be recharged with electricity after use. So the battery does not have to be replaced unless it becomes faulty. Cells that cannot be recharged are called primary cells; cells that can be recharged are called secondary cells. The lead-acid battery powers the car's electrical system. It is recharged by a device in a car called the alternator.

Find out more

BONDING P.28
TRANSITION METALS P.36
SEMIMETALS P.39
ELECTROLYSIS P.67
ENERGY SOURCES P.134
GENERATORS P.159
LIGHT P.190
MUSCLES P.355
FACT FINDER P.410

MAGNETISM

A MAGNET IS NOT STICKY, and yet objects made of iron or steel cling to it. A magnet is surrounded by an invisible field of force (its magnetic field) that affects certain materials nearby. All magnets have a south pole and a north pole; north poles are always attracted to south poles. When you think of a magnet, you probably picture a permanent magnet (one that keeps its magnetic power). But an ordinary piece of iron becomes magnetized when it is near a magnet, gaining a north and south pole. The first use of magnetism was in the magnetic compass. Today, magnetism is used in many other ways.

Each individual iron filing has been turned into a tiny magnet. They align with the big magnet's field.

BAR MAGNET
Iron filings around a bar magnet always arrange themselves into the same kind of pattern. They make the magnetic field around the magnet show up. The lines show the direction in which a compass needle would point when placed near the magnet. The Earth's magnetic field has little effect on the compass, because it is so close to the bar magnet.

EARTH'S MAGNETISM

The region around any magnet, where its magnetism can be detected, is called a magnetic field. The Earth has a magnetic field, just as if a permanent bar magnet is inside it. The field is caused by the iron core at the centre of the Earth.

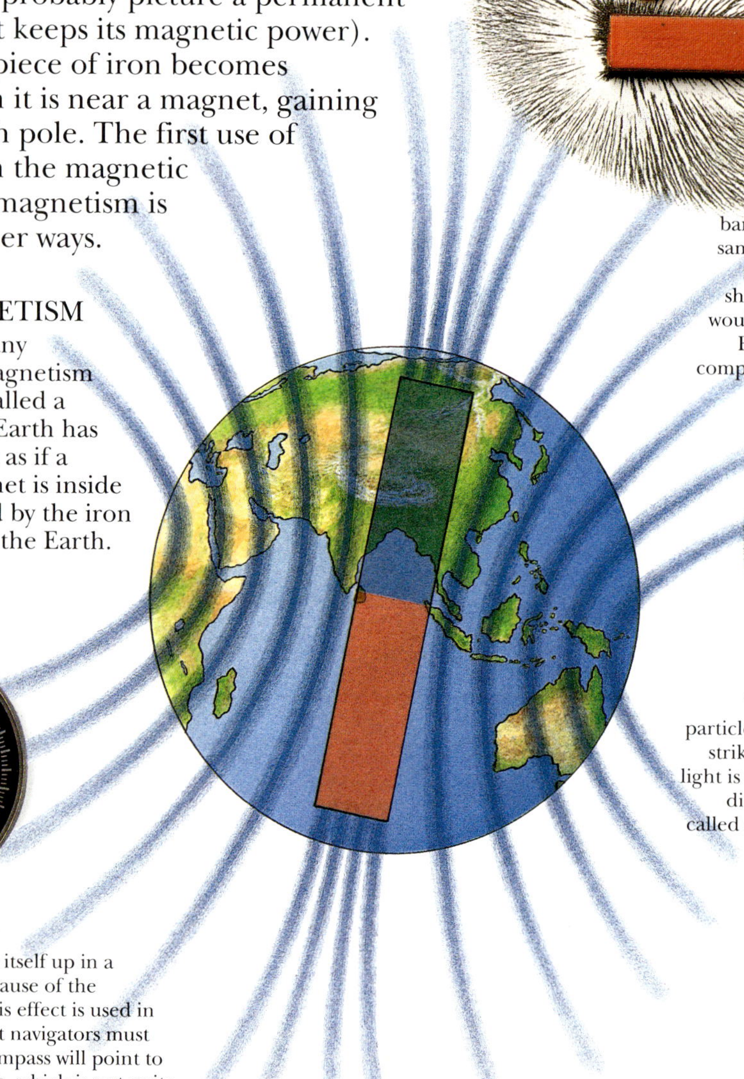

MAGNETIC COMPASS
A pivoted magnet will line itself up in a north-south direction, because of the Earth's magnetic field. This effect is used in the magnetic compass. But navigators must allow for the fact that a compass will point to the Earth's magnetic north, which is not quite the same as the geographical north.

AURORA
The Earth's magnetic poles attract charged particles emitted by the Sun. When these particles strike gas particles in the atmosphere, coloured light is radiated. In the Northern Hemisphere, the display of light, seen here in Alaska, U.S.A., is called aurora borealis, meaning "northern dawn". It is also called the northern lights.

POLES
Magnets show both attractive and repulsive forces. Every magnet has a north and a south pole, named according to which geographic Pole of the Earth they are attracted towards; opposite poles attract and like poles repel. A north pole of a compass points north because the Northern Hemisphere has a south magnetic pole. Iron filings can reveal attractive and repulsive forces between magnets.

Iron filings reveal the repulsive forces between like poles.

Iron filings reveal the attractive force between unlike poles.

SOLAR PROMINENCE
Using special telescopes, astronomers can photograph glowing streams of hydrogen gas hundreds of thousands of kilometres above the Sun's surface. These are called prominences. The gas contains moving charged particles, which are affected by the Sun's powerful magnetism. The enormous prominence shown here is being held up by magnetic forces.

What makes a magnet?

Inside a piece of steel are large numbers of tiny magnetized regions called domains. These are usually jumbled up, so their effects cancel out, and the steel is not magnetized. If the domains point in the same direction, the steel becomes a magnet. The end that the north poles of the domains point towards becomes a north pole, and the other end is a south pole.

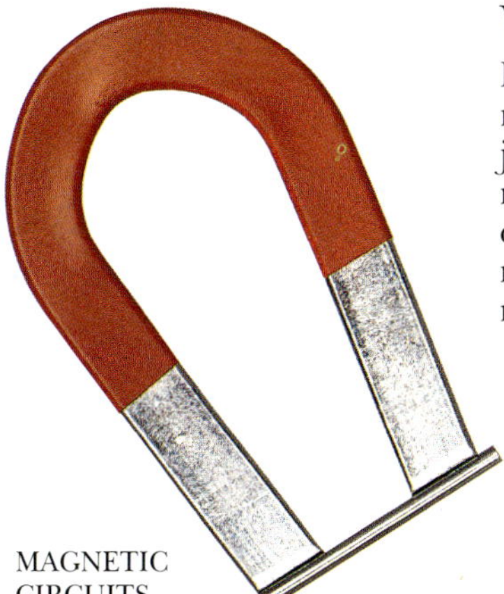

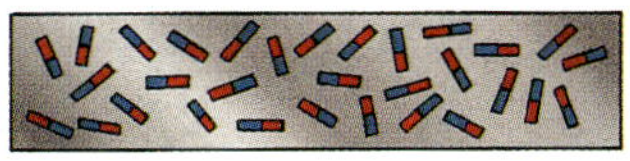

In unmagnetized steel, the magnetic domains are jumbled. Their north and south poles cancel each other out.

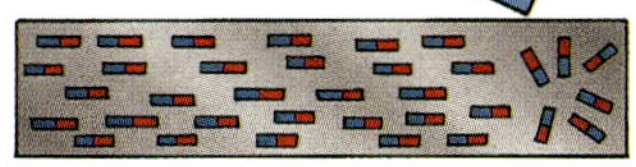

Stroking steel with a bar magnet magnetizes the steel. The magnet pulls the domains in the same direction.

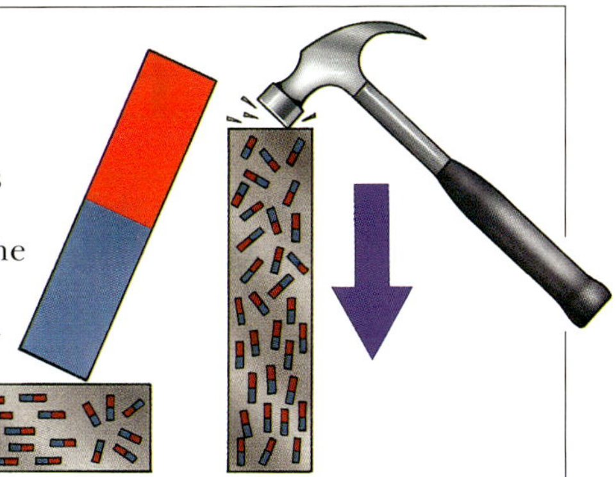

Striking a magnet with a hammer shakes up the domains. Their like poles push apart and the steel loses its magnetism.

MAGNETIC CIRCUITS

A magnet gradually loses its magnetism if it is stored by itself. The domains may gradually shift position (especially if the magnet gets hot or is shaken), so they are no longer lined up. To stop this happening, a piece of iron called a keeper is placed across the poles of a horseshoe magnet. Domains in the keeper are pulled into line by the magnet; domains in the magnet are kept in line by the keeper. This arrangement of domains is called a magnetic circuit; it prevents the magnet from losing its magnetism.

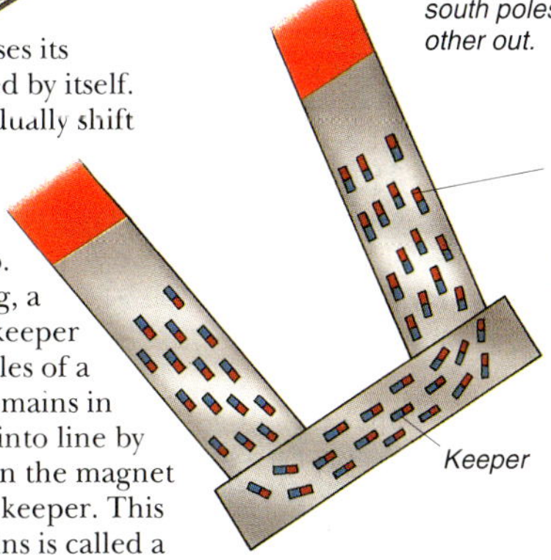

REFRIGERATOR MAGNET

A refrigerator magnet can hold a piece of paper to a fridge door, showing that magnetism can act through a non-magnetic solid. The fridge door acts like a keeper when a toy magnet clings to it. A magnetic circuit is set up between the refrigerator and the magnet; this preserves the magnetism of the magnet.

MAGNETIC TAPE

A cassette tape contains a plastic tape with a coating of iron oxide or chromium dioxide. Magnetic patterns can be applied to the tape by the head of a tape recorder. This changes electrical sound signals into a changing magnetic field, which induces patterns of magnetism on the tape. On replay, this magnetized tape causes or induces electrical signals in the head. These are reproduced as sound.

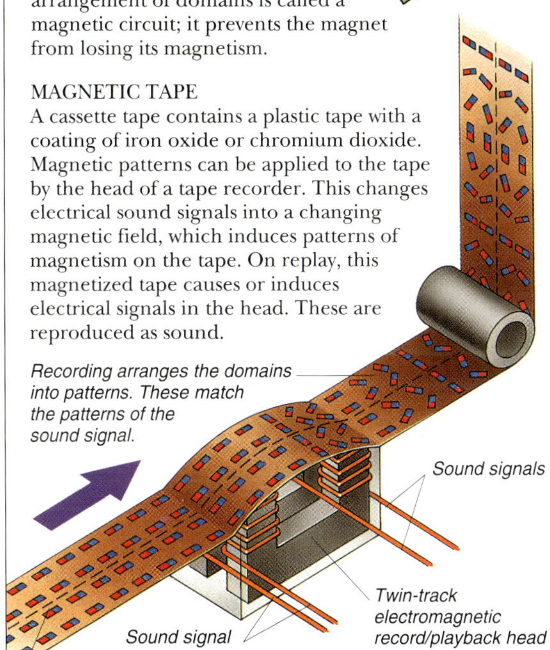

Information is stored on a disk as magnetic pulses that represent 1 (on) or 0 (off).

MAGNETIC DISKS

Computers store data on plastic disks that have a coating that can be magnetized. As in a tape recorder, the material to be recorded is in the form of electrical signals. The disk is spun, and a recording head passes over its surface. This head changes the electrical signals into magnetic pulses, leaving the information stored on the disk as magnetic patterns.

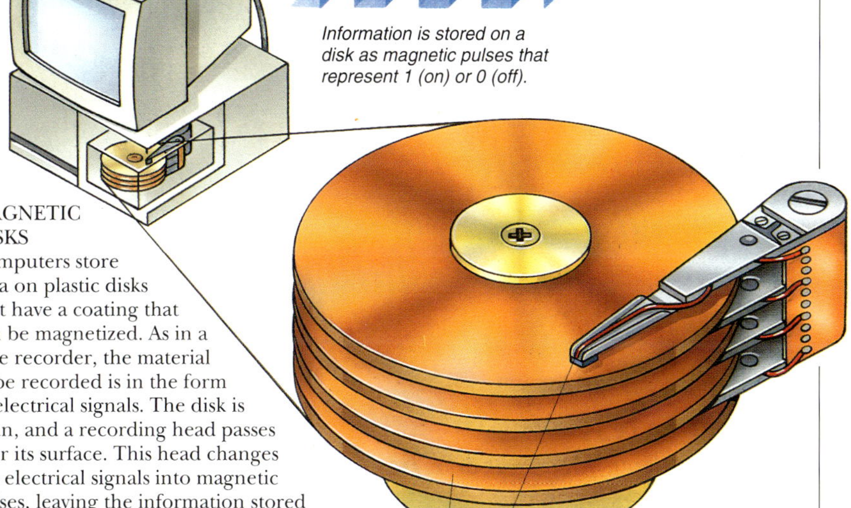

BURGLAR ALARM

A permanent magnet is mounted on the door, and a reed switch is mounted on the frame. When the door is closed, the magnet makes the two upper magnetic iron strips cling together. When the door is opened, the magnet moves away and the centre strip springs back. It touches the non-magnetic contact below, completing the circuit and activating the alarm.

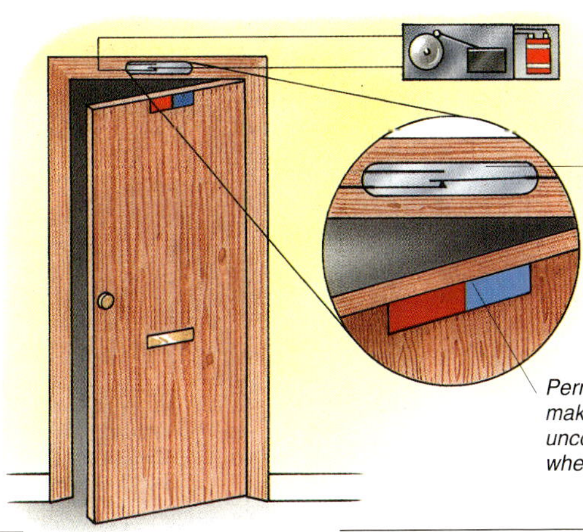

Find out more

TRANSITION METALS P.36
ELECTROMAGNETISM P.156
ELECTRIC MOTORS P.158
GENERATORS P. 159
STRUCTURE OF THE EARTH P.212
SUN P.284
FACT FINDER P.410

ELECTRIC MOTORS

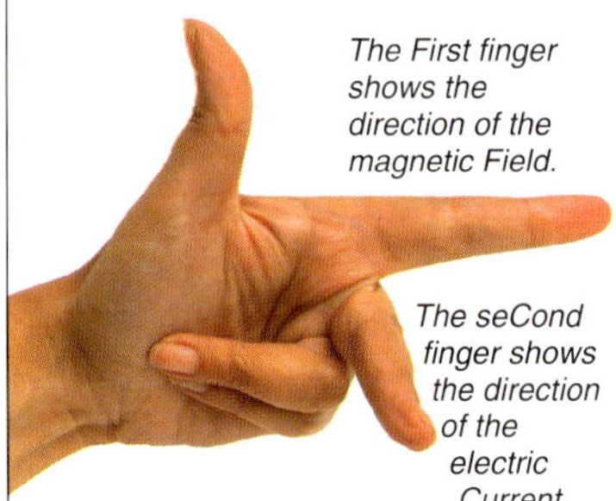

LEFT-HAND RULE
You can work out which way a wire carrying a current will move through a magnetic field by using a rule called Fleming's left-hand rule. Hold your left hand as shown, with the two fingers and thumb all at right angles to each other.

MANY OF THE MACHINES that we use every day are powered by an electric motor. Such a motor changes electricity into movement. It makes use of the fact that a wire carrying a current produces a magnetic field and so will feel a force in another magnetic field. This force can produce movement. Electric motors are convenient sources of power because they are clean, fairly quiet, and very versatile. Washing machines, food mixers, video recorders, and record players have electric motors that make them work. Cars use electric motors to start up and to operate windscreen wipers. But few cars run on electric motors because batteries of a reasonable size cannot store enough energy to power a modern car for long journeys.

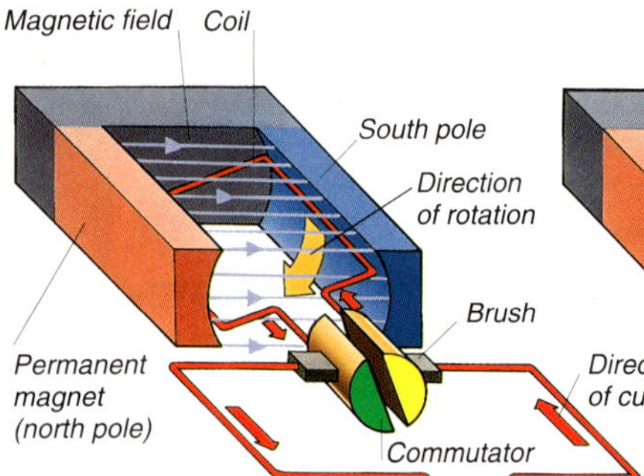

1. Current flows through the coil, and the field of the permanent magnet forces the right side of the coil down and the left side up, in accordance with Fleming's left-hand rule.

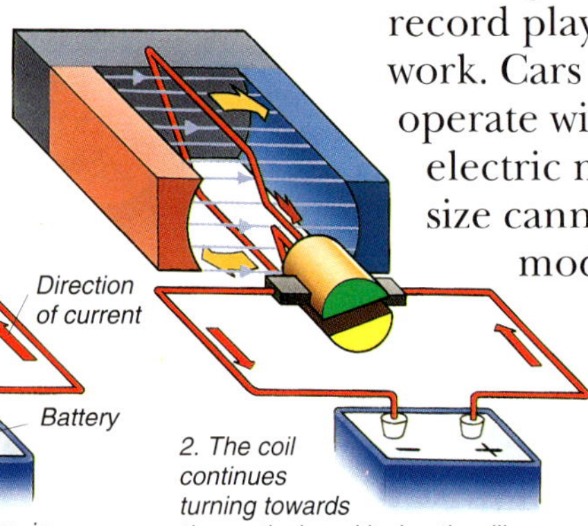

2. The coil continues turning towards the vertical, and its inertia will carry it beyond this position.

JOSEPH HENRY
American physicist Joseph Henry (1797-1878) made many important discoveries about electromagnetism. He improved the design of electromagnets, and in 1829 he built the first electric motor. This used electromagnets to make a pivoted beam rock up and down.

SIMPLE MOTOR

In a simple electric motor, direct current is fed into a coil by carbon rods called brushes. The coil sits between the north and south poles of a permanent magnet. The magnetic fields of the coil and the permanent magnet interact, forcing the coil to turn. To keep up the rotation, the current is reversed every half-turn by an attachment called a commutator. The continuous turning motion of the coil drives the motor.

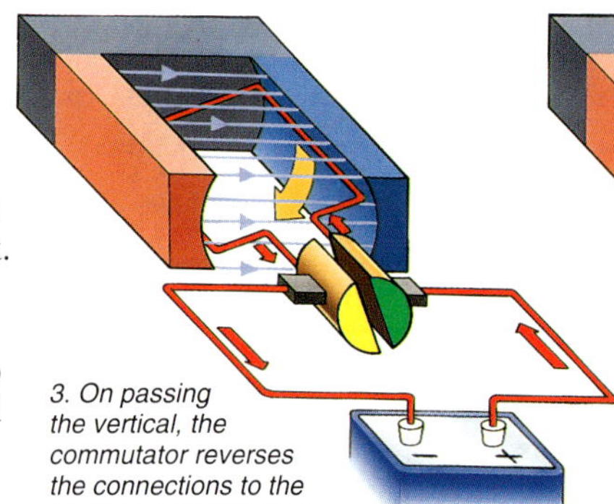

3. On passing the vertical, the commutator reverses the connections to the brushes and, therefore, also reverses the current in the coil. So the side that was moving up now moves down.

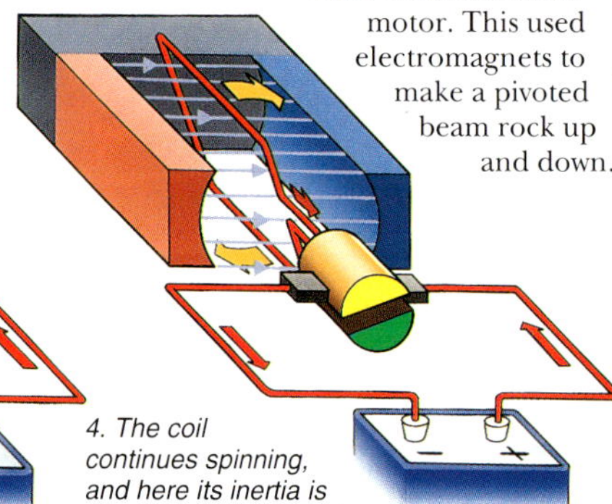

4. The coil continues spinning, and here its inertia is about to carry it past the vertical position again. The resultant reversal of current each half turn causes the coil to spin continuously.

MODEL TRAIN
An electric motor drives this model locomotive. It picks up electricity from the tracks through its wheels. Wires connect the wheels to the metal strips which touch the motor's commutator. A control unit can vary the voltage supplied to the tracks. The higher the voltage, the stronger the magnetic field made by the coils in the motor. This means the motor turns faster, so the locomotive speeds up.

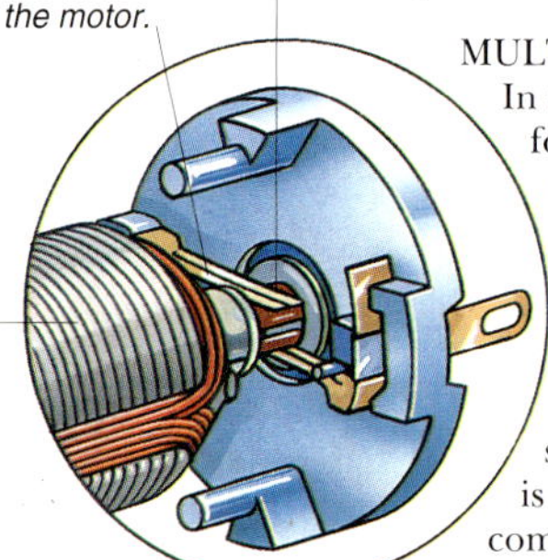

MULTIPOLE MOTORS
In a simple motor, the turning force on a coil carrying a current is greatest when the windings are in line with the magnetic field, and weakest when the windings are at right angles to the field. Most electric motors have several coils to give a smoother turning force. Current is supplied to the coils by a commutator with many sections.

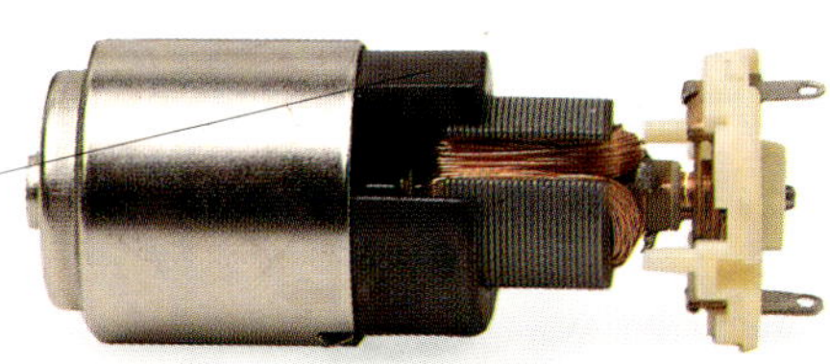

Find out more

FORCES AND MOTION P.120
ENGINES P.143
CURRENT ELECTRICITY P.148
ELECTROMAGNETISM P.156
FACT FINDER P.410

GENERATORS

EVERY DAY, WE USE ELECTRICITY made by powerful machines called generators. These work in the opposite way to electric motors; they turn movement into electricity. The principle they work on is called electromagnetic induction: electricity is produced in a wire when it moves in a magnetic field, or when a nearby magnetic field moves or changes in strength. Large generators are used in power stations to produce the mains supply that we take for granted in our homes. The movement is given by steam, moving water, or wind. Small generators called dynamos are used on bicycles to power the lights.

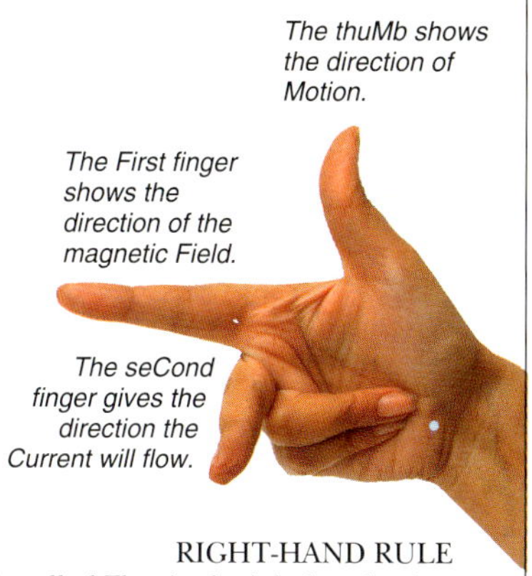

RIGHT-HAND RULE

A rule called Fleming's right-hand rule can show the direction in which current will flow in a wire when the wire moves in a magnetic field. Hold your right-hand thumb, first finger, and second finger at right-angles to one another.

BICYCLE DYNAMO

One type of bicycle dynamo has a small wheel touching the rear tyre of the bike. When the bike moves, the wheel turns; this movement makes a permanent magnet spin near a coil that is wound on an iron core. The wires in the coil experience a changing magnetic field from the spinning magnet, so electricity is generated in them. This effect is called electromagnetic induction – a voltage is induced in the coil.

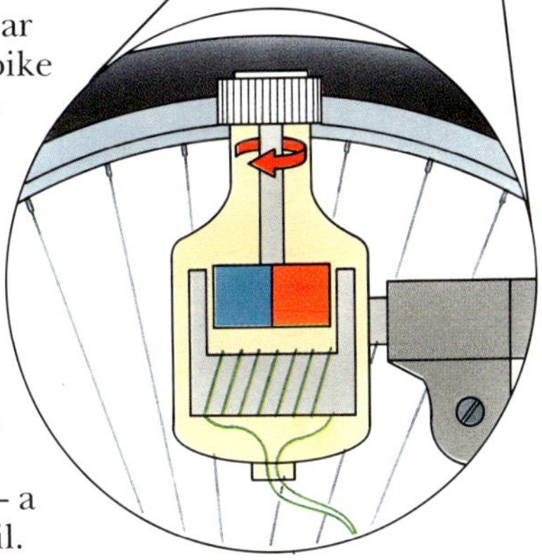

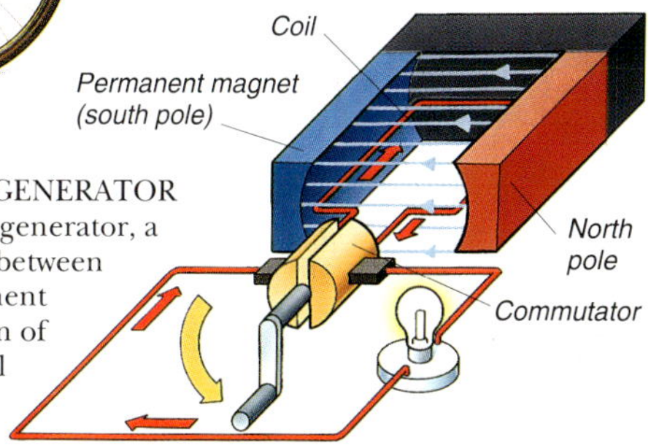

DIRECT CURRENT GENERATOR

In this direct current generator, a coil of wire is turned between the poles of a permanent magnet. The direction of the current in the coil reverses every half-turn, because each side of the coil alternately passes up and down through the magnetic field. But the current that passes through the bulb flows in one direction only, because the commutator changes the connections every half turn.

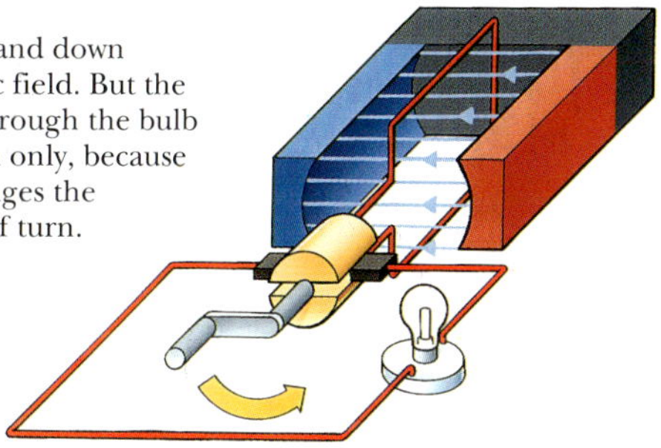

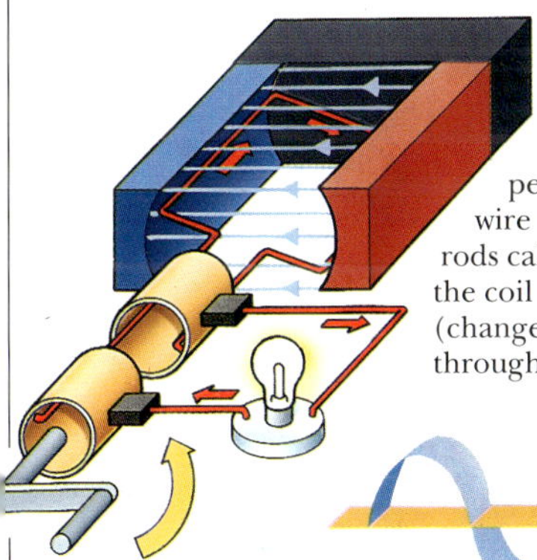

ALTERNATOR

A generator that produces alternating current is called an alternator. In this simple version, a coil of wire is spun between the poles of a permanent magnet. This creates a current in the wire that is carried to the lamp by carbon rods called brushes. The current through the coil and bulb continually alternates (changes direction); the current through the bulb is alternating too.

Direct current is produced in pulses that flow in one direction only.

Alternating current is produced in waves that flow first in one direction, then in the opposite direction.

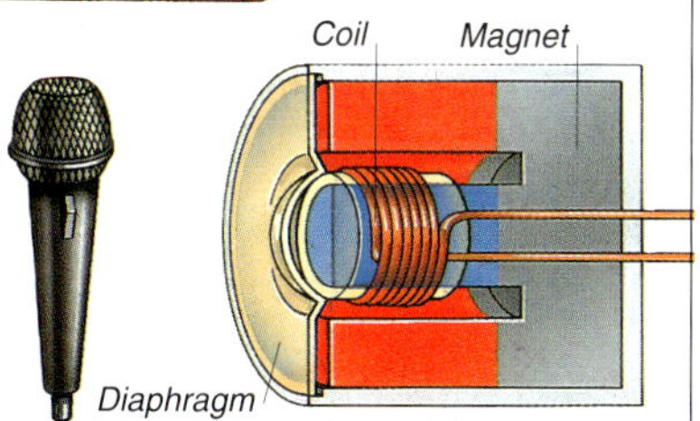

MOVING COIL MICROPHONE

A microphone generates electric signals from sounds. In a moving coil microphone, sound waves strike a diaphragm and vibrate a coil which is positioned between the poles of a permanent magnet. The voltage induced in the coil varies in strength and frequency in the same way as the sound waves.

MICHAEL FARADAY

Michael Faraday (1791-1867) was the son of an English blacksmith. He started work as a bookbinder. Inspired by the science books he bound, he took up physics and went on to make many discoveries. In 1821, he found that electricity could produce rotary motion; today's electric motors are based on this. In 1831, he showed that relative movement between a magnet and a coil of wire could induce electricity in the coil – an idea that gave birth to modern generators.

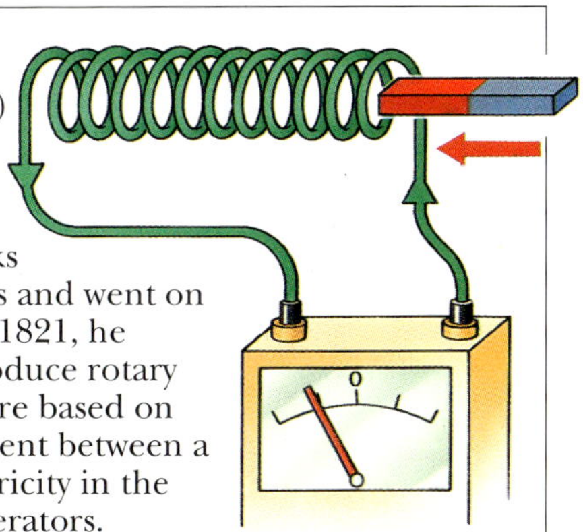

Find out more

NUCLEAR ENERGY P.136
ENGINES P.143
ELECTROMAGNETISM P.156
MAKING AND HEARING SOUND P.182
ELECTROMAGNETIC SPECTRUM P.192

ELECTRICITY SUPPLY

HOW CAN THE WALL SOCKETS in your home supply you with electricity? Because they are connected to power stations. In a power station, a turbine is driven by steam power (or water or wind power). The turbine then drives an electricity generator. So the generator converts kinetic energy (the movement of the turbine) into electrical energy. Most generators produce an alternating supply of electricity and are called alternators. Alternating current (a.c.) is more convenient than direct current (d.c.) because it can be changed to a higher or lower voltage by a device called a transformer. So the different voltages needed can be supplied to factories, offices, stores, and homes.

POWER PYLONS
The cheapest way to run cables across the country is to suspend them from towers called pylons. Insulators between the cables and the supports prevent the current from leaking away through the pylons. In towns, the cables are usually underground.

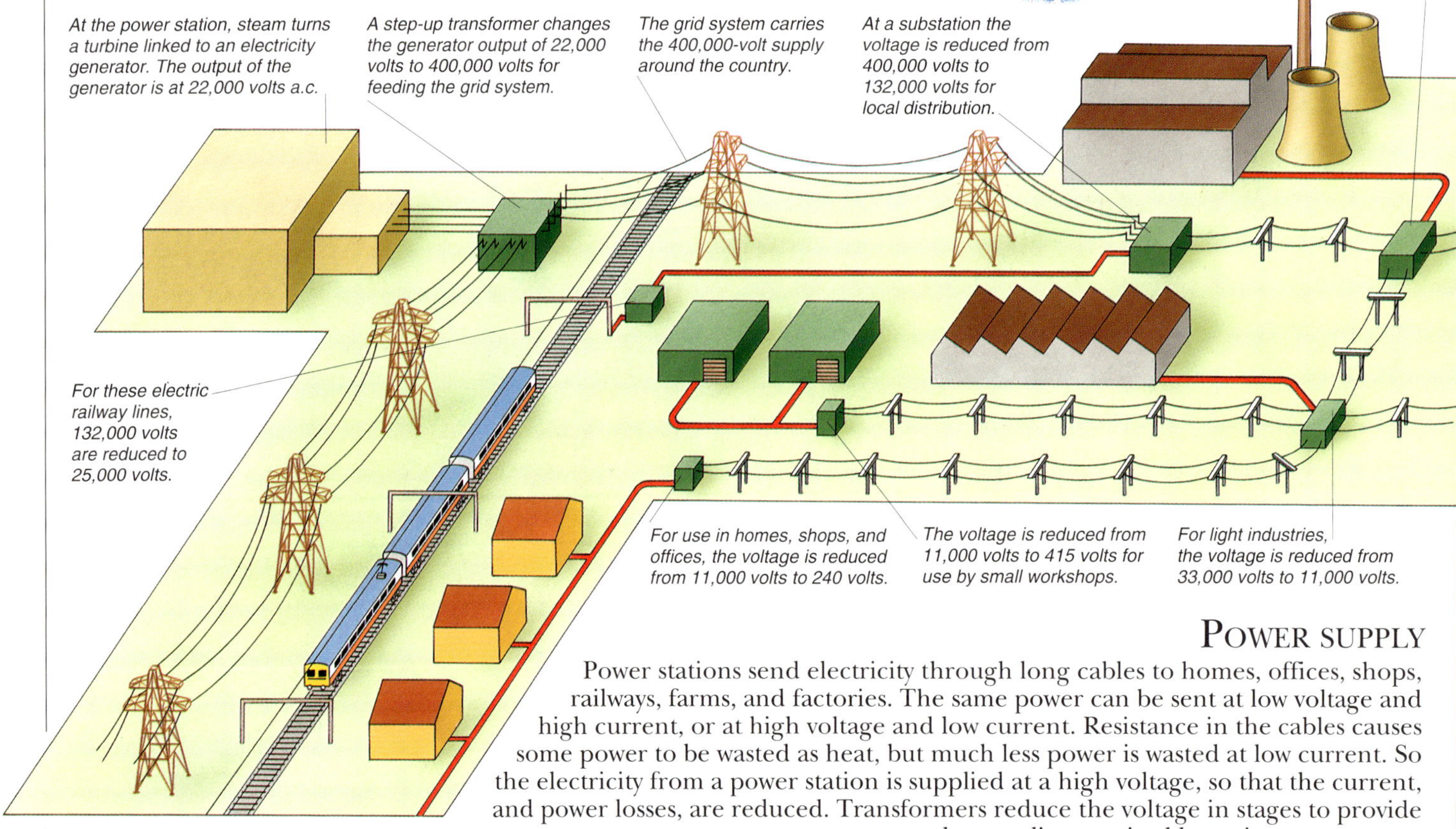

POWER SUPPLY

Power stations send electricity through long cables to homes, offices, shops, railways, farms, and factories. The same power can be sent at low voltage and high current, or at high voltage and low current. Resistance in the cables causes some power to be wasted as heat, but much less power is wasted at low current. So the electricity from a power station is supplied at a high voltage, so that the current, and power losses, are reduced. Transformers reduce the voltage in stages to provide the supplies required by various consumers.

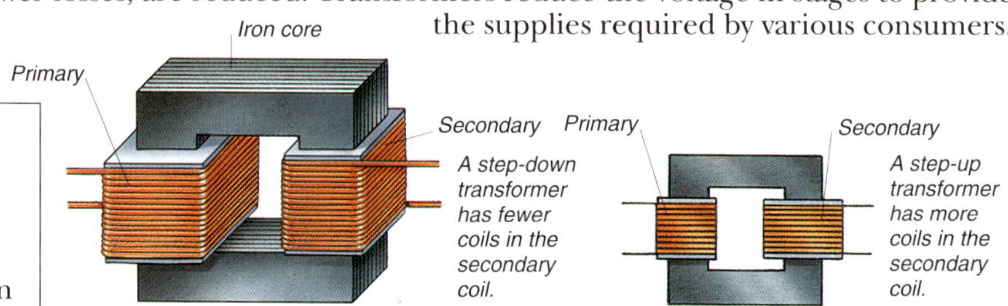

TRANSFORMERS
The high voltages from power cables need to be converted into levels that we can use in our homes. Transformers do this job. A simple transformer consists of two coils wound onto the same iron core. When an alternating voltage is applied to one coil (called the primary coil), it produces a changing magnetic field in the core. This induces an alternating voltage in the other coil (called the secondary coil).

NIKOLA TESLA
In 1887, the American inventor Nikola Tesla (1856-1943) patented a generating and distribution system that transmitted alternating current. It won over his former boss Thomas Edison's direct current system. The two men were to have been awarded a joint Nobel Prize in 1912. But Tesla refused to have anything to do with Edison, and neither man received the prize.

Find out more

POOR METALS P.38
WORK AND ENERGY P.132
ENERGY SOURCES P.134
CELLS AND BATTERIES P.150
GENERATORS P.159
FACT FINDER P.410

ELECTRICITY IN THE HOME

WITH ELECTRICITY READILY AVAILABLE at the flick of a switch, it is easy to forget how much we depend on it. The electricity supply runs our homes. This electricity has travelled from far-away power stations. When there is a power failure, we realize how many devices in the home depend on this supply. The lights go out, and suddenly you have to search for candles. The television no longer works – you have to listen to a battery-operated radio instead. Electric heaters, cookers, dishwashers, washing machines, dryers, and many other appliances can no longer be used.

LIGHT BULB

Most electric light bulbs have a thin tungsten wire called a filament, mounted in a sealed glass bulb. When a current flows through, the filament glows white hot. The wire takes some time to burn out because most of the oxygen (needed for burning) has been removed from the bulb.

DOMESTIC CIRCUITS

The electricity supply coming into our homes first passes through main fuses. It then reaches a meter that measures how much electricity we use. A consumer unit is connected to the other side of the meter. This contains fuses or circuit breakers to protect the house circuits.

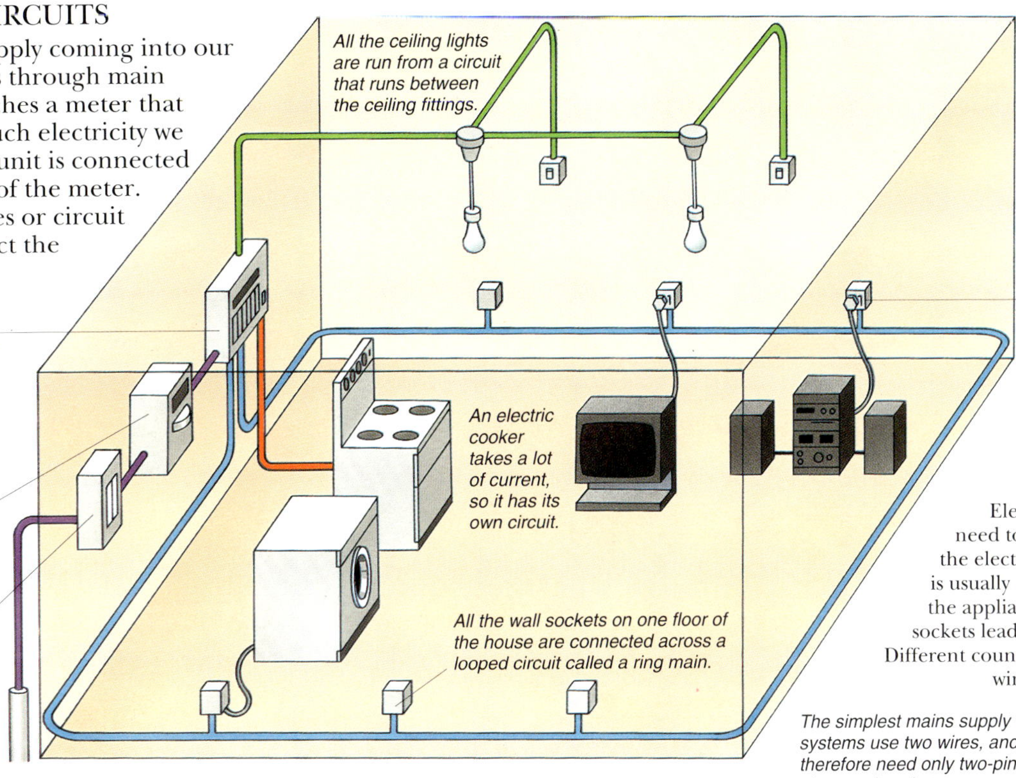

PLUGS AND SOCKETS

Electrical appliances need to be connected to the electricity supply. This is usually done via plugs on the appliance which fit into sockets leading to the supply. Different countries use different wiring colour codes.

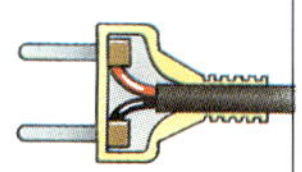

The simplest mains supply systems use two wires, and therefore need only two-pin plugs and sockets.

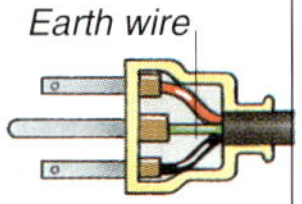

Many mains supply systems have a third wire, the earth wire. It is connected to a metal rod in the ground, and ensures that exposed metal parts can never become live and cause shocks.

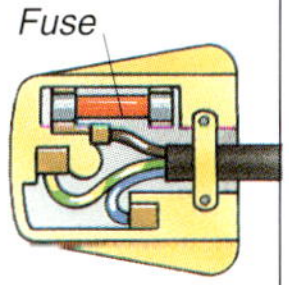

Some plugs have a fuse. If an appliance takes too much current, the fuse in the plug blows, rather than a fuse or a circuit breaker in the consumer unit. So power is still available at all the other sockets.

POWER AND ENERGY

Power, the rate of using energy, is measured in watts. When electricity flows through a resistor, the power equals the voltage multiplied by the current. A 240-volt cooker ring, taking a current of 4 amps, has a power of 960 watts. We can work out the total energy consumed by multiplying the power by the time that the ring is on; in two hours, the ring consumes 2 x 960 = 1920 watt-hours, or 1.92 kilowatt-hours (kWh) of electricity.

CIRCUIT PROTECTION

Electricity can accidentally cause a fire by heating a wire so much that it becomes red hot. This usually happens when a fault causes too much current to flow. To prevent this from happening, domestic circuits are protected by devices called fuses and circuit breakers. Both cut off the current if it increases to a dangerous level.

A circuit breaker is an electromagnetic switch that cuts off the current when it becomes too high.

A fuse is an enclosed length of wire that forms the weakest link in a circuit. It burns out safely to cut off the current when this becomes too high. Fuses are available to withstand various currents.

Find out more

WORK AND ENERGY P.132
CURRENT ELECTRICITY P.148
CELLS AND BATTERIES P.150
CIRCUITS P.152
SOURCES OF LIGHT P.193
FACT FINDER P.410

TELECOMMUNICATIONS

TELEGRAPHIC RECEIVER
In the 1830s, Samuel Morse invented a printer to record messages sent on his electric telegraph. A strip of plain paper moved slowly through the machine. Each pulse of current received made an electromagnet move an inked wheel, so that the dots and dashes of the Morse code were printed on the paper strip. Operators used a switch called a Morse key to send signals. Pressing the key allowed electricity to flow, which activated the inker (or a clicker) at the other end. Messages were received as they were being sent.

THE WONDER OF TALKING to someone who is thousands of miles away is only possible because of electricity. Electronic equipment converts sounds and pictures into electricity, which then travels with lightning speed to somewhere else to be changed back into sounds and pictures by other electrically powered equipment. A huge amount of information, from fax messages to telephone conversations, travels back and forth through telephone lines. Information can also be transmitted as light in fibreoptic cables or as radio waves, which are sent up to a satellite high up in space to be retransmitted to a receiving dish. Computers and other electronic machines can communicate with each other via telephone lines. All these forms of communication need three things: a transmitter to send out the information, something to carry the signals, and a receiver to convert signals back into a form that we can understand.

Morse code is sent as a combination of dots, dashes, and spaces that represent numbers and letters of the alphabet. Here the numbers 4 and 2 have been printed out.

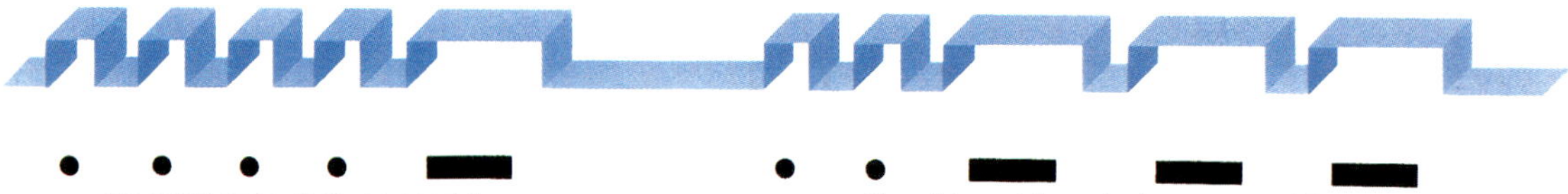

Four dots and a dash represent 4.

Two dots and three dashes represent 2.

RECEIVER
The receiver in the handset turns the incoming electrical signal into sound. The signal passes through an electromagnet, which attracts a thin iron disc called a diaphragm. As the strength of the signal varies, the pull on the disc varies, and this makes it vibrate. The vibrations pass through the air as sound waves, which you hear as speech.

TELEPHONE

When you dial or push buttons on a telephone, a series of dialling signals is sent out. These signals make automatic equipment connect your call. The bell or bleeper at the other end then sounds. When you speak, the microphone in the handset turns your speech into electrical signals, which are sent to the person at the other end of the line. Their receiver turns the incoming speech signals back into sounds.

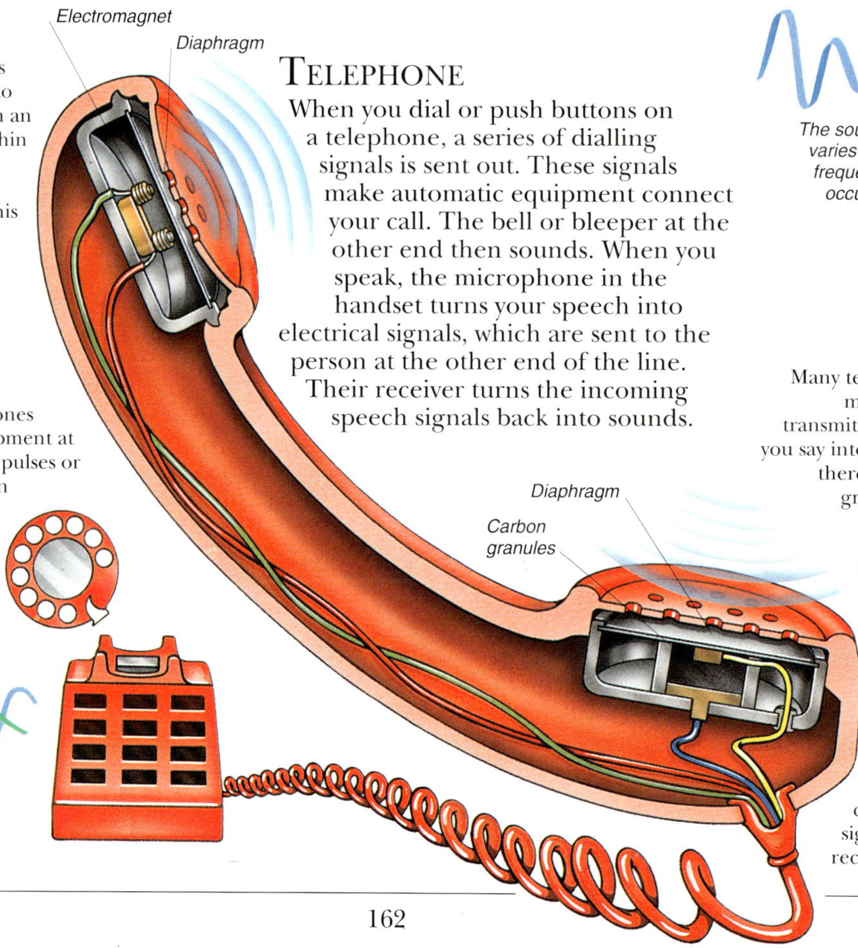

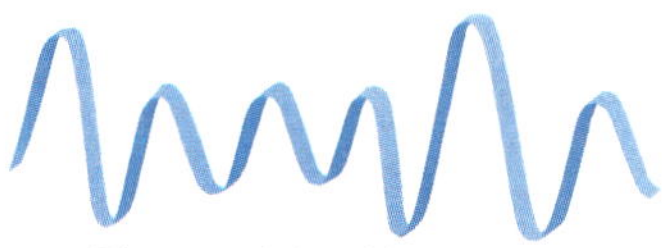

The sound signal from a telephone varies in amplitude (strength) and frequency (number of waves that occur in each second) to match the voice of the speaker.

DIALLING
Dialling signals are either simple electrical pulses or mixtures of tones (musical notes). Electronic equipment at telephone exchanges counts the pulses or recognizes the tones so that it can make the right connections.

When you dial one digit of a number, switches in the dial send pulses along the line.

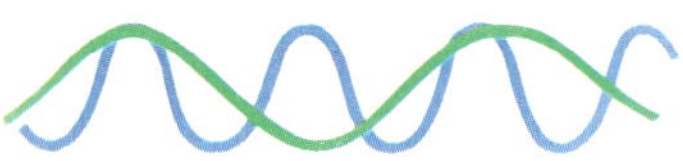

Some push-button phones send out mixtures of tones. A different combination is sent by each button. You can hear these when you press each button.

MICROPHONE
Many telephones have a carbon microphone, also called a transmitter, which converts what you say into electric signals. Inside, there is a capsule containing granules of carbon. When you speak, the sound waves vibrate a plastic diaphragm. This pushes on the granules. Every time they are pushed together, their resistance decreases. So a current passed through them varies in the same way as the sounds causing the vibrations. This varying current forms the sound signal which travels to the receiver in another phone.

ALEXANDER GRAHAM BELL

In 1876, Scottish-born American inventor and teacher Alexander Graham Bell (1847-1922) invented the telephone. Bell gave music lessons, taught deaf people how to speak, and studied how sounds are emitted by vibrating objects. He invented a form of electric telegraph that sent signals as musical notes made by vibrating reeds. This idea led Bell to devise a way of sending and receiving the frequencies present in the human voice. The result was the telephone.

COMMUNICATIONS LINKS

When you make a call, the dialling pulses pass along wires to your local telephone exchange. Equipment there recognizes the codes in the pulses. For a local call, the local exchange connects you. For a different area, you are connected with the exchange in that area. Equipment there then makes the connection to the number you want. International calls are sent through international exchanges. The whole system of connecting links is called a network.

SATELLITES

Calls sent via communications satellites, which are in orbit around the Earth, are transmitted by radio from huge dish-shaped aerials on the ground. The satellite, powered by solar cells, beams the signals back to an aerial in another part of the world.

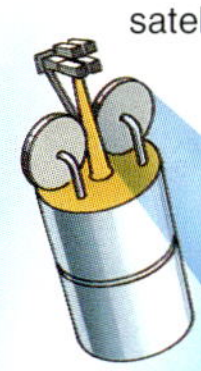

Have you noticed a slight delay when talking to someone on an overseas call? This can be because the call is going via a satellite. Radio signals take a little time to travel to and from the satellite.

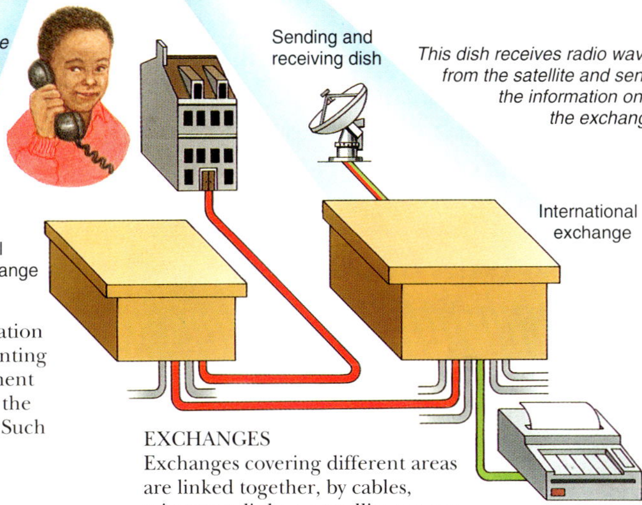

SATELLITE STATIONS

A satellite telecommunications station has a large dish-shaped aerial pointing at the satellite. Electronic equipment connected to the aerial amplifies the signals transmitted and received. Such stations are connected to local telephone exchanges.

EXCHANGES

Exchanges covering different areas are linked together, by cables, microwave links, or satellite systems. Such links enable people in one area to contact people in other areas.

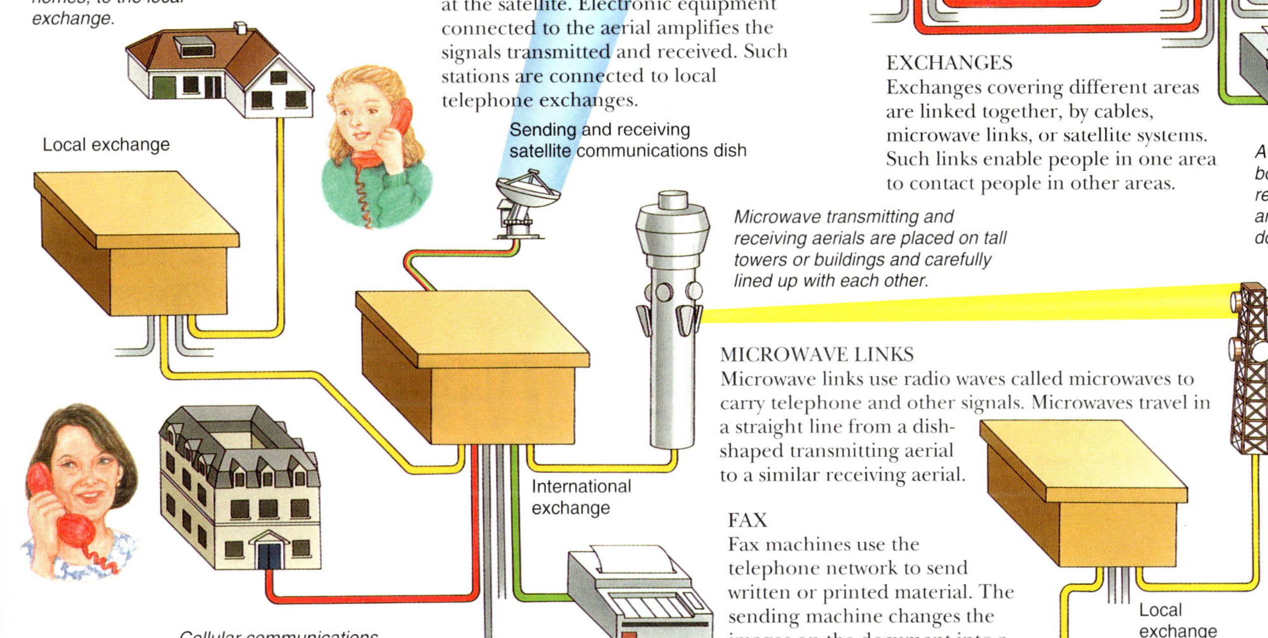

MICROWAVE LINKS

Microwave links use radio waves called microwaves to carry telephone and other signals. Microwaves travel in a straight line from a dish-shaped transmitting aerial to a similar receiving aerial.

FAX

Fax machines use the telephone network to send written or printed material. The sending machine changes the images on the document into a code of electrical signals and sends them down the telephone line. The receiving machine uses these to reproduce the original document.

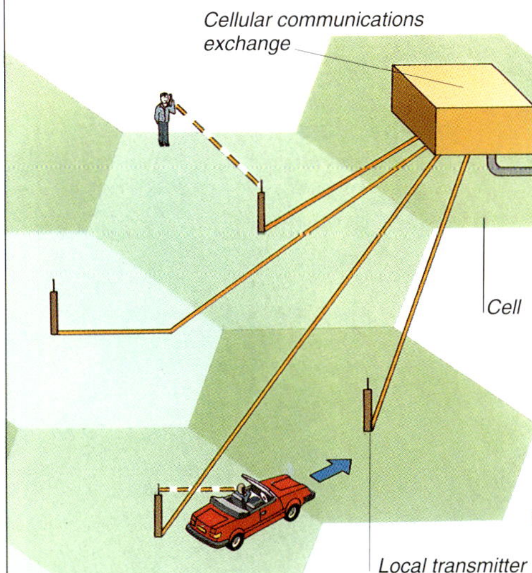

PORTABLE TELEPHONES

People driving along can talk to each other using portable telephones with built-in radio transmitters and receivers. A low-power transmitter in the telephone connects the call to permanent receiving equipment installed in the area, called a cell. From there, the call is connected into the telephone network. A local transmitter sends incoming signals to a radio receiver in the telephone. The whole system is called a cellular network.

Find out more

CELLS AND BATTERIES p.150
COMPUTERS p.173
SOUND AND LIGHT p.177
REFRACTION p.196
SATELLITES p.300
FACT FINDER p.410

TELEVISION

TELEVISION AFFECTS all our lives. We learn about places we shall never visit, we see important events as they take place; some programmes we watch purely for entertainment. Television became popular in the 1950s, but ideas for sending pictures over long distances date back to the 19th century. Thanks mainly to inventions such as valves, transistors, and the cathode-ray tube, we now have high-quality television systems. In many countries, television pictures and sound are transmitted nationally using UHF (ultra-high frequency) radio waves or electrical signals through cables. Television is also transmitted internationally via satellites. Closed-circuit television is used for security in banks and other buildings; the pictures travel straight from the camera to the screen.

TELEVISION STUDIO
Picture signals from the cameras and sound signals from the microphones go to a control room overlooking the studio. There, all the pictures are shown on screens. The programme director decides which picture to use and when to change to another shot.

LIVE TELEVISION
When a programme is broadcast live, a television camera changes light from the scene into electric signals. These are transmitted by radio and changed back into pictures by the television set.

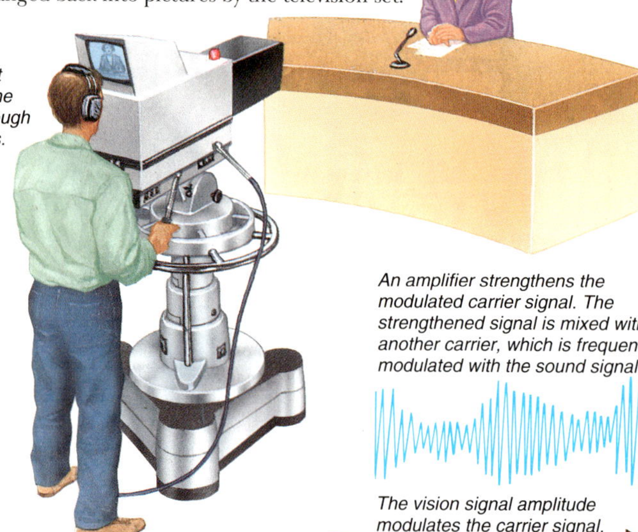

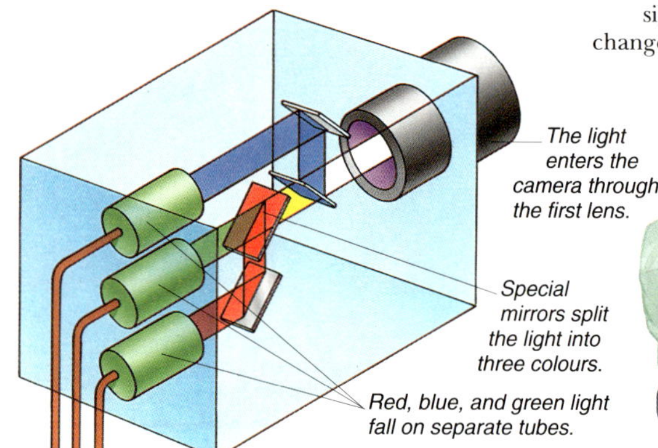

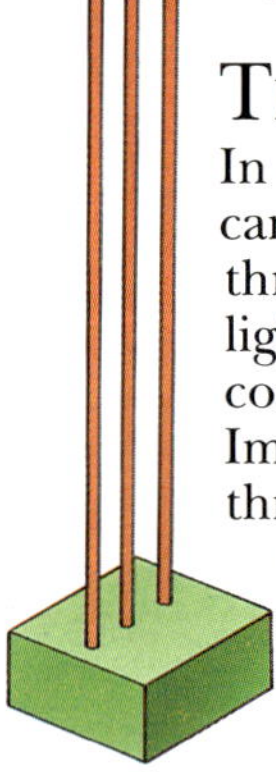

TELEVISION CAMERA

In one type of colour television camera, light from the scene passes through special mirrors that split the light into its primary colour components – red, green, and blue. Images in these colours are formed on three camera tubes. The tubes scan the images, line by line. Each tube then puts out an electric signal that varies with the brightness along each line of the image.

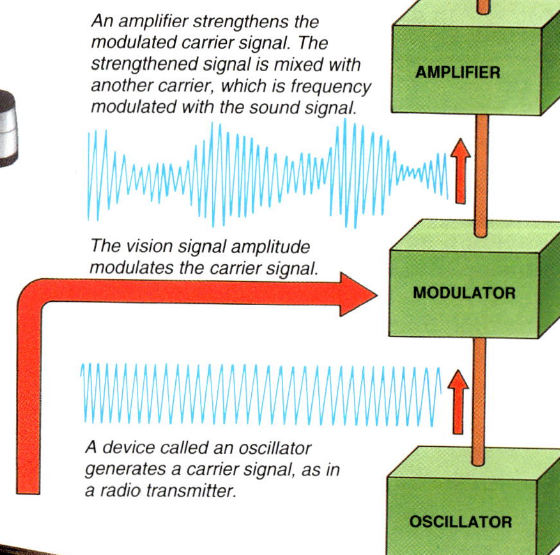

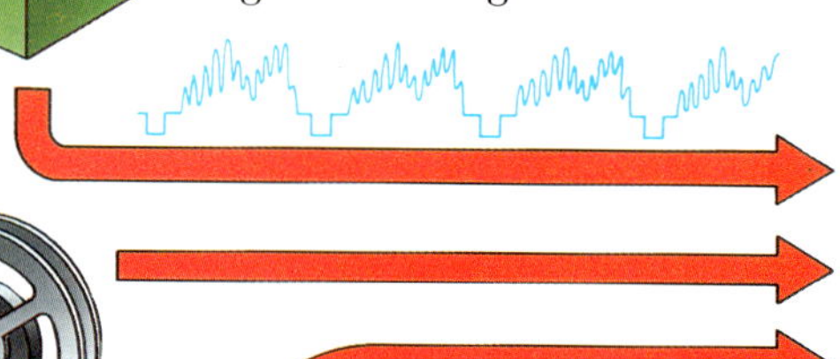

FILM AND TAPE
A cinema film is run through a telecine machine, which forms electric signals from the sounds and pictures recorded on the film. Programmes recorded on tape are played back on a videotape machine. The sound and vision signals from many sources go to the presentation suite. This is a control room with an adjoining announcers' studio.

PRESENTATION SUITE
Here, signals from live and recorded sources are selected and controlled. The pictures are displayed on screens called monitors. From the presentation suite, the sound signal, and a single vision signal containing all the colour information, are sent to the television transmitter. The vision signal also contains timing information called synchronizing pulses. These enable the receiver to reconstruct the picture correctly.

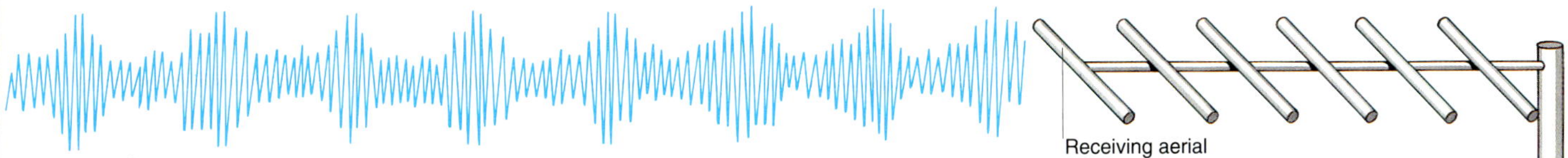

TELEVISION RECEIVERS

Signals from the television transmitter travel through the air at the speed of light. The aerial connected to a television set changes these radio waves back into electric signals. In the receiver, electronic circuits allow you to tune in to the television station you want. In a colour television, other circuits sort out the three colour components of the vision signal. The picture tube uses these to reproduce the picture in full colour. A loudspeaker reproduces the sound signal.

JOHN LOGIE BAIRD

In 1926, Scottish television pioneer John Logie Baird (1888-1946) demonstrated the first television system. He used a rotating disc with holes in it to transform light from a scene into lines. A photo-electric cell changed brightness variations into electric signals. In Baird's receiver, the signals made a bulb vary in brightness. The viewer saw a faint, fuzzy image through holes in another spinning disc. The system was soon replaced by a higher quality fully electronic system.

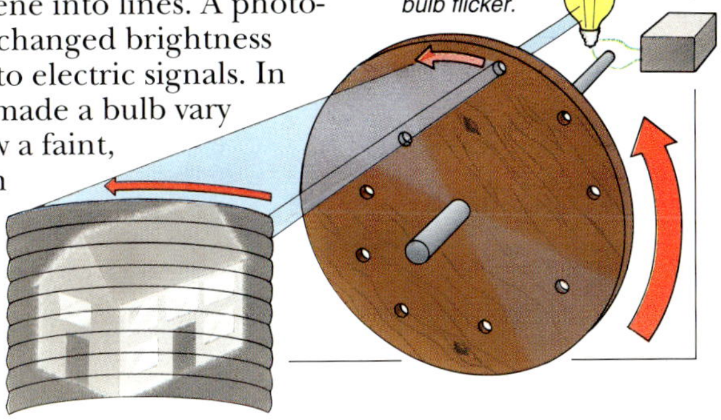

Baird's spinning disc was invented by Paul Nipkow (1860-1940) in 1884. This diagram shows how a nine-hole disc reproduces a picture when a vision signal makes the bulb flicker.

ELECTRON GUNS

Devices called electron guns inside the cathode-ray tube fire beams of electrons at the screen. Colour tubes have separate beams for each of the three primary colours. The beams vary in strength according to the brightness of the colour components in the original scene.

COLOUR PICTURES

Each electron beam varies in strength as it scans the screen, making the brightness of the phosphors (patches of chemicals) vary. The beams thus "paint" three colour images on the screen. These give the impression of one image in full colour.

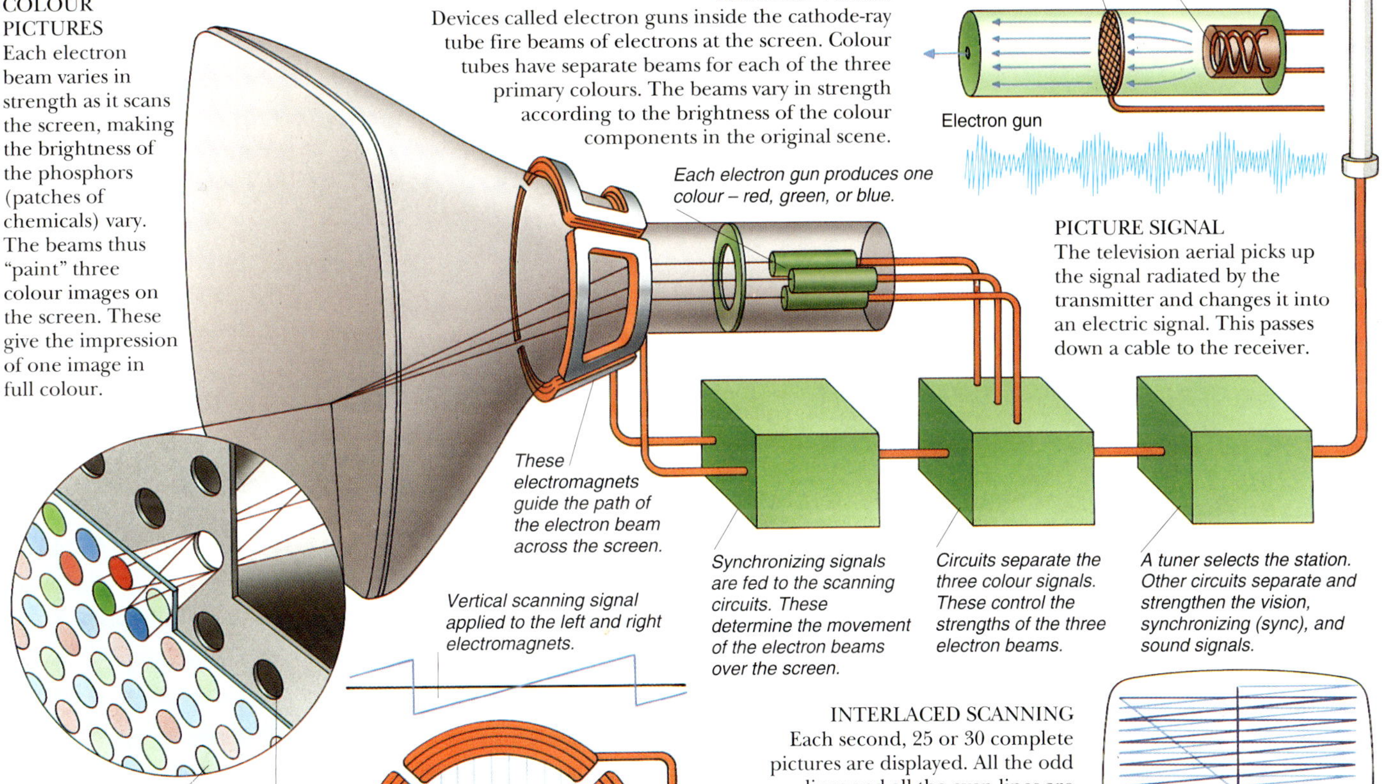

PICTURE SIGNAL

The television aerial picks up the signal radiated by the transmitter and changes it into an electric signal. This passes down a cable to the receiver.

SCREEN

Phosphors cover the television screen. These glow red, green, or blue when struck by an electron beam. Some colour tubes have a perforated plate called a shadow mask just behind the screen. The holes in the mask ensure that each beam strikes only one kind of phosphor. So each beam forms an image of one colour.

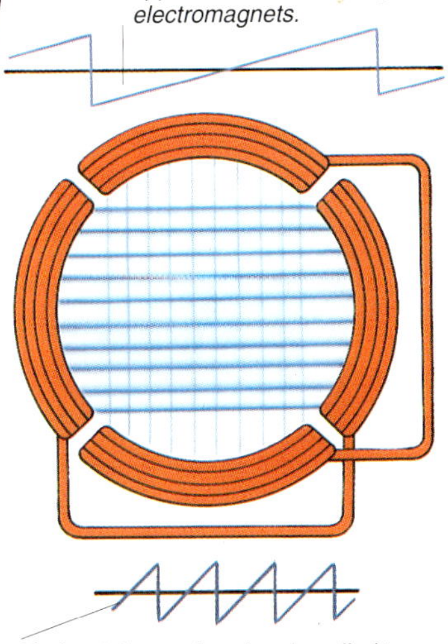

INTERLACED SCANNING

Each second, 25 or 30 complete pictures are displayed. All the odd lines and all the even lines are shown alternately, making 50 or 60 images per second. Increasing the image rate like this reduces flicker.

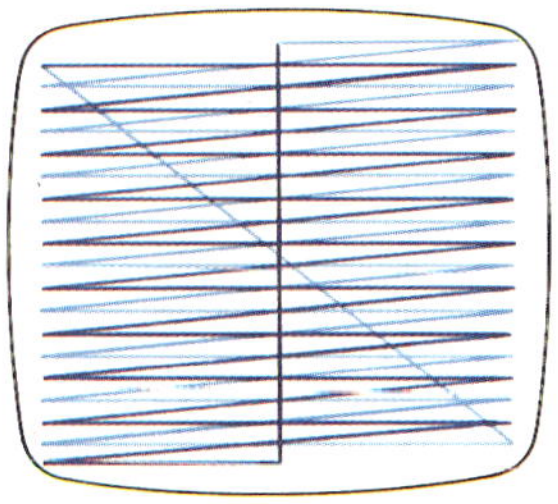

SCANNING

In a television receiver, beams of electrons are moved rapidly across the screen by pairs of electro-magnets called line and field deflection coils. Changing currents through the coils produce changing magnetic fields. These fields deflect the beams of electrons across and down the screen.

Find out more

ATOMIC STRUCTURE P.24
RADIO P.164
ELECTROMAGNETIC SPECTRUM P.192
COLOUR P.202
CINEMA P.208

ELECTRONIC COMPONENTS

ELECTRONICS AFFECTS OUR LIVES more than any other branch of technology. Radio and television sets, record players, and tape recorders were the first popular electronic devices to become available. They use parts called electronic components to control or change electric signals in some way. These parts include resistors, capacitors, transistors, and diodes. Today, many electronic components have been miniaturized (made tiny) so more and more devices can use them. Some watches, for example, contain complex electronic circuits that can tell us the time anywhere in the world. Electronic components in some cameras set the correct exposure and automatically focus the lens.

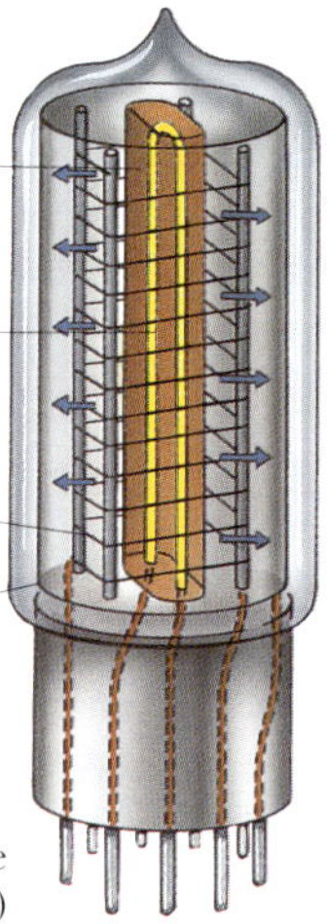

TRIODE VALVE
A component called a triode valve amplifies (strengthens) electric signals. It consists of a cathode and an anode with a wire grid between them. When a small signal is fed to the grid, the charge on the grid alters, which causes large changes in the electron flow to the anode. The signal to the anode is therefore an amplified version of the signal on the grid. Valves have been replaced in radios by transistors, which means that much smaller radios, called transistor radios, can be made.

PORTABLE RADIO

A modern portable radio contains many different electronic components to carry out many different jobs. The aerial picks up the signals from the radio stations. You can select the station you want using a tuning circuit consisting of a coil and a variable capacitor. Components called transistors amplify these signals. The volume is controlled by a variable resistor that adjusts the level of sound signals fed to the final amplifier and the loudspeaker.

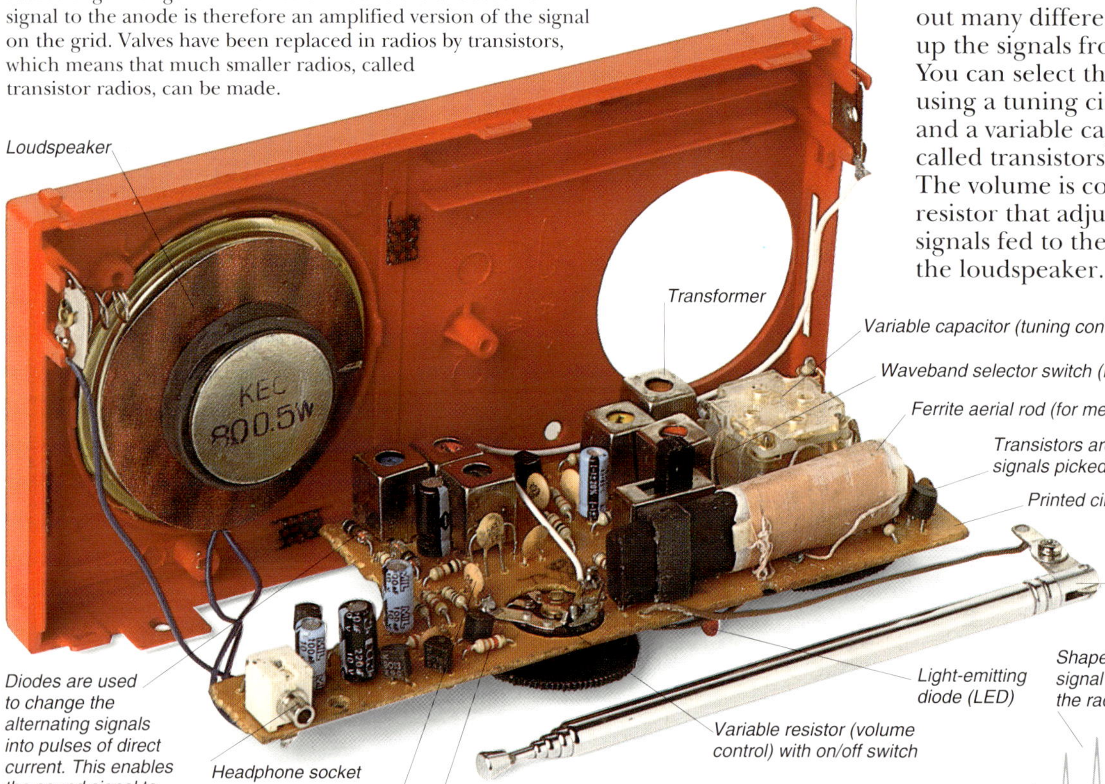

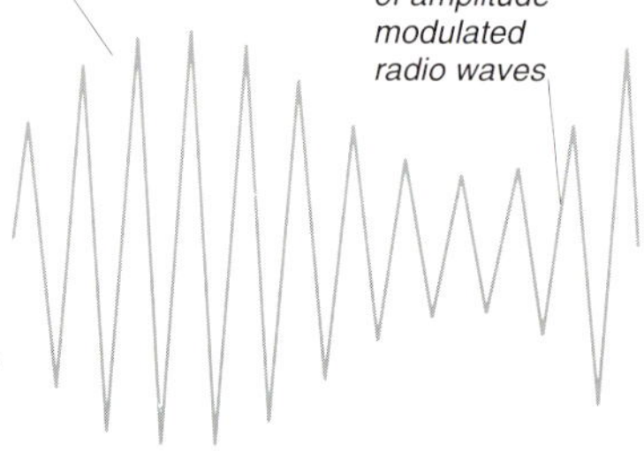

RECEPTION
The signals sent out by an AM radio transmitter are radio waves that vary in amplitude. The aerial of a radio receiver changes all received radio waves into matching electrical signals. A tuning circuit then selects the signal required.

DETECTION
The signal selected by the tuning circuit passes to a diode. This changes the waves into pulses of electricity, which charge a capacitor. As it retains most of the charge between pulses, the signal across the capacitor is like the original sound signal.

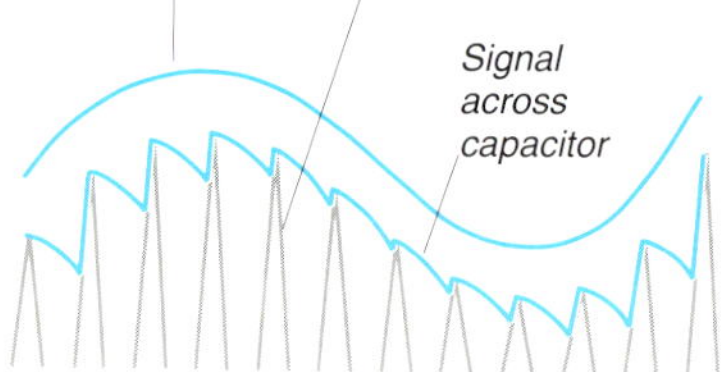

VARIABLE CAPACITOR
When you tune into a station on a radio, you may use a device called a variable capacitor. This has one or more sets of fixed plates and movable plates that can cross over without touching. The capacitance (ability to store charge) is greatest when the plates are fully crossed over each other. Changing the capacitance makes the radio select different frequency signals.

Modern components

Since the 1950s, many electronic components have been made much smaller, and new ones have been developed. They are now so small that miniature equipment is becoming more and more common. Tiny components called transistors, resistors, diodes, and capacitors are found in many common electronic gadgets. New technology has also produced more reliable components. For example, light-emitting diodes (LEDs) are often used instead of indicator bulbs because they hardly ever go wrong.

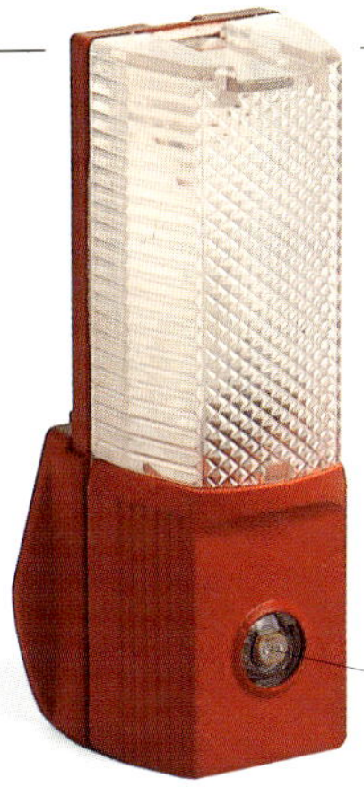

On the front of this night-light is a resistor that is sensitive to light. Its resistance increases when it gets dark. Electronic circuits detect this change and let the current through to switch the light on at night.

The circuit in a flash unit includes a capacitor that can hold an electric charge. When this charge is released to a special tube, a bright flash is produced.

RESISTORS

The amount of current flowing in a circuit can be controlled by resistors: a resistor with a high resistance will only let a relatively small current flow. Variable resistors, made from carbon or wire, have a sliding contact so that the resistance can be varied. Light-dependent resistors (LDRs) decrease in resistance with more light. Most thermistors decrease in resistance when their temperature rises.

RESISTORS

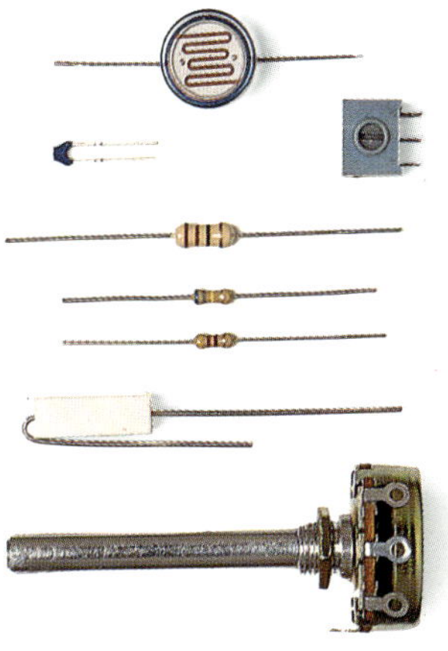

CAPACITORS

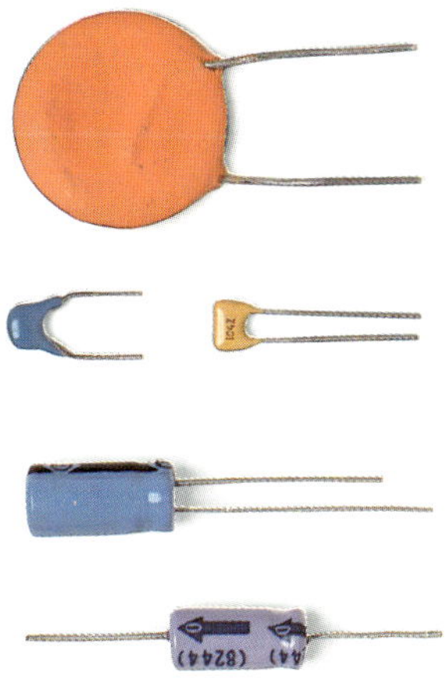

CAPACITORS

Capacitors are devices that can store an electric charge and release it when needed. They are made from two layers of metal separated by a layer of non-conducting material, such as plastic. Special capacitors, called electrolytic capacitors, are made by depositing a layer of insulating material on to aluminium plates by electrolysis. Different value capacitors hold different amounts of charge when the same voltage is passed across their plates.

AMPLIFIER

An amplifier contains a circuit that makes a small electric signal bigger. Transistors feed the amplified (stronger) signal to the loudspeaker.

TRANSISTORS

TRANSISTORS

Transistors are components that amplify electric current. They can also switch current on and off. Transistors vary in the frequency range of signals they can handle. Most transistors consume just a few milliamps from a supply of 12 volts or less. Transistors handling high power become hot and may have finned metal devices called heat sinks to help radiate the heat.

DIODES

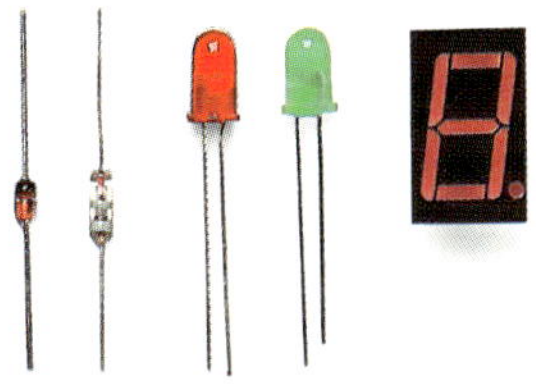

DIODES

Diodes will only let the current in an electronic circuit pass in one direction. This means they can change alternating current into pulses of direct current. Some diodes are designed to cope with weak currents; others can handle very high currents. Other diodes, called light-emitting diodes (LEDs), give off light.

LIGHT-EMITTING DIODES

Light-emitting diodes (LEDs) are used in some calculators for the numbers or as indicators on electronic panels. Columns of LEDs form the sound level indicators on some amplifiers. As the sound levels increase, more LEDs in a column light up.

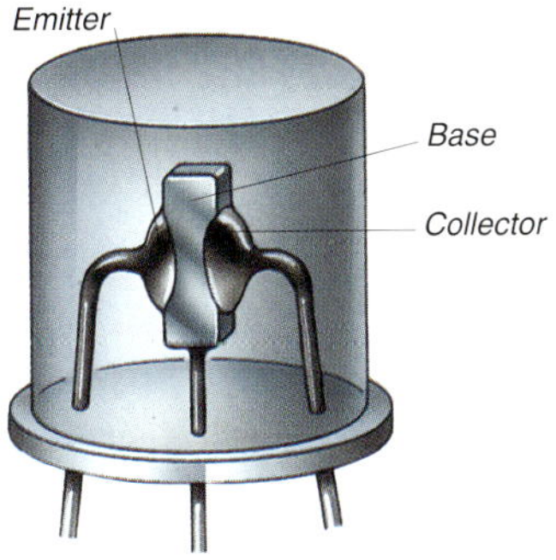

WHAT'S IN A TRANSISTOR

This transistor is made of a layer of p-type semiconductor sandwiched between two layers of n-type semiconductor. The middle layer is the base of the transistor and the outer layers are the emitter and the collector.

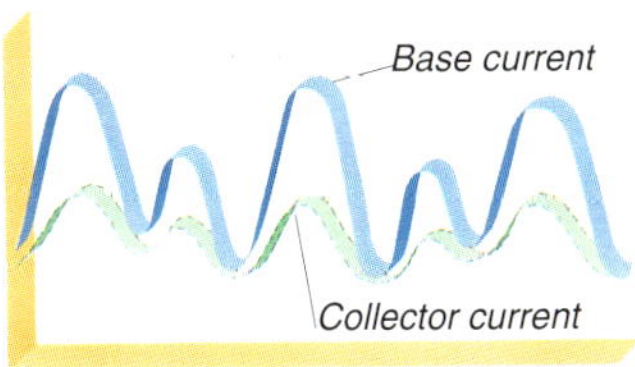

HOW A TRANSISTOR WORKS

A small change in the current flowing into the base causes a larger change in the current flowing through the collector. So when a small signal is applied to the base, a larger signal appears at the collector. Strengthening a signal in this way is called amplification.

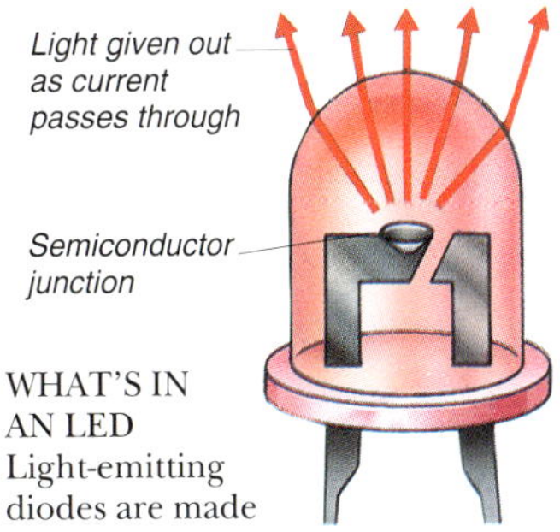

WHAT'S IN AN LED

Light-emitting diodes are made of a semiconductor junction encapsulated in plastic. It gives out light when a current passes through. LEDs hardly ever fail, and are used instead of bulbs.

Find out more

Electrolysis p.67
Current electricity p. 148
Circuits p.152
Radio p.164
Integrated circuits p.170
Calculators p.172
Fact finder p.410

INTEGRATED CIRCUITS

INSIDE AN ELECTRONIC GAME, one tiny part controls everything that the game can do: move characters around the screen, keep a record of the score, bleep when you win or lose. The tiny part is an integrated circuit (also called a silicon chip), which is a complete circuit in miniature; it is a few millimetres square. All the necessary electronic components are on the chip, and there are thousands of them on the one tiny slice of silicon. Integrated (all-in-one) circuits perform the same kinds of tasks as circuits made from separate electronic components. Chips are cheap to make, and are very reliable, so they have made electronic equipment cheaper, more efficient, and smaller.

ELECTRONIC TOY
Hand-held electronic games are dedicated electronic computers, which means that they are programmed and used to do one thing only. This game displays a space scene on the screen and allows players to fire at the enemy spacecraft.

CIRCUITS IN MINIATURE
Many integrated circuits are formed at the same time on a silicon wafer, which is a slice from a crystal of pure silicon. After manufacture, each individual circuit is tested electronically. Those that pass all the tests are mounted in protective plastic or ceramic capsules.

DESIGNING A CIRCUIT
Before an integrated circuit can be made, a large plan of the whole circuit is drawn and checked for accuracy. As integrated circuits are built up in layers, a plan for each layer is then designed and drawn up. A chip-sized version, called a mask, is made from these plans.

MAKING CHIPS
The components in a chip are made by laying p-type and n-type semiconductors and other materials on the silicon base, using masks as guides. Heat and chemicals are used to shape the materials. The different combinations produce different components, such as transistors, diodes, resistors, and low-value capacitors. These are three of the many stages involved in producing just one component on the chip, in this case a special type of transistor with an insulated central electrode.

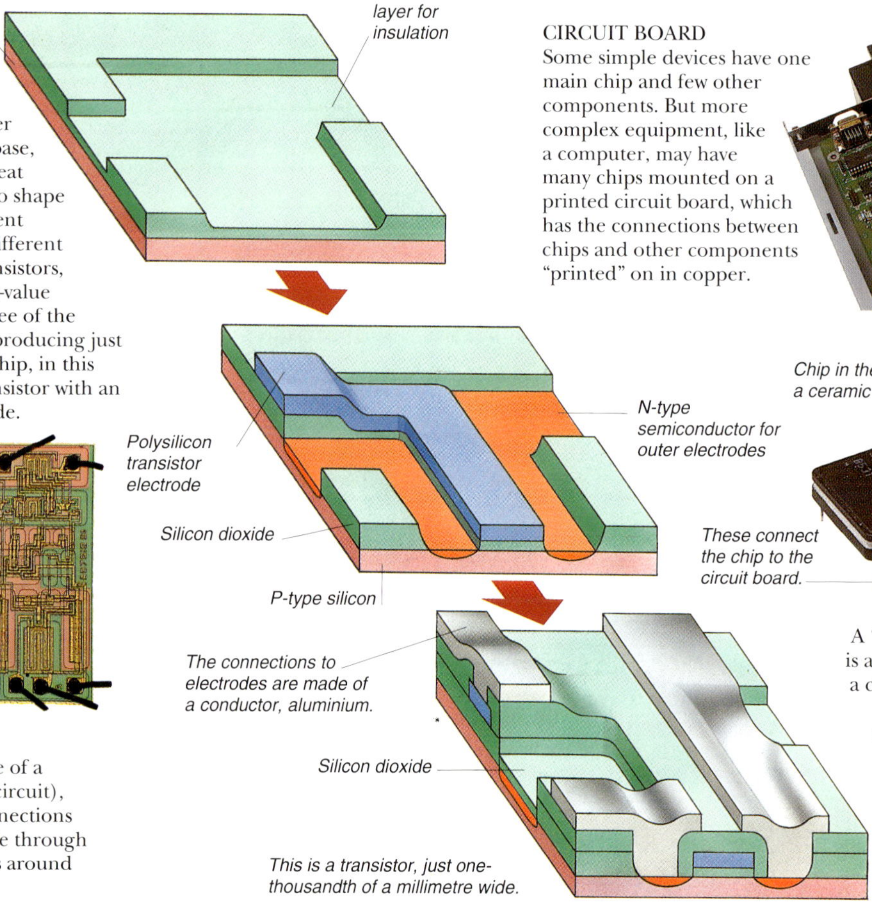

CIRCUIT BOARD
Some simple devices have one main chip and few other components. But more complex equipment, like a computer, may have many chips mounted on a printed circuit board, which has the connections between chips and other components "printed" on in copper.

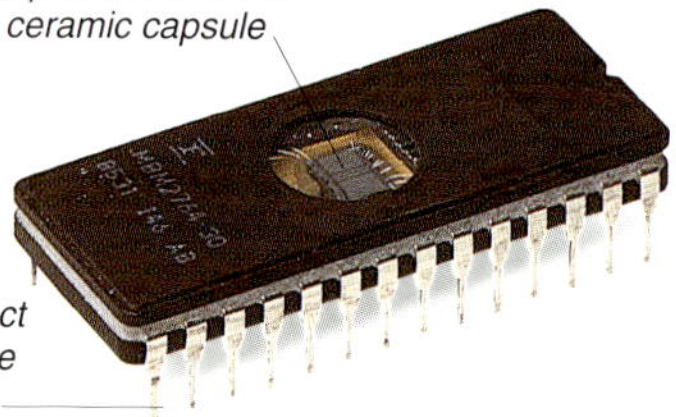

CHIP IN A CAPSULE
A "chip" seen on a circuit board is actually a capsule that protects a chip inside. Connections from the chip to the circuit board are made with fine gold wires connected to the metal pins that stick out of the capsule. These are soldered to the circuit board or plugged into sockets.

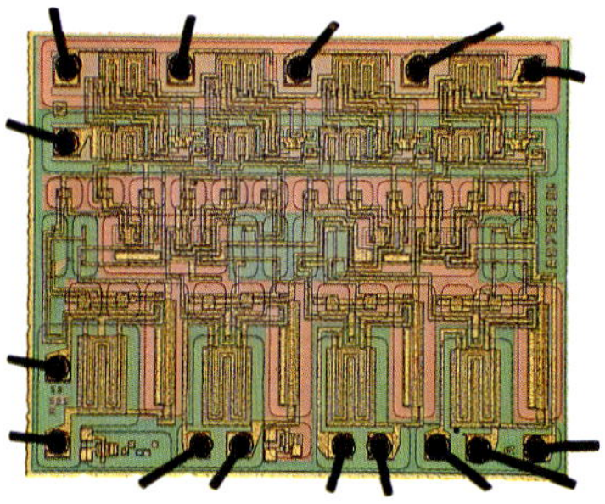

INSIDE A CHIP
This is part of the surface of a silicon chip (integrated circuit), magnified 40 times. Connections to other circuits are made through fine wires welded to pads around the edge of the chip.

Using integrated circuits

This pinball game uses a simple integrated circuit that contains several logic gates – each consisting of a few transistors and other components. A logic gate responds to the presence or absence of incoming signals and gives the appropriate output. The chip operates coloured light-emitting diodes (LEDs) to show which slots the balls enter, and to indicate win or lose. To win, you must get at least one ball in a blue slot and at least one in a yellow slot, but none in the red slot. The green light comes on if you win. A red light means you lose.

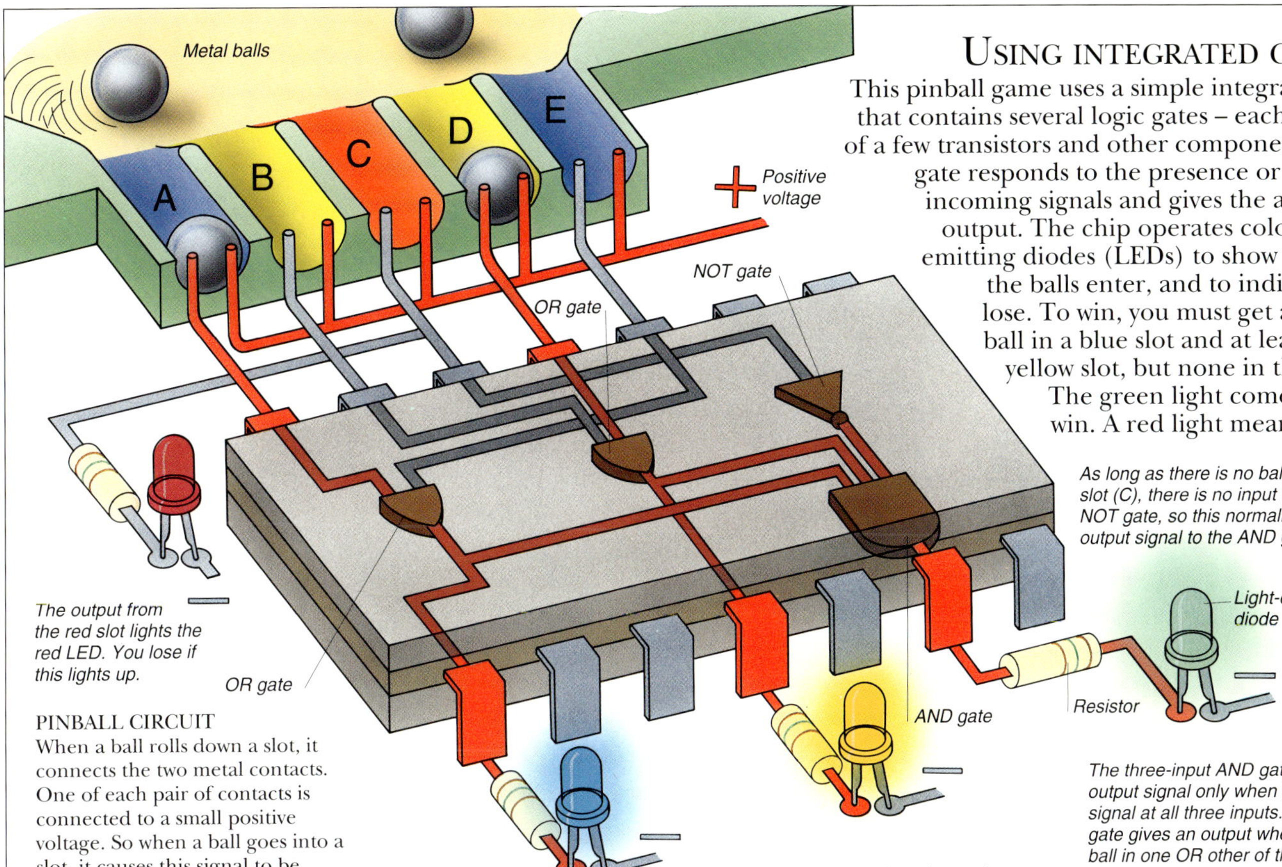

As long as there is no ball in the red slot (C), there is no input to the NOT gate, so this normally gives an output signal to the AND gate.

The output from the red slot lights the red LED. You lose if this lights up.

PINBALL CIRCUIT
When a ball rolls down a slot, it connects the two metal contacts. One of each pair of contacts is connected to a small positive voltage. So when a ball goes into a slot, it causes this signal to be applied to one of the gates. The circuit is arranged so that an LED of the right colour lights up when a ball is in a slot. The power supplies to the logic gates are not shown.

A ball in either blue slot sends a signal to the left-hand OR gate. This gives an output if there is an input signal at "A" OR "E" (OR both). This output lights the blue LED, and goes to the AND gate.

A ball in either yellow slot sends a signal to the right-hand OR gate. This gives an output if there is an input signal at "B" OR "D" (OR both). The output lights the yellow LED, and goes to the AND gate.

The three-input AND gate gives an output signal only when there is a signal at all three inputs. So the AND gate gives an output when you have a ball in one OR other of the blue slots, and in one OR other of the yellow slots, and NOT in the red slot. The output from the AND gate lights the green LED to show that you have won.

Logic gates

Logic gates work with digital signals – usually the presence or absence of a small positive voltage. Truth tables show what happens when logic signals are applied to logic gates. In a truth table, the presence of a signal is written as 1, and no signal is written as 0.

THE "AND" GATE
A two-input AND gate gives an output when a signal is applied to one input AND to the other input.

Input A	Input B	Output
0	0	0
1	0	0
0	1	0
1	1	1

THE "OR" GATE
A two-input OR gate gives an output when a signal is applied to one input OR to the other input OR to both.

Input A	Input B	Output
0	0	0
1	0	1
0	1	1
1	1	1

THE "NOT" GATE
A NOT gate gives an output when a signal is NOT applied to its input. It gives no output signal when an input signal is present. A NOT gate is sometimes called an inverter.

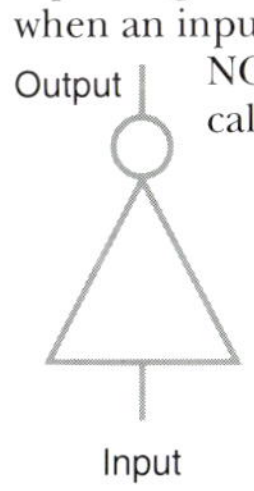

Input	Output
0	1
1	0

Analogue to digital

Specially designed integrated circuits are used to convert analogue signals, like a sound signal, to a digital form to be stored on a CD, for example. This gives a much better quality of sound because it doesn't get distorted when you amplify it, and it doesn't pick up noises like hiss from wear on a record. On reception or replay, digital signals are changed back into analogue form. Analogue signals are electrical copies of sound, vision, or other signals, so they vary continuously. Digital signals consist of simple pulses that are either on or off.

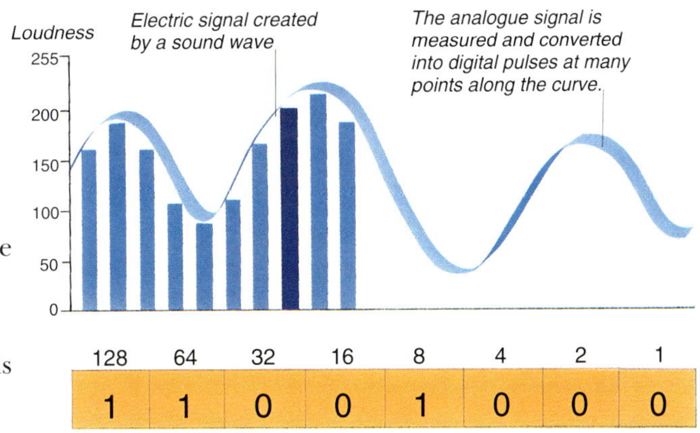

A digital signal is in binary form, which means that it is a sequence of on (1) and off (0).

The value of 200 is converted into the digital number 11001000, which represents 128 + 64 + 8.

MEASURING THE SIGNAL
To change an analogue signal into a digital one, an integrated circuit measures the strength of the analogue signal thousands of times each second. It then changes these measurements into the right pattern of digital signals.

Find out more

ELECTRONIC COMPONENTS P.168
CALCULATORS P.172
SOUND RECORDING P.188
FACT FINDER P.410

CALCULATORS

POCKET CALCULATOR
This pocket calculator has an extra memory to store numbers needed later while other calculations are carried out. The calculator can also work out square roots of numbers.

A MODERN ELECTRONIC CALCULATOR is a miracle of miniaturization, and it has more computing power than a room full of early electronic computing equipment. An electronic calculator is a computer that does calculations only. These calculations are done so quickly that the result appears almost as soon as you press the last key. Calculators have the basic functions of add, subtract, multiply, and divide; they can also have function keys that carry out complex calculations automatically. Some calculators can be programmed by the user to carry out specific calculations.

DIFFERENCE ENGINE
This early calculator was the first one designed by Charles Babbage. It had more than 2000 moving parts.

NUMBER COMPUTER

Some people use their fingers to help when counting and doing calculations. This is why our system of counting and numbering is based on tens. This decimal counting system uses the ten digits 0 to 9. Modern electronic calculators use the binary system, with two digits, 0 and 1, instead. This is because circuits designed to recognize just two signal levels, representing 0 and 1, are simpler and more reliable than circuits designed to recognize ten signal levels.

CHARLES BABBAGE

In the early 1830s, an English mathematician called Charles Babbage (1792-1871) designed a mechanical calculator called the Analytical Engine. It would have a store, or memory, to hold numbers. An arithmetic unit would do calculations according to instructions from a control unit. Instructions (programs) were to be fed into the machine in code, as patterns of holes on punched cards. In other words it would have been programmable (unlike his Difference Engines); modern computers still operate on these basic ideas. Babbage devoted many years and much of his fortune to this machine, but it was never completed.

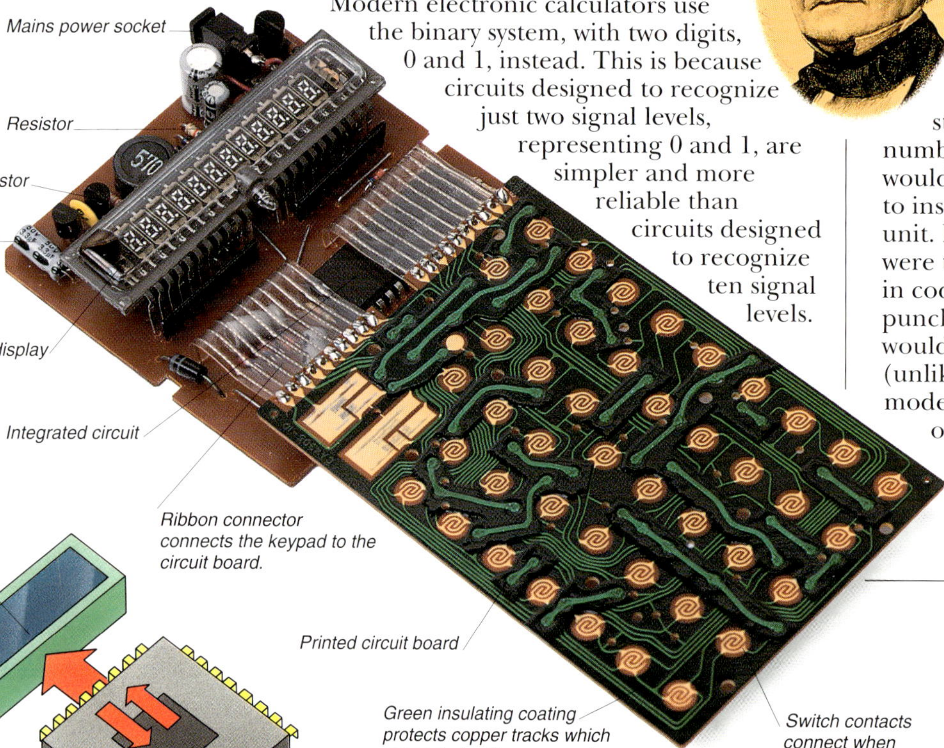

KEYPAD
Switches behind the keypad close briefly when you press the keys for numbers and instructions (such as +, −, ÷, or =). Electronic circuits detect what you key in and store it in binary form. Then other circuits carry out the calculations.

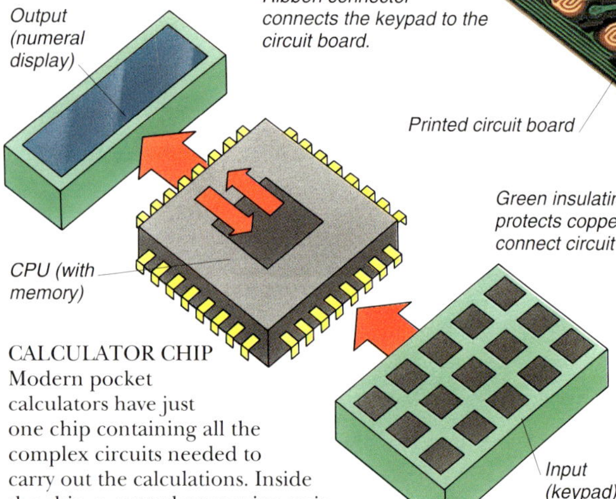

CALCULATOR CHIP
Modern pocket calculators have just one chip containing all the complex circuits needed to carry out the calculations. Inside the chip, a central processing unit (CPU) controls operations and uses an electronic memory to store numbers used in calculations and the results that are displayed.

BINARY SYSTEM
The decimal number 25, for example, is 11001 in binary. This represents 1 x 16, plus 1 x 8, plus 0 x 4, plus 0 x 2, plus 1 x 1. This may seem complicated to us, but it is very easy for a calculator to represent, store, and recognize each 0 or 1 as the absence or presence of an electrical voltage. The binary number calculated is automatically converted into the decimal number shown on the display.

Find out more

HOW SCIENTISTS WORK P.14
CELLS AND BATTERIES P.150
ELECTRONIC COMPONENTS P.168
INTEGRATED CIRCUITS P.170
COMPUTERS P.173
FACT FINDER P.410

COMPUTERS

COMPUTERS CAN HELP YOU write letters, draw pictures, play games, do calculations very quickly, and carry out many other tasks. For example, it would take hours to calculate and write down the 12 times table up to 3,000 times 12. But a computer can do this and produce a neatly printed and error-free table in minutes. Computers handle text by storing codes representing letters of the alphabet, spaces, and punctuation marks. Using a computer to write and edit text is called word processing. Computers also allow you to produce graphics (lines and pictures) without ever touching a pencil or paper. And in desk-top publishing, words and pictures are combined using a computer to produce newspapers, books, and magazines. With a suitable program (set of instructions) and hardware (computer equipment), you can do all these things and more besides.

MINIATURE COMPUTER
A laptop or notebook computer enables people to work while travelling. Some store the work in a memory that is continually powered, while others have a disk unit for storage.

HOME COMPUTER

A typical home computer system has input devices to put programs and data (information) into the computer. Electronic circuits inside the computer carry out the work and send the results to output devices. Programs on magnetic tapes or disks are fed into the computer by playing them on a suitable unit. Data may be fed into the computer from tape or disk, or by using a keyboard or some other input device. The computer's output is usually in the form of words, numbers, or pictures displayed on a screen or printed on paper, or as sounds made on a loudspeaker. The output can be stored on tape or disk.

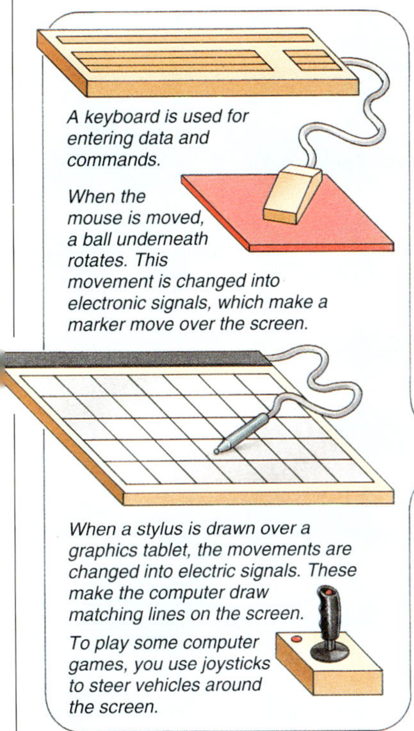

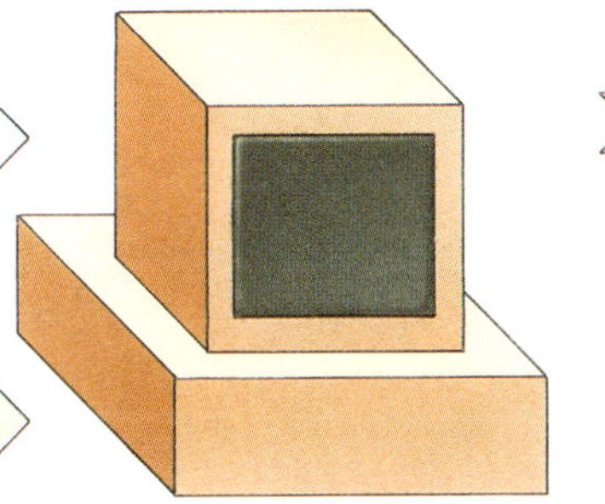

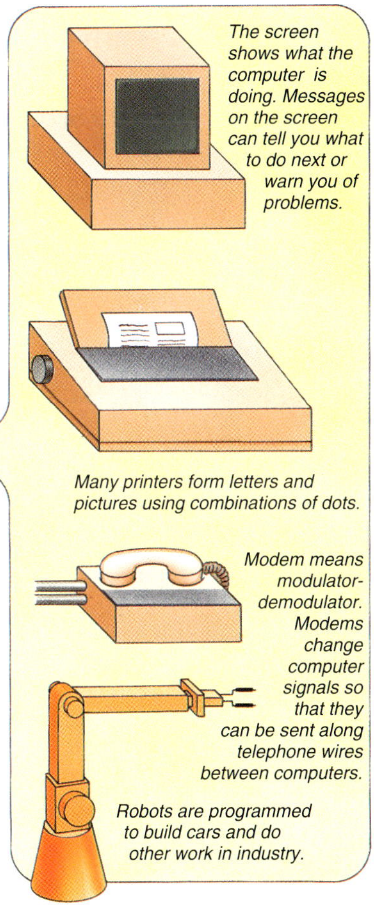

INPUT DEVICES
General-purpose computers have a keyboard. This has all the letters and numbers of a typewriter, plus a few extra keys. The keyboard is used to feed words and numbers into the computer. It is also used to type in commands, and to move players or objects around the screen when playing games. But other input devices are sometimes more useful. A joystick is better for controlling moving objects when playing games. A mouse may be moved around the desk to make a marker move on the screen. A mouse can also be used to draw a picture, but a graphics tablet is easier to use for this. Musical notes may be fed in from the "typewriter" keyboard, but it is easier to use a specially designed music keyboard.

STORAGE
The large amounts of information and instructions that computers handle have to be stored. The instructions that make up programs are usually stored as pulses on magnetic tapes or disks. These instructions are fed into the computer and stored there temporarily in memory chips. Other chips in the computer store information permanently, such as some messages that it displays on the screen to tell the user what to do next. Magnetic tapes and disks are often used also to store work done on the computer.

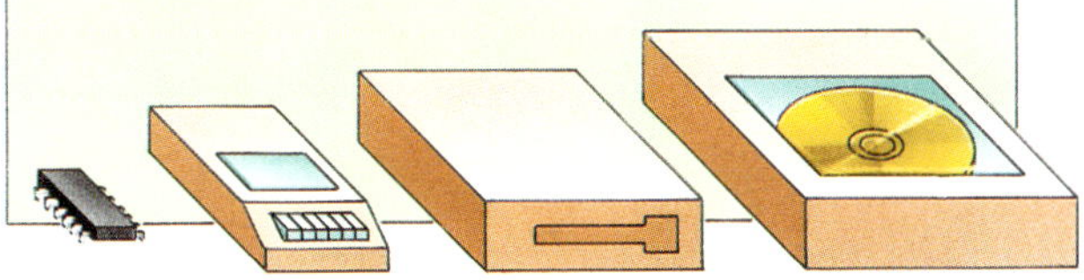

Chips store programs and information as electronic signals.

Cassettes can be used for storing programs and data.

Floppy disks work faster than tape cassettes.

One CD ROM (compact disc read-only memory) can store a lot of information, such as the contents of several books.

OUTPUT DEVICES
You can usually see what a computer is doing by looking at its monitor (screen). And you can usually obtain a permanent record, called a printout or hard copy, by sending the information in the computer to a printer. Sometimes the output of a computer is fed via a telephone line to another computer using a device called a modem. Computers can also interpret our instructions to make robots move as we want.

Continued on next page

Continued from previous page

Hardware and software

To make a computer do useful work, you need the equipment (hardware) and a set of instructions (called a program or software). Computers also need system software, which tells them how to operate. Computers work with information and instructions in the form of electronic signals representing the 1s and 0s of the binary code. Writing programs in this form would take a long time. So they are written instead in special programming languages that partly resemble English. These are automatically changed into the form that the computer understands.

MONITOR

The monitor, also called a VDU (visual display unit), is often a separate unit with a cable to connect it to the computer. Computer monitors are designed to give a high-quality picture so that words can be read from the screen without causing eye-strain. Some computers have a monitor permanently attached.

ECONOMY MONITORING

Some cheap computers have a modulator to make the signals from the computer similar to those that carry television programmes. This allows the signals to be tuned in and displayed on an ordinary television set. But the picture quality is not as good as that of a monitor designed for use with computers, and words may be hard to read.

COMPUTER

A personal computer is usually a box containing the main electronic units and fitted with sockets for connecting the mains supply, keyboard, monitor, printer, and other equipment. Disk units, called drives, are usually fitted inside this box, but sockets are usually provided for connecting other disk drives.

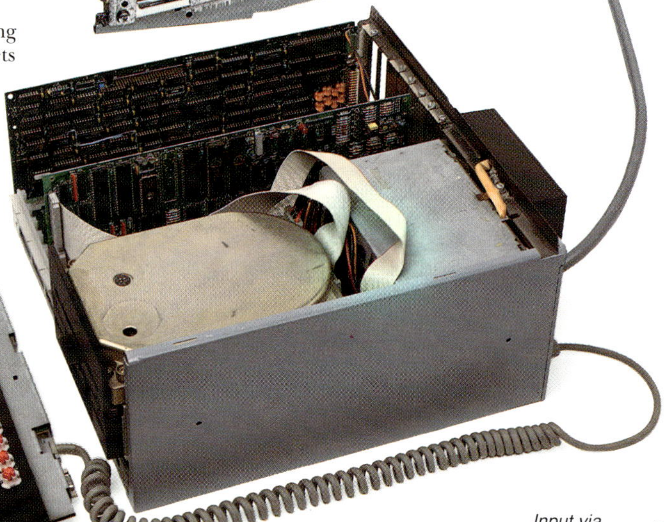

These red switches are under the keys on a keyboard.

KEYBOARD

The keyboard is simply lots of push-button switches marked with letters and other characters. What happens when you press a particular key depends on how the computer is programmed. For example, pressing the key may make a letter of the alphabet appear on the screen, or a character in an adventure game may move around.

Many computers have a built-in hard (rigid) magnetic disk drive to store programs and data. Most hard disks cannot be removed from the machine.

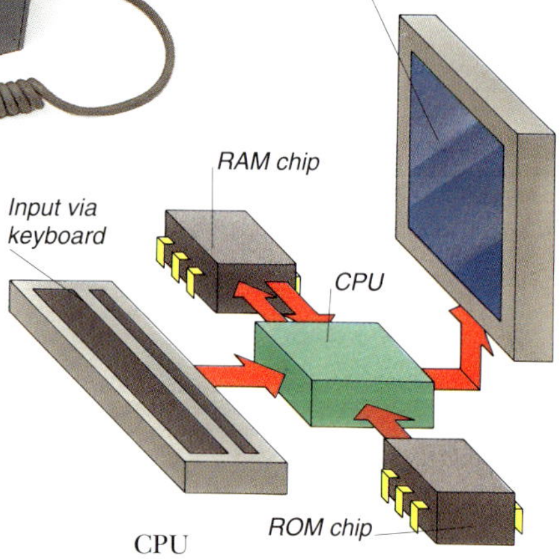

CPU

The central processing unit (CPU) is the computer's centre of operations. It consists of large numbers of electronic circuits, all contained in a single chip called a microprocessor. The CPU takes in data from the keyboard, the ROM, and the RAM. It can also send data to be stored in the RAM, and send data to the monitor (and other output devices).

Floppy disks, in protective plastic cases, and hard disk cartridges can be removed from the computer.

MEMORIES

Chips called the ROM (read-only memory) store information permanently needed by the computer. Other chips make up the RAM (random-access memory). The ROM is like a book: the computer gets information from it, but does not add to it. The RAM is like a notebook: the computer puts information in it and can use the information and alter it. But information in RAM is lost when the machine is switched off. Disks are also storage devices. Floppy disks are useful for transferring information between machines.

COMPUTERS

1642 Blaise Pascal (1623-62) builds a mechanical calculating machine.

1805 Joseph Jacquard (1752-1834) builds an automatic loom. The patterns are controlled by punched cards. Cards are later used in computers.

1833 Charles Babbage designs the first general-purpose programmable computer, the Analytical Engine.

1890 Herman Hollerith (1860-1929) uses a punched-card system to make the United States census calculations hundreds of times faster.

1946 Engineers in the United States build the first electronic digital computer.

1951 The same team build the first mass-produced computer, UNIVAC I.

Micrograph of an integrated circuit

Find out more

How scientists work p.14
Magnetism p. 154
Television p.166
Integrated circuits p.170
Calculators p.172
Using computers p.175
Fact finder p.410

USING COMPUTERS

MOST HOME COMPUTERS have several programs so they can be used in different ways, for games as well as word processing, for example. But many computers are dedicated machines. They do just one thing and look quite different. For example, a bank's cash-dispensing machine uses computer technology to check people's accounts and allow them to withdraw money. The machine at the bank is a computer terminal that is connected to the bank's central computer, where details of all accounts are stored. Dedicated computers are also used to control industrial processes and transport systems, and simulate real-life situations (like flying a plane) for research and training.

"REAL" WINDOWS
Computer graphics are used to create realistic views in the "windows" of a flight simulator. These change just like real views in a real aeroplane would. This is very important, to give the trainee pilots a proper sense of what it feels like to fly an aeroplane.

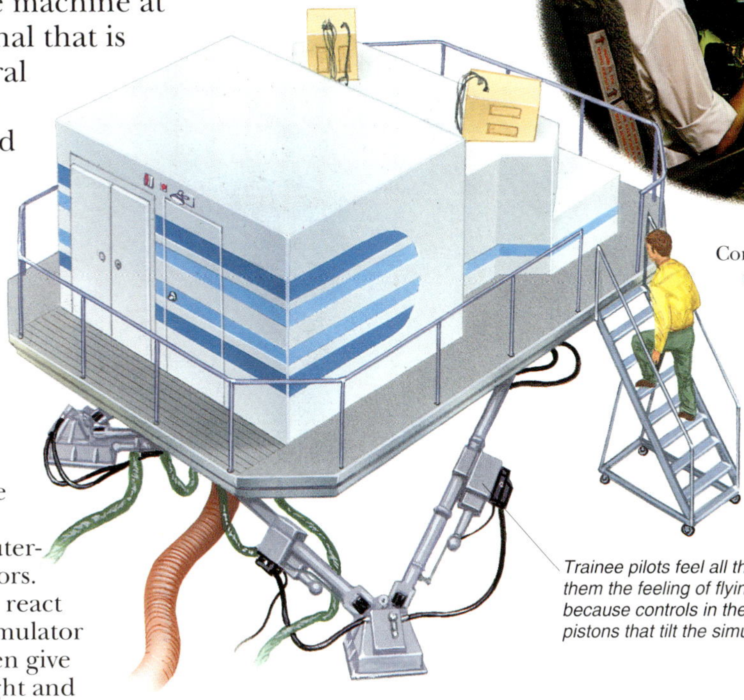

Trainee pilots feel all the forces that give them the feeling of flying a real aeroplane because controls in the cockpit move huge pistons that tilt the simulator.

SIMULATION

Pilots can become experts at flying complex modern aeroplanes before even getting into a real one. The trainee pilots are trained on computer-controlled machines called simulators. The computer makes the simulator react just like an aeroplane would: the simulator moves around, and the controls even give realistic readings of things like height and how much fuel is left in each tank.

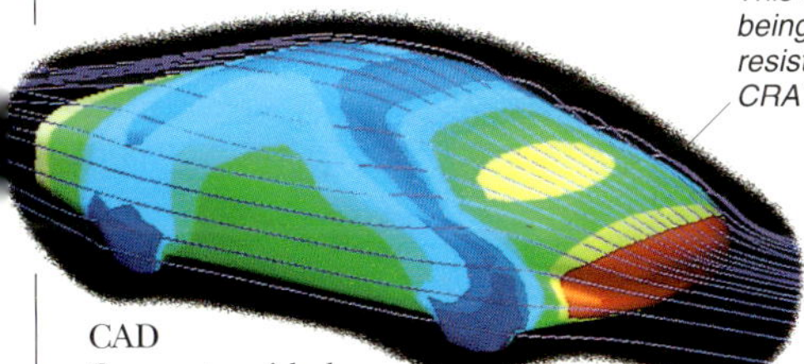

This car design is being tested for wind resistance using a CRAY supercomputer.

CAD
Computer-aided design (CAD) is a way of designing things using computer graphics. Information is fed into the computer which "constructs" the object on the screen. Different operating conditions are fed in too, and the design is tested. This helps to identify parts of the design that are not good enough so they can then be improved.

COMPUTER INTELLIGENCE
Are computers intelligent? Some chess computers can beat most people because their vast electronic memories allow them to work out all the possible moves ahead. Scientists just cannot agree whether that is intelligence. The main problem is that they cannot agree precisely what intelligence is. One important point is that computers do not understand what they are doing.

VIRTUAL REALITY
Virtual reality is a way of going into a world completely created by a computer. The computer creates 3-D images and stereo sound in a special helmet connected to a hand-held unit. Any move you make with the unit is translated to the headset, so that this man can move his arm and appear to be playing a racket game on screen. He even hears the sound of the racket hitting the ball.

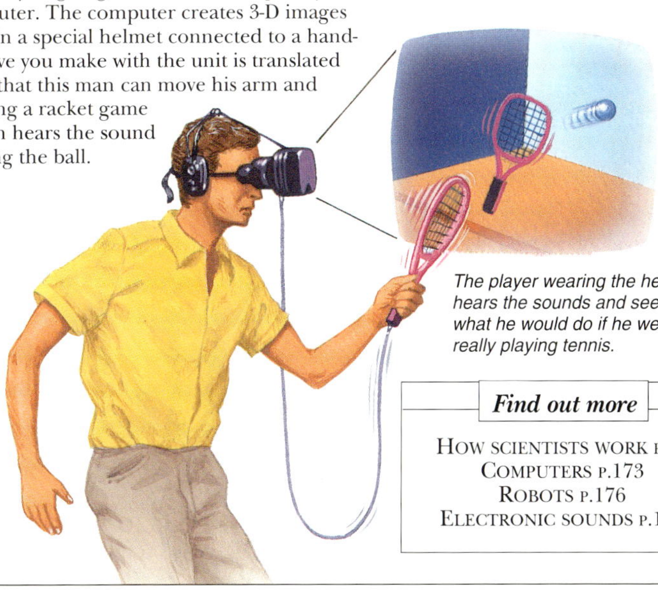

The player wearing the helmet hears the sounds and sees what he would do if he were really playing tennis.

ALAN TURING
The British mathematician Alan Turing (1912-54) was a major contributor to theories used in modern computing. He helped to develop the electronic device and the ideas used to decode German secret messages during World War II (1939-45). He was the first to suggest that computers could be "intelligent".

Find out more

HOW SCIENTISTS WORK P.14
COMPUTERS P.173
ROBOTS P.176
ELECTRONIC SOUNDS P.189

Robots

MOST ROBOTS YOU SEE in films look a bit like humans. They can walk and talk and, like humans, will tackle almost any problem that occurs. In real life, most robots work in factories, but they don't look at all like us. The most common kind of robot has one arm and no legs, and does just one job. Robots used in industry are controlled by computers and obey instructions stored in an electronic memory. One way of recording the required movement is for a skilled human worker to carry out a task first. The movements involved are stored as electronic signals so that the computer can make the robot copy them precisely. Different kinds of robots do other jobs, such as moving goods around factories, and exploring other planets.

ROBOTS IN FICTION
The robots from the film *Star Wars* are human-like: C3PO can communicate in three million ways, and R2D2 can repair spaceships. Real robots will never need to be so versatile, but some can already do simple translations and others can do repairs.

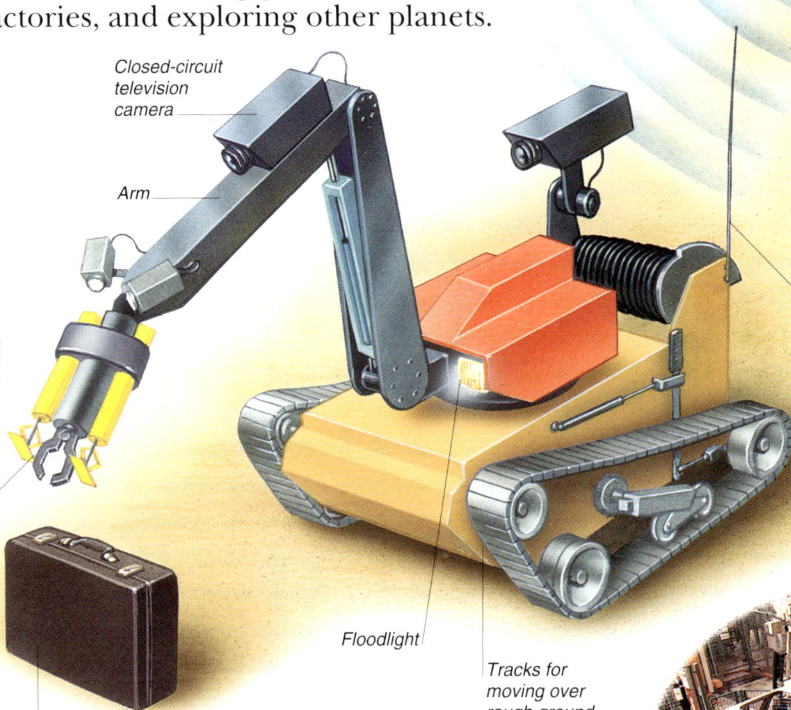

BOMB DISPOSAL
Bomb disposal experts can check safely for bombs, thanks to this mobile robot. Closed-circuit television cameras on the robot send back pictures to the controller. He or she uses the pictures to check objects suspected of being bombs. The robot also has floodlights for getting clear pictures at night. The remote-controlled grab on the end of the arm is used to pick up a suspicious object.

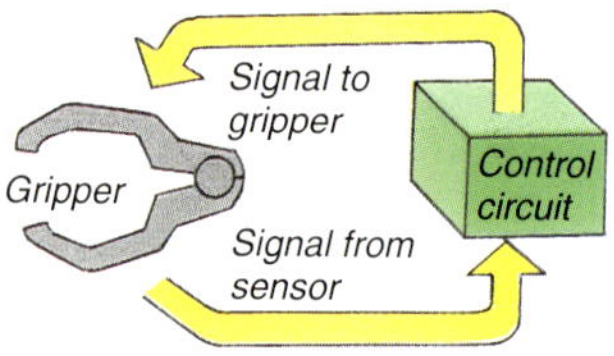

FEEDBACK
The grippers on a robot arm could crush fragile objects when picking them up. So pressure sensors are provided to detect when the grippers have a firm hold. The sensors feed an electric signal back to a control circuit, which then stops any further pressure being applied.

The Vikings were sent to Mars in two parts. An orbiter carried and protected the lander until reaching orbit around Mars.

The Viking *lander is the most complex robot to have been sent into space.*

MARS MISSION
Vikings landed on Mars in 1976! These Vikings were two robot landing craft, sent by American scientists to search for life on Mars. The machines scooped up soil and tested it for the presence of living organisms in a specially built biological laboratory. No life was found, but there could be life elsewhere on this red planet, and it could be in a different form – *Viking* looked only for life based on organic chemistry, as it is on Earth.

INDUSTRIAL ROBOTS
Robots like this weld together metal parts to make cars. Other robots spray the car bodies with paint. Unlike humans, robots never get fed up with doing the same work every day. They can also work for much longer without stopping.

Find out more

CARBON P.40
COMPUTERS P.173
MARS P.289
SPACE PROBES P.301

SOUND AND LIGHT

THE SOUNDS AND SIGHTS of the world are carried to us by energy in the form of sound and light. In some ways, sound and light are very similar. The energy of both is carried from one place to another by waves. The energy of sunlight warms the Earth, tans fair skin, and makes plants grow. The energy of the sonic boom – the bang made by a jet breaking the sound barrier – can shake buildings and shatter windows. In other ways, sound and light are different. Sound can only travel through matter – through gases such as the air, through liquids, and through solids. Light can travel through a vacuum. We see light from the stars that has been travelling for thousands of years before reaching our eyes.

THUNDER AND LIGHTNING

A lightning strike releases huge amounts of sound and light energy. The crash and flash of the storm can be heard and seen from a great distance. We see the lightning before we hear the thunder because light travels nearly a million times faster than sound. We see the flash within millionths of a second of it happening, but may not hear the thunder until several seconds later.

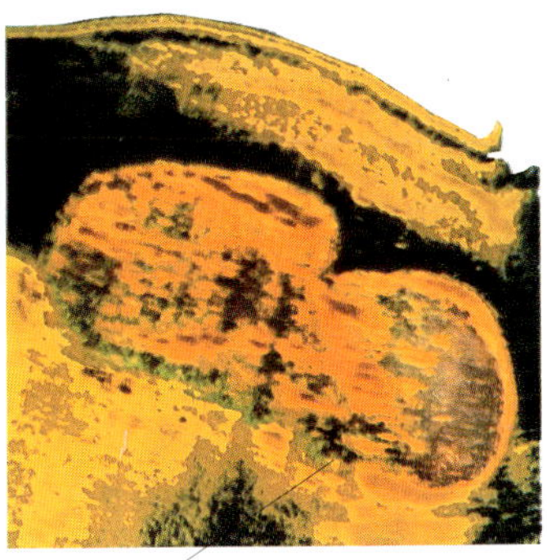

Image is artificially coloured.

SOUND PICTURES

Cameras collect light to create images on film and on television screens. Sound can produce images too. This image of a foetus inside the womb was made with sound echoes. The echoes are made when very high-pitched sound waves – ultrasonic waves – travel through the mother's body. These are recorded and used to build up a computer image of the unborn baby.

SILENT JAR

The Ancient Greek philosopher Aristotle believed that both sound and light travelled through the air like waves in the sea. He also believed that neither could travel through a vacuum. But it was not until the 17th century that scientists were able to create a vacuum to test Aristotle's theory. One experiment was by the Irish scientist Robert Boyle in 1658. He slowly pumped air out of a glass jar containing a ticking watch. The sound of the ticking disappeared completely as the jar was emptied. Boyle concluded that sounds are carried by air to our ears. Aristotle had been right about sound.

Robert Boyle

The sound of the ticking watch became fainter as air was pumped out of the jar.

This spray of optical fibres is made up of 2,000 individual strands.

COMMUNICATIONS

Both sound and light enable us to communicate. We use our voices to talk, and need light to see each other. Telephone systems convert the sounds of voices into electrical signals that are transmitted by cable and satellite to every part of the world. Modern communications networks use optical fibres to carry information. Pulses of light carry telephone calls, television pictures, and computer data along cables made from fine glass fibres.

QUIET SPACE

There is no air in space, so there are no sounds there. Astronauts talk to each other using radios because, unlike sound waves, radio waves can travel through space. Astronauts are able to see each other because light, like radio waves, can travel through a vacuum.

MAKING AND HEARING SOUND

IF YOU HAVE EVER LOST YOUR VOICE, you know how difficult it is to make people understand you without it. Speech is our main form of communication. When we speak, we produce vibrations that travel through the air as sound waves. These sound waves are changed into sounds we can recognize with our ears. Although our ears can detect sounds in the range of 20–20,000 Hz, they are most sensitive to sounds with frequencies of around 1,000 Hz. This is the frequency range of voices in normal conversation, although our voices may contain sounds as low-pitched as 50 Hz and as high-pitched as 10,000 Hz. Just as we use our voices to talk to other people, animals use the sounds they make to communicate with each other.

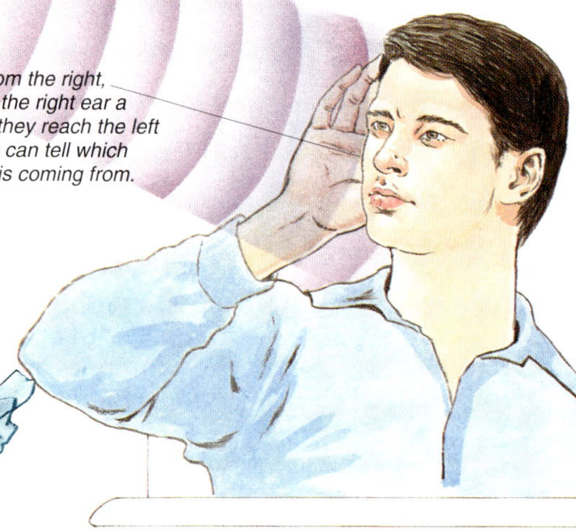

If a sound comes from the right, sound waves reach the right ear a split second before they reach the left ear. This is why you can tell which direction the sound is coming from.

MAKING SOUND

We produce our voices by forcing air from our lungs past the vocal cords in our throats. The rushing air makes the cords vibrate. When we speak and sing, we make constant adjustments to the tension of our vocal cords, the shape of our mouths, and the speed of the projected air. In this way, we control the pitch, quality, and loudness of our voices.

RESONANCE

Most objects can vibrate. The frequency at which an object vibrates naturally is called its resonant frequency. If a sound of exactly that frequency is played near the object, it picks up energy from the sound wave and vibrates in sympathy. This is resonance. You can often hear resonances when you play loud music in a room. A particular note will cause a door panel or an object near the speakers to resonate. If a singer sings with a frequency equal to the natural frequency of a wine glass, the glass may resonate so strongly that it shatters.

HEARING SOUND

Sound waves collected by the outer ear force the eardrum to vibrate. These vibrations are carried on to the inner ear through a series of tiny bones. Fluid inside a narrow tube, the cochlea, vibrates. These vibrations stimulate tiny hairs on nerves. These nerves send electrical impulses to the brain, which enables us to recognize the sound.

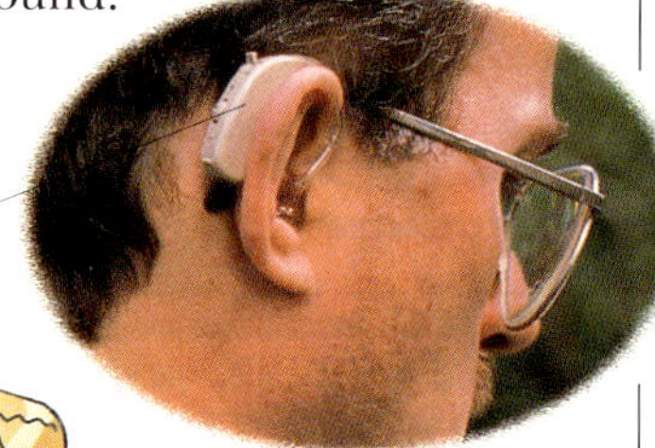

The aid can be adjusted to amplify particular sound frequencies.

AIR IN BOTTLES

You can see and hear how different amounts of air vibrate to give different sounds by blowing across the top of bottles. If you blow across the top of an empty bottle, the air inside vibrates at its resonant frequency. Pouring water into the bottle changes the volume of the air and alters the pitch of the note. Short columns of air vibrate more quickly and give a higher pitch than long air columns.

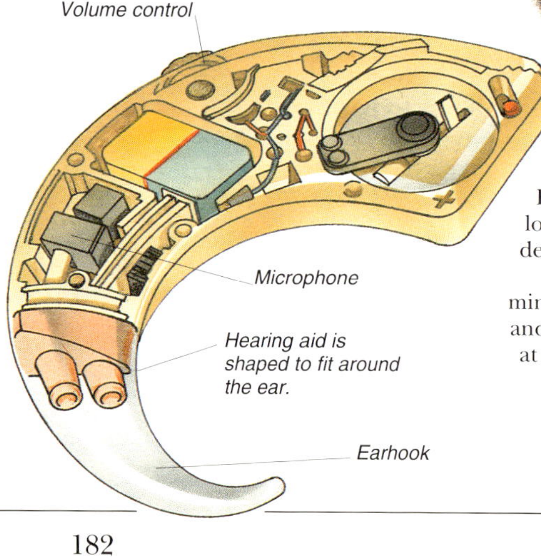

DEAFNESS

People who have some hearing loss, but who are not completely deaf, can be helped by wearing a hearing aid. This consists of a miniature microphone, amplifier, and loudspeaker. Sounds arriving at the microphone are amplified and fed into the earpiece.

ANIMAL SOUNDS

Animals are able to make a wide range of sounds. Despite their relatively small size, some frogs can produce very low-pitched croaks. They do this by puffing up an air sac under their throats until it is nearly as big as they are. Howler monkeys produce some of the loudest sounds in the animal kingdom. They have special spaces in the bones behind their nostrils that they force to resonate with powerful blasts of air. Insects do not have lungs, so they cannot blow air to make sounds. But grasshoppers can make a chirping sound by brushing stiff hairs on their legs.

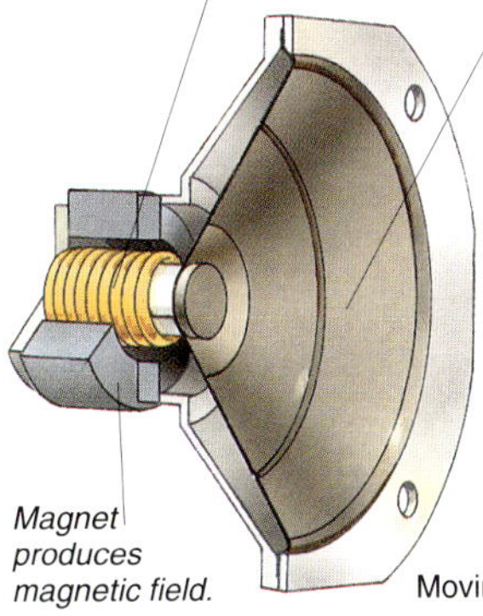

Moving-coil loudspeaker

LOUDSPEAKER

Sound is recorded and replayed by converting it to an electrical signal. Before we can listen to a record, tape, or compact disc (CD), these signals have to be converted back into sound by a loudspeaker. The electrical signals are fed to a wire coil surrounded by a magnetic field inside the loudspeaker. The changing signals cause the cone on the outside of the speaker to vibrate, generating sound.

HEARING RANGES

Most animals can hear more frequencies than they can produce, and can make sounds well outside the range of our hearing. The range of frequencies we can hear changes as we get older. A child can detect frequencies from 20 – 20,000 Hz. But a typical 60-year old can only hear sounds with frequencies up to about 12,000 Hz.

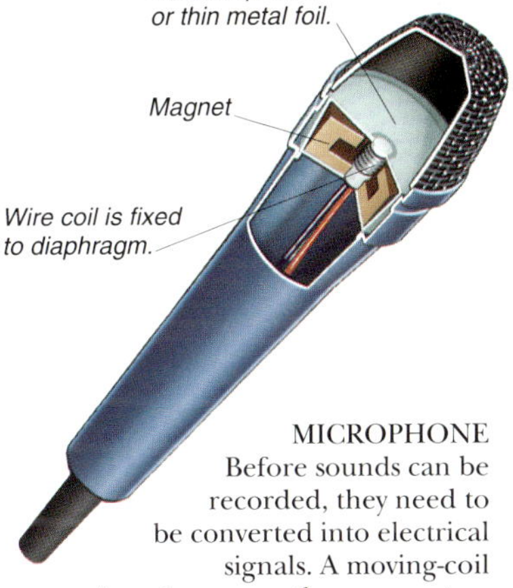

MICROPHONE

Before sounds can be recorded, they need to be converted into electrical signals. A moving-coil microphone uses the same system as a moving-coil loudspeaker, but in reverse. It contains a wire coil fixed to a flexible disc. Sound waves make the diaphragm and coil vibrate. The movement of the coil within a magnetic field generates an electric current in the coil. The current fluctuates in the same way as the sound wave.

VOICE ACTIVATION

A simple sound-activated toy, such as this dancing flower, has a microphone that triggers movement when it detects sounds above a certain level. A more sophisticated voice-activated system can give information about a customer's bank account when it is called by telephone. Recognizing words spoken by different people is very difficult, but computers that can respond to individual voice patterns are now being developed for everyday use.

Find out more

VIBRATIONS P.126
ELECTROMAGNETISM P.156
ELECTRONIC COMPONENTS P.168
MEASURING SOUND P.180
REFLECTION AND ABSORPTION P.184
SENSES P.358

REFLECTION AND ABSORPTION

HAVE YOU EVER WONDERED WHY your voice sounds fuller and more powerful than usual when you sing in the bath? It is because sound waves are reflected by smooth, hard surfaces such as the bathroom walls. They bounce off like a rubber ball bounces off the walls in a squash court. Although the direction of the sound waves changes, their pitch is not altered. As well as being fun, echoes (sound reflections) can be useful. Before the days of radar, sailors caught in fog could tell how far they were from dangerous cliffs by sounding the ship's fog horn and timing the interval before the reflection was heard. But sounds are not always reflected. If they meet a soft surface, such as a cushion, they will be absorbed and will not bounce back.

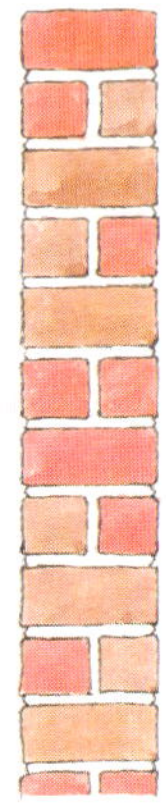

ECHOES
If you stand some distance away from a wall and make a sound, it will be reflected back to you shortly after. The time it takes depends on how far away the wall is. If you are standing 50 metres (164 ft) away, the sound has to travel there and back – a distance of 100 metres (328 ft). Dividing 100 metres by the time taken between making the sound and hearing the echo will give you the speed at which the sound is travelling.

ANECHOIC CHAMBER
The sound-absorbing panels in the walls and ceiling of an anechoic wind tunnel reduce reverberation. This enables scientists to measure accurately the noise generated by an aircraft propellor.

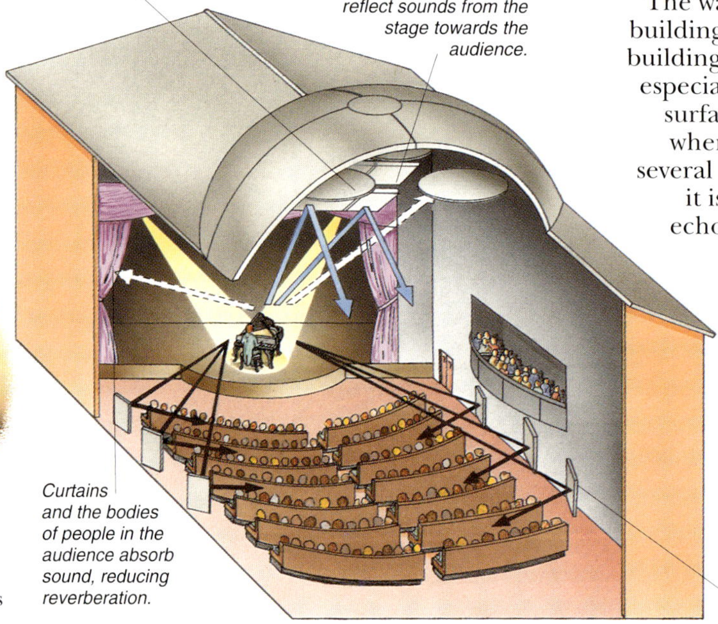

ACOUSTICS

The way sound echoes around a building is called acoustics. Large buildings can seem full of echoes, especially if they have many bare surfaces. Reverberation occurs when sounds echo around for several seconds. In a concert hall it is important to control the echoes. If there is not enough reverberation, the music sounds thin with no sparkle. Too much reverberation, and the sounds are jumbled. Special panels direct sound reflections towards the audience. Others, along with curtains, absorb excess reverberation.

SOUND DISHES

Parabolic dishes are used to collect and concentrate sound. Their special shape reflects and concentrates any sound coming from directly in front of the dish towards the microphone at the centre. In this way, the microphone receives more sound energy than it would without the dish. Parabolic dishes make it possible to record low-level sounds such as bird song.

SOUND ABSORPTION
Soft surfaces absorb sound energy in the same way as sand absorbs energy from a ball thrown onto it. In this room, the rug, curtains, sofa, and plant all absorb sound energy so that it does not bounce back.

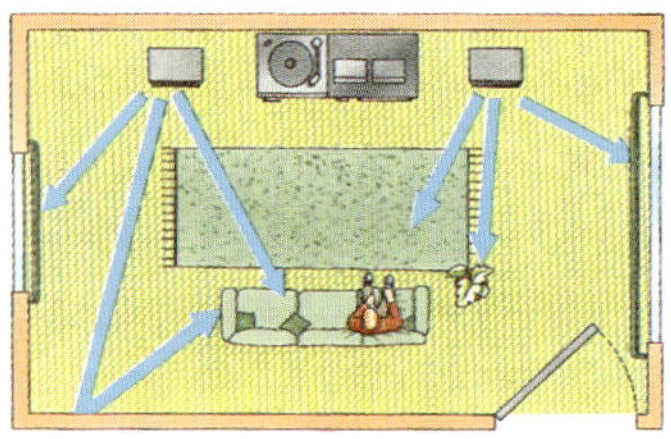

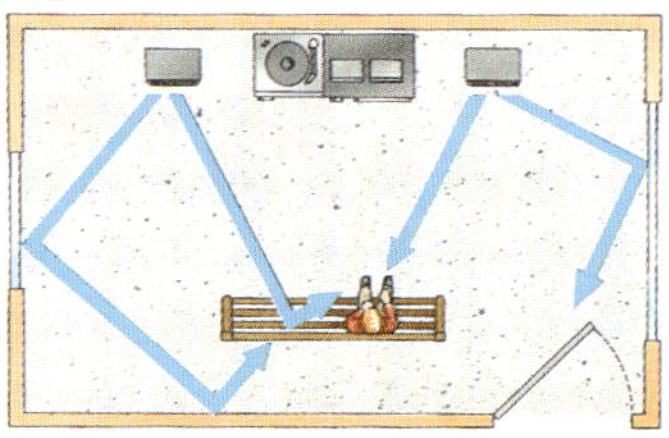

SOUND REFLECTION
Smooth, hard surfaces reflect sound energy in the same way as a ball bounces off concrete. In this room, the sound from the stereo speakers bounces off the floor, walls, and wooden chair.

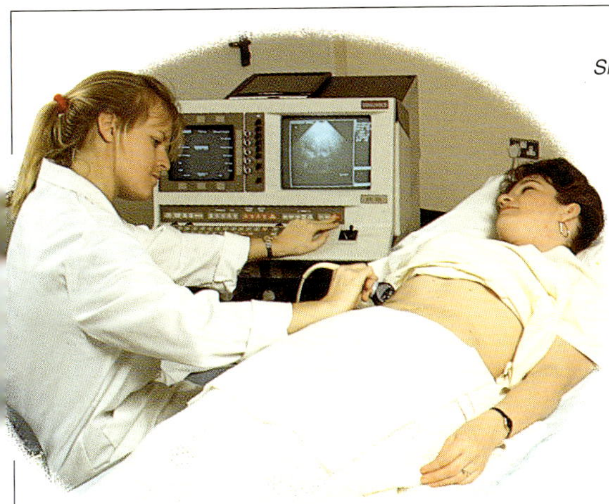

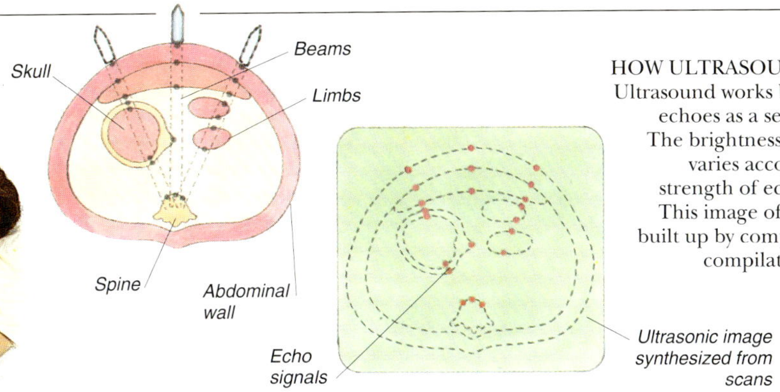

HOW ULTRASOUND WORKS
Ultrasound works by recording echoes as a series of spots. The brightness of each one varies according to the strength of echo received. This image of a foetus was built up by computer from a compilation of scans.

Ultrasound

Sound waves with frequencies above 20,000 Hz are beyond the range of human hearing. Sound with a frequency greater than this is described as ultrasound, or ultrasonic. Ultrasound is often used in medicine because, unlike X-rays, ultrasonic waves do not damage human tissue. A scanner transmits ultrasound waves into the body, where they are reflected by different organs. The scanner receives these reflections back and displays them as an image on a screen.

ECHOLOCATION

Dolphins use ultrasound frequencies to communicate with each other and also to locate fish and underwater obstacles. The loud clicking sounds the dolphins produce bounce off objects and make echoes. These echoes enable dolphins to tell the size and distance of objects in the water around them. This system is invaluable when it comes to detecting predators such as sharks.

Clicking sounds are produced by a special organ on the dolphin's head.

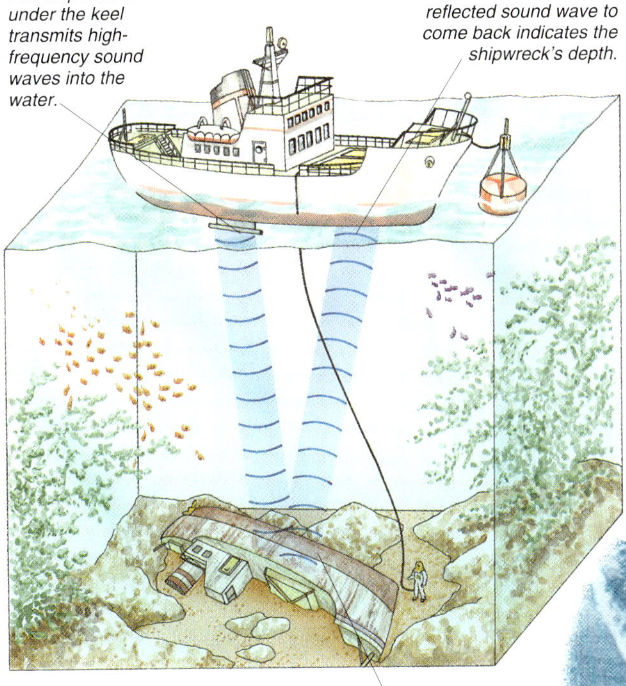

The ship's sonar under the keel transmits high-frequency sound waves into the water.

The time it takes the reflected sound wave to come back indicates the shipwreck's depth.

The shipwreck reflects the sound back.

ECHO-SOUNDING
As a result of the *Titanic* disaster in 1912, when the ship collided with an iceberg on her maiden voyage, French scientist Paul Langevin led research projects to develop sonar. Sonar uses reflected ultrasound waves to locate icebergs, shoals of fish, wrecks, submarines, and to measure the depth of water under a ship. Pulses of sound are transmitted into the ocean. Any echoes bouncing back from an object are monitored. The time delay between transmitting a pulse and receiving its echo indicates how far away the object is.

NON-DESTRUCTIVE TESTING
Important components in aircraft must not contain hidden flaws. Tiny internal cracks could grow and cause a component to fail when an aircraft is in flight. Non-destructive testing (NDT) uses ultrasound as a means of spotting such flaws without damaging the component. Pulses of ultrasound are reflected by any cracks, which show up in ultrasonic images on a screen.

Metal component is immersed in water, which acts as a conducting medium for the sound.

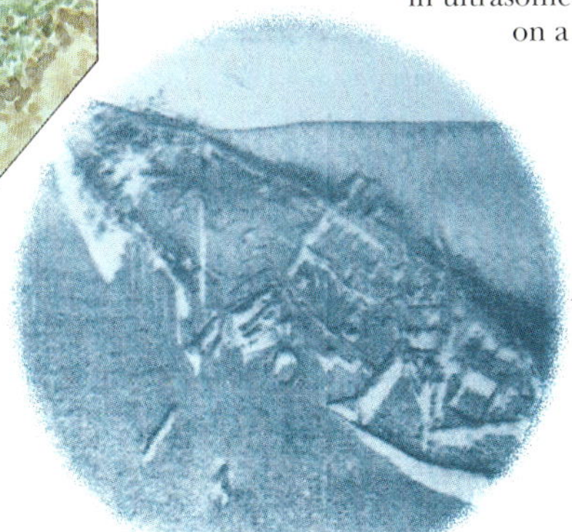

SCREEN IMAGE
This image of a shipwreck was produced by scanning the direction of the outgoing sound. The patterns of echoes were then gradually built up on a computer screen.

Find out more

Sound and light p.177
Measuring sound p.180
Making and hearing sound p.182
Mammals p.334

MUSICAL SOUNDS

ALL MUSICAL INSTRUMENTS work by making air vibrate. Players control the frequency and amplitude of the vibrations to play tunes and make rhythms. The distinctive timbre (quality of sound) of an instrument depends on the way the air vibrates. Musicians blow air into wind instruments either across a hole or past a flexible reed. The air inside a flute, which does not have a reed, vibrates simply to make a pure, sweet sound. Air blown past the reeds inside bagpipe tubes vibrates in a complex way to produce a rich, rasping sound. All acoustic (non-electric) string, wind, and percussion instruments are played by plucking or bowing, blowing, and striking.

STRING HARMONICS

Harmonics are the different frequencies at which something can vibrate. A string stretched between two supports can vibrate so that varying numbers of wavelengths fit along the string. The wave with the longest wavelength is called the fundamental. Other vibrations have shorter wavelengths and higher frequencies. This progressive series of frequencies is known as harmonics. The proportion of different harmonics gives an instrument its individual sound.

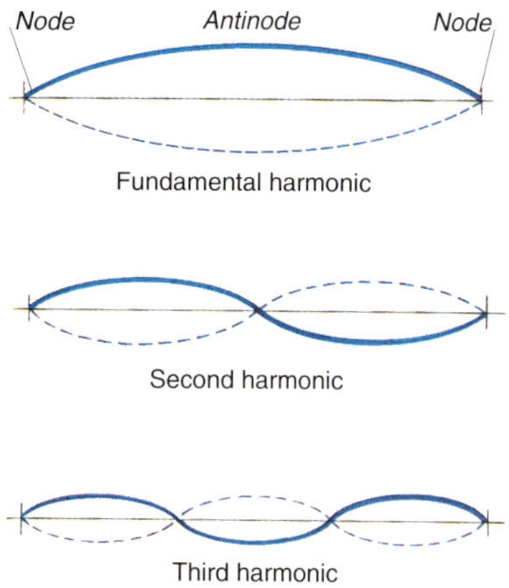

PIANO

Piano keys are connected to hammers that strike strings when the keys are pressed. The pianist can press several keys at once to play chords. Some combinations of notes are pleasing to the ear, but others are not. The effect of combining notes to make chords is called musical harmony.

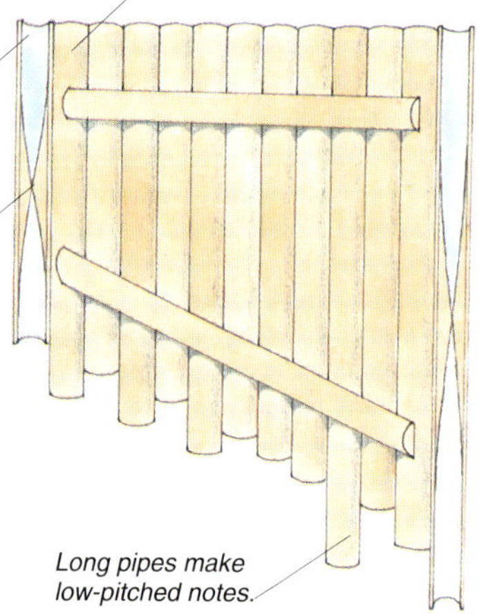

PIPES

The column of air inside a pipe vibrates by stretching and compressing. There is a point in the middle of the column where the air does not move. This is called the node. The air vibrates most at the ends of the column. These areas are called antinodes.

TRUMPET

A trumpeter vibrates his or her lips to make the air inside the tube resonate. Trumpeters can play different notes by changing lip tension and by opening and closing valves that alter the length of the tube. Long columns of air vibrate more slowly and make lower-pitched notes than shorter columns. Blowing harder makes the sound louder.

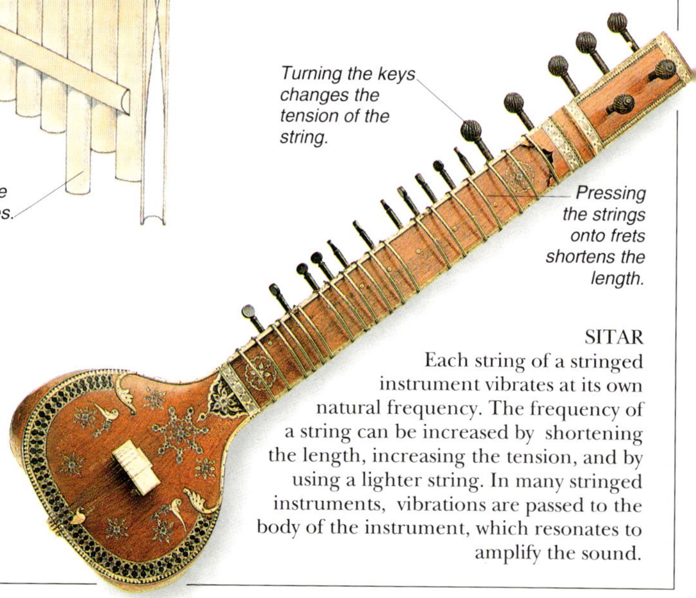

SITAR

Each string of a stringed instrument vibrates at its own natural frequency. The frequency of a string can be increased by shortening the length, increasing the tension, and by using a lighter string. In many stringed instruments, vibrations are passed to the body of the instrument, which resonates to amplify the sound.

ORCHESTRA

The combination of differently pitched string, wind, and percussion instruments in an orchestra produces a huge variety of harmony and timbre. It is a combination that has been carefully planned – each group of instruments has its own special part to play in the performance of a piece of music. An orchestra can play so softly that it can only just be heard but, when everyone plays together loudly, the sound level can reach 100 dB.

PYTHAGORAS

The Greek philosopher and mathematician Pythagoras (c. 582-500 B.C.) believed that beauty and harmony could be explained by numbers. He recognized the mathematical relationship between the pitch of a sound and the length of a string or pipe, or the size of a bell. He discovered that halving the length of a string doubles the frequency of its fundamental vibration, and raises the pitch by an octave.

MUSICAL SCALE

A scale is a sequence of notes of increasing frequency that progresses in a natural and pleasing way. The note at the top of the scale has exactly twice the frequency of the note at the bottom. Two notes, one of which has twice the frequency of the other, are said to be separated by an octave.

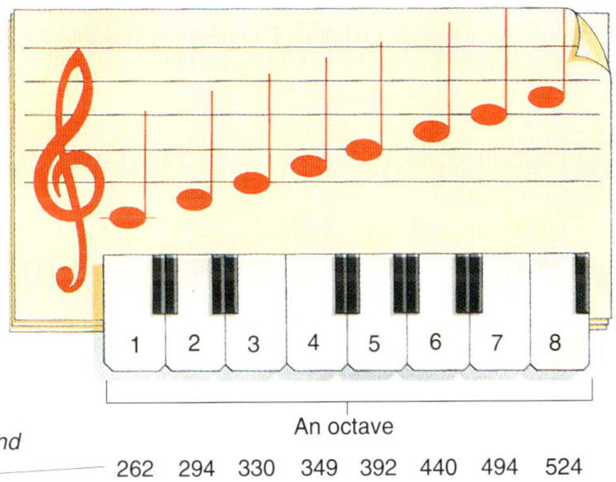

BANGING A DRUM

The regular beat and rhythm of percussion instruments, such as drums, helps to give an overall structure and mood to the music. Hitting the stretched drum skin makes it vibrate, but exactly the right amount of force must be used to make the instrument vibrate in the right way. A tighter skin gives a higher pitch, in the same way as a tighter string makes a higher note.

Find out more

VIBRATIONS P.126
MEASURING SOUND P.180
LOUDNESS P.181
MAKING AND HEARING SOUND P.182
REFLECTION AND ABSORPTION P.184
FACT FINDER P.412

SOUND RECORDING

JUST AS WORDS written on paper can be read again and again, sounds can be recorded and replayed. All sound recordings store sounds by making a copy of the sound waves. There are two types of sound recording: analogue and digital. Analogue recordings store sound wave patterns as a wavy line cut in a record or as magnetic patterns on a strip of tape. Digital recordings convert sound wave patterns into numbers that map the positions of all the points on a sound wave before being recorded. These numbers are stored as tiny pits on a compact disc (CD) or as magnetic patterns on digital audio tape (DAT), and then converted back into sound by a microprocessor chip.

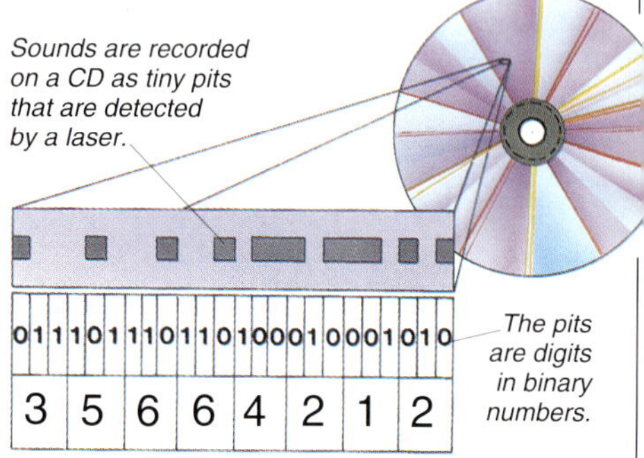

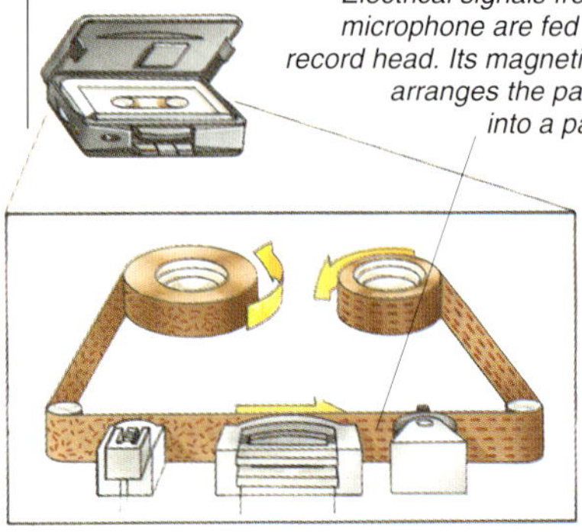

TAPE RECORDING
The tape inside a cassette is coated with a layer of oxide containing magnetic metals. On a blank tape, the magnetic particles point in random directions, but when a sound is recorded on the tape, the particles are arranged in a pattern that changes in step with the sound.

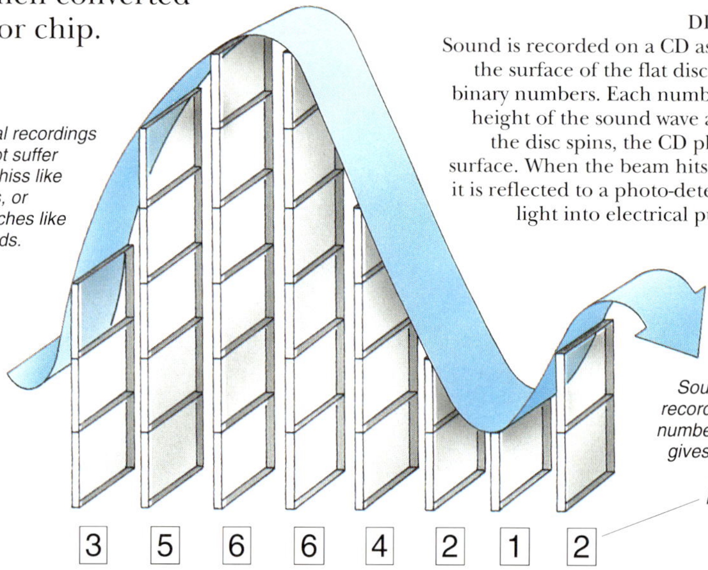

DIGITAL RECORDING
Sound is recorded on a CD as tiny pits pressed into the surface of the flat disc. The pits are digits in binary numbers. Each number is a measure of the height of the sound wave at a given moment. As the disc spins, the CD player's beam scans the surface. When the beam hits a flat part of the disc, it is reflected to a photo-detector that changes the light into electrical pulses. When the beam strikes a pit, it is reflected away.

RECORDING STUDIO

Recordings are made by mixing sounds from different instruments and vocalists. There is no need to record everything at once – the sound engineer can add sounds one on top of the other. The engineer mixes the sounds using sliders on the mixing desks.

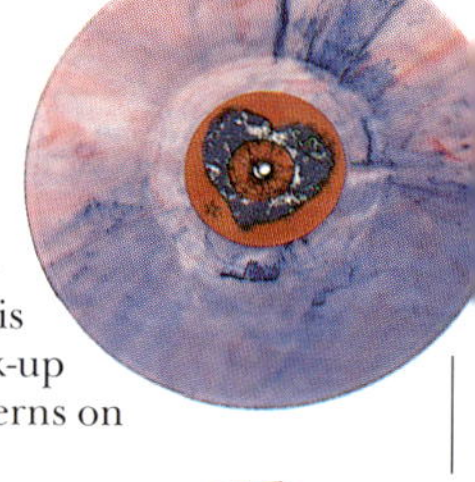

RECORDS
As the stylus in the pick-up head of the record player runs in the groove, it vibrates, following the pattern of the sound waves. This sets up electrical signals in the pick-up head. On a stereo record, the patterns on opposite sides of the groove are slightly different, so different sounds come from right- and left-hand speakers.

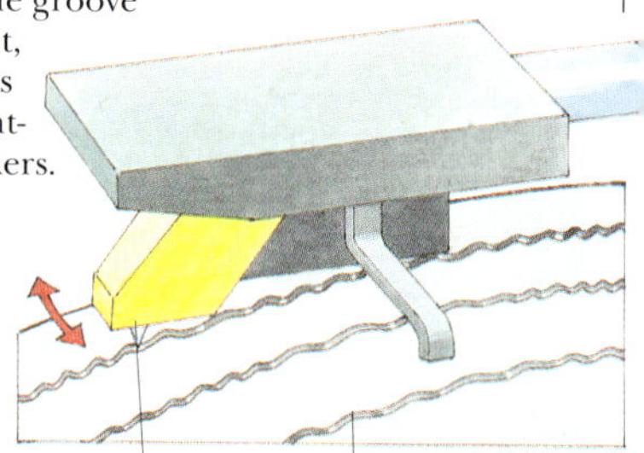

THOMAS EDISON
The first sound recording in 1877 was of the words "Mary had a little lamb..." spoken by Thomas Edison (1847-1931) into his phonograph. This recorded sound by scratching a groove in a wax cylinder. It had no electrical parts, and relied on the mechanical vibrations of a needle to record and reproduce sounds.

Find out more

SEMIMETALS P.39
MAGNETISM P.154
ELECTROMAGNETISM P.156
ELECTRONIC SOUNDS P.189

ELECTRONIC SOUNDS

EVERY SINGLE SOUND we know, including the sounds of the human voice, can be produced electronically by digital sound technology. Electronic instruments can also create completely new sounds. Acoustic instruments can be replaced by synthesized sounds or by sound samples – recordings that can be played forwards, backwards, at a different pitch, or processed in various ways by computer. Echoes and reverberation can also be added to sounds electronically. In fact, it is possible for one person working in a small room with a keyboard and computer to produce the sound of a whole orchestra.

SPECIAL EFFECTS

Electronic music and special effects are composed for radio and television in a radiophonic workshop. In the early days of broadcasting, the sounds of thunder were made by shaking a large metal sheet; and the sounds of horses' hooves by tapping coconut shells. Now these sounds can be synthesized.

ELECTRIC GUITAR

An electric guitar actually makes little sound of its own – the sound it produces is made possible by electricity. Plucking the metal strings makes them vibrate. These vibrations are changed into tiny electrical signals in the pick-ups beneath the strings. These signals are amplified and processed to make the guitar sound clear or fuzzy, harsh or sweet.

Words are entered into the computer through the keyboard and spoken by a synthesized voice.

SYNTHESIZED SOUNDS

A synthesizer is a musical instrument used to make sounds electronically. The Moog synthesizer, which was designed and developed by the American engineer Robert Moog in the 1950s, played one note at a time. Today's digital synthesizers can produce very complex arrangements of sounds. Professor Stephen Hawking cannot speak, but is able to communicate using a computer that synthesizes speech.

SAMPLING

A sampler records natural sounds and stores them digitally. When the sound is played back, the numbers can be altered to change the frequencies, and therefore the pitch, of the original sound. A sampler can even make a musical scale from the sound of a dog barking.

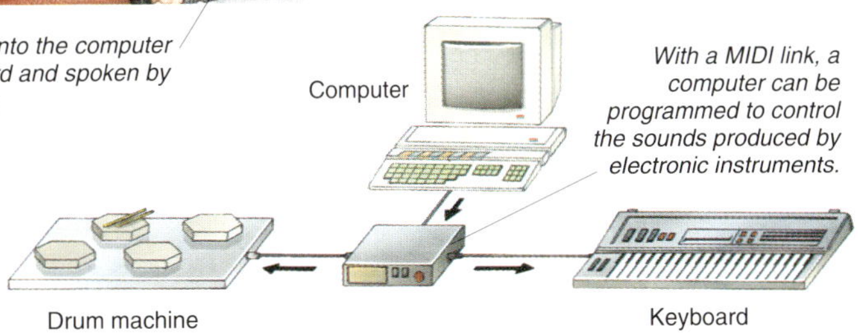

MIDI SYSTEM

A Musical Instrument Digital Interface (MIDI) system makes it possible for a computer to trigger instruments such as keyboards and drum machines to make sounds together or in sequence. This means that composers using a MIDI system can write film scores, music for television, and pop songs – without having to use a band or an orchestra.

Find out more

COMPUTERS P.173
MEASURING SOUND P.180
REFLECTION AND ABSORPTION P.184
MUSICAL SOUNDS P.186
SOUND RECORDING P.188

LIGHT

WHAT IS LIGHT? It is something we see and use every day, but do not often think about. Light is a form of energy. The energy from the Sun powers all of life on Earth. Light travels very fast. When we switch on a light bulb, light floods the room almost instantly. Almost, but not quite; it is actually travelling at about 300,000 km (186,000 miles) per second. In fact, the speed of light is the universal speed limit. Nothing can travel faster. Light sometimes seems to act as a wave, but unlike sound waves or water waves, it can travel through a vacuum. At other times, light seems to act as if it were a stream of particles. Light usually comes from hot objects – such as the Sun or flames – but it can be made in other ways too. Electricity can give off light, and some chemical reactions can too – such as those in a firefly which cause it to glow in the dark.

LIGHT ENERGY

Just by standing in sunlight, you can feel the energy that light carries. It heats your body, and causes chemical reactions which tan and burn skin. The light falling on each square metre of the Earth's surface could power ten electric light bulbs. Solar power stations harness this energy by using mirrors to focus sunlight on to a central receiver. This creates steam which can then generate electricity.

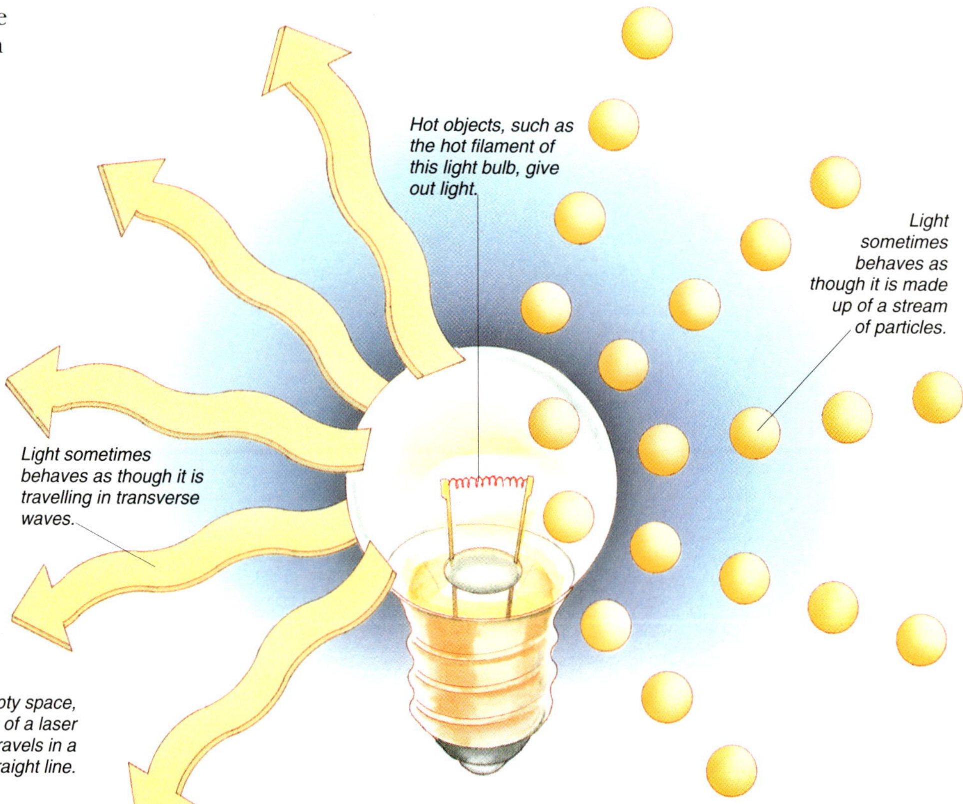

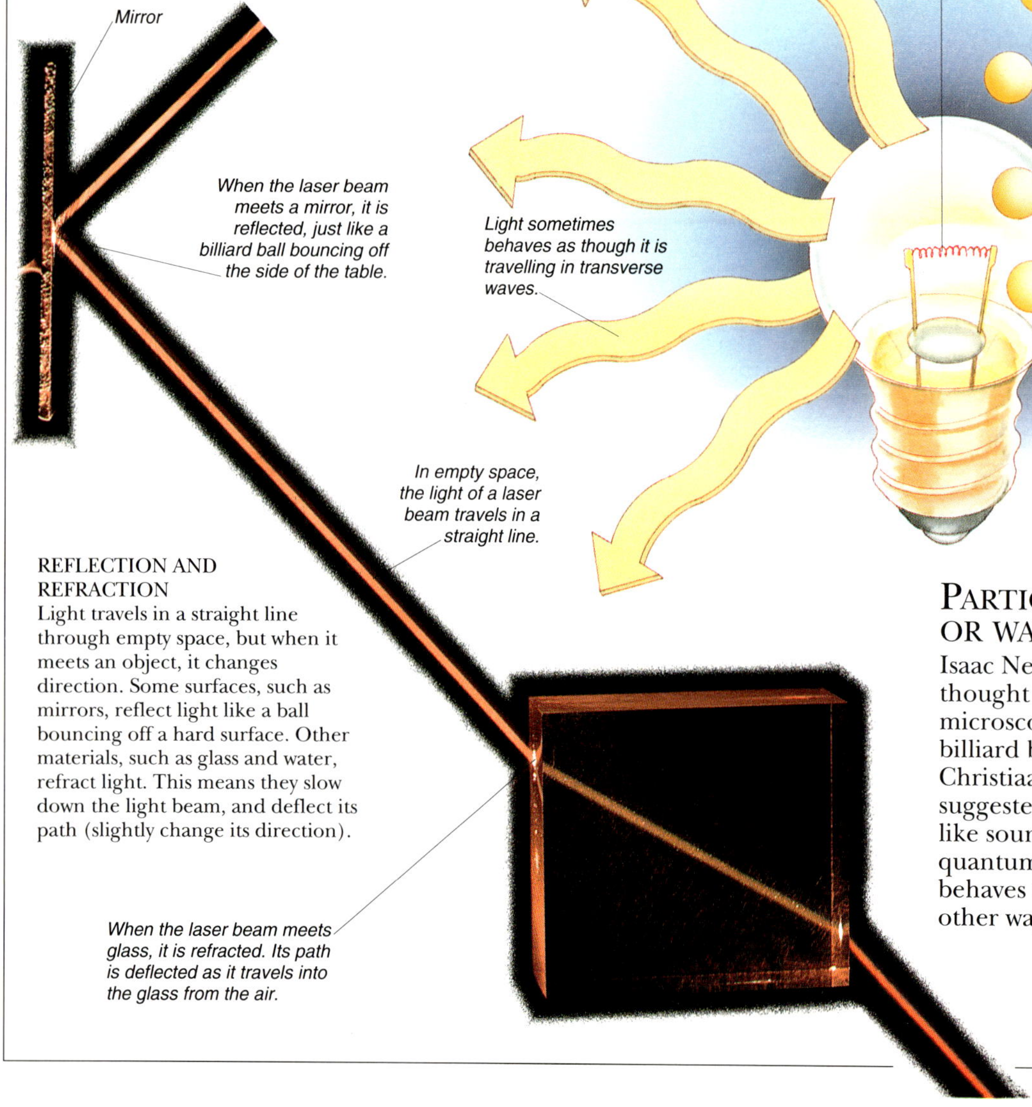

REFLECTION AND REFRACTION

Light travels in a straight line through empty space, but when it meets an object, it changes direction. Some surfaces, such as mirrors, reflect light like a ball bouncing off a hard surface. Other materials, such as glass and water, refract light. This means they slow down the light beam, and deflect its path (slightly change its direction).

PARTICLES OR WAVES?

Isaac Newton (1642-1727) thought that light was made of microscopic particles resembling tiny billiard balls. Dutch mathematician Christiaan Huygens (1629-95) suggested that light is a wave motion, like sound or water waves. Modern quantum theory describes how light behaves in some ways like waves, but in other ways like particles.

PHOTOELECTRIC EFFECT

If light is shone onto a metal, it can knock electrons out of metal atoms. This principle, called the photoelectric effect, is used in the photocells of a solar-powered calculator, which can generate electricity from light. But increasing the intensity of the light does not increase the speed of the ejected electrons, it just increases their number. This can only be explained by thinking of light as little packets of light energy called photons. When a photon strikes an atom it gives its energy to an electron, which flies out of the atom. More photons knock out more electrons.

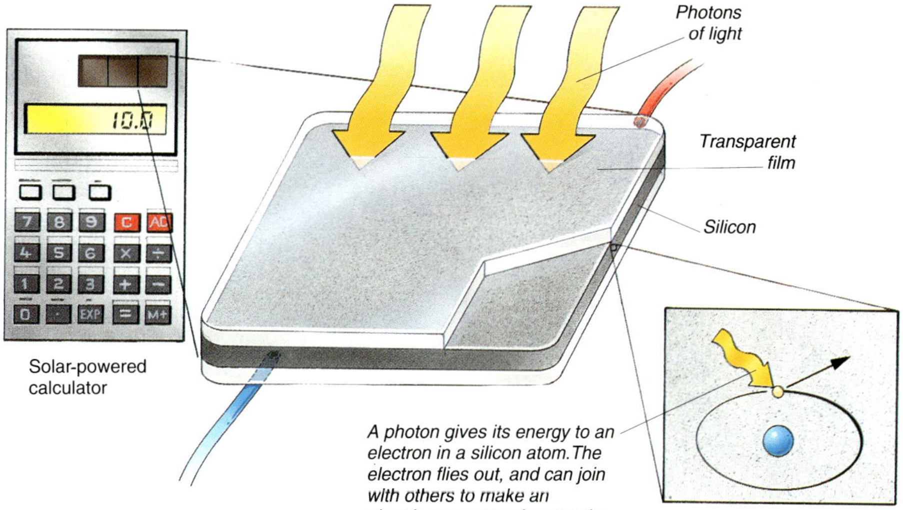

A photon gives its energy to an electron in a silicon atom. The electron flies out, and can join with others to make an electric current to show up the numbers.

DIFFRACTION AND INTERFERENCE

When a light beam passes through a narrow slit, it spreads out. The narrower the slit, the wider the spread. This is called diffraction. You can see this effect if you squint at street lamps through your eyelashes. If two diffracted light beams overlap, the pattern they make can only be explained if light is a wave made up of peaks and troughs. In some places, two peaks or two troughs will meet to form very bright spots. In other places, a trough will meet a peak; these cancel each other out leaving darkness. This is called interference.

QUANTUM THEORY

The German physicist Max Planck (1858-1947) was the first to suggest that light is neither purely a wave nor purely a particle, but has a combination of both properties. This theory was later expanded by Albert Einstein. To understand how light is reflected, refracted, and diffracted, we need to think of light as being like sound waves, with both a wavelength and a frequency. But to understand how atoms emit and absorb light, we must think of light as a stream of particles called photons, each carrying a certain amount of energy. This theory is called quantum theory.

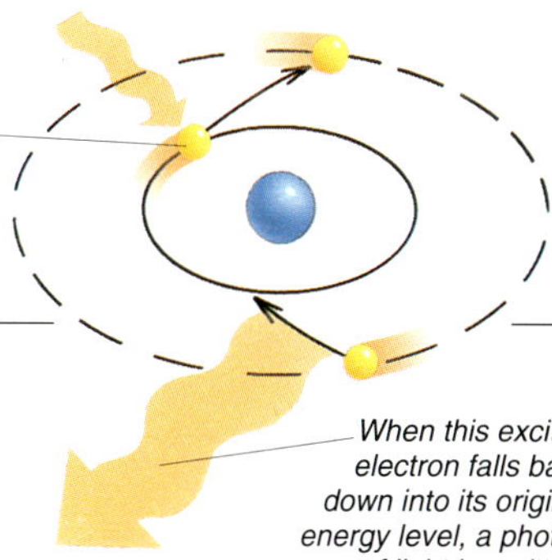

An atom is given energy which can "excite" an electron, causing it to jump into a higher energy level.

When this excited electron falls back down into its original energy level, a photon of light is emitted.

SPEED OF LIGHT

Light travels much too fast to be measured with an ordinary clock. French physicist Hippolyte Fizeau (1819-96) made an experimental measurement of the speed of light in 1849. He shone a light through a toothed wheel towards a mirror 9 km (5.5 miles) away. He speeded up the wheel until the reflected light beam could be seen through the gaps between teeth. Fizeau then knew that the light had travelled to the mirror and back in the time the wheel had turned by just one tooth.

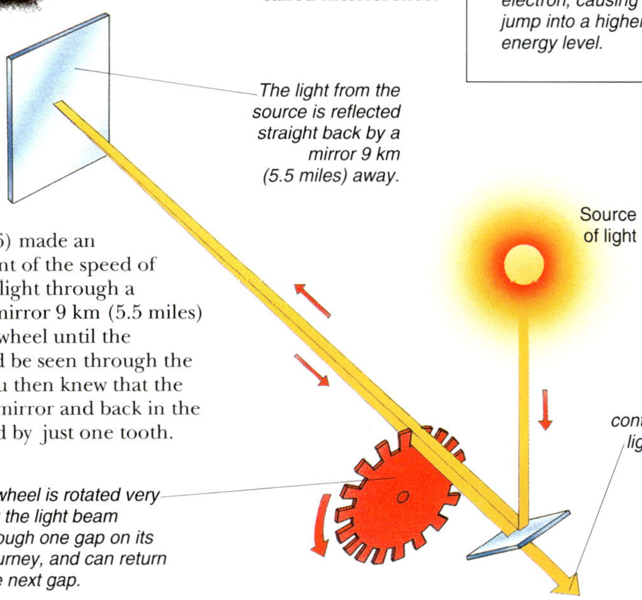

The light from the source is reflected straight back by a mirror 9 km (5.5 miles) away.

The observer speeds up the wheel until a continuous beam of light can be seen.

A toothed wheel is rotated very fast so that the light beam passes through one gap on its outward journey, and can return through the next gap.

Find out more

ELECTROMAGNETIC SPECTRUM

JUST AS LIGHT TRAVELS IN WAVES, so also do other forms of energy including radio waves, microwaves, and ultraviolet waves. These are all electromagnetic waves. The total range of electromagnetic waves is called the electromagnetic spectrum. The colours of the rainbow form the only part of this spectrum that we can see. All the other waves are invisible. Although all these waves travel at the speed of light, each group of waves has a different wavelength and carries a different amount of energy. Infrared, microwave, and radio waves have a longer wavelength and carry less energy than visible light. Ultraviolet, X-ray, and gamma rays have a shorter wavelength and carry more energy.

GAMMA RAYS
Gamma rays are very penetrating. They carry lots of energy and damage living cells as they pass through. Gamma rays are given out by the nuclei of radioactive atoms in nuclear reactions and explosions.

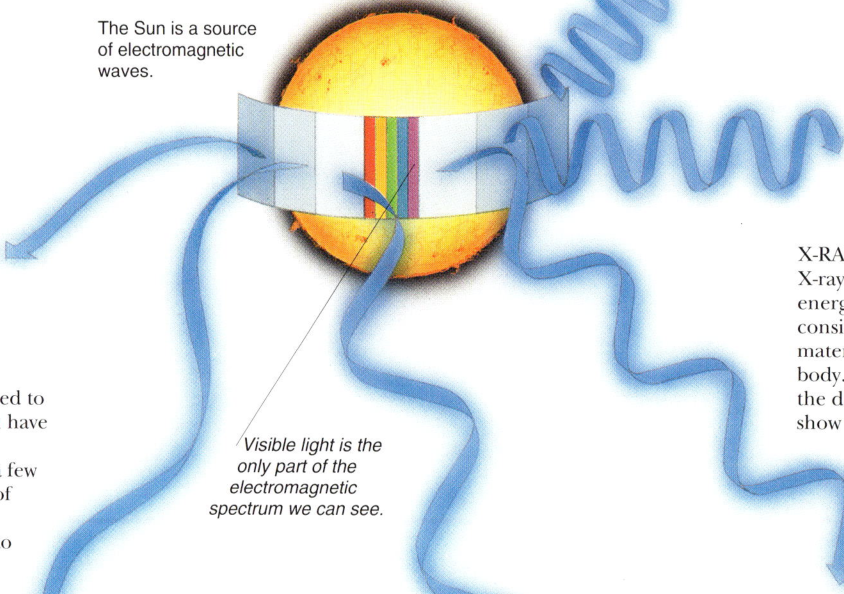

RADIO WAVES
The electromagnetic waves used to broadcast radio and television have wavelengths ranging from hundreds of metres down to a few tens of centimetres. The size of the aerial needed to detect a radio signal is closely related to the wavelength.

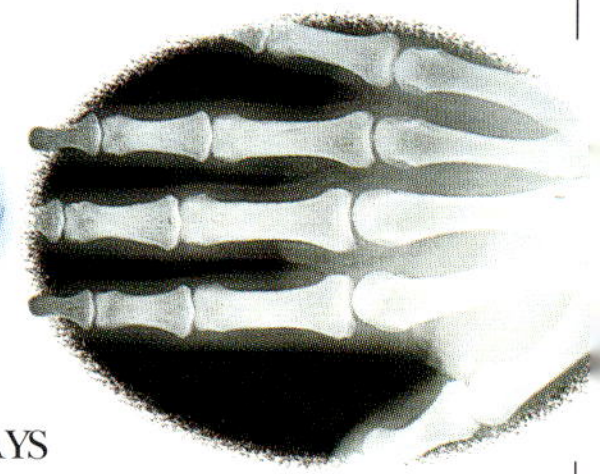

X-RAYS
X-rays have enough energy to travel through a considerable thickness of material – including the human body. On an X-ray photograph the denser parts of the body show up as shadows.

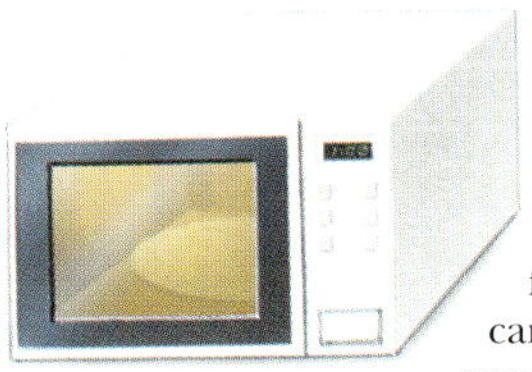

MICROWAVES
Microwaves are the shortest of the radio waves and are used to transmit radar signals. Some microwaves have the same frequency as water molecules, and can be used to cook moist food. The energy of the microwaves is converted into heat as the water molecules vibrate.

ULTRAVIOLET WAVES
Sunlight contains ultraviolet (UV) rays. Small amounts of UV rays are good for us, but large amounts can be bad for our eyes and cause skin cancer. It is these waves that tan and burn fair skins.

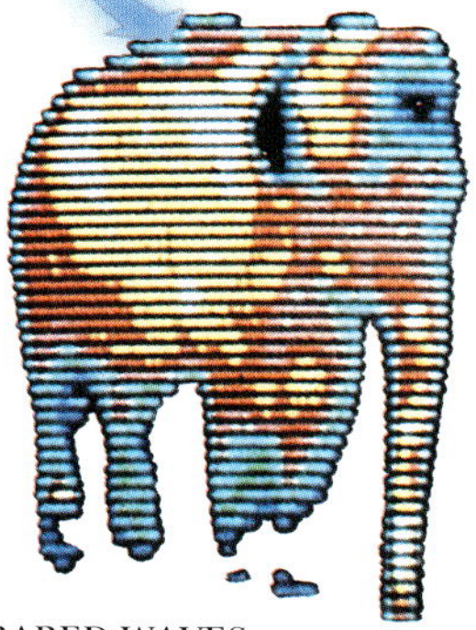

INFRARED WAVES
All warm objects give off infrared rays. Special photographs taken with infrared rays are called thermographs. Each colour represents a different skin temperature, ranging from yellow (hottest) through to blue (coldest).

JAMES CLERK MAXWELL
It was the Scottish physicist James Clerk Maxwell (1831-79) who formulated the equations of electricity and magnetism that predicted the existence of electromagnetic waves. Approximately 15 years after Maxwell published his equations, Heinrich Hertz first produced and detected radio waves.

Find out more

RADIOACTIVITY P.26
CRYSTALS P.30
RADIO P.164
TELEVISION P.166
FACT FINDER P.412

SOURCES OF LIGHT

EVERY OBJECT IN THE UNIVERSE gives off electromagnetic waves – stars, trees, and even our bodies. Most of the time these are invisible because their frequency is below that of visible light. But if an object is heated, the frequency of the radiation increases and visible light is produced. Objects start to glow dull red at about 500°C (900°F). At 2,000°C (3,500°F) they are bright orange, while at 5,000°C (9,000°F) they glow white hot, emitting all the colours of the visible spectrum. But it is not only hot objects that produce light. An electric current passed through a gas excites electrons which then lose their extra energy as light. Chemicals can also release light. The glowing patterns along the bodies of some deep-sea fish are produced by chemical reactions.

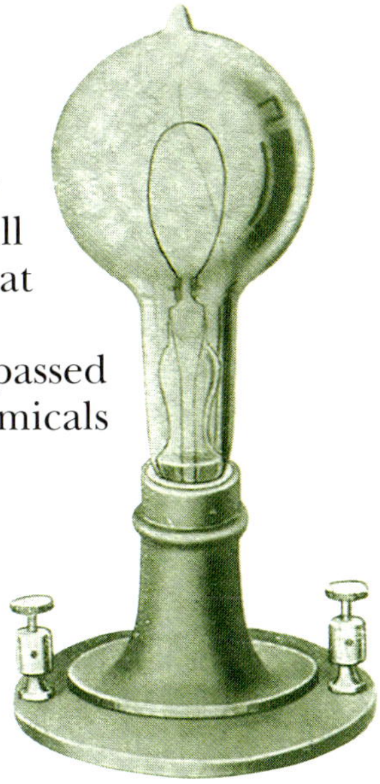

EDISON'S LIGHT BULB
American inventor Thomas Edison (1847-1931) made the first practical electric light bulb in 1879. He passed an electric current through a carbon filament to heat it so that it glowed brightly. Modern bulbs have a tungsten filament that heats up to about 3,000°C (5,500°F).

SOLAR SPECTRUM

The surface temperature of the Sun is 5,500°C (10,000°F). At this temperature all the colours of the visible spectrum are produced. But atoms in the cooler outer layers of the Sun's atmosphere absorb certain frequencies of the sunlight as it passes through. This causes dark lines on the solar spectrum, which are known as the Fraunhofer lines.

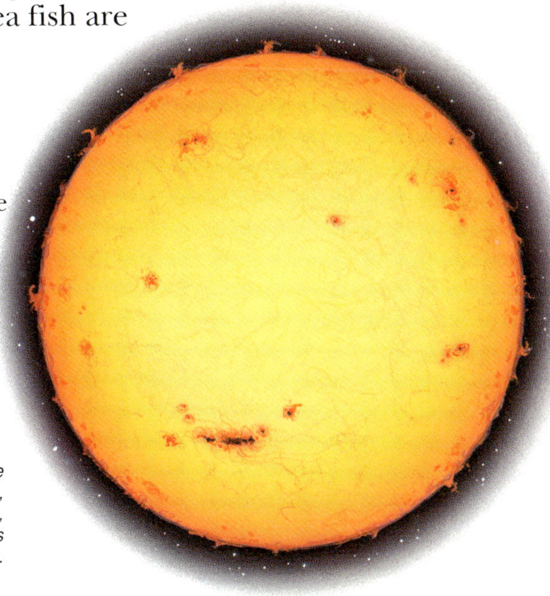

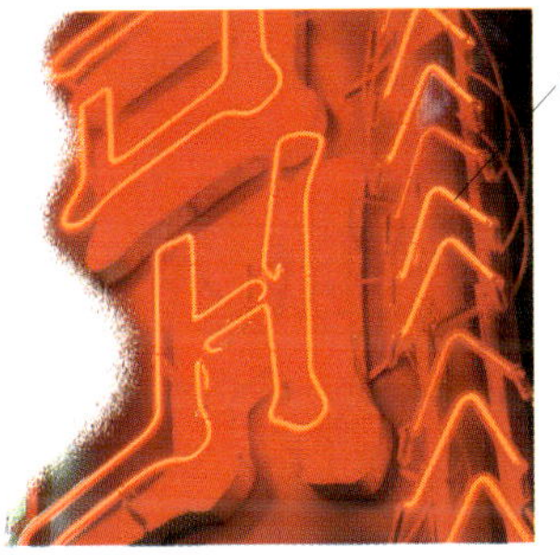

Different gases produce different coloured lights. Neon, for example, always gives out a red light.

NEON LIGHTS
A glass tube filled with gas produces light when an electric current flows through it. This is not because the gas is hot, but because the electrons of the gas are given energy that they lose by emitting it as light.

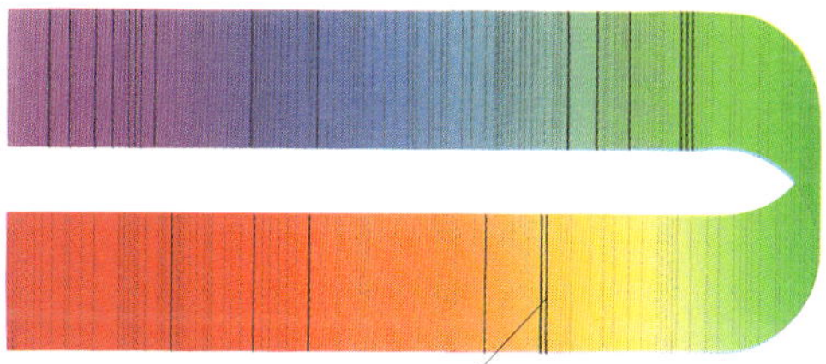

Positions of the Fraunhofer lines indicate which elements are present in the Sun's atmosphere.

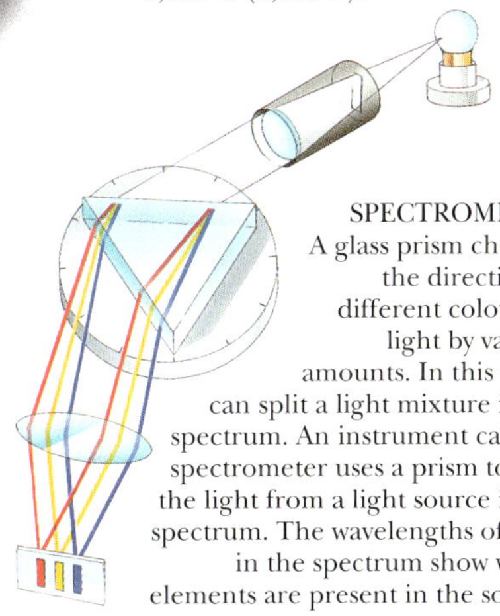

SPECTROMETER
A glass prism changes the direction of different colours of light by varying amounts. In this way it can split a light mixture into a spectrum. An instrument called a spectrometer uses a prism to split the light from a light source into a spectrum. The wavelengths of light in the spectrum show which elements are present in the source.

LEDs can produce red, orange, yellow, and green light.

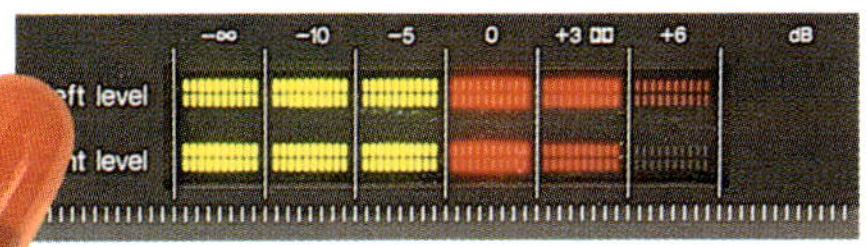

LEDs are sometimes used in displays in calculators, cash registers, and digital clocks.

LIGHT-EMITTING DIODES
Many modern hi-fi systems have a light-emitting diode (LED) display. LEDs change electrical energy into light energy – they give out light when a current flows through them. LEDs are small, need only a small current and last longer than filament lamps.

GUSTAV KIRCHOFF

German physicist Gustav Kirchoff (1824-87) studied light spectra using the spectrometer he developed with the chemist Robert Bunsen. He observed that individual atoms and molecules emit certain colours only when heated. Kirchoff realized that each element produces a distinct spectrum of coloured lines that can be used to identify the element.

Find out more

NOBLE GASES P.48
CHEMICAL REACTIONS P.52
ELECTRICITY SUPPLY P.160
COLOUR P.202

REFLECTION

The image in a plane mirror is laterally inverted. This means that the right side of the object appears as the left side of the image.

Virtual image is the same size as the object.

WE SEE SOME OBJECTS because they make their own light – like the Sun or a light bulb. But we can also see objects that do not give off their own light. They reflect light – light rays bounce off them. We see the Moon because it reflects the Sun's light. Gases are generally invisible because they are too thin to scatter enough light to be seen. But liquids and solids are clearly visible. The appearance of an object depends both on the amount of light it reflects and on the texture of its surface. A smooth white surface, for example, reflects more light than a rough dark one. If a surface does not reflect any light at all, it looks black.

MIRROR IMAGE

Have you ever noticed that the mirror image of an object appears to be as far behind a plane (flat) mirror as the object is in front? But it is not a real image; there is no light coming from behind the mirror – the reflected light just travels to our eyes as if it had come from an object where the image is. This type of image is called a virtual image.

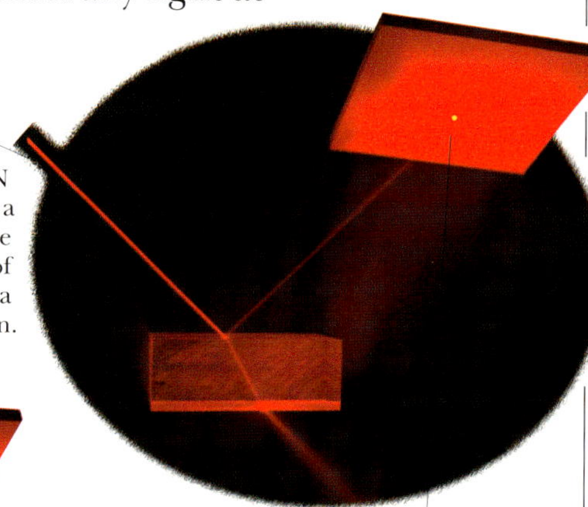

Light source

Specular reflection

SPECULAR REFLECTION
Light is reflected from a smooth surface at a definite angle. Specular reflection of a laser beam produces a bright spot on a screen.

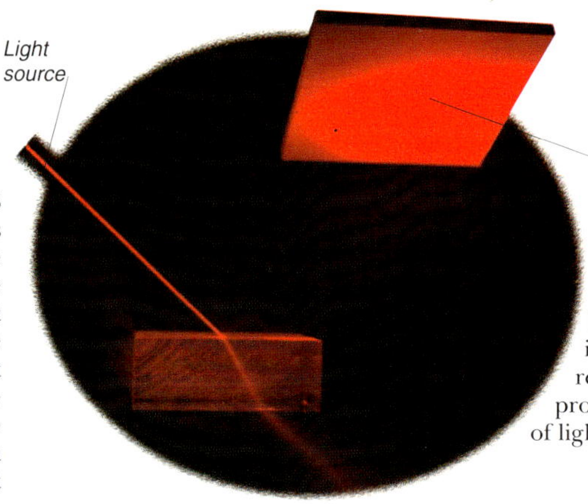

Light source

Diffuse reflection

DIFFUSE REFLECTION
Rough surfaces reflect light diffusely – scattering it in all directions. Diffuse reflection of a laser beam produces a fuzzy patch of light on a screen.

Reflected image

TWO-WAY MIRRORS
A glass sheet reflects about 5 per cent of the light falling on it. The other 95 per cent passes through. If the light is equally bright on both sides, the reflections look weak. But if it is dark on one side and bright on the other, the bright side looks like a mirror because there is no transmitted light swamping the reflection. People on the bright side can see themselves reflected. People on the dark side can see through the glass to the other side.

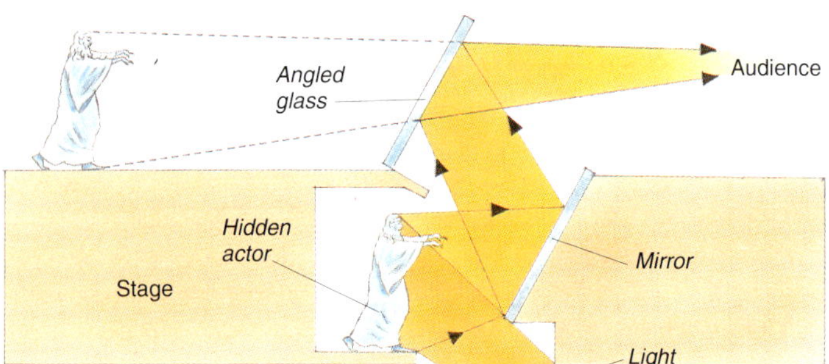

GHOSTLY APPARITION
A two-way mirror was used in 19th-century theatres to produce a ghostly image. Light shining on a hidden actor was reflected from a mirror onto a large sheet of angled glass, and then onto the stage. If the stage was dark, the audience could not see the glass. All they could see was the phantom appearing and disappearing!

HENDRIK LORENTZ
The Dutch physicist Hendrik Lorentz (1853-1928) used James Clerk Maxwell's theory of electromagnetic waves to explain how light is reflected. Light energy is absorbed by electrons, which then re-emit it at a new angle. Lorentz's theory confirms the law of reflection, which states that the angle of reflection is equal to the angle of incidence.

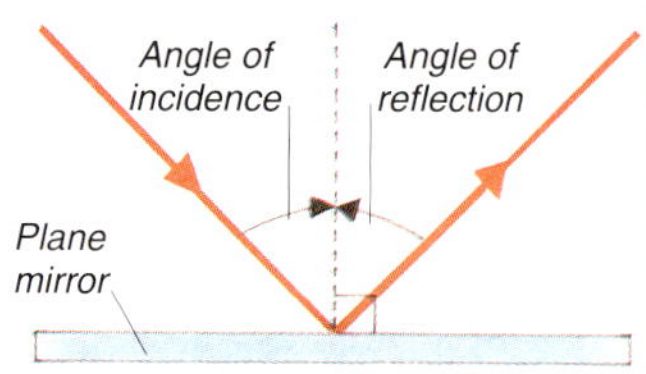

TELESCOPE MIRRORS
The world's largest optical telescopes use a large concave (dish-shaped) mirror to collect the light from distant stars. This curved mirror catches parallel light rays in such a way that they are concentrated to one point.

The large main mirror is a concave mirror several metres in diameter.

Light reflected from the concave mirror is sent to a smaller mirror. This smaller mirror reflects the light to a camera that produces either a photographic image or a television image.

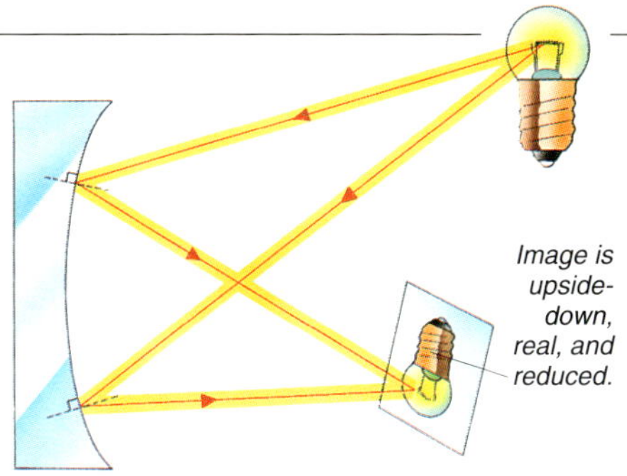

Image is upside-down, real, and reduced.

REAL IMAGE IN A CONCAVE MIRROR
A concave mirror can focus light from a distant object to project an upside-down image onto a screen. The size of the image depends on the distance between the object and the mirror. The nearer the object is to the mirror, the larger the image becomes.

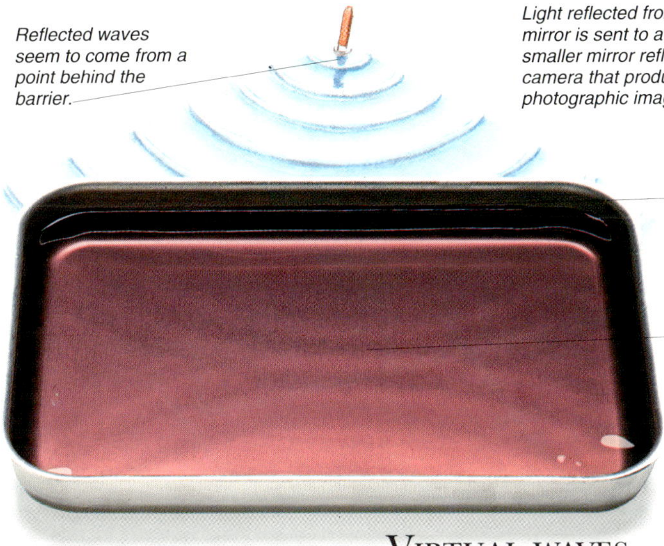

Reflected waves seem to come from a point behind the barrier.

Barrier

Reflected wave

VIRTUAL WAVES

The way in which a plane mirror produces an image can be demonstrated with water waves. Think of the barrier as a plane mirror. When the circular waves meet the barrier, they are reflected. These reflected waves appear to come from a point behind the barrier. As the waves do not really come from this point, it is called a virtual image.

DRIVING MIRROR
Driving mirrors are convex. They are curved outwards like the back of a spoon. Convex mirrors reflect light to produce an image that is always upright and reduced (smaller). This is useful if you want a wide field of view, such as in a car driving mirror. The driver can see farther out of the sides than with a flat mirror.

NOVELTY MIRRORS

A curved fairground mirror produces distorted images that can be both scary and amusing. In reality, it is the mirrors themselves that are distorted. Their concave and convex surfaces make the mirrors hollow in some places and bumpy in others. A bumpy convex surface makes things look smaller. A hollow concave surface magnifies. You may appear to have a long thin body and short fat legs. Other parts of you may be upside-down.

Image is upright and virtual, as well as magnified.

SHAVING MIRROR
If you put your face close to a concave mirror, the light is reflected, producing a magnified image of your face. But if you move further away from the mirror, the image becomes confused and then reappears upside-down and reduced. You can see the same effects by looking into the curved surface of a shiny spoon.

Find out more

ELECTROMAGNETIC SPECTRUM P.192
LENSES P.197
OPTICAL INSTRUMENTS P.198
LIGHT AND MATTER P.200

REFRACTION

LIGHT TRAVELS in straight lines. But when it passes from one transparent material to another, the light rays bend. This is called refraction, and is why a straw standing in a glass of water looks bent at the point where it enters the water. Refraction occurs because light travels at different speeds in different materials. Refraction was first investigated by a Dutch mathematician called Willebrord Snell in 1621. A number called the refractive index measures the amount a light beam bends when it travels from one substance to another. Relative to air, air has a refractive index of 1, water 1.3, and most glass 1.5. Light is not bent as much when it enters water as when it enters glass because it is not slowed down as much.

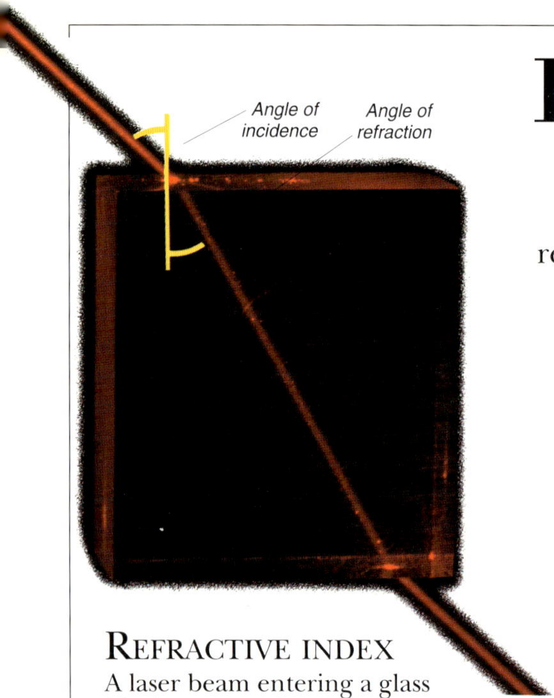

REFRACTIVE INDEX

A laser beam entering a glass block at an angle (the angle of incidence) is refracted because light travels more slowly in glass than in air. A number called the refractive index of a material gives the relationship between the two speeds. In this case, the speed of light in air divided by the speed of light in glass gives the refractive index of glass as compared with air.

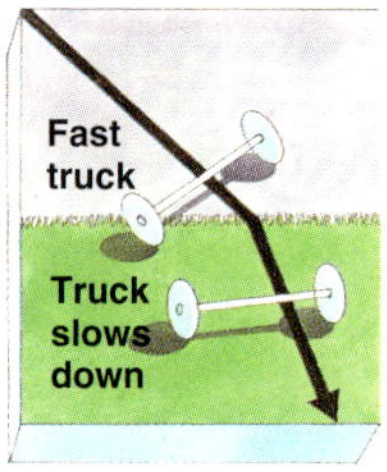

ALL CHANGE
When a truck's wheels move at an angle from a hard surface onto grass, the grass slows down the wheels of the truck on one side, causing the truck's path to bend. Light is refracted in the same way when it travels from air into glass.

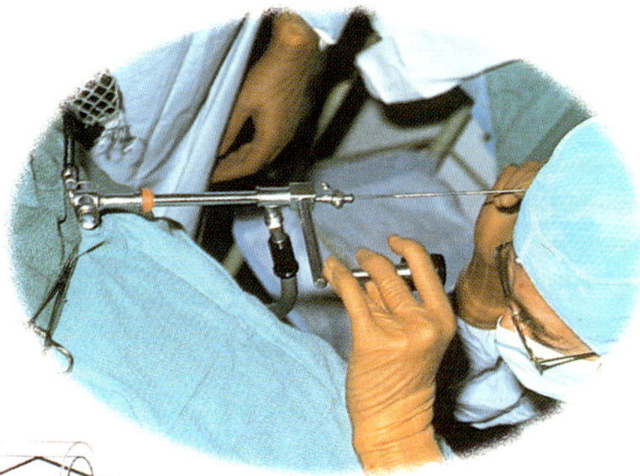

Each fibre is a fine strand of glass. Internal reflection channels light along the fibre even if it is bent or twisted.

ENDOSCOPE
The principle of internal reflection is put to good use in medicine. An endoscope is an optical device for inspecting the inside of the body without having to operate. It consists of a bundle of flexible optical fibres. Light is channelled along the fibres by internal reflections. A doctor can insert an endoscope down a patient's throat to examine the inside of the stomach.

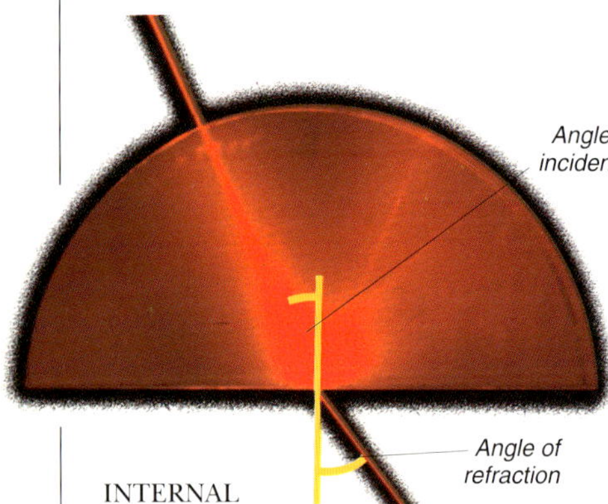

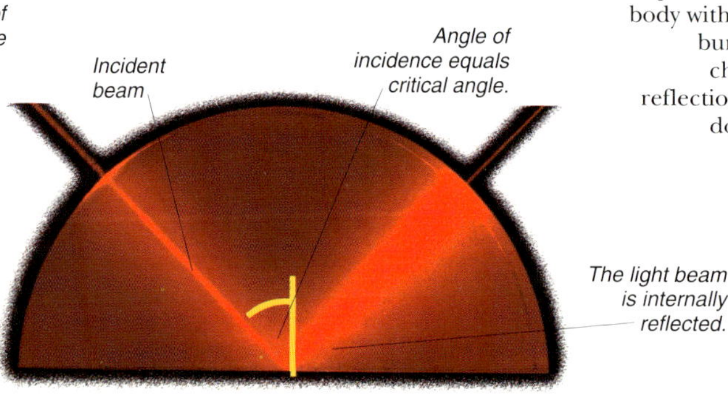

INTERNAL REFLECTION
The glass block above shows how light is refracted as it emerges from glass into air and its speed increases. When the angle of incidence is small, the beam emerges at a larger angle. But as the angle of incidence increases (right), the light beam becomes more and more refracted until, at a certain angle of incidence called the critical angle, the light is bent so much that it does not emerge from the glass at all – it is reflected inside. This is called internal reflection.

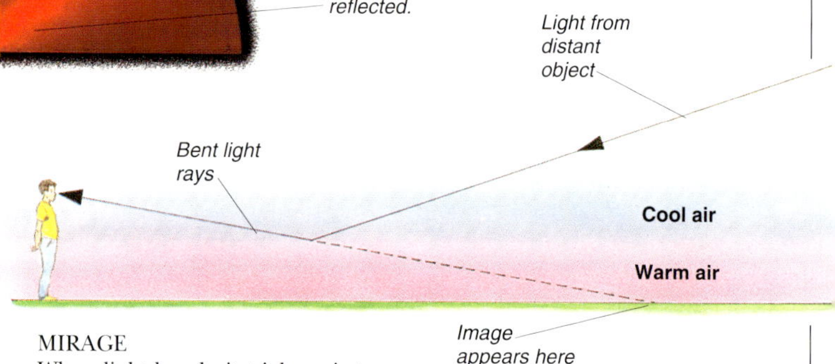

MIRAGE
When light bends, it tricks us into seeing things in the wrong place. A mirage is caused by light refraction in the atmosphere. Light travels more quickly through the warmer air near the ground than it does through the cooler air above. Light is refracted in a curved path, producing a false image of a distant object. Mirages are common in deserts where the air is very hot.

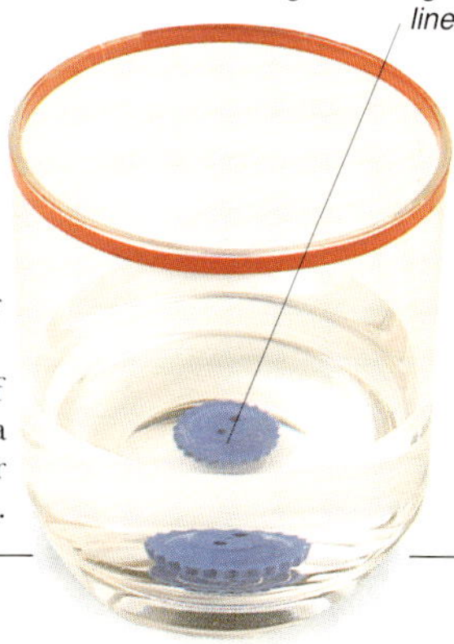

Light rays from the button are refracted as they leave the water. You see the button as though the light rays were travelling in a straight line.

DIFFERENT DEPTHS
Have you ever noticed that pools and ponds are always deeper than they look? This is because light is refracted as it leaves the water, making the bottom of the pool appear closer than it really is. You can see this effect in this glass of water. Light rays are refracted in such a way as to make the button look closer than it really is.

Find out more

SOUND AND LIGHT P.177
REFLECTION P.194
COLOUR P.202
VISION P.204
FACT FINDER P.412

LENSES

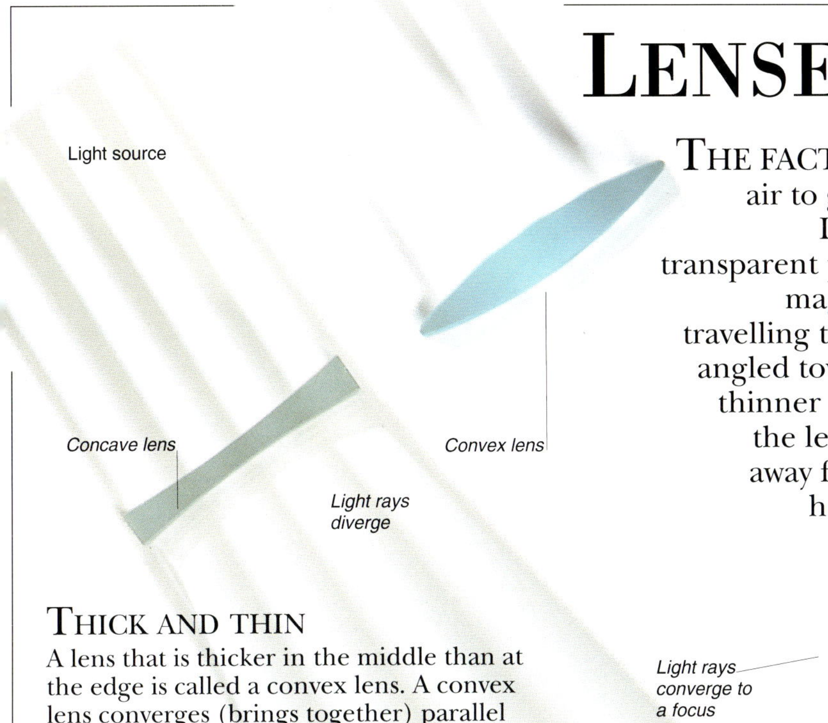

THE FACT THAT LIGHT BENDS when it passes from air to glass can be made to work to our advantage. Lenses are specially shaped pieces of glass or transparent plastic that focus light, produce images, and magnify or reduce a scene by bending the light travelling through them. A lens becomes steadily more angled towards the edge and may be either thicker or thinner at the centre than at the edge. The shape of the lens means that light is bent either towards or away from a single focus (point). Each of our eyes has a natural lens. You are using yours now to focus on these words.

THICK AND THIN

A lens that is thicker in the middle than at the edge is called a convex lens. A convex lens converges (brings together) parallel light rays to a focus after they have passed through the lens. A lens that is thinner in the middle is called a concave lens. This kind of lens diverges (spreads out) parallel light rays so that they appear to come from a focal point on the other side of the lens.

FRESNEL LENS
French physicist Augustin Fresnel (1788-1827) invented a lens made from a series of glass rings. Fresnel lenses are not suitable for producing images because they distort too much, but they are good for concentrating light beams. They are often used in lighthouses, car headlights, and projectors.

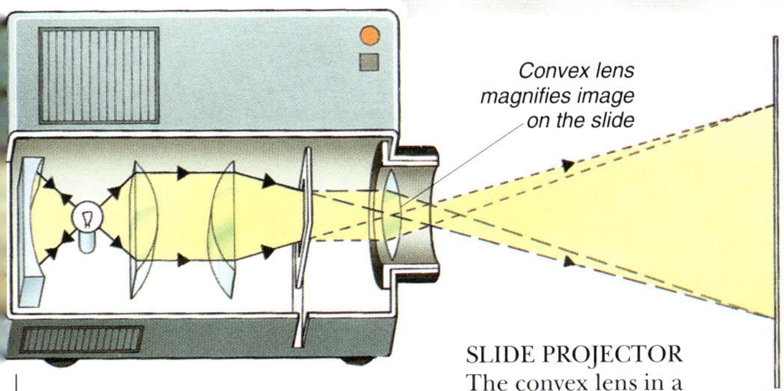

SLIDE PROJECTOR
The convex lens in a projector produces a magnified real image of the slide. The image is real because light passes through it and the image can be projected on a screen. The image is inverted (upside-down), so the slide must be put in upside-down to appear the right way up on the screen.

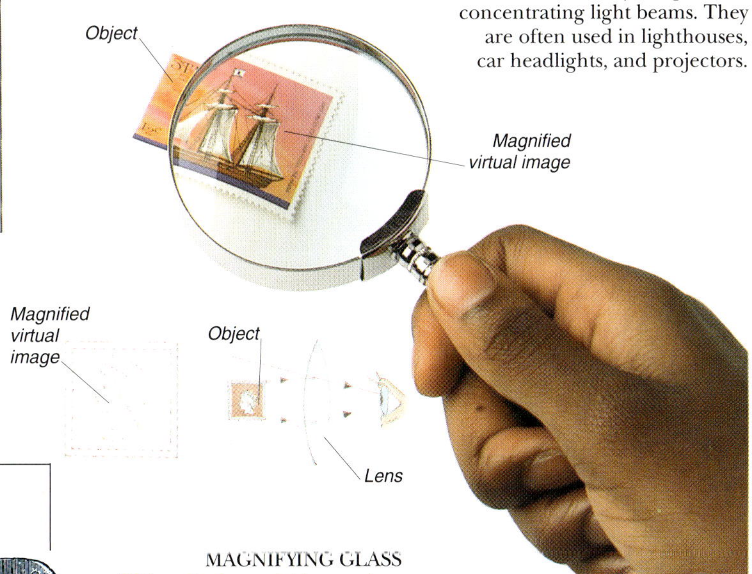

MAGNIFYING GLASS
Objects look much bigger when seen through the convex lens of a magnifying glass. Tracing the path of light beams through the lens shows how it produces a magnified virtual image of an object. The extent of the magnification depends on the focal length of the lens. The thicker the lens, the shorter the focal length. Lenses with shorter focal lengths are more powerful.

ANTONI VAN LEEUWENHOEK
Dutchman Antoni van Leeuwenhoek's (1632-1723) microscope made it possible to study bacteria and blood cells for the first time. This simple device was basically a powerful lens made from a glass bead mounted on a metal plate.

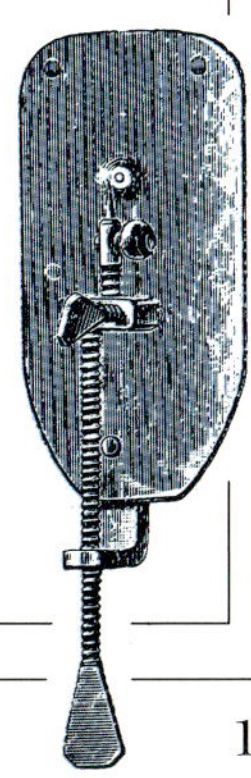

Find out more

POLYMERS P.100
GLASS P.110
OPTICAL INSTRUMENTS P.198
VISION P.204
PHOTOGRAPHY P.206

OPTICAL INSTRUMENTS

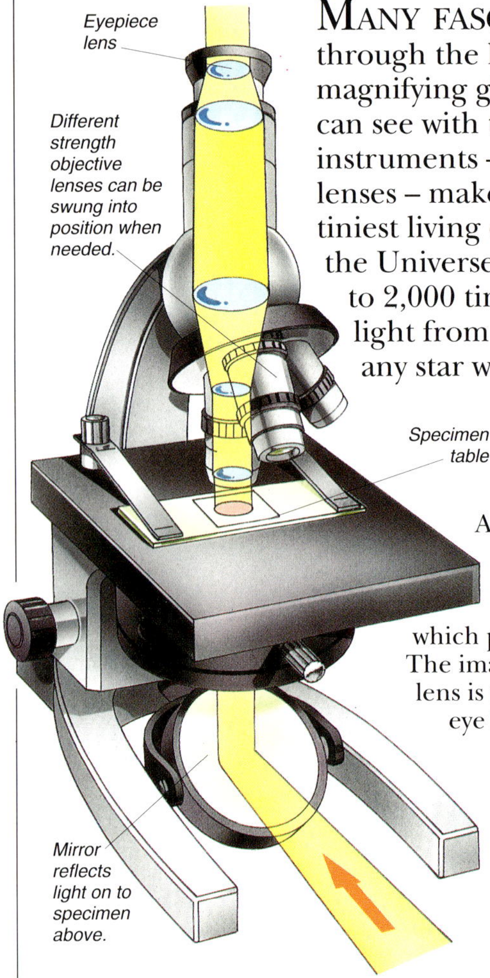

MANY FASCINATING DISCOVERIES have been made through the lens of an optical instrument. Even a simple magnifying glass reveals many times more detail than we can see with the naked eye. The more sophisticated instruments – made with a combination of mirrors and lenses – make it possible to study everything from the tiniest living organisms to the most distant objects in the Universe. Microscopes using light can magnify up to 2,000 times. Telescopes can capture and analyse light from objects a million times more distant than any star we can see in the night sky.

BINOCULARS
Binoculars consist of two refracting telescopes. Each contains an objective lens and eyepiece to form an image that appears much larger than the object being viewed.

COMPOUND MICROSCOPE

A compound microscope magnifies in two stages. Light from a mirror is reflected up through the specimen into the powerful objective lens, which produces the first magnification. The image produced by the objective lens is then magnified again by the eye lens, which acts as a simple magnifying glass.

Wasp at actual size

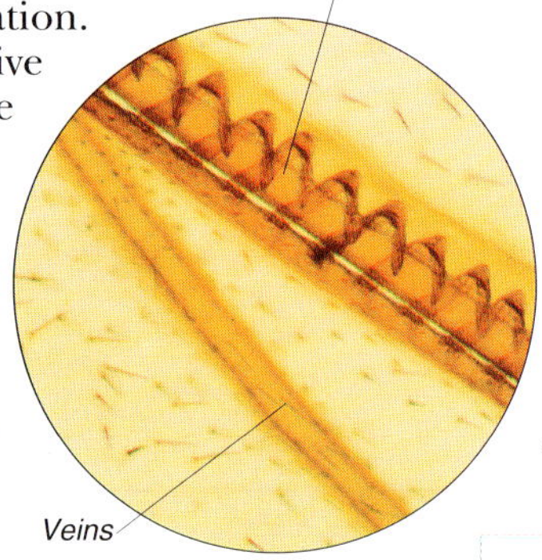

MICROSCOPE IMAGE
When a wasp's wing is magnified to 50 times its original size, details of the scales and veins are clearly visible. This photograph was taken through the lenses of a compound microscope.

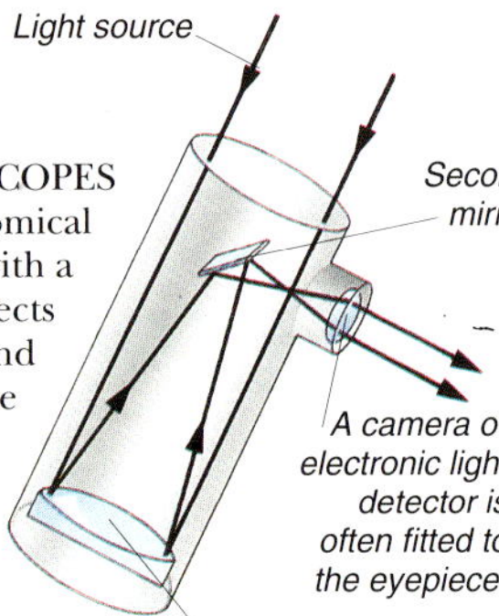

REFLECTING TELESCOPES
Most modern astronomical telescopes are reflectors, with a large concave mirror that collects and concentrates light. A second mirror reflects the light to the eye lens or camera.

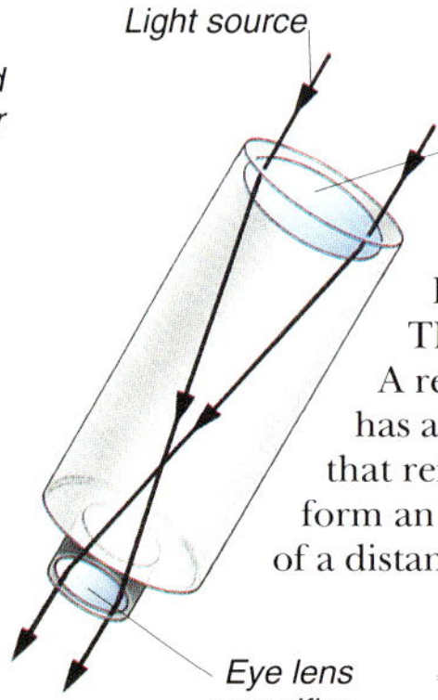

REFRACTING TELESCOPE
A refracting telescope has a large convex lens that refracts the light to form an upside-down image of a distant object.

IMPORTANT TELESCOPES

1789 William Herschel telescope, England, 1.23 m (4 ft) diameter.

1845 Lord Rosse telescope, Ireland, 1.83 m (6 ft) diameter.

1917 Mount Wilson telescope, California, USA, 2.54 m (8 ft) diameter.

1948 Hale Reflector, Palomar, California, USA, 5 m (16 ft) diameter.

1976 Mount Semirodriki telescope, CIS, 6 m (19.5 ft) diameter.

1992 Keck telescope, Hawaii, 10 m (33 ft) diameter.

HERSCHEL TELESCOPE
This 4.2 metre- (13 ft-) diameter reflecting telescope, named after William Herschel, has electronic cameras and computers to record and analyse starlight. It is situated in the clear atmosphere of the mountains of La Palma, one of the Canary Islands off Africa's northwest coast.

Find out more

REFLECTION P.194
REFRACTION P.196
LENSES P.197
STUDY OF ASTRONOMY P.296
TELESCOPES ON EARTH P.297
TELESCOPES IN SPACE P.298

LASERS

PENCIL BEAMS OF LASER LIGHT are now familiar sights at rock concerts. But as well as being used for entertainment, laser light is used in many practical ways, including eye surgery, surveying, cutting steel, carrying television and computer signals along optical fibres, and for reading information from bar codes and compact discs. The property of laser light that makes it so useful is its coherence (regularity). Ordinary light waves are jumbled and irregular, but laser light waves are all in step with each other – like marching soldiers. They can be directed in powerful beams that are both much brighter and more parallel than light from any other source.

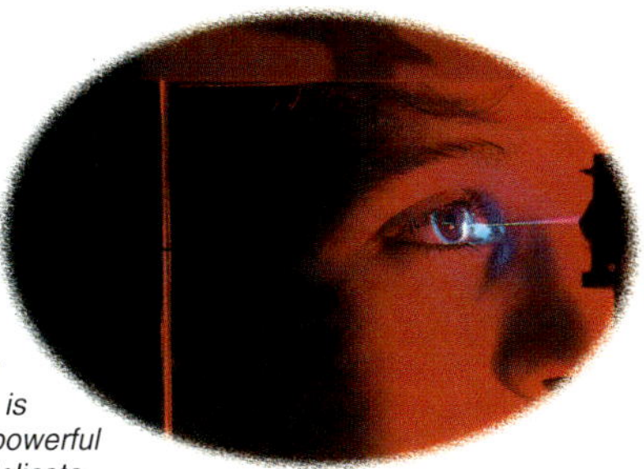

Laser beam is both powerful and delicate.

LASER SURGERY
Surgeons can control laser beams with great precision to make delicate cuts in the surface of a damaged eye or to burn cancer cells from a tumour.

Laser light can be produced by feeding energy into solids, liquids, or gases. The colour of laser light depends on the elements present in the material.

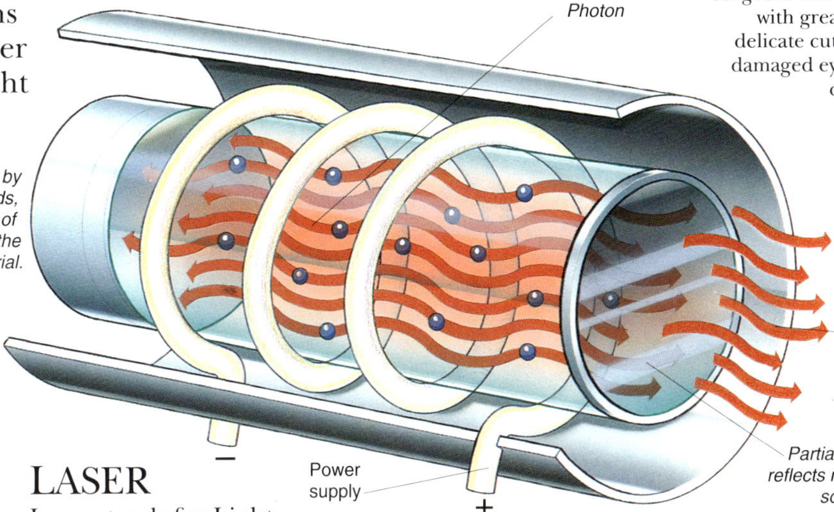

LASER

Laser stands for Light Amplification by the Stimulated Emission of Radiation. That is quite a mouthful! But what happens inside a laser is easily understood. Energy from a flash tube or an electric current excites atoms in the laser material. Some of the atoms emit photons which then stimulate more atoms to emit photons travelling in the same direction. Photons bounce up and down between the mirrors at either end of the tube.

SUPERMARKET CHECKOUT
The computerized information contained in the bar code of your shopping items is read by reflected laser light. The lasers in bar code readers are now made with semiconductors. Semiconductor lasers use much less power than the helium-neon gas lasers which were used in earlier machines.

INDUSTRIAL LASERS
High-power lasers cut through thick steel sheets as easily as a hot knife cuts through butter. Lasers are also valuable for surveying, because a laser beam travels in such a precise straight line. The course of the Channel Tunnel between France and England was plotted by laser.

THEODORE MAIMAN
The idea for the laser, which was based on Albert Einstein's theories of light, was developed by Gordon Gould in 1957. The first working laser was built by Theodore Maiman (born 1927) in 1960. Maiman's laser generated laser light by energizing a ruby crystal with light from a flash tube. Although only a few centimetres long, it worked very well.

A hologram is a 3-D picture taken with laser light. You can look around the image to view it from the side.

THREE-DIMENSIONAL IMAGES
An ordinary photograph is made by one set of light waves being reflected from the object on to film. But because laser light is so regular, it can be split into two to produce a three-dimensional (3-D) image. One set of waves is reflected by the object. The other set of waves arrives at the film from a different direction without meeting the object. Where the two sets of waves meet, an interference pattern is produced which is recorded on film. When the hologram is lit in the right way, a 3-D image is reproduced.

Find out more

SEMIMETALS P.39
NOBLE GASES P.48
SPEED P.118
CURRENT ELECTRICITY P.148
SOUND AND LIGHT P.177
LIGHT P.190

LIGHT AND MATTER

HAVE YOU EVER FELT THE HEAT given off by a tarmac road on a sunny day? The dark tarmac absorbs the light energy falling on it, and its temperature gradually rises. While black surfaces absorb light, white surfaces reflect light and heat up more slowly in the Sun. This is why light-coloured clothes are cooler than dark clothes in hot weather. As well as being absorbed or reflected, light can also be transmitted; it passes straight through transparent materials such as glass. The way that an object (matter) absorbs, reflects, or transmits light affects the way it looks.

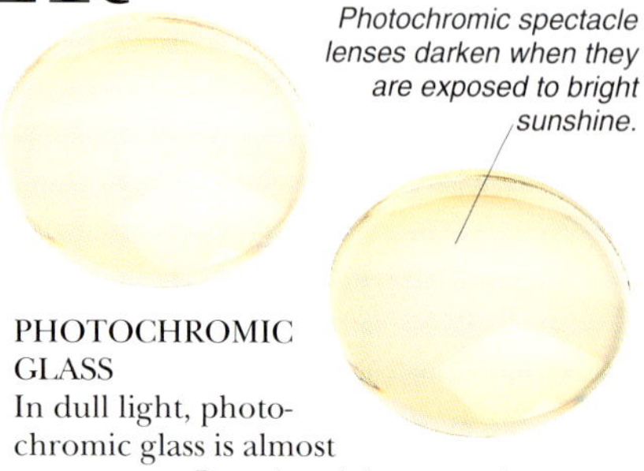

Photochromic spectacle lenses darken when they are exposed to bright sunshine.

PHOTOCHROMIC GLASS
In dull light, photochromic glass is almost transparent. But when it is exposed to brighter light, it darkens. The light energy changes the structure of some glass molecules so that they absorb more light. This process is reversible – away from bright light, the glass clears.

A transparent material transmits most of the light falling on it. A little is reflected, which is why we can see the surface of the glass.

A translucent material transmits light, but the light is scattered inside the material. This gives the material a milky appearance.

Light is reflected off the shiny spoon at the same angle as it arrives.

OPAQUE, TRANSPARENT, AND TRANSLUCENT

Everyday materials respond to light in different ways. Transparent materials transmit nearly all the light that falls on them. Other materials are translucent. Although they transmit light, the light is scattered in all directions by tiny particles inside the material. Opaque materials do not transmit any light. They either reflect it or absorb it.

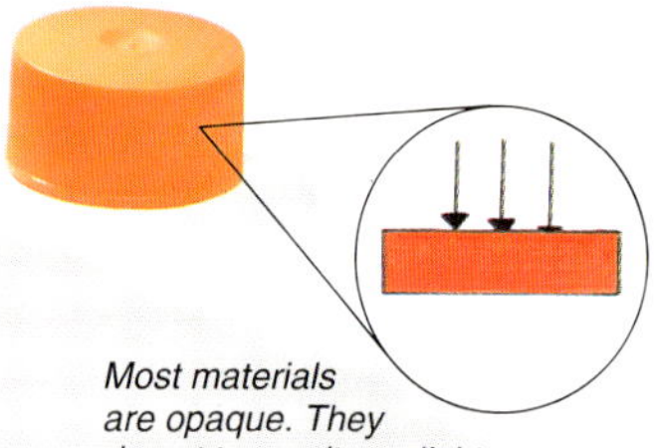

Most materials are opaque. They do not transmit any light and cast dark shadows.

FLUORESCENCE
Some chemicals absorb ultraviolet light and then release the energy as visible light. This is called fluorescence. These chemicals can be used to create "glowing" clothes, paints, crayons, and even make-up. Washing powder manufacturers put fluorescent chemicals in detergents to help white clothes appear even whiter in sunlight.

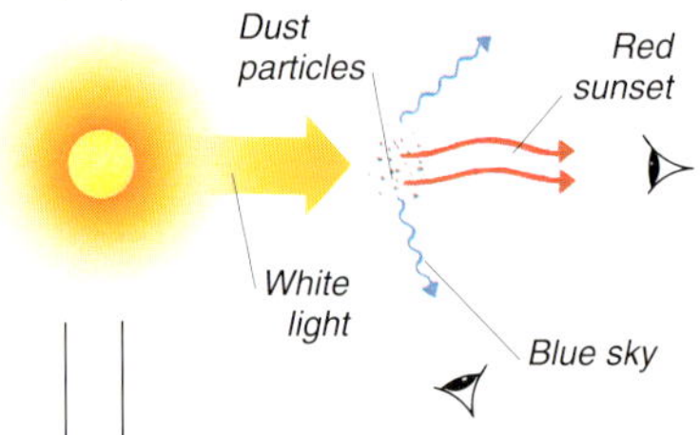

BLUE SKIES

Have you ever wondered why the sky appears blue? It looks blue because tiny particles of dust and water vapour in the atmosphere scatter the short wavelength blue light from the Sun more strongly than the longer wavelength red light. But when we look towards the setting Sun, we see the unscattered red light.

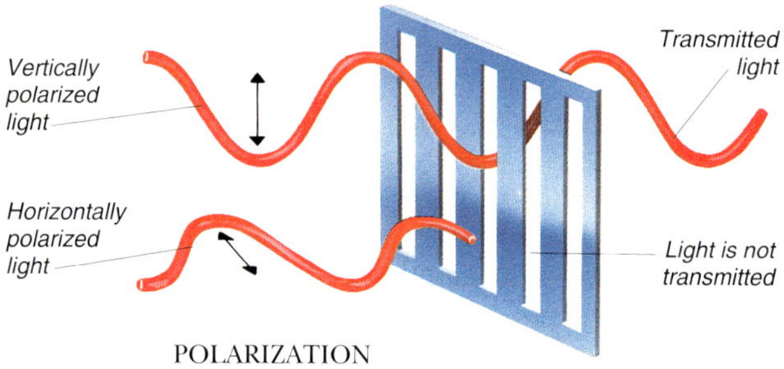

POLARIZATION
Light waves are transverse. This means that they vibrate at right angles to the direction in which they are travelling. Polarizing sunglasses only transmit light that is vibrating vertically. By absorbing horizontally polarized light, they help to reduce glare.

Find out more
SOUND P.178
ELECTROMAGNETIC SPECTRUM P.192
REFLECTION P.194
REFRACTION P.196

SHADOWS

SUNDIAL
The shadow cast by a sundial moves as the Sun appears to move through the sky. The motion of the shadow can be used to tell the time. The first sundials, which consisted of simple vertical poles, were used more than 4,000 years ago in China.

SHADOWS ARE FORMED because light rays travel in straight lines and cannot bend around opaque objects in their path. The sharpness of a shadow depends on the light source. A point (small, concentrated) source casts sharp shadows. An extended (large) source casts fuzzy shadows. The Sun is almost a point source because it is so far away; the shadows it casts are quite sharp at the edges. A more extended light source, such as a fluorescent tube, casts less distinct shadows. Perhaps the most spectacular shadows of all are eclipses – the shadows cast by the Earth and the Moon on each other when they block the light from the Sun.

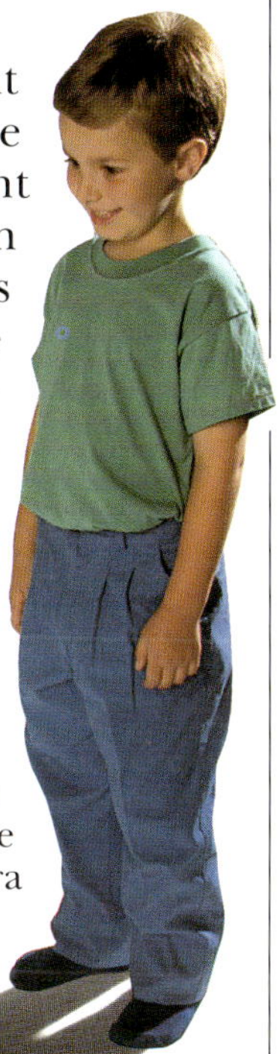

SHADOWS

When the Sun is directly overhead, it does not cast a shadow. But when it is lower in the sky, shadows lengthen and are much longer than the objects producing them. There are two parts to the shadow cast by the Sun – the umbra and the penumbra. The umbra is the region where the object blocks all of the Sun's light. The penumbra is where the object blocks light coming from some parts of the Sun but not from others.

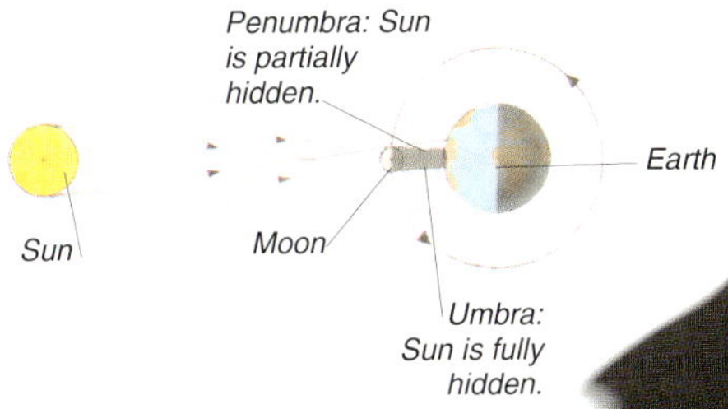

SOLAR ECLIPSE
During an eclipse of the Sun, the Moon passes between the Sun and the Earth, casting its shadow on the Earth's surface. At points lying in the penumbra, the eclipse is partial, and the Sun is only partly hidden. But in the umbra, day becomes night for a few minutes as the Sun disappears.

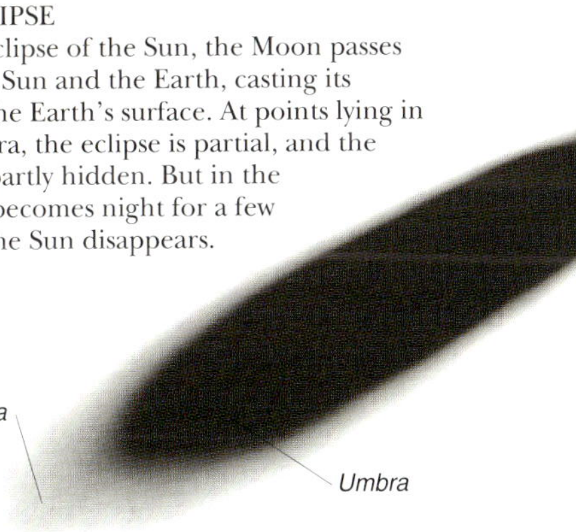

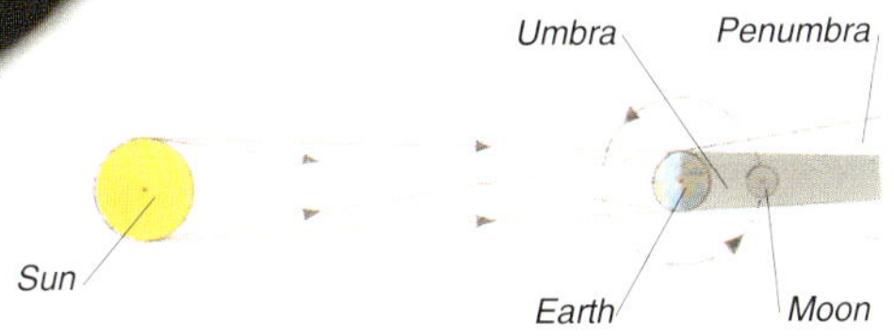

LUNAR ECLIPSE
Sometimes the Earth passes between the Sun and the Moon. This is called a lunar eclipse. When this happens, we see the Earth's shadow as it moves across the face of the Moon. At the centre of the eclipse, the Moon is blocked from view for more than an hour.

SOLAR CORONA
During a total eclipse, the Sun's atmosphere, called the solar corona, is visible. Scientists are able to study the activity of the gases in the corona. Prominences, which are normally invisible because they are swamped by sunlight, can be seen hanging above the Sun's surface.

ECLIPSES AND MYTHS

Before the scientific explanation was found, an eclipse was a frightening event. It seemed to early civilizations that a monster was swallowing the Sun. But as science developed, and astronomical records were kept, it became clear that the eclipses were regular events that could be predicted.

Find out more

LIGHT P.190
LIGHT AND MATTER P.200
SUN P.284
MOON P.288
STUDY OF ASTRONOMY P.296

COLOUR

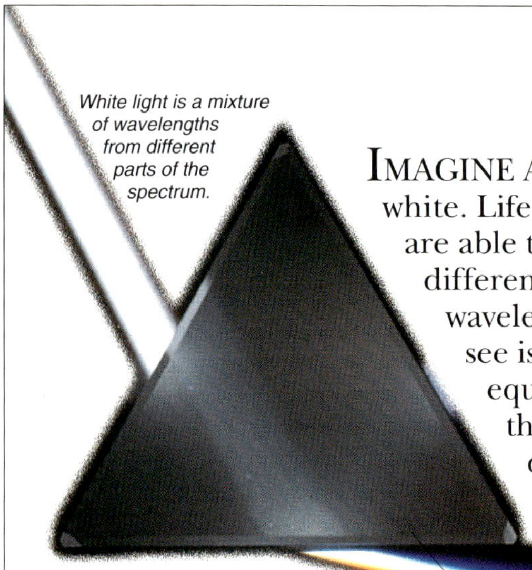

IMAGINE A WORLD in which everything was the "colour" of daylight – white. Life would be very drab. Luckily, our world is colourful. Our eyes are able to distinguish the different wavelengths of visible light as different colours. Each wavelength of light, or combination of wavelengths, is a particular colour. The longest wavelength that we can see is red light, and the shortest wavelengths are blue and violet. If equal amounts of all the wavelengths of light are mixed together, the result is white light. Many animals cannot distinguish between different wavelengths, so they live in a world in which everything is colourless.

RAINBOW COLOURS

The different colours that make up white light can be seen when a beam of light is split by a prism. The prism refracts the different wavelengths by different amounts, and disperses them (spreads them out) into a spectrum so that they can be seen. Red light is refracted least, violet light the most.

White light contains all the colours of the spectrum.

Magenta filter transmits red and blue light but absorbs green.

Green filter transmits only the green region. It absorbs red and blue regions.

FILTERS

A filter is a plastic sheet that absorbs some colours but lets others pass through. For example, a green filter absorbs the red and blue parts of the spectrum but transmits the green region. A magenta filter absorbs green light and transmits red and blue.

INTERFERENCE COLOURS

The brilliant colours you sometimes see on bubbles are caused by light interference. White light rays reflected from the inside of the soap film travel slightly further than those reflected from the outside. The waves in each ray interfere with each other where they meet. Some colours cancel each other out, while others combine to form bands of colours on the surface of the bubble.

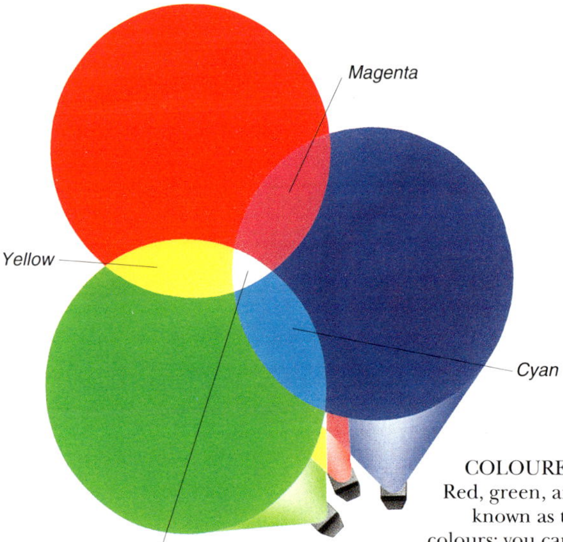

White light can be made by adding together just red, green, and blue light.

COLOURED LIGHTS

Red, green, and blue are known as the primary colours: you can mix these coloured lights together to make almost any other colour. If red, green, and blue lights are mixed together, we see them as white light. Where two primary colours overlap, they produce a secondary colour. Red and blue make magenta. Red and green make yellow. Green and blue make cyan.

Bar is emitting waves just within the red end of the visible spectrum.

As the bar is heated more, the hottest part of it turns yellow.

The bar is now emitting most colours of the visible spectrum, which add together to give white.

COLOUR TEMPERATURE

All objects give out electromagnetic waves. But they are often invisible to the eye. Heating an object gives the waves more energy, and they become shorter – short enough for us to see. At first, the heated steel bar above glows dull red. As it gets hotter, it turns to yellow. At the highest temperature, the bar gives out most colours of the visible spectrum, which mix together to give white.

Find out more

LIGHT P.190
ELECTROMAGNETIC SPECTRUM P.192
SOURCES OF LIGHT P.193
SPECIAL EFFECTS P.269

COLOUR SUBTRACTION

OBJECTS THAT DO NOT PRODUCE light themselves are coloured by a process called "colour subtraction". They subtract (absorb) light from some parts of the visible spectrum but not others. For example, a leaf looks green because it absorbs nearly all the colours in sunlight except one – green, which it reflects. Pigments and dyes are natural or artificial substances added to paints and inks to give them colour. A red pigment absorbs green and blue and reflects only red light. A blue pigment absorbs red and green light and reflects blue. By taking away colour, these substances actually add colour to our world!

Chameleon

NATURAL PIGMENTATION
The chameleon has pigmented skin cells that change size and shape to blend in with the colour of the background. In this way, it is excellently camouflaged when danger threatens. Cuttlefish have evolved a "language" based on patterns of colour change that ripple across their bodies.

When the colour images are printed on top of each other, a full-colour picture is reproduced.

Yellow

Magenta

Cyan

Black is treated as a separate colour so that text and outlines are reproduced sharply.

FOUR-COLOUR PRINTING

All colour photographs and illustrations are reproduced from just four coloured inks – magenta, cyan, yellow, and black. Mixing these colours in different proportions produces all the different colours you can see. When a book or magazine is prepared for printing, the colour images are scanned to separate the four colours photographically. The films are used to prepare a printing plate for each colour.

Yellow absorbs blue light, so reflects a mixture of red and green.

Magenta absorbs green light, so reflects a mixture of red and blue.

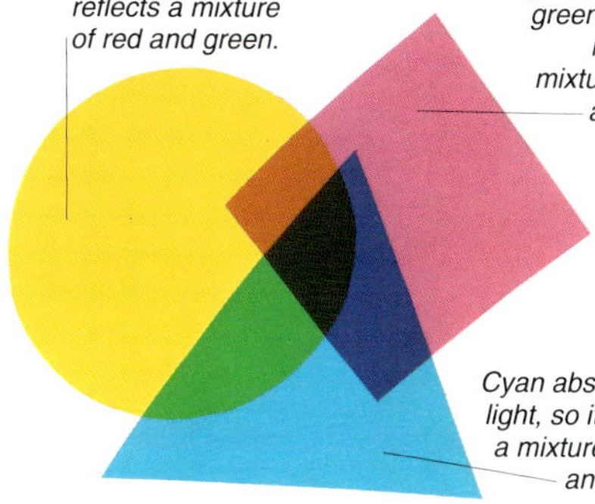

Cyan absorbs red light, so it reflects a mixture of blue and green.

MIXING PAINT
Colour mixing with paint works by subtraction. Magenta, cyan, and yellow ink absorb just one primary colour each from white light. Mixing any two of these colours produces a bright, primary-coloured paint. Mixing all three colours together produces black.

MUNSELL COLOUR TREE

If you have ever tried to match a colour exactly, you know how difficult it can be. Our eyes are incredibly sensitive to very slight colour differences. In fact, we can probably distinguish more than 10,000,000 various shades! The Munsell colour tree is a system of grading colours. The hue (basic colour), chroma (amount of colour), and value (lightness or darkness) are measured. Each colour is then put in position on the tree. Hue is shown by its place on the circumference; chroma by its distance from the trunk, and value by its position on the trunk.

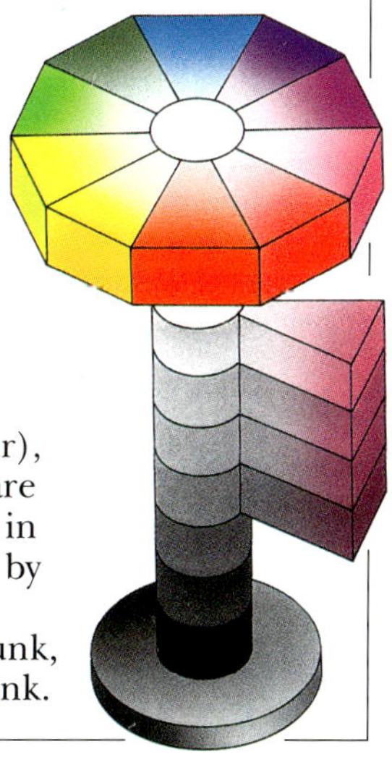

In daylight, sneakers reflect only red light and absorb all the other colours.

In blue light, the red pigment absorbs the blue light.

RED OR BLACK SHOES?
The sneakers above appear red in daylight or when lit by red light because they reflect only red light and absorb all the others. But what happens when they are lit by blue light? They look black (above right). This is because the red pigment in the sneakers absorbs all the blue light and there is no red light in the light source to be reflected.

Find out more

DYES AND PIGMENTS P.102
ELECTROMAGNETIC SPECTRUM P.192
REFLECTION P.194
COLOUR P.202

VISION

THE WAY THAT OUR EYES AND BRAIN work together to produce images is incredibly sophisticated. Imagine building a robot that could track a tiny baseball, hit at 160 km (100 miles) per hour into the air and run across a field to make a one-handed catch. The robot would need *at least* two eyes to see in three dimensions to judge the distance to the ball. But most important of all would be the robot's brain – the computer that interprets the images that the eyes create. When it comes to recognizing images, the human brain is still far more powerful than even the most powerful computers.

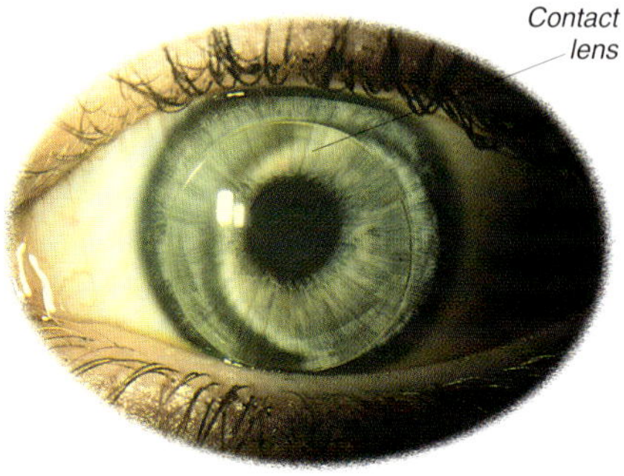

CONTACT LENSES

As an alternative to spectacles, many people wear contact lenses – thin lenses that fit over the cornea. These correct vision defects in the same way as conventional spectacles, but are virtually invisible. Modern lenses are made from a soft, almost jelly-like, material that floats on the surface of the eye.

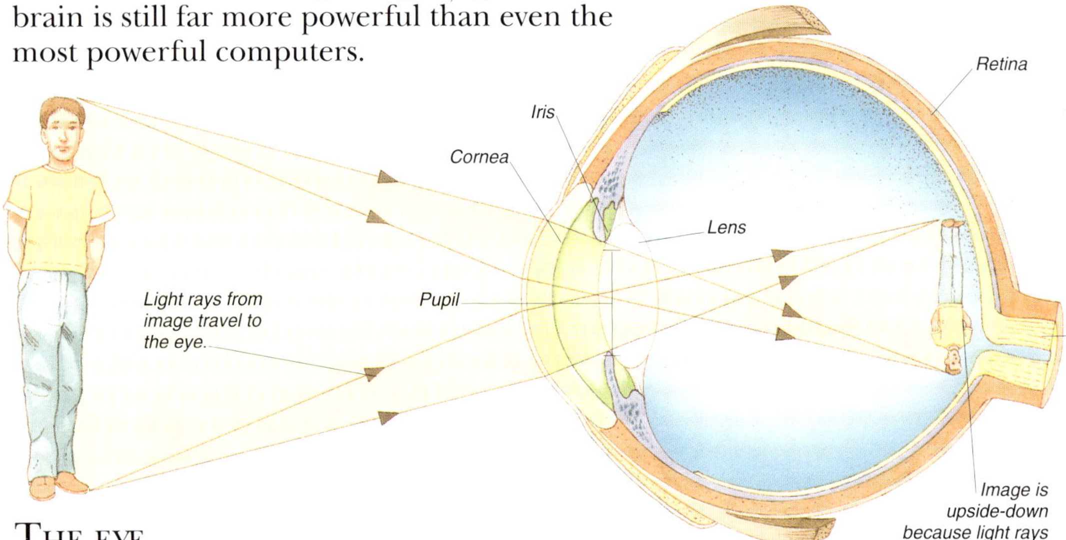

THE EYE

The human eye is a tough ball filled with fluid that sits in a bony socket. The cornea is the transparent, protective surface of the eye. It also focuses light. The iris controls the amount of light passing through the pupil. It closes up the pupil in bright light and opens it wide in dim light. The lens helps to focus light on the retina, which contains a layer of light-sensitive cells. These send signals via the optic nerve to the brain where they are interpreted to build up our view of the world.

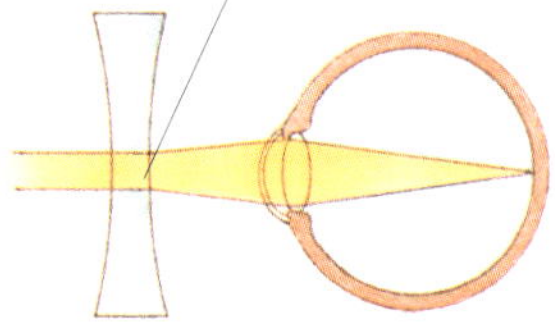

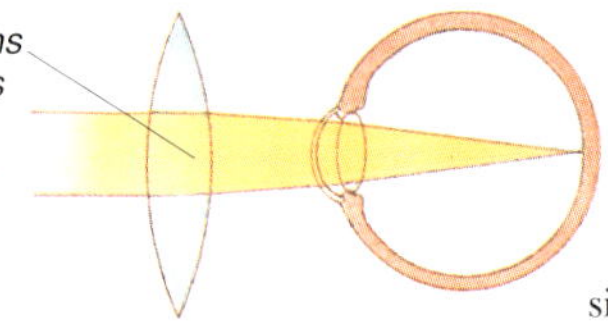

LONG AND SHORT SIGHT

Muscles change the shape of the lens to focus light onto the retina. In long-sighted people, the muscles are unable to make the lens strong enough; light rays are focused *behind* the retina. In short-sighted people, the muscles cannot relax the lens enough; light rays are focused *in front* of the retina. Lenses can correct both these conditions.

Chess board seen through left eye

Chess board seen through right eye

STEREO VISION

Having two eyes helps you to judge the distance to an object by giving you two view points. If you look at your finger, first through one eye and then through the other, it seems to move. The movement gets bigger as you move the finger closer to your eyes. Our brains combine our right- and left-eye views into a single 3-D image.

OPTICAL ILLUSIONS

Much of the information we gather from an image is based on our knowledge of how things *should* look. We judge the distance to an object because we are familiar with its size and know how big it should be at a certain distance. But we can be fooled! An optical illusion misleads us about the relative size or distance of an object by placing it in an unexpected situation. The two balls here look the same size, but the one behind is a football, the one in front, a golf ball.

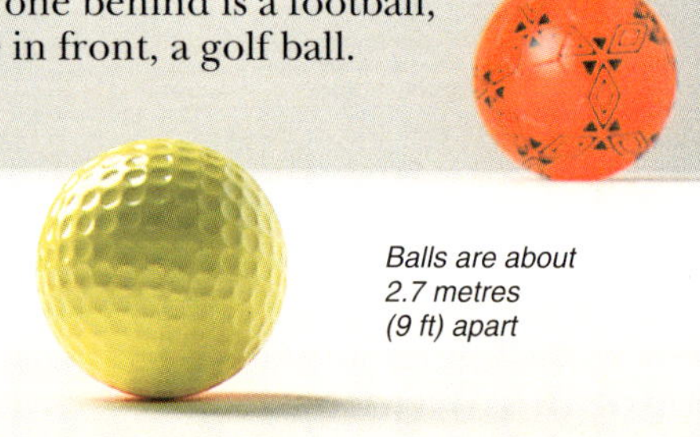

Balls are about 2.7 metres (9 ft) apart

Darkroom

A film is coated with chemicals that are sensitive to light, which is why film developing and printing has to be carried out in a darkroom. Producing a black and white photograph is a two-stage process – each stage consisting of several steps. When print film is developed, the result is a negative image. This then has to be turned into a positive image by printing it on photographic paper.

PHOTOGRAPHY LANDMARKS

1822 Joseph Nicéphore Niepce takes first photograph.

1839 Louis Daguerre takes first photograph of a person.

1841 William Fox-Talbot invents positive-negative process that allows photographs to be copied.

1861 James Clerk Maxwell takes the first colour photograph.

1888 George Eastman forms Kodak company to market flexible roll films and low-cost box cameras.

1948 Edwin Land markets the Polaroid instant picture camera.

DEVELOPING
The exposed film is taken out of its case and wound on a reel. It is then immersed in a tank containing chemicals that develop the image. The film is rinsed, after which more chemicals that fix the image are added.

ENLARGING AND PRINTING
After the negative has been rinsed and dried, it can be printed. The negative is placed in an enlarger. Light is shone through the negative, and a lens produces an enlarged image on light-sensitive paper. The print is then developed and fixed in the same way as the film.

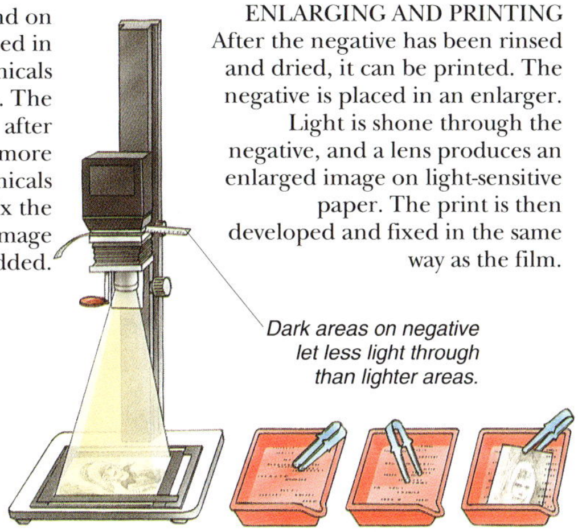

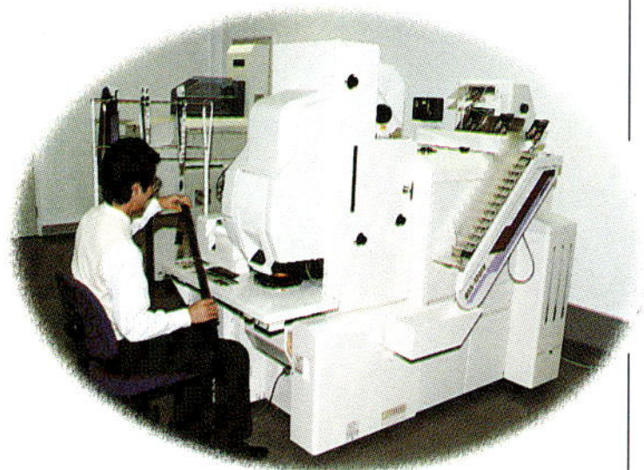

COLOUR PROCESSING
Colour film works in a similar way to black and white film, but the film has three layers, each of which is sensitive to either blue, green, or red light. When the film is processed, yellow, magenta, and cyan dyes are added to the layers. The result is a full-colour image.

JOSEPH NICÉPHORE NIEPCE

The first photographic image was produced by Joseph Nicéphore Niepce (1765-1833). He focused the view from his window onto a pewter sheet coated with light-sensitive bitumen and left it for eight hours. Niepce's partner, Louis Daguerre (1787-1851) later developed a more sensitive process (the Daguerreotype), requiring less than a minute's exposure.

COLOUR POSITIVE AND NEGATIVE
There are two kinds of colour film. When a colour positive film is processed, it reproduces the colours it was exposed to and gives a colour transparency or slide. When a colour negative is printed, the result is a negative image, which is then turned into a positive image by printing it on photographic paper.

POLAROID FILM
A Polaroid film produces almost instant pictures. When the exposed film is pulled from the pack, rollers squeeze chemicals onto the surface of the film and the image develops in about a minute. The film itself has nine separate layers, including three light-sensitive layers. Cyan, yellow, and magenta dyes spread through the image as it develops.

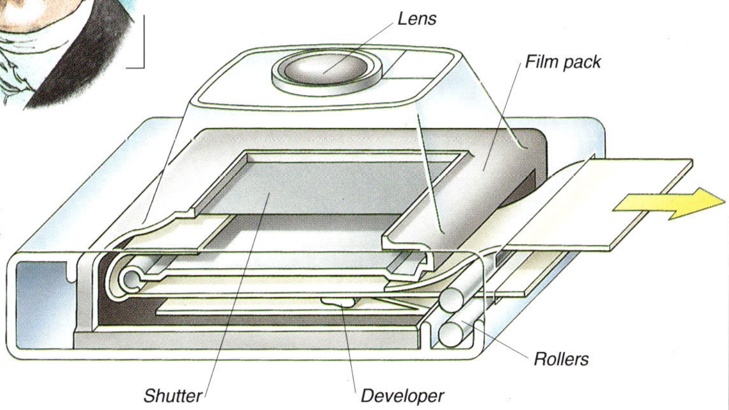

Find out more

Transition metals p.36
Halogens p.46
Lenses p.197
Colour p.202
Vision p.204
Fact finder p.412

Cinema

THE NOVELTY of being able to record images on film was so exciting that people soon began looking for a way to record *moving* images. The very first "movies" were made by Thomas Edison in 1893. But these 15-second films could only be seen by one person at a time through a machine called a kinetoscope. Two French brothers, Auguste and Louis Lumière, were the first to show a moving picture to an audience in 1895. Early films were flickery, black and white, and silent. The first Hollywood movie with a sound track was not shown until 1927; colour movie film became available in the 1930s. Today's filmakers not only have the creative ability to tell a story, they also understand the science of sound and light.

CINE FILM
Cinema film, or "cine" film, is actually a series of still photographs taken rapidly one after the other. A modern cine camera takes 24 frames (photographs) each second. When the images are projected at the same rate onto a screen, the illusion of movement is created.

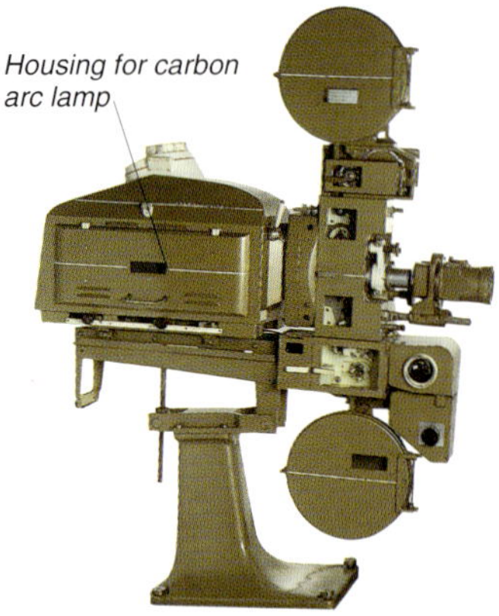

CINE PROJECTOR
Intense white light is generated when an electric current flows across a small gap between two carbon rods. A carbon arc lamp in this 1950s cine projector produced enough light to project a bright image onto a large screen.

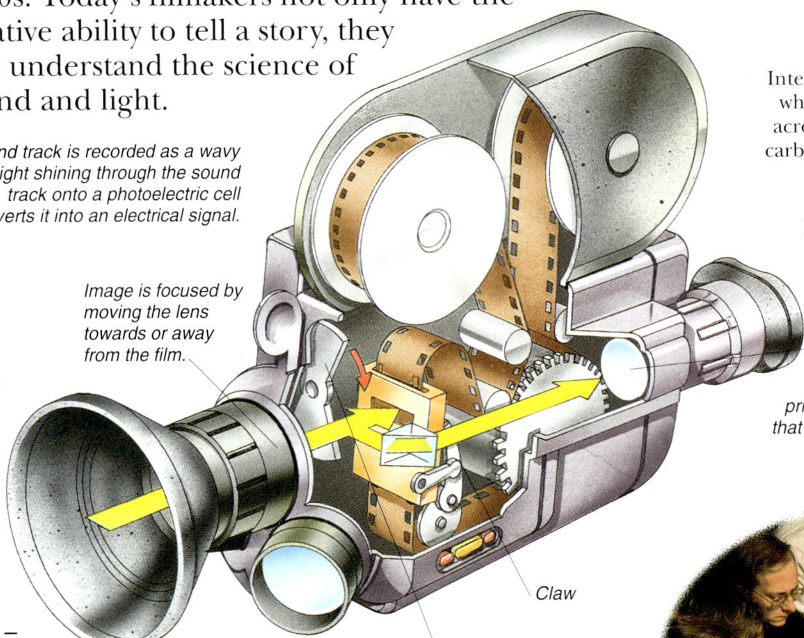

Cine camera

When the camera is running, the shutter rotates – opening and shutting 24 times a second to expose each frame of the film in turn. When the shutter is closed, a special mechanism called a claw hooks into the slots at the edge of the film and drags the next frame down into the gate to be exposed. The jerky motion of the claw and film makes the whirring noise you hear whenever a film camera or a projector is working.

FILM EDITING
Many more minutes of film are shot than are used in the final movie – and they are never shot in sequence! The film editor has to assemble the individual shots and link them together in the right order so that the film tells a story. This involves cutting up lengths of film and sticking them together with tape.

ZOETROPE
The zoetrope was a slotted drum lined with images. As it spun round, each picture was seen for a fraction of a second through a slot. If the drum spun fast enough, the pictures merged together and appeared to move.

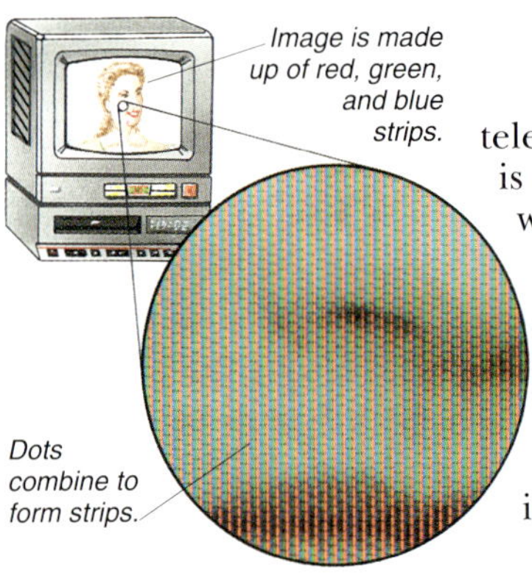

TV and video

Movement on the television and video screen is created in just the same way as cinema film. Most televisions show a complete picture 25 times every second. If you look at a television screen with a magnifying glass, you can see it is made up of tiny red, green, and blue dots.

Find out more

TELEVISION P.166
SOUND RECORDING P.188
LIGHT P.190
PHOTOGRAPHY P.206

EARTH

OF ALL THE PLANETS that have been discovered so far, Earth is the only one that contains life. From above, the Earth is seen as a mass of land, sea, and air. Each of these is changeable depending on the movement within Earth, and the energy from the Sun. The study of the Earth is ongoing, and scientists are constantly making new discoveries. The study of geology was once known as the observation of the rocks. However, during the late 20th century, geology began to broaden to the study of Earth and of all the sciences that deal with the Earth, known as "Earth sciences". This incorporates parts of modern technology, chemistry, physics, biology, and the applied sciences. Together, these teach us about the Earth.

A close look at minerals reveals the chemistry of the Earth and the different substances that are produced by geological processes. This is important in mining. The study of minerals is known as mineralogy.

Different types of minerals form different rocks. We use different kinds of rocks for buildings, for road surfacing, or as raw materials for chemicals. The study of rocks is known as petrology.

Skyscrapers are built of stone removed from the rocks, around frameworks of steel obtained from iron ore, and windows of glass made from sand. Oil is used to power the builders' machines. The use of geological principles to find usable materials is known as economic geology.

We must understand the structure of the rocks to discover how safe the foundations are before sinking our buildings into them, or tunnelling through mountains. The study of how rocks move and change shape is known as structural geology.

The location of farmland or towns depends on the geography and landforms of an area. The study of landforms produced by the rocks and their structures is known as geomorphology.

EARTH SCIENCE

Earth science includes the study of atoms and molecules in geochemistry, and of galaxies in cosmology. In this century, a vast range of information about the Earth has been collected by geographers, geologists, oceanographers, climatologists, astronomers, and so on. We are gradually relating all these new facts to one another, building a clear picture of the structure of the Earth and its evolution through time.

We can compare the geology of our home planet with that of our nearest neighbours, and contrast their histories. The study of the planets, including the Earth, is known as planetology.

This map of the world is dated Antwerpen, 1598.

OLD IDEAS OF THE EARTH

Some Hindus, about 1,500 years ago, believed that the world was supported on four elephants standing on a giant turtle. Myths such as these of how the Earth was created are part of the tradition and early scientific thought of any civilization. As technology advances, so does our knowledge of how the Earth formed. Every new investigation and analysis brings us closer to understanding our planet and everything it contains.

EARLY MAP

The 15th and 16th centuries were a time of exploration. Sailors set out from Europe to find new lands, to expand trading empires, and to circumnavigate (sail around) the globe. The observations that they made, the specimens they collected, and the tales that they brought back provided the foundations of the earliest understanding of the Earth.

FORMATION OF THE EARTH

AROUND 5,000 MILLION YEARS AGO, the Earth was no more than a spinning cloud of gas and dust in space, part of a much, much bigger cloud. Most of the material in this big cloud clumped together at the centre to form the Sun. Across the rest of the cloud, rings of material started to clump together to form planets, one of which was the Earth. Like all planets, the Earth has a layered structure, with lighter material on the outside and heavier material at the core. The original spin of the whole cloud is seen in the way Earth moves.

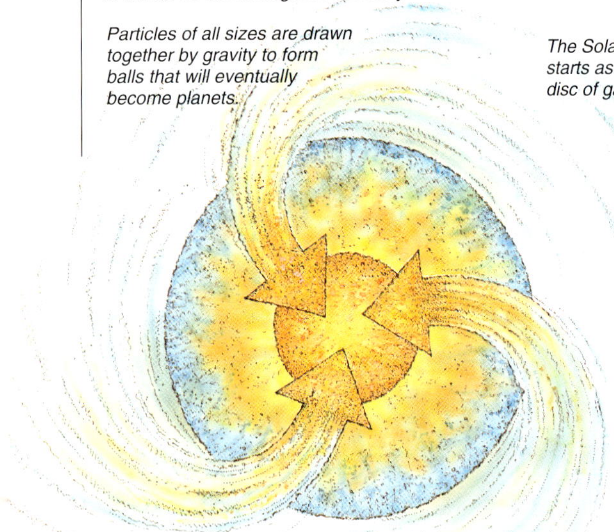

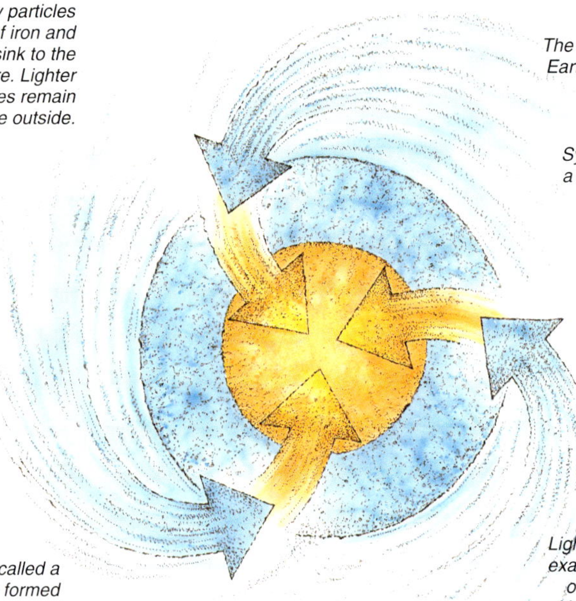

TWO THEORIES

Scientists are not quite sure just how a swirling cloud of gas and dust solidified to form the Earth. There are two theories. In the first, the homogeneous theory, the material that formed the Earth clumped together, and then separated out into different layers, with the lightest on the top. In the second, the heterogeneous theory, the core formed first from heavy materials, and then lighter materials gathered around it.

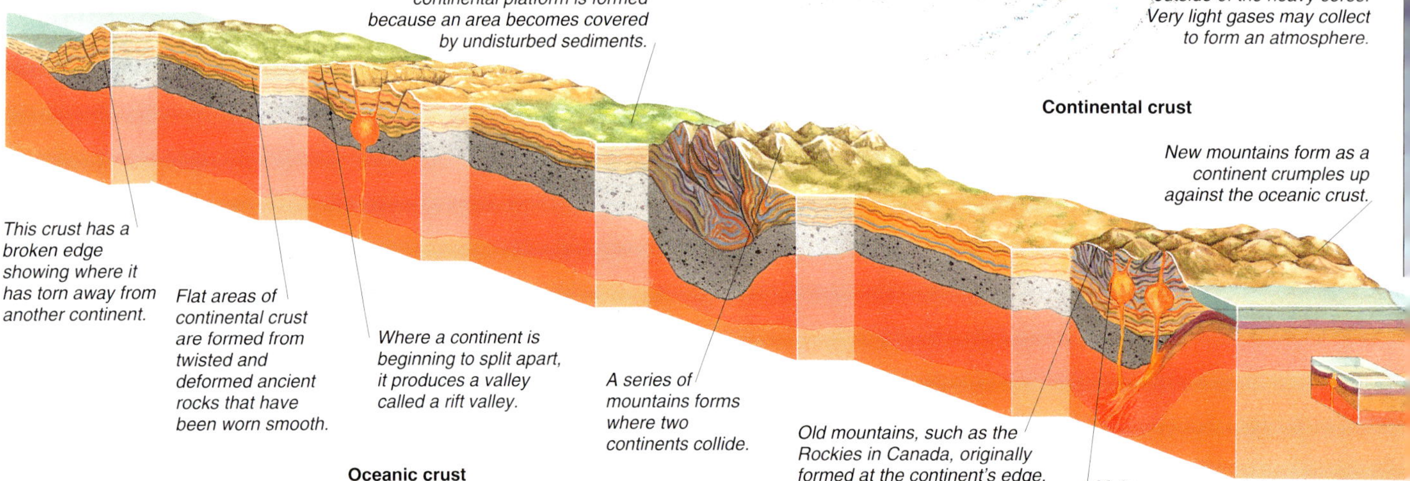

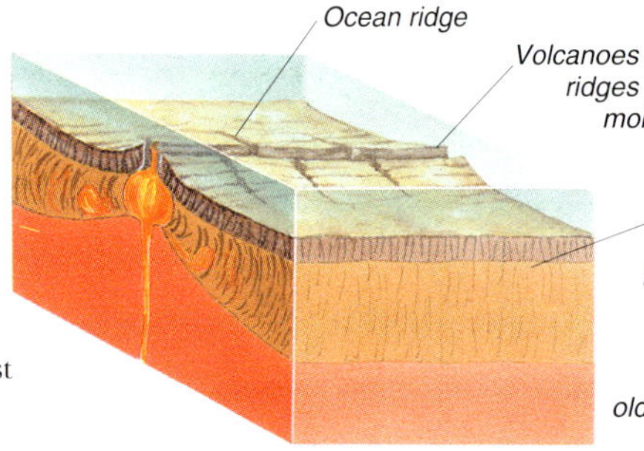

OCEANIC CRUST

The outermost layer of the Earth that lies beneath the oceans is called the oceanic crust. This crust is continually being produced by volcanoes at ridges under the ocean that push out molten rock. Older crust is destroyed as it drops into trenches beneath the ocean. The ocean crust is made up mainly of silica and magnesium (or SIMA for short).

CONTINENTAL CRUST

The outside layer of the Earth that forms the land masses is called the continental crust. It is mostly made of ancient rocks, with newer material that has clumped as mountain ranges around the edges. Each continent's complicated history is shown by its broken and twisted structure. The continental crust is made up mainly of silica and aluminium (or SIAL for short).

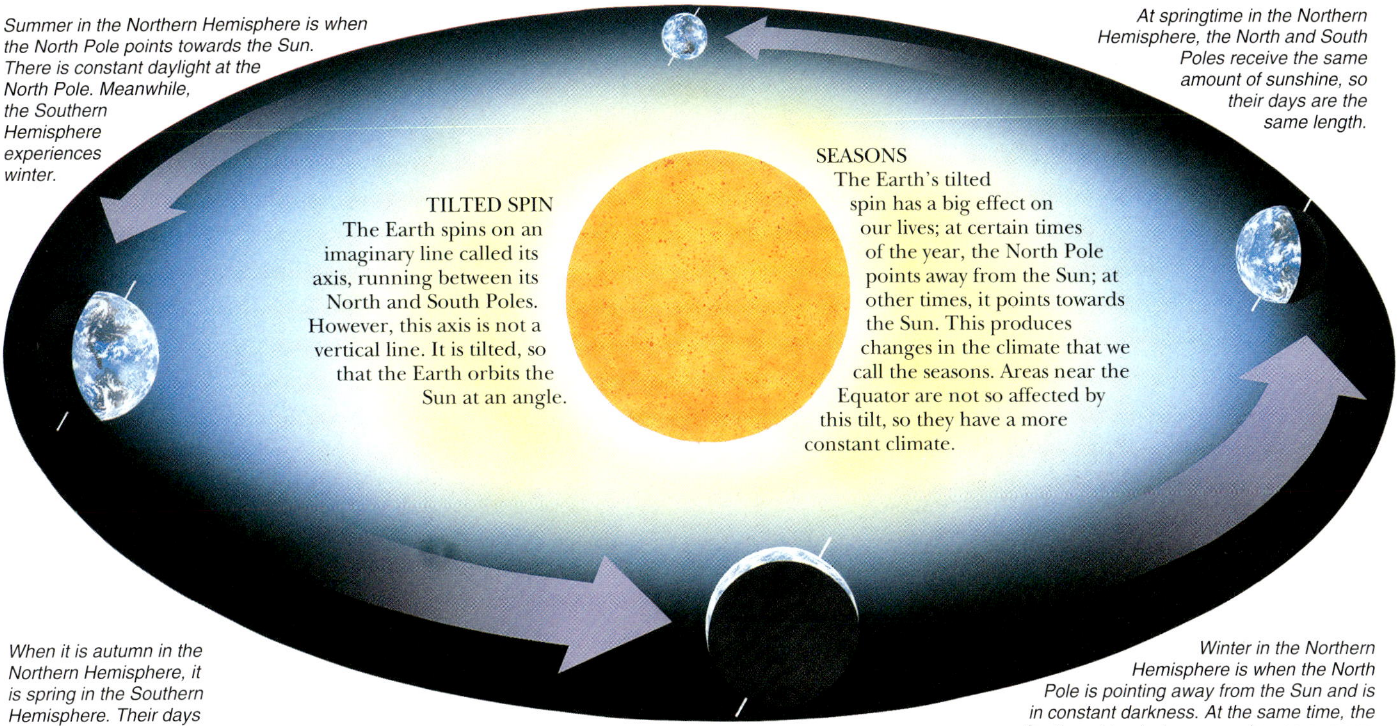

TILTED SPIN

The Earth spins on an imaginary line called its axis, running between its North and South Poles. However, this axis is not a vertical line. It is tilted, so that the Earth orbits the Sun at an angle.

SEASONS

The Earth's tilted spin has a big effect on our lives; at certain times of the year, the North Pole points away from the Sun; at other times, it points towards the Sun. This produces changes in the climate that we call the seasons. Areas near the Equator are not so affected by this tilt, so they have a more constant climate.

Spinning Earth

You might think you are standing still, but the Earth you are standing on is continually spinning in space; it is not only circling the Sun, but it is spinning on its own axis as well. A year is the time the Earth takes to make one complete circuit around the Sun. A day is the time the Earth takes to make one complete turn on its axis. When the part of Earth you are on is facing the Sun, it is day; when it is facing away from the Sun, it is night.

BULGING TUMMY

The Earth is not a perfect sphere shape. It bulges slightly in the middle. As the Earth spins, places on the Equator move much faster than places near the Poles. The faster the rotation, the stronger the force, called the centrifugal effect, which pushes material out from the centre of rotation. This is what happens when you spin around, and your hair is thrown outwards. This means the Earth is pushed out most around its middle.

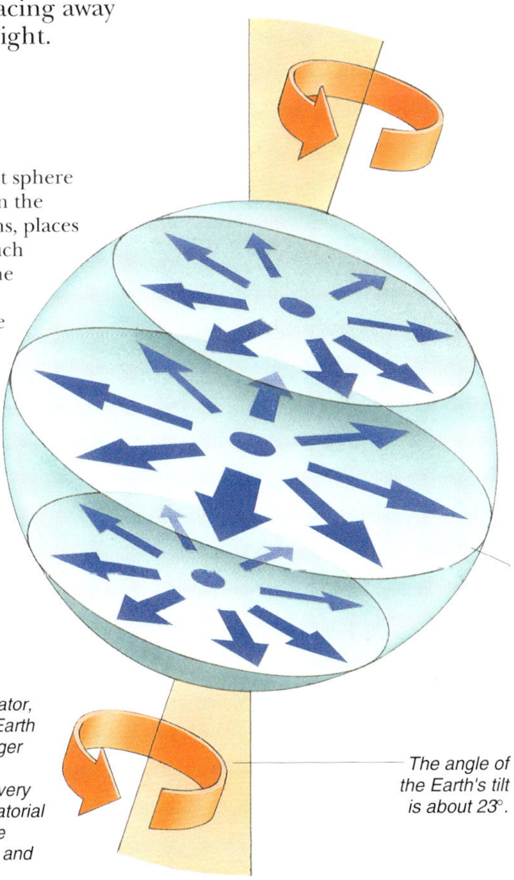

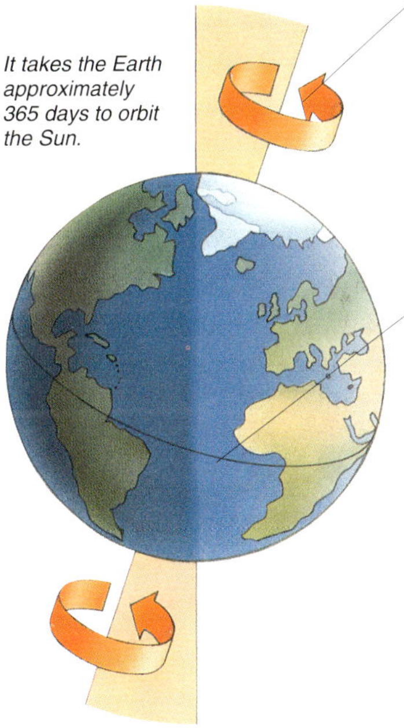

LONGER YEARS

The spin of Earth on its axis is very, very gradually slowing down. This is because of the friction of the tides dragging water back and forth around the surface. From growth lines on coral, scientists have worked out that 400 million years ago, a year was about 400 days long. This was because the Earth was spinning faster then, and so produced shorter days.

Find out more

Magnetism p.154
Structure of the Earth p.212
Rocks and minerals p.221
Origin of the universe p.275
Earth p.287

STRUCTURE OF THE EARTH

The Earth's layers

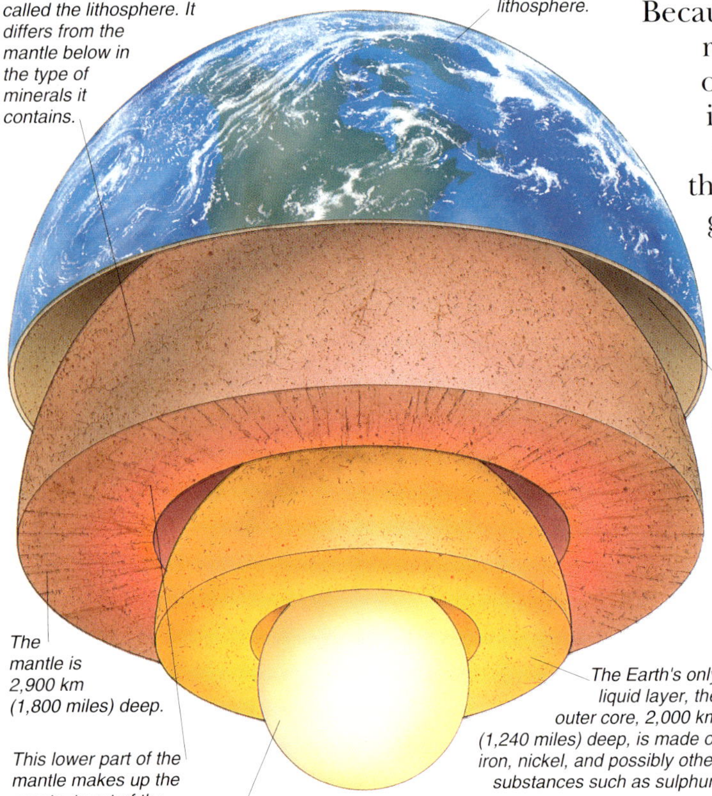

WHEN YOU PEEL AN APPLE, you remove only a thin, outer covering. Similarly, the surface of the Earth is only a thin layer compared to what is below. Because of the Earth's immense size, drilling does not reveal much of exactly what lies beneath. Instead, other methods have been used to discover what is inside the Earth. Most of what we know has come from the study of earthquake vibrations that run through the Earth. Over the years this has enabled geologists to build up a picture of a multi-layered Earth with a solid metal centre surrounded by lighter materials. The more that is known about the structure of the Earth, the more we are able to understand about the way it works.

Earthquake vibrations

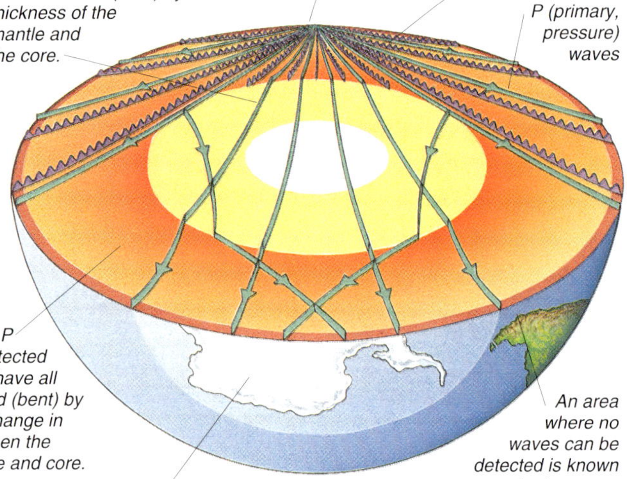

LAYER UPON LAYER

The Earth is made up of three main layers – the crust, the mantle, and the core. The outer layer, the crust, is a thin hard layer of rock. Heat from within the Earth causes some of the rock in the mantle to melt, whereas greater internal pressure in layers below compresses the rock into a solid state. The centre of the Earth, the core, has a liquid metal outer layer, and a solid metal interior.

SEISMIC WAVES

Vibrations caused by an earthquake are known as seismic waves and can be recorded by sensitive equipment. Two types run though the Earth's interior: fast-moving primary (P)waves and slower-moving secondary (S) waves. The time delay between them can provide geologists with valuable information about where the waves originate. The waves refract (bend) when they pass through different substances, revealing changes within the Earth's interior.

The deepest hole in the world, when compared to the layers of the Earth, gives an idea of how thick each layer is.

THE DEEPEST HOLE

In 1990 the deepest hole ever drilled was in the Kola peninsula, in the former U.S.S.R. It reached a depth of 12 km (7 miles) and is planned to go down to 15 km (9 miles). But drilling would have to continue for a further 6,355 km (3,947 miles) before the centre of the Earth could be reached!

MOHO

The crust and the mantle are divided by a boundary known as the Mohorovicic discontinuity, or Moho. The boundary is named after Andrija Mohorovicic (1857-1936), who discovered it in 1910. Moho was educated in Prague, Czechoslovakia, and taught in Zagreb, Yugoslavia. He noticed that earthquake waves changed when they passed through the two layers.

Earth's magnetic field

The Earth acts in the same way as a huge magnet. A magnet attracts certain materials towards it (such as iron) in an area known as the magnetic field. Each magnet has two magnetic poles. These are places around which magnetic materials tend to concentrate. The Earth's magnetic poles are situated near the geographical North and South Poles. The Earth's magnetic field is known as the magnetosphere. This reaches far out into space and protects our planet's life from harmful solar radiation. The magnetosphere is pulled into a teardrop shape by the continuous stream of electrically charged particles from the Sun, known as the solar wind.

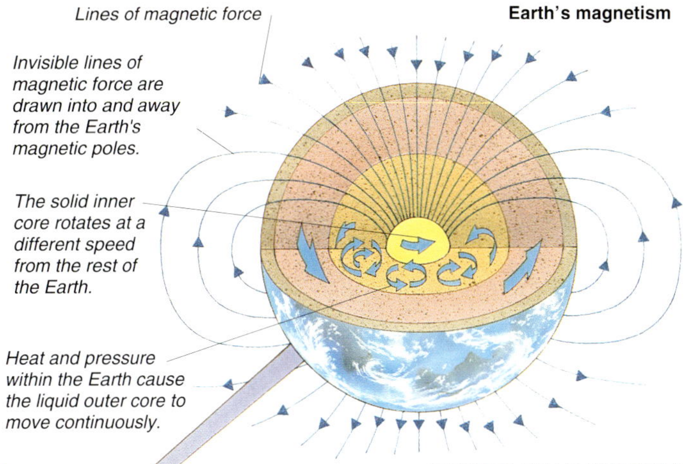

Effects of solar wind on Earth's magnetic field

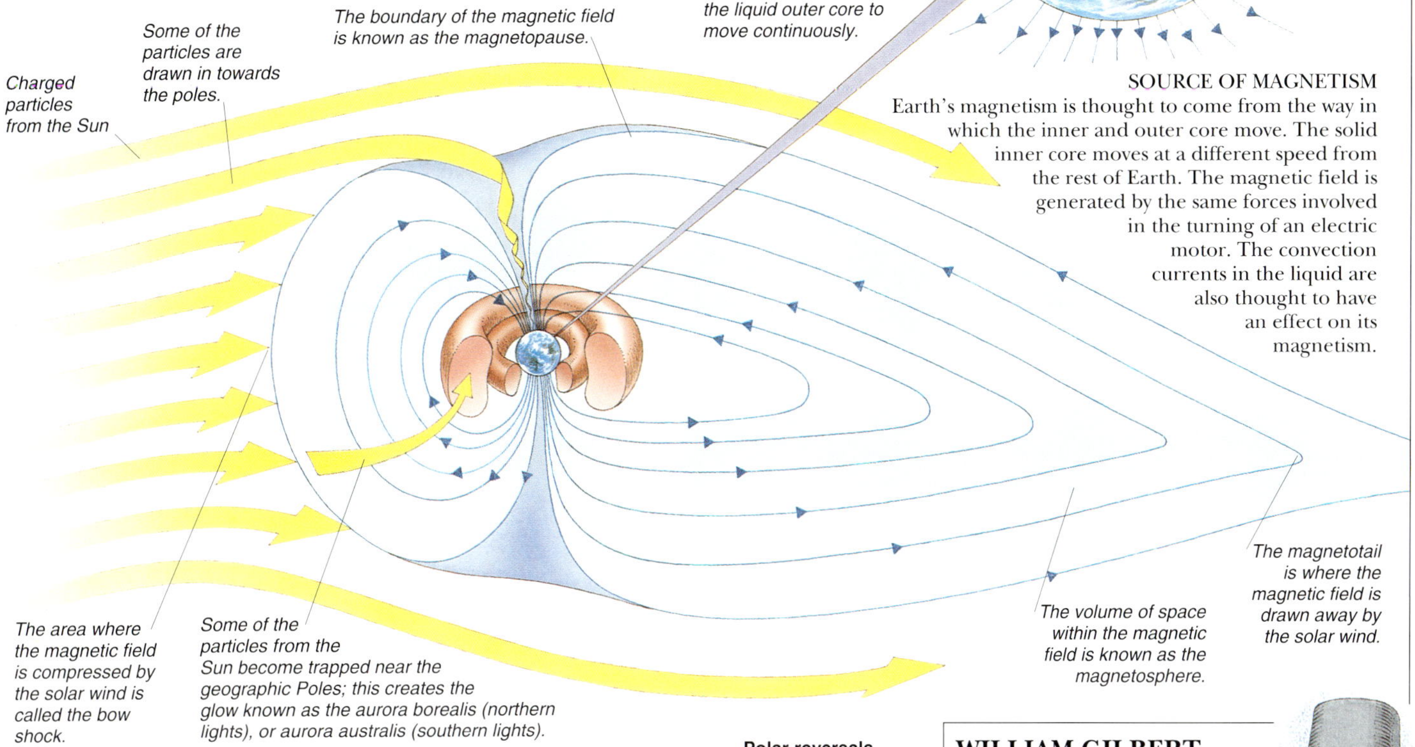

Source of magnetism

Earth's magnetism is thought to come from the way in which the inner and outer core move. The solid inner core moves at a different speed from the rest of Earth. The magnetic field is generated by the same forces involved in the turning of an electric motor. The convection currents in the liquid are also thought to have an effect on its magnetism.

Polar reversals

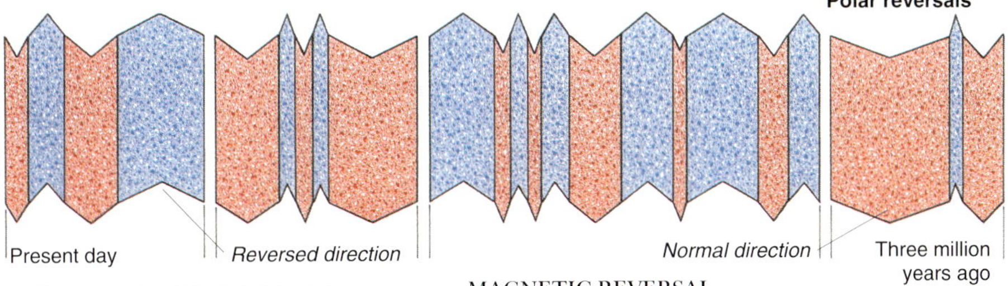

Magnetic reversal

The Earth's magnetic field varies constantly. On certain occasions, movement has been so dramatic that the magnetic field has completely reversed itself, with the North and South Poles changing place. This process is known as polar reversal. It is not clear how this happens, but we known that it has occurred about ten times in the past three million years.

William Gilbert

Queen Elizabeth I of England's physician, William Gilbert (1544-1603), first demonstrated how the Earth acts as a magnet. He did this using a magnetic compass needle. Gilbert used compass needles, which move up and down as well as from side to side to determine the magnetism at a point on the Earth, and the geographic and magnetic poles.

The ancient temple of Rameses II

Magnetic bricks

When a rock solidifies, the direction of the Earth's magnetic field at that time is recorded by its magnetic minerals and preserved. This means that the magnetic field can be detected in bricks baked 3,000 years ago, like those from this ancient temple of Rameses II.

Spinning top

A spinning top swings from side to side when it spins about its axis. The position of the north magnetic pole is continually moving in a similar way, and so maps need to be updated every few years. The magnetic pole differs from the geographical Pole by about 11 degrees – an angle known as the declination.

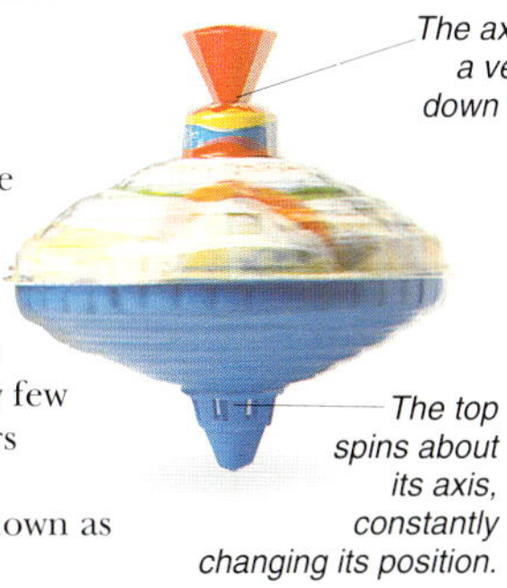

Find out more

Magnetism p.154
Formation of the Earth p.210
Moving continents p.214
Rocks and minerals p.221
Record in the rocks p.226

MOVING CONTINENTS

FOR THOUSANDS OF YEARS, people believed that the continents were fixed permanently into their positions. Then, in the 1960s, the opposite was proven. In fact, the continents are continually drifting around the surface of the Earth like logs floating on a syrupy sea. This is called continental drift. Also, the seabed is being recycled every 200 million years; at certain sites called ridges on the ocean floor, magma (molten rock) is rising from inner layers of the Earth. It then solidifies and moves outwards before being swallowed up at sites called ocean trenches. Nowadays, this idea of sea floor spreading is combined with the idea of continental drift in a theory called plate tectonics.

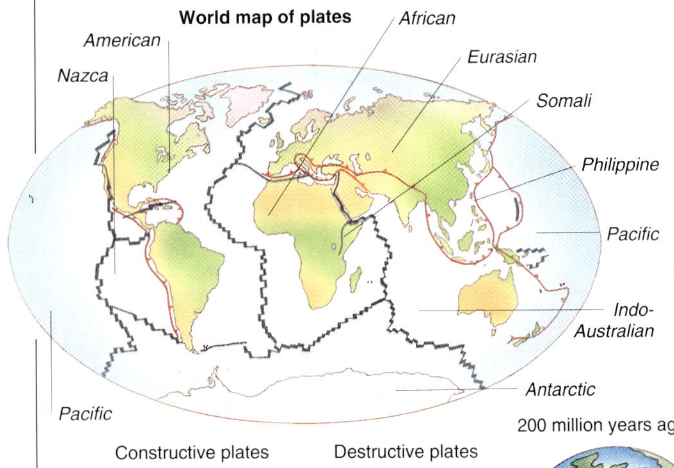

EARTH'S PLATES

The Earth's surface is divided into a number of plates, like the panels of a football. Each plate is growing at one of its edges, moving along, and then being destroyed at another. The edge of a plate where it is growing is called a constructive plate margin and these lie along the ocean ridges. The edge of a plate where it is being destroyed is called a destructive plate margin and these lie along the ocean trenches. The continents are embedded in these plates and are carried around by their movement.

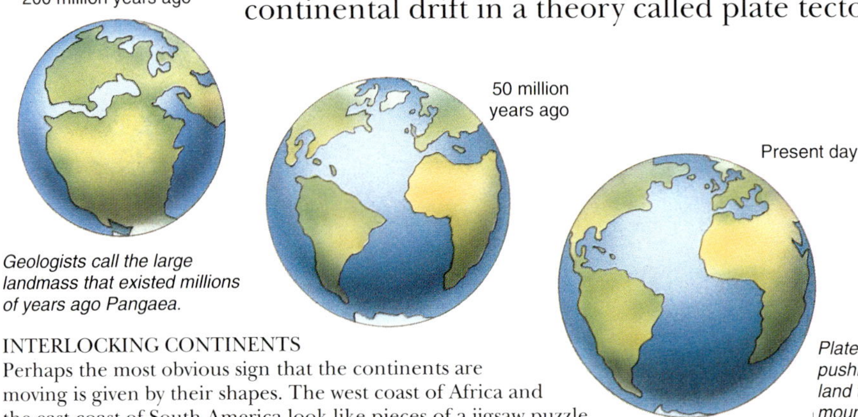

Geologists call the large landmass that existed millions of years ago Pangaea.

INTERLOCKING CONTINENTS

Perhaps the most obvious sign that the continents are moving is given by their shapes. The west coast of Africa and the east coast of South America look like pieces of a jigsaw puzzle that, if brought together, would fit snugly. This suggests that they were once part of a larger continent that has broken up. This was noticed as early as the 17th century, when mapmaking was becoming a more accurate science.

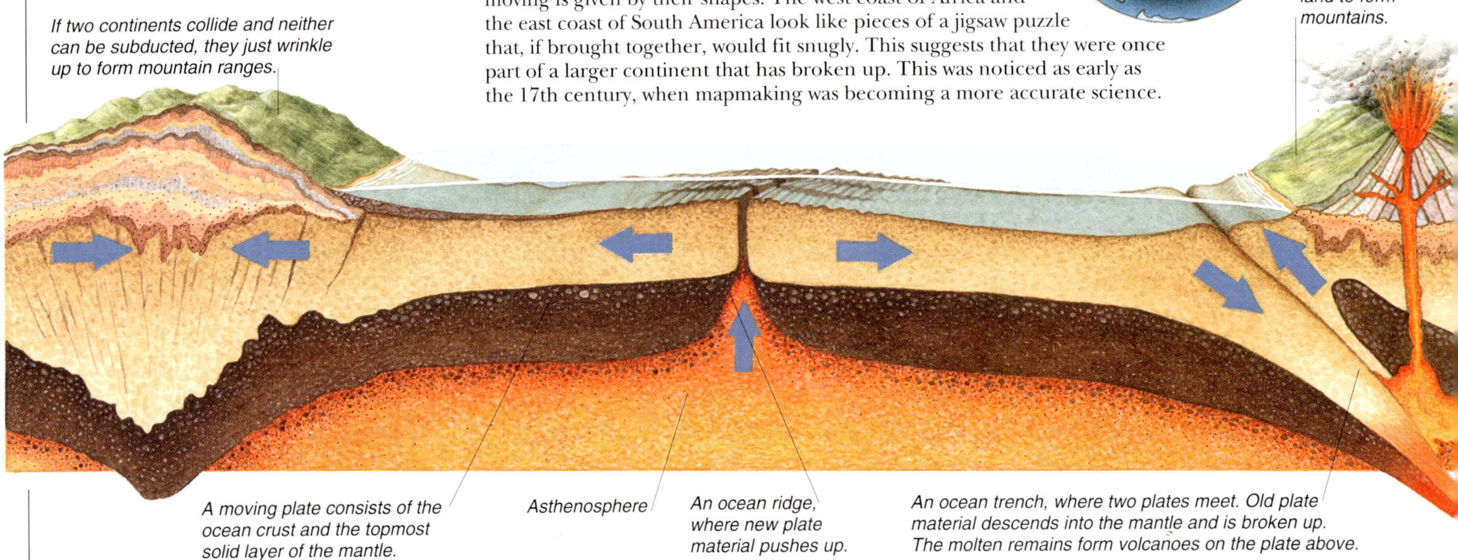

LITHOSPHERE

The Earth's plates consist of the crust and the topmost layer of the mantle. This layer is called the lithosphere. Below this is a layer of mantle called the asthenosphere which is quite soft, lubricating the movement of the solid plates above. At the ocean ridges, solidifying rock is created by volcanic action, and this pushes two plates apart. The ocean trenches are where two plates meet and one is swallowed up (subducted) beneath the other and destroyed.

F. Vine

D. Matthews

FREDERICK VINE AND DRUMMOND MATTHEWS

Evidence for the movement of continents is quite easy to find. But finding tell-tale signs of sea floor spreading is very difficult. In 1963, two British geophysicists, Fred Vine and Drummond Matthews, were the first to recognize the importance of one clue. They showed that the pattern of magnetic stripes in the rocks of the ocean floor was convincing evidence for sea floor spreading.

The movement of continents

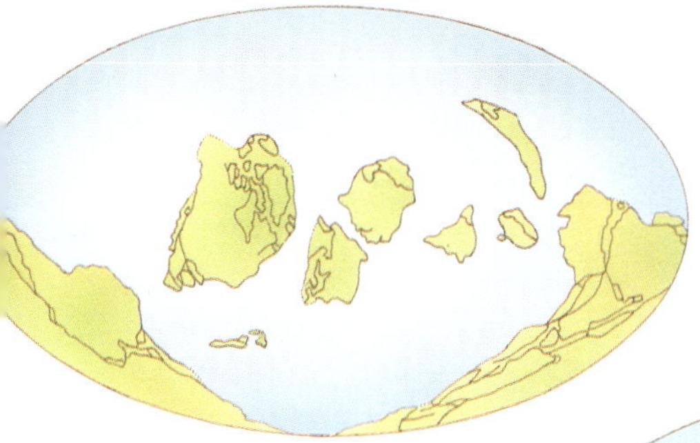

PRE-PANGAEA
Before Pangaea existed, the landmasses of the world were in separate continents. These continents were scattered across the globe, but were quite different from those of today. Very slowly, they were moving towards one another.

EVIDENCE FOR PANGAEA
How do we know that at one time the Earth held just one continent? Because there is lots of evidence to prove it. For example, geologists have found parts of the same ancient mountain range on different continents. Also, the same fossils have been found scattered over the globe, showing that the same animals existed over one big supercontinent.

Fossils of a freshwater swimming reptile, Mesosaurus braziliensis, *have been found in South Africa and Brazil.*

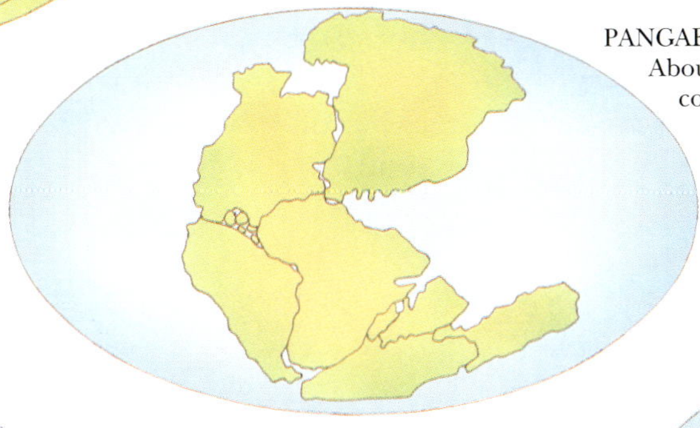

PANGAEA
About 300 million years ago, all the continents came together to form a single vast supercontinent that geologists call Pangaea. This supercontinent existed for about 100 million years. It then began to split into two parts – a northern section called Laurasia, and a southern section called Gondwana.

FOSSIL EVIDENCE
Fossils of an animal called *Mesosaurus* found in Brazil are identical to fossils found in South Africa. But such an animal could not have crossed the Atlantic. This indicates that the animal lived when America and Africa were joined together. The continents moved apart and the fossils were separated by the Atlantic Ocean. Also, fossils of the same plant and of the same age have been found in South America, Africa, India, Australia, and Antarctica.

Future of the continents

About 200 million years ago, Pangaea began to break up, and today's continents split away. Ever since, they have been moving at the rate of a few centimetres per year (about the same rate as your fingernails grow). The position in which the continents are today is just a temporary one. A map of the world of the future would be as strange to us as a map of the world of the past.

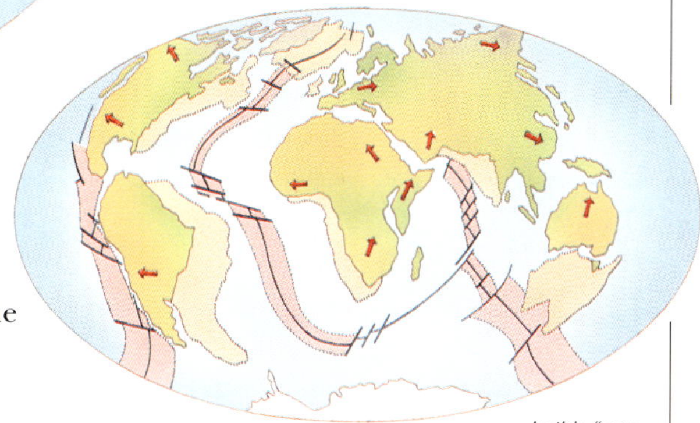

The way in which the continents are moving today has been "fast-forwarded" to create a map of Earth in the far future.

In this "new world", Australia has moved much further to the north, and North America has split away from South America.

This image shows magnetic stripes in each layer of the ocean ridge.

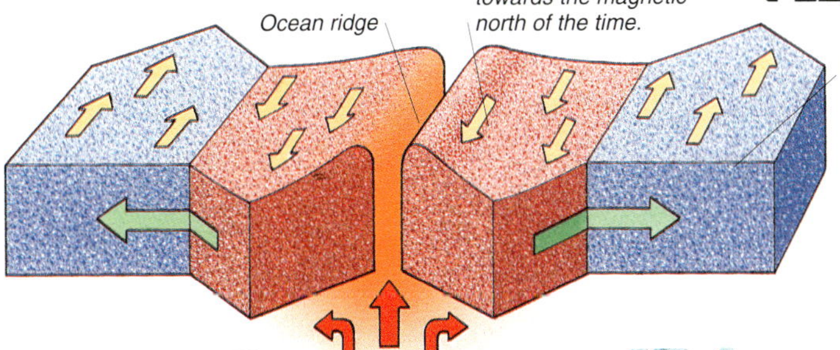

When rock wells up from the ridge, it is magnetized towards the magnetic north of the time.

Every few million years, the Earth's magnetic field reverses; north becomes south. Rocks formed during this period will have a reversed magnetic alignment.

MAGNETIC STRIPES
The rocks of the seabed are magnetized in stripes; a strip of rock magnetized towards today's magnetic north lies parallel to a strip magnetized in the opposite direction. This pattern of stripes is exactly the same either side of the ocean ridge. This is evidence of seafloor spreading.

COLUMBUS
In 1492, Italian-born explorer Christopher Columbus sailed across the Atlantic. The voyage took him 70 days. The same voyage today would take him a little longer. For today, North America and Europe are farther apart – the Atlantic ocean is 10 m (33 ft) wider now than it was 500 years ago!

Columbus' ship

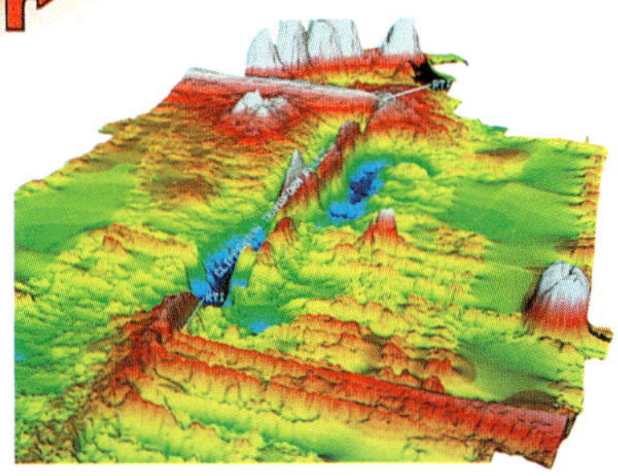

OCEAN FLOOR
The rocks close to the ocean ridge are quite clean, because they have had little time to collect sediment. But farther away from the ocean ridge, the rocks are piled with thick layers of sediment, showing the ocean floor is older there. This is more evidence of seafloor spreading.

Find out more

FORCES P.114
STRUCTURE OF THE EARTH P.212
MOUNTAIN BUILDING P.218
SEAS AND OCEANS P.234
EARTH P.287

VOLCANOES

POMPEII
In A.D. 79, Mount Vesuvius erupted and engulfed the Roman city of Pompeii in hot ash. This covered the bodies of victims and their pets. When the bodies decayed, they left hollows in the ground. These hollows are filled with plaster to make models of the victims.

IMAGINE SHAKING AND OPENING a can of fizzy drink. The pressure that forces the liquid to spray out of the can is similar to the pressure that causes a volcano to erupt. This violent explosion forms thick clouds of ash and red-hot lava that spray out of the volcano and flow down its sides. The eruption occurs when slabs of rock forming the Earth's surface, called plates, begin to move. When old plates collide, and one is ground down beneath the next, the plates melt and produce very violent volcanoes. Other types of volcanoes also exist, such as those that form as new plates grow. The molten material wells from the mantle, spurting up as quiet volcanoes. Some volcanoes lie away from the plate edges, above a very active spot in the Earth's mantle.

ANDESITIC VOLCANO

An andesitic volcano is a steep-sided cone. This forms as the melted plate material comes exploding out of the ground. The volcano gradually builds up from the slow-moving lava flows and ash layers. The thick lava it produces is called andesite.

Nuée ardente flowing down the side of a mountain in New Zealand, August 1968.

NUÉE ARDENTE
When the pressure in andesitic lava is suddenly released at the surface, it produces a *nuée ardente*. This is a glowing cloud which causes an avalanche containing a mixture of gases, fragments of rock, and white-hot ash. It crashes down the hill slopes and valleys at speeds up to 100 km/h (62 mph), smothering everything in its path.

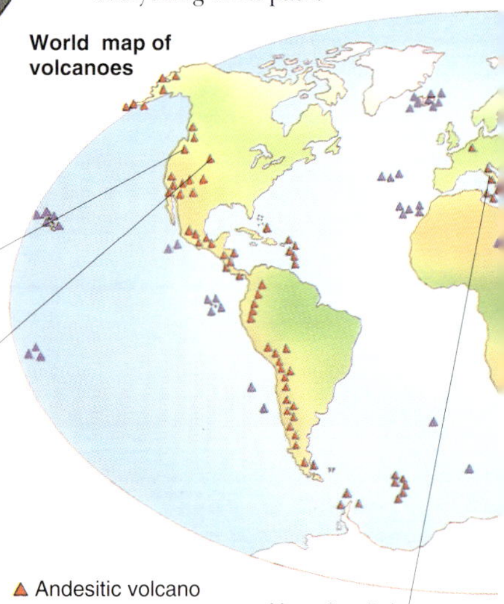

DISTRIBUTION
Andesitic volcanoes are named after the Andes mountains where they were first noticed. They are found in areas where each of the Earth's plates is swallowed up beneath the next.

ANDESITIC ERUPTION
An active andesitic volcano is extremely violent. The eruptions can happen at any time and the explosions cause considerable damage. This type of eruption can also send clouds of hot ash and dust over great distances. The image opposite is of an andesitic volcano after the eruption.

In 1980, Mount Saint Helens in the United States, an andesitic volcano, erupted, destroying miles of forest.

MUD POOL
Water seeping through the ground in a volcanic area may be heated by the hot rocks beneath. The rocks absorb volcanic gases, making them acidic. The hot acid absorbed by the rocks produces a sludge that comes to the surface as a boiling mud pool. The mud pools of Yellowstone National Park in the United States are popular tourist attractions.

HOT SPOTS

Deep within the Earth's mantle are areas of great heat and turbulence. These are known as hot spots. They create the right conditions for basaltic volcanoes to form on the crust above. Continuous plate movement produces a string of volcanoes.

An exploding hot spot island in Hawaii

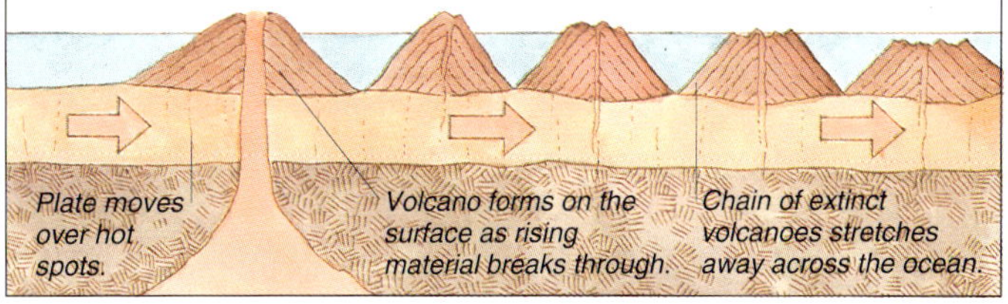

HOT SPRINGS
Water from the ground heated by volcanic rocks may come to the surface as steaming hot springs. Often a network of underground chambers forms and if water turns to steam in one of these, the expansion pushes water up and out at the surface. The reduced pressure allows even more steam to form, and the water is blasted upwards, gushing out of the ground as a boiling fountain called a geyser.

BASALTIC VOLCANO

Over areas such as hot spots, molten material rises up from the mantle. If it breaks through to the surface, it forms a dark runny lava called basalt. Unlike andesitic lava, basaltic lava usually flows for long distances before solidifying. The resulting volcano is broad and low, known as a shield volcano. Most basaltic volcanoes lie deep below the sea and the lava that erupts into the water cools quickly into blobs called pillow lavas. On land, molten basalt sprays into the air as a fire fountain. The drops may solidify in flight, forming volcanic bombs.

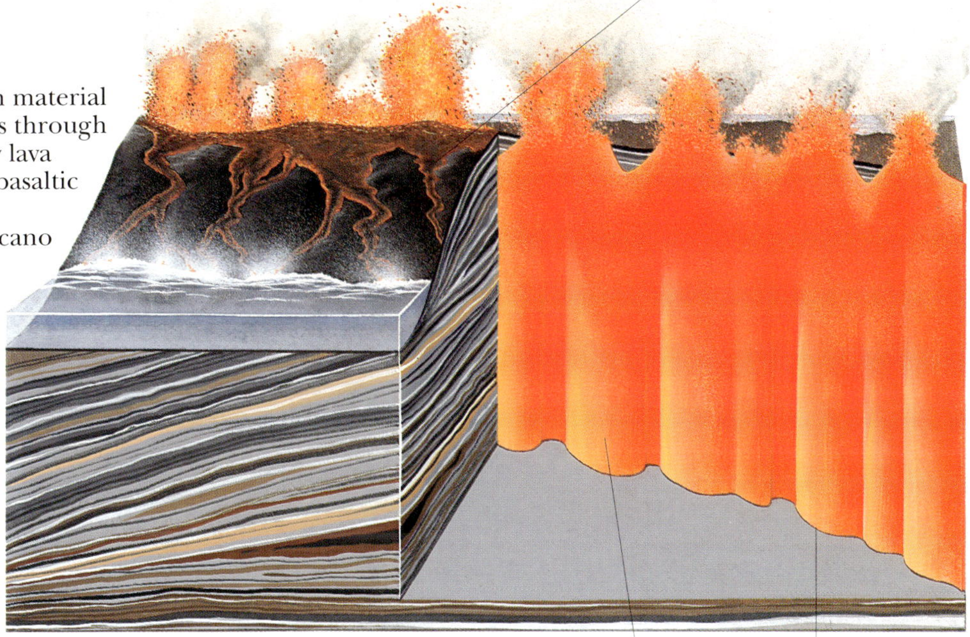

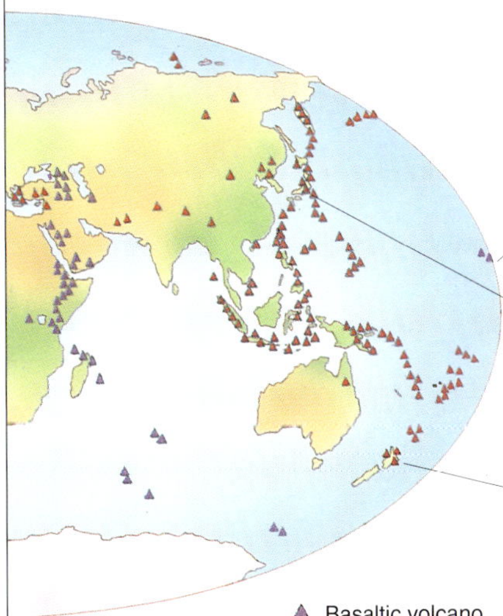

DISTRIBUTION
Basaltic volcanoes are found where the mantle material rises up to form new plates. They rarely appear above the sea surface. Hot spot volcanoes, such as those in Hawaii, may form a long way from the edge of the plate.

Molten lava flowing over rocks in Hawaii

LAVA SURFACES
Basaltic lava flows freely. Its cooling surface forms a skin, which wrinkles and puckers with the movement beneath. This ropy lava is known by its Hawaiian name *pahoehoe*. If this surface breaks up, it forms blocks of lava with rough surfaces, also known as *aa*.

Find out more

ACIDS p.68
MOVING CONTINENTS p.214
MOUNTAIN BUILDING p.218
EARTHQUAKES p.220
ROCKS AND MINERALS p.221
MAPPING THE EARTH p.240

MOUNTAIN BUILDING

World map of mountains

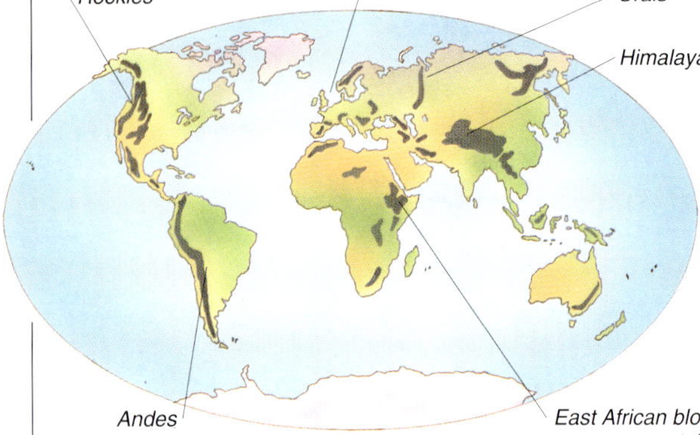

MOUNTAIN DISTRIBUTION

The major mountain ranges of the Earth are fold mountains. These are formed by compression at the edges of continents, or where continental plates have collided. Block mountains, caused by stretching, are less noticeable on the world scale. Volcanoes can be formed among either fold or block mountains.

LIKE YOU, MOUNTAINS ALSO GROW OLD, but not so quickly. The vast Himalayan mountain range in Asia began to grow 50 million years ago, but it is so young that it is still being formed. Mountains are formed by the forces of plate tectonics, movements that take place in the Earth's crust, pressing and squeezing against the edges of continents. These forces thrust mountains out of the Earth. Some ancient mountain ranges, such as the Urals in Russia and the Scottish Highlands, mark where continents collided at some time in the past. Great stresses are involved in mountain building: look for the twists and breaks of the rocks in mountainous areas.

Fold mountains: in theory

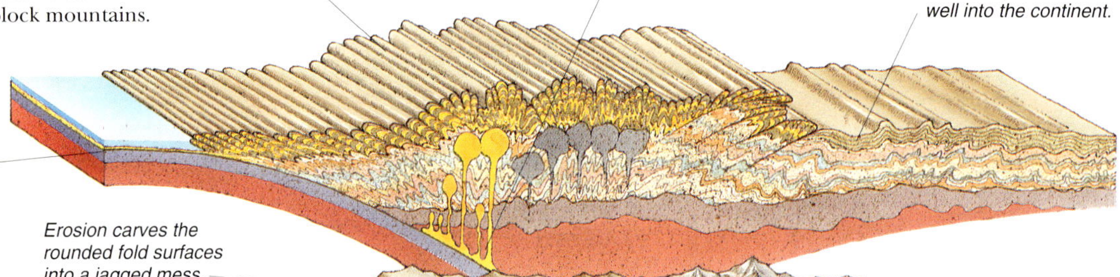

Fold mountains: in practice

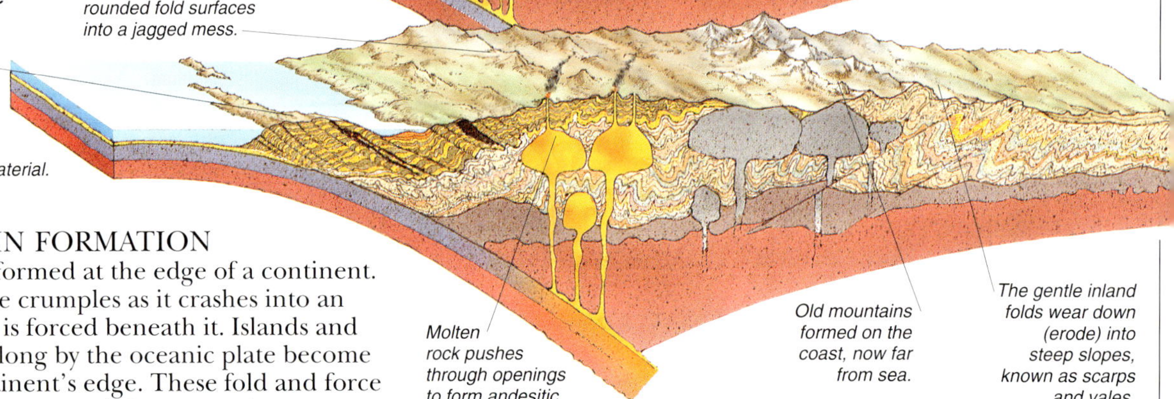

FOLD MOUNTAIN FORMATION

Fold mountains are formed at the edge of a continent. The continental plate crumples as it crashes into an oceanic plate, which is forced beneath it. Islands and sediments brought along by the oceanic plate become plastered to the continent's edge. These fold and force their way up to become part of the mountain range. The descending plate melts, and the liquid rises into the base of the mountains, raising them further and sending volcanoes to the surface.

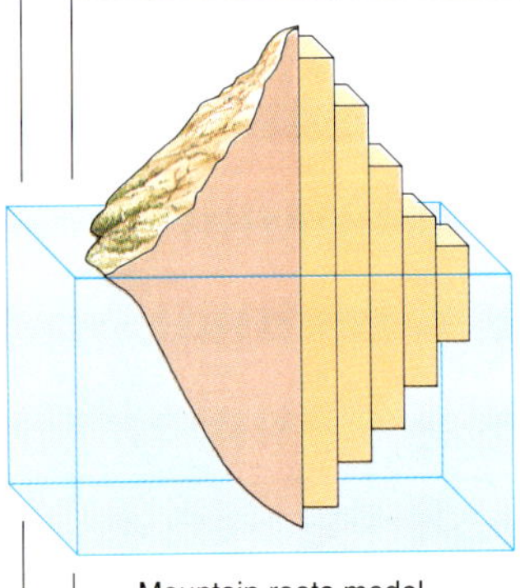

Mountain roots model

FLOATING MOUNTAINS

In 1855, G.B. Airy, the British Astronomer Royal, suggested that mountains behave like blocks of wood floating in water. The higher they are above the surface, the deeper they must be below it. Modern research shows that the continental crust is far thicker in mountainous areas than in flat regions and that mountains have deep roots stretching down into the mantle.

Block mountains

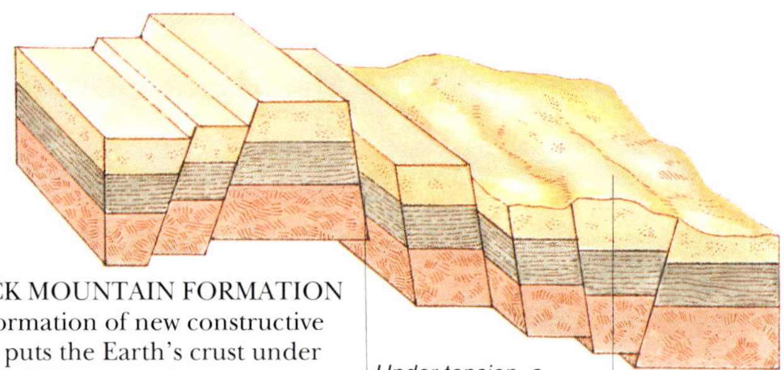

BLOCK MOUNTAIN FORMATION

The formation of new constructive plates puts the Earth's crust under tension. This causes the crust to split into blocks, separated by cracks called faults. Some of these blocks may subside, producing rift valleys, leaving the upstanding blocks between them as block mountains, such as those found in East Africa.

FORMATION OF A FOLD

When beds of rock are subjected to such pressures that they bend, the result is called a fold. A fold that sags downwards is a syncline, while one that arches upwards is an anticline. These two are usually found together. The line along which the rock bends is called the axis.

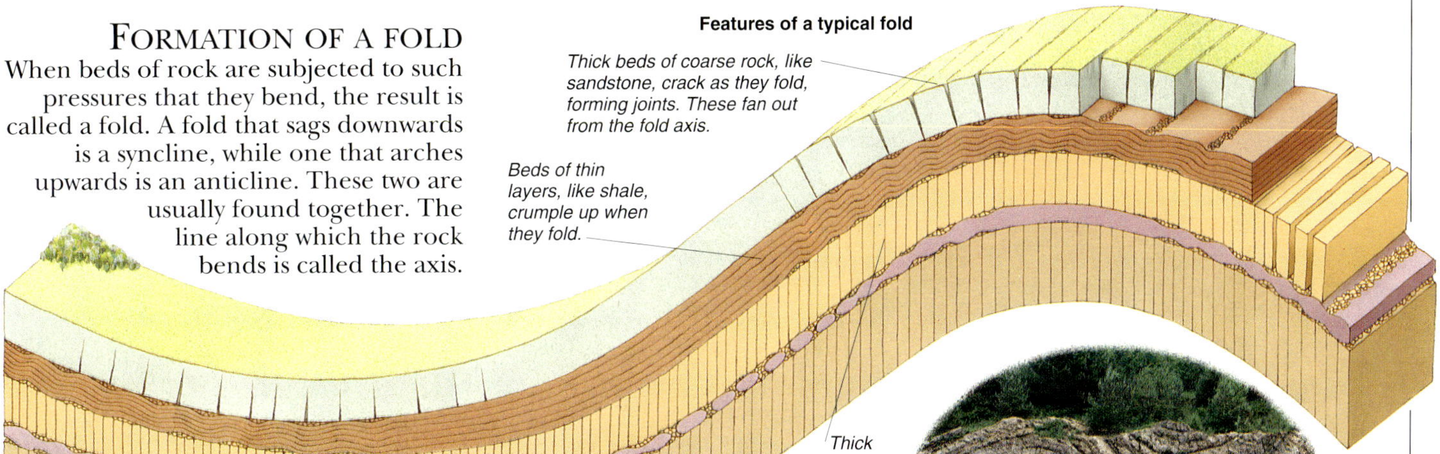

FOLD
This folded rock strata found in Newfoundland, New Jersey, U.S.A., shows the shapes formed by folds. A fold is recognizable in an outcrop by the rounded shape it produces in the rock strata.

TYPES OF FOLD
Rocks deform in different ways producing different types of fold. Those shown above are symmetrical, which means that the plane that the fold bends around is vertical. In asymmetrical folds, the fold appears to be tipping over because of the pressure applied to it. The pressures may become so great that the whole bed cracks and becomes a thrust.

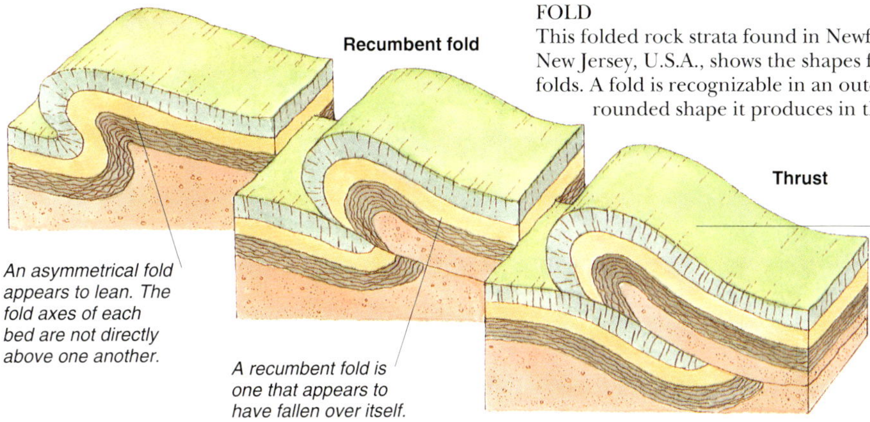

This rock found in Nikshahr, Iran, shows both normal and reversed faults.

FAULT
A fault can be seen as a crack, with the rocks at each side displaced in relation to each other.

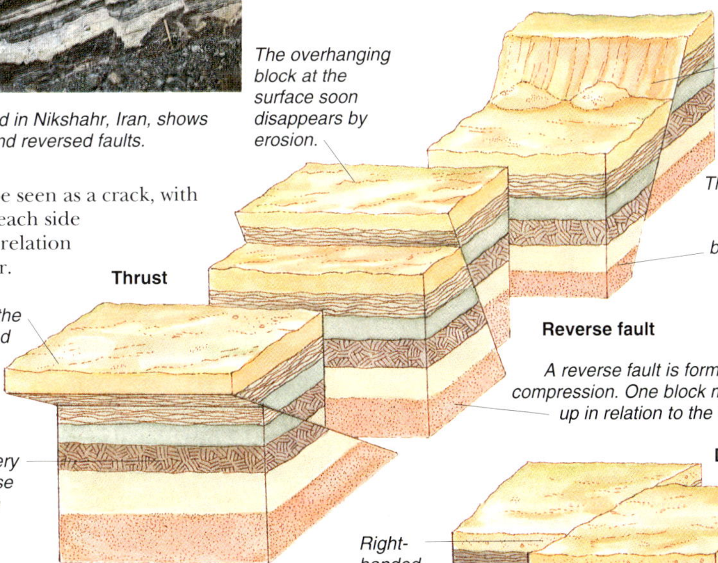

SAN ANDREAS FAULT
The spectacular San Andreas fault crosses the Carrizo Plain. It stretches across 450 km (300 miles) south of San Francisco and 160 km (100 miles) north of Los Angeles. It is an example of a seismic fault and is responsible for some major earthquakes in the United States.

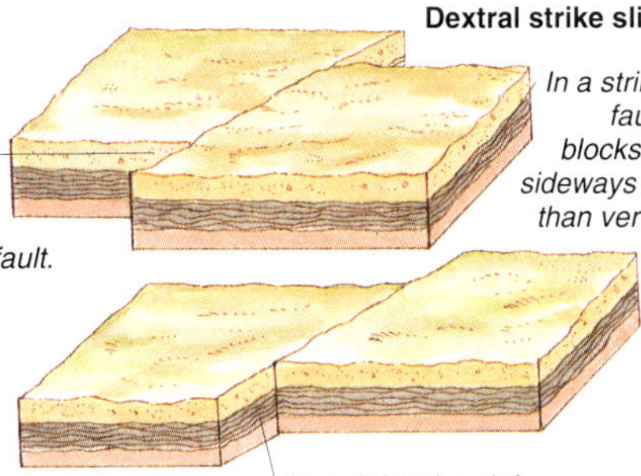

TYPES OF FAULTS

Sometimes, usually under tension rather than pressure, the rocks do not bend and fold. Instead, they crack into blocks that are moving in relation to each other or that have moved in the past. This is called faulting. The surface area on which the blocks slide past each other is known as the fault plane.

Find out more

PRESSURE P.127
STRUCTURE OF THE EARTH P.212
MOVING CONTINENTS P.214
WEATHERING AND EROSION P.230
FACT FINDER P.414

EARTHQUAKES

World map of earthquake zones

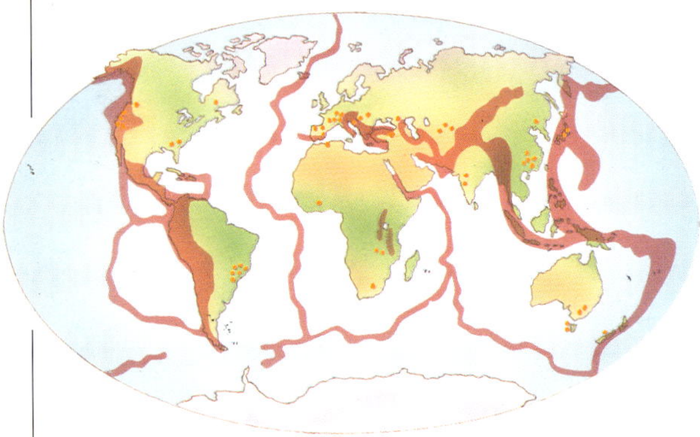

Deep earthquake zones

Shallow earthquake zones

IMAGINE THE FORCE used by two people to snap open a Christmas cracker. Now imagine the much greater force needed to snap open the layers of rock that make up the Earth's surface. Rocks do not bend or break easily. Tension, caused by movement of Earth's plates, builds up over the years until the rocks can take the strain no longer. Suddenly they crack and shift, sending out shock waves, and reducing anything built on the surface to rubble. This is what we call an earthquake. The shock of the initial earthquake may be followed by a series of aftershocks over the next few days. These fade as the rocks settle down into their new positions.

EARTHQUAKE ZONES
Earthquakes, like volcanoes, are found along the edges of the Earth's plates. Shallow earthquakes happen where the plates actually meet on the surface, while deeper earthquakes occur where one plate is sliding down beneath another.

At point II on the Mercalli scale, the earthquake shock is slight. You would notice it only if you were standing upstairs.

At point VI on the Mercalli scale, windows break, heavy furniture is moved, and chimney pots and plaster come tumbling down.

Mercalli scale

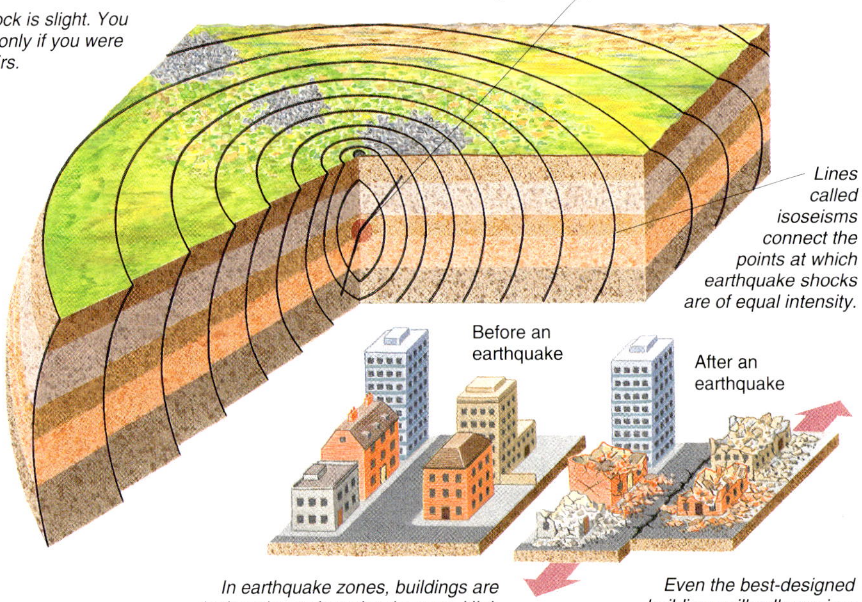

The greatest rock movement takes place at the focus.

Lines called isoseisms connect the points at which earthquake shocks are of equal intensity.

Before an earthquake

After an earthquake

In earthquake zones, buildings are designed to reduce the dangers. High buildings should swing without breaking. Low ones are made of lightweight materials.

Even the best-designed buildings will collapse in a severe earthquake. Taller buildings may survive better than low ones, and fire and disease are constant dangers afterwards.

MERCALLI SCALE

An earthquake's intensity, or the amount it shakes, is measured on the Mercalli scale. This scale is based on what is seen and felt during an earthquake. It runs from the very gentle tremor of point I, to point XII, which can cause total destruction. The point within the Earth where the earthquake takes place is called the focus. The greatest intensity is felt at the epicentre, the point on the Earth's surface just above the focus.

Vertical reading

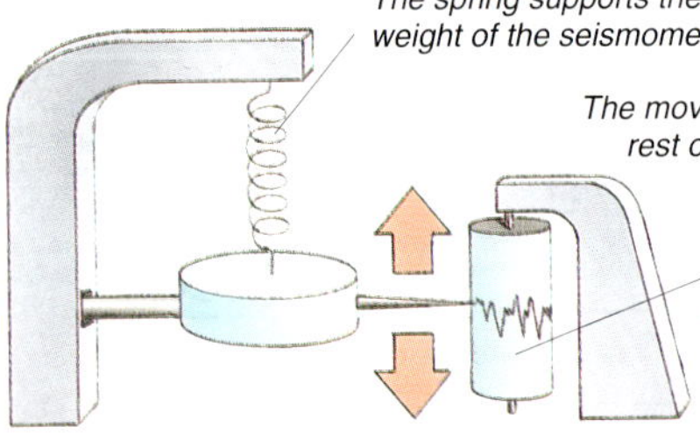

The spring supports the weight of the seismometer.

The movement of the rest of the room is magnified.

The revolving drum records the magnified movement.

Horizontal reading

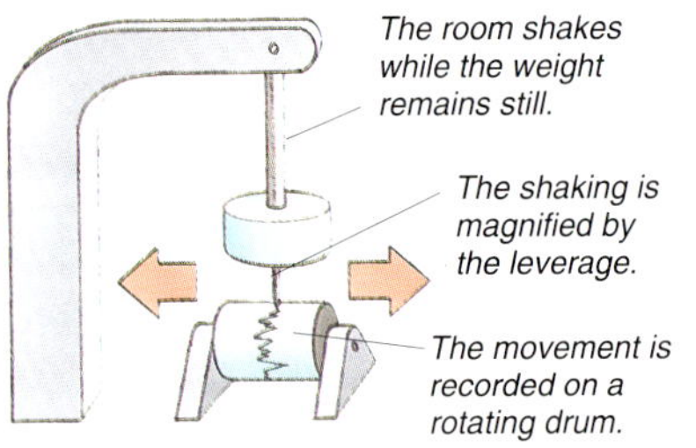

The room shakes while the weight remains still.

The shaking is magnified by the leverage.

The movement is recorded on a rotating drum.

SEISMOMETER
The seismometer is an instrument that records earthquakes. It contains a weight that is so heavy that it remains still while everything else shakes around it. The shaking is magnified by levers and recorded on rotating drums.

RICHTER SCALE

The size, as opposed to the intensity, of an earthquake is measured on the Richter scale using a seismometer. The scale was designed in 1935 by American seismologist C.F. Richter. Severe earthquakes reach a reading of 6 or more, but the most destructive have reached 8.9.

Earthquake scene in Erzicane, Turkey

TOTAL DESTRUCTION
At point XII on the Mercalli scale, destruction is widespread. The ground moves in ripples like waves in the sea. Objects are thrown into the air. Buildings are completely destroyed. The geography of an area is changed permanently, but, luckily, few earthquakes are this severe.

Find out more

FORCES AND MOTION P.120
VIBRATIONS P.126
STRUCTURE OF THE EARTH P.212
MOVING CONTINENTS P.214
MOUNTAIN BUILDING P.218
FACT FINDER P.414

ROCKS AND MINERALS

THE GROUND WE WALK ON, build on, and grow gardens on is made of rock. All the rocks in the world are made up of chemicals called minerals. Through a microscope, a rock shows that it is made of crystals of different minerals all growing together like a mosaic. Each mineral has its own chemical composition, and there are usually no more than half a dozen types in each rock. Three types of rock make up the Earth's crust. Rocks are formed in three different ways to produce igneous, metamorphic, and sedimentary rocks. Igneous rocks form when molten magma cools and solidifies. Metamorphic rocks form when a rock is chemically changed by heat or pressure to form a new rock type. Sedimentary rocks form when fragments of rocks and other debris are cemented together.

Grey quartz crystals

Pink granite

Biotite granite

Graphic granite

DIFFERENT GRANITE

In some rocks, such as granite, the crystals of mineral are big enough to be seen with the naked eye. Granite consists of the minerals quartz, feldspar, and mica. The rock can be pink or grey, depending on what type of feldspar it contains.

DOUBLE POLARIZED ROCK

When the same slice of rock is viewed through two polarized filters, the minerals show up in a spectacular range of colours. These colours change if the rock is turned under a microscope. The individual minerals can be identified by their appearance and by their colour changes.

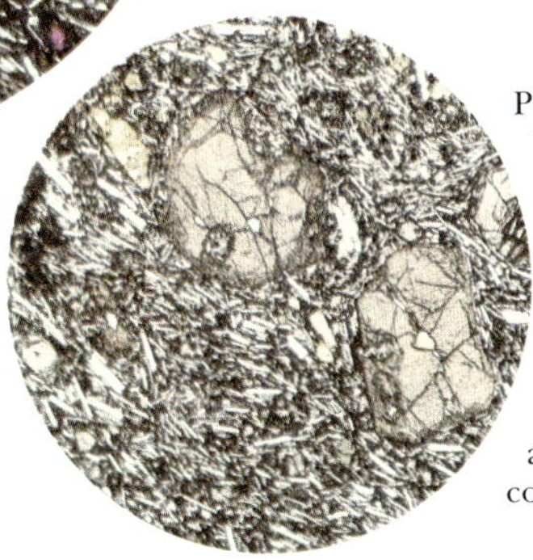

POLARIZED LIGHT

When a slice of rock is viewed through a microscope fitted with a single polarized filter (a special filter that only lets through certain light waves), the individual minerals are mostly transparent. Some may show a slight colour, and a few, such as iron, show up as completely opaque.

Hematite, iron ore

HEMATITE

The ore minerals contain a metal that can be removed quite easily. Hematite is an iron ore. Iron is both durable and flexible, and can combine with other metals to form an alloy. Its uses range from being made into pairs of scissors to industrial construction work.

JEWELLERY

Some minerals are very beautiful, and are used to make jewellery. Their value depends on how popular and rare they are.

Amethyst crystals forming a rim in the geode

GEODE

Minerals may dissolve out of the rock by water or by volcanic fluids passing through it. The minerals are then carried elsewhere. Those that build up along the sides of a hollow in the rock can produce a geode (a group of crystals that grow inside a cavity in a rock).

MOHS' SCALE

Minerals can be identified by their hardness. A mineral that can scratch another mineral must be harder than the mineral it scratches. Mohs' scale of hardness ranges from 1 to 10. Talc (the softest) is 1, gypsum 2, calcite 3, fluorite 4, apatite 5, orthoclase 6, quartz 7, topaz 8, corundum 9, and diamond 10 (the hardest).

Talc

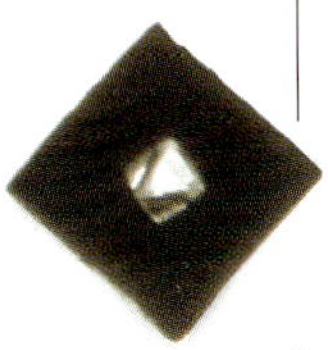

Diamond

Find out more

BONDING P.28
CRYSTALS P.30
ELEMENTS P.31
CERAMICS P.108
STRUCTURE OF THE EARTH P.212
FACT FINDER P.415

IGNEOUS ROCKS

WHEN A CANDLE BURNS, a runny wax is formed that trickles down its side and solidifies. Igneous rocks are formed in a similar way. The rocks solidify from a mass of molten rock, such as when a lava flow cools and hardens. Because of the heat needed to form igneous rocks, they are sometimes called "rocks of fire". There are two main types of igneous rock: extrusive and intrusive. Extrusive types form when molten rock comes to the surface and cools quickly, as with lava. This gives a very fine-grained rock. Intrusive rocks are those that have solidified underground, cooling slowly to produce coarse-grained rocks.

BASALT
A typical extrusive igneous rock is basalt, formed from lava. It is dense and dark, because of the minerals it contains, and fine-grained because of its quick cooling.

Basalt is formed when lava from a volcano cools on the Earth's surface.

Granite crystals are large enough to see without a microscope.

GRANITE
Granite is an intrusive igneous rock. There are several types of granite, but all are light-coloured because of the light-coloured minerals within them. Granite takes much longer to cool than basalt, forming larger crystals that are easier to see.

FORMATION

Molten material from the Earth's mantle forms an igneous rock low in silica, such as basalt. The molten material from the Earth's plates forms an igneous rock that is high in silica, such as granite, which solidifies in huge masses called batholiths, and in dome-shaped laccoliths. Or it forms in cracks, making vertical dykes or horizontal sills. It can also burst through the surface. The rock is only seen when overlying rocks are worn away.

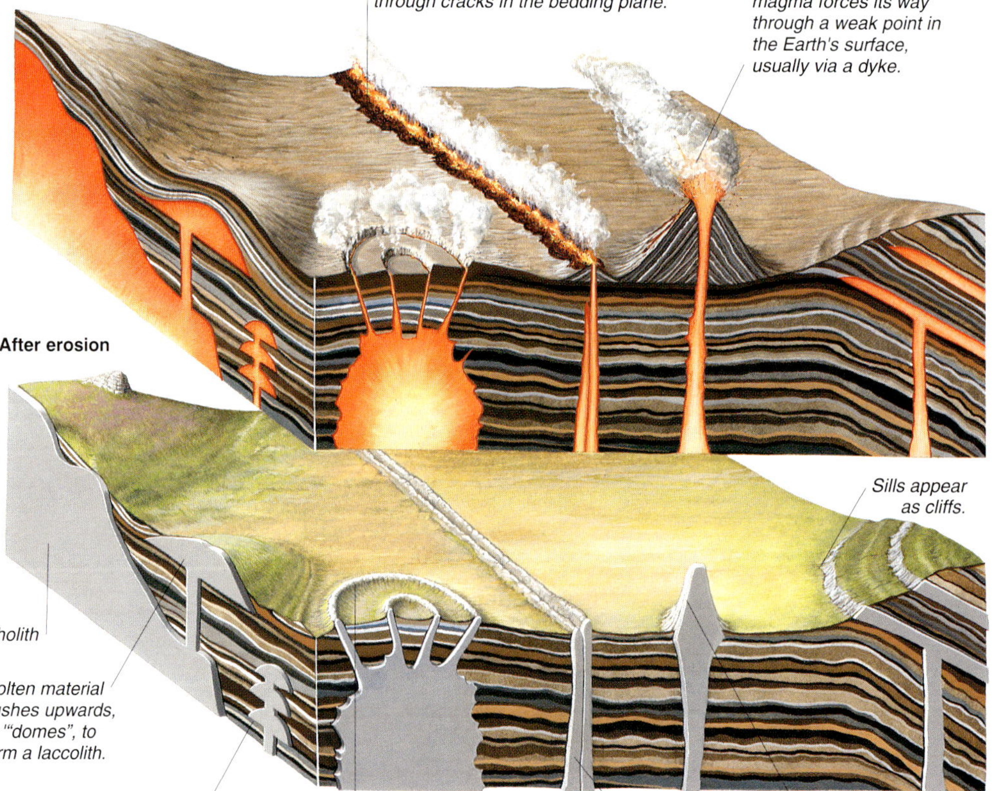

VOLCANIC DYKE
When molten material squeezes its way into a crack and solidifies, it produces a medium-grained intrusive rock. It is usually harder than the surrounding rocks, so after erosion, this intrusion stands out as a prominent landscape feature.

ROAD SURFACING
Igneous rocks tend to be very hard. When broken up, they make a good, strong road-surfacing material, especially when coated with tar. This prevents their silicate minerals (feldspars) from breaking down in the atmosphere.

A road surface is often made by adding granite chippings to hot tar.

Find out more

CARBON P.40
STRUCTURE OF THE EARTH P.212
VOLCANOES P.216
ROCKS AND MINERALS P.221
FACT FINDER P.415

SEDIMENTARY ROCKS

YOU NEVER KNOW what you might find in a sedimentary rock. Many rocks of this type are made up of lots of other rocks, or even animal remains, all stuck together. Sedimentary rocks are built up from particles laid down as layers, or beds, of sediment and later buried, compressed, and cemented into a solid mass. There are three types of sedimentary rock. Clastic sedimentary rock is made of broken bits of pre-existing rocks. Chemical sedimentary rock forms when salt and other substances dissolved in water are separated from the solution. And biogenic sedimentary rock is built up from the remains of living things.

Conglomerate

CONGLOMERATE
Fossilized shingle becomes the coarse clastic sedimentary rock called conglomerate. Other clastic sedimentary rocks include sandstone – made from layers of sand in deserts or in sea beaches – and shale, made from layers of mud.

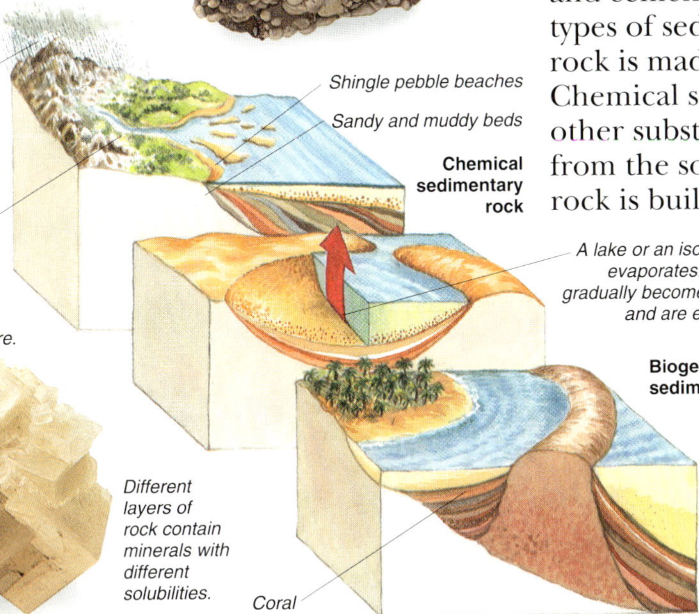

Rock salt

ROCK SALT
Seawater contains dissolved minerals. When an area of sea dries out, these minerals are deposited as a layer on the bottom. Rock salt and certain kinds of limestone are typical chemical sedimentary rocks.

LAYERS OF SEDIMENT
Sediments that eventually become sedimentary rocks may cover whole sea floors or small areas. Where two environments meet, as when a river delta runs into the sea, there is a mixture of sediment types.

Shelly limestone

SHELLY LIMESTONE
Biogenic rocks are made up of once-living material. The shelly limestone above is made up of broken seashells. Other examples of biogenic sedimentary rocks are reef limestone and coal.

FORMATION

The process that turns the loose sediments lying on the bottom of the sea or on a river bed into hard sedimentary rocks is known as lithification. There are two stages: first, the layers that continually build up on top of the bed compress it, squeezing out the air pockets, and interlocking the particles. Later, underground water seeping through the rocks deposits minerals – usually calcite or silica – as it goes. These minerals build up on the sediment particles, cementing them together into a solid mass.

BUILDING STONE
Bedding planes – the boundaries between the individual beds of rock – tend to make sedimentary rocks easy to split and to work. The harder, more thickly bedded sedimentary rocks, such as sandstone and limestone, are commonly used as building materials.

Brownstone house, New York City, U.S.A.

TODAY
Once the sediments are turned to sedimentary rock, they may be lifted by Earth movements and exposed at the surface. Harder rocks, like sandstone or limestone, may be resistant to erosion while softer rocks, like shale, may be quickly worn away. This will form a step-like landscape. This process is continually happening today.

Find out more

CRYSTALS P.30
MOUNTAIN BUILDING P.218
ROCKS AND MINERALS P.221
WEATHERING AND EROSION P.230
RIVERS P.233

METAMORPHIC ROCKS

MARBLE
Marble is a type of thermal metamorphic rock, formed when heat is applied to limestone. Its smooth texture and haphazard structure make it an attractive building and sculpting material. Its colour can vary from white to white streaked with brown, red, green, or grey.

Marble

WHEN YOU BAKE BREAD, you mix flour, yeast, and water together and bake it in a hot oven. In a similar way, heat and pressure from the overlying rocks may change the nature of the rocks below. This process is called metamorphosis, which means "change". There are two main types of metamorphic rock. The most common is known as regional (dynamic) metamorphic rock. This type involves vast volumes, and lies at the heart of mountain ranges and deep within the Earth's crust. The second kind of metamorphic rock is known as thermal (contact) rock. It is produced by heat from nearby igneous rock when the rocks come into contact with each other, and the volume involved may be no more than a few centimetres.

Slate

SLATE
Slate is dark grey, shiny, and splits easily into thin slices, because of the flat crystals of mica produced in it by metamorphism. A low-grade regional metamorphic rock, it is formed from a fine-grained rock such as shale.

FORMATION

Pressure and heat deep underground crush and bake existing sedimentary and igneous rocks, to form metamorphic rocks. These forces change the mineral content of the rock, sometimes completely, as in the case of gneiss, a high-grade metamorphic rock. The importance of this change is the change in the mineral composition that takes place in the solid state. If the rocks just melt and solidify again, the result is still an igneous rock. Regional metamorphic rock is only exposed after millions of years of erosion.

SCHIST
There are many varieties of schist, a high-grade regional metamorphic rock. None of the rock's original minerals are left unchanged.

Schist

Gneiss

GNEISS
Pronounced "nice", this is the highest grade of regional metamorphic rock. The minerals within it separate into distinct bands. The rock breaks in all directions, but not along the bands, as in the case of schist and slate.

SLATE IN USE
New materials have largely seen the decline of slate as a roofing material and as a chalkboard surface. However, one important property of slate is that its flat mica crystals enable it to be split easily.

Slate roof of a house in Britain

Find out more

CHANGES OF STATE P.20
MOUNTAIN BUILDING P.218
IGNEOUS ROCKS P.222
SEDIMENTARY ROCKS P.223
WEATHERING AND EROSION P.230
FACT FINDER P.415

FOSSILS

FOOTPRINTS
A trace fossil is one that does not contain parts of the original creature, just the marks that it made. These include dinosaur footprints, such as those opposite found in sandstone in Connecticut, United States. Ancient dung is sometimes preserved as fossils that geologists call coprolites.

A FLOWER PRESSED between heavy books, or in a flower press, can be preserved for many years. Rocks also do this by preserving plants and animals as fossils. A fossil is any part of a once-living thing preserved in a rock. It may be an entire body, a single bone, or just a set of footprints. Fossils tell us about life in the past and help us to date rocks and past environments. They show how mammoths walked the cold tundra wastes of the Ice Age a few million years ago. Tens of millions of years before that, dinosaurs ruled, and before then all life was in the sea. Many of these animals have left their remains in the Earth as fossils.

An insect trapped in tree resin becomes preserved when the resin turns to amber. The amber preserves the entire insect.

Leaves in shale may decay, leaving just a thin film of the original carbon in the leaf's shape. When this happens to entire forests, it produces coal.

TYPES OF FOSSILS

There are many types of fossil preservation. Only rarely is the whole plant or animal present. Usually it is just part of the hard skeleton, and even then the original material is often replaced by minerals. If the organic material rots away completely, there may be only a hole left in the shape of the original.

Sharks' teeth are hard and durable, so they can be preserved unaltered, unlike the rest of the skeleton.

If the original remains decay completely, they may leave a hole in the rock called a mould. If the mould later fills with minerals, it produces a fossil called a cast.

MARY ANNING
Fossil enthusiast Mary Anning (1799-1847) came from Dorset, in southern England. She became one of the most famous early professional fossil collectors. As children, she and her brother Joseph found the first complete skeleton of the swimming reptile *Ichthyosaurus*.

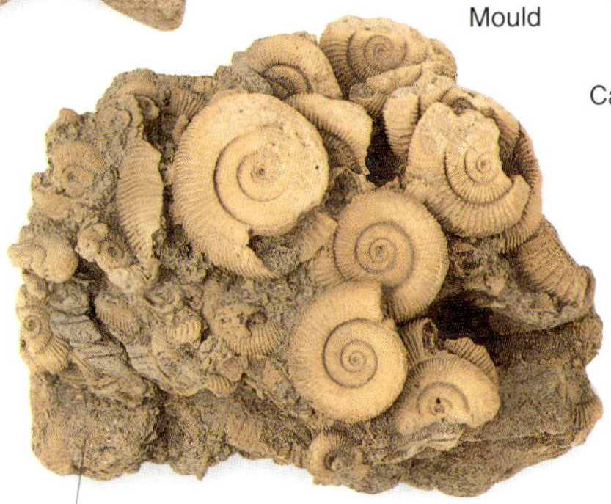

Fossilized animals that evolved quickly, and lived over a wide area, are the most useful for dating rocks. Ammonites, octopus-like animals that lived in coiled shells, are a good example of such creatures.

Fossils are rarely found on their own. More often, many are preserved together as assemblages. Fossil assemblages are useful in giving us an insight into ancient environments and how animals lived and survived under such conditions.

SABRE-TOOTHED TIGER
When an entire skeleton is preserved, a museum may mount it and put it on public display. One example is this fossilized skeleton of a sabre-toothed tiger found in the tar pits in Los Angeles, California, United States.

Ammonites in red chalk

Ammonites help to date rocks.

FOSSIL DATING

Fossils can tell us how old a rock is. If the rock contains a fossil of an animal that we know only lived during a certain period of time, the rock can be dated from that period. When several datable fossils are present in the rock, the dating becomes more accurate. This is because the rock would have formed when all the age ranges overlapped.

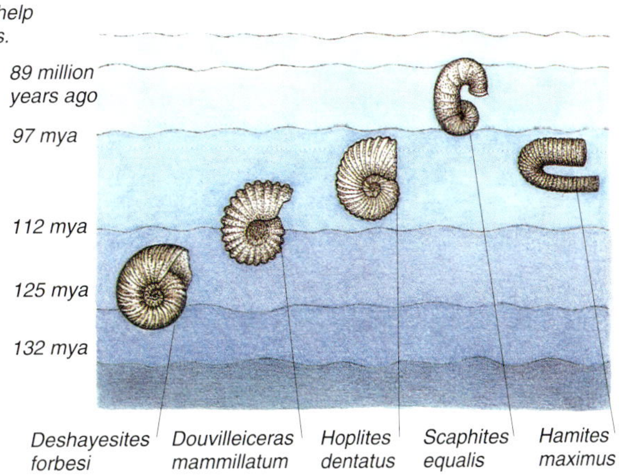

Find out more

CARBON p.40
ROCKS AND MINERALS p.221
SEDIMENTARY ROCKS p.223
RECORD IN THE ROCKS p.226
WEATHERING AND EROSION p.230
FACT FINDER p.415

RECORD IN THE ROCKS

THE ROCKS YOU SEE around you today are filled with clues from the past. Like pages in a book, they record much of the history of the Earth. Since layers of sedimentary rock are laid down one on top of the other, those at the bottom must be the oldest. A geologist, working like a detective, can make a study through these layers; each layer reveals the conditions under which it must have been laid down. The composition of a rock, its structure, and the fossils it contains all paint a picture of a certain environment from the far past. This study of rocks is called stratigraphy, or historical geology.

Unconformity between rocks in the Grand Canyon, Arizona, United States.

UNCONFORMITY

A break in a sequence of rocks is called an unconformity. It happens when a layer of rock is lifted into a mountain chain and erosion wears it down to a flat surface. This is covered by sea, and upper beds of rock are laid on top of it. A gap in the record of the Earth's history has been created.

ROCK SEQUENCE

A sequence of rocks can be used to work out the history of an area. If the column of rocks has been undisturbed, the beds of rock at the bottom will always be the oldest, and those at the top will be the youngest – this is the principle of superposition. The layers of rock then represent periods of time that follow on from one another. This example tells the story of a shallow sea that was laden with sand by a delta and eventually became a desert.

DISCOVERIES

1650 Archbishop Ussher of Ireland dates the creation of the Earth at 4004 B.C.

1669 Danish mineralogist Nicolaus Steno notes that sedimentary rocks were laid down in the sea and so the sea level must always be changing.

1788 Scottish geologist James Hutton realizes that sedimentary rocks are formed by erosion and deposition.

1830-33 British geologist Sir Charles Lyell publishes *Principles of Geology* which says that factors influencing landscape today have operated throughout Earth's history.

DESERT ENVIRONMENT

In a desert, the sand is carried around and set down by the wind to form sand dunes. The corners of the grains of sand are worn off. The iron they contain combines with oxygen to form a red colour.

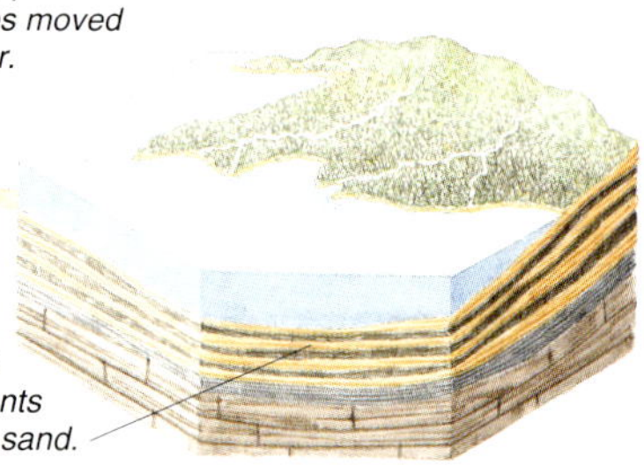

DELTA ENVIRONMENT

In a delta, the river channels bring sand down to the sea, covering up muddy sea deposits to form islands on which plants grow. These islands are only temporary as the sea often sweeps back again.

SEA FLOOR ENVIRONMENT

If the sea is warm and shallow, and the currents are gentle, the chemicals in sea water may form a deposit on the seabed. This will be mixed with the remains of animals that live there.

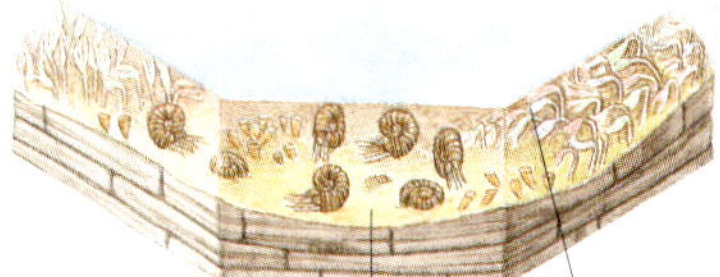

CURRENT MARKS

S-shaped bedding (called current marks) in a layer of sandstone, show that the sand was laid down in a river. The changing current in a river creates sandy "tongues" that are preserved.

Large scale current marks in Wealden sandstones, Sussex, England.

Dinsosaur bones found in Utah, U.S.A.

FOSSILS IN ROCK

Some animals may only live in very specific environmental conditions – for example, in mud that is very poor in oxygen. Their presence as fossils in a rock layer tell geologists about the conditions under which that rock formed.

QUATERNARY PERIOD
The time from 1.64 million years ago to the present day is called the Quaternary period, shown opposite. During this time, the Ice Age occurred, and human beings evolved.

TERTIARY PERIOD
The time stretching from 65 million to 1.64 million years ago is called the Tertiary period. This was the time when mammals and birds evolved to take the place of the dinosaurs and other great reptiles that had just become extinct. Forests gave way to grasslands, and the climate became cooler.

JAMES HUTTON

Scotsman James Hutton (1726-97) was a great historian of geology. In 1795, he published *Theory of the Earth* in which he explained that the Earth's features have developed over many years from changes that are still taking place today. He thought that there was no sign of Earth's beginning, nor an outlook for its end.

Geological time

The timing of events in Earth's history can be done in two ways. The most useful way is comparative dating, in which one event is placed either earlier or later than another. The other way is absolute dating, in which actual dates are given to events. Absolute dating is very difficult; any timescale produced in this way tends to change with every new piece of evidence.

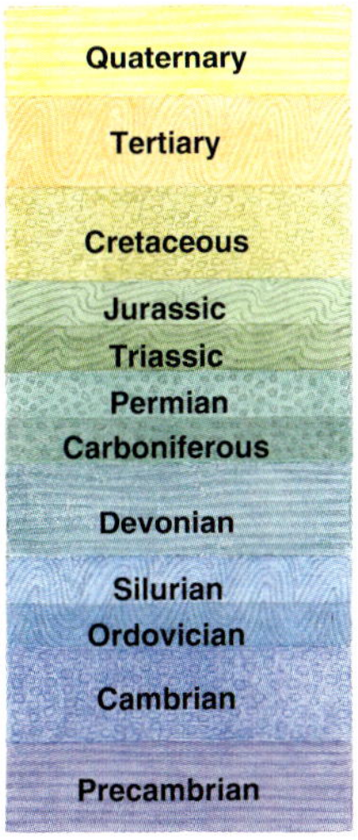

GEOLOGICAL COLUMN
Just as we date human history by naming periods after famous events, such as the Pre-Columbian age, so geological time is divided into periods depending on the kind of life that existed at that time. These periods are grouped together into eras.

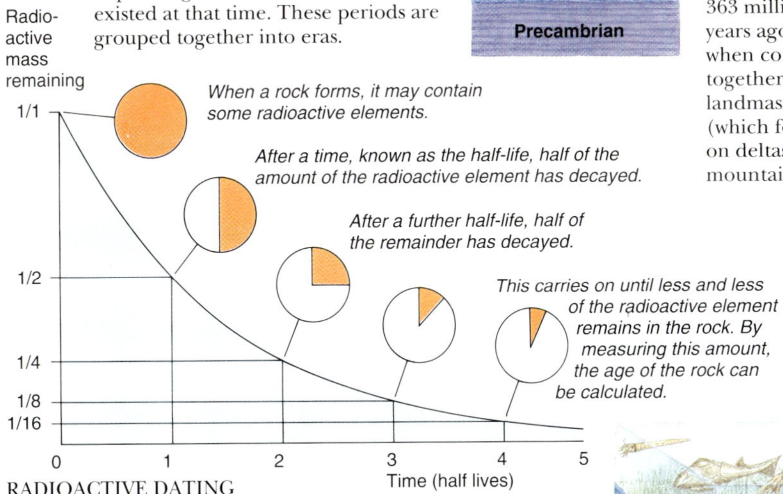

RADIOACTIVE DATING
In most rocks, there are tiny amounts of radioactive elements. Over the years, these break down into more stable elements. As scientists know the precise rate at which they do this, the age of a rock can be calculated from the proportion of radioactive elements it contains. The less it contains, the older it is. This is a type of absolute dating.

CRETACEOUS PERIOD
The Cretaceous period lasted from 146 million to 65 million years ago. The Earth was home to the great reptiles. Most of the modern continents had split away from the large land mass Pangaea; many were flooded by shallow chalk seas.

TRIASSIC AND JURASSIC PERIODS
The Triassic and Jurassic periods stretched from 250 million to 146 million years ago. Reptiles were beginning to evolve on Earth. Pangaea started to break up, and deserts gave way to forests and swamps.

CARBONIFEROUS AND PERMIAN PERIODS
These periods spanned from 363 million to 250 million years ago. This was the time when continents came together to form one big landmass, Pangaea. Forests (which form today's coal) grew on deltas around the new mountains, and deserts formed.

DEVONIAN PERIOD
The Devonian period lasted from 409 million to 363 million years ago. Continents started moving towards each other. At this time, the very first land animals, such as insects and amphibians, existed, and many fish swam in the seas.

ORDOVICIAN AND SILURIAN PERIODS
These periods spanned from 510 million to 409 million years ago. Sea life flourished at this time, and the very first fish evolved. The earliest land plants began to grow around shorelines and estuaries.

CAMBRIAN PERIOD
The Cambrian period stretched from 570 million to 510 million years ago. At this time, there was no life on land, but all kinds of sea animals existed. The animals with hard shells formed many of today's fossils.

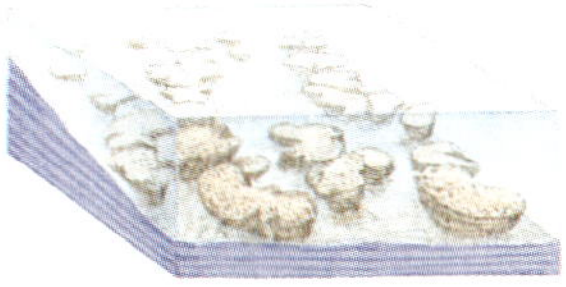

PRECAMBRIAN PERIOD
This is the largest length of geological time, covering seven-eighths of Earth's history right up to 570 million years ago. It is divided into the earlier Archaean period when there was no life, and the later Proterozoic period, when life of some sort existed.

Find out more

Radioactivity p.26
Structure of the Earth p.212
Rocks and minerals p.221
Fossils p.225
Weathering and erosion p.230

ICE AND GLACIERS

HAVE YOU EVER SQUEEZED some snow in your hands? It holds together because the pressure of your hands has turned the snow particles into ice crystals. The same thing happens when great masses of snow build up on top of each other, compressing the layers beneath. This may happen in a shady valley of a mountain range, where the snow does not melt from one year to the next. Snow compressed in a hollow forms a mass of ice, which moves slowly downhill towards the lower slopes of the valley. This is known as a glacier. On cold continents, the same thing happens, and the ice builds up into an ice cap.

Lake at 180 m (590 feet) in Valley of Velka Studena Dolina, Czechoslovakia

AFTER THE GLACIER

A valley glacier exerts such pressure on its base and sides that it wears them away. When the ice eventually melts, the valley is seen to be worn into a U-shape. This has vertical sides and a flat bottom.

VALLEY GLACIER

Glacier ice may start off smooth, clean, and snow-covered, but it soon breaks as it begins to move. It becomes stained by the rock fragments worn away from the valley sides. At its lower end (its snout), the glacier appears dirtier as once-buried rocks appear on the surface. Gullies and tunnels carved into the ice by the meltwater (ice melting into water) also make the ice look unclean.

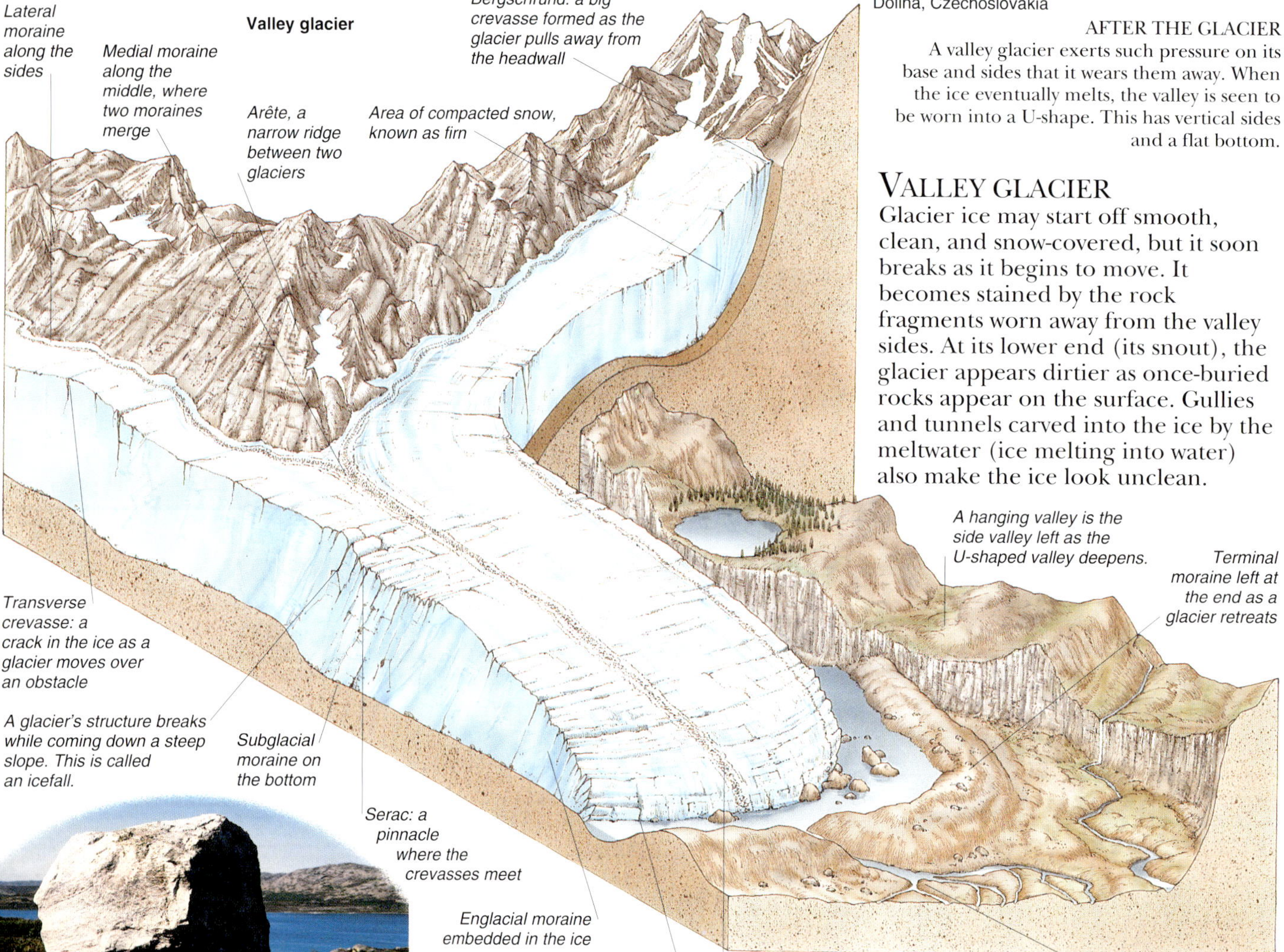

This rock was dropped in East Greenland by a glacier.

GLACIAL DEBRIS

The rocky material picked up, carried along, and dropped by a glacier is called a moraine. This may consist of mounds of clay, or gigantic boulders that have been carried for many miles. Much of the Northern Hemisphere landscape is formed by moraine left behind after the Ice Age.

NORTHERN HEMISPHERE ICEBERG

When a glacier reaches the sea, particularly along the Greenland coast, tides and waves heave it up and down. The strains exerted on it cause pieces to break off and float away, forming icebergs. This process of producing icebergs is known as calving.

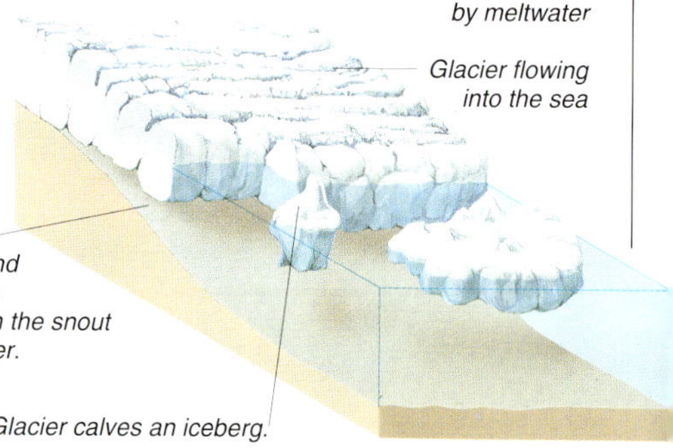

ICE AGES

At certain times in the Earth's history, the climate becomes so cold that extensive ice sheets are formed. Such periods are called ice ages. The most recent began about 1.6 million years ago and finally finished 20,000 years ago. Others took place in the distant past. There were four in Precambrian times, one in the Ordovician period, and one in the late Carboniferous and early Permian periods.

Ice age time line

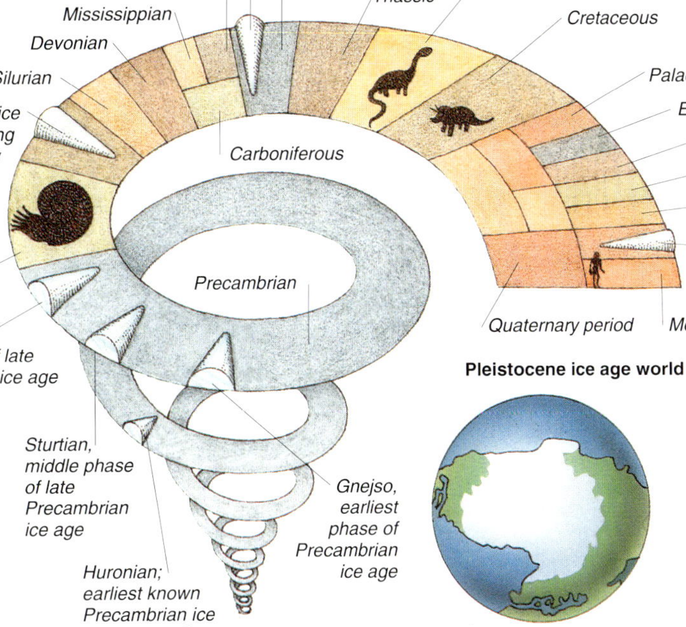

LOUIS AGASSIZ

The Swiss Louis Agassiz was the first to recognize that an ice age had taken place. He noted that some landscape features in Switzerland had been produced by glaciers. He also saw similar features in Scotland, where there are no glaciers. He deduced that at one time Scotland had been covered in ice.

Louis Agassiz (1807-1873)

Pleistocene ice age world | The world today

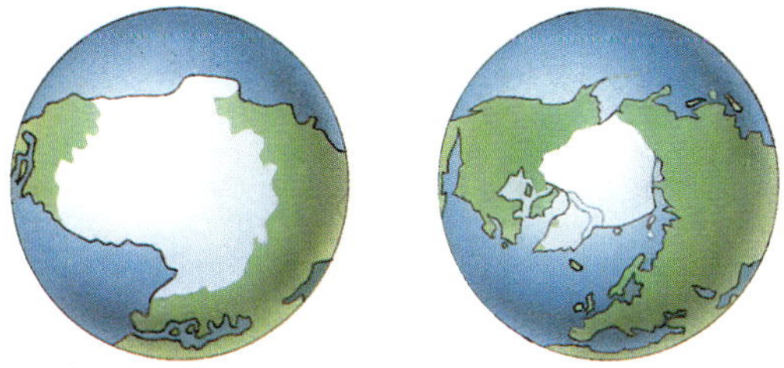

LAST ICE AGE
The Pleistocene ice age was very irregular. The glaciers advanced and, a few thousand years later, retreated again, giving an interglacial spell with warmer climates than now. This cycle took place about 20 times in the 1.6 million years of the ice age. It may not be over. We may just be living in another interglacial era.

ICE SHEET

In the far north and the far south, glaciers build up over continental areas, forming ice sheets or ice caps. These move outwards rather than downhill as valley glaciers do. The two main ice sheets are the Antarctic ice cap and the Greenland ice cap. These make up about 90 per cent of the Earth's fresh water. Snow in the centre of the continent will eventually find its way to the edge as ice.

Ice cap

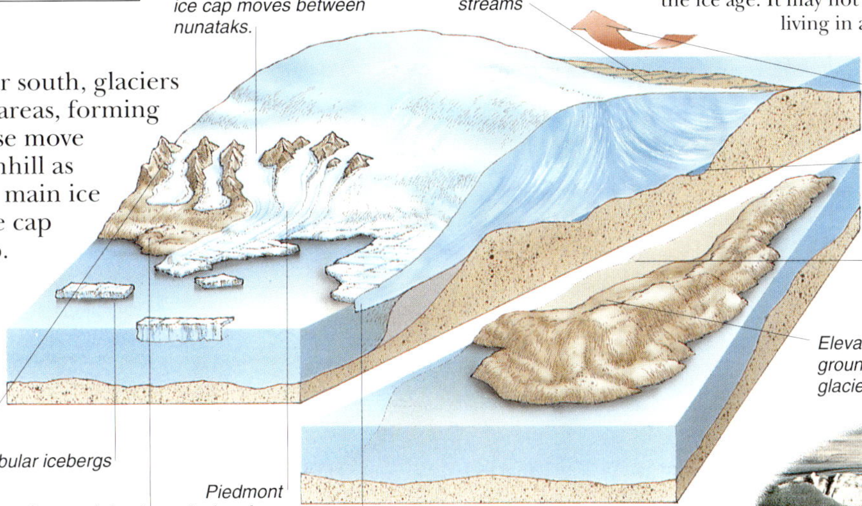

ICE CAP
The windswept surface of the ice cap may be over a kilometre above the bedrock. In Antarctica, only about 15 cm (6 in) of snow falls each year, but eventually it is all compressed into ice.

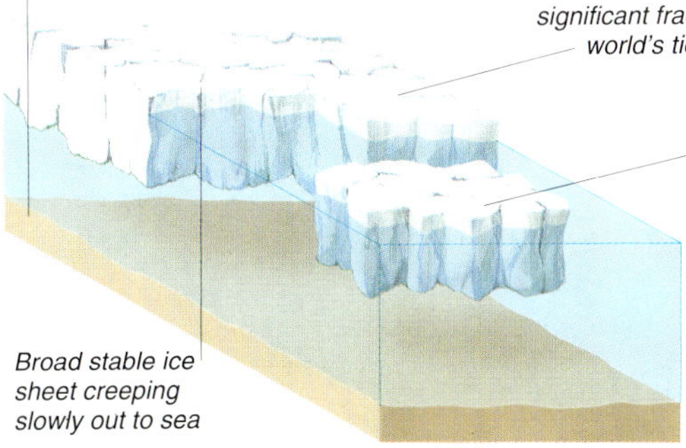

SOUTHERN HEMISPHERE ICEBERG
The icebergs that form in the southern ocean, broken off the ice shelves of Antarctica, are broad and tabular (flat). They may be many hundreds of kilometres long and exist for years before melting. Often these are tracked by satellite to help build up a picture of the world's oceans.

Find out more

PRESSURE P.127
FLOATING AND SINKING P.129
WEATHERING AND EROSION P.230
RIVERS P.233
SEAS AND OCEANS P.234
FACT FINDER P.414

WEATHERING AND EROSION

Effects of weathering and erosion on rocks

The rock falls away layer by layer. This is called onion skin weathering.

THE SURFACE OF THE EARTH is constantly changing. The movement of the Earth's plates pushes up mountains and builds up continents. At the same time, these new surfaces are worn back down again and ground to dust, in a process called erosion. It can be caused by many agents, but the most powerful one is that of the weather. There are two types of weathering – physical and chemical. Physical weathering is the buffeting of the wind, the washing of the rain, and the pull of gravity. An example of chemical weathering is when the acids in rainwater dissolve away rocks.

INSELBERGS

Rounded hills in dry regions, such as Uluru (Ayers Rock) in Australia, have been eroded by a combination of physical and chemical weathering. These are known as inselbergs. Infrequent rain eats into the surface layers of the rock. The hot days and cool nights cause daily expansion and contraction, which eventually splits the surface.

Pancake rocks, known as zeugens, found in Punakaiki, South Island, New Zealand

ZEUGENS

Sand flung about by the wind causes erosion. Exposed rocks are sandblasted into unusual shapes and polished smooth. Most erosion takes place near the ground, producing overhanging cliffs and top-heavy rock structures called zeugens.

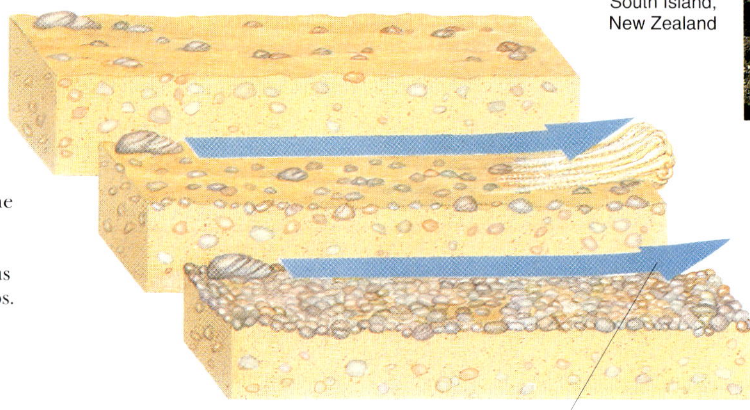

The arrows show the direction in which the wind is blowing.

DEFLATION EFFECT

Desert soil is a mixture of fine dust, sand, and coarse pebbles. Wind blows away the fine material leaving the heavier pebbles, which eventually form a continuous crust. The erosion then stops.

DESERT WINDS

Sand flung about by the wind is the most powerful erosional force in a desert. There are few plants in desert areas, so the soil is not held together by roots – nor is there much moisture to stick the particles to one another. The wind therefore easily picks up the loose sand and hurls it around in sandstorms. Rocks blasted by the sand are worn down to sand themselves; this is used by the wind for further erosion.

Formation of a mushroom rock

These arrows show how high the wind blows the sand and the direction it travels in.

DREIKANTER

Pebbles lying on the ground receive an intense blasting by sand. This wears away one side quickly, causing the pebble to overbalance. This exposes another pebble face. The result is a pebble that is polished flat on several sides – called a dreikanter. The larger pebbles that are found on beaches or dry river beds show this effect.

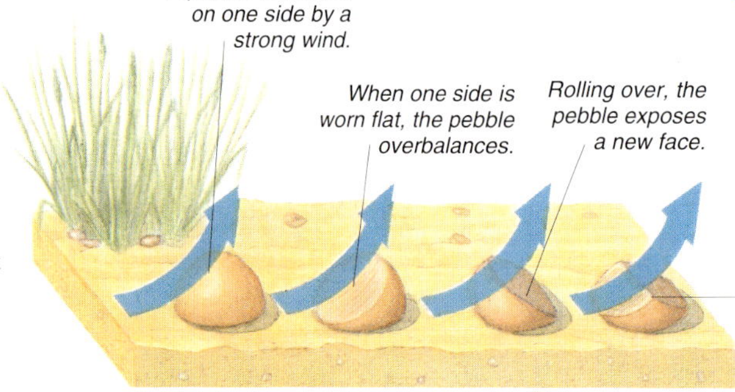

A pebble is blasted on one side by a strong wind.

When one side is worn flat, the pebble overbalances.

Rolling over, the pebble exposes a new face.

The resulting pebble has several flat, polished faces.

MUSHROOM ROCKS

Sand particles are usually bounced along by the wind close to the ground because of their weight. This process is called saltation. As a result, most erosion is done within around 1 m (3 ft) of the ground. Tall pinnacles of rock are only eroded at their base, leaving mushroom-shaped rock structures called zeugens.

SAND DUNES

The sand that is blown from loose desert soil usually builds up into heaps called dunes. Sand dunes are moved along gradually by the wind. Only about one-fifth of the world's desert areas consist of sand; in these areas the dunes can form in many different ways.

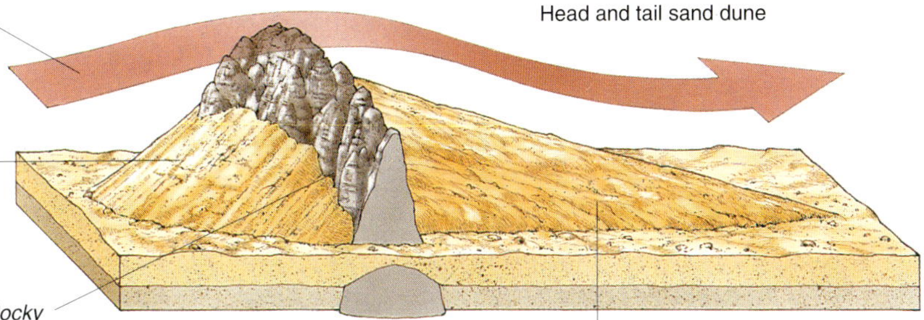

Head and tail sand dune

BARCHAN DUNES

The most familiar type of dune is the crescentic dune or the barchan. These dunes are shaped like a crescent. They form because the sand on the two ends is blown faster than that in the middle. Many of these barchans together form the typical sand and sea-like landscape seen in big deserts, such as the Sahara.

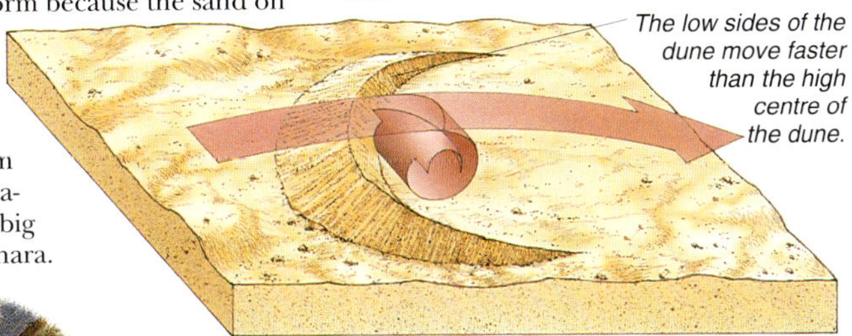

Barchan dune

Coastal sand dunes showing typical sand dune structures in England

HEAD AND TAIL DUNES

Head and tail dunes grow near an obstacle, such as a shrub. Sand builds up in front of the obstacle and forms a tail behind it. However, there are different types; an advanced dune, for example, may be deposited some distance before the obstacle, and wake dunes may line up at each side.

Decomposed granite in Cornwall, England

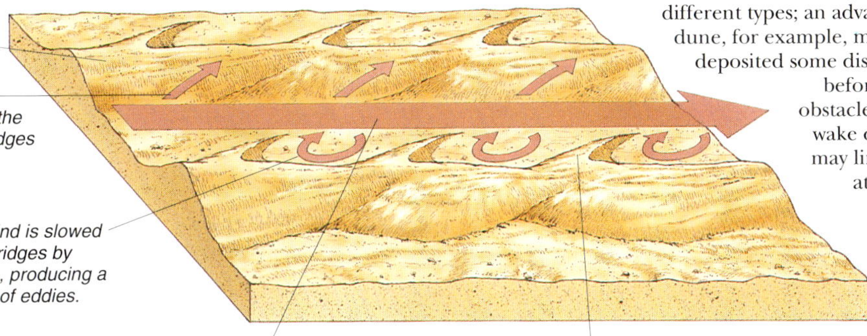

Seif dunes

ROTTING GRANITE

Minerals such as feldspar, one of the constituents of granite, are vulnerable to chemical weathering. Once the feldspar reacts to the acid in rainwater, the other minerals become loose and the granite crumbles.

SEIF DUNES

Dunes called longitudinal, or seif, dunes form as long ridges parallel to the direction of the wind. They are most obvious in places where the sand is being blown across bare rock.

FROST WEDGING

In cold climates, a type of physical weathering called frost wedging is common. Water seeps into cracks in the rock; as this water freezes, it expands and enlarges the cracks. Eventually chunks of rock fall away and pile against the mountainside as scree slopes, such as the one opposite in Camp Pont, in the Antarctic peninsular.

Clints and grikes in Yorkshire Dales, England

CLINTS AND GRIKES

Calcite suffers from chemical weathering. Where limestone is exposed to rain, the calcite decays on the surface and along cracks. This process erodes the rock into blocks called clints separated by enlarged cracks called grikes.

ACID RAIN

The natural acids in rainwater come from dissolved carbon dioxide. In built-up areas, the rain also contains acids from dissolved industrial gases, such as sulphur dioxide, causing acid rain. This increases the rate of chemical weathering, damaging buildings and statues such as this stone lion in Leeds, England.

Find out more

ACIDS P.68
FROST, DEW, AND ICE P.268
WEATHER WATCHING P.272
CYCLES IN THE BIOSPHERE P.372
DESERTS P.390

SOILS

WHEN WE LOOK at a landscape, we usually see grass, plants, and trees. Without soil, these would not exist. Soil is a complex mixture of fresh and eroded rocky material, dissolved and redeposited minerals, and the remains of once living things. These components are mixed together by the burrowing of animals, the pressure of plant roots, and the movement of water underground. The type of soil, its chemical composition, and the nature of its organic origin are all important to agriculture, and therefore to all our lives. Many different types of soils exist. Soils vary from one part of the world to the next, depending on the climate.

Different layers of soil

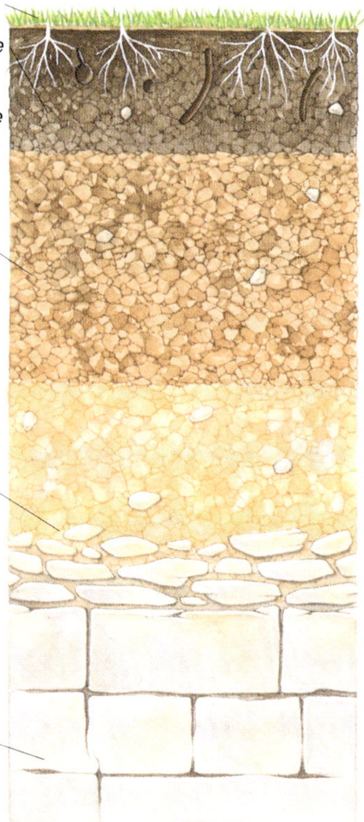

Horizon 0, humus layer: deposits of plant material

Horizon A, the topsoil: this is organically rich, but some minerals are taken out by groundwater.

Horizon B, the subsoil: this is less organic, but is rich in minerals brought down from the topsoil.

Horizon C, the parent rock: this is broken and weathered into loose chunks, and contains no organic material.

Horizon D, the underlying bedrock: the mineral content of the soil comes from this.

A sandy soil is light, and water drains through it easily. It only contains a small amount of organic matter, and so it is not very fertile.

Peat is a dark coloured soil containing a large proportion of humus that comes from the partial decay of bog plants. This soil tends to retain water.

Clay is a heavy soil and water cannot drain through it. It is sticky and plastic when wet, and can contain many nutrients.

Chalky soil is thin and stony, and drains water quickly. The organic material it contains decays quickly, and so it contains only a small amount of humus.

SOIL PROFILE

Soil is formed in a number of layers. Their sequence is called the soil profile. The layers, also called horizons, show the different things that go into making a soil – from the decay of rocks to the addition of material from living things. Not all soils have the same horizons, and their sizes vary from soil to soil.

A cloud forest in Venezuela

Hot climates can weather the bedrock to form thick soils rich in vegetable material.

Arctic landscape

Cold climates produce little weathering, so Arctic soils tend to be very thin.

SOIL THICKNESS

The depth of soil depends on a number of factors, such as the presence of a slope, where any soil formed may be washed away, and the nature of the bedrock. Limestone, for example, erodes more easily than sandstone, so it produces more decay products. But the most important factor is the climate and the erosional effect of the weather.

Small landslide in the Pindus mountains, Greece

SLOPES

Slopes are unstable because gravity pulls anything on them downwards. Any change in the soil adds to this downhill movement; the first frost pushes the soil downhill; raindrops dislodge particles downhill, and soil expansion caused by soaking takes soil downhill. As a result, artificial structures on a slope tend to lean, and growing trees are distorted.

Soil creep on slope

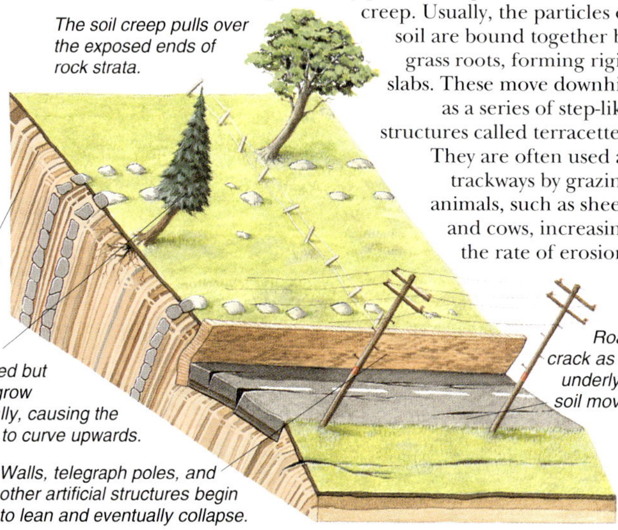

The soil creep pulls over the exposed ends of rock strata.

Weathered blocks move downhill.

Trees are tilted but try to grow vertically, causing the trunks to curve upwards.

Walls, telegraph poles, and other artificial structures begin to lean and eventually collapse.

Roads crack as the underlying soil moves.

SOIL CREEP

Soil on a slope moves gradually downhill, particle by particle – a process called soil creep. Usually, the particles of soil are bound together by grass roots, forming rigid slabs. These move downhill as a series of step-like structures called terracettes. They are often used as trackways by grazing animals, such as sheep and cows, increasing the rate of erosion.

Soil creep on the Chiltern Hills, England

Find out more

ORGANIC CHEMISTRY P.41
ROCKS AND MINERALS P.221
FOSSILS P.225
WEATHERING AND EROSION P.230
CLIMATES P.244

RIVERS

FLOOD
Rivers are important to people as a form of transport, as supplies of drinking and industrial waters, and as a source of irrigation. But they can also be a menace. A sudden increase in rainfall can produce floods that destroy the towns and cities that are built alongside the rivers.

A flood in Bangladesh. The river carries particles of sediment which give it its colour.

RAINWATER FALLS to form pools of water, or sinks into the soil and re-emerges as springs. This water is channelled into valleys and hollows, eventually forming the streams and rivers that flow down to the sea. Flowing water helps shape the landscape. It wears away the rocks of the mountains, redepositing the debris on the plains and lowlands, and eventually the floor of the sea. Most of the world's greatest rivers lie in tropical areas, where there is usually a constant supply of water because of heavy tropical rainfall.

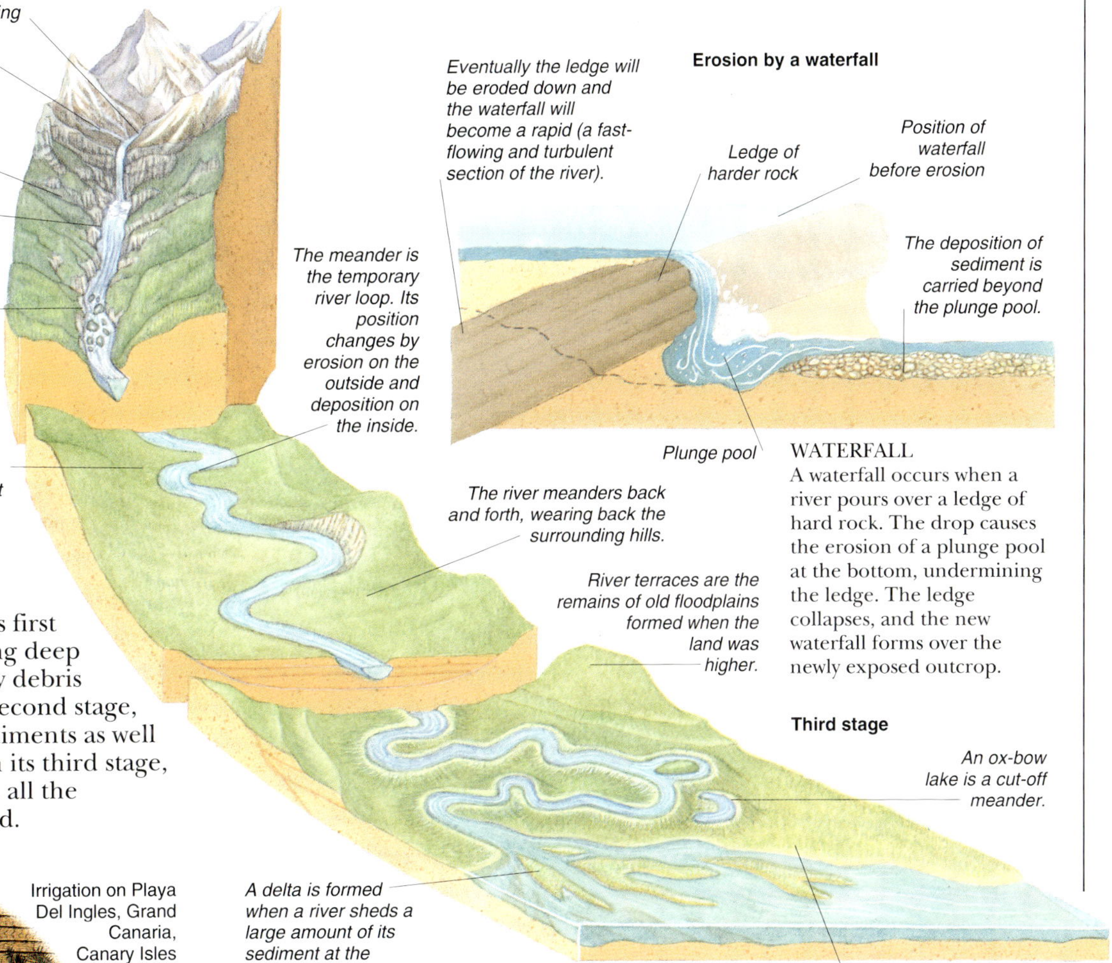

WATERFALL
A waterfall occurs when a river pours over a ledge of hard rock. The drop causes the erosion of a plunge pool at the bottom, undermining the ledge. The ledge collapses, and the new waterfall forms over the newly exposed outcrop.

RIVER STAGES

A river has three stages. In its first stage, it moves rapidly, cutting deep into its bed, picking up rocky debris and carrying it along. In its second stage, it slows down, depositing sediments as well as continuing the erosion. In its third stage, all its strength has gone, and all the transported debris is dropped.

Irrigation on Playa Del Ingles, Grand Canaria, Canary Isles

IRRIGATION
Crops need water to grow. Often the water from rivers is channelled to feed crops – a system known as irrigation. The early civilizations of Ancient Egypt produced complex irrigation systems fed from rivers such as the Nile.

HYDROELECTRIC POWER

The energy in moving water has been harnessed throughout history. Waterwheels once turned machinery that ground corn or worked looms. Today, water from dams can turn turbines that generate electricity for whole communities.

Sashta dam, a hydroelectric power station in Redding, California, U.S.A.

Find out more

WATER INDUSTRY P.83
GENERATORS P.159
WEATHERING AND EROSION P.230
SHORELINE P.236
RAIN P.264

SEAS AND OCEANS

DEEP BENEATH THE OCEAN waves, on the seabed, lies hidden land. There are mountain ranges, deep trenches, and vast open plains covering as much as two-thirds of the Earth's surface. The only way we can see them is by using complicated scientific equipment. The pattern of the land on the ocean bed is caused by the great movements of the Earth, called plate tectonics. The vast ocean ridges build up when the great plates at the Earth's surface are created. The great underwater trenches form when one plate is sucked down underneath another one and disappears.

World map of ocean ridges and trenches

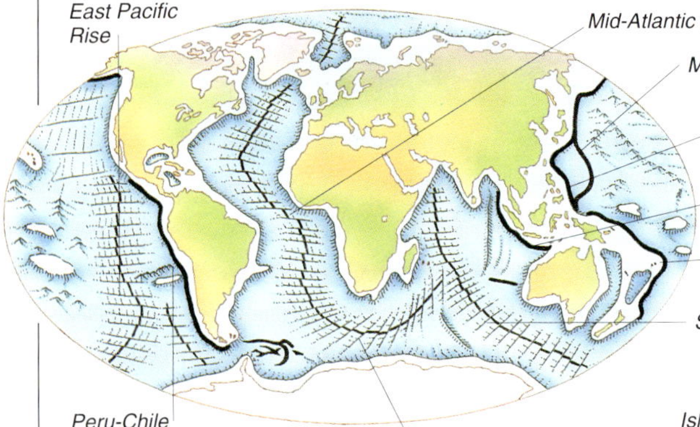

SEABED MAP
A few decades ago, the ocean floor was a mystery. Then, in the 1960s, scientists invented instruments that could detect shapes in the land from a distance. Today's maps of the seabed are made using these remote sensing images.

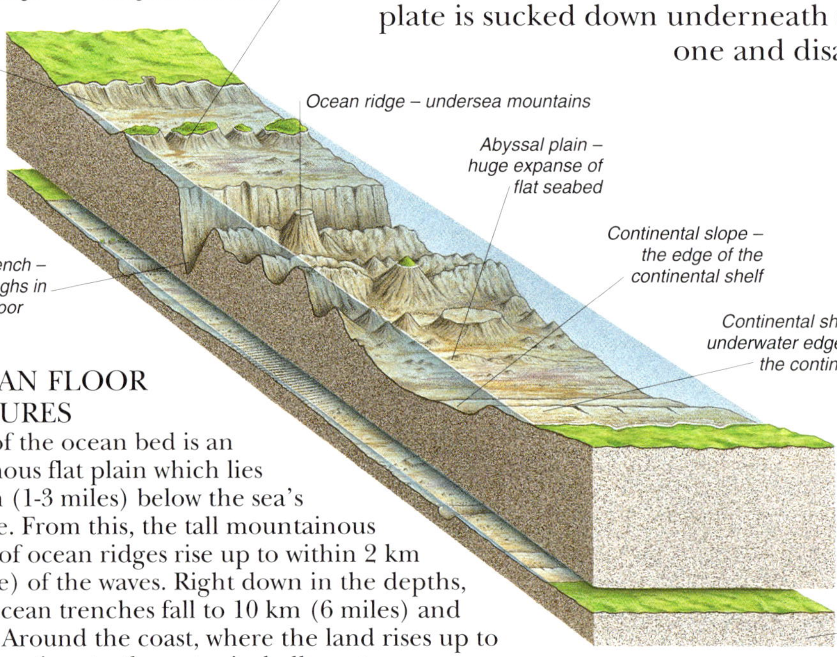

The lower part of the diagram shows the heights and depths in their true scale.

A coelacanth (*Latimeria chalumnae*) found in the Comores Islands

COELACANTH
Strange creatures lurk in the hidden depths of the oceans. The coelacanth is a fish that scientists thought had been extinct for 200 million years. In 1938, one was caught in the ocean waters off Madagascar and they have been caught there ever since. It is easier for ancient animals to survive in the ocean depths because living conditions do not change much.

OCEAN FLOOR FEATURES

Most of the ocean bed is an enormous flat plain which lies 3-4 km (1-3 miles) below the sea's surface. From this, the tall mountainous peaks of ocean ridges rise up to within 2 km (1 mile) of the waves. Right down in the depths, dark ocean trenches fall to 10 km (6 miles) and more. Around the coast, where the land rises up to form continents, the water is shallowest.

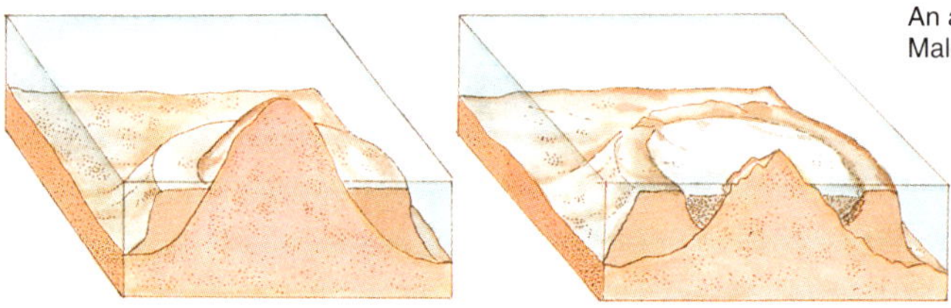

A coral reef begins to grow in the shallow water around a tropical island.

If the island sinks, the coral keeps growing and forms a barrier reef separated from the island.

An atoll in the Maldives

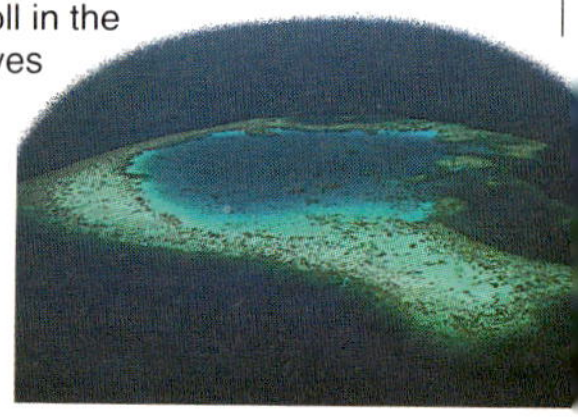

When the island disappears under the waves, it leaves a ring, an atoll, of coral with a lagoon in the centre.

SMOKER COMMUNITY
Hot volcanic waters bubble up along the ocean ridges. These are full of chemicals that attract bacteria. Animals that eat the bacteria have evolved there, and so have other animals that eat them. Creatures that have never seen sunlight live in these dark, distant waters, such as these crustacea and mussels in the Galápagos Islands.

CORAL REEFS
Coral will only grow where the water is clear, warm, and shallow. The shores of small, tropical islands are ideal. Each coral organism makes a limy shell that joins with others to form a firm foundation on which still more corals can grow. In this way, vast shelves, called reefs, build up to just below the water surface.

Find out more

CHEMISTRY OF WATER P.75
STRUCTURE OF THE EARTH P.212
ROCKS AND MINERALS P.221
WAVES, TIDES, AND CURRENTS P.235

WAVES, TIDES, AND CURRENTS

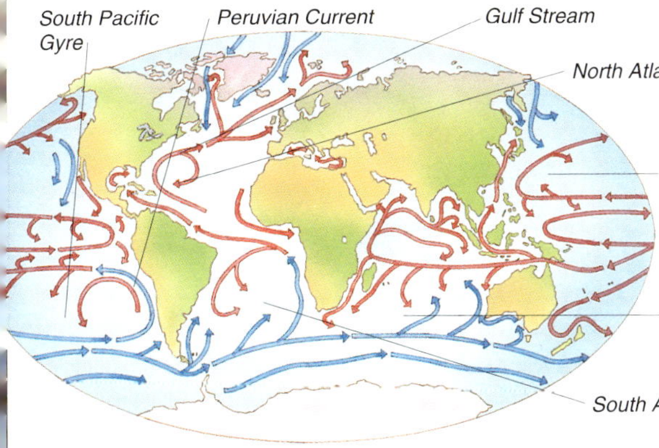

OCEAN CURRENTS
The huge swirling currents in the oceans are caused by prevailing winds. The Trade Winds in the South Pacific ocean sweep the cold Peruvian current up the west coast of South America.

THE OCEANS NEVER STAND STILL. Local winds push the surface of the sea into waves which pound onto the shore. The tides wash in and out of harbours twice a day, following the pull of the Sun and the Moon. At the same time, world winds sweep the seas into great ocean currents. As the Earth spins, the currents twist and flow around the oceans in huge circles called gyres. Warm currents travel away from the Equator, and cool ones flow back towards it. The winds that blow over these currents then carry warm or cool temperatures to the land nearby, so currents have a great effect on climate. The Gulf Stream in the Atlantic ocean keeps northwest Europe warm in winter.

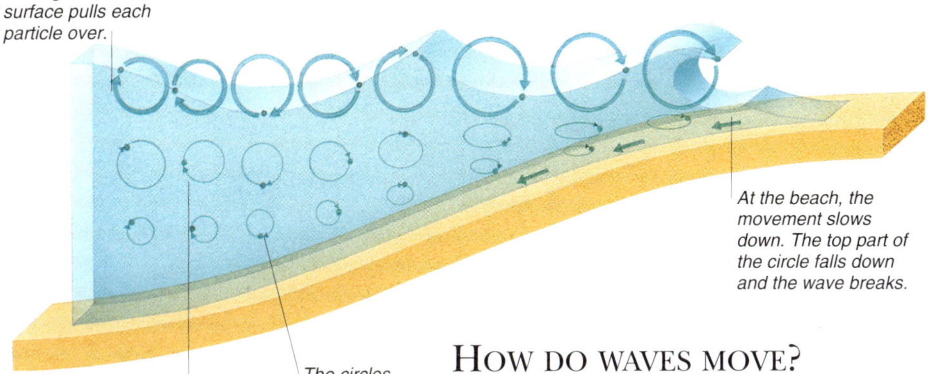

TSUNAMI

This giant wave is caused by an undersea earthquake. Vibrations rush through the ocean at hundreds of kilometres an hour. When they reach shallow waters they slow down and build up into vast waves, at times 76 m (250 ft) tall. The tsunami crashes onto the shore, sweeping away anything in its way.

Damage after a tsunami in Alaska, March 1964

HOW DO WAVES MOVE?

When the wind brushes the surface of the sea, it sends ripples through the water. Although the waves travel vast distances across the ocean, each water particle only goes around in a circle.

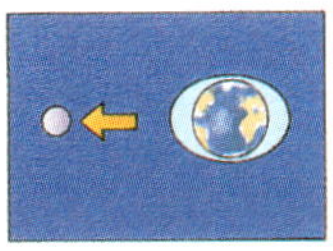
Moon pulls out a high tide on the Earth just beneath it.

Another high tide forms on the far side because of the Earth's spin.

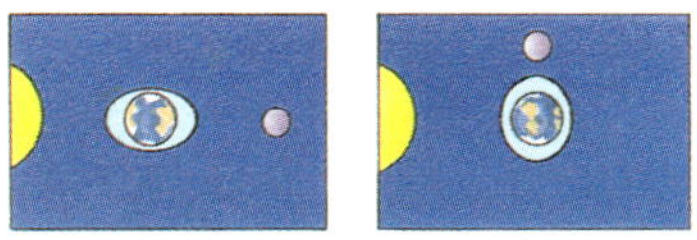
When the Sun and Moon line up, the high tides are very high and the low tides very low.

When the Sun and the Moon pull in different directions, the tides are not as high and low.

Child swings round in big circle like the Moon circling the Earth.

Mother swings in a smaller circle like the Earth pulled round by the Moon.

Skirt flies out behind like water flung away from the Moon.

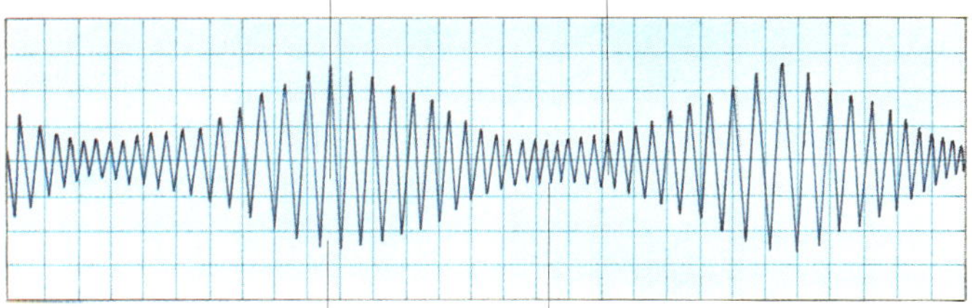

HOW THE TIDES WORK

Imagine a mother swinging her child around in circles. As they twirl, the mother's skirt flies out behind her. The child is like the Moon circling the Earth. The mother is like the Earth, and her skirt is like the high tide on the side of the Earth facing away from the Moon.

SUN, MOON, AND TIDES
The pull of the Moon makes the water bulge into a high tide on both sides of the Earth. As the Earth spins, each place has a high tide twice a day. The Sun pulls up the water too, but not so strongly. At one time of the month it adds to the Moon's pull. At another, it fights against it.

Find out more

CIRCULAR MOTION P.125
ROCKS AND MINERALS P.221
ICE AND GLACIERS P.228
WEATHERING AND EROSION P.230
SHORELINE P.236
UNIVERSE P.274

Shoreline

COASTLINE
The tremendous power of the sea is demonstrated here on this rocky coast at Kiwanda, Oregon, United States. Rocks form the basis of our landscape, but these are broken down and worn away by the continuous pounding of waves.

WHENEVER YOU GO PADDLING on a beach, you are standing on the edge of the sea, but on the beginning of the shore. Every piece of land has a shore, and each shore is unique. The features of a shore are determined by many factors, such as the strong winds, crashing waves, the temperature, climate, and the types of rocks that exist there. Shores can change from being sandy to rocky, or vice versa. The shoreline is shaped as the wind blows across the ocean surface, transferring some of its energy to the water. This energy is seen as waves that can travel for long distances. The energy of the waves is weakened as they hit the shoreline, but their destructive force can still wear away headlands and cliffs.

Headland erosion

Headlands are made up of hard rocks, but even these are eventually worn away. Waves approaching a headland curve around it, attacking it from the sides. This creates caves and arches, which are then further eroded. Erosion occurs in two main ways. Rock is damaged by stones flung up by the waves (a process known as corrasion or attrition), or cavitation may take place. In this process, cracks in the rock are enlarged, as air compressed by incoming water expands when the water retreats.

RIAS
If land subsides (sinks), or the sea level rises, coastal regions become flooded. At the end of the last ice age, ice caps melted in oceans worldwide and raised the sea level. Hills became islands, and river valleys flooded, creating indented coastlines with branching inlets called rias.

Rias and estuaries in Galicia, Spain

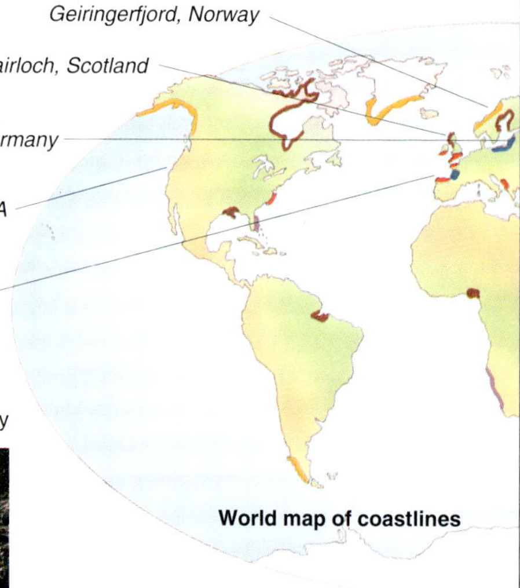

World map of coastlines

Geiringerfjord in Norway

FJORDS
When glaciers melt, they often leave U-shaped valleys. On the coast, rising sea levels flood these valleys, producing long narrow inlets with vertical sides. Deposits of rocks and other materials at the mouths of the valleys give the inlets very shallow entrances. Such inlets have the Norwegian name fjords or fiords, meaning a narrow strip of sea between steep cliffs.

CHANGING COASTLINES
The coastlines of the world do not always stay the same. They can change dramatically in a relatively short time as waves wear away the land and changing sea levels submerge or expose coastal areas.

Beach formation

Rocks worn away from headlands do not stay as rubble for long. They are ground down by waves into shingle (fragments of rock) and sand, dragged along the sea floor, and eventually deposited in a fairly sheltered place to form a beach. Even there, rock particles do not stop moving. They are constantly picked up and moved further by storm-generated waves, and the lightest pieces are shifted about by wind. Because of this continual movement, a winter beach may consist of coarse pebbles, while the same beach in the summer may be sandy. Today, special fences called groynes help stop this process.

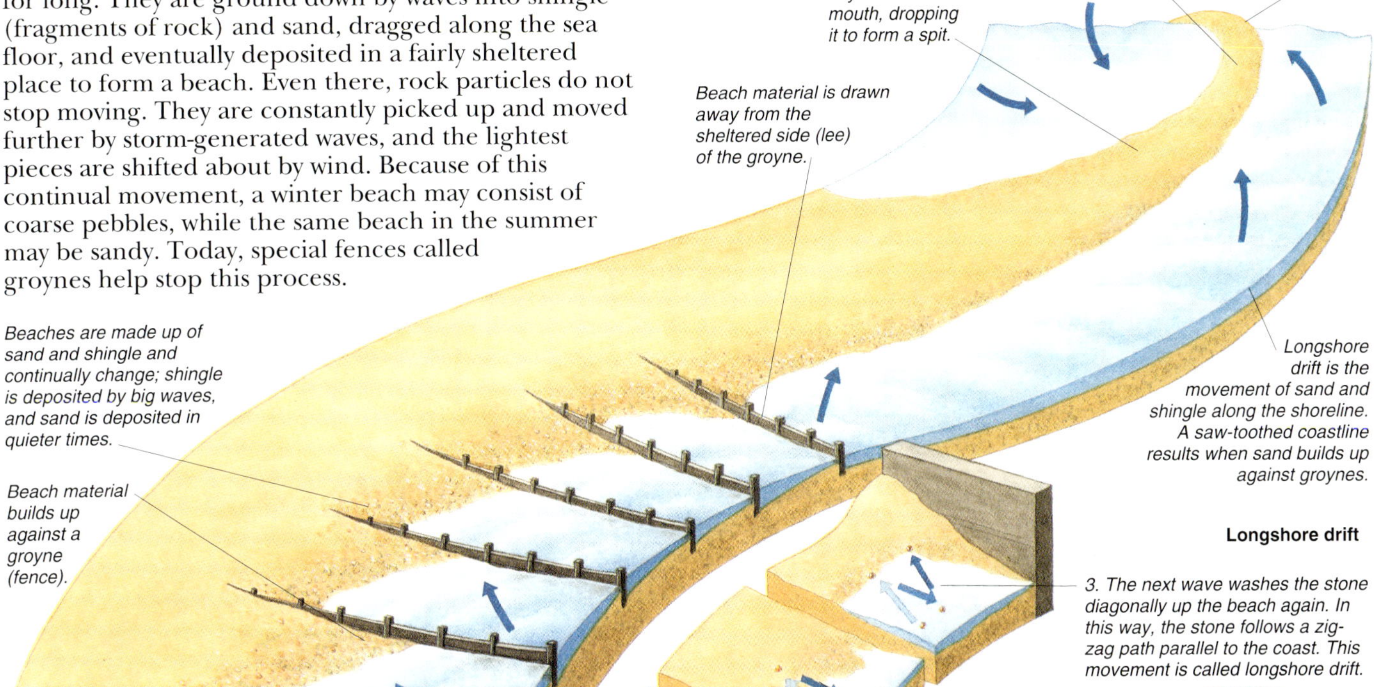
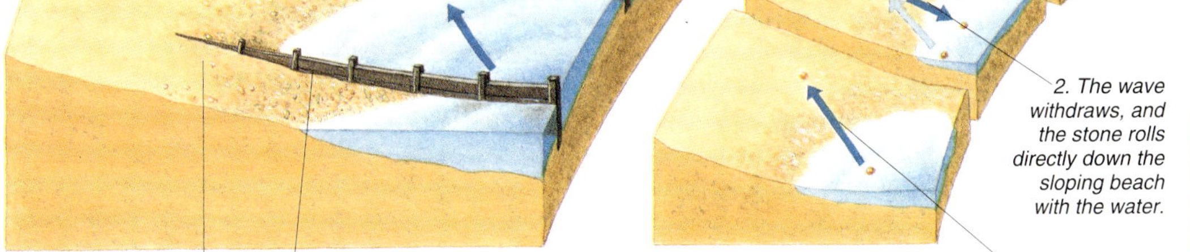

Moving beaches

Beach particles are continually moved by the ebb and flow of waves in a process called longshore drift. As they reach the shore, waves wash stones and sand grains backwards and forwards, and may cause them to drift along the beach to a new place.

A tombolo in Cha Bahar Makran, Iran

Sand spits

A sand spit forming outwards from the land across a bay may go right across to form a bar. If a spit forms between an island and the shore, it is given the name tombolo.

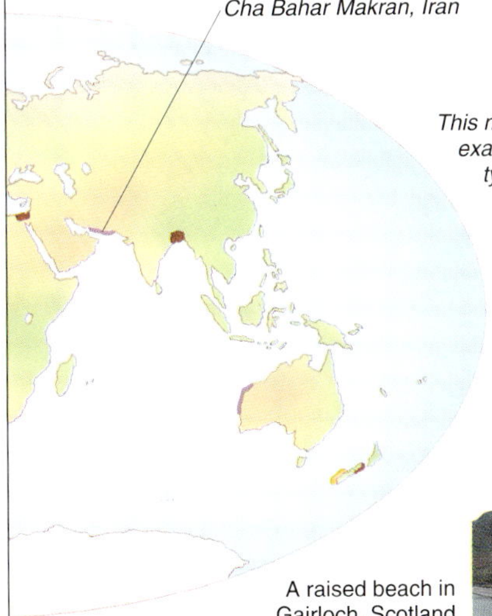

This map shows a few examples of the different types of coastlines found around the world. The colour coding helps identify each type.

A lowland beach in Sylt Island, Germany

Salt marshes

Areas of sand built up by waves can be moved about by wind to form dunes. The dunes may cut off areas of fresh or slightly salty (brackish) water, which then collect mud and develop into salt marshes.

A raised beach in Gairloch, Scotland

Making new land

The sea has the power to build up as well as destroy land. Eroded material deposited on beaches increases the land area, while lowering sea levels expose land that was once submerged.

Raised beach

When land rises or the sea level falls, the shoreline is left high and dry. This is known as a raised beach. Many raised beaches formed in northern Europe at the end of the last ice age. As ice melted, the land slowly began to rise up.

Find out more

Rocks and minerals p.221
Weathering and erosion p.230
Waves, tides, and currents p.235
Weather p.241

COAL

THE SUN'S ENERGY from millions of years ago has been preserved in a rock called coal. The Sun makes plants grow. If these plants are preserved under pressure for millions of years, they form a solid – coal. When coal is burned today, this ancient energy is released as heat. Coal contains the element carbon – wood contains about 50 per cent carbon; coal can contain up to 90 per cent carbon. Most coal began to form about 350 million years ago, during the Carboniferous period. The huge swampy forests that grew then are preserved today as the world's main coal deposits.

World distribution of coal

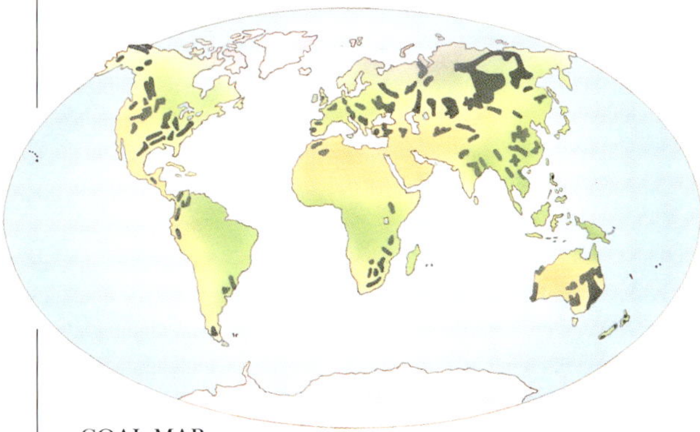

COAL MAP
Most of the world's coal comes from deposits laid down in the Carboniferous period, when the Earth's vegetation was most lush. However, some important coal seams (deposits of coal) of northern Europe are much younger, made of wood from the early Tertiary period, about 40 million years ago.

A peat cutting site in the Falkland Islands

PEAT
Before coal is formed, a fibrous material called peat develops. In fact, at this very minute, peat is developing in all the bogs of the world. It is sometimes used for fuel and as a rich plant food.

COAL FORMATION

As coal is a rock formed from the remains of living things, it is called a biogenic sedimentary rock. Millions of years ago, forests died and were buried in swamps before the wood had time to decay. As the mud and sand of the swamps slowly turned to stone, the make-up of the wood changed. Its components were carbon, hydrogen, and oxygen; the hydrogen and oxygen were removed, leaving a concentrated deposit of carbon.

Forests grow well in swampy conditions.

The trees eventually die, covered with swamp material. This is compressed into a layer.

Peat

As it loses its oxygen, the buried plant material is compressed into the fibrous material called peat.

Lignite

Sediments continue to be deposited that compress the peat into rock. More oxygen is removed from the peat, turning it into soft brown coal, called lignite.

Bituminous coal

Eventually the wood is compressed so much that it becomes the compact black glossy coal called bituminous coal. This is the most common type of coal used by industry.

MINING COAL
Coal is extracted from the ground by mining. If a coal seam emerges at the ground surface, miners can tunnel in horizontally. This is a drift mine. More often, a vertical tunnel is needed to reach coal deep underground. This is a shaft mine. If the coal occurs near the surface, the covering layers of ground are stripped off to reach the coal. This is an open-cast mine. Here extracted coal is being stacked in Australia.

DANGEROUS MINES
The Industrial Revolution in Europe during the 18th century depended on coal – it was vital as an energy source. But mining coal was very dangerous. Even children had to work down the mines in appalling conditions. One safety device was invented by a scientist named Humphry Davy. The Davy safety lamp detected when gases in a mine reached a dangerous level.

Davy lamp

Find out more

CARBON P.40
ORGANIC CHEMISTRY P.41
COAL PRODUCTS P.96
STRUCTURE OF THE EARTH P.212
SEDIMENTARY ROCKS P.223
FACT FINDER P.414

OIL AND GAS

WHAT HAPPENED to all the tiny plants and animals that died millions of years ago in the sea? They formed oil – the oil that drives cars, runs factories, and is used to make many useful chemicals. The animal matter that gathers on a seabed is broken down slowly by bacteria. This process gives off a gas called methane, or natural gas. If the material left heats up, it breaks down into light molecules called hydrocarbons that move through the rocks and gather as oil. Although natural gas is a by-product, the natural gas that is extracted from the rocks in places such as the North Sea is actually a breakdown product of coal.

World distribution of oil and gas

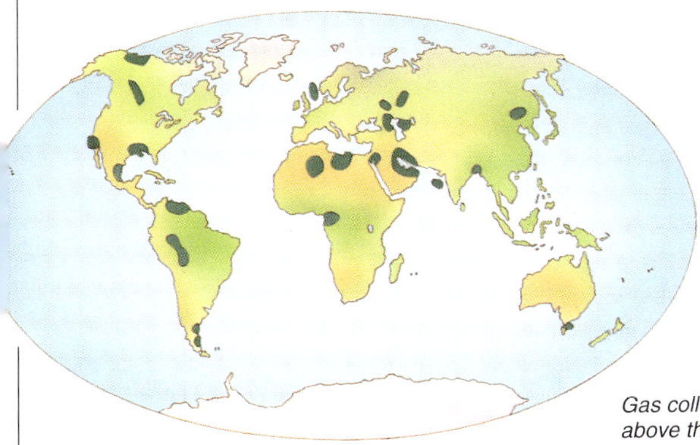

OIL MAP
The oil in the main oilfields of the world comes out of rocks that date from two periods in time: the Ordovician-Devonian period (400 to 350 million years ago) and the Jurassic-Cretaceous period (200 to 65 million years ago).

Gas collects above the oil.

Impermeable rock that the oil cannot travel through. Oil is trapped beneath it.

Porous rock that the oil can travel through

Oil collects in a porous rock called a reservoir rock, where it is trapped. Usually it is trapped by impermeable rock that will not let the oil pass.

One oil trap occurs when the reservoir rock is faulted against another rock.

In a stratigraphic trap, isolated beds of porous rock are embedded in impermeable rock. If these beds are tilted, the oil collects at one end.

OIL RESERVOIR

Animal matter collected in the rocks decays into oil droplets that float in the groundwater below. Because they are lighter than the groundwater, the droplets float upwards through pores in the rock, until they are trapped by a layer that will not let them pass – a cap rock. Here they collect to form an oil reservoir.

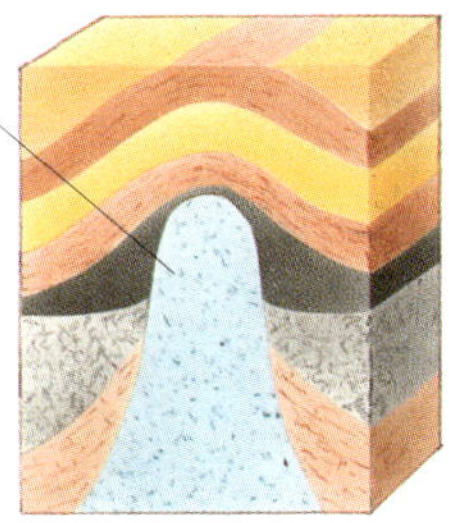

Beds of salt may bend under pressure and rise through the rocks above, pushing them into a dome. Oil can gather in this dome.

ALTERNATIVE THEORY

Although most scientists agree that oil has been made from living things, there is a theory that it is actually formed from metamorphic rocks. This may be proved or disproved by a borehole that is currently being drilled into metamorphic rocks in Sweden.

Siljan ring experiment

EXPLORATION RIGS
Possible oil reservoirs are found by studying the surface land and by a method called remote sensing – sound waves are sent into the Earth, and their reflections are recorded. However, the presence of oil can only be proved by drilling a hole into this ground. This work is done with a structure called an exploration rig.

Workers on an exploration rig in the North Sea

The oil rig floats low in the water, so that it is not affected by waves.

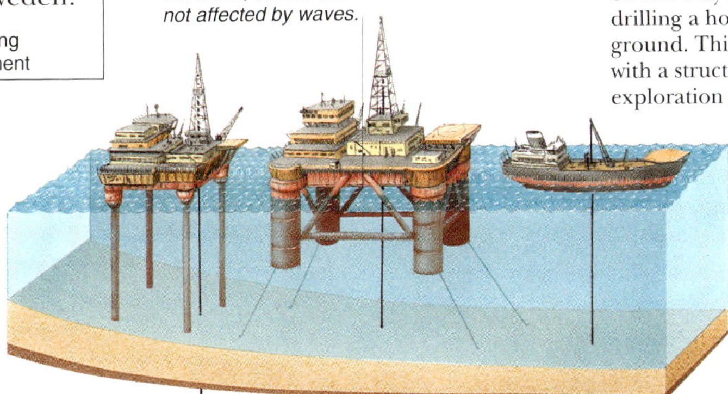

A jack-up rig is used in fairly shallow waters. It has legs that extend to the sea floor.

A tension-leg rig is used in deeper water. It floats but is secured to the seabed by tethers.

In very deep water, ships are used. The oil drill is put out through a hole in the hull.

PRODUCTION PLATFORM
Once it has been proved that a good amount of oil is present, it is extracted by means of a production platform. This sends down boreholes to the reservoir rocks, pumps up the oil, and channels it into pipelines or into tankers that transport it to a refinery.

Find out more

ORGANIC CHEMISTRY P.41
CHEMICAL INDUSTRY P.82
GAS PRODUCTS P.97
OIL PRODUCTS P.98
SEAS AND OCEANS P.234
FACT FINDER P.414

Mapping the Earth

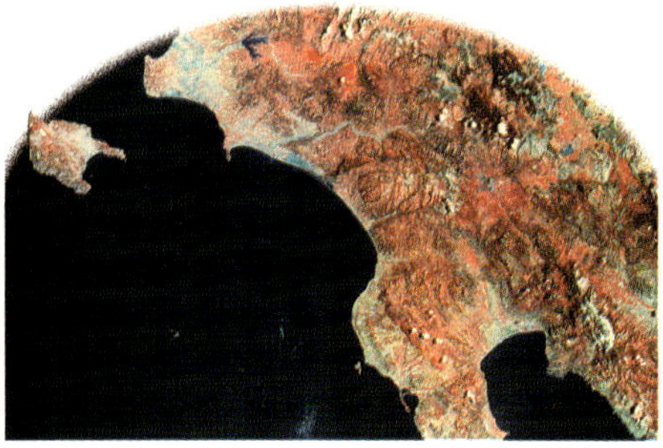

Landsat image of Peloponnesus in southern Greece

SATELLITE MAP
Modern space technology has revolutionized cartography (map-making). Maps are drawn from satellite photographs, which show how the Earth looks from space. Satellites are very sensitive and can pick out details such as types of crops grown in certain parts of the world, and the heat given off by factories.

IMAGINE TRYING TO SEE the whole world at a glance. This is what a map enables us to do. Without a map, it would be very difficult to get an idea of what the Earth looks like. For thousands of years, people have been creating maps to help them discover their surroundings. As maps have become more sophisticated, large-scale maps have been drawn that show geographical features, such as mountains and rivers, using symbols. Mapping the whole Earth, however, involves laying out the curved surface of the globe on a flat piece of paper. But any map that is created to do this will be distorted in some way.

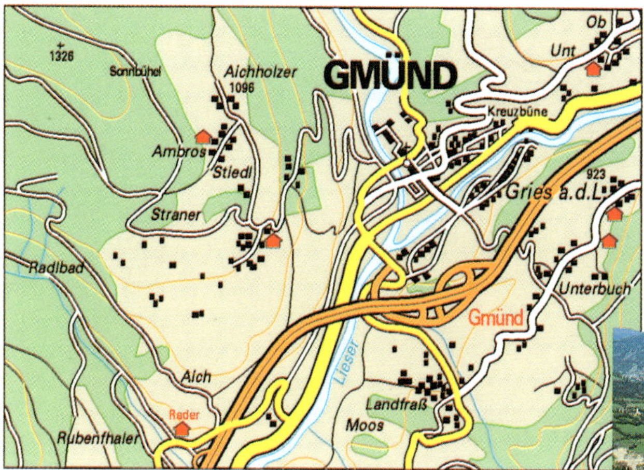

Key to symbols

Map

A map is a picture designed to show an area of the Earth's surface. There are many different types of maps available. The appearance and detail of each map depends on what it will be used for. Those used for route finding, for example, may emphasize the roads, showing different types of road represented by different symbols. Political maps will concentrate on boundaries and legal divisions.

Gmünd in Austria

AERIAL PHOTOGRAPH
A photograph of an area taken from an aeroplane gives an accurate representation of what an area looks like. However, this photograph will not show the conventional symbols that make a map usable.

Cylindrical projection

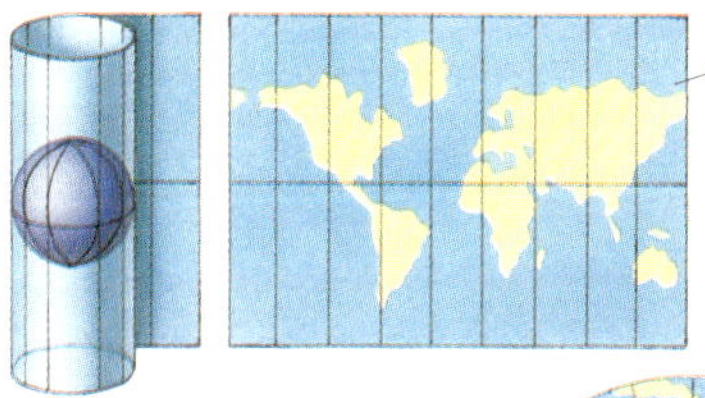

In the cylindrical projection, the imaginary sheet of paper is rolled around the Earth, touching it at the Equator. A map designed in this way always shows the north at the top, but the areas are distorted.

Conical projection

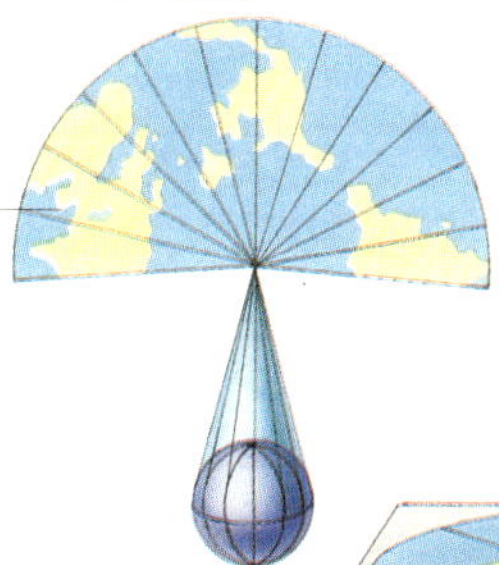

In the conical projection, the imaginary paper forms a cone, touching the Earth along a particular line of latitude. The map drawn in this way shows the least distortion to areas.

In the zenithal or azimuthal projection, the paper touches the globe at one point. If this point is the Pole, then the lines of longitude show their correct angles.

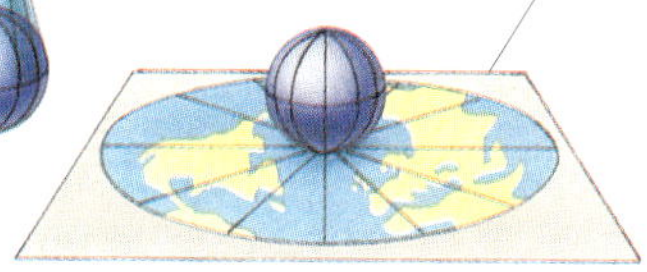

Zenithal projection

PROJECTIONS
To display the curved surface of the Earth accurately on a flat sheet of paper, a technique called projection is used. Imagine that the Earth is transparent and that there is a light at the centre. This light throws shadows of the Earth's surface features on a flat sheet of paper positioned nearby. The shadow image that falls on the sheet of paper is the basis of the map.

PETERS' MAP
The Peters' map was designed in 1977 by Arnos Peters. This map shows the true sizes of continents. But, for Peters to achieve this, the shapes of the continents have had to be stretched.

MERCATOR
The Mercator projection, first published in 1569, is based on the cylindrical projection. As directions are not distorted, it is useful for navigation and meteorological maps in which wind directions are important. However, the distortion of areas is so great that Greenland appears bigger than Africa, when in fact it has only about one-twelfth of its area.

Flemish geographer Gerardus Mercator, born Gerhard Kremer (1512-94)

Mercator's projection

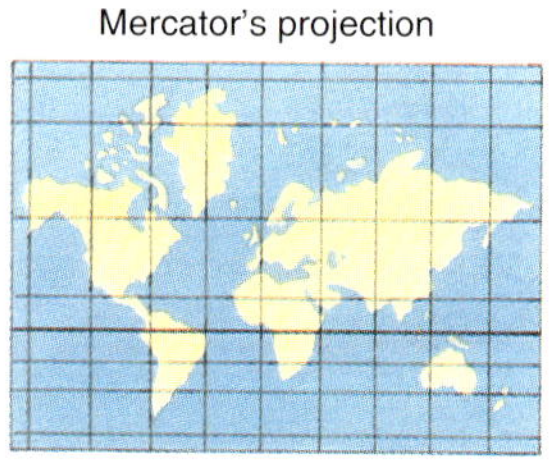

Peters' projection

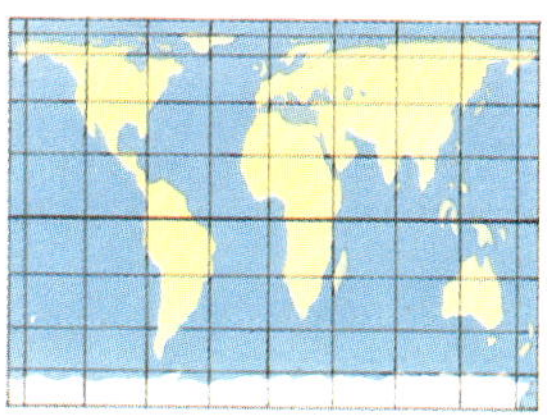

Find out more

TELESCOPES ON EARTH P.297
TELESCOPES IN SPACE P.298
SATELLITES P.300
SPACE PROBES P.301
SPACE STATIONS P.304
FACT FINDER P.414

WEATHER

THE LIVES OF US ALL are affected by the weather – what we eat and drink, what we wear, how we behave, and what our homes are like. Weather has even shaped the landscape. Wind and rain, snow and ice all wear away the rocks and grind down the mountains. Weather is with us all the time. It is the state of the air at any particular place and time. It can be hot, cold, windy, still, wet, or dry. In some places it changes from day to day; in others it stays much the same all year round. The usual weather of a place from year to year is called its climate. Climate depends mainly on how far north or south of the Equator a place is and therefore how much sun it gets.

RAIN
People who have a lot of rainy weather will know that a sky full of dark grey-black clouds means it's going to rain. Rain clouds are deep and filled with rain. They stop the Sun's rays from shining through to the ground. The deeper and darker the clouds, the more rain is likely to fall.

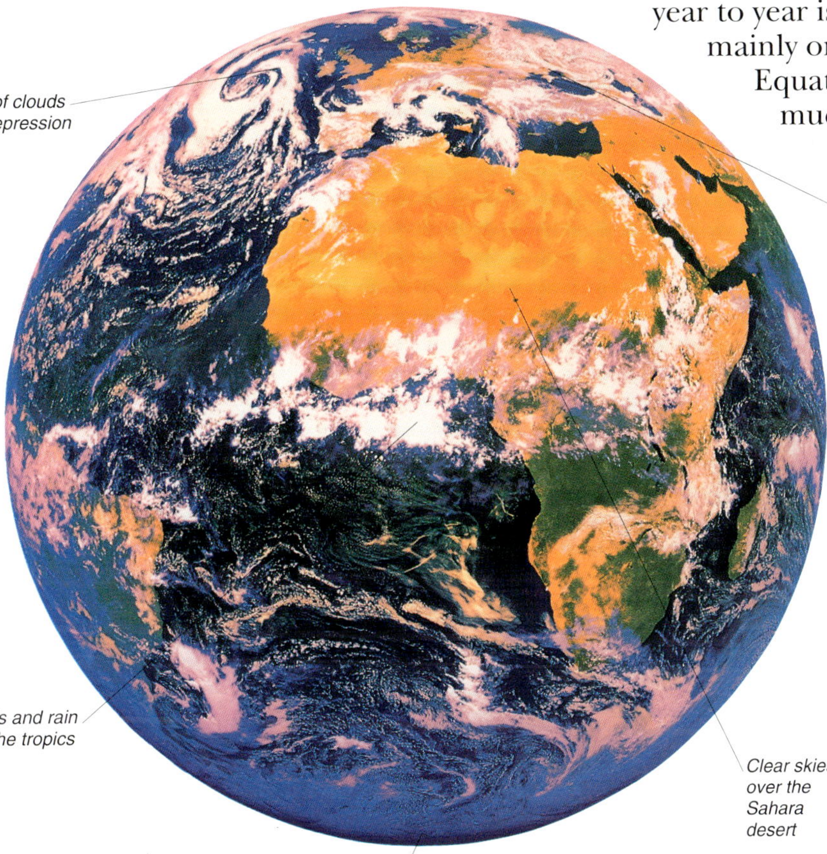

Swirl of clouds in a depression

Heavy clouds over Asia

Clouds and rain over the tropics

Clear skies over the Sahara desert

Clear skies over Antarctica

SUN
The places with the hottest weather in the world are the dry deserts, a little way away from the Equator. Here, there are no clouds to stop the sun getting through. The Sahara desert in Africa has cloudless skies nearly every day.

SUN GOD
Many ancient civilizations worshipped special gods who they thought were responsible for the weather. The Aztecs of Mexico worshipped the Sun god Tonatuich to ask for sunshine to ripen their crops. Without enough sunshine, the crops failed and there was famine. Tonatuich and all that he represented was so important to the Aztecs that they built temples and even sacrificed humans in their eagerness to please him.

CROP DAMAGE
Strong winds, rain, and hail are all bad news for farmers as crops can be severely damaged by them. Forecasters try to give farmers warning of bad weather so that they can take precautions. All the oranges in this pile from California, in the United States, have been spoiled and are unfit for sale.

SUNSHINE

IF THE SUN were surrounded by a shell of ice 1.5 km (about 1 mile) thick, the heat from the Sun would melt all the ice in just over two hours. All this heat comes from nuclear reactions inside the Sun. The surface of the Sun has a temperature of more than 5,500°C (9,900°F). The Sun pours out energy in all directions and our weather and climate depend on this energy. The Sun is so big that one million planets the size of the Earth could fit inside it. It looks so small because it is 150 million km (93 million miles) away. But even at this distance, the Sun is so bright that you must never look directly at it: it could damage your eyes.

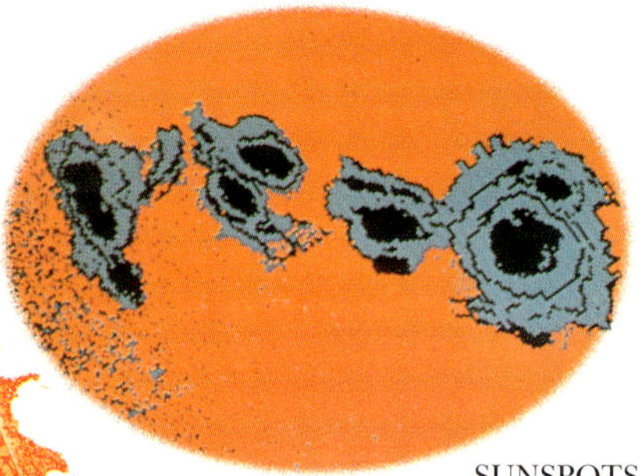

SUNSPOTS
Sometimes there are dark spots on the Sun. They are cooler than the rest of the Sun, but still as hot as 4,000 °C (7,000 °F). The number of these sunspots increases and decreases in an 11-year cycle. This photograph was taken on 1 September, 1989, a few months before maximum sunspot activity.

DROUGHT CYCLE
Some scientists think that sunspots affect the weather. In some parts of the world, the rains have failed roughly every 22 years – every two sunspot cycles – causing severe drought. This happened in North America in the 1930s, the 1950s, and the 1970s. If this sunspot theory is correct, the rains are due to fail again at the end of the 1990s. Drought can cause rivers to dry up completely.

MAKING WEATHER

All weather conditions happen because the heat from the Sun keeps the air constantly moving. As the surface of the Earth heats up, it heats the air. Hot air rises and cooler air moves in to take its place, stirring up winds. Heat from the Sun makes water evaporate from the seas and form clouds. When the clouds cool down, their moisture falls as rain.

EDWARD MAUNDER
The British astronomer Edward Maunder (1851-1928) was surprised to find that historical records of the Sun's activity showed there were no sunspots at all between 1645 and 1715. This is now called "the Maunder Minimum". At the same time, Europe was so cold that the period is known as the "Little Ice Age". Maunder married his assistant Annie Russell and worked closely with her. She was one of the world's first women astronomers and became famous in her own right.

The diameter of the Sun is 108 times bigger than the diameter of the Earth. But the Earth is a solid ball of rock, and the Sun is a ball of hot gas.

MAGNIFYING THE SUN
The power of the Sun's rays can be focused by an ordinary magnifying glass to burn holes in a piece of paper. Do not try this without an adult to help you. In hot, dry countries, special curved mirrors can be used to focus the Sun's rays to heat up a "hotplate" for cooking.

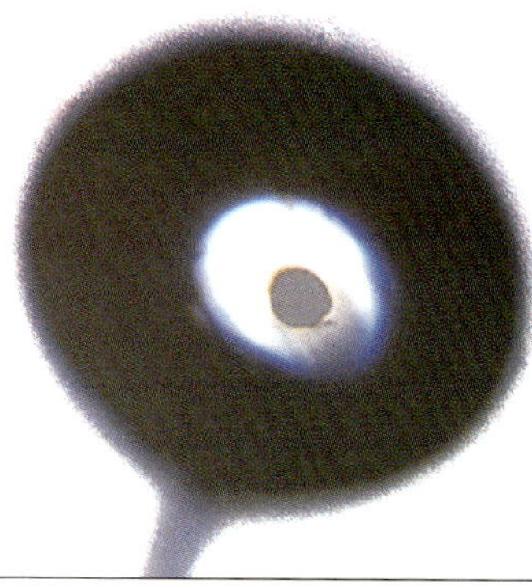

Find out more

CHANGING CLIMATES P.246
WINDS P.254
FORMATION OF CLOUDS P.262
RAIN P.264
SUN P.284
EARTH P.287

SEASONS

THE EARTH IS LIKE a spinning top moving in an orbit around the Sun. The spinning Earth leans over in its orbit, always tilting the same way. It takes 365.26 days to orbit the Sun completely. When the Earth is on one side of the Sun, the tilt leans the Northern Hemisphere towards the Sun. Six months later, when the Earth is on the other side of the Sun, the Southern Hemisphere leans towards the Sun. In the hemisphere leaning towards the Sun, the Sun rises high in the sky and the days are long and hot; it is summer. In the hemisphere leaning away from the Sun, the Sun rises lower in the sky and days are short; it is winter.

MIDNIGHT SUN
In regions near the North and South Pole, the Sun does not set for several months during the summer. In countries such as Finland it is daylight for 24 hours. This happens because of the tilt of the Earth. These areas are called the land of the midnight Sun. While one Pole has constant daylight, the other is shrouded in a dark mid-winter where the Sun never rises.

WHITE CHRISTMAS
At Christmas, in December, it is winter in the Northern Hemisphere. Countries such as Norway and Canada are cold and usually have snow. People have to wear warm clothes when they go outside.

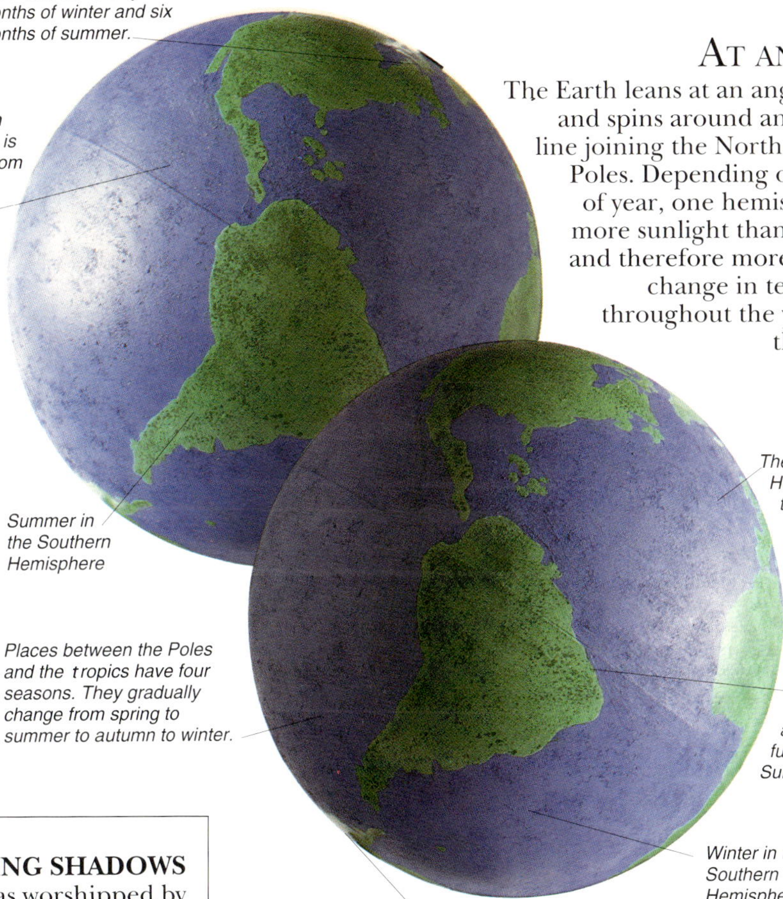

AT AN ANGLE

The Earth leans at an angle of 23.5° and spins around an imaginary line joining the North and South Poles. Depending on the time of year, one hemisphere gets more sunlight than the other, and therefore more heat. The change in temperature throughout the year causes the seasons.

CHRISTMAS ON THE BEACH
In the Southern Hemisphere, countries such as Australia have Christmas during the summer. The weather is just right for a dip in the sea.

CASTING SHADOWS

The Sun was worshipped by some Ancient civilizations. They knew the Sun's path changes. This stone in the Inca city of Machu Pichu in Peru is the *Intihuatana* – the seat of Inti the Sun Lord. The Incas noted how the length of the shadow the stone cast at noon changed during the year.

Find out more

FORMATION OF THE EARTH p.210
SUNSHINE p.242
SNOW p.266
SOLAR SYSTEM p.283
POLAR AND TUNDRA LANDS p.382

ATMOSPHERE

LIFE ON EARTH EXISTS only because of the atmosphere. It is like a blanket around the Earth, protecting it from the Sun and providing the necessary conditions in which animals and plants can live. Other planets have atmospheres, but these are very different. On Venus, the air is thick. It contains many more gas molecules than Earth's atmosphere and the pressure is 100 times greater than on Earth. The Sun's heat is trapped and temperatures reach 480°C (900°F). It is too hot for liquid water to exist. The atmosphere on Mars is thin. The Sun's heat bounces away and temperatures can fall to -120°C (-180°F). Liquid water cannot exist here either. Conditions on Earth are in between those on Mars and Venus. Earth is sometimes called the Goldilocks planet because the conditions are like Baby Bear's porridge – just right!

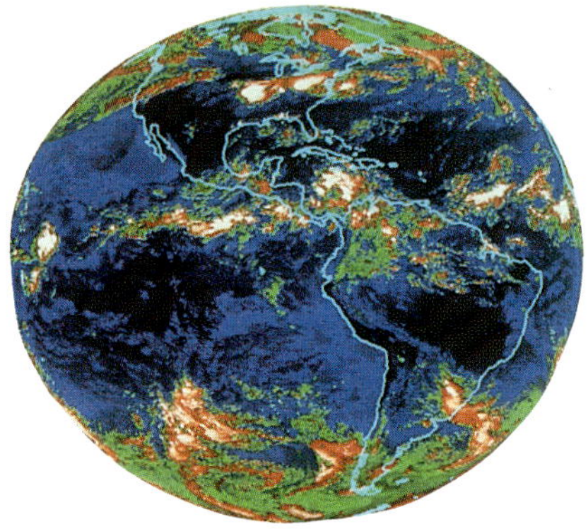

EARTH FROM SPACE
Satellites can take photos of the Earth at three different wavelengths at the same time. Infrared pictures show temperature changes – black, blue, green, red, and white showing hot to cold. Normal photos show the land and sea. Other pictures show how much water vapour is in the air.

LAYERS OF THE ATMOSPHERE

The atmosphere is made up of five main layers: the troposphere, stratosphere, mesosphere, thermosphere, and exosphere. The air gets thinner as you go higher, which is why climbers usually take oxygen with them when climbing high mountains. The troposphere is the only layer in which living things can breathe normally.

BELT ROUND THE EARTH
This photograph, taken from space as the Sun sets, shows bands of air of different heights (and different densities). The photo reveals how narrow the belt of atmosphere around the Earth is.

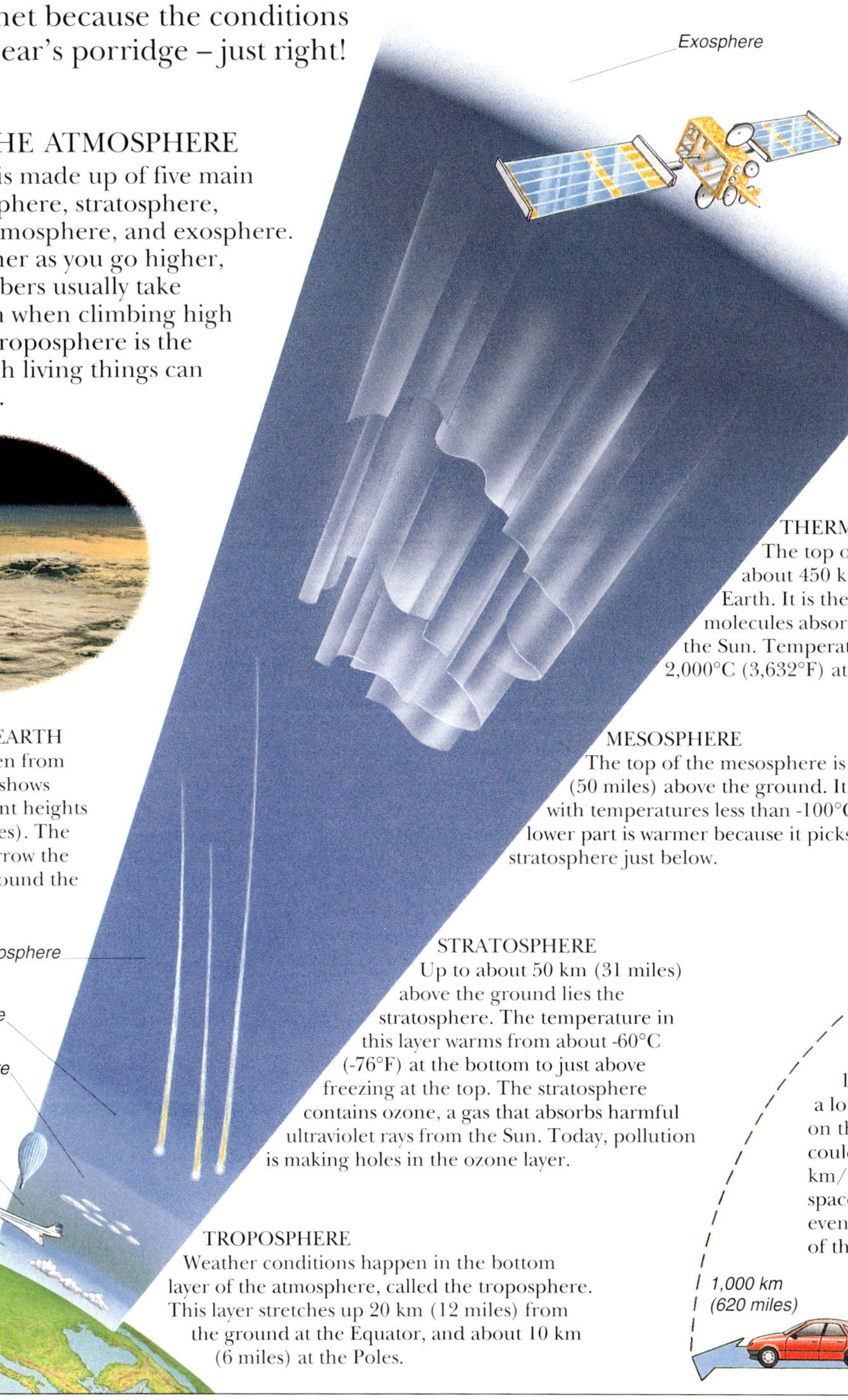

EXOSPHERE
The top layer of the atmosphere sits about 900 km (560 miles) above Earth. The air is very thin and gas molecules are constantly "exiting" into space. This is why it is called the exosphere.

THERMOSPHERE
The top of the thermosphere is about 450 km (280 miles) above the Earth. It is the hottest layer, as the few air molecules absorb radiation coming from the Sun. Temperatures reach as high as 2,000°C (3,632°F) at the top.

MESOSPHERE
The top of the mesosphere is about 80 km (50 miles) above the ground. It is very cold here, with temperatures less than -100°C (-148°F). The lower part is warmer because it picks up heat from the stratosphere just below.

STRATOSPHERE
Up to about 50 km (31 miles) above the ground lies the stratosphere. The temperature in this layer warms from about -60°C (-76°F) at the bottom to just above freezing at the top. The stratosphere contains ozone, a gas that absorbs harmful ultraviolet rays from the Sun. Today, pollution is making holes in the ozone layer.

TROPOSPHERE
Weather conditions happen in the bottom layer of the atmosphere, called the troposphere. This layer stretches up 20 km (12 miles) from the ground at the Equator, and about 10 km (6 miles) at the Poles.

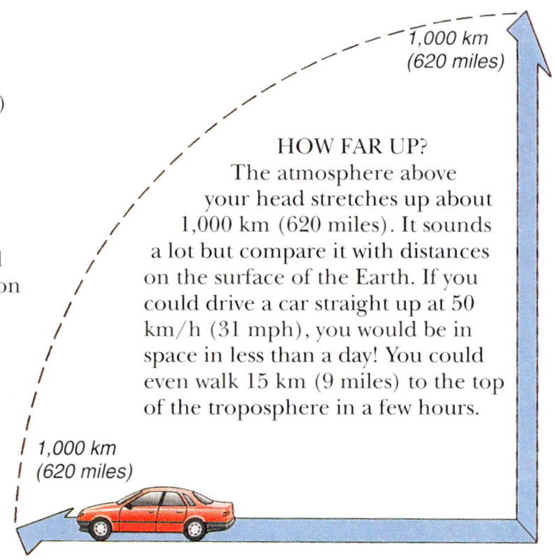

HOW FAR UP?
The atmosphere above your head stretches up about 1,000 km (620 miles). It sounds a lot but compare it with distances on the surface of the Earth. If you could drive a car straight up at 50 km/h (31 mph), you would be in space in less than a day! You could even walk 15 km (9 miles) to the top of the troposphere in a few hours.

Weather layer

The lowest layer of the atmosphere, the troposphere, is sometimes called the weather layer. It is the layer in which convection happens – warm air rises and cold air sinks to take its place. Clouds form in this layer too, bringing rain and snow. The clouds are trapped in the troposphere because the next layer up, the stratosphere, is warmer and acts like a lid. The troposphere cools from an average of 15°C (59°F)at the Earth's surface to -60°C (-76°F) at the tropopause (the top of the troposphere).

JAMES GLAISHER

A balloonist, Englishman James Glaisher (1809-1903), was also interested in the atmosphere. He and Henry Coxwell went up into the troposphere in a balloon and discovered that the air got cooler the higher they went. On one flight, Glaisher fainted because he had no oxygen equipment or protective clothes. In 1848, Glaisher started the first newspaper weather report in Europe for the London *Daily News*. He also made some of the first daily charts.

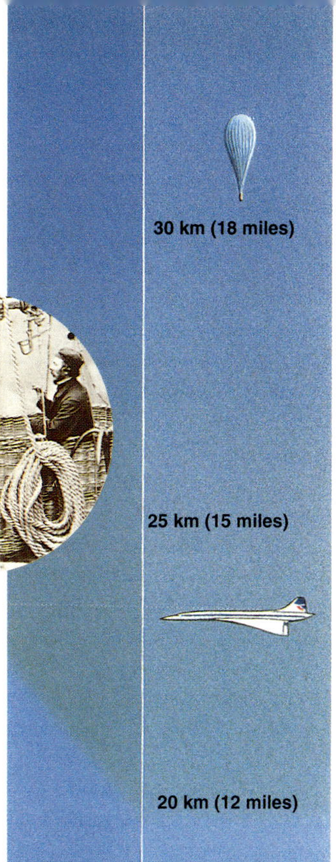

Storm clouds can reach up to 15,000 m (49,000 ft) high.

Cirrus clouds are the highest clouds. They form at the top of the troposphere.

Air has to rise to go over mountains. The weather on each side can be very different.

Flying though the troposphere can be bumpy because of the moving air.

Small, puffy, white clouds form when bubbles of warm air rise and cool.

Lightning is caused by the build-up of static electricity in storm clouds.

The air is full of water vapour, which turns to water droplets in some clouds and falls as rain.

Almost all clouds form in the bottom 10-12 km (6-7 miles) of the atmosphere.

ATMOSPHERIC POLLUTION

The rays of sunshine shining through this window in St Peter's Cathedral in Rome, Italy, show that the air is full of particles of dust and dirt which you cannot see most of the time. Try hanging a clean, white handkerchief outside your window on a dry, calm, cloudy day and look at it several hours later. You may find that your handkerchief has got dirtier just by being outside, especially if you live in a city. Smoke from factories and fumes from cars pollute the atmosphere. Some pollutants get trapped just above the ground and this causes people to have breathing problems and eye irritations.

Find out more

Chemistry of air p.74
Heat transfer p.142
Clouds p.260
Formation of clouds p.262
Forecasting p.270
Mercury and Venus p.286
Mars p.289
Cycles in the biosphere p.372
People and planet p.374

AIR PRESSURE

WE CANNOT SEE AIR, but it is all around us. Gravity pulls the atmosphere down on to the Earth. This is air pressure. You do not normally feel this pressure because there is an equal pressure inside your body pushing outwards. At ground level, the pressure is greatest because there is a large weight of air overhead pushing down. The higher you go, the less air there is so the less pressure it exerts. You have to boil an egg for longer to cook it at high altitudes because the lower air pressure allows water to boil at a lower temperature. Aeroplanes flying high in the sky have pressurized cabins so that there is enough air to breathe.

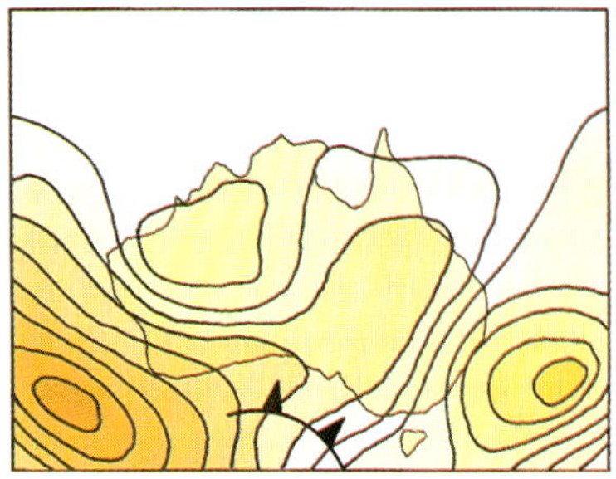

MAPPING PRESSURE
Pressure is measured in millibars (mb). On weather maps, all the areas of equal pressure are joined to make a curving line called an isobar. Areas of high and low pressure can then be easily identified.

HIGH AND LOW PRESSURE

Pressure is not the same everywhere. If the air is cold, it sinks, pushing down to create a higher pressure on Earth. As the air is squashed together, it warms up and so brings fine weather. If the air is warm, it rises and so there is a lower pressure on Earth. The warm air may also evaporate water from the sea and take it up to form clouds. This is why low pressure can bring rain.

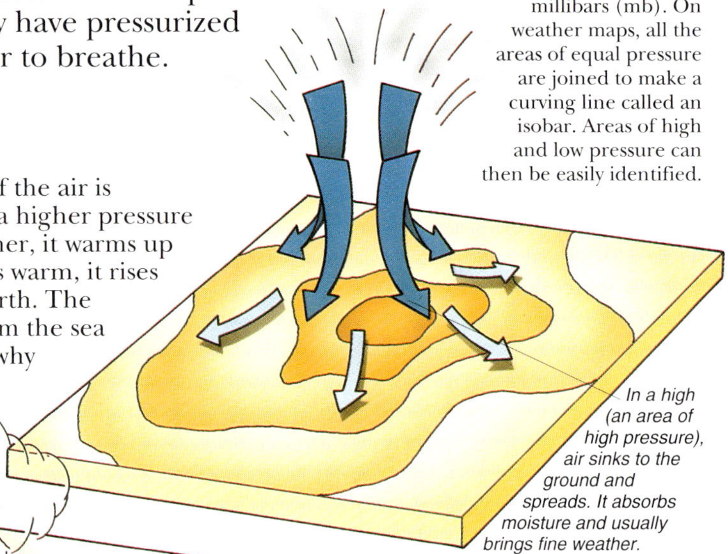

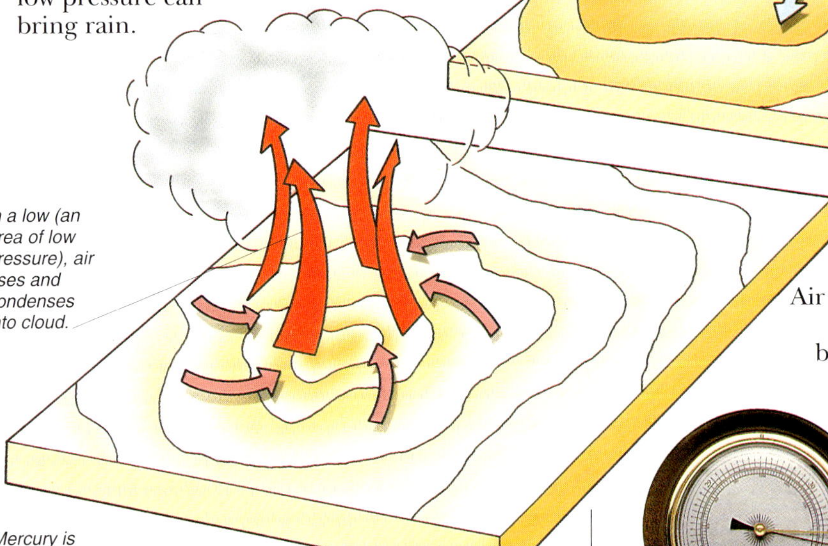

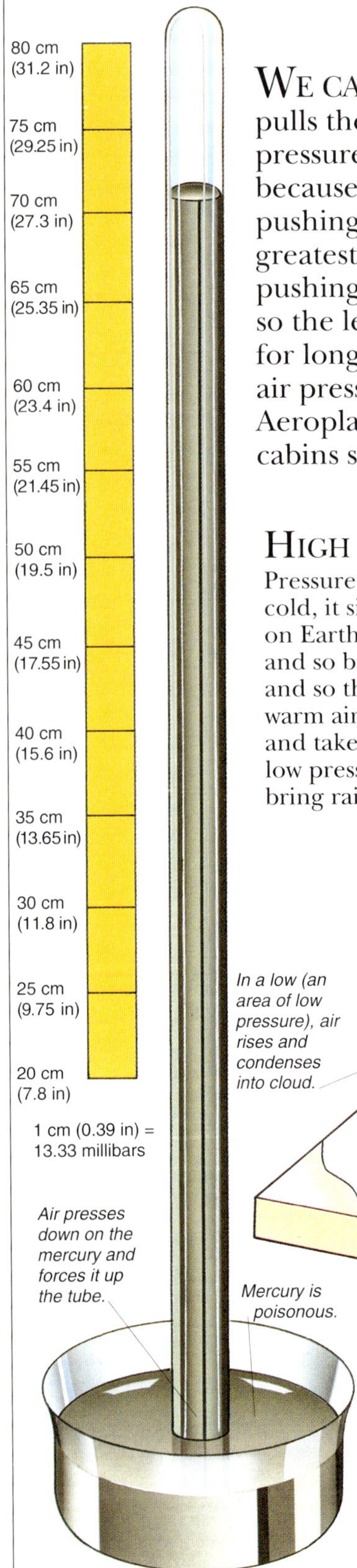

CHANGING PRESSURE
A glass tube standing in an open dish of mercury is a simple way of seeing how air pressure changes. As air pressure rises and falls, the level of mercury in the tube changes.

BAROMETERS

Air pressure is measured with barometers. An aneroid barometer looks a bit like a clock. It contains a sealed metal box with no air inside. The pointer is joined to the box. When air pressure rises, the box is squashed inwards and the pointer shows the change on a dial. Changing air pressure is a good indicator of weather to come.

Pressure is shown in millibars and pounds per square inch.

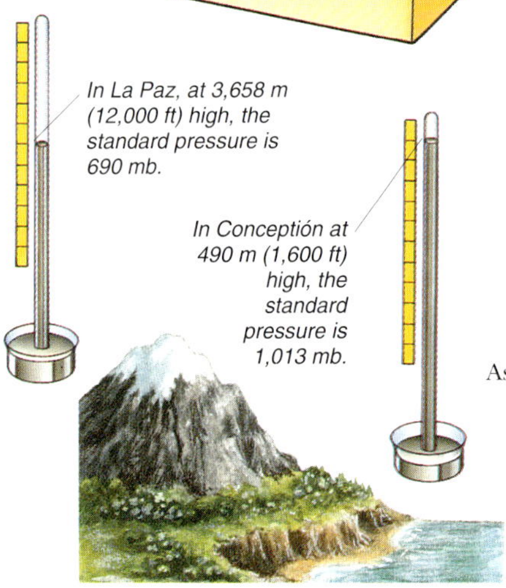

PRESSURE AND ALTITUDE
As you go up a mountain, the air pressure gets lower and lower. This is shown by the standard pressure of two cities in the Andes mountains in Bolivia – Conceptión and La Paz.

Find out more

GRAVITY P.122
PRESSURE P.127
ATMOSPHERE P.248
FRONTS P.253
FORMATION OF CLOUDS P.262
FORECASTING P.270

TEMPERATURE

DEPENDING ON WHERE YOU ARE, the Earth may be hot or cold. The average temperature at Dallol, Ethiopia, is 34 °C (93 °F). The average temperature at the Plateau research station, Antarctica, is -56 °C (-70 °F). Temperatures are always highest near the Equator and where there is no cloud so that heat from the Sun can easily reach the ground. They are lowest far from the Equator and where there is no cloud, so that heat can escape easily into space. The temperature also depends on how shiny the Earth's surface is – this is called its albedo. Areas of snow and ice have a high albedo so they reflect solar radiation back into space: temperatures remain low. Bare soil and forests absorb more radiation and keep warm.

HIGHEST TEMPERATURE
The highest temperature ever recorded was taken at al'Aziziyah, close to the Sahara Desert in Libya. It was 58 °C (136 °F) in the shade.

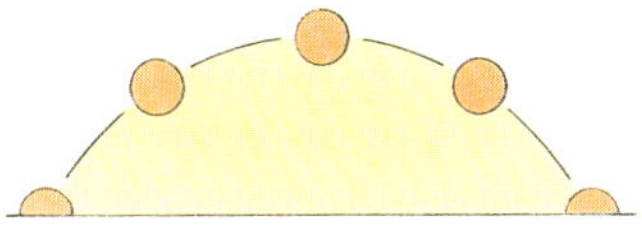

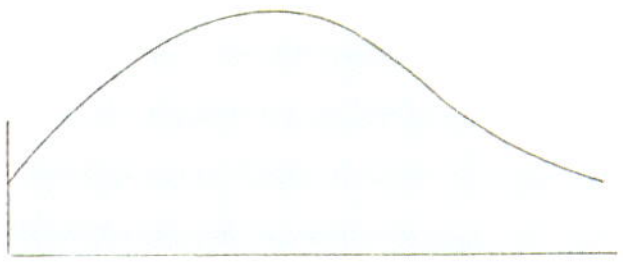

TEMPERATURE VARIATIONS
The temperature varies over the 24 hours of the day. It is colder at night and warmer in the daytime. In areas midway between the Equator and the Poles, the diurnal (daily) variation in temperature may be about 10 °C (18 °F).

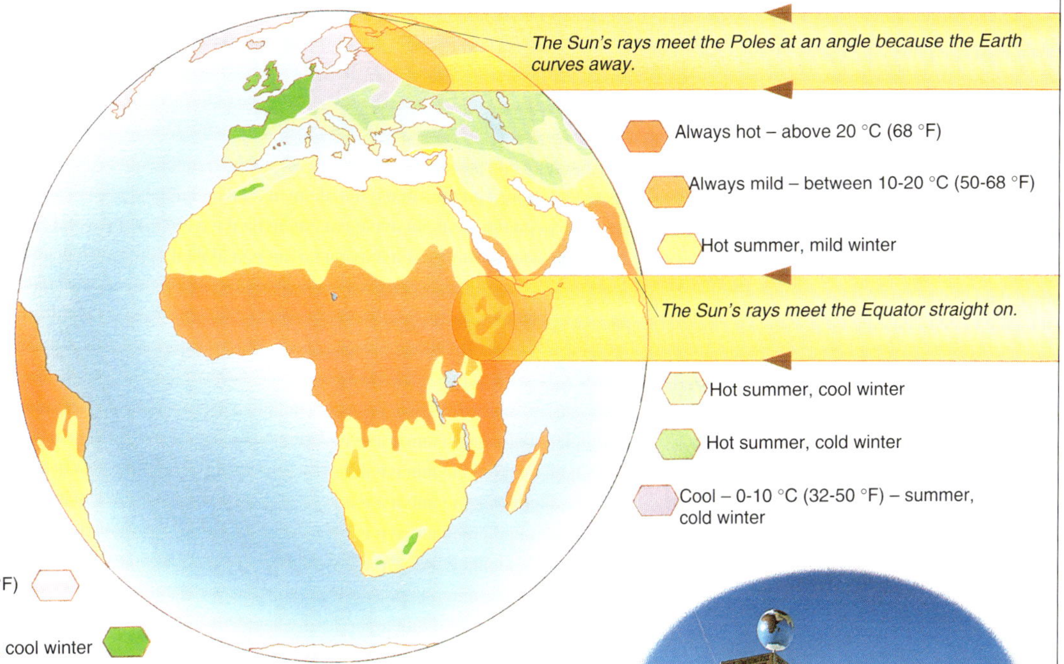

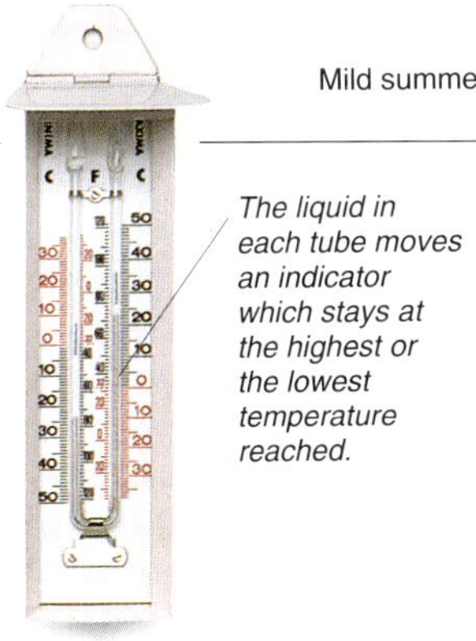

THERMOMETERS
Temperature should always be measured in the shade. The temperature change in a day can be measured with a maximum and minimum thermometer. This thermometer shows the highest and lowest temperature of the day.

HEAT FROM THE SUN

Temperature is different around the world because of the way the Sun's rays strike the surface. At the Equator, the Sun's rays hit the Earth straight on and so these areas are usually hot. At the Poles, the Sun's rays hit the Earth at a shallow angle so their heat is spread out.

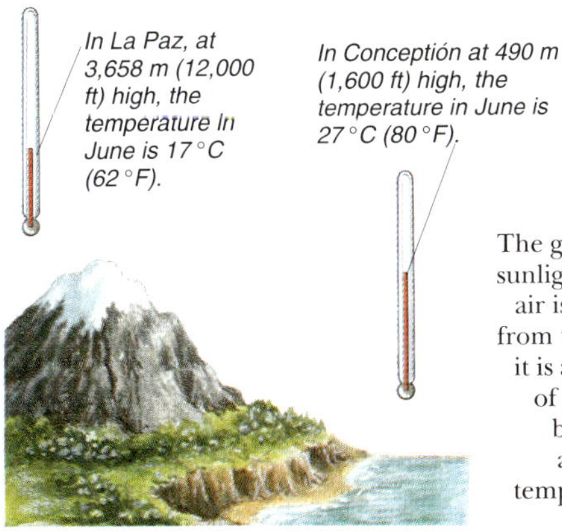

AIR TEMPERATURES
The ground is warmed up by sunlight falling on it. But the air is warmed by heat rising from the ground. This is why it is always colder at the top of a mountain than at the bottom, as shown by the average maximum June temperatures in La Paz and Conceptión in Bolivia.

COLDEST PLACE
The coldest temperature ever recorded was taken at Vostock Station, Antarctica, in July 1983. It was -89 °C (-129 °F) – colder than a freezer at home.

Find out more

HEAT TRANSFER P.142
SEASONS P.243
CLIMATES P.244
WEATHER WATCHING P.272
POLAR AND TUNDRA LANDS P.382
DESERTS P.390
FACT FINDER P.416

HUMIDITY

A twisted hair inside the house stretches when it is wet and shrinks when it is dry. As it stretches and shrinks, it turns a turntable.

WHEN THE AIR CONTAINS lots of water vapour, the weather is described as humid. The warmer the air is, the more moisture it can hold. If the air cannot carry any more water vapour, the humidity is 100 per cent. At this point the vapour condenses back into water and forms clouds, fog, or rain. Plants grow well in high humidity but it is uncomfortable for us. It is difficult for the body to cool down because sweat cannot evaporate into the air. Low humidity is better for us but it is hard to grow crops. Scientists often talk about relative humidity. This is the amount of water vapour in the air relative (compared) to the maximum it can hold at that temperature.

ADAPTING TO HUMIDITY
Hard physical work in humid air is exhausting if you are not used to it because your body finds it hard to keep cool. But with practice, the body gets more efficient. The British athlete Yvonne Murray trained in a greenhouse to become used to high humidity. She was going to compete in the World Championships in Tokyo, Japan, where it would be much more humid than in Britain.

The woman is outside the house when the humidity is low.

A model of a man and a woman stand on the turntable. In humid conditions, the stretched hair allows the turntable to turn, and the man appears. In dry conditions, the hair shrinks, pulling the turntable so that the woman appears.

MEASURING HUMIDITY

The amount of water vapour in the air can be measured with a hygrometer. This measures absorption or condensation of water from the air. There are different kinds of hygrometer. The earliest one was a sponge. When the air was humid, the sponge absorbed water and became heavier. A weather house is a simple hygrometer that indicates wet weather by the stretching of a hair.

FERDINAND II

Ferdinando de Medici, Duke of Tuscany, (1610-70) was an Italian experimenter who worked with Galileo. In 1655, he invented a condensation hygrometer. This instrument calculated the humidity of the air by measuring the amount of dew that appeared on a cool surface. He also invented the modern thermometer. A specially sealed glass tube made sure the results were not confused by the effect of air pressure.

Farming is difficult in deserts such as this one in Saudi Arabia. There is very little water for people, livestock, or crops.

Farming is successful in areas of medium humidity, such as Britain.

EFFECTS OF HUMIDITY
Water vapour in the air is important for life to survive. Deserts occur where humidity is low – less than 10 per cent. If the normal rains fail to fall in an area, the people may starve. At the opposite extreme where humidity is high, jungles grow.

Where humidity is very high, rainfall is heavy. This creates ideal conditions for plants. This rainforest is on the island of Grenada.

Find out more

CHANGES OF STATE P.20
HEAT P.140
FORMATION OF CLOUDS P.262
FOG, MIST, AND SMOG P.263
RAIN P.264
WEATHER WATCHING P.272
DESERTS P.390
TROPICAL RAINFORESTS P.394

FRONTS

THE WORLD'S WEATHER is carried around the Earth by huge swirling weather systems called highs and lows – areas of high and low pressure. Areas of high pressure, called anticyclones, are made by falling air. They move slowly causing the weather to be settled. The air is dry, bringing hot, dry weather in summer and cold, clear weather in winter. Areas of low pressure are called depressions. They are caused by rising air. The air is moist, bringing cloud, rain, or maybe snow. A depression is formed where a belt of warm and cool air collide. The two do not mix, but push into each other. Fronts form at the boundaries of the air masses and the weather becomes unsettled. A depression can be hundreds of kilometres across but usually passes overhead in less than 24 hours. A warm front is usually the first to arrive. When it has passed, a cold front follows close behind.

UNDER A WARM FRONT
When a warm front arrives, at first there is no change in the weather. The first sign is wispy clouds high in the sky, then some light drizzle.

UNDER A COLD FRONT
A cold front brings clouds and rain immediately. There may be strong gusts of wind, called squalls, or violent storms.

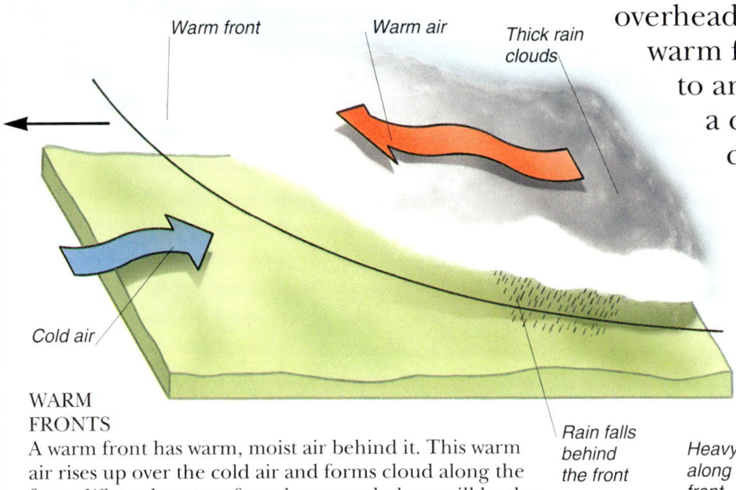

WARM FRONTS
A warm front has warm, moist air behind it. This warm air rises up over the cold air and forms cloud along the front. When the warm front has passed, there will be dry weather before the cold front arrives.

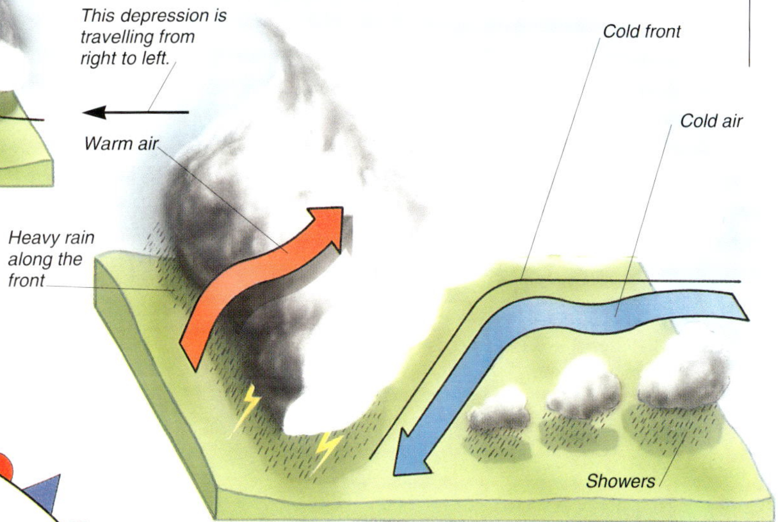

COLD FRONTS
A cold front has cold air behind it. The front is much steeper than a warm front. The cold air pushes underneath the warm air, and water vapour rises and condenses into cloud and rain. The air pressure drops and the wind gets stronger. As the front moves on, there are often showers from rain clouds trailing behind.

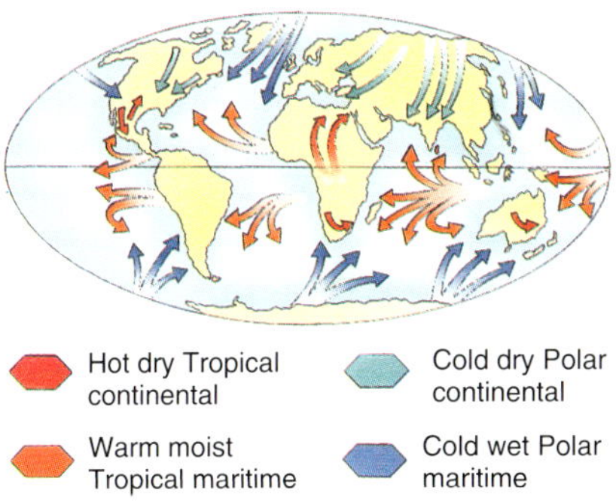

AIR MASSES

There are four main air masses that form over different parts of the Earth. These air masses affect the weather of the area over which they lie. They are blown by the winds and, where they meet and compete, the weather can be very changeable.

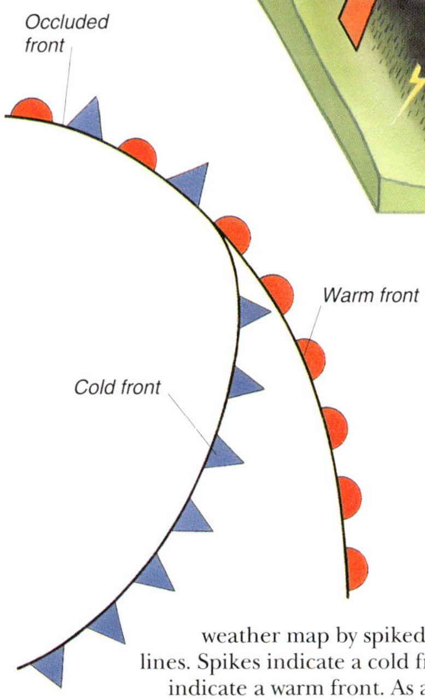

WEATHER MAP
Fronts are shown on a weather map by spiked and bumpy lines. Spikes indicate a cold front; bumps indicate a warm front. As a depression travels, the cold front often catches up the warm front. Then spikes and bumps alternate along the line. This is called an occluded front.

Find out more

CLIMATES P.244
AIR PRESSURE P.250
HUMIDITY P.252
CLOUDS P.260
FORMATION OF CLOUDS P.262
FORECASTING P.270

WINDS

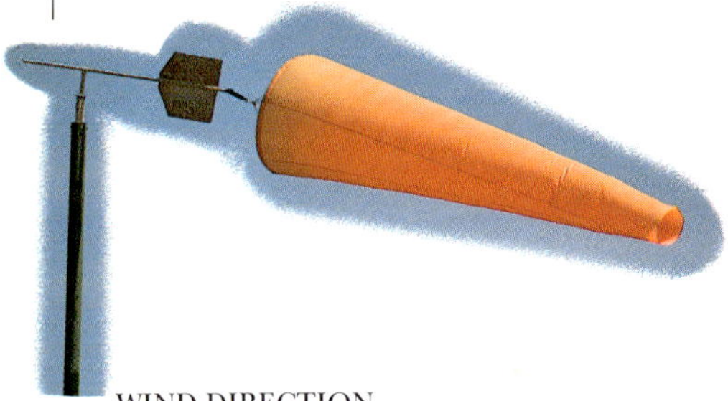

THE AIR NEVER STOPS MOVING. As it moves, it carries heat and water around the globe, giving us our weather. World winds blow because there is a difference in air pressure and temperature between one place and another. Winds blow from an area of high pressure to an area of low pressure. You can show this with a balloon. When you blow up a balloon you squeeze in more and more air until the balloon is under high pressure. If you let the air escape, it rushes out like a wind to where the pressure is lower. When air is warm, it is less dense than cold air and rises up into the sky causing an area of low pressure. Cold air sinks down to the Earth and moves in to fill the gap left by the warm air. It is this circulation of air that forms the winds.

WIND DIRECTION
Windsocks are used at small airports to show pilots the strength and direction of the wind. A floppy windsock means that the wind is only light. When strong winds blow, the sock is filled with moving air and billows in the direction the wind is blowing. A wind is described by the direction from which it is coming. For example, a west wind comes from the west; a north wind comes from the north.

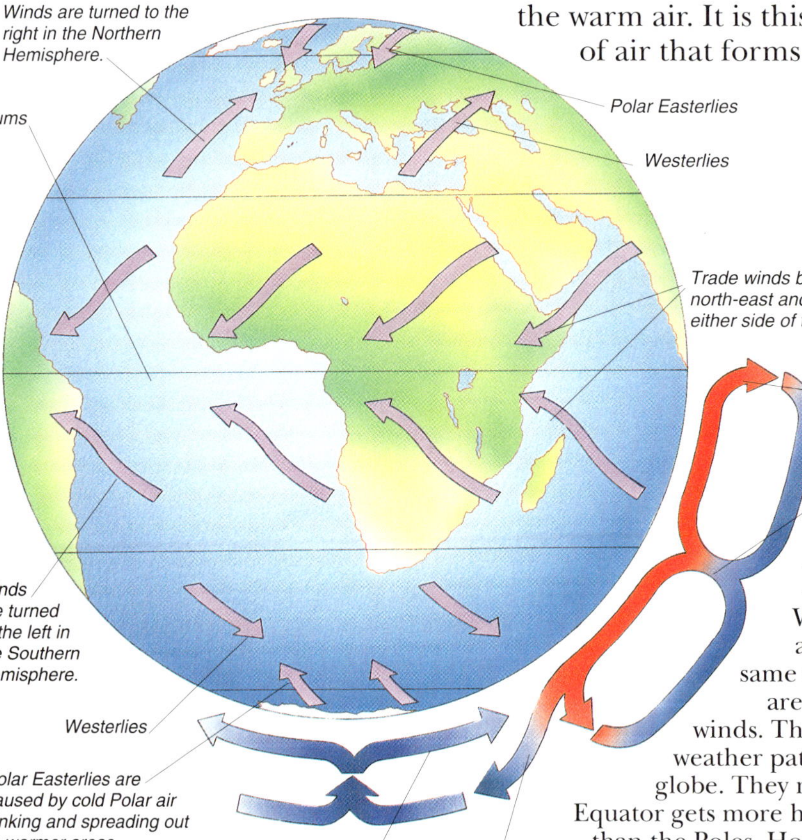

JET STREAMS
At about 10 km (6 miles) above the ground, strong winds called the jet streams circle the Earth – one in each hemisphere. This photograph from space shows jet stream clouds over Egypt. The jet streams are only a few hundred kilometres wide but sometimes stretch halfway round the Earth. They usually blow at about 200 km/h (125 mph), but can go twice as fast. The jet streams play a large part in moving the major air masses and therefore affect the weather considerably.

MAIN WINDS

Winds which blow all the time in the same area of the world are called prevailing winds. They determine the weather patterns around the globe. They move because the Equator gets more heat from the Sun than the Poles. Hot air moves north and south from the Equator, where it cools. The direction of the winds is also affected by the Earth's spin.

DOLDRUMS
Along the Equator there is an area of low pressure where the trade winds meet. In this area, called the doldrums, there is very little wind. When ships were powered only by sail they sometimes got stuck in the doldrums. Food and water began to run out and all they could do was wait until they drifted towards the trade winds.

LOCAL WINDS
All over the world there are regular local winds that have their own names. For example, the Föhn is a dry wind that blows from the Alps in Europe. This storm is blowing up over the Matterhorn in the Alps. Other local winds include the Chinook, a dry wind which blows down the east of the Rockies in North America. It creates rapid changes in temperature and humidity. The Doctor is a refreshing sea breeze that develops around midday in Fremantle, Australia. The Pampero is a cold, south-westerly wind blowing from the Andes in South America.

Sea breezes

Land and sea breezes happen only in hot, sunny weather. They are convection currents caused by the land and the sea heating up and cooling down at different rates. During the day, the land heats up more quickly than the sea. Warm air rises from the land and forms an area of low pressure. Air moves in from the sea to replace this rising air, causing a sea breeze. If there are no hills to act as a wind break, the breeze can blow up to 30 km (18 miles) inland.

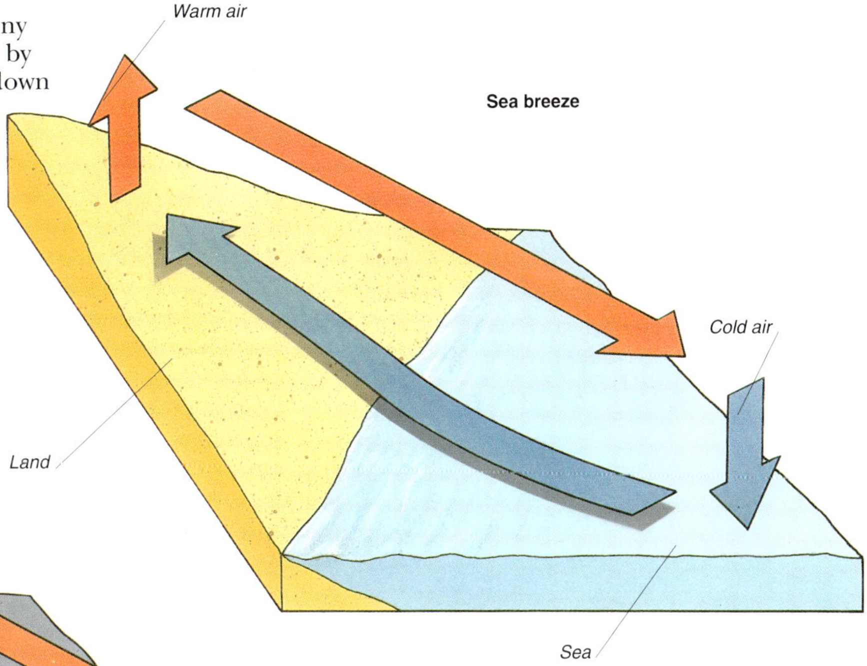

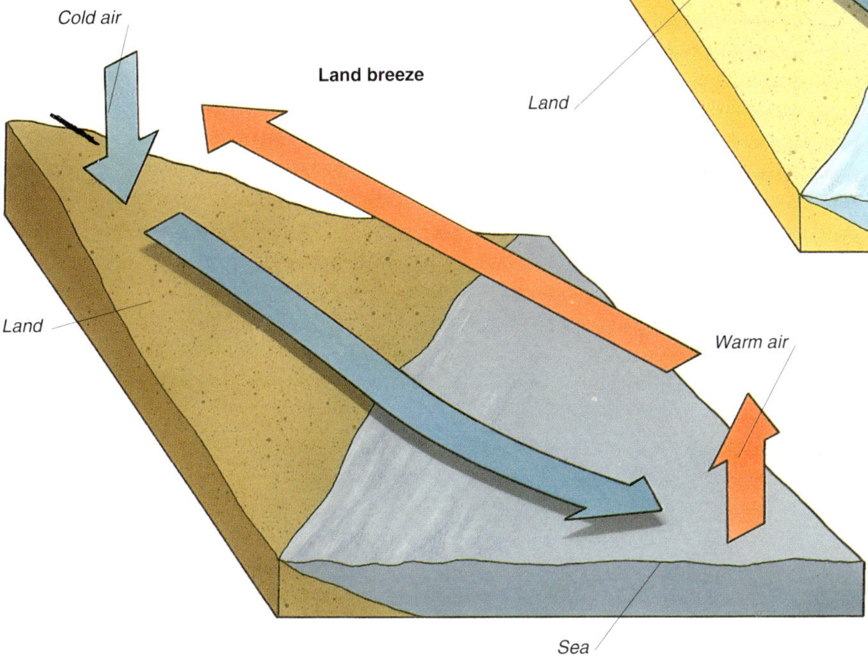

Land breezes

At night, the land cools down more quickly than the sea. Cold air sinks over the land and pushes out to sea. The air over the sea is still warm so it rises. The colder air moves in to replace it causing a land breeze.

WIND RECORD

The windiest place in the world is George V Coast in Antarctica – shown here. The winds regularly blow at 320 km/h (199 mph). The strongest wind ever recorded on the surface of the Earth was 371 km/h (231 mph) at Mount Washington, in New Hampshire, United States, on 12 April 1934.

TOWER OF WINDS

In the 1st century B.C. the Greek astronomer Andronicus built a Tower of Winds called a horologium. It had eight sides and on each one was carved a wind god. Each god showed off the style of his own wind. The god of the cold north wind was Boreus who was carved as an old man wearing warm clothes and playing a conch shell. The god of the warm east wind was in light clothes carrying fruit and grain.

WIND POWER

The wind can be captured to create electricity. In an experimental station in the United States, rows and rows of windmills are driven naturally by the forceful local winds. The windmills drive turbines which are connected to an electricity generator. They can collect enough energy to light and heat a small town. Unlike coal and nuclear power stations, wind turbines do not create any pollution.

Find out more

Energy sources p.134
Heat transfer p.142
Seasons p.243
Air pressure p.250
Temperature p.251
Fronts p.253

WIND STRENGTH

FRIEND AND FOE, the wind has a large effect on our lives. Sometimes it blows gently giving a refreshing breeze. At other times it blows strongly, creating storms, gales, and hurricanes in which widespread damage is caused and people are killed. The first attempt to standardize the reporting of winds was made by Admiral Sir Francis Beaufort in 1805. He devised a scale to help sailors estimate wind strength. In the past, the energy of the wind was used to drive windmills to grind corn. And even now, with all our modern technology, the wind's energy is still used. But now it drives wind turbines to generate electricity.

0. Calm. Chimney smoke rises straight up.

1. Light air – average wind speed 3 km/h (2 mph). Smoke drifts gently.

2. Light breeze – wind speed 9 km/h (5 mph). Leaves rustle. Wind felt on your face.

3. Gentle breeze – wind speed 15 km/h (10 mph). Leaves and twigs on trees move. Flags flutter.

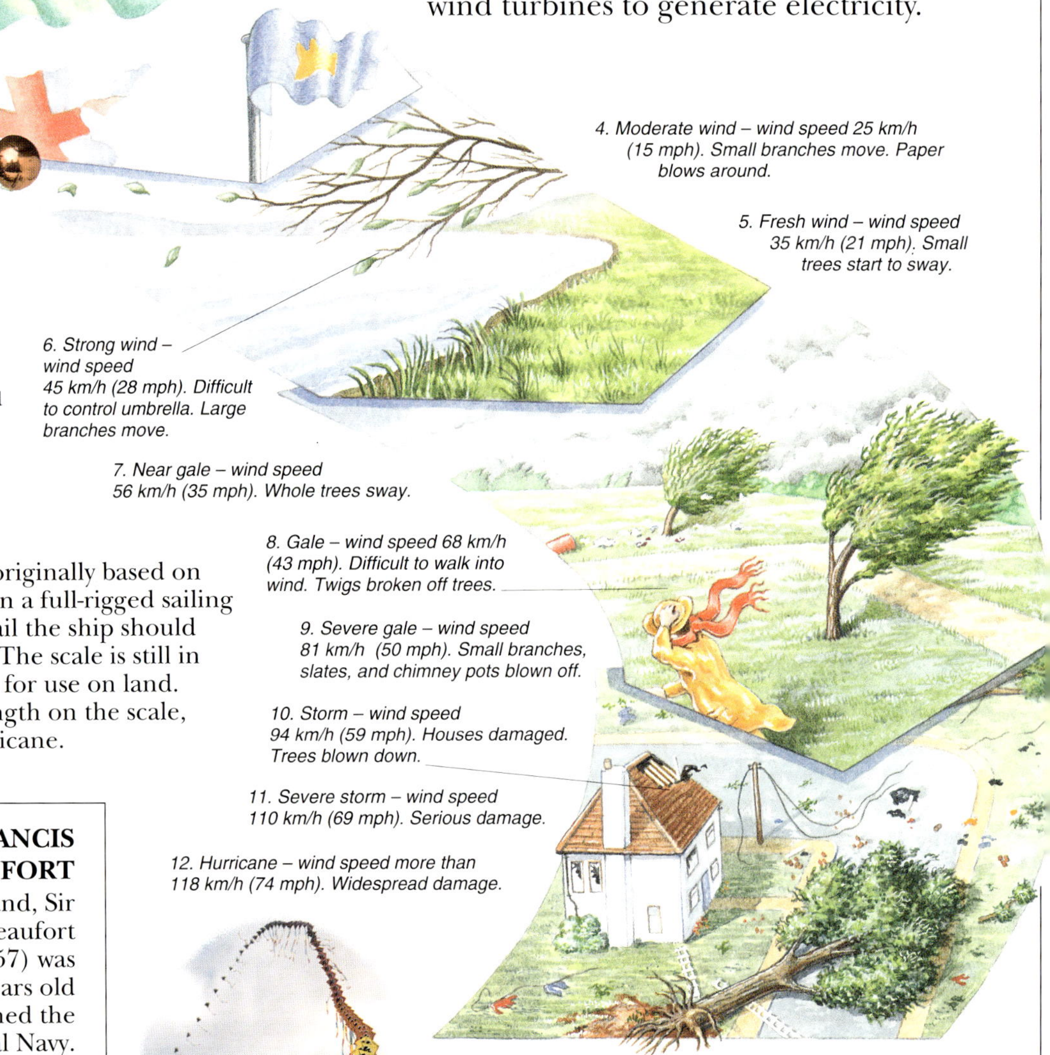

4. Moderate wind – wind speed 25 km/h (15 mph). Small branches move. Paper blows around.

5. Fresh wind – wind speed 35 km/h (21 mph). Small trees start to sway.

6. Strong wind – wind speed 45 km/h (28 mph). Difficult to control umbrella. Large branches move.

7. Near gale – wind speed 56 km/h (35 mph). Whole trees sway.

8. Gale – wind speed 68 km/h (43 mph). Difficult to walk into wind. Twigs broken off trees.

9. Severe gale – wind speed 81 km/h (50 mph). Small branches, slates, and chimney pots blown off.

10. Storm – wind speed 94 km/h (59 mph). Houses damaged. Trees blown down.

11. Severe storm – wind speed 110 km/h (69 mph). Serious damage.

12. Hurricane – wind speed more than 118 km/h (74 mph). Widespread damage.

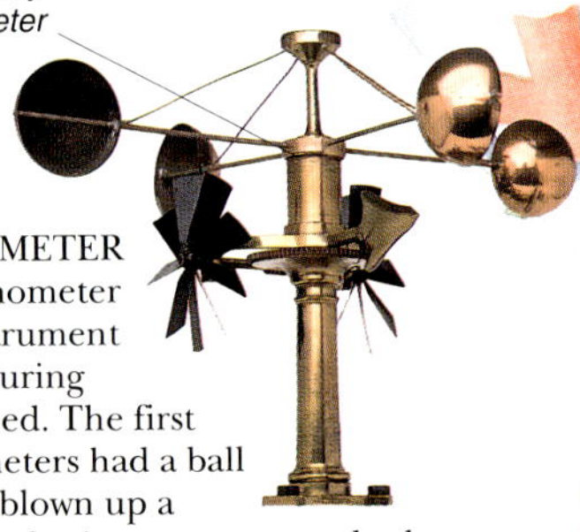

19th-century anemometer

ANEMOMETER
An anemometer is an instrument for measuring wind speed. The first anemometers had a ball that was blown up a curved scale. Anemometers today have three or more cups mounted on the end of arms that spin round a vertical pole. As the cups catch the wind, the arms spin round, and the speed is recorded.

BEAUFORT SCALE

This scale of wind strength was originally based on the effect that wind speed had on a full-rigged sailing ship and stated the amount of sail the ship should carry at different levels of wind. The scale is still in use today and has been adapted for use on land. There are 13 levels of wind strength on the scale, ranging from dead calm to hurricane.

SIR FRANCIS BEAUFORT

Born in Ireland, Sir Francis Beaufort (1774-1857) was only 12 years old when he joined the British Royal Navy. He was in active service for more than 20 years. He devised his wind scale after years of observation of ships at sea.

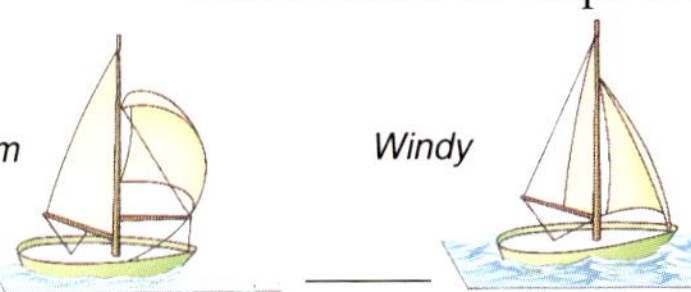

Calm *Windy*

KITE FESTIVAL
The Chinese flew kites 2,500 years ago. Today, people all over the world fly kites for fun. In Japan, traditional kites are decorated with legendary characters or animals that symbolize different things.

Find out more

ENERGY SOURCES P.134
WINDS P.254
HURRICANES P.258
TORNADOES P.259

THUNDER AND LIGHTNING

DARK THUNDERCLOUDS form on hot, humid days. A storm cloud is usually about 5 km (3 miles) across and 8 km (5 miles) high. Often, an individual thunderstorm is just one "cell" in a group of storms that may be 30 km (19 miles) across, and can last for five hours or more. Sometimes a single cell can become a "superstorm", more than 50 km (31 miles) across. This can produce large hailstones as well as thunder and lightning. If the storm is overhead, you can hear thunder at the same time as you see lightning. If it is not overhead, you can see the lightning first because light travels much faster than sound. If you count the seconds between the lightning and the thunder and divide by three, that gives you a rough idea of how far away the storm is in kilometres; for miles, divide by five.

SHEET LIGHTNING
When a flash of lightning lights up the sky, it is sheet lightning. This is a stroke of lightning that occurs within the storm cloud and doesn't come down to Earth.

THUNDERSTORM

Thunderclouds form when warm, wet air surges upwards into the sky and cools dramatically. Inside these clouds, some of the water freezes and strong air currents make the ice and water droplets bump together. This knocks tiny charged particles called electrons from the ice and so there is a build-up of electrical charge. This charge is released by a stroke of lightning. The lightning heats the air around it to an incredible 30,000 °C (54,000°F) – five times hotter than the surface of the Sun. This heat causes the air to expand very fast – in fact faster than the speed of sound. It is this which causes the crash of thunder.

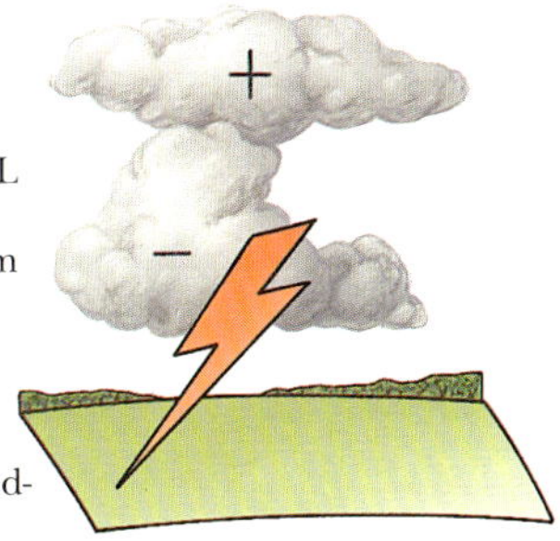

ELECTRICAL CHARGES
Inside a storm cloud, the bumping of water and ice particles creates a build-up of static electricity. Positive charge piles up at the top of the cloud; negative charge piles up at the bottom and tries to escape to the ground. When the difference between the charges is large enough, a lightning stroke flashes either from the bottom to the top of a cloud or from the bottom of the cloud to the ground.

FORKED LIGHTNING
Forked lightning begins when a "leader stroke" zigzags towards the ground at 100 km/second (62 mps), taking the easiest path. It creates a path of electrically charged air for a return, or main, stroke to shoot back immediately. It is this return stroke that we see.

GOD OF THUNDER

Thor was the Norse god of thunder, depicted here in a 10th-century bronze from Iceland. He was said to be a huge man with red hair and beard. He was a symbol of tremendous strength and power and was believed to make thunderbolts which fell from the clouds.

SAFE PLACE
If you are caught out in a storm, avoid sheltering under an isolated tall tree. Lightning looks for the quickest path to the ground and could strike the tree. One of the safest places to be is inside a car. If the car is struck by lightning, the steel frame conducts the electricity over the surface of the car to the ground.

Find out more

STATIC ELECTRICITY P.146
CURRENT ELECTRICITY P.148
SOUND P.178
LIGHT P.190
HAIL P.267
SUN P.284

HURRICANES

HURRICANE ANDREW
In 1992, hurricane Andrew swept across Florida, in the United States. A warning was issued and many people evacuated the area. The hurricane killed 15 people, and made 50,000 homeless.

SOMETIMES CALLED TROPICAL CYCLONES, typhoons, or willy-willies, hurricanes can rip up trees, destroy crops, and flatten buildings. Torrential rain causes flooding and coastal regions may be swamped by huge waves whipped up by winds that blow as fast as 300 km/h (185 mph). Hurricanes start to form when the Sun's heat stirs up moist air over the oceans, where the temperature is more than 27°C (80°F). At first, the ring of low pressure at the centre of the storm, called the eye, can be more than 300 km (185 miles) across and the winds only gale force. But as the eye narrows to about 50 km (30 miles) across, the winds begin to swirl around it at hurricane force.

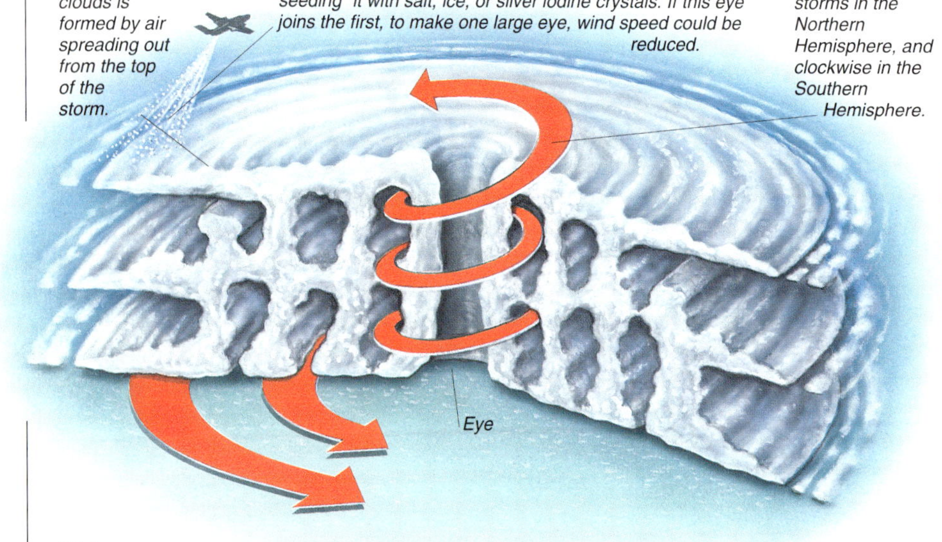

WHAT HAPPENS IN A HURRICANE?

At the eye in the centre of a hurricane, it is calm. A huge column of rising hot, moist air develops around the eye. As this humid air spirals up and cools, the water in it condenses into rain. Although the heaviest rain and strongest winds occur right next to the eye of the hurricane, lesser effects can be felt up to 400 km (240 miles) away.

1. At the beginning of a hurricane, air is sucked in towards the centre of the area of low pressure, creating fierce surface winds.

2. If the eye of the storm is very wide, the surrounding winds will be weak. As the eye becomes narrower, the wind speed increases violently.

3. As the hurricane progresses, the air moves even faster and swirls upwards in an enormous spiral.

4. At full strength, the winds spin round at over 118 km/h (74 mph). The hurricane only runs out of steam when it passes over land or over cooler water – below 27 °C (80 °F).

STORM OR HURRICANE?
Meteorologists are always on the look out for possible hurricanes. Satellites are used to take pictures of developing hurricanes. The satellite images help meteorologists to detect where a storm is likely to develop into a hurricane and to predict its likely path.

CLEMENT WRAGGE

Australian Clement Wragge (1852-1922) introduced the idea of naming hurricanes. He decided to give them women's names. It is said he used the names of people he disliked! Since 1970, an alphabetical list of alternating male and female names has been drawn up every year. Each time a hurricane is detected, it is given the next name on the list.

Find out more

AIR PRESSURE P.250
HUMIDITY P.252
WIND STRENGTH P.256
FORMATION OF CLOUDS P.262
RAIN P.264
FORECASTING P.270

TORNADOES

THE HIGHEST WINDSPEEDS on Earth occur in tornadoes. Winds whip round in a twisting funnel of air at maybe 500 km/h (310 mph), far higher than the windspeed inside a hurricane, although we cannot know exactly as meteorological instruments do not survive in the strongest tornadoes. Tornadoes are small, extremely powerful whirlwinds that form very suddenly and often occur in groups. They are most common and most violent in the United States, where more than 500 spring up every year. A tornado may measure anything from just a few metres to more than 100 metres (330 ft) across and can travel for more than 200 km (125 miles). As it goes, it can suck up anything in its path, including buildings, trees, and trains, and then drop them when its force fades.

Spiral forms in the water of the upper bottle.

TORNADO IN A BOTTLE
To see how a tornado works, take two plastic bottles with screw tops and glue the tops together. Make a small hole through both tops with a nail. Fill one bottle about three-quarters full with water, and screw the double top on. Screw the empty bottle on to the top of the full bottle. Turn the two bottles upside-down, and give the water a slight swirl to set it off. It will form a spiral in the middle, just like a tornado.

TORNADO FORMATION

Tornadoes form when a long funnel of quickly rising warm air stretches up from the ground, often to a thundercloud. They may happen when the ground gets very hot and a bubble of air starts rising. In North America, they form when cold, dry air from the Rocky Mountains flows east on top of warm, wet air moving north from the Gulf of Mexico. If the updraught of air is set spinning by strong winds, the updraught can become a tornado.

Whirling funnel of air stretches to the ground like a huge vacuum cleaner.

Pressure in the centre of the tornado is hundreds of millibars lower than normal atmosphere. Buildings can explode as air inside bursts out towards the area of low pressure.

SEA MONSTERS
If a tornado forms over sea, it is known as a waterspout. When it touches the surface of the ocean, water is sucked up inside the spinning wind. Waterspouts seem to rise up out of the sea like enormous dark grey serpents. They are probably the basis of legends about sea monsters.

TORRO SCALE

Tornadoes develop so suddenly that it is impossible to forecast the exact time and location of a tornado strike. When weather conditions that encourage tornadoes develop, general warnings are broadcast and then updated with more specific alerts as storms are identified. The Torro tornado intensity scale classifies the speed and destructive power of a moving tornado on a scale from 0 to 12. For example, Torro force 1 is described as mild: small trees will be uprooted and chimney pots removed. Torro force 12 is described as a super tornado: even steel-reinforced buildings will be seriously damaged.

STRANGE RAIN
As a tornado loses energy and disintegrates, things that it has picked up come crashing down. This could be the cause of strange "rain", such as frogs, falling. When a tornado passes over water, it can suck up small fish and frogs as well as the water. These can be carried a long way before being dropped.

Find out more

AIR PRESSURE P.250
WIND STRENGTH P.256
HURRICANES P.258
CLOUDS P.260
RAIN P.264

CLOUDS

CIRRUS

Cirrus clouds form high up in the sky – so high, that the water inside them is frozen to crystals of ice. Sometimes, cirrus clouds create a complete layer of white cloud.

CLOUDS ARE RESPONSIBLE for many aspects of weather. They therefore give some of the best clues as to what the weather will be like in the next few hours or days. If you look up and see a sky full of dark, menacing clouds, you know that it is likely to rain heavily. Fluffy, white clouds form on a warm sunny day and mean the weather will probably stay warm and dry. There are three basic types of cloud: cumulus, meaning heaped, stratus, meaning layered, and cirrus, meaning feathery. All the other many shapes and shades of cloud are a mixture or variation of these three.

WEATHER WITH CIRRUS
Cirrus clouds are often the first sign of fine weather coming to an end. The Sun and Moon can look as if they are surrounded by a halo when they shine through a layer of cirrus clouds. This is a strong indication that rain is on the way.

CUMULUS

Cumulus are puffy, white clouds with a flat base. They look a bit like pieces of cotton wool drifting about in the sky. They are sometimes called cauliflower clouds because of their shape. Cumulus clouds are produced by rising bubbles of warm air called thermals.

WEATHER WITH CUMULUS
Small, puffy, cumulus clouds are often seen on hot summer days. They disappear at night when the air is no longer heated by the ground, and warm air does not rise to form them.

STRATUS

Stratus clouds form in layers that build up and can reach across the whole sky. In hilly regions, a layer of stratus cloud often covers the ground as a wet mist.

LUKE HOWARD

In 1803, Luke Howard (1772-1864) devised a scheme for the classification of cloud types. He was a pharmacist and a keen amateur meteorologist. He tried, but failed, to find a link between the Moon's phases and the weather. Howard used Latin names to identify each type of cloud, as Latin names were being used in the classification systems for animals and plants. Howard's classification is based upon the shape of clouds and their height above the ground.

WEATHER WITH STRATUS
Stratus clouds form perhaps the most depressing types of cloud. They bring persistent drizzling rain or light falls of snow.

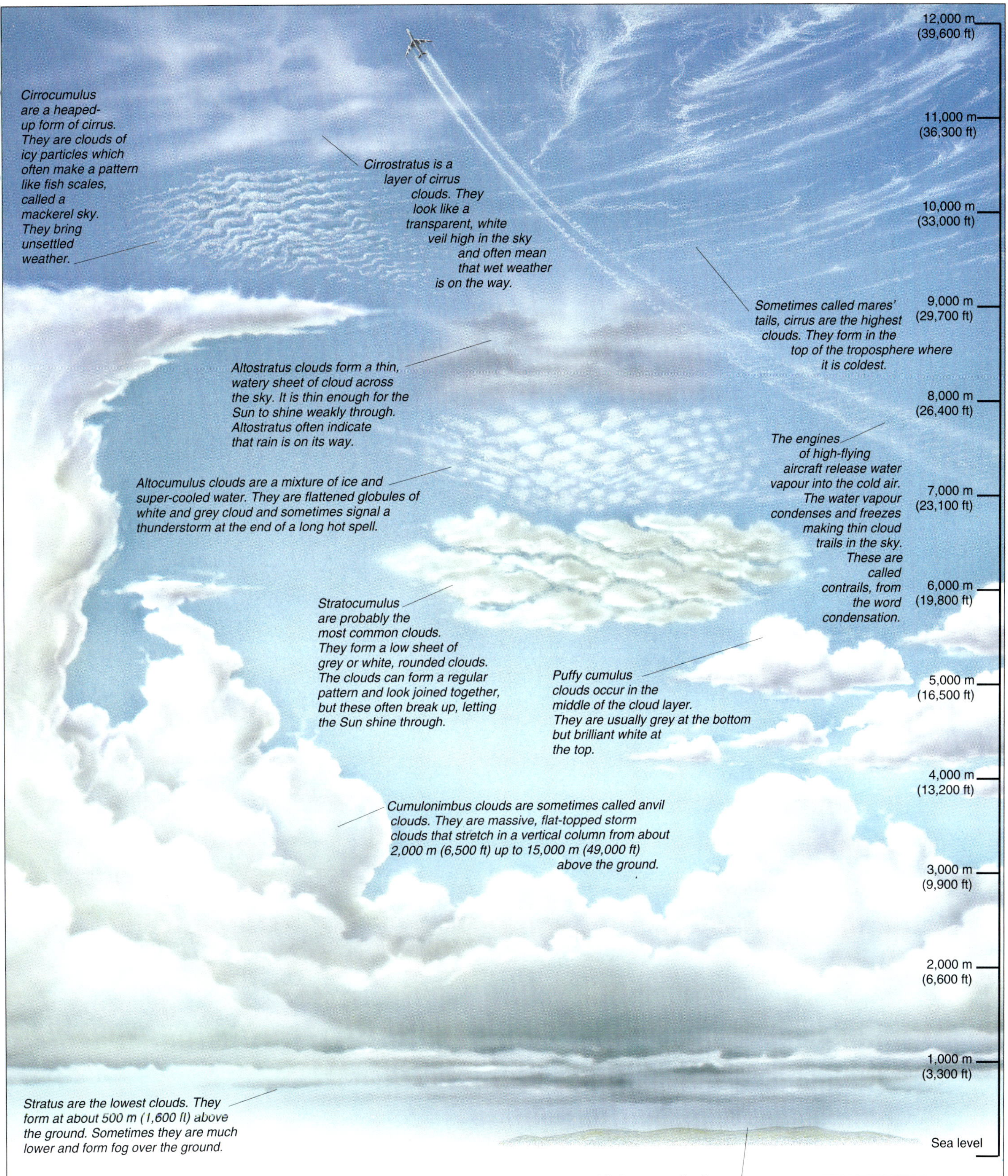

Classified clouds

There is a huge variety of clouds but only ten kinds are officially classified. Different clouds form at different levels in the sky – from sea level up to about 10,000 m (33,000 ft). Low-altitude clouds have a base below 2,000 m (6,600 ft), medium-altitude clouds form between 2,000-5,000 m (6,600-16,500 ft), and high-altitude clouds form above 5,000 m (16,500 ft).

Find out more

Formation of clouds p.262
Fog, mist, and smog p.263
Rain p.264
Special effects p.269
Moon p.288
Classifying living things p.310

FORMATION OF CLOUDS

THE AIR SOAKS UP WATER from rivers, lakes, and seas like a sponge. The water is in the form of an invisible gas called water vapour. It is this water vapour that forms the clouds, since clouds are made chiefly of water droplets. When the air near the ground rises into the sky, it cools and some of its water vapour condenses (turns into drops of liquid water). These gather together to form clouds. Air rises for several reasons. It may rise because it has been heated up by the warm ground. It may rise because cold air has pushed under warm air, lifting it higher. Or it may rise to pass over hills and mountains.

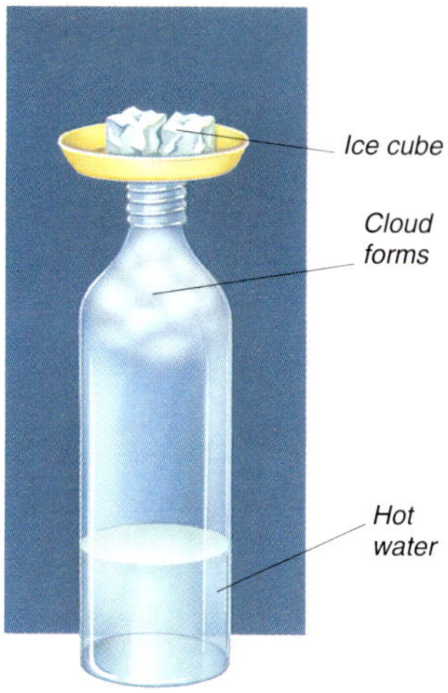

CLOUD IN A BOTTLE
You can create a cloud in a plastic bottle. Fill up the bottle with hot water (don't use boiling water because the bottle could melt). Leave it to stand for five minutes and then pour away three-quarters of the water. Lay an ice cube over the open top of the bottle and watch a cloud form. How does it work? Some of the water turns to water vapour in the warm air. When it meets the cold area by the ice cube, the water vapour turns into droplets to make a cloud.

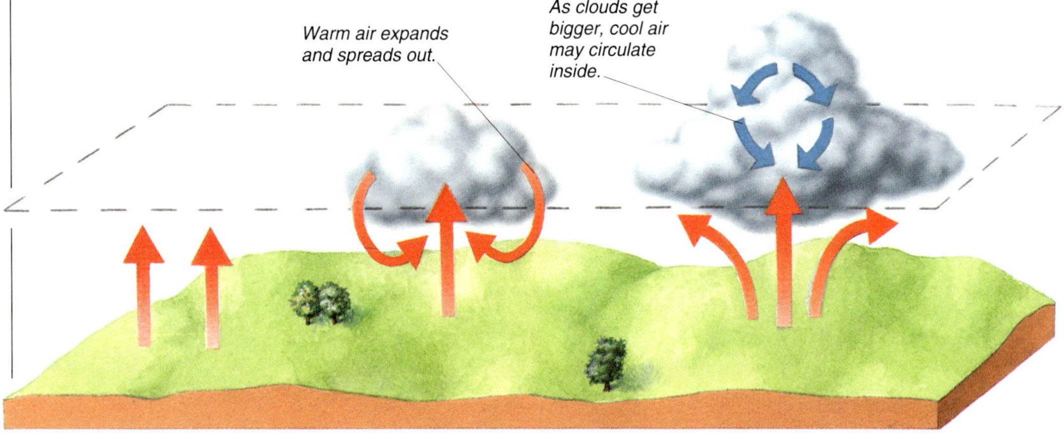

The Sun heats the ground. This warms the air nearby and the warm air rises into the sky.

As the air rises, it becomes cooler and the water vapour it contains condenses into droplets of water. These join together to form a cloud.

As the day goes on, more and more warm air rises and more water vapour condenses to form a bigger and bigger cloud.

CLOUDS AND DEW

Clouds form when the water vapour in the air is lifted high enough up into the sky for it to cool down and condense. The temperature at which this happens is called the dew point. Water vapour will turn to droplets only if the air contains small particles, such as dust or smoke, for it to condense on. If the air was clean, no clouds would form.

THERMALS

Cloud-forming is a useful sign to glider pilots of where warm air is rising. The pilots use pockets of rising air, called thermals, to give them lift. Birds of prey use thermals to help them stay up in the air while they circle round searching the ground for food.

On the okta scale, a vertical line across a circle represents 1 okta. This means there is a very fine cloud covering.

When the sky has 4 oktas of cloud, it means that about half the sky is covered by cloud. The circle is half shaded in.

8 oktas is the highest point on the okta scale. It means that the sky is completely covered by cloud. All of the circle is shaded in.

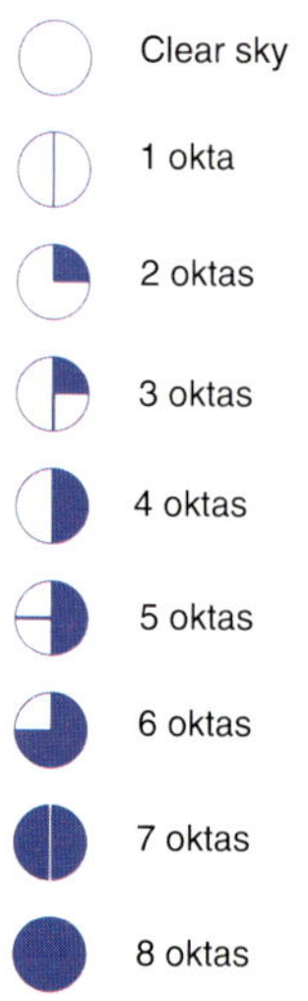

MEASURING CLOUD
Meteorologists measure the amount of clouds covering the sky in a unit called an okta. One okta represents one-eighth of cloud cover. The number of oktas of cloud cover are represented on a weather map by a partly shaded circle.

Find out more

CHANGES OF STATE P.20
FORCES IN FLUIDS P.128
HEAT TRANSFER P.142
AIR PRESSURE P.250
CLOUDS P.260
FROST, DEW, AND ICE P.268
CYCLES IN THE BIOSPHERE P.372

FOG, MIST, AND SMOG

CLOUDS THAT FORM near the ground are called fog or mist. Like other clouds, they are made when the air is full of water vapour. When the air comes into contact with cold ground, the water vapour condenses. If the distance we can see through the cloud is between one and two kilometres (0.6 and 1.25 miles), it is called mist. If the distance we can see is less than one kilometre (0.6 miles), the cloud is called fog. A dense fog is the most dangerous cloud. It is a hazard to all types of transport – cars, ships, and aeroplanes.

DRIVING IN FOG
Drivers in fog have to be very careful. Cars must use dipped headlights. If their lights are on full beam (directed straight ahead), the light reflects off the water droplets in the fog and the driver cannot see properly.

ICEBERG FOG
Icebergs are often shrouded in fog. This is because the air around them is cold but the water in which they float may be warmer. The water evaporates into water vapour, which condenses in the cold air to form fog. A ship called the *Titanic* collided with an iceberg in 1912. The crash may have been caused because the crew did not see the iceberg in the surrounding heavy fog.

RADIATION FOG

The most common kind of fog is radiation fog. On a night when there are no clouds in the sky to trap heat, the ground radiates heat so that it cools quickly. The air near the ground then cools too. If it cools to a low enough temperature, water vapour in the air will condense to form fog near the ground.

SMOG
Smog is smoky fog. In cities, the air contains many extra particles because of the smoke released by some industries. Water vapour condenses on these to form smog. This is worsened by an effect called an inversion – a layer of warm air prevents the surface air, and the pollutants it contains, from rising. This can happen in regions, such as Los Angeles, California, in the United States, where air is trapped by surrounding mountains.

PEA-SOUPERS
At one time, London in England had heavy yellow smogs, nicknamed "pea-soupers". This photograph was taken in 1952. These smogs were caused by smoke from the burning of coal in industry and in homes. The smog was no joke. It seeped into buildings, causing throat, eye, and breathing problems, and many people died because of it. Clean Air Acts agreed in the 1950s have made such pea-soupers a thing of the past.

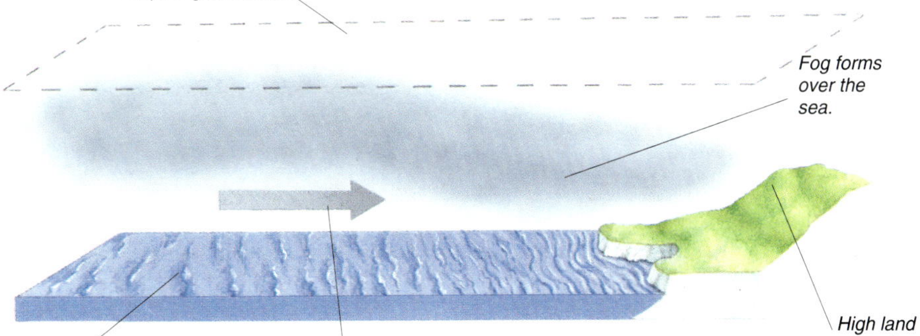

ADVECTION FOG
Fog and mist often form over rivers or seas. Water evaporates from the river or sea and early on a cold morning, it condenses into mist over the water. When warm air blows over a cold sea, a type of fog called advection fog is produced. A layer of fog forms just above the water, sandwiched between the sea and the warm air above. Advection fog will only push inland if the land around is low.

Find out more

CHANGES OF STATE P.20
HEAT TRANSFER P.142
REFLECTION P.194
FORMATION OF CLOUDS P.262
CYCLES IN THE BIOSPHERE P.372

RAIN

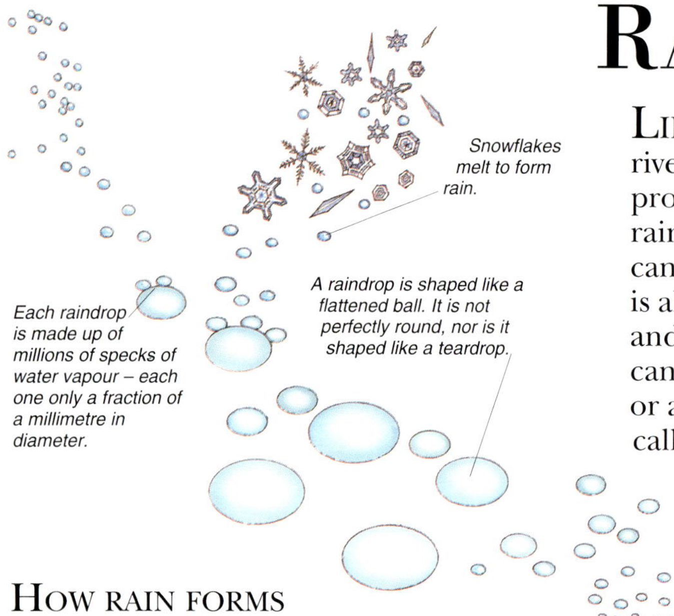

LIFE ON LAND DEPENDS ON RAIN. Rain fills the rivers and lakes, it lets seeds germinate and grow, and provides us with drinking water. In some areas, if the rains fail for just one season many thousands of people can die of starvation because crops fail. Too much rain is also a problem. Floods can destroy homes, farmland, and wildlife. Rain never falls from a clear, blue sky. It can only form in a cloud, usually either a nimbostratus or a cumulonimbus. Water that falls from a cloud is called precipitation. The temperature of the air, both inside and outside the cloud, determines whether precipitation is rain, snow, sleet, or hail.

HOW RAIN FORMS

Most rain outside the tropics starts off as snow, even in summer. High up in the clouds, the temperature is below freezing, and ice crystals form. The crystals grow bigger, form snowflakes, and fall from the cloud. If the temperature of the air nearer the ground is above freezing, the snow melts and turns into rain as it falls. In the tropics, where the clouds are warm, rain is formed when microscopic drops of water in the clouds collide and join together. When the drops are too heavy to stay up, they fall as rain. In thin clouds, fewer drops collide so the falling raindrops are smaller. Very small drops are known as drizzle.

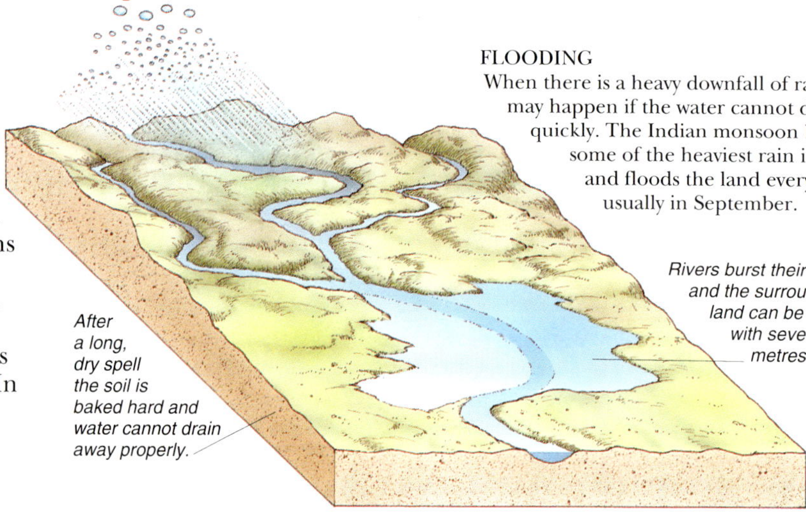

FLOODING
When there is a heavy downfall of rain, floods may happen if the water cannot drain away quickly. The Indian monsoon brings some of the heaviest rain in the world and floods the land every year, usually in September.

Key to map of annual rainfall

- *More than 3,000 mm (118 in)*
- *2,000-3,000 mm (78-118 in)*
- *1,000-2,000 mm (39-78 in)*
- *500-1,000 mm (20-39 in)*
- *250-500 mm (10-20 in)*
- *Less than 250 mm (10 in)*

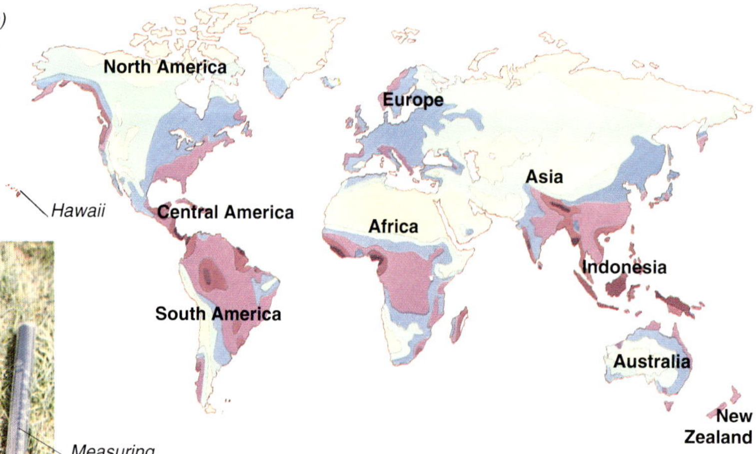

MEASURING RAINFALL
Rainfall is measured in millimetres or inches. It can be measured with a rain gauge. A funnel catches the rain and directs it down into a cylinder. The height of water in the cylinder is the amount of rain that has fallen.

ANNUAL RAINFALL AROUND THE WORLD
Different regions of the world get different amounts of rain. There are several reasons for this variation. For example, in the tropics, there is a lot of rain because a considerable amount of water evaporates from the warm sea and makes clouds. Land near the sea usually gets more rainfall than land far from the sea. Mountain ranges can block off the winds that bring rain clouds making it wet on one side and dry on the other. And there are dry deserts where air masses get hot and dry as they descend towards the ground.

RECORD RAINFALL
On the top of Mount Wai-ale-ali, on the island of Kauai in Hawaii, it rains on 350 days a year. The average annual rainfall is 15,000 mm (410 in). The moist south-east trade wind rises and cools as it passes over the mountain and this causes the rain.

MAKING RAIN
Clouds are sometimes "seeded" to make them rain. Aircraft drop dry ice or silver iodide crystals on to them. The chemicals provide "seeds" for snowflakes to grow on. The snowflakes turn into rain as they fall down to the ground. The effect on the clouds where the aircraft has just sprayed can clearly be seen in this photograph.

Drought

If, over about two weeks, there is less than 0.2 mm (1/100 in) of precipitation, there is said to be a drought. Without reservoirs, there is not enough water for people and crops. Some places have extreme drought which lasts for many years. It is said that Calama in the Atacama Desert in Chile did not have any rain for 400 years until 1972. In temperate Europe and North America, periods of drought are unexpected. But in Australia and parts of Africa, Central America, and Asia, drought happens regularly.

THE DUST BOWL
During the 1930s, there was a long period of prevailing Westerlies over North America. This meant that the Great Plains were in the "rain shadow" of the Rocky Mountains and had no rain. The drought was made worse because the farmers had ploughed up all the natural grasslands, letting the topsoil get dry and dusty. The Great Plains turned into the Dust Bowl. Crops could not grow and farming families were forced off the land.

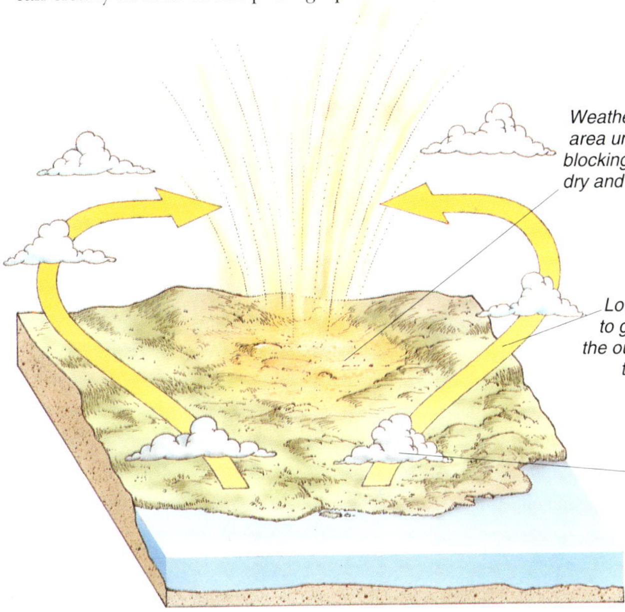

BLOCKING HIGH
A drought can be caused by an area of high pressure blocking the passage of moving low pressure systems. If the high pressure sticks in one place for a long time, it can prevent any change in the weather for weeks. Blocking highs are always dry. They bring clear, cold weather in winter and hot, dry weather in summer.

SURVIVING A DROUGHT
Flowers are blooming in this normally dry area in Australia, forming a pink carpet for a few days. Most plants cannot survive in the desert because it is so dry. But some seeds can survive for years in the soil. As soon as the rains come the seeds spring into life, flower, and quickly set new seeds before the ground dries up again.

THIRSTY PLANTS
Most plants need a constant supply of water to survive. If there is a drought, many plants will die, even established trees. You can tell when trees are not getting enough rain because their topmost branches will die.

BUSH FIRES
In hot, dry regions, bush fires often start. They clear the land, making room for new plants to grow, and the heat is necessary to make certain seeds germinate. Where people prevent bush fires, some kinds of plants die out. Nowadays, bush fires are often left to burn, provided that they do not threaten people's lives.

Find out more

CLOUDS P.260
SNOW P.266
HAIL P.267
CYCLES IN THE BIOSPHERE P.372
DESERTS P.390
FACT FINDER P.416

Snow

No two snowflakes are exactly the same. Each one is a collection of ice crystals, made of frozen water vapour, frozen together. Ice crystal shapes are divided into about 80 categories. They can be shaped like needles, prisms, plates, hexagons, and columns. The shape depends on the temperature, height, and water content of the cloud in which they form. Snow can be "wet" or "dry". Wet snow is made of large snowflakes and forms when the temperature is just about freezing. It is perfect for making snowballs but difficult to clear away. Dry snow is powdery and easy to clear. It forms when the temperature is well below freezing. Sleet is usually half-melted snow, but it can be half-frozen rain formed when raindrops evaporate and cool as they fall.

AVALANCHES
If a mountain slope is steeper than 22°, avalanches can happen. The snow piles up until a small amount starts to slip, collecting more and more snow as it goes down the slope. Avalanches may be set off by a heavy fall of snow on ice, a rise in temperature, a skier, or even by a loud noise.

All snowflakes form in a six-sided symmetrical pattern.

Ice caps have a shiny, white surface that reflects the Sun's heat. This helps to keep them cold even during the summer.

PERMANENT SNOW
Glaciers and ice caps are made from snow that has never melted. Instead, all the crystals and snowflakes have been squeezed together by the weight of more snow falling on top. Ice caps and glaciers form on mountain tops and near the Poles.

How snow forms

Ice crystals form in clouds where the temperature is between -20 °C and -40 °C (-4 °F and -40 °F). To form snowflakes, the crystals join together as they fall and become wet, and then re-freeze. When they fall out of the cloud, they will reach the ground as snow only if the temperature of the air is freezing all the way down. If it is too warm, the crystals may evaporate back into water vapour or melt and fall as sleet or rain. Sometimes, it can be snowing on the top of a tall skyscraper, while it is raining in the street below.

SNOW DRIFTS
When snow builds up in drifts, people can get stuck in cars or even inside their homes. If animals or people get buried in snow, they can survive for a long time. This is because freshly fallen snow contains air in the gaps between the ice crystals which the animals can breathe.

PINK SNOW
Snow is not always white! It can be pink, brown, or even red. This pink snow is in Greenland. The colour is caused by algae living in the snow. The pigment that makes the algae red also protects them in the extremely cold conditions.

Find out more

Heat transfer p.142
Ice and glaciers p.228
Temperature p.251
Clouds p.260
Polar and tundra lands p.382

HAIL

HAILSTONES ARE FROZEN drops of rain. They form inside tall cumulonimbus clouds which are much warmer at the bottom than at the top, where it is freezing. The temperature difference causes strong currents inside the cloud. These currents toss the raindrops up to the freezing top of the cloud and down again. In order for a hailstone to stay up in a cloud long enough to become even pea-sized, it needs to be swept up and down at speeds of about 30 m (100 ft) per second. As hailstones rise and fall inside a cloud, they crash into each other often causing electric charges to separate out and make lightning. Even when the hail is not falling to the ground, it can still make lightning inside the clouds.

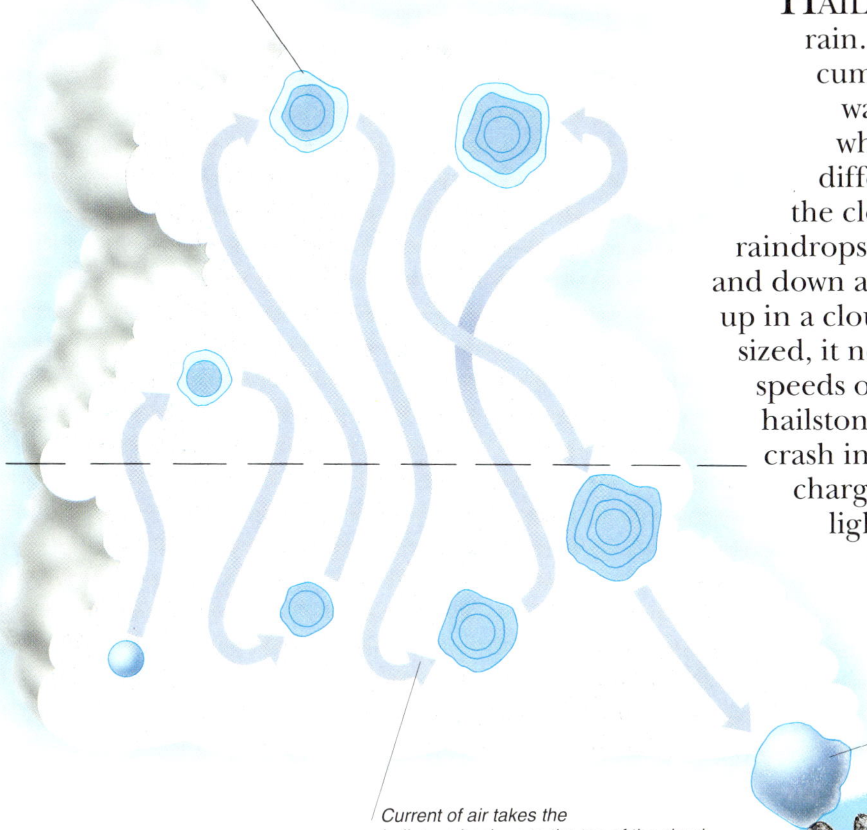

HOW HAIL FORMS

Hailstones develop inside cumulonimbus clouds which have grown to a height of about 10 km (6 miles). Strong, uprising air currents within a cloud can lift raindrops up into the frozen cloud top. The first time this happens the raindrop freezes and falls. When it is tossed upwards again a further layer of ice builds round it. The ice builds up, layer upon layer, until the hailstone finally falls to the ground.

LAYERS OF ICE
This cross-section of a hailstone clearly shows that a hailstone is made in layers, like the layers of an onion. Each layer represents one journey up to the top of a storm cloud and back down to the bottom.

RECORD HAILSTONES

Hailstones are often as big as marbles, and sometimes as big as tennis balls. Less common are those that fell in Bangladesh in 1986. They weighed 1.02 kg (2.25 lb). Shown here is a giant hailstone which fell in Kansas in the United States in 1970. It measured 43.6 cm (17.2 in) in circumference and weighed 765 g (1.7 lb).

HAIL DAMAGE
Hailstones can cause severe damage. They ruin crops, such as these apples, making them unfit to sell. Large hailstones can break windows and dent cars. Small birds, caught in a storm with no cover, have been killed by hailstones.

HAIL PREVENTION
Many attempts to prevent hail damage have been made, including firing guns into the clouds, as shown by this French magazine of 1910. More recently, silver iodide crystals have been fired into clouds. It is hoped that this will turn the hailstones into rain. But there is no proof that this works.

Find out more

HEAT TRANSFER P.142
STATIC ELECTRICITY P.146
THUNDER AND LIGHTNING P.257
CLOUDS P. 260
RAIN P.264

FROST, DEW, AND ICE

WHEN THE SUN HAS SET at night, the ground begins to lose its heat. The air does not lose heat so fast so the ground becomes colder than the air above it. On a clear, still night, water vapour in the air condenses on the ground as dew drops. The temperature at which dew starts to form is called the dew point. If the temperature of the air falls below freezing, the water vapour turns into ice crystals and coats everything with frost. Sometimes, a layer of transparent ice forms on the ground making roads slippery. It happens when rain falls through very cold air on to ground that is below 0°C (32°F), where it freezes into "black" ice. It is called black because the road can be seen through it.

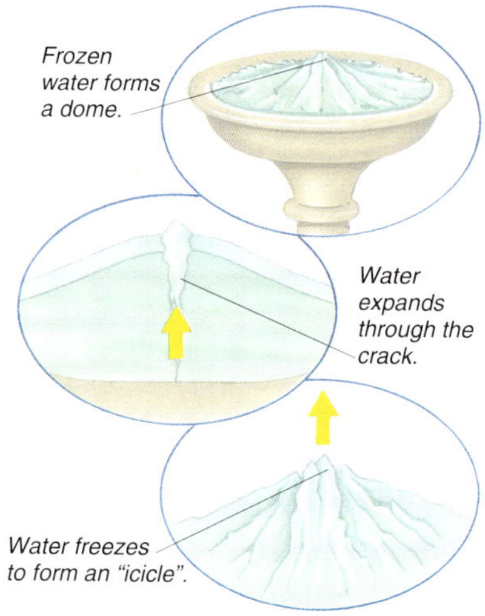

"UPSIDE-DOWN" ICICLES
Sometimes "icicles" form in shallow puddles or bird baths – sticking up. This happens because water expands when it freezes and pushes up a little dome of ice. If this cracks, water from underneath the dome pushes up through the crack and freezes. When this happens several times, the result is a spike of ice.

HOAR FROST

Frost usually occurs on a cold night when there is no blanket of cloud to stop warmth escaping from the ground. The most usual kind of frost is hoar frost. This coats the ground, leaves, branches, and even spiders' webs with a thin layer of tiny ice crystals. Sometimes hoar frost is so white and so deep on the ground that it looks like snow.

DEW POND
Dew that forms at night covers the ground in the early morning. When the Sun comes up, and it begins to get warmer, the dew evaporates into the air. Some farmers make dew ponds – hollows in the ground in low-lying parts of a field. Dew runs down and collects in the dew ponds for animals to drink first thing in the morning. Sometimes dew ponds occur naturally.

FROZEN WATER
If it is very cold, a layer of ice can form over rivers and lakes. This ice may seem strong and thick at the edges, but there will be weak spots where the ice is thinner. That is why it is dangerous to walk on water that is covered with ice. Fish survive because the ice acts like a lid, stopping the water underneath from freezing.

It is unusual for the ice on a river or lake to be thick enough to skate on.

FROZEN SEA
Seas do not often freeze because salt water freezes at a lower temperature than fresh water does. But if it is cold enough, ice can cover the sea, especially near the coast.

ICEFISH OF ANTARCTICA

The waters around Antarctica are so cold that they would freeze the blood of ordinary fish. Fish that live in these waters have evolved chemicals in their blood that act as a natural "antifreeze" – just like the antifreeze put in a car to stop the water freezing in the winter.

Find out more

CHANGES OF STATE P.20
HEAT TRANSFER P.142
ICE AND GLACIERS P.228
SNOW P.266
POLAR AND TUNDRA LANDS P.382

SPECIAL EFFECTS

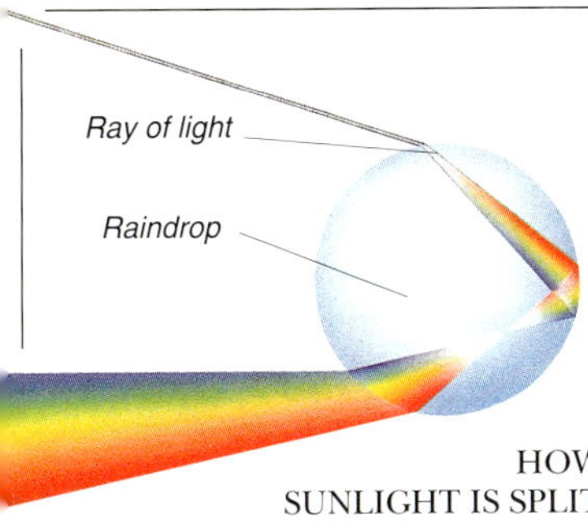

HOW SUNLIGHT IS SPLIT
A ray of light passing through a raindrop is bent on its way in and on its way out. It is also reflected off the inside of the raindrop.

THE COLOURED PATTERNS of a rainbow or a glorious sunset are familiar to everybody. But the changing patterns of weather can play other strange tricks on us. They produce pillars of light in the sky, rings around the Sun and Moon, and strange distortions of the shape of the Sun as it sets. The way stars twinkle in the sky has nothing to do with the stars themselves, but is caused by the effect of the air on light passing through it. And the atmosphere can even bend light, to bring you an image of a far-distant object.

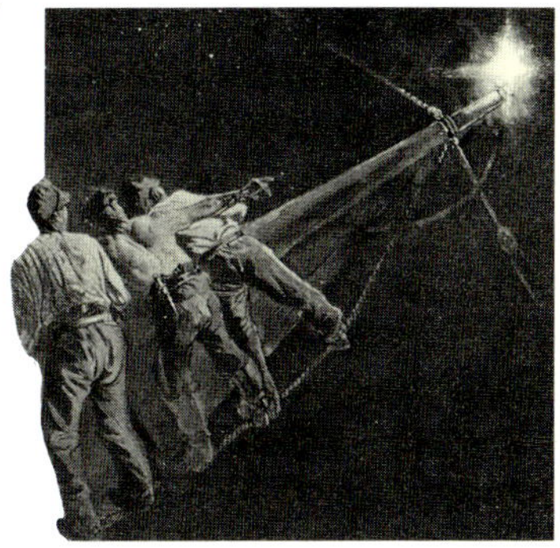

ST ELMO'S FIRE
In stormy conditions, an electric discharge, like lightning, may form a bluish-green ball of light on pointed objects. One of these on a ship's mast was known to sailors as St Elmo's Fire. It is sometimes seen today on the wingtips of aircraft, or lightning conductors.

The colours of a rainbow are, from the outside inwards, red, orange, yellow, green, blue, indigo, and violet.

RAINBOWS

You can only see a rainbow when the Sun is shining behind you and it is raining in front of you. Rainbows form when sunlight shines through millions of raindrops. Sunlight is a mixture of colours. When it passes through a raindrop, it is refracted (bent) and the light splits and spreads out into seven colours. All rainbows are part of a circle, but you can usually see only part of it, as the Earth is in the way. If you are lucky, you may see a complete circle from an aircraft.

MIRAGES
Mirages are associated with hot deserts, but you may see one on a hot road. Light bends from warmer air towards colder air. When air near the ground is hotter than air above, light rays are bent up so that they come to the eye from a different place to where they started. It can look as if there is a lake ahead, but this is really an image of the sky. You see light rays from the sky coming from near the ground.

JOHN TYNDALL
British scientist John Tyndall (1820-93) studied glaciers and was one of the first people to climb the Matterhorn mountain in the Swiss Alps. He studied light and how it is scattered by large molecules and dust. This effect, known as the Tyndall effect, is the cause of shafts of sunlight. Tyndall suggested that the sky is blue because the blue part of sunlight is scattered more easily around the sky than other colours. This was later proved by Einstein.

HALOES AROUND THE MOON
When light from the Moon passes through ice crystals high in the sky, haloes sometimes form around the Moon. Light reflecting off the ice crystals is bent at angles of either 22° or 46° to make two separate haloes. The haloes are often incomplete, and usually only the smaller one can be seen. You can also see haloes around the Sun.

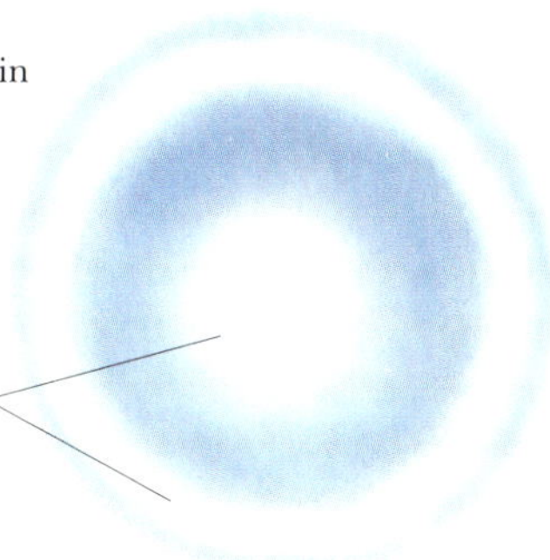

BROCKEN SPECTRE
An unusual effect can be seen, especially in mountains, when the Sun is low in the sky. The Sun casts a large shadow of objects or people on to low-lying mist or clouds. The shadow is called the Brocken spectre after the Brocken mountain in Germany.

Find out more

STATIC ELECTRICITY p.146
REFRACTION p.196
LIGHT AND MATTER p.200
SHADOWS p.201
COLOUR p.202
ATMOSPHERE p.248

FORECASTING

WHAT IS THE WEATHER going to be like today? To forecast the weather accurately, information must be gathered from all round the world. There are two types of forecast – long-range forecasts predict the weather for up to eight days ahead; short-range forecasts predict the weather for the next 24 hours. The biggest non-military customers for weather forecasts are civil aviation organizations, such as airlines and airports, which need to know conditions at different altitudes. Shipping needs to be warned of storms; power stations need to know if it is going to be cold, so that they can estimate the demand for energy. Farmers need forecasts so they can plan harvesting and protect crops. And you want to know what clothes to wear, or whether to take an umbrella out with you even if the Sun is shining!

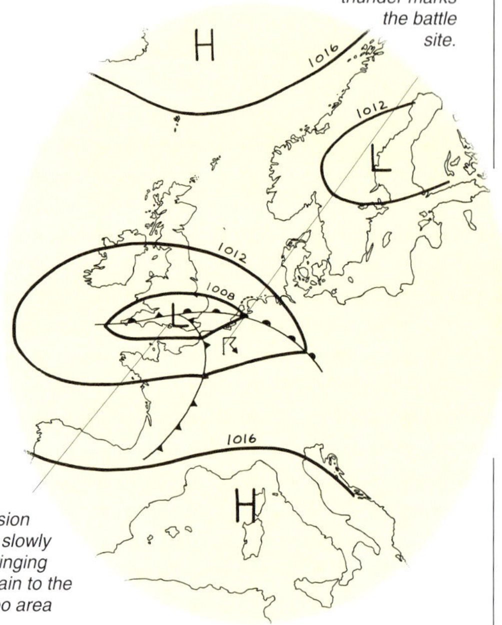

WEATHER IN HISTORY
Using old records, experts can draw up weather maps, or charts, for days in history. This map is of the night before the Battle of Waterloo, 17 June 1815. The battle was between the armies of the French emperor Napoleon and the Allied army commander the Duke of Wellington. Heavy rain made the ground muddy and delayed the French attack. This gave time for more troops to reach and support Wellington's army which won the battle.

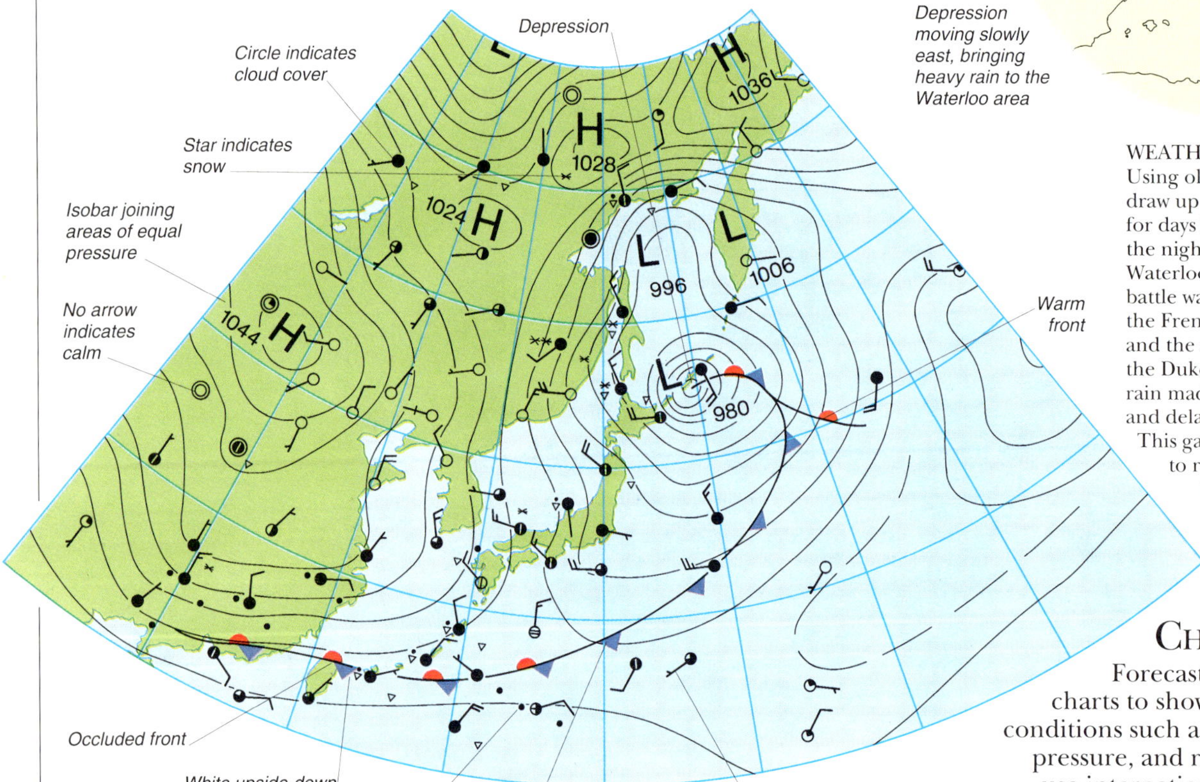

CHART FOR JAPAN

Forecasters draw up weather charts to show the picture of what conditions such as temperature, wind, pressure, and rainfall are like. They use internationally agreed weather symbols. This chart for 16 December, 1992 shows a developing low presure system, or depression, over Japan. Strong winds sweep anticlockwise around the low, swinging warm and cold fronts around with it. Japan has wet windy weather, while, to the west, high pressure means that the weather over China is cold and dry.

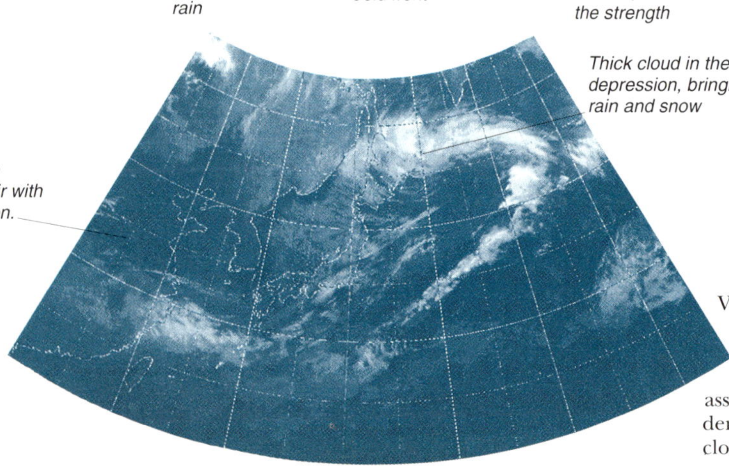

VIEW FROM SPACE
Photographs of clouds are taken from space by weather satellites. They show at a glance what the weather is like. This satellite picture shows the cloud patterns associated with the weather chart above. The cloud forms a dense knot near the centre of the depression, with more cloud spreading out along the line of the front.

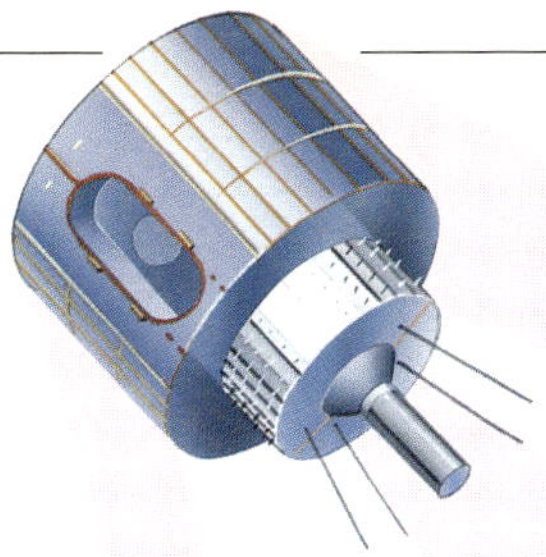

SATELLITES
Information from Earth is collected by satellites and sent down to weather stations every 30 minutes, with photos of cloud patterns.

COLLECTING INFORMATION

The World Meteorological Organization (WMO) has 150 member countries that share information in the World Weather Watch. Data from nearly 10,000 land stations, 7,000 ships, hundreds of aircraft and balloons, and several satellites are gathered each day at centres in Moscow in Russia, Washington DC in the United States, and Melbourne in Australia. Regional and worldwide forecasts are made and sent to members of the WMO. These send the data to national weather offices, which make the forecasts for their own countries.

SHIPS
Weather ships take measurements of pressure and temperature at sea level, and they measure the temperature of the sea itself. They launch weather balloons which send back information about the atmosphere at different heights.

AUTOMATIC BUOYS
Weather buoys are used in place of crewed ships. They record information about the local weather at sea level. The information is collected by satellites.

COMPUTERS
Information from around the world is fed into computer "models". The computers help make forecasts of future weather.

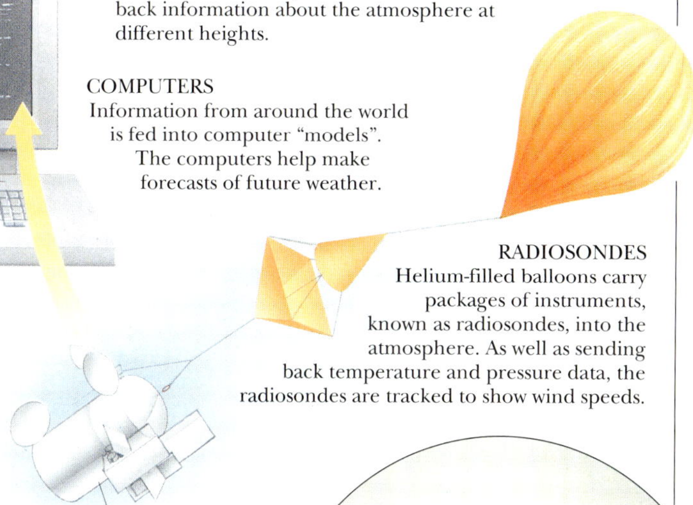

RADIOSONDES
Helium-filled balloons carry packages of instruments, known as radiosondes, into the atmosphere. As well as sending back temperature and pressure data, the radiosondes are tracked to show wind speeds.

Radiosondes are released at least twice a day.

AIRCRAFT
Specially adapted aircraft carry instruments up into the atmosphere. The measurements are sometimes immediately beamed back to the ground, and sometimes recorded and brought back.

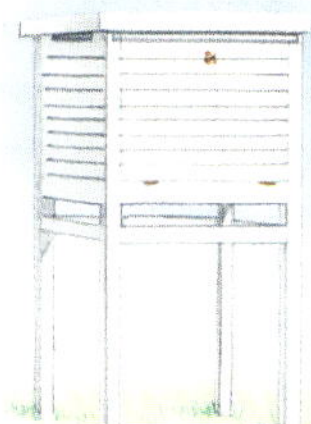

SMALL STATIONS
Individuals with a few simple instruments play an important part in weather forecasting. They send their information about local conditions to a main weather station.

USING FORECASTS
Airports need forecasts of bad weather so that equipment can be made ready to keep the runways open. Snow and ice are the worst hazards, but warnings of strong winds are also important.

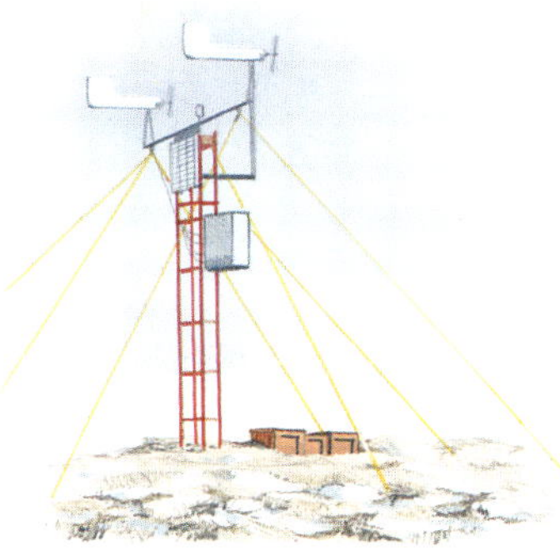

AUTOMATED STATIONS
Weather information in remote regions is collected at unstaffed stations. The information is sent automatically via satellite to the forecasting centres. Similar stations are set up on some offshore oil rigs.

LEWIS FRY RICHARDSON

British mathematician L F Richardson (1881-1953) worked out how to use mathematical techniques to forecast the weather. He worked on his theory while serving in the ambulance corps during the First World War. His manuscript was lost during a battle in 1917, but it turned up several months later under a heap of coal. Richardson's work was published in 1922, but his ideas could not be used until the electronic computer was invented twenty years later.

Find out more

AIR PRESSURE P.250
FRONTS P.253
WIND STRENGTH P.256
FORMATION OF CLOUDS P.262
WEATHER WATCHING P.272
SATELLITES P.300
FACT FINDER P.416

WEATHER WATCHING

FOR THOUSANDS OF YEARS, before weather-recording instruments were invented in the 16th century, people had to study natural signs to know what weather was coming. As well as the sky and clouds, animals, plants, the Sun, and the Moon all had their part to play. Many sayings arose from the signs and are now part of folklore. There are, of course, different signs and sayings in different parts of the world. Many of these are more than folklore – they work. Careful weather watching, combined with simple measurements of temperature and pressure, makes do-it-yourself local forecasting very reliable.

RED SKY

The sky is red every dawn and dusk. But when it is cloudy the sky's colour is hidden. In Europe and North America, winds usually bring weather from the west. If plenty of red sky is seen when the Sun is setting in the west, it means clear weather is on its way. Red sky in the morning means the good weather is on its way out.

STEVENSON SCREEN

Most weather stations and many schools have a Stevenson screen. This may contain a wet- and a dry-bulb thermometer to record humidity. The wet and dry thermometers show different temperatures according to the humidity. The humidity is worked out from a scale. There may also be a maximum and minimum thermometer and chart recorders of humidity and temperature.

JAPANESE CHERRY

In Japan, the dates on which the cherry trees blossom have been recorded for centuries. The records help weather watchers to know what the weather was like hundreds of years ago, and whether there was a harsh winter or an early spring in any year.

COWS

It is popularly thought that if cows lie down it means that rain is coming. The cows are supposed to be ensuring they have somewhere dry to lie. Even if this is true, cows lie down at all sorts of times. So a field full of cows lying down doesn't always indicate rain!

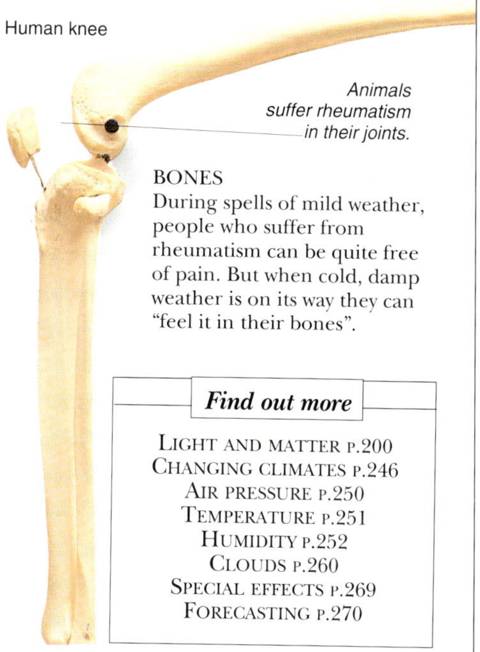

BONES

During spells of mild weather, people who suffer from rheumatism can be quite free of pain. But when cold, damp weather is on its way they can "feel it in their bones".

SEAWEED

A piece of seaweed brought back from the beach, such as this kelp, can help you to observe changes in the weather. When the weather is dry, the moisture in the seaweed evaporates, leaving it brittle and hard. In humid weather, the seaweed absorbs moisture from the air and it becomes plump and soft again. Seaweed changes tell us about the weather that we are having now, rather than what is coming.

Find out more

LIGHT AND MATTER P.200
CHANGING CLIMATES P.246
AIR PRESSURE P.250
TEMPERATURE P.251
HUMIDITY P.252
CLOUDS P.260
SPECIAL EFFECTS P.269
FORECASTING P.270

SPACE

LOOK UP INTO THE SKY and you are looking out into space. You can see stars and planets, as well as vast expanses of empty space in between. From the earliest times, people have tried to understand how we on Earth fit into our local part of space, and into the rest of the Universe that lies beyond. Early civilizations used the movements of objects in the sky (celestial objects) as a calendar, as a means of navigation, or to predict events in their lives. Early astronomers (people who study objects in space) tried to explain the movements of the celestial objects. Since the 19th century, they have tried to explain what the objects actually are. Today, astronomers have the most sophisticated technology available, which they use on Earth and in space, to pursue their quest.

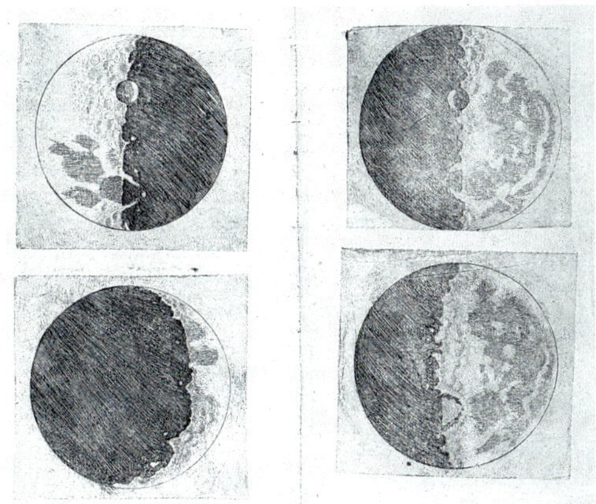

In 1609, the Italian astronomer Galileo Galilei was the first person to make a study of the skies with a telescope.

When Galileo studied the Moon with his telescope, he saw craters and mountains that were invisible to the naked eye.

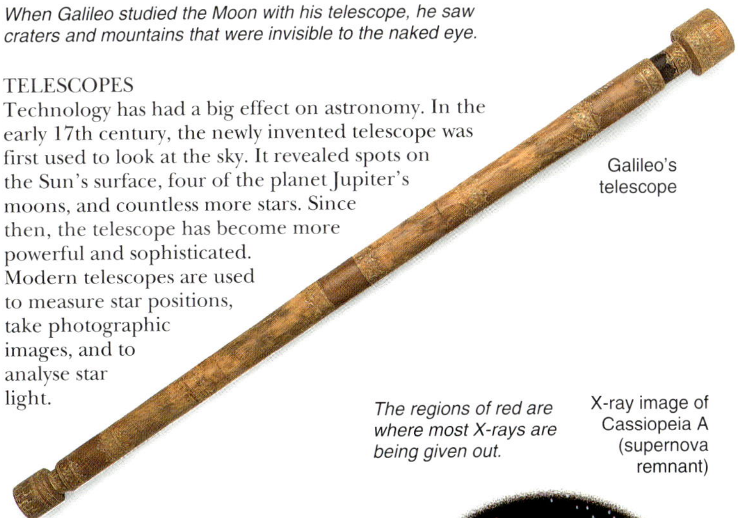

Galileo's telescope

TELESCOPES

Technology has had a big effect on astronomy. In the early 17th century, the newly invented telescope was first used to look at the sky. It revealed spots on the Sun's surface, four of the planet Jupiter's moons, and countless more stars. Since then, the telescope has become more powerful and sophisticated. Modern telescopes are used to measure star positions, take photographic images, and to analyse star light.

LONELY SPACE

The Universe is full of billions of stars and galaxies, but it is still a very empty place. The Universe is so vast that even the light from all the billions of stars doesn't illuminate it. In between the stars are billions of kilometres of empty, cold, and dark space. The only known intelligent life-form in the Universe is human. For humans, space is a very lonely place indeed.

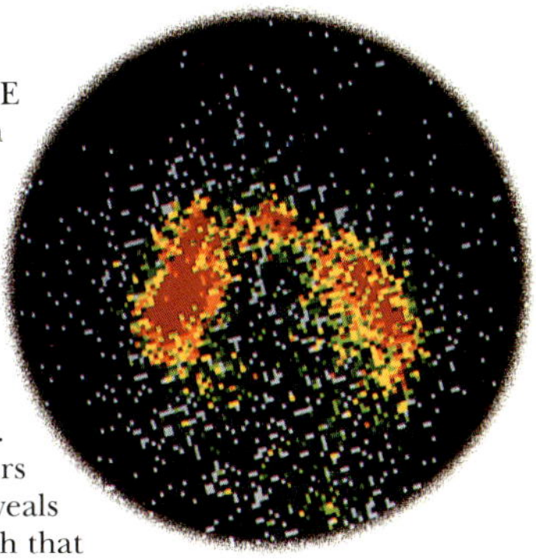

X-ray image of Cassiopeia A (supernova remnant)

The regions of red are where most X-rays are being given out.

PHOTOGRAPHS OF SPACE

For centuries, the only way to learn about the Universe was to collect and study the light waves given out by objects in space. Today, astronomers are able to collect and examine other types of radiation that are given out, such as X-rays, to build up a more complete picture of the Universe. This X-ray photograph of the leftovers of a supernova (exploding star) reveals clear, bright details. A photograph that captured only light waves would have shown just a dimly glowing gas.

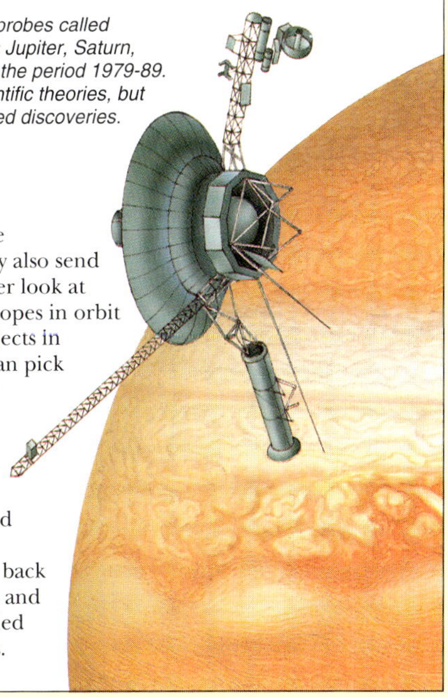

Between them, two space probes called Voyager visited the planets Jupiter, Saturn, Uranus, and Neptune over the period 1979-89. They confirmed some scientific theories, but also made some unexpected discoveries.

MODERN EQUIPMENT

Astronomers not only use equipment on Earth, they also send it into space to get a better look at our surroundings. Telescopes in orbit around Earth can see objects in space more clearly and can pick up radiation that cannot penetrate Earth's atmosphere. Robots called space probes are sent on lonely journeys to fly around and land on other planets, sending their discoveries back to Earth. Most telescopes and space probes are controlled from Earth by computers.

UNIVERSE

THE UNIVERSE IS EVERYTHING you can think of, and more besides. It includes all the stars, planets, moons, animals, plants, books such as this one, and you – it even includes all the empty space in between. Early people thought that the Universe only contained what they could see with their eyes from Earth. They thought of Earth as the central and most important part of the Universe. Today, we know just how vast the Universe is, and what a tiny part of it the Earth makes. Our present understanding of the Universe has been developed by astronomers and cosmologists working this century. Astronomers study specific parts of the Universe; cosmologists strive to explain the Universe's origin and development.

Universe
In all, there are around 100,000 million galaxies in the Universe.

Cluster of galaxies
The Milky Way lives in a cluster of about 30 galaxies. Clusters of such galaxies are loosely grouped into superclusters.

Milky Way
The Sun is just one of around 500,000 million stars in a galaxy called the Milky Way.

Solar System
Earth is one of nine planets that travel around a star called Sun.

Earth
Humans live on a planet called Earth.

Humans
Humans make up a tiny fraction of the Universe.

Astronomers believe there are millions of stars in the Universe with their own planets. But so far, the only such star known is our Sun.

The speed of light is the universal speed limit. Nothing can travel faster. Even so, the light from the nearest star to us (apart from the Sun) takes 4.3 years to reach us. It is 4.3 light years away. We see this star as it was 4.3 years ago.

CHANGING UNIVERSE

Everything in the Universe is changing. On Earth, humans or plants change as they live out their lives; stars in space have lives too, so they are also continually changing. Even the Universe as a whole does not stay the same. It too has a life of its own. Early this century, astronomers discovered that all galaxies (enormous collections of stars) are rushing away from each other. The Universe is getting bigger.

LIGHT YEAR

Distances in the Universe are so vast that a light year is used to measure them. This is the distance a ray of light travels in one year. As light travels at 300,000 km (186,000 miles) per second, it covers 9,460,000 million km (5,870,000 million miles) in one year.

RED SHIFT

Light travels as a wave. A squashed-up light wave is blue. A stretched-out light wave is red. In between are all the other colours of the spectrum. The light from a galaxy moving away from us will be stretched towards the red end of the spectrum. This is called a red shift. It will be more red-shifted if the galaxy is moving faster. From Hubble's law, astronomers know that the more distant galaxies move away faster than closer ones. The red-shift therefore shows how far away the galaxy is.

The orange-red light from this galaxy shows it is moving away from us.

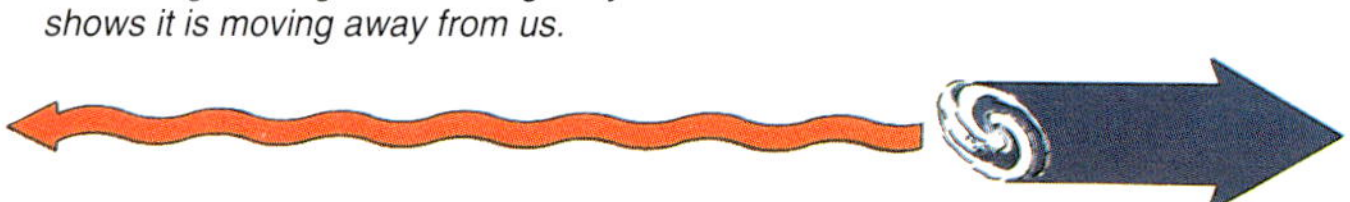

The light from this galaxy is shifted further towards the red end of the spectrum. This shows us that the galaxy is moving faster and is farther away than the galaxy above.

EDWIN HUBBLE

In 1924, an American astronomer, Edwin Hubble (1889-1953), showed that nebulae (fuzzy light patches in the sky) were distant galaxies. In 1929, he found the speed a galaxy moves away from Earth depends on its distance from Earth. If a galaxy is five times as far away as another, it is moving five times as fast. This is Hubble's law.

Find out more

MEASURING SOUND P.180
LIGHT P.190
ORIGIN OF THE UNIVERSE P.275
GALAXIES P.276
STARS P.278
SOLAR SYSTEM P.283
STUDY OF ASTRONOMY P.296

ORIGIN OF THE UNIVERSE

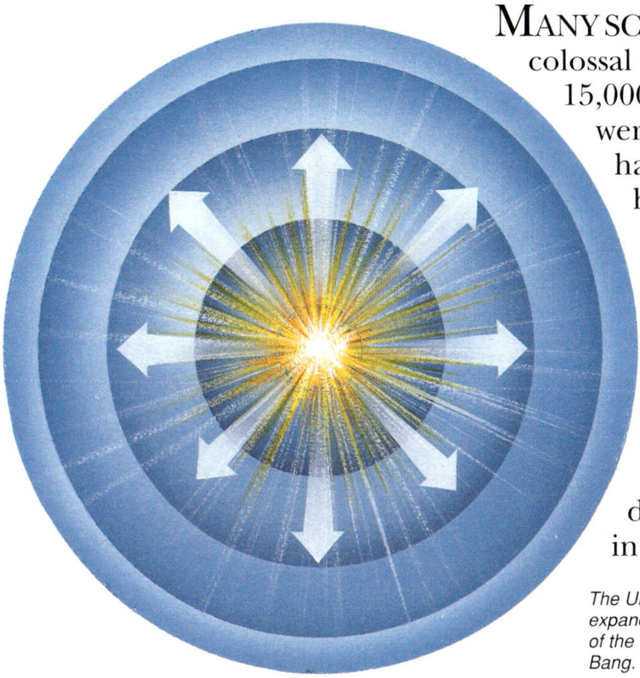

MANY SCIENTISTS THINK THAT the Universe was born in a colossal explosion called the Big Bang. In this explosion, 15,000 million years ago, all matter, energy, space, and time were created. Of course, no-one was there to tell us what happened. But discoveries in physics and astronomy have enabled scientists to trace the Universe's history to its first fraction of a second. They believe at that time, the Universe was squashed into a tiny volume, and it has been expanding ever since. The Big Bang Theory was put forward in 1933. Another idea, called the Steady State Theory, was suggested in 1948. This said that new material was continuously being created, and so overall the Universe would not change. The Steady State Theory has now been discounted. More recently, scientists have been looking into the future of the Universe. What happens next?

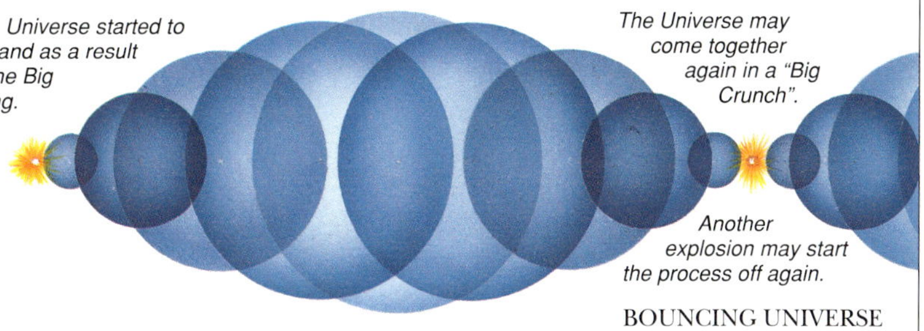

BOUNCING UNIVERSE

What will happen to the Universe? Scientists have different views about this. Some think it will have no definite end, but will gradually run down. This is the open Universe theory. Others think that it will stop expanding and start to contract until it is compressed and hot once more. This is the closed Universe theory.

BIG BANG

Around 15,000 million years ago, the Universe was very small and very hot. An explosion, the Big Bang, started off the process of expansion and change which still continues today. Within minutes of the explosion, atomic particles came together to make the gases helium and hydrogen, which over millions of years produced the galaxies, the stars, and the Universe as we know it today.

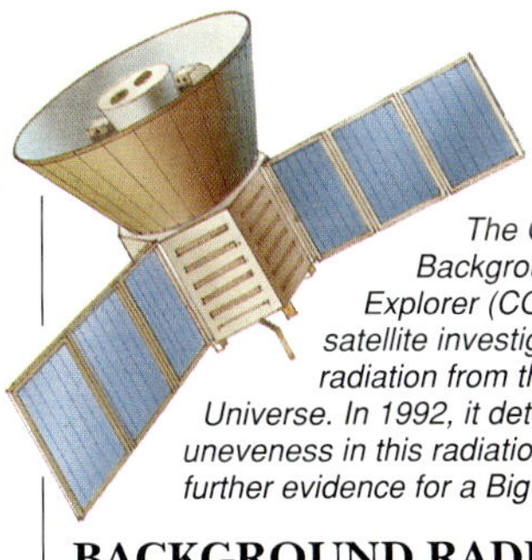

The Cosmic Background Explorer (COBE) satellite investigates the radiation from the early Universe. In 1992, it detected uneveness in this radiation – further evidence for a Big Bang.

BACKGROUND RADIATION

From the 1940s, scientists studied what the very young Universe was like. They realized it must have been full of radiation. As the Universe grew and cooled, the radiation would have cooled too. American astronomer George Gamow even worked out the temperature that it should now be. In 1965, two American scientists, Arno Penzias and Robert Wilson, detected exactly this type of radiation (called the background radiation). It provided evidence for a Big Bang.

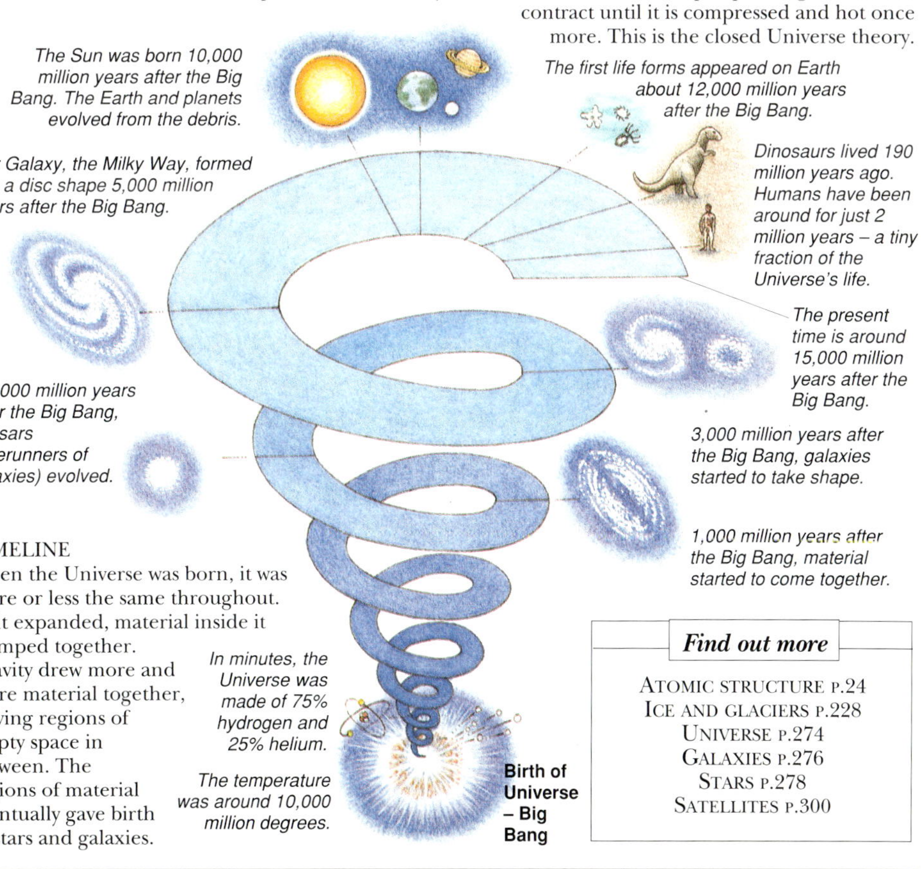

TIMELINE

When the Universe was born, it was more or less the same throughout. As it expanded, material inside it clumped together. Gravity drew more and more material together, leaving regions of empty space in between. The regions of material eventually gave birth to stars and galaxies.

Find out more

ATOMIC STRUCTURE P.24
ICE AND GLACIERS P.228
UNIVERSE P.274
GALAXIES P.276
STARS P.278
SATELLITES P.300

GALAXIES

STARS LIVE TOGETHER in "star cities" called galaxies. These enormous collections of stars started off as huge clouds of gas soon after the birth of the Universe. Gravity eventually pulled the gas into separate stars. Galaxies are so vast that it takes starlight hundreds of thousands of years to travel from one side to the other. The way the stars are arranged within a galaxy gives it a distinctive shape. Our star, the Sun, lives in a spiral-shaped galaxy called the Milky Way. Up until this century, astronomers thought that the Milky Way Galaxy was the only galaxy in the Universe. Today, we know it is just one of 100,000 million galaxies that exist.

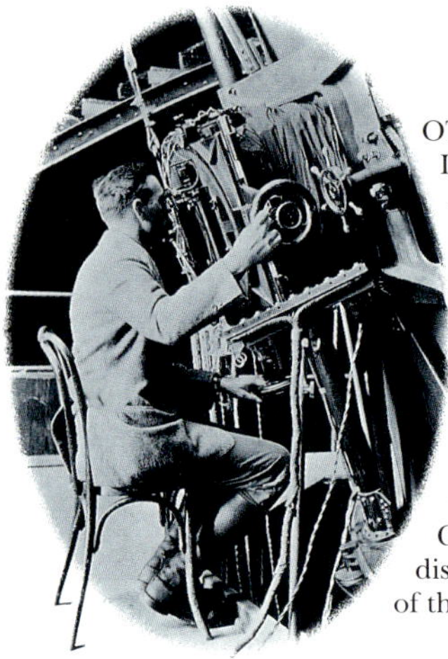

OTHER GALAXIES
In 1924, the American astronomer Edwin Hubble proved the existence of other galaxies. He showed that stars within the Andromeda Nebula (later called the Andromeda Galaxy) were too distant to be members of the Milky Way.

DISTANT WORLDS

By the start of the 20th century, astronomers had listed large numbers of dim, fuzzy patches in the sky which they called nebulae. Many of these had been seen for centuries. Some people thought they were just clouds of gas in the Milky Way. Others thought they might be distant galaxies. And indeed this is what many turned out to be. American astronomer Edwin Hubble studied them and classified them according to their shape. There are four main types of galaxies – spirals (like the Milky Way), barred spirals, ellipticals, and irregulars.

Galaxies start their lives as giant clouds of gas. The cloud spins, stars start to form, and the galaxy takes shape. The faster the spin, the flatter the galaxy.

Spiral galaxy NGC 5194

SPIRAL
Spiral galaxies contain young and old stars. They are disc-shaped with spiral arms. In a barred spiral, the arms come out from the ends of a bar across the centre of the galaxy.

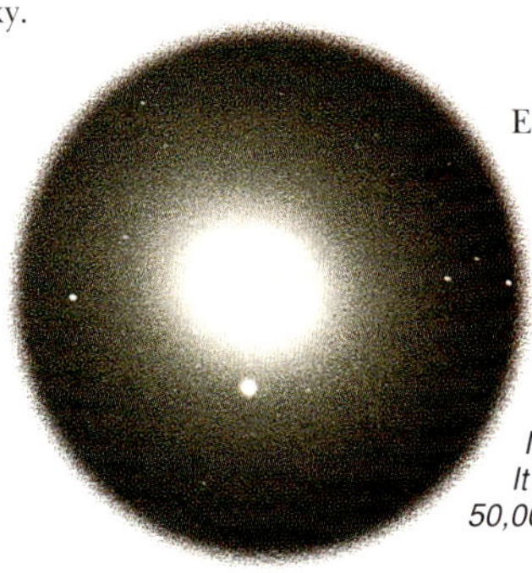

M49 elliptical galaxy. It has a diameter of 50,000 light years.

ELLIPTICAL
Elliptical galaxies are flattened ball-shaped collections of old stars (stars at the end of their life). They are the most common type of galaxy in the Universe.

Part of the Virgo cluster of galaxies, the nearest major cluster to our Local Group.

CLUSTERS
Galaxies tend to stick together. They are spread throughout the Universe in clusters. The Milky Way is in a cluster of about 30 galaxies called the Local Group. Other clusters can contain thousands of galaxies. Clusters may group together into superclusters.

IRREGULAR
Irregular galaxies are those that have not formed into a specific shape. They are the rarest type of galaxy in the Universe.

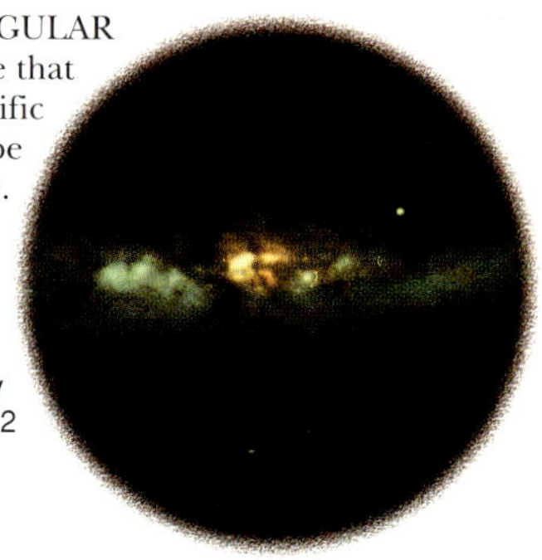

Irregular galaxy M82

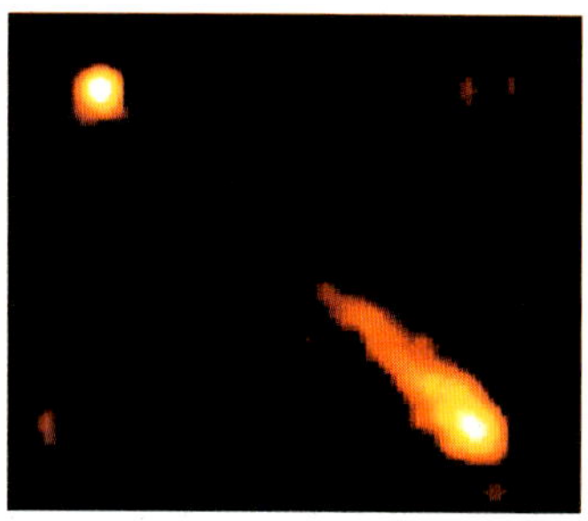

Radio image of quasar 3C 273. Its core (top left) and its tail (bottom right) are powerful emitters of radio waves.

QUASARS
In 1963, a new category of object – the quasar – was identified. We know these are very luminous, distant objects, moving away from us at great speed. However, many questions about them remain unanswered. At present, they are thought to be the cores of very young galaxies.

MILKY WAY

The Milky Way is a spiral galaxy with a concentration of stars at its centre. This gives the Galaxy a central bulge from which arms of stars radiate out. We live in one of these arms. This means that from the Southern Hemisphere of Earth, we look in towards the centre of the Galaxy; from the Northern Hemisphere, we look out to its edge. Like all galaxies, the Milky Way is moving. Not only is the whole galaxy travelling through space, but the stars within it are continuously moving around the galactic centre.

Photograph of Milky Way taken from New Zealand

Origin of the Milky Way by Tintoretto

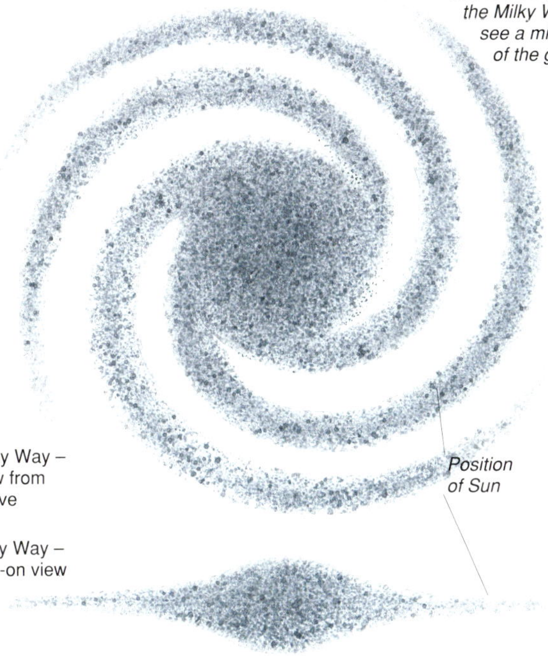

All the stars you can see in the night sky belong to the Milky Way. Sometimes, you can see a milky path made from the light of the galaxy's millions of stars.

Stars don't stay in the same position within the Galaxy. Over long periods of time, they move in and out of the spiral arms.

It would take a ray of light 100,000 years to travel from one side of the Galaxy to the other.

Milky Way – view from above

Position of Sun

The Sun takes around 220 million years to make one journey around the galactic centre.

Milky Way – side-on view

MYTHICAL ORIGIN

The Milky Way is so-called because it looks like a splash of milk in the night sky. In Ancient Greece, long before people understood the nature of the Milky Way, they explained that the Milky Way originated from milk spilt as young Hercules drank from the goddess Juno's breast.

SUN'S POSITION

Our Sun lives in one of the Milky Way's spiral arms, about two-thirds from the centre. It is just one of the estimated 500,000 million stars that make up the Galaxy. There are stars that live in between the spiral arms, but because the stars in the arms are younger and brighter, it is these that give the Galaxy its distinctive shape.

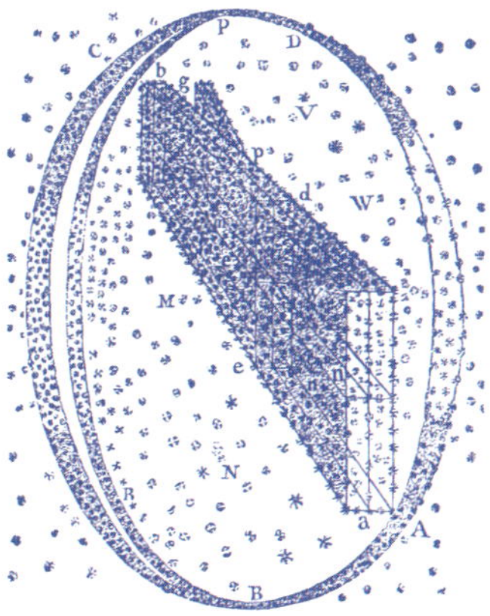

William Herschel's model of stars in the Milky Way

HERSCHEL'S MODEL

In the 18th century, the British astronomer William Herschel (1738-1822) surveyed the stars in the Milky Way. With the naked eye, you can see around 2,000 stars; with a telescope, you can see many millions – far too many to count. Herschel decided to count certain areas of stars and then average out the results. In this way, he made a fairly accurate model of the Milky Way. He also proposed that some nebulae might be star systems outside our own Galaxy. It was more than a century later before he was shown to be correct.

Photograph of light released from the Andromeda (M31) Galaxy. This is the closest major galaxy to our own.

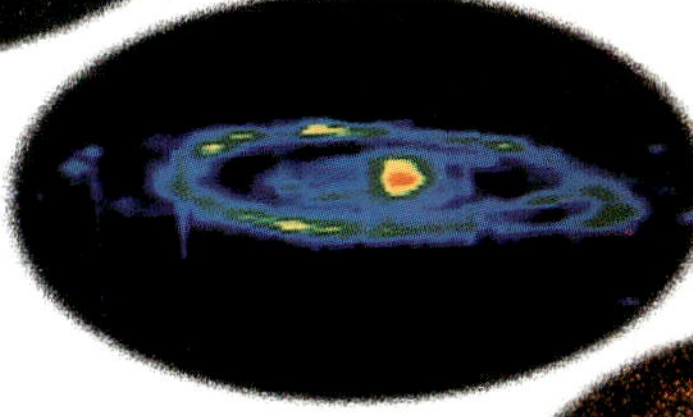

Infrared image of the Andromeda galaxy. These infrared rays have travelled for 2.2 million years before they reach Earth.

VIEWING GALAXIES

To build up a more complete picture of our Universe, we can gather other types of radiation from it as well as light. For example, X-ray views will show up very hot regions of energetic activity. Gamma-ray views reveal regions in which energy is released from nuclear reactions. Other wavelengths can pick out concentrated areas of hydrogen gas between stars and areas of cold dust.

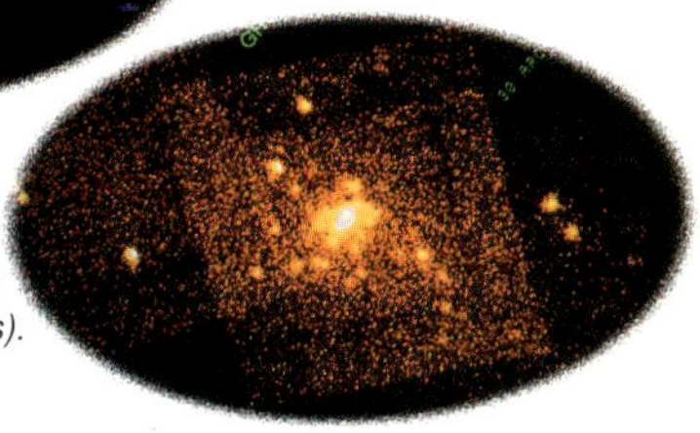

An X-ray image of the Andromeda Galaxy. The bright region in the centre is the core of the galaxy (the part that releases the most X-rays).

Find out more

UNIVERSE P.274
STARS P.278
LIFE CYCLE OF STARS P.280
CONSTELLATIONS P.282
SUN P.284
URANUS P.292
TELESCOPES IN SPACE P.298

STARS

EVERY ONE OF THE STARS you can see in the night sky is actually a violent, spinning ball of hot, luminous gas. The gases of a star are held together by gravity. Stars get their energy by "burning" their gases. This is not like burning coal, but it is a more efficient reaction called nuclear fusion. The amount of gas a star contains is very important as it influences the gravity, temperature, pressure, density, and size of the star. Stars live in galaxies and each galaxy contains many different types of stars. Astronomers have only understood the true nature of stars over this century. Until then, they were more concerned with the positions of stars.

STAR SPECTRA
Astronomers use special equipment to collect and then separate a star's light into its spectrum. On the spectrum are dark lines called absorption lines. These show which elements the star contains. Every star gives a different spectrum. An American astronomer called Annie Jump Cannon sorted the spectra of thousands of stars into different types. Each type is given a letter of the alphabet. The main types are O, B, A, F, G, K, M, where each star type is cooler than the previous one.

The gaps, or absorption lines, in a spectrum show which types of light the star has "used" or absorbed. This is an indication of which elements the star contains.

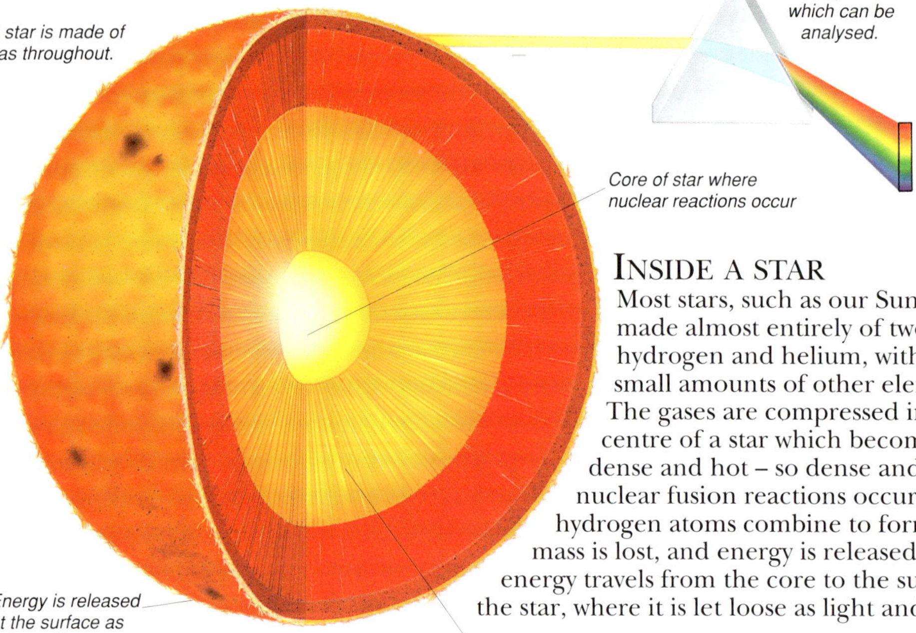

INSIDE A STAR

Most stars, such as our Sun, are made almost entirely of two gases, hydrogen and helium, with very small amounts of other elements. The gases are compressed in the centre of a star which becomes very dense and hot – so dense and hot that nuclear fusion reactions occur here: hydrogen atoms combine to form helium, mass is lost, and energy is released. This energy travels from the core to the surface of the star, where it is let loose as light and heat.

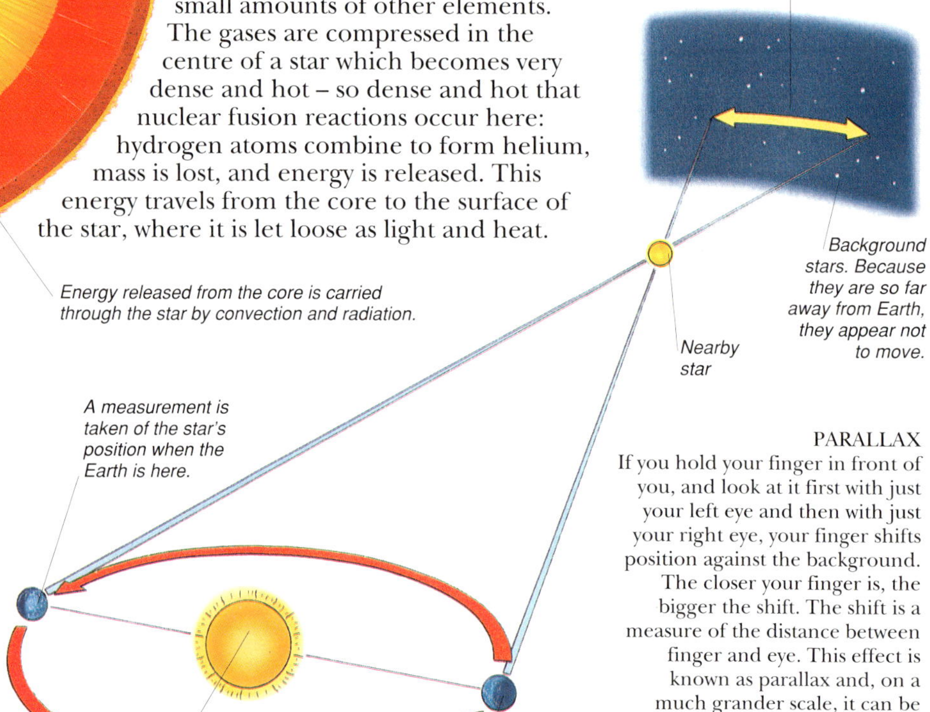

CECILIA PAYNE-GAPOSCHKIN

In the 19th century, the English astronomer William Huggins showed that stars are made of the same elements that exist on Earth. In the 1920s, a British astronomer named Cecilia Payne-Gaposchkin (1900-79) proved that stars are made mostly of hydrogen. She also found that the make-up of most stars is the same. These were great discoveries that made her a pioneer of stellar astrophysics (the study of the physical and chemical processes in stars).

PARALLAX
If you hold your finger in front of you, and look at it first with just your left eye and then with just your right eye, your finger shifts position against the background. The closer your finger is, the bigger the shift. The shift is a measure of the distance between finger and eye. This effect is known as parallax and, on a much grander scale, it can be used to calculate the distances of nearby stars. As the Earth orbits around the Sun, a star will appear to move slightly against the background of more distant stars. This produces a parallax angle which can be used to measure the distance of the star from Earth.

Blue giants are very bright and very hot stars. They are O-type stars with a temperature of around 35,000°C (63,000°F).

Main sequence stars

Stars at the top of the main sequence have 60 times the Sun's mass. Those at the bottom have just one-twelfth the Sun's mass.

This blue-white star is a B-type, with a temperature of about 20,000°C (36,000°F).

White stars are classified as A-types, with a temperature of about 10,000°C (18,000°F).

This yellow-white star is an F-type star, with a temperature of about 7,500°C (13,500°F).

The spectral types of stars, O, B, A, F, G, K, and M, relate to the star's colour and temperature. O-type stars are blue and hot, M-type stars are red and cooler.

JEWEL BOX
Most stars look like silver pinpoints of light in Earth's sky. But we can see the true colour of some stars. This colourful group of brilliant stars is called the Jewel Box cluster.

Main sequence stars

The colour of a star gives us an idea of its surface temperature. Blue stars are hot; red stars are cooler. If the temperature is plotted on a graph against the star's absolute magnitude (how much light it releases), most stars fall within a narrow band called the main sequence – the hotter the star, the brighter it shines. All stars on the main sequence are in a stable time of their lives – they are shining steadily because they are fusing hydrogen in their cores. When the hydrogen fuel has been used up, the star will move off the main sequence. More massive stars will move off more quickly than less massive stars.

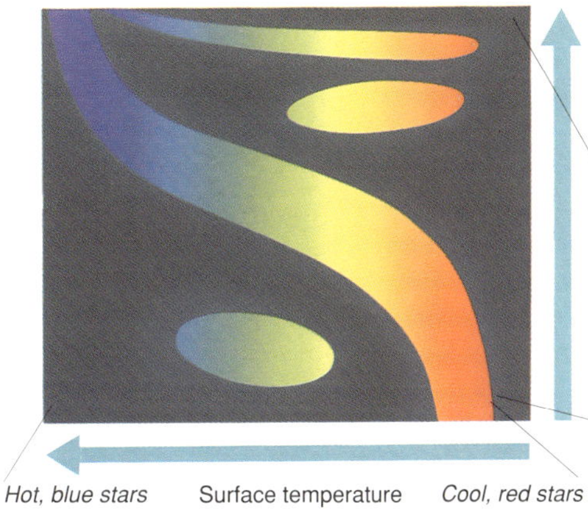

The graph is called a Hertzsprung-Russell diagram, after two astronomers, Enjar Hertzsprung from Denmark and Henry Norris Russell from America, who made it in 1913.

This yellow star is like our Sun – a G-type star, with a temperature of about 6,000°C (10,800°F).

This orange star is a K-type star, with a temperature of about 4,700°C (8,460°F).

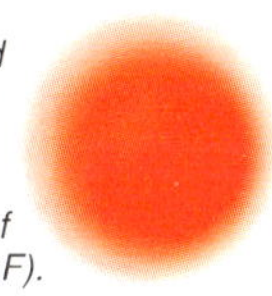

This tiny star is a red dwarf. It is a dim and fairly cool star. It is classified as an M-type, with a temperature of about 3,000°C (5,400°F).

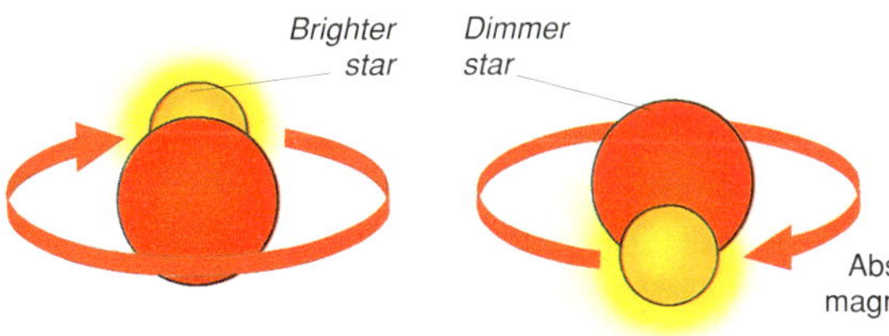

At this point, the binary system would appear dim from Earth because the dimmer star is blocking the brighter one.

From Earth, this binary system would appear bright, because the brighter star is in front of the dimmer star.

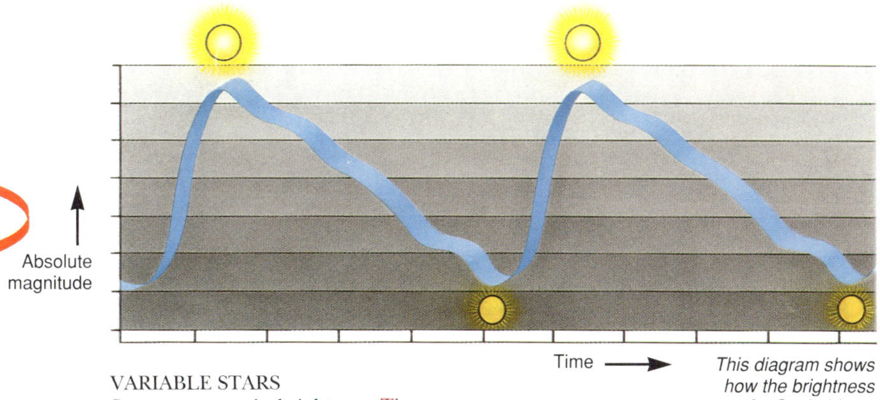

This diagram shows how the brightness of a Cepheid star varies with time.

ECLIPSING BINARIES
About half the stars in the Universe belong to a double or binary system in which two stars orbit about each other. The two stars can be close enough to almost touch or they can be millions of kilometres apart. We can detect binary systems in different ways. If we have a side-on view of a binary system from Earth, we can detect the changes in brightness as the two stars take it in turns to pass in front of each other. They are called eclipsing binaries.

VARIABLE STARS
Some stars vary in brightness. There are different types of these variable stars. Some, called RR Lyrae stars, change in less than a day. Others, called Cepheid stars, take one to 100 days to change. Still more, called Mira variables, can take up to two years to complete one cycle of change. Cepheid stars change in brightness because they change physically in size and temperature. They give off more light when they are expanding, and less when they are contracting. The star won't always be like this – it is just a normal star going through an unstable period in its life.

Find out more

NUCLEAR ENERGY P.136
SOURCES OF LIGHT P.193
REFRACTION P.196
GALAXIES P.276
LIFE CYCLE OF STARS P.280
SUN P.284
FACT FINDER P.418

LIFE CYCLE OF STARS

NOTHING IN THE UNIVERSE stays the same forever, and stars are no exception. However, we cannot see a star changing because it lives for billions and billions of years. The birthplaces of all stars are clouds of gas and dust that have slowly formed from the sparsely scattered atoms in space. Stars are born in groups, most of which break up, but others are kept together by gravity. The rest of a star's life depends on how massive it is. The more massive a star, the quicker it uses its hydrogen fuel, and the shorter and stormier its life is. Some are simply so massive they explode. But most, like our Sun, have a stable period in their lives when they shine steadily.

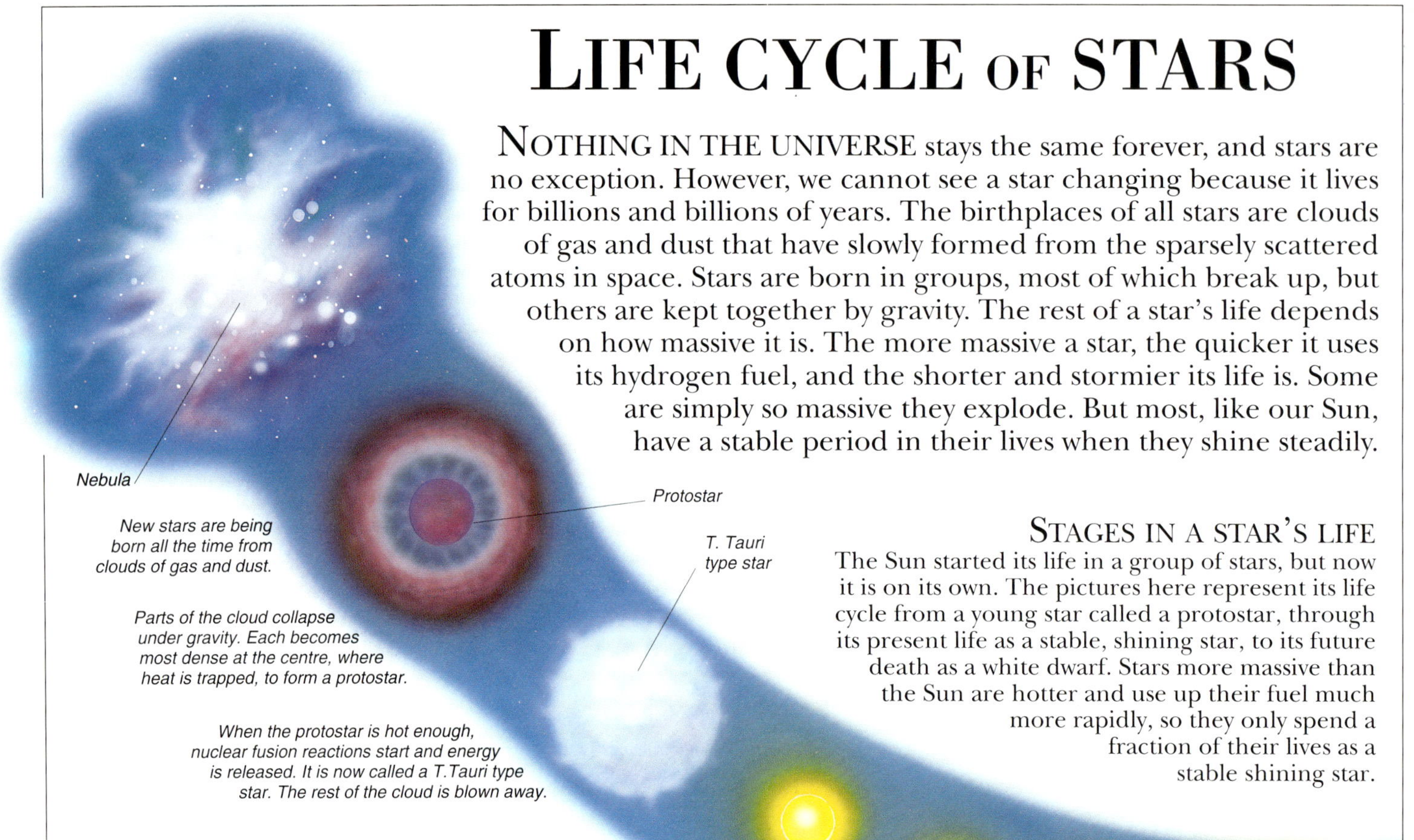

STAGES IN A STAR'S LIFE

The Sun started its life in a group of stars, but now it is on its own. The pictures here represent its life cycle from a young star called a protostar, through its present life as a stable, shining star, to its future death as a white dwarf. Stars more massive than the Sun are hotter and use up their fuel much more rapidly, so they only spend a fraction of their lives as a stable shining star.

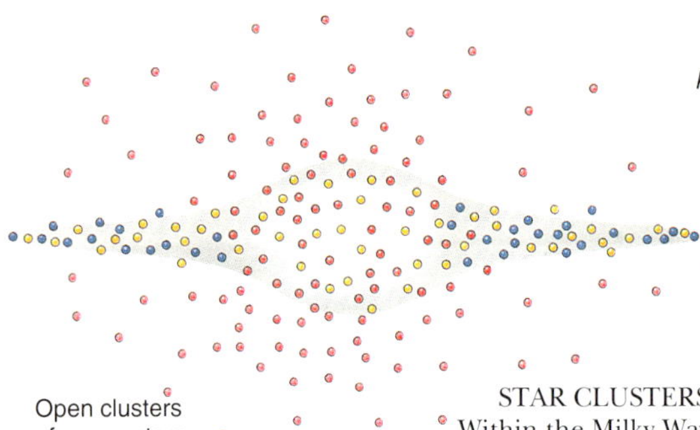

STAR CLUSTERS

Within the Milky Way Galaxy are concentrated groups of stars called star clusters. All the stars in a cluster were born from the same cloud, are the same age, and initially had the same composition. There are two types of cluster – open and globular. Open clusters contain up to a few hundred randomly arranged stars. They are found in the outer parts (the flat disc) of our Galaxy. Globular clusters contain hundreds of thousands of very old stars arranged in ball shapes. They are found in a huge sphere around the centre of our Galaxy.

47 Tucanae cluster of stars

GLOBULAR CLUSTER

Globular clusters contain very old stars. It is thought they were formed around the same time as the galaxies that they live in. This is why globular clusters can provide information on the early life of the Milky Way. This globular cluster, 47 Tucanae, is visible to the naked eye if you live in the Southern Hemisphere.

Pleiades cluster of stars

OPEN CLUSTER

The Pleiades is an open cluster of young stars that spreads across 30 light years in space (in star terms, "young" means around 60 million years old). To the naked eye, the Pleiades looks like a fuzzy patch of light with seven prominent stars. Through powerful telescopes, we can see many more of its bluish stars, as well as gas and dust that the stars have ploughed into.

NEUTRON STARS

When a star with between about 1.4 and 3 times the Sun's mass collapses, it leaves a core called a neutron star. The collapse is so violent that the electrons and protons within atoms are forced together to form neutrons. All the material is squashed into an incredibly dense sphere around 10 km (6 miles) across. It gives out energy. A pulsar is a fast-spinning neutron star that flashes a signal Earthwards as it spins (like a lighthouse). Pulsars were first detected in 1967 by British astronomers Jocelyn Burnell and Antony Hewish.

In 1054, the Chinese recorded a star bright enough to be seen in daylight. It was a supernova. Today, we see its remains in the Crab Nebula.The core of the exploding star is now a pulsar, rotating 30 times every second.

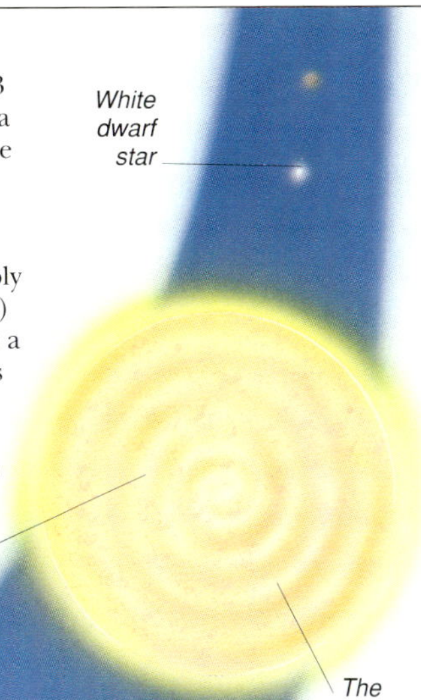

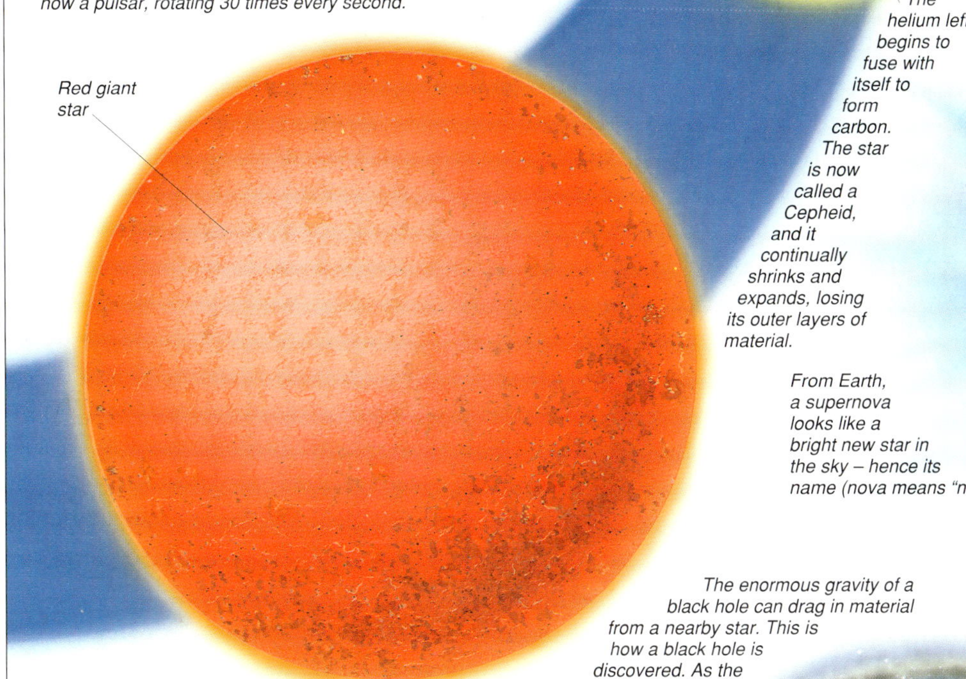

The outer layers of the star become unstable and puff away into space. The inner layers do not have enough energy to keep them expanded, and they collapse – so quickly that the atoms are pushed very close together. The star has become a white dwarf – this will slowly fade to become a black dwarf.

ALTERNATIVE DEATHS

Not all stars end their lives as white dwarfs. Some massive stars end their lives in spectacular fashion – they collapse so quickly that they explode. This explosion is called a supernova. The core may remain as a neutron star or a black hole. Its far-flung ashes will provide material for new stars to be born.

The helium left begins to fuse with itself to form carbon. The star is now called a Cepheid, and it continually shrinks and expands, losing its outer layers of material.

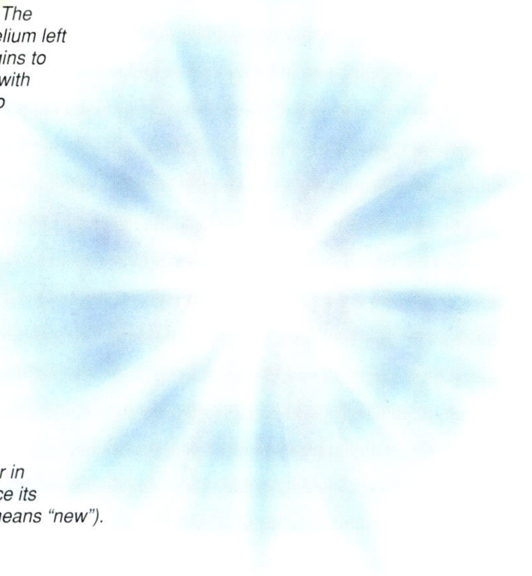

From Earth, a supernova looks like a bright new star in the sky – hence its name (nova means "new").

The hydrogen is used up. The centre is so hot by now that the star expands. The surface cools and turns red. Such a star is called a red giant.

The enormous gravity of a black hole can drag in material from a nearby star. This is how a black hole is discovered. As the material swirls into the black hole, it becomes very hot and gives off X-rays. These X-rays can be detected.

BLACK HOLES

Strange things happen to a star with more than three times the mass of the Sun. At the end of its life it will collapse, becoming more and more compact. The collapse continues until the star becomes so dense that nothing, not even light, can escape from its gravity. It has become a black hole, with a singularity (a point of infinite density) at its centre.

GENERAL RELATIVITY

In 1915, Albert Einstein published his startling but now famous theory called General Relativity. It gave a totally different view of gravity, proposing that it was a property of space, and not a force between bodies. Bodies of matter curve space, rather like a weight curves a trampoline, and so bodies "fall" towards other bodies. Even light "falls" into the curved space around a body and so its path is bent. This strange idea was put to the test during an eclipse of the Sun in 1919. The light from a distant star was indeed seen to be bent by the gravity of the Sun. Einstein was proved right.

The star appears to be in a different position from where it actually is because its light is bent by the Sun.

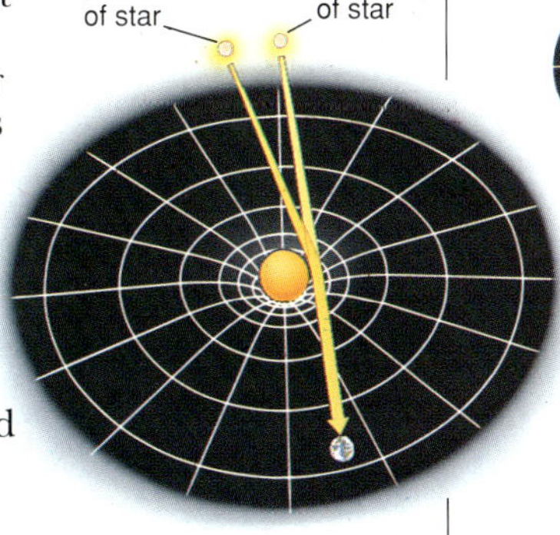

Around a black hole, light is bent so much that it cannot escape.

According to General Relativity, bodies of matter curve space. If the body of matter was very dense (a large amount of matter squashed into a small space), it would stretch space into an infinitely deep chasm – a black hole.

Find out more

ATOMIC STRUCTURE P.24
GRAVITY P.122
NUCLEAR ENERGY P.136
ORIGIN OF THE UNIVERSE P.275
GALAXIES P.276
STARS P.278
SUN P.284

CONSTELLATIONS

STAR TRAILS
From Earth, the stars appear to spin around two imaginary points in the sky – the north and south celestial poles. This photograph has captured the movements of the stars as trails in the night sky.

THE TWINKLING PINPOINTS of light in the night sky can all look the same at first. Thousands of years ago, early astronomers divided the stars into groups and drew imaginary pictures around them so they were easy to remember – pictures such as a scorpion or a bear. This is how our present-day system of constellations was born. The stars in a constellation are actually unrelated; they only appear to make these groups when viewed from Earth. The stars are all so far away that they appear to be at the same distance and to move together as if stuck on the inside of an enormous bowl – the celestial sphere.

ORION
Orion, the hunter, is an easy constellation to see. Four bright stars mark his shoulders and knees. Three more mark his belt, and one other, the Orion Nebula, marks his sword.

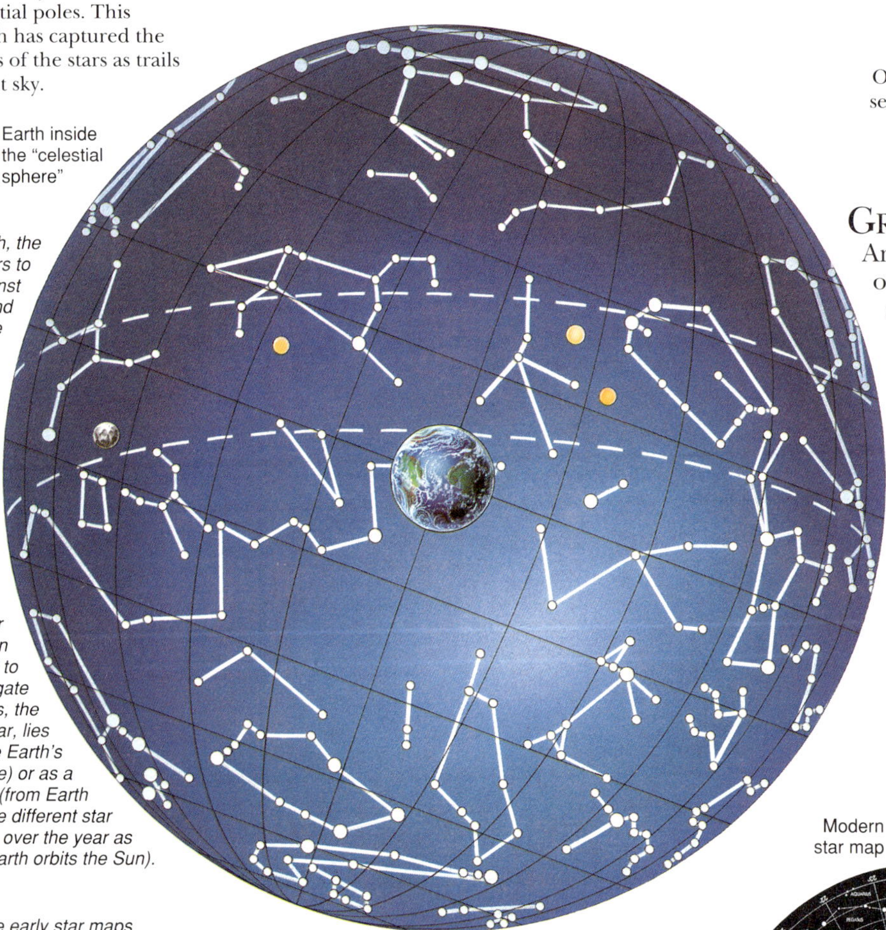

Earth inside the "celestial sphere"

From Earth, the Sun appears to move against a background of stars. The star groups it moves in front of are known as the Zodiac.

Star patterns can be used to navigate (Polaris, the North Star, lies above Earth's North Pole) or as a calendar (from Earth we see different star patterns over the year as the Earth orbits the Sun).

GROUPING STARS

An internationally agreed system of 88 constellations is used by astronomers today. Twelve of the constellations are together known as the zodiac. These form the backdrop against which the planets, the Moon, and the Sun move. Individual stars are identified within a constellation by a letter of the Greek alphabet. The brightest star is alpha, the next is beta, and so on.

MAGNITUDES
Astronomers use numbers to describe a star's brightness. The scale of apparent magnitude is so called because it doesn't describe how bright the star actually is, just how bright it is as seen from Earth. The larger the number given to the star, the fainter the star is. Stars classified 1-6 are visible with the naked eye.

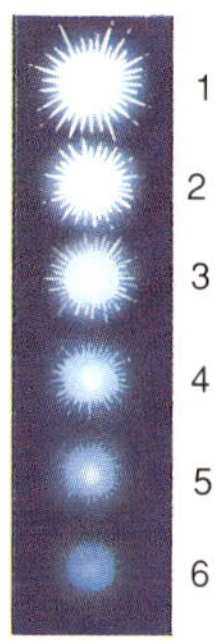

Some of the early star maps were more artistic than scientific.

STAR MAPS
Early star maps filled the northern sky with animals and mythical figures. As navigators voyaged south, more and more of the sky could be charted. Positions of the stars were pinpointed with increasing accuracy as the telescope and observing techniques improved; fewer charts with artistic representations of the constellations were produced. Celestial charts started to be made photographically and then with the aid of computers. Today, satellites plot positions of the stars with even greater accuracy and speed.

Modern star map

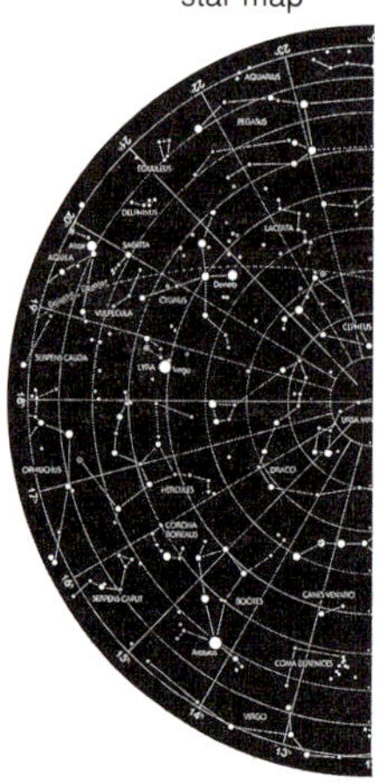

Find out more

UNIVERSE P.274
STARS P.278
LIFE CYCLE OF STARS P.280
STUDY OF ASTRONOMY P.296
TELESCOPES ON EARTH P.297
FACT FINDER P.418

SOLAR SYSTEM

MILLIONS OF YEARS AGO, a family was born around the Sun: balls of matter that we call the planets. The Sun and this system of planets that orbit (circle) around it make up the Solar System. Asteroids (minor planets between Mars and Jupiter), comets, moons (bodies that orbit around planets), and interplanetary dust also form part of this large family which extends over 12,000 million km (7,400 million miles) in space. The dominant body is the Sun which accounts for more than 99 per cent of the mass of the Solar System. Our Solar System was once regarded as the largest and central part of the Universe. Today, we know it is just a tiny speck compared with the rest of the Universe.

Astronomers have found discs of gas and dust around some young stars. So other planetary systems may exist.

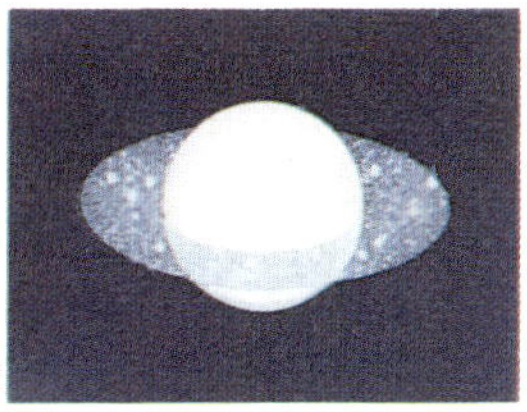

FORMATION

The planets and other bodies were formed 4,600 million years ago from material left over from the Sun's birth. The Sun was surrounded by a sphere of gas (hydrogen and helium) and dust (iron, rock, and snow) called the solar nebula, which formed into a flat rotating disc. The dust stuck together to form four lumps – Mercury, Venus, Earth, and Mars. Farther out, dust and snow combined with the gases to produce Jupiter, Saturn, Uranus, and Neptune. Pluto is different – it may be an escaped moon.

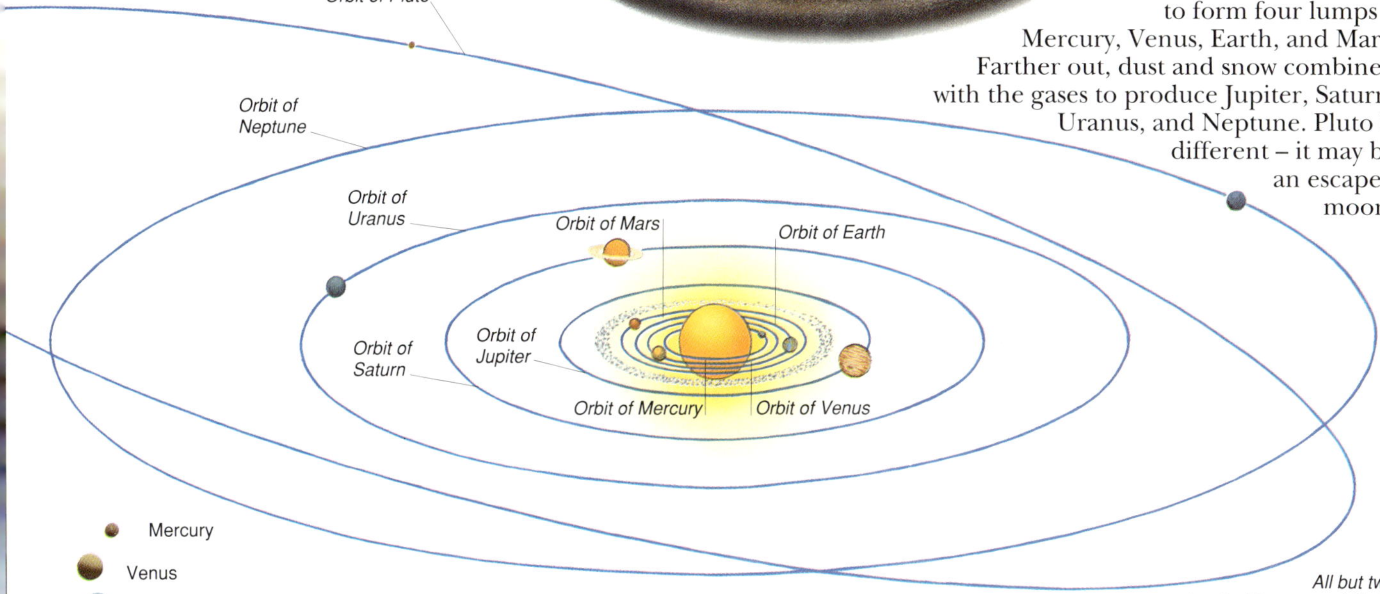

All but two planets, Mercury and Pluto, have orbits in the same plane.

PLANET SIZES

Astronomers are more interested in the mass of a body (the amount of material it contains) than its diameter (its size). Of all the planets, Jupiter has the largest mass as well as the biggest diameter.

GRAVITY IN THE SOLAR SYSTEM

What keeps the Solar System together? A force called gravity, which is an attraction between any two bodies that have mass. Its strength depends on how massive the bodies are and how far apart they are. Gravity keeps the material in a body together; if it is strong enough, it will pull gases towards a planet or moon to form an atmosphere. In the 17th century, the English scientist Isaac Newton investigated the motion of the Moon and the planets, and outlined a universal law of gravitation. It is one of the fundamental laws by which the Universe operates.

Gravity keeps the planets orbiting the Sun, and the moons orbiting the planets. The effect of gravity decreases with distance; the farther a planet is from the Sun, the slower it moves.

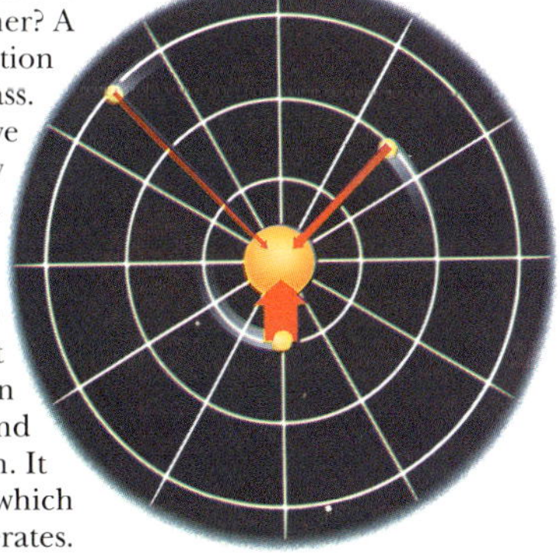

ORBITS

The Solar System is disc-like in shape. The Sun is at the centre and the planets follow individual paths called orbits around it. They all travel in the same direction, but move at different speeds and take different times to complete an orbit.

Find out more

GRAVITY P.122
SUN P.284
MERCURY AND VENUS P.286
EARTH P.287
MARS P.289
JUPITER P.290
SATURN P.291
URANUS P.292
NEPTUNE AND PLUTO P.293
FACT FINDER P.418

SUN

THE NEAREST STAR TO US is the Sun. By studying it, we can learn about the other stars in the Universe. Like all stars, the Sun is a huge, luminous ball of hot gas – mostly hydrogen, but some helium, with tiny amounts of other elements. Within the Sun, a process called nuclear fusion continuously generates energy such as light and heat; at its centre, the temperature is around 14,000,000°C (25,000,000°F). The Sun was born from a cloud of gas and dust about 5,000 million years ago. It was created in a group of stars which slowly broke up so that now the Sun is alone. It is the only star known to have a system of planets. But to one of these planets, the Earth, the Sun is not just any old star; it is a provider of energy for life.

Prominences are only visible during a total solar eclipse or by using special equipment.

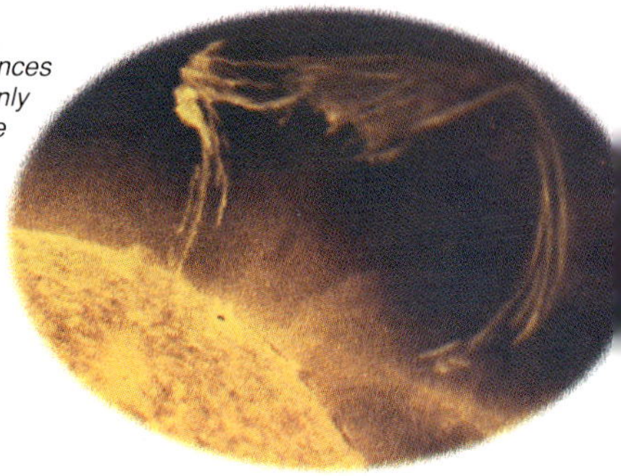

PROMINENCES
Huge, flame-like clouds of hot gas sometimes explode from the photosphere. These are called solar flares and prominences, and they are associated with sunspots. Flares are short-lived bursts of light. A large prominence may reach heights of 100,000 km (62,000 miles) and may last for months.

LAYERS OF SUN

The Sun is made of different layers of gas. The surface layer we see is called the photosphere. Here, gas swirls and bubbles about, giving the Sun a mottled look. Surrounding the photosphere is an unseen layer of gas called the chromosphere. Above this is a layer of gas called the corona (which means "crown").

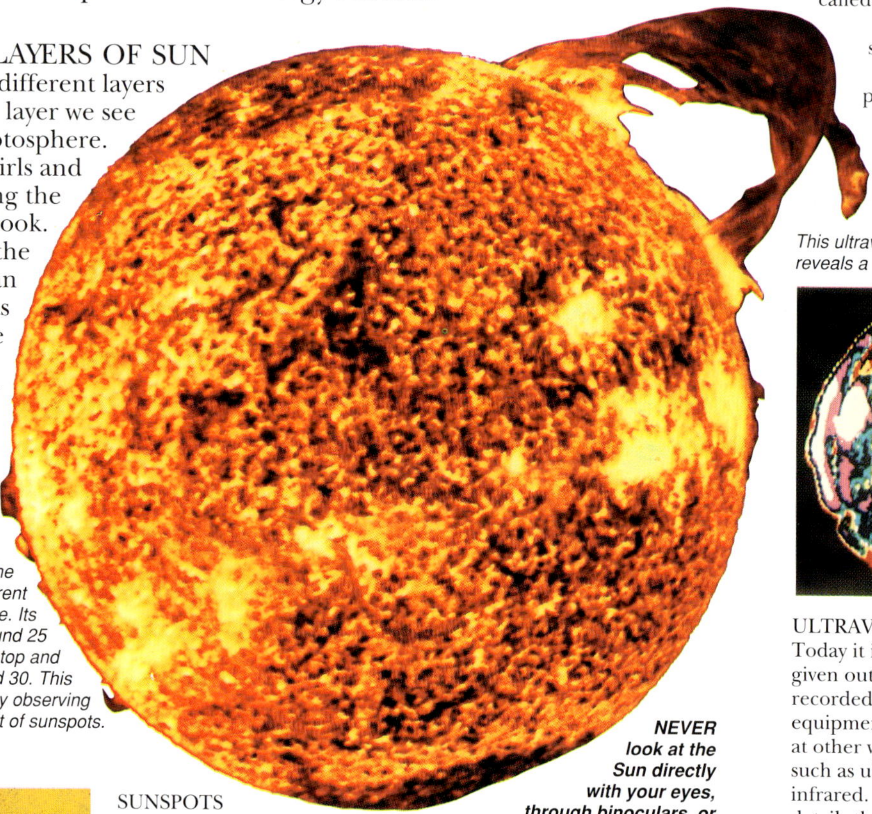

Different parts of the Sun take different times to rotate. Its middle takes around 25 days, while its top and bottom take around 30. This was discovered by observing the movement of sunspots.

NEVER look at the Sun directly with your eyes, through binoculars, or through a telescope.

This ultraviolet picture of the Sun reveals a hole in the corona.

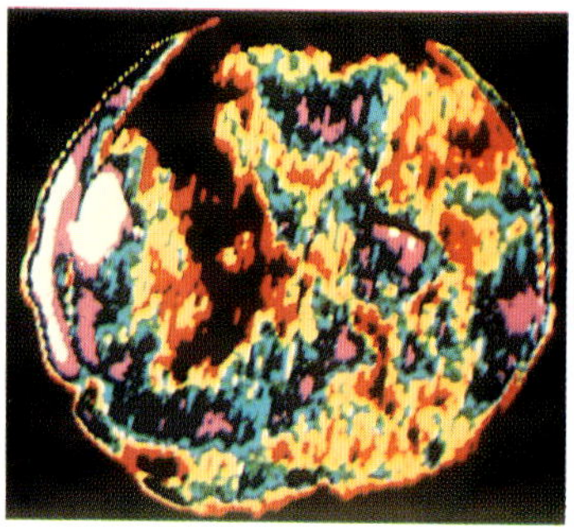

ULTRAVIOLET SUN
Today it is not only the visible light given out by the Sun that can be recorded. Astronomers have special equipment that can take photographs at other wavelengths, such as ultraviolet or infrared. These show up details that normal photographs cannot reveal.

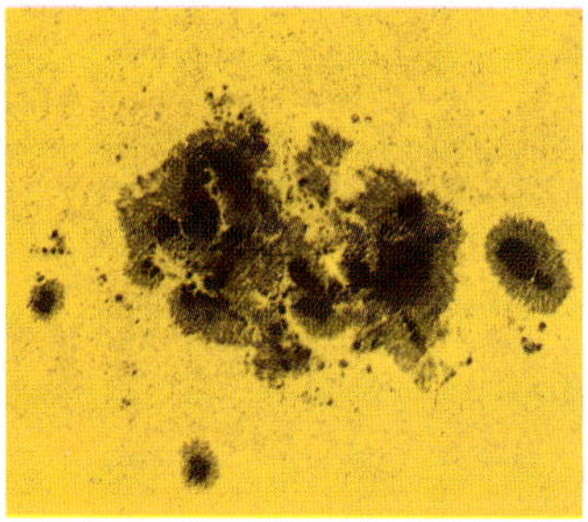

Group of sunspots

SUNSPOTS
On close inspection, the Sun's photosphere is at times riddled with dark patches. These are sunspots – patches of gas that look darker because they are cooler. Sunspots are caused by magnetic fields that slow down the flow of heat from the Sun's centre. They have a dark central region called the umbra, surrounded by a lighter region called a penumbra. They generally occur in pairs or groups.

Sunspots go through a cycle lasting 11 years. At the beginning, the Sun is free of spots. A few then appear high and low on the Sun's surface. These then disappear and new ones form nearer and nearer towards the Equator (middle).

SOLAR TELESCOPE
Astronomers use special instruments based on Earth, and others up in space, to study the Sun. The Sun's light is collected and then an instrument called a spectroscope is used to split it into its spectrum (the different wavelengths of light it emits). Astronomers have gained most of their knowledge about the Sun by studying its spectrum.

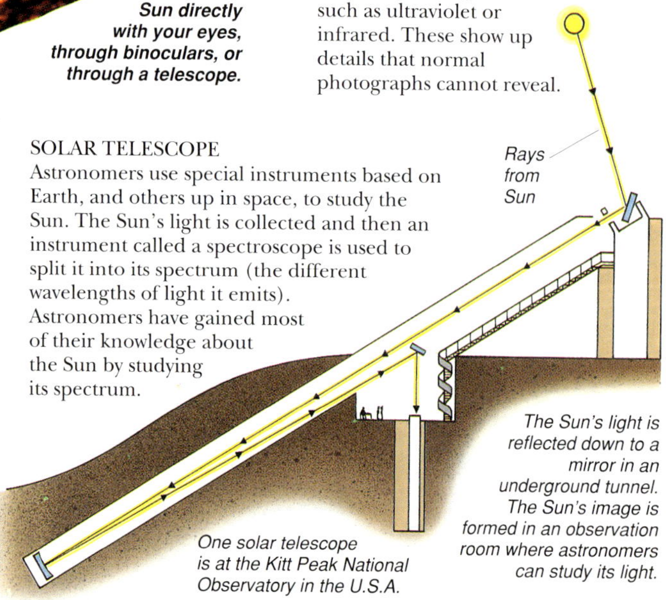

The Sun's light is reflected down to a mirror in an underground tunnel. The Sun's image is formed in an observation room where astronomers can study its light.

One solar telescope is at the Kitt Peak National Observatory in the U.S.A.

ARTHUR EDDINGTON

The English astronomer Sir Arthur Eddington (1882-1944) was the first to work out what the inside of a star was like. He discovered that the luminosity of a star (amount of light it gives out) depends on how massive it is. In 1919, he was the first person to find proof of Einstein's theory of relativity; during a total solar eclipse, he recorded the displacement (bending) of light from a distant star.

LIFE OF THE SUN

In star terms, our Sun is middle-aged and will die one day. But don't worry; it has another 5,000 million years of shining to do until it uses up its hydrogen fuel. It will then start using its helium; as it does so, it will turn into a red giant star, shining 1,000 times brighter than now, and it will be around 100 times larger in size. Next, it will shrink to become a white dwarf star, the size of the Earth. Thousands of millions of years later, it will cool down and end its life as a cold dark body called a black dwarf.

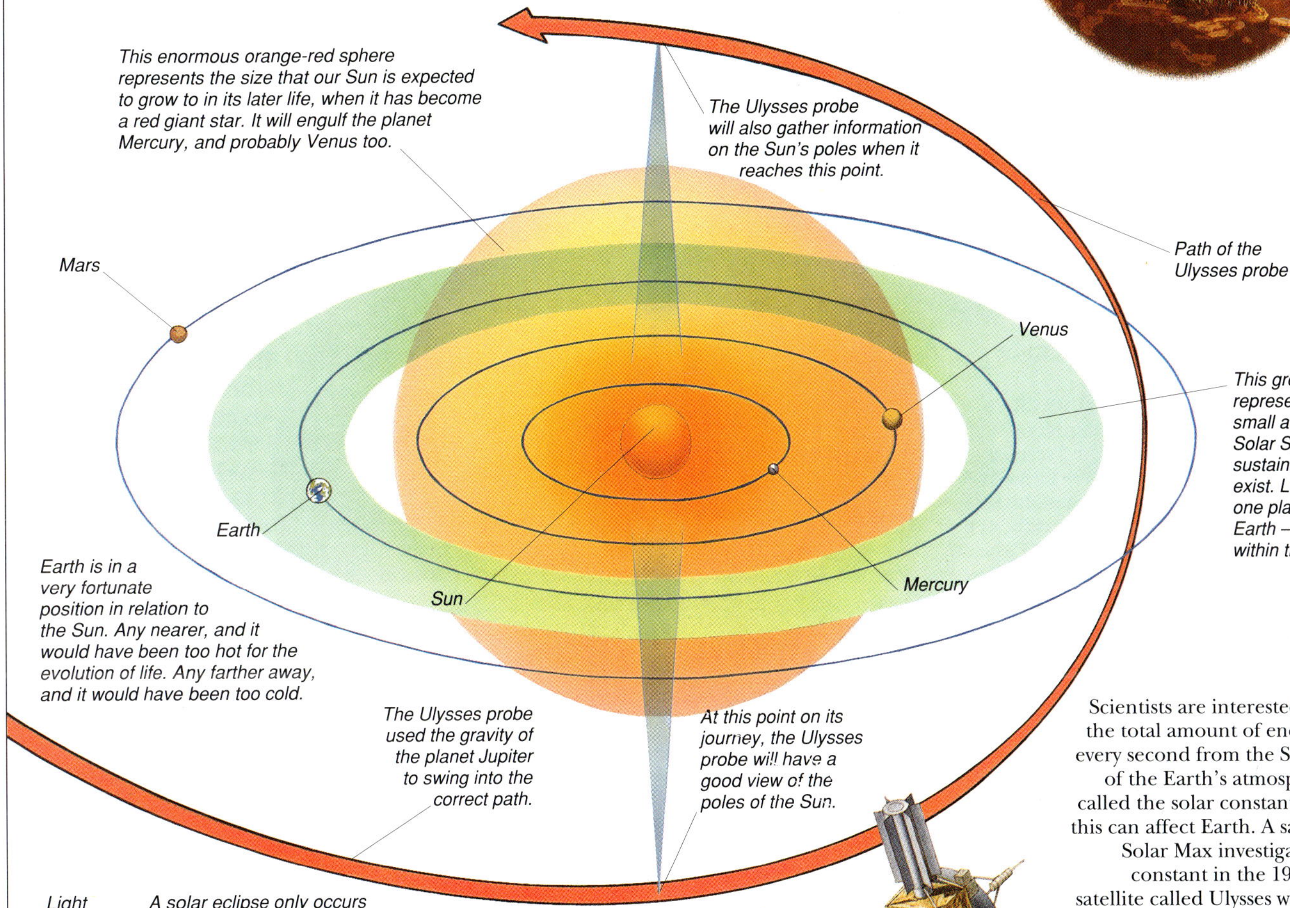

ULYSSES

Scientists are interested in knowing the total amount of energy received every second from the Sun at the top of the Earth's atmosphere. This is called the solar constant. Changes in this can affect Earth. A satellite called Solar Max investigated the solar constant in the 1980s. Another satellite called Ulysses will investigate the Sun further in 1994-5.

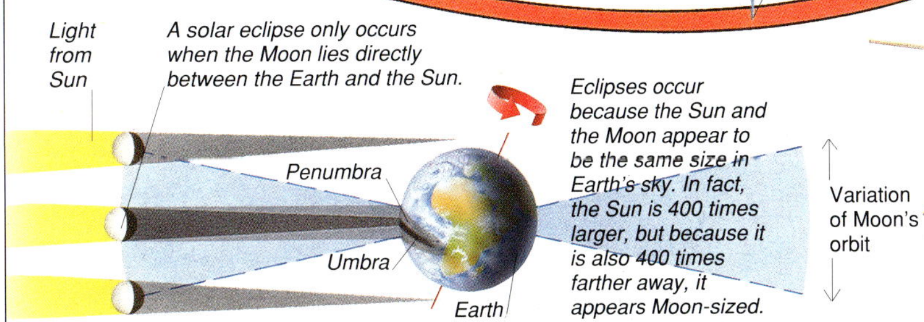

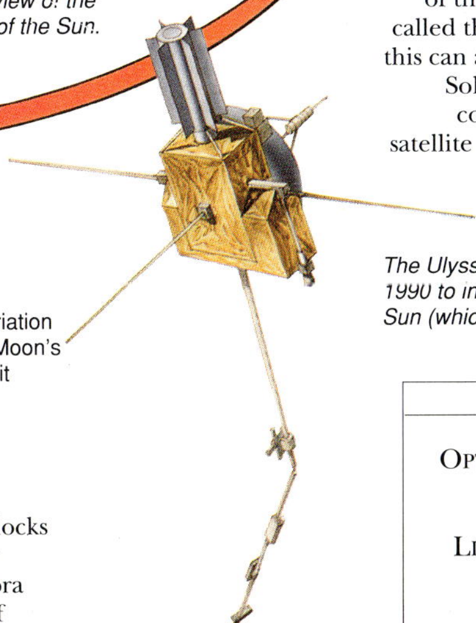

The Ulysses probe was launched in 1990 to investigate the poles of the Sun (which are invisible from Earth).

SOLAR ECLIPSE

Occasionally, the Earth, Moon, and Sun happen to line up so that the Moon blocks the Sun's light from Earth. This is called a solar eclipse.The Moon's shadow or umbra only covers a small area of Earth's surface. Anyone standing in this umbra sees the Sun totally eclipsed by the Moon. Surrounding the umbra is an area of partial shadow called the penumbra. From this area, the Sun is partially eclipsed.

Find out more

OPTICAL INSTRUMENTS P.198
SHADOWS P.201
STARS P.278
LIFE CYCLE OF STARS P.280
SOLAR SYSTEM P.283
FACT FINDER P.418

URANUS

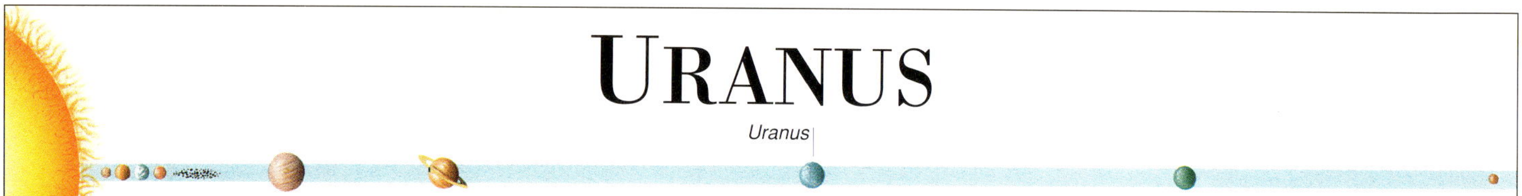

ASTRONOMERS WERE DUMBSTRUCK by the discovery of Uranus in 1781. Until then, it was thought that the Solar System consisted of the planets as far out as Saturn but no more. Its discovery doubled the size of the Solar System at a stroke – Uranus is twice as far from the Sun as Saturn. At such a distance, little was learnt about Uranus until a space probe called Voyager 2 flew by in 1986. It found a cold gas giant with a system of 15 moons and at least 11 thin, black rings surrounding it.

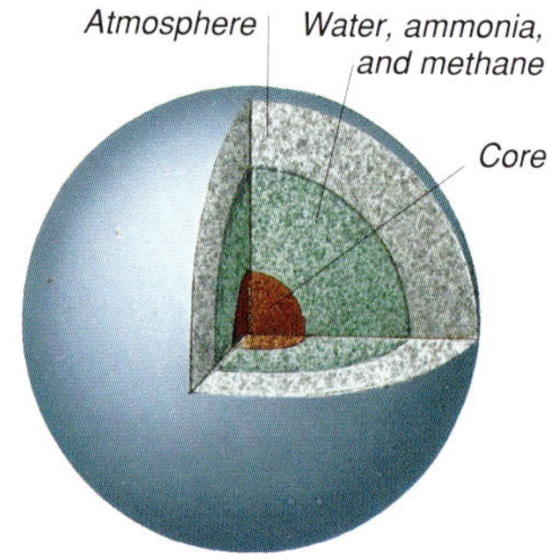

URANUS STRUCTURE
The rocky core of Uranus makes up about one-quarter of the planet's mass. Above this is a layer of water, ammonia, and methane, in ice and liquid form. The outer layer is made up of hydrogen and helium gases.

BLUE PLANET

Even through Earth's best telescopes, Uranus appears as a fuzzy bluish ball of gas; methane in its atmosphere reflects blue and green sunlight. Through the cameras on Voyager 2, Uranus still appears as a featureless globe. But computer processing has revealed occasional white clouds of methane ice crystals, carried around the planet by winds.

URANUS MOONS
Five of Uranus' fifteen moons were discovered from Earth. The ten smaller ones were revealed by Voyager 2's cameras in 1986. The farthest moon is called Oberon – it circles at 582,600 km (361,795 miles) out from Uranus.

Uranus' moons and rings circle around the middle of the globe.

URANUS LANDSCAPE
It doesn't get any warmer than -209°C (-344°F) on Uranus. The planet receives about 370 times less sunlight than Earth, although its atmosphere carries what heat there is around the planet. If you found yourself on Uranus, as well as being very cold, you would sink into the choking atmosphere of hydrogen, helium, and methane.

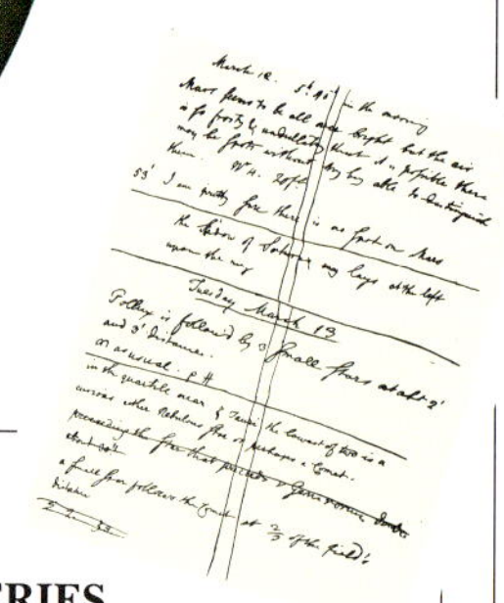

Page from Herschel's diary

DISCOVERIES

1781 Uranus discovered
German astronomer William Herschel was not looking for a planet; but during routine observations on 13 March he found Uranus. This led astronomers to believe other planets may lay beyond undetected.

1846 Neptune discovered
Neptune's position had been calculated and a search was carried out. Johann Galle from Germany located it on 23 September 1846.

1930 Pluto discovered
The American Clyde Tombaugh found Pluto when he was comparing photographic plates in January 1930.

TITANIA
The moons of Uranus are dark bodies of rock and ice. Titania is the largest. Craters and valleys cover its surface.

One of Uranus' moons, Miranda, is a hotch-potch of deep craters, high cliffs, and smooth planes. Most are ancient structures, but surprisingly some have been formed more recently.

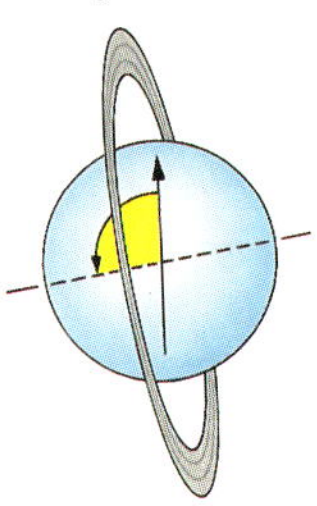

SIDEWAYS PLANET
Uranus appears to lie on its side. It is thought that the planet was tipped up when the last few huge chunks came together to form it.

Find out more

SOLAR SYSTEM P.283
SATURN P.291
NEPTUNE AND PLUTO P.293
SPACE PROBES P.301
FACT FINDER P.418

Neptune and Pluto

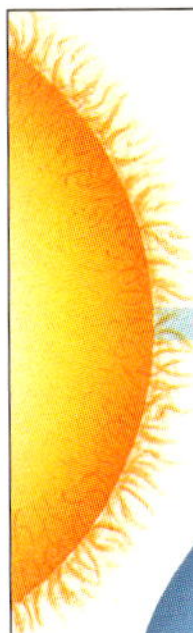

The two most distant planets are worlds of contrast. Neptune is the most distant gas giant. Pluto is a frozen world, the smallest of all the planets. Their existence was not known until fairly recently. Both were predicted and then discovered within the last 150 years. The two planets are so distant that very powerful telescopes are needed to see them. Details of Neptune were revealed when Voyager 2 flew by in 1989. Its images showed that Neptune had a thin, dim ring system. Pluto remains the only planet that has never been investigated by spacecraft.

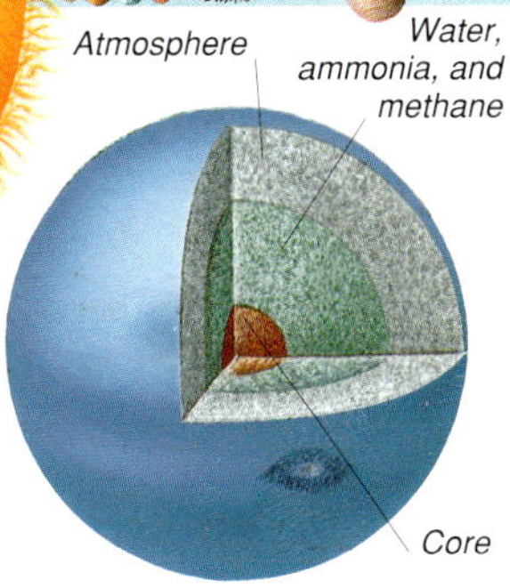

NEPTUNE STRUCTURE
Neptune has a small rocky core, surrounded by an ocean of water, ammonia, and methane. Its atmosphere is made of hydrogen, helium, and methane. The methane gives Neptune its intense blue colour.

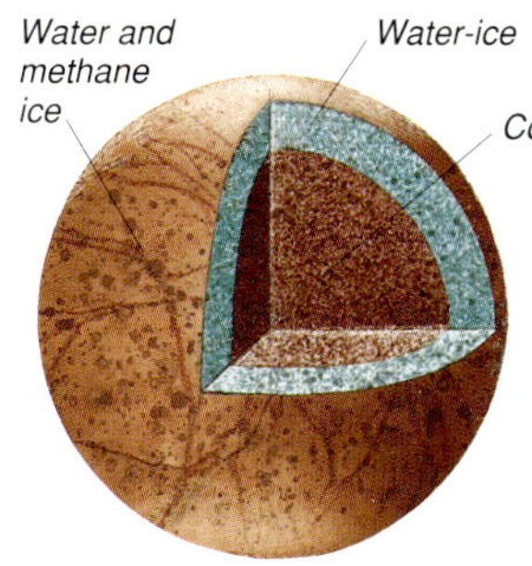

PLUTO STRUCTURE
The make-up of Pluto is very different from that of the other outer planets. Its density suggests that it has a rocky core. Its methane frost surface probably covers a water-ice layer below.

PLUTO
The unexplored planet Pluto is the smallest in the Solar System. It has one moon called Charon, which is fairly close to Pluto, and is about half its size. This makes it difficult to separate the two bodies when viewed from Earth.

Neptune

Voyager images of Neptune show a blue planet, flecked with white clouds of methane ice crystals. A point known as the Great Dark Spot in the Southern Hemisphere is in fact a huge storm which rotates around the planet.

PLUTO LANDSCAPE
If you were unlucky enough to land on Pluto, you would find a frozen, lonely, and very dark world. Because Pluto is nearly forty times farther from the Sun than the Earth, the Sun would probably just look like a very bright star.

NEPTUNE LANDSCAPE
Being on Neptune would be a very windy experience. The Voyager spacecraft has recorded winds of up to an incredible 2160 km/h (1340 mph).

Nereid, a moon of Neptune

Two of Neptune's moons, Triton and Nereid, were discovered from Earth. Six more were discovered by Voyager 2.

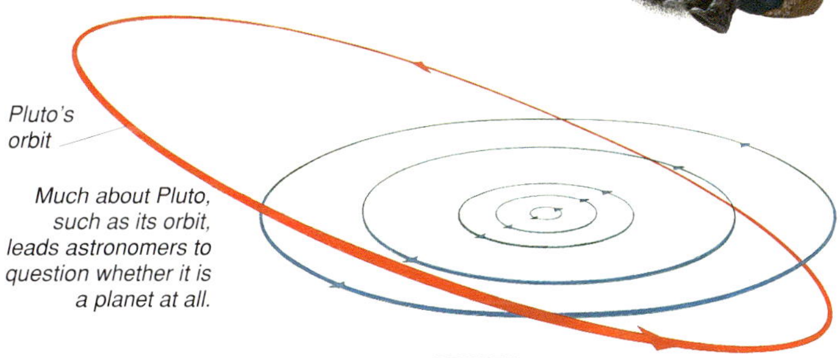

Much about Pluto, such as its orbit, leads astronomers to question whether it is a planet at all.

ORBITS
Pluto moves in strange ways. Its orbit is tilted further and is more elongated than that of any other planet. In fact, for part of its orbit, Pluto moves closer to the Sun than Neptune, so that for a time, Neptune is the most distant planet in the Solar System.

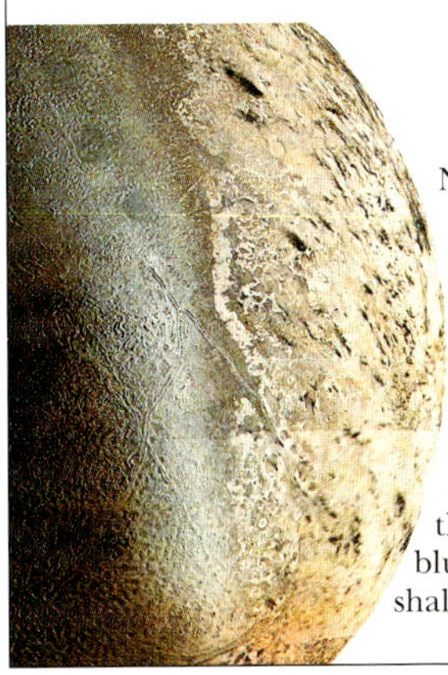

NEPTUNE MOONS
One of Neptune's eight moons, Triton, has two very different hemispheres. The south pole has active volcanoes and a pink cap of nitrogen and methane ice, while the north pole is bluish with many shallow valleys.

TENTH PLANET

Some astronomers believe that there could be another planet in the Solar System. This planet is usually referred to as Planet X. They believe this because the gravity of Pluto alone does not explain the orbits of Uranus and Neptune. A body with a much greater mass is needed to pull them around the paths they follow.

Scientists have worked out the mass they believe the Solar System contains. It is greater than the mass accounted for so far.

Find out more

Solar system p.283
Uranus p.292
Space probes p.301
Fact finder p.418

STUDY OF ASTRONOMY

Mayan observatory in Mexico dating from 1st century

ASTRONOMY IS THE oldest science. For thousands of years, people have sought to understand space and Earth's position in it. As long ago as 4000 B.C., the Egyptians developed a calendar, based on the movement of objects in space. Observation of the skies continued, and soon events such as eclipses could be predicted. Since the 17th century, the pace of discovery and understanding has quickened. We have learnt more about space this century than at any other time. Today, the astronomer is no longer a person working in many fields of science, but is a specialist who concentrates on one specific aspect of astronomical research.

ANCIENT ASTRONOMY

Ancient civilizations around the world relied on the movements of the bodies in space. The positions of the Sun and Moon were used to measure time – in days, months, seasons, and years. The Sun, Moon, and stars were also used to navigate on land and sea. As the bodies were not fully understood, some astronomical happenings were believed to be ill omens.

Tycho Brahe's observatory

USING TECHNOLOGY

Early astronomers had to work with their eyes alone. In the 16th century, Tycho Brahe made the most accurate measurements of the stars possible with the naked eye from his observatory. The telescope was first used in the 17th century, and over the years, it has remained the astronomer's fundamental tool. Today, powerful telescopes, satellites, and space probes are all used to collect information from space. Scientists then use sophisticated equipment to study the data.

CHANGE OF DIRECTION

During the 19th century, the focus of astronomy changed. Rather than cataloguing and trying to understand the movement of stars, astronomers thought about what stars actually were (the study of astrophysics). In the 1860s, a British astronomer, William Huggins, analysed the light from stars (their spectra). Others took up this work, and soon the stars were able to be classified by their spectra.

Astronomers use computers to analyse images, to calculate orbits, and to control instruments such as telescopes, satellites, and space probes.

JOHANNES KEPLER

Danish astronomer Tycho Brahe (1546-1601) spent years cataloguing the stars and planets with great accuracy. His assistant Johannes Kepler (1571-1630) put his observations to good use. He developed three important laws of astronomy. His first law describes the shapes of planetary orbits. His second law describes the speed at which the planets travel along their orbits. His third law relates the different planetary orbits to one another.

PRESENT-DAY ASTRONOMY

As astronomers answer questions that puzzle them, new problems take their place. For example, it is now accepted that the Universe started with the Big Bang. But how did the material from the Big Bang come together to form galaxies? Today's scientists can work faster on such problems with the help of computers. These can solve mathematical problems in hours rather than the weeks it would have taken a hundred years ago. Computers also enable astronomers around the world to link up so they can work together on our understanding of the Universe.

Find out more

STARS P.278
CONSTELLATIONS P.282
SOLAR SYSTEM P.283
SUN P.284
TELESCOPES ON EARTH P.297
TELESCOPES IN SPACE P.298
SPACE PROBES P.301

TELESCOPES ON EARTH

BEFORE THE TELESCOPE was invented, the only way people could observe the Universe was to look at it with just their eyes. From 1609, when Galileo first used the telescope to look into the sky, astronomers have been able to peer farther and farther into space. They can see surface details on planets and can look at stars which were once invisible to them. The first telescopes used lenses to gather the light from stars. These are called refracting telescopes. Telescopes that use mirrors rather than lenses are called reflecting telescopes. Today's telescopes have attachments that can take measurements and analyse starlight. The telescope is an astronomer's best friend.

Comet Halley, 1910

TELESCOPE IMAGES

Images from space (comets, for example) have been recorded photographically from the earliest days of photography. Today, astronomers take photographs through telescopes. The image is recorded on an electronic chip or photographic plate. Computers may be used to bring out detail in the image.

The Cerro Tololo Inter-American observatory is situated in the Andes mountain range.

Telescopes are so large and expensive that several countries join together to build and use one.

OBSERVATORIES

Telescopes need homes. Usually they are kept in observatories, special buildings that are always built high on mountain tops. This is so the telescope can obtain the very best view of space – away from city lights, and high enough so that Earth's atmosphere doesn't get in the way too much.

Radio image of the Crab Nebula, taken by the VLA telescope

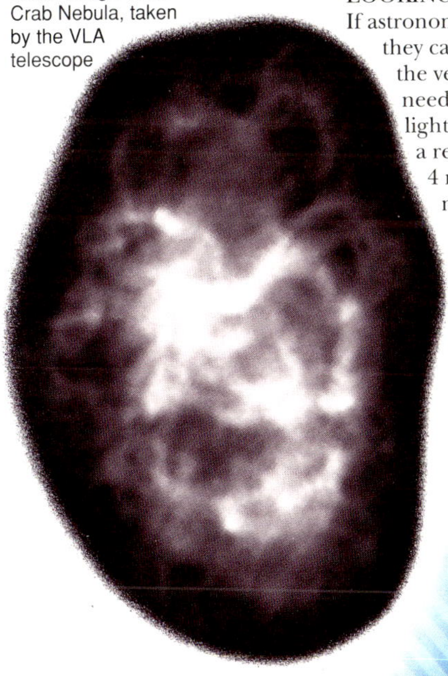

LOOKING BACK IN TIME

If astronomers observe more and more distant bodies, they can look further and further back in time towards the very beginning of the Universe. To do this, they need telescopes with very large mirrors to gather the light. The Cerro Tololo observatory in Chile houses a reflecting telescope with a huge mirror that is 4 m (13 ft) across. As it is very difficult to build a mirror bigger than this (because the glass breaks), multi-mirror telescopes have been developed. These use lots of small mirrors that are put together and have the same light-gathering power as one huge mirror.

Dawn over the enormous reflecting dish of the Arecibo radio telescope

TELESCOPES WORKING TOGETHER

Lots of small radio telescopes can be used to work like one enormous one. A computer combines the information received by each dish. This technique is called interferometry and it was first used in the 1960s. The biggest radio telescope of this type uses dishes positioned on different continents!

RADIO TELESCOPES

To collect radio waves from space, an astronomer uses a radio telescope. These work like optical telescopes (that collect light) – a dish faces the sky to collect and focus the waves. However, as radio waves have a larger wavelength than that of light waves, a radio telescope has to be much bigger than an optical one to collect the same amount of information. The largest single dish telescope in the world is at Arecibo, Puerto Rico. Its 305 m- (1,000 ft-) dish is built into a natural hollow in the jungle. As the Earth moves, the dish points to a different part of the sky.

RADIO IMAGE

Radio waves from space (sometimes called radio noise) were first detected in 1931. However, it wasn't until the end of the next decade that radio telescopes were built and used. The radio waves are changed into electrical signals that can be used to make radio images or pictures.

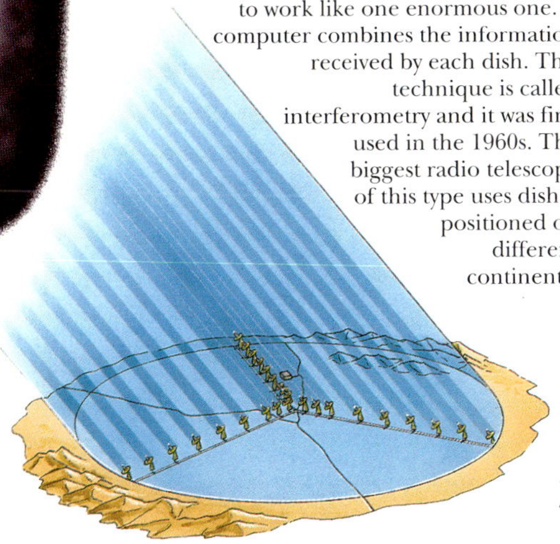

In New Mexico, the Very Large Array (VLA) radio telescope uses 27 dishes, each 25 m (82 ft) across.

Find out more

REFLECTION P.194
LENSES P.197
OPTICAL INSTRUMENTS P.198
TELESCOPES IN SPACE P.298

TELESCOPES IN SPACE

JUST AS SUNGLASSES protect our eyes, Earth's atmosphere prevents a lot of radiation from reaching Earth. It lets light through, but even this is affected – images are blurred and stars twinkle, when in reality they shine steadily. For this reason, from the middle of the 20th century, astronomers have been sending telescopes into space to get a better look at our surroundings. These telescopes can see views of the Universe that are invisible from Earth. They work day and night, recording data, and transmitting it to Earth to be analysed. Telescopes enable us to look into space with X-ray, ultraviolet, and infrared eyes.

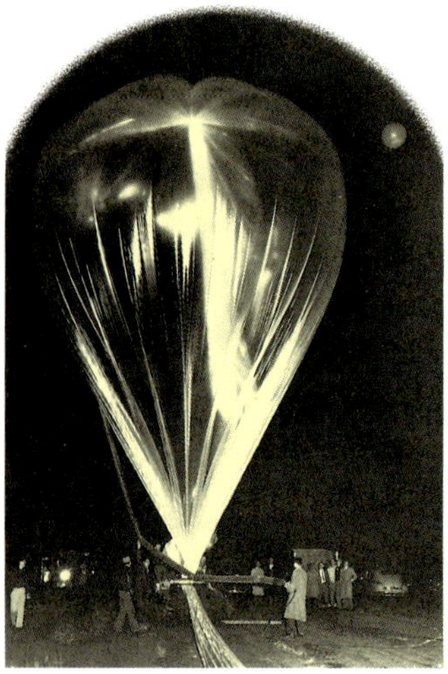

EARLY ATTEMPTS
During the 1930s and 1940s, balloons were one of the few ways to carry scientific instruments into space. Rockets were another option. Once high enough, they would have a few minutes in which to record a view, such as the Sun in X-rays, before plunging back down to Earth.

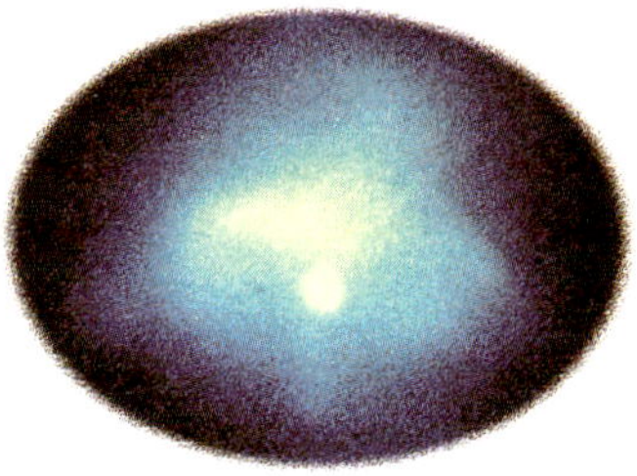

An X-ray image of the Crab Nebula

X-RAY PICTURES
From 1948, when the first X-rays from space were detected, astronomers have been looking at the X-ray universe. X-rays can reveal "hot spots" or areas of energetic activity in space. They can also help us to see otherwise dim objects such as pulsars.

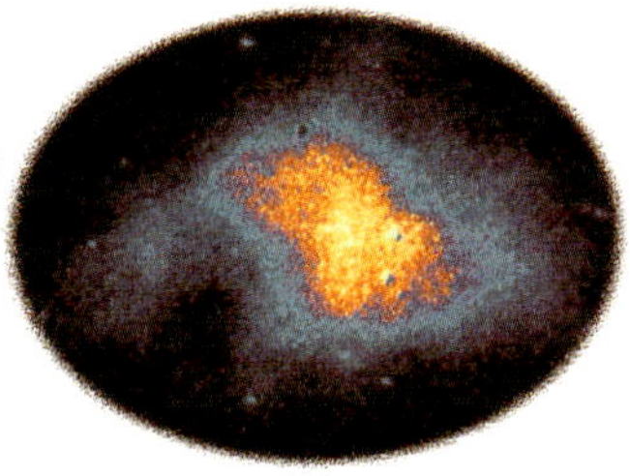

UV image of the Crab Nebula

ULTRAVIOLET PICTURES
Most ultraviolet (UV) light is absorbed by Earth's atmosphere (although some gets through to give us a suntan). Satellites for collecting UV waves were first launched in the 1960s. The International Ultraviolet Explorer (IUE) satellite has been used since its launch in 1978.

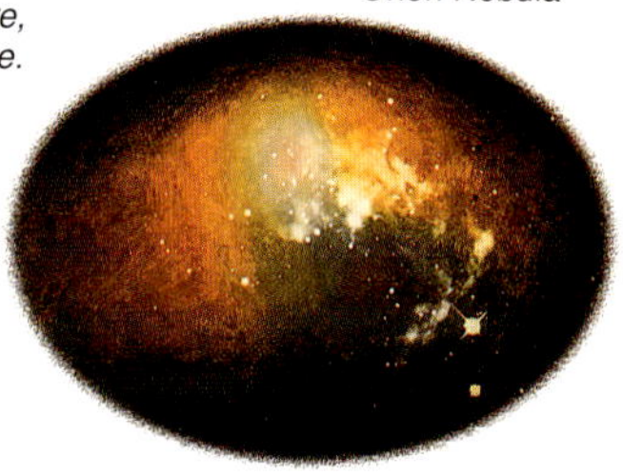

IR image of the Orion Nebula

INFRARED PICTURES
Although some infrared (IR) rays reach Earth from space, they get mixed up with the infrared rays that Earth itself produces. Therefore, astronomers like to have infrared telescopes out in space. These can detect heat sources that light-detecting telescopes would not show up.

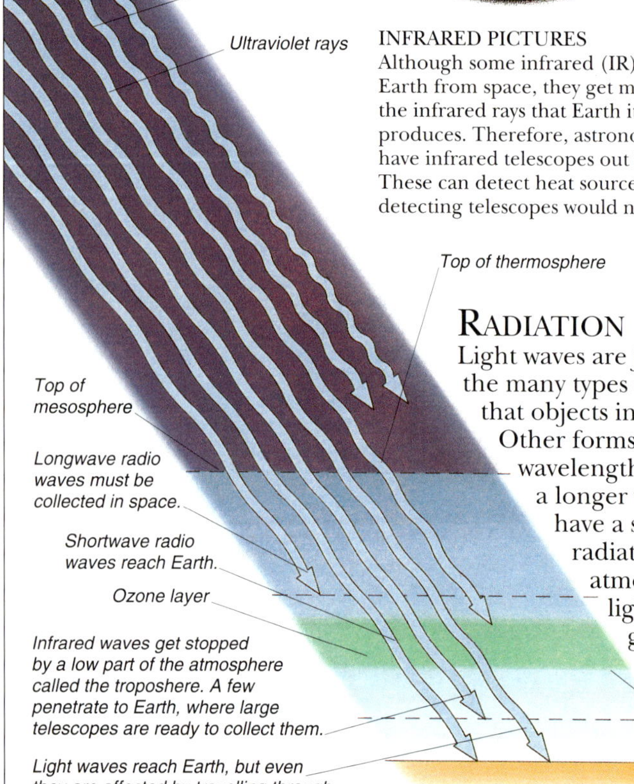

RADIATION

Light waves are just one of the many types of radiation that objects in space give out. Other forms have different wavelengths. Radio waves, for example, have a longer wavelength than light waves; X-rays have a shorter wavelength. Not all this radiation gets through Earth's atmosphere to reach the surface – most light does, some infrared does, but no gamma rays are able to get through. If astronomers want to collect such radiation, they must send their instruments into space.

HUBBLE TELESCOPE
The Hubble Space Telescope was launched in April 1990. It orbits Earth 500 km (310 miles) up in the sky. From its position, the Hubble collects images from millions of years ago, giving astronomers a chance to see the young Universe forming after the Big Bang. The telescope is maintained in space by astronauts from the space shuttle.

Find out more

ELECTROMAGNETIC SPECTRUM p.192
OPTICAL INSTRUMENTS p.198
ATMOSPHERE p.248
TELESCOPES ON EARTH p.297
ROCKETS p.299
SATELLITES p.300

Rockets

ANYTHING THAT WANTS TO GET AWAY from Earth must travel in a rocket. Rockets are used to propel satellites and astronauts into space. Without them, we would know little about Earth's surroundings, and we would not have all the benefits that satellites give our lives. Rockets burn fuel to make a thrust that pushes them upwards. In fact, most of a rocket is made up of fuel – its cargo or "payload" takes up a fairly small amount of room in comparison. In 1903, a Russian schoolmaster, Konstantin Tsiolkovskii, put forward the first scientific ideas on rocket propulsion. However, it wasn't until 1926, when an American engineer, Robert Goddard, launched the first liquid fuel rocket, that space travel was really born.

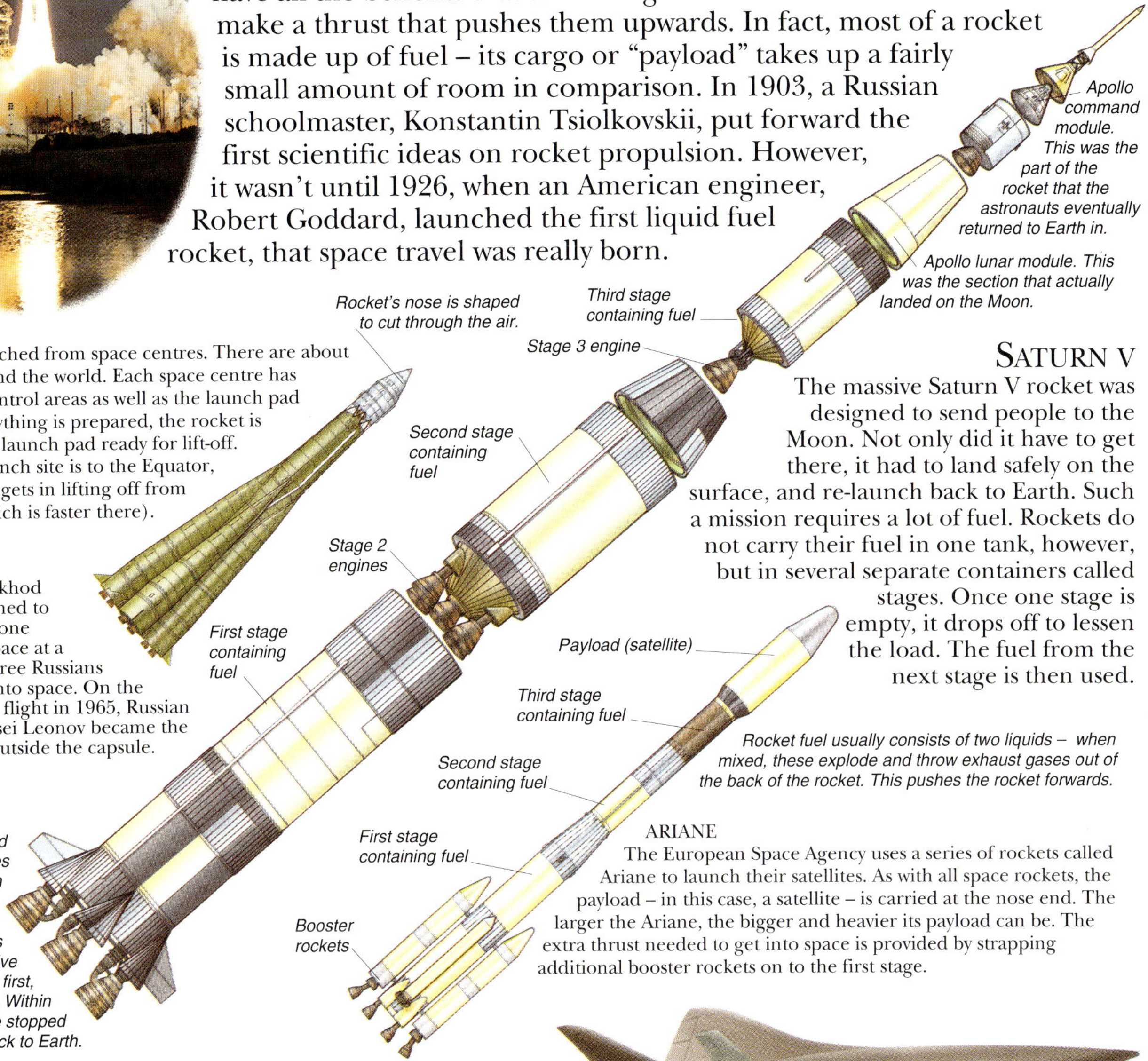

LAUNCH SITE
Rockets are launched from space centres. There are about 15 of these around the world. Each space centre has technical and control areas as well as the launch pad itself. Once everything is prepared, the rocket is mounted on the launch pad ready for lift-off. The nearer a launch site is to the Equator, the more help it gets in lifting off from Earth's spin (which is faster there).

VOSKHOD
The Russian Voskhod rocket was designed to send more than one astronaut into space at a time. In 1964, three Russians were launched into space. On the second Voskhod flight in 1965, Russian cosmonaut Aleksei Leonov became the first to venture outside the capsule.

Saturn V

The massive Saturn V rocket was designed to send people to the Moon. Not only did it have to get there, it had to land safely on the surface, and re-launch back to Earth. Such a mission requires a lot of fuel. Rockets do not carry their fuel in one tank, however, but in several separate containers called stages. Once one stage is empty, it drops off to lessen the load. The fuel from the next stage is then used.

ARIANE
The European Space Agency uses a series of rockets called Ariane to launch their satellites. As with all space rockets, the payload – in this case, a satellite – is carried at the nose end. The larger the Ariane, the bigger and heavier its payload can be. The extra thrust needed to get into space is provided by strapping additional booster rockets on to the first stage.

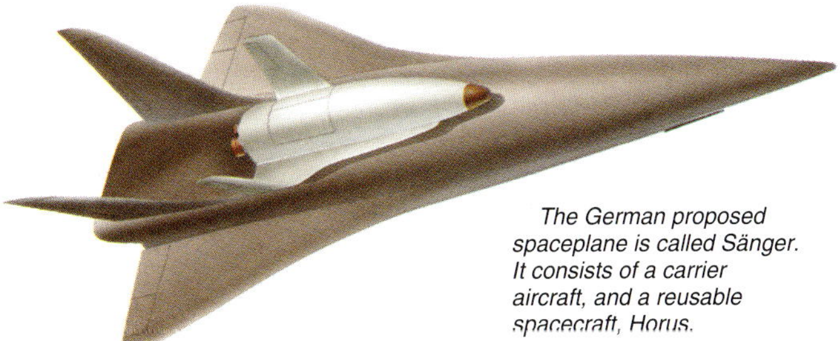

The German proposed spaceplane is called Sänger. It consists of a carrier aircraft, and a reusable spacecraft, Horus.

ESCAPE VELOCITY

If you throw a ball into the air, Earth's gravity will slow it down until it eventually falls back. If you could throw it as fast as 40,000 km/h (24,840 mph), it would be slowed down, but its speed would still be great enough to carry it out of the reach of Earth's gravity, and into space. This speed is called the escape velocity. Rockets must reach this speed if they are to escape from Earth.

The force with which a rocket moves away from Earth must be greater than the force of gravity pulling it towards Earth.

SPACEPLANE
The problem with multi-stage rockets is that they can only be used once. When the stages fall back to Earth, they burn up in the atmosphere and are destroyed. This is why scientists in several countries are trying to develop a reusable "spaceplane" that takes off horizontally. While in Earth's atmosphere, it would take in air to burn fuel (like a normal aeroplane). When in space, where there is no air, it would burn liquid hydrogen and oxygen (like a rocket).

Find out more

GRAVITY P.122
MOON P.288
TELESCOPES IN SPACE P.298
SATELLITES P.300
SPACE PROBES P.301
HUMANS IN SPACE P.302

SATELLITES

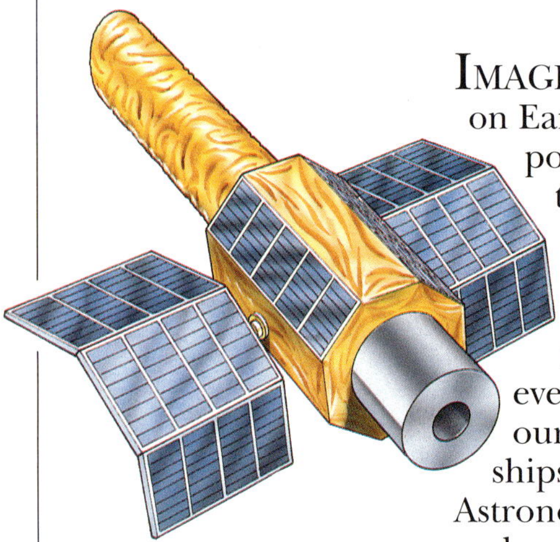

IMAGINE SOMETHING LOOKING DOWN on Earth that could tell us about the weather or point out areas such as mineral deposits. Such things exist. They are called satellites. There are many different types of satellite that are orbiting around the Earth, all performing different tasks. Some provide us with instant phone calls, others allow us to watch events happening around the world "live" on our television sets. Navigation satellites help ships or aeroplanes pinpoint their positions. Astronomers use satellites to look away from Earth and out into the Universe. The space around Earth is getting fuller as more and more satellites orbit and travel with Earth on its journey through space.

REPAIRING SATELLITES
What happens when something goes wrong with a satellite in orbit? It can be mended in space by astronauts. If the fault is a major one, the satellite is brought back to Earth for repair and re-launch. In November 1984, the crew of the space shuttle *Discovery* recovered a telecommunications satellite and returned it to Earth.

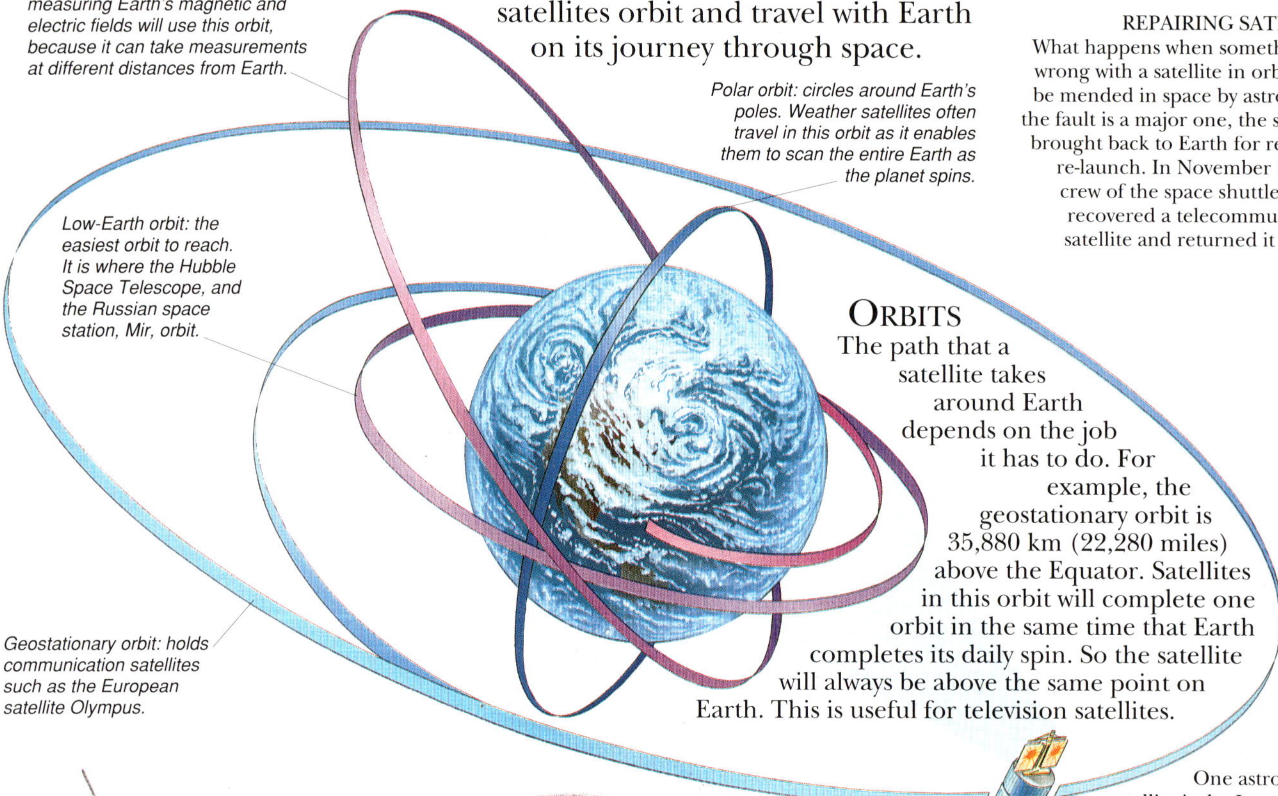

ORBITS

The path that a satellite takes around Earth depends on the job it has to do. For example, the geostationary orbit is 35,880 km (22,280 miles) above the Equator. Satellites in this orbit will complete one orbit in the same time that Earth completes its daily spin. So the satellite will always be above the same point on Earth. This is useful for television satellites.

IUE
One astronomical satellite is the International Ultraviolet Explorer (IUE). This monitors ultraviolet radiation coming from space. It was launched in 1978 and expected to last three years, but it is still going strong. The satellite takes only eight minutes to transmit a picture to either of the ground stations that monitor it: one in America, and one in Spain.

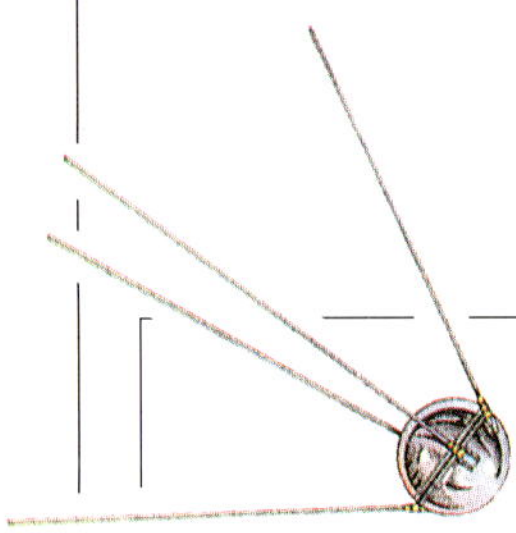

Sputnik 1 was an aluminium sphere measuring only 58 cm (23 in) across.

SPUTNIK

Russia put the first ever artificial satellite into orbit in October 1957. During its short time in space, it investigated Earth's atmosphere. Just a month later, Sputnik 2 was launched. On board was the first living thing in space – a dog called Laika.

SATELLITE DISH
Once an astronomical satellite is in orbit, it can start its work. Ground stations track the satellite. They monitor its condition and redirect it if necessary. They also receive and process the data from the satellite ready to pass on to scientists. Signals from the satellite are collected by dishes on the ground. These are similar to satellite television dishes but are much larger.

Find out more

TELECOMMUNICATIONS P.162
REFLECTION P.194
WEATHER WATCHING P.272
TELESCOPES IN SPACE P.298
ROCKETS P.299
SPACE PROBES P.301

SPACE PROBES

MOVING THROUGH SPACE like roving reporters, space probes are unstaffed spacecraft that are sent to investigate and report back on our Solar System. They have made many discoveries that would be impossible from Earth. Space probes are highly sophisticated robots. Once launched, they follow a pre-arranged route to a target, such as a planet. As they fly near or orbit around the planet, instruments on board set to work. Results are sent back to Earth by radio. Some of this data is made into pictures to give close-up views of distant worlds. The Sun, comets, asteroids, and all the planets except for Pluto have been visited by different probes.

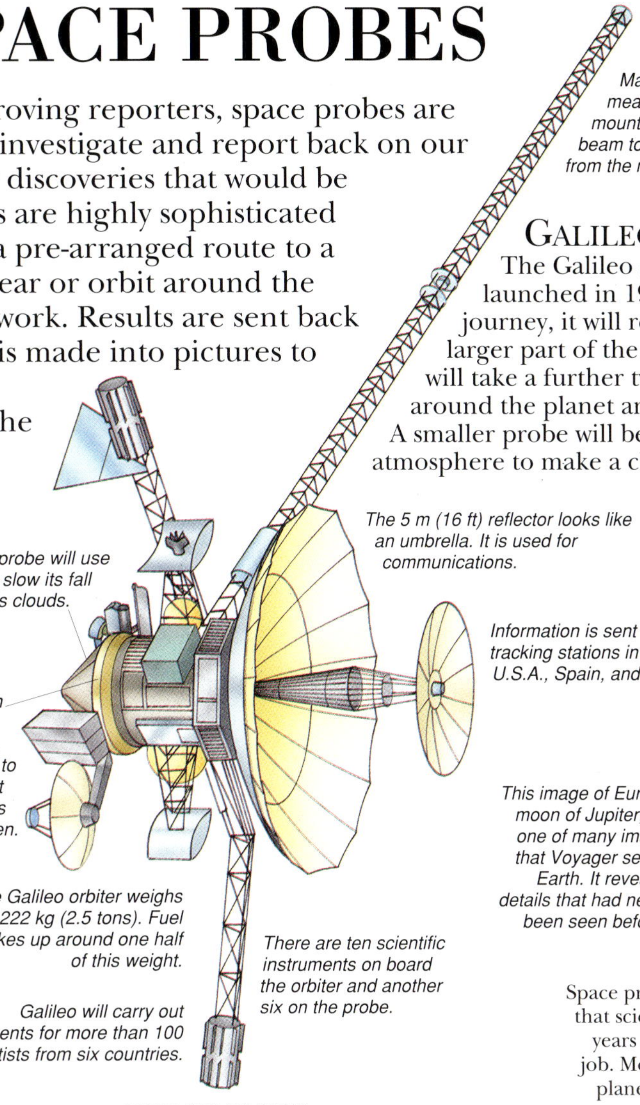

GALILEO PROBE

The Galileo space probe was launched in 1989. After a six-year journey, it will reach Jupiter. The larger part of the craft – the orbiter – will take a further two years to tour around the planet and its major moons. A smaller probe will be sent into Jupiter's atmosphere to make a close examination.

PROBE VISITS

1959 First successful probe, Luna 2, reaches the Moon.

1962 First successful planetary probe, Mariner 2, flies by Venus.

1969 Apollo 11 is first probe to bring back samples from the Moon to Earth.

1973 Launch of Mariner 10; first probe to visit two planets, Venus and Mercury.

1976 Viking 1 and Viking 2 probes land on Mars.

1977 Voyager 1 and Voyager 2 sent to Jupiter, Saturn, Uranus, and Neptune.

1985 Five probes sent to investigate Comet Halley.

1990 Launch of Ulysses probe to fly over the poles of the Sun.

This image of Europa, a moon of Jupiter, was one of many images that Voyager sent to Earth. It revealed details that had never been seen before.

IMAGES

Space probes provide so much data that scientists have to analyse it for years after a craft has finished its job. Moons of all four of the giant planets have been discovered by space probes. Scientists are sure that more smaller moons are still waiting to be found.

VOYAGER PROBES

The twin Voyager space probes, Voyager 1 and Voyager 2, were launched in 1977. Their task was to find out more about the four gas giants. They both flew by Jupiter and Saturn. Then Voyager 2 alone travelled on to Uranus and Neptune. Each spacecraft had 11 instruments on board, including two television cameras.

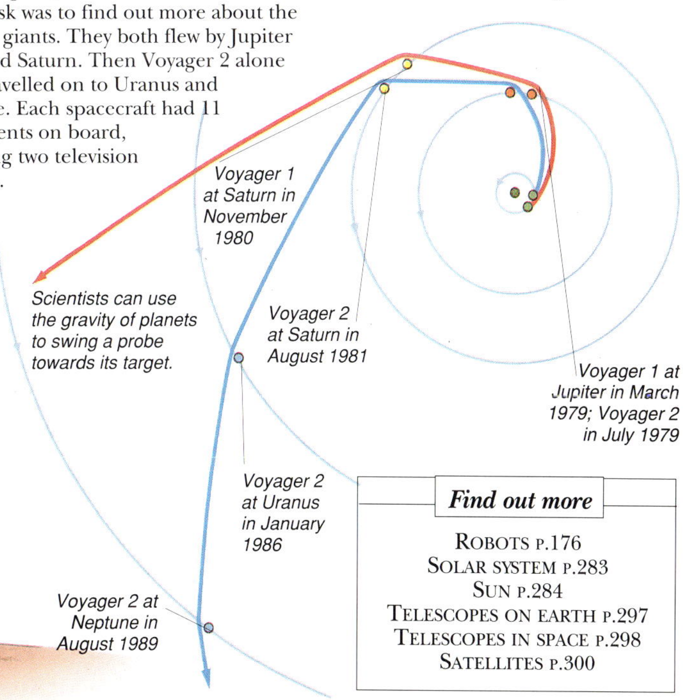

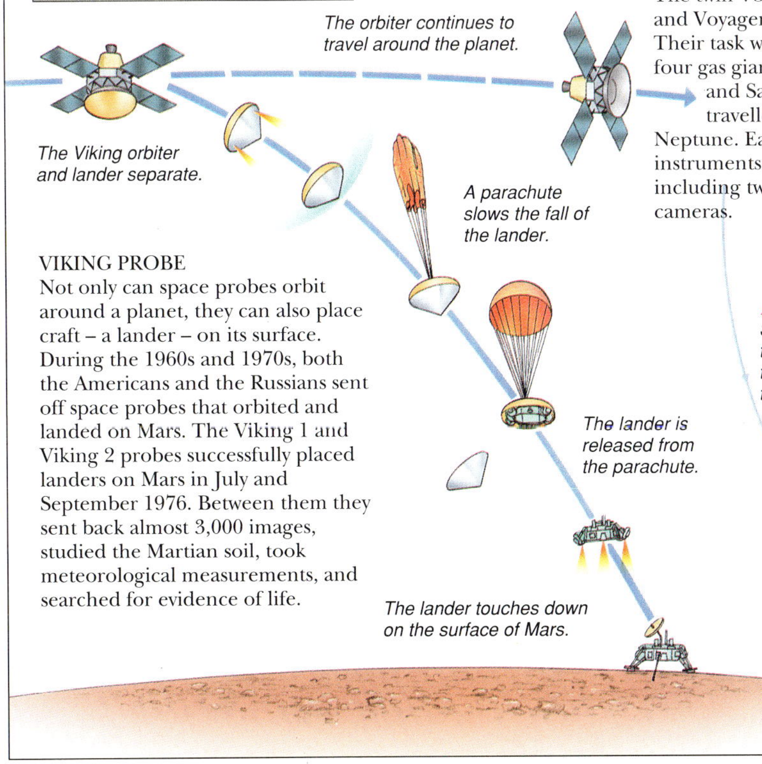

VIKING PROBE

Not only can space probes orbit around a planet, they can also place craft – a lander – on its surface. During the 1960s and 1970s, both the Americans and the Russians sent off space probes that orbited and landed on Mars. The Viking 1 and Viking 2 probes successfully placed landers on Mars in July and September 1976. Between them they sent back almost 3,000 images, studied the Martian soil, took meteorological measurements, and searched for evidence of life.

Find out more

ROBOTS P.176
SOLAR SYSTEM P.283
SUN P.284
TELESCOPES ON EARTH P.297
TELESCOPES IN SPACE P.298
SATELLITES P.300

HUMANS IN SPACE

FOR CENTURIES, humans have dreamed of travelling in space. But the dream only became a reality in 1961 when a Russian astronaut called Yuri Gagarin rocketed into space and orbited around the Earth. Today, many men and women travel into space; most go just for a few days, but others go for months at a time. Even so, space remains a hostile environment for humans. Spacesuits are needed for protection and to provide air to breathe. If humans are to live and work more permanently in space, and to land on Mars in the next century, we must learn all we can about the long-term effects of space travel.

TRAINING FOR SPACE
For journeying into space, astronauts need to be physically and mentally fit. They undergo very long and hard periods of training in conditions that are similar to those in space. For example, astronauts may train in large swimming pools so that they have some idea of what feeling weightless is like. They wear special suits and practise the jobs they will do in space.

WOMEN IN SPACE
The United States and the Soviet Union dominated the first two decades of space exploration. In 1963, the Russian astronaut Valentina Tereshkova became the first woman to travel into space.

SPACE WEAR

The first astronauts had just one spacesuit per journey. But today, astronauts wear different clothes for the different jobs they do. One suit is for travelling to and from space. Then, in orbit, they wear specially designed casual clothes. If they are working outside their spacecraft, they wear a suit called an extravehicular mobility unit (EMU). On top of this is a strap-on motor called a manned manoeuvring unit (MMU) that can fly the astronaut around.

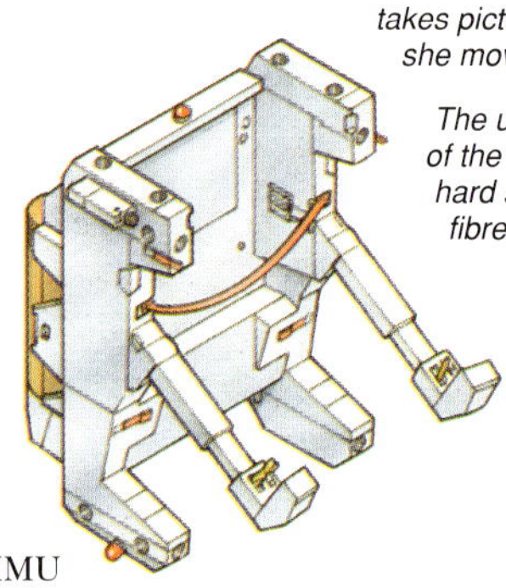

MMU
A manned manoeuvring unit (MMU) is a cross between a backpack and a chair. It runs on nitrogen and can be recharged from the spacecraft. The astronaut controls the MMU from the arm-rests. This unit was first used by the American astronaut Bruce McCandless in February 1984.

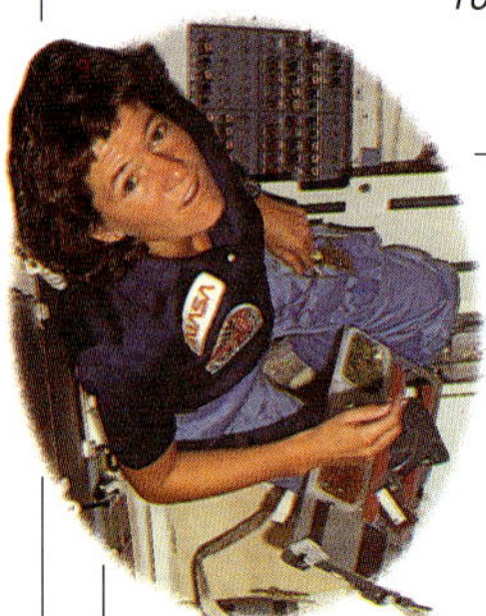

SALLY RIDE
Until 1983, all the American astronauts were male. When the Space Shuttle programme was introduced in the 1970s, both men and women could apply to be astronauts. Then in 1983, Sally Ride (born 1951) became the first American woman in space. Today, there are many other women astronauts.

On 20 July 1969, Neil Armstrong became the first human to step on anything other than the Earth. His colleague Buzz Aldrin joined him 19 minutes later.

MOON MISSIONS
During the late 1950s, there was a race to conquer space by sending up humans: the space age had begun. In 1961, the Americans promised to land a man on the Moon by the end of the decade. They did. In 1969, Neil Armstrong became the first person to walk on the Moon. Between 1969 and 1972, there was a flurry of activity to and from the Moon. Over this time, astronauts spent nearly 80 hours on the Moon's surface.

LIVING IN SPACE

Space travel has changed since Yuri Gagarin's day. In orbit, astronauts move about their craft in casual clothes and eat their favourite meals. When they are not working, they relax with taped music and a good book. They even take it in turns to do "housework". But all of this is done in a state of weightlessness. As bodies are not working against gravity, bones and muscles may weaken (which is why astronauts must exercise every day). So far, the effects of weightlessness on the human body have reversed once the astronaut is back on Earth. But scientists are monitoring the effects as astronauts spend longer and longer in space.

MONITORING ASTRONAUTS

In March 1992, Russian astronaut Sergei Krikalev returned to Earth after spending 313 days in space. On his return, his physical health was closely examined. In space, astronauts can expect their heartbeat to slow and to suffer from space sickness.

Sergei Krikalev

In space, astronauts may feel dizzy and sick as their bodies move around.

Astronauts suck drinks through straws but eat snacks such as chocolate or nuts in the usual way. Meals are oven warmed before being placed in a special tray to stop them floating away as they are eaten.

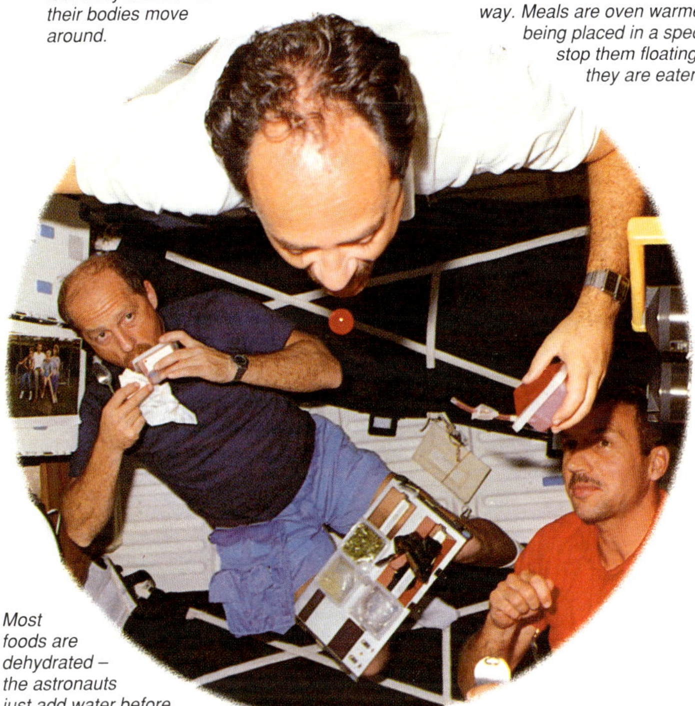

Most foods are dehydrated – the astronauts just add water before eating. Other foods are sealed in tins or pouches just as on Earth. Fresh food may be available for the first part of a trip.

In space, liquids are very difficult to control. This water has formed into a floating ball.

WEIGHTLESSNESS

The gravity of Earth continually pulls on our bodies to give us weight. But if you are in a lift that is speeding downwards, you feel lighter. This effect is exaggerated in a spacecraft; as it is falling in a gravitational field, the astronauts inside it are falling at the same rate and become weightless. Experiments on animals and plants are carried out in space to learn of the effects of weightlessness. Certain experiments, impossible on Earth, can also be performed.

SPACE SHUTTLE

The first astronauts were sent into space in small capsules that sat on top of rockets. They returned by splashing into the sea. These missions were expensive as the rockets could only be used once. Today, American astronauts are transported into space by the Space Shuttle. The main parts – the orbiter spacecraft, and the rocket boosters – are reusable. The orbiter returns to Earth like a plane, and can be used over and over again.

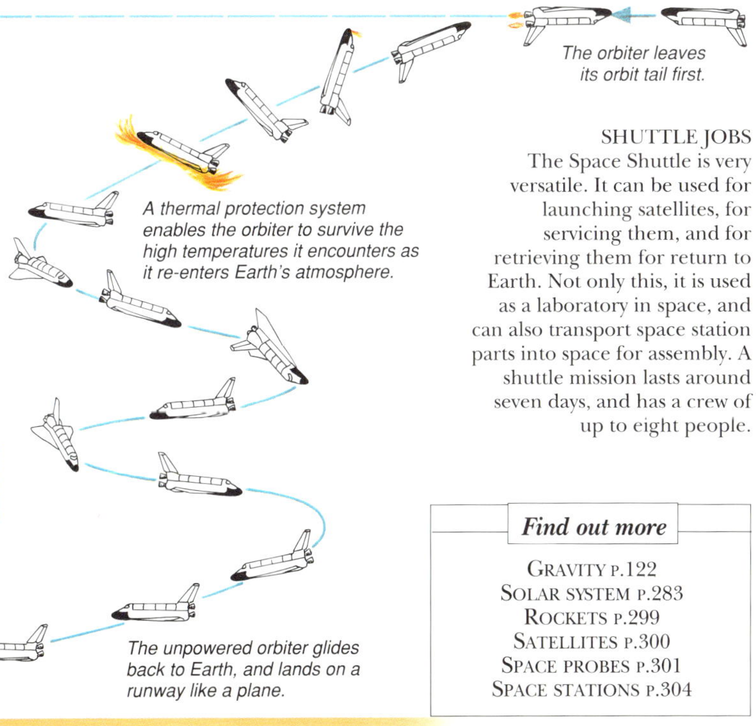

The orbiter leaves its orbit tail first.

A thermal protection system enables the orbiter to survive the high temperatures it encounters as it re-enters Earth's atmosphere.

The unpowered orbiter glides back to Earth, and lands on a runway like a plane.

A braking system brings the orbiter to a halt.

After landing, new fuel tanks are fitted for the next launch.

SHUTTLE JOBS

The Space Shuttle is very versatile. It can be used for launching satellites, for servicing them, and for retrieving them for return to Earth. Not only this, it is used as a laboratory in space, and can also transport space station parts into space for assembly. A shuttle mission lasts around seven days, and has a crew of up to eight people.

Find out more

GRAVITY P.122
SOLAR SYSTEM P.283
ROCKETS P.299
SATELLITES P.300
SPACE PROBES P.301
SPACE STATIONS P.304

SPACE STATIONS

TRIPS INTO SPACE need no longer be short stays. Astronauts can now stay in a space station. This is a large satellite orbiting around Earth with room on board for people to live and work. It can act as both home and office for weeks or months at a time. In the future, it will also be used as a hotel where astronauts can stop off before travelling farther into the Solar System, or before coming back to Earth. Space stations are important because experiments in microgravity (conditions of very low gravity) can be carried out there by a person rather than a machine. The astronauts also perform experiments on themselves to see how humans cope in space.

SKYLAB
For five years in the 1970s, Skylab, the first American space station, became a "drop-in" centre for visiting astronauts. Skylab was the size of an average house. It offered astronauts the first chance of comfortable surroundings in space.

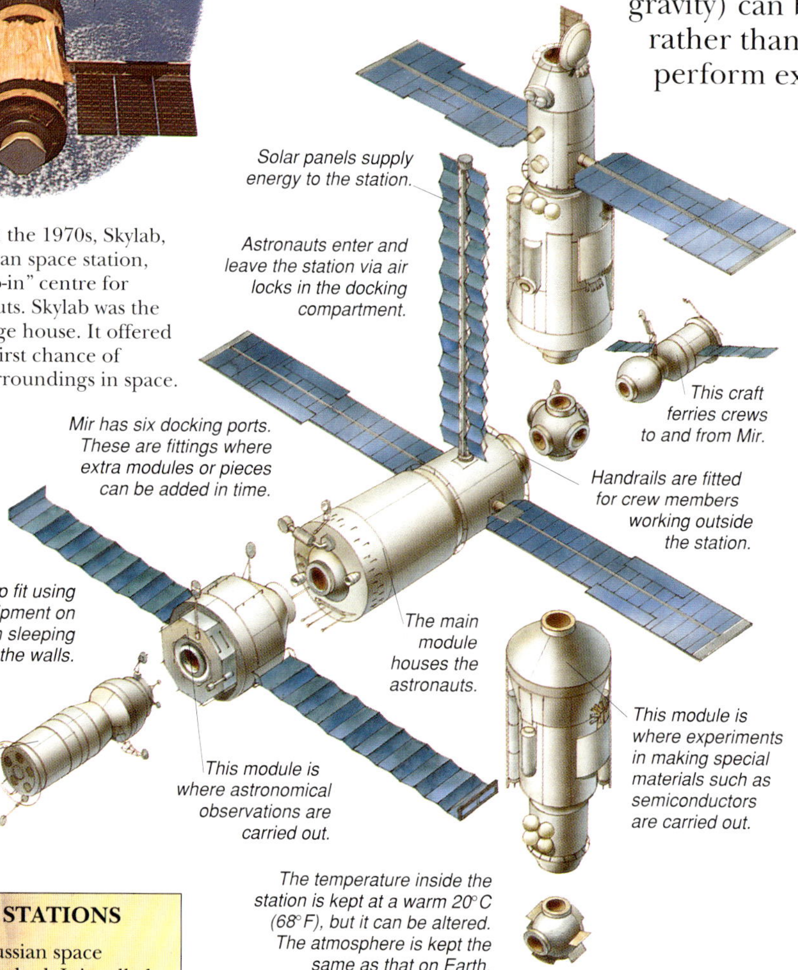

MIR

A Russian space station called Mir was launched in February 1986 and boarded by astronauts three months later. Spacecraft take astronauts to and from the station by docking (connecting) with one of its six ports. At present, the station has room for up to six crew members. But the size of the station can be changed by adding new modules, such as laboratories, to the basic structure.

EXPERIMENTS
Chemists, biologists, and physicists will all benefit from having a laboratory in space. They will be able to work in conditions of microgravity, where they can process and produce materials (such as drugs or electrical components) to a level of purity that is not possible on Earth.

SPACE STATIONS

1971 First Russian space station is launched. It is called Salyut.

1973 First American space station is launched. It is called Skylab.

1980 Skylab re-enters Earth's atmosphere and disintegrates.

1983 First purpose-built space laboratory is launched. It is called Spacelab.

1986 The largest space station, Mir, is launched from Baïkonour in Russia.

1987 Russian astronaut Yuri Romanenko returns to Earth from Mir after a record 326 days in space.

Photograph of solar prominence taken from space station Skylab

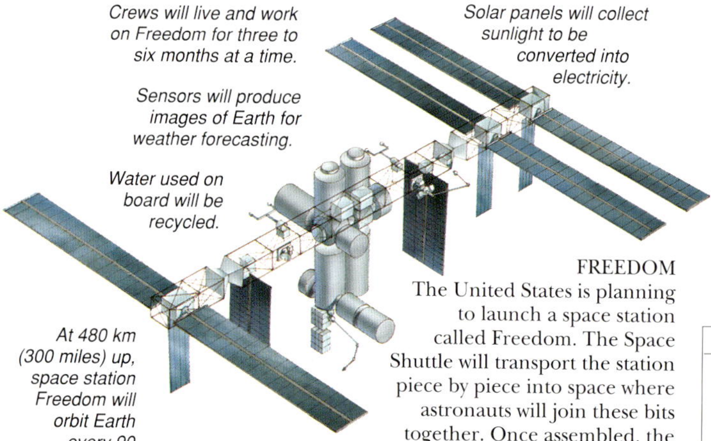

FREEDOM
The United States is planning to launch a space station called Freedom. The Space Shuttle will transport the station piece by piece into space where astronauts will join these bits together. Once assembled, the station will be longer than a football field and staffed by a permanent crew of six.

Find out more

GRAVITY P.122
SATELLITES P.300
SPACE PROBES P.301
HUMANS IN SPACE P.302

LIVING THINGS

YOU WILL FIND living things almost everywhere you look. A single crumb of bread can support a tiny mould. A spoonful of river water may be home to many different microscopic forms of life. Living things are spread across vast land masses and throughout the oceans between them. Even where conditions seem extremely hostile – in scorching dry deserts, or on freezing mountain tops, for example – some forms of life survive and multiply. Biology is the study of all living things, from those that can be seen only with a microscope to those that are much bigger than we are. Biologists study living things to find out how they work and how they are linked together in the complex pattern of life on Earth.

Moths from the *Arctiidae* family

HOW BIOLOGISTS WORK
During the 19th century, scientists often studied animals by killing and collecting them. These moths are part of a typical museum collection that contains thousands of specimens. Collecting can provide useful information, but it can also harm rare species. Because today's biologists are more aware of the need for conservation, they spend more time studying animals in the wild. In this way, they can learn about an animal without harming it or changing its natural behaviour.

ORGANISMS AND SPECIES

To biologists, the word "organism" means anything that is alive. A bacterium (singular of bacteria) is an organism, and so too is a plant, an insect, or a human being. Another word that is often used in biology is "species". A species is a group of organisms that are able to breed with each other, such as lions or ostriches. The organisms above belong to different species. They can breed with members of their own species, but not with members of any other species. Organisms usually live separately, but sometimes members of the same species live together very closely in a colony (large group).

FRIEDRICH WÖHLER

All living things contain carbon compounds. Until the 19th century, most scientists believed that carbon compounds in living things were quite separate from those in non-living things. But in 1828, the German chemist Friedrich Wöhler (1800-82) disproved this idea, which was known as "vitalism". He made urea, a carbon compound formed by animals, from a compound that is found only in non-living matter.

HIDDEN LIFE
Although this plant looks quite lifeless, it is actually very much alive. *Lithops* (*Lithops aucampiae*), known as the "living stone" plant, grows in dry parts of southern Africa. For most of the year, the *Lithops* plant is well camouflaged. But it has to reproduce. To do this, it grows brightly coloured flowers. These flowers attract insects that transfer pollen from one plant to another. After the plant has been pollinated, it produces seeds.

EXPLORING NATURE
The English naturalist Henry Bates (1825-92) was one of the first European people to investigate the wildlife of the Amazon rainforest in South America. He collected many new species and studied the ways in which they compete for survival. Today, scientists are still discovering new species. At the same time, many species are becoming extinct because of the damage we are doing to the natural world.

WHAT IS LIFE?

LIVING THINGS EXIST in many different shapes and sizes. They range from trees that are higher than a 20-storey building to bacteria that are far too small to see. Plants spend their lives in the same place, but many animals travel huge distances through the air, over land, or in the sea. Despite these differences, all forms of life share some important characteristics. They all take in raw materials, either in the form of food, or in the form of simpler substances. They all use chemical reactions to get energy from these raw materials, and they all make waste products from this process. The energy they obtain enables them to grow, to reproduce, and to respond to the world around them.

PLANT LIFE
Plants cannot move about, but they are just as alive as we are. An oak tree collects energy from sunlight, and builds it into food. It uses this food to grow and to reproduce. Although the tree does not have any special sense organs, it can detect and respond to light.

Chemical reactions inside a mouse's body enable it to move and stay warm.

A female mouse uses the energy and nutrients (raw materials) from food to make milk for her young.

When it breathes, a mouse takes in oxygen and gives out carbon dioxide as a waste product.

Young mice use energy and nutrients from food to grow.

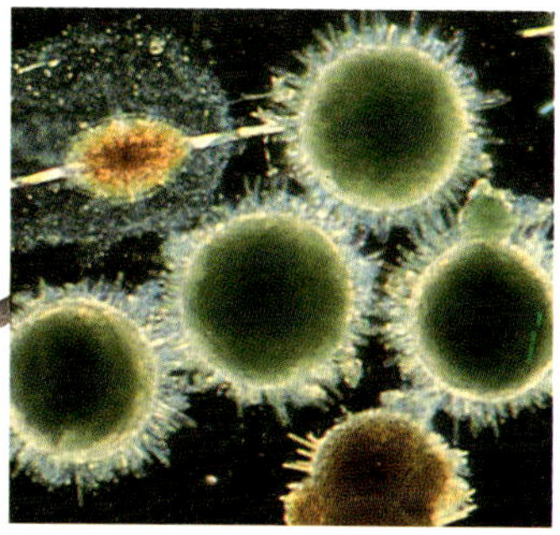

PLANKTONIC LIFE
Most forms of life are far smaller than we are. These tiny planktonic organisms drift with the currents in the open sea. Each member of the plankton is very small, but together they weigh millions of tonnes.

CHARACTERISTICS OF LIFE

The most important daily task for these mice is to find food to fuel their bodies. They use their senses to track down anything they can eat, and to check for danger. A mouse obtains energy by combining its food with oxygen. When it does this, carbon dioxide is formed as a waste product. It also uses the nutrients in food to build new body parts. Within six weeks of being born, a mouse is ready to reproduce.

This shell was once home to a nautilus – a mollusc that lives in the sea. As the mollusc grew, it made sure the shell grew too by secreting calcium, which gradually crystallized to form new shell.

ORDER FROM CHAOS

A wind-up toy will gradually lose its energy if you do not turn its key. After a few years, it may also rust and break. It is typical of non-living things. Living things work the other way around. They take in energy, and use it to build structures such as cells or shells. This ability to create order from chaotic matter is unique. Only living things can do this. When they die, this ability is lost.

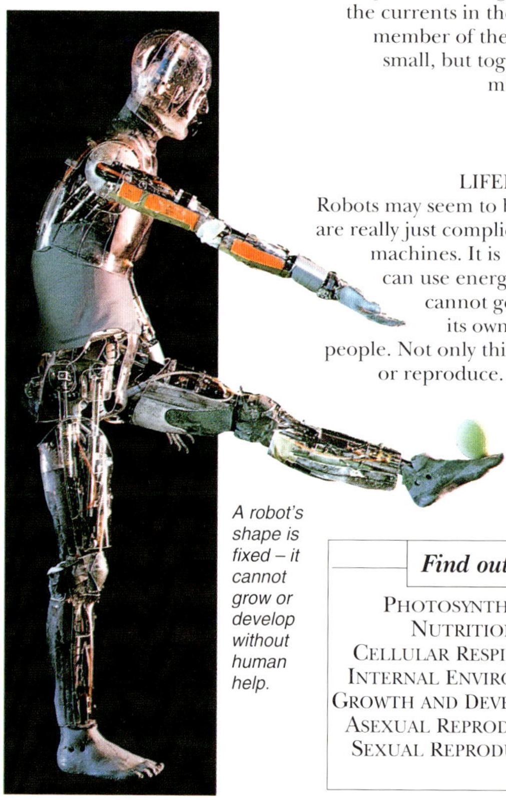

A robot's shape is fixed – it cannot grow or develop without human help.

LIFELESS MACHINE
Robots may seem to be alive, but they are really just complicated, non-living machines. It is true that a robot can use energy to move. But it cannot get this energy on its own – it depends on people. Not only this, it cannot grow or reproduce. Without regular maintenance, a robot will eventually break down and fall apart.

Find out more

PHOTOSYNTHESIS P.340
NUTRITION P.342
CELLULAR RESPIRATION P.346
INTERNAL ENVIRONMENT P.350
GROWTH AND DEVELOPMENT P.362
ASEXUAL REPRODUCTION P.366
SEXUAL REPRODUCTION P.367

HOW LIFE BEGAN

OUR PLANET has been around for about 4,500 million years. In its early years, it was far too hot and dangerous to support life. It was bombarded by meteors and torn apart by volcanic explosions. But as the Earth cooled, its surface became calmer. Steamy water vapour from the constant eruptions formed clouds and rain fell. In this water, life appeared over 3,500 million years ago. Some people believe that living things were specially created, but most scientists think life came about through a series of chemical reactions that happened by chance. Over millions of years, these reactions slowly built living things from simple chemical substances.

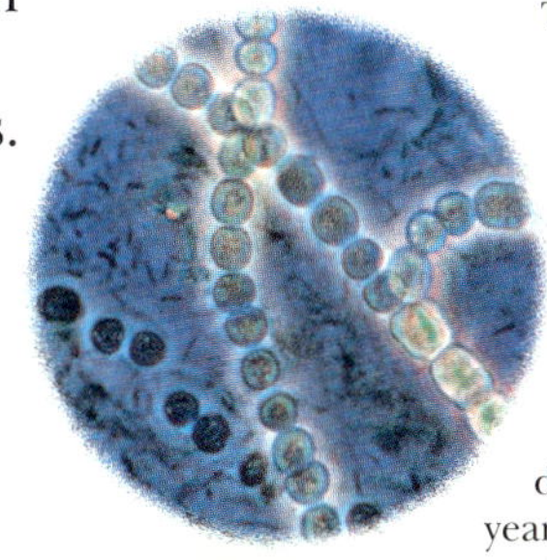

OLDEST LIFE FORMS
These simple plant-like blue-green algae are called cyanobacteria. They usually live in shallow water, and make their food by photosynthesis. Geologists have found fossilized mats of cyanobacteria that date from 3,500 million years ago. These life forms must have been among the earliest on Earth.

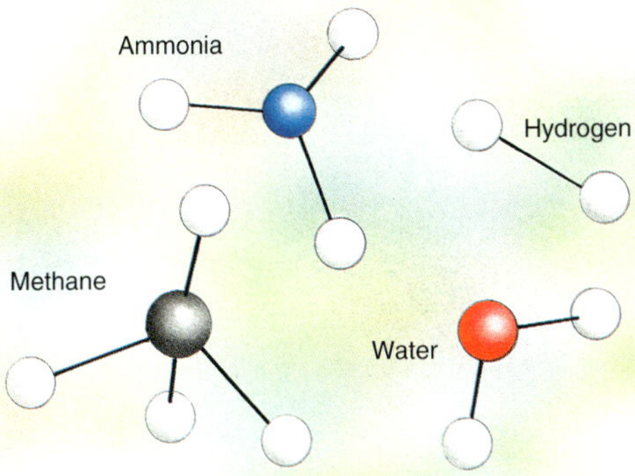

RAW INGREDIENTS
The ocean and atmosphere of the early Earth contained simple chemicals, such as water, methane, ammonia, and hydrogen. In their famous experiment, Urey and Miller sealed a mixture of these chemicals in a container. They wanted to see what would happen when the chemicals were allowed to react.

Energy produced by electrical spark caused chemicals in container to react with each other.

Water, methane, ammonia, and hydrogen chemicals were sealed in a container.

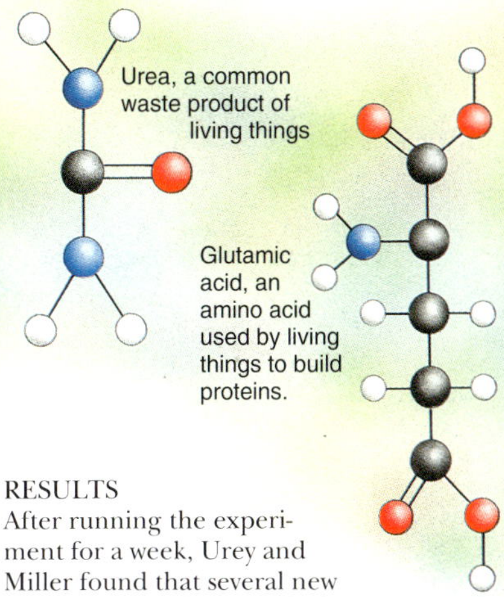

RESULTS
After running the experiment for a week, Urey and Miller found that several new and complex substances had formed. Among them were amino acids. These are important chemicals that link together to form proteins, the building blocks of life.

LIFE FROM LIFE

At one time, people thought that living things could suddenly appear from lifeless substances.They thought, for example, that maggots developed from decaying meat. Experiments by Italian scientist Lazzaro Spallanzani (1729-99) and French scientist Louis Pasteur (1822-95) showed that this idea was wrong. Living things are now always formed by reproduction.

By laying her eggs on meat, this female bluebottle fly (Calliphora vomitoria) ensures a plentiful supply of food for the maggot larvae when they hatch.

CRADLE OF LIFE

Imagine a young Earth covered with oceans that contained simple chemicals. Energy from sunlight and from strikes of lightning would have made these chemicals react with each other. Eventually, some of these reactions may have created chemicals that could copy themselves, or membranes (coatings) that would shield them from the outside world. In 1953, American chemists Harold Urey and Stanley Miler tested this idea. They found that complex substances could be built up from simpler ones.

LIFE BEYOND EARTH?
If life arose on Earth by random chemical reactions, it is possible that it has evolved elsewhere in the Universe in the same way. Life on Earth is based on carbon compounds, such as amino acids. Scientists have found traces of amino acids in some meteorites. Astronomers have also detected simpler carbon-based chemicals in the dust that is scattered throughout space.

This iron meteorite fell from space about 20,000 years ago.

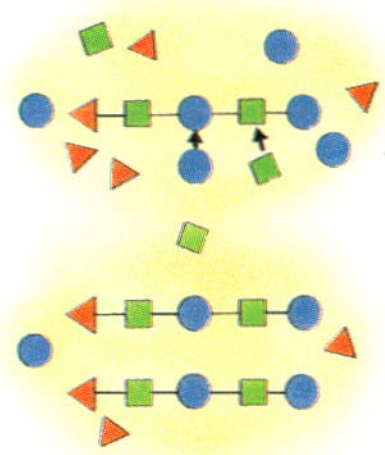

Original chemical attracts other chemicals and reacts with them.

After several reactions, a copy of the original chemical is formed.

CHEMICAL REPRODUCTION
Life may have started in a simple way. By chance, a chemical may have entered into a series of reactions that resulted in it making a copy of itself. This copy, through the same reactions, could then make a copy of itself. The chemical was able to reproduce.

Find out more

CARBON P.40
HYDROGEN P.47
EARTH P.209
CELLS P.338
PHOTOSYNTHESIS P.340
GENETICS P.364

EVOLUTION

IMAGINE BEING ABLE to go back in time to see what living things looked like millions of years ago. Sadly, this is impossible, but we can find out a lot about the past by looking at fossils. A fossil is created when something that was once alive becomes buried by mud or sand. The soft parts of the plant or animal often rot away without trace, but the harder parts, such as stems, bones, teeth, and shells, very slowly turn to stone. Fossils from all over the world show that living things have gradually changed over many millions of years. Some kinds have become extinct (ceased to exist), and new kinds have developed from older ones. This process of slow change is called evolution.

REPTILE OR BIRD?

Very occasionally, a fossil is found that shows how one major group of living things may have evolved from another. One such fossil is that of *Archaeopteryx*, which means "ancient wing". The fossil shows an animal that had scales and teeth like a reptile, but that also had feathers like a bird. From this evidence, biologists can be almost certain that birds evolved from reptiles.

FOSSIL RECORD
This *Archaeopteryx* fossil was found in Germany in 1861. It is thought that *Archaeopteryx* evolved from small dinosaurs (a type of reptile) that ran on two legs.

EVOLUTION OF THE HORSE

Fossil evidence shows that the modern horse has evolved from smaller ancestors, which lived quite differently. The earliest horse, *Hyracotherium*, was about the size of a small dog. It had four-toed hooves on its front feet and browsed on the leaves of bushes. Over millions of years, its descendants became bigger, and their diet changed from leaves to grass. They developed longer legs with fewer toes, enabling them to run away from their enemies on open grassland.

Hyracotherium *lived over 50 million years ago. It probably hid from its enemies because it was small and could not run fast.*

Mesohippus, *which lived about 30 million years ago, had longer legs and just three toes on its front feet.*

Merychippus *appeared about 20 million years ago. It was the first horse to eat grass. It also had three toes, but one of the toes formed a large hoof.*

Equus, *the modern horse, evolved about 2 million years ago. It lives on grass, and it has just a single toe on each foot, forming a hoof.*

GEORGES-LOUIS BUFFON

In the 17th century, most people believed that living things had been specially created. They thought that each kind of plant or animal had fixed characteristics, a view still held by some people today. Count Georges-Louis Buffon (1707-88) was a wealthy French naturalist who gradually came to doubt this idea. During research for his 44-volume work *Natural History*, he decided that some species of plants or animals must have given rise to others. He was one of the first people to write about the idea of evolution.

A SHARED PATTERN

Evolution works by adapting things that already exist. One species may evolve into others that look very different, but they all share the same basic pattern. Mammals are a good example. They have front limbs of many different shapes and sizes, and they carry out many different functions – from swimming to flying. But each one is built on the same basic pattern. This suggests that mammals have evolved from a common ancestor.

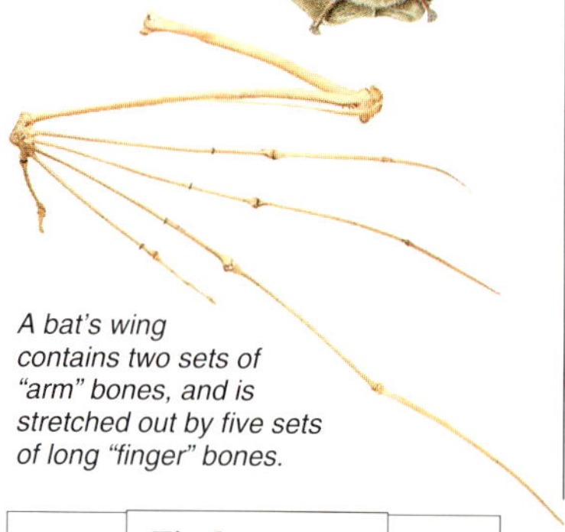

A bat's wing contains two sets of "arm" bones, and is stretched out by five sets of long "finger" bones.

A porpoise's front flipper contains two sets of short "arm" bones, and five sets of "finger" bones.

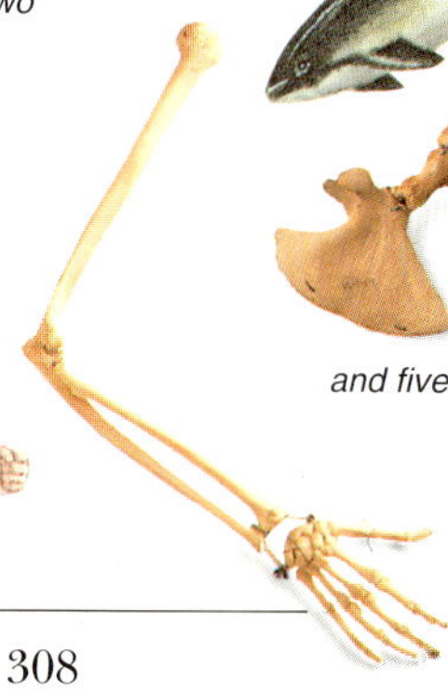

A human arm contains two sets of long bones. The hand is made up of five sets of finger bones.

Find out more

FOSSILS P.225
HOW EVOLUTION WORKS P.309
CLASSIFYING LIVING THINGS P.310
REPTILES P.330
BIRDS P.332
GENETICS P.364
FACT FINDER P. 420

How evolution works

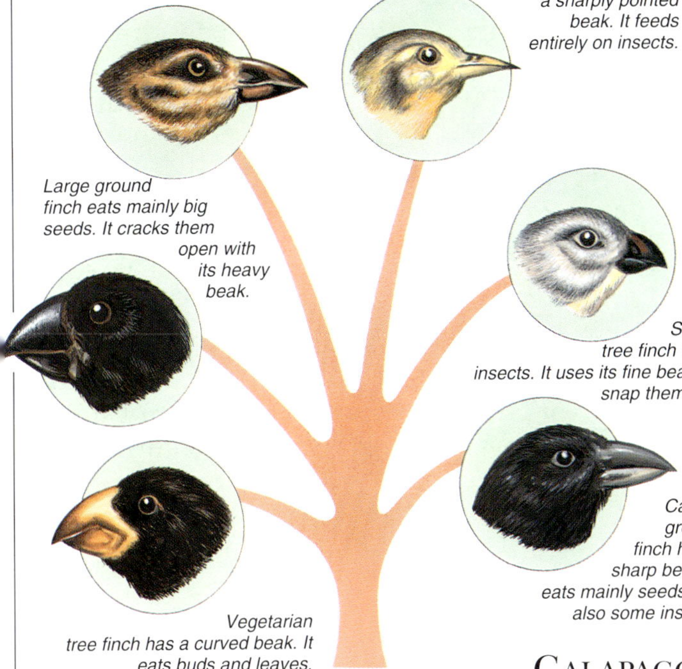

Tool-using finch holds a cactus spine in its beak to pick out insects from bark crevices.

Warbler finch has a sharply pointed beak. It feeds entirely on insects.

Large ground finch eats mainly big seeds. It cracks them open with its heavy beak.

Small tree finch eats insects. It uses its fine beak to snap them up.

Cactus ground finch has a sharp beak. It eats mainly seeds, but also some insects.

Vegetarian tree finch has a curved beak. It eats buds and leaves.

WHY SHOULD PLANTS or animals slowly change as one generation follows another? Two 19th-century biologists, Charles Darwin and Alfred Russel Wallace, quite separately hit upon the answer. They knew that members of a species vary from each other slightly, and that these differences can be passed on to the next generation. They also knew that all living things have to compete for resources, such as food. Darwin and Wallace realized that the young born with the most useful differences would produce the most offspring. As a result, the species would evolve, or become better adapted to its way of life. This process is called natural selection.

Galapagos finches

During a round-the-world voyage on board *HMS Beagle*, Charles Darwin landed in 1832 on the remote Galapagos Islands, off the west coast of South America. Here he saw many unique animals, including 13 species of finch. Darwin studied the finches carefully, noting their similarities and differences. It became clear to him that they must all have descended from one species of finch that had arrived from the mainland. The original finch ate seeds and lived on the ground, but its offspring had gradually evolved different beak shapes and different ways of life. Seed-eating finches usually have big, powerful beaks, while insect-eating finches have thinner, pointed beaks.

Charles Darwin and Alfred Russel Wallace

Wallace

Darwin

The theory of natural selection, also called "survival of the fittest", was conceived by Darwin (1809-82) and Wallace (1823-1913). Before they published their work in 1858, many people thought that plants or animals evolved by changing *during* their lives. It was thought that these changes were passed on to offspring by their parents, causing evolution. Darwin and Wallace put forward evidence to support the theory of natural selection. In 1859, Darwin outlined this idea in his bestselling book, *The Origin of Species.*

Adult spider carries her offspring around on her back.

Struggle for survival

This female spider laid hundreds of eggs. Not all of the baby spiders have survived, and more will die before they can reproduce. If these spiderlings did not have to compete for food and shelter, the world would soon be overrun by spiders!

Rabbit flea (Spillopsyllus cuniculi) *feeding on a rabbit.*

Evolution of the flea

Natural selection does not always make things bigger or more complicated. It often "doubles back" on itself. Long ago, the ancestors of fleas evolved wings. But wings are not particularly useful to fleas. As a result of natural selection, fleas have lost their wings. Instead, they have developed powerful back legs so that they can leap aboard their hosts.

Artificial selection

Variations within a species do not always happen naturally. The stripes on these flowers are artificial – they were brought about by exposing a plant to X-rays. The X-rays changed the plant's own chemical "blueprint" (genetic make-up), so that the stripes were passed on to the next generation. The stripy characteristic can be made more common by deliberately breeding these plants. This way of spreading changes in plants and animals is called artificial selection.

Stripes on petunia are a result of artificial selection.

Find out more

BIRDS P.332
MOVEMENT P.356
GENETICS P.364
SEXUAL REPRODUCTION P.367
DESERTS P.390
FACT FINDER P. 420

CLASSIFYING LIVING THINGS

KINGDOM ANIMALIA
The animal kingdom is one of five major groups of living things. The kingdom is divided into about 30 groups. Each group is called a phylum. Some of these groups contain many species, while others contain just a few. The Roman snail belongs to the mollusc phylum, or Phylum Mollusca.

This chart shows some of the animal kingdom phyla.

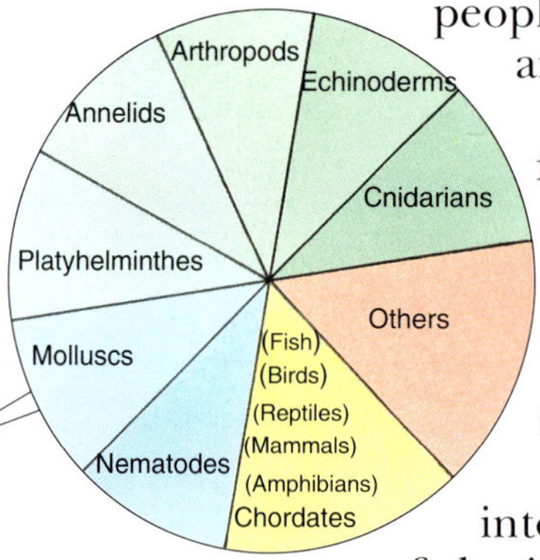

LONG BEFORE BIOLOGY became a science, people used ordinary names for common plants and animals. These names usually described what something looked like, where it was found, or how it was used. But these names do not work for scientists because they vary between languages. Even in one language, some things have several names, while others have none. The 18th-century Swedish botanist Linnaeus devised a way of naming living things and classifying them into groups. In his binomial (two-part) system of classification, every species has its own name. As well as identifying the species, it also shows where it fits into the world of living organisms.

PHYLUM MOLLUSCA
The mollusc phylum contains about 90,000 species, making it one of the largest phyla (plural of phylum) in the animal kingdom. A mollusc has a special body layer, called a mantle, that can produce a shell. The mollusc phylum is divided into seven groups called classes. The Roman snail belongs to the Class Gastropoda, which means "stomach-foot".

CLASS GASTROPODA
Gastropods have a single, sucker-like foot, and most move by creeping along on it. The majority have well-developed heads, and eyes on tentacles. The Class Gastropoda consists of three subclasses. The Roman snail has a lung, and so is a member of the Subclass Pulmonata, which means "with lung".

SUBCLASS PULMONATA
The Subclass Pulmonata is split into two groups, called orders. The Roman snail lives on land. It has eyes at the tips of its tentacles, and so is included in the Order Stylommatophora.

Heb. Reem, Rhinoceros, *Neushoorn.*

NAMES TO REMEMBER
Even before Linnaeus devised his binomial system, educated people were using Latin to name plants and animals. This engraving of a rhinoceros appeared in a medieval "book of beasts".

CHANGING NAMES
Scientific names often change as biologists find out more about how living things are related. The bluebell was originally named by Linnaeus, who included it in the genus *Hyacinthus.* It has been renamed many times as a result of scientific studies, and it is now classified as belonging to another genus, *Scilla.*

CLASSIFICATION
Here you can see how one species, the Roman snail, is classified. As you work down the page, you will notice that the classification starts with the animal kingdom, and then narrows down until it picks out just one species – according to various characteristics. These categories have been devised by biologists, and work like divisions in a vast filing system. Biologists often use additional divisions, such as subphylum and superorder, that are not shown here.

ORDER
STYLOMMATOPHORA
This order contains many kinds of air-breathing molluscs that live on land and that have eyes on tentacles. It is divided into several groups, called families. These include families of both snails and slugs, which are similar, although most slugs do not have a shell. The Roman snail belongs to a family of snails called the Helicidae.

FAMILY HELICIDAE
In biological classification, a family means a collection of species. Within a family, there are groups of species called genera (plural of genus). The Roman snail belongs to the genus *Helix* because of its shell's *helical* (coiled) shape.

GENUS HELIX
The genus *Helix* contains many species that are very similar. Each one has a binomial scientific name. The first part of the name identifies the genus that all the species belong to – in this case, *Helix.* The second part identifies the species itself. The species name of the Roman snail is *pomatia,* meaning " apple-shaped". The Roman snail's full scientific name is therefore *Helix pomatia.*

SPECIES *Helix pomatia*

MONERANS

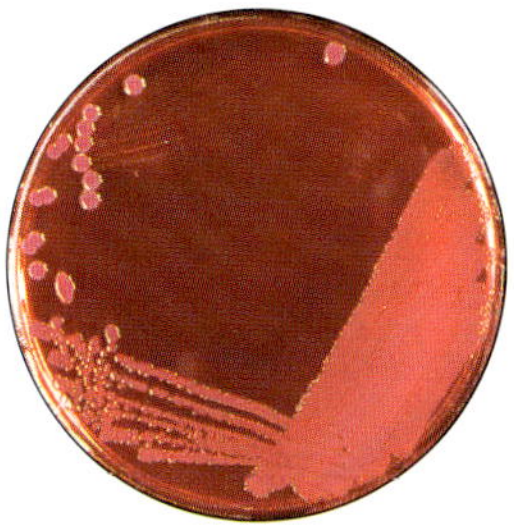

The moneran kingdom consists of the single-celled organisms, bacteria, and the blue-green algae called cyanobacteria. A moneran cell is prokaryotic (simple, with no nucleus). All other living things have eukaryotic cells that have a nucleus.

PROTISTS

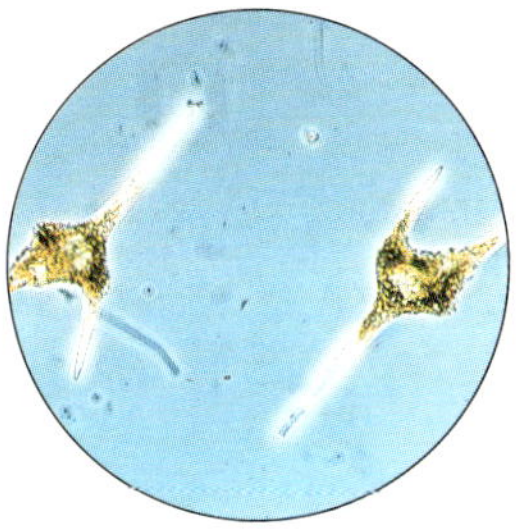

The protist kingdom is made up of organisms that have a single eukaryotic cell. Protists are extremely varied. Some biologists include single-celled algae in this kingdom, while others think that they belong to the plant kingdom.

FUNGI

The fungi kingdom consists of organisms that absorb substances originally produced by other living things. Fungi are sometimes treated as if they were plants. However, the structure of their cells and their way of life are quite different.

PLANTS

The plant kingdom contains organisms that use chlorophyll (green pigment) to harness the energy in sunlight in order to make food. Plant cells have rigid walls made of a substance called cellulose.

ANIMALS

The animal kingdom contains organisms made of many cells that live by taking in food. Most animals can move, but some spend a large part of their lives anchored to one spot. Their cells do not have rigid walls.

FIVE KINGDOMS OF LIVING THINGS

At one time, biologists divided the living world into just two groups: the plant kingdom and the animal kingdom. Telling the difference between a plant and an animal seemed easy. Plants were green, rooted in one place, and needed light to live. Animals usually moved about, and fed by eating other things. However, biologists have since discovered that the living world is not that simple. In any handful of soil, or bucket of water, there are vast numbers of tiny living things that do not belong to either kingdom. Today, the living world is usually divided into five kingdoms. As ideas change about how living things are related, the way that they are classified changes too.

HOW MANY SPECIES?

Biologists still have no real idea how many species of living things exist on Earth. Almost two million have been discovered and described, but there may be ten times that number. We know of about 550 species of conifers, and nearly 400,000 species of beetles.

These are just five of the thousands of beetle species.

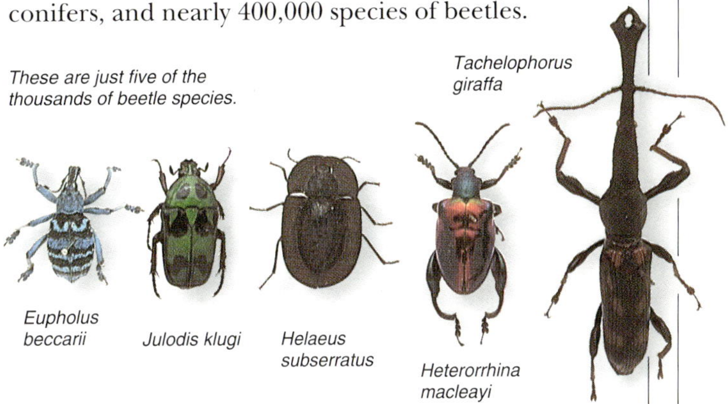

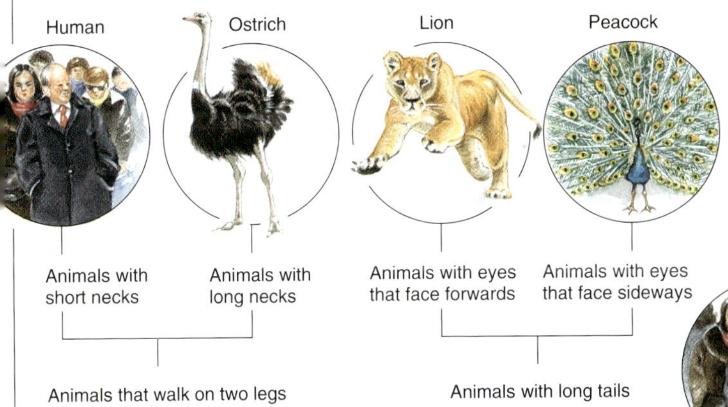

UNIMPORTANT CHARACTERISTICS

Biologists try to classify species in a way that shows how they are linked through evolution. To do this, they have to choose characteristics that different species share. But which characteristics are the most important? The family tree above shows one way of classifying four animals, based mainly on their shape. It does not work very well.

IMPORTANT CHARACTERISTICS

The first family tree suggests that an ostrich is more closely related to a human than to a peacock. Common sense tells you that this is unlikely, because ostriches and peacocks both have feathers and beaks, while we do not. The family tree above is more sensible. It is based on features such as feathers and bone structure, which give a much better guide to classification.

CHOOSING A NAME

The first person to discover a new species often has the honour of choosing its name. This is the skull of a dinosaur called *Baryonyx walkeri*. The first part of the name refers to the dinosaur's heavy claws. The second part commemorates the discoverer – Bill Walker.

Find out more

EVOLUTION P.308
HOW EVOLUTION WORKS P.309
MOLLUSCS P.324
CELLS P.338
PHOTOSYNTHESIS P.340
SKELETONS P.352
FACT FINDER P.420

VIRUSES

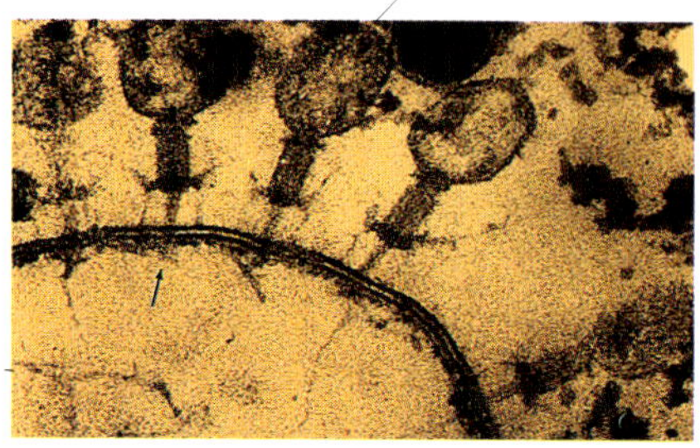

BACTERIOPHAGES
Some viruses, called bacteriophages, attack bacteria in order to reproduce. This bacterium has been attacked by T4 bacteriophages. Empty viruses, which have injected their DNA (deoxyribonucleic acid) into the bacterium, are attached to the outside of the cell.

THE UNPLEASANT SYMPTOMS of a cold are caused by a virus that attacks your nose and throat. A virus is a tiny package of chemicals coated by protein that breaks into living animal or plant cells. Once inside, it "hijacks" the cell's chemical processes, so that instead of working normally, the cell makes copies of the virus. Scientists do not consider viruses to be fully alive because they cannot reproduce on their own – they need the help of living cells. As well as the common cold, viruses cause many other diseases. These include chicken-pox, mumps and measles, and also AIDS (Acquired Immune Deficiency Syndrome), which is thought to be caused by HIV (Human Immunodeficiency Virus). This virus puts the body's natural defences out of action, so that other viruses or bacteria can attack.

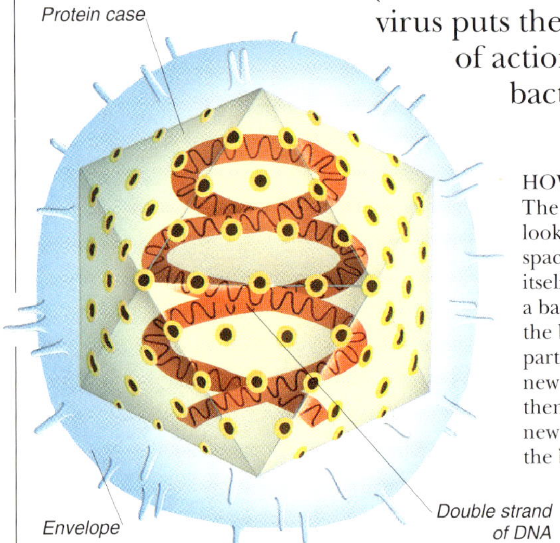

HOW VIRUSES ARE COPIED
The T4 bacteriophage virus looks like a miniature spaceship. It forms copies of itself by injecting its DNA into a bacterium. The DNA makes the bacterium build all the parts needed to assemble new viruses. The parts are then put together, and the new viruses break out of the bacterial cell.

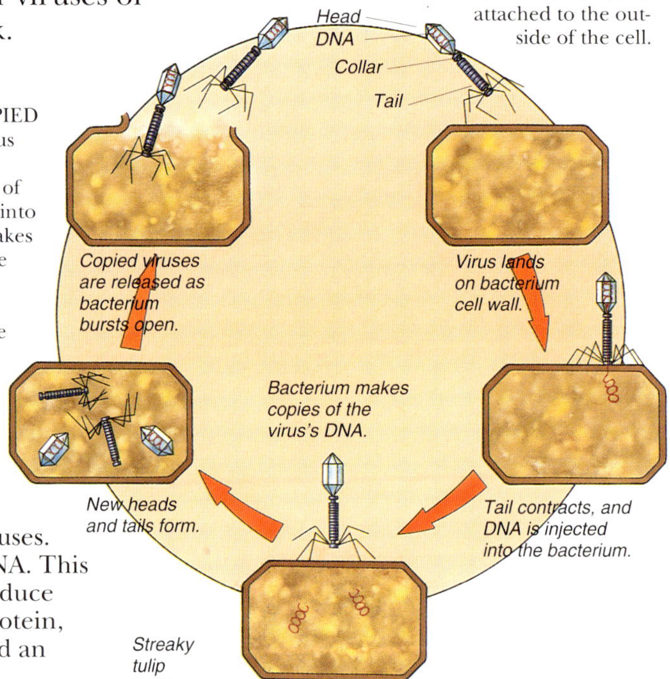

HERPES VIRUS

Chicken-pox, shingles, and cold sores are caused by herpes viruses. Inside each virus is a double strand of the genetic chemical DNA. This contains all the "instructions" needed to make a living cell produce copies of the virus. The DNA is protected by a case made of protein, which has 20 identical sides. Around the case is a coating called an envelope. When the virus encounters a suitable cell, its envelope links up with the cell's membrane – rather like two bubbles joining together. The rest of the virus then enters the cell, where it is copied. Herpes viruses sometimes live in the human body for many years without causing any harm.

SMALLER AND SMALLER

Viruses are not the only chemical particles that can infect living cells. Viroids are similar to viruses, but they are even smaller. A viroid is made of a short length of the genetic chemical RNA (ribonucleic acid), without a protein coat. Prions are smaller still. Unlike viruses or viroids, they are thought to be made of proteins. Viroids cause several diseases of plants, while prions cause scrapie, a disease of sheep and cattle.

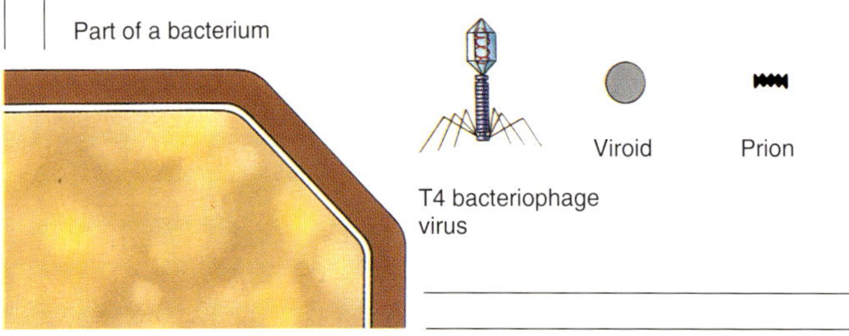

Vase of Flowers by Jan van Huysum (1682-1749).

TREASURED VIRUS
Tulip mosaic virus creates beautiful streaks in the petals of tulips. In 17th-century Holland, tulips infected with this virus were highly prized. People traded tulips like stocks and shares, and the price of a single tulip bulb was often more than an ordinary person's yearly income.

RUNNY NOSES
Cold viruses give you a "runny nose". When you sneeze, droplets of moisture containing millions of viruses are sprayed into the air. If someone close breathes in some of these droplets, they may catch the cold as well.

Find out more

BACTERIA P.313
CELLS P.338
INTERNAL ENVIRONMENT P.350
GROWTH AND DEVELOPMENT P.362
GENETICS P.364

BACTERIA

IF YOU HAVE EVER LEFT MILK OUT in warm weather, you will know how quickly it turns sour. This change is caused by the rapid growth of microscopic moneran organisms called bacteria. Bacteria are the most widespread living things on Earth. They are found in the air, in the ground, and all over plants and animals, including humans. A few kinds even live in hot springs and ice. There are many different bacteria – some harmful, some very beneficial. Harmful bacteria include those that cause dangerous diseases, such as tetanus and septicaemia (blood poisoning). Beneficial bacteria include those that break down waste, and those that live in plant roots, gathering nitrogen from the air.

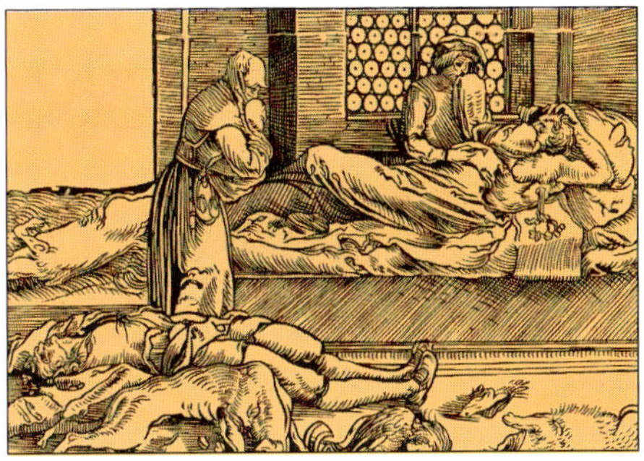

BUBONIC PLAGUE
Before antibiotics were invented, bacterial diseases sometimes swept vast areas in terrifying epidemics. During the 13th and 17th centuries, the bubonic plague, known as the Black Death, killed millions of people in Europe. Bubonic plague is caused by a bacterium that lives in rats, and which is spread to humans by fleas.

BACTERIAL CELLS

A typical bacterium is about 1,000 times smaller than an animal cell, and can only be seen in detail with an electron microscope. It has a thick cell wall, but does not have a nucleus. Bacteria live either by using energy from chemicals or sunlight, or by absorbing food substances. Bacteria can absorb food from dead matter, such as plant and animal remains, or from living cells.

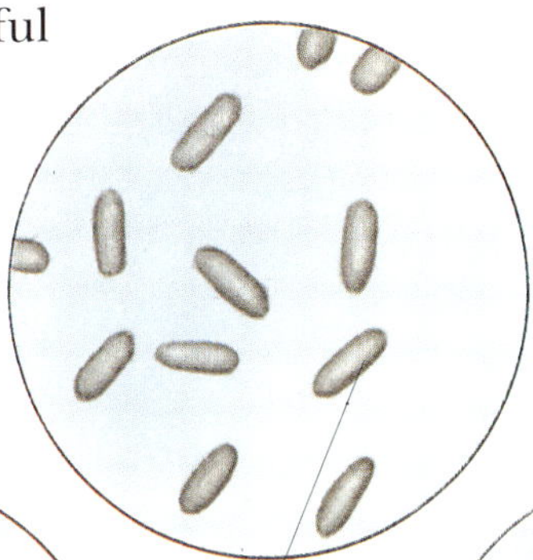

A bacillus is a rod-shaped bacterium. Bacilli live singly or in chains.

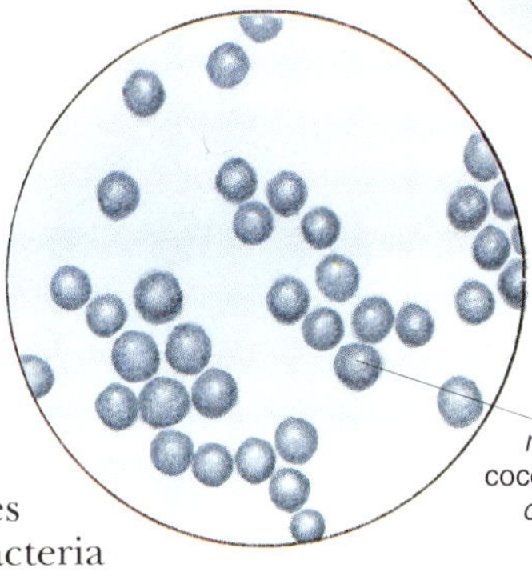

A coccus has a round cell. Some cocci live in clusters or in long chains.

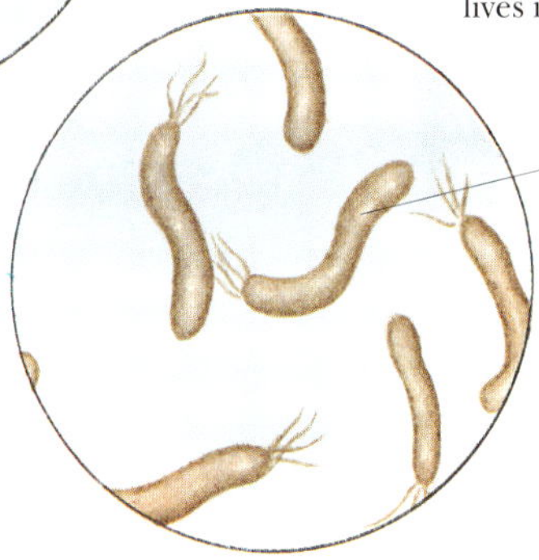

A spirillum has a corkscrew shape. Some form chains.

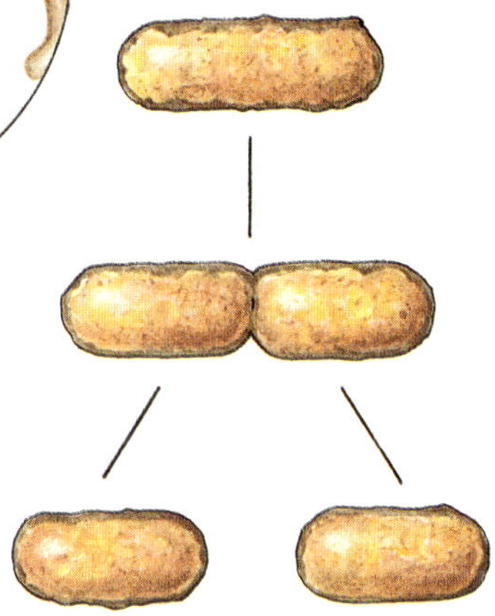

BACTERIAL REPRODUCTION
Bacteria reproduce mainly by dividing in two. With good conditions – warmth, moisture, and food – they do this every 20 minutes. This means that three generations of bacteria can be produced within just one hour. In 24 hours, repeated divisions would produce nearly 5,000 billion billion offspring!

MAKING WASTE SAFE
Bacteria play an important part in processing our body waste and in preventing it from causing pollution. In a sewage farm, liquid waste is slowly trickled through beds of clinker (lumps of solid ash) or fine gravel. Bacteria living on the surface of the clinker digest the waste, breaking it down into simpler substances. These can be released into streams and rivers without harming wildlife.

ROBERT KOCH
A German doctor named Robert Koch (1843-1910) helped to establish the study of bacteria as a medical science. In 1876, he discovered that the bacterium that produced anthrax, a disease of cattle and humans, could be cultured (grown) in a laboratory. He also identified the bacteria that cause tuberculosis and cholera.

TOOTH DECAY
We all have many kinds of bacteria living on and in our bodies. Your mouth contains bacteria that digest traces of leftover food. If you do not brush your teeth regularly, these bacteria build up, forming a white coating called plaque. Acids produced by the bacteria attack the hard outer covering of teeth. If the acid gets through to the soft layer underneath, the teeth decay more.

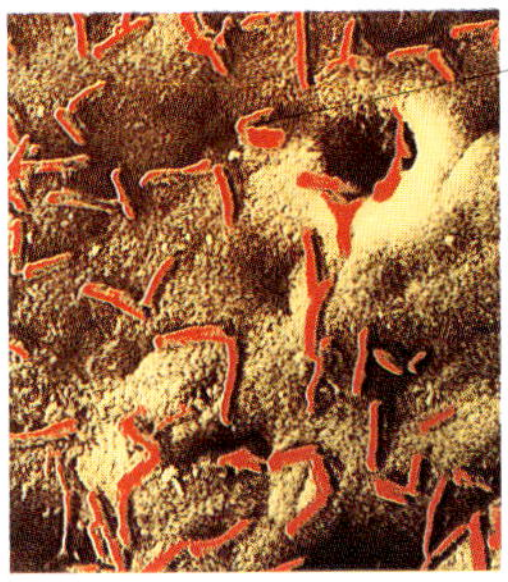

Bacteria on surface of tooth

Find out more

CELLS P.338
PHOTOSYNTHESIS P.340
TEETH AND JAWS P.344
INTERNAL ENVIRONMENT P.350
GROWTH AND DEVELOPMENT P.362
FACT FINDER P.420

SINGLE-CELLED ORGANISMS

WET PLACES such as the sea, ponds, or damp ground, are alive with tiny single-celled organisms called protists. Although protists are bigger than bacteria, most are still far too small to see with the naked eye. Each protist cell is quite different from those of bacteria. It contains a nucleus, and also has special structures called organelles that carry out various tasks to keep the cell alive. Protists feed in two ways. Some make their food like plants – by using the energy in sunlight. Others, called protozoa ("first animals"), catch and eat prey. But protists cannot always be separated neatly into plant-like or animal-like forms. Some can do both: they can make food using sunlight *and* eat other organisms.

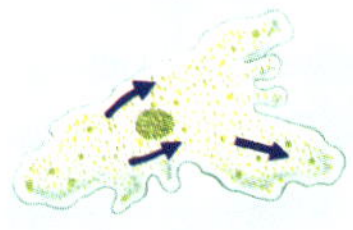

Liquid cytoplasm flows through the pseudopods, carrying organelles with it.

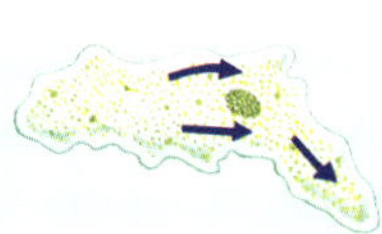

An amoeba's top speed is about 2 cm (just under 1 inch) in an hour.

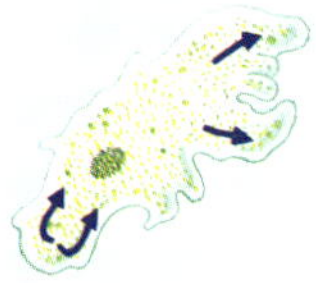

The amoeba sends out pseudopods in the direction of motion.

HOW AN AMOEBA MOVES

An amoeba can change parts of its cytoplasm (cell fluid) into a jelly-like solid and back to a fluid again. It does this to make temporary "feet", called pseudopods. As the amoeba moves, the sides of the pseudopods become solid and stay still, while the front and inside flow forwards.

AMOEBA

An amoeba is a special kind of protist that does not have a fixed shape. Its single bag-like cell moves by flowing in any direction. Amoebas live in water, and feed by engulfing their prey. Their food becomes locked up in bubbles called food vacuoles, where it is eventually digested. To reproduce, an amoeba simply divides itself in two.

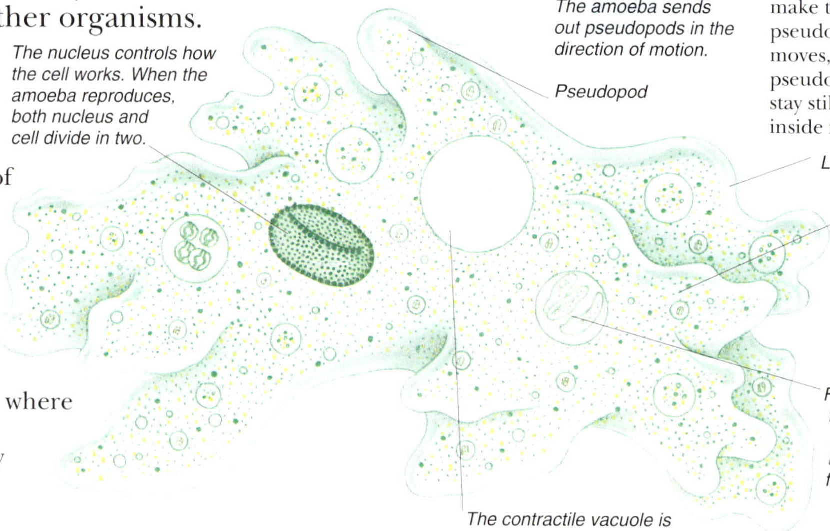

The nucleus controls how the cell works. When the amoeba reproduces, both nucleus and cell divide in two.

Pseudopod

Liquid cytoplasm

Jelly-like cytoplasm

Food vacuoles digest things that the amoeba has engulfed. Any remains are then ejected from the cell.

The contractile vacuole is like a pump. It collects surplus water and then squirts it out of the cell.

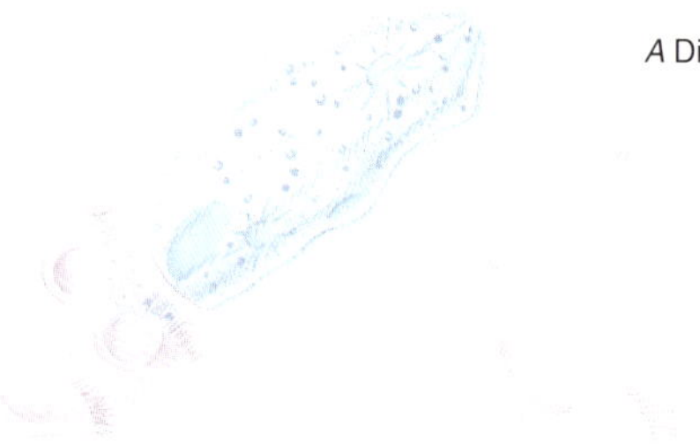

A Didinium swims about looking for food.

The Didinium *has bumped into a* Paramecium. *The* Didinium *stretches wide to take in its enormous meal. Within two or three hours, it will be ready to feed again.*

PROTIST BATTLE

Protists may be small, but their world includes some ferocious predators. Here, a protist called *Didinium* is attacking another called *Paramecium*. The battle begins when *Didinium* fires poisonous threads at its prey. Although much smaller than its meal, the *Didinium* then swallows the *Paramecium*. Both these protists are ciliates – organisms that "row" through water by beating tiny hairs called cilia.

ROCK-MAKING PROTISTS

Foraminiferans ("hole-bearers") are protists that live in microscopic shells rich in calcium. Each shell is covered with tiny holes through which special "feet" project to gather food. Foraminiferans live in huge numbers in the sea. When they die, their shells pile up on the seabed. Eventually, they turn into rocks such as the chalk seen in these white cliffs.

MOSQUITOES AND MALARIA

Malaria is a dangerous disease that is particularly widespread in the tropics. It is caused by a protist called *Plasmodium*. People catch malaria when they are bitten by a mosquito carrying this protist. Once inside a human, *Plasmodium* lives and reproduces inside liver and red blood cells. Every few days, the new protist cells break out of the red blood cells, producing bouts of fever.

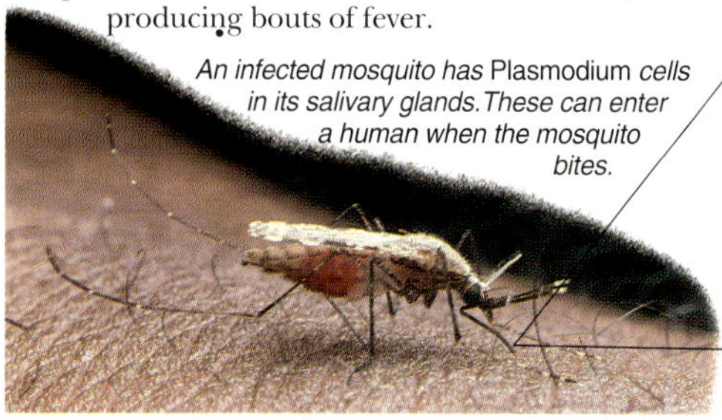

An infected mosquito has Plasmodium *cells in its salivary glands. These can enter a human when the mosquito bites.*

Mosquito (*Anopheles arabiensis*)

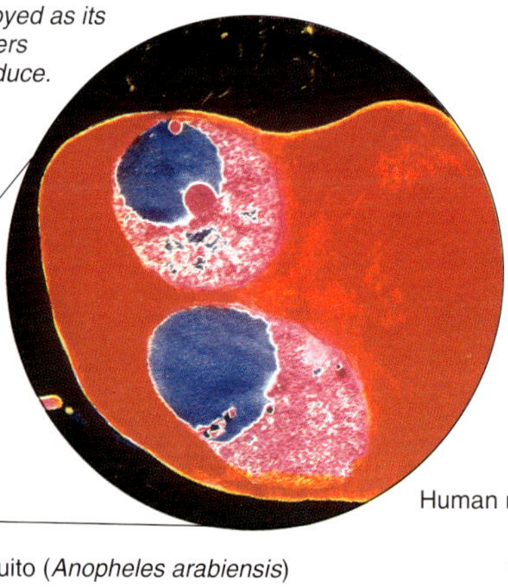

The blood cell is destroyed as its invaders reproduce.

Human red blood cell infected with *Plasmodium*.

Find out more

BACTERIA P.313
CELLS P.338
PHOTOSYNTHESIS P.340
ASEXUAL REPRODUCTION P.366
FACT FINDER PP.420, 422

FUNGI

FOR MANY PEOPLE, a fungus is a mushroom or a toadstool. But mushrooms and toadstools are just the visible parts of fungi. The rest of a fungus is made up of a mass of tiny threads called hyphae, which are usually hidden in the ground, or in organic matter such as dead wood. Unlike green plants, fungi cannot make food by capturing sunlight energy. Instead, they use their threads to absorb chemicals that have already been made by other living things that have died. Together with bacteria, fungi are important decomposers. They break down the remains of dead plants and animals, releasing chemicals that can be recycled. Fungi do not only feed on dead matter. Some attack living plants and animals and often cause diseases.

FLAVOUR FROM FUNGI
Although some fungi are poisonous, many harmless species are used to flavour food. These cheeses have been infected with *Penicillium* fungus. It grows through the cheese, giving it a special taste.

FLY AGARIC

The fly agaric (*Amanita muscaria*) is a poisonous fungus that reproduces by forming toadstools. The toadstool has flaps called gills that hang from its cap. The gills make spores, which are like tiny seeds. These spores are shed into the air, and if one lands in a suitable place, it produces a new mass of fungal threads.

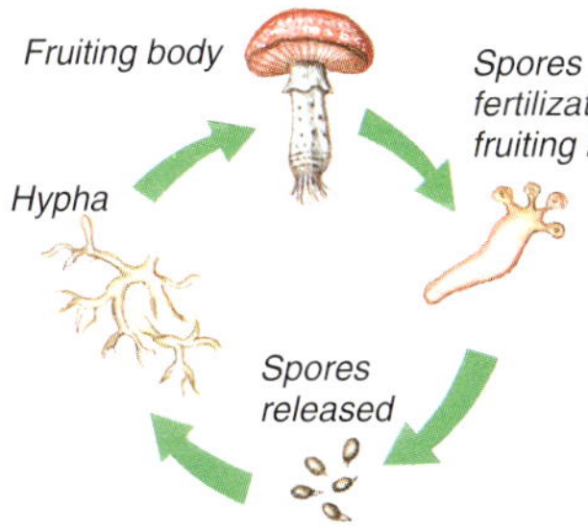

Life cycle of a typical fungus

Black mould (Cladosporium cladosporiodes) growing on damp wall.

FUNGI AROUND THE HOME
Many kinds of fungi grow on and around houses. Cool, damp walls are often colonized by a mould that forms black patches. Timbers in old houses can be eaten away by dry rot (*Serpula lacrimans*), while mildews and rusts attack garden plants and farm crops.

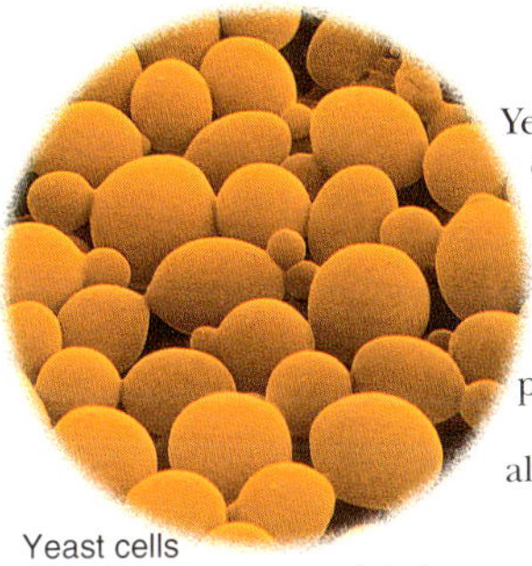

Yeast cells (*Saccharomyces cerevisiae*)

SINGLE-CELLED FUNGI
Yeasts are microscopic single-celled fungi that reproduce mainly by budding. They feed on sugars, turning them into alcohol or other substances through a process called fermentation. Yeasts are used to produce alcoholic drinks and to make bread rise.

SIR ALEXANDER FLEMING
Scotsman Alexander Fleming (1881-1955) studied medicine. In 1928, he noticed that a dish of bacteria in his laboratory had accidentally become infected by a fungus. Fleming saw that the fungus had killed the bacteria near it, and he isolated the substance that the fungus produced. He called it "penicillin" – the first antibiotic drug. As a result of later research, pencillin has saved millions of lives.

POTATO FAMINE
In the middle of last century, a fungus changed the course of history. The fungus concerned was potato blight (*Phtyophthora infestans*), which rots potato plants. It ruined much of the potato crop in Ireland for several years, and forced thousands of starving people to emigrate to North America.

Puffball (*Lycoperdon pyriforme*)

PUFFBALL
A puffball's spores form inside a round head that gradually dries out and becomes a hollow bag. If an animal or a raindrop strikes the bag, spores are puffed out of a hole in the top.

Find out more

BACTERIA P.313
PHOTOSYNTHESIS P.340
FEEDING P.343
ASEXUAL REPRODUCTION P.366
CYCLES IN THE BIOSPHERE P.372
WASTES AND RECYCLING P.376
FACT FINDER PP.420, 422

PLANTS WITHOUT FLOWERS

PLANTS ARE DIFFERENT from fungi because they can make their own food using the chlorophyll (green pigment) in their leaves. Plants fall into two main groups: plants without flowers, and plants with flowers. Plants without flowers grew more than 300 million years ago. They included algae, ferns, and mosses, and some of them reached great sizes. Today, plants without flowers still exist, but those on land are often quite small, and are usually tucked away in shady places. Plants without flowers spread by shedding spores. Many of them, ferns for example, exist as two different kinds of plant. One kind, the sporophyte, makes the spores. The spores then germinate to make a second kind of plant, the prothallus, that produces gametes (sex cells).

UNDERWATER GIANT

Giant kelp (*Macrocystis pyrifera*) is the largest alga in the world, and is also one of the fastest-growing. This seaweed can grow from a single cell to a plant 50 m (165 ft) long in one year. Older plants may reach 200 m (650 ft). Giant kelp grows in the cool water off California, United States, where it forms underwater "forests". The tangle of kelp fronds provides home and food for many animals, including fish and sea otters.

A kelp does not have true leaves. It has pointed fronds.

Instead of a stem, kelp has a tough rubbery stipe.

Giant kelp is clamped to the sea bottom by a root-like anchor called a holdfast.

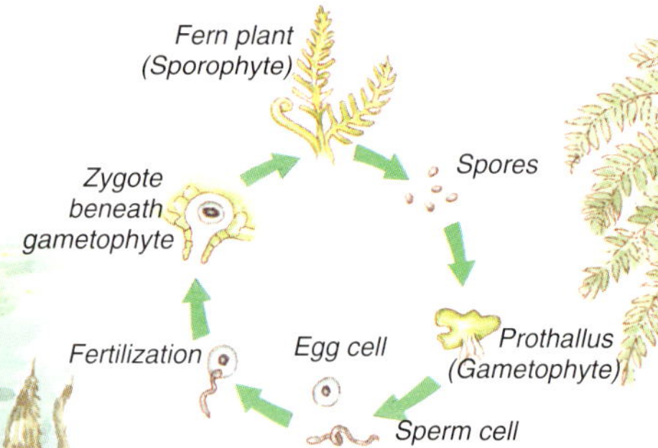

Life cycle of a typical plant without flowers

TREE-FERNS

Tree-ferns are the tallest non-flowering plants on land. They grow mainly in the tropics, although some are found in cooler places such as New Zealand.

Ferns have special tissues that carry water through the plant.

WEALTH OF ALGAE

There are more than 20,000 species of alga. They vary in size from this microscopic water plant called *Volvox* to the giant kelp. *Volvox* is made of a ball of cells set in jelly. Daughter colonies are produced within the parent colony and released when they are large enough.

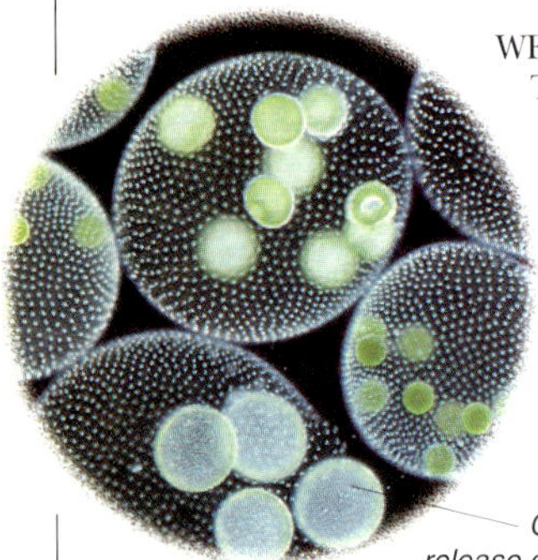

Colony ruptures to release daughter colonies.

LIVERWORTS

Liverworts are closely related to mosses. They are low-growing plants that look like pieces of green ribbon. As the plant grows forwards, the ribbon keeps dividing in two. Liverworts like places that are very damp, such as rocky hollows and the banks of streams.

Liverworts either have flat ribbons, or ribbons made of pieces that look like leaves.

USES OF SEAWEED

You probably encounter seaweeds every day without knowing it. Extracts from seaweeds are often used to thicken ice-cream. They are also used in soft drinks, glue, toothpastes – and even explosives. Seaweeds contain large amounts of useful minerals. They are sometimes harvested and used to make fertilizer.

Carrageenan and alginate from seaweeds are used as thickeners in foods.

Mosses are anchored with root-like hairs called rhizoids.

MOSSES

A clump of moss is made up of a number of plants growing closely together. Mosses release their spores from capsules held on little stalks. You can sometimes see these capsules if you look closely.

Find out more

CELLS P.338
PHOTOSYNTHESIS P.340
TRANSPORT IN PLANTS P.341
CELLULAR RESPIRATION P.346
ASEXUAL REPRODUCTION P.366
SEXUAL REPRODUCTION P.367
FACT FINDER P.420

CONIFERS

YOU WILL NEVER SEE a conifer with flowers, and it does not grow from spores. So how does a conifer reproduce? The answer is that it forms cones. Each cone makes either male or female cells, and the male cells are carried to the female ones to produce seeds. Conifers were among the first plants to make seeds. Unlike spores, these seeds are complete with their own food supply. There are about 550 species of conifer, and nearly all of them are trees, such as firs and pines. Most have narrow, tough leaves known as scales or needles, and many are good at coping with severe cold. In parts of the world that have hard winters, conifers can form forests that stretch from one horizon to another.

MONKEY PUZZLE
The Chile pine (*Araucaria auracana*), also known as the monkey puzzle, is an unusual conifer that comes from South America. It has sharp, leathery leaves, and the male and female cones grow on separate trees.

Each soft male cone sheds millions of pollen grains (male cells) into the air.

Young female cones sit upright on the branches. Their female cells are fertilized by male pollen grains that fall on them from the air.

Mature female cones hang from the branches. When the winged seeds are released, they flutter away.

Scales close in damp weather.

Pine cone scales open in dry weather to release the seeds.

Each scale protects a pair of winged seeds.

CONES AND SEEDS
Mature seed-bearing cones grow in many shapes and sizes. Most are woody, but some are soft and look like berries. The cones of pines and spruces usually fall to the ground in one piece, but the cones of cedars and firs slowly break up while still on the tree.

AMBER TRAP
This spider is millions of years old. It has been preserved in amber – the fossilized remains of a sap called resin. Resin is extremely sticky, and conifers use it to stop small animals eating their wood. If a conifer's bark is wounded, resin oozes out, trapping any insects or spiders that it touches.

ANCIENT PINES
The North American bristlecone pines (*Pinus longaeva*) are the world's oldest living trees. Some surviving examples took root more than 6,000 years ago! Scientists study the width of growth rings in their wood to see how the world's climate has changed.

Life cycle of a typical conifer

SITKA SPRUCE
The Sitka spruce (*Picea sitchensis*) is a North American conifer that is now grown in plantations all over the world – both for its timber and for making paper. The male and female cones grow on the same tree. Spruces are easy to recognize because their stiff needles are attached to small pegs on the branches. You can feel these pegs on an old branch that has shed its leaves.

Yew (Taxus baccata) *has flat needles that grow on opposite sides of the stems.*

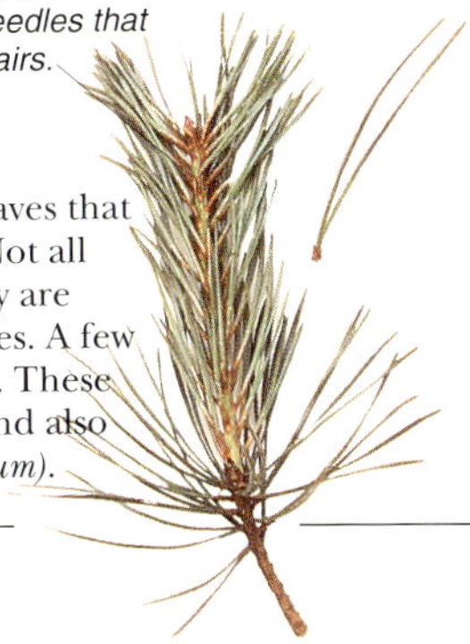

Scots pine (Pinus sylvestris) *has narrow needles that grow in pairs.*

The needles of the larch (Larix decidua) *grow in bunches. They fall in autumn.*

Giant sequoia (Sequoiadendron giganteum) *has tiny, scale-like leaves that lie almost flat against the stems.*

CONIFER LEAVES
Most conifers have small, leathery leaves that stay on the tree for a year or more. Not all these leaves are needle-shaped. Many are short and flat, and are known as scales. A few conifers shed their leaves in autumn. These include the larches (*Larix* species) and also the swamp cypress (*Taxodium distichum*).

Find out more

CHANGING CLIMATES P.246
FLOWERING PLANTS P.318
TRANSPORT IN PLANTS P.341
GROWTH AND DEVELOPMENT P.362
TEMPERATE FORESTS P.396
FACT FINDER PP. 420, 422

FLOWERING PLANTS

WE ALL LOVE the beautiful shapes, colours, and scents of flowers. But flowers have not evolved for our pleasure. They have developed as a way of spreading pollen (male cells) to other flowers of their own kind. Flowers receive pollen so that their own ovules (female egg cells) can be fertilized. There are more than 250,000 species of flowering plant on Earth, and these are divided into two main groups: monocotyledons and dicotyledons. Monocotyledons have one cotyledon (a special leaf packed inside the seed), and long adult leaves with parallel veins. Dicotyledons have two cotyledons and adult leaves with a branching network of veins.

WIND POLLINATION
Grasses are pollinated by the wind. Their anthers dangle in the air so that the pollen is blown away. Grasses make up one of the largest families of monocotyledon plants.

Cucumber plant

SEPARATE SEXES
Unlike the poppy flower, which contains both male and female parts, the cucumber plant (*Cucumis sativus*) has separate male and female flowers. Kiwi fruit plants (*Actinidia chinensis*) are either male or female.

TREES AND FLOWERS
A tree is a plant with a single tall, woody stem. Some trees are conifers. Hundreds of others are broadleaved (flowering) plants. Cherry trees belong to the rose family of flowering plants.

Flowering cherry tree *(Prunus serrulata)*

COMMON POPPY

The common poppy (*Papaver rhoeas*) is a typical annual flowering plant. It flowers, sets seed, and dies in a single season. Annual plants grow rapidly, and are quick to make use of any patch of bare ground. Once the seeds are scattered, they remain dormant (inactive) until conditions are right for germination. This can sometimes take several years. Perennial plants live for more than one season. They have well-developed roots, and often store food underground in bulbs or tubers. Some perennials flower just once, but most flower every year.

PARASITIC PLANTS

Some plants get all or part of their food by stealing it from others. The roots of mistletoe (*Viscum album*) penetrate the wood on trees, and take water and mineral salts from the tree. But because mistletoe has green leaves, it can also make its own food from sunlight. The *Rafflesia* plant, the giant flower of which is shown on the opposite page, is completely parasitic.

MANY FLOWERS IN ONE
A daisy (*Bellis perennis*) is not a single flower. The flowerhead is made of many tiny flowers called florets, packed together. It is a composite flower. The disc florets in the middle are yellow and tubular. The ray florets around the edge have a single white petal each.

INSECT POLLINATION

Compared to a poppy, a foxglove (*Digitalis purpurea*) has quite complicated flowers. The petals are joined together to form a tube, and the male and female parts of the flower lie under the tube's roof. This shape has evolved so that one kind of insect, a bumblebee, can pollinate the flower. The anthers and stigma in each flower mature at different times, so a foxglove cannot pollinate itself. When a bumblebee enters the flower, it either collects pollen off the ripe male anther, or brushes pollen from another flower onto the ripe female stigma. When the bee visits another flower, the process is repeated.

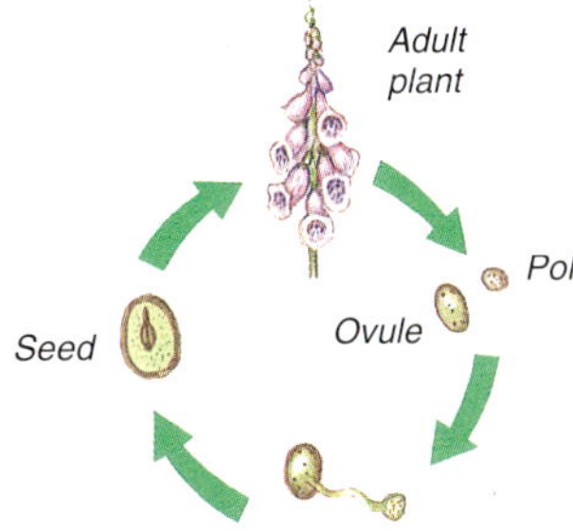

Life cycle of a typical flowering plant

FLORAL GIANT

The parasitic *Rafflesia* plant of Southeast Asia lives on the roots of vines. Its flowers, which can measure as much as 1 m (3 ft) across, are the heaviest in the world. They give off a powerful smell of rotting meat to attract pollinating flies.

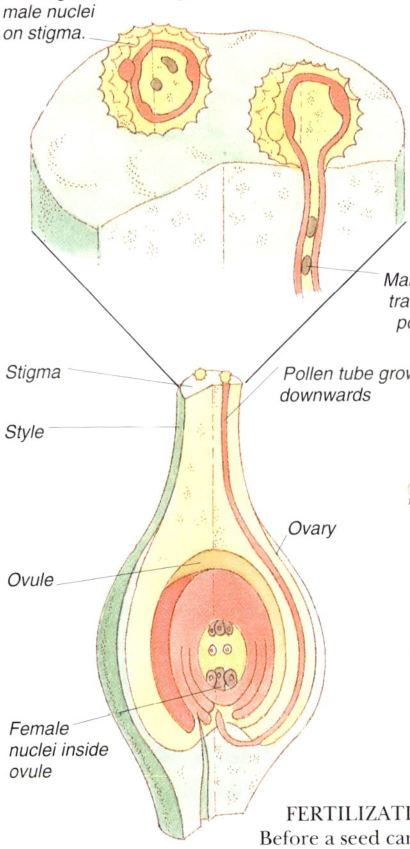

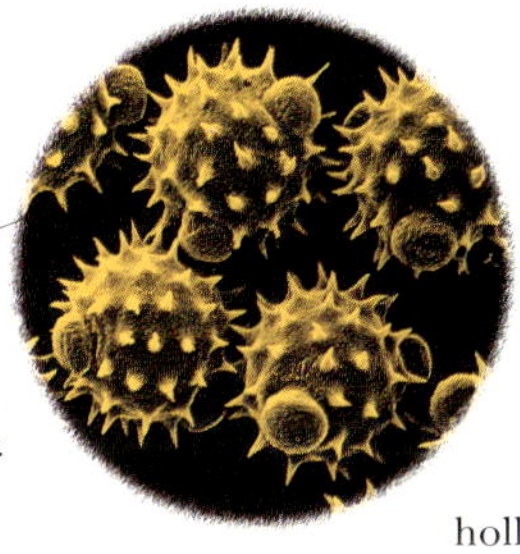

Sharp spines of this Colt's foot (Tussi lago farfara) pollen get caught in insects' fur.

POLLEN

Although pollen grains are microscopic, they are very tough. Their surfaces are covered with a complicated pattern of projections and hollows, which varies according to the species of plant. Pollen grains that are spread by the wind sometimes have tiny "sails" to keep them airborne.

(Tarsipes rostratus)

ANIMAL POLLINATION

The pocket-sized honey possum of western Australia (*Tarsipes rostratus*) lives entirely on nectar and pollen. It feeds with a long, brush-like tongue that reaches deep into flowers. As it feeds, the anthers brush pollen onto its fur, while the stigma collects pollen from other flowers. The flowers of many kinds of tropical tree are pollinated by bats.

SCATTERING SEEDS

Plants cannot move, but they have evolved unusual ways of spreading their seeds far and wide. The seeds of the primrose (*Primula vulgaris*) have special food-bodies called elaiosomes attached to them. Ants eat these food-bodies and "plant" the seeds by discarding them.

Ants carrying away primrose seeds.

FERTILIZATION

Before a seed can be made, nuclei from male and female cells have to join together. When a pollen grain lands on the stigma of a flower of the same species, the grain grows a fine tube that makes its way through the stigma and style until it meets an ovule. Male nuclei from the pollen grain then combine with the female nuclei in the ovule, and fertilization occurs.

Find out more

CELLS P.338
PHOTOSYNTHESIS P.340
TRANSPORT IN PLANTS P.341
GROWTH AND DEVELOPMENT P.362
SEXUAL REPRODUCTION P.367
FACT FINDER PP.420, 422

JELLYFISH, ANEMONES, AND CORALS

JELLYFISH, SEA ANEMONES, AND SPONGES are all invertebrates (without a backbone). Invertebrates make up about 97 per cent of the animal species on Earth. They have evolved a great range of body forms, and many different ways of feeding and reproducing. Many invertebrates live in water. Some spend their adult lives swimming or drifting with the current, while others stay anchored to one spot. Bryozoans (moss-like animals) and sponges filter food from the water. Jellyfish, sea anemones, and corals – which belong to a group of animals called the cnidarians – attack their food with tiny stinging threads. They all have circular bodies without a head or a tail, and a digestive cavity with only one opening.

BRYOZOAN COLONY
Without a microscope, a bryozoan colony looks like a plant. It is actually a collection of thousands of tiny animals. Each one lives in a hard case, and traps food with a ring of tentacles. If disturbed, a bryozoan pulls in its tentacles, and shuts the case.

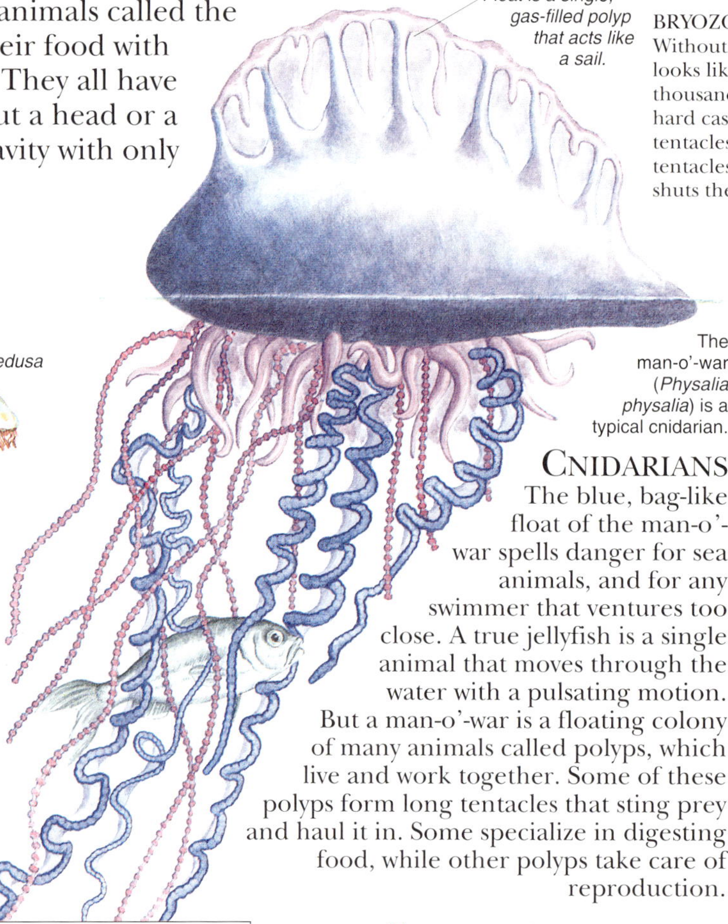

Float is a single, gas-filled polyp that acts like a sail.

The man-o'-war (Physalia physalia) is a typical cnidarian.

The man-o'-war's tentacles reach up to 20 m (65 ft) when they are fully extended. If a tentacle catches a fish, it contracts and pulls the food upwards.

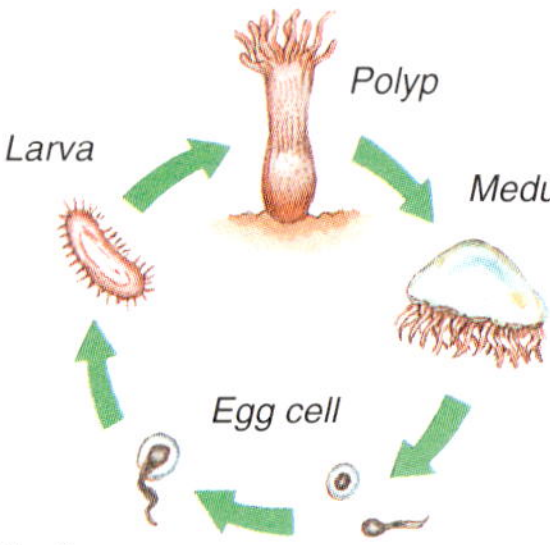

Life cycle of a typical cnidarian

CNIDARIANS

The blue, bag-like float of the man-o'-war spells danger for sea animals, and for any swimmer that ventures too close. A true jellyfish is a single animal that moves through the water with a pulsating motion. But a man-o'-war is a floating colony of many animals called polyps, which live and work together. Some of these polyps form long tentacles that sting prey and haul it in. Some specialize in digesting food, while other polyps take care of reproduction.

SPONGES
Do you realize that some bath sponges were once living animals in the sea? A living sponge is lined with special cells that work like pumps. Water flows in through the holes in the sponge, and out through a vent. Any food in the water is trapped by tiny sieves and then absorbed.

CORALS
Some corals live on their own. Others grow in large colonies and very slowly build up, layer upon layer, to make coral reefs. A coral usually feeds at night. It catches food particles with its tentacles and pulls them into its digestive cavity.

HOW A JELLYFISH STINGS

The tentacles of a jellyfish are covered with special cells that contain tightly coiled stinging threads called nematocysts. If a passing animal brushes one of these cells, the nematocysts explode outwards. Within a fraction of a second, the threads turn inside out and stab the victim with their sharp tips. Most nematocysts inject a poison, but some wrap themselves around the prey to prevent it escaping.

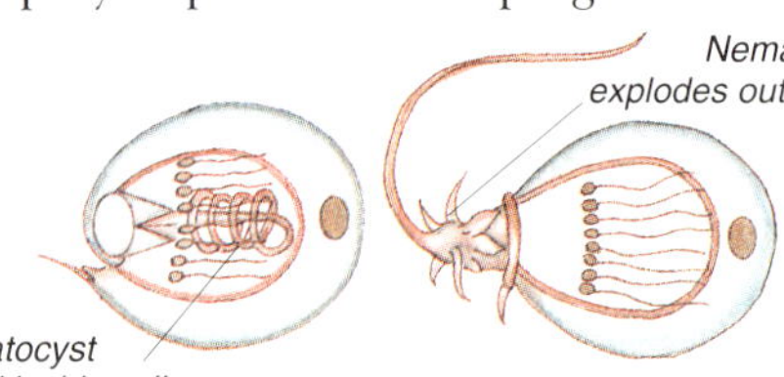

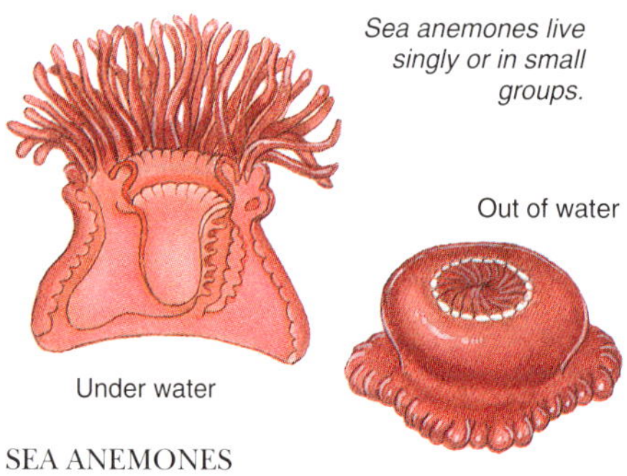

SEA ANEMONES
If you explore a rocky shore at low tide, you may sometimes find small, jelly-like blobs attached to rocks . These are probably sea anemones. A sea anemone grips the rock with a sucker-like disc. When it is under water, it spreads out its ring of tentacles to catch passing animals, which it attacks with nematocysts (stinging threads). As the tide goes out, the anemone withdraws its tentacles to prevent them from drying out.

Find out more

LIVING THINGS P.305
GROWTH AND DEVELOPMENT P.362
ASEXUAL REPRODUCTION P 366
SEXUAL REPRODUCTION P.367
SEASHORES P.385
FACT FINDER P.420

WORMS

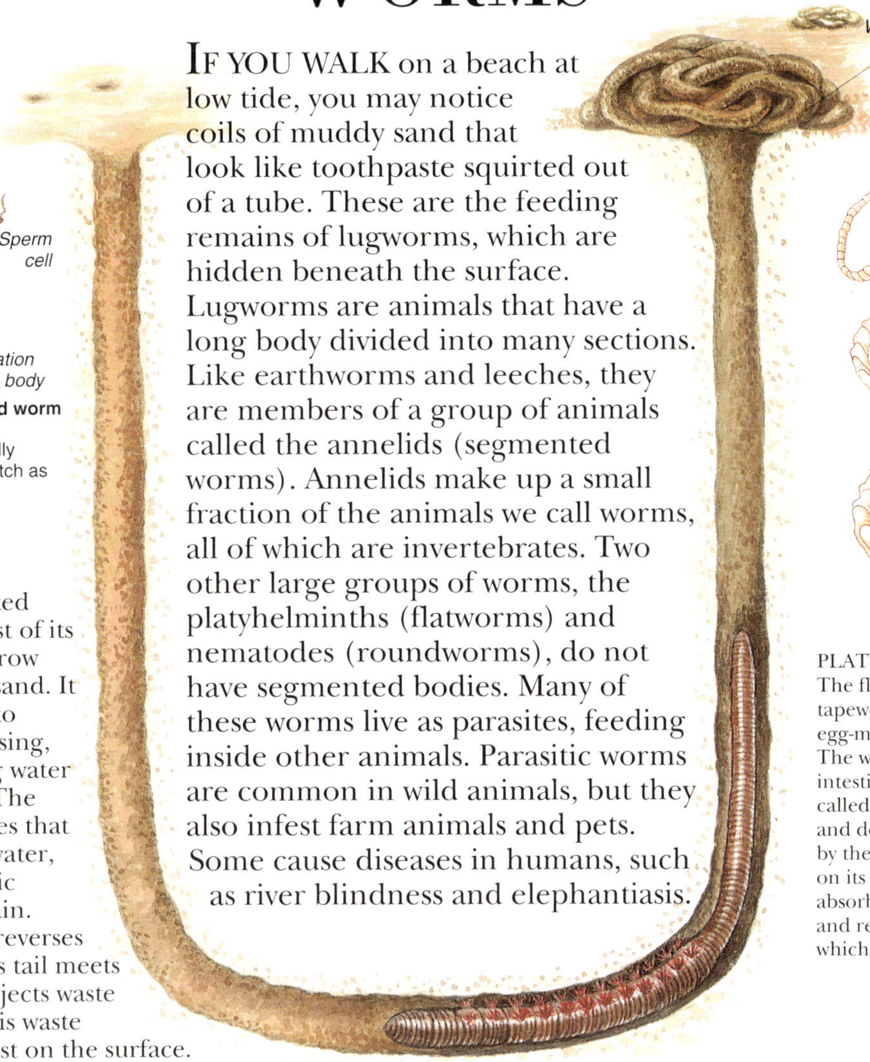

IF YOU WALK on a beach at low tide, you may notice coils of muddy sand that look like toothpaste squirted out of a tube. These are the feeding remains of lugworms, which are hidden beneath the surface. Lugworms are animals that have a long body divided into many sections. Like earthworms and leeches, they are members of a group of animals called the annelids (segmented worms). Annelids make up a small fraction of the animals we call worms, all of which are invertebrates. Two other large groups of worms, the platyhelminths (flatworms) and nematodes (roundworms), do not have segmented bodies. Many of these worms live as parasites, feeding inside other animals. Parasitic worms are common in wild animals, but they also infest farm animals and pets. Some cause diseases in humans, such as river blindness and elephantiasis.

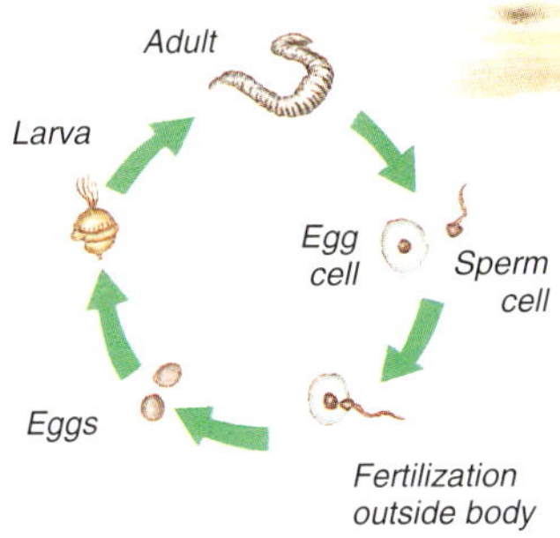

Life cycle of a typical annelid worm

Annelids that live on land usually develop inside the egg, and hatch as fully formed worms.

ANNELIDS

A lugworm (*Arenicola maritima*) is a segmented worm that spends most of its life in a U-shaped burrow that it digs in muddy sand. It lines this with mucus to prevent it from collapsing, and feeds by pumping water through the burrow. The worm swallows particles that are carried in by the water, and digests any organic matter that they contain. From time to time, it reverses up the burrow until its tail meets the surface, where it ejects waste sand and mud. It is this waste matter that forms a cast on the surface.

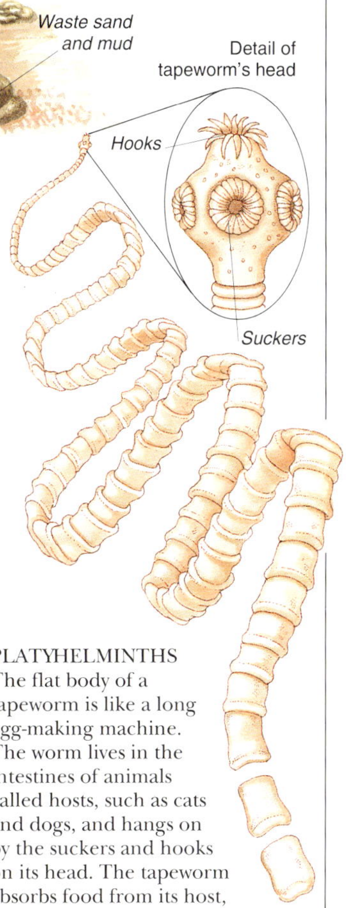

PLATYHELMINTHS

The flat body of a tapeworm is like a long egg-making machine. The worm lives in the intestines of animals called hosts, such as cats and dogs, and hangs on by the suckers and hooks on its head. The tapeworm absorbs food from its host, and releases eggs in packets which break off from its body.

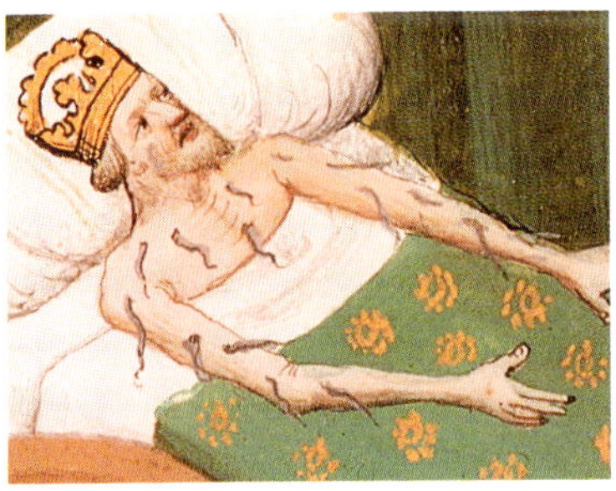

LEECH TREATMENT

A leech has a segmented body with a sucker at either end. Many species of leech feed on blood. When a leech bites, it produces a chemical that stops blood clotting. Leeches were once used by doctors to drain blood from patients.

A leech can rapidly take in three or four times its own weight in blood.

GIANT EARTHWORM

Australia is the home of the giant earthworm (*Megascolides australis*), which can reach a length of over 3 m (10 ft). These worms live in the same way as their smaller relatives – by swallowing soil and digesting the organic matter it contains.

Earthworms help to keep soil fertile. As they burrow, they mix the soil layers and allow air and water to soak in.

SEA MOUSE

The segmented sea mouse (*Aphrodite aculeata*) is a very unwormlike worm. It is about the size of an adult's hand, and has a broad, flat body fringed with bristles. Sea mice burrow through mud and sand on the seabed, eating any small animals they find on the way.

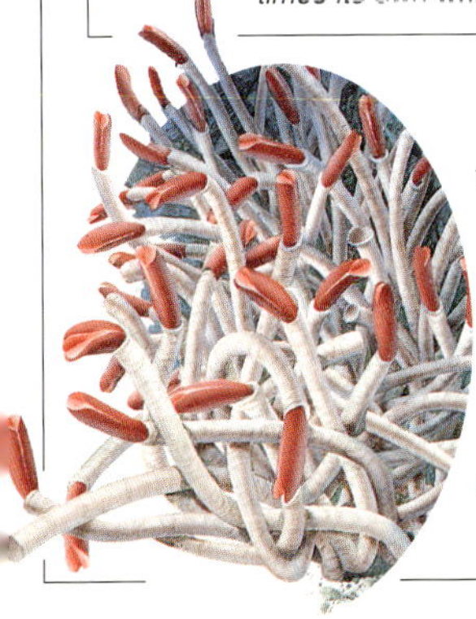

RIFTIA WORMS

Giant riftia worms like these were only seen for the first time in 1977. They live around vents on the seabed, where volcanically heated water gushes out of the Earth's crust. The worms contain bacteria that obtain energy from chemicals in the water.

Human roundworms (Ascaris lumbricoides)

NEMATODES

Roundworms live either as parasites or as independent animals. They are often hidden away, and exist in vast numbers in soil and in plants. Biologists often say that if all the trees in a forest were taken away, but the roundworms from the trees left behind, you would still be able to see the outline of the forest.

Find out more

SKELETONS P.352
NERVES P.360
GROWTH AND DEVELOPMENT P.363
SEXUAL REPRODUCTION P.367
OCEANS P.386
FACT FINDER P.420

ARTHROPODS

THE LARGEST GROUP of invertebrates is made up of arthropods – animals that have a segmented body and an exoskeleton (hard case on the outside). This case has special hinges that bend so that its owner can move. As an arthropod grows, it moults (sheds its case) from time to time so that its body can expand. Well over a million species of arthropods are known to biologists, making this the largest group of animal species on Earth. Of these species, nearly 90 per cent are insects. The remainder of arthropods are either arachnids (mainly spiders), crustaceans – such as crabs and lobsters – or diplopoda (millipedes) and chilopoda (centipedes).

Giant spider crabs live on the seabed. Their body cases are reinforced with calcium, making them hard and very strong.

Arthropods do not have internal skeletons.

CRUSTACEANS

Most crustaceans live in the sea. Sea-living crustaceans can grow bigger than arthropods that live on land because their big body cases are supported by the water. The largest crustaceans of all are spider crabs (*Macrocheira kaempferi*), which can measure up to 3.5 m (11 ft) with their legs stretched out. But not all crustaceans are as big as this. The water fleas that live in fresh water are also crustaceans, but they are about the size of a full-stop. A few crustaceans, including woodlice, live on land and breathe air, but they usually need damp conditions.

Life cycle of a typical crustacean

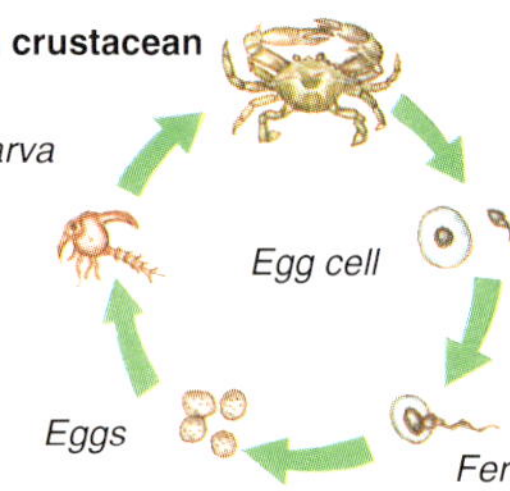

The centipede's first pair of legs are modified to act as a pair of poisonous fangs.

DIPLOPODA AND CHILOPODA

From a distance, centipedes and millipedes look quite similar. But if you look more closely, it is easy to tell them apart. A centipede has just one pair of legs on each body segment, while a millipede has two. Centipedes are hunters. They paralyse their prey with poisonous fangs. Millipedes live on decaying plants. Both animals prefer dark, moist areas.

A millipede's body is made up of many ring-shaped segments. Each segment has two pairs of legs.

SCORPIONS

Some arachnids look after their young until they can fend for themselves. A female scorpion gives birth to fully formed young. The tiny scorpions climb onto their mother's back, where they are protected by the poisonous sting in her tail. After they have shed their skin for the first time, the young scorpions climb down from their perch.

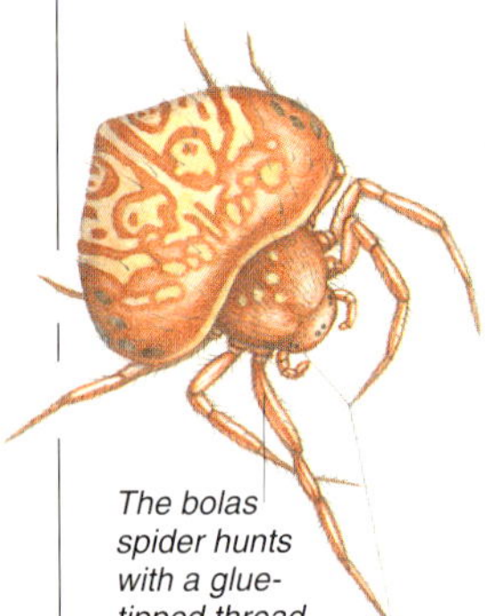

The bolas spider hunts with a glue-tipped thread instead of a web.

ARACHNIDS

Spiders, scorpions, ticks, and mites make up a group of arthropods called the arachnids. Nearly all arachnids live on land, and most of them are hunters. Bolas spiders hunt by whirling a silk thread tipped with glue around in the air. If the glue sticks to a passing insect, the spider pulls it in.

SPINNING A WEB

A spider builds its web out of silk, which is rich in protein. The silk is formed by special glands in the spider's abdomen, and is squeezed out through tiny nozzles called spinnerets. The liquid silk solidifies when it meets the air. An orb (round) web like this one can take up to an hour to make.

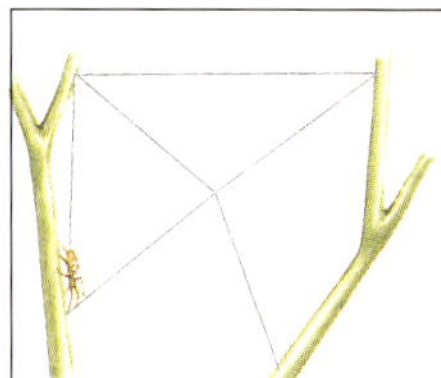

A spider begins its web by stretching strands of silk between solid supports. It climbs along the silk using the hooks and bristles on its feet.

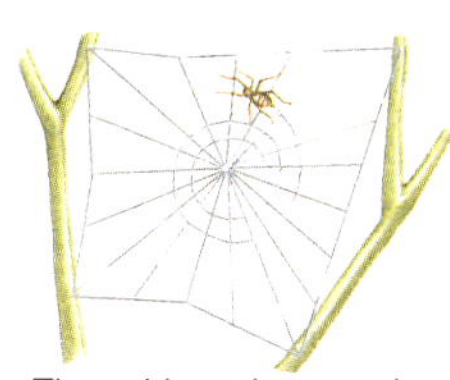

The spider spins round and round in a spiral until the web is finished. The web is covered with blobs of glue that trap insects.

INSECTS

Insects have been very successful on land, mainly because they have evolved the ability to fly. Insects with wings can travel larger distances than wingless insects, and so can find more food. A wasp is a typical flying insect. Its body is divided into three sections – the head, thorax, and abdomen. It also has two pairs of wings. Like beetles and butterflies, a wasp undergoes a complete metamorphosis (change in shape). Young wasps are raised in a nest by adults, but the young of most insects must fend for themselves. Insect parents and young often live in different habitats. An adult dragonfly lives in air, but a young dragonfly lives in water. Some insects spend their whole life in water.

Each nest contains a single queen wasp who lays eggs. The other wasps are her offspring. They collect food and look after the eggs and young.

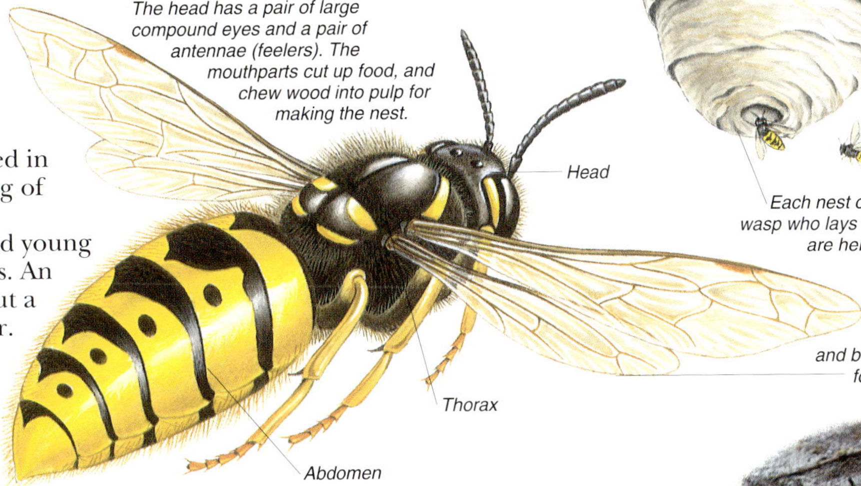

The head has a pair of large compound eyes and a pair of antennae (feelers). The mouthparts cut up food, and chew wood into pulp for making the nest.

Hind wings of wasps and bees are attached to the forewings by tiny hooks.

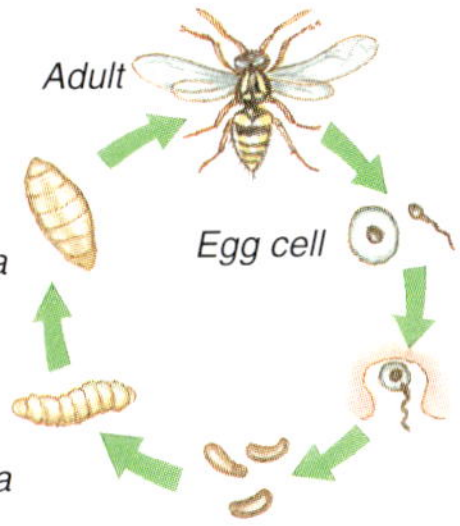

Life cycle of a typical insect

This life cycle is typical of insects that undergo complete metamorphosis.

WINGLESS INSECTS

Despite its name, the silverfish is not a fish at all, but a small, wingless insect. There are about 300 species of silverfish. Like other wingless insects, silverfish feed mainly on dead plants. They sometimes live indoors, where they eat leftover food.

INSECTICIDES

Some insects are very useful because they pollinate flowering plants. But others are voracious plant eaters that cause tremendous damage to crops. Farmers often spray fields with insecticides to prevent insect damage. Unfortunately, these chemicals often kill helpful insects as well as the harmful ones.

BOMBARDIER BEETLE

The insect world is full of animals that have unusual ways of repelling attackers. If a bombardier beetle is threatened, it tucks up its abdomen and mixes together a brew of special chemicals. These react with each other and explode out of the beetle, giving the attacker a hot, poisonous shower.

Wings of praying mantis look like leaves.

Legs look like stems

Sharp spines on the legs grip the trapped insect.

MANTIS ATTACK

A praying mantis relies on stealth and camouflage. A hunting mantis flutters onto a plant and folds up its wings. It then waits. If another insect comes within striking range, the mantis stabs it with its front legs. The legs have sharp spines that grip the insect so that it cannot escape the jaws of its predator.

JEAN-HENRI FABRE

Fabre (1823-1915) was a French entomologist (scientist who studies insects). He researched insect life extensively, and described his work in a series of books. Fabre's observations, and his gift for writing and painting, helped to create great interest in the insect world.

Find out more

VISION P.204
FLOWERING PLANTS P.318
BLOOD P.348
GROWTH AND DEVELOPMENT P.362
SKELETONS P.352
MOVEMENT P.356
SEXUAL REPRODUCTION P.367
FACT FINDER PP.420,422

MOLLUSCS

MOLLUSCS MAKE UP the second-largest group of invertebrates. There are more than 90,000 species of mollusc, most of which live in water, although some live on land and breathe air. All molluscs have a soft body, which is often protected by a hard shell. There are three main groups of molluscs. Gastropods, which include limpets, snails, and whelks, usually have a coiled or pyramid-shaped shell. Bivalves, such as clams and mussels, have a shell that is made of two parts joined by a hinge. Slugs are gastropod molluscs, but they usually do not have shells. The third group, cephalopods, which includes octopuses and squids, have a small shell that is hidden inside their bodies.

MATING SLUGS
These two slugs are mating as they hang from a thread of mucus. Each slug is hermaphrodite (both male and female). When slugs mate, they exchange sperm through special organs, and each slug then lays eggs. Being hermaphrodite is not unusual in the mollusc world. Some molluscs even start life as one sex, and then change to another.

Great slug (*Limax maximus*)

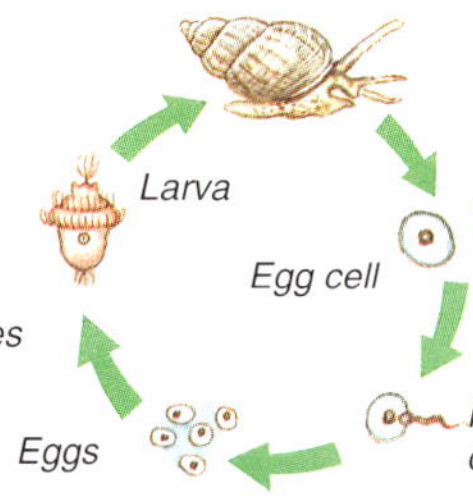

Life cycle of a typical mollusc

Land snails have internal fertilization. Their young develop inside the egg and hatch as miniature snails.

GASTROPODS

The common whelk (*Buccinium undatum*) is a typical gastropod ("stomach-foot") mollusc. It has a large, muscular foot and a shell that coils in a clockwise direction. Only a few gastropod shells coil in the other direction. The whelk's shell is made by a special body layer called the mantle. The whelk lives underwater, and breathes using gills. The siphon on top of its head funnels water into the chamber that contains the gills.

KILLER CONE
Cone shells are gastropods that attack their prey with a deadly poison. If an animal comes within range, the cone flicks out its proboscis (tubular mouthpart). This stabs the victim like a harpoon, and injects a paralysing poison. The poison of some cones is powerful enough to kill humans.

Common octopus (*Octopus vulgaris*)

INTELLIGENT MOLLUSC
Octopuses have good eyesight and large brains. They are probably the most intelligent of all invertebrate animals. They can remember shapes and colours, and are able to work out quickly how to reach food. Like squids, octopuses can move fast by squirting a jet of water backwards through a funnel.

Common mussel (*Mytilus edulis*)

BIVALVES

Mussels spend most of their lives anchored to rocks by very tough byssus threads. Like most bivalves, they pump water through their gills and feed on the small food particles that become trapped as the water flows past. Some bivalves can burrow and move about. A few – like the scallop – can even swim.

CEPHALOPODS

Giant squids are the largest cephalopod molluscs. They are also the largest invertebrate animals. Giant squids live in the depths of the sea, where they catch their prey with sucker-covered tentacles. There are many stories about giant squids, but little is really known about them. The largest specimens found measure over 15 m (50 ft).

Find out more

SKELETONS P.352
MOVEMENT P.356
BRAINS P.361
GROWTH AND DEVELOPMENT P.362
SEXUAL REPRODUCTION P.367
FACT FINDER P.420

STARFISH AND SEA SQUIRTS

STARFISH AND THEIR RELATIVES, which include sea urchins and sea cucumbers, make up a group of invertebrate creatures called echinoderms ("spiny skins"). Echinoderms are easy to recognize because their bodies are built around the number five. A starfish, for example, usually has five arms. It has five sets of reproductive organs, and a digestive system that is divided into five branches. All echinoderms have a skeleton made of chalky plates. Sea squirts belong to a different group of animals, the tunicates. They have soft, bag-like bodies and tadpole-shaped larvae.

TUBE FEET
The underside of a starfish's arms carry two rows of water-filled tube feet connected by a system of internal canals. Each tube foot ends in a sucker, and can be moved independently. The starfish uses its tube feet to move and to hold its prey.

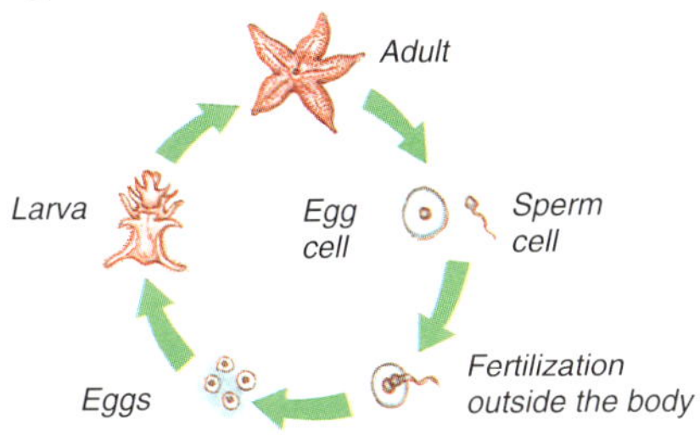

Life cycle of a typical echinoderm

ECHINODERMS

Like all echinoderms, starfish have a skeleton made of chalky plates covered by a thin layer of cells. The plates have small bumps and spines, and also tiny pincers that stop small animals settling on the starfish's body. The plates are hinged to allow the starfish to bend. A starfish's mouth is on the underside of its body. When it feeds, the starfish pushes its stomach out through its mouth, turning it inside out.

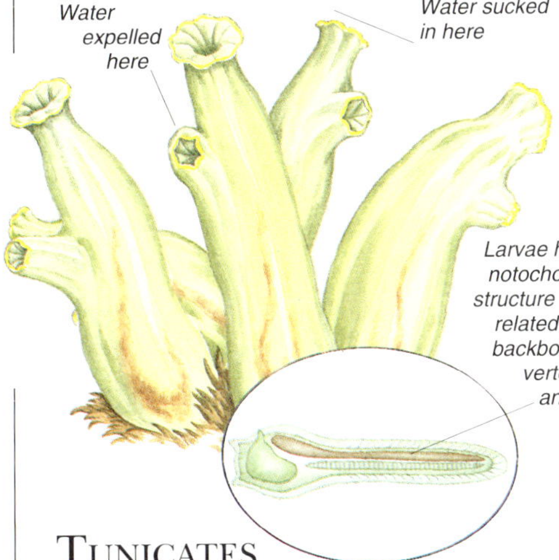

Shallow water starfish

STARFISH SHAPES
There are about 2,000 species of ordinary starfish. Like all echinoderms, they live only in sea water. The starfish of shores and shallow water feed mainly on living animals. They use their tube feet to prise open the shells of bivalve molluscs, and feed by pushing their stomachs between the shell halves. Brittlestars and featherstars live in deeper water. They use their long tube feet to collect tiny particles of food, which they then push to their central mouth.

Brittlestar

Crown-of-thorns starfish

Featherstar

Cushion star

TUNICATES

Adult sea squirts are small animals that filter food from sea water. They live either singly or in groups, usually attached to rocks. Their larvae are free-swimming and look quite different. They are shaped like tadpoles.

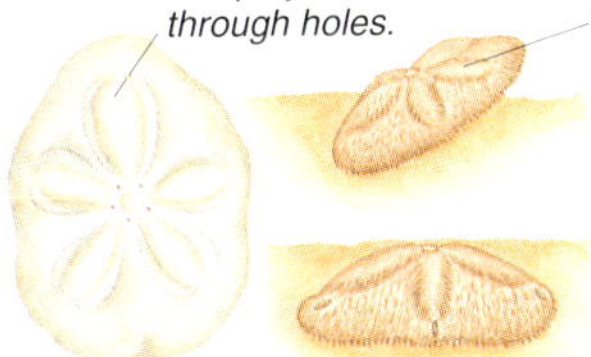

SAND DOLLARS
A sand dollar is a sea urchin that has short spines and a very flattened test, making it look like a biscuit or a large coin. When the spines have rubbed off after death, you can see an intricate pattern of holes where the tube-feet once poked out.

SEA URCHINS
Sea urchins look very different from starfish, but underneath their spines they also have a body divided into five similar parts. A sea urchin has a rounded test (skeleton), with a mouth on the underside. It feeds by creeping over rocks, scraping off small plants and animals with its five teeth.

Find out more

GROWTH AND DEVELOPMENT P.362
SEXUAL REPRODUCTION P.367
SEASHORES P.385
OCEANS P.386
FACT FINDER P.420

FISH

STRANGE ARMOURED ANIMALS called ostracoderms swam in the world's seas more than 400 million years ago. They did not have jaws or fins, but they did have backbones, making them the first vertebrates (animals with a backbone) on Earth. Today, their aquatic descendants – fish – live throughout the world's seas, lakes and rivers. Fish are exothermic (cold-blooded)– their body temperature changes according to their surroundings. The colder the surroundings, the less active they are. There are more than 21,000 species of fish. Most have jaws. Their bodies are streamlined and are usually covered with scales. Fish absorb dissolved oxygen from water through gills.

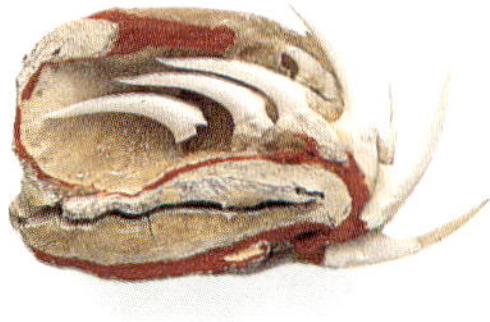

SHARK'S TEETH
A shark's teeth are larger, sharper versions of the scales that cover its body. The teeth grow on a non-stop production line that starts at the back of the jaw. Each tooth gradually swings forwards until it reaches the front of the mouth. If it breaks off, it is soon replaced by the tooth behind it.

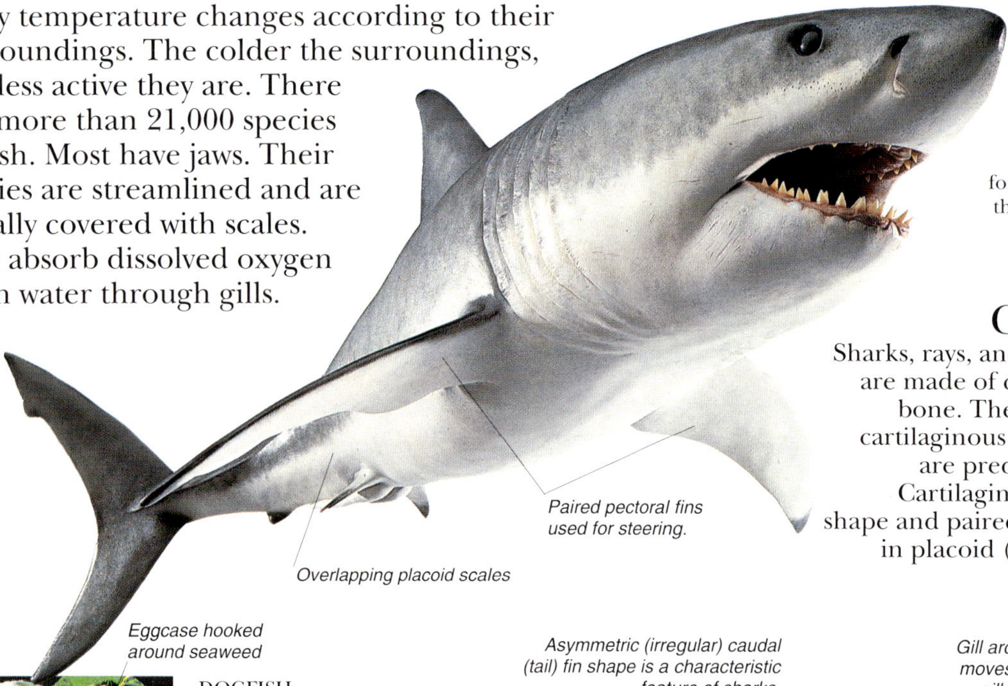

CARTILAGINOUS FISH

Sharks, rays, and skates have skeletons that are made of cartilage (gristle) instead of bone. There are about 700 species of cartilaginous fish, and nearly all of them are predators that live in salt water. Cartilaginous fish have a streamlined shape and paired fins. Their skin is covered in placoid (tooth-like) scales that gives them a rough texture.

DOGFISH
Dogfish are small sharks that live in shallow water. The male mates with the female, fertilizing her eggs while they are inside her body. The female then lays her eggs in leathery cases that hook around seaweed. The parent dogfish do not guard the eggs.

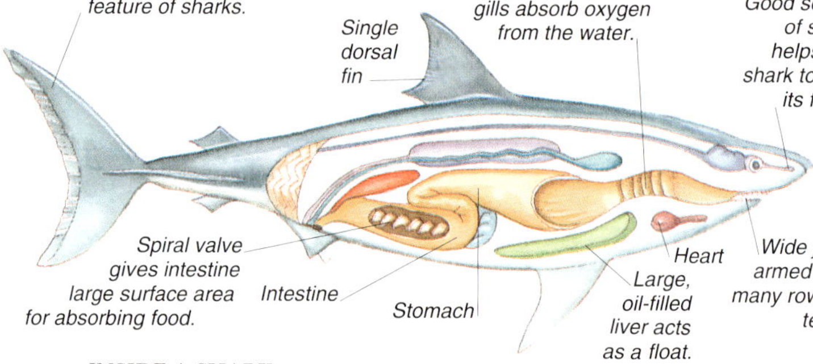

INSIDE A SHARK
Most of a shark's body is made up of the muscles that it uses to swim. As in all vertebrates, these are arranged in blocks called myotomes. Part of a shark's intestine is coiled into a spiral, which gives the short intestine a large surface area for absorbing food. The shark's large liver helps to keep it afloat.

JAWLESS FISH

This group, which includes lampreys and hagfish, has some features in common with the very first fish. They do not have jaws or paired fins, and their gills have openings like portholes, rather than slits. There are only about 70 species of jawless fish. Adult lampreys live parasitically on other fish, while young lampreys filter particles of food from water.

An adult lamprey has a mouth that is ringed with hooks. It clamps itself to another fish and sucks its blood.

FISH SPEEDS

Generally, the more streamlined a fish is, the faster it swims. Most fish swim faster than humans, who have an average speed of 6 km/h (4 mph) over a short distance.

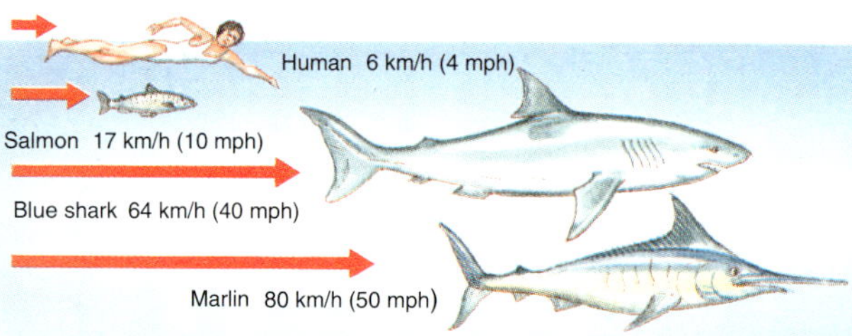

BONY FISH

This trout, and all the other fish shown on this page, belong to a group called the bony fish – the largest of the three groups of fish. These fish have bony skeletons, and a special gas-filled bag, called a swim bladder, which works like an inbuilt float. Their bodies are usually covered with cycloid (slippery, flat) scales, and their gills are tucked away behind a flap called an operculum. During the last 250 million years, bony fish have evolved an amazing variety of shapes and sizes.

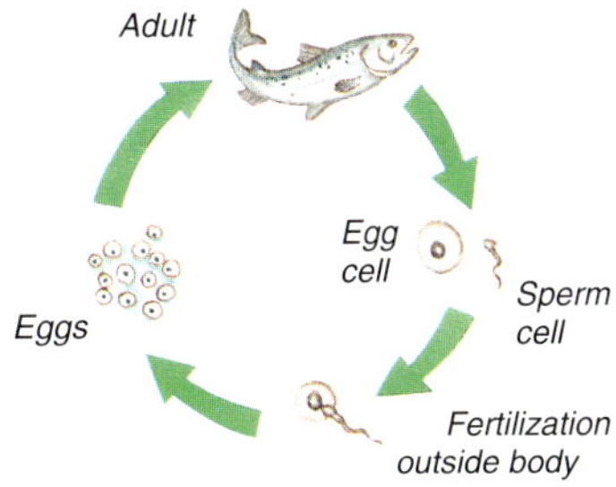

Life cycle of a typical bony fish

Most cartilaginious fish have internal fertilization. They lay eggs, or give birth to live young.

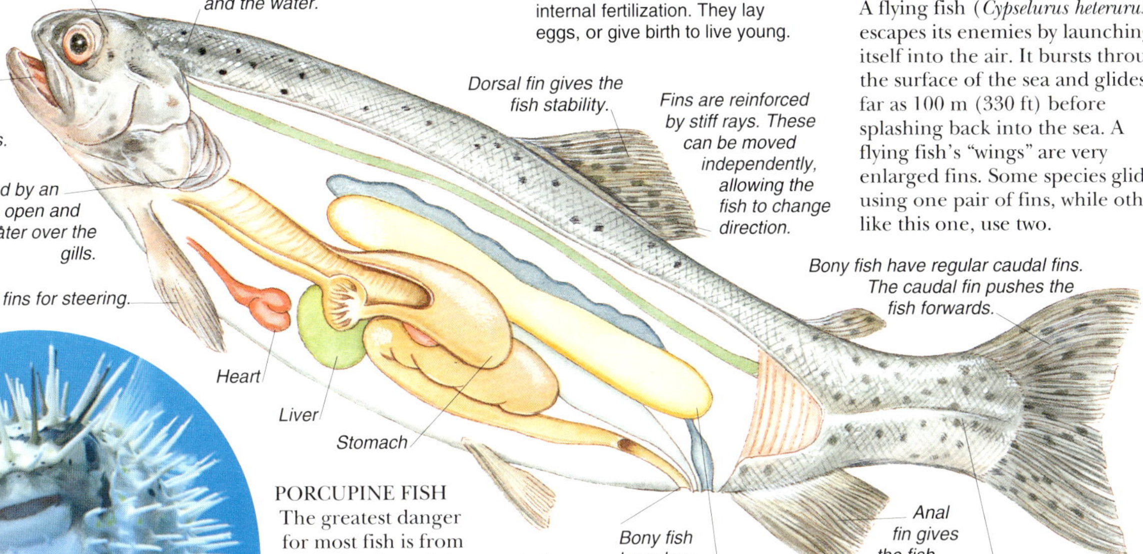

FISH THAT FLY

A flying fish (*Cypselurus heterurus*) escapes its enemies by launching itself into the air. It bursts through the surface of the sea and glides as far as 100 m (330 ft) before splashing back into the sea. A flying fish's "wings" are very enlarged fins. Some species glide using one pair of fins, while others, like this one, use two.

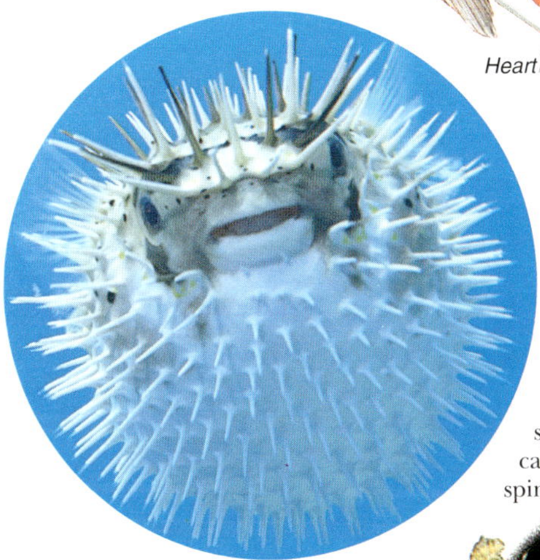

PORCUPINE FISH

The greatest danger for most fish is from other predator fish around them. When threatened, the porcupine fish (*Diodon hystrix*) protects itself by gulping water. This makes it swell up like a balloon, and its spines stand up on end. Although it can hardly swim when it is inflated, its spines make it almost impossible to attack.

SEAHORSES

Many bony fish lay vast numbers of eggs, but take no part in looking after their young. Seahorses are different. The female lays a small number of eggs in a special pouch on the male's abdomen. The male seahorse looks after the eggs until they hatch, and continues to look after the young seahorses. Although seahorses lay fewer eggs, each one has a better chance of survival.

White's seahorse (*Hippocampus whitei*)

DEEP-SEA FISH

There is no light or plant life at the bottom of the sea. Everything that lives here has to feed either on "leftovers" that fall from above, or on other animals. The batfishes are among the strangest fish of the seabed. They eat invertebrates and small fish, and shuffle fowards using their fins.

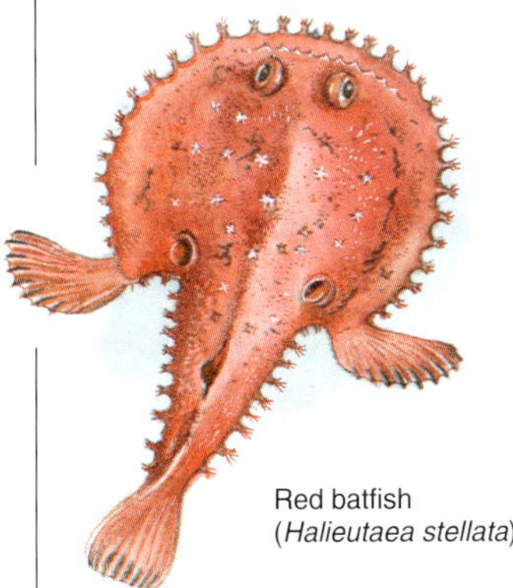

Red batfish (*Halieutaea stellata*)

Eels have paired pectoral fins, but no pelvic fins.

EELS

Some eels look like snakes, but their fins and gills show that they are fish. The green moray (*Gymnothorax prasinus*) is a typical eel. It lurks in rocky hideouts and attacks passing animals with its sharp teeth. Eels start life as tiny larvae that look quite different from adults. It can take several years for a larva to develop into an adult.

Find out more

BREATHING P.347
CIRCULATION P.349
INTERNAL ENVIRONMENT P.350
SKIN P.354
MOVEMENT P.356
SENSES P.358
FACT FINDER PP.420, 422

AMPHIBIANS

AMPHIBIANS HAVE A SPECIAL PLACE in the evolution of life on Earth. Their ancestors were the first vertebrates to emerge from water and spend some of their time on land. Most of today's 4,000 species of amphibian still divide their time between water and land, but in different ways. A few amphibians, such as the axolotl, spend nearly all their lives in water, but most spend their adult lives on land and return to water only to breed. Amphibians do not usually have scales, and their skin is generally loose-fitting and moist. All amphibians are exothermic (cold-blooded) and are divided into three groups: the anurans (frogs and toads), the urodeles (newts and salamanders), and a small third group without legs, the caecilians, or apoda.

FLYING FROGS
The flying frog (*Rhacophorus nigropalmatus*) hunts for small animals on trees in southeast Asia. To move from one tree to another, it launches itself into the air. The frog spreads out its webbed feet – which work like small parachutes – and angles them to steer as it glides.

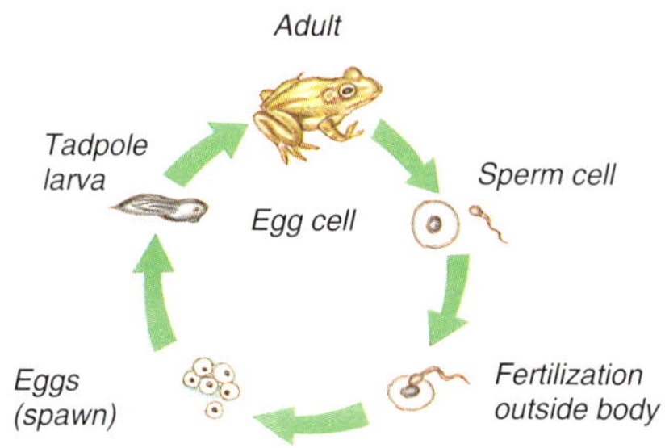

Life cycle of a typical amphibian

ANURANS

Amphibians in this group have short bodies, strong legs, and no tails. This South African bullfrog (*Pyxicephalus adspersus*) is a powerful predator. It feeds on small mammals and reptiles, and also on smaller frogs. Like all frogs, it has a thin skin that has to be kept moist. Toads usually have drier skins, and are usually covered with warts. On land, frogs usually move by hopping, while toads often walk. Frogs and toads both have simple, internal lungs.

WATER-HOLDING FROG
Some frogs and toads survive drought by burrowing underground and sealing themselves in a waterproof membrane. The Australian water-holding frog (*Cyclorana* species) spends most of its adult life underground. As soon as it rains, the frog breaks out of the membrane and digs its way to the surface.

POISON-ARROW FROGS
The thumb-sized poison-arrow frog (*Phyllobates terribilis*) that lives in the forests of Central and South America is one of the most dangerous of all amphibians. The frog's bright colours warn other animals that its skin produces a deadly poison. Forest Indians use this to make poison-tipped arrows that kill other animals.

EARLIEST AMPHIBIAN

The oldest amphibian fossils that have been discovered belong to a creature called *Ichthyostega*, which lived about 375 million years ago. This animal was about 1 m (3 ft) long. It had a streamlined, fish-like body, but strong legs that supported its weight on land.

LOOKING AFTER EGGS
Most frogs and toads lay hundreds or thousands of eggs, and then abandon them. Other species lay fewer eggs, but look after them more carefully. The male midwife toad (*Alytes obstetricans*) wraps the female's eggs around his legs. When the tadpoles are ready to hatch, he carries the eggs to water.

Urodeles

These amphibians have longer bodies and smaller legs than anurans. Some have flattened tails that they use for swimming. The fire salamander (*Salamandra salamandra*) has bright colours for the same reason as the poison-arrow frog – to warn that its skin is poisonous. Newts and salamanders are found mainly in the Northern Hemisphere, and they live in water or in damp places, such as the woodland floor. Fire salamanders mate on land. The eggs develop and hatch inside the mother's body.

Fire salamander's skin secretes a toxic chemical.

Salamanders have small toes, and their feet are not webbed.

Unlike frogs and toads, newts and salamanders do not lose their tails as they grow up.

1. The smooth newt's underwater dance begins when the male approaches the female and touches her side-on. He is able to smell "scent" chemicals that she releases into the water.

2. The male then swims in front of the female, and settles at right angles so that he is blocking her way. The male waves his tail, pumping his scent towards the female.

3. After a series of moves, the male settles in front of the female. When the female touches his tail, he deposits his sperm packet. The female drops down onto it so that the sperm are taken into her body.

Female

Male

COURTSHIP DANCE
When newts or salamanders mate, the male deposits a packet of sperm and the female picks it up. In the case of the fire salamander, the male carries the female and then lowers her onto his sperm packet so that the sperm are taken up into her body. The smooth newt (*Triturus vulgaris*), shown here, mates underwater. The male dances in front of his partner before mating occurs.

Olm belongs to the urodeles group.

Caecilians

Caecilians are aquatic or burrowing animals that live in the tropics. They have no legs, and their cylindrical shape makes them look more like worms or small, rubbery snakes than amphibians. But some caecilians lay eggs that develop into tadpoles with gills, linking them directly to salamanders and other amphibians.

Most caecilians have a covering of keratin plates.

Although caecilians have eyes, they are nearly blind.

AXOLOTL

The axolotl (*Ambystoma mexicanum*) is sometimes called the "Peter Pan" of the amphibian world because it never grows up. Axolotls are salamanders that come from one particular lake in Mexico. Like many salamanders, they begin life as tadpoles with feathery gills. But instead of losing their gills and taking up life on land, axolotls usually stay in water, and breed without changing shape.

LIFE IN THE DARK
The deep limestone caves of southern Europe are home to the olm (*Proteus anguinus*). This aquatic relative of salamanders has a pencil-thin body with tiny legs, and is almost completely blind. Olms live in underground pools and rivers, where they feed on small water animals. A similar cave-dwelling salamander lives in the caves of southern Texas, United States.

Find out more

Circulation p.349
Internal environment p.350
Skin p.354
Muscles p.355
Brains p.361
Sexual reproduction p.367
Fact Finder pp.420, 422

REPTILES

THERE ARE ABOUT 6,500 SPECIES of reptile alive today. Further back in time, there were many more. For about 200 million years, prehistoric reptiles dominated life on Earth, and they included the largest plant eaters and predators ever to live on land – the dinosaurs. Reptiles were the first vertebrates to become properly adapted to life on land. They do not need moist conditions in which to live. Their dry, scaly skin stops them from losing too much body water and their eggs, which they lay on land, have thick, leathery shells that stop them drying out. Because reptiles are exothermic (cold-blooded), they usually live in warm parts of the world where the Sun warms their bodies and makes them active.

The cobra's hollow fangs are positioned at the front of its mouth. It can squirt venom through the air towards an attacker.

Flexible ligaments and joints allow the two parts of the lower jaw to move apart during swallowing.

When threatened, the cobra spreads out the ribs behind its head.

Snakes sometimes have over 400 pairs of ribs, but usually just one working lung. A snake's kidneys lie one behind the other so that they fit into the narrow body.

Small, overlapping scales

Like all reptiles, the boa is exothermic. When cold, it basks in the sun. If it gets too hot, it retreats into the shade.

BOA CONSTRICTOR
A boa constrictor (*Constrictor constrictor*) kills its prey by suffocating it. The snake coils its body around the victim, preventing it from breathing. The snake waits until its prey is completely dead before swallowing it head-first. Boas produce eggs, but the mother snake keeps them in her body until they are ready to hatch.

SQUAMATES

Today's reptiles are split into three major groups. By far the largest group is the squamates (snakes and lizards). Although snakes look very different from lizards, they probably evolved from lizard-like ancestors by gradually losing their legs. The Indian cobra (*Naja naja*) is a typical front-fanged snake. It kills its prey by injecting a poison, and swallows its food whole. Cobras lay about 20 leathery eggs, and the female guards the eggs until they hatch.

GIANT LIZARDS
The Komodo dragon (*Varanus komodensis*) is the world's largest lizard. An adult can measure 3 m (nearly 10 ft) from head to tail, and can weighmore than a person. Komodo dragons live on islands in Indonesia, and feed on animals as large as deer.

SHEDDING SKIN

Lizards and snakes shed the outermost layer of their skin from time to time so that they can grow. This process often takes several days to complete. The skin starts to split around the head, and then begins to peel away along the rest of the body. Snakes often shed their skin in a single piece.

This slow worm (Anguis fragilis) is shedding its skin in very large pieces.

DIVING LIZARD
The Galapagos Islands in the eastern Pacific are the home of the marine iguana (*Amblyrhynchus cristatus*), the only lizard that feeds in the sea. When a marine iguana dives, its heartbeat slows down. This helps it to save oxygen, and also prevents too much of the iguana's blood being chilled by the cold water outside.

Marine iguana feeds on algae growing on submerged rocks.

Geckos have large eyes, like many nocturnal hunters.

CLIMBING LIZARDS
Geckos are nocturnal lizards that hunt small insects. They can run up walls, and can even walk upside-down on ceilings. Geckos are able to do this because they have special pads on their toes. These are covered with tiny bristles that hook into small cracks on the surface they are climbing.

CROCODILIANS

Crocodiles, together with their relatives the alligators, caimans, and gavials, belong to a group of reptiles called the crocodilians. Crocodiles look like giant lizards, but the arrangement of bones in their skulls shows that they are more closely related to dinosaurs than to any living reptile. There are about 21 species of crocodilian, and all live partly in water. The largest species, the estuarine or saltwater crocodile (*Crocodylus porosus*), can reach a length of more than 6 m (nearly 20 ft), making it the biggest reptile in the world.

Life cycle of a typical reptile

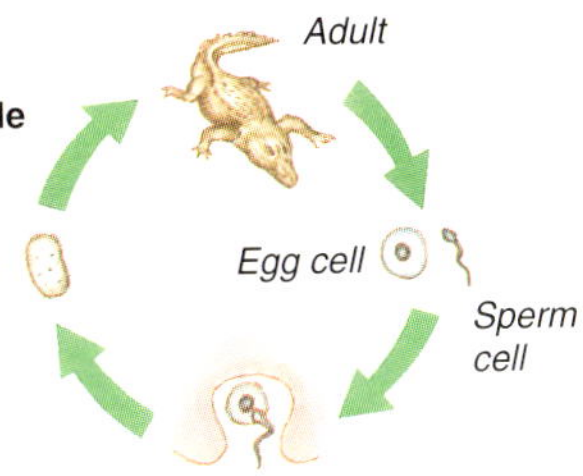

The eggs of some reptiles develop inside the body. The young are born after hatching.

REPTILE SKULLS

The estuarine crocodile's skull is broad, and its jaw muscles are extremely powerful. It feeds on large animals, dragging its prey underwater and tearing off pieces, which it swallows whole. The smaller gavial (*Gavialis gangeticus*), which lives in rivers in the Indian subcontinent, eats fish. Its skull has very narrow jaws, and it catches its food by snapping like a bird.

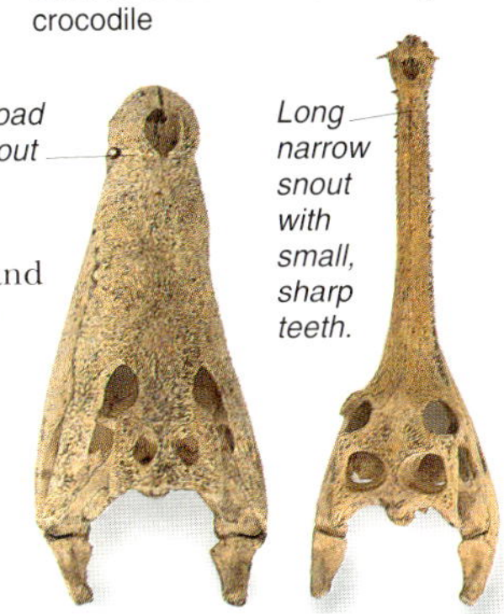

TUATARA

Tuataras are the only living descendants of the sphenodonts – a group of reptiles that were common millions of years ago. Unlike other reptiles, tuataras can remain active in quite low temperatures. Wild tuataras (*Sphenodon punctatus*) live under special protection on small islands off New Zealand.

A fully grown tuatara is about 60 cm (2 ft) long. Tuataras live in burrows, and feed on insects, eggs, frogs, and young seabirds.

CHELONIANS

Tortoises, turtles, and terrapins make up a group of reptiles called chelonians. These animals usually have a bony shell covered in scales made of horn. Chelonians feed on both plants and small animals, and have horn-covered jaws instead of teeth. This Galapagos tortoise (*Geochelone elephantopus*) is a giant species that can weigh as much as three people.

RULING REPTILES

Reptiles were once the most successful vertebrates on land. Dinosaurs ranged from chicken-sized animals to the giant herbivore *Brachiosaurus*. The dinosaurs, together with many other forms of life, died out during a mass extinction. Some scientists think this was caused by the impact of a giant meteorite.

This dinosaur is called *Deinonychus*

Find out more

BREATHING P.347
INTERNAL ENVIRONMENT P.350
SKELETONS P.352
MOVEMENT P.356
SENSES P.358
SEXUAL REPRODUCTION P.367
FACT FINDER PP.420,422

PRIMATES

WE BELONG to a group of mammals called the primates. Primate means "the first", although there is really no top place in the evolution of living things. The primates are divided into two groups: the anthropoids (humans, apes, and monkeys) and the prosimians (which include lemurs, bushbabies, and aye-ayes). Humans are all members of one species, *Homo sapiens*. We live on the ground and walk on two legs, but most primates live in trees, and use all four legs. Primates have forward-pointing eyes, which help in judging distances, and flexible fingers and toes that can grip branches. Anthropoids have large brains and are highly intelligent.

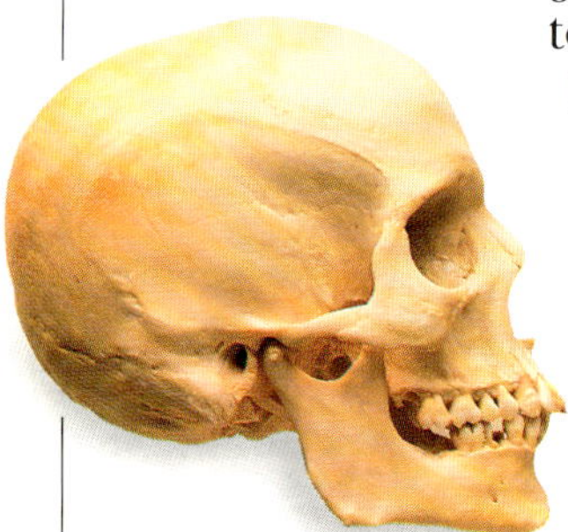

Compared to an ape's skull, a human skull has a very large brain-case, short jaws, and small teeth.

ORANG-UTAN

Most primates live in the tropics and subtropics. There are about 180 species altogether. The orang-utan (*Pongo pygmaeus*) is a member of the ape family, which also includes gorillas and chimpanzees. Orang-utans live in the rainforests of southeast Asia. Like many primates, they are under threat because their forest home is being cleared for timber and for farmland.

ORIGIN OF *HOMO SAPIENS*

The shape of the human skull is important in deciding how the human species evolved, because it can be compared directly with the fossilized skulls of our distant relatives. Humans almost certainly evolved from ape-like ancestors. Fossils show that several species of human-like animals, called hominids, existed between one and five million years ago. Today, only our species survives.

PROSIMIAN PRIMATE

The aye-aye (*Daubentonia madagascariensis*) is an endangered prosimian that is found only on the island of Madagascar in the Indian Ocean. It is a nocturnal tree-dweller and feeds on insect grubs and young leaves. The aye-aye's front hands have extra long third fingers, which it uses to pick out grubs from bark crevices.

Chimpanzee (Pan troglodytes) *using tool to dig out insects from bark.*

CHIMPANZEES

We often use tools to carry out particular tasks. So, too, do some other primates. Chimpanzees, for example, use sharp sticks and blades of grass to probe for food. Baboons sometimes squash small animals with stones. Several other kinds of animal use tools, but they do this mainly by instinct. Primates can learn how to make tools by watching each other at work.

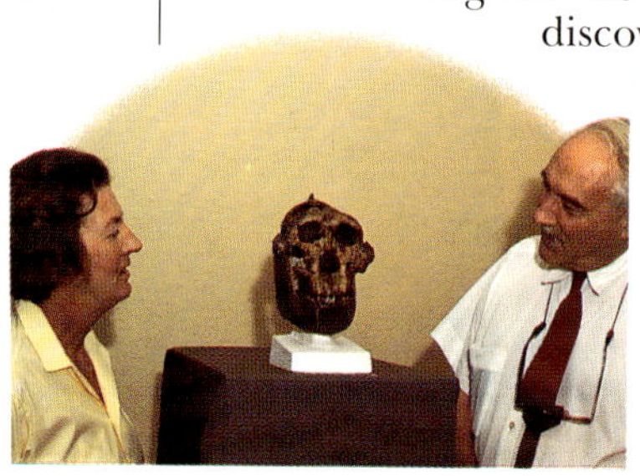

LOUIS AND MARY LEAKEY

The work of the Leakey family has helped to piece together the story of how our species has evolved. Louis Leakey (1903-72) discovered hominid fossils in East Africa, and suggested that humans originated in this region. His wife Mary (1913-) has discovered several fossils of human ancestors and human footprints that date back nearly 3 million years. Richard Leakey (born 1944), their son, has also made several important fossil finds.

HUMAN SUCCESS

Humans are by far the most numerous of all primates. In the last 300 years, the human population has grown from about 1,000 million to nearly 6,000 million. Never in the history of the world has a single species had such a wide-ranging effect on other living things.

Find out more

EVOLUTION P.308
MAMMALS P.334
SKELETONS P.352
PEOPLE AND PLANET P.374
FACT FINDER P.422

HOW LIVING THINGS WORK

WHY ARE PLANTS GREEN? What is blood for? Is your skin dead or alive? In many cases, the answers to these questions lie in the make-up of living matter: living things contain different parts, which fit together amazingly well to make them work. In plants and animals, some of these parts are big enough to see, but others are so small that they can only be looked at through a microscope. In all living things, even the smallest parts can be very complicated. By finding out exactly how the small parts work, scientists have been able to see how whole organisms work.

Each kind of living thing is adapted to the world around it. A gibbon's long arms enable it to swing through the treetops. Forward-pointing eyes make it good at judging distances as it swings from one branch to the next.

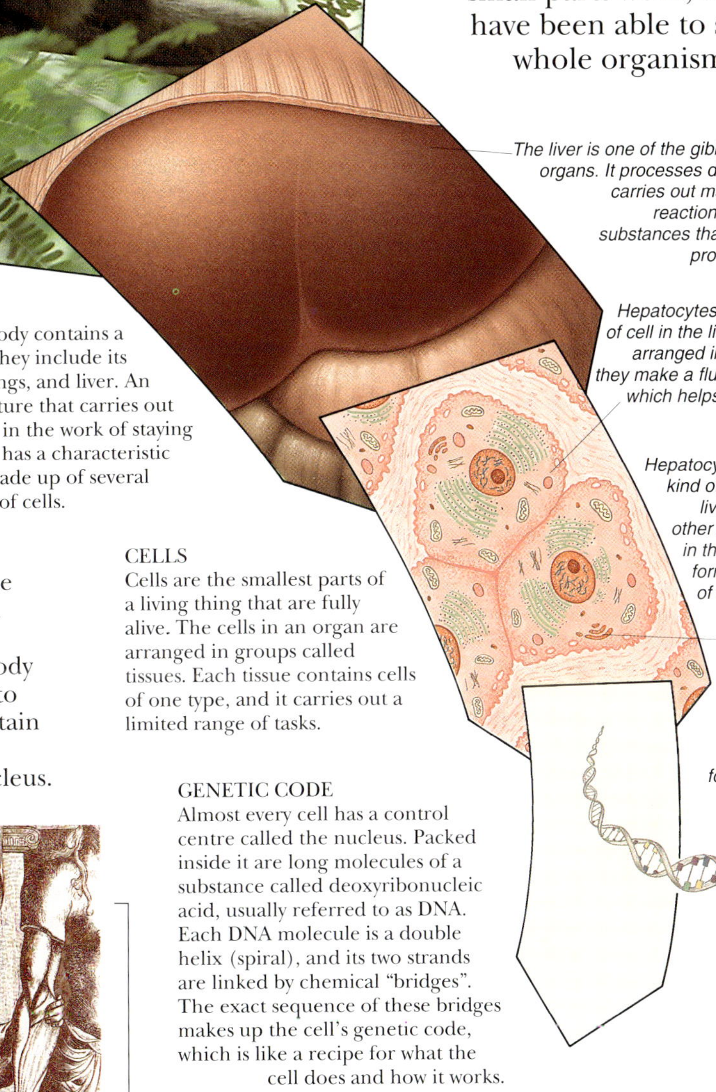

The liver is one of the gibbon's biggest organs. It processes digested food, carries out many chemical reactions, and stores substances that are used to produce energy.

Hepatocytes are one kind of cell in the liver. They are arranged in sheets, and they make a fluid called bile, which helps in digestion.

Hepatocytes form one kind of tissue in the liver. There are other kinds of cells in the liver, which form other kinds of tissues, such as blood vessels.

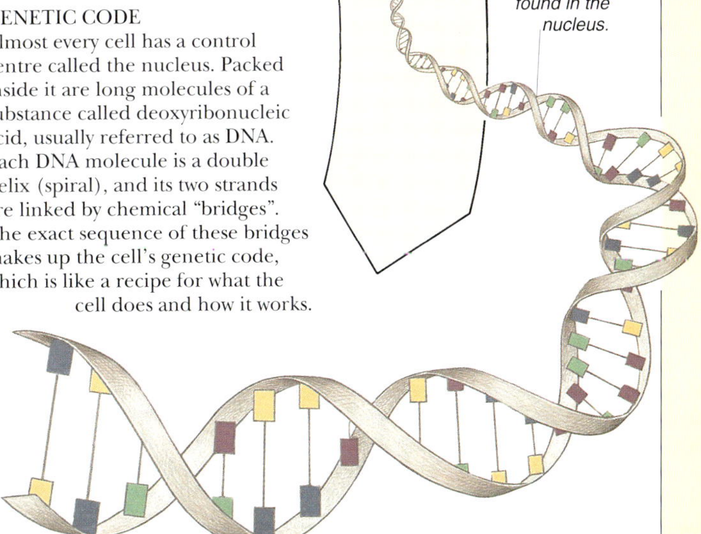

Strands of DNA are found in the nucleus.

ORGANISMS AND THEIR ENVIRONMENT
All living things, or organisms, need to fit in with their environment. They take in food from the world around them. They put the food to many uses, including producing energy for moving, and raw materials for growing and reproducing. Through evolution, living things have developed different ways of getting their food. A gibbon is good at reaching leaves and fruit high in the treetops. Its body can break down this food to release the nutrients and energy that it contains.

ORGANS
The gibbon's body contains a set of organs. They include its brain, heart, lungs, and liver. An organ is a structure that carries out particular tasks in the work of staying alive. Each one has a characteristic shape, and is made up of several different kinds of cells.

THE BODY MACHINE

An animal's body is like a gigantic city of separate parts. The smallest of these parts are called cells. There are many types of cells in living things. Together they provide all the services that the body needs, from energy supply and communication to waste disposal. A single animal or plant may contain billions of cells arranged in a very precise way. Everything each cell does is controlled by its nucleus.

CELLS
Cells are the smallest parts of a living thing that are fully alive. The cells in an organ are arranged in groups called tissues. Each tissue contains cells of one type, and it carries out a limited range of tasks.

GENETIC CODE
Almost every cell has a control centre called the nucleus. Packed inside it are long molecules of a substance called deoxyribonucleic acid, usually referred to as DNA. Each DNA molecule is a double helix (spiral), and its two strands are linked by chemical "bridges". The exact sequence of these bridges makes up the cell's genetic code, which is like a recipe for what the cell does and how it works.

ANDREAS VESALIUS

Vesalius (1514-64) founded the modern science of anatomy, which looks at the structure of living things. He was Belgian, but he did his most important work in Italy. He became a professor of anatomy at the age of 23, and in 1543 he published a book called *The Structure of the Human Body*. It was based on careful observation, and was beautifully illustrated. This was the first book to show details of the body in an accurate way.

CELLS

EVERY LIVING THING is made up of cells. Each one is like a microscopic factory, where thousands of chemical reactions happen in a carefully controlled way. Cells use these reactions to perform all the tasks involved in being alive. Cells can divide in two over and over again. Some living things, such as amoebas, are just one cell. Others, such as ourselves, have millions of cells that all work together. Within an organism, the cells in different tissues are slightly different. Plant cells are different to animal cells in in two ways. They have stiff cell walls and can make their own food.

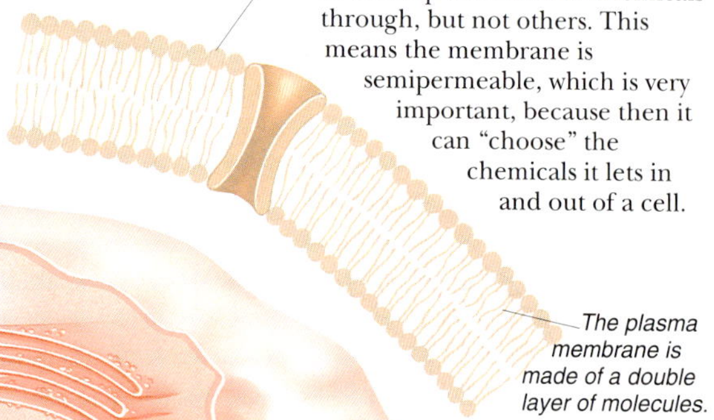

PLASMA MEMBRANE

The plasma membrane encloses the whole cell, but it has pores in it. These pores let some chemicals through, but not others. This means the membrane is semipermeable, which is very important, because then it can "choose" the chemicals it lets in and out of a cell.

ANIMAL CELLS

An animal cell is like a tiny, fluid-filled, squashy bag. The cell is held together by a thin, flexible layer called a plasma membrane. The membrane is semipermeable, meaning that it allows some chemicals to pass through it, but not others. At the heart of the cell is the nucleus, which controls everything that happens inside the cell. Around the nucleus is a jelly-like fluid called cytoplasm. The cytoplasm contains tiny structures, called organelles. Each kind of organelle carries out a different set of tasks.

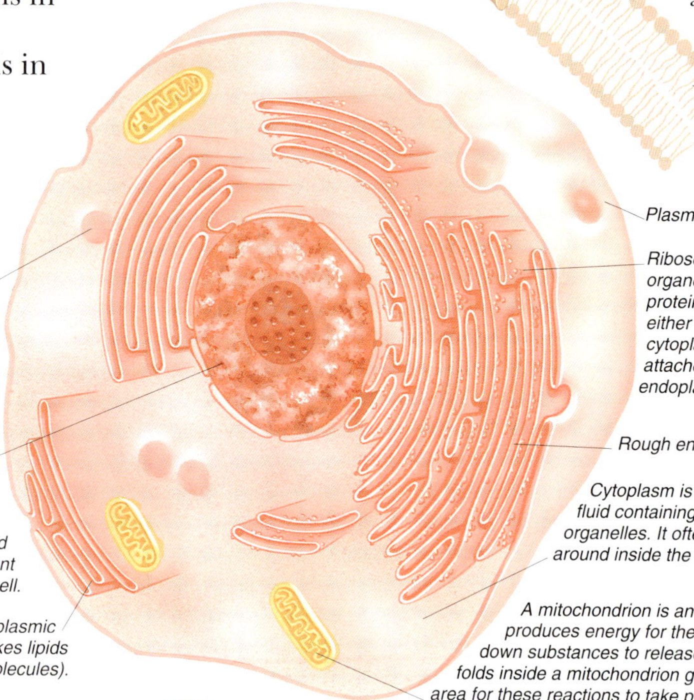

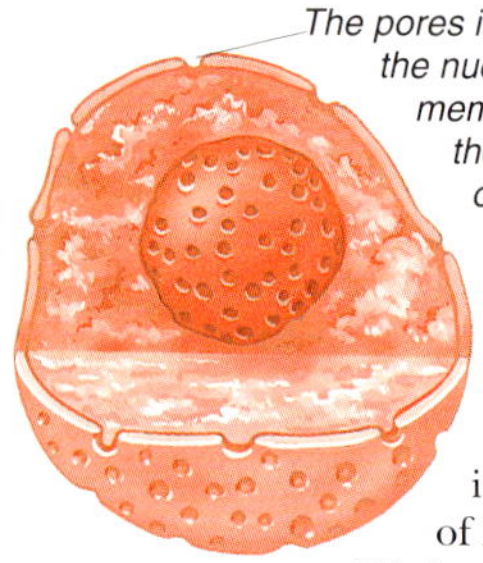

NUCLEUS

The nucleus is the cell's command centre. It contains chemical instructions in molecules of DNA (deoxyribonucleic acid) for everything that the cell does. Normally, the DNA is spread out in long strands. The nucleolus is a round "blob" inside the nucleus. It makes organelles called ribosomes.

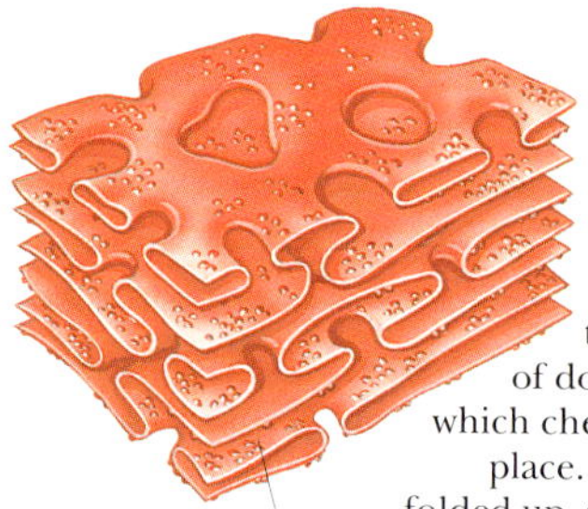

ENDOPLASMIC RETICULUM

The endoplasmic reticulum (ER) is the work surface of the cell. It is a system of double membranes on which chemical reactions take place. The membranes are folded up, and packed together like the layers in a sandwich. They link up with the membrane around the nucleus, and with the plasma membrane that encloses the cell.

HOW BIG IS A CELL?

Most animal cells are between 10 and 20 micrometres (1/100th to 1/50th of a millimetre) across, while plant cells are slightly larger. But cells vary enormously in size. The smallest free-living cells are bacteria called mycoplasmas. Their cells are about 0.1 micrometres (1/10,000th of a millimetre) across. Eggs are giant cells. An ostrich egg cell can be up to 25 cm (10 in) long, which makes it the largest cell that we know of.

Rod cells from a human eye measure 40 micrometres long, compared to ostrich eggs, which measure 250,000 micrometres across.

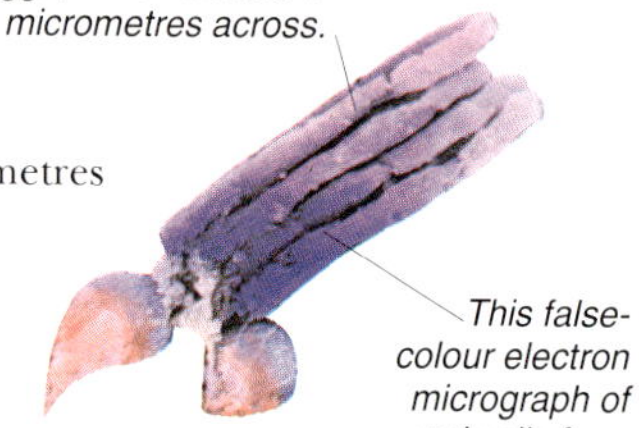

This false-colour electron micrograph of rod cells from the eye shows four cells. The two round cells are nerve cells.

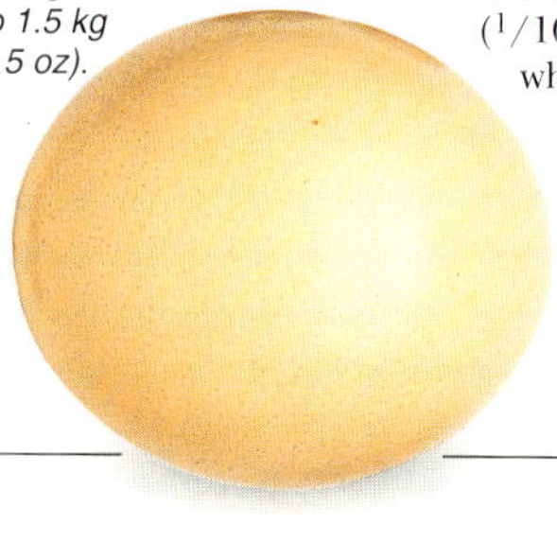

An ostrich egg weighs up to 1.5 kg (3 lb 5 oz).

CELLS

1590 The Dutch optician Zacharias Janssen invents the compound microscope (a microscope with more than one lens). This makes tiny objects visible for the first time.

1665 The English scientist Robert Hooke (1635-1703) looks at thin slices of plants through his microscope. He sees box-like shapes, and calls them "cells".

1838 Two German doctors, Theodor Schwann (1810-82) and Jakob Mathias Schleiden (1804-81), suggest that all living things are made of cells.

1937 Edouard Chatton, a French biologist, notices that some microorganisms (prokaryotes) have cells that are quite different to those of all other living things.

Nerve cell

Plant cells

A plant cell is different from an animal cell in two important ways. As well as being surrounded by a plasma membrane, it also has a stiff cell wall. A plant cell also contains organelles called chloroplasts, which give it a green colour. Chloroplasts catch the energy in sunlight for the cell to make its own food. Most plant cells also contain large vacuoles, which store cell sap. The sap presses against the walls of the cell, keeping it in shape. A plant wilts when it lacks water and the sap does not press against the cell wall.

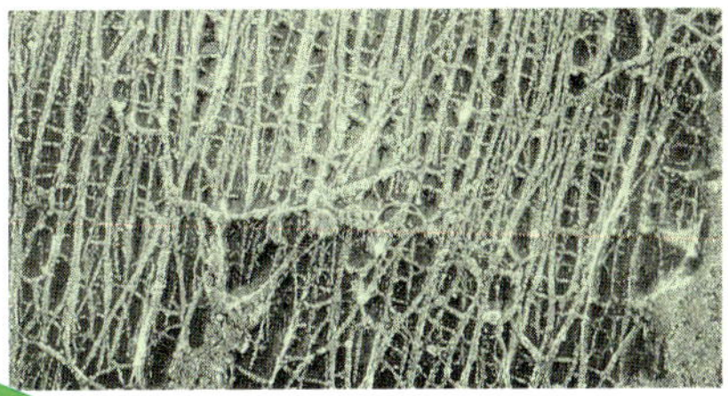

BUILDING A WALL
Plant cell walls are made of a tough material called cellulose. The cell makes tiny cellulose fibres, and builds them up in criss-cross layers on the outside of its plasma membrane. The cellulose layers make a strong, stiff box. Without their tough cell walls, most plants would collapse into a green sludge.

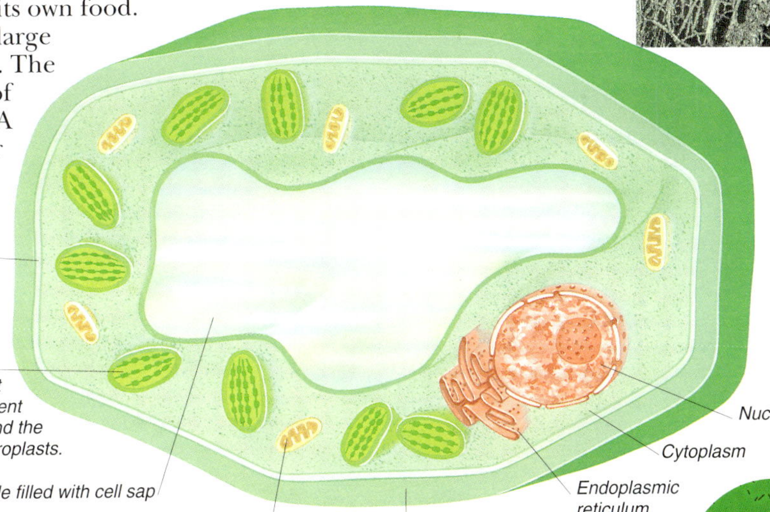

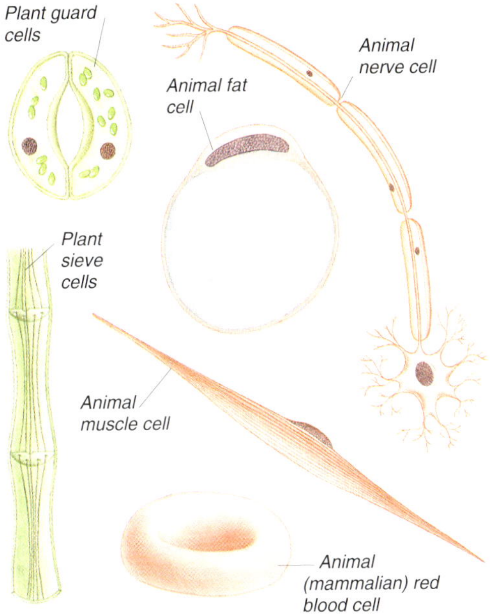

DIFFERENT SHAPES FOR DIFFERENT WORK

The different cells in plants and animals are specialized, meaning that they can carry out only one kind of work. A fat cell is filled with fat either permanently or until it is needed for energy. A nerve cell carries messages from one part of the body to another, and a muscle cell contracts to make part of the body move. Red blood cells carry oxygen in animals, and sieve cells carry nutrients in plants. Unlike most cells, these two kinds do not have nuclei. Guard cells are found in plant leaves, controlling the pores that allow air into the leaf. They also have chloroplasts to harness the energy in sunlight.

LOOKING AT CELLS
Most cells are far too small to see with eyes alone. To look at them, biologists have to use microscopes. A light microscope can magnify clearly up to about 2,000 times. Special stains or lighting are used to make different parts of the cell stand out. An electron microscope works in a different way. It can magnify over a million times, but normally it cannot be used with living specimens. A scanning electron microscope gives an almost three-dimensional image.

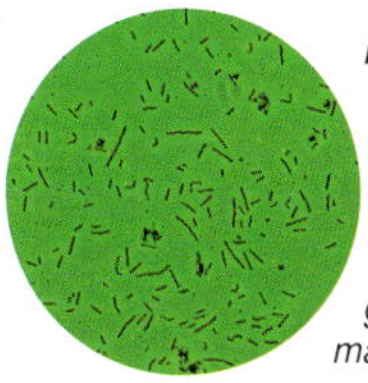

Light micrograph of Lactobacillus bulgaricus, a bacterium found in live yoghurt. It is illuminated with green light and magnified 400 times.

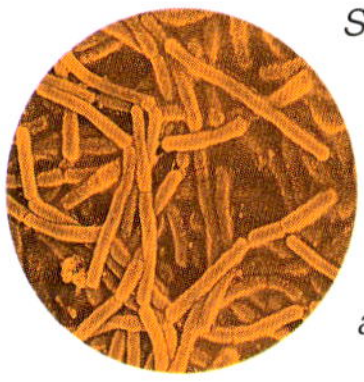

Scanning electron micrograph of Lactobacillus bulgaricus magnified 1,000 times. Electron microscopes produce a black and white image. Here, the image has been artificially coloured by a computer.

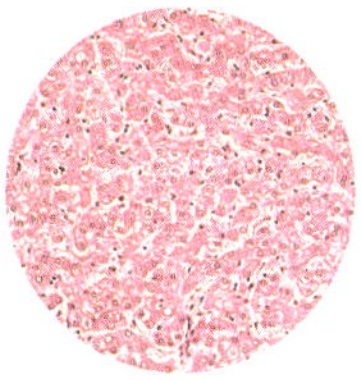

Light micrograph of hepatocytes (liver cells) magnified 56 times. The cells have been stained to make them easier to see. The nuclei absorb the dye, giving them a dark colour.

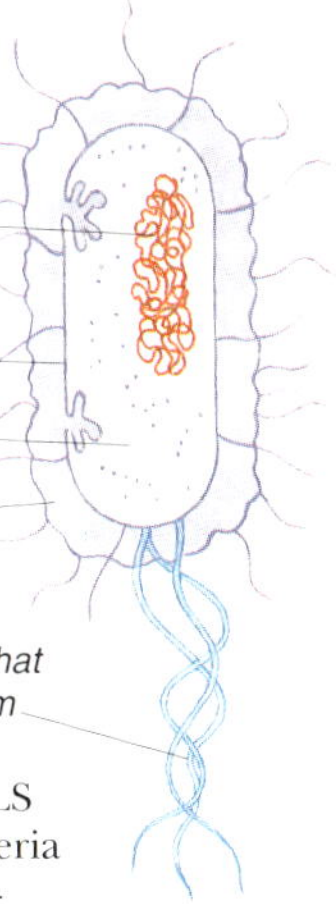

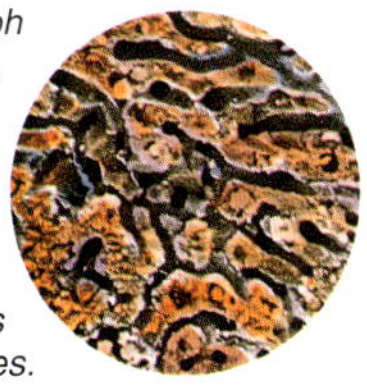

Electron micrograph of liver cells, magnified 90 times and artificially coloured. Electron microscopes can produce small magnifications as well as large ones.

SIMPLEST CELLS
The cells of bacteria and other micro-organisms do not have nuclei or mitochondria. They are called prokaryotic. Other cells, such as plant and animal cells, do have nuclei, and are called eukaryotic cells. They are more common.

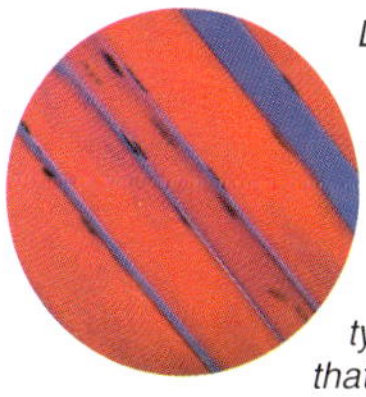

Light micrograph of muscle fibres, magnified 140 times. Several nuclei can be seen, as well as the striations (stripes) that are typical of muscles that pull on bones.

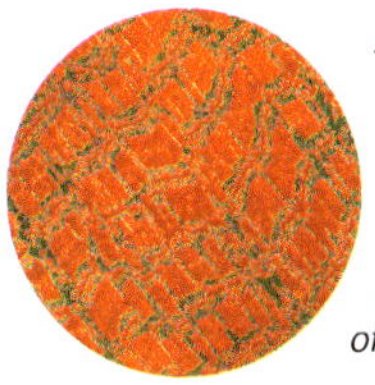

Artificially coloured electron micrograph of a single muscle fibre, magnified 1,940 times. The fibre is made up of many parallel fibrils. Each fibril is just 1/500th of a millimetre across.

Find out more

How scientists work p.14
Vision p.204
Single-celled organisms p.314
Bacteria p.313
Photosynthesis p.340
Cellular respiration p.346

PHOTOSYNTHESIS

IMAGINE BEING ABLE TO MAKE FOOD just by standing in sunlight. This is what plants do when they carry out photosynthesis. The word photosynthesis means "putting together by light". During this process, plants collect energy from sunlight. They use this energy to turn water and carbon dioxide into a simple sugar called glucose. Plants then use glucose to fuel their cells, and also to make other substances, such as starch and cellulose. Plants are not the only living things that carry out photosynthesis. Some protists and monerans also make food in this way.

WHY ARE MOST LEAVES GREEN?
Sunlight is made of many colours. Most plants contain a green pigment called chlorophyll, which reflects the green part of light. It captures the blue and red parts of sunlight, and uses them to drive photosynthesis. Plants such as the copper beech in the woodland above, and red and brown seaweeds, also use other pigments as well as chlorophyll to capture different colours in light. That is why they are not green.

Photosynthesis takes carbon dioxide and water and produces glucose and oxygen. The equation is: $6CO_2 + 6H_2O \longrightarrow C_6H_{12}O_6 + 6O_2$.

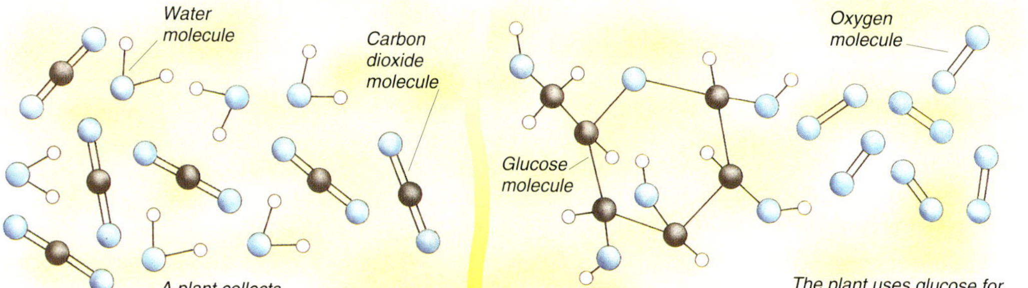

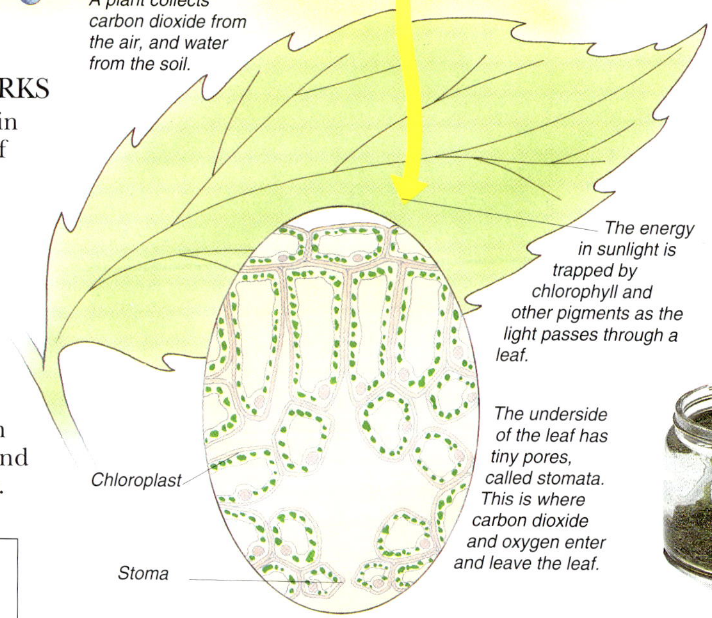

HOW PHOTOSYNTHESIS WORKS

Most plants carry out photosynthesis in their leaves. Many of the cells in a leaf contain tiny organelles called chloroplasts. Chlorophyll and other pigments in the chloroplasts trap the energy in sunlight. Once the energy has been trapped, it powers a complicated series of chemical reactions. During these reactions, water molecules are split apart into hydrogen and oxygen atoms. The hydrogen atoms combine with carbon dioxide molecules to make glucose, and oxygen is given off as a waste product.

JAN INGENHOUSZ

At one time, people thought that plants grew simply by absorbing substances from the soil. But in the 18th century, it was found that they needed air as well. The Dutchman Jan Ingenhousz (1730-99) discovered that plants take in carbon dioxide and release oxygen when sunlight shone on them. He found that the gases travel in the opposite direction when it is dark.

CHLOROPLASTS
Most cells inside a leaf contain dozens of chloroplasts. Each one is made of piles of tiny discs. The surface of each disc contains chlorophyll and other pigments, which trap the energy in sunlight.

MAKING OXYGEN
Normally, we cannot see the oxygen that is released by plants. But when water plants carry out photosynthesis, oxygen sometimes forms bubbles on the surface of their leaves. Water plants get carbon dioxide dissolved in the water around them.

AUTUMN LEAVES
In autumn, many trees break down the chlorophyll in their leaves. The leaves are then coloured by any pigments left behind. These include carotenoids, which make carrots orange, and anthocyanins, which make some apples red.

Find out more

DESCRIBING REACTIONS P.53
LIGHT P.190
COLOUR P.202
DIGESTION P.345
CELLULAR RESPIRATION P.346
GROWTH AND DEVELOPMENT P.362

TRANSPORT IN PLANTS

IF YOU FORGET TO WATER an indoor plant, it will eventually wilt and die. This happens because plants need water to survive. Water travels upwards through a plant's roots and stems, and it evaporates into the air from its leaves and flowers. This movement is called transpiration. It keeps the plant's cells firm, and it also carries dissolved minerals up from the soil. Plants also have another transport system, called translocation, which often works in the other direction. It carries food substances away from the leaves into the buds, shoots, and roots.

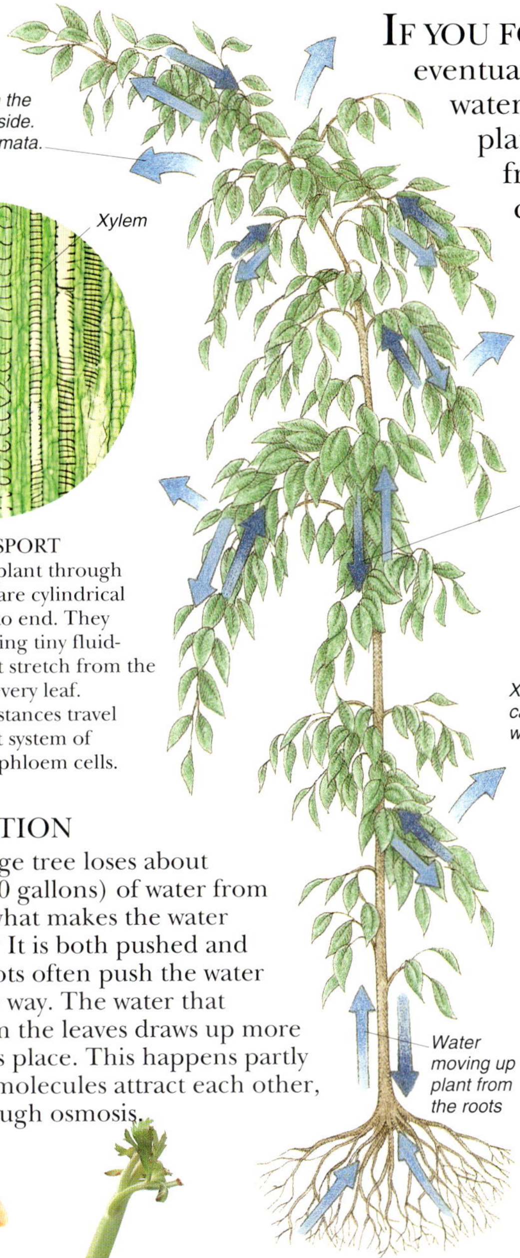

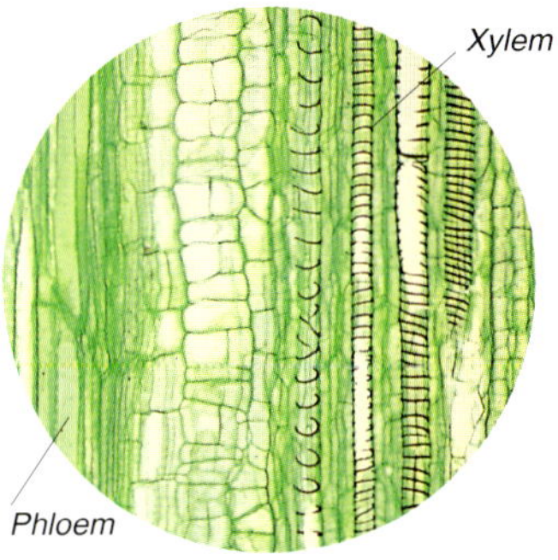

TWO-WAY TRANSPORT

Water travels up a plant through xylem cells. These are cylindrical cells that link end to end. They eventually die, leaving tiny fluid-filled pipelines that stretch from the roots and up into every leaf. Dissolved food substances travel through a different system of pipelines made by phloem cells.

TRANSPIRATION

Every day, a large tree loses about 1,000 litres (220 gallons) of water from its leaves. But what makes the water move upwards? It is both pushed and pulled. The roots often push the water upwards a little way. The water that evaporates from the leaves draws up more water to take its place. This happens partly because water molecules attract each other, and partly through osmosis.

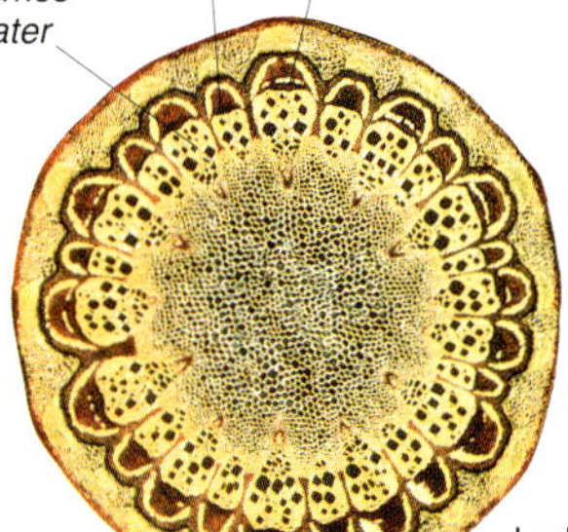

FEEDING ON SAP

The sugary fluid in phloem cells makes an energy-rich food for sap-sucking insects. Aphids pierce the stem and phloem cells with their sharp mouthparts, and then drink the fluid which oozes out. Sometimes there is too much sugar for an aphid to digest. The leftover sugar passes out of its body in drops of sticky liquid called honeydew.

TUBES FOR TRANSPORT

Xylem and phloem cells are clustered together in groups called vascular bundles. The xylem is on the inside, and the phloem on the outside. Xylem cells are often strengthened, which keeps the tubes open so that liquids can pass up them easily.

Lady's mantle (*Alchemilla vulgaris*)

Slice of celery stem, showing xylem cells stained by dye

Evaporation from leaves draws water and dye up through celery stem.

SEEING TRANSPIRATION

You can see transpiration at work by putting a stick of celery into some water containing a food dye. As water evaporates from the leaves, water travels up the celery and carries the dye with it. The dye shows that the water moves upwards through narrow channels, which are the xylem cells.

OSMOSIS

If you put a peeled potato in very salty water, water will be sucked out from its cells. If you put it in tap water, the cells will absorb water. This flow of water into and out of cells is called osmosis. During osmosis, water always flows through a semipermeable membrane. It always flows from the side that contains a bigger proportion of water molecules to the side that contains a lower proportion of water molecules and more dissolved substances.

A cube of potato was left in very salty water for a day, and shrunk slightly because water was sucked out of it by osmosis.

A cube of potato of the same size was left in tap water for a day, and it swelled slightly because water was absorbed by osmosis.

GUTTATION

In low-growing plants, water is sometimes pumped upwards by the roots faster than it is lost by the leaves. When this happens, water droplets form around the leaf edges because the water does not evaporate fast enough. This is guttation. It usually occurs after dark, and only when the air is still and humid.

Find out more

KINETIC THEORY P.50
COLOUR P.202
FLOWERING PLANTS P.318
CELLS P.338
PHOTOSYNTHESIS P.340
ASEXUAL REPRODUCTION P.366

NUTRITION

EVERY LIVING THING needs nutrients (raw materials) to stay alive. Nutrition is the process by which they get these substances, and put them to work. Like all animals, we get our nutrients by eating food. This is called being heterotrophic. Food contains three main kinds of nutrients: proteins, fats, and carbohydrates. We use proteins to build and repair our bodies, and fats and carbohydrates mainly for fuel. We need other nutrients, but in smaller amounts. These substances are minerals, used to build important molecules in the body, or vitamins, which enable particular chemical reactions to take place. Plants live in quite a different way. They make their own food, which is called being autotrophic. They only need simple nutrients, such as carbon dioxide, water, and mineral salts from the soil.

KEEPING A BALANCE
Good nutrition means eating the right food in the right proportions. Here is a meal that has a range of different foods, which gives a balance of proteins, fats, and carbohydrates, as well as a range of minerals and vitamins. That's why it is important to eat a wide variety of food, rather than too much "junk" food, such as crisps, which mainly provide fats and carbohydrates.

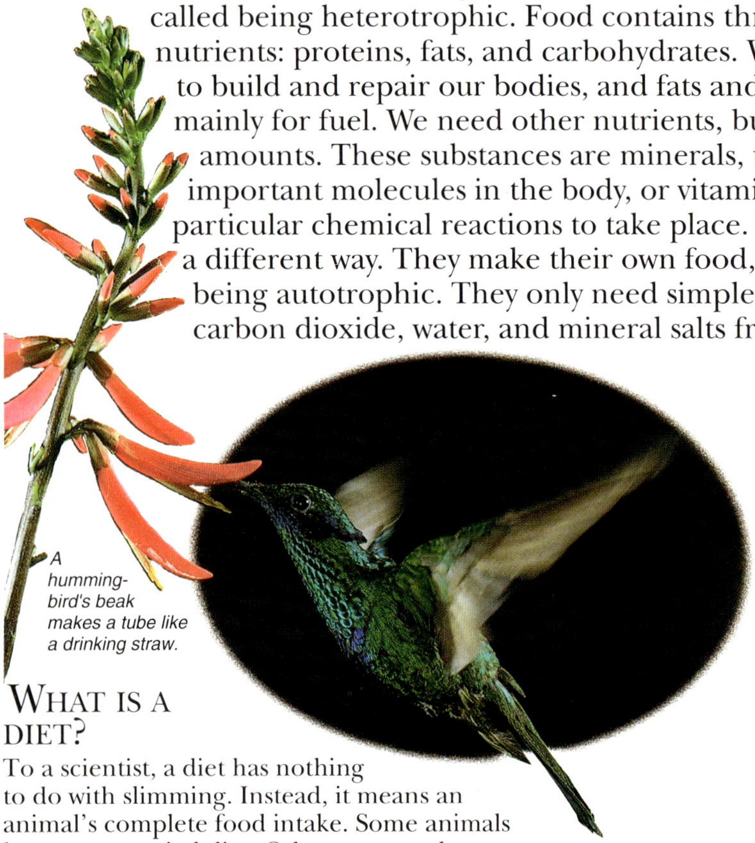

A hummingbird's beak makes a tube like a drinking straw.

Hummingbirds get the energy to hover in front of flowers from nectar, which is rich in sugars. But nectar contains very little protein, so hummingbirds also eat a few insects.

WHAT IS A DIET?

To a scientist, a diet has nothing to do with slimming. Instead, it means an animal's complete food intake. Some animals have a very varied diet. Others are much more choosy. An adult hummingbird lives mainly on nectar, a sugary liquid made by flowers. Nectar is packed with carbohydrates, which means that it is a good source of energy.

This swallowtail butterfly caterpillar (Papilio machaon) eats almost all the time it is awake.

HERBIVORES

Many kinds of animal, from caterpillars to elephants, live entirely on plant food. They are called herbivores. Their food is often not very nutritious, and to get enough energy and nutrients to live, they have to spend a large part of their lives eating. Some herbivores, like camels, have bacteria in their digestive systems to help them release the nutrients from their food.

CARNIVORES

A pike is a carnivore – an animal that feeds on other animals. Its food is rich in nutrients, so a single meal can last for a long time. However, its food is not always easy to obtain. Carnivores such as the pike often have to put a lot of energy and time into finding and catching a meal.

OMNIVORES

Raccoons, bears, and humans are omnivores, meaning that they can feed on both plant and animal food. Omnivorous animals are not very choosy, so they can usually find something to eat. Raccoons are particularly good at living on people's leftovers.

MALNUTRITION

If an animal's diet is missing a particular kind of nutrient, it becomes malnourished. Its health declines, and it may suffer from a "deficiency disease". In some parts of the world, children suffer from kwashiorkor, which is a deficiency disease caused by a lack of protein. Plants, too, become unhealthy if important minerals are missing in the soil. These cherry leaves are suffering from magnesium deficiency.

Find out more

CHEMISTRY OF FOOD P.78
ARTHROPODS P.322
FISH P.326
FEEDING P.343
TEETH AND JAWS P.344
DIGESTION P.345
FOOD CHAINS AND WEBS P.377
FACT FINDER P.422

FEEDING

LONG AGO, PEOPLE GOT THEIR FOOD by gathering seeds and fruit, and by hunting animals. Nowadays, most of our food is produced by farming. Instead of gathering food ourselves, people who live in towns and cities buy it in shops. But in the natural world, things are very different. Wild animals spend a large part of their time either feeding, or trying to find their next meal. The way that they do this depends on what they eat. Herbivores (animals that eat plants) do not usually have to look far for their food, because plants are rooted in one spot and cannot run away. Carnivores (animals that eat meat) usually have to track down their prey, and overpower it. However, some animals, such as barnacles or sea anemones, stay in one place and wait for their food to come within reach.

SAFETY IN A HERD
Gazelles feed on grass, in the open country of the African plains. They have many enemies, and their only defence is to run away. Gazelles make themselves safer by living in herds. While some of the gazelles are eating, others keep a watchful eye for any signs of danger.

PREDATOR AND PREY

The common shrew (*Sorex araneus*) is one of the smallest of all predatory mammals (mammals that hunt). It measures just 7.5 cm (3 in) from head to tail, and is about as heavy as a sugar cube. Despite its tiny size, it is a fierce hunter with a large appetite. It overpowers earthworms with its sharp teeth, and quickly starts to feed. A shrew needs to eat its own body mass in food every day, or it will die. Larger predatory mammals eat much less, because their bodies use energy at a much slower rate.

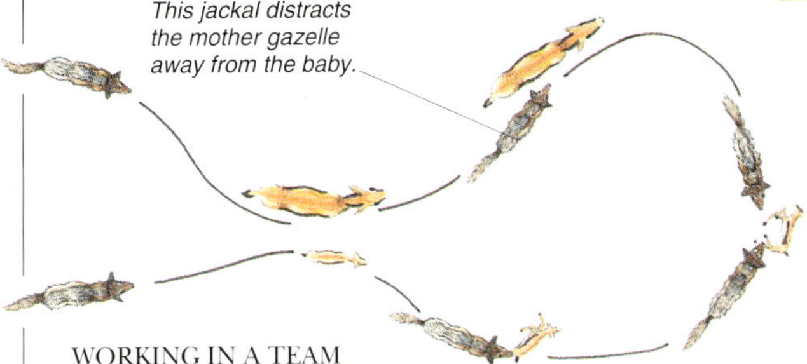

WORKING IN A TEAM
Some hunting mammals catch their prey by working together. Here, one jackal attacks the mother gazelle, even though an adult gazelle is too big for it to kill. While the mother is distracted, the other jackal pounces on her youngster. By working as a team, the jackals get a meal that one jackal could not catch on its own.

FILTER FEEDING
This fanworm (*Protula intestinum*) lives by filtering tiny particles of food from water. Its "fans" are rings of tentacles. The tentacles trap particles of food, and tiny hairs then push the food towards the worm's mouth. Many different animals live by filtering food. They include molluscs, such as oysters and mussels, and sponges and sea squirts. Small filter-feeding animals usually spend their adult lives in one place. The biggest filter-feeders of all, whales, filter food as they swim along.

FEEDING ON LEFTOVERS

Several different fungi are living on food substances in this piece of bread. Instead of eating whole pieces of bread, they absorb food chemicals through a mass of tiny threads. Fungi and bacteria are important because they help to break down the dead remains of living organisms. Those that do this are called saprophytes, or saprobes. Other fungi live on things that are still alive.

UNDERWATER NET
The larvae of caddisflies live in streams. Most of them find their food by crawling about, but some have a different technique. They make nets from silk, and then sit inside the neck of the net. Small animals are swept into the net and then eaten.

Find out more

CHEMISTRY OF FOOD P.78
FUNGI P.315
JELLYFISH, ANEMONES, AND CORALS P.320
MOLLUSCS P.324
MAMMALS P.334
TEETH AND JAWS P.344
GROWTH AND DEVELOPMENT P.362
FOOD CHAINS AND WEBS P.377
FACT FINDER P.422

CELLULAR RESPIRATION

ALL LIVING THINGS NEED ENERGY to survive. Your energy comes from food. After you digest a meal, food substances travel in your blood and then into your cells. Here, they are respired, which means that they are broken down so that their energy can be released and put to work. In anaerobic respiration, food substances (mainly glucose) are split apart without using oxygen, and a small amount of energy is released. In aerobic respiration, food substances are combined with oxygen, and carbon dioxide and water are produced as waste products. This kind of respiration takes place inside a cell's mitochondria, and releases a lot more energy. Aerobic respiration supplies most of the energy that your body needs.

Respiration works like a turnstile: it releases energy as and when it is needed.

MANAGEABLE ENERGY

Aerobic respiration is very like burning, because it combines food substances (the fuel) with oxygen to release energy. But there is an important difference. Burning happens very quickly, and it releases energy in a sudden rush. Aerobic respiration involves many chemical reactions, and it releases energy in a much more controlled and manageable way.

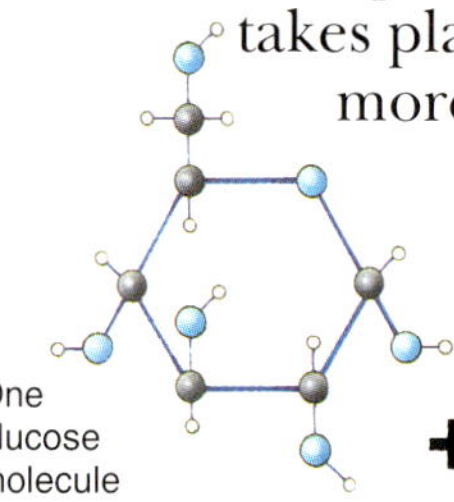

One glucose molecule

+

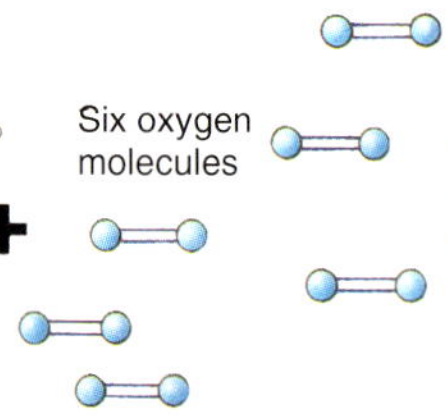

Six oxygen molecules

Respiration takes glucose and oxygen and produces energy, carbon dioxide, and water. The equation is: $C_6H_{12}O_6 + 6O_2$ —> energy + $6CO_2 + 6H_2O$.

During respiration, one molecule of glucose is combined with six molecules of oxygen.

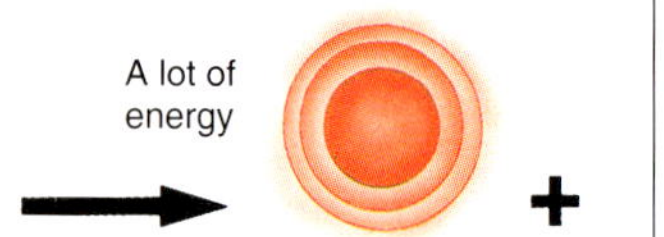

A lot of energy

+

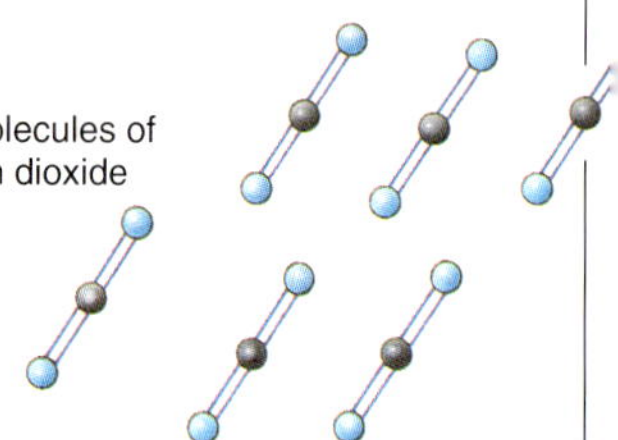

Six molecules of carbon dioxide

+

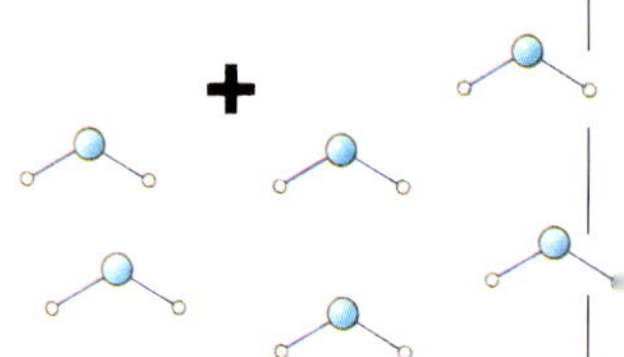

Six molecules of water

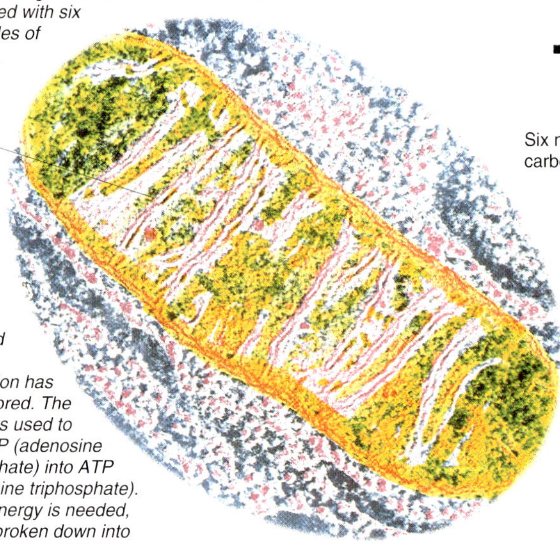

A mitochondrion contains folded membranes that create large work surfaces on which reactions can take place.

Energy released during respiration has to be stored. The energy is used to turn ADP (adenosine diphosphate) into ATP (adenosine triphosphate). When energy is needed, ATP is broken down into ADP to release it.

Chinese hibiscus (*Hibiscus rosa-sinensis*)

RESPIRATION IN PLANTS

During daylight hours, a plant builds up food (glucose and starch) by photosynthesis. It also breaks down some food by respiration. It makes more food than it breaks down, so its leaves take in carbon dioxide. At night, photosynthesis stops. Then the plant only breaks down food by respiration, so its leaves take in oxygen.

WHAT HAPPENS DURING RESPIRATION

The human body is powered mainly by glucose. This is a sugar that you get by digesting starch and other carbohydrates in your food. Before glucose can be respired, it has to be broken down into a simpler substance, pyruvic acid. This travels into the cell's mitochondria, where it is combined with oxygen to produce carbon dioxide and water. During this process, lots of energy is released. The energy can be used to make muscles work, for example. Aerobic respiration is exactly the opposite of photosynthesis, which uses energy to make glucose.

HANS KREBS

The German biochemist Hans Krebs (1900-81) discovered exactly what happens when glucose is respired by cells. Krebs knew that a glucose molecule was split to make pyruvic acid, a simpler substance. However, no-one knew what happened to the pyruvic acid. Krebs dicovered that it joins an endless cycle of chemical reactions, now known as the citric acid cycle or Krebs cycle. Energy is released at each turn of the cycle.

ANAEROBIC RESPIRATION

If you sprint very quickly, your muscles run out of oxygen. Without oxygen, your muscles cannot turn glucose into water and carbon dioxide. Instead, they turn glucose into a substance called lactic acid (too much of this gives you cramp). This is anaerobic respiration, because it does not use oxygen. Later, when you have stopped running, the lactic acid is broken down using oxygen. Some organisms, such as yeasts and bacteria, can live entirely by anaerobic respiration.

Find out more

PHOSPHORUS P.43
OXYGEN P.44
FERMENTATION P.80
CELLS P.338
PHOTOSYNTHESIS P.340
DIGESTION P.345
FACT FINDER P.422

BREATHING

EVERY TIME YOU TAKE A BREATH, you suck air into your lungs. The oxygen in the air diffuses (spreads) through the thin lining of the lungs, until it reaches the blood in the tiny blood vessels in your lungs. It is then loaded on to red blood cells, and carried to all parts of your body. At the same time, the waste gas carbon dioxide (from cellular respiration) moves in the other direction, so that your body can get rid of it. Mammals, birds, amphibians, and reptiles all have lungs. Fish breathe through thin flaps called gills, and insects have tiny air pipes running through their bodies.

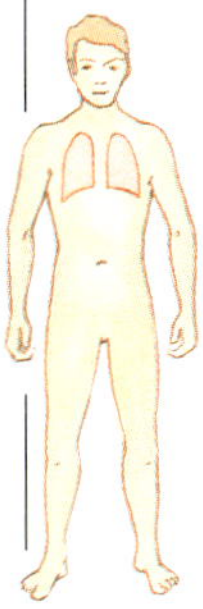

You have two lungs, but they are not the same shape. Your right lung is broader, and has three lobes. The left lung has just two lobes.

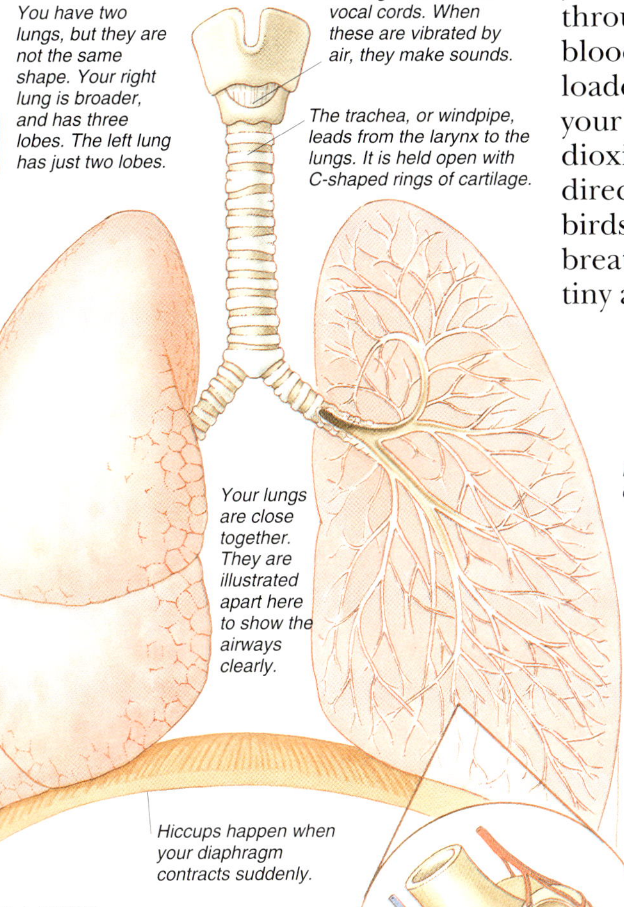

BREATHING

Your lungs are surrounded by your ribs, and they sit on a dome of muscle called the diaphragm. When you breathe, your ribs and diaphragm change the shape of your lungs. Air is either sucked into the lungs, or squeezed out. The amount of air that moves depends on what you are doing. When you sit still, only a little air moves with each breath. When you exercise, you breathe faster and more deeply. Each deep breath moves up to six times more air as when you sit still.

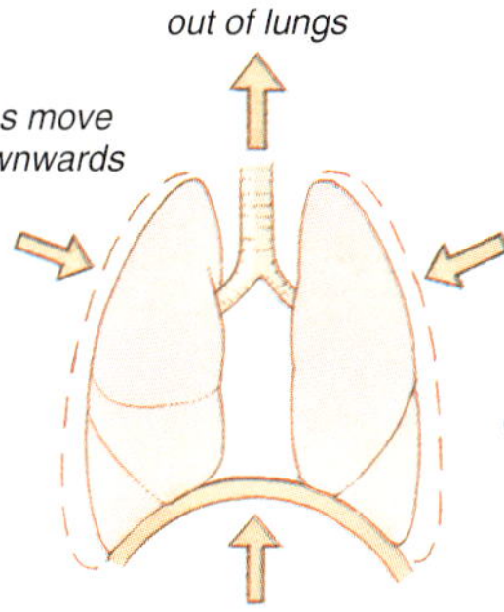

When you breathe out, your ribs move downwards and your diaphragm springs upwards. This reduces the space around the lungs, so that air is squeezed up through the trachea (windpipe).

INSIDE A LUNG

Your lungs are like a pair of large sponges. They have a very rich supply of tiny blood vessels called capillaries, and they are filled with a network of branching air passages. The smallest passages end in dead-end spaces, each called an alveolus, where the air and blood are brought close together. All the alveoli put together have a huge surface area – about 40 times that of your skin. This enables large amounts of oxygen and carbon dioxide to pass into or out of your body.

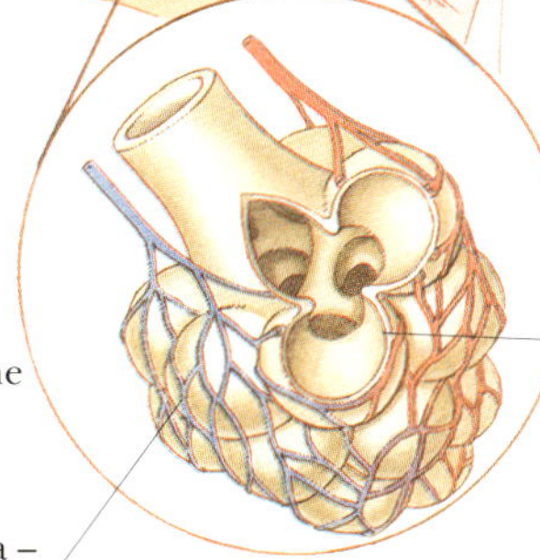

In an alveolus, blood and air are so close together that oxygen and carbon dioxide can easily move between them.

Bush cricket (*Ephippiger* species)

TRACHEAL SYSTEM

Insects breathe through a network of air-filled tubes, called tracheae. These lead deep into the insect's body, and divide into branches that are fine enough to reach right into its muscles. The tracheae are sometimes connected to air sacs, which can change shape just like our lungs. Each trachea opens to the outside through a small hole called a spiracle in the insect's body case.

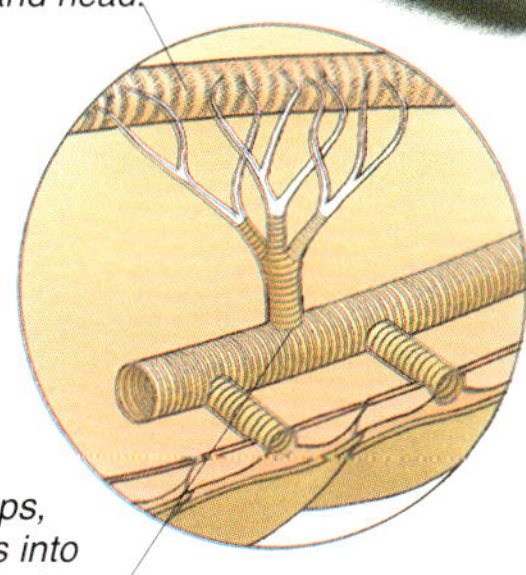

Tracheae carry oxygen directly to an insect's cells.

A fish's gills are just behind its head.

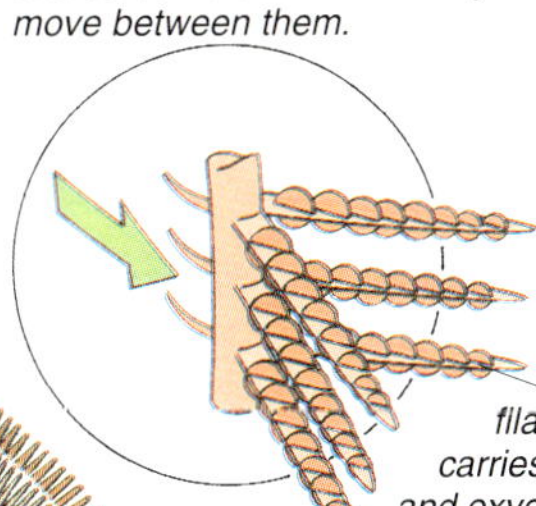

Gills are made up of curved arches, which have feathery projections called filaments.

BREATHING WITH GILLS

Water contains oxygen, although much less than air does. Fish collect oxygen using their gills. A gill is a series of tiny flaps that have a rich blood supply, like our lungs. The fish takes in water through its mouth. As the water washes over the gills, the gills collect oxygen, and give up carbon dioxide. The water then flows out through one or more slits on the fish's body.

Find out more

MAKING AND HEARING SOUND P.182
CELLULAR RESPIRATION P.346
BLOOD P.348
CIRCULATION P.349
INTERNAL ENVIRONMENT P.350

Blood

BLOOD IS AN AMAZING SUBSTANCE. It is like a fluid conveyor belt that carries oxygen to every living cell in your body. It also transports food substances, hormones, waste products, and warmth, and it acts as your body's main defence against disease. If you look at a drop of blood, it seems to be just a red liquid. But under a microscope, the same drop turns out to be packed with millions of cells, floating in a watery fluid. The red blood cells carry oxygen, and the white cells attack anything that invades the body from outside. The plasma (the liquid part) carries most of the carbon dioxide. You have about 4 litres (6½ pints) of blood. Its cells are squashed, squeezed, and battered. Every day, millions of them are replaced.

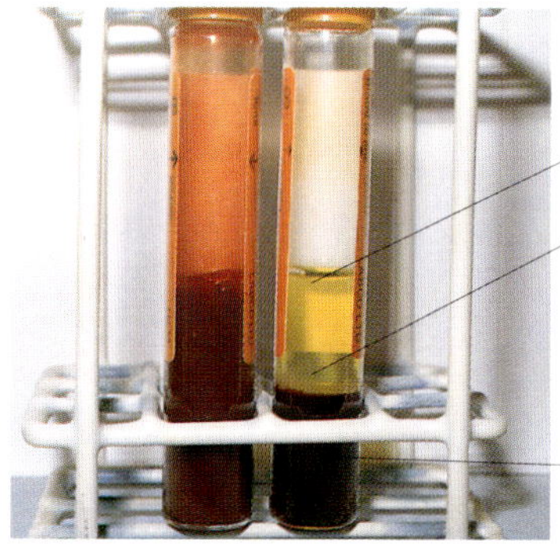

In most people, the plasma makes up over half the blood's volume.

Thin layer of white blood cells and platelets

Red blood cells packed closely together

COMPOSITION OF BLOOD

If a sample of blood is spun around very quickly in a test tube, the cells settle to the bottom. At the top is a yellowish liquid, called the blood plasma. Plasma is 90 per cent water. The rest of it is mainly dissolved food substances and salts, and also proteins such as fibrinogen, which forms blood clots. Cells make up just under half the blood's volume, and red blood cells usually outnumber white cells by 500 to 1.

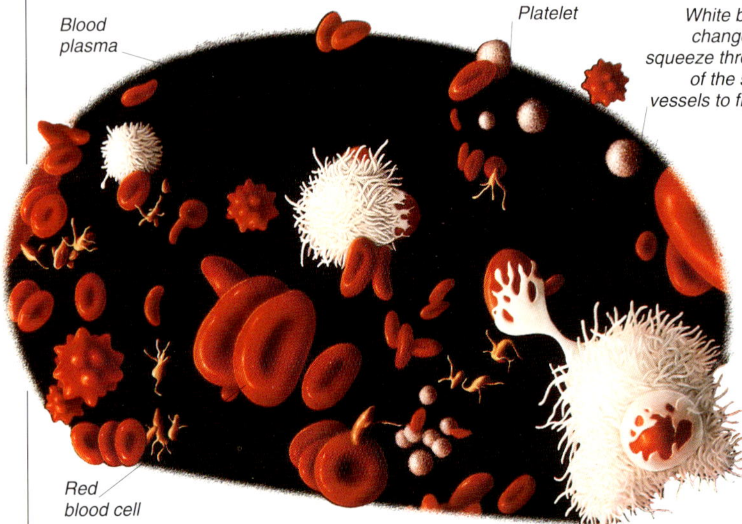

Blood plasma

Platelet

White blood cells can change shape. They squeeze through the walls of the smallest blood vessels to fight infections.

Red blood cell

HAEMOGLOBIN

Haemoglobin is a pigment that gives red blood cells their colour. It contains iron, and it is very special because it can make temporary bonds with gas molecules. Haemoglobin combines with oxygen when red blood cells travel through the lungs. It gives up the oxygen in other parts of the body, and collects some carbon dioxide. When it reaches the lungs once more, it releases the carbon dioxide, and the cycle starts again.

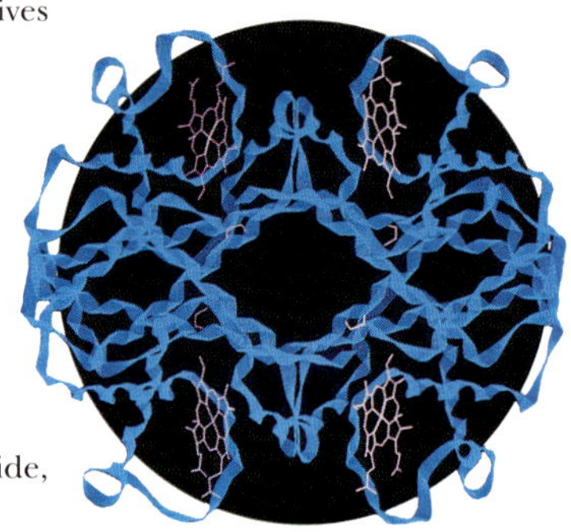

This computer-generated image shows a molecule of haemoglobin. The pink parts are the iron-containing groups that link with oxygen.

Blood in close-up

A single drop of blood contains millions of cells. Most of these are red blood cells, which contain a protein called haemoglobin. This boosts the amount of oxygen that the blood can carry by about 100 times. White blood cells are larger and fewer in number. They engulf foreign cells (such as bacteria) and attack intruders (such as viruses) by releasing antibodies. The blood also contains cell fragments, called platelets, which help it to form clots.

HOW BLOOD CLOTS

If you cut yourself, your blood eventually seals the wound. Blood platelets near the wound become sticky, and they join together to form a plug. While this is happening, a blood protein called fibrinogen changes into fibrin. It makes a dense network of threads, which contract and bind the red blood cells to form a clot.

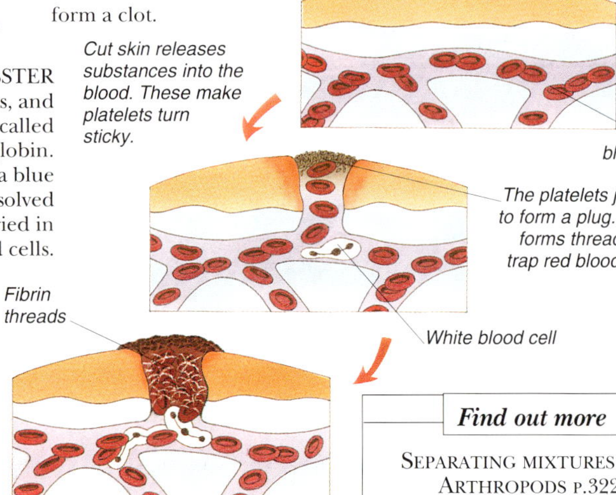

Cut skin releases substances into the blood. These make platelets turn sticky.

Red blood cell

The platelets join up to form a plug. Fibrin forms threads that trap red blood cells.

Fibrin threads

White blood cell

The fibrin and red blood cells form a clot, which hardens to make a scab. When the skin has healed, the scab falls off.

BLUE-BLOODED LOBSTER

Crustaceans, such as crabs and lobsters, and some molluscs, use a pigment called haemocyanin instead of haemoglobin. This substance gives their blood a blue colour. In crustaceans, haemocyanin is dissolved in the blood plasma, instead of being carried in blood cells.

Haemocyanin contains copper instead of iron and, as shown in this Common lobster (Homarus vulgaris), makes blood blue not red.

BLOOD GROUPS

Blood is slightly different from one person to another, because of special proteins on the surface of its red cells and in its plasma. People who have the same proteins share the same blood group. If blood from different groups is mixed, the proteins can make red blood cells stick together, which is dangerous. So if someone has to have blood replaced by a transfusion, the new blood must be of the right group.

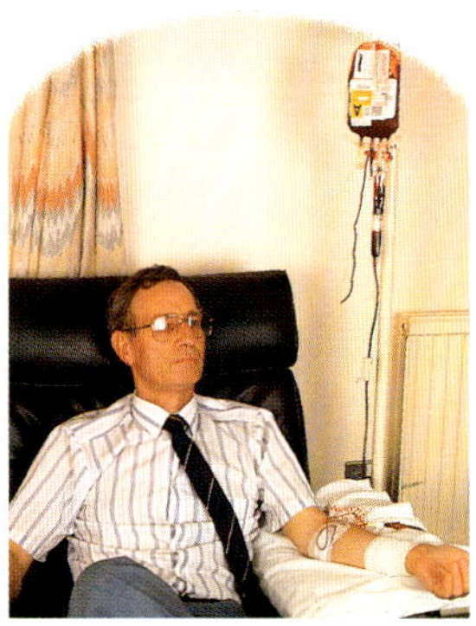

Find out more

SEPARATING MIXTURES P.61
ARTHROPODS P.322
CELLULAR RESPIRATION P.346
CIRCULATION P.349
INTERNAL ENVIRONMENT P.350

CIRCULATION

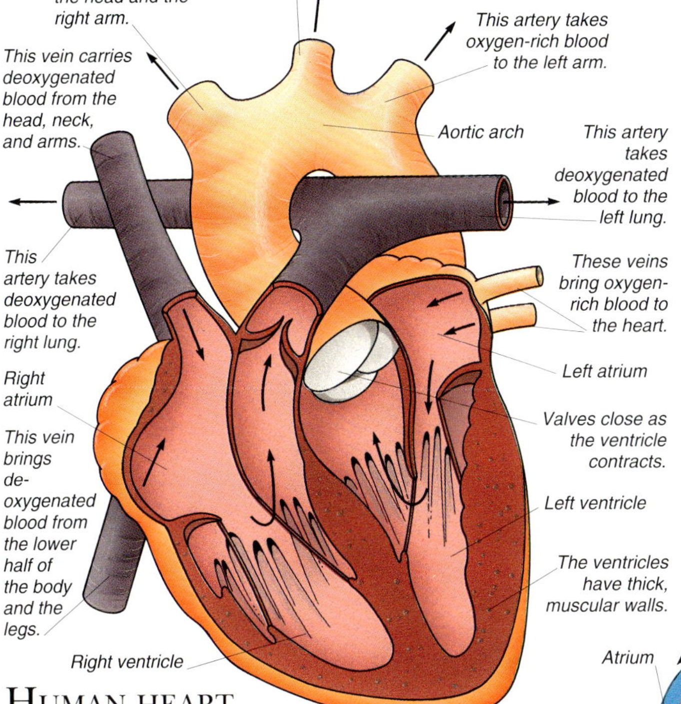

YOUR HEART BEATS 100,000 times every day. It squeezes your blood through a network of tubes that take it on a journey around your body. Humans have a "closed" circulation, which means that our blood travels in special vessels all the way round. When blood is pumped out of the heart, it surges forwards under high pressure, which you can feel as a pulse. Blood circulates at an amazing speed: a single blood cell can take just one minute to travel from your heart to your knee and back to your heart. Simpler animals, such as snails, have "open" circulations. Their blood flows mainly through large body spaces, instead of through narrow vessels. It is not pumped with such pressure, and it moves quite slowly.

HUMAN HEART

Your heart is like two pumps working side by side. Each one is made of two muscular parts: an atrium at the top, and a ventricle at the bottom. During a heartbeat, the atrium contracts, and forces blood into the ventricle. The ventricle contracts a split-second later, forcing blood out of the heart and into the arteries. The right side of the heart pumps blood from the body to the lungs. The left side takes oxygen-rich blood from the lungs and pumps it to the rest of the body.

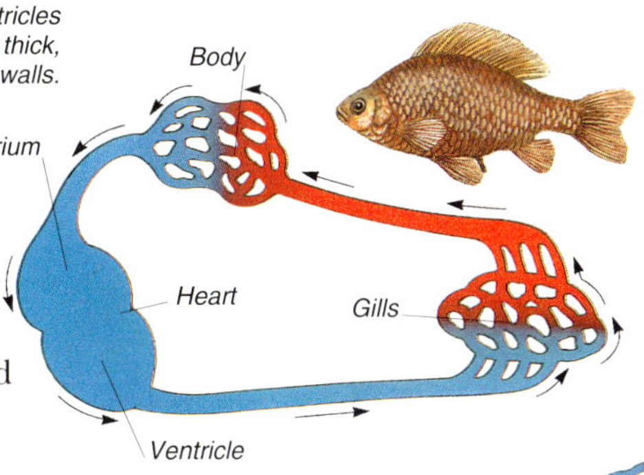

FISH CIRCULATION

A fish has a heart with just two chambers, and its blood flows in a single loop. The blood travels through the gills, where it collects oxygen. It then flows around the body to deliver the oxygen and collect carbon dioxide, which it then takes back to the gills.

WILLIAM HARVEY

The Arab doctor Ibn An-Nafis (c.1205-88) was the first person to describe how blood circulates through the lungs, but his work did not become known in Europe. It was not until 1628 that the English doctor William Harvey (1578-1657) published a full account of how the blood circulates around the body. He could not see capillaries, but he deduced that they must exist.

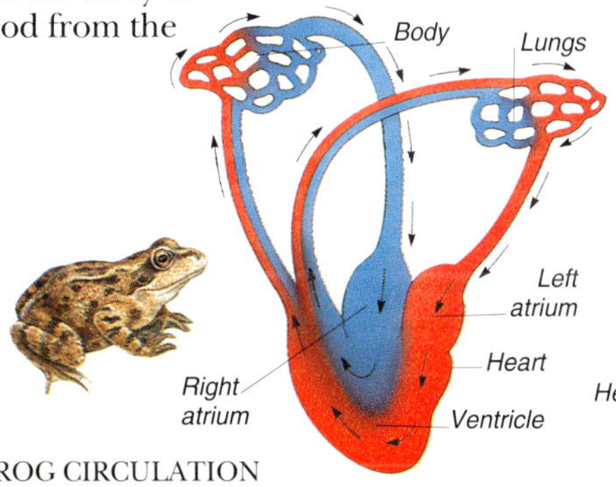

FROG CIRCULATION

A frog's heart has three chambers, two atria, and one ventricle. Its blood flows in two loops – one through the lungs to gain oxygen, and one around the body to give up oxygen. When blood from both loops returns to the heart, it becomes partly mixed.

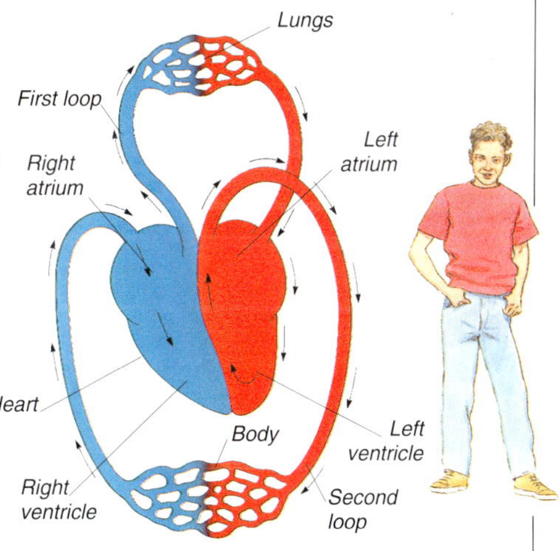

HUMAN CIRCULATION

Like all mammals and birds, we have a double circulation. In the first loop of its journey, the blood travels from the right half of the heart through the lungs, gains oxygen, and is bright red. On the second loop, it travels from the left half of the heart, around the body to lose oxygen and gain carbon dioxide; it is now a darker red because it is deoxygenated.

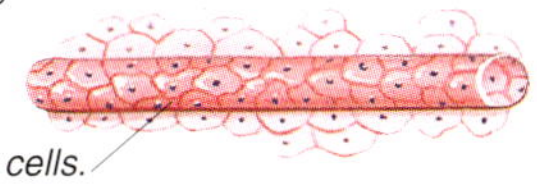

Capillaries are the only vessels whose walls are thin enough to let substances, such as oxygen or hormones, pass out of blood to the cells.

BLOOD VESSELS

Your body contains about 100,000 km (60,000 miles) of blood vessels. Arteries take blood away from the heart, while veins carry it back. Arteries and veins are linked by a dense network of tiny capillaries, which can only be seen through a microscope. Capillaries form a network right through your body.

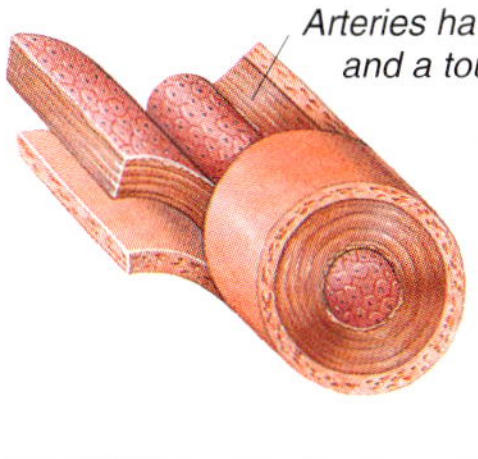

Arteries have muscular walls and a tough outer coating. This helps them to withstand high pressures.

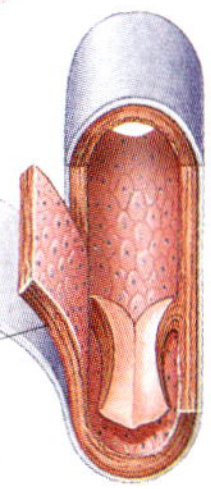

Veins have thin walls, and valves that keep the blood flowing in one direction.

Find out more

BREATHING P.347
BLOOD P.348
INTERNAL ENVIRONMENT P.350

INTERNAL ENVIRONMENT

THE WORLD AROUND US is always changing. The air can get warmer or colder, and it may pour with rain, or stay sunny and dry. But inside your body, things stay much the same from one day to another. The temperature is always about the same, and a constant mixture of chemicals keeps your cells alive. This does not mean that your body never changes. Instead, it makes tiny adjustments to its internal environment all the time. Nerves and hormones (chemical messengers) work together to keep your body in a stable state. This process is called homeostasis, and it happens in all living things.

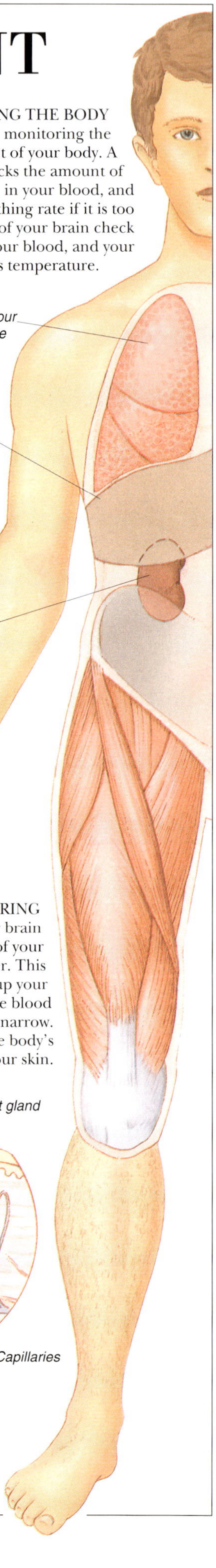

MONITORING THE BODY
Your brain is always monitoring the internal environment of your body. A part of the brain checks the amount of carbon dioxide in your blood, and increases your breathing rate if it is too high. Other parts of your brain check the water level in your blood, and your body's temperature.

Every time you breathe out, your lungs give off carbon dioxide and water vapour (this vapour makes glass go misty if you breathe on it).

Your liver works like a filter and a chemical factory. It removes worn-out red blood cells, and stores the iron that they contain. It also makes sure that your blood contains the right level of glucose, and it makes the proteins that make blood clot.

Your kidneys filter your blood. They drain off its fluid part as it passes through them and then make urine from the waste that it contains.

Sweat helps to cool you down. It contains salt, which is why your skin tastes salty if you have been sweating.

SHIVERING
If your body is too cold, your brain sends signals to some of your muscles to contract, or shiver. This produces heat, which warms up your body. At the same time, the blood vessels near your skin become narrow. This prevents too much of the body's heat escaping through your skin.

EXCRETION

All living things have to get rid of waste. This is called excretion. We excrete carbon dioxide and water through our lungs. We excrete nitrogen compounds, salts, and water in our urine, and some salt and water in sweat. We also get rid of the undigested parts of food – but this is not true excretion, because undigested food never passes through our cells. Excretion is important because waste can poison the body. In a healthy body, the nervous system and hormones make sure that waste products never build up.

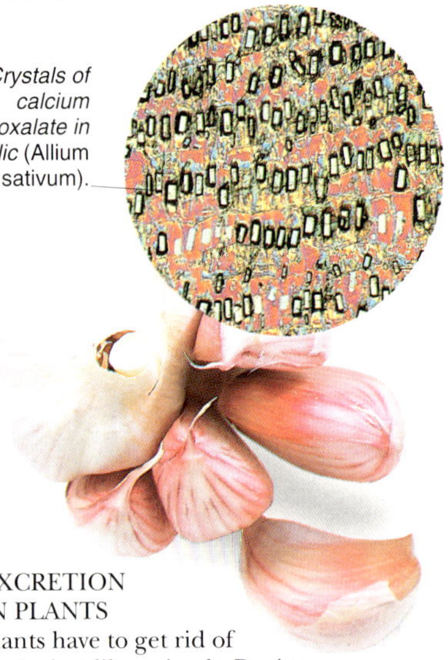

Crystals of calcium oxalate in garlic (Allium sativum).

EXCRETION IN PLANTS
Plants have to get rid of waste, just like animals. During photosynthesis, plants release waste oxygen from their leaves. Some plants store solid waste in their cells.The cells shown here are from a clove of garlic. They have stored crystals of calcium oxalate as a waste product.

Lizard basking on a rock

"COLD-BLOODED" BODIES
Fish, amphibians, and reptiles are exothermic ("cold-blooded") animals. But their bodies are not always cold. Instead, their temperature rises and falls with the temperature of their surroundings. Many exothermic animals alter their body temperature through their behaviour. A lizard will lie in the sun when it is cold, and it will hide in the shade to cool down when it is too hot.

"WARM-BLOODED" BODIES
Mammals and birds are endothermic ("warm-blooded") animals. They can keep their bodies at a set temperature,which is usually warmer than their surroundings. Endothermic animals can stay active even when it is very cold, but their bodies need lots of fuel to do this.

This robin (Erithacus rubecula) *has fluffed up its feathers to keep warm.*

TEMPERATURE REGULATION

Unless you are ill, your body temperature stays at 37°C (98.6°F). Heat is produced by breaking down food during cellular respiration. At the same time heat is lost. If you lose more heat than you make, your brain signals your body to step up your heat production, and prevents some heat escaping by shutting off blood vessels near the skin, and making your body hair stand on end. If you produce too much heat, you begin to sweat.

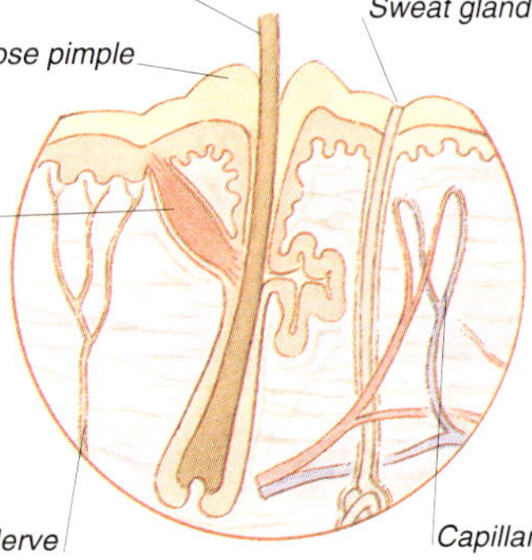

GOOSE PIMPLES
One of the first signs of feeling cold are goose pimples – tiny bumps on your skin. These appear when tiny muscles lift your body hairs upright.

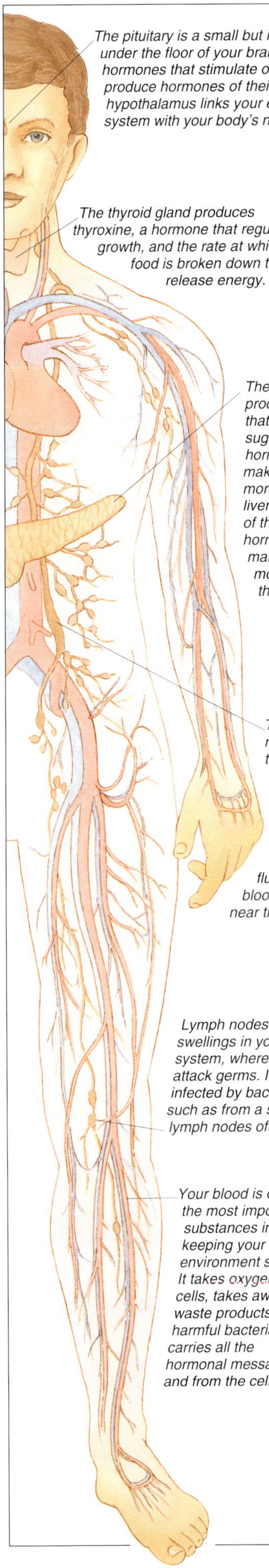

The pituitary is a small but important gland just under the floor of your brain. It produces many hormones that stimulate other glands to produce hormones of their own. The nearby hypothalamus links your endocrine (hormonal) system with your body's nervous system.

The thyroid gland produces thyroxine, a hormone that regulates growth, and the rate at which food is broken down to release energy.

The pancreas produces hormones that control blood sugar levels. The hormone insulin makes the cells use more glucose and the liver take glucose out of the blood. The hormone glucagon makes the liver put more glucose into the blood.

Throughout the body, a network of tubes called the lymphatic system drains fluid that seeps out of the capillaries. The fluid, called lymph, is filtered to remove foreign cells and particles. The filtered fluid then rejoins the blood through a duct near the heart.

Lymph nodes are spongy swellings in your lymphatic system, where white blood cells attack germs. If your body is infected by bacteria or poison, such as from a snake bite, the lymph nodes often swell up.

Your blood is one of the most important substances in keeping your internal environment stable. It takes oxygen to the cells, takes away waste products, kills harmful bacteria, and carries all the hormonal messages to and from the cells.

Hormones

Hormones are substances that carry a message. In animals, they are made by glands. A gland releases a hormone into the bloodstream to travel around the body. When it reaches the target cells, its message is put into action. Your body produces more than 50 different hormones. Some regulate the levels of important substances in your blood, and others control the way that you grow and develop. They often work in pairs, with each hormone having an opposing effect.

HORMONES IN PLANTS
If you put some seedlings on a windowsill, they will bend towards the light. This happens because their growth is controlled by hormones. Hormones gather on the side of a stem that is away from the light, making it bend. Plant hormones mainly control growth and development. Some slow down a plant's growth, and others make leaves fall in autumn.

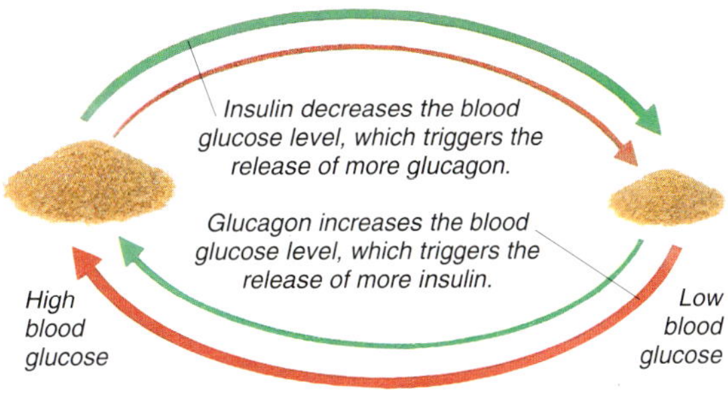

FEEDBACK LOOPS
Insulin and glucagon are hormones that control the level of glucose in blood. Insulin decreases the blood glucose level, while glucagon increases it. The hormones form a feedback loop, because each hormone affects what the other one does.

Honey bees (Apis mellifera)

Queen bee

CHEMICAL COMMUNICATION
Some animals release chemicals that send messages to others. These chemicals are called pheromones. Social insects, such as bees, ants, and termites, pass pheromones to each other through the air and by touching. A queen bee controls a hive by making a special substance containing pheromones.

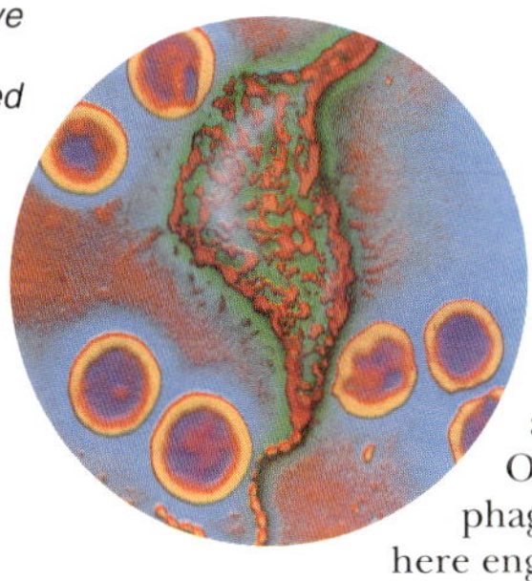

MOBILE DEFENCES
The white cells in blood are the body's guards against invasion. One kind, called phagocytes, are shown here engulfing a string of *Streptococcus* bacteria. They move through the blood and body and engulf germs. Other white blood cells, called lymphocytes, make antibodies. These protein chemicals stick to invaders and kill them.

CLAUDE BERNARD

The French scientist Claude Bernard (1813-78) was one of the first people to study physiology, which is the study of how all the organs in the body work together and keep the internal environment stable. He discovered that glucose, the main source of energy for the body, is stored in the liver as glycogen, and released as and when it is needed. He also studied digestion, how drugs change the way the body works, and the nervous system.

Fighting disease

For microscopic organisms like bacteria, your body is an ideal place to live. It offers warmth and food. To stay in a stable state, your body uses its immune system to fight these germs. Your blood and lymphatic system are very important for doing this. Many of the germs that manage to get into your body are engulfed by white blood cells. Others are attacked by immune system proteins, called antibodies. Once you have been attacked by a certain bacterium, your immune system "remembers" its chemical make-up, so it can respond very quickly to a second attack. This is called immunity.

Find out more

Bacteria p.313
Cellular respiration p.346
Blood p.348
Growth and development p.362
Fact finder p.422

SKELETONS

A SKELETON SUPPORTS an animal's body. It makes up a framework that protects and keeps the body in shape, and gives its muscles something to pull against. Most familiar animals have skeletons that are made of something hard, such as bone or shell. The larger an animal is, the stronger the support system has to be. Many small animals also have skeletons, but they are not always made from hard parts. An earthworm does not have a single bone in its body, and instead it supports itself by pressure from inside. Its body fluid presses against its skin like air inside a tyre, making what is called a hydrostatic skeleton; that is what allows it to burrow through earth.

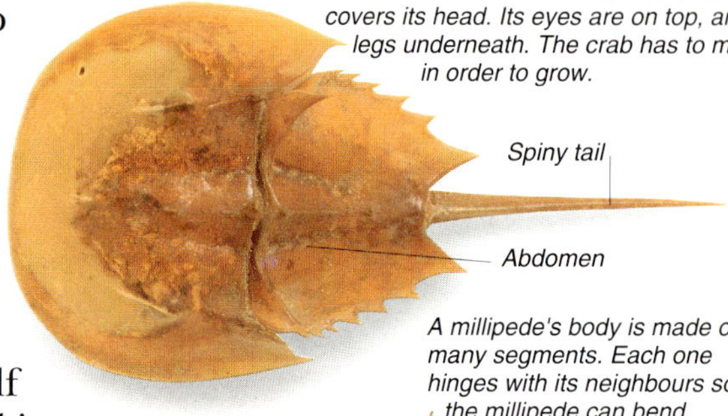

The horseshoe crab has a domed shield that covers its head. Its eyes are on top, and its legs underneath. The crab has to moult in order to grow.

A millipede's body is made of many segments. Each one hinges with its neighbours so the millipede can bend. Millipedes have to moult to grow.

Unlike an insect or a crustacean, a mussel does not have to moult. Its shell gets bigger with the rest of its body.

EXOSKELETONS

Many invertebrate animals have an exoskeleton, which is a hard case that supports their bodies from outside. In insects and other arthropods, the exoskeleton is made of stiff plates that meet at flexible joints. The plates cannot change size once they have formed. To grow, an insect has to shed its exoskeleton and make another one. In beetles, the forewings have evolved into a pair of hard plates, or elytra. These cover the wings underneath.

LIVING IN A CASE

An exoskeleton has several advantages, and two important drawbacks. It protects its owner from injury, and it also makes it harder for disease-causing organisms to attack. In land animals, it also helps to stop the body drying out. However, an exoskeleton can be heavy, particularly on land. Some exoskeletons also have to be moulted (shed) as their owners grow. During moulting, the exoskeleton splits and the animal wriggles out of it, exposing a new soft one underneath. Until this one enlarges and hardens, the animal has to hide as it is vulnerable to its predators.

These horns are very hard because they are made of chitin.

Rhinoceros beetle

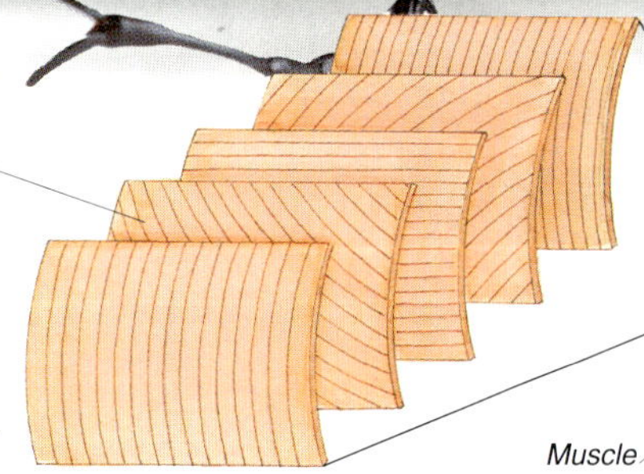
Layers of chitin laid on top of each other.

CHITIN

Insect exoskeletons are made from a substance called chitin. This is laid down in layers of parallel fibres. The fibres in the different layers often run in different directions, which makes the exoskeleton very strong.

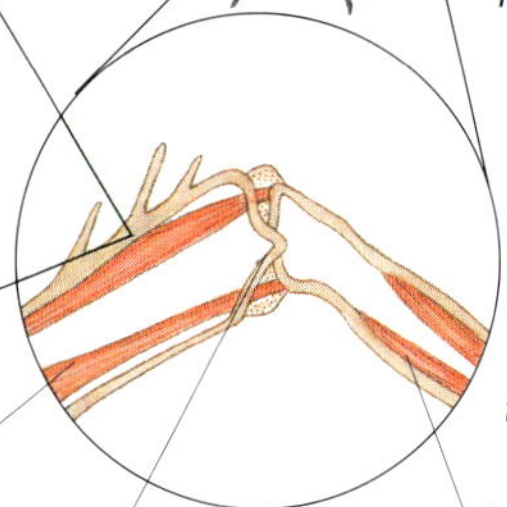

The joints are made of flexible tissue so that the animal can move the different sections of its body easily.

A beetle's legs are covered with hard chitin plates, like the rest of its body. The muscles that move its legs are attached to the inside of the plates in the next segment.

Young shell with few turns

Older shell with more turns

SHELLS

Molluscs have hard exoskeletons, their shells, which are made from the mineral calcium carbonate. As a mollusc grows, it keeps laying down the mineral to the lip of its shell. This gradually adds extra turns, so that the space inside the shell gets bigger. By enlarging its shell, a mollusc can keep the same exoskeleton for the whole of its life. Unlike an insect or a crustacean, it does not have to moult.

SUPPORT IN PLANTS AND SINGLE-CELLED ORGANISMS

All plant cells are supported by cellulose, but many of the cells in wood also have a tough substance called lignin. Trees stay upright because they have evolved this very strong support material. In the sea, single-celled diatoms make beautiful skeletons from silica, the same mineral that sand is made of. Each species of diatom makes a skeleton in a different shape.

Diatoms

Palm trees

Endoskeletons

Like all vertebrates, humans have an endoskeleton – a skeleton that supports the body from inside. Most endoskeletons are made of bone and cartilage. Bone provides the strength, while cartilage at the joints lets bones slide over each other so that the body can move. The human skeleton is made up of about 206 bones, ranging in size from the thighbone to the tiny bones of the inner ear. Unlike an insect's body case, our skeleton grows in step with the rest of our body.

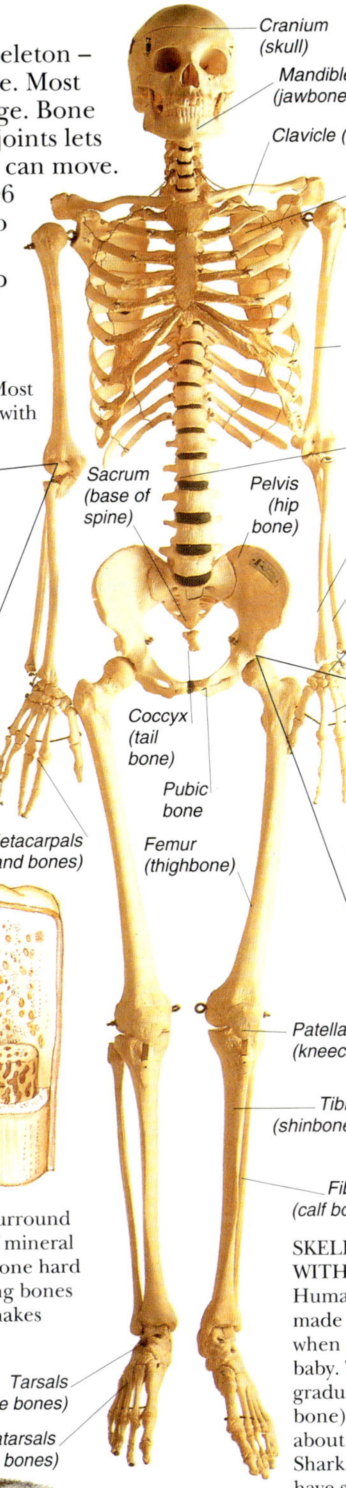

JOINTS

The area where different bones meet is called a joint. Most joints are movable, and in these the bones are covered with a layer of cartilage. They slip over each other easily because the cartilage is smooth and lubricated with a special fluid. The whole joint is enclosed in a tough membrane.

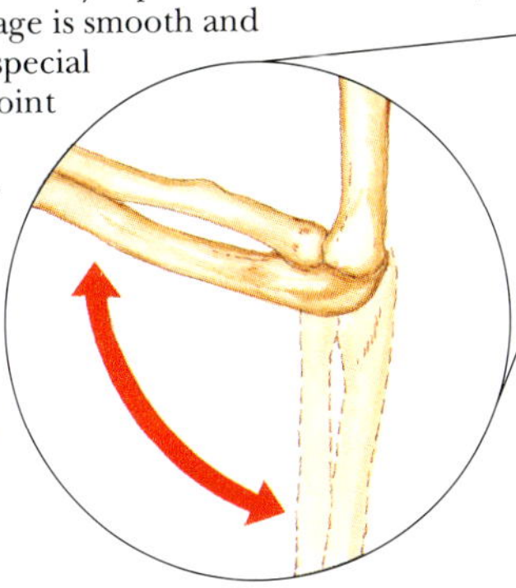

HINGE JOINTS

Your elbow is a hinge joint. It can swing up and down, but not from side to side.

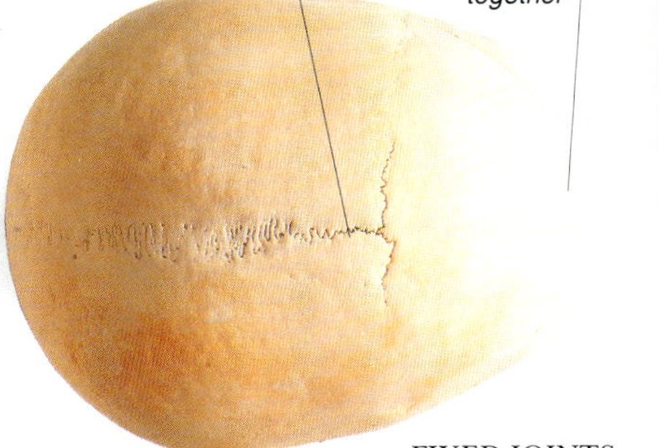

FIXED JOINTS

Some joints are locked together and cannot move. These are found between the bones that protect your brain, in your skull. When the skull first forms, its bones are separate. They gradually grow together, forming wiggly lines called suture lines. The two bones that make your forehead join together completely for added strength.

BALL AND SOCKET JOINTS

Your hip and shoulder joints can move in almost any direction. Each one contains a long bone that ends in a ball, and a socket that the ball fits into. The two bones are held together by strong fibres called ligaments.

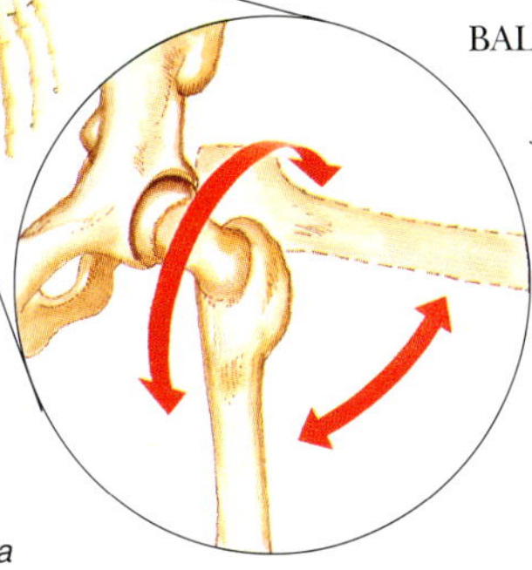

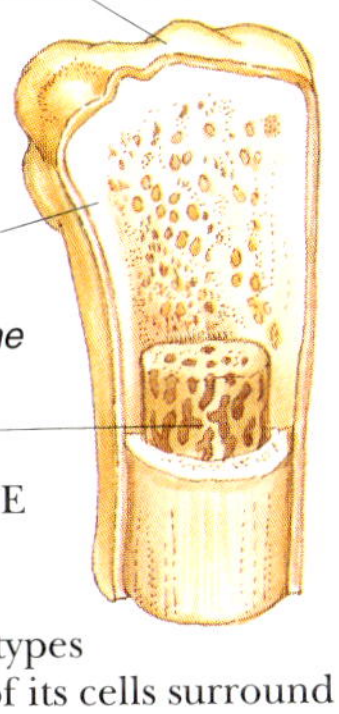

INSIDE A BONE

Bone is a living tissue that contains many types of cells. Some of its cells surround themselves with crystals of mineral salts, and this makes the bone hard and stiff. The inside of long bones contains marrow, which makes blood cells and stores fat.

SKELETONS WITHOUT BONES

Human skeletons are made entirely of cartilage when they first form, in a baby. The cartilage gradually ossifies (turns into bone) until we are about 25 years old. Sharks and rays have skeletons that never ossify. Because they live in water, cartilage alone is strong enough to support their bodies.

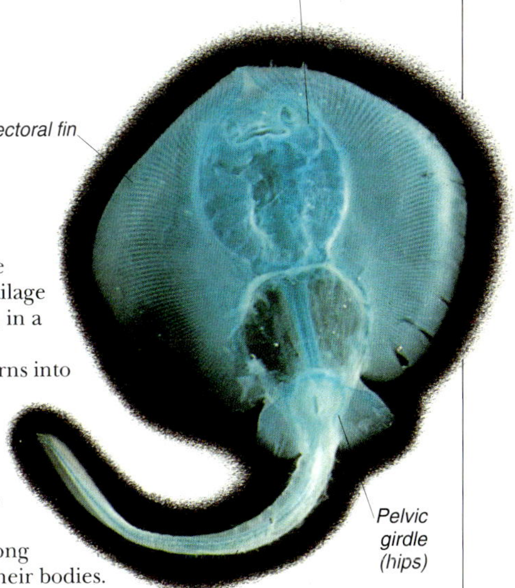

Cartilaginous skeleton of a ray

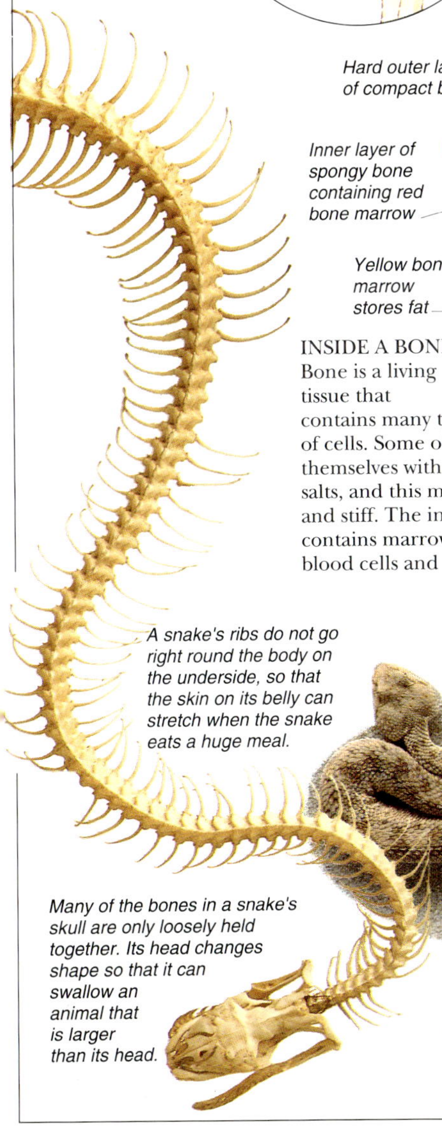

SKELETON WITHOUT LEGS

A snake's skeleton is almost entirely skull, spine, and ribs. It contains hundreds of vertebrae (the individual bones that make up the spine). A snake can coil up its body because its spine contains a huge number of joints, and each can bend a little way. Snakes have no arm or leg bones, and most snakes have also lost all traces of their shoulder and hip bones as well.

Find out more

Single-celled organisms p.314
Arthropods p.322
Muscles p.355
Movement p.356

SKIN

SKIN IS A TOUGH, FLEXIBLE COVERING that protects your body, and helps to keep it at the right temperature. Although it feels alive, its outer surface is completely dead. Without this dead layer, your body would soon dry out or be invaded by bacteria. Your skin renews its outer surface all the time, and quickly repairs itself when it gets cut or scratched. If part of your skin, such as the soles of your feet, gets more wear than normal, it gets thicker. Most of your skin is covered with hair, but most mammals have much more hair. Your skin is very good at cooling you down. If you are hot, the capillaries in your skin fill with blood so that heat is lost to the air, and you sweat, which cools you down when the sweat evaporates. Skin is your largest organ; in an adult it covers about 2 sq m (21 sq ft).

FEEDING ON SKIN
Every day, people shed millions of dead cells from the surface of their skin. These cells are found in house dust, and they provide food for tiny house dust mites. The mites are usually harmless, but some people can be allergic to their droppings.

INSIDE THE SKIN

Skin is made of two layers, the epidermis and the dermis. The epidermis is the outer layer. At its base is a single layer of cells that divide all the time. As the new cells are pushed upwards they die, forming a tough layer on the surface. The dermis is the lower layer and is much thicker. It contains elastic fibres that make the skin stretchy. It also has hair follicles, blood vessels, sensitive nerve endings, fat, and sweat glands. Sweat glands send sweat to the surface of your skin through little holes called pores.

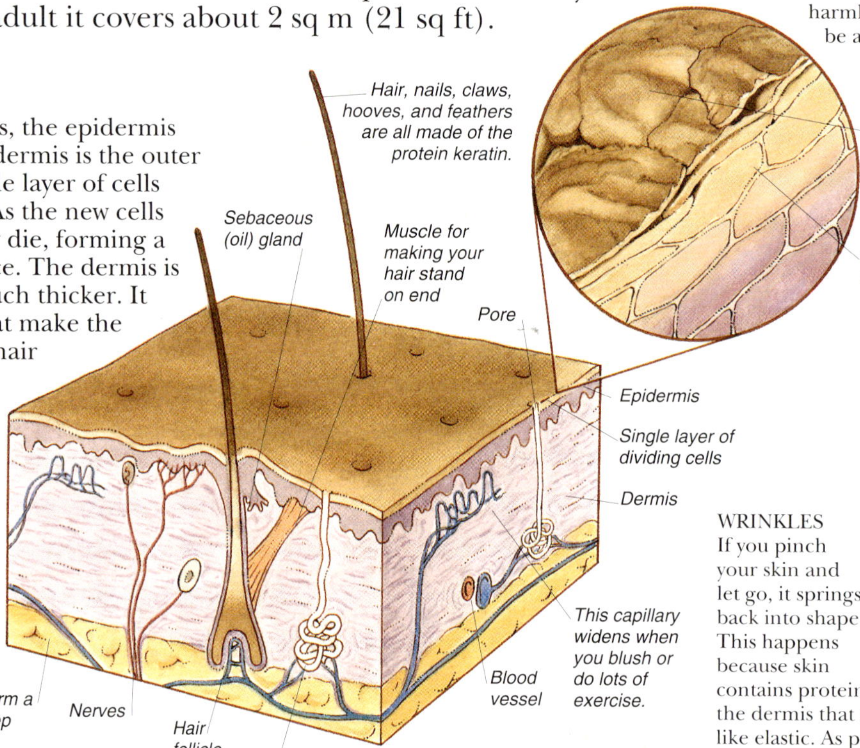

Section through human skin

WRINKLES
If you pinch your skin and let go, it springs back into shape. This happens because skin contains proteins in the dermis that stretch like elastic. As people get older, their skin becomes less elastic, so it begins to form wrinkles.

SCALES
Most fish are covered in overlapping scales to protect their skin. They grow out from the dermis, and are made from bone and other tissues. Most bony fish have round scales that make them shiny and smooth, while sharks have small pointed scales that give their skin a sandpapery texture.

SKIN COLOUR
Some animals can change the colour of their skin. For example, the cuttlefish changes its colour by changing the size of special droplets in its skin. Humans get their skin colour mainly from a pigment called melanin, which is made just beneath the skin's surface. Some people also have carotene in their dermis. So everyone's skin is the same except for the amount of pigment it contains.

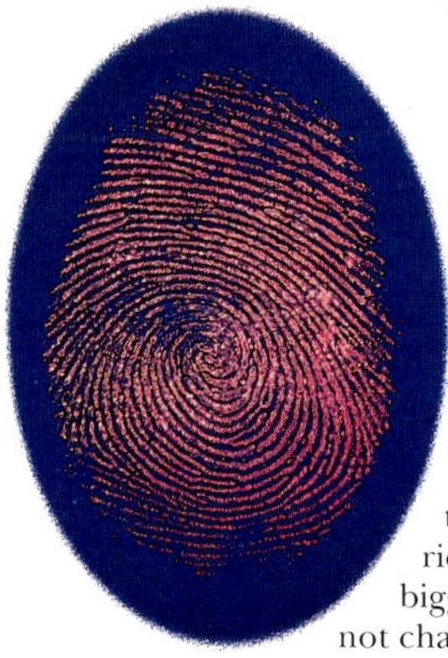

FINGERPRINTS
The skin on the palms of your hands and the soles of your feet has tiny ridges. These give your skin a better grip for holding on to things. Every person has their own unique pattern of ridges. The pattern gets bigger as you grow, but it does not change shape.

Find out more

HEAT TRANSFER P.142
MOLLUSCS P.324
FISH P.326
REPTILES P.330
BIRDS P.332
INTERNAL ENVIRONMENT P.350

MUSCLES

ABOUT HALF THE WEIGHT of your body is taken up by muscles. They make your body move. Muscles can pull, but they cannot push. To make up for this, most of your muscles are arranged in pairs or groups, so that they pull in opposite directions. Vertebrates (animals with backbones) have three different types of muscles. Voluntary or skeletal muscles are attached to your bones by tough tendons, and when they contract, part of your body moves. These muscles are easy to feel, because you can make them move whenever you want to. You also have other muscles that work automatically. These are called involuntary or smooth muscles. They squeeze food through your digestive tract, for example. A third kind of muscle is found only in your heart. Cardiac or heart muscle contracts automatically, and never gets tired.

HUMAN MUSCLES

The human body contains about 660 voluntary muscles (muscles you can move when you want to). They have a rich blood supply, which provides them with oxygen and glucose. Muscles get warm when they contract, and they supply about four-fifths of your body's heat.

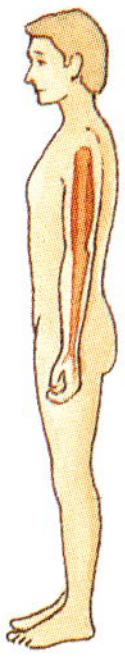

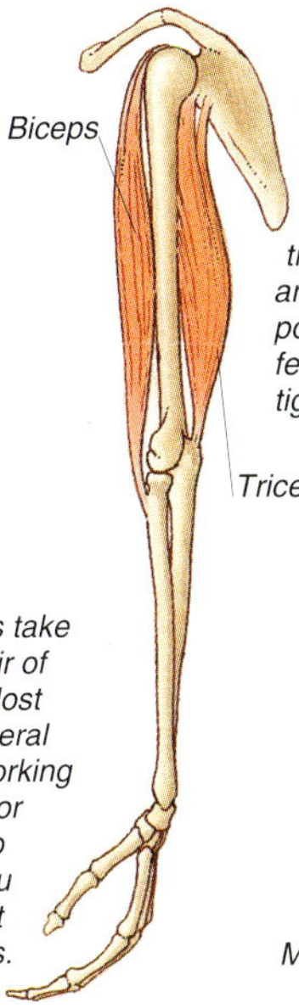

When you lower your arm, your biceps muscle relaxes. If you now try to make your arm as straight as possible, you can feel your triceps tighten up.

Very few movements take just one pair of muscles. Most involve several muscles working together. For example, to swallow you use at least six muscles.

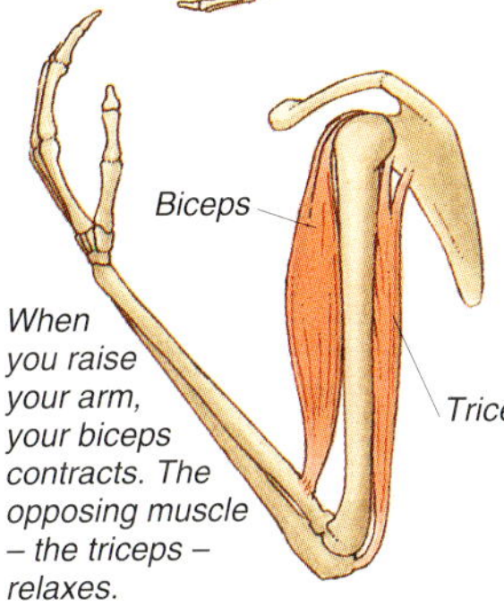

When you raise your arm, your biceps contracts. The opposing muscle – the triceps – relaxes.

MAKING A MOVE

When a frog jumps, signals flash from its brain through its nerves to the muscles in its legs. The signals cross from the nerves to the muscle fibres, and the fibres contract. Even when the frog is not moving, some of its muscle fibres contract while others relax. This makes each muscle firm (toned) which keeps the frog's body in shape. Muscle tone is important in our bodies as well, and it is improved by regular exercise.

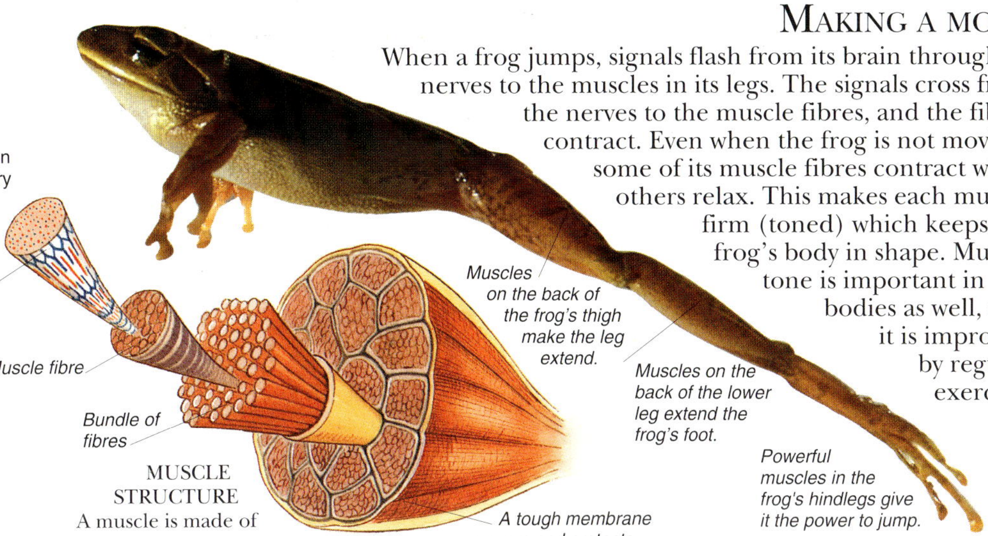

Muscles on the back of the frog's thigh make the leg extend.

Muscles on the back of the lower leg extend the frog's foot.

Powerful muscles in the frog's hindlegs give it the power to jump.

A tough membrane covers and protects the muscle.

MUSCLE STRUCTURE

A muscle is made of lots of fibres arranged in bundles. Each fibre is a single cell. The cells are unusual because they have many nuclei, and can be more than 1 cm (1/2 in) long. The fibres (cells) are made of even smaller filaments, called myofibrils. These contain chemicals that slide past each other and make the muscle contract.

HOW A MUSCLE CONTRACTS

A myofibril contains bunches of two proteins, actin and myosin. Each one is made of separate filaments, and these are packed in overlapping layers. When the myofibril is relaxed, the actin and myosin filaments overlap slightly. If the myofibril is triggered by an electric signal from a nerve, the myosin filaments are attracted to the actin filaments, and they slide past each other. The myofibril shortens, and so the muscle contracts.

LUIGI GALVANI

By accident, the Italian Professor of Anatomy Luigi Galvani (1737-98) discovered that a dead frog's legs contracted if they were pegged to an iron frame with brass pins. Galvani thought that frogs' muscles made electricity, which caused the contractions. Galvani was right to think that electricity made the muscles move, but in fact it was the two metals reacting together that made the electricity. We now know that in living animals, electrical signals from nerves make muscles contract.

Rough limpet (Collisella seabla)

LOCKING SHUT

If you lift a heavy weight, your arms will quickly get tired. But after the muscle in a limpet's foot contracts, it locks in position. Once locked, it does not need any more energy to stay contracted, although it does need energy to unlock. This is a special sort of voluntary muscle called catch muscle.

Find out more

CELLS AND BATTERIES P.150
MOLLUSCS P.324
AMPHIBIANS P.328
CELLS P.338
CIRCULATION P.349
MOVEMENT P.356
NERVES P.360

MOVEMENT

EVEN WHEN YOU SIT VERY STILL, parts of your body are moving. Your heart beats to send blood around your body, and food is moved through your digestive system. This is involuntary movement, because you do it without thinking about it. Like most animals, you use voluntary movement to move part of your body, or carry your entire body from place to place. Moving your whole body from one place to another is called locomotion. The way an animal moves about depends on the shape of its body, its surroundings, and its size. Small animals generate more power in proportion to their weight, so in relative terms, they move faster than large ones. If a cockroach was as large as a human, and its speed was scaled up in proportion, it would race along at 140 km/h (85 mph).

MOVEMENT IN PLANTS

Some plants, such as daisies, open their flowers when the Sun rises, and close them when it sets. This is known as sleep movement, and happens because of pressure changes inside the plants' cells. Leaf-folding is another common form of sleep movement. It happens, for example, in clovers and other members of the pea family.

Daisies (Bellis perennis) *closing their flowers as the Sun goes down.*

PERISTALSIS

When you swallow, muscles at the back of your mouth contract to push food down your oesophagus. This movement, called peristalsis, carries food through the whole of your digestive system. You decide when to swallow, but after that your food is moved by automatic peristalsis – an involuntary movement.

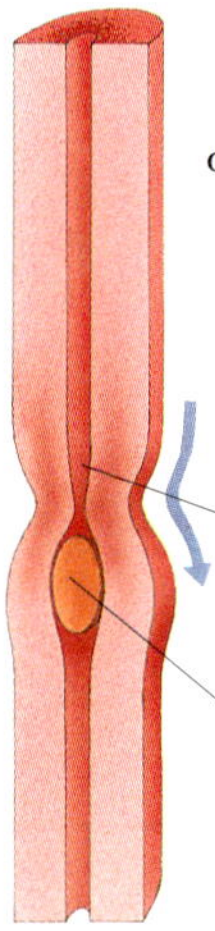

Peristalsis happens in reverse when the stomach rejects food. When this happens, you vomit.

Garden snail (*Helix aspersa*)

SNAIL TRAIL

Snails and slugs have a single sucker-like foot. The foot is made of muscle, which contracts in waves to allow the animal to creep forwards. Mucus (slime) enables a snail to grip and move over rough surfaces.

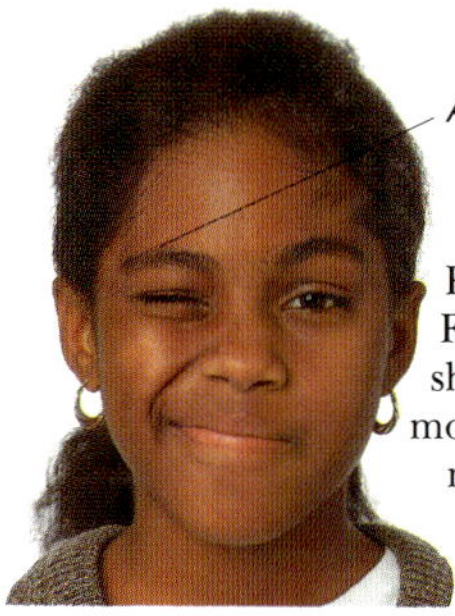

A wink is a conscious movement that is relatively slow. Blinking is a very fast automatic movement that cleans your eyeballs.

FACIAL EXPRESSIONS

Facial expressions, such as looking shocked, or smiling, are tiny voluntary movements made by more than 30 different muscles. Although they are voluntary, you often make these movements with hardly any thought.

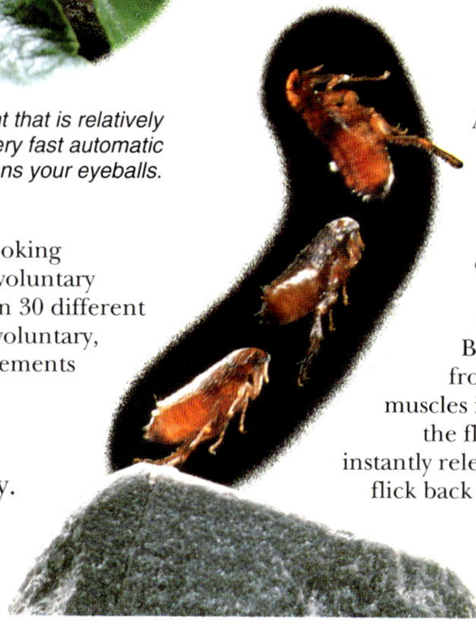

ELASTIC POWER

A flea can leap over 100 times its own height because of tiny pads of resilin, a rubber-like protein that stores energy. The pads are in the joints between the flea's legs and its body. Before each leap, energy from the flea's contracted muscles is stored in the pads. As the flea jumps, this energy is instantly released, causing its legs to flick back suddenly, throwing the flea into the air.

MOVING ON LEGS

Animals with legs have to move them in a carefully co-ordinated way. We move our legs alternately. A walking cheetah moves its front right leg and back left leg together, then the opposite pair. When it is running at top speed, it moves its front legs together and then its back legs together.

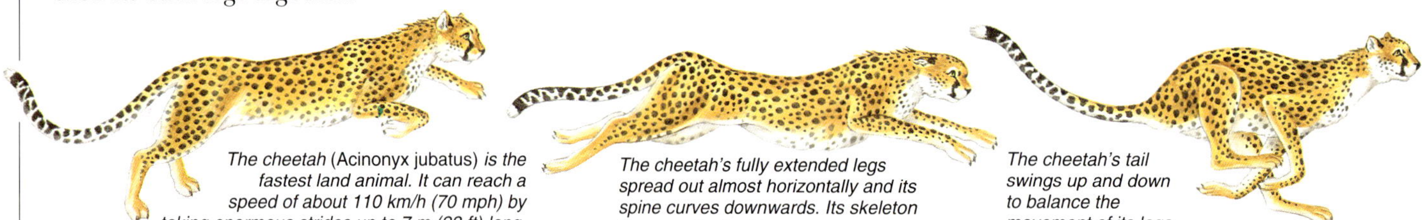

The cheetah (Acinonyx jubatus) *is the fastest land animal. It can reach a speed of about 110 km/h (70 mph) by taking enormous strides up to 7 m (23 ft) long.*

The cheetah's fully extended legs spread out almost horizontally and its spine curves downwards. Its skeleton is unusually flexible.

The cheetah's tail swings up and down to balance the movement of its legs.

The cheetah's spine curves upwards so that its back legs can come as far forwards as possible, ready for the next leap.

MOVING WITHOUT LEGS

Snakes move by four different methods. In the most common way, a snake curves its body. This is called serpentine motion. Each curve pushes against the ground so that the snake slides forwards. In tight spaces, a snake anchors its tail, and then stretches forwards. Its tail then catches up in a concertina motion. Heavy snakes creep along in a straight line, by raising and lowering their belly scales. This is called rectilinear motion. Some snakes throw themselves forwards in a special movement called sidewinding.

This common garter snake (Thamnopis sirtalis) *is moving along using serpentine motion.*

Flying and swimming

Flying and swimming are ways of moving through two quite different fluids. Animals fly and swim by pushing backwards. A force called reaction acts in the opposite direction, so that they travel forwards. The bodies of most swimming animals are as dense as the water around them, so they do not rise or sink. Flying animals have bodies that are far denser than air. They have to use their wings for staying up, as well as for moving along.

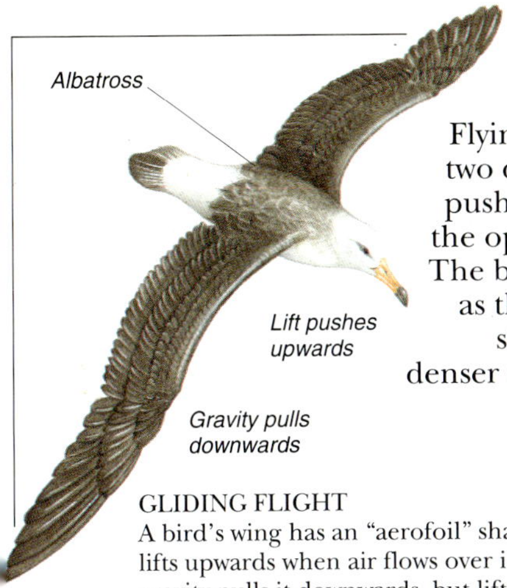

Albatross

Lift pushes upwards

Gravity pulls downwards

Gliding flight

A bird's wing has an "aerofoil" shape, which means that it lifts upwards when air flows over it. When a bird glides, gravity pulls it downwards, but lift opposes the downward force. Birds use gliding flight to cover long distances with little effort, especially in warm rising air.

Flapping flight

A bird flaps its wings to push itself through the air. As it moves forwards, the air flowing over its wings creates lift, which holds the bird up. If the bird stops flapping, it slows down. The lift decreases, so it begins to drop. Birds use flapping flight to travel at speed or in a set direction.

5. The wings are ready to be pulled down again by powerful muscles in the bird's chest.

4. The wings begin to move up once again. Lift counteracts gravity, so the bird stays up as its flies along.

Steering in the air

Many flying insects have two pairs of wings. Craneflies and house flies have just one pair. Their hindwings have evolved into tiny club-shaped organs called halteres. The halteres vibrate as the insect flies, and they produce nerve signals that keep the insect on course.

Halteres help this cranefly keep its balance as it flies along.

3. During the downstroke, the wings push down and backwards against the air. Reaction makes the bird move up and forwards.

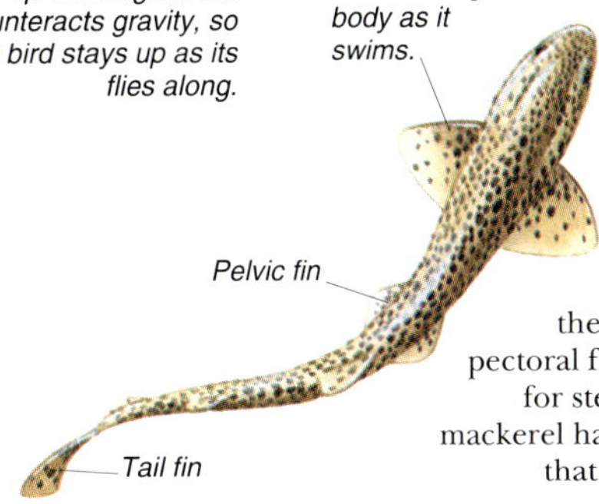

A dogfish uses its pectoral (front) fins to alter the angle of its body as it swims.

Pelvic fin

Tail fin

Swimming

A fish swims by pushing against the water with its fins or with its whole body. Most cartilaginous fish, such as this dogfish, bend their bodies as they swim, but bony fish, such as a goldfish, often propel themselves just with their tail or pectoral fins. They use their other fins for steering. Fish such as tuna and mackerel have special groups of muscles that are used for bursts of speed.

2. During the upstroke, the bird raises its wings so that they almost touch.

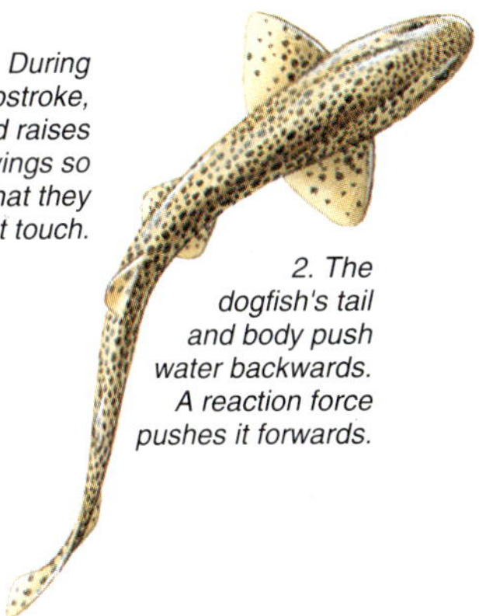

2. The dogfish's tail and body push water backwards. A reaction force pushes it forwards.

Jet propulsion

A squid's body contains a cavity that is normally filled with water. The squid can make the cavity contract very rapidly, so that the water squirts outwards through a tube called a siphon. The force of the moving water pushes the squid in the opposite direction. The squid changes direction by altering the position of its siphon. Cuttlefish and octopuses also move by this kind of jet propulsion.

1. The woodpigeon's streamlined body reduces its friction with the air as it flies along.

Flapping flight

The cilia on a sea gooseberry's body are for locomotion. The cilia on its tentacles help it catch food particles.

Moving by hairs

Sea gooseberries, also called comb jellies, do not have any legs or fins. Instead, they move by beating tiny hairs, called cilia. The cilia are arranged in clusters that work like paddles. A sea gooseberry uses its cilia to stay the right way up, and to keep near the sea's surface.

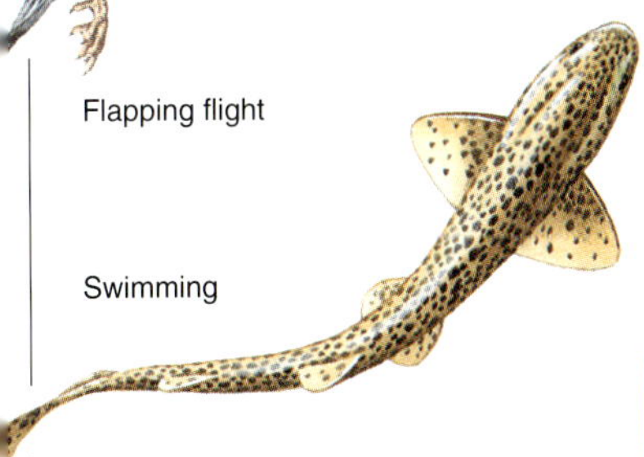

Swimming

1. A swimming dogfish contracts the muscles on either side of its body in turn. This makes its body curve from side to side.

Staying in one place

Barnacles are marine animals that glue themselves to hard surfaces. They feed by beating their feathery legs, and collecting any food that becomes trapped in them. Barnacles spend their entire adult lives in one place. Like all sessile animals (animals that are fixed in one place), their larvae can swim or drift from one place to another.

Find out more

Speed p.118
Forces and motion p.120
Molluscs p.324
Fish p.326
Reptiles p.330
Birds p.332
Digestion p.345
Muscles p.355

Senses

IF YOU HAVE EVER TRIED to find a friend who is hiding, you will know how important your senses are. If your friend makes just one accidental sound, or moves something, it will be enough to let you know where she is. Senses keep us in touch with our surroundings, and also with our bodies. Sense organs like eyes and ears send a stream of information along nerves to the brain. The brain sorts out the signals, and then makes the body react to them. Different animals rely on different senses according to their way of life. Some, such as cats, have very good eyesight and hearing; others, such as dogs, have a strong sense of smell.
Some animals find out about their surroundings by detecting pressure, heat, or even electricity.

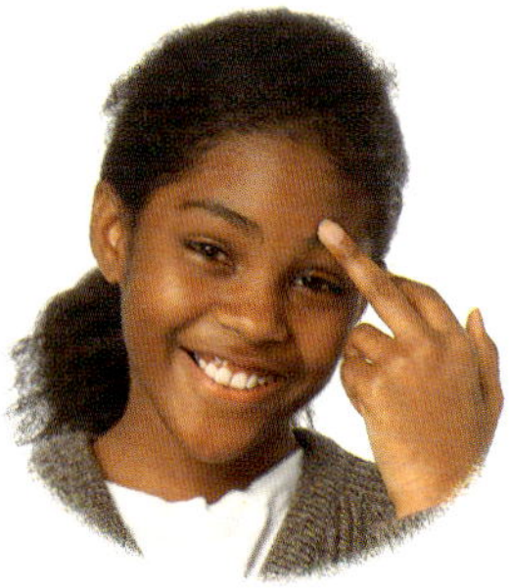

ALL THE SENSES
People often refer to the five senses, but you have many more than this. Touch is actually several senses. Special nerve endings in your skin detect pressure, pain, heat, and cold. You can feel where your arms and legs are, and your sense of balance helps you stay upright.

WHISKERS
When there is no light to see by, you may walk with your arms out in front to feel your way. Other animals, such as this crested porcupine (*Hysterix africaeaustralis*), feel with their whiskers. These are long stiff hairs on an animal's head. They will brush against anything in the way before the animal bumps into it.

LATERAL LINE
Many fish have a line of sensors along their sides, called a lateral line. These sensors detect waves of pressure travelling through the water. A fish's lateral line enables it to feel the movement of other animals around it.

Sensing movement and pressure

Many sense organs detect movement and pressure, which includes touch, sound, and vibrations. Most of a grasshopper's body is sensitive to touch. Its body also has cells that detect vibrations in the ground, and these warn it to hop out of the way when another animal approaches. Sound is another form of pressure, and the grasshopper detects this through its ears.

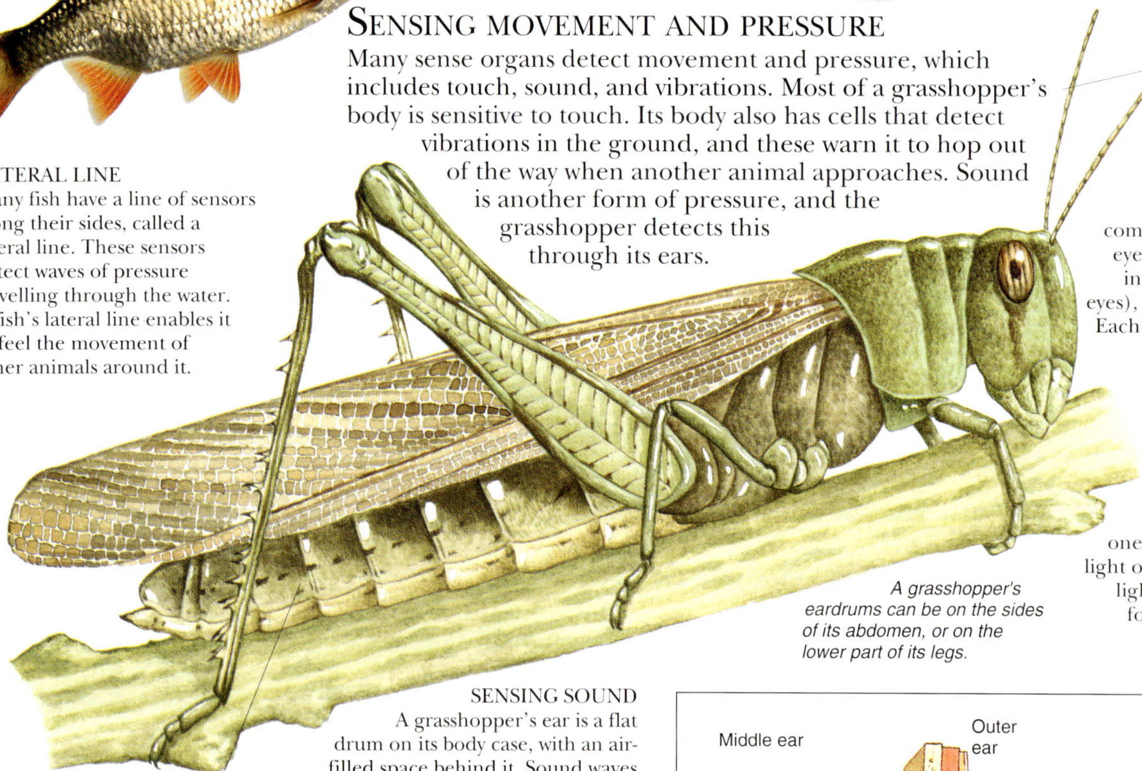

SENSING LIGHT
A grasshopper has compound eyes. These are eyes which are divided up into many facets (simple eyes), each with its own lens. Each facet has a lens, and it forms a tiny image. The grasshopper combines these images to see the world around it. Our eyes work in a different way. They each have just one lens. The lens focuses light onto a curved screen of light-sensitive nerve cells, forming just one image.

SENSING SOUND
A grasshopper's ear is a flat drum on its body case, with an air-filled space behind it. Sound waves vibrate the drum. Cells attached to the drum sense the vibration, and send signals to the brain. Small insects, such as midges and mosquitoes, can detect sound with their antennae.

BODY SENSORS
The hard plates around a grasshopper's body are linked by flexible joints. Each joint has special cells on either side, which are either squashed or stretched, depending on the joint's position. The cells send signals to the grasshopper's brain, and from these signals the animal can sense the way the body is positioned. Like nearly all animals, a grasshopper also has other cells that detect the pull of gravity. This tells it which way up it is.

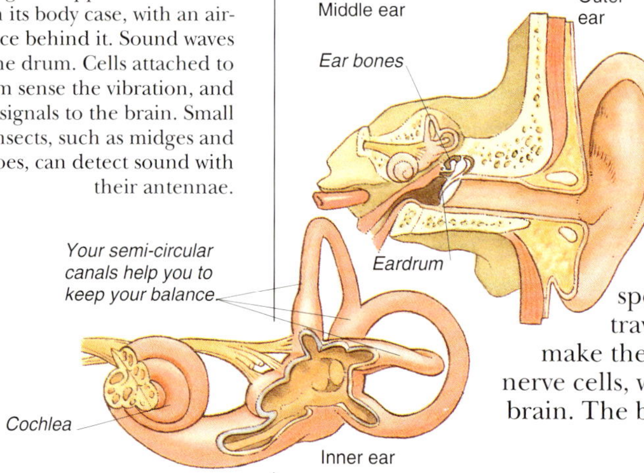

HUMAN EAR
Your outer ear channels sound waves into the eardrum, making it vibrate. Three tiny bones in the middle ear carry the movement to the cochlea. This contains a fluid and cells with special hairs. The vibrations travel through the fluid, and make the hairs move. This triggers nerve cells, which send signals to your brain. The brain sorts the signals into sounds that you hear.

Taste and smell

Animals use the senses of taste and smell to detect chemicals. When you taste something, groups of cells on your tongue, called taste-buds, detect chemicals dissolved in your saliva. When you smell something, cells at the top of your nose detect chemicals dissolved in the moist lining of your nose. Taste-buds detect only what we describe as sweet, sour, salt, and bitter. Flavours are combinations of these four, so they are much more varied. Taste is linked to the sense of smell, which is why it is hard to tell different foods apart if your nose is blocked.

Adder (*Vipera berus*)

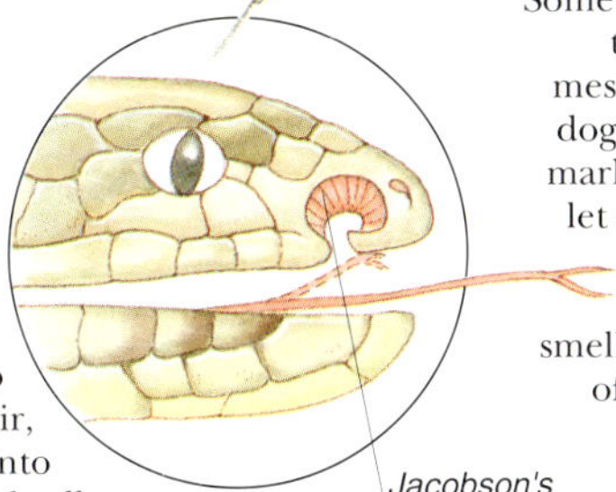

Jacobson's organ

JACOBSON'S ORGAN

A snake detects different smells in a pit in the roof of its mouth called a Jacobson's organ. The snake flicks out its tongue to collect chemicals from the air, then presses the forked tip into the Jacobson's organ. Special cells lining the pit detect the chemicals picked up from the air.

SMELL

Some animals use scents to send and receive messages. For example, dogs leave their scent to mark their territory, or to let other dogs know they are around. Dogs use their sense of smell to build up a "picture" of the world around them.

Most taste-buds lie in tiny grooves in the surface of the tongue.

TASTE

Different taste-buds on an animal's tongue detect different tastes, such as sweet or sour. An animal's sense of taste enables it to tell if something is good or bad to eat. Animals use this sense to choose food to eat, and to avoid eating something poisonous.

JUDGING DISTANCES

Many animals, including humans, have "binocular vision" which allows them to judge distances. Binocular vision means having two eyes facing forwards, which gives two slightly different views of the same object. The tiny jumping spider (*Lyssomanes viridis*) has four pairs of large eyes. Some of its eyes point sideways, but one pair looks directly forwards. This pair of eyes enables the spider to judge how far away its prey is before it jumps on to it.

A male cockchafer's antennae unfold like fans.

FINDING A MATE

Female insects often let male insects know where they are by releasing tiny amounts of chemicals called pheromones which spread through the air. These are detected by a male of the same species, which then follows the pheromone trail to track down the female in order to mate. The male cockchafer (*Melolontha melolontha*) detects the female's pheromones with its feathery antennae.

PLANT SENSES

Plants do not have special sense organs, but they can respond to the world around them. All plants detect light and gravity, and some plants also sense nearby objects. The sensitive plant (*Mimosa pudica*) has very quick reactions. Its leaves go limp if they are touched. The tendrils of climbing plants can "feel" things that they touch. They respond by coiling up, to attach the plant to a support.

The folding leaves of the sensitive plant may help the plant escape being eaten.

Tendrils of climbing plants, such as this pea plant, are modified leaves.

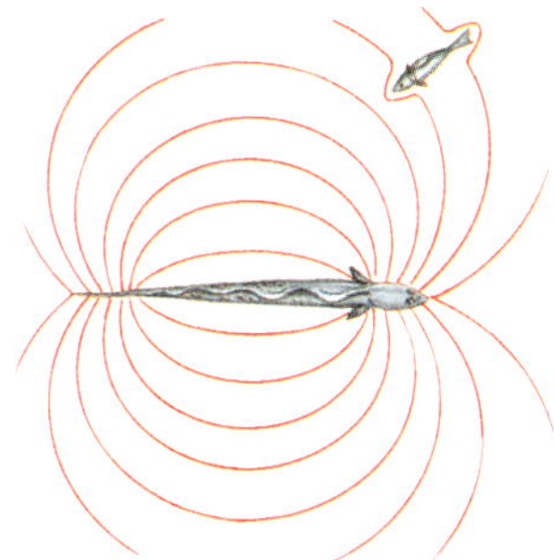

ELECTRIC FIELDS

In muddy water it is difficult to see. Some fish, such as this *Gymnarchus niloticus* use an electric field, produced by special muscles, to detect things nearby. If something disturbs the field, the fish can tell what it is by the size and position of the disturbance.

Find out more

Making and hearing sound p.182
Vision p.204
Arthropods p.322
Fish p.326
Skin p.354
Movement p.356
Nerves p.360
Brains p.361

NERVES

WHEN YOU PICK UP this book, lots of things happen very quickly. Your arms adjust to the book's weight, so that they lift it with just the right force. Muscles in your back contract, so that you do not tip forwards, and the lenses in your eyes change shape, so that your eyes focus on the pages. Thanks to your nerves, you are now ready to read. Nerves are bundles of long, thin cells called neurons which carry fast-moving electrical signals. The sensory neurons carry signals from different parts of your body to your brain or spinal cord. The motor neurons, carry signals from your brain or spinal cord to your muscles to make them contract. Between them are different neurons: the association neurons, which pass signals to motor neurons, and send messages to your brain.

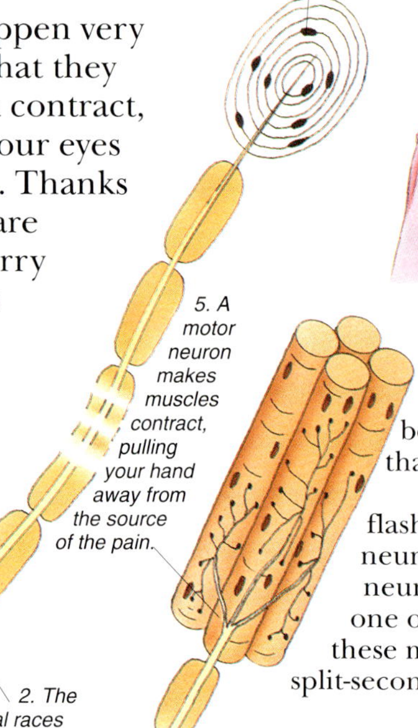

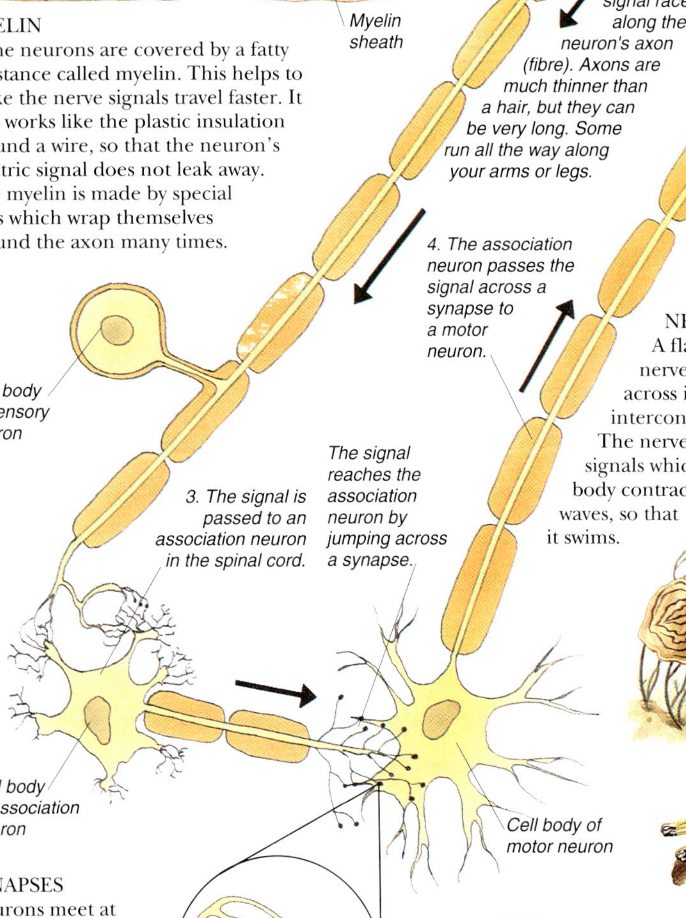

HOW NERVES WORK

You have three types of neuron (nerve cell) in your body. If you touch something that hurts, the pain is detected by a sensory neuron. This flashes a signal to an association neuron in your spinal cord. This neuron then passes the signal to one or more motor neurons, and these make you move. This kind of split-second reaction is called a reflex.

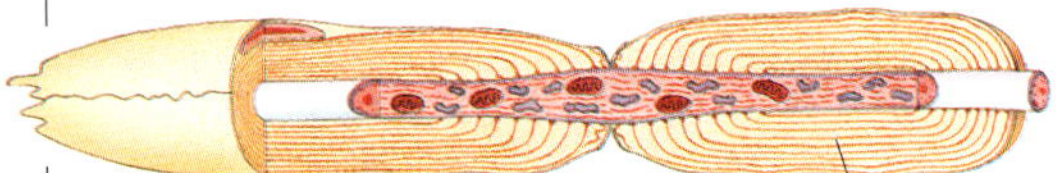

MYELIN

Some neurons are covered by a fatty substance called myelin. This helps to make the nerve signals travel faster. It also works like the plastic insulation around a wire, so that the neuron's electric signal does not leak away. The myelin is made by special cells which wrap themselves around the axon many times.

HUMAN NERVOUS SYSTEM

Your nervous system consists of the central nervous system (spinal cord and brain), and the peripheral nerves. Your brain co-ordinates almost everything that your body does. Some of your nervous system is under your control. The rest works automatically, so that your body runs smoothly without you telling it what to do.

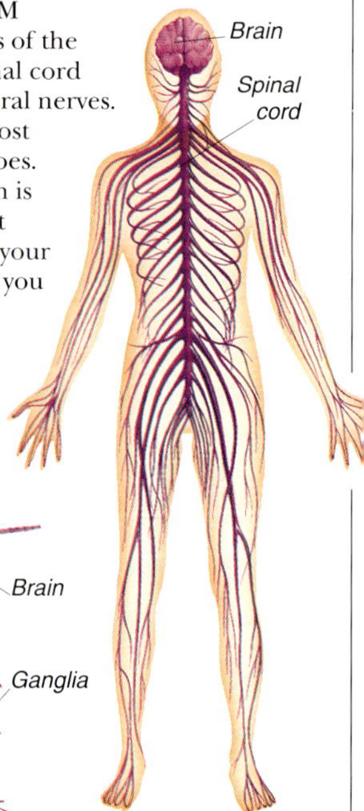

NERVE NETS

A flatworm's nerves are scattered across its body in an interconnecting net. The nerves produce signals which make its body contract in waves, so that it swims.

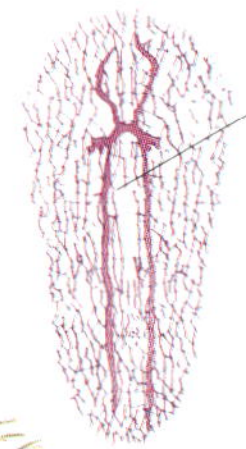

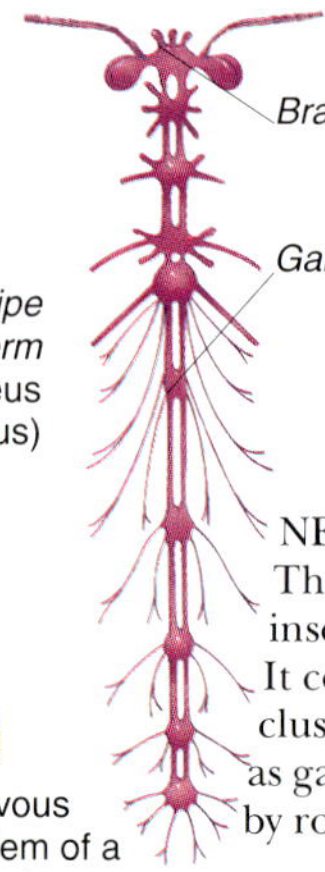

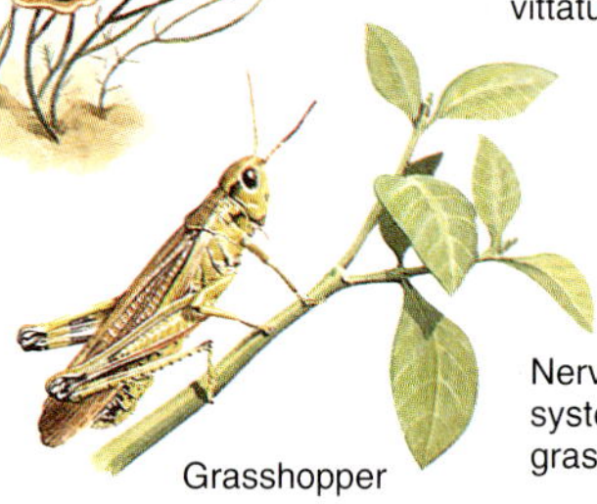

NERVES IN INSECTS

The nervous system of an insect is simpler than ours. It consists of a brain and clusters of neurons, known as ganglia. These are joined by rows of nerve fibres.

SYNAPSES

Neurons meet at tiny gaps, called synapses. Nerve signals jump across the gap in one direction. Some neurons pass on a signal as soon as they receive it. Others wait for a number of signals to arrive before sending one of their own.

GIANT NERVES

An earthworm has special giant neurons that run from its tail to its head. These cells carry signals about 50 times faster than the rest of its nerves. If a bird pecks at a worm's tail, signals race along the giant nerves and make the worm contract almost instantly.

Find out more

WORMS P.321
ARTHROPODS P.322
INTERNAL ENVIRONMENT P.350
MUSCLES P.355
SENSES P.358
BRAINS P.361

BRAINS

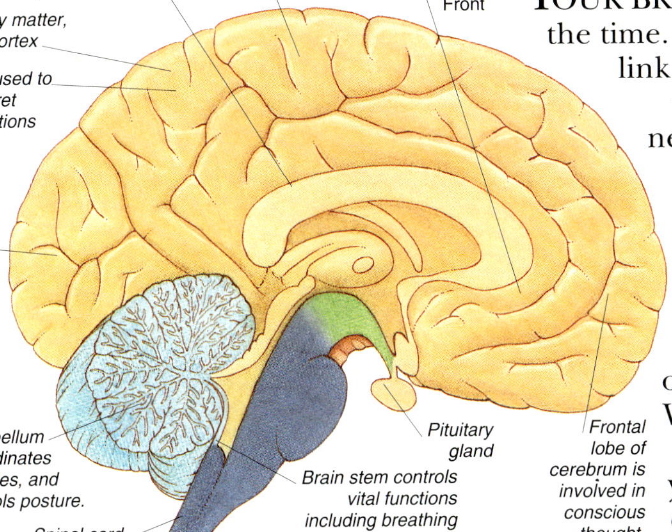

YOUR BRAIN IS IN TOUCH with the rest of your body all the time. It contains billions of neurons (nerve cells) that link up with each other, and with all of the nerves in your body. Scientists know a lot about individual neurons, but the way that the whole brain works is not fully understood. Experts are only just beginning to discover how we think or how we remember things. But it is known that our brains are divided up into separate areas. Some areas deal with the general running of the body. Others are involved in co-ordinating our movements, or understanding spoken words. While you are awake, you are conscious, or aware of what you are doing. When you fall asleep, your conscious brain shuts down, but other parts continue the essential work of keeping you alive.

HUMAN BRAIN

Your brain is divided into three main regions. Two of them, the brain stem and cerebellum, look after the running of your body. They control your breathing, your circulation, and your posture. The cerebrum, which is much larger, processes information. It is this part of your brain that you use to think. Your brain contains about 1,000 billion nerve cells when you are born. This number slowly decreases as you get older, because neurons die and cannot be replaced.

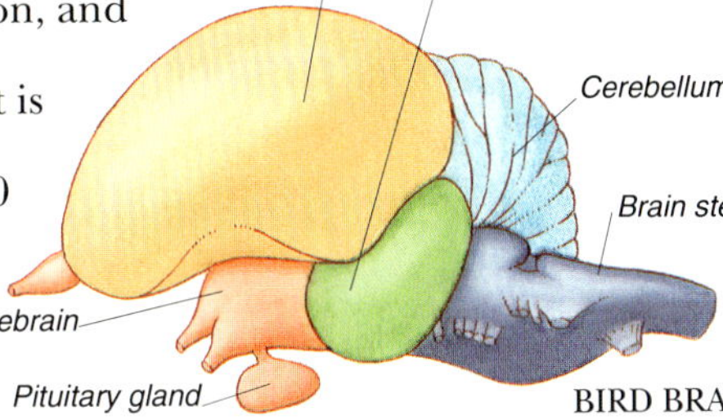

BIRD BRAIN

In a bird's brain, the cerebrum does not cover the cerebellum. The brain has a large optic lobe – the part that processes information from its eyes.

IVAN PAVLOV

Pavlov (1849-1936) was a Russian physiologist who investigated the way reflexes work. He knew that all animals have inbuilt reflexes, but he found that new reflexes could be conditioned (learned). Pavlov conditioned dogs to expect food after a bell was rung. He found that their new reflex made them salivate (drool) after the bell sounded, even if there was no food.

FROG BRAIN

A frog's cerebrum is quite small, while its cerebellum is tiny. Its brain stem makes up about half of the brain's volume. Vision is important to a frog because it hunts by sight. Its optic lobes are not as large as a bird's, but they are still a major part of its brain.

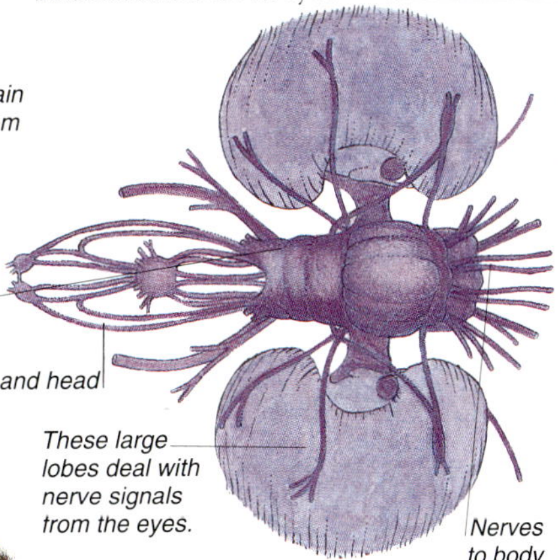

OCTOPUS BRAIN

An octopus has one of the largest brains of all invertebrates. It is built on a completely different plan from the brains of vertebrates, and has many connected lobes. Octopuses have good eyesight, and a large part of their brain deals with signals from their eyes. Experiments have found that octopuses are intelligent animals. They can work out how to reach food, even if this means taking the stopper out of a submerged bottle.

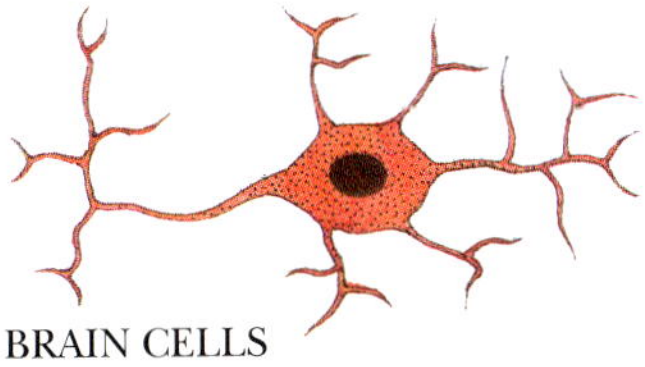

BRAIN CELLS

The nerve cells in the brain can have synapses with over 200,000 neighbouring cells. Signals from their neighbours may either make a group of cells send a message (like making you swallow), or prevent them from doing so (like taking a breath while you are swallowing).

INSTINCT AND LEARNING

A male great bower bird (*Chlamydera nuchalis*) builds an extraordinary bower (an alleyway) out of sticks, and decorates it with bright objects. If he is lucky, it will attract a mate for him. The male bower bird does not have to learn how to do this complicated work. Instead he does it by instinct. Instinct is a kind of behaviour that is inherited, rather than learned.

Find out more

MOLLUSCS P.324
AMPHIBIANS P.328
BIRDS P.332
SENSES P.358
NERVES P.360

GROWTH AND DEVELOPMENT

MOST LIVING THINGS GET BIGGER as they get older. They do not do this by having bigger cells, but by making more of them. When a cell gets to a certain size, it makes a copy of itself to make two new cells. The two new cells can also divide, and so many cells build up. This is cell division. Some living things, such as plants, carry on growing by cell division all their lives. But in most animals, including humans, cells divide more slowly once the adult body has taken shape.

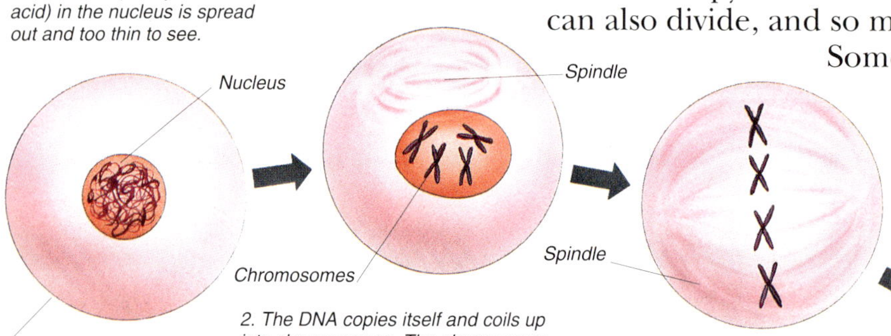

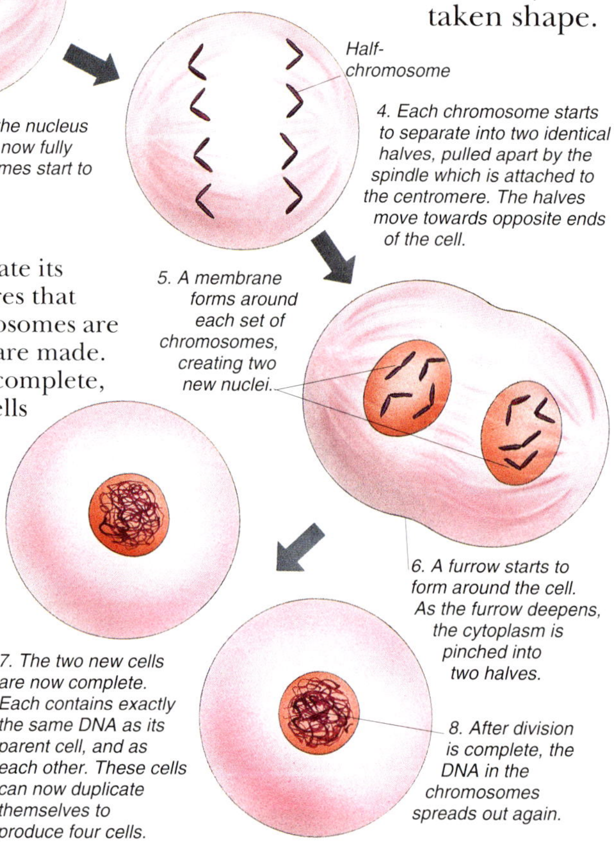

CELL DIVISION

Before a cell can divide, it must duplicate its chromosomes (the thread-like structures that contain DNA). The duplicated chromosomes are then pulled apart and two new nuclei are made. This is called mitosis. When mitosis is complete, the cell divides, so that two identical cells are made. This kind of cell division is used for growth. Another kind of division, called meiosis, occurs before sexual reproduction. It does not make identical cells.

DIVISION IN ACTION

In this thin layer of cells from an onion root, each cell is surrounded by a cell wall. The dividing cells have clearly visible chromosomes. In the other cells, the chromosomes are spread out in the nucleus. Plant and animal cells divide in a very similar way, although plant cells have to make a cellulose cell wall after they are formed.

GROWTH IN TREES

A tree grows in two different ways. Cells at the tips of its branches and roots divide so that the branches and roots grow longer. At the same time, cells just underneath the bark, called the cambium, divide to make the trunk and branches thicker.

As a sapling grows, its lowest branches drop off to leave a bare trunk. The trunk thickens but does not stretch upwards – an old branch scar will always stay at the same height.

Growth rings are formed by a burst of growth every spring, slower growth in summer, and none in winter.

Food stored in the seed gives it the energy to germinate.

SEEDLINGS

Growth needs lots of energy. A seedling can grow quickly because it has a store of food in a tissue in the seed called the endosperm. Sometimes the seed-leaves (cotyledons) also have a store of food. In many seedlings, the cotyledons quickly open up so that photosynthesis can begin.

CELL CYCLE

Many of the cells in your body divide according to a fixed timetable. A cell inside your cheek, for example, divides about once every 24 hours. Not all cells divide this quickly. In some cells, division is "switched off" during a long gap period. In nerve cells, division stops altogether after the cell is formed in a baby in the womb.

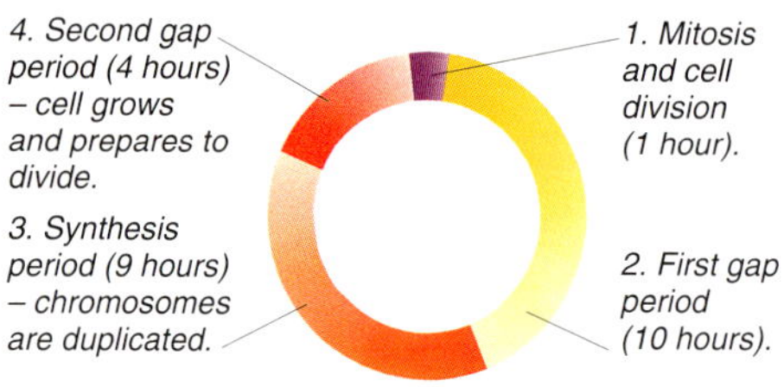

Division cycle of a cell from the inside of a cheek

Growing up

The cells in your body do not all divide at the same rate. As you grow up, many of your cells, particularly those in your arms and legs, divide faster than those in your head. As a result, your body slowly changes shape. This is development. Growth and development are controlled by hormones – chemical messengers which are carried by your blood to the different parts of your body. Some of these hormones make your body put on a sudden burst of growth from the age of about 12 or 13, and make you stop growing altogether at around 21.

Human development

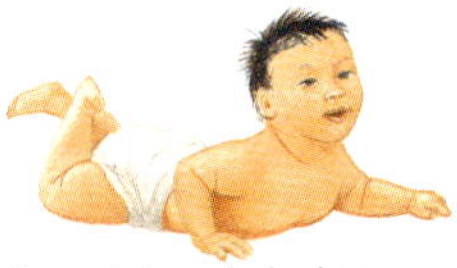

A newly born baby has a very large head, and short arms and legs.

A two-year-old's legs and arms have grown a lot. Its legs are now strong enough for walking.

By the age of five, the arm and leg muscles have got much stronger. A five-year-old can walk and run.

A 10-year-old has longer limbs, and has learned how to make precise movements, such as writing, or catching a ball.

At the age of 13, many changes are taking place in the body. It is growing quickly, and preparing for adulthood.

Most 20-year-olds are fully grown. The head is now a smaller part of the body. The wisdom teeth are one of the last parts to finish growing.

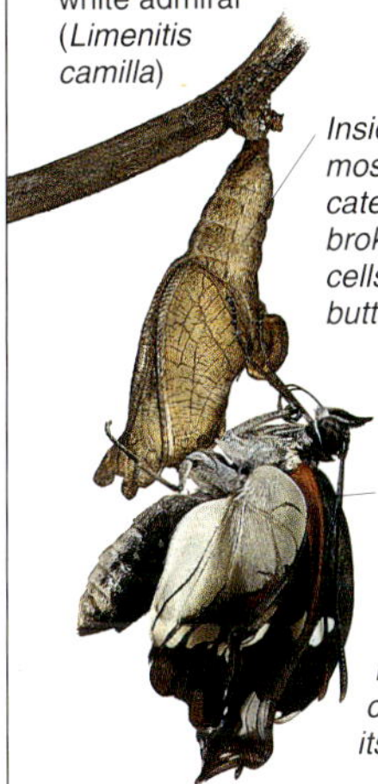

Southern white admiral (*Limenitis camilla*)

Inside a chrysalis, most of a caterpillar's cells are broken down. New cells then form the butterfly.

A caterpillar has powerful jaws but a butterfly has tubular mouthparts and can only drink its food.

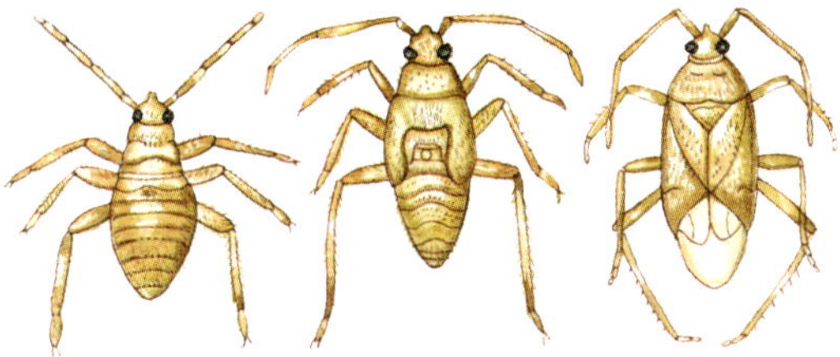

A mirid bug (leaf bug) in the second, fifth, and adult phases of incomplete metamorphosis.

Incomplete metamorphosis

A bug gradually changes shape as it grows up. When it hatches, it has no wings or reproductive organs. As it grows up, it moults (sheds its case). After each moult, its body changes slightly, and after the fifth moult it becomes an adult. This slow change of body shape is called incomplete metamorphosis. Cockroaches and grasshoppers also develop in this way.

Taking to the air

By changing shape, the same animal can use different kinds of food, and move in different ways. A caterpillar eats leaves, and spends all its time on plants. But when it turns into a butterfly, it feeds on nectar. It can now fly far away to search for new food plants, on which it will lay its eggs if it is a female.

A crab's zoea larva has a long tail, and a curved spine on its back. It beats its legs to keep near the surface.

A megalopa larva has well developed legs, no spine, and a shorter tail. It lives partly on the seabed.

An adult crab has a short tail, which is folded up underneath its body. It has strong legs, but is not a good swimmer. This is a shore crab (Carcinus maenas).

Complete metamorphosis

A crab changes shape completely as it grows up. It starts life as a tiny zoea larva, which floats in the upper waters of the sea. After moulting its body case several times, the zoea turns into a megalopa larva, which can walk as well as swim. Finally, the megalopa moults and becomes a young crab.

GROWING MISSING PARTS

If you cut yourself, cells in your skin start to divide until the cut has healed. This kind of growth is called regeneration. We can regenerate skin and bone, but some animals can regenerate entire parts of themselves, including legs and tails.

Starfish can grow a new leg if one breaks off.

Find out more

Flowering plants p.318
Arthropods p.322
Starfish and sea squirts p.325
Cells p.338
Internal environment p.350
Genetics p.364

GENETICS

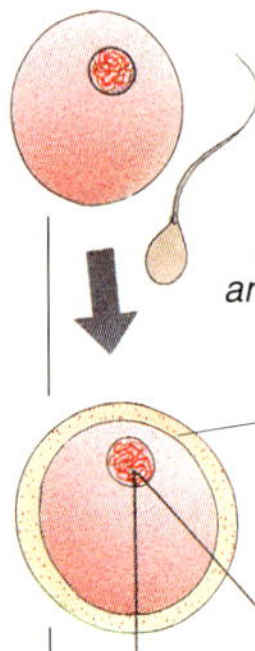

EVERY FORM OF LIFE, from an elephant to an alga, is put together and controlled by a chemical "recipe". Instead of being written down, this recipe is in the form of a chemical code. The code is contained in helical (spiral-shaped) molecules of deoxyribonucleic acid (DNA), which are packed away inside the cells of all living things. The chemical code is very complex. The code inside one human cell contains 50,000 to 100,000 separate instructions, called genes, and each one controls a different characteristic. Genetics is the study of the way that inherited characteristics are passed on.

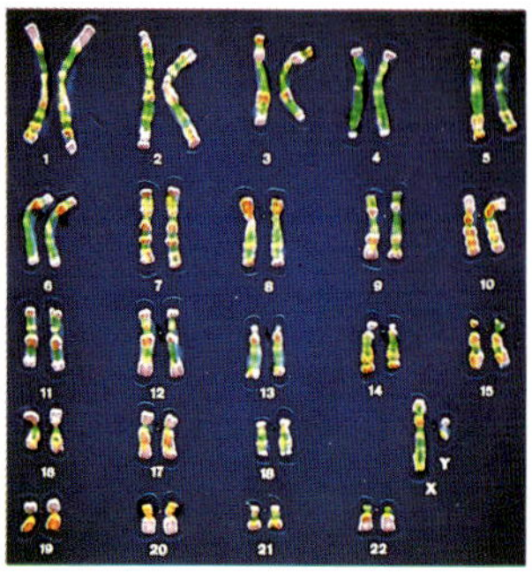

HUMAN CHROMOSOMES
This photograph shows all the 46 chromosomes in a single human cell. They have been treated with a special dye and arranged in pairs. (The X and Y chromosomes are on the lower right.) Every species of plant and animal has a characteristic chromosome number. Some have less than ten, others over a thousand.

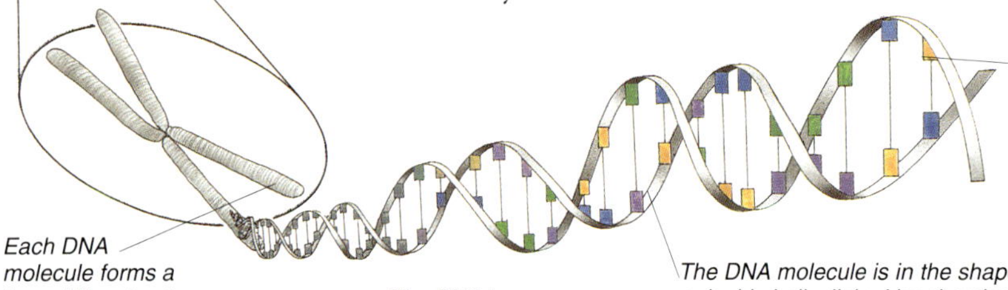

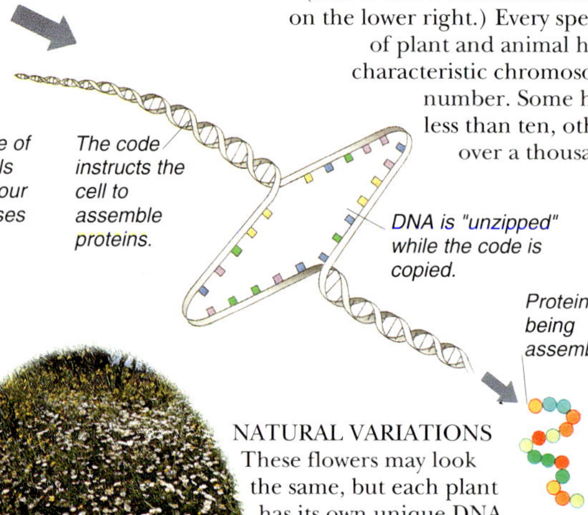

CHROMOSOMES, GENES, AND DNA

In a cell's nucleus, there are several lengths of DNA. Each one is called a chromosome. A gene is one area of a chromosome that has the instructions to make one protein. DNA works by telling a cell how to make the many different proteins that your cells need to work. To do this, part of the DNA helix is temporarily "unzipped", so that its code can be copied. The copy moves out of the nucleus. Once outside, it instructs the cell to assemble a particular protein, which could be an enzyme, or collagen (a protein in your skin), for example.

These flowers are chamomile (Anthemis chia).

NATURAL VARIATIONS
These flowers may look the same, but each plant has its own unique DNA, because it was formed by sexual reproduction. This gives the plant a distinctive set of characteristics. It might have more flowers than others, or it might put slightly more energy into growing roots. Tiny variations like this are important, because they mean a species evolves (changes with time). Some DNA variations are more successful than others, so as one generation succeeds another, their more successful genes become more common.

ROSALIND FRANKLIN

The final break-through in the study of DNA's structure. was made in 1953, by British bio-physicist Francis Crick (born 1916) and American geneticist James Watson (born 1928). They suggested that DNA was a double helix – a conclusion they reached after studying X-ray photographs taken by British X-ray crystallographer Rosalind Franklin (1920-58). She used X-rays to look at DNA crystals. Crick, Watson, and Maurice Wilkins (born 1916) got the Nobel Prize for Physiology or Medicine in 1962. Franklin died before her contribution was properly credited.

GENES AND PEOPLE
Unless you are an identical twin, you are unique, because nobody else has exactly your combination of genes. Genes control all the inherited characteristics of your body. Sometimes a single gene controls a characteristic that we can see, such as the colour of your eyes, but usually several genes are involved. Many of the characteristics you inherit are modified by the way you live. For example, your height depends on what you eat, as well as on your genes.

MUTATIONS
DNA is an extremely long molecule, and it is frequently damaged. Normally, this damage is automatically repaired. But if the damage is extensive, it creates a permanent new piece of genetic code, called a mutation. Mutations normally have little effect if they occur in body cells. But if they occur in gametes (sex cells), they can be passed on from one generation to another. Mutations create new characteristics in living things.

Albino (white) colour is a common type of mutation in animals and plants. This is an albino red squirrel.

Meiosis

Meiosis is a special kind of cell division that produces gametes (sex cells). During meiosis, a cell divides twice, so that it makes four new cells. The new cells have only half the amount of DNA in the original cell. Each of their chromosomes has a new and unique pattern, because the original cell's chromosomes swap pieces just before division begins. Unlike mitosis (ordinary cell division), meiosis makes cells that have new genetic instructions. A female gamete is usually called an egg cell, and the male gamete is a sperm cell.

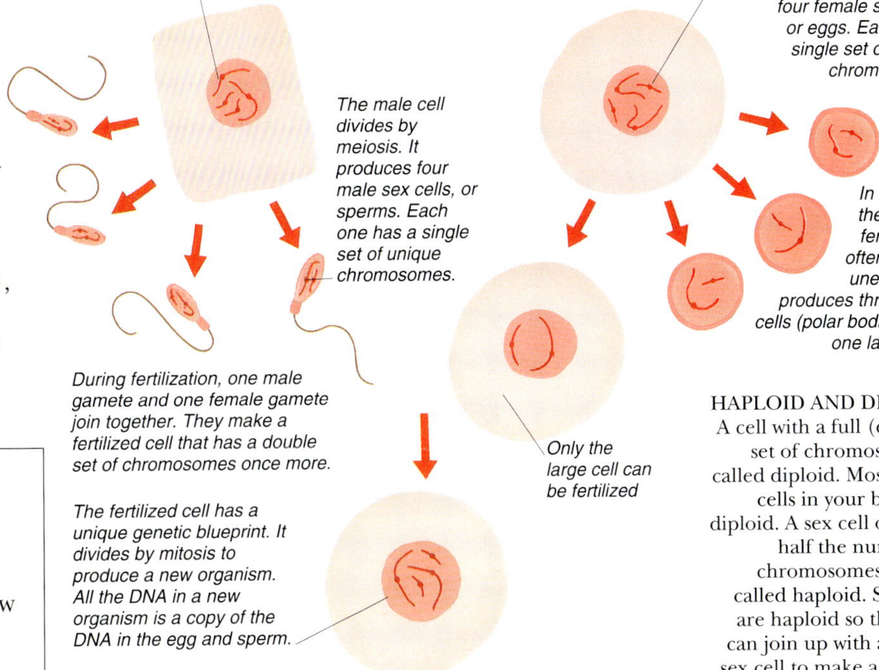

The original male cell has a double set of chromosomes.

The original female cell also has a double set of chromosomes.

The female cell divides by meiosis. It produces four female sex cells, or eggs. Each has a single set of unique chromosomes.

The male cell divides by meiosis. It produces four male sex cells, or sperms. Each one has a single set of unique chromosomes.

In animals, the original female cell often divides unequally. It produces three small cells (polar bodies), and one large one.

During fertilization, one male gamete and one female gamete join together. They make a fertilized cell that has a double set of chromosomes once more.

Only the large cell can be fertilized

The fertilized cell has a unique genetic blueprint. It divides by mitosis to produce a new organism. All the DNA in a new organism is a copy of the DNA in the egg and sperm.

GREGOR MENDEL

Mendel (1822-84) was an Austrian monk and botanist who discovered how characteristics are inherited. He patiently carried out thousands of experiments on pea plants, cross-fertilizing particular parents, and studying the results. He found out that inheritance does not work by blending characteristics together, as people then thought. Instead, they are inherited in pairs. In each pair, only one characteristic is usually expressed (shown). Mendel worked out the basic rules of genetics, but it was not until the 20th century that scientists rediscovered his work.

HAPLOID AND DIPLOID

A cell with a full (double) set of chromosomes is called diploid. Most of the cells in your body are diploid. A sex cell only has half the number of chromosomes, so it is called haploid. Sex cells are haploid so that they can join up with another sex cell to make a diploid cell. This cell can then grow into a new organism.

Ginger cats are usually male (XY). The gene for ginger is carried on the X chromosome, but it is often masked if another X chromosome is present, as it is in a female (XX).

Tortoiseshell cats are always female, because this colour can only be produced by two X chromosomes. Only females have the XX combination.

GENES AND SEX

In cats, humans, and many other animals, two differently shaped chromosomes decide what sex an individual will be. The chromosomes are known as X and Y. An animal can either have two X chromosomes, making it female, or it can have an X and Y chromosome, making it male. It cannot have two Y chromosomes, because it always receives one X chromosome from its mother. As well as sex, these chromosomes also determine some other characteristics. In cats, they include fur colour, while in humans, they include colour blindness.

HOW CHARACTERISTICS ARE INHERITED

Most cells contain two sets of chromosomes, one from each parent. This means they have two sets of genes. Normally one gene in every pair is dominant, meaning that it masks (hides) the effects of its recessive partner. Here, you can see how a pair of genes controls the colour of pea flowers. The dominant gene (labelled R) makes flowers red. The recessive gene (labelled r) makes the flowers white. However, its effects are masked, unless there are two of them.

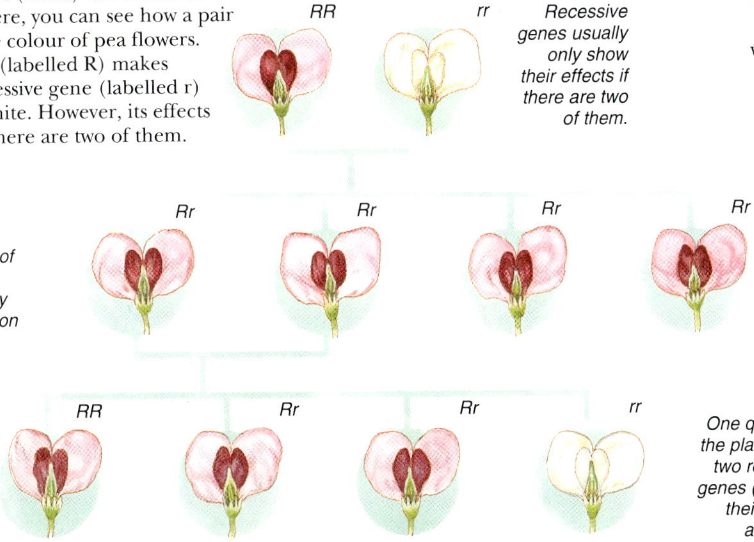

One parent plant has two dominant genes (RR), so its flowers are red. The other parent has two recessive genes (rr), so its flowers are white.

Recessive genes usually only show their effects if there are two of them.

Each offspring plant receives one flower colour gene from each of its parents. In the first generation, there is only one possible combination of genes: Rr.

The first generation offspring all have red flowers. Although each has a recessive gene for white flowers, its effects are masked by the dominant gene.

In the second generation, there are four possible combinations of genes: RR, Rr, rR, and rr.

One quarter of the plants have two recessive genes (rr). Only their flowers are white.

Find out more

How evolution works p.309
Cells p.338
Growth and development p.362
Sexual reproduction p.367
Human reproduction p.368

ASEXUAL REPRODUCTION

ALL LIVING THINGS REPRODUCE. Reproduction and continuing the species is a basic feature of all living things. But living things reproduce in two quite different ways. Here, you can find out about one way. It is called asexual reproduction, because it does not involve sex. In asexual reproduction, there is just one parent. Part of the parent buds off or splits away, and this becomes a new individual. Asexual reproduction is simple and quick, but it does have one result which can be a drawback under certain conditions. The parent and young share the same genetic material, so they have exactly the same characteristics. If the parent has a disadvantage, such as low resistance to a disease, its offspring will have it too.

BUDDING YEAST
Yeasts are microscopic single-celled fungi. They reproduce asexually by budding off parts of their cells. A yeast cell can bud every two hours. The new cells sometimes start to bud before they have completely separated from their parent, so a branching chain is produced.

ASEXUAL REPRODUCTION IN ANIMALS

Asexual reproduction is widespread in plants, but it is less common in animals. The first person to see an animal reproduce in this way was Antoni van Leeuwenhoek, one of the earliest users of the microscope. In 1701, he was watching a tiny animal called a hydra, which lives in ponds. He saw how parts of it bud off to become new animals.

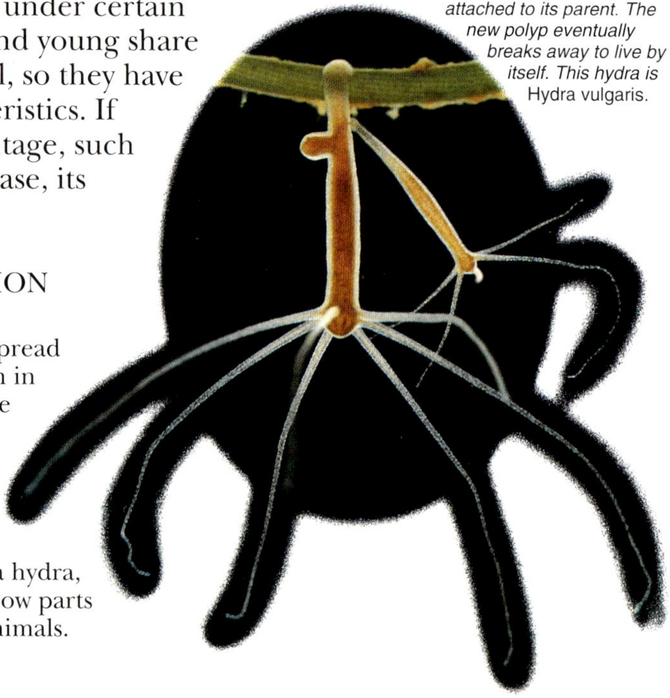

A young hydra polyp attached to its parent. The new polyp eventually breaks away to live by itself. This hydra is Hydra vulgaris.

PRODUCTION LINE BIRTH
In spring and summer, female aphids are often surrounded by dozens of young. The females produce babies by parthenogenesis (without mating), and they multiply very rapidly. This means that there are lots of aphids when there is plenty of food. Later, as the food supply starts to dwindle, their young reproduce sexually.

An anemone gradually pulls itself apart as the two halves creep in different directions.

The two new animals are genetically identical to their "parent", which is the original anemone.

CLONES
Sea anemones usually reproduce sexually by releasing eggs into the water, but they can also multiply by breaking off parts of themselves, or by pulling themselves in two. Some species concentrate on this form of reproduction. They spread over rocks, forming a group of identical animals that share exactly the same genes. Groups like this are called clones.

PROPAGATING CROPS
Bananas are never grown from seed. Instead, a farmer simply cuts off new shoots, and plants them. With crops like this, the plants will all have the same characteristics. If one catches a disease, the rest may do so as well. This lack of variety is a major problem of asexual reproduction.

SPREADING BY RUNNERS
Many plants reproduce in two different ways at the same time. Strawberries have flowers, which make seeds by sexual reproduction. They also send out horizontal stems, called runners, which form new plants by asexual reproduction. Each runner develops several young plants, and these gradually take root. If a strawberry patch is left untended, new strawberry plants soon cover the ground.

NEW BULBS
Bulbs contain food, which is stored in special leaves that are packed tightly together. As a bulb grows, it forms new small bulbs called bulbils around its base.

Daffodil bulb with bulbil

Find out more

SINGLE-CELLED ORGANISMS P.314
GROWTH AND DEVELOPMENT P.362
FACT FINDER P.422

SEXUAL REPRODUCTION

THERE ARE ALWAYS TWO PARENTS in sexual reproduction. Each parent makes gametes (sex cells) by a special kind of cell division called meiosis. The male gamete (the sperm) and the female gamete (the egg) are brought together, and a new cell is formed. This is fertilization. From this fertilized cell, a whole new organism develops. Sexual reproduction is more complicated than asexual reproduction, but it has an important advantage. Instead of being the same as one of their parents, sexually produced offspring are unique. They have a unique combination of genes, so that they have a completely new mixture of characteristics. This means that some of them may be better equipped in the struggle to survive.

Great crested grebes (*Podiceps cristatus*)

COURTSHIP AND MATING

Before grebes mate, they carry out a series of complicated dances. This kind of behaviour, called courtship, is common in many animals. It helps both partners to get used to each other, and ensures that they choose a suitable and healthy mate. Courtship is then followed by mating.

Californian mountain kingsnakes (*Lampropeltis zonata*) mating

INTERNAL FERTILIZATION

For sexual reproduction to work, the male and female sex cells have to be brought together. In some animals, this happens through mating. Snakes and many other land animals have internal fertilization: when two snakes mate, the male injects his sperm into the female so that fertilization of her eggs takes place inside her body. Animals that have internal fertilization produce fewer eggs and sperms, as these are more likely to come together.

EXTERNAL FERTILIZATION

In some animals, the eggs and sperm join together outside the female's body, but the animals still have to come together. The male stickleback (*Gasterosteus aculeatus*) makes a nest, in which the female lays her eggs. The male then adds his sperm to the eggs. Most animals with external fertilization have to produce lots of eggs so that enough will be fertilized.

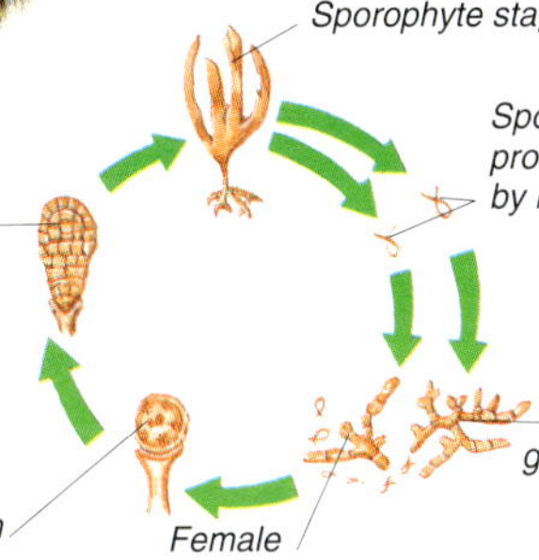

ALTERNATING GENERATIONS

In some plant life cycles there are two different forms of the plant. In the brown algae *Laminaria*, the "adult" form (called the sporophyte) produces spores by meiosis. These develop into male and female plants called gametophytes. It is this stage that produces the gametes (sex cells). The eggs and sperm come together in the water to produce a fertilized cell. This grows into a sporophyte, and the cycle starts again.

SEX CELLS

Sex cells (gametes) have exactly half the amount of genetic material of ordinary cells. They are specially shaped so that they can join together. In some plants and animals, the sex cells are the same size. But more often, the female sex cell is much larger than the male. Female sex cells (eggs) stay in one place, while male sex cells (sperms) swim towards them.

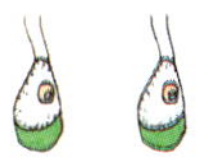

The sea lettuce (Ulva lactuca) *has identical male and female sex cells.*

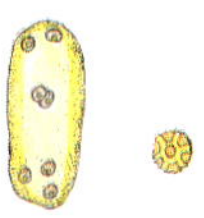

Flowering plants have several female sex cells in an embryo sac. The male cells are contained in pollen grains.

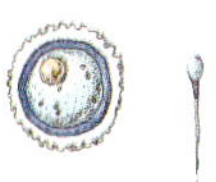

In most animals, the egg is far bigger than the sperm.

In "thrum" primrose flowers the stamens (which produce the pollen) are high up, and the stigma is short.

"Pin" primrose flowers have a long stigma (the female part). The stamens are low down.

ENSURING CROSS-FERTILIZATION

Many plants have both male and female parts in their flowers. They can often fertilize themselves, but they usually have features that encourage cross-fertilization (fertilization with sex cells from another plant). Cross-fertilization is useful, because it makes a plant's offspring more varied. Primroses (*Primula vulgaris*) have two types of flowers, but only one type is found on a plant. Each flower type can only fertilize the other, so cross-pollination is guaranteed.

Find out more

PLANTS WITHOUT FLOWERS P.316
FLOWERING PLANTS P.318
FISH P.326
REPTILES P.330
BIRDS P.332
CELLS P.338
GENETICS P.364
HUMAN REPRODUCTION P.368
FACT FINDER P.422

HUMAN REPRODUCTION

LIKE EVERY PERSON ON EARTH, you started life as a tiny fertilized cell. This cell was formed when one of your father's sperms (sex cells) joined up with an egg cell in a tube that leads into your mother's womb (uterus) called the fallopian tube. Almost immediately, the fertilized cell began to change. It started to divide, and it then settled on the lining of the womb. Nourished by your mother's blood, it divided again and again, and slowly your body began to take shape. After nine months in the warmth and darkness of your mother's body, you were ready to be born.

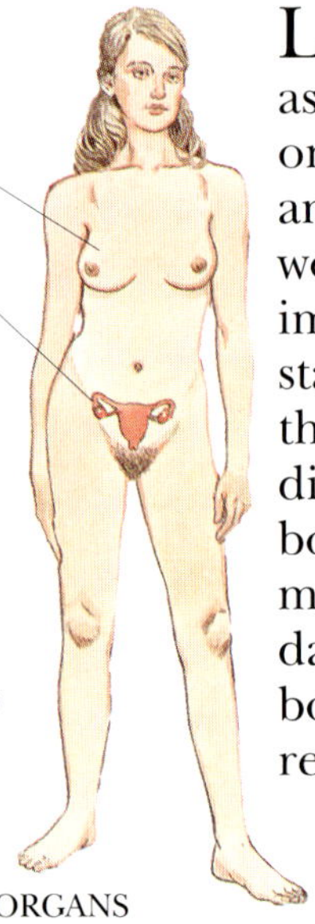

FEMALE SEX ORGANS
A woman's egg cells are stored inside two glands called ovaries. From the age of about 13, one egg cell is released every 28 days.

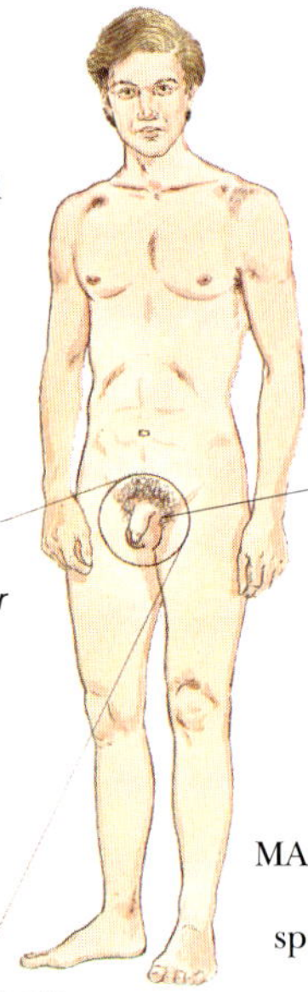

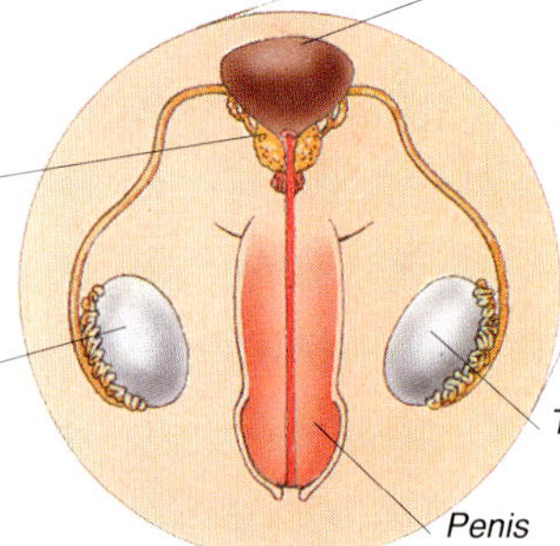

MALE SEX ORGANS
Male sex cells, or sperms, are made in two glands called testes. During lovemaking, the sperms are mixed with liquid from the prostate gland that makes the sperms swim. This means they can reach the egg in the woman's uterus.

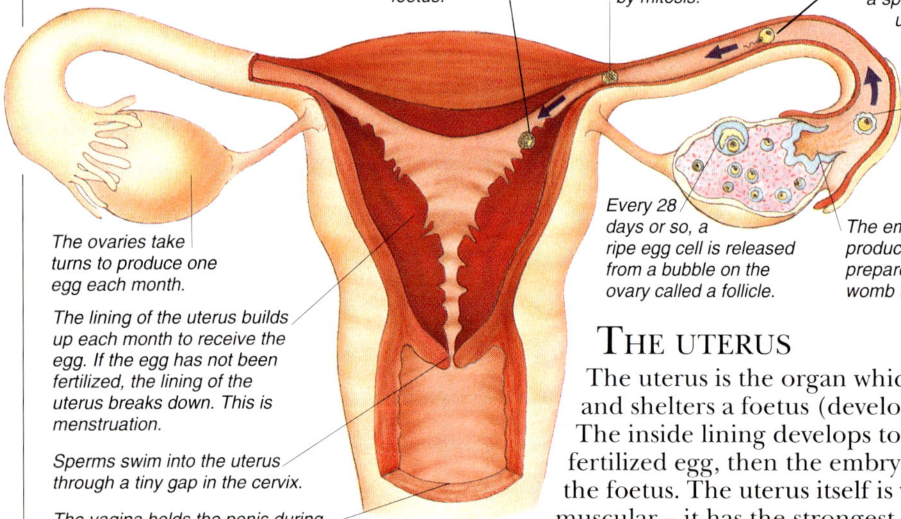

THE UTERUS
The uterus is the organ which feeds and shelters a foetus (developing baby). The inside lining develops to feed a fertilized egg, then the embryo, and later the foetus. The uterus itself is very muscular – it has the strongest muscles in the human body. These push the baby out during labour, with help from the mother's other muscles in her abdomen and chest.

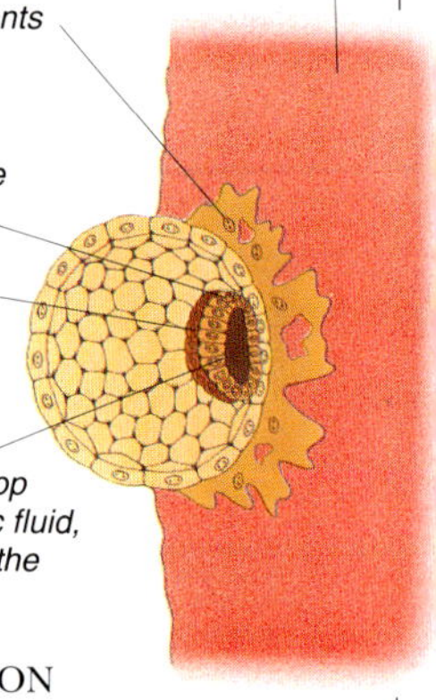

IMPLANTATION
When a fertilized egg lands on the wall of the uterus, it starts to break down some of the mother's cells. To begin with, it is nourished by these cells. Later, it gets oxygen and nutrients from its mother's blood through a spongy organ called the placenta. This is connected to the foetus by a long cord called the umbilical cord. These two organs take the foetus's waste products back to the mother. The placenta also produces hormones in pregnancy.

CHANGES IN PREGNANCY
To begin with, the foetus (developing baby) takes up little room, but by the ninth month it fills the whole of the uterus and this pushes up against the mother's stomach and diaphragm. The mother's body adapts to these changes. Her heart pumps more blood to nourish her growing child. She eats much more to feed it, and her breasts grow in preparation for breast-feeding after it is born. She also prepares herself mentally for the new baby.

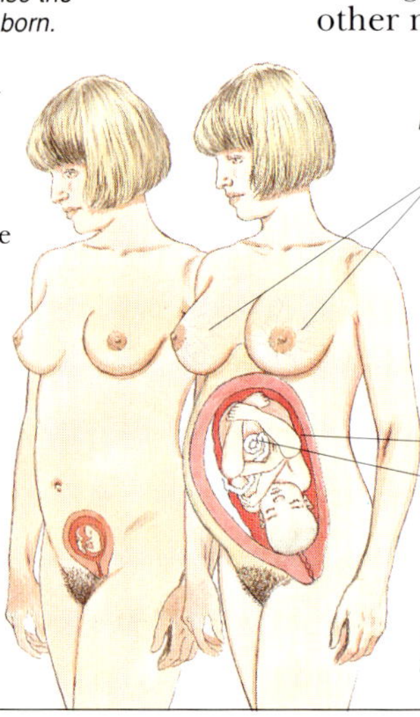

BREAST FEEDING
Most baby mammals are fed with milk from their mother's breasts. Milk contains a perfectly balanced mixture of nutrients designed for the baby, and it is easily digested. Milk also has the advantage of being readily available.

Find out more

MAMMALS P.334
PRIMATES P.336
GROWTH AND DEVELOPMENT P.362
GENETICS P.364
SEXUAL REPRODUCTION P.367

ECOLOGY

The weather is part of the rabbit's environment. The rabbit has to survive in different conditions. It needs clean air to breathe and water to drink.

THE STUDY OF LIVING THINGS in their natural surroundings is called ecology. And their surroundings are called their environment. Ecology is about seeing the whole picture as well as the pieces. By studying an animal's environment, ecologists can begin to understand why the animal behaves in a particular way. But ecology is still a "new" science, and the natural world is very complex. Ecologists know that problems exist but are not always sure how serious they are or how to solve them.

Animals that eat rabbits, such as foxes and stoats

Animals that live in the rabbit's fur, such as fleas, or organisms inside its body, such as bacteria

Plants that the rabbit eats such as grass, dandelions, and clover

Soil in which the rabbit digs burrows for shelter from the weather and predators, and to protect its young

Other animals, such as squirrels and mice, that eat the same food as the rabbit

Other rabbits that live together in the same warren (several burrows). Rabbits breed together to produce more rabbits and help each other to survive.

Animals that live in the same place, such as worms in the soil

RABBIT'S ENVIRONMENT

The conditions in which an animal lives, and the other species of animals and plants that live in its area, all affect the animal's own life. This is why, when ecologists study the environment of an animal such as a rabbit, they study everything living and non-living that is connected with it. This includes animals that hunt it, its food, other rabbits, the weather, air, and soil.

HUMAN ENVIRONMENT
Unlike most other animals, humans can change their environment to suit their way of life. This does not always help plants and other animals. Human ecology is the study of how humans change the environment and how these changes affect humans themselves.

ERNST HAECKEL

German biologist Ernst Haeckel (1834-1919) was, in 1869, the first to use the word ecology. He defined it as "the study of the economy, of the household, of animal organisms". He took the word from the Greek *oikos,* meaning "house" or "place to live in". Haeckel supported Darwin's theory of evolution by natural selection. His idea of ecology was forgotten until about 1900 when biologists began to study it seriously.

GATHERING FACTS AND FIGURES
The information that ecologists need to collect involves a lot of counting, weighing, and measuring – on land and under water. Sometimes figures are fed into computers that work out the possible effects of certain changes to an area. Ecologists can then advise people how to treat the environment.

THE BIOSPHERE

THE EARTH is a complicated system. The part in which life exists is called the biosphere. *Bios* is an Ancient Greek word meaning "life". The biosphere extends a little way above and below the surface of the planet. The habitat is made up of distinct areas, each with its own characteristic climate, soils, and living communities of plants and animals. These areas are called ecosystems. Each one consists of a number of parts which are related in such a way as to keep the whole system going. Although distinct, each ecosystem is not closed. Sunlight and rain enter it, water drains from it, nutrients enter and leave through the soil, and plant seeds and animals come and go.

NICHE
A niche is the position of a living thing within an ecosystem, including where it lives, what it absorbs or eats, how it behaves, and how it is related to other living things. The niche has been called the "profession" of a species.

LARGE AND SMALL
An ecosystem can be as small as a drop of rainwater on a leaf, or as large as an ocean. Both have different characteristics from the surrounding area, and both contain groups of living things, which interact with each other. A single tree and a huge forest are also ecosystems. Human skin can even be studied as an ecosystem as colonies of bacteria and mites live here.

HABITAT
A habitat is the natural home of a group of plants and animals. This group of living things is called a community. The habitat is sometimes called the "address" of a species. It contains several niches. Trees are an example of a habitat.

UNITS WITHIN THE BIOSPHERE

To make the biosphere easier to study, ecologists break it down into smaller units. Information about each unit can then be fitted together to give a more complete picture. One ecosystem can be studied as a whole, or the living things within it can be studied individually.

ECOSYSTEM
An ecosystem is a distinct area in the biosphere which contains living things. It includes the rocks and soil underneath the ground, the surface of the ground, and the air above it. It contains several habitats. A forest is an example of an ecosystem. The largest ecosystems, such as rainforests and deserts, are called biomes.

BIOSPHERE
The biosphere covers the whole surface of the Earth. It is the living part of the planet, and includes the atmosphere. It contains many different ecosystems.

THE EARTH
The Earth is the only planet known to have life. It has an atmosphere that contains the elements needed by living things for survival, and which protects the planet's surface from the harmful rays of the Sun.

JAMES E. LOVELOCK
British scientist, James Lovelock (born 1919) put forward his "Gaia hypothesis" in the 1970s. *Gaia* is an old Greek term for "Mother Earth", or "Earth goddess". After studying the atmosphere on Mars, Lovelock began to study Earth's atmosphere. He suggested that the atmosphere is regulated by the biosphere. All living things on Earth can be thought of as part of one being that can change its environment to suit its needs. Gaia will ensure conditions are right for its own survival, even if humans make the Earth unfit for themselves.

The world's ecosystems

Ecosystems are distributed over the Earth mainly according to climate. There are zones of different climates ranging from cold and dry at the Poles, to hot and wet at the Equator. Plants and animals are adapted to the conditions and are associated with each other to form communities. They have particular roles within each ecosystem, competing for the resources to survive.

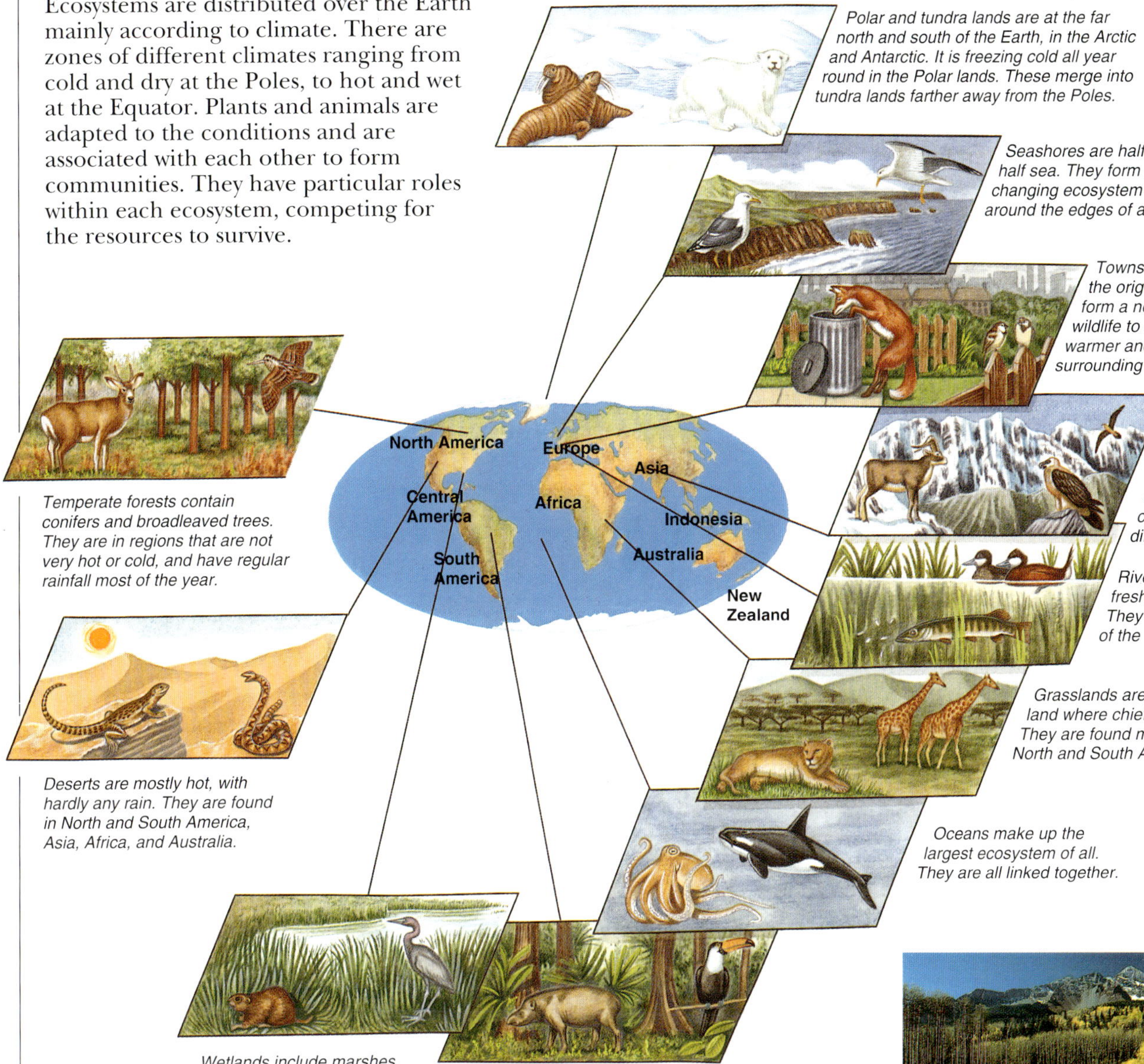

Polar and tundra lands are at the far north and south of the Earth, in the Arctic and Antarctic. It is freezing cold all year round in the Polar lands. These merge into tundra lands farther away from the Poles.

Seashores are half land and half sea. They form a constantly changing ecosystem found around the edges of all continents.

Towns and cities replace the original ecosystems, and form a new ecosystem for wildlife to adapt to. They are warmer and less windy than the surrounding countryside.

Mountains are found on all the continents. They include most of the major ecosystems because climatic conditions change at different heights.

Rivers and lakes are freshwater ecosystems. They are found over most of the world's land surface.

Grasslands are huge areas of land where chiefly grasses grow. They are found mainly in Asia, North and South America, and Africa.

Oceans make up the largest ecosystem of all. They are all linked together.

Temperate forests contain conifers and broadleaved trees. They are in regions that are not very hot or cold, and have regular rainfall most of the year.

Deserts are mostly hot, with hardly any rain. They are found in North and South America, Asia, Africa, and Australia.

Wetlands include marshes, swamps, and bogs, both freshwater and saltwater. They are found on all continents except Antarctica.

Tropical rainforests grow in Central and South America, central Africa, Southeast Asia, and northern Australia. They are mostly near the Equator, so are hot and wet most of the year.

Ecosystem boundaries

Each ecosystem is different from its surroundings in some way. Its surroundings are parts of other ecosystems. Some ecosystems have distinct boundaries, such as between a forest and a lake. The habitats and niches suddenly change. But many ecosystems merge together. The area where they merge is called an ecotone. It contains animals and plants from both ecosystems.

SUCCESSION

Communities develop until they reach a stable form known as the climax community. The process of change, for example from grassland to woodland, is called succession. This example is primary succession. Secondary succession is when an ecosystem is destroyed by nature or by people, and then, after a time, recovers.

Grazing animals keep grassland as it is, by eating tree seedlings.

If the number of animals decreases, trees may start to grow and stop sunlight reaching the grass.

Eventually, the trees take over the area and form woodland.

Find out more

Climates p.244
Atmosphere p.248
Earth p.287
Cycles in the biosphere p.372

CYCLES IN THE BIOSPHERE

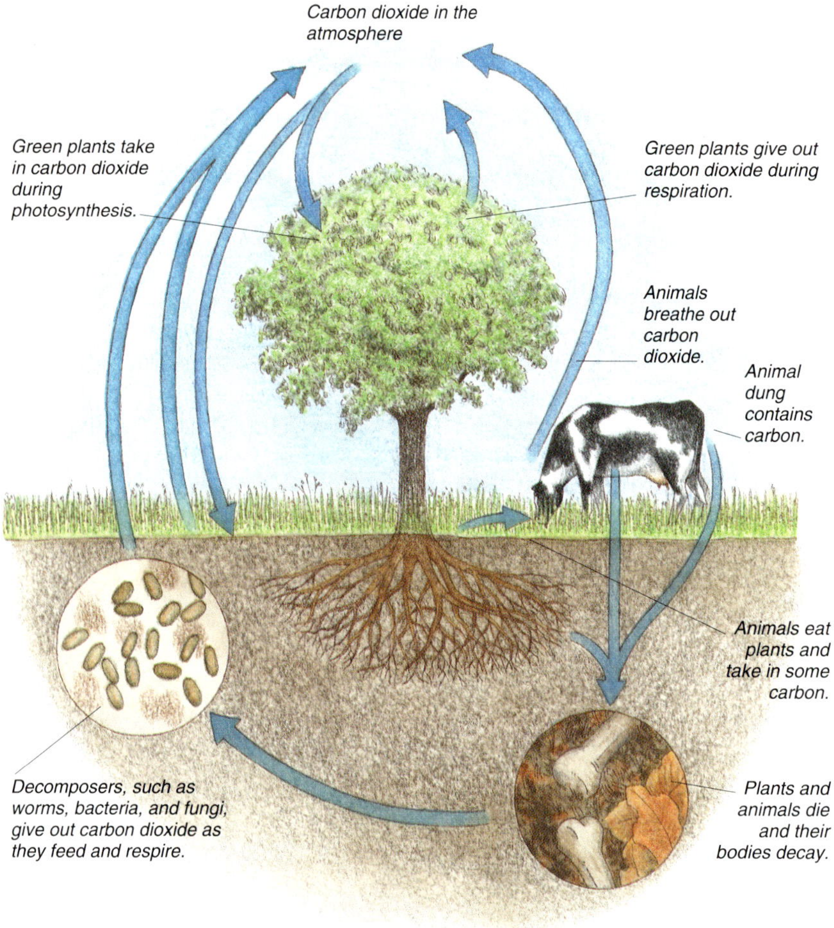

PART OF YOU might once have been part of a dinosaur. This is because the basic substances in your body have been recycled and used by other animals, and plants, before you used them. Living things take in water, carbon, nitrogen, and oxygen and use them to live and grow. If these resources were used only once, they would run out. All animals and plants respire (breathe), grow, and eventually die and decompose. Decomposition releases the substances in their bodies back into the biosphere to be used again.

LEAD POISONING

Fumes from traffic are responsible for releasing more than 225,000 tonnes of lead into the atmosphere every year. The lead is mixed into the air and absorbed by humans and other animals, poisoning their bodies. Children are especially at risk.

CARBON CYCLE

The bodies of all living things are based on the element carbon. The carbon comes originally from carbon dioxide gas in the atmosphere. Green plants and some bacteria take this in, and use it to make food. When animals eat the plants, they take in some of the carbon. Carbon dioxide goes back into the atmosphere when living things breathe out, or when they produce waste, die, or decay.

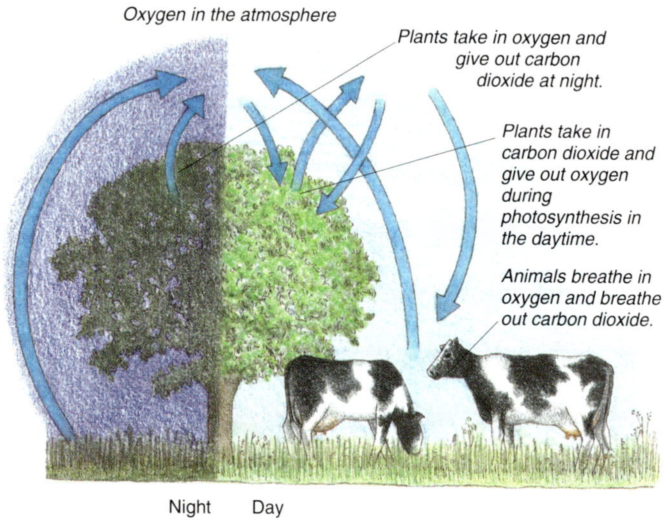

GLOBAL WARMING

When we burn oil, coal, and wood, we release carbon dioxide into the atmosphere. All this extra carbon dioxide is creating a "blanket" around the Earth. Most of the short-wave radiation from the Sun can get through the blanket. But most of the long-wave radiation from Earth cannot escape, causing the Earth to get hotter and hotter. This is called the "greenhouse effect" and causes global warming.

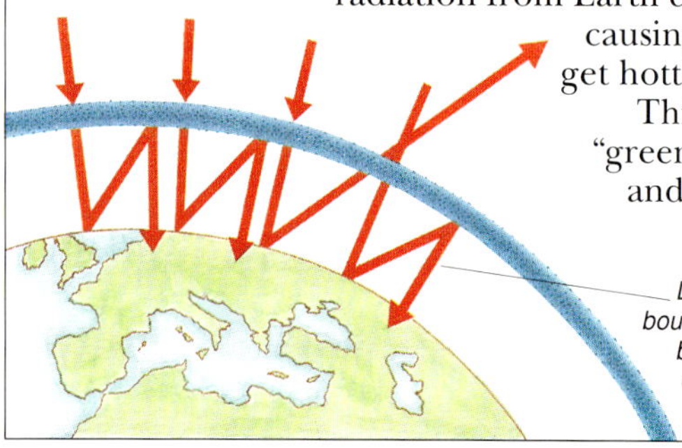

OXYGEN CYCLE

Living things take in oxygen from the air. They use it to release energy from the food they eat. They may also use it, together with carbon, hydrogen, and nitrogen, to build new molecules in their bodies. Oxygen is released back into the atmosphere by green plants during photosynthesis, and by plants and animals as part of carbon dioxide.

Nitrogen cycle

All living things need nitrogen to make proteins. But most cannot make use of nitrogen gas in the air directly. The nitrogen has to be fixed, or combined with other elements, to form compounds called nitrites and nitrates. Plants can take in nitrates and animals get their nitrogen by eating the plants. This fixing process is carried out by special nitrifying bacteria, algae, and lichens. The bacteria live in the soil or on the roots of plants such as peas, beans, and clover. Denitrifying bacteria break down animal waste and dead plants and animals, to release nitrogen back into the atmosphere.

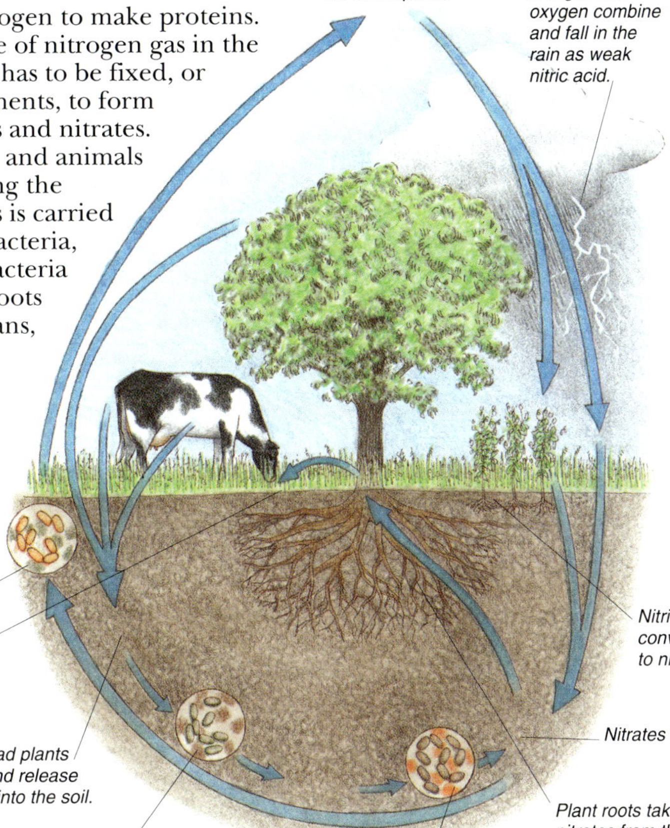

EUTROPHICATION

Farmers add nitrates to the soil, as fertilizers, to make better crop yields. These can get washed into waterways. Then too many plants and animals grow in the water, affecting the ecosystem there. This is called eutrophication.

POLLUTION

Factory waste has polluted many rivers and lakes, killing the wildlife. And oil spilt at sea is very dangerous to wildlife. It clogs animals' feathers and fur, gets inside them, and stops them finding food. They then die of cold and hunger.

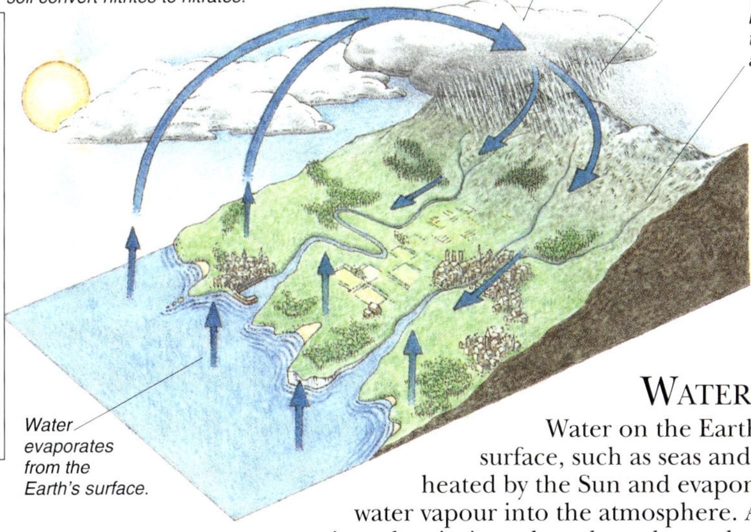

Water cycle

Water on the Earth's surface, such as seas and rivers, is heated by the Sun and evaporates as water vapour into the atmosphere. As it rises up into the air, it cools and condenses back into water again. Water droplets collect together to form clouds and then fall back to the surface as rain.

ACID RAIN

Poisonous gases from power stations and vehicles mix with water in the air. This then falls as acid rain and becomes part of the water cycle. Acid in the rain can damage wildlife in all ecosystems where it falls. It also affects stone, causing statues and buildings to crumble away. Gases can be carried long distances by the wind, so pollution produced in one country can fall as acid rain in another.

Find out more

Carbon p.40
Nitrogen p.42
Oxygen p.44
Changing climates p.246
Formation of clouds p.262
Rain p.264
Photosynthesis p.340
Transport in plants p.341
Cellular respiration p.346

PEOPLE AND PLANET

THE EARTH IS THOUSANDS of millions of years old. If this time was fitted into one day, humans would have been around for less than a second. But by the end of the 20th century, there will probably be more than 8,000 million of us. People need food and water, space in which to live, air to breathe, and energy to drive their machines. This leaves less and less space and food for other animals and plants. Many environmental problems have been caused by people. Global warming, acid rain, and holes in the ozone layer are just three. There are no simple solutions to these problems. But we are becoming more aware of what harm we are doing.

DANGEROUS CHEMICALS
Some of the chemicals we spray on crops are poisonous to people as well as to the environment. Protective clothing should be worn but it is not always available in developing countries.

GIVE AND TAKE

People take many resources from the planet, but put back mainly harmful things, such as waste and pollution. Coal, gas, oil, and metals will run out. We need to find some renewable resources before the non-renewable ones are all gone.

POPULATION EXPLOSION
It took thousands of years, until the 1830s, for the number of people in the world to reach 1,000 million. But it took only 100 more years for there to be more than 2,000 million. The world population has doubled in the last 40 years and it is thought that it will probably reach 10,000 million towards the end of the 21st century. This picture shows houses huddled together on a hillside in Rio de Janeiro, Brazil.

POLLUTION DISASTERS

1953-60 Mercury poisoning in shellfish in Minimata Bay, Japan, causes brain damage to people.

1976 Herbicide leak in Seveso, Italy, poisons hundreds of people. Domestic animals in the area have to be killed.

1984 Leak of chemicals from factory in Bhopal, India, kills 2,500 people.

1986 Nuclear reactor accident at Chernobyl, Russia, affects a wide area with radioactive poisoning.

1989 Tanker spills 40,000 tonnes of oil off the coast of Alaska which kills thousands of animals.

1993 Tanker spills 84,000 tonnes of oil into the sea off Shetland Islands, Scotland, polluting farms and beaches, and killing wildlife.

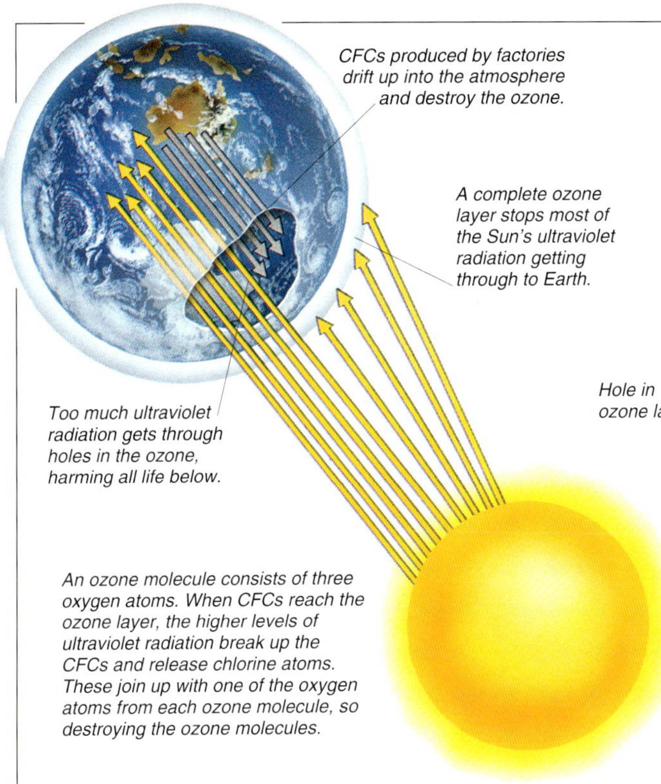

HOLE OVER ANTARCTICA

In the 1980s, scientists discovered a hole in the ozone layer over Antarctica, as big as the United States. This special photograph, taken from space, shows the hole clearly. A smaller hole has also been found over the Arctic and the ozone layer is becoming thinner over other parts of the planet too. Scientists blame mainly gases called chlorofluorocarbons (CFCs) for the destruction of the ozone. CFCs are used in some refrigerators, aerosols, air conditioners, fire extinguishers, and in the production of some kinds of polystyrene and cleaning substances.

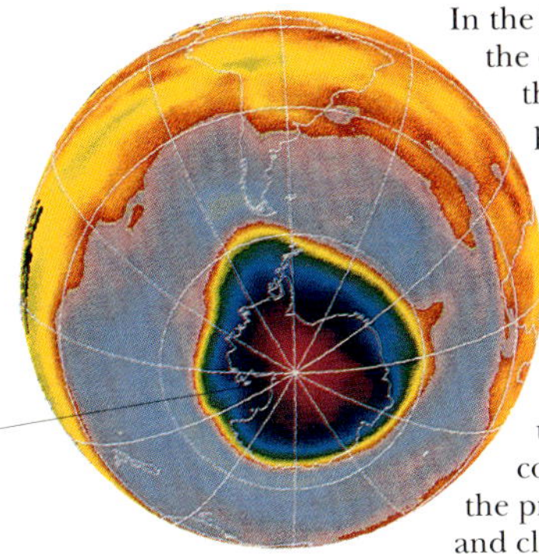

OZONE LAYER

About 15-50 km (9-30 miles) above the Earth is a layer of ozone. This ozone layer shields the Earth from most of the Sun's harmful ultraviolet radiation. Too much ultraviolet can change the genetic structure of plants and animals and cause skin cancer in people. Holes have formed in the ozone layer, allowing more of the ultraviolet rays through to the Earth. In the Antarctic, high levels of ultraviolet are stopping plankton from photosynthesizing (making food using sunlight) which disrupts the food chains in the sea.

LIVING POLLUTION CLUES

By studying living things, we can tell how polluted the air or water is. Some living things can stand a lot of pollution while others thrive only where the air is clean. Lichens are very sensitive to air pollution because they absorb minerals from rainwater all over their surface. Poisons in the rain soon build up in their tissues and kill them.

Find out more

CATALYSTS P.56
ENERGY SOURCES P.134
ATMOSPHERE P.248
PHOTOSYNTHESIS P.340
CYCLES IN THE BIOSPHERE P.372
WASTES AND RECYCLING P.376
FACT FINDER P.424

Wastes and Recycling

IN THE NATURAL WORLD, nothing is wasted. Living things called decomposers eat dead and decaying material. The decomposers break everything down so it can be recycled and used again. The material is said to be biodegradable. But this natural recycling is upset by the huge amounts of wastes produced by people. Most of this, such as tin, glass, and most plastic, is not biodegradable. When we throw it away, it stays for hundreds of years. Even if it rusts or breaks into tiny little pieces, it cannot be eaten by the decomposers. It pollutes the atmosphere, the land, and the water. We can recycle material by sending it back to be used again instead of throwing it away. And we can try to avoid using non-biodegradable material and buy only items with biodegradable, or very little, packaging.

DECOMPOSERS
When an animal dies, it is recycled by nature. The larvae of the flies – maggots – will be the decomposers on this dead shrew. Decomposers help to clean up the environment and make material available for other plants and animals to use. When material has been broken down into small enough pieces, bacteria and fungi, the most important decomposers, can work on it.

Rubbish dumps

Human rubbish has to be put somewhere. Most methods of disposing, or getting rid of it, could harm the environment. A lot of our rubbish is dumped into holes in the ground, called landfill sites. Heavy vehicles spread it out and squash it so it takes up less space. Soil is put on top of the rubbish each day to stop birds and animals feeding there, and spreading disease. Although this hides the rubbish, poisonous liquids can leak out, the rubbish can get hot and catch fire, and gases are produced which can explode.

AVERAGE RUBBISH

In highly industrialized countries, where most people have a modern way of life, an average family throws away over 1 tonne of rubbish every year. Most of their rubbish consists of paper from packaging and kitchen waste. A lot of this could be recycled and used again.

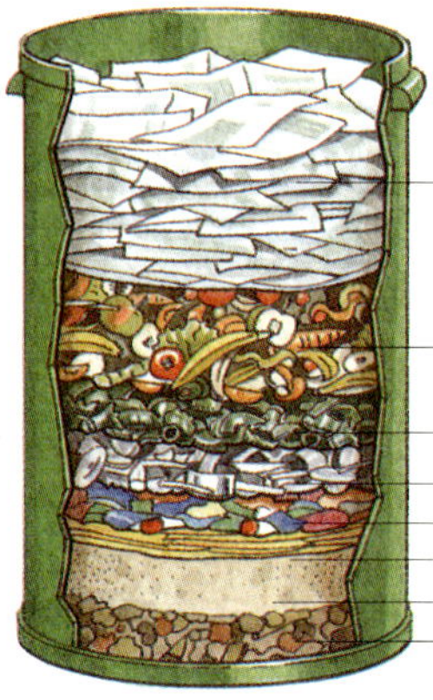

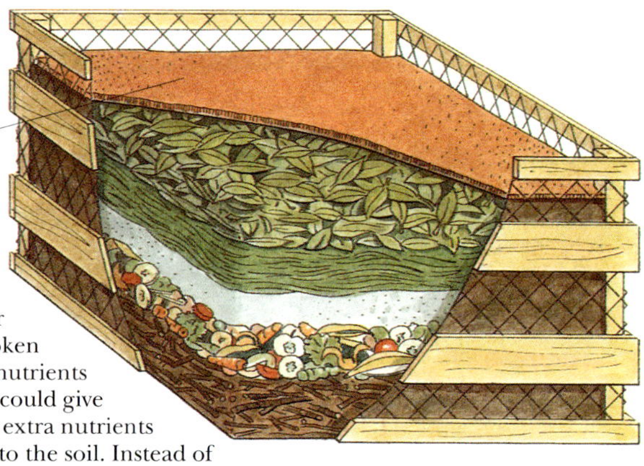

BUILDING A COMPOST HEAP
Dead leaves and other plant material are broken down in the soil into nutrients for plants to use. You could give plants in your garden extra nutrients by mixing compost into the soil. Instead of throwing away all your vegetable peelings, dead flowers, and leaves from the garden, make a compost heap. Collect layers of plant waste in a large container outside. Cover each layer with soil to keep in the heat caused by decomposers eating the dead plants. Keep the compost heap damp because decomposers like warm, wet conditions. It will take several months for the compost to form. Be careful as the heap can get very hot inside, and even catch fire.

Find out more

Bacteria p.313
Fungi p.315
Nutrition p.342
Cycles in the biosphere p.372
People and planet p.374
Conservation p.400

FOOD CHAINS AND WEBS

THE LIVING THINGS in a community are linked through their food. For example, a fox, a rabbit, and a plant are linked because the rabbit eats the plant and the fox then eats the rabbit. These links are called food chains. Animals and plants get the energy they need from their food. Plants use the Sun's energy to make their own food. They are called producers. Animals cannot make their own food, so they have to eat plants or other animals. They are called consumers. Animals often eat more than one kind of food so they are part of a number of food chains. Several food chains can be joined together into a food web.

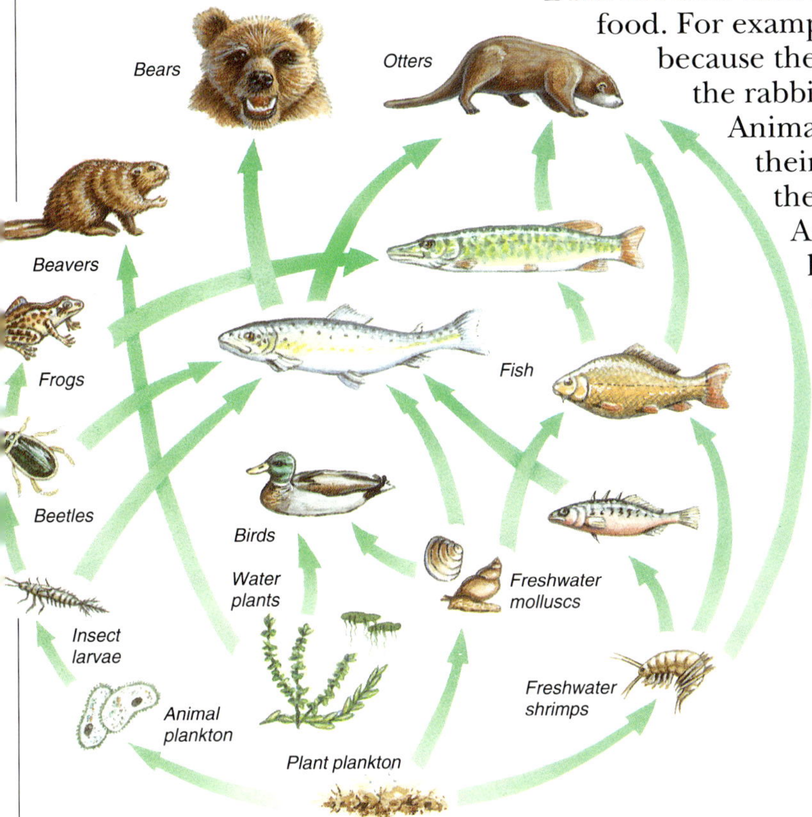

FOOD CHAIN
A food chain is a series of living things linked together because each one is food for the next, for example, plant to rabbit to fox. Most food chains have only three or four links. By the fourth link, all the energy has been used up.

FOOD WEB

A food web can include living things from several ecosystems. In this food web in a lake community, some animals and plants live in the water, and some live on land. The producers are water plants and plant plankton. These are eaten by herbivores (plant eaters), such as animal plankton, snails, insects, and some fish. The herbivores are eaten by carnivores (meat eaters), such as other insects, fish, and mammals. A change in the number of a species at one link will affect the plants and animals in the whole web.

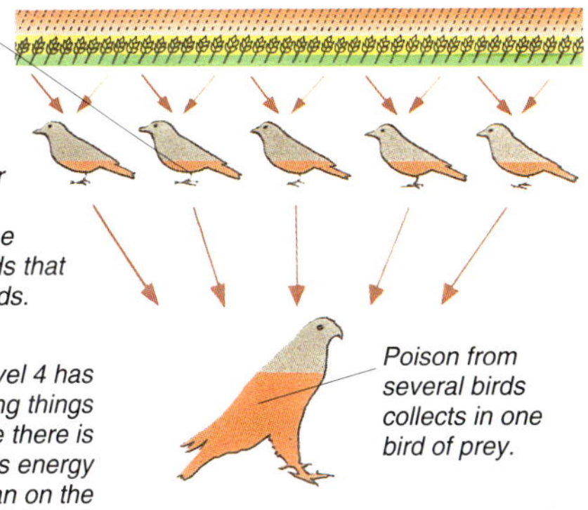

POISON IN A FOOD CHAIN
Poisons build up as they are passed along a food chain. Chemicals sprayed on to a field of crops to kill insects are taken in by birds that eat seeds from the crops. If a bird of prey eats several of the smaller birds, it takes in a large amount of poison. This may be enough to kill it or cause it to lay eggs with thin shells. These break when the parent bird sits on them in the nest. The build-up of poisons is called bioamplification.

A pyramid of energy

TROPHIC LEVELS
One way of studying a community is to group the living things into feeding levels called trophic levels. *Trophe* is a Greek word meaning nourishment. Trophic levels are based on the numbers or mass (biomass) of living things at the same stage in a food web, or on the amount of energy stored by a group of living things at one stage. They are drawn as steps, usually forming a pyramid, because the amount of energy in living things decreases as it is transferred to each successive level.

JONATHON PORRITT

British lecturer and writer, Jonathon Porritt (born 1950) is one of the leading activists in educating people about the importance of looking after the Earth and its wildlife. He became involved in "green politics", stood as a candidate for the British Green Party, and became Director of Friends of the Earth. In 1990, he stood down from his position in order to concentrate on lecturing, broadcasting, and writing on green issues around the world.

Find out more

PHOTOSYNTHESIS P.340
NUTRITION P.342
FEEDING P.343
DIGESTION P.345
THE BIOSPHERE P.370
WILDLIFE IN DANGER P.398

ANIMAL GROUPS

A PACK OF WOLVES, a herd of deer, a school of fish, and a flock of birds are all examples of animal groups. Animals may live in groups all the time or just come together to nest or feed in a particular area at a certain time of year. Members of a group are often related to each other. They may share out the jobs, such as collecting food, caring for the young, and defending the group. Living as a group allows the young animals to learn skills and behaviour from the adults. In this way they are more likely to survive and can pass on their knowledge to the next generation.

WOLF PACK

The members of a pack of wolves (*Canis lupus*) help each other to survive by hunting together and defending the cubs. Within a pack, each wolf knows its own place. The high-ranking wolves tell the others that they are dominant, or superior, with special positions of the body, called body language. The low-ranking wolves also use body language to show that they are submissive – they know who's in charge. The top male and female wolf are both large and healthy. The top female is usually the only female to have cubs.

BIRD COLONIES
Many seabirds, such as gannets (*Sula bassana*), nest in large groups called colonies. They sit just out of pecking distance of each other. Nesting in numbers is safer as enemies are less likely to attack and birds warn each other of danger.

JANE GOODALL

English scientist Jane Goodall (born 1934) began to study chimpanzees at the Gombé Stream Game Reserve in Tanzania, Africa. After years of research, following chimp groups through the forest, Goodall began to piece together details of their family life. She could then work out the best way to protect the chimps. The Jane Goodall Institute focuses attention on the plight of chimpanzees. They are an endangered species due to destruction of their habitat, hunting, and illegal trade.

BEE DANCE
Honeybees (*Apis mellifera*) run in a figure-of-eight pattern to tell other bees in the hive where to find a good supply of food. The speed of the "dance" tells the other bees how far away the food is. The faster the dance, the nearer the food.

Find out more

BIRDS P.332
PRIMATES P.336
FEEDING P.343
WILDLIFE IN DANGER P.398
FACT FINDER P.424

PARTNERSHIPS

DIFFERENT SPECIES OF PLANTS and animals can live together. In some cases, the partnership helps both species. This is called mutualism. In other cases, one of the partners is worse off. For example, a flea living on a dog does not help the dog. The dog is bitten and gets itchy skin. The flea is described as a parasite. In some partnerships, one of the species gains and the other is neutral – neither gaining nor losing. A partnership in which food is shared is called commensalism, which means "eating at the same table". Usually one partner benefits and the other is neutral. Animals that raid our rubbish bins, such as foxes, possums, and raccoons, have this kind of partnership with us.

MUTUAL PROTECTION
Acacia ants (*Pseudomyrmex* species) protect the bull's horn acacia tree (*Acacia cornigera*) in Costa Rica. They bite animals that try to eat parts of the tree. In return, the tree provides the ants with a safe place to nest inside its large thorns. It also produces parcels of a sweet substance that the ants eat.

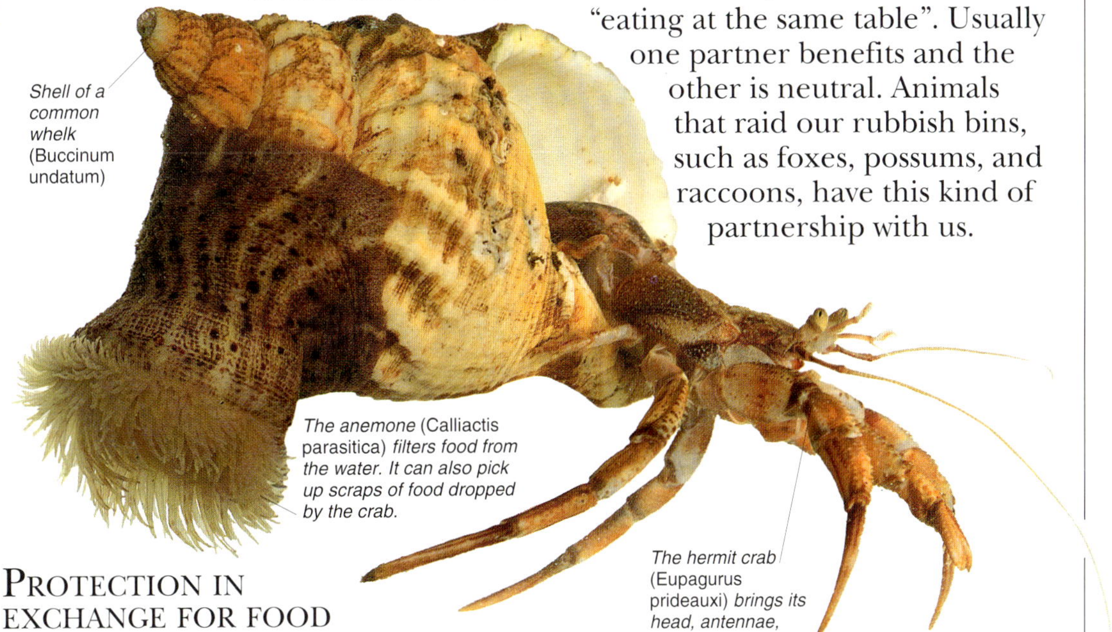

Shell of a common whelk (Buccinum undatum)

The anemone (Calliactis parasitica) *filters food from the water. It can also pick up scraps of food dropped by the crab.*

The hermit crab (Eupagurus prideauxi) *brings its head, antennae, front claws, and first two pairs of legs out of the shell when it is moving about.*

PROTECTION IN EXCHANGE FOR FOOD

Hermit crabs do not have their own hard shell. They live in the empty shells of dead shellfish. As a crab grows, it moves on to a larger shell. Some sea anemones live on the shells inhabited by hermit crabs. The crab carries the anemone to new feeding grounds and provides it with leftover scraps of food. In return, the anemone's stinging tentacles protect the crab from attack.

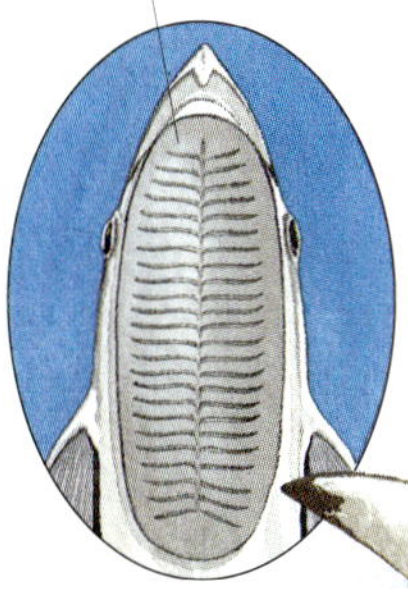

A remora's suction disc has a series of plates.

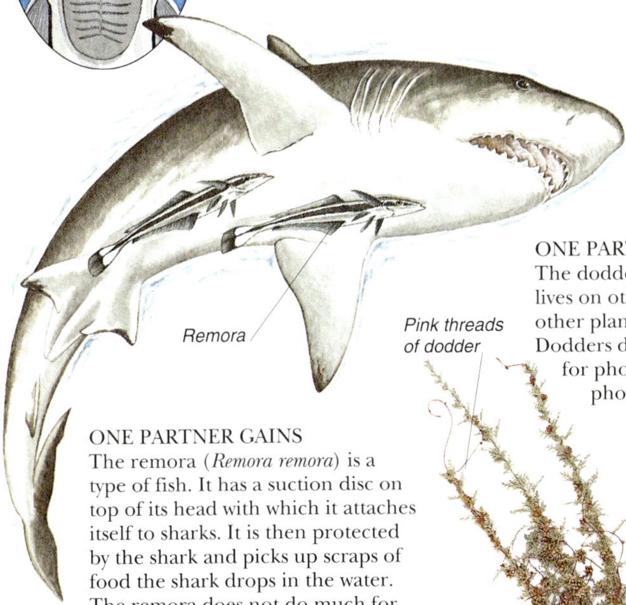

Remora

ONE PARTNER GAINS
The remora (*Remora remora*) is a type of fish. It has a suction disc on top of its head with which it attaches itself to sharks. It is then protected by the shark and picks up scraps of food the shark drops in the water. The remora does not do much for the shark, although it may remove parasites from its body.

BOTH PARTNERS GAIN
The red-billed oxpecker (*Buphagus erythorhynchus*) climbs over the skin of large African animals, such as giraffes, searching for ticks and blood-sucking flies to eat. The giraffe (*Giraffa camelopardalis*) gains because the oxpecker takes away irritating pests.

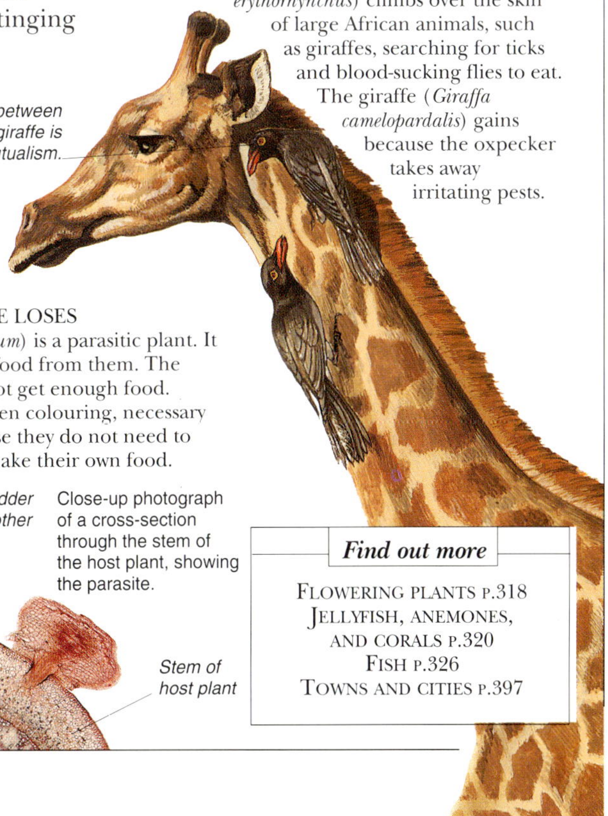

The partnership between an oxpecker and a giraffe is an example of mutualism.

ONE PARTNER GAINS, ONE LOSES
The dodder (*Cuscuta epithymum*) is a parasitic plant. It lives on other plants, taking food from them. The other plant therefore does not get enough food. Dodders do not have any green colouring, necessary for photosynthesis, because they do not need to photosynthesize and make their own food.

Pink threads of dodder

The roots of the dodder penetrate into the other plant's tissue.

Close-up photograph of a cross-section through the stem of the host plant, showing the parasite.

Stem of host plant

Find out more

FLOWERING PLANTS P.318
JELLYFISH, ANEMONES, AND CORALS P.320
FISH P.326
TOWNS AND CITIES P.397

COLOUR AND CAMOUFLAGE

ANIMALS AND PLANTS look the way they do for a reason. Plants have bright colours that attract animals, which then carry the plant's pollen or seeds away to make new plants. Animals have bright colours that attract a mate or warn that the animal is poisonous. Dull colours camouflage, or hide, animals against their background. This helps hunting animals to creep up on their prey, and helps prey to hide from the hunters.

Hoverflies are harmless, but they look like bees or wasps which makes predators think they can sting.

The wings of the male common blue butterfly are bright blue on top which attracts a mate.

The bright colours of ladybirds warn predators that they taste nasty.

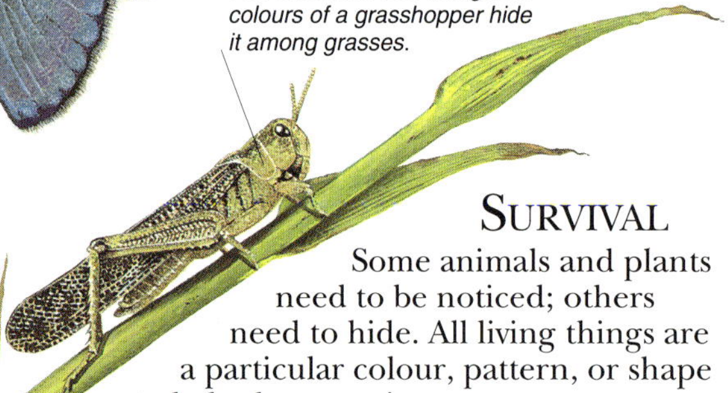

The mottled brown and green colours of a grasshopper hide it among grasses.

The wings of the common blue butterfly (Polyommatus icarus) are dull underneath for camouflage on some plants.

The bright flowers of foxgloves attract bumblebees, which feed on their nectar. The bees also collect pollen, some of which pollinates the next flower they visit.

The caterpillar of the privet hawk moth (Sphinx ligustri) is bright green with diagonal stripes. This helps it hide on the privet leaves on which it feeds.

SURVIVAL

Some animals and plants need to be noticed; others need to hide. All living things are a particular colour, pattern, or shape to help them survive.

CHANGE OF COLOUR

Some animals change colour with the seasons so that they are camouflaged all year round. The stoat (*Mustela erminea*) is brown and black for most of the year. In winter, in places where it snows, the stoat turns white, except for the black tip of its tail.

COLOURFUL MALES

Male birds of many species are more colourful than the females. Females usually have to sit on the nest and look after the chicks, so bright colours would make it easy for predators to see them. The male frigate bird (*Fregata minor*) has a red throat pouch. During courtship, he puffs out his pouch to impress a female.

HENRY WALTER BATES

English naturalist and explorer Henry Bates (1825-92) studied camouflage in animals. He suggested that some harmless insects looked like unpleasant ones so that predators would not attack them. This is now known as Batesian mimicry. He suggested that mimicry was the result of evolution by natural selection.

SPOTS AND STRIPES

Patterns, such as spots and stripes, help to break up the outline of an animal's body. The leopard and bongo can be hard to see in the shadows of the forests where they live. Some young animals have spots or stripes when the adults do not. This camouflages them until they can defend themselves or run away from danger.

Clouded leopard (Neofelis nebulosa)

Bongo (Boocercus euryceros)

Find out more

EVOLUTION P.308
FLOWERING PLANTS P.318
ARTHROPODS P.322
BIRDS P.332
FEEDING P.343
SENSES P.358

MIGRATION AND HIBERNATION

WHEN FOOD IS HARD TO FIND, in cold, hot, or dry seasons, many animals migrate, or move to another place, to find food and water. Other animals find a safe place, such as a burrow or cave, and go into a deep sleep for many months. This sleep is called hibernation. Before migrating or hibernating, animals eat as much as they can to build up extra reserves of fat in their body. In this way they can survive long periods without food. Migrating animals also feed when they can during the journey.

MIGRATION

Animals migrate to find food, warmth, water, space, or a safe place to raise their young. The champion long-distance migrators are birds, such as the Arctic tern, and butterflies. In the African dry season, wildebeest (*Connochaetes taurinus*) move in their thousands to find fresh grass to eat. They follow their parents, but many animals have to make the first journey on their own. Then they remember landmarks or the position of the Sun or stars. Some sense the Earth's magnetic field. Fish and whales may recognize ocean currents.

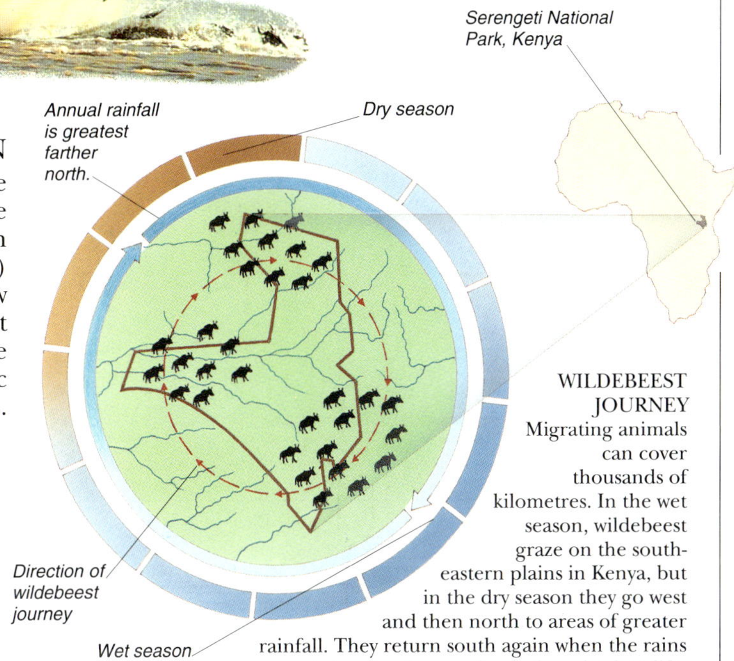

WILDEBEEST JOURNEY

Migrating animals can cover thousands of kilometres. In the wet season, wildebeest graze on the south-eastern plains in Kenya, but in the dry season they go west and then north to areas of greater rainfall. They return south again when the rains bring the dry grasslands there back to life. Predators of wildebeest, such as lions, have to follow them, otherwise they would go hungry too.

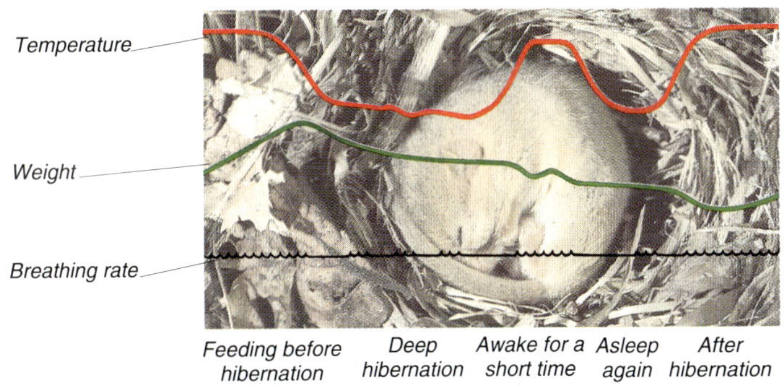

HIBERNATION

Body processes slow down in hibernation, so the animal is just alive. Body temperature falls to a few degrees above the air temperature, and there are fewer, weaker heartbeats. This chart shows a hibernating dormouse (*Muscardinus avellanarius*).

LENGTHS OF HIBERNATION

Marmots, such as this yellow-bellied marmot (*Marmota flaviventris*), are called true hibernators. They remain inactive during hibernation otherwise they would lose too much energy. Some animals, such as bears, are inactive for long periods. But their heartbeat hardly slows at all and, if there is a warm spell, they wake up and feed.

South American lungfish (*Lepidosiren paradoxus*)

SURVIVING DROUGHT

Lungfish live in swamps where the water disappears during the dry season. They survive by burrowing in the mud and curling up inside a cocoon of wet, mucus. This stops their body losing too much water by evaporation. The lungfish breathes through a mud lid to its cocoon. When the rains return, the lungfish breaks out and swims off. This kind of hibernation, in hot, dry conditions, is called aestivation.

Find out more

STRUCTURE OF THE EARTH P.212
SEASONS P.243
CLIMATES P.244
NUTRITION P.342
FACT FINDER P.424

POLAR AND TUNDRA LANDS

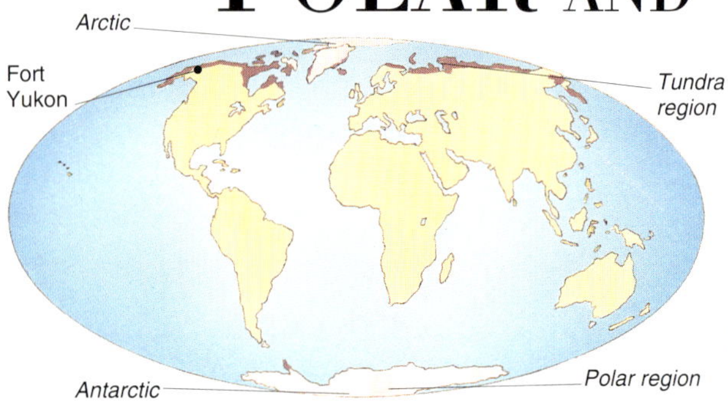

World distribution of Polar and tundra lands

AT THE TOP AND BOTTOM of the world are some of the harshest ecosystems on Earth. The region around the North Pole is called the Arctic, and the region around the South Pole is called the Antarctic. The Antarctic is the coldest place on Earth. Temperatures can be as low as -80°C (-112°F) and the wind can blow at 320 km/h (200 mph). There is not a large variety of life, so food webs are simple and can be easily upset. The wildlife is adapted for surviving the climate.

POLAR LANDS

A huge area around each Pole is covered by ice. In the Arctic, the ice floats on top of the sea and is often only a few metres thick. In the Antarctic, the ice is on top of a rocky landmass and in places is about 4 km (2.5 miles) thick. Animals survive the cold because they have thick fur, dense feathers, or layers of fatty blubber under the skin. All these help to stop body warmth escaping. Large numbers of birds, such as penguins and eider ducks, migrate to the Polar regions in summer. There are few predators and plenty of food at this time of year.

WALRUS
Tough skin and thick layers of fat protect the walrus (*Odobenus rosmarus*) in the Arctic against the cold and from attacks by other walruses. The length of a walrus's tusks may indicate its status in the group. It uses its tusks to dig up shellfish from the seabed.

ARCTIC TERN
Arctic terns (*Sterna paradisaea*) raise their young in the Arctic summer, then migrate to the other end of the world for the Antarctic summer. They see more hours of daylight than any other living creature.

WHITE WHALE
The beluga, or white whale, (*Delphinapterus leucas*) may stay in Arctic waters all year round, although most whales only visit the Arctic in the summer. Belugas feed mainly on fish such as cod, halibut, and haddock.

POLAR BEAR
Thick fur and layers of blubber help to keep the polar bear (*Thalarctos maritimus*) warm in the Arctic. The blubber is a source of energy. Male polar bears may hunt seals all through the winter.

Monthly temperature and rainfall in Fort Yukon, Alaska

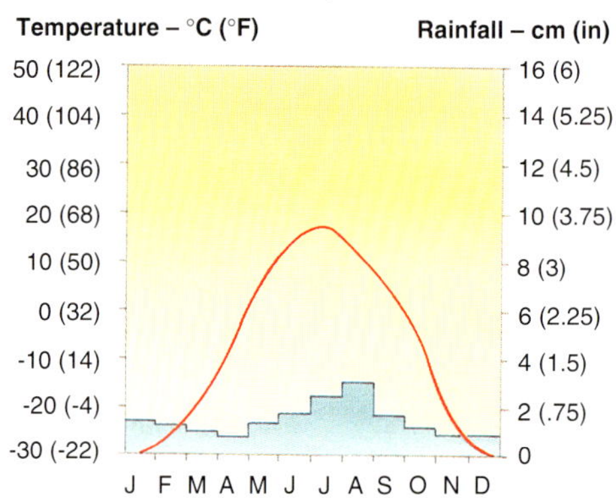

CLIMATE
The Polar and tundra regions are very cold. There is little rain or snow because the cold air cannot hold much moisture. Less snow falls around the Poles than rain falls in the Sahara desert. In winter, the Polar regions are dark all the time and, in summer, the sun shines for 24 hours.

TUNDRA LANDS

The tundra is a barren landscape on the edge of the Polar ecosystem. The ground is covered with lichens, and small bushes that grow in low, dense cushions out of the wind. The plants have small leaves to stop them losing too much water. In summer, insects such as mosquitoes and blackflies hatch from eggs laid in the soil. The insects feed on the blood of large mammals, such as reindeer, and are themselves eaten by birds.

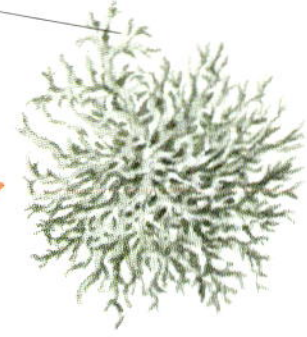

Reindeer moss (Cladonia species) absorbed radioactivity from the air.

Reindeer (Rangifer tarandus) ate the lichens, making their meat unfit for the Lapland people to eat.

POLLUTION CHAIN

In 1986, there was a serious nuclear accident at a power station in Chernobyl in the Ukraine. The air was polluted with massive doses of dangerous radioactivity which was absorbed by plants and passed on in the food chain. For example, radioactivity in a lichen called reindeer moss was passed on to reindeer and then to humans.

STUDYING THE OZONE

Scientists go to the Arctic and Antarctic to study the ozone layer. They perform ground and balloon-based experiments to test the air for pollutants, and for the amount of ozone. The ozone problem is bad over the Poles because of the extreme weather conditions. High levels of ultraviolet rays are getting through to the Earth, and harming plankton in the sea, so disrupting the start of many food chains.

MUSK OXEN

Musk oxen (*Ovibos moschatus*) live in the Arctic tundra. They have a woolly coat, and thick layers of fat. In winter they grow a long overcoat of windproof hair. The oxen huddle together, with the young in the middle, for warmth and protection from predators.

EIDER DUCK

In the summer the eider duck (*Somateria mollissina*) migrates to the Arctic to nest. The female plucks feathers from her breast to line the nest and keep the eggs from losing heat.

A little way below the surface of the tundra is a frozen layer, called permafrost, which never thaws out. The soil above the permafrost thaws in summer but the water cannot drain away. It collects on the surface, forming marshy pools.

PENGUINS

Penguins live only in the Southern Hemisphere. They cannot fly, but are excellent swimmers, using their wings as flippers. They come ashore to lay eggs and to raise their young. Some, such as these Adelie penguins (*Pygoscelis adeliae*), march over 350 km (220 miles) from the sea to reach their nest site.

NORWAY LEMMING

Lemmings, such as the Norway lemming (*Lemmus lemmus*), spend most of their time sheltering among plants or in a burrow just under the soil. In winter, they tunnel beneath the snow, which acts like a blanket and keeps out extreme cold. The number of lemmings rises and falls, and peaks about every four years.

THREATS TO POLAR REGIONS

The Trans-Alaska oil pipeline stretches for 1,300 km (800 miles). It avoids the nesting places of rare birds and is raised in some places so that migrating animals can go underneath it. But the building of the pipeline damaged the environment and upset traditional migration routes. And roads near the pipeline opened up the area to poachers.

Find out more

NUCLEAR ENERGY P.136
SEASONS P.243
CLIMATES P.244
TRANSPORT IN PLANTS P.341
PEOPLE AND PLANET P.374
FOOD CHAINS AND WEBS P.377
MIGRATION AND HIBERNATION P.381

Mountains

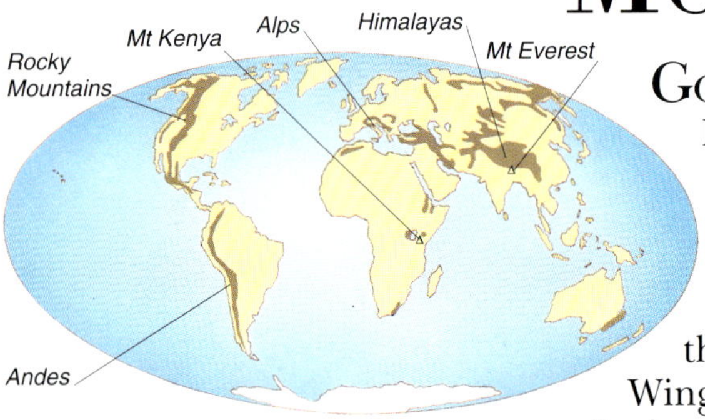

World distribution of major mountains

GOING UP A MOUNTAIN is like making a journey across the Earth from the Equator to the Poles. You go through all the main ecosystems, from forests on the lower slopes to grassland, tundra, and snow. The wildlife of the higher slopes has to cope with freezing temperatures, fierce winds, and thin air. Plants grow in dense cushions and have thick, hairy leaves that trap heat and reduce water loss. Wingless insects are common because the winds are too strong for insects to fly. Some mountain mammals have large hearts and lungs to help them get enough oxygen from the thin air. They may also have thick fur to keep out the cold. Some animals turn white in winter, for camouflage in the snow and ice.

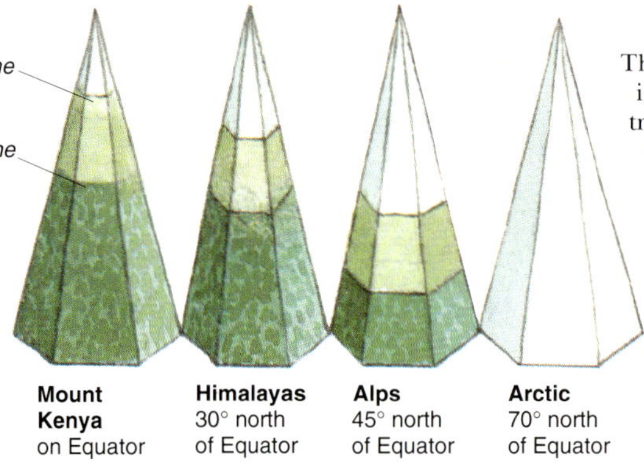

TREE LINE

The height above which it is too cold and windy for trees to grow is called the tree line. The snow line is the lower edge of the part where snow stays all year round. The height of the snow and tree line depends on the weather and how near a mountain is to the Equator.

Mountain zones

All mountains have broad bands, or zones, each with its own typical plants and animals. In the Himalayas, on the border of Nepal and India, the bottom zone is a warm deciduous forest. Above this is a band of cooler coniferous forest. The tree line is at about 3,400 m (11,200 ft). Higher than this, there are only low-growing bushes and shrubs, which merge into grassland and bare rock just below the snow-covered peaks.

THREATS TO MOUNTAINS

Mountain ecosystems are not as threatened as many others. Many mountains are the last refuge for rare species. But some mountain forests and scrublands are being destroyed by the construction of ski resorts. Unique alpine plants and fragile soils have to be cleared away to make ski runs, and new roads and holiday villages can upset the natural mountain life.

Find out more

CLIMATES P.244
SNOW P.266
CONIFERS P.317
COLOUR AND CAMOUFLAGE P.380
POLAR AND TUNDRA LANDS P.382
GRASSLANDS P.392
TEMPERATE FORESTS P.396

SEASHORES

WHERE THE LAND MEETS THE SEA there is an ecosystem rich in food. Some food is washed down by rivers; more is brought in from the sea by the tides. Animals and plants are adapted to survive these difficult conditions. The environment is constantly changing as waves and tides move water, sand, and pebbles up, down, and along the beach. When the tide goes out, the plants and animals are exposed to air, winds, strong sunlight, and rainwater. On tropical and polar shores, the animals and plants have to tolerate extreme temperatures.

ESTUARIES

The place where a river meets the sea is called an estuary. Birds known as waders, such as these redshank (*Tringa totanus*), walk through the shallow water searching for food in the mud with their long beaks. Estuaries are important to migrating birds in winter. Many birds break their journey to rest and feed there.

Seabirds such as shags (Phalacrocorax aristotelis) *and puffins* (Fratercula arctica)*, far right, nest on cliffs where they are safe from enemies.*

The roots of marram grass (Ammophila arenaria) *spread out under the sand in a thick network which holds the sand together.*

During the day, the masked crab (Corystes cassivelaunus) *stays under the sand. It breathes by taking in water through its tube-like antennae. Only the tips of these stick up into the water.*

SHIFTING SANDS

Beneath the surface of a sandy beach is a mass of worms and shellfish. There they are protected from pounding waves and drying air. Many sandy shore animals filter fragments of food from the sand and the seawater. Microscopic algae coat the surface of the sand or float in the water.

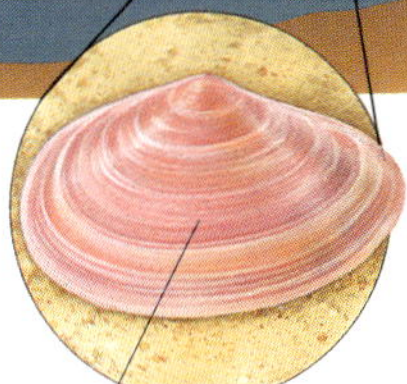

Thin tellins (Tellina tenuis) *burrow in the sand from the middle shore to shallow water. They suck in food from the seabed using a siphon like a vacuum cleaner.*

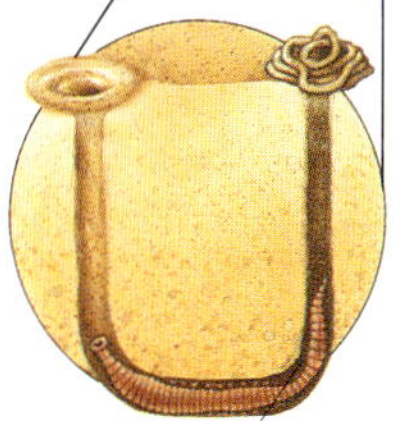

Lugworms (Arenicola marina) *live in a U-shaped burrow under the sand.*

THREATS TO SEASHORES

Beaches can be at risk from people building hotels and airports, dropping litter, and dumping oil and sewage into coastal seas. Birds and reptiles that nest on beaches are disturbed by the noise and bright lights in tourist areas. Loggerhead turtles (*Caretta caretta*) come ashore to lay their eggs on the beaches of the Greek island of Zakynthos. Their numbers have decreased but naturalists are now protecting their nesting sites.

Young loggerhead turtle

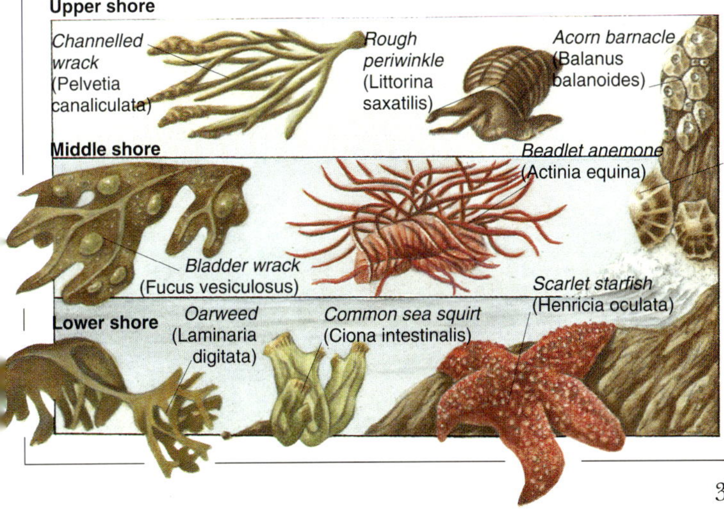

ROCKY SHORE ZONES

Zones on a rocky shore are often clearly marked by the types of seaweed. Green seaweeds grow near the top of the shore, and brown ones grow near the lower shore. Different animals also live in each zone, according to the amount of time they can survive out of the water.

Find out more

SHORELINE P.236
MIGRATION AND HIBERNATION P.381
OCEANS P.386
RIVERS AND LAKES P.388
FACT FINDER P.424

OCEANS

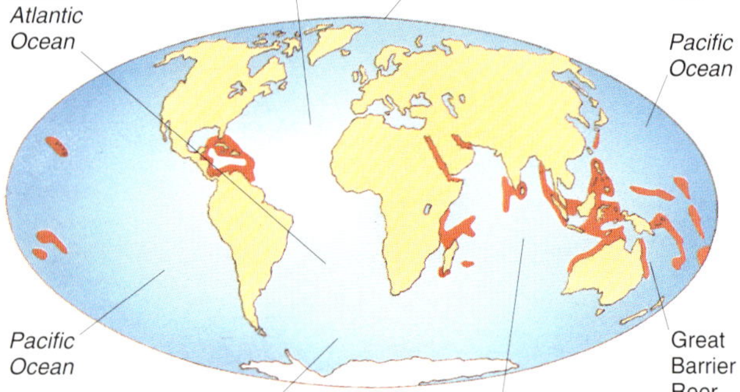

World distribution of oceans and major coral reefs

MORE THAN 70 PER CENT of the Earth's surface is covered by ocean. This makes the oceans the largest ecosystem. Life exists at depths of 4 km (2.5 miles) or more. Dead plants and animals, food scraps, and droppings fall down on the ocean floor, making it rich in nutrients. There are many different habitats in the oceans, from sandy underwater deserts and huge mountains to coral reefs and open water. The oceans do not contain a great variety of species – only about 20 per cent of the Earth's species live there, and nine out of ten of these live on the ocean floor.

PLANKTON

Most ocean food chains start with the microscopic plankton in the euphotic zone. Tiny plants (phytoplankton), such as diatoms, are eaten by tiny animals (zooplankton). Zooplankton include a large number of larvae of animals such as shrimps and crabs. They provide food for a variety of fish, which are in turn eaten by other fish and marine mammals.

OCEAN ZONES

There are two main habitats in the ocean – the water itself, called the pelagic habitat, and the ocean floor, called the benthic habitat. The pelagic habitat is divided into several depth zones. Sunlight reaches down through only about 100 m (330 ft) and in very muddy waters it may reach down less than a metre. This thin zone, where plants can photosynthesize, is called the euphotic zone. Below this, down to about 2,000 m (6, 500 ft), is the bathyal zone, where there is little or no light. The vast ocean deeps, or abyssal zone, go down to 6,000 m (19,500 ft) and more.

DEEP-SEA CHEMICALS

On the floor of the Pacific Ocean there are cracks in the Earth's crust where hot, sulphur-rich water gushes out of tall vents. Animals live nearby, absorbing chemicals dissolved in the water. Bacteria in their body tissues convert the chemicals into the energy that the animals need.

The food chain near the deep-sea vents begins with bacteria that do not need light for photosynthesis.

Giant worms (*Riftia pachyptila*) up to 3 m (10 ft) long live near the deep-sea vents.

FINDING FOOD

Food is hard to find in the dark ocean depths. Deep-sea fish, such as this angler fish (*Melanocoetus johnsoni*), can have lights that attract prey, and large stomachs to hold as much food as possible.

JACQUES-YVES COUSTEAU

Frenchman Jacques Cousteau (born 1910) is famous for his underwater explorations. In the early 1940s, he developed the aqualung, a portable breathing apparatus for divers, with the French engineer Emile Gagnan. This encouraged more people to explore the oceans, which has greatly increased our knowledge of underwater life. Cousteau helped to develop an underwater camera, and has made many films of life under the sea, including *The Silent World*. Cousteau has also campaigned to stop mining in Antarctica.

CORAL REEFS
The Great Barrier Reef of Australia is the largest coral reef in the world. Coral reefs contain a great variety of wildlife. The waters are not rich in nutrients but the reef inhabitants recycle them very quickly so that nothing is wasted. Corals can live only in clean, warm, salty water less than 30 m (100 ft) deep, so that sunlight reaches them. Algae live in the bodies of the corals and they need sunlight to make food. Coral reefs are threatened by pollution, mining, and rising sea levels due to the greenhouse effect.

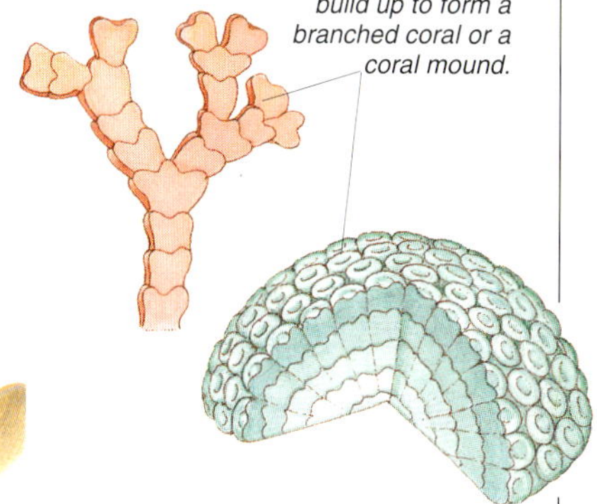

Corals are tiny animals that filter food from the water with waving tentacles. Skeletons of coral can build up to form a branched coral or a coral mound.

Most of our fishing is done in shallow waters near the edges of continents.

The shallow waters near continents are rich in nutrients because they are washed off the land, and storms mix up the water, bringing nutrients to the surface.

A coral reef is built up over thousands of years from coral skeletons.

A narrow ledge of land called the continental shelf sticks out from continents under the oceans. The shallow water on the continental shelf is called the neritic (near shore) zone.

OCEAN MAMMALS
The largest animals on Earth, whales live in the oceans where the water supports their massive bodies. They are mammals so although they can stay underwater for a long time, they have to come to the surface to breathe air. They blow out the used air through nostrils on top of their head, called spouting, then take in fresh air.

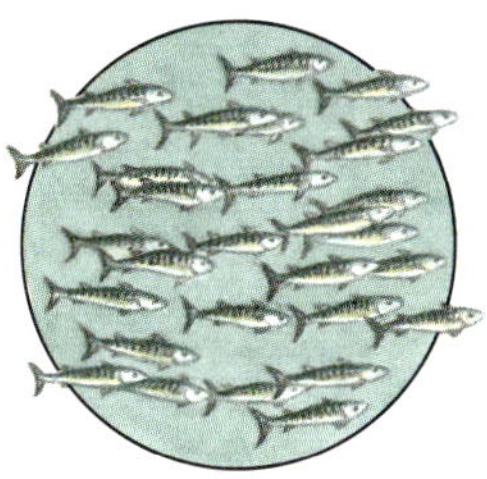

SHOALS OF FISH
Fish such as mackerel (*Scomber scombrus*), swim near the surface in shallow waters. They filter small pieces of food from the water with their brush-like gill rakes.

THREATS TO OCEANS

The biggest threat to ocean ecosystems is pollution from oil, sewage, and industrial waste. People also hunt fish, whales, and other wildlife. As the number of people in the world grows, so more food is needed. In some places, there are no more fish left to catch. Strong nets stretch for up to 60 km (37 miles) across the oceans. With these nets and new technology to find fish, they have little chance of escape. But some countries have set limits on how many fish can be caught. Others use nets with large holes so that young fish can escape and grow into the next generation.

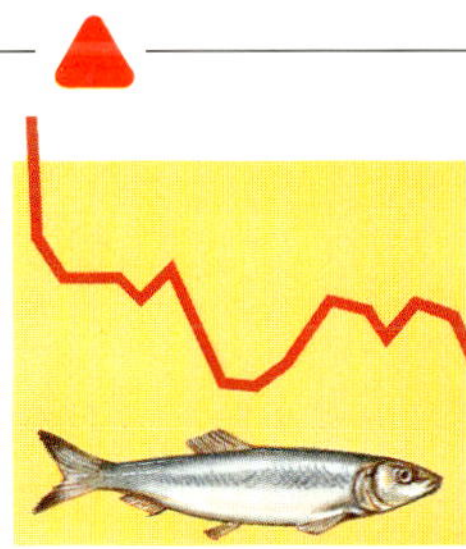

Herring numbers have fallen dramatically in the last 20 years.

Find out more

SULPHUR P.45
SEAS AND OCEANS P.234
SINGLE-CELLED ORGANISMS P.314
JELLYFISH, ANEMONES, AND CORALS P.320
FISH P.326
MAMMALS P.334
PHOTOSYNTHESIS P.340
FEEDING P.343

RIVERS AND LAKES

Fast mountain stream

The horse leech (Haemopis sanguisuga) *clings on to stones with suckers. It eats insect larvae, snails, and worms.*

Brown trout (Salmo trutta) *like cool water with plenty of oxygen. They are good swimmers and can move easily against the strong currents.*

THE STILL WATERS OF TINY POOLS and great lakes, and the flowing waters of mountain streams and wide rivers, are all freshwater ecosystems. Some of these change with the seasons; others are changing all the time. The weather and natural processes, such as erosion, affect the amount of water in each area. Rivers change their course and new lakes form. They can also fill up with silt, material deposited by the water, and turn into dry land. Some pools and rivers appear only in a wet season, so only simple communities live there. But large rivers and lakes contain complex communities that have developed over hundreds of years.

Young swift river

Adult dragonflies lay their eggs on plants, and the larvae, called nymphs, live in the water until they change into adults.

The Eurasian kingfisher (Alcedo atthis) *nests in holes in the bank. It dives into the water up to 100 times a day to catch fish.*

Water plantain (Alisma plantago-aquatica) *provides shelter for birds. It grows up to 1 m (3.3 ft) tall.*

Slow mature river

FROM SOURCE TO SEA

In fast-flowing water near the source (the start) of a river, there is plenty of oxygen but few plants for animals to eat. Most food chains start with dead material in the water. In the middle part of the river, the water flows more slowly. Plants take root and provide food and shelter for animals. The water in the lower part of the river, towards the sea, can be muddy. It flows slowly and contains less oxygen. Vertebrates, such as fish, are an important part of the community.

Greater reedmace (Typha latifolia) *grows over 2 m (6.6 ft) tall. It can survive if the water level rises.*

The otter (Lutra lutra) *has webbed feet to help it swim underwater. It can close its ears to stop water getting in.*

Dams are built across rivers to provide water, to generate electricity, or to stop flooding. Villages and farmland can be covered by lakes that are formed.

THREATS TO RIVERS

When dams are built across rivers, huge lakes are formed and the nature of the river is changed. The lakes provide a new habitat for fish, but make it difficult for some other animals and plants to survive. The Aswan dam, across the Nile in Egypt, also stops silt flowing down the river. The silt used to flood over the land and enrich the soil.

TROPICAL RIVERS

The black caiman (*Melanosuchus niger*) lives in the Amazon in South America. It is related to crocodiles and alligators. It is the top carnivore in its ecosystem, eating everything from fish to wild pigs. Hunting by humans means it is now in danger of extinction.

RECORD-BREAKING LAKE

Lake Baikal, in Siberia, is the deepest and oldest freshwater lake in the world. It reaches a depth of 1,620 m (5,314 ft) and is at least 25 million years old. The lake contains more than 1,000 species of animals that are found nowhere else in the world. Sadly, this ecosystem is threatened by pollution from factories, towns and agriculture around the lake.

Find out more

WEATHERING AND EROSION P.230
RIVERS P.233
WORMS P.321
ARTHROPODS P.322
FISH P.326
REPTILES P.330
FOOD CHAINS AND WEBS P.377

WETLANDS

SIX PER CENT OF THE EARTH'S SURFACE is covered by wetlands. They can be fresh or saltwater, and include wet grasslands, called marshes, wet peatlands, called bogs, and waterlogged forests called swamps. Wetlands are some of the world's richest ecosystems. They produce more plant material than most other ecosystems on Earth. A variety of small mammals, birds, insects and other invertebrates live there. Birds flock to wetlands to nest because they do not have many enemies there. Large mammalian predators would sink into the wet ground. Water levels change with the seasons so the wildlife has to be able to survive in dry and wet conditions.

SITATUNGA
To stop it sinking into the swampy ground, the sitatunga (*Tragelaphus spekei*) of Africa has long splayed-out hooves. It can swim well and, in times of danger, hides underwater with only the tip of its nose showing, so that it can breathe.

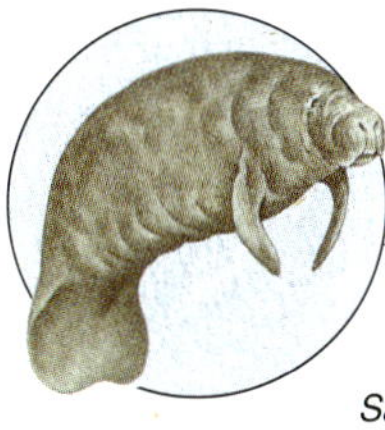

The manatee is a mammal so has to breathe air, but it can stay underwater for up to 15 minutes.

The zebra butterfly (Heliconius charitonius) *flies slowly on long, narrow wings. At night, large groups gather on bare twigs.*

The anhinga (Anhinga anhinga) *dives underwater to catch fish. It then perches with its wings half-open to dry them in the sun.*

Stunted bald cypress (Taxodium distichum)

Sawgrass dotted with islands of trees

Slash pines (Pinus elliottii) *and saw-palmetto* (Serenoa repens) *grow on higher ground.*

Mangrove swamp on the coast

The water moccasin (Agkistrodon piscivorus) *is a poisonous snake that hunts at night.*

THE EVERGLADES

At the southern tip of Florida in the United States is a huge area of cypress swamp called the Everglades. It is home to rare species such as the manatee (*Tricheus manatus*) and the Florida panther (*Felis concolor coryi*). It is now a national park but is threatened by chemicals used in agriculture, and by drainage, pollution, and tourism. Fast boats kill more than 100 manatees every year.

The American alligator (Alligator mississippiensis) *is the largest and loudest reptile in North America. In the spring, the male bellows to attract females.*

The garpike (Lepisosteus osseus) *has gills for breathing underwater, but can also breathe air if the water dries up.*

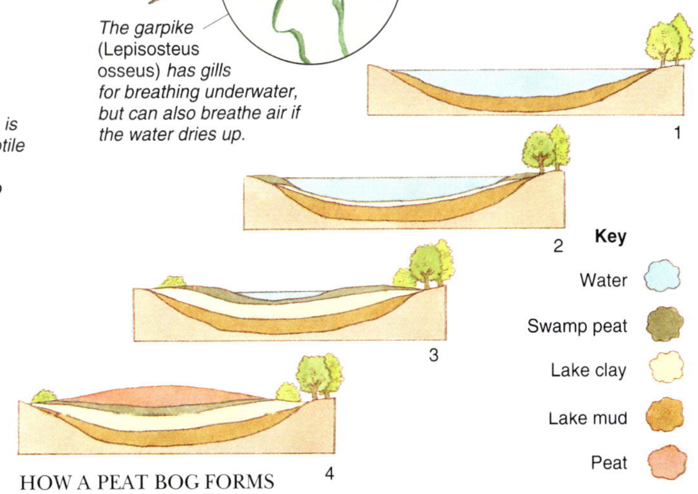

HOW A PEAT BOG FORMS
A peat bog may form where a lake fills in with mud and plants. (1) The water is clear, with mud on the bottom. (2) Mud collects around roots of plants. (3) Mosses grow and build up mounds of peat. (4) The lake disappears and is replaced by a dome of peat. Peat bog forming is an example of succession.

MANGROVES

The most common trees in tropical fresh and saltwater swamps are mangroves. They can survive in waterlogged mud because they have breathing pores in their roots. Some mangroves have roots that grow up into the air and get oxygen. The red mangrove (*Rhizophora mangle*) grows in coastal swamps and estuaries. It protects them from storms and tidal waves.

Find out more

PRESSURE P.127
REPTILES P.330
MAMMALS P.334
THE BIOSPHERE P.370
WILDLIFE IN DANGER P.398

DESERTS

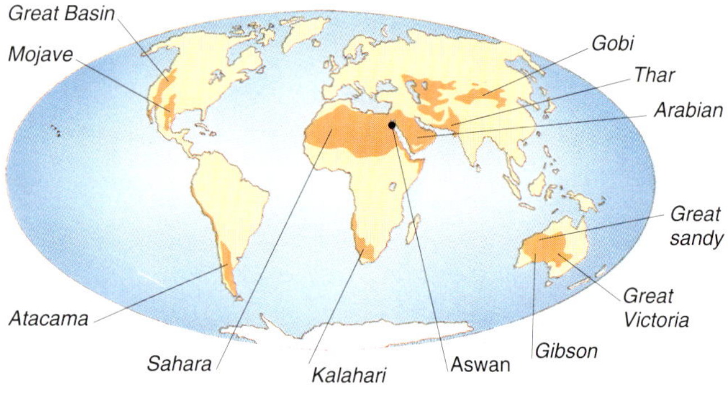

World distribution of major deserts

DESERTS ARE THE DRIEST PLACES on Earth. Most have less than 10 cm (4 in) of rain a year. Some may have no rain at all for several years. Most deserts are hot, so more water evaporates into the air than falls as rain. Desert plants have deep or wide-spreading roots, tough skins, small leaves or spines, and special ways of storing water. Many animals may never drink, getting all their water from their food. Only a few species of plants and animals can survive in the desert so there is little dead material to make the soil rich. The few nutrients that are present take a long time to cycle through the ecosystem.

DESERT BY DAY

Daytime temperatures in hot deserts may reach more than 50°C (120°F) and the surface of the sand can be as hot as 90°C (195°F). Most animals hide away in burrows or beneath rocks where the air is cooler and more moist. Some desert plants have hairy leaves that reflect strong sunlight. The pores of most stay shut during the day so less water escapes.

The huge ears of the fennec fox (Vulpes zerda) *help it to hear the faintest sound of prey moving nearby. The ears also help the fox to keep cool by giving off heat like a radiator.*

The kit fox (Vulpes macrotis) *comes out at night to hunt. It runs fast to catch small animals before they escape down a burrow.*

CONVERGENT EVOLUTION

Animals living in the same habitats in different parts of the world often look similar, for example, the kit fox of North America and the fennec fox of Africa. This is because both foxes have adapted to survive in the same kind of ecosystem, where environmental conditions are similar. This is called convergent evolution.

Chuckwallas (Sauromalus obesus) *bask in the morning sun until they are warm enough to crawl off in search of flowers, fruits, and seeds to eat.*

On its powerful back legs, the black-tailed jack-rabbit (Lepus californicus) *can leap away from danger at speeds of up to 56 km/h (35 mph).*

Kangaroo rats (Dipodomys deserti) *get all the water they need from the seeds they eat. They carry seeds back to their burrow in cheek pouches.*

STORAGE TANKS

Desert plants and animals have to survive long dry spells. Some animals can store fat in their body. The fat can be broken down to provide energy and water.

A camel, such as the one-humped Arabian camel (Camelus dromedarius), *can go without water for weeks. A camel can drink up to 114 litres (25 gallons) of water in one go.*

The gila monster (Heloderma suspectum) *stores fat in its thick tail to help it survive hard times.*

Because water is lost through leaves, cacti such as this Mammillaria elongata *do not have any – just spines, which prevent them from being eaten. They store water in their thick stems.*

SIDE-WINDING

Several snakes that live in sandy deserts, such as this sidewinder adder (*Bitis peringueyi*), move by throwing themselves over the sand in "S"-shaped curves. This is called side-winding because the snakes travel sideways rather than forwards. The advantage of this type of movement is that only two parts of the snake's body touch the hot surface of the sand at any one time. The snake also is less likely to sink into the soft sand.

Desert at night

At night, the desert is much cooler and the air becomes more moist. Many animals come out to hunt and the desert comes to life. Food is still hard to find, and many desert hunters, such as spiders and scorpions, are very poisonous. If a meal does come their way, they have to deal with it as quickly as possible and must not let it escape.

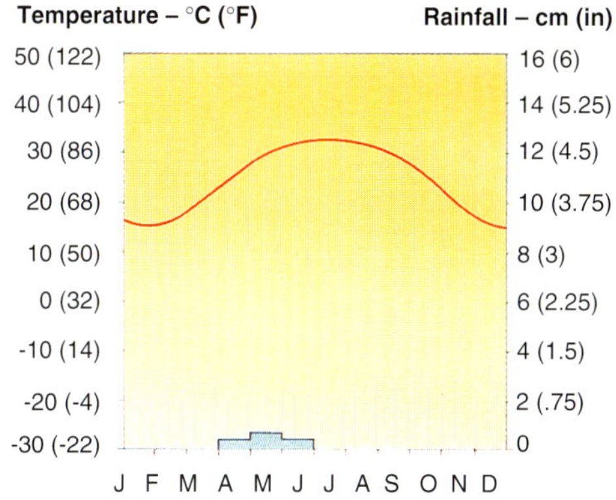

Monthly temperature and rainfall in Aswan, Egypt

CLIMATE

The largest deserts are near the Equator. They are hot and dry all year round because the winds that blow across them contain very little moisture. Deserts in colder parts of the world, such as the Gobi desert in central Asia, are hot in summer and cold in winter. Deserts also occur in the shelter of high mountains, such as the Atacama desert in South America.

OASES

In a few places in a desert, water seeps through the ground to form a moist area called an oasis where plants can grow. Oases are a vital lifeline for animals, including people travelling across the desert. The water in an oasis comes from water-filled rocks near the surface. It may have fallen as rain many kilometres away and drained down through the rocks under the desert. But oases do not last forever; the water may run dry or sand dunes may be blown over the oasis. People and animals then have to move on.

Oasis in Australia

SPREADING DESERTS

The spread of deserts is a major threat. It is partly caused by people who live on the desert edges. The grazing of animals, and the cutting down of wood for building, can cause the land to turn to desert. This is called desertification. It is a particular problem in areas where several years have passed without any rain.

Find out more

Heat transfer p.142
Climates p.244
Evolution p.308
Transport in plants p.341
Movement p.356

Grasslands

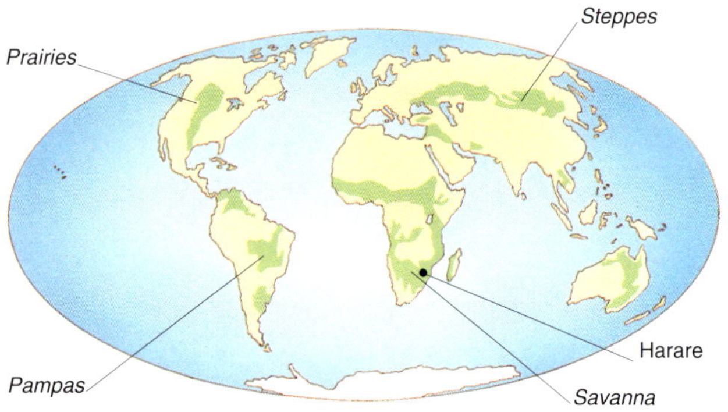

World distribution of major grasslands

Where the climate is too dry, and the soils too poor for most trees, grasses grow. These areas are called grasslands. Grass is the start of many food chains. It is able to survive nibbling by animals because it sprouts from the bottom, and not from the tips as other plants do. The more the grass is bitten off, the more it grows. Grass also grows back well after fires, which are common in this ecosystem. In dry or cold seasons, animals have to migrate long distances to find enough food and water to survive.

Food for all

The tropical grasslands of East Africa are called the savanna. More than 40 species of grazing mammals live here and share out the food. There is usually enough to go round because the animals feed on different parts of the grasses, shrubs, and trees. For example, zebras eat the top of the grass stems, wildebeest eat the middle part, and Thomson's gazelles eat the bottom part. Dik-diks concentrate on small bushes near the ground while giraffes feed high up in the trees.

Monthly temperature and rainfall in Harare, Zimbabwe

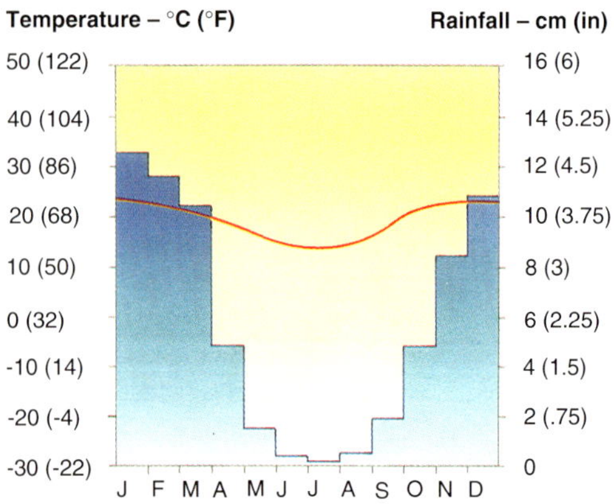

Climate

Tropical grasslands are warm all year round, but there is a long dry season in summer. Temperate grasslands have very cold winters, with hard frosts, and hot, dry summers. This graph shows the climate for a city in a tropical grassland area.

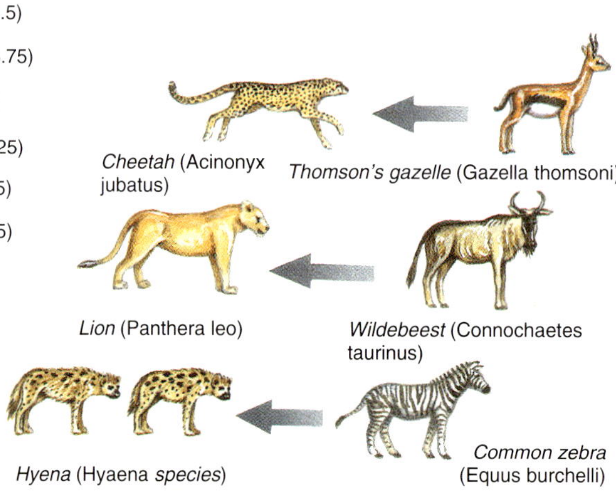

Hunters

The large number of herbivores on the African savanna are food for a whole range of predators. Each predator tends to have a favourite food because of the way it hunts. Cheetahs can chase gazelles at up to 100 km/h (62 mph) but for a short time only. Lions cannot run so fast. They have to get close to their prey. But they are strong and hunt in groups so can kill large animals such as wildebeest. Hyenas also hunt in groups but usually kill animals only as large as a zebra.

ASIAN STEPPES

Temperate grasslands called the Steppes stretch across central Asia from Europe to China. Large herds of grazing animals, such as bison (*Bison bonasus*), and saiga antelope (*Saiga tatarica*) used to graze here. They trod seeds into the ground so that they could grow, encouraged fresh growth by biting off the grasses, and fertilized the soil with their droppings. Hunting and farming have killed most of these animals, although saiga antelope are now increasing due to conservation measures.

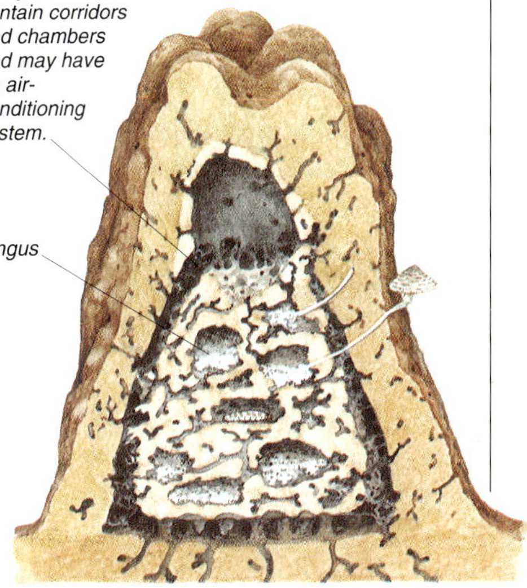

TERMITES

Insects called termites are a vital part of decomposition in grasslands. They eat dead material or take it inside their tall mud nests. They use it as compost for the fungus they grow for food. Termite nests can be up to 2.5 m (8 ft) high and contain up to 20 million individuals.

Burrowing animals of the South American pampas

BURROWING ANIMALS

On the pampas of South America, huge numbers of small mammals live underground where they are safe from fires and predators. Their burrowing helps to mix up the soil layers and stops all the minerals building up on the surface. This makes the soil rich and helps the grasses and other plants to grow. On the North American prairies, ground squirrels, called prairie dogs (*Cynomys* species) live in huge groups and have a whole "town" of interconnected burrows. They keep the ground grazed all around the burrows so that they can see enemies coming.

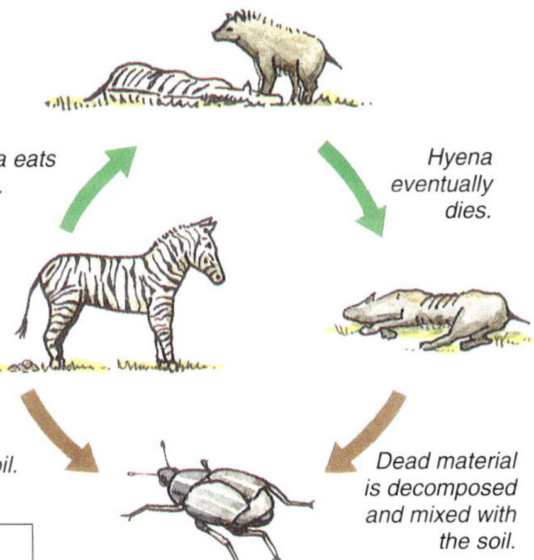

NUTRIENT CYCLE

Many grassland animals, bacteria, and fungi feed on dead plants or animals or animal dung. Some of the nutrients become part of the decomposers' bodies and some eventually enrich the soil. This means that nothing is wasted, and the nutrients go round and round in an endless cycle.

GEORGE AND JOY ADAMSON

British game warden George Adamson (1906-89) worked to protect and conserve wildlife in Kenya, Africa. He worked with his wife Joy (1910-80) who was especially interested in lions. She is famous for looking after the lioness Elsa as a cub, and the story of Elsa's return to the wild was made into the film *Born Free* in 1960. Both George and Joy Adamson were murdered in Kenya.

THREATS TO GRASSLANDS

Hunting has drastically reduced the number of grazing animals and their predators on grasslands. Where hunting is banned, people still poach, or hunt illegally. At least 85 per cent of the worlds's rhinoceroses have been killed by poachers during the last 30 years. Gamewardens such as these in Kenya have to look out constantly for hunters. Sometimes they rescue animals that have been illegally trapped.

Find out more

CLIMATES P.244
NUTRITION P.342
DIGESTION P.345
FOOD CHAINS AND WEBS P.377
MIGRATION AND HIBERNATION P.381

TROPICAL RAINFORESTS

MORE THAN HALF of all animal and plant species in the world live in tropical rainforest ecosystems. But these forests cover less than 10 per cent of the Earth's land surface. Tropical rainforests grow in regions near the Equator in South America, Africa, Asia, and Australia. They are so rich in life because they are wet and warm, and have bright sunlight overhead – all conditions that encourage life. The trees grow fast and reach great heights as they compete with each other to get as much light as possible.

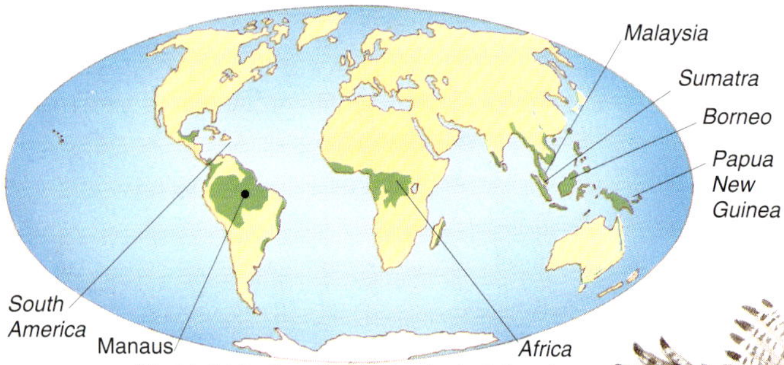

World distribution of major tropical rainforests

LOOKING AFTER THE FORESTS
This family in the Brazilian rainforest are making baskets from natural materials. Over thousands of years, rainforest peoples have lived in harmony with their surroundings. They grow a mixture of crops in small areas to make the best use of nutrients. After a few years, the soil is left to rest and recover.

LAYERS OF LIFE

The wildlife in Amazonian rainforests lives at different levels. Most lives near the top of the trees, in the canopy, where there is lots of sunlight, warmth, and food. Below the canopy, in the understorey, it is darker and cooler, and wildlife is less varied. The largest animals live on the forest floor.

The harpy eagle (Harpia harpyja) *is the biggest eagle in the world. It soars over the canopy hunting for monkeys and sloths to eat.*

Toucans feed on fruit, leaves, and seeds.

Spider monkeys (Ateles *species*) *use their tails to grip the branches.*

Sloths (Brabypus tridactylus) *hang upside-down in the trees, using their long curved claws as hooks.*

Emerald tree boa (Corallus caninus)

Tree frogs are common because they can lay their eggs in pools of water that collect in the trees.

In the understorey, climbing plants, such as lianas and vines, twine around the trees and bushes.

The spotted coat of the jaguar (Panthera onca) *camouflages it as it preys on animals such as agoutis and peccaries.*

Army ants move through the forest in columns of up to 200,000 ants. They march to find food for their larvae.

Peccaries (Tayassu *species*) *feed on plants at the forest edge.*

Fungi can live on the forest floor because they do not need light to make their food.

Agouti (Dasyprocta *species*)

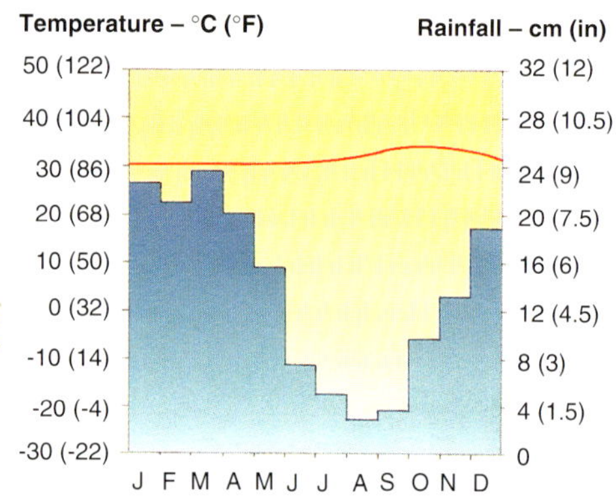

Monthly temperature and rainfall in Manaus, Brazil

CLIMATE
Rainforests are warm all year round, with temperatures between about 20°C and 28°C (68°F and 82°F). This is the wettest ecosystem, with rain nearly every day. Up to 4 m (160 in) of rain falls in a year.

MINI ECOSYSTEM
Plants called bromeliads live on the branches of trees. Pools of water collect in them, creating a mini-ecosystem. Rotting leaves and animal droppings provide food for bacteria and insects, which are in turn eaten by small animals.

Moving through the forest

Rainforest animals have special features to help them move through the trees. Birds have short, broad wings so they can twist and turn between the branches. Some animals have flaps of skin that unfold like wings and enable them to glide from branch to branch. Monkeys use their hands and feet to climb through the trees. Some can grasp branches with their tail, too, like an extra hand. This is called a prehensile tail.

BIRD OF PARADISE
The Raggiana bird of paradise (*Paradisea raggiana*) lives in the rainforests of Papua New Guinea. It has short wings to fly through the trees and strong feet to grasp branches. The male, shown here, may hang upside-down on a branch while he tries to impress females with his brilliant-coloured feathers.

ORANG-UTAN
With their long arms and strong fingers, orang-utans (*Pongo pygmaeus*) swing quickly, hand over hand, through the trees. They live in the rainforests of Borneo and Sumatra. The name orang-utan is a Malysian word meaning "man of the forests".

FLYING GECKO
The flying gecko (*Ptychozoon kuhli*) lives in the rainforests of Malaysia. Folds of skin along the sides of its body, tail, and legs allow it to glide from tree to tree. The folds also camouflage the gecko when it is resting on tree bark. The gecko has ridges of scales on its feet and sharp claws, which help it cling to the slippery tree trunks.

Rainforest cycles

Water, oxygen, minerals, and nutrients all pass through the trees. Due mainly to the warmth and moisture in a tropical rainforest, nutrients are recycled from the soil via the trees to the canopy quickly. This means that the soil is surprisingly poor, and attempts to farm on the land usually fail.

THREATS TO RAINFORESTS

Since 1945, more than half the world's rainforests have been destroyed. Hundreds of species of animals and plants are now extinct. An area of forest the size of a soccer pitch disappears every second. The main threats come from people cutting down the trees for timber, to use the land for cattle ranches and farms, or to mine for oil and metals.

LUNGS OF THE PLANET
Rainforests are sometimes called the lungs of the planet. Large areas of rainforest, such as this one in Malaysia, take in huge amounts of carbon dioxide, and give out lots of oxygen and water during photosynthesis. This influences the climate of the whole Earth.

STUDYING THE RAINFOREST
There are thousands of species of animals and plants living in rainforests that scientists know nothing about. Ecologists are studying there all the time. They use mountaineering equipment to climb up to the canopy, and build permanent walkways through the trees.

Find out more

Climates p.244
Photosynthesis p.340
Transport in plants p.341
Cycles in the biosphere p.372
Colour and camouflage p.380
Wildlife in danger p.398

TEMPERATE FORESTS

CONIFERS AND BROADLEAVED TREES grow in temperate forests. The forests are found in north temperate regions, such as parts of Europe and North America, which have a mild climate. There are distinct seasons, with cold winters and warm summers, but nothing too extreme. Conifer forests tend to grow in the north, and broadleaved forests farther south. Temperate forests provide food and shelter for a large number of plants and animals. More light reaches through the trees than it does in a rainforest because the trees are not as tightly packed. Small plants can survive without having to grow as creepers up trees to get sunlight. In colder areas, it can take years for dead material to be broken down, so the cycles of nutrients are slower.

The beak tips of the common crossbill (Loxia curvirostra) *are crossed, enabling the bird to open pine cones to reach the seeds inside.*

Acid rain badly affects conifers, making the needles drop off.

CONIFEROUS FORESTS

Conifers are more common where it is colder. Trees cannot take up water from the frozen soil in winter. But the needles of conifers lose less water than broad, flat leaves, so they can stay on the trees all year round. The pyramid shape of many conifers allows the snow to slide off their branches so the trees are not crushed by the weight of the snow.

Oak marble galls form when gall wasps (Andricus kollari) *lay their eggs on the buds of the oak tree in spring. Larvae develop into adult wasps inside the galls and eat their way out in autumn.*

OAK TREE ECOSYSTEM

An oak tree is a broadleaved tree. It is an ecosystem on its own. It makes its own food, and its leaves, flowers, fruit, bark, and wood are eaten by insects, birds, and small mammals. These creatures are in turn eaten by bigger animals. All the animals eventually die and rot back into the soil. The nutrients in their bodies are taken up by the tree again and used for growth. The ecosystem changes with the seasons as the tree sprouts leaves in spring and drops them in autumn. In winter the tree rests and the animals hibernate, migrate, or become less active.

Great spotted woodpeckers (Dendrocopus major) *nest in holes in the tree and chisel into decaying trunks to search for insects to eat.*

THREATS TO FORESTS

Many temperate forests have been cut down to make way for farms and houses. Conifers from other countries are often planted in place of broadleaved forests. These conifers grow faster and their straight trunks are easier to saw into planks for timber. But the wildlife is often unable to live on the new trees.

Spruce and larch plantations in Scotland

Grey squirrels (Sciurus carolinensis) *bury acorns to eat in winter. They do not find them all so some acorns sprout into new trees.*

The fruiting bodies of honey fungus (Armillaria mellea) *sprout from tree stumps and dead trees in autumn.*

Woodlice (Porcellio scaber) *live in damp, dark places under leaves, stones, bark, and logs. They feed on decaying leaves, bark, and fungi.*

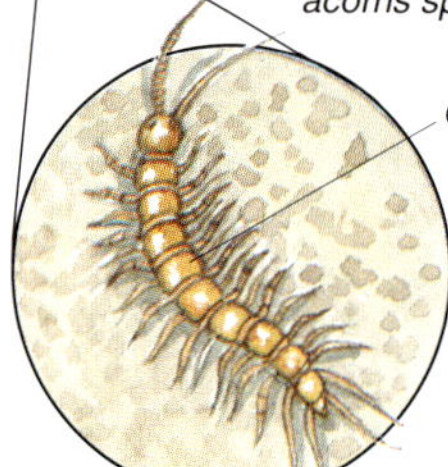

Centipedes (Lithobius forficatus) *live in damp places such as leaf litter. They come out at night to hunt for food such as spiders, worms, and woodlice.*

Find out more

CLIMATES P.244
CONIFERS P.317
FLOWERING PLANTS P.318
TRANSPORT IN PLANTS P.341
CYCLES IN THE BIOSPHERE P.372
MIGRATION AND HIBERNATION P.381

TOWNS AND CITIES

AS THE HUMAN POPULATION GROWS towards 6,000 million, more and more of the Earth's surface is taken over by towns and cities. The original wildlife of the areas now covered by buildings has been driven out, but some animals and plants have managed to take advantage of the new shelters. The edible rubbish we throw away is a major source of food for animals, and city climates can protect animals and plants in cold parts of the world. Temperatures can be several degrees higher than they are in the surrounding countryside, and there is less wind, except round tall buildings.

LIFE IN AN URBAN ECOSYSTEM

A house and garden, such as this one in a British urban ecosystem, provide a variety of living spaces for plants and animals. Birds such as starlings roost and nest in the roof, together with bats and squirrels. Smaller creatures, such as cockroaches, ants, beetles, and moths, feed and shelter behind walls, under floors, and in cupboards. Mice and rats live in drains and sewers.

House martins (Delichon urbica) nest under the eaves of roofs.

The common pipistrelle bat (Pipistrellus pipistrellus) roosts in roofs.

Ivy (Hedera helix) climbs up walls. It clings on to the stone or bricks.

Spiders spin webs to trap insects for food.

Food left out on bird tables helps birds – and squirrels – to survive through the winter.

Part of a garden can be made into a sanctuary for wildlife if left to grow wild. Long grass, weeds, compost heaps, and rotting logs will encourage wildlife to feed and shelter there.

Bees nest in holes in walls or in old flower pots.

Common toads (Bufo bufo) hide under stones during the day and come out at night to eat worms, snails, and woodlice.

RED FOX
The intelligent red fox (*Vulpes vulpes*) has adapted well to living in a city. It has a varied diet and will eat almost anything it can find, often raiding bins for food thrown out by humans.

POSSUMS

The species of animals that live in towns and cities vary in different parts of the world because of the different conditions. The brush-tailed possum (*Trichosurus vulpecula*) has adapted well to urban life in Australia. In the wild it shelters in burrows, caves, or tree hollows, but in towns it has learnt to nest in the roofs of buildings. Colonies of possums live in parks and they sometimes become tame enough to take food from people's hands.

Find out more

CLIMATES P.244
PEOPLE AND PLANET P.374
WASTES AND RECYCLING P.376
PARTNERSHPS P.379
FACT FINDER P.424

WILDLIFE IN DANGER

HUNDREDS OF MILLIONS OF SPECIES of plants and animals have become extinct (died out) since life began on Earth. Some of these have died out due to the natural process of evolution. But, in the last 300 years, people have speeded up the extinction process more than 1,000 times by destroying habitats, polluting the environment, and by hunting and collecting species. It is difficult to work out exactly how quickly species are becoming extinct, but one estimate suggests that about 100 species a day, or one species every quarter of an hour, disappear for ever. There are probably one million species that are in danger of dying out within the next 20 years unless we act now to save unecessary extinction.

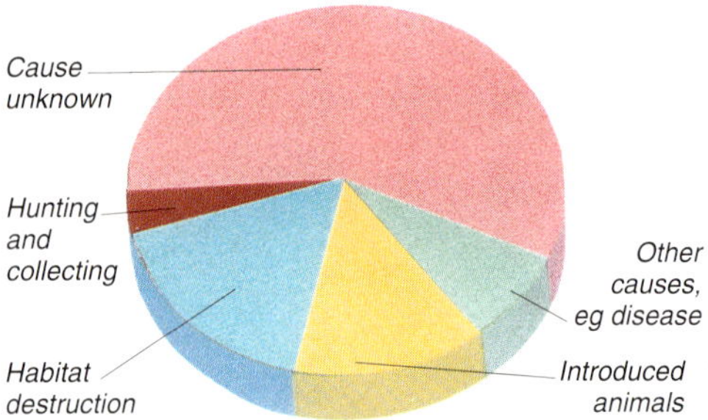

REASONS FOR EXTINCTION
We do not know the exact reason for many animal extinctions. This pie chart shows that habitat destruction and animals introduced from one place to another are two major reasons. Hunting and collecting are also responsible for the disappearance of many animals.

Untouched wetlands, such as swamps and marshes, are a rich habitat for wildlife, especially insects, fish, and birds.

Reasons for wetland destruction include: drainage and filling in for farms, towns, ports, and factories; pollution; mining for peat, fuels, and minerals; cutting trees for timber.

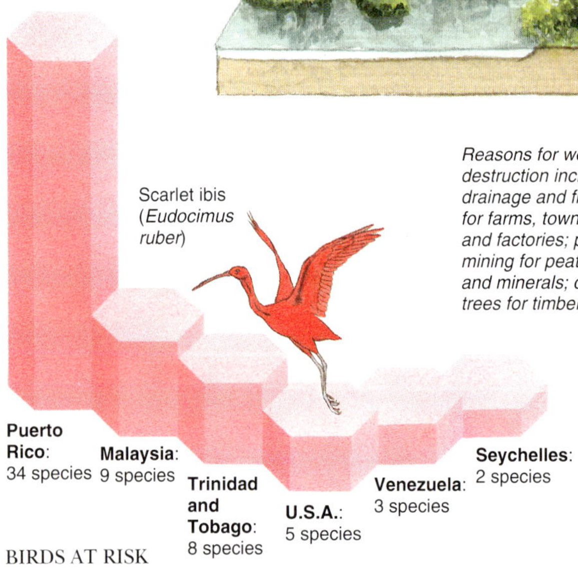

BIRDS AT RISK
Mangrove swamps are a type of wetland on tropical coasts. Birds are especially at risk from the destruction of mangrove swamps. This chart shows the estimated number of bird species in danger of exinction in mangrove swamps around the world today.

DESTRUCTION OF WETLANDS

Wetlands are one of the world's most threatened ecosystems. More than half have already been destroyed. Some have disappeared due to natural causes, such as rises in sea level, drought, and violent storms. But many more have been destroyed by people. If they are drained, floods and insects can be controlled to make it safer for people to live nearby. But then the wildlife has nowhere to go.

PLANTS AT RISK
About a quarter of all the plant species in the world are thought to be threatened. They are in danger from habitat destruction, and many plants are taken from the wild to sell. The endangered silver sword (*Argyroxilphrum kauense*) from Hawaii, shown here, is threatened by introduced goats, which eat it, and plant collectors.

RARE PANDA
The giant panda (*Ailuropoda melanoleuca*) lives in the bamboo forests of southwestern China. But most of the original bamboo has been cut down and replaced with villages and rice fields. It is thought that there are now only 300-400 giant pandas left. They live in small areas of bamboo forest separated by farmland.

Native frogs are not a pest to sugar-cane farmers.

The cane toad eats small frogs.

Mice can be a pest to farmers, but they were not the intended prey for the cane toad.

The cane toad eats mice and other small rodents.

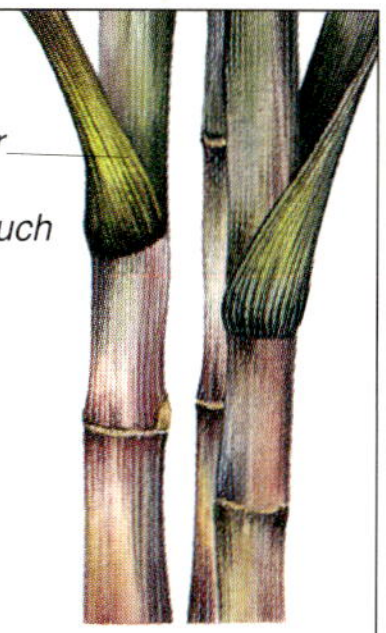

The Australian sugar cane harvest is damaged by pests such as the cane beetle.

The cane beetle (Dermolepida albohirtum) eats the sugar cane.

The cane toad eats the cane beetle and other insects.

Lizards and geckos help the farmers by eating insects.

The cane toad eats geckos and other lizards.

The cane toad (Bufo marinus) was introduced into the food web.

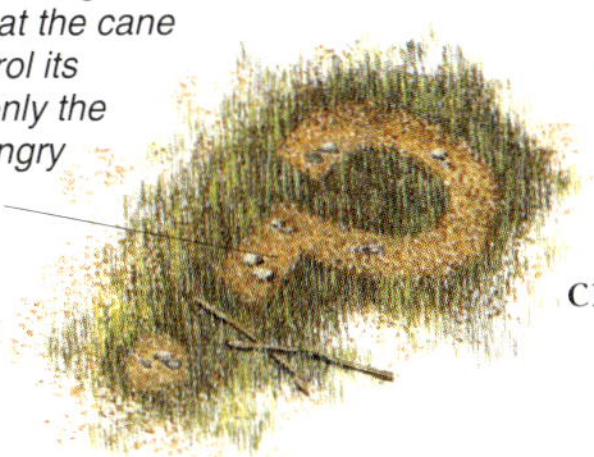

There are not enough predators to eat the cane toad and control its population – only the occasional hungry snake or bird.

Species Introduction

In 1935, a species of toad from Central and South America was introduced into Queensland, Australia. It was thought that the toads would eat beetles that were destroying the sugar cane. But the toads ate many other creatures as well. And because they had no natural predators, the toads multiplied into huge populations which are now destroying the native Australian wildlife.

GEORGE SCHALLER

The research done by American zoologist Dr George Schaller (born 1933) has helped scientists to devise conservation methods. He studied the behaviour of many animals in the wild, including pandas in China, gorillas and lions in Africa, orang-utans in Sarawak, and tigers in India. His many books include *The Deer and the Tiger* and *The Year of the Gorilla*.

MONK SEAL

Monk seals (*Monachus* species) are some of the rarest seals in the world. There are less than 500 Mediterranean monk seals and 1,500 Hawaiian monk seals left, and the Caribbean monk seal is now extinct. Pollution of the sea, fishing, motorboats, and aeroplanes have disturbed the seals and caused them to stop breeding properly.

CATSKIN TRADE
Many animals are still hunted, often illegally, for their fur, horns, or tusks. Some people like to wear the skins of large cats, such as leopards and tigers, as coats. This chart shows the total world export of catskins. The amount decreased considerably during the 1980s, but many cats are still in danger of extinction.

ZOOS
For a long time, animals were taken from the wild to fill zoos. Many of these animals were rare and, by collecting them, zoos were driving them closer to extinction. Today, most zoos breed their animals. Some zoos have bred rare animals, such as the Arabian oryx, golden lion tamarin, and red wolf, and then released them into the wild.

Find out more

CYCLES IN THE BIOSPHERE P.372
PEOPLE AND PLANET P.374
WASTES AND RECYCLING P.376
FOOD CHAINS AND WEBS P.377
WETLANDS P.389
CONSERVATION P.400
FACT FINDER P.424

CONSERVATION

Koala (Phascolarctos cinereus) – *hunting banned and protected in wildlife parks*

Hawaiian goose (Branta sandvicensis) – *bred in captivity and reintroduced into the wild*

Southern sea otter (Enhyaris lutra) – *hunting banned and protected in reserves*

Heath fritillary (Mellicta athalia) – *special needs studied and reintroduced into the wild*

Przewalski's horse (Equus ferus) – *bred in captivity and reintroduced into the wild*

BY BANNING HUNTING, protecting habitats, setting up nature reserves, and reducing pollution, many rare species of animals and plants can be saved. People are starting to realize how important it is to save wildlife from extinction. Organizations, such as the Worldwide Fund for Nature (WWF), and the International Union for the Conservation of Nature and Natural Resources (IUCN), make people aware of problems and raise money to protect species and habitats. The wildlife shown around this page are some of those being saved.

Red wolf (Canis rufus) – *bred in zoos and reintroduced into the wild*

Grey whale (Eschrichtius robustus) – *hunting banned*

EARTH SUMMIT

In 1992, there was a conference on the environment in Rio de Janeiro, Brazil. Representatives from governments of most countries in the world discussed what should be done to save the planet. A special "Tree of Life" was created in Rio to which paper "leaves" were attached. Written on the leaves were things people promised to do and what they thought governments should do.

European bison (Bison bonasus) – *protected in nature reserves in Poland*

WILDLIFE RESERVES

The Yellowstone National Park in the United States was the world's first National Park. Today, there are areas of countryside all over the world that have been set aside as wildlife reserves. The plants and animals are protected, as much as possible, from human hunters, collectors, and developers who may want to build on the land. Some of these reserves cover thousands of square kilometres. Others are just a small wood, or piece of undeveloped land in a city.

Polar bear (Thalarctos maritimus) – *habitat protected and hunting controlled*

Recycling symbol

HOW YOU CAN HELP

Everyone can do something to help conserve wildlife. You can collect paper, tins, and bottles for recycling. This will help reduce the number of trees cut down, and mines dug under rare habitats. You can stop buying things made from rare animals and plants, and try to avoid packaging that cannot be recycled.

Arabian oryx (Oryx leucoryx) – *bred in zoos and reintroduced into the wild*

Pere David's deer (Elaphurus davidiensis) – *reintroduced into the wild in China from reserves in the West*

New Zealand brush lily (Xeronema callistemon) – *protected on island reserves*

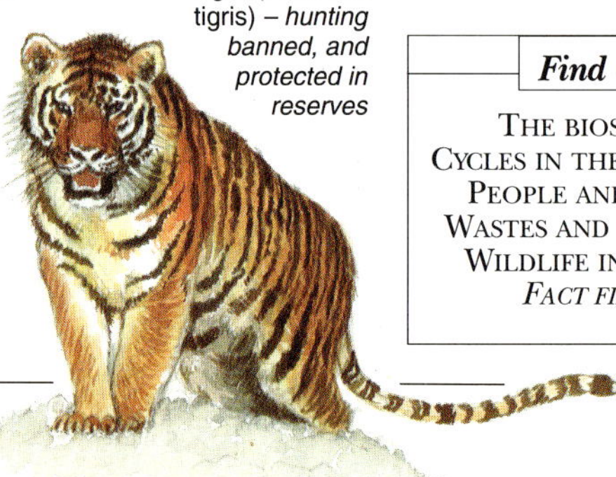

Tiger (Panthera tigris) – *hunting banned, and protected in reserves*

Find out more

THE BIOSPHERE P.370
CYCLES IN THE BIOSPHERE P.372
PEOPLE AND PLANET P.374
WASTES AND RECYCLING P.376
WILDLIFE IN DANGER P.398
FACT FINDER P.424

FACTFINDER SECTION

This section contains charts, tables, and maps full of important scientific information and statistics. The page numbers in this mini - index will help you look up the things you need to know.

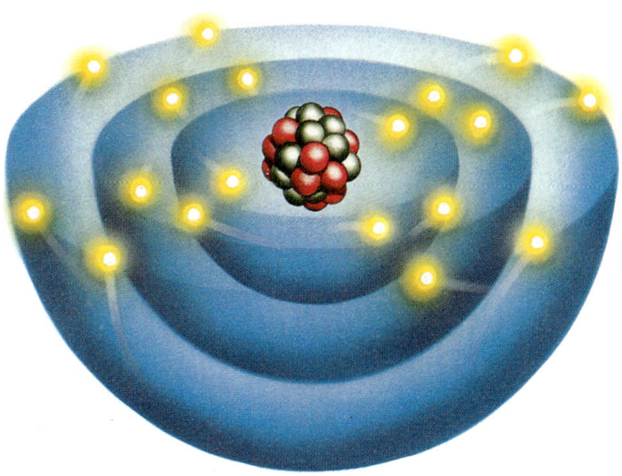

MATTER

PERIODIC CHART

In this chart, the elements are arranged in order of increasing atomic number, as they are in the traditional periodic table. The relative atomic mass shown is for the most common isotope or, for radioactive elements, the most stable isotope. Where no data is shown, the element is so short-lived and has been made in such small amounts that it has not been possible to discover its properties. See pp. 22, 24, 31, 32.

Atomic number	Element	Symbol	Relative atomic mass	Melting point °C	Melting point °F	Boiling point °C	Boiling point °F	Valency	Date of discovery	Physical description
1	Hydrogen	H	1	-259	-498	-253	-487	1	1766	colourless gas
2	Helium	He	4	-272	-522	-269	-516	0	1868/1895	colourless gas
3	Lithium	Li	7	179	354	1317	2403	1	1817	silvery-white metal
4	Beryllium	Be	9	1283	2341	2487	4509	2	1798	grey metal
5	Boron	B	11	2200	3992	2550	4622	3	1808	dark brown powder
6	Carbon	C	12					2,4		
	graphite			3500	9500	3900	10220		ancient	black solid
	diamond			3500	6332	4827	8721		ancient	colourless solid
7	Nitrogen	N	14	-210	-410	-196	-385	3,5	1885	colourless gas
8	Oxygen	O	16	-219	-426	-183	-361	2	1772	colourless gas
9	Fluorine	F	19	-220	-428	-188	-370	1	1886	pale green-yellow gas
10	Neon	Ne	20	-249	-480	-246	-1015	0	1898	colourless gas
11	Sodium	Na	23	98	208	890	1634	1	1807	silvery-white metal
12	Magnesium	Mg	24	650	1202	1105	2021	2	1808	silvery-white metal
13	Aluminium	Al	27	660	1220	2467	4473	3	1825	silvery metal
14	Silicon	Si	28	1420	2588	2355	4271	4	1824	dark grey solid
15	Phosphorus	P	31					3,5	1669	
	white			44	111	280	536			waxy solid
16	Sulphur	S	32					2,4,6	ancient	
	rhombic			119	246	445	833			yellow solid
17	Chlorine	Cl	35	-101	-214	-34	-93	1,3,5,7	1774	yellow-green gas
18	Argon	Ar	40	-189	-372	-186	-367	0	1894	colourless gas
19	Potassium	K	39	64	147	754	1389	1	1807	silvery-white metal
20	Calcium	Ca	40	848	1558	1487	2709	2	1808	silvery-white metal
21	Scandium	Sc	45	1541	2806	2831	5128	3	1879	metallic
22	Titanium	Ti	48	1677	3051	3277	5931	3,4	1795	silvery metal
23	Vanadium	V	51	1917	3483	3377	6111	2,3,4,5	1801	silvery-grey metal
24	Chromium	Cr	52	1903	3457	2642	4788	2,3,6	1797	silvery metal
25	Manganese	Mn	55	1244	2271	2041	3706	2,3,4,6,7	1774	red-white metal
26	Iron	Fe	56	1539	2802	2887	5229	2,3	ancient	silvery-white metal
27	Cobalt	Co	59	1495	2723	2877	5211	2,3	1735	red-white metal
28	Nickel	Ni	58	1455	2651	2837	5139	2,3	1751	silvery-white metal
29	Copper	Cu	63	1083	1981	2582	4680	1,2	ancient	pink metal
30	Zinc	Zn	64	420	788	907	1665	2	1746	blue-white metal
31	Gallium	Ga	69	30	86	2403	4357	2,3	1875	grey metal
32	Germanium	Ge	74	937	1719	2355	4271	4	1886	grey-white metal
33	Arsenic	As	75	817	1503	613	1135	3,5	1250	steel-grey solid
34	Selenium	Se	80	217	423	685	1265	2,4,6	1817	grey solid
35	Bromine	Br	79	-7	-45	59	138	1,3,5,7	1826	red-brown liquid
36	Krypton	Kr	84	-157	-315	-152	-306	0	1898	colourless gas
37	Rubidium	Rb	85	39	102	688	1270	1	1861	silvery-white metal
38	Strontium	Sr	88	769	1416	1384	2523	2	1808	silvery-white metal
39	Yttrium	Y	89	1522	2772	3338	6040	3	1794	steel-grey metal
40	Zirconium	Zr	90	1852	3366	4377	7911	4	1789	steel-white metal
41	Niobium	Nb	93	2467	4473	4742	8568	3,5	1801	grey metal
42	Molybdenum	Mo	98	2610	4730	5560	10040	2,3,4,5,6	1778	silvery metal
43	Technetium	Tc	97	2172	3942	4877	8811	2,3,4,6,7	1937	silvery-grey metal
44	Ruthenium	Ru	102	2310	4190	3900	7052	3,4,6,8	1844	blue-white metal
45	Rhodium	Rh	103	1966	3571	3727	6741	3,4	1803	steel-blue metal
46	Palladium	Pd	106	1554	2829	2970	5378	2,4	1803	silvery-white metal
47	Silver	Ag	107	962	1764	2212	4014	1	ancient	shiny white metal
48	Cadmium	Cd	114	321	610	767	1413	2	1817	blue-white metal
49	Indium	In	115	156	313	2000	3632	1,3	1863	blue-silvery metal
50	Tin	Sn	120	232	450	2270	4118	2,4	ancient	silvery-white metal
51	Antimony	Sb	121	631	1168	1380	2516	3,5	ancient	silvery metal
52	Tellurium	Te	130	450	842	990	1814	2,4,6	1782	silver-grey solid
53	Iodine	I	127	114	237	184	363	1,3,5,7	1811	purple-black solid
54	Xenon	Xe	132	-112	-234	-107	-225	0	1898	colourless gas

Atomic number	Element	Symbol	Relative atomic mass	Melting point °C	Melting point °F	Boiling point °C	Boiling point °F	Valency	Date of discovery	Physical description
55	Caesium	Cs	133	29	84	671	1240	1	1860	silvery-white metal
56	Barium	Ba	138	725	1337	1640	2984	2	1808	silvery-white metal
57	Lanthanum	La	139	921	1690	3457	6255	3	1839	metallic
58	Cerium	Ce	140	799	1470	3426	6199	3,4	1803	dark grey solid
59	Praseodymium	Pr	141	931	1708	3512	6354	3	1885	steel-grey metal
60	Neodymium	Nd	142	1021	1870	3068	5554	3	1885	yellow-white metal
61	Promethium	Pm	145	1168	2134	2700	4892	3	1947	metallic
62	Samarium	Sm	152	1077	1971	1791	3256	2,3	1879	light grey metal
63	Europium	Eu	153	822	1512	1597	2907	2,3	1896	steel-grey metal
64	Gadolinium	Gd	158	1313	2395	3266	5911	3	1880	silvery-white metal
65	Terbium	Tb	159	1356	2473	3123	5653	3	1843	silvery metal
66	Dysprosium	Dy	164	1412	2574	2562	4644	3	1886	metallic
67	Holmium	Ho	165	1474	2685	2695	4883	3	1878-9	silvery metal
68	Erbium	Er	168	1529	2784	2863	5185	3	1843	grey-silver metal
69	Thulium	Tm	169	1545	2813	1947	3537	2,3	1879	metallic
70	Ytterbium	Yb	174	819	1506	1194	2181	2,3	1878	silvery metal
71	Lutetium	Lu	175	1663	3025	3395	6143	3	1907	metallic
72	Hafnium	Hf	180	2227	4041	4602	8316	4	1923	steel-grey metal
73	Tantalum	Ta	181	2996	5425	5427	9801	3,5	1802	silvery metal
74	Tungsten	W	184	3410	6170	5660	10220	2,4,5,6	1783	grey metal
75	Rhenium	Re	187	3180	5756	5627	10161	1,4,7	1925	white-grey metal
76	Osmium	Os	192	2700	4892	5297	9567	2,3,4,6,8	1804	grey-blue metal
77	Iridium	Ir	193	2410	4370	4130	7466	3,4	1804	silvery-white metal
78	Platinum	Pt	195	1772	3222	3827	6921	2,4	1735	blue-white metal
79	Gold	Au	197	1064	1947	3080	5576	1,3	ancient	shiny yellow metal
80	Mercury	Hg	202	-39	-102	357	675	1,2	ancient	silvery metallic liquid
81	Thallium	Tl	205	303	577	1457	2655	1,3	1861	blue-grey metal
82	Lead	Pb	208	328	622	1744	3171	2,4	ancient	steel-blue metal
83	Bismuth	Bi	209	271	520	1560	2840	3,5	1450	red-silvery metal
84	Polonium	Po	209	254	489	962	1764	2,3,4	1898	metallic
85	Astatine	At	210	300	572	370	698	1,3,5,7	1940	metallic
86	Radon	Rn	222	-71	-160	-62	-144	0	1900	colourless gas
87	Francium	Fr	223	27	81	677	1251	1	1939	metallic
88	Radium	Ra	226	700	1292	1737	3159	2	1898	silvery metal
89	Actinium	Ac	227	1050	1922	3200	5792	3	1899	metallic
90	Thorium	Th	232	1750	3182	4787	8649	4	1828	grey metal
91	Protactinium	Pa	231	1597	2907	4027	7281	4,5	1917	silvery metal
92	Uranium	U	238	1132	2070	3818	6904	3,4,5,6	1789	blue-white metal
93	Neptunium	Np	237	637	1179	4090	7394	2,3,4,5,6	1940	silvery metal
94	Plutonium	Pu	244	640	1184	3330	6026	2,3,4,5,6	1940	silvery metal
95	Americium	Am	243	994	1821	2607	4724	2,3,4,5,6	1944	silvery-white metal
96	Curium	Cm	247	1340	2444	3190	5774	2,3,4	1944	silvery metal
97	Berkelium	Bk	247	1050	1922	710	1310	2,3,4	1949	silvery metal
98	Californium	Cf	251	900	1652	1470	2678	2,3,4	1950	silvery metal
99	Einsteinium	Es	254	860	1580	996	1825	2,3	1952	silvery metal
100	Fermium	Fm	257					2,3	1952	metallic
101	Mendelevium	Md	258					2,3	1955	metallic
102	Nobelium	No	255					2,3	1958	metallic
103	Lawrencium	Lr	256					3	1961	metallic
104	Unnilquadium	Unq	260						1964,1969	
105	Unnilpentium	Unp	262						1970	
106	Unnilhexium	Unh	263						1974	
107	Unnilseptium	Uns	262						1976	
108	Unniloctium	Uno	265						1984	
109	Unnilennium	Une	266						1982	

DECAY OF MATTER

Radioactive elements decay at different rates. A half-life is the time it takes for half of the original amount of radioactive element to decay. Different elements emit different types of radiation when they decay – alpha particles (α), beta particles (β), and gamma rays (γ).

Uranium-238 (α) 4,500 million years	Plutonium-239 (α) 24,400 years	Carbon-14 (β) 5,700 years	Radium-226 (α) 1,600 years	Strontium-90 (β) 28 years	Hydrogen-3 (β) 12.3 years
Cobalt-60 (γ) 5.3 years	Phosphorus-32 (β) 14.3 days	Iodine-131 (β) 8.1 days	Radon-222 (α) 4 days	Lead-214 (β) 27 minutes	Unnilpentium-105 (α) 32 seconds

REACTIONS

GAS LAWS

The gas laws predict how a gas will behave if you change its conditions – that is, its temperature (T), its pressure (P), or its volume (V). In the equations below, the symbol K represents a constant number.

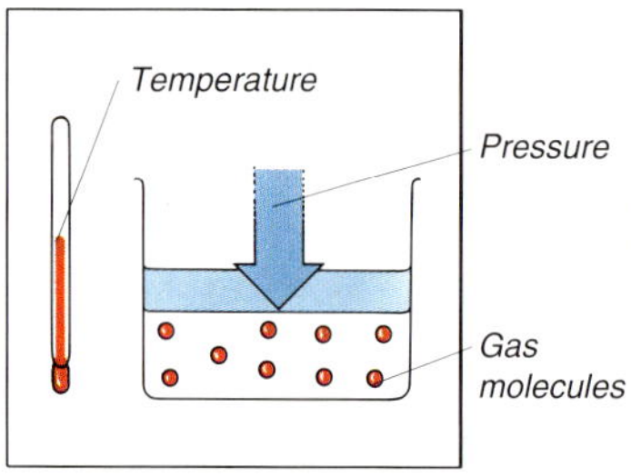

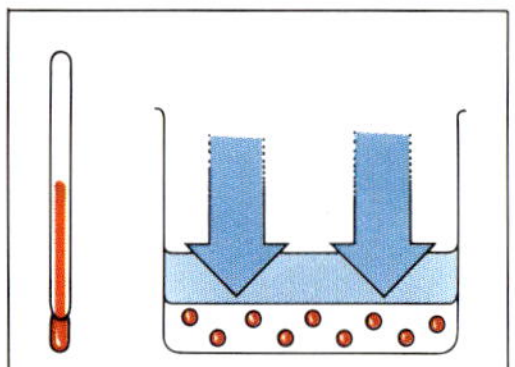

Boyle's Law
If the temperature is constant, the pressure of a gas is inversely proportional to the volume (the gas will contract if the pressure is raised): PV=K

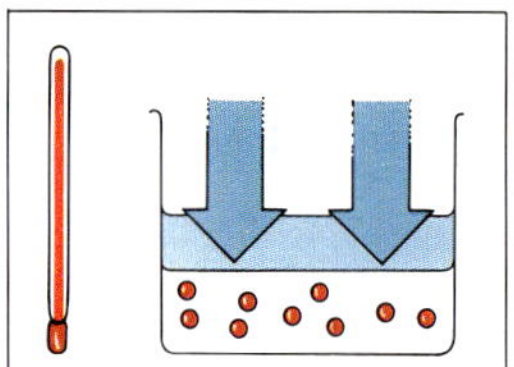

Pressure Law
If the volume is constant, the pressure of a gas is directly proportional to the temperature (the pressure increases if the temperature rises): P/T=K

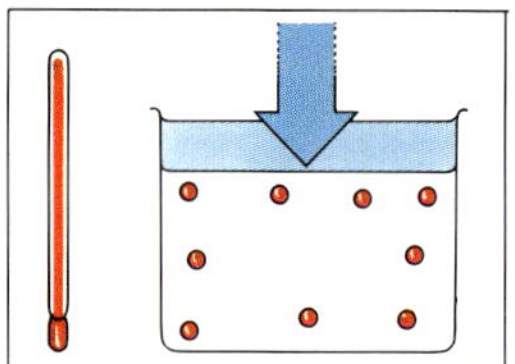

Charles' Law
If the pressure is constant, the volume of a gas is directly proportional to the temperature (the gas will expand if the temperature is raised): V/T=K

Ideal Gas Law
The ideal gas law combines Boyle's Law, Charles' Law, and the Pressure Law into one equation. All the gas laws will work best for gases that have small, widely spaced molecules – gases that are said to behave like an ideal gas. (R is the gas constant. It is the same for all gases.)

PV=RT

Graham's Law of Diffusion
If the temperature and pressure are constant, the rate of diffusion of a gas depends on its density. A high density gives a low rate of diffusion. So gases with light molecules will diffuse faster than gases with heavy molecules.

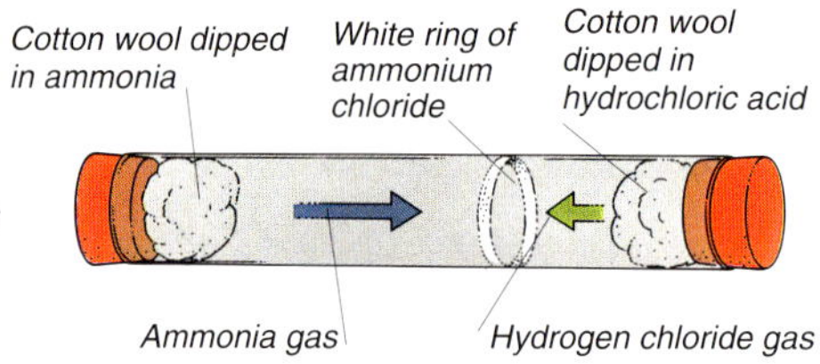

A white ring of ammonium chloride forms where the gases meet. Ammonia molecules are lighter than hydrogen chloride molecules, and so they diffuse faster. This means the white ring forms nearer to the right-hand end of the tube.

Avogadro's Law
At the same temperature and pressure, equal volumes of all gases contain the same number of molecules.

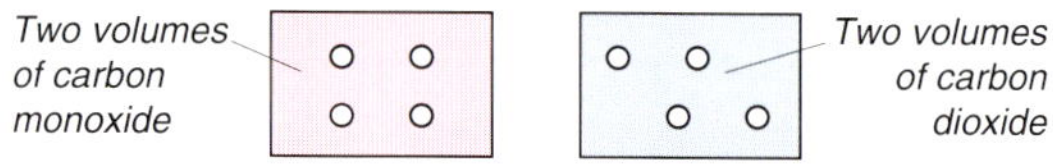

Two volumes of carbon monoxide gas would contain exactly the same number of molecules as two volumes of carbon dioxide gas (even though carbon dioxide molecules are much heavier).

Gay-Lussac's Law
If the temperature and pressure are constant, when gases react to produce other gases, the volumes of the reactants and the products are in a ratio of simple whole numbers.

$$2CO_{(g)} \;(400\ cm^3) + O_{2(g)} \;(200cm^3) \rightarrow 2CO_{2(g)} \;(400cm^3)$$

Two volumes of carbon monoxide gas will always react with one volume of oxygen gas to produce two volumes of carbon dioxide gas.

COLLECTING A GAS

If a gas is a product of a reaction, it is not easy to collect it. The set-up of apparatus below shows how it can be done.

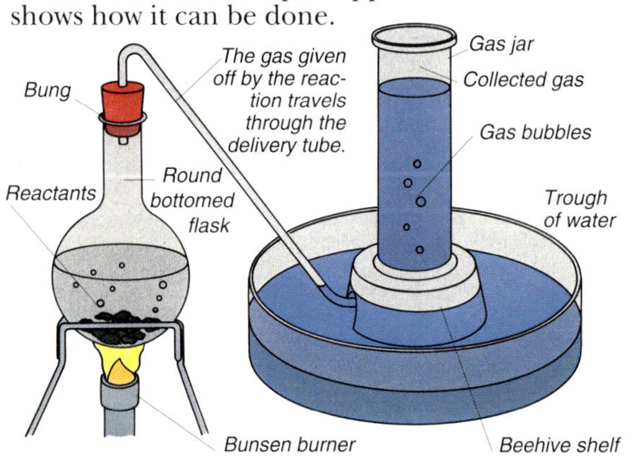

To make carbon dioxide gas, for example, the reacting chemicals would be marble chips (calcium carbonate) and dilute hydrochloric acid.

IDENTIFYING A GAS

Carbon dioxide
If you bubble a gas through limewater (calcium hydroxide solution), and the limewater turns cloudy, it proves the gas is carbon dioxide.

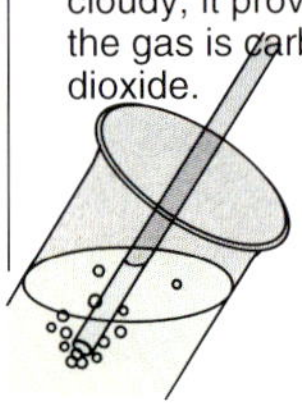

Hydrogen
If you put a lighted splint into a small sample of a gas, and the gas ignites with a "pop", it proves the gas is hydrogen.

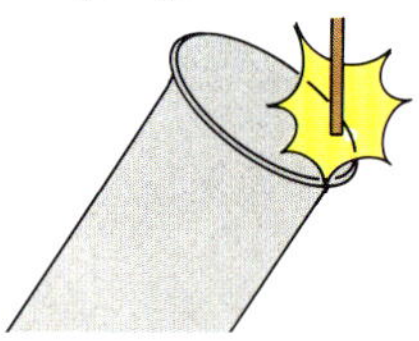

Oxygen
If you put a glowing splint into a small sample of a gas and the splint relights, it proves the gas is oxygen.

ENDINGS AND PREFIXES

A chemical name can tell us about the elements the chemical contains. One way of obtaining this information is by looking at the endings and the prefixes in a name.

Compound ending in	Description	Example
-ide	Contains just the two elements in the name.	Iron sulphide FeS
-ite	Contains oxygen as well as the other elements in the name.	Iron sulphite $FeSO_3$
-ate	Contains oxygen as well as the other elements in the name. Contains more oxygen than is found in -ites.	Iron sulphate $FeSO_4$

Prefix	Number of atoms in prefix	Example
Mono-	1	Carbon monoxide CO
Di-	2	Dinitrogen oxide (Nitrous oxide) N_2O Nitrogen dioxide NO_2
Tri-	3	Boron trichloride BCl_3

REACTIVITY SERIES

This is a series that compares the reactivity of different metals. Those at the top are the most reactive; those at the bottom are the least reactive.

Increasing reactivity ↑ | Increasing power of displacement ↑

Metal		Reaction when heated in air	Reaction with water	Reaction with dilute acid
Potassium	K	Burn vigorously to form oxides.	React with cold water to form hydrogen gas and alkaline hydroxide solution. React with decreasing vigour down the series.	Violent reaction to give hydrogen gas and salt solution.
Sodium	Na			
Calcium	Ca	Burn with decreasing vigour down the series.		React to form hydrogen gas and salt solution with decreasing vigour down the series.
Magnesium	Mg			
Aluminium	Al		Do not react with cold water. React with steam to form hydrogen gas and oxide, with decreasing vigour down the series.	
Zinc	Zn			
Iron	Fe			
Lead	Pb	React slowly to form oxide layer on surface.	No reaction.	
Copper	Cu			No reaction.
Silver	Ag			
Gold	Au			

APPARATUS

Here are some of the most common pieces of chemical equipment used in a laboratory.

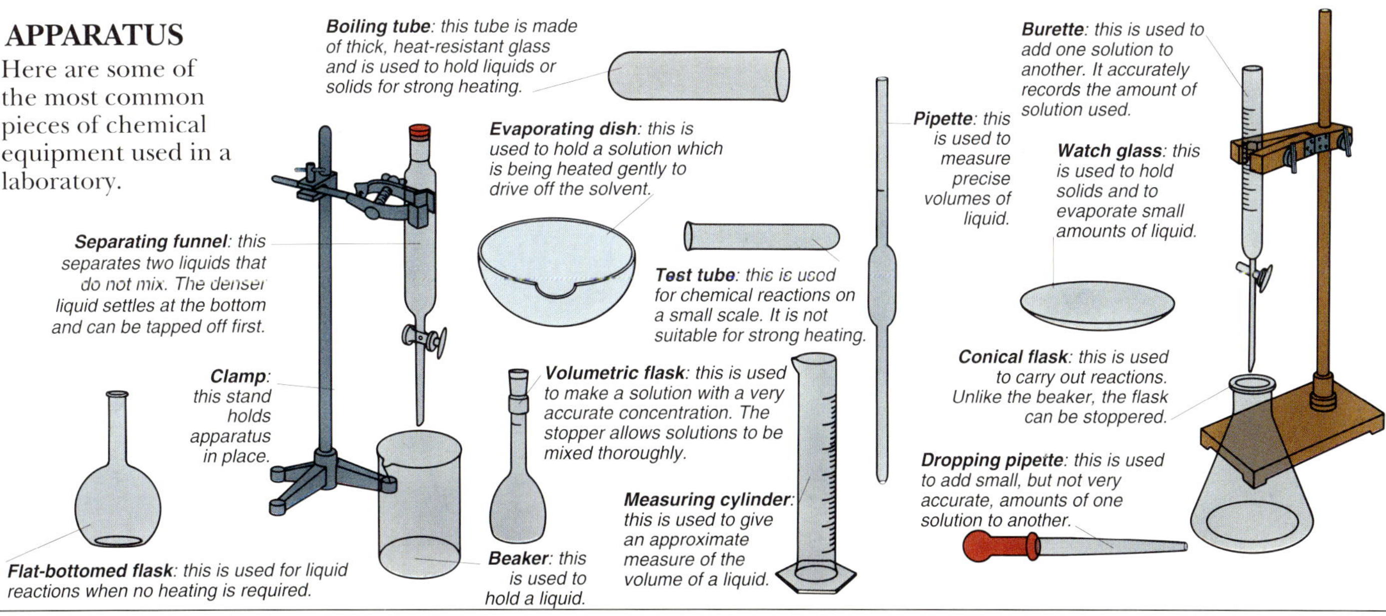

MATERIALS

ALKANES AND ALKENES

Alkanes and alkenes are chemical compounds of hydrogen and carbon. Although their hydrogen and carbon atoms are arranged in a similar way, alkanes have only a single bond between the carbon atoms, whereas alkenes have a double bond. This difference means that alkenes react with more substances than alkanes do (see Uses of Ethene, right). Alkanes are used mainly as fuels. The properties of alkanes and alkenes change according to the number of carbon atoms they contain.

ALKANES

Carbon atoms in chain	Name	Physical state at 22°C (77°F)	Molecular formula
1	methane	gas	CH_4
2	ethane	gas	C_2H_6
3	propane	gas	C_3H_8
4	butane	gas	C_4H_{10}
5	pentane	liquid	C_5H_{12}
6	hexane	liquid	C_6H_{14}
7	heptane	liquid	C_7H_{16}
8	octane	liquid	C_8H_{18}
9	nonane	liquid	C_9H_{20}
10	decane	liquid	$C_{10}H_{22}$

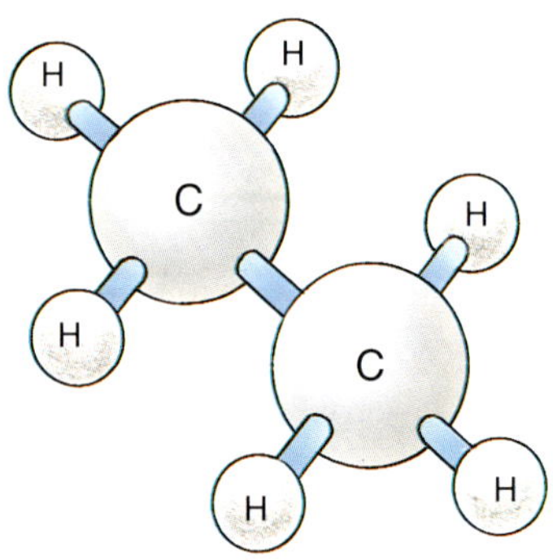

Ethane is an example of an alkane containing a single bond between its carbon atoms.

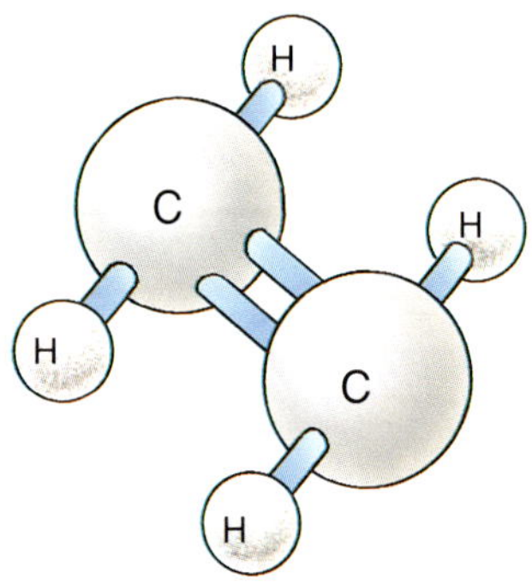

Ethene is a typical alkene containing a double bond between its carbon atoms.

ALKENES

Carbon atoms in chain	Name	Physical state at 22°C (77°F)	Molecular formula
2	ethene	gas	C_2H_4
3	propene	gas	C_3H_6
4	butene	gas	C_4H_8
5	pentene	liquid	C_5H_{10}
6	hexene	liquid	C_6H_{12}
7	heptene	liquid	C_7H_{14}
8	octene	liquid	C_8H_{16}
9	nonene	liquid	C_9H_{18}
10	decene	liquid	$C_{10}H_{20}$

USES OF ETHENE

The chemical ethene is obtained during the refining of petroleum, or crude oil, by a process known as cracking. This process is carried out in huge chemical plants, where heat is used to break, or crack, a mixture of hydrocarbons known as naphtha. By-products are then used for fuel, or as important raw materials for use in other chemical processes. Ethene is used on its own to ripen fruit artificially, but when reacted with the chemicals below, it forms new materials which have hundreds of uses in the manufacturing industry.

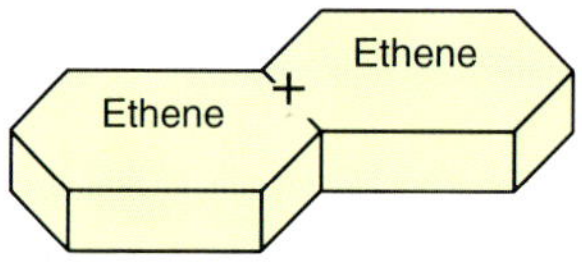

Polyethene
Packaging (cling film, carrier bags, bottles); moulded articles (buckets, beakers, kitchenware); other (pipes, insulating cables, clothing, photographic film)

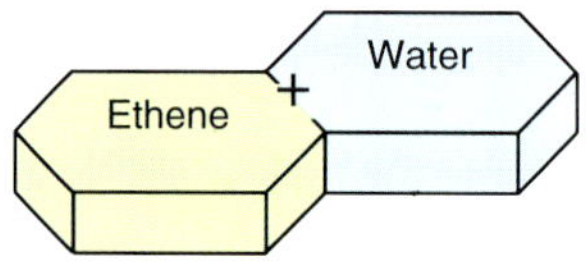

Ethanol
Solvent for after-shave lotions, perfumes, and cosmetics; methylated spirits; solvent for paints, resins, soaps, and dyes; other (plastics, drugs – such as anaesthetics, textiles)

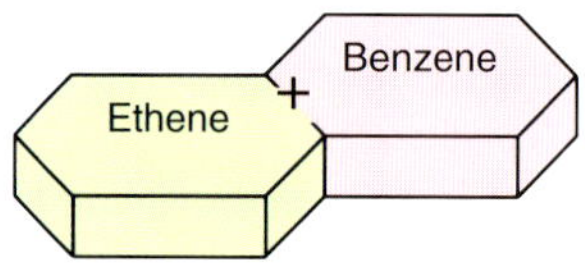

Polystyrene
Ceiling tiles, cavity wall insulation, cups, bowls, packaging (yogurt pots); nylon (clothes, carpets, tennis racket strings, fishing nets); other (car tyres, latex paints, computer disks, toys)

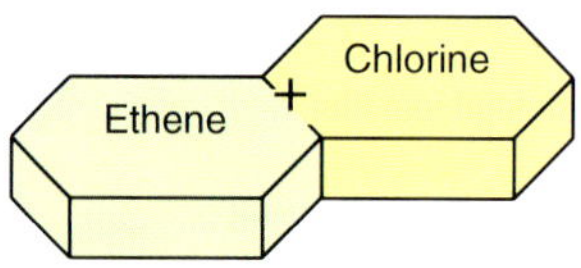

PVC
Insulating material and protective covering (gas and water pipes, hosepipes, insulating cables, roof fittings, window frames, floor tiles); wallpaper, curtains, furniture upholstery, car interior trim, rainwear, protective clothing, shoes, handbags; chemicals (fumigant, degreaser), refrigerant; other (toys, records, recording tape)

SODIUM CARBONATE

This important industrial chemical, also known as soda ash ($Na_2 CO_3$), is made from limestone and salt. Its major use is in the production of glass. To make glass, soda ash is heated together with limestone and sand. Glass is not expensive to produce because there is an abundance of these raw materials.

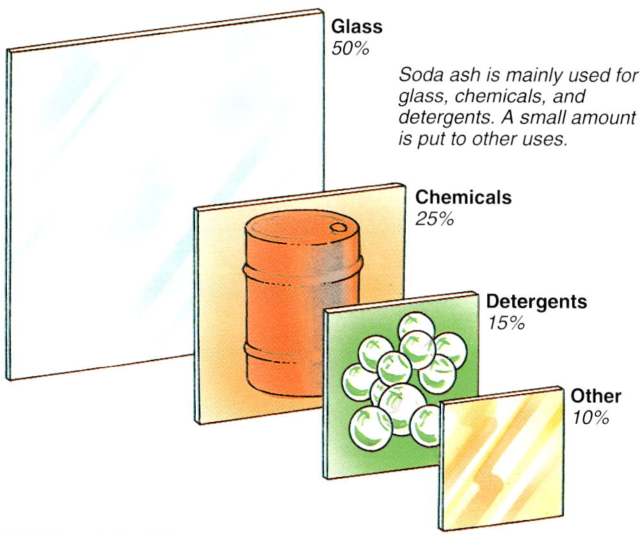

Soda ash is mainly used for glass, chemicals, and detergents. A small amount is put to other uses.

WORLD DISTRIBUTION OF RAW MATERIALS

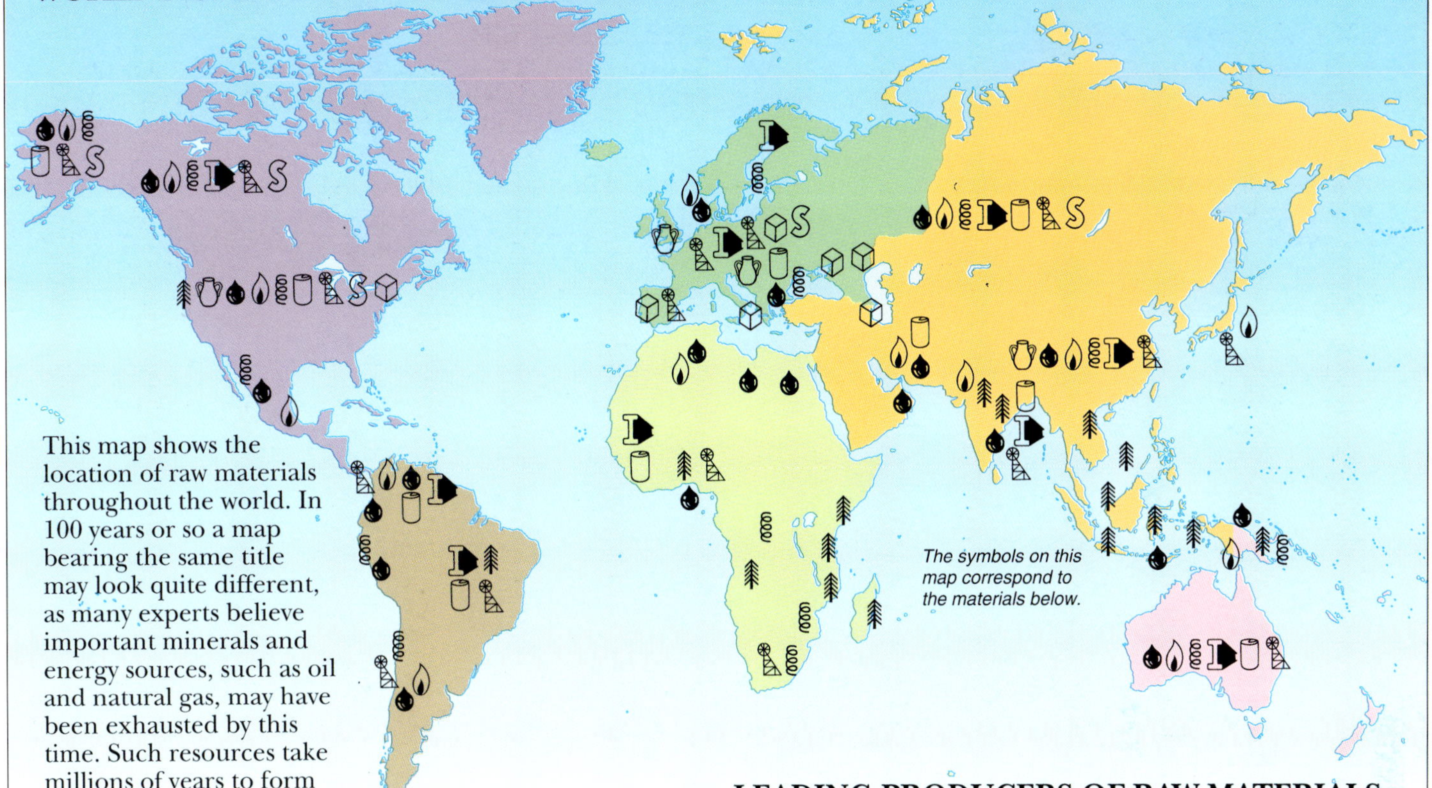

This map shows the location of raw materials throughout the world. In 100 years or so a map bearing the same title may look quite different, as many experts believe important minerals and energy sources, such as oil and natural gas, may have been exhausted by this time. Such resources take millions of years to form and once they are used up they cannot be renewed.

USES OF RAW MATERIALS

Raw Materials	Uses
Bauxite (aluminium oxide)	Aluminium is extracted from bauxite and used for aircraft, foil wrapping, cars, paints, and kitchen utensils.
Coal	Coal is mainly made of carbon and is used as fuel. This fuel is used to heat homes, and to generate electricity.
Copper	Copper is used to conduct electricity in wires and cables, and to make a range of alloys such as brass.
Natural gas	This is used to make ammonia. It is also used in the home as a fuel for heating and cooking.
Iron ore	Engine parts for cars are made out of iron, and so are magnets. Iron is also used to make steel. Steel is stronger than iron and is one of the main materials for building bridges.
Kaolin (clay)	This is used in the manufacture of bricks to build houses, ceramics to make pottery, and cement.
Oil	Oil is used to make plastics, and as a fuel for for aeroplanes and cars.
Salt	This is used as a food flavouring, and to make sodium hydroxide (caustic soda) and sodium carbonate.
Sulphur	This is used to make sulphuric acid, which is used to make paints, detergents, plastics, and fibres.
Wood	Wood is used to make buildings, beams, doors, and furniture. It is also the raw material for making paper.

LEADING PRODUCERS OF RAW MATERIALS

Material	Top producers	World total
Bauxite (aluminium oxide)	Australia 37.4 million Guinea 16.5 million	1,064 million
Coal	China 1,054 million U.S.A. 889 million	5,882 million
Copper	Chile 1.6 million U.S.A. 1.5 million	9.2 million
Natural Gas	C.I.S. 796,000 million m^3 U.S.A. 488,749 million m^3	2,100,000 million m^3
Iron ore	C.I.S. 241 million China 165 million	984 million
Kaolin (clay)	C.I.S. 2 million Republic of Korea 1.3 million	23.1 million
Oil	C.I.S. 607 million U.S.A. 373 million Saudi Arabia 257 million	2,987 million
Salt	U.S.A. 35.5 million China 28.3 million	189 million
Sulphur	U.S.A. 11.6 million China 7.4 million	60.3 million
Wood	U.S.A. 1,109 million m^3 C.I.S. 862 million m^3	7,147 million m^3

All figures in tonnes
Except m^3 = cubic metres

FORCES AND ENERGY

EQUATIONS

The following equations are commonly used in physics. Some of the units used to calculate these equations can be found in the metric and imperial measurement table opposite.

Average speed (m/s)	$\frac{\text{distance moved (m)}}{\text{time taken (s)}}$
Force (kgm/s^2 or N)	mass (kg) x acceleration (m/s^2)
Acceleration (m/s^2)	$\frac{\text{change in velocity (m/s)}}{\text{time taken for this change (s)}}$
Momentum (kgm/s)	mass (kg) x velocity (m/s)
Impulse (Ns)	force(N) x time (s)
Work done (Nm or J)	force (N) x distance moved in the direction of the force (m)
Average power (J/s or W)	$\frac{\text{work done (Nm)}}{\text{time taken (s)}}$ or $\frac{\text{energy change (J)}}{\text{time taken (s)}}$
Efficiency (%)	$\frac{\text{work output (Nm) x 100\%}}{\text{work input (Nm)}}$
Pressure (N/m^2)	$\frac{\text{force (N)}}{\text{area (m}^2\text{)}}$
Density (kg/m^3)	$\frac{\text{mass (kg)}}{\text{volume (m}^3\text{)}}$

Key:
J - joule kg - kilogram m - metre N - newton s - second W - watt

TEMPERATURE SCALES

Temperature is measured using a thermometer. This measures how hot or cold an object or person is. The higher the reading on the scale, the hotter the object. Some objects measure below zero degrees Celsius, the freezing point of water, below which the Celsius reading becomes a minus figure.

Centre of Sun 14 million°C (25 million°F)

Water boils 100°C (212°F)

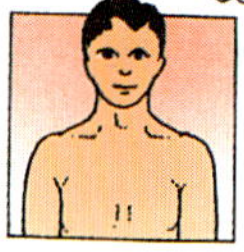

Maximum temperature a naked body can stand 74°C (165°F)

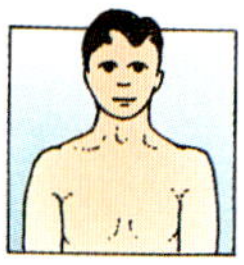

Normal body temperature 37°C (98.6°F)

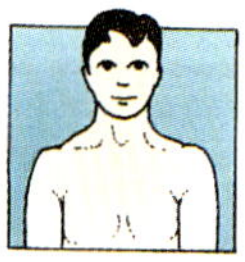

Minimum temperature a naked body can stand 10°C (50°F)

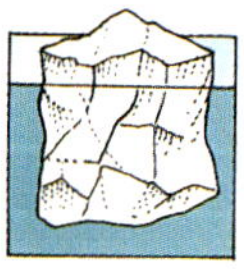

Water freezes 0°C (32°F)

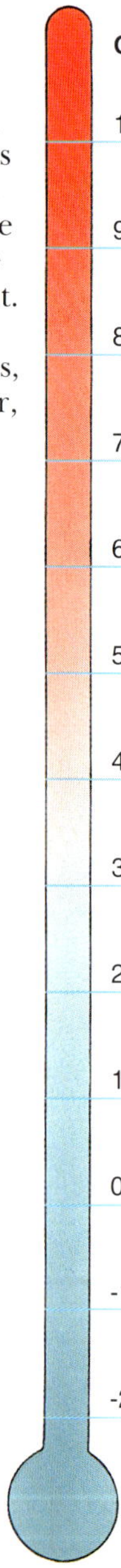

Celsius	Fahrenheit	Kelvin
100	212	373
90	194	363
80	176	353
70	158	343
60	140	333
50	122	323
40	104	313
30	86	303
20	68	293
10	50	283
0	32	273
-10	14	263
-20	-4	253

AVERAGE DAILY USE OF ENERGY BY A PERSON

This chart shows how the energy used by a person each day can vary considerably from one country to the next. The values include all sources of energy e.g. food, electricity, gas and petrol.

PLIMSOLL LINE

Ships float because their average density is less than that of water. They have a mark painted on the hull called a Plimsoll line. It shows the maximum load a ship can carry. If the line lies below the surface of the water, it means the load is too heavy.

The letters on the Plimsoll line indicate the safe load levels a ship can carry in different climates.

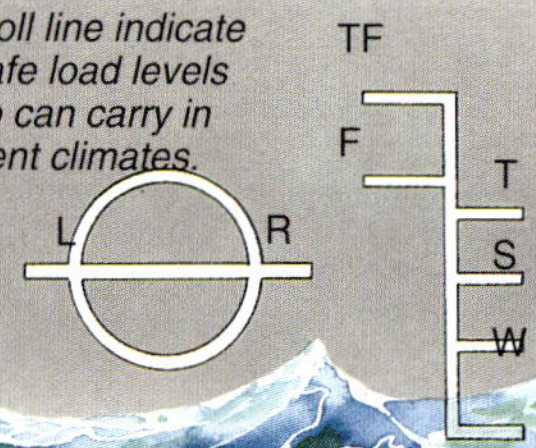

METRIC AND IMPERIAL MEASUREMENT

UNITS OF MEASUREMENT

Metric unit	Equivalent
Length	
1 centimetre (cm)	10 millimetres (mm)
1 metre (m)	100 centimetres
1 kilometre (km)	1,000 metres
Area	
1 square centimetre (cm^2)	100 square millimetres (mm^2)
1 square metre (m^2)	10,000 square centimetres
1 hectare (ha)	1,000 square metres
1 square kilometre (km^2)	1 million square metres
Volume	
1 cubic centimetre (cc or cm^3)	1 millilitre (ml)
1 litre (l)	1,000 millilitres
1 cubic metre (m^3)	1,000 litres
Mass	
1 kilogram (kg)	1,000 grams (g)
1 tonne (t)	1,000 kilograms

Imperial unit	Equivalent
Length	
1 foot (ft)	12 inches (in)
1 yard (yd)	3 feet
1 mile	1,760 yards
Area	
1 square foot (ft^2)	144 square inches (in^2)
1 square yard (yd^2)	9 square feet
1 acre	4,840 square yards
1 square mile	640 acres
Volume	
1 pint	34.68 cubic inches (in^3)
1 quart	2 pints
1 gallon	4 quarts
Mass	
1 pound (lb)	16 ounces (oz)
1 ton	2,240 pounds

METRIC UNITS INTO IMPERIAL UNITS

To convert	Into	Multiply by
Length		
centimetres	inches	0.39
metres	feet	3.28
kilometres	miles	0.62
Area		
square cm	square inches	0.16
square metres	square feet	10.76
hectares	acres	2.47
square km	square miles	0.39
Volume		
cubic cm	cubic inches	0.061
litres	pints (imperial)	1.76
litres	gallons (imperial)	0.22
Mass		
grams	ounces	0.04
kilograms	pounds	2.20
tonnes	tons (imperial)	0.98

IMPERIAL UNITS INTO METRIC UNITS

To convert	Into	Multiply by
Length		
inches	centimetres	2.54
feet	metres	0.30
miles	kilometres	1.61
Area		
square inches	square cm	6.45
square feet	square metres	0.09
acres	hectares	0.40
square miles	square km	2.59
Volume		
cubic inches	cubic cm	16.39
pints (imperial)	litres	0.57
gallons (imperial)	litres	4.55
Mass		
ounces	grams	28.35
pounds	kilograms	0.45
tons (imperial)	tonnes	1.02

CHANGING ENERGY SUPPLIES

The following diagram shows how the world's energy supply has changed since 1850. Using the key below, it becomes clear that the increasing sources of energy are oil, gas, and nuclear energy.

Power source

- Muscles
- Wood
- Coal
- Oil
- Gas
- Nuclear

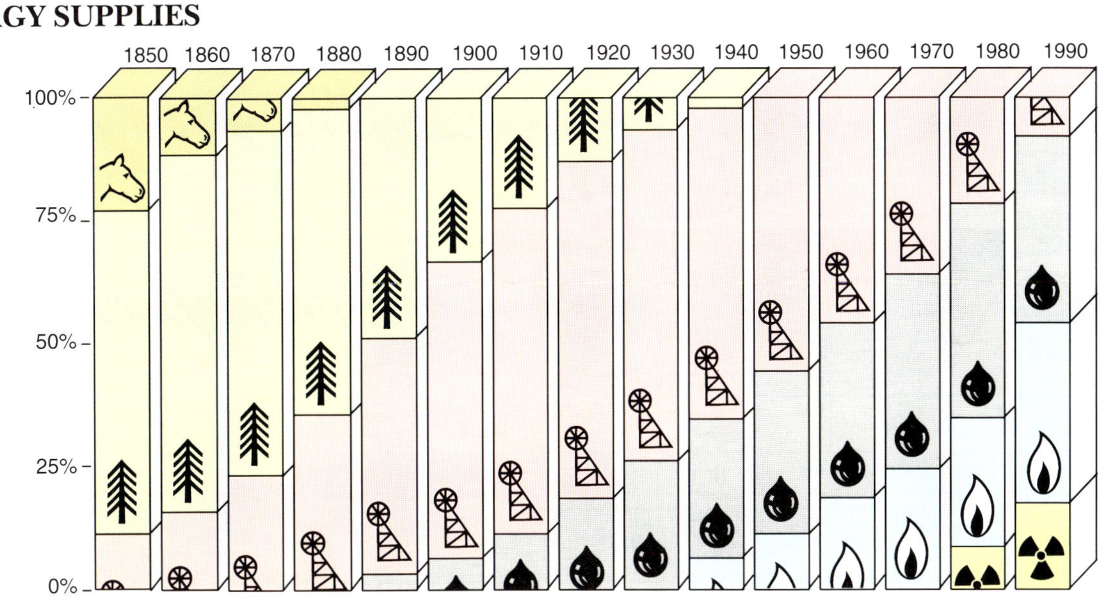

EARTH

GEOLOGICAL TIMESCALE

The history of Earth is outlined in the geological timescale, and calculated by studying the ages of the various layers of sedimentary rock.

Era	Period	Epoch	Time began
Cenozoic	Quarternary	Holocene	0.01
		Pleistocene	1.6
	Tertiary	Pliocene	5.3
		Miocene	23
		Oligocene	34
		Eocene	53
		Palaeocene	65
Mesozoic	Cretaceous		135
	Jurassic		205
	Triassic		250
Palaeozoic	Permian		300
	Carboniferous (divided into Lower Mississippian and Upper Pennsylvanian in United States)		355
	Devonian		410
	Silurian		435
	Ordovician		510
	Cambrian		570
Precambrian			4600

Time began: millions of years ago

LATITUDE AND LONGITUDE

At 0° latitude lies the line of the Equator, 0° longitude runs through Greenwich, London, England. The positions of places are calculated by the degrees of latitude and longitude. Each degree is divided into 60 minutes.

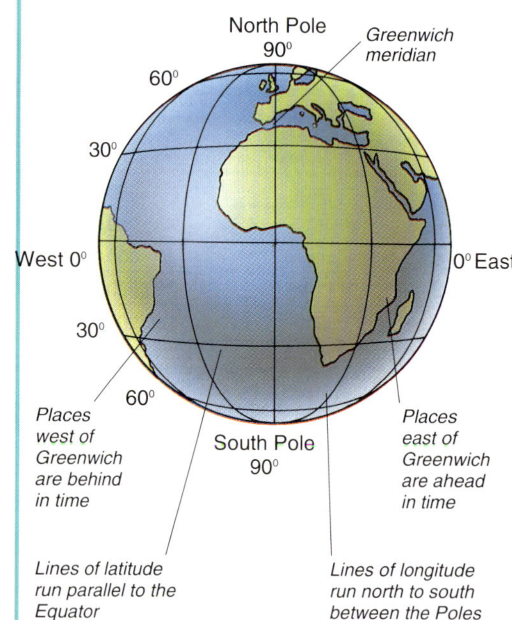

STRUCTURE OF THE EARTH

The Earth contains four layers. The outer layer, the crust, is made of different types of rocks such as basalt and granite. The mantle also contains rocks but these are heavier and darker than those found in the crust. The outer core is liquid and is thought to contain liquid iron, sulphur, and silicon. The inner core probably contains solid iron.

Depth (km)	Pressure (k bar)	Density (kg/m³)	Temperature (°C)
50	100	3,000	500
400	150	3,500	1,750
1,000	325	4,500	2,000
2,900	1,325	10,000	3,000
5,100	3,300	12,100	3,600
6,300	3,750	12,100	4,000

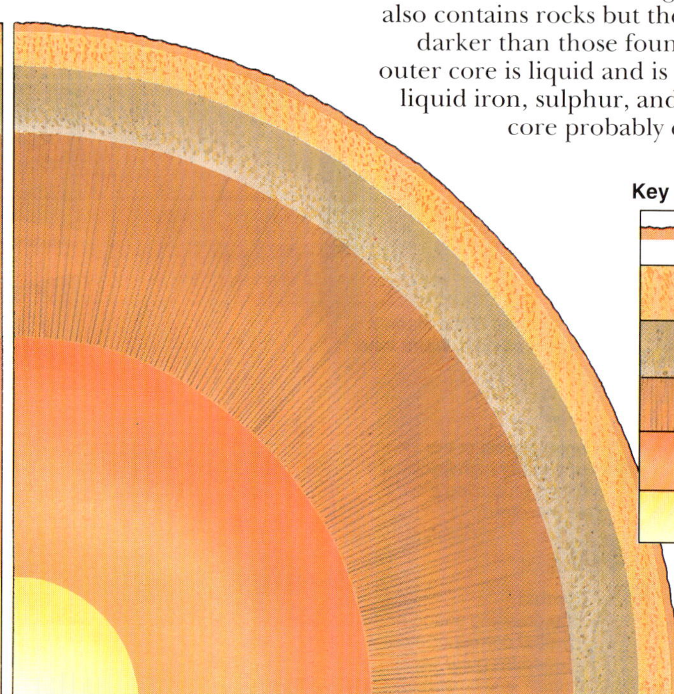

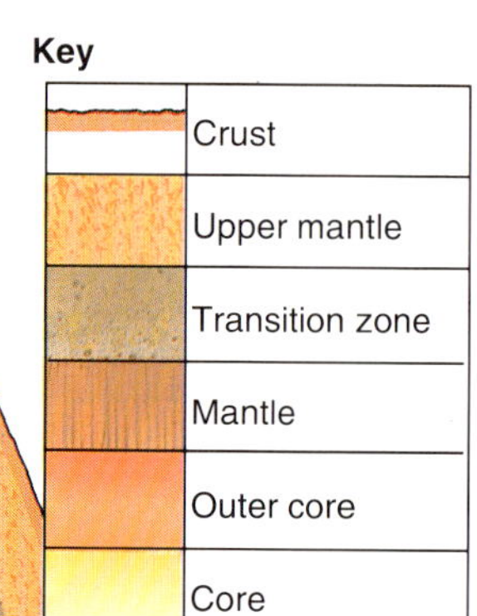

MOHS' SCALE OF HARDNESS

Friedrich Mohs, a German minerologist, created a table of ten minerals to show their hardness. The higher the number, the harder the mineral. Each mineral can scratch those of a lower number.

THE MOST COMMON ROCKS

All the rocks that make up the Earth are igneous, sedimentary, or metamorphic rocks. Igneous rocks form when molten rock is cooled. Sedimentary rocks are fragments of rock, sand, and silt compressed to form a solid mass. Metamorphic rocks form when heat and pressure change the mineral content of a rock. Below are ten common examples of each.

Igneous	Sedimentary	Metamorphic
Granite	Limestone	Slate
Syenite	Dolomite	Phyllite
Gabbro	Sandstone	Schist
Dolerite	Conglomerate	Gneiss
Basalt	Breccia	Hornfels
Andesite	Evaporite	Marble
Obsidian	Siltstone	Quartzite
Diorite	Mudstone	Migmatite
Porphyry	Shale	Amphibolite
Rhyolite	Clay	Tactite

THE ROCK CYCLE

The Earth's crust is made of recycled rocks. These are formed by external factors such as heat, pressure, and weathering. These factors are continually breaking up and rebuilding sedimentary, igneous, and metamorphic rocks in a process known as the rock cycle.

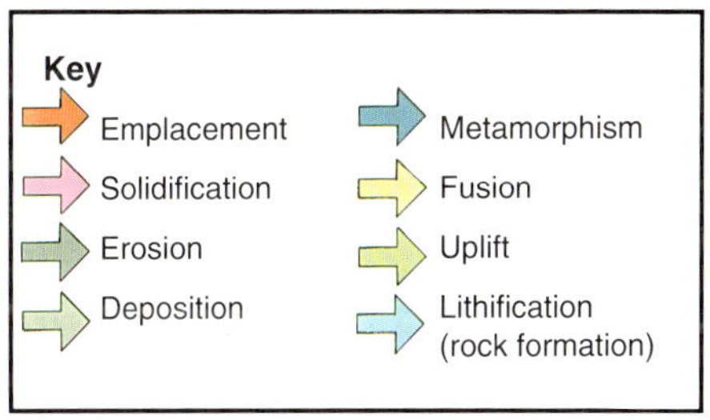

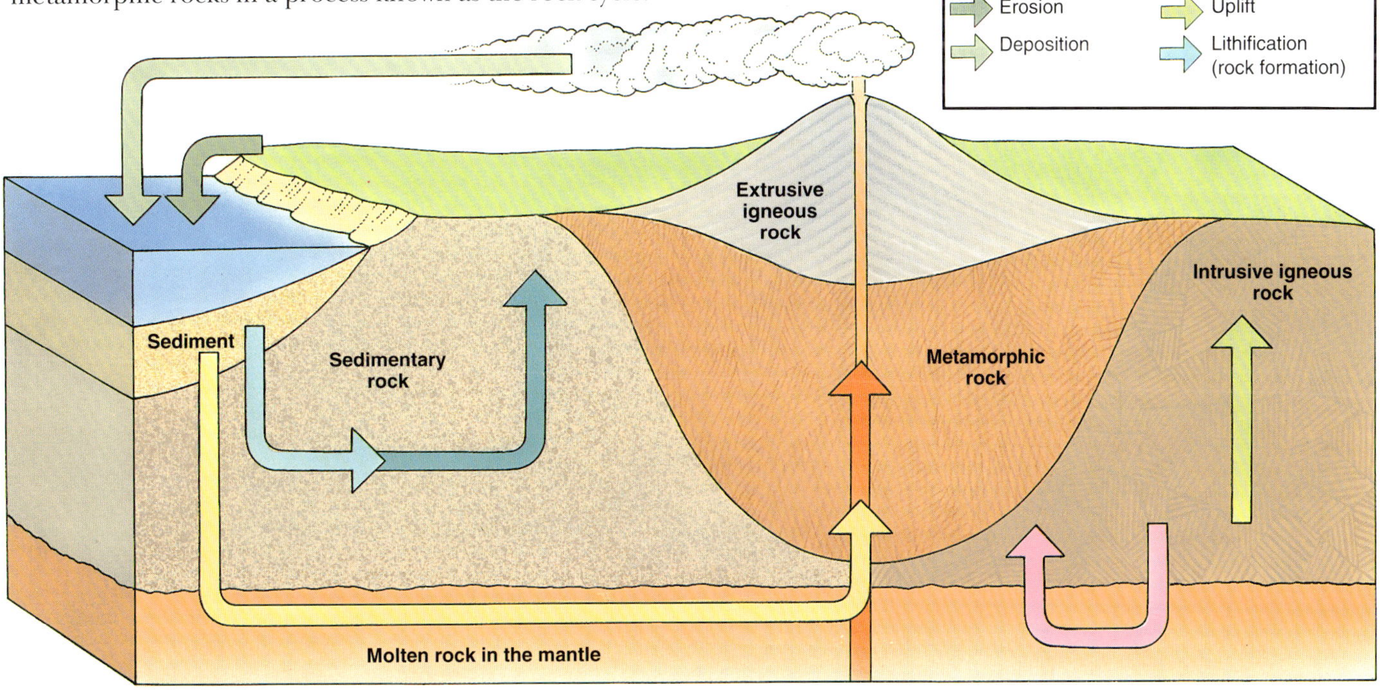

WEATHER

WORLD METEOROLOGICAL ORGANIZATION

The World Meteorological Organization consists of a network of about 10,000 permanent weather stations all over the world. Reports from these stations are sent by telephone every three hours (called 'synoptic hours') to the thirteen main weather centres shown on this world map. This weather information is then continually passed around the world to countries that make up their own weather forecasts.

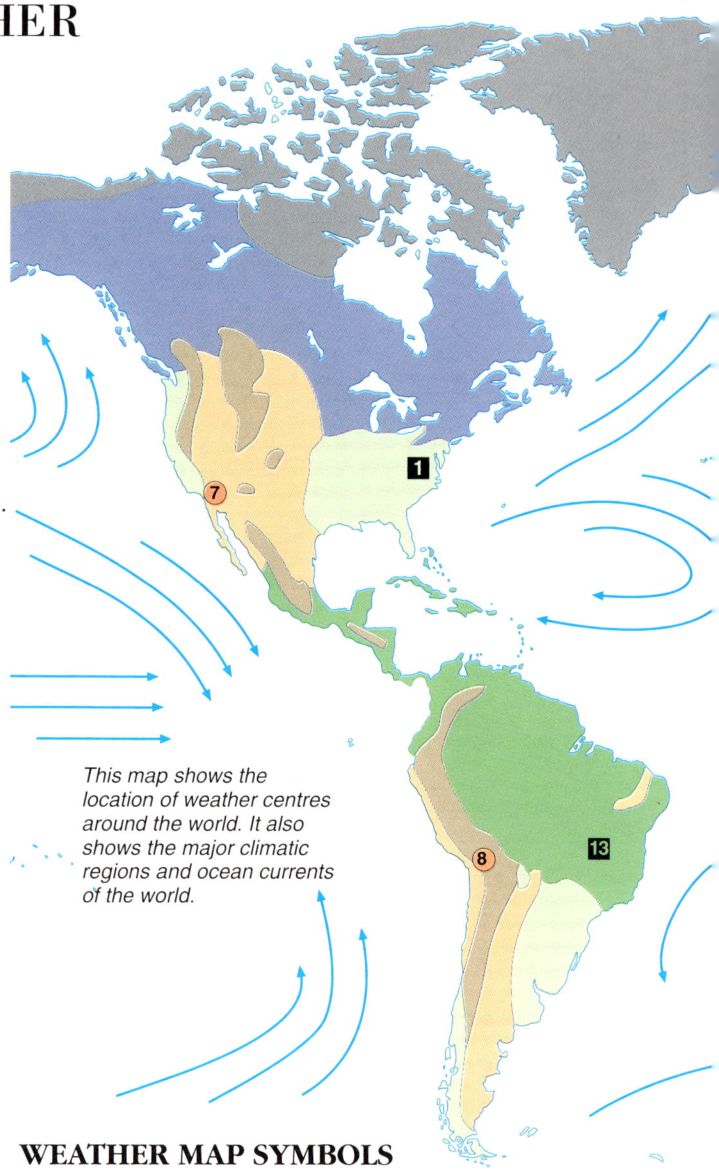

This map shows the location of weather centres around the world. It also shows the major climatic regions and ocean currents of the world.

EXTREMES IN WEATHER CONDITIONS

This chart shows the extreme weather conditions recorded around the world. In some places, extreme conditions are part of the normal seasonal weather pattern for that area. In others, conditions such as floods and droughts can interrupt the usual pattern.

Greatest snowfall
(12 months) 31,102 mm (1,224.5 in). Paradise, Mount Rainier, Washington State, U.S.A. 19/2/1971 to 18/2/1972.

Greatest rainfall
(24 hours) 1,870 mm (73.62 in). Cilaos, Reunion, Indian Ocean. 15/3 to 16/3/1952.

Driest place/longest drought
(Annual average) Nil, in the Atacama Desert, near Calama, Chile. 400 years to 1972, also in the Atacama Desert.

Highest surface wind speed
371 km/h (231 mph), Mount Washington (alt. 1,916 m/6,288 ft). New Hampshire, U.S.A. 12/4/1934.

Maximum sunshine
97% (0ver 4,300 hours). Eastern Sahara.

Minimum sunshine
Nil, North Pole – for winter stretches of 182 days.

Highest shade temperature
58°C (136°F). al' Aziz yah, Libya (alt. 111 m/367 ft). 13/9/1922.

Hottest place
(Annual average) 34.4°C/94°F. Dallol, Ethiopia.

Coldest place
(Coldest measured average) -89°C (-129°F). Plateau Station, Antarctica.

Most rainy days
(Year) up to 350 per year, Mount Wai-ale-ali (alt. 1,569 m/5,148 ft) Kaunai, Hawaii.

Windiest place
Where gales reach 320 km/h (199 mph). Commonwealth Bay, George V Coast, Antarctica.

READING WEATHER SYMBOLS

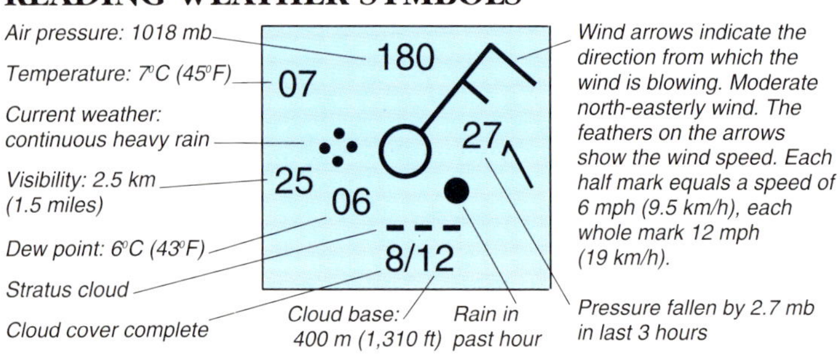

WEATHER MAP SYMBOLS

Meteorologists use a list of symbols to indicate weather and wind speed. The symbols shown are recognized internationally. Once plotted on weather maps they provide essential information used in making weather forecasts. Television weather forecasters use simplified versions of these symbols.

Mist	Fog	Drizzle
Rain	Rain and drizzle	Rain and snow
Snow	Rain shower	Rain and snow shower
Snow shower	Hail shower	Thunderstorm
Cold front	Warm front	Occluded front
Light to strong winds: Calm … Gale		

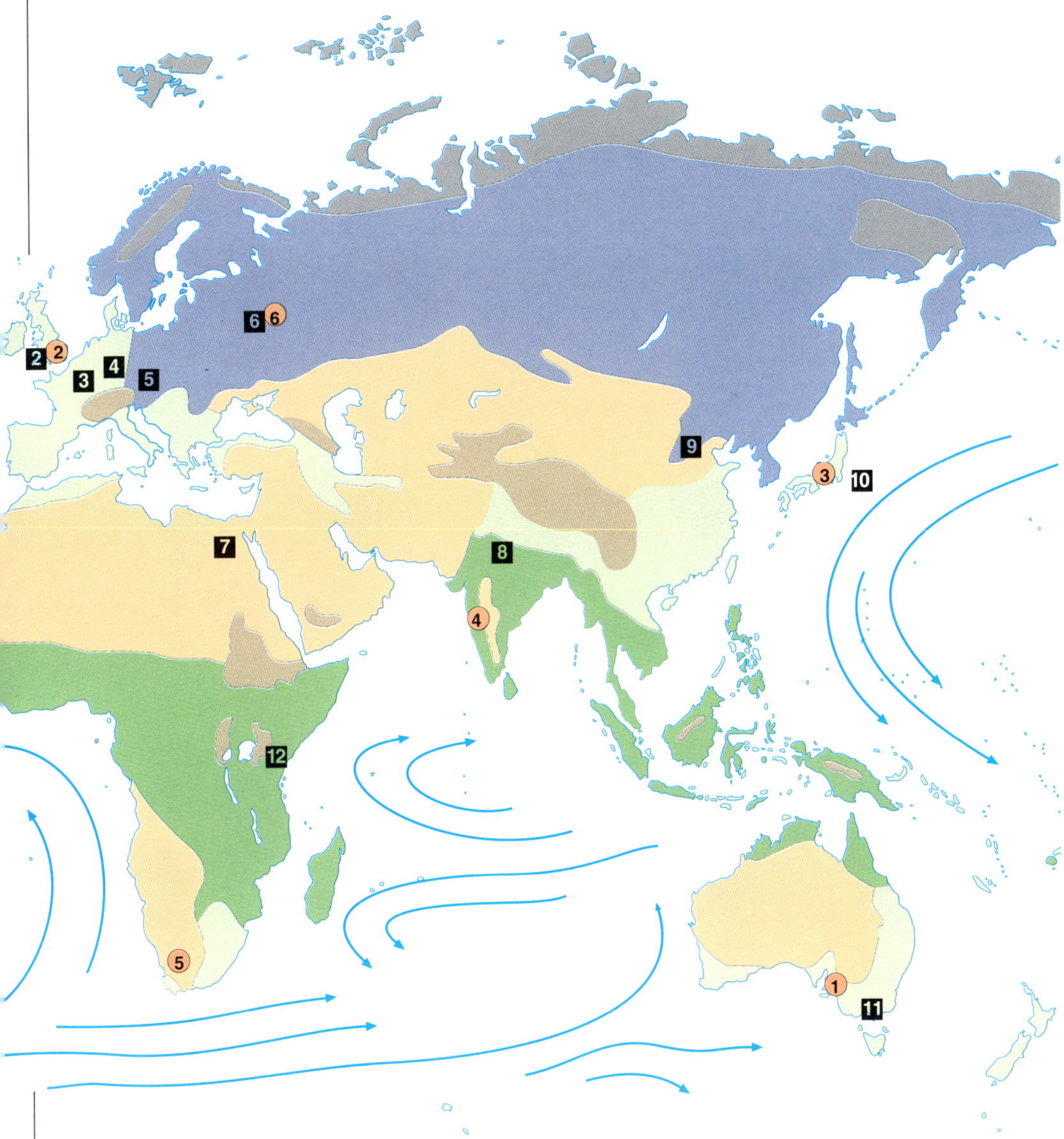

WEATHER CENTRES

The location of the thirteen main weather centres listed below is shown on the world map.

1. Washington, D.C., U.S.A.
2. Bracknell, U.K.
3. Paris, France
4. Offenbach, Germany
5. Prague, Czechoslovakia
6. Moscow, Russia
7. Cairo, Egypt
8. New Delhi, India
9. Beijing, China
10. Tokyo, Japan
11. Melbourne, Australia
12. Nairobi, Kenya
13. Brasilia, Brazil

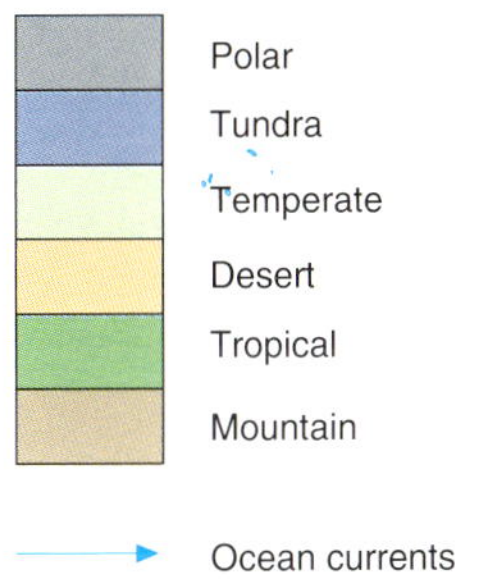

CLIMATES OF MAJOR CITIES

These graphs show the average temperature and rainfall statistics for various cities around the world (the locations of these cities are shown on the world map above).

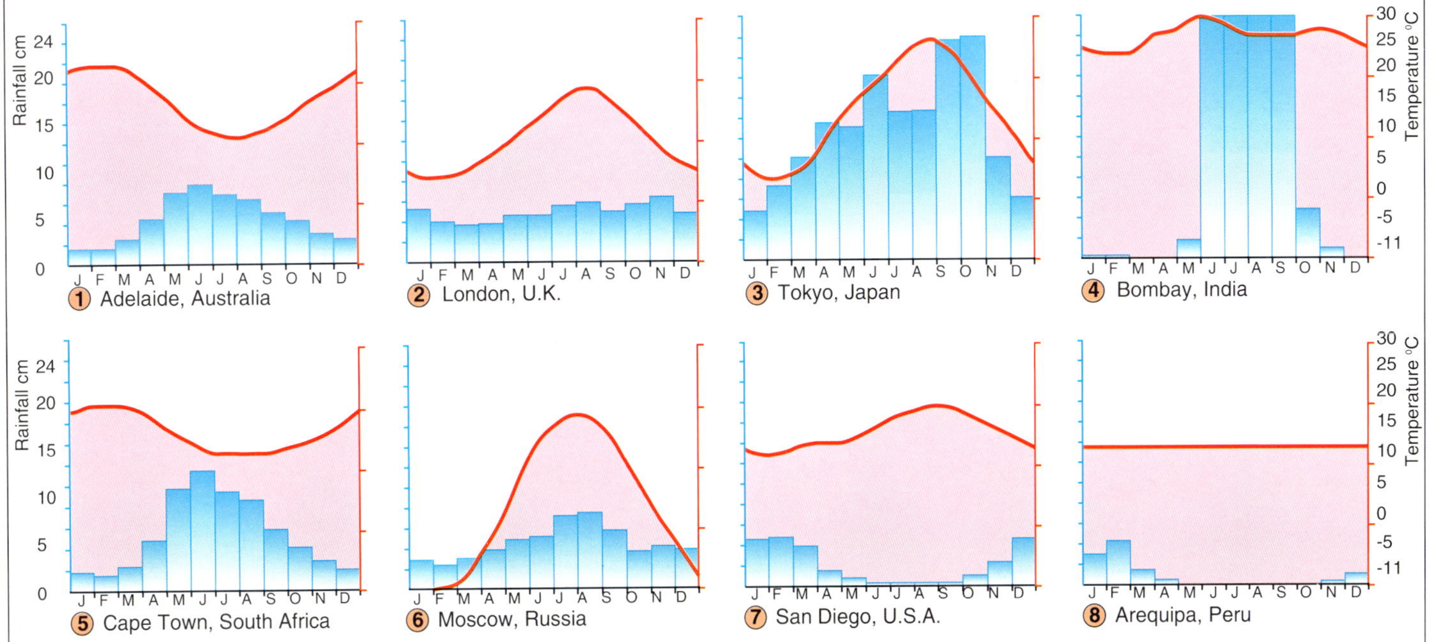

SPACE

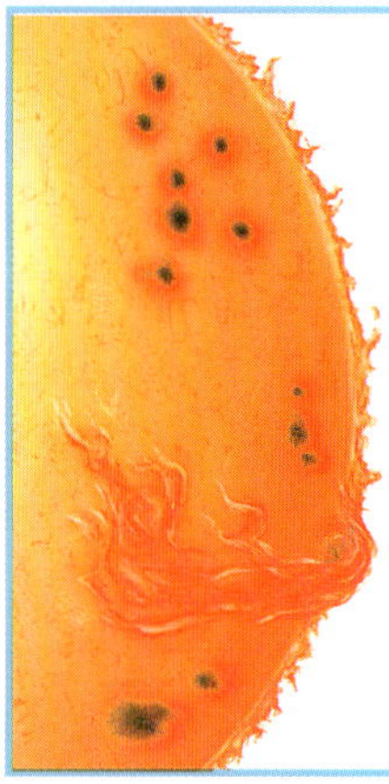

THE SUN

By far the brightest star in our sky is the Sun because of its closeness to Earth. Even so, the light leaving it takes 8.3 minutes to reach us; the Sun we see is 8.3 minutes old.

Mass	1.99 x 10^{33}g
Surface temperature	6,000°C
Core temperature	14,000,000°C
Diameter	1,392,000 km

BRIGHTEST STARS

The brightness of a star is measured by its magnitude. The brighter the star, the lower the magnitude number. The apparent magnitude of a star is its brightness as seen from Earth. The absolute magnitude is how much light a star actually gives out.

Name	Magnitude Apparent	Magnitude Absolute	Distance from Sun (light years)
Sirius	–1.46	+1.4	8.65
Canopus	–0.73	–4.6	1200
Alpha Centauri	–0.1	+4.1	4.38
Arcturus	–0.06	–0.3	36
Vega	+0.04	+0.5	26
Capella	+0.08	–0.5	42
Rigel	+0.10	–7.0	900
Procyon	+0.35	+2.6	11.4
Betelgeuse	+0.49	–5.7v	310
Achernar	+0.51	–2.5	117
Hadar	+0.63	–4.6	490
Altair	+0.77	+2.3	16
Aldebaran	+0.85	–0.7	69
Acrux	+0.90	–3.7	370
Antares	+0.92	–4.5	430
Spica	+0.96	–3.6	260
Pollux	+1.15	+1.0	35
Fomalhaut	+1.16	+1.9	23
Deneb	+1.25	–7.1	1800
Beta Crucis	+1.25	–5.1	489
Regulus	+1.35	–0.7	85
Adhara	+1.50	–4.4	681

LARGEST METEORITES

Name	Country	Approximate tonnage
Hoba West	South West Africa	60
The Abnighito Tent	Greenland	30.4
Bacuberito	Mexico	27
Mbosi	Tanzania	26
Agpalik	West Greenland	20.1
Armanty	Outer Mongolia	20
Chupaderos	Mexico	14
Willamette	U.S.A.	14
Campo del Cielo	Argentina	13
Mundrabilla	Australia	12

THE PLANETS

There are nine planets in the Solar System. They fall roughly into two groups. Closest to the Sun are four rocky planets. These are Mercury, Venus, Earth, and Mars.

Farther from the Sun are the gas giants. These are Jupiter, Saturn, Uranus, and Neptune. Pluto is the odd one out – it is the smallest planet and is made of rock and ice.

Planet	Mercury	Venus	Earth	Mars	Jupiter	Saturn	Uranus	Neptune	Pluto
Distance from Sun millions of km (miles)	57.9 (36.0)	108.2 (67.2)	149.6 (93)	227.9 (141.5)	778.3 (483.3)	1,427 (886.1)	2,870 (1,782)	4,497 (2,774)	5,913 (3,672)
Diameter at equator km (miles)	4,879 (3,033)	12,104 (7,523)	12,756 (7,928)	6,786 (4,222)	142,984 (88,784)	120,536 (74,914)	51,118 (31,770)	49,528 (30,757)	2,284 (1,419)
Mass (Earth =1)	0.056	0.82	1	0.107	318	95	14.5	17	0.002
Volume (Earth =1)	0.056	0.86	1	0.15	1,319	744	67	57	0.01
Surface temperature °C (°F)	–180 to +430 (–356 to +800)	+480 (+896)	–70 to +55 (–158 to +133)	–120 to +25 (–248 to +77)	–150 (–238)	–180 (–292)	–214 (–353)	–220 (–364)	–230 (–382)
Surface gravity (Earth=1)	0.38	0.9	1	0.38	2.64	0.925	0.79	1.12	0.05
Time to orbit Sun ("year")	87.97 days	224.7 days	365.26 days	686.98 days	11.86 years	29.46 yrs	84.01 yrs	164.8 yrs	248.5 yrs
Time to turn 360° ("day")	58.65 days	243.01 days	23 h 56 m 4 s	24 h 37 m 23 s	9 h 55 m 30 s	10 h 39 m	17 h 14 m	16 h 7 m	6 days 9 h
Orbital velocity km/s (miles/s)	47.9 (29.7)	35 (21.8)	29.8 (18.5)	24.1 (15)	13.1 (8.1)	9.6 (6)	6.8 (4.2)	5.4 (3.4)	4.7 (2.9)
Number of moons	0	0	1	2	16	18	15	8	1

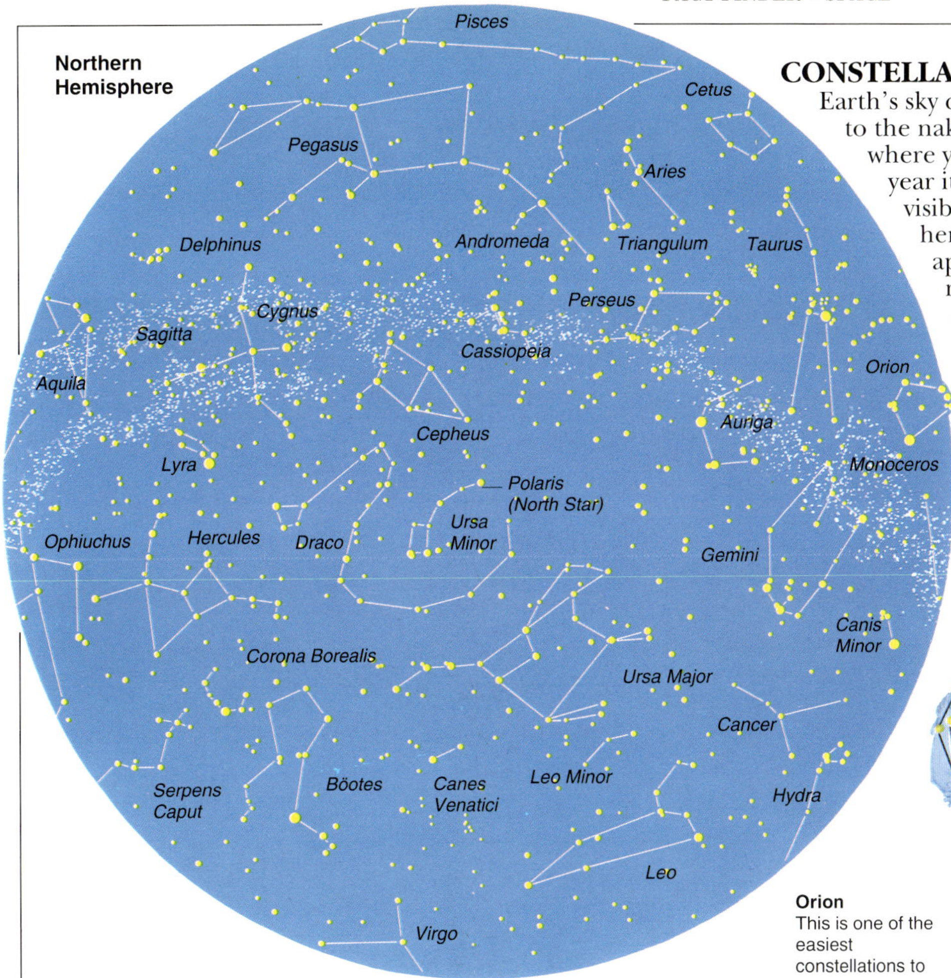

CONSTELLATIONS

Earth's sky contains around 6,000 stars that are visible to the naked eye. The stars that you see depend on where you are standing on Earth and what time of year it is. These star maps show the stars that are visible from the Northern and Southern hemispheres. As the Earth spins, the stars appear to move across the sky and so these maps will need to be rotated too. The stars in the centre of the maps can be seen all year round; those at the edge may only be seen at certain times of the year.

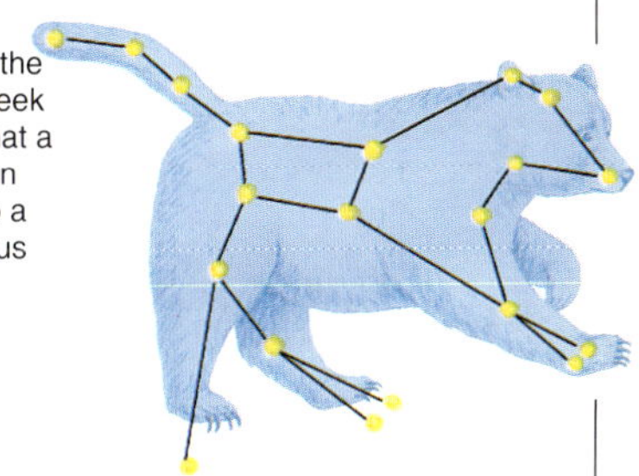

Ursa Major
Also known as the Great Bear. Greek legend has it that a beautiful woman was turned into a bear by a jealous goddess.

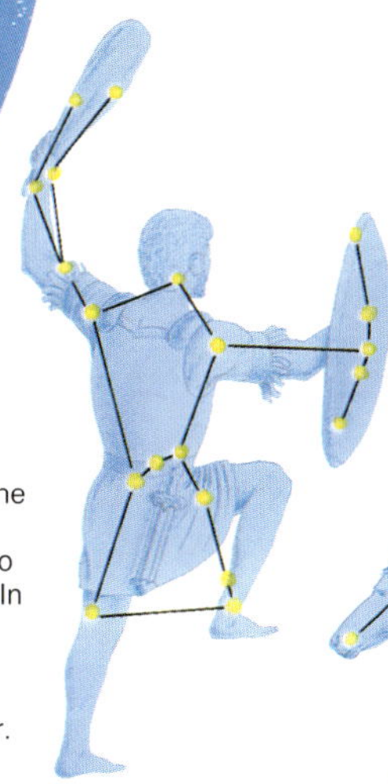

Orion
This is one of the easiest constellations to find in the sky. In Greek legend, Orion was a successful but arrogant hunter.

Pegasus
This constellation takes the form of a winged horse. In Greek legend, the horse sprang from the blood of a monster called Medusa, after it was killed by Perseus.

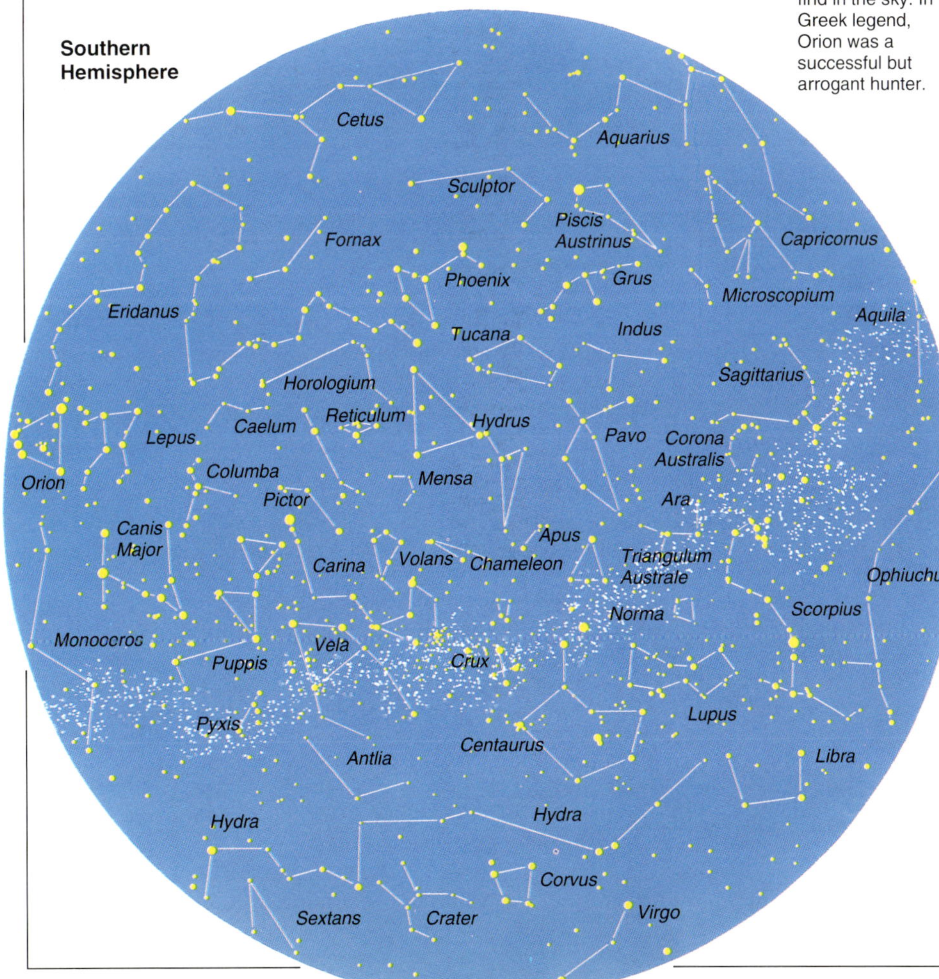

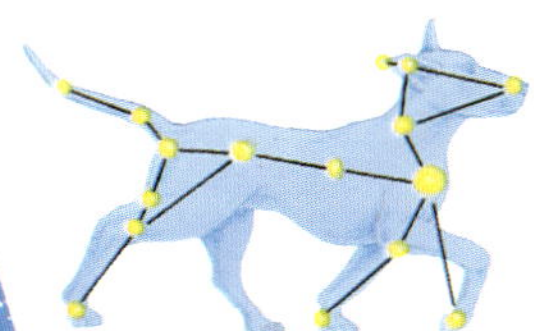

Canis Major
This constellation represents one of the two dogs that are snapping at Orion's heels. One of the stars that makes up Canis Major is Sirius, the brightest star in the sky.

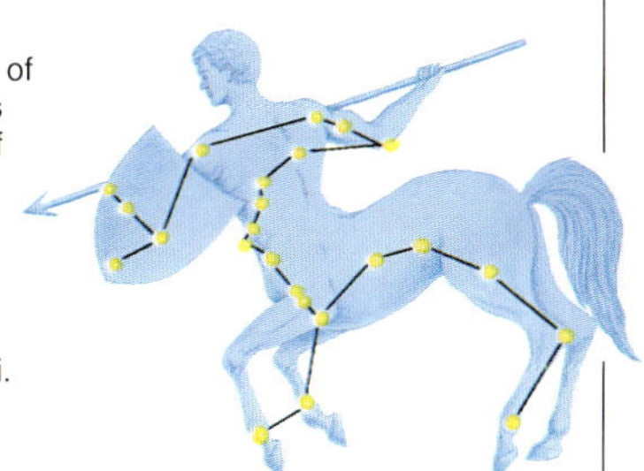

Centaurus
The constellation of Centaurus shows the centaur – half man and half horse. It contains the nearest star (apart form the Sun) to Earth – Proxima Centauri.

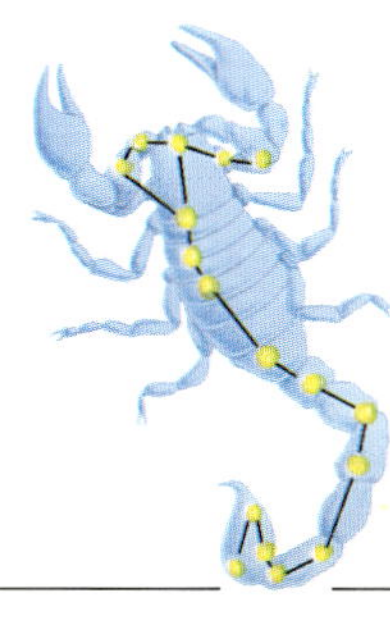

Scorpius
In Greek legend, this scorpion was sent to kill Orion. The characters are now at opposite ends of the sky. As Orion sets, the scorpion rises.

LIVING THINGS

This chart shows how biologists classify the different forms of life on Earth. It is divided into five major groups, called kingdoms, and the kingdoms are themselves broken down into several smaller units. Each organism in the chart contains two pieces of information about it. First, you will be able to discover which group of the living world it belongs to. Second, you will be able to see what other living things are most closely related to it through the process of evolution.

HOW TO USE THE CHART

The chart is colour-coded so that you can quickly tell the classification level of any group shown.

- **Kingdom** – *The largest grouping in the classification of living things.*
- **Phylum** – *A major group within a kingdom. This is sometimes called a division when used in the classification of plants.*
- **Subphylum** – *Part of a phylum, or division, in the classification of plants.*
- **Class** – *A major part of a phylum or subphylum.*
- **Subclass** – *A large group within a class.*
- **Order** – *Part of a class or subclass. Some classes are split into many orders.*
- **Family** – *A large collection of species that have several features in common.*
- **Genus** – *A small collection of species that have many features in common.*
- **Species** – *A group of living things that can breed together in nature.*

Green algae
Chloropyhta – *Scientific name*
6,000 – *Number of species*
Non-vascular – *Further information*

MONERANS

This kingdom includes the simplest forms of life on Earth. There are over 4,000 species.

Bacteria
2,000

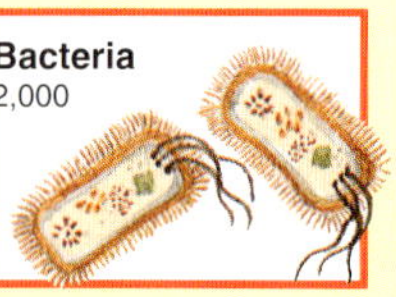

Blue-green algae
2,000

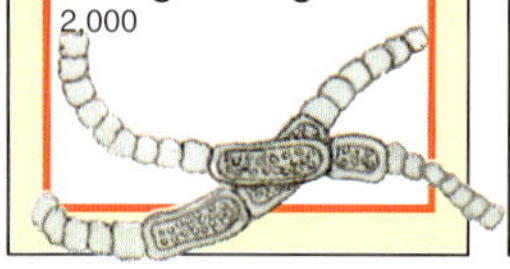

PROTISTS

This kingdom contains single-celled organisms. There are about 50,000 species and most live in water.

Amoebas
10,000

Diatoms
10,000

Euglenas
10,000

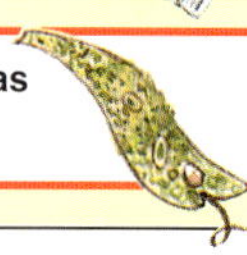

FUNGI

Fungi absorb food made by plants or animals. There are over 100,000 species. Many are microscopic.

Slime moulds
10,000

True fungi
100,000

PLANTS

The plant kingdom contains organisms that produce their food using sunlight, together with some species that have since lost this ability. The kingdom contains more than 400,000 species. Plants cannot move, but they reproduce by making spores or seeds. These often spread far from the parent plant. The simplest plants reproduce by making spores. The most advanced plants, which include conifers and flowering plants, reproduce by making seeds.

NON-FLOWERING PLANTS

This general category includes simple, non-vascular plants, which do not have transport systems for water, salts, or food. It also includes some vascular plants, which transport these substances in special vessels. Non-vascular plants mostly live in water, or in damp places. Vascular plants can survive in drier habitats. Some biologists classify all forms of algae as protists.

Green algae
Chlorophyta
6,000
Non-vascular

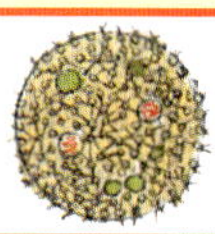

Red algae
Rhodophyta
4,000
Non-vascular

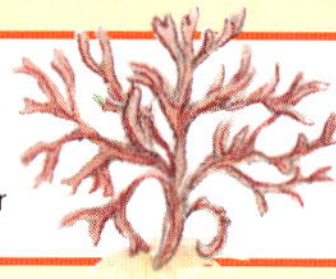

Brown algae
Phaeophyta
2,000
Non-vascular

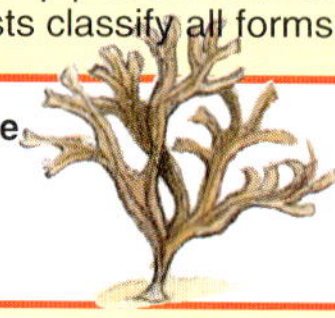

Mosses and liverworts
Bryophyta
25,000
Non-vascular

Ferns
Pteridophyta
12,000
Vascular

Club mosses
Lycopodiophyta
400
Vascular

Horsetails
Sphenophyta
550
Vascular

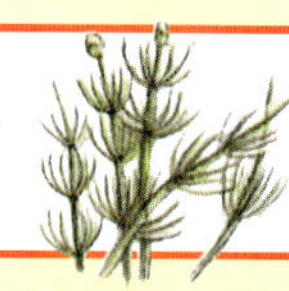

Conifers
Coniferophyta
550
Vascular

FLOWERING PLANTS

There are more than 250,000 species of flowering plant. They are all vascular, and all produce seeds. Flowering plants such as buttercups have flowers made of many separate parts arranged symmetrically around the flower stem. Advanced flowering plants such as foxgloves have fewer parts. These are often fused together to form funnels or tubes, and the flower shape is often irregular.

Monocotyledons
Plants whose seeds have one cotyledon (seed-leaf), and leaves with parallel veins. Flower parts usually in threes, or multiples of three. Rarely woody.

Irises
Iridaceae
1,850

Grasses
Graminae
8,000

Orchids
Orchidaceae
17,500

Dicotyledons
Plants whose seeds have two cotyledons (seed-leaves), and leaves with a branching network of veins. Flower parts usually in fours or fives, or multiples of these numbers. Many species have woody stems. There are over 250 families of "dicots". Some of the most important are shown here.

Elms
Ulmacaeae
140

Legumes
Leguminosae
18.400

Daisies
Compositae
21,000

Roses
Rosaceae
3,100

Cacti
Cactaceae
1,650

Foxgloves
Scrophulariaceae
4,500

Parsley and carrots
Umbelliferae
3,100

Cabbages
Cruciferae
3,000

Oaks
Fagaceae
1,050

Heathers
Ericaceae
3,350

ANIMALS

The animal kingdom contains organisms that feed on plants, on other animals, or on their remains. Most animals can move about, but some spend their adult lives in one place. There may be about 10 to 20 million species.

INVERTEBRATES

This informal category contains all animals that do not have a backbone, and it includes over nine-tenths of all animal species. Many invertebrates are soft-bodied and live in water, or in damp habitats. One phylum, the arthropods, has been outstandingly successful in water and on land.

Cnidarians
Cnidaria
9,500
Mainly marine

- **Corals**
- **Jellyfish**
- **Sea anemones**
- **Hydras**

Flatworms
Platyhelminthes
10,000

- **Free-living flatworms**
- **Flukes**
- **Tapeworms**

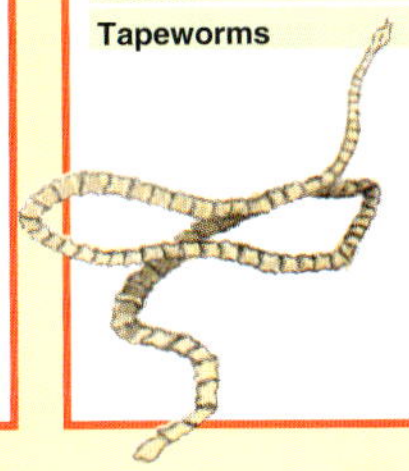

Molluscs
Mollusca
90,000
Aquatic and terrestrial

- **Chitons**
- **Slugs and snails**
- **Clams, scallops**
- **Tusks or tooth shells**
- **Octopuses, squids, and cuttlefish**

Annelid worms
Annelida
12,000
Aquatic and terrestrial

- **Earthworms and bloodworms**
- **Leeches**
- **Lungworms and other marine worms**

Echinoderms
Echinodermata
6,000
Marine

- **Brittle stars**
- **Sea urchins**
- **Sea cucumbers**
- **Starfish**
- **Sea lilies and feather stars**

Small phyla
Ctenopora, Rotifera, Nemertea
3,000+

- **Comb jellies**
- **Rotifers**
- **Nemertean worms**

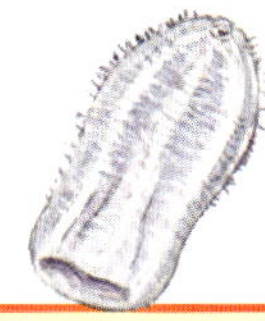

Sponges
Porifera
5,000
Mainly marine

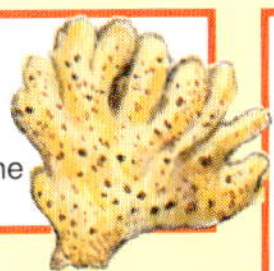

Nematode worms
Nematoda
12,000

Bryozoans
Bryozoa
4,000
Mainly marine

Arthropods

Arthropods (Arthropoda) This large phylum contains animals with a jointed body that is covered by an external skeleton, and divided into a number of segments. The skeleton supports and protects the body and, on land, it helps to prevent it from drying out.

Millipedes
Diplopoda
7,000

Centipedes
Chilopoda
1,700

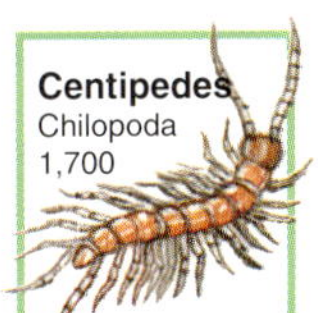

Crustaceans
Crustacea
40,000
Mainly marine

- **Water fleas**
- **Wood lice**
- **Crabs and lobsters**
- **Fish lice**
- **Barnacles**

Arachnids
Arachnida
70,000
Mainly terrestrial

- **Scorpions**
- **Spiders**
- **Mites**
- **Harvestmen**

Insects
Insecta 1,000,000+ Mainly terrestrial

- **Springtails**
- **Silverfish and bristletails**
- **Dragonflies and damselflies**
- **Butterflies and moths**
- **Grasshoppers and crickets**
- **Earwigs**
- **Stick insects**
- **Cockroaches**
- **Mantids**
- **Termites**
- **Lice**
- **True bugs**
- **Thrips**
- **Lacewings**
- **Beetles**
- **Flies**
- **Fleas**
- **Bees, wasps and ants**

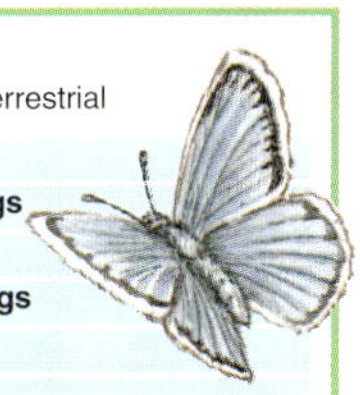

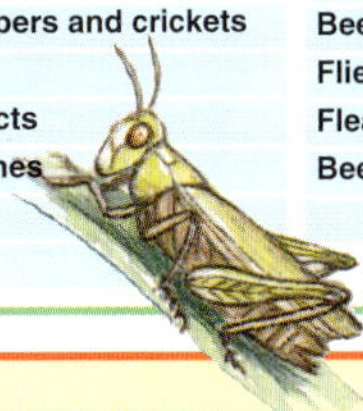

CHORDATES

CHORDATES (Chordata) This phylum contains animals that have a stiff cord which runs down their bodies. There are about 44,000 species, and almost all are vertebrates (animals with backbones). The lancelets and sea squirts, two subphyla, have a stiff cord but not a true backbone.

Jawless fish
Agnatha
70
Marine; skeleton made of cartilage

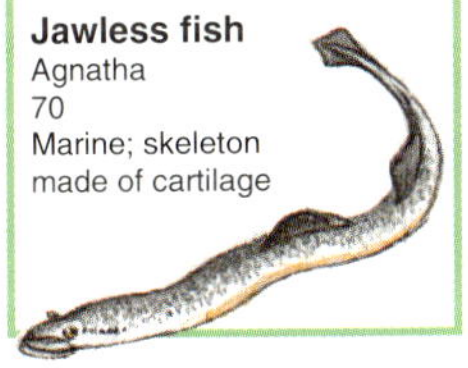

Cartilaginous fish
Chondrichthyes
700
Marine; skeleton made of cartilage

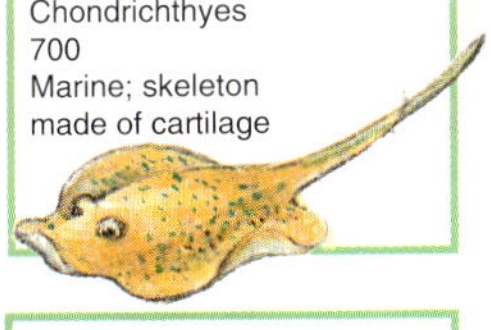

Amphibians
Amphibia
4,000
Freshwater or terrestrial

- **Frogs and toads**
- **Newts and salamanders**
- **Caecilians (Apodans)**

Bony fish
Osteichthyes
21,000
Marine and freshwater; skeleton made of bone

- **Coelacanth**
- **Lungfish**
- **Birchirs**
- **Sturgeons, paddlefish**
- **Eels**
- **Herrings, anchovies**
- **Salmon, trout**
- **Carp**
- **Catfishes**
- **Perches, marlins, swordfishes, tunas**
- **Anglerfish**
- **Cods**
- **Flying fishes**
- **Grunions**
- **Sticklebacks**
- **Seahorses**

Reptiles
Reptilia 6,500 Mainly terrestrial; skin covered with scales

- **Snakes and lizards**
- **Turtles and tortoises**
- **Crocodiles, alligators**
- **Tuatara**

Birds
Aves 9,000 All breed on land; skin covered in feathers

- **Divers**
- **Grebes**
- **Albatrosses, petrels**
- **Penguins**
- **Pelicans, gannets, cormorants**
- **Herons, storks**
- **Ducks, geese, swans**
- **Eagles, hawks, vultures**
- **Pheasants, partridges**
- **Gulls, plovers**
- **Pigeons, doves**
- **Parrots**
- **Cuckoos, roadrunners**
- **Owls**
- **Hummingbirds**
- **Kingfishers, bee-eaters, rollers**
- **Perching birds (e.g. finches)**

Mammals
Mammalia 4,000 Terrestrial or aquatic; suckle young on milk

Marsupials
Marsupialia
250
Mammals that raise their young in a pouch

- **Opossums**
- **Koalas**
- **Bandicoots**
- **Kangaroos, wallabies**

Monotremes
Montremata
3
Egg-laying mammals

- **Duck-billed platypus**
- **Echidnas**

Placentals
Eutheria
3,810
Mammals that nourish their young through a placenta

- **Hedgehogs, shrews, moles**
- **Bats**
- **Rabbits, hares**
- **Lemers, monkeys, apes, humans**
- **Anteaters, armadillos**
- **Rodents**
- **Whales, dolphins**
- **Dogs, cats, bears**
- **Seals, sea lions, walruses**
- **Elephants**
- **Hyraxes**
- **Manatees, dugongs**
- **Horses, tapirs, rhinoceroses**
- **Pigs, deer, sheep, antelope, cattle**

HOW LIVING THINGS WORK

LIFESPANS

Here you can see how long different kinds of organisms live. With most living things, lifespan is closely linked to reproduction. Most plants and animals do not survive for long after their reproductive life has ended. Bacteria and protists often reproduce by dividing in two, so their cells stay alive, even though they have split apart.

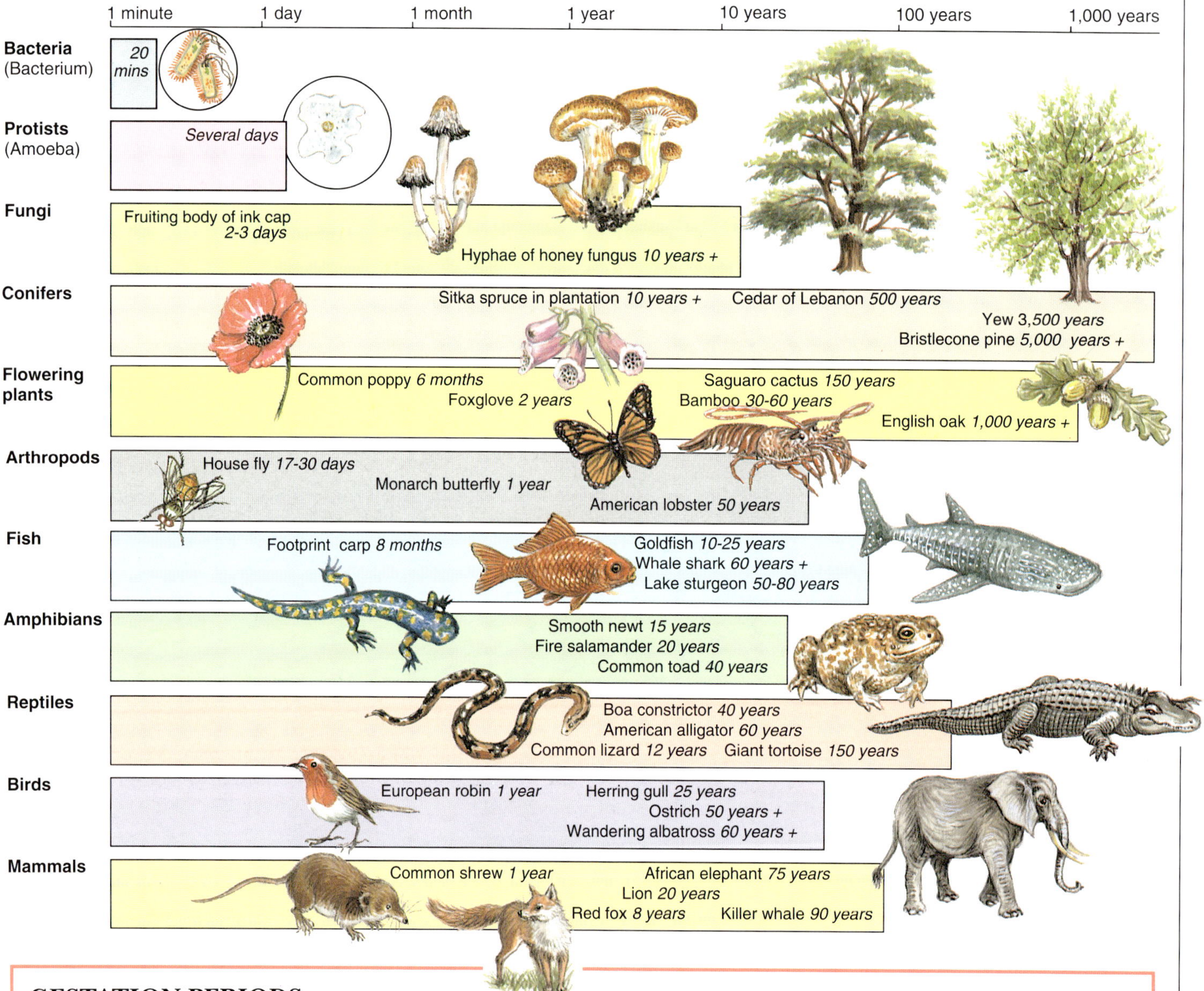

GESTATION PERIODS

A gestation period is the time between fertilization and birth. In most mammals, it is a precise length of time. Large mammals usually have long gestation periods, but there are exceptions, such as the kangaroo, which has a very short gestation period.

Key
15 days — Gestation period
(6-8) — Average number of young

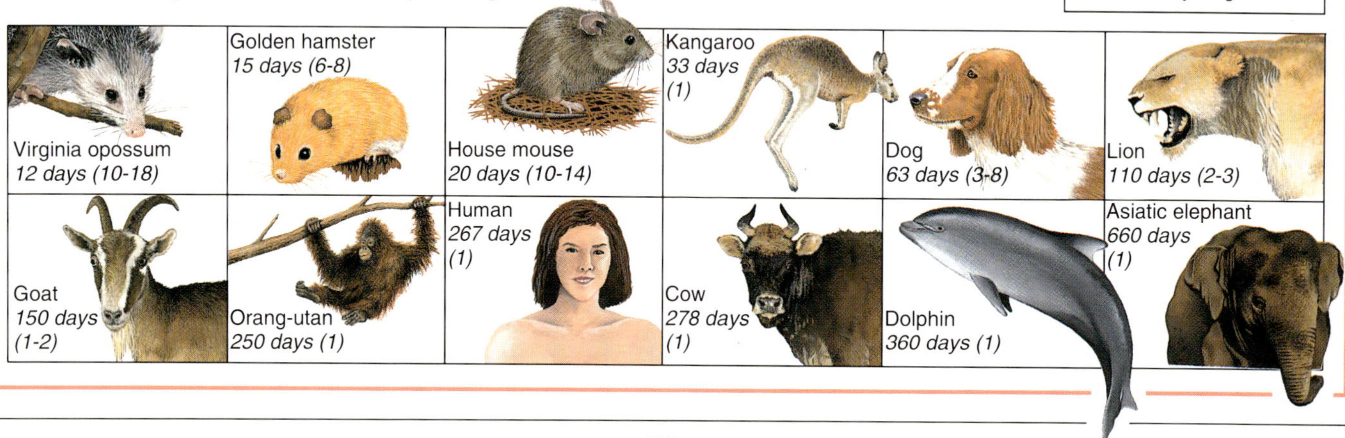

BODY TEMPERATURE

"Warm-blooded" and "cold-blooded" are two terms that can be misleading. A desert pupfish is "cold-blooded", like all fish. However, it lives in hot springs, so its blood is actually warm. A "warm-blooded" hibernating bat has a much colder body temperature.

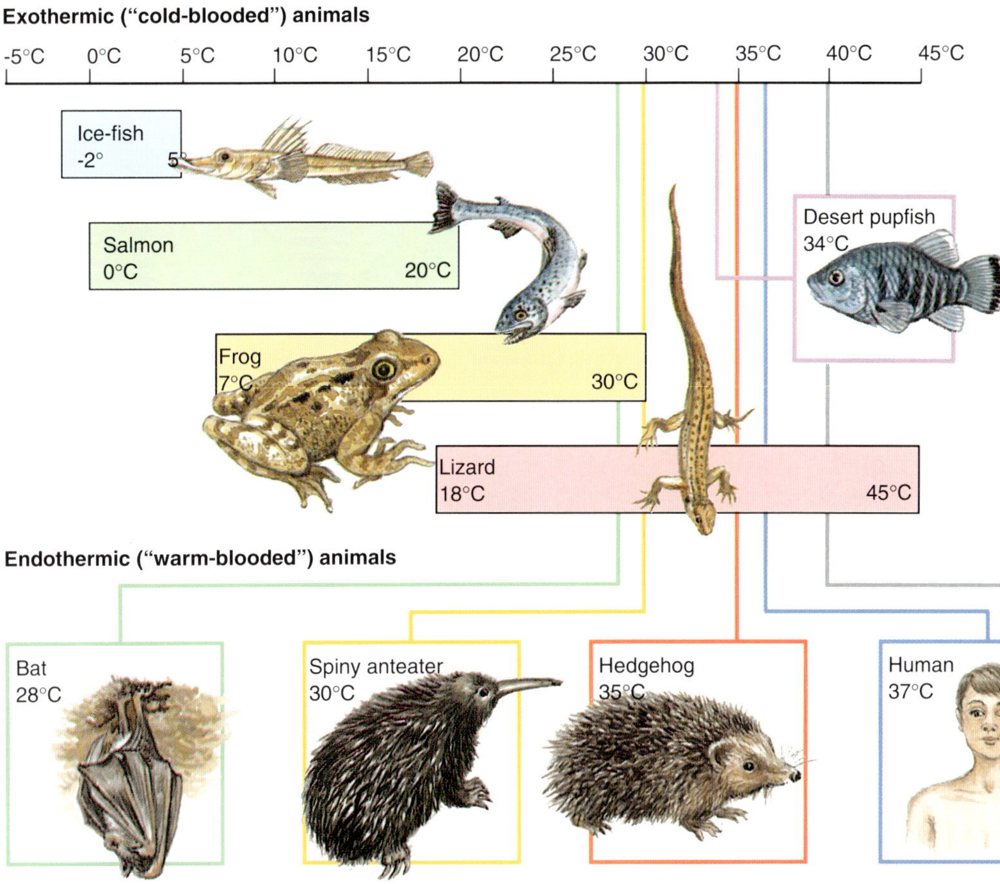

VITAMINS

Vitamins are essential nutrients that are needed in very small amounts. This list shows the daily vitamin requirements of an adult.

Vitamins that dissolve in fats

Vitamin A	1 milligram
Vitamin D	7.5 micrograms
Vitamin E	10 milligrams
Vitamin K	100 micrograms

Vitamins that dissolve in water

Vitamin B_1	1.5 milligrams
Vitamin B_2	1.7 milligrams
Niacin	19 milligrams
Vitamin B_6	2.2 milligrams
Vitamin B_{12}	3 micrograms
Pantothenic acid	6 milligrams
Folic acid	400 micrograms
Biotin	200 micrograms
Vitamin C	60 milligrams

METABOLIC RATE

An animal's metabolic rate is the rate at which it "burns" its food to release energy. Here you can see the metabolic rates of a range of different mammals, compared to that of humans. Small mammals have to burn their food at a high rate in relation to their volume; they have a high surface area of skin, through which their bodies quickly lose heat.

This chart shows how quickly animals burn their food for each unit of their body weight. The rate for humans is set at one.

ECOLOGY

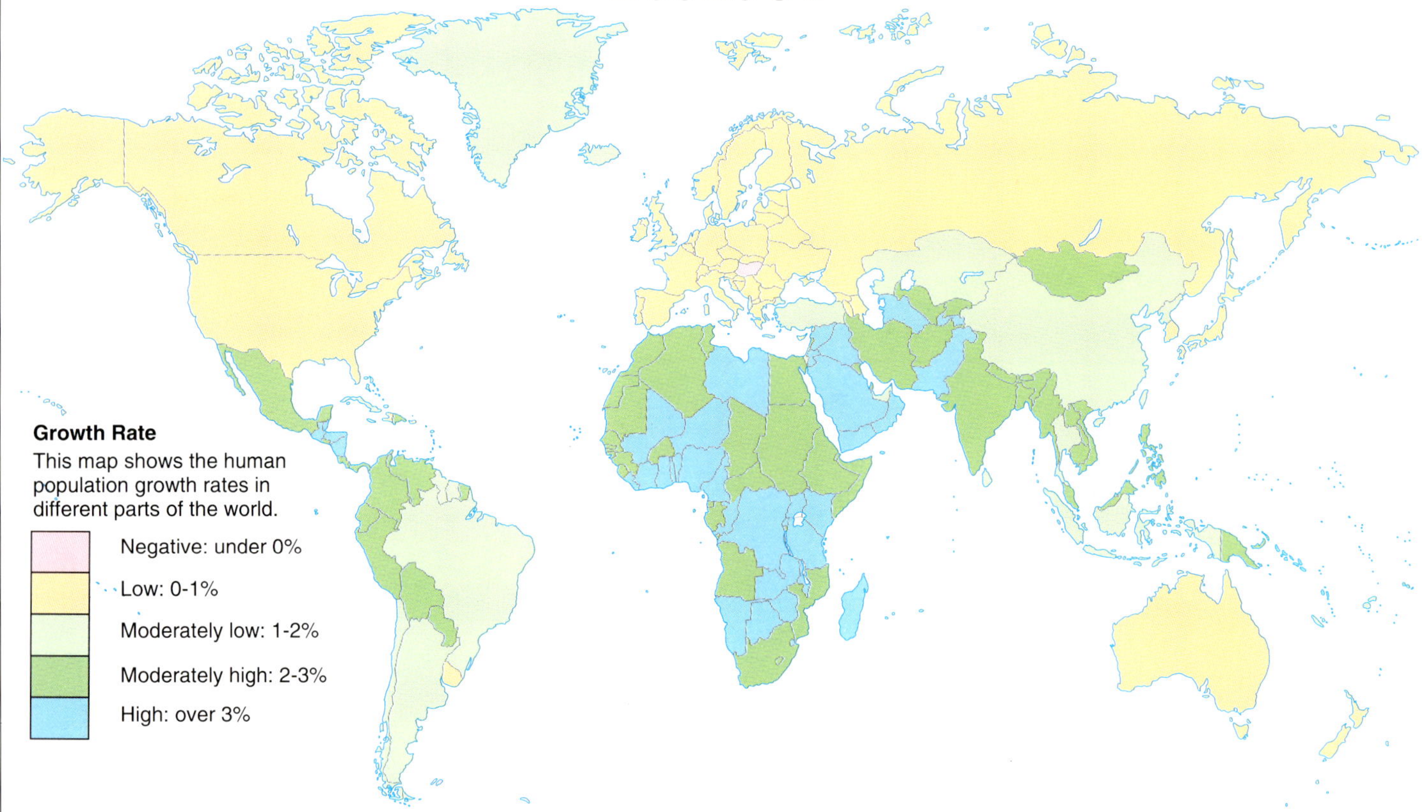

POPULATION GROWTH

The world's human population has steadily increased over the years, and is expected to double over the next 40 years. This chart shows the increase in the world's population, in millions, through the last 1,000 years. As you can see, Asia has the highest population growth.

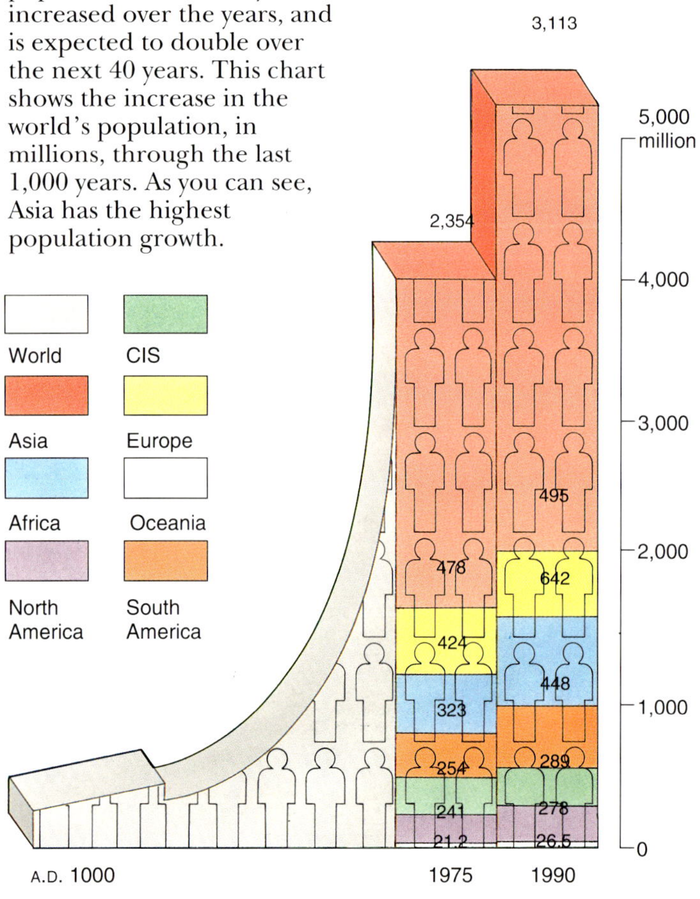

POLLUTION

Our wildlife and forests are damaged by acid rain. This is caused by the sulphur dioxide and nitrogen oxides in the fuels we burn. As they burn, they form gases that dissolve in water droplets in moist air. This in turn falls as rain or snow that damages the environment.

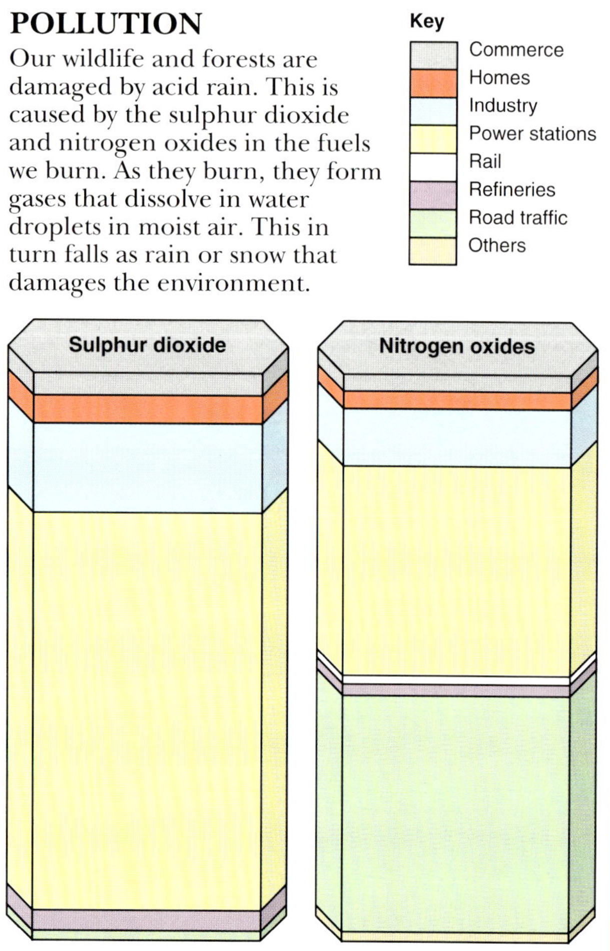

THREATENED SPECIES

Many species of animal are threatened with extinction, such as those shown below, because of habitat destruction, pollution, hunting, and competition from introduced species.

Animal	Where found	Numbers remaining
Asiatic buffalo	India, Nepal	2,200
European bison	Poland	About 1,000
Mountain gorilla	Rwanda, Africa	600
Mediterranean monk seal	Mediterranean sea	500
Chinese river dolphin	China	300
Giant panda	China	300
Whooping crane	North America	200
Golden lion tamarin	South America	200
Pygmy hog	Assam, India	100
Javan rhino	Java, Indonesia	50
Kakapo	New Zealand	50

RATE OF EXTINCTION

The rate of extinction traces how rapidly a species becomes extinct (dies out). A species is thought to be extinct if it has not been found in the wild for the past 50 years. The rate of extinction has increased over the past 300 years by human interference. Some species are becoming extinct 1,000 times faster than they did before people started to inhabit the Earth.

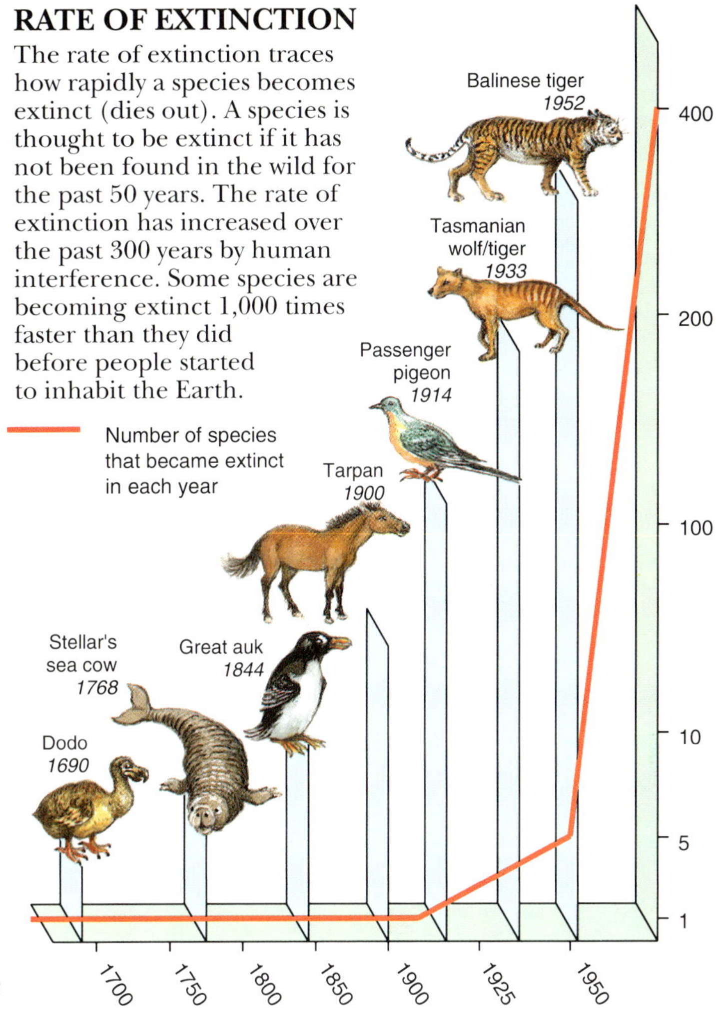

MIGRATION ROUTES

At certain times of the year, some animals travel from one area to another. This is known as migration. The average distances travelled are shown in the box below.

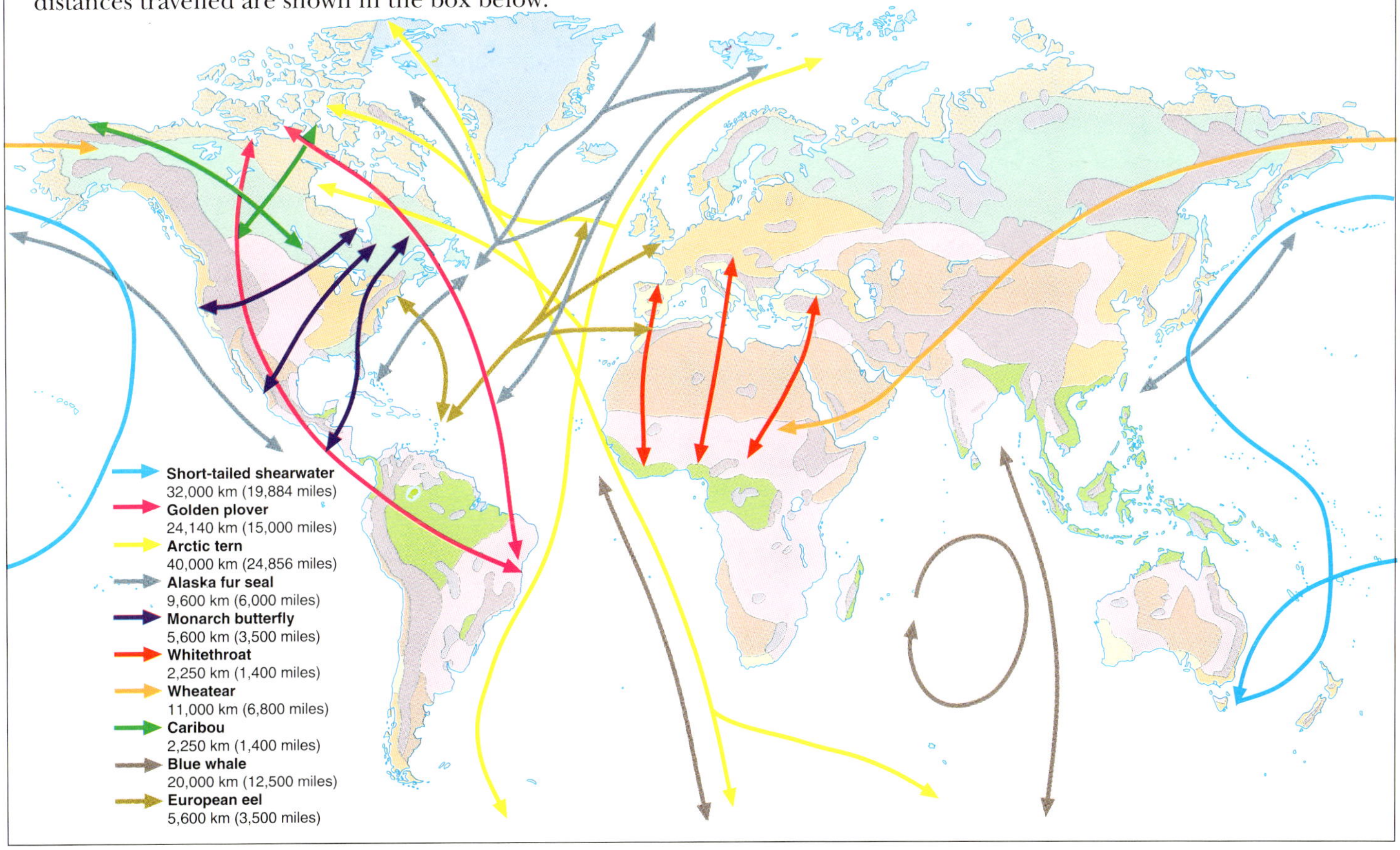

GLOSSARY

Words in *italic* have their own entry in the glossary.

A

aa Volcanic lava with a rough surface.
absolute magnitude A measure of the actual *luminosity* of a star. (Compare to *apparent magnitude.*)
absolute scale A scale of temperature, also known as the Kelvin scale, that begins at *absolute zero.* Its unit of measurement is the kelvin.
absolute zero The lowest possible temperature – 0 °K or -273.15 °C (-459.67 °F)
acceleration The rate of change of *velocity.*
acid A compound containing hydrogen which splits up in water to give hydrogen *ions.*
acid rain Rain that has become acid due to water in the air reacting with acids from power stations and car exhausts. When acid rain falls it can damage plants and erode buildings.
acoustics 1. The study of sound. 2. How sound travels around a room — a concert hall, for example, must have good acoustics.
activation energy The energy needed to start a chemical *reaction.* A different amount is needed for every reaction.
adaptation The way in which a plant or animal changes over many generations to survive better in a particular *environment.*
additive Any substance added in small amounts, especially to food or drink, to improve it, e.g. to change colour or taste.
adhesion The force of attraction between the *atoms* or molecules of two different substances.
adhesive A sticky substance, such as paste or glue, used to join two surfaces together.
ADP Adenosine diphosphate. A *compound* formed when *ATP* releases energy.
advection fog or **sea fog** A type of fog that forms where warm moist air moves over a colder surface.
aerobic respiration A type of *respiration* that needs oxygen.
aerofoil The special shape of an aircraft wing – more curved on the top than the bottom. It produces *lift* as it moves through the air.
aestivation The deep sleep or immobility that some animals go into when the weather is very hot and dry.
air resistance The force that resists the movement of an object through the air.
albedo How much an object, especially a planet or moon, reflects the light that hits it, i.e. its reflecting power.
alchemy A medieval science that tried, among other things, to find a way of changing metals such as lead into gold.
algae (singular **alga**) Simple plants found in water. They are non-flowering and do not have proper stems or roots.
aliphatic compound An organic compound made up of chains, not rings, of carbon *atoms.*
alkali A *base* that dissolves in water.
alkaline Describes a solution with a *pH* greater than 7.

allotropes Different forms of the same *element,* e.g. diamond and graphite are allotropes of carbon.
alloy A mixture of two or more metals, or of a metal and a non-metal.
alternating current (AC) An electric current whose direction reverses at regular intervals. (Compare to *direct current.*)
alternator An electric *generator* that produces *alternating current.*
alveoli (singular **alveolus**) Tiny air sacs in the lungs.
AM Amplitude modulation. The transmission of a signal by changing the *amplitude* of the carrier wave.
amalgam An *alloy* of mercury and another metal, such as tin.
ammeter An instrument that measures electric current.
amp (ampère) The unit that measures electric current.
amplitude The size of a *vibration,* or the height of a wave, such as a sound wave.
anabolism A series of chemical *reactions* in living things that builds up large *molecules* from small ones.
anaerobic respiration A type of *respiration* that does not require oxygen. It produces less energy than *aerobic respiration.*
analogue Representing a quantity by a varying electrical voltage. (Compare to *digital.*)
andesite Fine-grained brown or greyish volcanic rock.
angle of incidence The angle a light ray makes with the perpendicular to the surface it hits.
angle of reflection The angle a reflected light ray makes with the perpendicular to the reflecting surface.
anion A negatively charged *ion.*
anode A positive *electrode.*
anodizing The process of coating a metal object with a thin protective layer of oxide by *electrolysis.*
anthracite Hard coal that burns with hardly any flame or smoke.
antibodies Proteins in the blood which protect the body by fighting foreign bodies such as bacteria and viruses.
anticyclone An area of high pressure air which often produces fine weather.
antioxidant A compound added to foods and plastics to prevent them oxidizing and so going stale or breaking down.
antiseptic Able to kill bacteria.
apparent magnitude The brightness of a star as seen from Earth. (Compare to *absolute magnitude.*)
arteries Blood vessels that carry blood from the heart to other parts of the body.
artificial selection The process by which humans change the genetic make-up of a species. (Compare to *natural selection.*)
asexual reproduction Reproduction that involves only one parent.
asteroid or **minor planet** or **planetoid**. A rocky body that circles the Sun. Most asteroids are in the **asteroid belt**, between Mars and Jupiter.
asthenosphere A soft layer of the Earth's *mantle.*
astrology The study of how the movements of the stars and planets may affect our lives.
astronaut A person trained to be a crew member in a spacecraft.
astronomy The study of the stars, planets, and other bodies in space.
atmosphere The layer of gases that surrounds a planet.
atom The smallest part of an *element* that can exist. It consists of a *nucleus* of protons and neutrons, surrounded by orbiting electrons.
atomic number The number of protons in the nucleus of an *atom.*
ATP Adenosine triphosphate. A chemical in plant and animal *cells* that stores energy.
autoclave A strong, steam-heated container used for carrying out chemical *reactions* and *sterilization* at high temperature and pressure.
autotrophic A plant that makes its own food by *photosynthesis.*
axis 1. An imaginary line around which an object rotates. 2. The line along which rock bends in a *fold.*

B

background radiation 1. Low-intensity *radiation* emitted by *radioactive* substances in and around the Earth. 2. Radiation (in the form of *microwaves*) detected in space that may have come from the *Big Bang.*
bacteriophage A *parasitic* virus that lives on a bacterium.
bacterium (plural **bacteria**) A micro-*organism* that is a single *cell.*
barchan (say bar-can) A sand dune with a crest.
basalt A dark volcanic rock.
base A compound that reacts with an *acid* to give water and a *salt.*
batholith A dome of *igneous rock* that solidifies in a huge underground mass.
battery A series of two or more electrical *cells* which produce and store electricity.
Beaufort scale A scale used to measure wind speed, ranging from 0 to 12 (calm to *hurricane* force)
Big Bang The theory that the Universe began with a massive explosion of matter. It is thought that everything in the Universe is still moving apart because of the explosion.
binary system A number system with only two digits, 0 and 1.
binocular vision The ability of some animals to see objects in three dimensions and so judge distance.

binomial system A system of giving an *organism* two names. The first is the genus and the second the species.
biodegradable A substance that can *decompose* and become harmless naturally.
biogas A gas made when plant or animal waste rots down without the presence of air.
biogenic Produced by *organisms.*
biology The study of living things.
biomass 1. The total number of living *organisms* in a given area. 2. Plant material used as a source of energy, e.g. wood that is burnt to provide heat.
biome A large *ecosystem,* e.g. a tropical forest or a desert.
biosphere The region of the Earth and its *atmosphere* in which living things are found.
bituminous Containing bitumen, a tar-like substance produced from petroleum.
black dwarf The faded remains of a dead star. See also *white dwarf.*
black hole A highly dense object in space. Its gravity is so strong that it pulls in anything around it, even light, so that it looks black.
black ice Thin, hard, transparent ice, especially on the surface of a road.
blastocyst A hollow ball of *cells.*
boiling point The temperature at which a liquid becomes a gas.
bond The attraction between *atoms* or *ions* which holds them together in a *crystal* or *molecule.*
bone Hard tissue that is part of an animal's *skeleton.*
brine A strong *solution* of *salt* in water.
Brownian motion The random movement of tiny particles in a liquid or a gas, caused by *molecules* colliding with them.
buffer 1. A *solution* that is resistant to changes in *pH.* 2. An electric circuit used to join two other circuits.

C

CAD Computer-aided design.
caecum (say ky-kum) A pouch in an animal's intestines where plant food is digested.
calorie A unit of energy. The calorie used in food science is in fact a kilocalorie =1,000 calories.
camouflage The colour, markings, or body shape that helps to hide an animal or plant in its surroundings.
capacitance The ability to store electric charge.
capacitor A device used to store electric charge temporarily.
capillaries Tiny blood vessels which carry blood to and from *cells.*
capillary action The movement of a liquid up or down a tube due to attraction between its *molecules* and the molecules of the tube.
carbohydrate An energy-giving compound made up of carbon, hydrogen, and oxygen, found in foods such as potatoes.
carbon cycle The circulation of carbon (contained in carbon dioxide) from the atmosphere, through plants (by being trapped in *carbohydrates* by *photosynthesis*) and animals (which eat the plants), and back into the atmosphere (through *respiration* and *decomposition).*
carnivore A meat-eater.
cartilage Gristly connective tissue which makes up the soft parts of the skeleton and is present in some joints. The skeletons of some fish, e.g. sharks and rays, are made entirely of cartilage.
cartography The science of map-making.
cast A hollow in a rock, formed around a since decomposed animal or plant. The cast is a mould in which minerals collect and solidify to form a *fossil.*
catabolism A series of chemical *reactions* in living things that breaks down large *molecules* into small ones. This releases energy.
catalyst A chemical that speeds up a chemical *reaction* without being changed itself at the end of the reaction.
catalytic converter A device in a car that uses a *catalyst* to change toxic exhaust gases into less harmful gases.
cathode A negative *electrode.*
cation A positively charged *ion.*
cavitation The enlarging of cracks in rock by *compressed* air.
celestial body A natural object in space, such as a planet or star.
celestial pole One of two points in the *celestial sphere* about which stars appear to revolve when seen from Earth.
celestial sphere The imaginary sphere in which the stars seem to lie when seen from Earth.
cell 1. The smallest unit of an *organism* that can exist on its own. 2. (Voltaic) cell A device which produces electricity by chemical change.
cell division The process where one *cell* splits to produce two cells, called **daughter cells.**
cellulose A *carbohydrate* that forms the walls of plant *cells.*
centrifugal force (or **centrifugal effect**) The force that appears to push outwards on a body moving in a circle.
centrifuge A device used to separate substances of different densities, by spinning them round at high speed.
centripetal force The force that pulls inwards to keep an object moving in a circle.
Cepheid (say see-fee-id) **star** A type of star that has a cycle of varying brightness.
ceramics Objects made of clay or porcelain fired in a kiln.
cerebellum The part of the brain at the back of the skull that controls muscle movement and balance.
cerebrum The main part of the brain in the top of the skull that processes information.
cermet A material made from *ceramic* and *metal.* Cermets can withstand very high temperatures.
CERN Conseil Européen pour Recherches Nucléaires. The research centre of the European Organization for Nuclear Research in Geneva.
CFC Chlorofluorocarbon. Gases, which if allowed to escape into the atmosphere, e.g. from refrigerators and aerosols, will cause holes in the *ozone* layer.
chain reaction A reaction which continues on its own, e.g. a *nuclear reaction* in which neutrons from the splitting of one atom go on to split other atoms.
chemical bond See *bond.*
chemical Any substance that can change when joined or mixed with another substance.
chemistry The study of matter.
chlorophyll The green *pigment* found in many plants which absorbs light to provide the energy for *photosynthesis.*
chloroplasts Tiny bodies in some plant cells which contain *chlorophyll.*
chromatography A method of separating a mixture by running it through a medium e.g. filter paper. Different parts of the mixture move through the medium at different speeds.
chromosome A structure made up of *genes,* which carries the genetic information in a *cell.* Chromosomes are arranged in pairs in the *nucleus* of a cell.
chromosphere A layer of gases in the Sun's atmosphere that shines red.
cilia (singular **cilium**) Tiny "hairs" on the surface of many small *organisms.*
circuit A path around which an electric current can flow.
climate The normal weather conditions in an area over a long period of time.
clone Two or more identical *organisms* that share exactly the same *genes.*
cohesion The force of attraction between two particles of the same substance.
coke A fuel made by baking coal. It is mostly carbon and gives off much more heat than coal.
colloid A mixture made up of tiny particles of one substance dispersed in another in which it does not dissolve.
colony A large group of the same species of *organism* that live together.
coma A cloud of gas and dust that surrounds the centre of a *comet.*
combustion (or **burning**) A chemical *reaction* in which a substance combines with oxygen, producing heat energy.
comet A ball of frozen gas and dust that travels around the Sun. Some of the dust streams out from the comet to make a "tail".
commensalism Where two or more *organisms* live together, and neither causes harm to the other.
community A group of people or animals who live in the same place.
commutator A device which reverses the direction of an electric current.
compound A substance containing *atoms* of two or more *elements.*
compression 1. Being pressed together or bunched up (e.g. the crest of a sound wave). 2. The increase in *density* of a *fluid* .
concave lens A lens that curves inwards.
concentration A measure of the strength of a solution, ie the amount of *solute* dissolved in a certain amount of *solvent.*
condensation The change of a gas or vapour into a liquid.
conduction The movement of heat or electricity through a substance.
conductor A substance through which heat or electric current flows easily.
cones Light-sensitive *cells* in the retina of the eye that enable us to see colours.
constellation A pattern made by a number of stars when seen from Earth.
convection The transfer of heat through a *fluid* by currents within the fluid.

converging lens See *convex lens.*
convergent evolution The way in which different species *evolve* similar features because they are subjected to similar *environmental* conditions.
convex lens A lens that curves outwards.
coprolites Fossilised dung.
corona The outer layer of hot gases surrounding the Sun.
corrasion The wearing away of a surface by the action of rocks carried in ice or water.
corrosion Chemical attack of the surface of a metal.
cosmology The study of the structure and origin of the Universe.
cotyledon A simple leaf which forms part of a developing plant. Also called a seed-leaf.
covalent bond A chemical *bond* formed by *atoms* sharing one or more electrons.
CPU Central processing unit. The "brain" of a computer.
cracking The process of splitting larger *molecules* into smaller ones by heating under pressure.
cross-fertilization *Fertilization* of a plant with *gametes* from another species of plant.
crust The rocky outer surface of the Earth.
crystal A solid substance with a regular shape.
crystal lattice The repeating pattern of *atoms* or *ions* that forms a crystal.
crystallogram A pattern formed on a photographic plate by passing a beam of X-rays through a *crystal.*
cyclone Another name for a *hurricane* especially over the Indian Ocean.
cytoplasm The contents of a *cell,* except the *nucleus.*

D

decant To separate a mixture of a solid and a liquid by allowing the solid to settle and pouring off the liquid.
decibel A unit used to measure the loudness of a sound.
decomposer A tiny *organism,* such as a *bacterium,* which breaks down dead matter.
decomposition 1. *Organic* decay.
2. Breaking larger *molecules* into smaller ones.
density The *mass* per unit volume of a substance.
depression An area of low air pressure, which often brings bad weather.
dermis The thick layer of tissue in the skin below the *epidermis.*
desalination The removal of salt from sea water.
desertification The formation of a desert.
desiccate Dry out a substance by removing water from it.
desiccator A sealed container used to desiccate and keep substances dry.
detector The circuit in a radio receiver that separates a sound signal from a radio wave.
detergent A substance which, when added to water, helps the water to remove grease and oil.
dicotyledon A flowering plant with two *cotyledons.*
diffraction The spreading out of waves, e.g. light waves, when they pass through a narrow slit.
diffusion The mixing of two or more different substances because of the random movement of the molecules.
digestion The breaking down of food in the stomach into simple *molecules* which can pass into the bloodstream.
digital Representing a quantity by electrical signals which are either on or off. (Compare to *analogue.*)
diode An electronic component that lets electricity flow in one direction only.
diploid cell A *cell* with two complete sets of *chromosomes.*
direct current (DC) An electric current that flows in one direction only. (Compare to *alternating current.*)
discharge The release or conversion of stored energy.
displacement A chemical reaction in which one kind of *atom* or *ion* in a *molecule* is replaced by another.
distillation A process in which a liquid is boiled and then *condensed.* It is used to separate mixtures of liquids or purify liquids.
DNA Deoxyribonucleic acid. The chemical which makes up *chromosomes* and is present in all *cells.* DNA can replicate itself to transmit genetic information from parent to offspring.
doldrums Area along the Equator where the *trade winds* meet and form an area of very little wind.
drag The force that slows down an object as it travels through a liquid or gas.
drought A long period with no rain.
dye A substance which colours a material.
dynamo A *generator* that produces *direct current.*

E

Easterlies Major winds which blow from the east.
echo When a sound is heard again because it reflects off a solid object.
eclipse The shadow caused by a body blocking the light from another. See *lunar eclipse* and *solar eclipse.*
ecology The study of the relationships between *organisms* and their *environment.*
ecosystem A distinct area in the *biosphere* which contains living things, e.g. a lake or a forest
effort A force applied to move a load.
elasticity The ability of a material to stretch and then return to its original shape.
electrode A piece of metal or carbon that collects or releases *electrons* in an electric circuit.
electric current The flow of *electrons* or *ions.*
electrolysis Chemical change in an *electrolyte* caused by an electric current flowing through it.
electrolyte A substance that conducts electricity when molten or in *solution.*
electromagnetic spectrum The complete range of electromagnetic radiation – *gamma rays, X-rays, ultraviolet radiation,* visible light, *infrared radiation, microwaves,* and radio waves.
electromotive force (e.m.f.) The *potential difference* of a *battery* or cell. It pushes an electric current around a circuit.
electron A particle with a negative electrical charge outside the *nucleus* in all *atoms.*
electron gun A device which produces a stream of *electrons,* called a cathode ray, for use in a television, for example.
electron micrograph A magnified image of an object made by an *electron microscope.*
electron microscope A *microscope* that uses a beam of *electrons* to produce a magnified image of an object.
electrophoresis The separation of charged particles in a mixture.
electroplating The coating of a metal object with a thin layer of another metal by *electrolysis.*
electroscope An instrument that detects electric charge.
electrostatic field The field of force surrounding an electrically charged object.
element A substance which cannot be broken down into more simple substances by chemical *reactions.*
emulsifier A substance used to make *immiscible* liquids blend.
emulsion Tiny particles of one liquid dispersed in another liquid.
endoplasmic reticulum (ER) A system of *membranes* in a *cell* on which chemical *reactions* take place.
endoscope An instrument used to examine the inside of the body.
endoskeleton The internal skeleton of *vertebrates.*
endosperm The tissue in a seed that stores food.
endothermic reaction A chemical *reaction* during which heat is absorbed from the surroundings.
energy The capacity to do *work.*
environment The surroundings of an animal or plant.
enzyme A *catalyst* in living things that increases the speed of reaction in natural chemical processes.
epidermis The outer layer of the skin.
Equator An imaginary circle around the middle of the Earth, midway between the Noth and South Poles.
equilibrium A state of physical or chemical balance.
erosion The wearing away of the Earth's surface due to the effects of weather, water, or ice.
erythrocytes Red blood *cells.*
escape velocity The minimum speed that a space rocket must reach to escape the Earth's gravity.
eukaryotic cell A cell with a nucleus. (Compare to *prokaryotic cell.*)
eutrophication Where an excess of nutrients, from fertilizers for example, gets into water, causing the overgrowth of aquatic plants. This creates a shortage of oxygen in the water, killing animal life.
evaporation The changing of a liquid into a vapour by the escape of *molecules* from its surface.
evolution The gradual process by which life develops and changes.
evolve To undergo evolution.
excretion The elimination of waste by *organisms.*
exosphere The outermost part of the Earth's *atmosphere,* about 900 km (560 miles) above the surface of the Earth.

exoskeleton The hard outer "skin" of many *invertebrates*, such as insects.
exothermic A chemical *reaction* which produces heat.
extinction The death of all the members of a species.

F

fault A break in the Earth's *crust*.
fermentation The process in which yeast converts sugars in plant material to alcohol and carbon dioxide.
fertilization The joining of male and female *gametes*.
fibre An elongated, thick-walled plant *cell*.
filter A device that removes the solid material from a liquid.
fluid A substance which can flow, i.e. either a gas, a vapour, or a liquid.
fluorescence Light given off by certain *atoms* when they are hit by *ultraviolet radiation*.
FM Frequency modulation. The transmission of a signal by changing the *frequency* of the carrier wave, such as a radio wave.
fold A bend in rock layers.
food chain A series of *organisms*, each of which is eaten by the next.
food web The system of *food chains* in an *ecosystem*.
force Something which changes the movement or shape of an object.
force field The area in which a force can be felt.
formula (plural **formulae**) A set of chemical symbols which shows the make-up of a chemical.
fossil The remains of an animal or plant turned to stone.
fossil fuel A fuel which has been formed over millions of years from the remains of living things, e.g. coal and oil.
Fraunhofer lines Dark lines on the Sun's *spectrum* caused by elements in the Sun's gases absorbing certain wavelengths of light.
freezing point The temperature at which a substance turns from liquid to solid.
frequency The number of waves that pass a point every second.
friction A force which slows down or stops the movement of one surface against another.
front The first part of an advancing mass of cold or warm air.
fuse A safety device used in electrical circuits. It is a thin wire which melts if too much current passes through it.

G

Gaia (Say guy-a) **hypothesis** The theory that all the living things on the Earth form a huge "*organism*" which controls the *biosphere*.
galaxy A large group of stars, dust, and gas, all loosely held together by gravity. Our galaxy is called the Milky Way.
galvanize To coat iron with zinc to protect it from rust.
gamete A reproductive *cell*, such as a sperm or egg.
gamma rays A type of *electromagnetic radiation* with a very short *wavelength*.
ganglion (plural **ganglia**) A group of nerve *cells* enclosed in a casing of connective tissue.
Geiger counter An instrument used to detect and measure certain forms of *radiation*.
gene Part of the *chromosome* which controls a particular characteristic of an individual.
generator A device which converts mechanical energy into electricity.
geochemistry The study of the chemistry and composition of the Earth.
geomorphology The study of the physical features on the Earth's surface.
geothermal energy Energy harnessed from the hot rocks inside the Earth.
germination The early stages in the growth of a seed.
gland An organ or group of *cells* which produces substances used by the body.
global warming The heating of the Earth's atmosphere caused by the *greenhouse effect*.
gluons Particles within protons and neutrons that hold *quarks* together.
gravity The force of attraction between any two masses. It is what attracts all objects towards the Earth, giving them *weight*.
greenhouse effect The way in which certain gases in the Earth's *atmosphere*, especially carbon dioxide, trap heat. The build up of these gases leads to *global warming*.
grike An enlarged crack in limestone produced as the rock gradually dissolves in rainwater.
groynes Low walls or fences built along the seashore to prevent coastal *erosion*.
guttation The loss of water from the surface of a plant as liquid rather than vapour.
gyroscope A fast-spinning wheel whose axis stays pointing in the same direction, once it is spinning. A gyrocompass is used in the navigation of ships and aircraft.

H

habitat The natural home of an animal or plant.
haemoglobin A compound in red blood *cells* which carries oxygen around the body.
haploid cell A cell with a single set of *chromosomes*.
hard water Water which contains calcium and magnesium salts.
hardware The mechanical and electronic parts of a computer.
hemisphere One half of a sphere. The Earth is divided into the Northern and Southern Hemisphere by the *Equator*.
herbivore A plant-eating animal.
Hertz (Hz) The unit of *frequency*. One Hertz is one cycle per second.
hibernation The deep sleep or period of inactivity that some animals go into during the winter.
holography A method of producing a three-dimensional image of an object on a flat surface, using a split beam of *laser* light.
homeostasis The way an animal keeps it internal environment (temperature, blood pressure, etc.) stable.
hominid Any member of the primate family Hominidae, including humans.
hormones Chemical "messengers" which move around in the blood stream and control the functions of the body.
humidity The amount of water vapour in the air.
hurricane A huge, circular tropical storm in which there are wind speeds of 120 km/h (75 mph) or more.
hydraulic Describes a machine that operates by transferring pressure through a liquid.
hydrocarbon A chemical compound made up of hydrogen and carbon only.
hydroelectricity The generation of electricity by harnessing the energy in flowing water.
hydrometer An instrument used to measure the *density* of a liquid.
hyphae (say hi-fee) (singular **hypha**) Tiny threads that form the main body of a fungus.

I

igneous rock Rock formed when molten *magma* cools and solidifies.
immiscible Describes two liquids which do not blend together, e.g. water and oil.
indicator A substance which shows the *pH* of a *solution* by its colour.
induction The production of an electric current by a changing *magnetic field*.
industrial plant The land, buildings, and machinery used to carry out an industrial process.
inertia The tendency of an object to remain at rest or keep moving in a straight line until a force acts on it.
infrared radiation (IR) The type of electromagnetic *radiation* produced by hot objects.
inhibitor A substance that slows down a chemical *reaction*.
inorganic Not created by natural growth. (Compare to *organic*.)
inorganic chemistry The branch of chemistry which deals with chemicals except those that contain carbon. (Compare to *organic chemistry*.)
input Information fed into a computer.
insulator A material that reduces or stops the flow of heat, electricity, or sound.
integrated circuit A tiny electric circuit made of components built into the surface of a silicon chip.
interference The disturbance of signals caused where two or more waves meet.
interglacial The period of warmer weather between two ice ages.
internal reflection The reflection of some of the light in a ray that passes from a *dense* to a less dense medium, e.g. from glass to air.
invertebrate An animal with no backbone.
inverter A device used to convert *direct current* into *alternating current*.
ion An *atom* or group of atoms that has lost or gained one or more electrons to become electrically charged.
ionic bond A chemical *bond* made when one or more electrons are passed from one atom to another, forming two ions of opposite charge which attract each other.
ionosphere The part of the atmosphere, from 50-400 km (30-250 miles) above the Earth's surface, that reflects radio waves.

irradiation The use of *radiation* to preserve food.
isobar A line on a weather map which connects points with the same air pressure.
isomers Compounds which contain the same *atoms*, but in different arrangements.
isoseism A line on a map connecting places with equal strengths of earthquake shock.
isotopes *Atoms* of the same element which have the same number of protons, but a different number of neutrons.

J

jet propulsion The pushing forward of a machine by a stream of *fluid*.
jet stream Strong winds that circle the Earth about 10 km (6 miles) above the surface.
joule (J) A unit of energy.

K

Kelvin scale See *absolute scale*.
keratin A *protein* which makes up hair, horns, hoofs, nails, and feathers.
kinetic energy The energy which an object has because of its movement.

L

laccolith A mass of *igneous rock* which pushes the rock above into a dome shape.
lactose A sugar that occurs in milk.
larva (plural **larvae**) The second stage in the life of an insect, between the egg and the adult (e.g. a caterpillar).
laser Light Amplification by the Stimulated Emission of Radiation. A device that emits an intense beam of light.
latent heat The heat needed to change a solid to a liquid or a liquid to a gas without a change of temperature.
latitude A measure of distance from the Equator (the Poles are at 90° latitude and the Equator is at 0°). **Lines of latitude** are imaginary lines drawn around the Earth, parallel with the Equator.
LDR Light-dependent resistor. A *resistor* whose *resistance* increases when the amount of light which hits it increases.
leaching The extraction of a soluble material from a mixture by passing a *solvent* through the mixture.
LED Light-emitting diode. A *diode* which emits light when a current flows through it.
leucocytes White blood cells.
lift The upward force produced by an aircraft's wings which keeps it in the air.
ligaments Short bands of flexible tissue which connect bones together in joints.
light year The distance travelled by light in a year. It is equal to 9.5 million, million km (5.9 million, million miles).
lignin A *polymer* in the walls of the *cells* of trees and shrubs. It makes the plant woody.
lithosphere The layer of the Earth that includes the *crust* and the upper *mantle*.
longitude A measure of distance around the Earth, measured in degrees. **Lines of longitude** are imaginary lines drawn on the Earth's surface between the Poles.
longitudinal wave A wave in which the particles of the medium vibrate in the direction in which the wave is travelling.
luminosity The amount of light given out by an object, such as a star.
lunar eclipse When the moon moves into the Earth's shadow so that it cannot be seen from Earth.
lymphocytes White blood *cells* which fight disease.
lymphatic system A network of tubes and small *organs* which carries a fluid called **lymph** from the body's cells into the bloodstream.

M

magma Liquid molten rock in the Earth's *mantle* and *crust*. It cools to form igneous rock.
magnetic field The area around a magnet in which its effects are felt.
magnetic poles The two points on a magnet where magnetic effect is strongest.
magnetism The invisible force of attraction or repulsion between some substances, especially iron.
magnetosphere The *magnetic field* around a star or planet.
manned manoeuvring unit (MMU) A backpack used by astronauts to move about in space.
mantle A thick, *dense* layer of rock under the Earth's *crust*.
mass The amount of matter in an object.
matter Anything that has *mass* and occupies space.
meiosis *Cell* division which produces four *gametes*, each of which has half the number of *chromosomes* as the original cell.
melanin A brown *pigment* found in the skin, hair, and eyes.
melting point The temperature at which a solid turns to a liquid.
membrane A thin skin.
meniscus The curved upper surface of a liquid in a thin tube.
Mercalli scale The scale used to measure an earthquake's intensity.
mesopause The part of the *atmosphere* about 80 km (50 miles) above the Earth's surface. It is the upper limit of the *mesosphere*.
mesosphere The part of the *atmosphere* from about 50-80 km (30-50 miles) above the Earth's surface.
metal Any of several elements that are usually shiny solids and good *conductors* of electricity and heat.
metallic bond A *bond* formed between metal *atoms*. The metal's electrons flow freely around the atoms.
metamorphic rock Rock that has been changed by great heat and pressure underground.
metamorphosis A change of form, e.g. from a caterpillar to a *pupa*.
meteor A tiny piece of dust from space, which burns up as it enters the Earth's *atmosphere*, producing a streak of light.
meteorite A piece of rock or metal from space which enters the Earth's *atmosphere* and reaches the ground without burning up.
meteorology The study of the weather.
microclimate The particular climate of a small area, e.g. a valley.
micrograph A photograph taken using a microscope.
microorganism A tiny *organism* which can be seen only with the aid of a *microscope*.
microscope An instrument that enlarges the image of an object through a system of lenses.
microwave A type of electromagnetic *radiation*. Microwaves are very short radio waves.
migration The movement of some animals to find food, warmth, space, or a place to breed.
mimicry Where a species of plant or animal *evolves* to look like another.
mineral A naturally occurring substance not formed from plant or animal material, e.g. rock and metal.
mineralogy The study of minerals.
mirage An optical illusion produced by light bending through layers of air with different *densities*.
miscible Describes two or more liquids which can be blended together.
mitochondrion (plural **mitochondria**) An *organelle* that produces energy for a cell.
mitosis *Cell* division where the *nucleus* divides to produce two cells, each with the same number of *chromosomes* as the parent cell.
mixture A substance which contains two or more *elements* or compounds which are not combined chemically.
modulation The transmission of a signal by changing the characteristics of a radio wave (called the carrier wave).
mole The amount of a substance that contains the same number of *atoms* or *molecules* as there are in 12 g (0.4 oz) of carbon-12.
molecule The smallest unit of an *element* or *compound*. A molecule is made up of at least two *atoms*.
momentum The tendency of a moving object to keep on moving until a force stops it. See also *inertia*.
monocotyledon A flowering plant with a single *cotyledon*. See also *dicotyledon*.
monomer A *molecule* that is the building block of a *polymer*.
monsoon A strong wind that changes direction according to the season, bringing torrential rain from the sea to areas such as India and Bangladesh.
moon A small body that *orbits* a planet.
moraine Rocks and debris that have been deposited by a glacier.
mordant dyes *Dyes* that need another chemical to be added to fix them to a fabric.
mouse A hand-held device that is used to control a cursor on a computer monitor.
mutation A random change in the *chromosomes* of a cell.
myelin A fatty material found around nerve fibres.
myofibril Stretchy threads found in muscle cells.

N

natural selection The process by which the characteristics that help a *species* to survive are passed on to the next generation.
nebula (plural **nebulae**) A cloud of dust and gas in space.
nectar A sugary liquid found in the flowers of some plants.

nematocyst A long, coiled thread which shoots out of a stinging *cell*, e.g. in a sea anemone.
nerve Part of a network of tiny "cables" that pass messages from the body to the brain and from the brain to the muscles.
neuron A nerve *cell*.
neutralize Make an acid or alkali into a neutral solution, i.e. make it neither acid nor alkaline.
neutron A particle in the *nucleus* of an atom which has no electrical charge.
newton (N) A unit of force.
niche (say neesh) The position that a living thing occupies in an *ecosystem*.
nocturnal An animal which is active at night and sleeps during the day.
nuclear fission A *nuclear reaction* in which the *nucleus* of an atom splits into two smaller nuclei, releasing energy.
nuclear fusion A *nuclear reaction* in which the nuclei of light atoms (e.g. hydrogen) fuse to form a heavier nucleus, releasing energy.
nuclear reaction A change in the *nucleus* of an atom.
nucleolus A small, dense, round body inside the *nucleus* of a cell.
nucleus 1. The central part of an atom, made up of protons and neutrons. 2. A body found in most plant and animal *cells* that contains the genetic material of the cell.
nutrients Substances in food which are used by plants and animals for growth.

O

observatory A building from which astronomers study space.
occlusion Where a cold *front* catches up with a warm front.
ohm (Ω) A unit of electrical *resistance*.
okta scale A scale for measuring cloud cover. One okta equals one-eighth cloud cover.
omnivore An animal that eats both plants and animals.
opaque Does not let light through.
optical fibres Thin glass fibres along which light travels. They are used in communications.
orbit The path of one body, such as a planet or satellite, around another body, such as a star or planet.
ore A naturally occurring rock from which metals can be extracted.
organ A self-contained part of an organism with a special function, e.g. the brain and the heart.
organelle Specialized structure that forms part of a plant or animal cell.
organic 1. A compound containing carbon. 2. Food production without the use of chemical fertilizers.
organism A living thing consisting of one or more *cells*.
oscillator An instrument that produces an *alternating current* of known *frequency*.
oscilloscope An instrument that shows electrical signals on a screen.
osmosis The movement of water through a semi-permeable *membrane* from a weak *solution* to a strong one.
ossify Turn to bone.
output Information from a computer.
oxidation When a substance gains oxygen or loses hydrogen, or an atom loses electrons in a chemical *reaction*.
oxide A *compound* formed between an element and oxygen.
oxidizing agent A substance that causes the *oxidation* of another substance.
ozone An *allotrope* of oxygen found in the Earth's upper *atmosphere*, where it forms the ozone layer. A *molecule* of ozone contains three oxygen *atoms*.

P

parabolic dish A specially shaped dish that collects and concentrates waves, such as sound or *electromagnetic* waves.
parallax The apparent movement of objects against each other as the observer moves, e.g. the movement of nearby trees against background hills.
parasite An *organism* that lives on and feeds off another organism, called the host, often until it destroys the host.
particle A tiny speck of *matter*.
parthenogenesis Reproduction without mating.
pasteurization The heating of food to destroy disease-carrying bacteria.
payload The equipment, e.g. a satellite, carried into space by a spacecraft.
penumbra A partial shadow, especially round the shadow of the moon or Earth in an *eclipse*.
periodic table A table of all the elements arranged in order of their *atomic numbers*.
pesticide A substance used to kill pests such as insects.
petrochemical Any chemical made from petroleum or natural gas.
petrology The study of rocks.
pH A measure of acidity or alkalinity of a *solution*.
phases 1. The changes in the apparent shape of a moon or planet caused by the reflection of sunlight. 2. The three states in which matter occurs – solid, liquid, and gas or vapour.
pheromones Chemical substances released by an animal to communicate with another by smell.
phloem Tissue that carries food in a plant.
photocell An electronic device which generates electricity when light falls on it, e.g. in a solar-powered calculator.
photochromic The ability of an object, e.g. a spectacle lens, to darken or change colour when exposed to light, and to return to its original colour when the light is removed.
photoelectric effect The emission of *electrons* from the surfaces of some substances when light hits them.
photon The particle which makes up light and other *electromagnetic radiation*.
photosphere The visible surface of the Sun, which gives out almost all of its light.
photosynthesis The method by which plants make food from water and carbon dioxide using energy from the Sun.
physics The science of the properties and nature of *matter* and the interactions of energy and matter.
physiology The study of how *organisms* work.
phytoplankton Tiny plants which are part of *plankton*.
piezoelectric effect The production of electricity by applying stress to certain *crystals*, e.g. quartz.
pigment A substance that gives colour to a material, but unlike a *dye*, does not dissolve in it.
pitch The property of a sound that makes it high or low.
placebo (say plas-see-bo) An inactive substance given to a patient to compare its effects with a real drug.
planet A large body that *orbits* a star.
plankton Tiny plants and animals which live near the surface of the seas and inland waters.
plant Any *organism* that contains *chlorophyll*.
plaque (say plark) A deposit on teeth where bacteria thrive.
plasma 1. The liquid part of the blood. 2. A hot, electrically charged gas, in which the *electrons* are free from their atoms.
platelet An irregular-shaped disc in the blood which releases chemicals to coagulate the blood.
plate tectonics The study of continental drift and the spreading of the sea floor.
polar reversal The reversal of the direction of the Earth's *magnetic field*.
pollution Substances, such as waste chemicals from factories, that dirty or poison the air, land, and water.
polymer An *organic* compound that has very long molecules, made up from many *monomers*.
potential difference The difference in energy between two places in an electric field or circuit.
potential energy 1. Energy stored for use at a later time. 2. The stored energy that a body has because of its position or state.
power The rate of change of energy.
precipitate Tiny particles of solid in a liquid, made by a chemical *reaction*.
precipitation Rain, snow, sleet, or hail.
predator An animal which lives by hunting and eating other animals.
pressure The amount of force pushing on a given area.
prey An animal that is hunted or eaten by another animal.
prism A block of transparent material e.g. glass with a triangular cross-section.
program A series of coded instructions to operate a computer.
prokaryotic cell A cell with no *nucleus*.
prominence A mass of glowing gas reaching out from the surface of the Sun.
protein A substance found in foods such as meat, fish, cheese, and beans, which the body needs for growth and repair.
proton A particle in the *nucleus* of an atom which has a positive electric charge.
protostar A gas cloud about to turn into a star.
pulsar A *dense* star which emits regular pulses of *radiation*, usually radio waves.

Q

qualitative analysis Finding out what a substance is made of.
quantitative analysis Finding out how much of each ingredient is in a substance.

quantum theory The theory that light and other electromagnetic *radiation* is made up of a stream of photons, each carrying a certain amount of energy.
quark (say kwark) One of a group of small particles that make up *protons* and *neutrons*.
quasar (say kway-zar) The brilliant core of a young galaxy, probably a disc of hot gas around a massive *black hole*.

R

radar Radio detection and ranging. A way of detecting objects by sending out radio waves and collecting the "echoes".
radiation 1. An electromagnetic wave. 2. A stream of particles from a source of *radioactivity*. See also *electromagnetic spectrum*.
radioactive dating A method of estimating the age of an object by measuring how much the radioactive *isotopes* in it have decayed.
radioactivity The disintegration of the *nuclei* in an atom, causing *radiation* to be given off.
radiosonde A package of instruments carried into Earth's upper *atmosphere* by a weather balloon to gather meteorological information.
RAM Random access memory. Computer memory chips where information can be stored and retrieved. The information is lost when the computer is turned off.
rarefaction Areas along a longitudinal wave, such as a sound wave, where the *pressure* and *density* of the *molecules* is decreased. (Compare to *compression*.)
reactants The substances which take part in a chemical *reaction*.
reaction 1. A force that is the same in magnitude, but opposite in direction to another force. Every force has a reaction. 2. (Chemical reaction) Any change that alters the chemical properties of a substance or that forms a new substance.
reactivity The ability of a substance to take part in a chemical *reaction*.
real image An image formed where light rays focus. It can be seen on a screen. (Compare to *virtual image*.)
recycling Using waste material again, thus saving resources and energy.
red giant A star near the end of its life, which has swelled and cooled.
red shift The stretching out of light (moving it towards the red end of the *spectrum*) from a galaxy moving away from the Earth.
reducing agent A substance that causes the *reduction* of another substance.
reduction When a substance gains hydrogen or loses oxygen, or an atom gains electrons in a chemical *reaction*.
reflection The bouncing back of light, heat, or sound from a surface.
reflex An automatic reaction to something.
refraction The change of direction of a light beam as it passes from one medium to another of different *density*, e.g. from air to glass.
refractive index The ratio of the speed of light in one medium to the speed of light in a second medium when a light ray is *refracted*.
resistance A measure of how much an electrical component opposes the flow of an electric current.
resistor A component in an electric circuit that opposes the flow of electricity.
resonance When the *vibrations* of an object become large because it is being made to vibrate at its "natural" *frequency*.
resource A substance that can be used to make or do something useful. Oil and coal are natural resources.
respiration The process in which oxygen is taken in by living things and used to break down food. Carbon dioxide and energy are produced.
resultant The overall force which results from two or more forces acting on an object.
reverberation Where an echo reaches a listener before the original sound has finished. It makes a sound seem to last longer.
rheostat A *resistor* whose *resistance* can be changed.
ria (say ree-a) A long, narrow sea inlet caused by the flooding of a river valley.
ribosomes Tiny spherical bodies in the *cytoplasm* of cells, where *proteins* are made.
Richter (say rik-tur) **scale** A scale used to measure the strength of earthquakes.
robot A machine that performs jobs automatically.
ROM Read only memory. Computer memory in which information is stored permanently, so that it can be retrieved, but not altered.

S

salt 1. A compound formed from the *reaction* of an acid with a base. 2. The common name for sodium chloride.
sap The liquid that flows through a plant, carrying food and water.
saprophyte An organism, such as a fungus or bacterium, that lives on dead or decaying matter.
satellite An object which *orbits* a planet. There are natural satellites, e.g. a moon, and artificial satellites, e.g. a craft used for reflecting radio signals.
satellite dish A dish-shaped aerial which receives signals broadcast from satellites.
saturation When no more *solute* can be dissolved in a *solution*.
scalar quantity A quantity that has only magnitude, e.g. *mass* and time. (Compare to *vector quantity*.)
secretion The release of specific substances from plant and animal *cells*.
sedimentary rock Rock formed when fragments of material settle on the floor of a sea or lake in layers and are cemented together over time.
seismic wave A wave that travels through the ground, e.g. from an earthquake or explosion.
seismometer A device that records vibrations in the ground, such as those caused by earthquakes.
semiconductor A substance which has a *resistance* somewhere between that of a *conductor* and an *insulator*.
semipermeable membrane A *membrane* which lets small *molecules* through, but stops large molecules.
sessile 1. Describes animals that cannot move around, e.g. sea anemones. 2. Describes plants with no stalks e.g. algae.
sex cell See **gamete.**
sexual reproduction Reproduction that involves the combination of male and female *gametes*.
sial The *silica*- and aluminium-rich upper layer of the Earth's *crust*.
silica A white or colourless *compound* of silicon that occurs naturally, eg quartz.
sima The *silica*- and magnesium-rich lower layer of the Earth's *crust*.
skeleton The frame of bone and cartilage in *vertebrates* which supports the body and protects its *organs*.
smog A poisonous mixture of smoke and fog.
soft water Water free of dissolved calcium and magnesium salts.
software The *programs* used by a computer.
solar constant The amount of heat energy from the Sun which hits a certain area of the Earth's surface.
solar eclipse An *eclipse* in which the moon passes between the Earth and the Sun so that the Sun, or part of it, cannot be seen from Earth.
solar flare A sudden burst of *radiation* from the Sun.
solar panel An object which collects energy from the Sun and uses it to heat water, for example, or to produce electricity.
Solar System The Sun, the planets that orbit the Sun, their moons, and the other bodies in space whose movements are controlled by the Sun's gravity.
solder An *alloy* (often made of tin and lead) used to join metal surfaces together.
solenoid A coil of wire which produces a *magnetic field* when an electric current flows through it.
solubility The ability of a *solute* to be dissolved.
solute The substance which dissolves in a *solvent* to form a *solution*.
solution A mixture in which the molecules of a *solute* are mixed with the molecules of a *solvent*.
solvent The substance (usually a liquid) in which a *solute* dissolves to form a *solution*.
sonar Sound navigation and ranging. A way of detecting objects and of navigating underwater by sending out sound waves.
sonic boom The loud explosive noise made by the shockwave from an object travelling faster than the speed of sound.
space age The era of space travel.
space probe An unmanned spacecraft sent from Earth to investigate the *Solar System*.
space station A spacecraft, big enough for people to live and work on, which *orbits* the Earth.
species A group of *organisms* which look alike and can breed with one another.
spectroscope An optical instrument which divides the light given off by an object into its *spectrum*.
spectrum (plural **spectra**) A particular distribution of *wavelengths* and *frequencies*, e.g. the *electromagnetic spectrum*.
specular reflection When light bounces off a surface at exactly the same angle as that at which it hits.

spinal cord A bundle of nerves running from the brain down through the spine.
star A *celestial body* that releases energy from the *nuclear reactions* in its core.
starch A *polymer* found in plants which is an important part of the human diet.
static electricity An electric charge held on an object, caused by the gain or loss of *electrons*.
sterilization The removal of bacteria from an object.
stoma (plural **stomata**) A tiny opening in a plant's leaf or stem through which gases and water vapour pass.
stratigraphy The study of rock layers.
stratopause The boundary between the *stratosphere* and the *mesosphere* in the Earth's atmosphere.
stratosphere The part of the Earth's atmosphere between the *troposphere* and the *mesosphere*.
subatomic particle A particle smaller than an *atom*, e.g. a proton or a neutron.
sublimation When a solid turns straight from a solid into a gas without becoming a liquid first.
substance Any kind of *matter*.
succession The process of change from one *ecosystem* to another, eg from grassland to woodland.
sugars A group of soluble, sweet-tasting *carbohydrates*.
sunspot A cooler patch on the Sun's surface which appears darker than its surroundings.
superconductor A substance that has no electrical *resistance* at very low temperatures.
supernova (plural **supernovae**) The explosion of a very large star at the end of its life.
supersonic Faster than the speed of sound.
surface tension An effect that makes a liquid seem as though it has an elastic "skin". It is caused by *cohesion* between the surface molecules.
suspension A mixture of tiny particles of solid matter in a liquid.
synapse A junction of two nerve *cells*.
synthesis The building of larger *molecules* from smaller molecules or atoms.
synthesizer A musical instrument that creates sound electronically.

T

temperate Describes a climate which has mild summers and cool winters.
temperature A measure of how hot or cold something is.
terminal A connecting point on an electrical component.
thermal A current of rising hot air in the *atmosphere*.
thermistor A *resistor* whose *resistance* changes with temperature.
thermoplastic A material which can be repeatedly softened by heating and hardened by cooling.
thermoset A soft material which sets hard when heated.
thermosphere A part of the Earth's atmosphere between the *mesosphere* and the *exosphere*.
timbre The quality of a musical sound.
tissue A group of similar *cells* which carries out a function, e.g. muscle tissue.
titration A method of finding the *concentration* of a solution.
trace elements Substances, such as minerals, that are needed by living things in minute amounts.
trachea The main tube which carries air to and from the lungs.
trade winds Winds that blow steadily towards the Equator from the northeast and southeast.
transformer A device that increases or decreases *voltage*.
translocation The movement of *fluids* through a plant.
translucent Allows some light through, but is not "see-through".
transparent Allows nearly all light through, so that it is "see-through".
transpiration The loss of water from a plant by *evaporation*.
transverse wave A wave in which the particles of the medium vibrate at right angles to the direction of travel of the wave.
trophic level The level at which an animal is in a *food chain*.
tropical Describes a climate which is hot with periods of heavy rainfall.
tropopause The boundary between the *troposphere* and the *stratosphere*.
troposphere The lowest layer of the Earth's *atmosphere*, between the surface and the *stratosphere*. It is about 13 km (8 miles) thick on average.
turbine A machine which is made to rotate by a *fluid* in order to drive a *generator*.
typhoon The name given to a *hurricane* in the Pacific Ocean.

U

UHF Ultra-high-*frequency* radio waves.
ultrasound Sound with a *frequency* above that which the human ear can detect.
ultraviolet (UV) A type of electromagnetic *radiation* with a wavelength shorter than visible light.
umbra The dark central part of a shadow, where no light falls.
Universe The whole of space and everything it contains.
upthrust The upward push on an object in a *fluid*.

V

vacuole A small *fluid*-filled sac in the *cytoplasm* of a cell.

vacuum A space in which there is no *matter*.
valency The number of chemical *bonds* that an *atom* can make with another atom.
vector quantity A quantity which has both magnitude and direction, e.g. a force. (Compare to *scalar quantity*.)
veins Tubes which carry blood from all parts of the body back to the heart.
velocity Speed in a particular direction.
vertebrate An animal with a spine.
VHF Very-high-*frequency* radio waves.
vibration A quick back-and-forth movement. For example, an earthquake causes the Earth to vibrate; sound causes the air to vibrate.
virtual image An image formed where light rays appear to be focused, e.g. a reflection in a mirror. (Compare to *real image*.)
virus A microscopic particle which invades *cells* to reproduce, and often cause disease.
viscosity A measure of how easily a substance flows.
vitamin An *organic* compound found in foods which is essential for good health.
volt The unit of *potential difference*.
voltaic cell See *cell*
voltmeter or **voltammeter** A device used to measure *potential difference*.
volume 1. The space occupied by *matter*. 2. The loudness of a sound.
vulcanization The hardening of rubber by heating it with sulphur.

W

waterspout A column of water sucked up by a tornado moving over the sea.
watt (W) A unit of power (1 watt = 1 *joule* per second).
wavelength The distance between the crest of one wave and the crest of the next.
weight The force with which a *mass* is pulled towards the centre of the Earth.
Westerlies Major winds blowing from the west.
whirlwind A column of air spinning rapidly in a funnel shape over land or water.
white dwarf The small, *dense* remains of a dead star.
WMO World Meteorological Organization
work The energy transferred when a force moves an object or changes its shape.

X

X-ray A type of electromagnetic *radiation* with a *wavelength* shorter than *ultraviolet radiation*.
xylem (say zy-lem) The tissue which carries water through a plant.

Z

zeolite A natural or synthetic compound with an open structure that can act as a *catalyst* or a filter for individual *molecules*.
zeugen A ridge of hard rock formed by *erosion*.
zodiac The 12 *constellations* that are seen in the sky.
zooplankton The tiny, often microscopic, animals in the sea which form part of *plankton*.

INDEX

Page numbers in **bold** type refer to main entries. Numbers in *italics* refer to pages in the Fact Finder

D

G

N

O

P

Q

R

S

T

PICTURE SOURCES

Abbreviations: t = top; b =bottom; c = centre; l = left; r = right; a = above

Albright & Wilson 43cl
Allsport 141bl/Gray Mortimer 116br, 346bc
Ardea 124tr, 127tl, 136bl/Anthony & Elizabeth Bomford 184bl
Aspect Picture Library/Mike Wells 134tr
Associated Press 199bl
Aviation Photographers International/Jeremy Flack 48tl, 128tr

BASF 90r
BBC Radiophonic Workshop/David Darby 189tr
Biofotos/Heather Angel 341cr, 351tr, 357bl
Biofoto Associates 35cl, 198c & cr, 352bc
Biosphere Associates 348tr
BOC Ltd. 42br
Bodleian Library, Oxford 17bl
Bridgeman Art Library 14cl, 282bl, 312bc/Bodleian Library, Oxford, Ms Add.A.287.fol.78r, 31tl; British Museum, London 64tc; Christie's, London 64br; Louvre, Paris 63bc
British Alcan Aluminium plc. 87tl, 87bl
British Coal 96cl
Paul Brierley 37bc, 109tr, 191cl
British Museum/Peter Hayman 27bl, 81cl
Bruel & Kjaer 181br
Bubbles 105r/Jacqui Farrow 140br

Cambridge Botanic Gardens 140tl
Cambridge University Press, Star Atlas 2000.0 by Wil Tirion 282br
Ciba Geigy Plastics 106tc
Cleanair Transport 151br
Bruce Coleman 306tl, 316cl, 329cb, 336b/Bartlett 331cb; Stephen Bond 314crb; Jane Burton 324clb, 347bl, 356c, 363bl, 380cl; Neville Coleman 52cr; Eric Crichton clb; Gerald Cubitt 393cr, 395cl; Peter Davey 336clb; A.J.Deane 203tr; Jeff Foott 355bc, 373bl, 381bl, 387cr; CB & DW Frith 361bc; Francisco Futil 399br; J.S.Grove 331bc; Udo Hirsch 328bc; Carol Hughes 75br, 390br; Johnny Johnson 154cr; Steven C. Kaufman 397bl; Frans Lanting 399bl; Leonard Lee Rue 380cr; L.C.Marigo 334cb, 374bl; Norman Myers 374tr; C. Martin Pampaloni 373tr; Goetz D.Plage 106tl; Fritz Prenzel 335cl; Andrew Purcell 324cb; Timm Rautert 399cr; Marie Read 379tl; Hans Reinhard 342br, 381bc; Carl Roessler 325cb; Frieder Sauer 311tlc & tcr, 320tr, 257br, 343bc, 363cl; Nancy Sefton 320cra; Kim Taylor 363c, 366tr, 366c, 367cr; Michel Viard 317c; Paul R.Wilkinson 42cl; Rod Williams 389tr; Conrad Wottle 336c; J.T.Wright 336cr
Colorific!/T.Spencer 86tr; Ann Purcell 153tr; Carl Purcell 195cb
Colorsport 118t, 120cl, 141bl
Copper Development Association 86cl

Derby Museums & Art Gallery 60bl
Deutsches Museum, Munich 90tc & cl

E.T. Archive 65tl, 100br
Mary Evans Picture Library 25tl, 28bl, 30bl, 55tl, 61tl, 71b, 74bl, 81b, 86cr, 108t, 188bl, 193tr, 201bc & crb, 206cl, 295tl, 297tr, 305bl, 308cr, 324cr, 337bl, 380bl

Barry Finch Photography 89bl, 107bl & cl
Martyn Foote 130cl, 249bl, 260cl, 260br, 262cr, 262cr, 262br

Geoscience Features 30cl, 39c, 43c, 46tr, 178bc
Jane Goodall Institute 378bl
Dr. Julian Goodfellow, Birkbeck College 30bc
Greenpeace/Morgan 400cr
Derek Hall 364c
Robert Harding Picture Library 23tl, 35bl, 72cla & cl, 87br, 113t, 114br, 117bc, 122b, 179cr, 192tl, 201tl/Walter Rawlings 113cr
Courtesy of Harvard University Archives 278bl
Stuart Hildred 149br
Hitachi Scientific Instruments 15cr
Michael Holford 80r, 138tr
Holt Studios International/Nigel Cattlin 90b, 91bl; Primrose Peacock 71cr
Hulton-Deutsch Collection 32br, 47bl, 57tl, 104cr, 115tr, 121cr, 285tl, 351br, 369bl
Henry Huntington Library 276tl
Hutchison Library/Edward Parker 395cr; Philip Wolmoth 96bl

IBM Research Laboratory, Zurich 149bl
ICI Katalco 56cr
The Image Bank 48tr, 74c/Anthony A. Boccaccio 44br; Paolo Curto 52tr; Arthur D'Arazieu 43tr; Jon Davison/Stockphotos 88tr; Mel Digiacomo 199tr; Grant V. Faint 113bl, 193cl, 197; Nicholas Foster 46c; Gregory Heisler 93bl; Laurence Hughes 343tl; Don Landwehrle 177tr; David de Lossy 99bl; Leo Mason 43bl; Eric Meola 140c, 140cr; J.Ramey/Stockphotos 84tl; Co. Rentmeester 337t; Al Satterwhite 44tl; Erik Leigh Simmons 92cl; Paul Trummer 55bl; Pete Turner 103tr; Anne van der Vaeren 37c; Hans Wendler 52cl; Ernst Wrba 130br
Institute of Agricultural History & Museum of English Rural Life, University of Reading 96tr

Jet Propulsion Laboratory 294bl & crb

Kobal Collection 176tl

Frank Lane Picture Agency 322cr/David T. Grewc 367tl; Eric & David Hosking 343cr, 360bc; Steve McCutcheon 205tc, 205tr, 383bc; F.Polking 121bl; John Tinning 391bl; D.P.Wilson 386tl
London Transport Museum 124b
Lowell Observatory 289 tr & cra

Mansell Collection 290clb, 315crb, 323bc
John Marmaras/Du Pont 101bl
Memtek International 182c

NASA 56bc, 59tc, 70cl, 97bl, 177br, 277clb, 284c & tr, 286br & cl, 287cr, 288tr, c & crb, 289crb, 291c, crb, br & bc, 292cr, cb, bc & ca, 293c, clb & bl, 294cb, 298c, clb, crb & crb, 299tl, 300tr, 301cl & cr, 302tl, c, bl, & br, 303cra, cl & bl, 304tl, bl & crb
NHPA 321crb/ANT 321cr, 332clb, 333cb, 335crb br, 395tc; ANT Kelvin Aitkin 327bl; Anthony Bannister 314bc, 345tr; G.I.Bernard 21tr; Laurie Campbell 356tr; James Carmichael Jnr.325cb; Stephen Dalton 341cr, 342cl, 344bc, 356cr, 376tr; R.J.Erwin 400cl; Stephen Krasemann 398bl; Michael Leach 318bl; Tsueneo Nakamura 327cl; Peter Parks 306cr; Otto Rogge 391bc; Carl Roessler 325cb; Kevin Schafer 395bc; Philippa Scott 393tl, 341tl; John Shaw 332bl, 335br; Karl Smith 332clb; Martin Wendler 323cl
National Gallery 277cra
National Medical Slide Bank 88bl, 192tr, 204tr
Nature Photographers 370tl/Christopher Grey-Wilson 354cr; Richard Mearns 396br; Paul Sterry 350bc, 378br, 381cl, 384br

Omega 118cl
Oxford Scientific Films 19cr, 132c, 134bl, 201cl, 201bl, 305cb, 326cl, 327tr, 341tl/Doug Allan 51t; Eyal Bartov 352br; Fred Bavendam 102tr; Stuart Bebb 340tl; G.I.Bernard 308crb, 323cr; Deni Brown 78bc; Cambridge Productions Ltd. 68cr; N.M.Collins 345tl; Jal Cooke 320crb; Gilbert S.Grant 385br; Rudi Kuiter 354bl; Leonard Lee 344tl; London Scientific Films 50bl; Sean Morris 323crb; Stan Osolinski 364br; Richard Packwood 315bc; Peter Parks 327tr; Ronald Toms 366cr; Babs & Bert Wells 319crb; Kim Westerskov 151cr; David Wright 70b

Panos Pictures/Ron Gining 87cl
Photos Horticultural 342cr
Pictor International 54tl
Planet Earth Pictures 328crb, 371cr, 389bl/Sean Avery 94b; Gary Bell 387tc; Richard Coomber 351cr; Walter Deas 363cr; J.Duncan 387cb; Wayne Harris 357cl; Robert Hessler 386bl; Chris Huxley 357cr; P.Losse 347br; Richard Matthews 388bcr; Christian Petron 369bc; Mike Potts 385tr; Flip Schulke 387tl; Jonathan Scott 381tl, 393bl; Peter Stephenson 61bl; James D.Watt 185cr; Norbert Wu 353br
Popperfoto 191c
Premaphotos Wildlife/K.G.Preston-Mafham 369br

QA Photos 179tl, 181c
Quadrant Picture Library 148bc

Redferns/David Redfern 188c
Rentokil 315cr
Rex Features 47bc, 55cl & br/P.Villard 42tr, 65br
Rockwell International 111r
Roger-Viollet 107b
Rolls Royce plc. 88r
Ann Ronan at Image Select 34tr, 74bc, 96tc, 96br, 145br, 187cl, 208bc, 277crb, 287clb, 310cr
Royal Astronomical Society Library 291tl, 292cr, 296cl

St.Paul's School 364bl
Santapod Dragways 119c
Peter Saunders 113br
Scala/Biblioteca Nationale 273cl
Science Museum 194cl
Science Photo Library 37br, 48bl, 50br, 54cr, 63tl, 84tr, 102bl, 106br, 137br, 138br, 144cr, 179bl, 180tr, 192bl, 194cbr, 274crb, 282tl, 305tr, 312tr, 313c & bc, 321bc, 346bl, 349bl, 354tr, 355bl, 365cl, /Michael Abbey 339c; Doug Allan 18tr; Jodrell Bank crb; Alex Bartel 112bl; Biofoto Associates 61cr; Dr.Jeremy Burgess 29cra, 70tl, 71bc & cl, 75c, 80tl & tr, 93cl, 95ca & c, 123bl, 296bl, 315cl, 340cr; CERN 25tr; Jean-Loup Charmet 31c, 49c, 139cr, 296cra, 321clb; Dr.Ray Clark & Mervyn Goff 142tl, 192bc; CNRI 27br, 105tl, 177tl, 314bl, 346cr, 364tr; Tony Craddock 112tl; Martin Dohrn 27bc, 44tr; John Durham 311tl; Earth Satellite Corporation 44c; Bob Edwards 62tr; Ray Ellis 184cl; Fred Espenak 277tr; Dr.Brian Eyden 339; Vaughan Fleming 48tl; Simon Fraser 36br, 69b, 348bc; David Frazier 117cr; Clive Freeman, The Royal Institution 56c, 77tl; David Gayon, The BOC Group PLC 40br; Roberto de Gugliemo 43cl; John Hadfield 182br; Adam Hart-Davis 39br, 63bl, 88c, 177bl, 205c; G.J.Hills, John Innes Institute 29tl; James Holmes 14br, 81cr, 82tl/Cellmark Diagnostics 62bc/Hays International 94tl/Fulmer Research 185br; Anthony Howarth 370br; Manfred Kage 354bc,

362cl, 366tc; Richard Kirby, David Spears Ltd. 341c; Klein Associates Inc.185b; Mehan Kulyk 29cl; Laboratory for Atmospheres, NASA Goddard Space Flight Center 57cr; Martin Land 45cl; Francis Leroy, Biocosmos 348cl; Dr. A. Lesk 15crb; Charles Lightdale 196tr; R.E.Litchfield 319c; Patrice Loiez, CERN 17br; Marcos Lopez 92tr; Andrew McClenaghan 37tc; Will & Deni McIntyre 82cr; Mike McNamee 84bl; John Mead 64c; Richard Megna, Fundamental Photos 72bc; Peter Menzel 190tl, 300bc; Astrid & Hans-Frieder Michler 57tc, 79c; Moredun Animal Health Ltd.80bl, 339; Hank Morgan 14tr, 39c, 82cl, 101br, 104cl, 111bc, 145tr, 199bc; Prof. P.Motta, Dept. of Anatomy, University La Sapienza, Rome 338b, 339; G.Muller, Struers GMBH 86br; NASA 37cl, 92tl, 125bl, 277bc, 286ca & cr, 290cr & cb, 298cra, 375tl; NOAO 276cb, 295bc; NRAO/AVI 297clb; National Library of Medicine 26br, 313clb; Novosti Press Agency 302tr, 361cr; Claude Nuridsany & Marie Perennou 350c; Omikron 351bc; David Parker 31bl, 62bl, 126tr; Dr.David Patterson 45bc; Dept. of Physics, Imperial College 63c; Philippe Plailly 25tc, 199cr, 296crb, 383tcr; Max Planck Institute Fur Physik und Astrophysik 273bca; Chris Priest 181bc, 185tl; Roger Ressmeyer 195tl/Starlight 297crb; J.C.Revy 348cr; Royal Greenwich Observatory 198bl, 295clb; Royal Observatory, Edinburgh 276bl; Rev.Ronald Royer 295tr; Sandia National Laboratories 137cr; John Sanford 295bc, 297cl; Françoise Sauze 208bl & br; Science Source 75bc; Smithsonian Institute 277, 296tl; SOPEXA, Food & Wine from France 315tl; St.Mary's Hospital Medical School 315clb; Sinclair Stammers 49br, 112tr, 307tr, 321crb; Dr.Tony Stone 77cl; Survival Anglia 329crb; Andrew Syred 339; David Taylor 30cr; Sheila Terry 135br; Geoff Tompkinson 55cr, 85cl; Alexander Tsiaras 37cr; U.S. Dept. of Energy 26tr, 136tr, 306bc; U.S. Geological Survey 289bc; U.S.Library of Congress 118bl; U.S.Naval Observatory 276clb; Dr.David Wexler, coloured by Dr.Jeremy Burgess 88bc; Williams & Metcalf 112br; Dr.Arthur Winfree 54b
Shell 82b, 98br, 99tl
Courtesy of Dr.W.D.A. Smith 42bl

Frank Spooner Pictures 136br/David Gaywood 189c
Sporting Pictures(UK)Ltd 73tr, 77br, 87tr

TASS/Pushkara 303tr; V. Kozherukov 48br

Telegraph Colour Library 39cl, 74tr/ Susan Griggs Agency 65c; J. Young 142c
Topham Picture Source 137tl, 199cl, 200cl

UPI/Bettmann 298tl

Water Research Council/Water Bulletin 21b, 83b
Wildlife Matters 91cl
Trevor Wood 133bl

ZEFA 22br, 34cr, 38tr, 46tl, 66tr, 72tl, 104cb, 111tl, 139cl, 147tl, 388cb/Abril 67tr; Berssfnbr.83tr; Big Mike 376cl; W.Braun 60br; Damm 58br; W.F.Davidson 73b; W.Fuchs 394tl; Gunter Heil 187b; Kalt 50tc; Mandelstein 50tr; Orion Press 192br; Hans Schmied 372cr; Stockmarket 104c; Streichan 38c, 99tr; Ung.Werbestudio 101tr; Art Wolfe 383cr
Zinc Development Association 66br

Every effort has been made to trace the copyright holders; we apologize in advance for any unintentional omissions. We will be pleased to insert the appropriate acknowledgment in any subsequent edition of this publication.

ILLUSTRATORS

Evi Antoniou: 333 cl, c, l, 335 bl, tr, 345 cl

Lesley Alexander: 313 c, cr

Craig Austin/Garden Studios: 210 bc, c, 356 b, 357c

Rick Blakely: 20 tr, 21 bl, 26 t, 27 tr, tl, c, 34 bl, 36 cl, 37 bl, 38 cl, 39 bl, cl, 57, 65, 67 c, 68 bl, 70 c, 71 bl, 83 bl, c, 84 tl, 87 c, 93 cr, cl, 94 c, 95 tr, 97 m, 105 bl, 107 br, 109 bl, b/cl, 110 c, 111 c, 116 tr, 117 c, 121 cb, 126 cb, 127 tr, 128 ct, 131 ct, 134 cl, tl, cr, br, 137 c, 141 tl, 142 tr, cb, 143 c, cl, 144 br, ct, c, 147 ct, 178 br, 179 br, 180 cl, c, bl, 181 cl, 182 cb, 183 ct, 184 c, br, 185 l, 186 cr, 187 cr, 188 c, cl, tr, 189 br, 191 tr, 198 cb, 207 tr, 208, bl, 215 c, 226 bl, 308 bc, 310 ct, 346 cr, 367 bl, 375 b, 381 c, 408 br, 411 cl, 416 l, 424 bl

Bill Botten: 310 bl, br, 413 tr

Peter Bull: 193 cr, 195 tr, cl, 204, 205 tl, bl, 217 tr, 218 br, 219 cb, 220 bl, 229 c, 234 cb, 235 br, 250 l, 251 cl, c, 252 tl, 253 cb, bl, 254, 263 cl, 269 br, 315 cr, 316 c, bl, cr, 317 c, 319 tl, bl, 320 bl, cl, cb, 321 tl, tr, 324 c, 325 tr, 326 cr, br, 327 ct, cb, tr, 328 cr, 331 c, 332 ct, 334 c, 344 cr, br, 345 b, cr, 352, 353, 362 br, 363 c, 366 cl, 367 cr, 372 bl, 387 cb, bl, 388 bl, 389 br, 391 tr, bl, 394, 400

Lynn Chadwick/Garden Studios: 214 cb

Julia Cobbold: 268 c

Richard Coombes: 256, 349 cb, 371 cb, 375 b, 378 cb, 383 tr, 394

Luciano Corbella: 218 tl, 220 tl, 234, tl, 235 tl, 236 cb, 238 tl, 239 273 br, 275 cl, 277 cl, 283 bl, tr, 284 bl, 285 br, 286 tl, tr, 287 tl, 288 tl, cl, 289 tl, cr, 290 tl, cb, 291 tr, cr, 292 tr, 293 tl, tr, cr, 295 cr, 299 br, 304 tl, 244 br, 244-45, 264 cl, cb, 381 cr, 382 tl, 386 tl, 390 tl, 394 tl

Bill Donohoe: 209 c, 210 t, 211 t, 213 , 218 c, 228, 229 c, 231 , 264 , 265 c

Angelika Elsebach: 308 c, b, cr, 311 c, 333 bl, 336 tr, 357 tl

Eugene Fleury: 214 tl, 215, 216 br, 217 bl

Jeremy Gower: 286 t, 287 t, 289 t, 290 t, tl, 291 t, 292 t, 293 t, cb, 299 c, 300 tl, 301 bl, c, 302 cl

Taurus Graphics: 146 br, 149 cl, 152 cl, 154 br, 156 cl, 159 c, 167 ct, 171 tc, 172 bl, 174 cr, tr, 294 cb, cl, 303 b, 349 tl, 404 t, bl, 405 b

Elizabeth Gray: 380 cb, 385 bl

Mike Grey: 148 cl, bl, 150 bl, cl, 151, bl, ct, 153 ct, cl, 156 tr, 157 tr, c, bl, 155 t, cb, tl, tr, cl, c, 158 cb, 159 br, cb, 164 br, 168 tl, 169 b, 170 cb, 247 cr, tl, 250 cb, 251 cb, 262 tr, cl, 263 br, 268 tr, 279 c, br, bl, 280 cl, 282 br, 291, 292 bl, 299 bl, 301 br, 338 tr, bl, c, 339 t, 343 cl, 347 cb, 365 tr

Sheila Hadley: 318 cl, 319 rt, 325 bl, 386 br, 387 bl

Nick Hall: 180 tl, 186, 187, 226, 227

John Hutchinson: 45 cr, 405 t, 406 c, br, 408 c, tr, bl, 412 bl, tl, cr, 413 bl, 414, 415, 418 b

Nick Hewetson: 16, 19 bl, 21 tl, 31 cb, 40 bl, 41 c, 44 bl, 50 br, 52 tl, 56 tr, 65 cb, 76 bl, 77 tr, 81 bl, 102 tl, 103 tl, 104 br, 105 tr, c 110 tr, 116 cl, 117 tl, 118 tr, 119 cl, 120 t, 122 cr, 123 c, 124 tl, 125 br, 130 bl, 131 bl, 132 br tr, 133 cr, 138 c, 178 cl, 179 t, 181 tr, 182 tc, 183 tl, cr, 184 t, 185 ct, 186 c, 188 br, 189 tl, 194 br, bl, 196 c, br, c, 197 br, 201, 206 br, 235 bl, 348 br, 349 c, 356 cl, 360 tl, tr, 361 bl, 398 tl, cl, 399 cb

Mark Iley: 370, 371

Marks Illustration: 347, cb, c, 354 c, 355 tl, cb, 361 br, t, c

R. Johns: 117 cr

Karen Johnson/Garden Studios: 324 tr, tl

Norman Lacey: 258, 260, 261, 266 tl, 385 c, 388 c

Adrian Lascomb: 386-87

Jason Lewis: 135 t, 144 tr

Richard Lewis: 218 bl, 219 t, 227 bl, 228 br, 229 bl, 267 tl

Linden Artists: 21 c, 96 tl, 146 tl, 151 cl, 156 cl, b, cr

Ruth Lindsay: 120 c, 128 ct, 232 tl, 330

Stuart Mackay: 18 br, c, 20 c, 24 cl, br, 28, 29 tr, cr, 33 c, 40, 41 bl, cb, tr, 47 c, 52 c, 53 br 54 c, 56 cl, 57 br, 59 c, tr, 60 tr, 64 br, c, 65 tr, 68 c, cr, 76 bl, 95 cl, br, 96 cb, 97 c, 98 c, 99 c, 102 cb, 103 bl, 106 cl, 109 tr, 119 b, 128 cl, 136 tl, 137 bl, 140 c, 148 c, cl, 149 tr, cb, 151 c, 181 tr, 183 cr, tl, 191 cb, 200 c, br, bl, 202 cb, 203 cb, 269 tl, 272 ct, 307 c, 360, 364, 401

Andrew Macdonald: 225 cb, 229 ct, 275, 372 br, tl, 373 cr, ct

Kevin Maddison: 23 br, 25 cr, 40 c, 45 c, 46 cb, 47, 47, cl, 51 bl, bcl, br, 52 bl, 53 tl, br, cl, 54 tr, cb, 55 bc, cr, 56 bl, br, 58 c, 67 br, 68 t, 71 t, 78 c, 119 tr, 131 cl, 132 tl, 135 c, 139 c, 141 cr, cb, 207 c,

Sergio Momo: 40 cb, 42 c, 50 tr, 57 cr, 73 cr, 86 c, 102 c

Liz Pepperell: 319 tr, cb

Daniel J Pyne: 230 c, br, cb, tl, 233 cr, 236

Jim Robins: 17 cb, 27, 41 cl, 43 br, 44 br, 47 cr, 49 cl, bl, 58 bl, 67, 89 cr, 128 cr, 129 cr, 133 tr, 140 br, 143 br, 177 c, 193 cb, 197 bl, 207 bl

Colin Salmon: 154 c, 165 br, 212 cr, 213 bl, 215 bl, 234 cr, 248 c, br, 249 cr, 382-3

Pete Serjeant: 158 c, 159 cr, bl, 183 c, 197 cl, 199, 281br, 283 cb, 285, c, 292 l

Sue Sharples: 328 br, 379 br, 385

Guy Smith: 146 bl, 147 bl, 173, 274 cb, 278 br, 282, 287 br, 297 cb, 298 bl, 300, 360 br, cr, 375 tl

Clive Spong: 387 tr

Roger Stewart: 157 br, 164 cb, 165 cl, 166 c, 175 c, br, 176 c, 285 tr, 286 cb, bl, 287 cb, 288, 289 bl, 290 cl, 291 bl, 292 c, 293 cr, cl, 312, 346 tl, 363 t

G Thompson: 329 tr, c

Gill Tomblin: 223, 238 c, 251, 262 bl, 265 bl, 266 cr, 268 cb, 272 cb, 316, 317 tl, 318 r, c, 321, 326 br, 342 cb, 349 c, 352 bl, 362 cb, 366 bl, 367, 369, 378, 384 c, bl, 388, 389, 390-91, 395 c, 396 tr, bl, 397, 398, 400, 420, 421, 422, 423, 425 tr

Kevin Toy: 328 bl, 329 bl, tl, 380, 399, 422 bc

Raymond Turvey: 165 t, 166 cr, 167 c, 274, 278c, 279, 281

Richard Ward: 21 br, 22 cl, cr, 26, 27 c, 31 tr, 32 c, 35 br, 36 bl, 45 bl, 47 cl, c, 48 cb, 59 cb, 60 c, 66 cl, cb, 72 tr, 78 tl, 89 bl, c, 92 c, 94 96 cr, 108 c, 113 cl, 114 c, 115 ct, 117 bl, 118 c, cb, 119 tr, 121 tr, 122 tr, 129 bl, cl, 130 c, 132 br, 135 bl, 138 bl, 144 c, cl, 159 c, 162 cl, 164 t, c, 171 bl, c, 178 c, 179 c, 181 cb, 189 bl, 191 br, 192, 206 tr, 285 bl, 288

L. Warren: 120 br

Brian Watson/Linden Artists: 273 tr, 275 tl, cr, 276 cr, 296 ct

David Webb: 320, 325 cl, 332 tr, 379 bl, 389

Steve Weston/Linden Artists: 224 cl, 235 cr, 239 cr, cb

Paul Williams: 76-77 c, 82 c, 84-85, 112 c, 211 cb, 212 bl, 214 cr, 229 tr, 240 b, 270 cl, 374

Gerald Wood: 148 tr

Debra Woodward: 237, 312 cl, cl, bl, 314 tr, cr, cl, c, 418 tl, 419 r

Martin Woodward: 207 cb, 153, 244 cl, 245 cb, 246 c, 247 c, cb, 250 ct, 255, 256 bl, 257 cr, cb, 263 tr

John Woodcock: 147 cl, 149 tl, 150 cb, 152-3 bl, 156 br, 213 br, 225 c, 227 tr, 240 br, 246 br, 252 cr, 256 bl, 260 cb, 308 bl,

Dan Wright: 205 bl, 217 cr, 222 cr, 232 cb, 233

ACKNOWLEDGMENTS

Additional editorial assistance from
Claire Bampton, Claire Calman, Gill Cooling, Rosanne Hooper, Michele Lynch, Miranda Smith, and Jill Somerscales

Additional design assistance from
Phil Lord on the initial stages of the book, and Susan St. Louis

Index
Hilary Bird

Special photography
Gary Kevin and Tim White

In addition, the publishers would like to thank the following people and organizations for their assistance in the production of this book.
Peter Barry; Dr. Tim Beales; University of Cambridge; Jack Challoner; The Crafts Council; The Definitive Laser Company; Dr. John Emsley, Dr. Chris Swan, and Chris Sausman, Imperial College, London; Dr. Gramshaw, Dept. of Food Science, University of Leeds; John Hirst, Rutherford Appleton Laboratory; Gordon Howes; International Automotive Design; Japan Meteorological Agency; John Kington, Climatic Research Unit, University of East Anglia; Barry Mills, ICI, Northwich; Dr. Philip Monroe, Hampshire Advisory and Technical Services; Nirmala Patel; Dr. David Robinson; The Royal Society of Chemistry; The Science Museum; Worldwide Fund for Nature, and The Youth Hostel Association.